SPACE
MANIFOLD 2

By the same author

THE TIME SHIPS
VOYAGE
TITAN
ANTI-ICE
TRACES
MOONSEED

Novels and stories in the Xeelee Sequence
RAFT
TIMELIKE INFINITY
FLUX
RING
VACUUM DIAGRAMS

Novels in the Manifold Sequence
TIME

Voyager

STEPHEN BAXTER

SPACE

MANIFOLD 2

HarperCollins*Publishers*

Voyager
An Imprint of HarperCollins*Publishers*
77–85 Fulham Palace Road,
Hammersmith, London W6 8JB

www.voyager-books.com

Published by *Voyager* 2000
3 5 7 9 8 6 4 2

A catalogue record for this book
is available from the British Library

ISBN 0 00 225771 8 (HB)
ISBN 0 00 710672 6 (TPB)

Set in PostScript Linotype Sabon and Gill Sans by
Rowland Phototypesetting Ltd, Bury St Edmunds, Suffolk

Printed and bound in Great Britain by
Clays Ltd, St Ives plc

To my nephew, Thomas Baxter, and
Simon Bradshaw and Eric Brown

ACKNOWLEDGEMENTS

Sections of this novel appeared in substantially different versions in *Science Fiction Age* magazine and in *Moonshots*, an anthology edited by Peter Crowther.

Innumerable suns exist; innumerable earths
revolve around these suns in a manner similar to
the way the seven planets revolve around our
sun. Living beings inhabit these worlds . . .
GIORDANO BRUNO (1548–1600)

If they existed, they would be here.
ENRICO FERMI (1901–1954)

PROLOGUE

My name is Reid Malenfant.

You know me. And you know I'm an incorrigible space cadet.

You know I've campaigned for, among other things, private mining expeditions to the asteroids. In fact, in the past I've tried to get you to pay for such things. I've bored you with that often enough already, right?

So tonight I want to be a little more personal. Tonight I want to talk about why I gave over my life to a single, consuming project.

It started with a simple question:

Where is everybody?

As a kid I used to lie at night out on the lawn, soaking up dew and looking at the stars, trying to feel the Earth turning under me. It felt wonderful to be alive – hell, to be ten years old, anyhow.

But I knew that the Earth was just a ball of rock, on the fringe of a nondescript galaxy.

As I lay there staring at the stars – the thousands I could pick out with my naked eyes, the billions that make up the great wash of our Galaxy, the uncounted trillions in the galaxies beyond – I just couldn't believe, even then, that there was nobody out *there* looking back at me down *here*. Was it really possible that this was the *only* place where life had taken hold – that only *here* were there minds and eyes capable of looking out and wondering?

But if not, *where are they*? Why isn't there evidence of extraterrestrial civilization all around us?

Consider this. Life on Earth got started just about as soon as it could – as soon as the rocks cooled and the oceans gathered. Of course it took a good long time to evolve *us*. Nevertheless we have to believe that what applies on Earth ought to apply on all the other worlds out there, like or unlike Earth; life ought to be popping up everywhere. And, as there are *hundreds of billions* of stars out there in the Galaxy, there are presumably hundreds of billions of opportunities for life to

I

come swarming up out of the ponds – and even more in the other galaxies that crowd our universe.

Furthermore, life spread over Earth as fast and as far as it could. And already we're starting to spread to other worlds. Again, this can't be a unique trait of Earth life.

So, if life sprouts everywhere, and spreads as fast and as far as it can, how come nobody has come spreading all over *us*?

Of course the universe is a big place. There are huge spaces between the stars. But it's not *that* big. Even crawling along with dinky ships that only reach a fraction of lightspeed – ships we could easily start building now – we could colonize the Galaxy in a few tens of millions of years. One hundred million, tops.

One hundred million years: it seems an immense time – after all, a hundred million years ago the dinosaurs ruled Earth. But the Galaxy is a hundred times older still. There has been time for Galactic colonization to have happened *many* times since the birth of the stars.

Remember, all it takes is for *one* race somewhere to have evolved the will and the means to colonize; and once the process has started it's hard to see what could stop it.

But, as a kid on that lawn, I didn't see them. I seemed to be surrounded by emptiness and silence.

Even *we* blare out on radio frequencies. Why, with our giant radio telescopes we could detect a civilization no more advanced than ours anywhere in the Galaxy. But we don't.

More advanced civilizations ought to be much more noticeable. We could spot somebody building a shell around their star, or throwing in nuclear waste. We could probably see evidence of such things even in other galaxies. But we don't. Those other galaxies, other reefs of stars, seem to be as barren as this one.

Maybe we're just unlucky. Maybe we're living at the wrong time. The Galaxy is an old place; maybe They have been, flourished, and gone already. But consider this: even if They are long gone, surely we should see Their mighty ruins, all around us. But we don't even see that. The stars show no signs of engineering. The solar system appears to be primordial, in the sense that it shows no signs of the great projects we can already envisage, like terraforming the planets, or tinkering with the sun, and so on.

We can think of lots of rationalizations for this absence.

Maybe there is something that kills off every civilization like ours before we get too far – for example, maybe we all destroy ourselves in nuclear wars or eco collapse. Or maybe there is something more sinister, plagues of killer robots sliding silently between the stars, which for their own antique purposes kill off fledgling cultures.

Or maybe the answer is more benevolent. Maybe we're in some kind of quarantine – or a zoo.

But none of these filtering mechanisms convinces me. You see, you have to believe that this magic suppression mechanism, whatever it is, works for *every* race in this huge Galaxy of ours. All it would take would be for *one* race to survive the wars, or evade the vacuum robots, or come sneaking through the quarantine to sell trinkets to the natives – or even just to start broadcasting some Eetie version of *The Simpsons*, anywhere in the Galaxy – and we'd surely see or hear them.

But we don't.

This paradox was first stated clearly by a twentieth-century physicist called Enrico Fermi. It strikes me as a genuine mystery. The contradictions are basic: life seems capable of emerging everywhere; just one starfaring race could easily have covered the Galaxy by now; the whole thing seems inevitable – but it hasn't happened.

Thinking about paradoxes is the way human understanding advances. I think the Fermi paradox is telling us something very profound about the universe, and our place in it. Or was.

Of course, everything is different now.

I
—

FOREIGNERS

AD 2020–2042

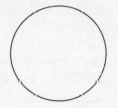

. . . And he felt as if he was drowning, struggling up from some thick, viscous fluid, up towards the light. He wanted to open his mouth, to scream – but he had no mouth – and no *words*. What would he scream?

I.

I am.

I am Reid Malenfant.

He could see the sail.

It was a gauzy sheet draped across the crowded stars of this place – where, Malenfant? why, the core of the Galaxy, he thought, wonder breaking through his agony – and within the sail, cupped, he could see the neutron star, an angry ball of red laced with eerie synchrotron blue, like a huge toy.

A star with a sail attached to it. Beautiful. Scary.

Triumph surged. I won, he thought. I resolved the *koan*, the great conundrum of the cosmos; Nemoto would be pleased. And now, together, we're fixing an unsatisfactory universe. Hell of a thing.

. . . But if you see all this, Malenfant, then what are *you*?

He looked down at himself.

Tried to.

A sense of body, briefly. Spread-eagled against the sail's gauzy netting. Clinging by fingers and toes, monkey digits, here at the centre of the Galaxy. A metaphor, of course, an illusion to comfort his poor human mind.

Welcome to reality.

The pain! Oh, God, the *pain*.

Terror flooded over him. And anger.

And, through it, he remembered the Moon, where it began . . .

Chapter 1

GAIJIN

A passenger in the HOPE-3 tug, Reid Malenfant descended towards the Moon.

The Farside base, called Edo, was a cluster of concrete components – habitation modules, power plants, stores, manufacturing facilities – half-buried in the cratered plain. Comms masts sprouted like angular flowers. The tug pad was just a splash of scorched Moon-dust concrete, a couple of kilometres further out. Around the station itself, the regolith was scarred by tractor traffic.

Robots were everywhere, rolling, digging, lifting; Edo was growing like a colony of bacilli in nutrient.

A *hi-no-maru*, a Japanese sun flag, was fixed to a pole at the centre of Edo.

'You are welcome to my home,' Nemoto said.

She met him in the pad's airlock, a large, roomy chamber blown into the regolith. Her face was broad, pale, her eyes black; her hair was elaborately shaved, showing the shape of her skull. She smiled, apparently habitually. She could have been no more than half Malenfant's age, perhaps thirty.

Nemoto helped Malenfant don the suit he'd been fitted with during the flight from Earth. The suit was a brilliant orange. It clung to him comfortably, the joints easy and loose, although the sewn-in plates of tungsten armour were heavy.

'It's a hell of a development from the old EMUs I wore when I was flying Shuttle,' he said, trying to make conversation.

Nemoto listened politely, after the manner of young people, to his fragments of reminiscence from a vanished age. She told him the suit had been manufactured on the Moon, and was made largely of spider silk. 'I will take you to the factory. A chamber in the lunar soil, full of immense spinnerets. A nightmare vision! . . .'

7

Malenfant felt disoriented, restless.

He was here to deliver a lecture, on colonizing the Galaxy, to senior executives of Nishizaki Heavy Industries. But here he was being met off the tug by Nemoto, the junior researcher who'd invited him out to the Moon, just a kid. He hoped he wasn't making some kind of fool of himself.

Reid Malenfant used to be an astronaut. He'd flown the last Shuttle mission – STS-194, on *Discovery* – when, ten years ago, the space transportation system had reached the end of its design life, and the International Space Station had finally been abandoned, incomplete. No American had flown into space since – save as the guest of the Japanese, or the Europeans, or the Chinese.

In this year 2020, Malenfant was sixty years old and feeling a lot older – increasingly stranded, a refugee in this strange new century, his dignity woefully fragile.

Well, he thought, whatever the dubious politics, whatever the threat to his dignity, he was *here*. It had been the dream of his long life to walk on another world. Even if it was as the guest of a Japanese.

And even if he was too damn old to enjoy it.

They stepped through a transit tunnel and directly into a small tractor, a lozenge of tinted glass. The tractor rolled away from the tug pad. The wheels were large and open, and absorbed the unevenness of the mare; Malenfant felt as if he were riding across the Moon in a soap bubble.

Every surface in the cabin was coated with fine, grey Moon dust. He could smell the dust; the scent was, as he knew it would be, like wood ash, or gunpowder.

Beyond the window, the Mare Ingenii – the Sea of Longing – stretched to the curved horizon, pebble-strewn. It was late in the lunar afternoon, and the sunlight was low, flat, the shadows of the surface rubble long and sharp. The lighting was a rich tan when he looked away from the sun, a more subtle grey elsewhere. Earth was hidden beneath the horizon, of course, but Malenfant could see a comsat crawl across the black sky.

He longed to step through the glass, to touch that ancient soil.

Nemoto locked in the autopilot and went to a little galley area. She emerged with green tea, rice crackers and dried *ika* cuttlefish. Malenfant wasn't hungry, but he accepted the food. Such items as the fish were genuine luxuries here, he knew; Nemoto was trying to honour him.

The motion of the tea, as she poured it in the one-sixth gravity, was complex, interesting.

'I am honoured you have accepted my invitation to travel here, to Edo,' Nemoto said. 'You will of course tour the town, as you wish. There is even a *Makudonarudo* here. A McDonald's. You may enjoy a *bifubaaga!* ... soya, of course.'

He put down his plate and tried to meet her direct gaze. 'Tell me why I've been brought out here. I don't see how my work, on long-term space utilization, can be of real interest to your employers.'

She eyed him. 'You do have a lecture to deliver, I am afraid. But – no, your work is not of primary concern to Nishizaki.'

'Then I don't understand.'

'It is I who invited you, I who arranged the funding. You ask why. I wished to meet you. I am a researcher, like you.'

'Hardly a researcher,' he said. 'I call myself a consultant, nowadays. I am not attached to a university.'

'Nor I. Nishizaki Heavy Industries pay my wages; my research must be focused on serving corporate objectives.' She eyed him, and took some more fish. 'I am *salariman*. A good company worker, yes? But I am, at heart, a scientist. And I have made some observations which I am unable to reconcile with the accepted paradigm. I searched for recent scientific publications concerning the subject area of my – hypothesis. I found only yours.

'My subject is infrared astronomy. At our research station, away from Edo, the company maintains radiometers, photometers, photopolarimeters, cameras. I work at a range of wavelengths, from twenty to a hundred microns. Of course a space-borne platform is to be preferred: the activities of humankind are thickening the Moon's atmosphere with each passing day, blocking the invisible light I collect. But the lunar site is cheap to maintain, and is adequate for the company's purposes. We are considering the future exploitation of the asteroids, you see. Infrared astronomy is a powerful tool in the study of those distant rocks. With it we can deduce a great deal about surface textures, compositions, internal heat, rotation characteristics –'

'Tell me about your paradigm-busting hypothesis.'

'Yes.' She sipped her green tea. She said calmly, 'I believe I have observational evidence of the activity of extraterrestrial intelligences in the solar system.'

The silence stretched between them, electric. Her words were shocking, quite unexpected.

But now he saw why she'd brought him here.

Since his retirement from NASA, Malenfant had avoided following

9

his colleagues into the usual ex-astronaut gravy ponds, lucrative aero-space executive posts and junior political positions. Instead, he'd thrown his weight behind research into what he regarded as long-term thinking: SETI, using gravitational lensing to hunt for planets and Eetie signals, advanced propulsion systems, schemes for colonizing the planets, terraforming, interstellar travel, exploration of the venerable Fermi paradox.

All the stuff that Emma had so disapproved of. *You're wasting your time, Malenfant. Where's the money to be made out of gravitational lensing?* . . .

But his wife was long gone, of course. Struck down by cancer: the result of a random cosmic accident, a heavy particle that had come whizzing out of an ancient supernova and flown across the universe to damage her *just* so . . . It could have been him; it could have been neither of them; it could have happened a few years later, when cancer had been reduced to a manageable disease. But it hadn't worked out like that, and Malenfant, burnt out, already grounded, had been left alone.

So he had thrown himself into his obsessions. What else was there to do?

Well, Emma had been right, and wrong. He was making a minor living on the lecture circuit. But few serious people were listening, just as she had predicted. He attracted more knee-jerk criticism than praise or thoughtful response; in the last few years, he'd become regarded as not much more than a reliable talk-show crank.

But now, *this*.

He tried to figure how to deal with this, what to say. Nemoto wasn't like the Japanese he had known before, on Earth, with their detailed observance of *reigi* – the proper manner.

She studied him, evidently amused. 'You are surprised. Startled. You think, perhaps, I am not quite sane to voice such speculations. You are trapped on the Moon with a mad Japanese woman. The American nightmare!'

He shook his head. 'It's not that.'

'But you must see that my speculations are not so far removed from your own published work. Like myself, you are cautious. Nobody listens. And when you do find an audience, they do not take you seriously.'

'I wouldn't be so blunt about it.'

'Your nation has turned inward,' Nemoto said. 'Shrunk back.'

'Maybe. We just have different priorities now.' In the US, flights into space had become a hobby of old men and women, dreams of an age of sublimated warfare which had left behind only images of charmingly antique rocket craft, endlessly copied around the data nets. Nothing to do with *now*.

She said, 'Then why do you continue, to argue, to talk, to expose yourself to ridicule?'

'Because –' Because if nobody thinks it, it definitely won't happen.

She was smiling at him; she seemed to understand. She said, 'The *kokuminsei*, the spirit of your people, is asleep. But in you, and perhaps others, curiosity burns strong. I think we two should defy the spirit of our age.'

'Why have you brought me here?'

'I am seeking to resolve a *koan*,' she said. 'A conundrum that defies logical analysis.' Her face lost its habitual smile, for the first time since they'd met. 'I need a fresh look – a perspective from a big thinker – someone like you. And –'

'Yes?'

'I am afraid, I think,' she said. 'Afraid for the future of the species.'

The tractor worked its way across the Moon, following a broad, churned-up path. Nemoto offered him more food.

The tractor drew up at an airlock at the outskirts of Edo. A big NASDA symbol was painted on the lock: NASDA for Japan's National Space Development Agency. With the minimum of fuss, Nemoto led Malenfant through the airlock and into Edo, into a colony on the Moon.

Here, at its periphery, Edo was functional. The walls were bare, of fused, glassy regolith. Ducts and cables were stapled to the roof. People wore plain, disposable paper coveralls. There was an air of bustle, of heavy industry.

Nemoto led him through Edo, a gentle guided tour. 'Of course the station is a great achievement,' she said. 'No less than ninety-five flights of our old H-2 rockets were required to ferry accommodation modules and power plants here. We build beneath the regolith, for shelter from solar radiation. We bake oxygen from the rocks, and mine water from the polar permafrost . . .'

At the centre of the complex, Edo was a genuine town. There were public places: bars, restaurants where the people could buy rice, soup, fried vegetables, *sushi, sake*. There was even a tiny park, with shrubs and bamboo grass; a spindly lunar-born child played there with his parents.

Nemoto smiled at Malenfant's reaction. 'At the heart of Edo, ten metres beneath lunar regolith, there are cherry trees. Our children study beneath their branches. You may stay long enough to see *ichibuzaki*, the first state of blossoming.'

Malenfant saw no other Westerners. Most of the Japanese nodded politely. Many must have known Nemoto – Edo supported only a few hundred inhabitants – but none engaged her in conversation. His impression of Nemoto as a loner, rather eccentric, was reinforced.

As they passed one group he heard a man whisper, '*Wah! – gaijin-kusai.*'

Gaijin-kusai. The smell of foreigner. There was laughter.

Malenfant spent the night in what passed for a *ryokan*, an inn. His apartment was tiny, a single room. But, despite the bleak austerity of the fused-regolith walls, the room was decorated Japanese style. The floor was *tatami* – rice straw matting – polished and worn with use. A *tokonoma*, an alcove carved into the rock, contained an elaborate data net interface unit; but the owners had followed tradition and had hung a scroll painting there – of a dragonfly on a blade of grass – and some flowers, in an *ikebana* display. The flowers looked real.

There was a display of cherry blossom, fixed to the wall under clear plastic. The contrast of the pale living pink with the grey Moon rock was the most beautiful thing he had ever seen.

In this tiny room he was immersed in noise: the low, deep rumblings of the artificial lungs of the colony, of machines ploughing outward through the regolith. It was like being in the belly of a huge vessel, a submarine. Malenfant thought wistfully of his own study: bright Iowa sunlight, his desk, his equipment.

Edo kept Tokyo time, so Malenfant, here on the Moon, suffered jet lag. He slept badly.

Rows of faces.

'. . . How are we to populate the Galaxy? It's actually all a question of economics.' Over Malenfant's head a virtual image projected in the air of the little theatre, its light glimmering from the folded wooden walls.

Malenfant stared around at the rows of Japanese faces, like coins shining in this rich brown dark. They seemed remote, unreal. Many of these people were NASDA administrators; as far as he could tell there was nobody from Nishizaki senior management here, nominally his sponsors for the trip.

The virtual was a simple schematic of stars, randomly scattered. One star blinked, representing the sun.

Malenfant said, 'We will launch unmanned probes.' Ships, little dots of light, spread out from the toy sun. 'We might use ion rockets, solar sails, gravity assists – whatever. The first wave will be slow, no faster than we can afford. It doesn't matter. Not in the long term.

'The probes will be self-replicating: Von Neumann machines, essentially. Universal constructors. Humans may follow, by such means as generation starships. However it would be cheaper for the probes to manufacture humans in situ, using cell synthesis and artificial womb technology.' He glanced over the audience. 'You wish to know if we can build such devices. Not yet. Although your own Kashiwazaki Electric has a partial prototype.'

At that there was a stir of interest, self-satisfied.

As his virtual light-show continued to evolve, telling its own story, he glanced up at the walls around him, at the glimmer of highlights from wood. This was a remarkable place. It was the largest structure in Edo, serving as community centre and town hall and showpiece, the size of a ten-storey building.

But it was actually a *tree*, a variety of oak. The oaks were capable of growing to two hundred metres under the Moon's gentle gravity, but this one had been bred for width, and was full of intersecting hollowed-out chambers. The walls of this room were of smooth polished wood, broken only subtly by technology – lights, air vents, virtual display gear – and the canned air here was fresh and moist and alive.

In contrast to the older parts of Edo – all those clunky tunnels – this was the future of the Moon, the Japanese were implicitly saying. The living Moon. What the hell was an American doing here on the Moon, lecturing these patient Japanese about colonizing space? The Japanese were *doing* it, patiently and incrementally working.

But – yes, *incrementally*: that was the key word. Even these lunar colonists couldn't see beyond their current projects, the next few years, their own lifetimes. They couldn't see where this could all lead. To Malenfant, that ultimate destination was everything.

And, perhaps, Nemoto and her strange science would provide the first route map.

The little probe-images had reached their destination stars.

'Here is the heart of the strategy,' he said. 'A target system, we assume, is uninhabited. We can therefore program for massive and destructive exploitation of the system's resources, without restraint, by the probe. Such resources are useless for any other purpose, and are therefore economically free to us. And so we colonize, and build.'

13

More probes erupted from each of the first wave of target stars, at greatly increased speeds. The probes reached new targets; and again, more probes were spawned, and fired onwards. The volume covered by the probes grew rapidly; it was like watching the expansion of gas into a vacuum.

He said, 'Once started, the process is self-directing, self-financing. It would take, we think, ten to a hundred million years for the colonization of the Galaxy to be completed in this manner. But we must invest merely in the cost of the initial generation of probes. Thus the cost of colonizing the Galaxy will be less, in real terms, than that of our Apollo program of fifty years ago.'

His probes were now spreading out along the Galaxy's spiral arms, along lanes rich with stars. His Japanese audience watched politely.

But as he delivered his polished words he thought of Nemoto and her tantalizing hints of otherness – of a mystery which might render all his scripted invective obsolete – and he faltered.

Trying to focus, feeling impatient, he closed with his cosmic-destiny speech. '. . . This may be a watershed in the history of the cosmos. Think about it. *We know how to do this.* If we make the right decisions now, life may spread beyond Earth and Moon, far beyond the solar system, a wave of green transforming the Galaxy. We must not fail . . .' And so on.

Well, they applauded him kindly enough. But there were few questions.

He got out, feeling foolish.

The next day Nemoto said she would take him to the surface, to see her infrared spectroscopy results at first hand.

They walked through the base to a tractor airlock, and suited up once more. The infrared station was an hour's ride from Edo.

A kilometre out from Edo itself, the tractor passed one of the largest structures Malenfant had yet seen. It was a cylinder perhaps a hundred and fifty metres long, ten wide. It looked like a half-buried nuclear submarine. The lunar surface here was scarred by huge gullies, evidently the result of strip-mining. Around the central cylinder there was a cluster of what looked like furnaces, enclosed by semi-transparent domes.

'Our fusion plant,' Nemoto said. 'Edo is powered by the fusion of deuterium, the hydrogen isotope, with helium-3.'

Malenfant glared out with morbid interest. Here, as in most technological arenas, the Japanese were way out ahead of Americans. Twenty per cent of the US's power now came from the fusion of two hydrogen isotopes, deuterium and tritium. But hydrogen fusion processes, even with such relatively low-yield fuel, had turned out to be unstable and expensive: high-energy neutrons smashed through reactor walls, making them brittle and radioactive. The Japanese helium-3 fusion process, by contrast, produced charged protons, which could be kept away from reactor walls with magnetic fields.

However, the Earth had no natural supply of helium-3.

Nemoto waved a hand. 'The Moon contains vast stores of helium-3, locked away in deposits of titanium minerals, in the top three metres of the regolith. The helium came from the sun, borne on the solar wind; the titanium acted like a sponge, soaking up the helium particles. We plan to begin exporting the helium to Earth.'

'I know.' The export would make Edo self-sufficient.

She smiled brightly, young and confident in the future.

Out of sight of Edo, the tractor passed a cairn of piled-up maria rubble. On the top there was a *sake* bottle, a saucer bearing rice cakes, a porcelain figure. There were small paper flags around the figure, but the raw sunlight had faded them.

'It is a shrine,' Nemoto explained. 'To *Inari-samma*. The Fox God.' She grinned at him. 'If you close your eyes and clap your hands, perhaps the *kami* will come to you. The divinities.'

'Shrines? At a lunar industrial complex?'

'We are an old people,' she said. 'We have changed much, but we remain the same. *Yamato damashi* – our spirit – persists.'

At length the tractor drew up to a cluster of buildings set on the plain. This was the Nishizaki Heavy Industries infrared research station.

Nemoto checked Malenfant's suit, then popped the hatch.

Malenfant climbed stiffly down a short ladder. As he moved, clumsily, he heard the hiss of air, the soft whirr of exoskeletal multipliers. These robot muscles helped him overcome the suit's pressurization and the weight of his tungsten anti-radiation armour.

His helmet was a big gold-tinted bubble. His backpack, like Nemoto's, was a semi-transparent thing of tubes and sloshing water, six litres full of blue algae that fed off sunlight and his own waste products, producing enough oxygen to keep him going indefinitely. In theory.

Actually Malenfant missed his old suit: his Space Shuttle EMU, Extravehicular Mobility Unit, with its clunks and whirrs of fans and pumps. Maybe it was limited compared to this new technology. But he hated to wear a backpack that *sloshed,* for God's sake, its mass pulling him this way and that in the low gravity. And his robot muscles – amplifying every impulse, dragging his limbs and tilting his back for him – made him feel like a puppet.

He dropped down the last metre; his small impact sent up a little spray of dust, which fell back immediately.

And here he was, walking on the Moon.

He walked away from the tractor, suit whirring and lurching. He had to go perhaps a hundred metres to get away from tractor tracks and footsteps.

He reached unmarked soil. His boots left prints as crisp as if he had stepped out of Apollo 11.

There were craters upon craters, a fractal clustering, right down to little pits he could barely have put his fingertip into, and smaller yet. But they didn't look like craters – more like the stippling of raindrops, as if he stood in a recently ploughed and harrowed field, a place where rain had pummelled the loose ground. But there had been no rain here, of course, not for four billion years.

The sun cast brilliant, dazzling light. Otherwise the sky was empty, jet black. But he was a little surprised that he had no sense of openness, of immensity all around him, unlike a desert night sky at home. He felt as if he was on a darkened stage, under a brilliant spotlight, with the walls of the universe just a little way away, just out of view.

He looked back at the tractor, with the big red sun of Japan painted on its side. He thought of a terraformed Moon, of twin blue worlds. He felt tears, hot and unwelcome, prickle his eyes. Damn it. We were here first. We had all this. And we let it go.

Nemoto waited for him, a small figure on the Moon's folded plain, her face hidden behind her gold-tinted bubble of glass.

She led him into the cluster of buildings. There was a small fission power plant, tanks of gases and liquids. A living shelter was half-buried in the regolith.

The centre of the site was a crude cylindrical hut, open to the sky, containing a battery of infrared sensors and computer equipment. The infrared detectors themselves were immersed in huge vessels of liquid helium. Robots crawled between the detectors, monitoring constantly, their complex arms stained by Moon dust.

Nemoto walked up to a processor control desk. A virtual image appeared, hovering over the compacted regolith at the centre of the hut. The virtual was a ring of glistening crimson droplets, slowly orbiting.

Nemoto said, 'Here is a summary of my survey of the asteroid belt.

16

Or "belts", I should say, for there are gaps between the sub-belts – the Kirkwood gaps, swept clear by resonances with Jupiter's gravity field.' The Kirkwood gaps were dark bands, empty of crimson drops. 'Of course Nishizaki Heavy Industries is very interested in asteroids. There is a mine in Sudbury, Ontario, which for a long time was a rich source of nickel. The nickel seam is disc-shaped. It is almost certainly the scar of an ancient asteroid collision with the Earth.'

'Mineral extraction, then.'

'There is a scheme to retrieve a fragment of the asteroid Geographos, which crosses Earth's orbit. We may cleave it with controlled explosions. Perhaps we can deliver fragments to orbit, using lunar gravity assists and grazes against the Earth's atmosphere. Or we may initiate a controlled impact with the Moon. This exercise alone would yield more than nine hundred billion dollars' worth of nickel, rhenium, osmium, iridium, platinum, gold – so much, in fact, the planet's economy would be transformed, making estimates of wealth difficult.'

Malenfant walked around the instrument hut. The novelty of his Moonwalk was wearing off; his suit scratched, his helmet was hot, and his condom was itching. 'Nemoto, it's time you got to the point.'

'The *koan*,' she said. The virtual ring shone in her visor, making her face invisible. 'Let us look at the stars.'

She took his gloved hand in hers – through the thick layers of glove he could barely feel the pressure of her fingers – and she led him out of the building. The virtual asteroid ring, eerily, followed them out.

They stood in the deep shadow of the structure. With a motion, she indicated he should lift his visor.

He raised his head so he couldn't see the ground or the buildings, and he turned around and around, as he used to as a kid, on the darkest Moonless nights back home.

The stars, of course: thousands of them, peppering the sky all around him, crowding out the bright-star constellations seen from Earth. And now, at last, came that elusive feeling of immensity. From the Moon it was *much* easier to see that he was just a mote clinging to a round ball of rock, spinning endlessly in an infinite, three-dimensional starry sky.

'Look.' Nemoto, pointing, swept out an arc of the sky, where dusty light shone.

Despite the crowding stars, Malenfant recognized one or two constellations – Cygnus and Aquila, the swan and the eagle. And, where she pointed, a river of light ran through the constellations, a river of stars. It was the Milky Way: the Galaxy, the disc of stars in which Sol and all its planets were embedded, seen edge on and turned into a band of light that wrapped around the sky. But, as it passed through Cygnus and Aquila, that band of light seemed to split into two, twin streams separated by a dark gap. In fact the rift was a shadow, cast by dark clouds blocking the light from the star banks behind.

Nemoto pointed. 'See how the darkness starts out narrow in Cygnus, then broadens in Aquila, sweeping wider through Serpens and Opiuchus. This is the effect of perspective. We are seeing a band of dust as it comes from the distance in Cygnus, passing closest to the sun in Aquila and Opiuchus. Malenfant, we live in a spiral arm of this Galaxy – a small fragment, in fact, called the Orion Arm. And spiral arms typically have lanes of dust on their inside edges.'

'Like that one.'

'Yes. *That* is the inner edge of our spiral arm, hanging in the sky for all to see.' Her shadowed eyes glimmered, full of starlight. 'It is possible to make out the Galaxy's structure, you see: to witness that we are embedded in a giant spiral of stars – even with the naked eye. *This* is where we live.'

'Why are you showing me this?'

'Look at the Galaxy, Malenfant. It appears to be a giant machine – no, an ecology – evolved to make stars. And there are hundreds of millions of galaxies beyond our own. Is it really conceivable, given all of that immensity, all that structure, that we are truly alone? – that life emerged here, and nowhere else?'

Malenfant grunted. 'The old Fermi paradox. Troubled me as a kid, even before I heard of Fermi.'

'Me too.' He could see her smile. 'You see, Malenfant, we have much in common. And the logic behind the paradox troubles me still –'

'Even though you think you have found aliens.'

She let that hang, and he found he was holding his breath.

Cautiously, she said, 'How would it make you feel, Malenfant, if I was right?'

'If you had proof that another intelligence exists? It would be wonderful. I guess.'

'Would it?' She smiled again. 'How sentimental you are. Listen to me: humanity would be in extreme danger. Remember, by your own argument, the assumption on which such a colonizing expedition operates is that it is appropriating an empty system. Such a probe could destroy our worlds without even noticing us.'

He shivered; his spider-web suit felt thin and fragile.

'Think it through further,' she said. 'Think like an engineer. If an alien replicator probe were to approach the solar system, where would it seek to establish itself? What are its requirements?'

He thought about it. You'll need energy; plenty of it. So, stay close to the sun. Next: raw materials. The surface of a rocky planet? But you wouldn't want to dip into a gravity well if you didn't have to . . . Besides, your probe is designed for deep space –

'The asteroid belt,' he said, suddenly seeing where all this was leading. 'Plenty of resources, freely floating, away from the big gravity wells . . . Even the main belts aren't too crowded, but you'd probably settle in a Kirkwood gap, to minimize the chance of collision. Your orbit would be perturbed by Jupiter, just like the asteroids', but it wouldn't require much station-keeping to compensate for that. And some kind of ship or colony out there, even a few kilometres across, would be hard for us to spot.' He looked at her sharply. 'Is that what this is about? Have you found something in the belt?'

'The plain facts are these. I have surveyed the Kirkwood gaps with the sensors here. And, in the gap which corresponds to the one-to-three resonance with Jupiter, I have found –' She pointed to her virtual model, to a broad, precise gap.

At the centre of the gap, a string of rubies shone, enigmatic, brilliant in the shadows.

'These are sources of infrared,' she said. 'Sources I cannot explain.'

Malenfant bent to study the little beads of light. 'Could they be asteroids that have strayed into the gap after collisions?'

'No. The sources are too bright. In fact, they are each emitting more heat than they receive from the sun. I am, of course, seeking firmer evidence: for example, structure in the infrared signature; or perhaps there will be radio leakage.'

He stared at the ruby lights. My God. She's right. If these are *emitting* heat, this is unambiguous: it's evidence of industrial activity . . .

His heart thumped. Somehow he hadn't accepted what she had said to him, not in his gut, not up to now. But now he could see it, and his universe was transformed.

He made out her face in the dim light reflected from the regolith, the smooth sweep of human flesh here in this dusty wilderness. Though it must have been a big moment for her to show him this evidence – a moment of triumph – she seemed troubled. 'Nemoto, why did you ask me here? Your work is a fine piece of science, as far as I can see.

19

The interpretation is unambiguous. You should publish. Why do you need reassurance from me?'

'I know this is good science. But the answer is *wrong*. Very wrong. The *koan* is not resolved at all. Don't you see that?' She glared up at the sky, as if trying to make out the signature of aliens with her own eyes. '*Why now?*'

He glimpsed her meaning.

They must have just arrived, or we'd surely see their works, the transformed asteroids swarming . . . But why should they arrive *now*, just as we ourselves are ready to move beyond the Earth – just as we are able to comprehend them? A simple coincidence? Why shouldn't they have come here long ago?

He grinned. Old Fermi wasn't beaten yet; there were deeper layers of the paradox here, much to unravel, new questions to ask.

But it wasn't a moment for philosophy.

His mind was racing. '*We aren't alone.* Whatever the implications, the unanswered questions – my God, what a thought. We'll need the resources of the race, of all of us, to respond to this.'

She smiled thinly. 'Yes. The stars have intervened, it seems. Your *kokuminsei*, your people's spirit, must revive. It will be *satori* – a reawakening. Come.' She held out her hand. 'We should go back to Edo. We have much to do.'

He squinted, trying to make out the constellations against the glare of the regolith. There was *gaijin-kusai* there, the smell of foreigner, he thought. He felt exhilarated, awakened, as if a hiatus was coming to an end. *This changes everything.*

He took Nemoto's hand, and they walked back across the regolith to the tractor.

Chapter 2

BAIKONUR

The priest was not what Xenia Makarova had expected.

Xenia herself wasn't religious. And Xenia's family, emigrant to the United States four generations ago, had been Orthodox. What did she know about Catholic priests? So she had expected the cliché: some gaunt old man, Italian or Irish, shrivelled up by a lifetime of celibacy, dressed in a flapping black cassock that would soak up the toxic dust and prove utterly unsuitable for the conditions here at the launch site.

Her first surprise had come when the priest had expressed no special accommodation requirements, but had been happy to stay in the town of Baikonur, along with the technicians who worked for Bootstrap here at the old Soviet-era launch station. Baikonur – once called Leninsk, at the heart of Kazakhstan – was a place of burned-out offices and abandoned, windowless apartments, of roads and roofs coated with strata of gritty brown powder, blown from the pesticide-laden salt flats of the long-dead Aral Sea a few hundred kilometres away. Baikonur was a relic of Soviet dreams, plagued by crime and ill-health. Not a good place to stay.

So Xenia wasn't sure what to expect by the time the bus drew up to the security gate, and she went out to greet her holy guest.

The priest must have been sixty, small, compact: fit-looking, though she showed some stiffness climbing down from the bus. Camera drones, glittering toys the size of beetles, whirred out in a cloud around her head.

Her, yes: of course it would be a female, one of the Vatican's first cadre of women priests, that would be assigned to this most PR-friendly of operations.

And no black cassock. The priest, dressed in loose, comfortable-looking therm-aware shirt and slacks, could have held any one of a number of white collar professions: an accountant, maybe, or a space scientist of the kind Frank Paulis had recruited in droves, or even a lawyer like Xenia herself. It was only the dog collar, a thin band of white at the throat, that marked out a different vocation.

From the shadows of her broad, sensible sun-hat the priest smiled out at Xenia. 'You must be Ms Makarova.'

'Call me Xenia. And you –'

'Dorothy Chaum.' The smile grew a little weary. 'I'm neither Mother, nor Father, thankfully. You must call me Dorothy.'

'It's a pleasure to have you here, Ms – Dorothy.'

Dorothy flapped at the drones buzzing around her head like flies. 'You're a good liar. I'll try to trouble you as little as I can.' And she looked beyond Xenia, into the rocket compound, with questing, curious eyes.

Maybe this won't be so bad after all, Xenia thought.

Xenia, in fact, had been against the visit on principle, and she had told her boss so. 'For God's sake, Frank. This is a space launcher development site. It's a place for hard hats, not haloes.'

Frank Paulis – forty-five years old, squat, brisk, bustling, sleek with sweat even in his air-conditioned offices – had just tapped his softscreen. 'Just like it says in the mail here. This character is here on behalf of the Pope, to gather information on the mission –'

'And bless it. Frank, the *Bruno* is a mission to the asteroids. We're going out to find Eeties, for God's sake. To have some quack waving incense and throwing holy water over our ship is – ridiculous. Mediaeval.'

Frank had got a look in his eyes she'd come to recognize. *You have to be realistic, Xenia. Live in the real world.* 'The Vatican are one of our principal sponsors. They've a right to access.'

'The Church is using us as part of its repositioning,' she'd protested sourly. It was true; the Church had spent much of the new millennium rebuilding, after the multiple crises that had assailed it after the turn of the century: sexual scandals, financial irregularities, a renewed awareness of the horrors of Christian history – the Crusades and the Inquisition chief amongst them. 'Not to mention,' Xenia said bitterly, 'the Church's refusal to acknowledge female reproductive rights and to address the issue of population growth, a position not abandoned until 2013, a historic wrong which must be on a par with –'

'Nobody's arguing,' Frank said gently. 'But – who are you suggesting is cynical? Us or them? Look, I don't care about the Church. All I care about is its money, and there's still a hell of a lot of *that*.

And, just like any other corporate sponsor, the Church is entitled to its slice of the PR pie.'

'Sometimes I think you'd take money from the Devil himself if it got your Big Dumb Booster a little closer to the launch pad.'

'Since we have a bunch of those apocalyptic cultists here – the ones who think the Gaijin are demons sent to punish us, or whatever – I suppose I *am* taking money from the other guy. Well, at least it shows balance.' Frank put his arm around her – he had to reach up to do it – and guided her out of his office. 'Xenia, this witch doctor isn't going to be with us for long. And, believe me, a priest is going to be a lot easier for you to entertain than some of the fat cats we have to put up with.'

'*Me* . . . Frank, if you knew how much I resent the implication that my time isn't valuable –'

'Bring her to the lecture. That will eat up a couple of hours.'

'What lecture?'

He frowned. 'I thought you knew. Reid Malenfant, on the philosophy of extraterrestrial life.'

She had to retrieve the name from deep memory. 'The dried-up old coot from the talk shows?'

'Reid Malenfant, the ex-astronaut. Reid Malenfant, the co-discoverer of alien life five years back. Reid Malenfant, modern icon, come to give our grease monkeys a pep talk.' He grinned. 'Lighten up, Xenia. Maybe it will be interesting.'

'Are *you* going?'

'Of course I am.' And, gently, he had closed the door.

Xenia and Dorothy were SmartDriven around Baikonur, the standard-issue corporate tour.

Baikonur, the Soviet Union's long-hidden space centre, had been pretty much a derelict by the time Frank Paulis took it over and began renovation. Stranded at the heart of a chill, treeless steppe, connected to the Russian border by a single antique rail line, it was like a run-down military base, dotted with hangars and launch pads and fuel tanks. Even after years of work by Bootstrap here, there were still piles of rusty junk strewn over the more remote corners of the base – some of it said to be the last relics of Russia's never-successful Moon rockets.

But Dorothy's attention was diverted, away from Xenia's sound bites on the history and the engineering and the mission of Bootstrap, by the folks Frank Paulis referred to as the Sports Fans: adherents of one view or another about the Gaijin, seemingly attracted here irresistibly.

The Sports Fans lived at the fringe of the launch complex in semi-permanent camps, contained by tough link fences. They spent their time chanting, costume-wearing, leafleting, performing protests of one baffling kind or another, right up against the fences, carefully watched over by Bootstrap security staff and drone robots. They were funded, presumably, by savings, or sponsors, or by whatever they could sell of their experiences and their witness on the data nets, and they were a fat, easy revenue source for the local Kazakhs – which was why they were tolerated here.

Xenia tried to guide Dorothy away from all this, but Dorothy demurred. And so they began a slow drive around the fences, as Dorothy peered out, and Xenia struggled to contain her impatience.

Public reaction to the Gaijin – as it had developed over the five years since the announcement of the discovery by Nemoto and Malenfant – had bifurcated. There were two broad schools of thought. The technical terms among psychologists and sociologists, Xenia had learned, were 'millennialists' and 'catastrophists'.

The millennialists, taking their lead from thinkers like Carl Sagan – not to mention Gene Roddenberry – believed that no star-spanning culture could possibly be hostile to a more primitive species like humanity, and the Gaijin must therefore be on their way to educate us or uplift us or save us from ourselves. The more intellectual millennialists had at least produced some useful, if slanted, material: careful studies of parallels with intercultural contact in Earth's past, ranging from the dreadful fall-out of western colonialism through to the essentially benevolent impact of the transmission of learning from Arabian and ancient Greek cultures to the medieval west.

But some millennialists were more direct. Various giant, elaborate structures had been cut or burned or painted on Earth's surface – featuring the peace sigil, the yin and yang, the Christian cross, a human hand – giant graffiti, Dorothy thought, painted in the deserts of America and Africa and Asia and Australia and even, illegally, on the Antarctic ice cap, its creators wistfully hoping to catch the eye of the anonymous, toiling strangers out in the belt.

Others were even less subtle. Right here before her now there was a circle of people, hands open and faces raised to the desert sky, all steadily praying. She knew there had been similar gatherings, some in continuous session, at many of the world's key religious and mystic sites: Jerusalem, Mecca, the pyramids, the European stone circles. *Take me! Take me!*

Meanwhile, the catastrophists believed that the aliens represented terrible danger.

Much of their fear and anger was directed at the aliens themselves, of course, and there were elaborate schemes for military assaults on their supposed asteroid bases – justified, in some cases, by appeal to the evident malice of most of the aliens reported in UFO abduction cases of the past. There was even one impressive presentation – complete with animation and sound effects, emanating from softscreen posters draped over Bootstrap's link fence – from a major aerospace cartel. The military-industrial-complex types were as always seeking to turn the new situation into lucrative new contracts, and how better than to be asked to build giant asteroid-belt battle cruisers?

But the catastrophists had plenty of rage left over to be directed at other targets, healthily fuelled by conspiracy theorists. There were still some who held that the US government had been collaborating with the aliens since Roswell, 1947 – 'I wish they had been,' Frank once said tiredly; 'it would make life a lot easier' – and there were protests aimed at government agencies at all levels, the United Nations, scientific bodies, and anybody thought to be involved in the general cover up. The most spectacular of the related assaults had been the grenade attack which had caused the destruction of the decrepit, never-flown Saturn V Moon rocket which had lain for decades as a monument outside NASA's Johnson Space Center.

It kept the Bootstrap guards watchful.

'Intriguing,' Dorothy murmured. 'Disturbing.'

Xenia said gently, 'But places like this always concentrate the noise. The vast majority of people out there in the real world are simply indifferent to the whole thing. When the news about the Gaijin first broke it was an immediate sensation, taking over every media outlet – for a day or two, perhaps a week. I was already working with Frank at the time. He was electrified – well, we both were; we thought the news the most significant of our lifetimes. And the business opportunities it might open up sent Frank running around in circles.'

Dorothy smiled. 'That sounds like the Frank Paulis I've read about.'

'But then there was no more fresh news . . .'

After a couple of weeks, the Gaijin had been crowded off the front pages. Politics had assumed its usual course, and all the funds hastily promised in that first startling morning after the Nemoto–Malenfant discovery – for deeper investigations and robot probes and manned missions and the rest – had soon evaporated.

'But the news was too – lofty,' Dorothy murmured. 'Inhuman. It

25

changed everything. Suddenly the universe swivelled around us; suddenly we knew we weren't alone, and how we felt about ourselves, about the universe and our place in it, could never be the same again.

'And yet, *nothing* changed. After all the Gaijin didn't *do* anything but crawl around their asteroids. They didn't respond to any of the signals they were sent, whether by governments or churches or ham-radio crackpots.'

Frank had gotten involved in some of that, in fact; the early messages had been framed using a universal-language methodology that dated back to the 1960s, called Lincos: lots of redundancy and framing to make the message patterns clear, a simple primer which worked up from basic mathematical concepts through physics, chemistry, astronomy . . . A lot of beautiful, fascinating work, none of which had raised so much as a peep from the Gaijin.

'And meanwhile,' Dorothy went on, 'there were still babies to deliver, crops to grow, politicking to pursue and wars to fight. As my father used to say, the next morning you still had to put your pants on one leg at a time.

'You know,' she said thoughtfully, 'I'm generally in favour of all this activity. Your Sports Fans, I mean. The only way we have to absorb such changes in our view of the world, and ourselves, is like this: by talking, talking, talking. At least the people here care enough to express an opinion. Look at that.' It was a softscreen poster showing a download from the net: a live image returned by some powerful telescope, perhaps in orbit or on the Moon, of the asteroid belt anomalies: a dark, grainy background, a line of red stars, twinkling, blurred. 'Alien industry, live from space. The most popular Internet site, I'm told. People use it as wallpaper in their bedrooms. They seem to find it comforting.'

Xenia snorted. 'Sure. And you know who makes most use of that image? The astrologers. Now you can have your fortune told by the lights of Gaijin factories. I mean, Jesus . . . Sorry. But it says it all.'

Dorothy laughed good-naturedly.

They drove away from the Sports Fans' pens, and approached the pad itself: the true centre of attention, bearing Bootstrap's first interplanetary ship, Frank Paulis's pride and joy.

Xenia could see the lines of a rust-brown external tank, the slim pillars of solid rocket boosters. The stack was topped by a tubular cover that gleamed white in the sun. Somewhere inside that fairing rested the *Giordano Bruno,* a complex robot spacecraft that would

26

some day ride out to the asteroids, and seek out the Gaijin that lurked there – if Frank could drive the test program to completion, if Xenia could guide the corporation through the maze of legislation that still impeded them.

As Xenia studied the ship, Dorothy studied her.

Dorothy said, 'Frank Paulis relies on you a lot, doesn't he? I know that formally you are head of Bootstrap's legal department . . .'

'I'm the first name on Frank's call list. He relies on me to get things done.'

'And you're happy with your role.'

'We do share the same goals, you know.'

'Umm. Your ship looks something like the old Space Shuttle.'

'So it should,' said Xenia, and she launched into a standard line. 'This is what we here at Bootstrap call our Big Dumb Booster. It's actually comprised largely of superannuated Space Shuttle components. You'll immediately see one benefit over the standard Shuttle design, which is in-line propulsion; we have a much more robust stack –'

Dorothy said with smooth humour, 'I'm no more an engineer than you are, Xenia.'

Xenia allowed herself a grin. 'Sorry. It's hard to change the script after doing this so many times . . . This is primarily a launcher to the planets. Or the asteroids.'

Dorothy smiled. 'You have built a rocket ship for America.'

Xenia bristled. 'It does seem rather a scandal that America, first nation to land a human being on another planet, has let its competence degrade to the point that it has no heavy-lift space launch capability at all.'

'But the Chinese are in Earth orbit, and the Japanese are on the Moon. There's even a rumour that the Chinese are preparing a flight of their own out to the asteroids.'

Xenia squinted at the washed-out, dusty sky. 'Dorothy, it's five years since the Gaijin showed up in the solar system. But you can't call it contact. Not yet. As you said, they haven't responded to any of our signals. All they do is build, build, build. Maybe if we do manage to send a probe there, we'll achieve real contact, the kind of contact we've always dreamed of.'

'And you think America should be first.'

'If not us, who? The Chinese? . . .'

A siren sounded: an engine test was due. With smooth efficiency, the car's SmartDrive cut in and swept them far from danger.

*   *   *

27

'. . . We used to think that life was pretty unlikely – maybe even unique to Earth,' Malenfant was saying. 'An astronomer called Fred Hoyle once said that the idea that you could shuffle organic molecules in some primeval soup and, purely by chance, come up with a DNA molecule is about like a whirlwind passing through an aircraft factory and assembling scattered parts into a 747.' Laughter. 'But now we think those notions are wrong. Now we think that the complexity that defines and underlies life is somehow hardwired into the laws of physics. Life is *emergent*.

'Imagine boiling a pan of water. As the liquid starts to convect, you'll see a regular pattern of cells form, kind of like a honeycomb – just before the proper boiling cuts in and the motion becomes chaotic. Now, all there is in the pan is water molecules, billions of them. Nobody is *telling* those molecules how to organize themselves into those striking patterns. And yet they do it.

'That's an example of how order and complexity can emerge from an initial uniform and featureless state. And maybe life is just the end product of a long series of self-organizing steps like that . . .'

Malenfant was giving his lecture in Bootstrap's roomy, air-conditioned public affairs auditorium: the one place Frank had been prepared to spend some serious money, aside from on the engineering itself. Xenia and Dorothy arrived a little late. To Xenia's surprise, the auditorium was pretty nearly full, and she had to squeeze them into two seats at the back.

The stage was bare save for a lectern and a plastic mock-up, three metres tall, of the Big Dumb Booster – that, and Malenfant.

To Xenia, Reid Malenfant – a lithe but sun-wrinkled sixty-something, his polished-bald head shining under the overhead lights – was an unprepossessing sight. Even as he spoke he seemed oddly out of place, blinking at his audience as if he wasn't sure what he was doing here.

But the audience, mostly of young engineers, seemed spellbound. She spotted Frank himself in the front row, a dark, hulking figure before the grounded astronaut, gazing raptly with the rest. That old space dust still carried some magic, she supposed; there was something primal here, about wanting to be close to the wizard, the sage who had been involved in that first wondrous discovery – as if, just by being close, it was possible to soak up a little of that marvellous light.

Malenfant went on, 'We'd come to believe, even before the Gaijin showed up, that life must be common. We believe nature is uniform, so the laws and processes that work here work everywhere else. And

28

now we hold to the Copernican principle: we believe that we aren't in any unique place in space or time. So if life is here, on Earth, it must be everywhere – in one form or another.

'So the fact that living things have come sailing into the asteroid belt from the stars (if they *are* living, that is) isn't much of a surprise. But what is a surprise is that they should be *just* arriving, here, now. If they exist, why weren't they here before?

'It is good scientific practice, when you're facing the unknown, to assume a condition of *equilibrium*: a stable state, not a state of change. Because change is unusual, special.

'Now, maybe you see the problem. What we seem to face with the Gaijin is the arrival – the very first arrival we can detect – of alien colonists in the solar system. And so we find ourselves – not in a time of equilibrium – but at a time of *transition*, in fact of possibly the most fundamental change of all. It's so unlikely it isn't true.

'To put it another way, this is the question that was avoided by all those terrible alien-invasion sci-fi movies I grew up with as a kid.' Laughter, a little baffled, from the younger guys. *What's a 'movie'?* 'Why should these bug-eyed guys arrive *now*, just when we have tanks and nukes to fight them with?'

Malenfant gazed around at his audience, his eyes deep-sunken, tired-looking, wary. 'I'm telling you this because you people are the ones who have taken up the challenge, where governments and others have shamefully failed, to get out there and figure out what's going on. There are obvious mysteries about the Gaijin – some of which might be resolved as soon as we get our first good look at them. But there are other, deeper questions which their very presence here poses, questions which go right to the heart of the nature of the universe itself, and our place in it. And right now, only *you* are doing anything which might help us tackle those questions.

'You have my support. Do your work well. Godspeed. Thank you.'

The applause began, politely at first.

It was a polished performance, Xenia supposed. She imagined this man thirty years ago giving pep talks at Space Shuttle component factories. *Do good work!*

But, to her surprise, the applause was continuing, even growing thunderous. And to her deeper surprise, she found herself joining in.

Xenia and Dorothy had some trouble reaching Frank Paulis and Malenfant, so walled off was the astronaut by a crowd of eager young engineer types.

Dorothy studied Xenia's expression. 'You don't quite go for all this hero worship, do you, Xenia?'

'Do you think I'm cynical?'

'No.'

Xenia grimaced. 'But it – frustrates me. We're living through first contact, an era unique in the human story, whatever the future holds. At least Bootstrap is trying to respond. Away from here, aside from what we're doing, all I see is irrationalism. That, and positioning. Various bodies trying to use this discovery for their own purposes.'

'Like the Church?'

'Well, isn't it?'

'We all must pursue our own goals, Xenia. At least the Church's involvement in this project of yours represents a tangible demonstration that we are working our way through the crisis of faith the Gaijin have caused us.'

'What crisis?'

'The Vatican began its first modern evaluation of the implication of extraterrestrial life for Christianity back in the '90s. But the debate has been going on much longer than that. We seem to have believed there were other minds out there long before we even had any clear notion of what *out there* actually was ... This intuition seems to be an expression of our deep embedding in the universe; if the cosmos created us, it could surely create others. Did you know that Saint Augustine, back in the sixth century, speculated about Eeties?'

'He did?'

'Augustine decided they couldn't exist. If they did, you see, they would require salvation – a Christ of their own. But that would remove the uniqueness of Christ, which is impossible. Such theological conundrums plague us to this day ... You can laugh if you like.'

Xenia shook her head. 'The idea that we might go out there and try to convert the Gaijin does seem a little odd.'

'But we don't know *why* they are here,' Dorothy pointed out. 'Would seeking truth be such an invalid reason?'

'And now you're here to bless the BDB,' Xenia said.

'Not exactly. Perhaps you've already done that, by naming it after Giordano Bruno. I take it you know who he was.'

'Of course.' The first thinker to have expressed something like the modern notion of a plurality of worlds – planets orbiting suns, many of them inhabited by beings more or less like humans. Earlier thinkers on other worlds had imagined parallel versions of a Dante's-*Inferno* pocket universe, centred on a stationary Earth. 'You have to imagine other worlds before you can conceive of travelling there.'

'But Bruno was anticipated,' Dorothy said gently. 'A cardinal we know as Nicolas of Cusa, who lived in the fifteenth century . . .'

Dorothy's lecturing tone seemed quite inappropriate to Xenia, making her impatient. 'Whatever his antecedents, Bruno was killed by the Church for his heresy.'

Dorothy said, 'He was burned, in 1600, for a mystical attack on Christianity, not for his argument about aliens, or even his defence of Copernicus.'

'That makes it okay?'

Dorothy continued to study her quietly.

At last the crowd of techic acolytes was breaking up.

'. . . You can't know how much I admire you, Colonel Malenfant,' Frank was saying. 'I'm twenty years younger than you. But I modelled myself on you.'

Malenfant eyed him dubiously. 'Then I'm in hell.'

'No, I mean it. You started a company called Bootstrap. You had plans to exploit the asteroids.'

'It failed. I was a lousy businessman. And when I lost my wife –'

'Sure, but you had the right idea. If not for that –'

Malenfant was looking longingly at the BDB mock-up. 'If not for that, if the universe was a different shape – yes; maybe *I'd* have done all this. And who knows what I'd have found?'

The silence stretched. Dorothy Chaum was frowning, Xenia noticed, as she studied Malenfant's cloudy, troubled expression.

Chapter 3

DEBATES

It was four more years before Malenfant encountered Frank J Paulis again.

In 2029, Malenfant was invited to the Smithsonian at Washington, DC as a guest at the annual meeting of the American Association of the Advancement of Science – or at least, a stream of it supported by the SETI Institute, a privately funded outfit based in Colorado and devoted to the study of the Gaijin, the search for extraterrestrial intelligence, and other good stuff.

Despite the subject matter of the conference, Malenfant had come here with some reluctance.

He had grown wary of appearing in public. As Paulis's robot probe swung relentlessly out from Earth, the unwelcome notoriety he had attracted nine years back was picking up again. He thought of it as the Buzz Aldrin syndrome: *But you were there* . . . When people looked at him, he thought, they saw a symbol, not a human being; they saw somebody who was incapable of doing original work ever again. It was a regard that was embarrassing, paralysing, and it made him feel very old. Not only that, Malenfant had found himself the target of unwelcome attention of the most extreme factions from either side of the spectrum, both the xenophobes and xenophiles.

But he had been invited here by Maura Della, a now-retired Congresswoman he'd encountered in the course of the unravelling of that initial discovery.

Maura Della was about Malenfant's age, small, neat and spry. She had served as part of the President's science advisory support at the time of the Gaijin announcement, when Malenfant and Nemoto had been dragged before the President himself, the Secretary of Defense, the Industrial Relations Council, and various Presidential task forces, as the Administration sought an official posture concerning the Gaijin. Unlike some of the Beltway apparatchiks Malenfant had encountered in those days, Della had proved to be tough but straightforward in her dealings with Malenfant, and he had grown to respect her sense of responsibility about SETI and other issues. It would be good to see her again.

And, he hoped, maybe she was still close enough to the centre of power to give him a genuine insight into anything *new*.

In that, as it turned out, he would not be disappointed.

At first, though, the conference – summing up what was known about the Gaijin, nine long years after discovery – proved to be meagre stuff. In the absence of new fact the proceedings were dominated by presentations on the impact of the Gaijin's existence on philosophical principles.

Thus, the first talk Maura Della escorted him to was on the brief and unrewarding history of SETI, the search for extraterrestrial intelligence.

Since the 1950s appropriately tuned radio telescopes had been turned on promising nearby stars, like Tau Ceti and Epsilon Eradini. Over the years the search was taken up by NASA and upgraded and automated, until it was possible to search thousands of likely radio frequencies at very high speed.

But decades of patient, longing search had turned up nothing but a few evanescent, tantalizing whispers of pattern.

As Malenfant listened to the stream of detail and acronyms, of project after project – Ozma, Cyclops, Phoenix – he became consumed with pity for these patient, hungry listeners, hoping to hear the faintest of whispers from beyond the stars. For, of course, it had always been futile, wrong-headed. *Equilibrium*, he thought: either the sky is silent because it is empty, or else the aliens should be everywhere. There should have been no need to seek out whispers; if we weren't alone, the sky should, metaphorically, have been blazing with light.

The next speaker impressed Malenfant rather more. She was a geologist from Caltech called Carole Lerner – no older than thirty, spiky, argumentative. She had tried to come up with a new answer to the conundrum of the arrival of the Gaijin. Maybe there had been no sign of the Gaijin before, said Lerner, because they had only recently evolved – and not among the stars, but where they had been found, in the asteroid belt itself.

There had been suggestions for some decades that life could get a foothold in comets – perhaps in pockets of liquid water, drenched with the organic compounds that laced cometary interiors – and, of course, some asteroids were believed to be burned-out comets, or at least to

33

have a comparable composition to comets. The coincidence of the emergence of a spacefaring alien race in the asteroids *now*, just as we reached a similar state, might be explained by a convergence of timescales. Perhaps it simply took this long, a few billion years, for life to crawl its way from the ponds to the stars, no matter where it originated.

It was a nice hypothesis, Malenfant reflected, but he judged that the coincidence of timescales was surely too neat to be convincing. Still, this was the first speaker Malenfant had heard at the conference who had attempted to address the deeper issues which obsessed the likes of Nemoto. He glanced at his softscreen, seeking presenters' bio details.

Lerner's general specialism was the volcanic history of the planet Venus. Malenfant wasn't surprised to learn she was having trouble finding funding to continue her work. One side-effect of the arrival of the Gaijin had been a decline of interest in the sciences. It seemed to be generally assumed that the Gaijin would eventually hand over the answers to any questions humans could possibly pose; so why spend time – and, more significantly, money – seeking out answers now? No genuine scientist Malenfant had ever met would have been satisfied with such passivity, of course; it seemed to him this Carole Lerner might be consumed with exactly that impatience.

The next paper, given by a heavy-set academic from the SETI Institute, turned out to have his own name in the title: 'The Nemoto–Malenfant Contact – An Example of How Not to Do It'.

Maura Della sat back to listen with an expression of intense enjoyment.

The presentation was based on a bureaucratic protocol devised to cover the event of alien contact. The protocol was first worked out by NASA in the 1990s, and then, after the cancellation of government funding for SETI and the NASA project's take-over by private institutions, developed further by the UN and national governments.

Malenfant – as one of only two people in all history to have been placed in the situation covered by the protocol – had never bothered to read it. He wasn't surprised to learn now that it was top-down, officious and almost comically foolish in its optimism that central control could be maintained:

'After concluding that the discovery appears to be credible evidence of extraterrestrial intelligence, and after informing other parties to this declaration, the discoverer should inform

34

observers throughout the world through the Central Bureau for Astronomical Telegrams of the International Astronomical Union, and should inform the Secretary General of the United Nations in accordance with Article XI of the Treaty on Principles Governing the Activities of States in the Exploration and Use of Outer Space, Including the Moon and Other Bodies. Because of their demonstrated interest in and expertise concerning the question of the existence of extraterrestrial intelligence, the discoverer should simultaneously inform the following international institutions of the discovery and should provide them with all pertinent data and recorded information concerning the evidence: the International Telecommunication Union, the Committee on Space Research, of the International Council of Scientific Unions, the International Astronautical Federation, the International Academy of Astronautics, the International Institute of Space Law, Commission 51 of the International Astronomical Union and Commission J of the International Radio Science Union . . .'

Malenfant and Nemoto, by comparison, had gone straight on the talk shows.

Playfully, Maura slapped Malenfant's wrist. 'Naughty, naughty. All those Commissions you skipped. You made a lot of enemies there.'

'But,' he said, 'I did get to sleep in the Lincoln Bedroom at the White House. You know, this guy makes it sound as if he'd rather we hadn't made the discovery at all, rather than making it the wrong way.'

'Human nature, Malenfant. You took away his toy.'

Now the speaker opened the floor for comments.

The discussion soon turned to how the situation should be managed from here. There were plenty of calls for behavioural scientists to study ways in which the public response to the news could be somehow anticipated and controlled, for research into popular public images of Eeties, discussion of analogies with the response to missions like Apollo to the Moon and Viking to Mars, and suggestions that SETI proponents should make use of media like webcasts, games and music to present SETI and Eetie themes 'responsibly'.

Maura pulled an elaborate face. 'Don't these people realize the cat is already out of the bag? You can't control the public's access to information any more – and you certainly can't control their response. Nor should you try, in my opinion.'

35

At last the speaker cleared off the stage, and Malenfant's spirits lifted a little. As an engineer, he knew that a bucket-load of philosophical principles wasn't worth a grain of good hard fact. And that was why the next item, by Frank Paulis, was a breath of fresh air. After all, it was Paulis, with his money and his initiative, who was actually going out there to look.

Paulis's images of his en-route spacecraft, the *Bruno*, showed a gangly, glittering dragonfly of solar-cell panels and gauzy antennae and sensors mounted on long booms, surrounded by a swarm of microsats devoted to fly-around inspections and repairs.

The launch had been uneventful, the first years of the long flight enlivened only by the usual hardware glitches and nail-biting techie dramas. It struck Malenfant as remarkable how little space technology seemed to have progressed in seventy years since the first Sputnik; the design of the *Bruno* would probably have been recognizable, give or take a few sapphire-based quantum chips, to Wernher von Braun. But flying in space had always been a conservative business; if you had only one shot, you wanted your ship to work, not to serve as the test bed for new gadgets and ideas.

Anyhow, the *Bruno* had survived its man-made crises. The ship was still a year away from its rendezvous with what appeared to be the primary construction site – or colony, or nest – of the Gaijin. The asteroid belt was a broad lane of rubble; already the probe had encountered a number of those dusty wanderers, never visited before or seen in close-up. But – Paulis promised, standing before slide after slide of coal-dark, anonymous rocks – the best was yet to come. For, in the darkness, the Gaijin awaited.

After a morning of such thin gruel, Malenfant retreated to his hotel room.

He travelled light these days: just bathroom stuff, a couple of self-cleaning suits and sets of underwear, a softscreen that was all he needed to connect him to the rest of the species – and a single ornament, a piece of unbelievably ancient rock from the far side of the Moon, carved into an exquisite fox god. He had become minimal. The time he spent on the Japanese Moon, he supposed, had changed him, no doubt for the better.

He spent a half hour watching heavily filtered and interpreted news on his softscreen. He needed to know what was going on, but he was too old to have any patience with the evanescent buzz of instant commentaries.

A corner of his softscreen rippled with light: an incoming message.

It was Nemoto. It was the first time she'd contacted Malenfant in years.

'Nemoto! Where are you?'

There was a delay of a few seconds before her reply came back, her face creasing into a thin smile. That could place her on the Moon. But the delay could be a fake . . .

'You should know better than to ask me that, Malenfant.'

'Yeah. Sorry.'

She was still under forty, but she wasn't ageing well, he thought. Her hair remained thick and jet black, but her oval face had shed its prettiness: grown angular, the bones showing, her eyes dark and sunken with suspicion. Her voice, from the softscreen's tiny speakers, was an insect whisper. 'You are enjoying the conference?'

'Not much.' He shared with her his gripe over too many philosophers.

'But there are worse fools. Here is some more philosophy for you. "This is the way I think the world will end – with general giggling by all the witty heads, who think it is a joke." Kierkegaard.'

'He got it right.' Whoever he was.

'And philosophy can sometimes guide us, Malenfant.'

'For instance –'

'For instance, the notion of equilibrium . . .'

It was like resuming a conversation they had pursued, on and off, for nine years; a slow teasing-out of the *koan*.

After their notoriety following the announcement of the aliens in the belt, Nemoto had recoiled completely. She'd refused all offers of public appearances, had quit her job, had turned down offers of research positions from a dozen of the world's most prestigious universities and corporations, and had effectively disappeared. All this while Malenfant had slogged around the public circuit with diminishing enthusiasm, enduring the brickbats and bouquets that came from his sliver of fame. She had been an Armstrong, he sometimes thought wryly, to his own Aldrin.

But she was continuing her researches – though what her purpose was, and where her money was coming from, he couldn't have said.

She didn't like the Gaijin, though. That much was obvious.

She said softly, 'We imagined only two possible equilibrium states: no aliens, or aliens everywhere. We have diagnosed this moment, the moment of first contact, as a transition between equilibriums, brief and therefore unlikely for us to be living through. But what if that's wrong? What if *this* is the true state of equilibrium?'

Malenfant frowned. 'I don't get it. Contact changes everything. How can a *change* be described as an equilibrium?'

'If it happens more than once. Over and over and over. In that case it's no coincidence that I happen to be alive, here and now, to witness this. It's no coincidence that we happen to have a technical culture capable of detecting the signals, even initiating contact, of a sort, just at this moment. *Because this isn't unique.*'

'You're saying this happened before? That others have been here? Then where did they go?'

'I can't think of any answers that don't scare me, Malenfant.'

He studied her. Her eyes were almost invisible, her face an expressionless mask. The background was dark, anonymous, no doubt scrambled beyond the reach of image enhancement routines.

He considered what to say. *You're spending too much time alone. You need to get out more.* But he was scarcely a friend to this strange, obsessive woman. 'You've spent a lot of time thinking about this, haven't you?'

She seemed offended. 'This is the destiny of the species.'

He sighed. 'What is it you called me about, Nemoto?'

'To warn you,' she said. 'It isn't quite true that we are waiting on Frank Paulis and his space probe for new data. There are two items of interest. First, a fresh interpretation. I've been able to deduce patterns from the infrared signature of the Gaijin's activity in the belt. I believe I have determined their pattern of propagation.'

Her face disappeared, to be replaced by the virtual display of the type she'd first shown him in the silence of the Moon. It was a ring of glistening crimson droplets, slowly orbiting: the asteroid belt, complete with dark Kirkwood gaps. And there was the gap with the one-to-three resonance with Jupiter, with its string of rubies, enigmatic, brilliant.

'Watch, Malenfant . . .'

Malenfant bent close to the screen and studied the little beads of light. The images cycled with small vector arrows, which showed velocity and acceleration. The rubies weren't in simple orbits about the sun, he saw; they seemed to be spreading around the belt, some of them actually moving retrograde, against the motion of the rest of the belt.

The motion was intriguing.

Nemoto said, 'Imagine the arrows projected backwards.'

'Ah,' Malenfant said. 'Yes. They might converge.'

Nemoto cut in a routine to extrapolate back from the Gaijin sites' velocity vectors. 'This is rough and ready,' she admitted. 'I had to make a lot of assumptions about how the objects' trajectories had deviated from simple orbits through the sun's gravitational field. But it did not take long before I found an answer.'

The projected paths arced out of the asteroid belt – out, away from the sun, into the deeper darkness, before converging.

Malenfant tapped the screen. 'You found it. The prime radiant. Where these probes, or factories, or whatever the hell they are, are emanating from.'

Nemoto said, 'It is one point four times ten to power fourteen metres from the sun. That is –'

'About a thousand astronomical units out.' A thousand times as far as Earth from the sun. 'Somewhere in the direction of Virgo . . . But why there?'

'I do not know. I need more data, more work.'

'And your second item?'

She eyed him. 'You are meeting Maura Della. Ask her about Rigil Kent.'

Rigil Kent. Also known as Alpha Centauri, nearest star system to the sun, four light years away

'Nemoto –'

But the softscreen had already filled up with the everyday froth of the online news channels; Nemoto had receded into darkness.

He was taken to lunch by former Congresswoman Della.

After lunch they strolled around the conference hall, glancing at poster presentations and the fringe sessions. Malenfant felt uncomfortable being out in public like this.

'I wouldn't be too concerned,' Maura said. 'Not here; you have to be afraid of the ones who stay at home polishing the telescope sights on their rifles.'

'Not funny, Maura.'

'Perhaps not. Sorry.'

She hadn't said a significant word during lunch; now he couldn't contain himself any more. 'Rigil Kent,' he said.

She slowed to a halt. Her voice low, she said, 'You spoiled my surprise. I should have known you'd find out.'

'What's going on, Maura?'

For answer she took him to a small, over-priced coffee bar. On a handheld softscreen she showed him images of the great radio telescope at Arecibo, various microwave satellites, activity in the Main Bay at

JPL: arcs of consoles, young, excited engineers on roller chairs, information flickering over screens before them.

'Malenfant, we've picked up a signal. From Alpha Centauri.'

'What – how –'

She pressed a finger to his lips.

As it turned out – though this bit of news had been Maura's true motive for inviting him here – there was little more to tell. Maura had gotten the news from her contacts in the government. The signal was faint, first picked up by an orbital microwave satellite. But it was nothing like the neatly structured Lincos signals humans had been sending to the asteroid belt. It was heavily compressed, a mush of apparently incoherent noise, with only evanescent hints of structure – much what Earth might have sounded like, from four light years away.

'Or it may be an efficient signal,' Malenfant said hoarsely. 'It can't be cheap to signal between the stars. You'd take out as much redundancy – repetitive structure – as possible. If you don't know how to decode it, such a signal must look like noise . . .' Either way the implication was clear. This wasn't a signal meant for humans.

But whoever was there, at Alpha Centauri, had only just started to broadcast – or rather, only four years in the past, given the time it took for signals to crawl to Earth.

In fact the signal's existence and nature were still being verified. '*This* time we're following the protocols, Malenfant . . .'

'Is it the Gaijin? Or somebody else?'

'We don't know.'

'Keep me informed.'

'Oh, yes,' she said. 'But keep it to yourself.'

Malenfant stayed in his hotel room the rest of the night, unable to relax, pacing back and forth until Nemoto called again.

He was furious Nemoto had known all about Centauri. But he controlled his irritation.

'At least,' he said, 'this discovery demolishes theories that the Gaijin might be native to our solar system. If they came from Centauri –'

'Of course they don't come from Centauri,' Nemoto said. 'Why would they suddenly start making such a radio clatter if that was so? No, Malenfant. They only just arrived in the Centauri system. Just as they only just arrived *here*. Apparently we are watching the vanguard of a wave of colonization, Malenfant, extending far from our system.'

'But –'

Nemoto waved a delicate hand before her face. 'But that isn't important, Malenfant. None of this is. Not even the activity in the asteroids.'

'Then what is?'

'I have determined the nature of the Gaijin's prime radiant, here in the solar system.'

'The nature? You said it is a thousand AU out. What's out there to have a nature at all?'

'A solar focus,' Nemoto said.

'The what?'

'That far out is where you will find the focal points of the sun's gravitational field. Images of remote stars, magnified by gravitational lensing. And the star that is focussed at the Gaijin prime radiant is –'

'Alpha Centauri?' The stubbly hairs on the back of his neck stood on end.

She said grimly, 'You see, Malenfant? Any number of probes to the belt won't answer the fundamental questions.'

'No.' Malenfant shook his head, mind racing. 'We've got to send somebody out there. Through a thousand AU; out to the solar focus . . . But that's impossible.'

'Nevertheless that is the challenge, Malenfant. *There* – at the solar focus – is where the answers will be found. *That* is where we must go.'

Chapter 4

ELLIS ISLAND

Maura was flying around an asteroid.

The asteroid – whimsically christened Ellis Island by the Bootstrap flight controllers at JPL – was three kilometres wide, twelve long. The compound body looked like two lumpy barbecue potatoes stuck end-to-end, dark and dusty. Maura could see extensions of the *Bruno*'s equipment ahead of her: elaborate claws and grapples, lines that coiled out across space to where rocket-driven pitons had already dug themselves into the asteroid's soft, friable surface.

With an effort she turned her head. Her viewpoint swivelled. The asteroid shifted out to the left; the image, heavily enhanced and extrapolated from the feed returned by *Bruno*, blurred slightly as the processors struggled to keep up with her wilfulness.

She was suspended in a darkness that was broken only by pinpoints of light. There were stars all around her: above, below, behind. Here she was in the middle of the asteroid belt, but there was not a single body, save for Ellis itself, large enough to show a disc. Even the sun had shrunk to a yellow dot, casting long shadows, and she knew that it shed on this lonely rock only a few per cent of the heat and light it vouchsafed Earth.

The asteroid belt had turned out to be surprisingly empty, a cold, excessively roomy place. And yet it was here the Gaijin had chosen to come.

Xenia Makarova, Bootstrap's VIP host for the day, whispered in her ear. 'Ms Della, are you enjoying the show?'

She suppressed a sigh. 'Yes, dear. Of course I am. Very impressive.'

And so it was. In her time as part of the President's science advisory team, she'd put in a lot of hours on spaceflight stunts like this, manned and unmanned. She had to admit that being able to share the experience vicariously – to be able to sit in her own apartment wearing her VR headband, and yet to ride down to the asteroid with the probe itself

42

– was a vast improvement on what had been on offer before: those cramped visitors' booths behind Mission Control at the Johnson Space Center, that noisy auditorium at JPL.

And yet she felt restless, here in the dark and cold. She longed to cut her VR link to the *Bruno* feed, to drink in the sunlight that washed over the Baltimore harbour area, visible from her apartment window just a metre away.

She said to Xenia, 'It's just that space operations are always so darn slow.'

'But we have to take it slow,' Xenia said. 'Encountering an asteroid is more like docking with another spacecraft than landing; the gravity here is so feeble the main challenge is not to bounce off and fly away.

'We're coming down at the asteroid's north pole. The main Gaijin site appears to be at the other rotation pole, the south pole. What we intend is to land out of sight of the Gaijin – assuming we haven't been spotted already – and work our way around the surface to the alien. That way we may be able to keep a measure of control over events . . .'

'This is a terribly dark and dusty place, isn't it?'

'That's because this is a C-type asteroid, Ms Della. Ice, volatiles and organic compounds: just the kind of rock we might have chosen to mine for ourselves, for life support, propellant.'

Yes, Maura thought with a flicker of dark anger. This is our belt, *our* asteroid. Our treasure, a legacy of the solar system's violent origins for our future. And yet there are Gaijin here – strangers, taking our birthright.

Her anger surprised her; she hadn't suspected she was so territorial. It's not as if they landed in Antarctica, she told herself. The asteroids aren't yet ours; we have no claim here, and therefore shouldn't feel threatened by the Gaijin's appropriation.

And yet I do.

The Alpha Centauri signal – though the first, picked up a year ago – was no longer unique. Whispers in the radio wavebands had been detected across the sky: from Barnard's Star, Wolf 359, Sirius, Luyten 726–8 – the nearby stars, the sun's close neighbours, the first destinations planned in a hundred interstellar-colonization studies, homes of civilizations dreamed of in a thousand science fiction novels.

One by one, the stars were coming out.

There were patterns to the distribution. No star further than around nine light years away had yet lit up with radio signals. But the signals weren't uniform. They weren't of the same type, or even on the same frequencies; such differences were just as confusing as the very existence

43

of the signals. And meanwhile the Gaijin, the solar system's new residents, remained quiet: they seemed to be producing no electromagnetic output but the infrared of their waste heat.

It was as if a wave of colonization had abruptly reached this part of the Galaxy, this remote corner of a ragged spiral arm, and diverse creatures – or machines – were busily digging in, building, perhaps breeding, perhaps dying. Nobody knew how the colonists had gotten here. Nobody could even guess why they had come *now*.

But it seemed to Maura that already one fact was clear about the presumed Galactic community: it was messy and diverse, just as much as the human communities of Earth, if not more. In a way, she supposed, that was even healthy. If communities separated by light years had turned out to be identical, it would be an oppressive sky indeed. But it was sure going to make figuring out the meaning of it all a lot more difficult.

And, for Maura, that was a matter to regret.

She was never short of work, of invitations like this. She knew that as part of the amorphous community of pols and workers who never really got the stink of the Beltway out of their nostrils, she was prized by corporations like Bootstrap as an opinion-former, perhaps a conduit to power. But she was, officially, retired. Perhaps she should sit back and stop thinking so hard, and just let the pretty light shows from the sky wash over her.

But that wasn't in her nature. And, after all, Reid Malenfant was older than she was, and she knew he continued to agitate for a deeper engagement with the mystery of these Gaijin, for more probes, other missions. If *he* was still active, then perhaps she should be.

But, in this complicated universe, she was too damn *old*. The more complicated it was, the more likely it was that she would never live to see this puzzle – perhaps the greatest mystery ever to confront humanity – unravelled.

Now a technical feed faded up in Maura's other ear. 'Closing with the target at two metres per second, range just under a klick, one metre per second cross-range. Hydrazine thruster tests in progress: +X, –X, +Y, –Y, +Z, –Z, all check out. Counting down to the thruster burn to null our approach and cross-range velocities a klick above the ground. Then we're on gyro-lock to touchdown . . .'

With an effort of will, Maura tuned out the irrelevant voices.

The asteroid became a wall that approached her in slow, dusty silence; the tether lines twisted before her, retaining their coils in the absence of gravity. She made out surface features, limned by sunlight:

44

craters, scarps, ridges, valleys, striations where it looked as if the aster-oid's surface had been crumpled or stretched. Some of the craters were evidently new, relatively anyhow, with neat bowl shapes and sharp rims. Others were much older, little more than circular scars overlaid by younger basins and worn down, presumably by a billion years of micrometeorite rain.

And there were colours on Ellis's folded-over landscape, spectral shades that emerged from the dominant grey-blackness. The sharper-edged craters and ridges seemed to be slightly bluish, while the older, low-lying areas were more subtly red. Perhaps this was some deep space weathering effect, she thought; perhaps aeons of sunlight had wrought these gentle hues.

She sighed. It really was lovely, in a quite unexpected way – like so much of the universe she found herself in. By God, I love it all, she thought. How can I retire? If I did, I would miss *this*.

And now, with a kiss of dust, the *Bruno* reached its destination.

The techs began cheering tinnily.

A year before the *Bruno*'s arrival – after the AAAS meeting – Malenfant had returned to the Johnson Space Center, for the first time in two decades.

The campus looked pretty much unchanged: the same blocky black and white buildings, with those big nursery-style numbers on their sides, scattered over square kilometres of grassy plain here at the south east suburban edge of Houston, all contained by a mesh fence from NASA Road One. (But it wasn't called the NASA Road any more.) In the surrounding streets there were still run-down strip malls and fast food places and Seven-Elevens.

But inside the campus itself, there was no sign of the tourists who used to ride between the buildings in their long tram trains. And though there were plenty of historic-marker plaques, nobody was making his-tory here any more.

The cherry trees were still here, though, and the green grass still seemed to glow.

He wasn't here to sight-see. He had come to meet Sally Brind, who ran a NASA department called the Solar System Exploration Division. He made his way to Building 31.

Inside, the air conditioning was ferocious, a hell of a contrast to the flat moist Houston heat outside. Malenfant welcomed the plummeting temperature; it was like old times.

*   *   *

45

Reid Malenfant had loomed over Sally Brind. He was leaning on her desk, resting his weight on big, bony knuckles. He was around twice Brind's age and he was a legend out of the past. And, to her, he was as intimidating as hell.

'We got to get out to the solar focus,' he began.

'Hello, good morning, nice to meet you, thanks for giving up your time,' she said dryly.

He backed off a little, and stood up straight. 'I'm sorry,' he said.

'Don't tell me. At your time of life, you don't have time to waste.'

'No, I'm just a rude asshole. Always was. Mind if I sit down?'

She said, 'Tell me about the solar focus.'

He moved a pile of glossies from a chair; they were digitized artist's impressions of a proposed, never-to-be-funded, unmanned mission to Io, Jupiter's moon. 'What I'm talking about, specifically, is a mission to the solar focus of Alpha Centauri – the nearest star system.'

'I know about Alpha Centauri.'

'Yes . . . The sun's gravitational field acts as a spherical lens, which magnifies the intensity of the light of a distant star. At the point of focus, out on the rim of the system, the gain can be hundreds of millions; at the right point, it would be possible to communicate across stellar distances with equipment no more powerful than you'd need to talk between planets. The Gaijin may be using the Centauri solar focus as a communication node. The theorists are calling it a Saddle Point. Actually there is a separate Saddle Point for each star. All roughly at the same radius, because of –'

'All right. And why do we need to go to Alpha Centauri's focus?'

'Because Alpha was the first source of extrasolar signals. And because the Gaijin are *there*. We have evidence that the Gaijin entered the system at the Alpha solar focus. From there, they sent a fleet of some kind of construction or mining craft into the asteroid belt. Sally, we now have infrared signatures, showing the activity in the asteroid belt, going back ten years.'

'There is an unmanned probe en route to the asteroid belt. Maybe we should wait for its results.'

Malenfant flared. 'A private initiative. Not relevant, anyhow. The solar focus – *that* is where the action is.'

'You don't actually have any direct evidence of anything out at the solar focus, do you?'

'No. Only what we've inferred from the asteroid belt data.'

'But there's no signature of any huge interstellar mother ship out there, at the rim. As there would have to be, if you're right.'

'I don't have all the answers. That's why we have to get out there and see. And to tell the damn Gaijin we're here.'

'I don't see how I can help you.'

'This is NASA's Solar System Exploration Division. Right? So, now we need to go do some exploring.'

'NASA doesn't exist any more,' she said. 'Not as you knew it, when you were flying Shuttle. The JSC is run by the Department of Agriculture –'

'Don't patronize me, kid.'

She sighed. 'I apologize. But I think you have to be realistic about this, sir. This isn't the 1960s. I'm really just a kind of curator, of the grey literature.'

'Grey?'

'Studies and proposals that generally never made it to the light of day. The stuff is badly archived; a lot of it isn't yet digitized, or even on fiche . . . Even this building is seventy years old. I bet it would be closed for good if it wasn't for the Moon rocks.'

That was true; elsewhere in this building, fifty per cent of the old Apollo samples still lay sealed in their sample boxes, still awaiting analysis, after six decades. Now that there were Japanese living on the Moon, Brind suspected the boxes would stay sealed forever, if only so they could serve as samples of the Moon as it used to be in its pristine, prehuman condition. An ironic fate for those billion-dollar nuggets.

'I know all that,' he said. 'But I used to work for NASA. Where else am I supposed to go? Look – I want you to figure out how it could be done. *How can we send a human to the solar focus?* It will all come together, once we have a viable scheme to fix on. I can get the hardware, the funding.'

She arched an eyebrow. 'Really?'

'Sure. And the science will be good. After all, we still haven't sent a human out beyond the orbit of the Moon. We can drop probes on Jupiter, Pluto en route. We'll get sponsorship from the Europeans and Japanese for that. The US government ought to contribute, too.'

You make it sound so easy, Colonel Malenfant . . . 'Why should these organizations back you? We haven't sent a human into orbit, other than as a passenger of NASDA or ESA, in twenty years.'

'Otherwise,' said Malenfant, 'we'll have to let the Japanese do this alone.'

'True.'

'Also there'll be a lot of media interest. It will be a hell of a stunt.'

'A stunt is right,' she said. 'It would be a spectacular one-shot. Just like Apollo. And look where that got us.'

'To the Moon,' he said severely, 'forty years before the Japanese.'

She chose her next words carefully. 'Colonel Malenfant, you must be aware that it will be difficult for me to support you.'

He eyed her. 'I know I'm thought of as an obsessive. Twenty years after Shuttle was grounded, I'm still working out a kind of long, lingering disappointment about the shape of my career. I want to pursue this Gaijin hypothesis because I'm obsessed with them, because I want America to get back into space. I have an agenda. Right?'

'I – yes. I guess so. I'm sorry.'

'Hell, don't be. It's true. I was never too good at the politics here. Not even in the Astronaut Office. I never got into any of the cliques: the spacewalkers, the sports fans, the commanders, the bubbas who hung out at Molly's Pub. I was never *interested* enough. Even the Russians mistrusted me because I wasn't enough of a team player.' He slapped his leathery hand on her desk. 'But the Gaijin are *here*. Sally, I've waited ten years for our government, *any* government, to act on that lunar infrared evidence. Only Frank Paulis responded – a private individual, with that one damn probe. Now, I've decided to do something about it, before I drop dead.'

'How far away is the solar focus?'

'A thousand astronomical units.' A thousand times as far as the distance between Earth and sun.

She whistled. 'You're crazy.'

'Sure.' He grinned, showing even, rebuilt teeth. 'Now tell me how to do it. Treat it as an exercise, if you like. A thought experiment.'

She said dryly, 'Do you have an astronaut in mind?'

His grin widened. 'Me.'

Dark, crumpled ground, a horizon that was pin-sharp and looked close enough to touch, a sky full of stars dominated by a single bright spark . . .

Maura felt herself lurch as the probe began to make its way across the folded-over asteroid earth. She saw pitons and tethers lance out ahead of her field of view, extruding and hauling back, tugging the robot this way and that. Her viewpoint swivelled up and down, and some augmentation routine in the virtual generators was tickling her hind brain, making her feel as if she was riding right along with the robot over this choppy, rocky sea. With a sub-vocalized command, she told the software to cut it out; some special effects she could live without.

Xenia whispered to her audience of VIPs. 'As we move we're being extremely cautious. The surface gravity is even weaker than you might expect for a body this size. Remember this "dumbbell asteroid" is a contact binary, a compound body; imagine two pool balls snuggled up against each other, spinning around their point of contact. We're a fly crawling over the far side of one of those pool balls. The dumbbell is spinning pretty rapidly, and here, at the pole, centrifugal force almost cancels out the gravity. But we modelled all these situations; *Bruno* knows what he's doing. Just sit tight and enjoy the ride.'

And now something was looming beyond that close horizon. It was like the rise of a moon – but this moon was small and dark and battered, a twin of the world over which she crawled. It was the other lobe of the dumbbell.

Xenia said, 'We're studying the ground as we travel. As we don't know what to look for, we've carried broad-spectrum surveying equipment. For instance, if the Gaijin came here to extract light metals such as aluminium, magnesium or titanium, they would most likely have used processes like magma electrolysis or pyrolysis. The same processes could be used for oxygen production. In the case of magma electrolysis the main slag component would be ferrosilicon. From a pyrolysis process we would expect to find traces of elemental iron and silicon, or perhaps slightly oxidized forms . . .'

We are crawling across a slag heap, Maura thought, trying to figure out what was made here. But are we being too anthropomorphic? Would a Neandertal conclude that *we* must be unintelligent because, searching our nuclear reactors, she could find no chippings from flint cores?

But what else can we do? How can we test for the unknowable?

The asteroid's second lobe had all but 'risen' above the horizon now. It was a ball of rock, black and battered, that hung suspended over the land, as if in some Magritte painting. She could even see a broad band of crushed, flattened rock ahead, where one flying mountain rested against the other.

The second lobe was so close it seemed Maura could see every fold in its surface, every crater, even the grains of dust there. How remarkable, she thought.

The probe's mode of travel had changed now, she noticed; the pitons were applying small sideways or braking tweaks to an accelerating motion towards the system's centre of gravity, that contact zone. Gravity must be decreasing in strength the tug of the rock below her balanced by the equal mass of rock above, so that the net force was becoming more and more horizontal, and the probe was simply pulled across the surface.

Now the second lobe was so close, in this virtual diorama, it was over her head. Its crumpled inverted landscape formed a rocky roof. It was dark here, with the sun occluded, and the slices of starlight in the gap between the worlds were growing narrower.

Lamps lit up on the probe, and they played on the land beneath, the folded roof above. She longed to reach up and touch those inverted craters, as if a toy Moon had been hung over her head, a souvenir from some Aristotelian pocket universe.

'. . . I think we have something,' Xenia said quietly.

Maura looked down. Her field of view blurred as the interpolation routines struggled to keep up.

There was something on the ground before her. It looked like a blanket of foil, aluminium or silver, ragged-edged, laid over the dark regolith. Aside from a fringe a metre or two wide, it appeared to be buried in the loose dirt. Its crumpled edges glinted in the low sunlight.

It was obviously artificial.

Brind had next met Malenfant a few months later, at Kennedy Space Center.

Malenfant found KSC depressing; most of the launch gantries had been demolished or turned into rusting museum pieces. But the visitors' centre was still open. The Shuttle exhibit – artefacts, photographs and virtuals – was contained within a small geodesic dome, yellowing with age.

And there, next to the dome, was *Columbia*, a genuine orbiter, the first to be flown in space. A handful of people were sheltering from the Florida sun in the shade of her wing; others were desultorily queuing on a ramp to get on board. *Columbia*'s main engines had been replaced by plastic mock-ups, and her landing gear was fixed in concrete. *Columbia* was forever trapped on Earth, he thought.

He found Brind standing before the astronaut memorial. This was a big slab of polished granite, with names of dead astronauts etched into it. It rotated to follow the sun, so that the names glowed bright against a backdrop of sky.

'At least it's sunny,' he said. 'Damn thing doesn't work when it's cloudy.'

'No.' The granite surface, towering over them, was mostly empty. The space program had shut down leaving plenty of room for more names.

Sally Brind was short, thin, intense, with spiky, prematurely grey hair; she was no older than forty. She affected small round black glasses, which looked like turn-of-the-century antiques. She seemed bright, alert, engaged. Interested, he thought, encouraged.

He smiled at her. 'You got any answers for me?'

She handed him a folder; he leafed through it.

'Actually it was a lot of fun, Malenfant.'

'I'll bet. Gave you something real to do.'

'For the first time in too long. First we looked at a continuous nuclear fusion drive. Specific impulse in the millions of seconds. But we can't sustain a fusion reaction for long enough. Not even the Japanese have managed that yet.'

'All right. What else?'

'Maybe photon propulsion. The speed of light – the ultimate exhaust velocity, right? But the power plant weight and energy you'd need to get a practical thrust are staggering. Next we thought about a Bussard ramjet. But it's beyond us. You're looking at an electromagnetic scoop that would have to be a hundred kilometres across –'

'Cut to the chase, Sally,' he said gently.

She paused for effect, like a kid doing a magic trick. Then she said: 'Nuclear pulse propulsion. We think that's the answer, Malenfant. A series of micro-explosions – fusion of deuterium and helium-3 probably – set off behind a pusher plate.'

He nodded. 'I've heard of this. Project Orion, back in the 1960s. Like putting a firecracker under a tin can.'

She shaded her eyes from the sun's glare. 'Well, they proved the concept, back then. The Air Force actually ran a couple of test flights, in 1959 and 1960, with conventional explosives. And it's got the great advantage that we could put it together quickly.'

'Let's do it.'

'Of course we'd need access to helium-3.'

'NASDA will supply that. I have some contacts . . . Maybe we should look at assembly in lunar orbit. How are you going to keep me alive?'

She smiled. 'The ISS is still up there. I figure we can cannibalize a module for you. Have you decided what you want to call your ship?'

'The *Commodore Perry*,' he said without hesitation.

'Uh huh. Who – ?'

'Perry was the guy who, in 1853, took the US Navy to Japan and demanded they open up to international trade. Appropriate given the nature of my mission, don't you think?'

'It's your ship.' She glanced about. 'Anyhow, what are you doing out here?'

He nodded at the Shuttle exhibit. 'They've got my old EMU in there, on display. I'm negotiating to get it back.'

'EMU?'

'My EVA Mobility Unit. My old pressure suit.' He patted his gut, which was trim. 'I figure I can still get inside it. I can't live with those modern Jap designs full of pond scum. And I want a manoeuvring unit . . .'

She was looking at him oddly, as if still unable to believe he was serious.

'Not ours,' whispered Xenia. 'Nothing to do with *Bruno*.'

Suddenly Maura found it difficult to breathe. This is it, she thought. This unprepossessing blanket: the first indubitably alien artefact, here in our solar system. Who put the blanket there? What was its purpose? Why was it so crudely buried?

A robot arm reached forward from the probe, laden with sensors and a sample-grabbing claw. She wished that was her hand, that she could reach out too, and stroke that shining, unfamiliar material.

But the claw was driven by science, not curiosity; it passed over the blanket itself and dug a shallow groove into the regolith that lay over it, sampling the material.

Within a few minutes the results of the probe's analysis were coming in, and she could hear the speculation begin in Bootstrap's back rooms.

'These are fines, and they are ilmenite-rich. About forty per cent, compared to twenty per cent in the raw regolith.' 'And the agglutinate has been crushed.' 'It's as if it has been beneficiated. It's just what we'd do.' 'Not like *this*. So energy-intensive . . .'

She understood some of this. Ilmenite was a mineral – a compound of iron, titanium, and oxygen – that was common in long-exposed regolith on airless bodies like the Moon and the asteroids. Its importance was that it was a key source of volatiles: light and exotic compounds implanted there over billions of years by the solar wind, the thin, endless stream of particles that fled from the sun. But ilmenite was difficult to concentrate, extract and process; the best mining techniques the lunar Japanese had thought up were energy-intensive and relied on a lot of heavy-duty, unreliable equipment.

'I knew it!' somebody cried. 'There's no helium-3 in the processed stuff! None at all!' 'None to the limits of the sensors, you mean.' 'Sure, but –' 'You mean they're processing the asteroids for helium-3? Is that *all*?'

Maura felt oddly disappointed. If the Gaijin were after helium-3, did that mean they used fusion processes similar to – perhaps no more advanced than – those already known to humans? And if so, they can't be so smart – can they?

In her ears, the speculation raged on.

'. . . I mean, how dumb can these guys be? Helium-3 is *scarce* in asteroid regolith because you're so far from the sun, which implants it. The Moon is a *lot* richer. If they came in a couple of astronomical units –' 'They could just buy all they want from the Japanese.'

Laughter.

'But maybe they can't come in any closer. Maybe they need, I don't know, the cold and the dark.' 'Maybe they are scared of *us*. You thought about that?'

'They aren't so dumb. You see any rock-crushers and solar furnaces here? That's what *we'd* have to use to get as efficient an extraction process. Think about that blanket, man. It *has* to be nanotech.'

She understood what that meant too: there was no brute force here, no great ugly machines for grinding and crushing and baking as humans might have deployed, nothing but a simple and subtle reworking of the regolith at a molecular, or even atomic, level.

'That blanket must be digging its way into the asteroid grain by grain, picking out the ilmenite and bleeding the helium-3. Incredible.' 'Hey, you're right. Maybe it's extending itself as it goes. The ragged edge –' 'It might eat its way right through that damn asteroid.' 'Or else wrap the whole thing up like a Thanksgiving turkey . . .' 'We got to get a sample.' '*Bruno* knows that . . .'

Nanotechnology: something, at last, beyond the human. Something *other*. She shivered.

But now there was something new, at the corner of her vision, something that shouldered its way over the horizon. It was glittering, very bright against the dark sky. Huge.

It was as if a second sun had risen above the grimy shoulder of Ellis. But this was no sun.

The prattling, remote voices fell silent.

It was perhaps a kilometre long, and wrought in silver. There was a bulky main section, a smoothly curved cylinder, with a mess of silvery ropes trailing behind. Dodecahedral forms – perhaps two or three metres across, silvered and anonymous – clung to the tentacles. There were hundreds of them, Maura saw. Thousands. Like insects, beetles.

53

A ship. Suddenly she remembered why they were here: not to inspect samples of regolith, not to pick at cute nanotechnological toys. They were here to make contact.

And this was it. She imagined history's view swivelling, legions of scholars in the halls of an unknown future inspecting this key moment in human destiny.

She found she had to force herself to take a breath.

The ship was immense, panning out of her view, cutting the sky in half. Its lower rim brushed the asteroid's surface, and plasma sparkled.

The Bootstrap voices in her ear buzzed. 'My God, it's beautiful.' 'It looks like a flower.' 'It must be a Bussard ramjet. That's an electromagnetic scoop –' 'It's so beautiful, a flower-ship . . .' 'Yeah. But you couldn't travel between the stars in a piece of junk like that!'

Now those shining beetles drifted away from the ropes. They skimmed across space towards the *Bruno*. Were these dodecahedra individual Gaijin? What was their intention?

Silver ropes descended like a net across her point of view now, tangling up the *Bruno*, until the view was criss-crossed with silver threads. The threads seemed to tauten. To cries of alarm from the insect voices at Bootstrap's mission control, the probe was hauled backwards, and its gentle grip on the asteroid was loosened, tethers and pitons flying free in a slow flurry of sparkling dust.

The brief glimpse of the Gaijin ship was lost. Stars and diamond-sharp sun wheeled, occluded by dust specks and silver ropes.

Maura felt her heart beat fast, as if she was herself in danger. She longed for the *Bruno* to burst free of its restraints and flee from these grasping Gaijin, running all the way back to Earth. But that was impossible. In fact, she knew, the *Bruno* was designed to be captured, even dissected; it contained cultural artefacts, samples of technology, attempts to communicate based on simple diagrams and prime number codes. *Hello. We are your new neighbours. Come over for a drink, let's get to know each other* . . .

But this did not feel like a welcoming embrace, a contact of equals. It felt like capture. Maura made a stern effort to sit still, not to struggle against silver ropes that were hundreds of millions of kilometres away.

Chapter 5

SADDLE POINT

The *Commodore Perry* was assembled in lunar orbit.

The fuel pellets were constructed at Edo, on the Moon, by Nishizaki Heavy Industries, and hauled up to orbit by a fleet of tugs. Major components like the pusher plate and the fuel magazine frame were manufactured on Earth, by Boeing. The components were lifted off Earth by European and Japanese boosters, Ariane 12s and H-VIIIs.

After decades in orbit the old International Space Station module had a scuffed, lived-in look. When the salvage crew had moved in the air had been foul and the walls covered with a scummy algae, and it had taken a lot of renovation to render it habitable again.

The various components of the *Perry* were plastered with sponsors' logos. That didn't matter a damn to Malenfant; he knew most of his paintwork would be scoured off in a few months anyhow. But he made sure that the Stars and Stripes was large, and visible.

Malenfant prepared himself for the trip.

In her cramped office at JSC, Brind challenged him, one last time. She felt, obscurely, that it was her duty.

'Malenfant, this is ridiculous. We know a lot more about the Gaijin now. We have the results returned by the probe –'

'The *Bruno*.'

'Yes. The glimpses of the beautiful flower-ship. Fascinating.'

'But that was two years ago,' Malenfant growled. 'Two years! The Gaijin still won't respond to our signals. And we aren't even going back. The government shut down Frank Paulis's operation after that one shot. National security, international protocols . . .'

She shrugged.

'Exactly,' he snapped. 'You shrug. People have lost interest. We've got the attention span of mayflies. Just because the Gaijin haven't come storming into the inner system in flying saucers –'

'Don't you think that's a good point? The Gaijin aren't doing us any harm. We're over the shock of learning that we aren't alone. What's the big deal? We can deal with them in the future, when we're ready. When *they* are ready.'

'No. Colonizing the solar system is going to take centuries, minimum. The Gaijin are playing a long game. And we have to get into the game before it's too late. Before we're cut out, forever.'

'What do you think their ultimate intentions are?'

'I don't know. Maybe they want to dismantle the rocky planets. Maybe take apart the sun. What would you do?'

Oddly, in her mundane, cluttered office, her security badge dangling at her neck, she found herself shivering.

The *Perry* looped through an elliptical two-hour orbit around the Moon. On the lunar surface, the lights of the spreading Japanese colonies and helium-3 mines glittered.

The completed ship was a stack of components fifty metres long. At its base was a massive, reinforced pusher plate, mounted on a shock-absorbing mechanism of springs and crushable aluminium posts. The main body of the craft was a cluster of fuel magazines. Big superconducting hoops encircled the whole stack.

Now pellets of helium-3 and deuterium were fired out of the back of the craft, behind the pusher plate. They formed a target the size of a full stop. A bank of carbon dioxide lasers fired converging beams at the target.

There was a fusion pulse, lasting two hundred and fifty nanoseconds. And then another, and another.

Three hundred micro-explosions each second hurled energy against the pusher plate. Slowly, ponderously, the craft was driven forward.

From Earth, the new Moon was made brilliant by fusion fire.

The acceleration of the craft was low, just a few per cent of G. But it was able to sustain that thrust for a long time – years, in fact – and once the *Perry* had escaped lunar orbit, its velocity mounted inexorably.

Within, Reid Malenfant settled down to the routines of long-duration spaceflight.

His hab module was a shoebox, big enough for him to stand up straight. He drenched it with light from metal halide lamps, hot white light like sunlight, to keep the blues away. The walls were racks which held recovery units, designed for easy replacement. There were wires and cables and ducts, running along the corners of the hab module and across the walls. A robot spider called Charlotte ran along the wires, cleaning and sucking dust out of the air. Despite his best efforts, the whole place was soon messy and cluttered, like an overused utility room. Gear was scattered everywhere, stuck to the floor and walls and ceiling with straps and Velcro. If he brushed against a wall he could cause an eruption of gear, of pens and softscreens and clipboards and data discs and equipment components, and food cans and toothpaste and socks.

Much of the key equipment was of Russian design – the recycling systems, for instance. He had big generators called Elektrons which could produce oxygen from water distilled from his urine. Drinking water was recovered from humidity in the air. There was a system of scrubbers called Vozdukh that removed carbon dioxide from the air. He had a backup oxygen generator system based on the use of 'candles', big cylinders containing a chemical called lithium perchlorate which, when heated, gave off oxygen. He had emergency oxygen masks that worked on the same principle. And so on.

It was all crude and clunky, but – unlike the fancier systems American engineers had developed for the Space Station – it had been proven, over decades, actually to work in space, and to be capable of being repaired when it broke down. Still, Malenfant had brought along two of most things, and an extensive tool kit.

Malenfant's first task, every day, was to swab down the walls of his hab module with disinfected wipes. In zero gravity micro-organisms tended to flourish, surviving on free-floating water droplets in the air. It took long, dull hours.

When he was done with his swabbing, it was exercise time. Malenfant pounded at a treadmill bolted to a bracket in the middle of the habitation module. After an hour Malenfant would find pools of sweat clinging to his chest. Malenfant had to put in at least two hours of hard physical exercise every day.

On it went. *Boring a hole in the sky,* the old astronauts had called it, the dogged cosmonauts on *Salyut* and *Mir*. *Looking at stars, pissing in jars.* To hell with that. At least he was going someplace, unlike those guys.

He communicated with his controllers on Earth and Moon using a ten-watt optical laser, which gave him a data rate of twenty kilobits a second. He followed the newscasts that were sent up to him, which he picked up with his big, semi-transparent main antenna.

As the months wore on, interest in his mission faded. Something else he'd expected. Nobody followed his progress but a few Gaijin obsessives – including Nemoto, he hoped, who had, deploying her shadowy, vast resources, helped assemble the funding for this one-shot mission – not that she ever made her interest known.

Sometimes, even during his routine comms passes, there was nobody to man the other end of the link.

He didn't care. After all they couldn't call him back, however bored they were.

While he worked his treadmill, his only distraction was a small round observation port, set in the pressure hull near him, and so he stared into that. To Malenfant's naked eye, the *Perry* was alone in space. Earth and Moon were reduced to star-like points of light. Only the diminishing sun still showed a disc.

The sense of isolation was extraordinary. Exhilarating.

He had a sleeping nook called a *kayutka*, a Russian word. It contained a sleeping bag strapped to the wall. When he slept he kept the *kayutka* curtained off, for an illusory sense of privacy and safety. He kept his most personal gear here, particularly a small animated image of Emma, a few seconds of her laughing on a private NASA beach close to the Cape.

He woke up to a smell of sweat, or sometimes antifreeze if the coolant pipes were leaking, or sometimes just mustiness – like a library, or a wine cellar.

Brind had tried another tack. 'You're seventy-two years old, Malenfant.'

'Yeah, but seventy-two isn't so exceptional nowadays. And I'm a damn fit seventy-two.'

'It's pretty old to be enduring a many-year spaceflight.'

'Maybe. But I've been following lifespan-extending practices for decades. I eat a low fat, low calorie diet. I'm being treated with a protein called co-enzyme Q10, which inhibits ageing at the cellular level. I'm taking other enzymes to maintain the functionality of my nervous system. I've already had many of my bones and joints rebuilt with biocomposite enhancements. Before the mission I'm going to have extensive heart bypass surgery. I'm taking drugs targeted at preventing the build-up of deposits of amyloid fibrils, proteins which could cause Alzheimer's –'

'Jesus, Malenfant. You're a kind of grey cyborg, aren't you? You're really determined.'

'Look, microgravity is actually a pretty forgiving environment for an old man.'

'Until you want to return to a full Earth gravity.'
'Well, maybe I don't.'

After two hundred and sixty days, half-way into the mission, the fusion-pulse engine shut down. The tiny acceleration faded, and Malenfant's residual sense of up and down disappeared. Oddly, he felt queasy; a new bout of space adaptation syndrome floored him for four hours.

Meanwhile, the *Perry* fired its nitrogen tet and hydrazine reaction control thrusters, and turned head over heels. It was time to begin the long deceleration to the solar focus.

The *Perry*, at peak velocity now, was travelling at around seven million metres per second. That amounted to two per cent of the speed of light. At such speeds, the big superconducting hoops came into their own. They set up a plasma shield forward of the craft, which sheltered it from the thin interstellar hydrogen it ran into. This turnaround manoeuvre was actually the most dangerous part of the trajectory, when the plasma field needed some smart handling to keep it facing ahead at all times.

The *Perry* was by far the fastest man-made object ever launched, and so – Malenfant figured, logically – he had become the fastest human. Not that anyone back home gave a damn.

That suited him. It clarified the mind.

Beyond the windows now there was only blackness, between Malenfant and the stars. At five hundred astronomical units from the sun, he was far beyond the last of the planets; even Pluto reached only some forty astronomical units. His only companions out here were the enigmatic ice moons of the Kuiper Belt, fragments of rock and ice left undisturbed since the birth of the sun, each of them surrounded by an emptiness wider than all the inner solar system. Further beyond lay the Oort cloud, the shadowy shell of deep space comets; but the Oort's inner border, at some thirty thousand astronomical units, was beyond even the reach of this attenuated mission.

When the turnaround manoeuvre was done, he turned his big telescopes and instrument platforms forward, looking ahead to the solar focus.

'You must want to come home. You must have family.'
'No.'
'And now –'
'Look, Sally, all we've done since finding the Gaijin is talk, for twelve years. Somebody ought to *do* something. Who better than me?

And so I'm going to the edge of the system, where I expect to encounter Gaijin.' He grinned. 'I figure I'll cross all subsequent bridges when I come to them.'

'Godspeed, Malenfant,' she said, chilled. She sensed she would never see him again.

The *Perry* slowed to a relative halt. From a thousand AU, the sun was an overbright star in the constellation Cetus, and the inner system – planets, humans, Gaijin and all – was just a puddle of light.

Malenfant, cooped up in his hab module, spent a week scanning his environment. He knew he was in the right area, roughly; the precision was uncertain. Of course, if some huge interstellar mother craft was out here, it should be hard to miss.

There wasn't a damn thing.

He went in search of Alpha Centauri's solar focus. He nudged the *Perry* forward, using his reaction thrusters and occasional fusion-pulse blips.

The focusing of gravitational lensing was surprisingly tight. Alpha Centauri's focal point spot was only a few kilometres across, in comparison with the hundred *billion* kilometres Malenfant had crossed to get here.

He took his time, shepherding his fuel.

At last he had it. In his big optical telescope there was an image of Alpha Centauri A, the largest component of the multiple Alpha system. The star's image was distorted into an annulus, a faintly orange ring of light.

He recorded as much data as he could and fired it down his laser link to Earth. The processors there would be able to deconvolve the image and turn it into an image of the multiple-star Alpha Centauri system, perhaps even of any planets hugging the two main stars.

This data alone, he thought, ought to justify the mission to its sponsors.

But he still didn't turn up any evidence of Gaijin activity.

A new fear started to gnaw at him. For the first time he considered seriously the possibility that he might be wrong about this. What if there was nothing here, after all? If so, his life, his reputation, would be wasted.

And then his big supercooled infrared sensors picked up a powerful new signature.

The object passed within a million kilometres of him.

His telescopes returned images, tantalizingly blurred. The thing was tumbling, sending back glimmering reflections from the remote sun; the reflections helped the processors figure out its shape.

The craft was maybe fifty metres across. It was shaped something like a spider. A dodecahedral central unit sprouted arms, eight or ten of them, which articulated as it moved. It seemed to be assembling itself as it travelled.

It wasn't possible to identify its purpose, or composition, or propulsion method, before it passed out of sight. But, he was prepared to bet, it was heading for the asteroid belt.

It was possible to work out where the drone had come from. It was a point along the sun's focal line, further out, no more distant from the *Perry* than the Moon from Earth.

Malenfant turned his telescopes that way, but he couldn't see a thing.

Still, he felt affirmed. Contact, by damn. I was right. I can't figure out how or what, but there sure is something out here.

He powered up his fusion-pulse engine, one more time. It would take him twenty hours to get there.

It was just a hoop, some kind of metal perhaps, facing the sun. It was around thirty metres across, and it was sky blue, the colour dazzling out here in the void. It was silent, not transmitting on any frequency, barely visible at all in the light of the point-source sun.

There was no huge mother-ship emitting asteroid-factory drones. Just this enigmatic artefact.

He described all this to Sally Brind, back in Houston. He would have to wait for a reply; he was six light-days from home.

After a time, he decided he didn't want to wait that long.

The *Perry* drifted beside the Gaijin hoop, with only occasional station-keeping bursts of its thrusters.

Malenfant shut himself up inside the *Perry*'s cramped airlock. He'd have to spend two hours in here, purging the nitrogen from his body. His antique Shuttle-class EVA Mobility Unit would contain oxygen only, at just a quarter of sea level pressure, to keep it flexible.

Malenfant pulled on his thermal underwear, and then his Cooling and Ventilation Garment, a corrugated layering of water coolant pipes. He fitted his urine collection device, a huge, unlikely condom.

He lifted up his Lower Torso Assembly; this was the bottom half of his EMU, trousers with boots built on, and he squirmed into it. He fitted a tube over his condom attachment; there was a bag sewn into his Lower Torso Assembly garment big enough to store a couple of pints of urine. The LTA unit was heavy, the layered material awkward and stiff. Maybe I'm not quite the same shape as I used to be, forty years ago.

Now it was time for the HUT, the Hard Upper Torso piece. His HUT was fixed to the wall of the airlock, like the top half of a suit of armour. He crouched underneath, reached up his arms, and wriggled upwards. Inside the HUT there was a smell of plastic and metal. He guided the metal rings at his waist to mate and click together. He fixed on his Snoopy flight helmet, and over the top of that he lifted his hard helmet with its visor, and twisted it into place against the seal at his neck.

The ritual of suit assembly was familiar, comforting. As if he was in control of the situation.

He studied himself in the mirror. The EMU was gleaming white, with the Stars and Stripes still proudly emblazoned on his sleeve. He still had his final mission patch stitched to the fabric, for STS-194. Looking pretty good for an old bastard, Malenfant.

Just before he depressurized, he tucked his snap of Emma into an inside pocket.

He opened the airlock's outer hatch.

For twenty months he'd been confined within a chamber a few metres across; now his world opened out to infinity.

He didn't want to look up, down or around, and certainly not at the Gaijin artefact. Not yet.

Resolutely he turned to face the *Perry*. The paintwork and finishing over the hull's powder-grey meteorite blanket had pretty much worn away and yellowed; but the dim sunlight made it look as if the whole craft had been dipped in gold.

His MMU, the Manned Manoeuvring Unit, was stowed in a service station against the *Perry*'s outer hull, under a layer of meteorite fabric. He uncovered the MMU and backed into it; it was like fitting himself into the back and arms of a chair. Latches clasped his pressure suit. He powered up the control systems, and checked the nitrogen-filled fuel tanks in the backpack. He pulled his two hand controllers round to their flight positions, and released the service station's captive latches.

He tried out the manoeuvring unit. The left hand controller pushed him forward, gently; the right hand enabled him to rotate, dip and roll. Every time a thruster fired a gentle tone sounded in his headset.

He moved in short straight lines around the *Perry*. After years in a glass case at KSC, not all of the pack's reaction control thrusters were working. But there seemed to be enough left for him to control his flight. And the automatic gyro stabilization was locked in.

It was just like working around Shuttle, if he focused on his immediate environment. But the light was odd. He missed the huge, comforting presence of the Earth; from low Earth orbit, the daylit planet was a constant overwhelming presence, as bright as a tropical sky. Here there was only the sun, a remote point source that cast long, sharp shadows; and all around he could see the stars, the immensity which surrounded him.

Now, suddenly – and for the first time in the whole damn mission – fear flooded him. Adrenaline pumped into his system, making him feel fluttery as a bird, and his poor old heart started to pound.

Time to get with it, Malenfant.

Resolutely, he worked his right hand controller, and he turned to face the Gaijin artefact.

The artefact was a blank circle, mysterious, framing only stars. He could see nothing that he hadn't seen through the *Perry*'s cameras, truthfully; it was just a ring of some shining blue material, its faces polished and barely visible in the wan light of the sun.

But that interior looked jet black, not reflecting a single photon cast by his helmet lamp.

He glared into the disc of darkness. What are you for? Why are you here?

There was, of course, no reply.

First things first. Let's do a little science here.

He pulsed his thrusters and drifted towards the hoop itself. It was electric blue, glowing as if from within, a wafer-thin band the width of his palm. He could see no seams, no granularity.

He reached out a gloved hand, fabric encasing monkey fingers, and tried to touch the hoop. Something invisible made his hand slide away, sideways.

No matter how hard he pushed, how he braced himself with the thrusters, he could get his glove no closer than a millimetre or so from the material. And always that insidious, soapy feeling of being pushed sideways.

He tried running his hand up and down, along the hoop. There were – ripples, invisible but tangible.

He drifted back to the centre of the hoop. That sheet of silent darkness faced him, challenging. He cast a shadow on the structure from the distant pinpoint sun. But where the light struck the hoop's dark interior, it returned nothing: not a highlight, not a speckle of reflection.

Malenfant rummaged in a sleeve pocket with stiff gloved fingers. He held up his hand to see what he had retrieved. It was his Swiss Army knife. He threw the knife, underarm, into the hoop.

The knife sailed away in a straight line.

When it reached the black sheet it dimmed, and it seemed to Malenfant that it became reddish, as if illuminated by a light that was burning out.

The knife disappeared.

Awkwardly, pulsing his thrusters, he worked his way around the artefact. The MMU was designed to move him in a straight line, not a tight curve; it took some time.

On the far side of the artefact, there was no sign of the knife.

A gateway, then. A gateway, here at the rim of the solar system. How appropriate, he thought. How iconic.

Time to make a leap of faith, Malenfant. He fired his RCS, and began to glide forward.

The gate grew, in his vision, until it was all around him. He was going to pass through it – if he kept going – somewhere near the centre.

He looked back at the *Perry*. Its huge, misty main antenna was pointed back towards Earth, catching the light of the sun like spider-web. He could see instrument pallets held away from the hab module's yellowed, cloth-clad bulk, like rear-view mirrors. The pallets were arrays of lenses, their black gazes uniformly fixed on him.

Just one press of his controller and he could stop right here, go back.

He reached the centre of the disc. An electric blue light bathed him. He leaned forward inside his stiff HUT unit, so he could look up.

The artefact had come to life. The electric blue light was glowing from the substance of the circle itself. He could see speckles in the light. Coherent, then. And when he looked down at his suit, he saw how the white fabric was criss-crossed by the passage of dozens of points of electric blue glow.

Lasers. Was he being scanned?

He said, 'This changes everything.'

The blue light increased in intensity, until it blinded him. There was a single instant of pain –

Chapter 6

TRANSMISSION

'We think a Gaijin flower-ship is a variant of the old Bussard ramjet design,' Sally Brind said. She had spread a fold-up softscreen over one time-smoothed wall of Nemoto's lunar cave. Now – Maura squinted to see – the 'screen filled up with antique design concepts: line images of gauzy, unlikely craft, obsessively labelled with captions and arrows. 'It is a notion that goes back to the 1960s . . .'

Nemoto's home – here on the Japanese Moon, deep in Farside – had turned out to be a crude, outmoded subsurface shack close to the infrared observatory where she'd made her first discovery of Gaijin activity in the belt. Here, it seemed, Nemoto had lived for the best part of two decades. Maura thought *she* couldn't stand it for more than a couple of hours.

There wasn't even anywhere to sit, aside from Nemoto's low pallet, Maura had immediately noticed, and both Sally and Maura had carefully avoided *that*. Fortunately the Moon's low gravity made the bare rock floor relatively forgiving, even for the thin flesh that now stretched over Maura's fragile bones. There were some concessions to humanity – an ancient and worn scrap of *tatami,* a *tokonoma* alcove containing a *jinja,* a small, lightweight Shinto shrine. But most of the floor and wall space, even here in Nemoto's living area, was taken up with science equipment: anonymous white boxes that might have been power sources or sensors or sample boxes, cables draped over the floor, a couple of small, old-fashioned softscreens.

As Sally spoke, Nemoto – thin, gaunt, eyes invisible within dark hollows – pottered about her own projects. Walking with tiny, cautious steps, she minutely adjusted her equipment – or, bizarrely, watered the small plants that flourished on brackets on the walls, bathed by light from bright halide lamps.

Still, the languid flow of the water from Nemoto's can – great fat droplets oscillating as they descended towards the tiny green leaves – was oddly soothing.

Sally continued her analysis of the Gaijin's putative technology. 'The ramjet was always seen as one way to meet the challenge of interstellar journeys. The enormous distances even to the nearest stars would require an immense amount of fuel. With a ramjet, you don't need to carry any fuel at all.

'Space, you see, isn't empty. Even between the stars there are tenuous clouds of gas, mostly hydrogen. Bussard, the concept originator, proposed drawing in this gas, concentrating it, and pushing it into a fusion reaction – just as hydrogen is burned into helium at the heart of the sun.

'The trouble is, those gas clouds are *so* thin your inlet scoop has to be gigantic. So Bussard suggested using magnetic fields to pull in gas from an immense volume, hundreds of thousands of kilometres around.'

She brought up another picture: an imaginary starship startlingly like a marine creature – a squid, perhaps, Maura thought – a cylindrical body with giant outreaching magnetic arms, preceded by darting shafts of light.

'The interstellar gas would first have to be electrically charged, to be deflected by the magnetic scoops. So you would pepper it with laser beams, as you see here, to heat it to a plasma, as hot as the surface of the sun. It's an exotic, difficult concept, but it's still easier than hauling along all your fuel.'

'Except,' Nemoto murmured, labouring at her gadgets, 'that it could never work.'

'Correct . . .'

Maura had been privy to similar breakdowns and extrapolations emanating from the Department of Defense and the US Air & Space Force, and – given that Sally's summary was based on no more than piecework by various space buff special-interest groups and NASA refugees in various corners of the Department of Agriculture – Maura thought it hung together pretty well.

The problem with Bussard's design was that only a hundredth of all that incoming gas could actually be used as fuel. The rest would pile up before the accelerating craft, clogging its magnetic intakes; Bussard's beautiful ship would expend so much energy pushing through this logjam it could never achieve the kind of speeds essential for interstellar flight.

Sally presented various developments of the basic proposal to get around this fundamental limitation. The most promising was called RAIR – pronounced 'rare' – for Ram-Augmented Interstellar Rocket. Here, the intake of interstellar hydrogen would be greatly reduced, and used only to top up a store of hydrogen fuel the starship was already carrying. It was thought that the RAIR design could perform two or three times better than the Bussard system, and achieve perhaps ten or twenty per cent of the speed of light.

'And, as far as we can tell from the *Bruno* data,' said Sally, 'that Gaijin flower-ship was pretty much a RAIR design: exotic-looking, but nothing we can't comprehend. *Bruno* actually passed through what seemed to be a stream of exhaust, before it ceased to broadcast.' A nice euphemism, thought Maura, for *trapped and dismantled*. 'The exhaust was typical of products of a straightforward deuterium–helium-3 fusion reaction, of the type we've been able to achieve on Earth for some decades.'

Sally hesitated. She was a small woman, neat, earnest, troubled. 'There are puzzles here. *We* can think of a dozen ways the Gaijin design could be improved – nothing that's in our engineering grasp right now, but certainly nothing that's beyond our physics. For instance the deuterium–helium fusion reaction is about as low-energy and clunky as you can get. There are *much* more productive alternatives, like reactions involving boron or lithium. I think I always imagined that when Eetie finally showed up, she would have technology beyond our wildest dreams – beyond our imagining. Well, the flower-ships are pretty, but they aren't the way *we'd* choose to travel to the stars –'

'Especially not in this region,' Nemoto said evenly.

Maura said, 'What do you mean?'

Nemoto smiled thinly, the bones of her face showing through papery skin. 'Now that we are, like it or not, part of an interstellar community, it pays to understand the geography of our new terrain. The interstellar medium, the gases that would power a ramjet, is not uniform. The sun happens not to be in a very, umm, cloudy corner of the Orion Spiral Arm. We are moving, in fact, through what is called the ICM – the intercloud medium. Not a good resource for a ramjet. But of course the flower-ships are not interstellar craft.' She eyed Maura. 'You seem surprised. Isn't that obvious? These ships, with their small fraction of lightspeed, would take many decades even to reach Alpha Centauri.'

Maura said, 'But time dilation – clocks slowing down as you speed up –'

Nemoto shook her head. 'Ten per cent of lightspeed is much too slow for such effects to become significant. The flower-ships are inter-planetary cruisers, designed for travel at speeds well below that of light, within the relatively dense medium close to a star. The Gaijin are interplanetary voyagers; only accidentally did they become interstellar pioneers.'

'Then,' asked Maura reasonably, 'how did they get here?'

Nemoto smiled. 'The same way Malenfant has departed the system.'

'Just tell me.'

'Teleportation.'

Maura had brought Sally Brind here because she'd grown frustrated, even worried, by the passage of a full year since Malenfant's disappearance: a year in which nothing had happened.

Nothing obvious had changed about the Gaijin's behaviour. The whole thing had long vanished from the mental maps of most of the public and commentators, who had dismissed Malenfant's remarkable jaunt as just another odd subplot in a slow, rather dull saga that already spanned decades. The philosophers continued to debate and agonize over the meaning of the reality of the Gaijin for human existence. The military were, as always, wargaming their way through various lurid scenarios, mostly involving the Gaijin invasion of Earth and Moon, huge armed flower-ships hurling lumps of asteroid rock at the helpless worlds.

Meanwhile, the various governments and other responsible authorities were consumed by indecision.

Truthfully, the facts were still too sparse, questions still proliferating faster than answers were being obtained, mankind's image of these alien intruders still informed more by old fictional images than any hard science. The picture was not converging, Maura realized with dismay, and history was drifting away from meaningful engagement with the Gaijin.

Which was why she had set up this meeting. Nemoto had, after all, been the first to detect the Gaijin – she had quickly understood the implications of her discovery – and she had immediately selected the one person, Reid Malenfant, who had, in retrospect, been best placed to help articulate her discovery to the world, and even to do something about it.

If anybody could help Maura think through the jungle of possibilities of the future, it was surely Nemoto.

But still – teleportation?

*   *   *

68

Maura closed her eyes. So I have to imagine these Gaijin e-mailing themselves from star to star. She suppressed a foolish laugh.

Nemoto continued to tinker with her apparatus, her plants.

Sally Brind said slowly, 'Let's be clear. You think the hoop Malenfant found was some kind of teleportation node. Then why not locate this – gateway – in the asteroid belt? Why place it all the way out on the rim of the system, with all the trouble and effort that causes? . . .'

Nemoto kept her counsel, letting the younger woman think it through.

Sally snapped her fingers. 'But if you teleport from another star you must basically fire a stream of complex information by conventional signal channels – that is, light or radio waves – at the solar system, the target. And the place to pick that up with greatest fidelity is the star's solar focus, where the signal gain is in the hundreds of millions . . . But Malenfant can't have known this. He can't have deduced the mechanism of teleportation.'

'But his intuition is strong,' Nemoto said, smiling. 'He recognized a gateway, and he stepped through it. Contact had been his purpose, after all.'

'I thought,' Maura said doggedly, 'teleportation was impossible. Because you'd need to map the position and velocity of every particle making up the artefact you want to transmit. And that violates the Uncertainty Principle.' The notion that, because of quantum fuzziness, it was impossible to map precisely the position and momentum of a particle. And if you couldn't make such a map, how could you encode, transmit and reconstruct such a complex object as a human being?

'If you did it so crudely as that, yes,' Nemoto said. 'In a quantum universe, no such classical process could possibly work. Even in principle we know only one way to do this, to teleport. An unknown quantum state can be disassembled into, then later reconstructed from, purely classical information and purely non-classical correlations . . .'

Maura said tightly, 'Nemoto, please.'

'*This* is a teleport machine,' Nemoto said, waving her hand at her strung-out junk. 'Sadly I can only teleport one photon, one grain of light, at a time. For the moment.'

'Sally, do you understand any of this?'

'I think so,' Sally said. 'Look, quantum mechanics allows for the long-range correlation of particles. Once two objects have been in contact, they're never truly separated. There is a kind of spooky entanglement, called EPR correlation.'

'EPR?'

'For Einstein–Podolsky–Rosen, the physicists who came up with the notion.'

'I do not transport the photon,' Nemoto said. 'I transmit a *description* of the photon. The quantum description.' She tapped two boxes. 'Transmitter and receiver. These contain a store of EPR-correlated states – that is, they were once in contact, and so are forever entangled, as Sally puts it.

'I allow my photon to, umm, interact with ancillary particles in the receiver. The photon is absorbed, its description destroyed. But the information I extract about the interaction can then be transmitted over to the receiver. There I can use the other half of my entangled pair to reconstruct the original quantum state.'

Sally said, still figuring it out, 'The receiver has to be entangled with the transmitter. What the builders must have done is send over the receiver gate – the hoop Malenfant found – by some conventional means, a slower-than-light craft like a flower-ship. The gate is EPR-correlated with another object back home, a transmitter. The transmitter makes a joint measurement on itself and the unknown quantum system of the object to be teleported. The transmitter then sends the receiver gate the classical result of the measurement. Knowing this, the receiver can convert the state of its EPR twin into an exact replica of the unknown quantum state at the transmitter . . .'

'So now you have two photons,' Maura said slowly to Nemoto. 'The original and the version you've reconstructed.'

'No,' said Nemoto, with strained patience. 'I explained this. The original photon is destroyed when it yields up its information.'

Sally said, 'Maura, quantum information isn't like classical information, the stuff you're used to. Quantum information can be transformed, but not duplicated.' She studied Maura, seeking understanding. 'But, even if we're right about the principle here, there is a lot here that is far beyond us. Think about it. Nemoto can teleport a single photon; the Gaijin gateway can teleport something with the mass of a human being. Malenfant's body contained –'

'Some ten to power twenty-eight atoms,' Nemoto said. 'That is ten billion billion *billion*. And therefore it must take the same number of kilobytes, to order of magnitude, to store the data. If not more.'

'Yes,' Sally said. 'By comparison, Maura, all the books ever written probably amount to a mere thousand billion kilobytes. The data compression involved must be spectacular. If we could get hold of that technology alone, our computing and telecoms industries would be transformed.'

'And there is more,' Nemoto said. 'Malenfant's body was effectively destroyed. That would require the extraction and storage of an energy equivalent of some one thousand megaton bombs . . .'

His body was destroyed. Nemoto said it so casually.

'So,' Sally said slowly, 'the signal that encodes Malenfant is currently being transmitted between a transmitter-receiver link –'

'Or links,' said Nemoto.

'Links?'

'Do you imagine that such a technology would be limited to a single route?'

Sally frowned. 'You're talking about a whole network of gateways.'

'Perhaps placed in the gravitational foci of every star system. Yes.'

And now, all at once, Maura saw it: a teleport network spanning the huge gaps between the stars, grand data highways along which one could travel – and without being aware even of the passing of time. 'My God,' she murmured. 'The roads of empire.'

'And so,' Sally said, working her way through Nemoto's thinking, 'the Gaijin built the gateways. Right?'

'Oh, no,' said Nemoto gently. 'The Gaijin are much too – *primitive*. They were limited to their system, as we are to ours. In their crude ramjet flower-ships, exploring the rim of the system, they stumbled on a gateway – or perhaps they were guided to look there by others, as we have been by the Gaijin in turn.'

Maura said, 'If not the Gaijin, then who?'

'For now, that is unknowable.' Nemoto gazed at her clumsy apparatus, as if studying the possibilities it implied.

Sally Brind got to her feet and moved slowly around the cramped apartment, drifting dreamily in the low lunar gravity. 'It takes years for a signal, even a teleport signal, to travel between the stars. This must mean that nobody out there has developed faster-than-light technology. No warp drives, no wormholes. Kind of low tech, don't you think?'

Nemoto said, 'In such a Galaxy, processes – cultural contacts, conflicts – will take decades, at least, to unfold. If Malenfant is heading to a star, it will take years for his signal to get there, more years before we could ever know what became of him.'

'And so,' Maura said dryly, 'what must we do in the meantime?'

Nemoto smiled, her cheekbones sharp. 'Why, nothing. Only wait. And try not to die.'

*　　*　　*

71

In the silent years that followed, Maura Della often thought of Malenfant.

Where *was* Malenfant?

Even if Nemoto was right, with his body destroyed – as the detailed information about the contents and processes of his body and brain shot towards the stars – *where was his soul*? Did it ride the putative Gaijin laser beam with him? Was it already dispersed?

And would the thing that would be reconstructed from that signal actually *be* Malenfant, or just some subtle copy?

Still, in all this obscure physics there was a distinct human triumph. Malenfant had found this mysterious gateway. And passed through. She remembered the resentment she had felt while watching the Gaijin's calm appropriation of solar system resources in the asteroid belt, their easy taking of the *Bruno*. Now Malenfant had fired himself back through the transport system the Gaijin themselves had used, back to the nest of the Gaijin, and Maura felt a stab of savage satisfaction.

Hey, Gaijin. You have mail . . .

But these issues weren't for Maura.

She had done her best to use Nemoto's insights and other inputs to rouse minds, to shape policy. But the time had come for her to retire, to drive out of the Beltway at last. She went home, to a small town called Blue Lake, in northern Iowa, her old state, the heart of the Midwest.

Her influence was ended. Too damn old.

I don't have decades left; I don't have the strength to stay alive, waiting, like Nemoto, while the universe ponderously unfolds; for me, the story ends here. You'll just have to get along by yourself, Malenfant.

Godspeed, Godspeed.

Chapter 7

RECEPTION

The blue light faded.

He realized he'd been holding his breath. He let it out, gasping; his chest ached. He was grasping the MMU hand controllers compulsively. He flexed his hands; the gloves were stiff.

The blue artefact was all around him, inert once more. He couldn't see any difference; the sun's light glimmered from its polished surface, casting double shadows –

Double?

He looked up, to the sun, and flipped up his gold visor.

The sun seemed a little brighter, a strong yellow-white. And it was a double pinprick now, two jewels on a setting of velvet. The light was actually so bright it hurt his eyes, and when he looked away there were tiny double spots on his retina, bright yellow against red mist.

It wasn't the sun, of course. It was a binary star system. There was a misty lens-shaped disc around the twin stars: a cloud of planetary material, asteroids, comets – a complex inner system, illuminated by double starlight. Even from here, just from that smudge of diffuse light, he could see this was a busy, crowded place.

He worked his controller and swivelled. Beyond the gate, the *Perry* was gone.

No. Not gone. Just parked a few light years away, is all.

He had no idea how the artefact had worked its simple miracle. Nor, frankly, did he care. It was a gateway – and it had worked, and taken him to the stars.

Yes, but where the hell, Malenfant?

He looked around the sky. The stars were a rich carpet, overwhelming the familiar constellations.

After some searching he found Orion's belt, and the rest of that great constellation. The hunter looked unchanged, as far as he could see. Orion's stars were scattered through a volume of space a thousand

73

light years deep, and the nearest of them – Betelgeuse, or maybe Bellatrix, he couldn't recall – was no closer than five hundred light years from the sun.

That told him something. If you moved across interstellar distances your viewpoint would shift so much that the constellation patterns would distort, the lamps scattered through the sky swimming past each other like the lights of an approaching harbour. He couldn't have come far, then, not on the scale of the distances to Orion's giant suns: a handful of light years, no more.

And, given that, he knew where he was. There was only one system like this – two Sol-like stars, bound close together – in the sun's immediate neighbourhood. This was indeed Alpha Centauri, no more remote from Sol than a mere four light years plus change. Just as he had expected.

Alpha Centauri: the dream of centuries, the first port of call beyond Pluto's realm – a name that had resonated through a hundred starship studies, a thousand dreams. And here he was, by God. He felt his mouth stretch wide in a grin of triumph.

He blipped his thrusters and swivelled, searching the sky until he found another constellation, a neat, unmistakable W-shape picked out by five bright stars. It was Cassiopeia, familiar from his boyhood astronomy jags. But now there was an extra star to the left of the pattern, turning the constellation into a crude zigzag. He knew what that new star must be, too.

Suspended in immensity, here at the rim of the Alpha Centauri system, Malenfant looked back at the sun.

The sun is a star – just a star. Giordano Bruno was right after all, he thought.

But if it took light four years to get here, it had surely taken him at least as long, however the portal worked. *Suddenly I am four years into the future. And, even if I was to step home now – assuming that was possible – it would be another four years before I could feel the heat of the sun again.*

How strange, he thought, and he felt subtly cold.

Movement, just ahead of him. He rotated again.

It was a spider robot, like a scaled-down copy of the one he had seen on the other side of the portal. There was a puff of what looked like reaction control engines, little sprays of crystals that glittered in the remote double light. *Crude technology,* he thought, making assessments automatically. It was heading towards the gate, its limbs writhing stiffly.

It seemed to spot him.

It stopped dead, in another flurry of crystals, a good distance away, perhaps a kilometre. But distances in space were notoriously hard to estimate, and he had no true idea of the robot's size.

Those articulated limbs were still writhing. Its form was complex, shifting – obviously functional, adaptable to a range of tasks in zero gravity. But overall he saw that the limbs picked out something like a W shape, like the Cassiopeia constellation, centred on a dodecahedral core. He had no idea what it was doing. Perhaps it was studying him. He could barely see it, actually; the device was just an outline in Alpha Centauri light.

Malenfant calculated.

He hadn't expected a reception committee. This was just a workaday gateway, a portal for unmanned robot worker drones. Maybe the Gaijin themselves were off in the warmth of that complex, crowded inner system.

He reckoned he had around five hours life support left. If he went back – assuming the portal was two-way – he might even make it back to the *Perry*.

Or he could stay here.

It would be one hell of a message to send on first contact, though, when the inhabitants of the Centauri system came out to see what was going on, and found nothing but his desiccated corpse.

But you've come a long way for this, Malenfant. And if you stay, dead or alive, they'll sure know we are here.

He grinned. Whatever happened, he had achieved his goal. Not a bad deal for an old bastard.

He worked his left hand controller; with a gentle shove, the MMU thrust him forward, towards the drone.

He took his time. He had five hours to reach the drone. And he needed to keep some fuel for manoeuvring at the close, if he was still conscious to do it.

But the drone kept working its complex limbs, pursuing its incomprehensible tasks. It made no effort to come out to meet him.

And, as it turned out, his consumables ran out a lot more quickly than he had anticipated.

By the time he reached the drone, his oxygen alarm was chiming, softly, continually, inside his helmet. He stayed conscious long enough to reach out a gloved hand, and stroke the drone's metallic hide.

When he woke again, it was as if from a deep and dreamless sleep.

The first thing he was aware of was an arm laid over his face. It was his own, of course. It must have wriggled free of the loose restraints around his sleeping bag.

Except that his hand was contained in a heavy spacesuit glove, which was not the way he was accustomed to sleeping.

And his sleeping bag was light years away.

He snapped fully awake. He was floating in golden light. He was rotating, slowly.

He was still in his EMU – but, Christ, his helmet was gone, the suit compromised. For a couple of seconds he fumbled, flailing, and his heart hammered.

He forced himself to relax. You're still breathing, Malenfant. Wherever you are, there is air here. If it's going to poison you, it would have done it already.

He exhaled, then took a deep lungful – filtered through his nose, with his mouth clamped closed. The air was neutral temperature, transparent. He could smell nothing but a faint sourness, and that probably emanated from himself, the cramped confines of a suit he'd worn for too long.

He was stranded in golden light, beyond which he could make out the stars, slightly dimmed, as if by smoke. There was the dazzling-bright pairing of Alpha Centauri. He hadn't come far, then.

Were there walls around him? He could see no edges, no seams, no corners. He stretched out his feet and gloved fingers. His questing fingers hit a soft membrane. Suddenly the wall snapped into focus, just centimetres from his face: a smooth surface, overlaid by what felt like cables the width of his thumb, but welded somehow to the wall. The cables were a little hard to grip, but he clamped his fingers around them.

Anchored, he felt a lot more comfortable.

The wall itself was soft, neither warm nor cold, smooth beyond the discrimination of his touch. It curved tightly around him. Perhaps he was in some kind of inflated bubble; it could be no more than a few metres across. And it wasn't inflated to maximum tension. When he pushed at the wall it rippled in great languid waves, pulses of golden light that briefly occluded the stars.

He picked at the membrane with one fingernail. It felt like some kind of plastic. He had no reason to believe it was anything more advanced; the Gaijin had not shown themselves to be technological super-beings. He could have easily taken a scraping of this stuff, analysed it with a small portable lab. Except he didn't have a portable lab.

Something bumped against his leg. 'Shit,' he said. He whirled, scrabbling at the embedded ropes, until he was backed up against the wall.

It was the helmet from his Shuttle EMU.

He picked it up and turned it over in his gloved hands. The helmet had a snap-on metal ring, to fit it to the rest of the suit – or rather, it used to. The attachment had been cut, as if by a laser.

The Gaijin – or their robot drones, here on the edge of the Alpha system – had found him in a shell of gases: air that roughly matched what they must have known, from some equivalent of spectrograph studies, of the composition of Earth's atmosphere. So they had provided more of the gases in this containment, and broken open his suit – and then, presumably, hoped for the best.

He took off his gloves. He found he was still wearing his lightweight comms headset. He pulled it off and tucked it inside the helmet. There was no sign of his manoeuvring unit.

. . . And now a kind of after-shock cut in. He rested against the slowly rippling wall, lit up by gold-filtered Centauri light, four light years from home. The robots had been smart, he realized with a shiver. After all the robots, if not the Gaijin themselves, shared nothing like human anatomy. What if they'd decided to see if his whole head was detachable? He felt very old, fragile, and unexpectedly lonely – as he hadn't during the long months of his *Perry* flight to the Saddle Point.

What now?

First things first. You need a bio break, Malenfant.

He forced himself to take a leak into the condom he still wore. He felt the warm piss gather in the sac inside his suit. Piss that had been magically transported across four light years. He probably ought to bottle it; if he ever got back home he could probably sell it, a memento of man's first journey to the stars.

There was movement, a wash of light beyond the bubble wall. Something immense, bright, cruising by silently.

He swivelled, still pinching hold of the embedded ropes, until he faced outwards. He pressed his face against the bubble wall, much as he used to as a kid, staring out of his bedroom window, hoping for snow.

The moving light was a flower-ship.

The Gaijin craft sailed across the darkness, heading for the warm glow at the heart of the Centauri system. The cables and filaments that shaped the maw of its electromagnetic scoops were half-furled, and they waved with slow grace as the ship slowly swivelled on its long

77

axis, perhaps intent on some complex course correction. Dodecahedral shapes swarmed over its flanks, reduced by distance to toy-like specks, fast-moving, intent, purposeful. They almost looked as if they were rebuilding the ship as it travelled – as perhaps they were; Malenfant imagined a flexible geometry, a ship that could adjust its form to the competing needs of the cold stillness here at the rim of this binary system, and the crowded warmth at its heart.

But still, despite its strangeness, he felt a tug at his heart as the flower-ship receded. Don't leave me here, drifting in space.

But he wasn't adrift, he saw now. There were ropes embedded in the outer surface of his shell, ropes which gathered in a loosely plaited tether, as if this bubble of air had been trapped by spider-web. The tether, loosely coiled, led across space – not to the flower-ship – but to something hidden by the curve of the bubble.

He pushed himself across the interior of the bubble to look out the other side.

In the dim light of the distant Alpha suns, he made out only an outline: a rough ball that must have been kilometres across, the glimmer of what looked like frost from crater dimples and low mountains.

From one spacesuit pocket he dug out a fold-up softscreen, unpacked it and plastered it against the wall of the bubble. This 'screen had been designed as a low-light and telescopic viewer. Soon its enhancement routines were cutting in, and it became a window through which he peered, angling his head to change his view.

The object seemed to be a ball of ice. It might have been an asteroid, but he was a long way from those double suns. This was more likely the Alpha equivalent of a Kuiper object, an ice moon – or maybe he was even in this system's Oort cloud, and this was the head of some long-period comet.

And now he made out movement on that icy surface: continual, complex, almost rippling. He tapped at the softscreen, instructing it to magnify and enhance some more.

He saw drone robots, swarming everywhere, their complex limbs working like cockroach legs. The drones moved back and forth in files and streams, endless traffic. Here and there in the flow there were islands of stillness, nodes where the swirl gathered in knots and eddies. And in a few places he saw the gleam of silvery blankets, perhaps like the nano-blankets Frank Paulis's probe had found on that belt asteroid back home. Maybe they were making more flower-ships. Or perhaps these were von Neumann machines, he thought, replicators engaged primarily on making more copies of themselves, and they would continue until every gram of this remote ball of ice and rock had been converted into purposeful machinery.

But everywhere he looked, as he scanned his 'screen, he could see endless, purposeful movement – perhaps millions of drones, the toiling community making up a glinting, robotic sea. His overwhelming impression was of cooperation, of blind, unquestioning, smoothly efficient obedience to a higher communal goal. These robots had more in common with hive insects, he thought, ants or termites, than with humans.

. . . But perhaps I should have expected this, he thought. Humans were competitive. But there was no reason to suppose that everybody else had to be that way. Maybe a competitive technological community could only reach a certain point before it became unstable and destroyed itself. Arms races could only take you so far. Perhaps only the cooperative could survive. In which case, he thought, what we are going to find as we move further out is, inevitably, more of *this*. Termite colonies. And, perhaps, nobody like us.

Damn, he thought. I might be the only true individual in this whole star system. What a bleak and terrifying notion.

But if the robots were replicators they weren't very good ones.

They all seemed to be based on the design of the type he had first met, with that chunky dodecahedral body, limbs sprouting in a variety of configurations, apparently specialized. But otherwise these toiling drones appeared somewhat diverse. The differences weren't great: a few extra limbs here, a touch of asymmetry there, each dodecahedron slightly diverging from the geometric ideal – but they were there.

Perhaps the authentic von Neumann vision – of identical replicators spawning each other – was impossible without true nanotech, a command of materials and manufacturing right down to the atomic level. He imagined a fleet of these limited, imperfect robots being unleashed on the Galaxy, ordered to travel from star to star, to build others of their kind . . . and, with each generation, getting it subtly wrong.

But for there to be such a wide variety of 'mutations' as he saw here, there surely had to have been an awful lot of generations.

Or, he thought, what if these *are* the Gaijin?

He had been assuming that behind these 'mere' machines there had to be something bigger, something smarter, something more complex. Lack of imagination, Malenfant. Anthropomorphic. Deal with what you see, not what you imagine might be waiting for you.

He tired of watching the incomprehensible swarming of the robots, and he turned his enhancement softscreen on Alpha Centauri.

Each of the near-twins looked hauntingly like the sun – but if the brighter star, Alpha A, were set in place of the sun, its companion, Alpha B, would be within the solar system: closer than planet Neptune, in fact.

And there were planets here. The interpretative software built into his softscreen began to trace out orbits – one, two, three of them, tight around bright Alpha A – of small rocky worlds, perhaps twins of Earth or Venus or Mars. A couple of minutes later, similar orbits had been sketched out around the companion, B.

Alpha Centauri wasn't just a twin star; it was a twin solar system. If Earth had been transplanted here the second sun would be a brilliant star. There would be double sunrises, double sunsets, strange eclipses of one star by the other; the sky would be a bright and complex place. And there would have been a whole other planetary system a few light-hours away: so close humans would have been able to complete interstellar journeys maybe as early as the 1970s. He felt an odd ache of possibilities lost, nostalgia for a reality that had never come to be.

The double system contained only one gas giant – and that was small compared to mighty Jupiter, or even Saturn. It was looping, it seemed, on a strange metastable orbit that caused it to fly, on decades-long trajectories, back and forth between the two stars. And as the stars followed their own elliptical orbits around each other, it seemed highly likely that within a few million years the rogue planet would be flung out into the dark, from whence, perhaps, it had come.

If there were few giants, the Alpha sky was full of minor planets, asteroids, comet nuclei. Unlike the orderly lanes of Earth, these asteroid clouds extended right across the space between the stars, and into the surrounding volume. As the 'screen's software began to plot density contours within the glittering asteroid clouds, Malenfant made out knots and bands and figure-of-eight loops, even what looked like spokes radiating from each star's central system: clouds of density marked out by the sweeping paths of flocks of asteroids, shepherded by the competing pulls of the stars and their retinues of planets. From an Earth orbiting Alpha A or B, there would be a line across the sky, marking out the plane of the ecliptic: dazzling, alluring, the sparkle of trillions of asteroids, the promise of unimaginable wealth.

The pattern seemed clear. The mutual influence of A and B had prevented the formation of giant planets. All the volatile material that had been absorbed into Sol's great gas giants had here been left uncon-solidated. Malenfant, who had spent half his life arguing for the mining of space resources, felt his fingers itch as he looked at those immense

clouds of floating treasures. Here it would have been easy, he thought
with some bitterness.

But this was not a place for humanity, and perhaps it never would
be. For now the software posted tiny blue flags, all around the rim of
the system. These were points of gravitational-lensing focus, Saddle
Points, far more of them than in Sol's simple unipolar gravity field.
And there was movement within those dusty lanes of light: bright
yellow sparks, Gaijin flower-ships, everywhere.

The solar system is impoverished by comparison, he thought. *This*
is where the action is in this part of space: Alpha Centauri, riddled
with so many Saddle Points it's like Grand Central Station, and with
a sky full of flying mines to boot. He felt humbled, embarrassed, like
a country cousin come to the big city.

There was a blur of motion, washing across his magnified vision.

He rocked back, peering out of his bubble with naked eyes.

It was a robot, skittering this way and that on its attitude thrusters,
crystals of reaction gas sparkling in Alpha light. It came to rest and
hovered, limbs splayed, no more than ten metres from the bubble.

Malenfant pushed himself to the wall nearest the robot, pressed his
face against the membrane, and stared back.

Its attitude suggested watchfulness. But he was probably anthropomorphizing again.

That dodecahedral core, fat and compact, must have been a couple
of metres across. It glistened with panels of complex texture, and
there were apertures in the silvery skin within which more machinery
gleamed, unrecognizable. The robot had various appendages. A whole
forest of them no more than centimetres long bristled from every surface of the core, wiry, almost like a layer of fur. But two of the limbs
were longer – ten metres each, perhaps – and articulated like the robot
arms carried by the old Space Shuttle, each ending in a knot of machinery. He noticed small attitude thruster nozzles spread along the arms.
The whole thing reminded him of one of the old space probes – Voyager, perhaps, or Pioneer – that dense solid core, the flimsy booms, a
spacecraft built like a dragonfly.

The robot showed signs of wear and age: crumpled panels on the
dodecahedral core; an antenna-like protrusion that was pitted and
scarred, as if by micrometeorite rain; one arm that appeared to have
been broken and patched by a sheath of newer material. This is an
old machine, he thought, and it might have been travelling a long,
long time; he wondered how many suns had baked its fragile skin,

how many dusty comet trails clouds had worn away at those filmy structures.

Right now the two arms were held upwards, as if in an air of supplication, giving the robot an overall W-shape – like the first robot he'd seen.

Could this be the same machine I met when I came through the hoop? Or, he wondered, am I anthropomorphizing again, longing for individuality where none exists? After all, this thing could never be mistaken for something alive – could it? If nothing else its lack of symmetry – one arm was a good two metres longer than the others – was, on some profound level, deeply disturbing.

He gave in to his sentimentality.

'Cassiopeia,' he said. 'That's what I'll call you.'

Female, Malenfant? But the thing did have a certain delicacy and grace. Cassiopeia, then. He raised a hand and waved.

He half-expected a wave back from those complex robot arms, but they did not move.

. . . But now there was a change. An object that looked for all the world like a telephoto lens came pushing out of an aperture in the front of Cassiopeia's dodecahedral torso, and trained on him.

He wondered if Cassiopeia had just manufactured the system, in response to its – her – perceived need, in some nano factory in her interior. More likely the technology was simpler, and this 'camera' had been assembled from a stock of parts carried within. Maybe Cassiopeia was like a Swiss Army knife, he thought: not infinitely flexible, but with a stock of tools that could be deployed and adapted to a variety of purposes.

And then, once again, he was startled – this time by a noise from within his bubble.

It was a radio screech. It had come from the comms headset tucked inside his helmet.

He grabbed the helmet, pulled out the headset and held one speaker against his ear. The screech was so loud it was painful, and, though he thought he detected traces of structure in the signal, there was nothing resembling human speech.

He glanced out at the robot, Cassiopeia, still patiently holding her station alongside his membrane.

She's trying to communicate, he thought. After years of ignoring the radio and other signals we beamed at her colleagues in the asteroid belt, she's decided I'm interesting enough to talk to.

He grinned. Objective achieved, Malenfant. You made them notice us, at least.

. . . Yes, but right now it wasn't doing him much good. The signal he was being sent might contain whole libraries of interstellar wisdom. But he couldn't decode it; not without banks of supercomputers.

They still have no real idea what they're dealing with here, he thought, how limited I am. Maybe I'm fortunate they didn't try hitting me with signal lasers.

If we're going to talk, it will have to be in English. Maybe they can figure that out; we've been bombarding them with dictionaries and encyclopaedias for long enough. And it will have to be slow enough for me to understand.

He dug in a pocket on the leg of his suit until he found a thick block of paper and a propelling pencil.

Another moment of contact, then: the first words exchanged between human being and alien. Words that would presumably be remembered, if anybody ever found out about this, long after Shakespeare was forgotten.

What should he say? Poetry? A territorial challenge? A speech of welcome?

At last, he grunted, licked the pencil lead, and wrote out two words in blocky capitals. Then he pressed the pad up against the clear membrane.
THANK YOU

With its – her – telescopic eye, Cassiopeia peered at the paper block for long minutes.

From her angular body Cassiopeia extruded a new pseudopod. It carried a small metal block the size and shape of his note pad.

The block bore a message. In English. The text was in a neat, unadorned font.

COMMUNICATION DYSFUNCTION. REPAIRS MANDATED. REPAIRS PERFORMED. DECISION CONSTRAINED.

He frowned, trying to figure out the meaning. *We don't understand. Why are you thanking us? You would have died. We had no choice but to help you.*

He thought, then wrote out: IT SHOWED GOODWILL BETWEEN OUR SPECIES. Not the right word, that *species*; but he couldn't think of anything better. MAYBE WE WILL UNDERSTAND EACH OTHER IN THE FUTURE. MAYBE WE WILL LIVE IN PEACE.

The reply: DECISION CONSTRAINED BUT NOT SINGLE-VALUED. INFORMATION REQUIRED CONCERNING OBJECTIVE: REPLICATION; RESOURCE APPROPRIATION; ACTIVITY PROHIBITION; EXOTIC. WHICH.

We didn't have to keep you alive, asshole. We didn't know what the hell you were doing here, and we needed to find out. Maybe you wanted to make lots of little Malenfants from Centauri asteroids. Maybe you wanted to take away our resources for some other purposes. Maybe you wanted to stop us doing what we're doing. Or maybe something else we can't even guess. What are you doing here?

Take care with your answer, Malenfant. Most of those options, from a Gaijin point of view, aren't too healthy; you mustn't let them think you're some kind of von Neumann rapacious terminator robot yourself, or they'll slit open this air sac, and then your belly.

I'M HERE OUT OF CURIOSITY.

A pause. COMMUNICATION DYSFUNCTION.

What??

He wrote, WHERE DID YOU COME FROM? WHO MADE YOU? ARE THEY NEARBY?

Another, longer pause. SEVERAL THOUSAND ITERATIONS SINCE INITIALIZATION. *We are thousands of generations removed from those who began the migration.*

Then these *are* the Gaijin, he thought. They don't know who made them. They've forgotten. Or maybe *nobody* made them. After all, you believe *you* evolved, Malenfant; why not them?

He wrote out, WHAT IS YOUR PURPOSE HERE?

REPLICATION. CONSTRUCTION. SEARCH.

So they did come here from somewhere else . . . and that last word, finally, gave him hope he was dealing with something more than a fixed machine here, more than simple mechanical goals.

SEARCH, he wrote. SEARCH FOR WHAT?

The answer chilled him. SEARCH OBJECT: OPTION TO AVOID COMING STERILIZATION EVENT. EXISTENCE OF OPTION QUERY.

My God, he thought. We always thought the aliens would come and teach us. Wrong. These guys are coming to *us* for answers.

Answers to whatever it is they are fleeing. The 'sterilization event'.

For long minutes he gazed at Cassiopeia's crumpled, complex hide. Then he wrote carefully, WE MUST TALK. BUT I NEED FOOD.

OPTION: RETURN BEFORE EXPIRATION. *We can take you home before you die.*

WHAT ELSE?

OPTION: MANUFACTURE FOOD. ITERATIVE PROCESS, SUCCESS ANTICIPATED.

Reassuring, he thought dryly.

COROLLARY: CONTINUE.

He wrote, CONTINUE? YOU MEAN I CAN GO ON?

OPTION: ORIGIN NODE. OPTION: OTHER NODES. *We can take you home. Or we can take you further. Other places. Even further than this.*

Even deeper in time, too. My God.

He thought about it for sixty seconds.

I WANT TO GO ON, he said. MAKE ME FOOD.

Then he added, PLEASE.

Maura Della died eight years after Malenfant's disappearance into the Gaijin portal, a few months before a signal at lightspeed could have completed the journey to Alpha Centauri and back.

But when those months had passed – when the new signals arrived, bearing news from Alpha Centauri – the great asteroid belt flower-ships at last opened up their electromagnetic wings, and a thousand of them began to sail in towards the crowded heart of the solar system, and Earth.

II

TRAVELLERS

AD 2061–2186

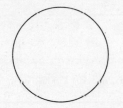

He told himself: All this – the neutron star sail, the toiling community – is a triumph of life over blind cosmic cruelty. We ain't taking it any more.

But when he thought of Cassiopeia, anger flooded him. Why?

It had been just minutes since she had embraced him on that grassy simulated plain . . . hadn't it?

How do you *know*, Malenfant? How do you know you haven't been frozen in some deep data store for ten thousand years?

And . . . how do you know this isn't the first time you surfaced like this?

How *could* he know? If his identity assembled, disintegrated again, what trace would it leave on his memory? What *was* his memory? What if he was simply restarted each time, wiped clean like a reinitialized computer? How would he *know*?

But it didn't matter. I did this to myself, he thought. I wanted to be here. I laboured to get myself here. Because of what we learned, as the years unravelled. That the Gaijin would be followed by a great wave of visitors. And that the Gaijin were *not even the first* – just as Nemoto had intuited from the start. And nothing we learned about those earlier visitors, and what had become of them, gave us comfort.

Slowly, as they began to travel the stars, humans learned to fear the universe, and the creatures who lived in it. Lived and died.

Chapter 8

AMBASSADORS

Madeleine Meacher barely got out of N'Djamena alive.

Nigerian and Cameroon troops were pushing into the airstrip just as the Sänger's undercarriage trolley jets kicked in. She heard the distant crackle of automatic fire, saw vehicles converging on the runway. Somewhere behind her was a clatter, distant and small; it sounded as if a stray round had hit the Sänger.

Then the spaceplane threw itself down the runway, pressing her back into her seat, its leap forward sudden, gazelle-like. The Sänger tipped up on its trolley, and the big RB545 engines kicked in, burning liquid hydrogen. The plane rose almost vertically. The gunfire rattle faded immediately.

She shot into cloud and was through in a second, emerging into bright, clear sunshine.

She glanced down: the land was already lost, remote, a curving dome of dull desert-brown, punctuated with the sprawling grey of urban development. Fighters – probably Nigerian, or maybe Israeli – were little points of silver light in the huge sky around her, with contrails looping through the air. They couldn't get close to Madeleine unless she was seriously unlucky.

She lit up the scramjets, and was kicked in the back, hard, and the fighters disappeared.

The sky faded down to a deep purple. The turbulence smoothed out as she went supersonic. At thirty thousand metres, still climbing, she pushed the RB545 throttle to maximum thrust. Her acceleration was a Mach a minute; on this sub-orbital hop to Senegal she'd reach Mach 15, before falling back to Earth.

She was already so high she could see stars. Soon the reaction control thrusters would kick in, and she'd be flying like a spacecraft.

It was the nearest she'd ever get to space, anyhow.

For the first time since arriving in Chad with her cargo of light artillery shells, she had time to relax. The Sänger was showing no evidence of harm from the gunfire.

The Sänger was a good, solid German design, built by Messerschmitt–Boelkow–Blohm. It was designed to operate in war zones. But Madeleine was not; safe now in her high-tech cocoon, she gave way to the tension for a couple of minutes.

While she was still shaking, the Sänger logged into the nets and downloaded her mail. Life went on.

That was when she found the message from Sally Brind.

Brind didn't tell Madeleine who she represented, or what she wanted. Madeleine was to meet her at Kennedy Space Center. Just like that; she was given no choice.

Over the years Madeleine had received a lot of blunt messages like this. They were usually either from lucrative would-be employers, or some variant of cop or taxman. Either way it was wise to turn up.

She acknowledged the message, and instructed her data miners to find out who Brind was.

She pressed a switch, and the RB545s shut down with a bang. As the acceleration cut out she was thrust forward against the straps. Now she had gone ballistic, like a hurled stone. Coasting over the roof of her trajectory in near-silence, she lost all sensation of speed, of motion.

And, at her highest point, she saw a distant glimmer of light, complex and serene: it was a Gaijin flower-ship, complacently orbiting Earth.

When she got back to the States, Madeleine flew out to Orlando. To get to KSC she drove north along US 3, the length of Merritt Island. There used to be security gates; now there was nothing but a rusting fence, with a new smart-concrete road surface cut right through it.

She parked at the Vehicle Assembly Building. It was early morning. The place was deserted. Sand drifted across the empty car park, gathering in miniature dunes.

She walked out to the old press stand, a wooden frame like a baseball bleacher. She sat down, looking east. The sun was in her eyes, and already hot; she could feel it draw her face tight as a drum. To the right, stretching off to the south, there were rocket gantries. In the mist they were two-dimensional, colourless. Most of them were disused, part-dismantled, museum pieces. The sense of desolation, abandonment, was heavy in the air.

Sally Brind had turned out to work for Bootstrap, the rump of the corporation which had sent a spacecraft to the Gaijin base in the asteroid belt, three decades earlier.

Madeleine was not especially interested in the Gaijin. She had been born a few years after their arrival in the solar system; they were just a part of her life, and not a very exciting part. But she knew that four decades after the first detection of the Gaijin – and a full nineteen years after they had first come sailing in from the belt, apparently prompted by Reid Malenfant's quixotic journey – the Gaijin had established something resembling a system of trade with humanity.

They had provided some technological advances: robotics, vacuum industries, a few nanotech tricks like their asteroid mining blankets, enough to revolutionize a dozen industries and make a hundred fortunes. They had also flown human scientists on exploratory missions to other planets: Mars, Mercury, even the moons of Jupiter. (Not Venus, though, oddly, despite repeated requests.) And the Gaijin had started to provide a significant proportion of Earth's resources from space: raw materials from the asteroids, including precious metals, and even energy, beamed down as microwaves from great collectors in the sky.

Humans – or rather, the governments and corporations who dealt with the Gaijin – had to 'pay' for all this with resources common on Earth but scarce elsewhere, notably heavy metals and some complex organics. The Gaijin had also been allowed to land on Earth, and had been offered cultural contact. The Gaijin had, strangely, shown interest in some human ideas, and a succession of writers, philosophers, theologians, and even a few discreditable science fiction authors had been summoned to converse with the alien 'ambassadors'.

The government authorities, and the corporations who were profiting, seemed to regard the whole arrangement as a good deal. With the removal of the great dirt-making industries from the surface of the Earth – power, mining – there was a good chance that eco recovery could, belatedly, become a serious proposition.

Not everybody agreed. All those shut-down mines and decommissioning power plants were creating economic and environmental refugees. And there were plenty of literal refugees too, for instance, all the poor souls who had been moved out of the great swathes of equatorial land that had been given over to the microwave receiving stations.

Thus the Gaijin upheaval had, predictably, caused poverty, even famine and war.

It was thanks to that last Madeleine made her living, of course. But everybody had to survive.

'. . . I wonder if you know what you're looking at, here.' The voice had come from behind her.

A woman sat in the stand, in the row behind Madeleine. Her bony wrists stuck out of an environment-screening biocomp bodysuit. She must have been sixty. There was a man with her, at least as old, short, dark and heavy-set.

'You're Brind.'

'And you're Madeleine Meacher. So we meet. This is Frank Paulis. He's the head of Bootstrap.'

'I remember your name.'

He grinned, his eyes hard.

'What am I doing here, Brind?'

For answer, Brind pointed east, to the tree line beyond the Banana River. 'I used to work for NASA. Back when there was a NASA. Over there used to be the site of the two great launch complexes: 39-B to the left, 39-A to the right. 39-A was the old Apollo gantry. Later they adapted it for Shuttle.' The sunlight blasted into her face, making it look flat, younger. 'Well, the pads are gone now, pulled down for scrap. The base of 39-A is still there, if you want to see it. There's a sign the pad rats stuck there for the last launch. *Go, Discovery!* Kind of faded now, of course.'

'What do you *want*?'

'Do you know what a burster is?'

Madeleine frowned. 'No kind of weapon I've ever heard of.'

'It's not a weapon, Meacher. It's a *star*.'

Madeleine was, briefly, electrified.

'Look, Meacher, we have a proposal for you.'

'What makes you think I'll be interested?'

Brind's voice was gravelly and full of menace. 'I know a great deal about you.'

'How come?'

'If you must know, through the tax bureau. You have operated your –' she waved a hand dismissively '– *enterprises* in over a dozen countries over the years. But you've paid tax on barely ten per cent of the income we can trace.'

'Never broken a law.'

Brind eyed Madeleine, as if she had said something utterly naive. 'The law is a weapon of government, not a protection for the likes of you. Surely you understand that.'

Madeleine tried to figure out Brind. Her biocomposite suit looked efficient, not expensive. Brind was a wage slave, not an entrepreneur. She guessed, 'You're from the government?'

Brind's face hardened. 'When I was young, we used to call what you do gun-running. Although I don't suppose that's how you think of it yourself.'

The remark caught Madeleine off guard. 'No,' she said. 'I'm a pilot. All I ever wanted to do is fly; this is the best job I could get. In a different universe, I'd be –'

'An astronaut,' said Frank Paulis.

The foolish, archaic word got to Madeleine. *Here,* of all places.

'We know about you, you see,' Sally Brind said, almost regretfully. 'All about you.'

'There are no astronauts any more.'

'That isn't true, Meacher,' Paulis said. 'Come with us. Let us show you what we're planning.'

Brind and Paulis took her out to Launch Complex 41, the old USASF Titan pad at the northern end of ICBM Row. Here, Brind's people had refurbished an antique Soviet-era Proton launcher.

The booster was a slim black cylinder, fifty-three metres tall. Six flaring strap-on boosters clustered around the first stage, and Madeleine could pick out the smaller stages above. A passenger capsule and hab module would be fixed to the top, shrouded by a cone of metal.

'Our capsule isn't much more sophisticated than an Apollo,' Brind said. 'It only has to get you to orbit and keep you alive for a couple of hours, until the Gaijin come to pick you up.'

'Me?'

'Would you like to see your hab module? It's being prepared in the old Orbiter Processing Facility . . .'

'Get to the point,' Madeleine said. 'Where are you planning to send me? And what exactly is a burster?'

'A type of neutron star. A very interesting type. The Gaijin are sending a ship there. They've invited us – that is, the UN – to send a representative. An observer. It's the first time they've offered this, to carry an observer beyond the solar system. We think it's important to respond. We can send our own science platform; we'll train you up to use it. We can even establish our own Saddle Point gateway in the neutron star system. It's all part of a wider trade and cultural deal, which –'

'So you represent the UN?'

'Not exactly.'

Paulis said, 'We need somebody with the qualifications and experience to handle a journey like this. You're about the right age, under forty. You've no dependants that we can trace.' He sighed. 'A hundred years ago, we'd have sent John Glenn. Today, the best fit is the likes of you. You'll be well paid.' He eyed Madeleine. 'Believe me, very well paid.'

Madeleine thought it over, trying to figure the angles. 'That Proton is sixty years old, the design even older. You don't have much of a budget, do you?'

Paulis shrugged. 'My pockets aren't as deep as they used to be.'

Brind prickled. 'What does the budget matter? For Christ's sake, Meacher, don't you have any wonder in your soul? I'm offering you, here, the chance to *travel to the stars*. My God – if I had your qualifications, I'd jump at the chance.'

'And you aren't truly the first,' Paulis said. 'Reid Malenfant –'

'– is lost. Anyhow it's not exactly being an astronaut,' Madeleine said sourly. 'Is it? Being live cargo on a Gaijin flower-ship doesn't count.'

'Actually a lot of people agree with you,' Paulis said. 'That's why we've struggled to assemble the funding. Noone is interested in human spaceflight in these circumstances. Most people are happy just to wait for the Gaijin to parachute down more interstellar goodies from the sky . . .'

'Why don't you just send along an automated instrument pallet? Why send a human at all?'

'No.' Brind shook her head firmly. 'We're deliberately designing for a human operator.'

'Why?'

'Because we want a human there. A human like you, God help us. We think it's important to try to meet them on equal terms.'

Madeleine laughed. 'Equal terms? We limp into orbit, and rendezvous with a giant alien ramjet capable of flying to the outer solar system?'

'Symbolism, Meacher,' Paulis said darkly. 'Symbols are everything.'

'How do you know the Gaijin respond to symbols?'

'Maybe they don't. But *people* do. And it's people I'm interested in. Frankly, Meacher, we're seeking advantage. Not everybody thinks we should become so completely reliant on the Gaijin. You'll have a lot of discretion out there. We need someone with – acumen. There may be opportunities.'

'What kind of opportunities?'

'To get humanity out from under the yoke of the Gaijin,' Paulis said. For the first time there was a trace of anger in his voice, passion.

Madeleine began to understand.

There were various shadowy groups who weren't happy with the deals the governments and corporations had been striking with the Gaijin. This trading relationship was *not* between two equals. And besides the Gaijin must be following their own undeclared goals. What about the stuff they were keeping back? What would happen when the human economy was utterly dependent on the trickle of good stuff from the sky? And suppose the Gaijin suddenly decided to turn off the faucets – or, worse, decided to start dropping rocks?

Beyond that, the broader situation continued to evolve, year on year. More and more of the neighbouring stars were lighting up with radio and other signals, out to a distance of some thirty light years. It was evident that a ferocious wave of emigration was coming humanity's way, scouring along the Orion-Cygnus spiral arm. Presumably those colonists were propagating via Saddle Point gateways, and they were finding their target systems empty – or undeveloped, like the solar system. And as soon as they arrived they started to build, and broadcast.

Humans knew precisely nothing about those other new arrivals, at Sirius and Epsilon Eridani and Procyon and Tau Ceti and Altair. Maybe humans were lucky it was the Gaijin who found them first, the first to intervene in the course of human history. Or maybe not. Either way, facing this volatile and fast-changing future, it seemed unwise – to some people – to rely entirely on the goodwill of the first new arrivals to show up. Evidently those groups were now trying, quietly, to do something about it.

But Madeleine's first priority was the integrity of her own skin.

'How far is it to this burster?'

'Eighteen light years.'

Madeleine knew the relativistic implications. She would come back stranded in a future thirty-six years remote. 'I won't do it.'

'It's that or the Gulf,' Brind said evenly.

The Gulf. *Shit.* After twenty years of escalating warfare over the last oil reserves the Gulf was like the surface of Io: glassy nuke craters punctuated by oil wells which would burn for decades. Even with biocomp armour, her life expectancy would be down to a few months.

She turned, and lifted her face to the Florida sun. It looked like she didn't have a choice.

But, she suspected, she was kind of *glad* about that. Something inside her began to stir at the thought of this improbable journey.

And crossing the Galaxy with the Gaijin might be marginally safer than flying Sängers into N'Djamena, anyhow.

Paulis seemed to sense she was wavering. 'Spend some time,' he said. 'We'll introduce you to our people. And –'

'And you'll tell me how you're going to make me rich.'

'Exactly.' He grinned. He had very even, capped teeth.

She was flown to Kefallinia, the Ionian island which the Gaijin had been granted as a base on planet Earth. From the air the island looked as if it had been painted on the blue skin of the sea, a ragged splash of blue-grey land, everywhere indented with bays and inlets, like a fractal demonstration. Off the coast she spotted naval ships, grey slabs of metal, principally a US Navy battle group.

On the ground the sun was high, the air hot and still and very bright, like congealed light, and the rocks tumbled from a spine of mountains down to the tideless sea.

People had lived here, it was thought, for six thousand years. Not any more, of course: not the natives anyhow. When the UN deal with the Gaijin had been done, the Kefallinians were evacuated by the Greek government, most to sites in mainland Greece, others abroad. Those who came to America had been vocal. They regarded themselves as refugees, their land stolen, their culture destroyed by this alien invasion. Rightly so, Madeleine thought.

But the Kefallinians weren't the only dispossessed on planet Earth, and their plight, though newsworthy, wasn't attention-grabbing for long.

At the tiny airport she saw her first piece of close-up genuine Gaijin technology: a surface-to-orbit shuttle, a squat cone of some shimmering metallic substance. It looked too fragile to withstand the rigours of atmospheric entry. And yet there it was, large as life, sitting right next to the Lear jets and antiquated island-hoppers.

From the airport she was whisked to the central UN facility, close to the old capital of Argostoli. The facility was just a series of hastily prefabricated buildings and bunkers, linked by walkways and tunnels. The central building, containing the Gaijin themselves, was a crude aluminium box.

Surrounding the Gaijin shelter there were chapels and temples and mosques, embassies from various governments and inter-governmental bodies, a science park, representatives of most of the world's major corporations. All of these groups, she supposed, were here trying to get a piece of the action, one way or another.

The senior US government official here, she learned, was called the Planetary Protection Officer. The PPO post had been devised in the 1990s to coordinate quarantine measures to handle samples of Mars rock returned to Earth, and such-like. With the arrival of the Gaijin, the joke post had become somewhat more significant.

The military presence was heavy, dug in all over the complex. There were round-the-clock patrols by foot soldiers and armoured vehicles. Copters hovered overhead continually, filling the languid air with their crude rattle, and fighter planes soared over the blue dome of the sky, flight after flight of them.

To some extent this show of military power, as if the Gaijin were being contained here by human mil technology, was a sop for public opinion. Look: we are dealing with these guys as equals. We are in control. We have *not* surrendered . . . Madeleine had even heard senior military officers describing the Gaijin as 'bogeys' and 'tin men', and seeking approval to continue their wargaming of hypothetical Gaijin assaults. But she'd seen enough warfare herself to believe that there was no way humans could prevail in an all-out conflict with the Gaijin. The hoary tactic of dropping space rocks on the major cities would probably suffice for them to win. So the smarter military minds must know that mankind had no choice but to accommodate.

But there was a splash of darkness on the concrete, close to the Gaijin facility: apparently a remnant of a near-successful protest assault on the Gaijin, an incident never widely publicized. Happily the Gaijin had shown none of the likely human reaction to such an incident, no desire to retaliate. It made Madeleine realize that the military here were looking two ways: protecting mankind from its alien visitors, and vice versa.

She stood on heat-soaked concrete and looked up at the sky. Even now, in the brightness of a Mediterranean day, she could see the ghostly shapes of flower-ships, their scoops hundreds of kilometres wide, cruising above the skies of Earth. At that moment, the idea that humans could contain the Gaijin, engage them in dialogue, control this situation, seemed laughable.

They had to put on paper coveralls and overboots and hats, and they were walked through an airlock. The Gaijin hostel worked to about the cleanliness standard of an operating theatre, Madeleine was told.

Inside the big boxy buildings, it was like a church, of a peculiarly stripped-down, minimalist kind: there was a quiet calm, subdued light, and people in uniform padded quietly to and fro in an atmosphere of reverence.

In fact, Madeleine found, that church analogy was apt. For the Gaijin had asked to meet the Pope.

'And other religious leaders, of course,' said Dorothy Chaum, as she shook Madeleine's hand. 'Strange, isn't it? We always imagined the aliens would make straight for the Carl Sagan SETI-scientist types, and immediately start "curing" us of religion and other diseases of our primitive minds. But it isn't working out that way at all. They seem to have more questions than answers . . .'

Chaum turned out to be an American, a Catholic priest who had been assigned by the Vatican to the case of the Gaijin from their first detection. She was a stocky, sensible-looking woman who might have been fifty, her hair frizzed with a modest grey. Madeleine was shocked to find out she was over one hundred years old. Evidently the Vatican could buy its people the best life-extending treatments.

They walked towards big curtained-off bays. The separating curtain was a nearly translucent sheet stretched across the building, from ceiling to floor, wall to wall.

And there – beyond the curtain, bathed in light – was a Gaijin.

Machinery, not life: that was her first impression. She recognized the famous dodecahedral core. It was reinforced at its edges – presumably to counter Earth's gravity – and it was resting, incongruously, on a crude Y-frame trailer. A variety of instruments, cameras and other sensors, protruded from the dodecahedron's skin, and the skin itself was covered with fine bristly wires. Three big robot arms stuck out of that torso, each articulated in two or three places. Two of the arms were resting on the ground, but the third was waving around in the air, fine manipulators at the terminus working.

She looked in vain for symmetry.

Humans had evolved to recognize symmetry in living things – left-to-right, anyhow, because of gravity. Living things were symmetrical; non-living things weren't – a basic human prejudice hard-wired in from the days when it paid to be able to pick out the predator lurking against a confusing background. In its movements this Gaijin had the appearance of life, but it was angular, almost clumsy-looking – and defiantly not symmetrical. It didn't fit.

Human researchers were lined up with their noses pressed against the curtain. A huge bank of cameras and other apparatus was trained on the Gaijin's every move. She knew a continuous image of the Gaijin was being sent out to the net, twenty-four hours a day. There were bars which showed nothing but Gaijin images on huge wall-covering softscreens, all day and all night.

The Gaijin was reading a book, turning its pages with cold efficiency. Good grief, Madeleine thought, disturbed.

'The Gaijin are deep space machines,' said Brind. 'Or life forms, whatever. But they're hardy; they can survive in our atmosphere and gravity. There are three of them, here in this facility: the only three on the surface of the planet. We've no way of knowing how many are up there in orbit, or further out, of course . . .'

Dorothy Chaum said to her, 'We think we're used to machinery. But it's eerie, isn't it?'

'If it's a machine,' Madeleine said, 'it was made by no human. And it's operated by none of us. Eerie. Yes, you're right.' She found herself shuddering, oddly, as that crude mechanical limb clanked. She'd lived her life with machinery, but this Gaijin was spooking her, on some primitive level.

Dorothy Chaum murmured, 'We speak to them in Latin, you know.' She grinned, dimpling, looking younger. 'It's the most logical human language we could find; the Gaijin have trouble with all the irregular structures and idioms of modern languages like English. We have software translation suites to back us up. But of course it's a boon to me. I always knew those long hours of study in the seminary would pay off.'

'What do you talk about?'

'A lot of things,' Brind said. 'They ask more questions than they volunteer answers. Mostly, we figure out a lot from clues gleaned from inadvertent slips.'

'Oh, I doubt that anything about the Gaijin is inadvertent,' Chaum said. 'Certainly their speech is not like ours. It is dull, dry, factual, highly structured, utterly unmemorable. There seems to be no rhythm, no poetry – no sense of *story*. Simply a dull list of facts and queries and dry logic. Like the listing of a computer program.'

'That's because they are machines,' Paulis growled. 'They aren't conscious, like we are.'

Chaum smiled gently. 'I wish I felt so sure. The Gaijin are clearly intelligent. But are they conscious? We know of examples of intelligence without consciousness, right here on Earth: social insects like ant colonies, the termites. And you could argue there can be consciousness without much intelligence, as in a mouse. But is *advanced* intelligence possible without consciousness of some sort?'

'Jesus,' said Paulis with disgust. 'You gave these clanking tin men

99

a whole island, they've been down here for five whole years, and you can't even answer questions like that?'

Chaum stared at him. 'If I could be sure *you* are conscious, if I even knew for sure what it meant, I'd concede your point.'

'Conscious or not they are different from us,' Brind said. 'For example, the Gaijin can turn their brains off.'

That startled Madeleine.

'It's true,' Chaum said. 'When they are at repose, as far as we can tell, they are deactivated. Madeleine, if you had an off-switch on the side of your head – even if you could be sure it would be turned back on again – would you use it?'

Madeleine hesitated. 'I don't think so.'

'Why not?'

'Because I don't see how I could tell if I was still me, when I rebooted.'

Chaum sighed. 'But that doesn't seem to trouble the Gaijin. Indeed, the Gaijin seem to be rather baffled by our big brains. Madeleine, your mind is constantly working. Your brain doesn't rest, even in sleep; it consumes the energy of a light bulb – a big drain on your body's resources – all the time; that's why we've had to eat meat all the way back to *Homo Erectus*.'

Madeleine protested, 'But without our brains we wouldn't be us.'

'Sure,' said Chaum. 'But to be *us*, to the Gaijin, seems to be something of a luxury.'

'Ms Chaum, what do *you* want from them?'

Frank Paulis laughed out loud. 'She wants to know if there was a Gaijin Jesus. Right?'

Chaum smiled without resentment. 'The Gaijin do seem fascinated by our religions.'

Madeleine was intrigued. 'And do *they* have religion?'

'It's impossible to tell. They don't give away a great deal.'

'That's no surprise,' Paulis said sourly.

'They are very analytical,' Chaum said. 'They seem to regard our kind of thinking as pathological. *We* spread ideas to each other – right or wrong, useful or harmful – like an unpleasant mental disease.'

Brind nodded. 'This is the old idea of the meme.'

'Yes,' said Chaum. 'A very cynical view of human culture.'

'And,' Paulis asked dryly, 'have your good Catholic memes crossed the species barrier to the Gaijin?'

'Not as far as I can tell,' Dorothy Chaum said. 'They think in an orderly way. They build up their knowledge bit by bit, testing each new element – much as our scientists are trained to do. Perhaps their minds are too organized to allow our memes to flourish. Or perhaps they have their own memes, powerful enough to beat off our feeble intruder notions. Frankly I'm not sure what the Gaijin make of our answers to the great questions of existence. What seems to interest them is that we *have* answers at all. I suspect they don't . . .'

Madeleine said, 'You sound disappointed with what you've found here.'

'Perhaps I am,' Chaum said slowly. 'As a child I used to dream of meeting the aliens: who could guess what scientific and philosophical insights they might bring? Well, these Gaijin do appear to be a life form millions of years old, at least. But, culturally and scientifically, they are really little evolved over us.'

Madeleine felt herself warming to this earnest, thoughtful woman. 'Perhaps we'll find the really smart ones out there among the stars. Maybe they are on their way now.'

Chaum smiled. 'I certainly envy you your chance to go see for yourself. But even if we did find such marvellous beings, the result may be crushing for us.'

'How so?'

'God shows His purposes through us, and our progress,' she said. 'At least, this is one strand of Christian thinking. But what, then, if our spiritual development is far behind that of the aliens? Somewhere else He may have reached a splendour to which we can add nothing.'

'And we wouldn't matter any more.'

'Not to God. And, perhaps, not to ourselves.'

They turned away from the disappointing aliens, and walked out into the flat light of Kefallinian noon.

Later, Frank Paulis took Madeleine to one side.

'Enough bullshit,' he said. 'Let's you and me talk business. You're fast-forwarding through thirty-six years. If you're smart, you'll take advantage of that fact.'

'How?'

'Compound interest,' he said.

Madeleine laughed. After her encounter with such strangeness, Paulis's blunt commercial calculation seemed ludicrous. 'You aren't serious.'

'Sure. Think about it. Invest what you can of your fee. After all you won't be touching it while you're gone. At a conservative five per cent you're looking at a five-fold payout over your thirty-six years. If you can make ten per cent that goes up to *thirty-one* times.'

'Really.'

'Sure. What else are you going to do with it? You'll come back a few months older, subjectively, to find your money has grown like Topsy. And think about this. Suppose you make *another* journey of the same length. You could multiply up that factor of thirty-fold to nearer a thousand. You could shuttle back and forth between here and Sirius, let's say, getting richer on every leg, just by staying alive over the centuries.'

'Yeah. If everything stays the same back home. If the bank doesn't fail, the laws don't change, the currency doesn't depreciate, there's no war or rebellion or plague, or a take-over of mankind by alien robots.'

He grinned. 'That's a long way off. A lifetime pumped by relativity is a whole new way of making money. *You'd be the first*, Meacher. Think about it.'

She studied him. 'You really want me to take this trip, don't you?'

His face hardened. 'Hell, yes, I want you to make this trip. Or, if you can't get your head sufficiently out of your ass, somebody. We have to find our own way forward, a way to deal with the Gaijin and those other metal-chewing cyborgs and giant interplanetary bugs and whatever else is heading our way from the Galactic core.'

'Is that really the truth, Paulis?'

'Oh, you don't think so?'

'Maybe you're just *disappointed*,' she goaded him. 'A lot of people were disappointed because the Gaijin didn't turn out to be a bunch of father figures from the sky. They didn't immediately start beaming down high technology and wisdom and rules so we can all live together in peace, love and understanding. The Gaijin are just *there*. Is that what's really bugging you, Paulis? That infantile wish to just give up responsibility for yourself –'

He eyed her. 'You really are full of shit, Meacher. Come on. You still have to see the star of this freak show.' He led her back into the facility. They reached another corner, another curtained-off Gaijin enclosure. 'We call *this* guy Gypsy Rose Lee,' he said.

Beyond the curtain was another Gaijin. But it was in pieces. The central dodecahedron was intact, save for a few panels, but most of those beautiful articulated arms lay half-disassembled on the floor. The last attached arm was steadily plucking wiry protrusions off the surface of the dodecahedron, one by one. Lenses of various sizes lay scattered over the floor, like gouged-out eyeballs.

Human researchers in white all-over isolation gear were crawling over the floor, inspecting the alien gadgetry.

'My God,' Madeleine said. 'It's taking itself apart.'

'Cultural exchange in action,' Paulis said sourly. 'We gave them a human cadaver to take apart – a volunteer, incidentally. In return we get this. A Gaijin is a complicated critter; this has been going on six months already.'

A couple of the researchers – two earnest young women – overheard Paulis, and turned their way.

'But we're learning a lot,' one of the researchers said. 'The most basic question we have to answer is: *are the Gaijin alive*? From the point of view of their complexity, you'd say they are; but they seem to have no mechanism for heredity, which we think is a prerequisite for any definition of a living thing –'

'Or so we thought at first. But seeing the way this thing is put together has made us think again –'

'We believed the Gaijin might be von Neumann machines, perfect replicators –'

'But it may be that *perfect* replication is impossible in principle. Uncertainty, chaos –'

'There will be drift in each generation. Like genetic drift. And where there is variation, there can be selection, and so evolution –'

'But we still don't know what the *units* of replication are here. It may be a lower level than the individual Gaijin –'

'The subcomponents that comprise them, perhaps. Maybe the Gaijin are a kind of vehicle for replication of their components, just as you could say we humans are a vehicle to enable our genes to reproduce themselves . . .'

Breeding, evolving *machines*? Madeleine found herself shuddering.

Paulis said, 'Do you see now? We are dealing with the truly alien here, Madeleine. These guys might spout Latin in their synthesized voices, but they are *not* like us. They come from a place we can't even imagine, and we don't know where they are going, and we sure as hell don't know what they are looking for here on Earth. And that's why we have to find a way to deal with them. Go ahead. Take a good long look.'

The Gaijin plucked a delicate panel of an aluminium-like soft metal off its own hide; it came loose with a soft sucking tear, exposing jewel-like innards. Perhaps it would keep on going until there was only that grasping robot hand left, Madeleine thought, and then the hand would take itself apart too, finger by gleaming finger, until there was nothing left that could move.

Chapter 9

FUSION SUMMER

Brind drew up contracts. Madeleine tidied up her affairs; preparing for a gap of thirty-six years, at minimum, had a feeling of finality. She said goodbye to her tearful mother, rented out her apartment, sold her car. She took the salary up front and invested it as best she could, with Paulis's help.

She decided to give her little capsule a call-sign: *Friendship-7*.

And, before she knew it, before she felt remotely ready for this little relativistic death, it was launch day.

Friendship-7's protective shroud cracked open. The blue light of Earth flooded the cabin. Madeleine could see fragments of ice, shaken free of the hull of the booster; they glittered around the craft like snow. And she could see the skin of Earth, spread out beneath her like a glowing carpet, as bright as a tropical sky. On the antique Proton, it had been one mother of a ride. But here she was – at last – in orbit, and her spirits soared. To hell with the Gaijin, to hell with Brind and Paulis. Whatever else happened from here on in, they couldn't take this memory away from her.

She travelled through a single orbit of the Earth. There were clouds piled thickly around the equator. The continents on the night side were outlined by chains of city lights.

She could see the big eco-repair initiatives, even from here, from orbit. Reforestation projects were swathes of virulent green on the continents of the northern hemisphere. The southern continents were filled with hot brown desert, their coasts lined grey with urban encrustation. Patches of grey in the seas, bordering the land, marked the sites of disastrous attempts to pump carbon dioxide into the deep oceans. Over Antarctica, laser arrays glowed red, labouring to destroy tropospheric chlorofluorocarbons. The Gulf was just a sooty smudge, drowning in petrochemical smog. And so on.

From here she could see the disturbing truth: that space was doing Earth no damn good at all. Even though this was a time of off-world colonies and trade with interstellar travellers, most of mankind's efforts were directed towards fixing up a limited, broken-down ecology, or dissipated on closed-economy problems: battles over diminishing resources in the oceans, on the fringes of the expanding deserts.

She wondered, uneasily, what she would find when she returned home, thirty-six years from now.

Madeleine would live in an old Shuttle Spacelab – a tiny reusable space station, seventy years old and flown in orbit twice – dug out of storage at KSC, gutted and refurbished. At the front was her small pressurized hab compartment, and there were two pallets at the rear fitted with a bunch of instruments which would be deployed at the neutron star: coronagraphs, spectroheliographs, spectrographic telescopes.

Brind gave her a powerful processor to enable her to communicate, to some extent, with her Gaijin hosts. It was a bioprocessor, a little cubical unit. The biopro was high technology, and it was the one place they had spent serious amounts of Paulis's money. And it was human technology, not Gaijin. Madeleine was fascinated. She spent a long time going over the biopro's specs. It was based on ampiphiles, long molecules with watery heads and greasy tails, that swam about in layers called Langmuir–Blodgett films. The active molecules used weak interactions – hydrogen bonding, van der Waals forces and hydrophobic recognition – to assemble themselves into a three-dimensional structure, supramolecular arrays thousands of molecules long.

Playing with the biopro was better than thinking about what was happening to her, where she was headed.

She wasn't so happy to find, though, when she first booted up the biopro, that its human interface design metaphor was a two-dimensional virtual representation of Frank Paulis's leathery face.

'Paulis, you egotistical bastard.'

'Just want to make you feel at home.' The image flickered a little, and his skin was blocky – obviously digitally generated. It – he – turned out to be backed up by a complex program, interactive and heuristic. He could respond to what Madeleine said to him, learn, and grow.

He would be company, of a sort.

'Are you in contact with the Gaijin?'

He hesitated. 'Yes. In a way. Anyhow I'll keep you informed. In the meantime, the best thing you can do is follow your study program.'

He started downloading some kind of checklist; it chattered out of an antique teletype.

'You have got to be kidding.'

'You've a lot of training on the equipment still to complete,' virtual Paulis said.

'Terrific. And should I study neutron stars, bursters, whatever the hell they are?'

'I'd rather not. I want your raw reactions. If I coach you too much it will narrow your perception. Remember, you'll be observing on behalf of all mankind. *We may never get another chance.* Now. Maybe we can start with the spectroheliograph deployment procedure . . .'

When she flew once more over the glittering east coast of North America, the Gaijin ship was waiting to meet her.

In Earth orbit, the Gaijin flower-ship didn't look so spectacular. It was laid out something like a squid, a kilometre long and wrought in silver, with a bulky main section as the 'head' and a mess of 'tentacles' trailing behind.

Dodecahedral forms, silvered and anonymous, drifted from the cables, and clustered around Madeleine's antique craft. Her ship was hauled into the silvery rope stuff. Strands adhered to her hull, until her view was criss-crossed with shining threads, and she had become part of the structure of the Gaijin ship. She felt a mounting claustrophobia as she was knit into the alien craft. How did Malenfant stand all this?

Then the flower-ship unfolded its petals. They made up an electromagnetic scoop, a thousand kilometres wide. The lower edge of the scoop brushed the fringe of Earth's atmosphere, and plasma sparkled.

Madeleine felt her breath shortening. This is real, she thought. These crazy aliens are really going to do this. And I'm really *here.*

She fought panic.

After a couple of widening loops around the planet Madeleine sailed out of Earth's orbit, and she was projected into strangeness.

Eating interplanetary hydrogen, it took the flower-ship one hundred and ninety-eight days to travel out to the burster's Saddle Point, eight hundred AU from the sun.

Saddle Point gateways must destroy the objects they transport.

For eighteen years a signal crossed space, towards a receiver gateway which had been hauled to the system of the burster neutron star. For eighteen years Madeleine did not exist. She was essentially dead (though not legally).

Thus, Madeleine Meacher crossed interstellar space.

There was no sense of waking – *is it over?* – she was just *there*, with the Spacelab's systems whirring and clicking around her as usual, like a busy little kitchen. Her heart was pounding, just as it had been a second before – eighteen years before.

Everything was the same. And yet –

'Meacher.' It was virtual Paulis's voice. 'Are you all right?'

No. She felt extraordinary: renewed, revived. She remembered every instant of it, that burst of exquisite pain, the feeling of reassembling, of *sparkling*. Was it possible she had somehow retained some consciousness during the transition?

My God, she thought. *This could become addictive.*

A new, complex light was sliding over the back of her hand. She suddenly remembered where she was. She made for her periscope.

From the dimly-lit, barren fringe of the solar system, she had been projected immediately into a crowded space. She was, in fact, sailing over the surface of a star.

The photosphere, barely ten thousand kilometres below, was a flat-infinite landscape, encrusted by granules each large enough to swallow the Earth, and with the chromosphere – the thousand-kilometre-thick outer atmosphere – a thin haze above it all. Polarizing filters in the viewport periscope dimmed its light to an orange glow. As she watched, one granule exploded, its material bursting across the star's surface; neighbouring granules were pushed aside, so that a glowing, unstructured scar was left on the photosphere, a scar which was slowly healed by the eruption of new granules.

From the tangled hull of the flower-ship, an instrument pod of some kind uncoiled on a graceful pseudopod. Gaijin instruments peered into the umbra of a star-spot below her. 'This is an F-type white dwarf star, Meacher,' Paulis said. 'A close cousin of the sun, the dominant partner of the binary pair in this system.'

I mightn't have come here, she thought. She felt an odd, retrospective panic. Brind might have picked on somebody else. I might have turned them down. I might have died, without ever imagining this was possible.

. . . But I just lost eighteen years, she thought. Nearly half my life. Just like that. She tried to imagine what was happening on Earth, right now. Tried and failed.

Virtual Paulis had issues of his own. 'Remarkable,' he said.

'What?'

Paulis sounded wistful. 'Meacher, we didn't want to emphasize the point overmuch before you left, but you're the first human to have passed through a Saddle Point teleport – except for Malenfant, and he never reported back. We didn't know what would happen.'

'Maybe I would have arrived here as warm meat. All the lights on but nobody at home. Is that what you expected?'

'It was a possibility. Philosophically.'

'The Gaijin pass back and forth all the time.'

'Ah, but perhaps they don't have souls, as we do.'

'*Souls,* Frank?' She was growing suspicious. 'It isn't just you in there, is it? I can't imagine Frank Paulis discussing theology.'

'I'm a composite.' He grinned. 'But I – that is, Paulis – won the fight to be front man.'

'Now *that* sounds like Frank.'

'For thousands of years we've wondered about the existence of a soul. Does the mind emerge from the body, or does the soul have some separate existence, somehow coupled to the physical body? Consider a thought experiment. If I made an exact duplicate of you, down to the last proton and electron and quantum state, but a couple of metres to the left – would that copy be *you*? Would it have a mind? Would it be conscious?'

'But that's pretty much what we've done. Isn't it? But rather than a couple of metres . . .'

'Eighteen light years. Yes. But still, as far as I can tell you – I mean the inner you – have emerged unscathed. The teleport mechanism is a purely physical device. It has transported the machinery of your body – and yet your soul appears to have arrived intact as well. All this seems to prove that we are after all no more than machines – no more than the sum of our parts. A whole slew of religious beliefs are going to be challenged by this one simple fact.'

She looked inward. 'I'm still Madeleine. I'm still conscious.' But then, she reflected, I would think so, wouldn't I? Maybe I'm not truly conscious. Maybe I just think I am.

The ship surged as the flower scoop thumped into pockets of richly ionized gas; the universe was, rudely, intruding into philosophy.

'I don't understand how come the Saddle Point wasn't out on some remote rim, like in the solar system.'

'Meacher, the gravitational map of this binary system is complex, a lot more than Sol's. There is a solar focus point close to each of the system's points of gravitational equilibrium. We emerged from L4, the stable Lagrange point which precedes the neutron star in its orbit, and that's where we'll return.'

'There must be other foci, on the rim of the system. Other Saddle Points which would be a lot safer to use.'

'Sure.' Virtual Frank grinned. 'But the Gaijin aren't human, remember. They seem to have utter confidence in their technology, their shielding, the reliability and control of their ramjets. We have to assume that the Gaijin know what they're doing . . .'

Madeleine turned to the consoles. Soon her monitors showed that data was starting to come in on hydrogen alpha emission, ultraviolet line spectra, ultraviolet and X-ray imaging, spectrography of the active regions, zodiacal light, spectroheliographs. Training and practice took over as she went into the routine tasks, and as she worked, some of her awe went away.

'Meacher. Look ahead.'

She reached for the periscope again. She looked at the approaching horizon – over which dawn was breaking. Dawn, on a star?

A great pulse of torn gas fled towards her over the horizon. It subsided in great arcs to the star's surface, the battered atoms flailing in the star's magnetic field – and again, a few seconds later – and once again, at deadly regular intervals. And the breaths of plasma grew more violent.

'My God, Frank.'

'Neutron star rise,' Paulis said gently. 'Just watch. Watch and learn. And *remember*, for all of us.'

The neutron star came over the horizon now, stalking disdainfully over its companion's surface, their separation only a third that between the Earth and its Moon. The primary rose in a yearning tide as the neutron star passed, glowing gas forming a column that snaked up, no more than a few hundred metres across at its neck. Great lumps of glowing material tore free and swirled inwards to a central point, a tiny object of such unbearable brightness that the periscope covered it with a patch of protective darkness.

And then the explosion came.

Blackness.

Madeleine flinched. 'What the hell –'

The smart periscope had blanked over. The darkness cleared slowly, revealing a cloud of scattered debris through which the neutron star sailed serenely.

'*That's* a burster,' said Paulis dryly.

The cloak of matter around the neutron star was building up again. *Flash*.

The periscope blacked out once more.

'You'll get used to it,' Paulis said. 'It comes every fourteen seconds, regular as your heartbeat. An X-ray flash bright enough to be seen from Earth.'

She studied her instruments. The data was flowing in, raw, uninterpreted. 'Paulis, I'm no double-dome. Tell me what's happening. The primary's star-stuff –'

Flash.

'– fuses when it hits the neutron star, right?'

'Yes. Hydrogen from the primary fuses to helium as it trickles to the neutron star's surface. In seconds, the helium collects over the crust into a kind of atmosphere, metres thick. But it is a transient atmosphere which abruptly fuses further, into carbon and oxygen and other complex molecules –'

Flash.

'– blasting away residual hydrogen as it does so.'

The neutron star roared towards the flower-ship, dragging its great hump of star-stuff beneath it, and –

Flash.

– bellowing out its fusion yells. The Gaijin pulled the flower-ship's petals in further; the mouth of the ram closed to a tight circle.

A circle which dipped towards the neutron star.

'What are they doing?'

'Try not to be afraid, Meacher.'

The flower-ship swooped closer to the primary; red vacuoles fled beneath Madeleine like crowding fish. She sailed *beneath* the neutron star, skirting the mouth of fire it tore open in the flesh of the primary.

Her body decided it was time for a fresh bout of space adaptation syndrome.

The Waste Management Station was another Shuttle-era veteran, and it took some operating. When she came out, she opened her medical kit and took a scopalomine/Dexidrene.

'Meacher, you're entitled to a little nausea. You're earning us a first-hand view of a neutron star. I'm proud of you.'

'Frank, I've been flying for twenty years, fifteen professionally. I've flown to the edge of space. I have *never* had a ride like this.'

'Of course not. No human has, in all of history.'

'No human except Reid Malenfant.'

'Yes. Except him.'

She looked inside herself, and found, despite the queasiness, she was hooked.

Maybe it didn't matter what she would find, back home. Maybe she would choose to go on, like Reid Malenfant. Submit herself to the beautiful blue pain, over and over. And travel on to places like this . . .

'Listen, Meacher. You'll have to prepare yourself for the next encounter with the burster. The neutron star's orbit around its parent is only eleven minutes.' His image seemed to be breaking up.

'Frank, I think I'm losing you.'

'No. I'm just diverting a lot of processing resources right now . . . I have something odd, from that neutron star flyby. I need some input from you.'

'What kind of input?'

'Interpretation. Look at this.'

He brought up an image of the neutron star, at X-ray wavelengths. He picked out a section of the surface, and expanded it. Bands of pixels swept over the image, enhancing and augmenting.

'Do you know anything about neutron stars, Meacher? A neutron star is the by-product of a supernova, the violent, final collapse of a massive star at the end of its life. This specimen is as heavy as the sun, but only around twenty kilometres wide. The matter in the interior is degenerate, the electron shells of its atoms collapsed by the pressure. The surface gravity is billions of G, although normal matter – bound by atomic bonds – can exist there. The surface is actually rigid, a metallic crust.'

She looked more closely at the image. 'Looks like there are patterns on the surface of the neutron star.' There were hexagons, faintly visible.

'Yeah,' Paulis said. 'Now look at this.'

He flicked to other wavelengths. The things showed up at optical frequencies, even: patterns of tidy hexagons each a metre or so across. In a series of shots shown in chronological order, she could see how the patterns were actually spreading, their six-fold symmetry growing over the crystalline surface of the neutron star.

Growing, to her unscientific mind, like a virus. Or a bacterial colony.

Life, she thought, and she dissolved into wonder.

'The Gaijin don't seem surprised,' virtual Frank said.

'Really?'

'*Life emerges everywhere it can.* So they say . . . The star creatures' metabolism is based on atomic bonds. Just as is ours – *yours.* Their growth paths follow the flux lines of the neutron star's magnetic field, which is enormously powerful. Evidently the complex heavy atoms deposited by the fusion processes assist and stimulate their development. But eventually –'

'I think I can guess.'

On multiple softscreens, hexagons split and multiplied into patterns of bewildering complexity, ever-changing. The images grew more blurred as the star's rudimentary, and transient, atmosphere built up.

'Think of it, Meacher,' Paulis said. His image was grainy, swarms of blocky pixels crossing his face like insects; nearly all the biopro's immense processing power was devoted to interpreting the neutron star data. 'The very air they move through betrays them; it grows too thick and explodes – wiping the creatures clean from the surface of their world.'

'Well, not quite,' Madeleine said. 'They survive somehow, for the next cycle.'

'Yes. I guess the equivalent of spores must be deposited on or below the surface of the star. To survive these global conflagrations, every fourteen seconds, they must be pretty rudimentary, however – probably no more advanced than lichen. I wonder how much these frenetic little creatures might achieve if the fusion cycle was removed from their world . . .'

She watched the surges of the doomed neutron star lichen, the hypnotic rhythm of disaster on a world like a trap.

She stirred. Did it *have* to be this way?

Paulis said, 'Meacher –'

'Shut up, Frank.'

Maybe she wasn't going to turn out to be just a passive observer on this mission after all. But she doubted if John Glenn would have approved of the scheme she was planning.

The Gaijin told Paulis, by whatever indirect channels they were operating, that they planned two more days in orbit.

Madeleine called up Paulis. 'We have a decision to make,' she said.

'A decision?'

'On the siting of our UN-controlled teleport gateway.'

'Yes. Obviously the recommendation is to place the gateway at L5, the trailing Lagrange stable point –'

'No. Listen, Frank. This system must have a Saddle Point on the line between the neutron star and its parent – somewhere in the middle of that column of hydrogen attracted from the primary.'

'Of course.' He looked at her suspiciously. 'There's a gravitational equilibrium there, the L1 Lagrange point.'

'That's where I want the gateway.'

He looked thoughtful – or rather his face emptied of expression, and she imagined mips being diverted to the data channel connecting him to the Gaijin. 'But L1 is unstable. It would be difficult to maintain the gateway's position. Anyway, there would be a net flow of hot hydrogen through the gateway, into the transmitter at the solar system end. We won't be able to use the gateway for two-way travel.'

'Frank, for Christ's sake, that's hardly important. We can't get out to the solar system Saddle Points anyhow without the Gaijin hauling us there. Listen – you sent me on this mission to seek advantage. I think I found a way to do that. Trust me.'

He studied her. 'Okay.' He went blank again. 'The Gaijin want more justification.'

'All right. We'll be disrupting the flow of hydrogen from the primary to its neutron-star companion. What will be the effect on the neutron star?'

Paulis said slowly, 'Without the steady drizzle of fusing hydrogen onto the surface, the helium layer will cease its cycle of growth and explosion. The burster will die.'

'*But the lichen life forms will live.* Won't they? No more fusion blow-outs every fourteen seconds.'

He thought it over. 'You may be right, Meacher. And, free of the periodic extinction pulse, they may advance. My God. What an achievement. It will be as if we'll have fathered a whole new race . . . But what's the benefit to the Gaijin?'

She said briskly, 'They say they've come to us seeking answers. Maybe this is a place they will find some. A new race, new minds.'

There was motion beyond her windows. She looked out, pressing her nose to the cool glass. The Gaijin were swarming over the hull of their flower-ship like metallic beetles, limbs flailing angularly. They were *merging*, she saw, becoming a gruesome metallic sea that writhed and rippled.

'The Gaijin seem . . . intrigued,' Paulis said carefully.

She waited while he worked his data stream to the Gaijin.

'They agree, Meacher. I hope you know what you're doing,' he said.

'Me too, Frank. Me too.'

The Gaijin opened up the flower-ship's petals, and once more Madeleine swooped around the thin column of star-stuff.

As soon as the UN Saddle Point gateway was established and operational, the result was extraordinary.

The gateway was set at the thinnest point of the column of hot hydrogen torn from the primary. The gateway flared lurid blue, continually teleporting. At least fifty per cent of the primary's hydrogen – according to Paulis – was disappearing into the maw of the teleport gate. It looked as if the column of material had been neatly pruned by some cosmic gardener, capped with an almost flat surface.

'Good,' Madeleine said. 'It's worked . . . We're moving again.' She returned to her periscopes.

The ship approached the neutron star. The star's ruddy surface sparkled softly as residual material fell into its gravity well. Once more the elaborate hexagonal patterns flowed vigorously across the surface of the star – but the lichen seemed, oddly, to pause after a dozen seconds or so, as if expectant of the destruction to come.

But the fusion fire did not erupt, and the creatures surged, as if with relief, to new parts of their world.

A fourteen-second cycle to their growth remained, but that was soon submerged in the exuberant complexity of their existence. Flowing along magnetic flux lines, the lichen quickly transformed their star-world; major sections of its surface changed colour and texture.

It was stunning to watch.

She felt a surge of excitement. The data she would take back on this would keep the scientists busy for decades. Maybe, she thought, this is how the double-domes feel, at some moment of discovery.

Or an intervening god.

. . . Then, suddenly, the growth failed.

It started first at the extremes; the lichen colonies began shrivelling back to their heart lands. And then the colour of the patterns, in a variety of wavelengths, began to fade, and the neat hexagonal structure became chaotic.

The meaning was obvious. Death was spreading over the star.

'Frank. What's happening?'

'I expected this,' the interface metaphor said.

'You did?'

'Some of my projections predicted it, with varying probability.

114

Meacher, the lichen can't survive without their fusion cycle. Our intervention from orbit was somewhat crude. Kind of anthropocentric. Maybe the needs of the little creatures down there are not as simple as we imagined. What if the fusion cycle is *necessary* to their growth and existence, in some way we don't understand?'

The fusion cycle had delivered layers of complex molecules to the surface. Maybe the crystalline soil down there needed its fusion summer, to wipe it clean and invigorate it, regularly. After all, extinction events on Earth led to increased biodiversity in the communities that derived from their survivors.

And Madeleine had destroyed all that. Guilt stabbed at her stomach.

'Don't take it hard, Madeleine,' Paulis said.

'Bullshit,' she said. 'I'm a meddler.'

'Your impulse was honourable. It was worth a try.' He gave her a virtual smile. '*I* understand why you did it. Even if the real Frank won't . . . I think we're heading for home, Meacher. We'll be at the Lagrange point gateway in a couple of minutes. Prepare yourself.'

'Thanks.' Thank God. Get me out of here.

A couple of minutes, and eighteen years into the future . . .

'And, you know,' Paulis said, 'maybe there are deeper questions we haven't asked here.' *That* didn't sound like Frank Paulis, but one of his more reflective companions. A little touch of Dorothy Chaum, perhaps. 'The Gaijin could have brought you – the first human passenger, after Malenfant – anywhere. Why *here*? Why did they choose to show you this? Nothing the Gaijin do is without meaning. They have layers of purpose.'

She thought of that grisly, slow dismantling in Kefallinia, and shuddered.

The Paulis composite said, 'Perhaps we are here because *this is the truth*. The truth about the universe.'

'*This*? This dismal cycle of disaster, helpless life forms crushed back into the slime, over and over?'

'On some symbolic level, perhaps, this is the truth for us all.'

'I don't understand, Frank.'

'Maybe it's better that you don't.'

The truth? No, she thought. Maybe for these wretched creatures, here on this bizarre star relic. Not for us; not for humans, the solar system. Even if this is the cosmos's cruel logic, why do we have to submit to it? Maybe we ought to find a way to fix it.

Maybe Reid Malenfant would know the answer to such questions by now – wherever he was, if he was still alive. She wondered if it would ever be possible to find him.

. . . But none of that mattered now, for electric blue light enveloped her, like fusion summer.

Chapter 10

TRAVELS

And, far from home, here was Malenfant, all alone save for a sky full of Gaijin, orbiting a planet that might have been Earth, circling a star that might have been the sun.

He peered down at the planet, using the telescopic features of his softscreen, for long hours. It might have been Earth, yes: a little heavier, a little warmer, but nevertheless compellingly familiar, with a jigsaw arrangement of grey-brown continents and blue oceans and streaky white clouds and even ice caps, all of it shining unbearably brightly. Was that textured greenery really forest? Did those equatorial plains breed some analogy of grass? And were those sweeping shadows great herds of herbivores, the buffalo or reindeer of this exotic place?

But, try as he might, he found no sign of intelligent life: no city geometries, no glowing artificial light, not even the thread of smoke or the sprinkling of firelight.

This wasn't a true copy of Earth. Of course not, how could it be? He knew there was no Africa here, no America, no Australia; these strange alien continents had followed their own long tectonic waltz. But those oceans really were made of liquid water – predominantly anyhow – and the air was mainly a nitrogen–oxygen mix, a bit thicker than Earth's.

Oxygen was unstable; left to itself it should soon combine with the rocks of the planet. So something had to be injecting oxygen into the atmosphere: free oxygen was a sure sign of life – life that couldn't be so terribly dissimilar to his own.

But that atmosphere looked deeper, mistier than Earth's; the blue of the oceans, the grey of the land, had a greenish tinge. And if he looked through the atmosphere towards the edge of the planet, he could see a pale yellow-green staining, a sickly, uncomfortable colour. The green was the mark of chlorine.

He tried to explain to his Gaijin companion, Cassiopeia, what it was that kept him staring down at this new world, long after he had exhausted the analytic possibilities of his eyeball scrutiny. 'Look down there.' He pointed, and he imagined interpretative software aligning his finger with the set of his eyes.

IT IS A PENINSULA.

'True . . .' Pendant from a greater continent, set in a blue equatorial sea, and surrounded by blue-white echoes of its outline, echoes that must be some equivalent of a coral reef. 'It reminds me of Florida. Which is a region of America –'

I KNOW OF FLORIDA. THIS PENINSULA IS NOT FLORIDA. Over the months (subjective) they'd been together, Cassiopeia's English had got a *lot* better, and now she spoke to him using a synthesized human voice relayed over his old Shuttle EMU headset.

'But it's *like* Florida. At least, enough to make me feel . . .'

WHAT?

He sighed.

It had taken him forty years to get here from Alpha Centauri – including around six months of subjective time, as he had coasted between various inner systems and Saddle Point gateways. System after system, world after world. Six months as he had tried to get to know the Gaijin, and they to know him.

It seemed very important to them that they understood how he saw the universe, what motivated him. As for himself, he knew that understanding was going to be the only way humans were ever going to deal with these strangers from the sky.

But it was hard.

Cassiopeia would *never* have picked out that peninsula's chance resemblance to Florida. Even if some mapping routine had done it for her, he supposed, it would have meant nothing, save as an example of convergent processes in geology. The Gaijin sought patterns, of course – it was hard to imagine a science which did not include elements of pattern recognition, of correlation and trend analysis – but they were not *distracted* by them, like humans.

No doubt this was simply a product of differing evolutionary origins. The Gaijin had evolved in the stately stillness of deep space, where there was, in general, time to think things through; humans had evolved in fast-moving, crowded environments where it paid to be able to gaze into the shadows of a tree, a complex visual environment of dapples and stripes, and pick out the tiger *fast*.

But the end-result was that he simply could not communicate to

Cassiopeia why it pleased him to pick out an analogue of Florida off the shore of some unnamed continent, on a planet light years from Earth.

Cassiopeia was still waiting for a reply.

'Never mind,' he said. He opaqued the membrane and began his routine for sleep.

Talking to aliens:

It didn't help that he didn't really have any idea who, or what, he was talking *to*.

He had no idea how complex an individual Gaijin was. Was Cassiopeia equivalent to a car, a bacterium, a person, something more?

And the question might have no meaning, of course. Just because he communicated with a discrete entity *he* called Cassiopeia, it didn't mean there had to be anything like a corresponding person behind his projection. Maybe he was talking to a limb, or a hand, or a digit, of some greater organism – a super-being, or some looser Internet of minds.

Still, he had found places to start. His first point of contact had been navigation.

Both he and Cassiopeia were finite, discrete creatures embedded in a wider universe. And that universe split into obvious categories – space, stars, worlds, you, me. It had been straightforward to agree on a set of labels for Sol, Earth and the nearby stars – even if that wasn't the custom of the Gaijin. They thought of each star as a point on a dynamic four-dimensional map, defined not by a *name* but by its orientation compared to some local origin of coordinates. So their label for Sol was something like get-to-Alpha-Centauri-and-hang-a-left-for-four-light-years . . . except that Alpha Centauri, the local centre of Gaijin operations, was itself defined by an orientation compared to another, more remote origin of coordinates – and so on, recursively back, until you reached the ultimate origin: the starting point, the home world of the Gaijin.

And this recursive web of directions and labelling was, of course, subject to constant change, as the stars slid through the sky, changing their orientations to each other.

It was a system of thinking that was logical, and obviously useful for a species who had evolved to navigate among the stars – a lot more so than the Earthbound human habit of seeking patterns in the random lamps of the sky, patterns called constellations, which shifted because of perspective if you moved more than a couple of light years from

Earth. But it was a system that was far beyond the capacity of any human mind to absorb.

Another point of contact: *You. Me. One. Two.* In this universe, it seemed, it was impossible not to learn to count.

Malenfant's math extended (shakily) as far as differential calculus, the basic tool mathematicians used to model reality. It did appear that Cassiopeia thought of the world in similar terms. Of course, Cassiopeia's mathematical models were smarter than any human's. The key to such modelling was to pick out the right abstractions from a complex background: close enough to reality to give meaningful answers, not so detailed they overwhelmed the calculations. For the Gaijin, the boundaries of abstraction and simplification were *much* further back than any human's, her models much richer.

And there were more fundamental differences. Cassiopeia seemed much smarter at *solving* the equations than Malenfant, or any human. He managed to set out for her the equations of fluid mechanics, one of his specialities at college, and she seemed to understand them qualitatively: she could immediately *see* how these equations, which in themselves merely described how scraps of flowing water interacted with each other, implied phenomena like turbulence and laminar flow, implications it had taken humans years – using sophisticated mathematical and computational tools – to tease out.

Could Cassiopeia look at the equations of relativity and *see* an implied universe of stars and planets and black holes? Could she look at the equations of quantum mechanics and *see* the intricate chemistry of living things?

Of course, that increased smartness must lead to a qualitative jump in understanding. A chimp didn't think about things more simply than Malenfant did; it couldn't grasp some of his concepts at all. There were clearly areas where Cassiopeia was simply working above Malenfant's wretched head.

Cassiopeia had spent time trying to teach him about a phenomenon just a little beyond his own horizon – as chaos theory might have been to an engineer of, say, the 1950s. It was something to do with the emergence of complexity. The Gaijin seemed able to *see* how complexity, even life, naturally emerged from the simplest of beginnings: not fundamental physical laws, but something even deeper than that – as far as he could make out, the essential mathematical logic which underlaid all things. Human scientists had a glimmering of this. His own DNA somehow contained, in its few billion bases, enough information to generate a brain of three *trillion* connections . . .

But for the Gaijin this principle went further. It was like being given a table of prime numbers and being able to deduce atoms and stars and people, as a *necessary* consequence of the existence of the primes. And since prime numbers, of course, existed everywhere, it followed there was life and people, humans and Gaijin, everywhere there could be.

Life sprouting everywhere, like weeds in the cracks of a pavement. It was a remarkable, chilling thought.

'Take me to your home,' he'd said one day.

Cassiopeia's choice of a human label for her remote home was Zero-Zero-Zero-Zero, the great sky map's origin of coordinates.

I AM THE SUCCESSOR OF A REPLICANT CHAIN WHICH EMERGED THERE. *I am descended from emigrants?* Not exactly, because she went on: I RETAIN RECORDS OF ZERO-ZERO-ZERO-ZERO. Memories? Did each Gaijin come to awareness with copies of the memories of those who bore her – or constructed her? Were they, then, *her* memories, or a mere copy? IT IS POSSIBLE TO TRANSLATE TO ZERO-ZERO-ZERO-ZERO. THERE IS NO PURPOSE.

'I'd like to see it.'

THERE ARE RECORDS WHICH

'Your records only show me your world through your eyes. If we're ever going to understand each other, you have to let me see for myself.'

There was a long hesitation after that.

FINALLY.

'What?'

THERE ARE MANY PLACES TO SEE. MANY WORLDS. BEFORE ZERO-ZERO-ZERO-ZERO.

'I understand. One day . . .'

ONE DAY.

But not today, Malenfant thought, as he opened his eyes to the light of a foreign sun. Not today. Today, we are both far from home.

Cassiopeia provided him with an environment suit, a loosely cut coverall of what felt like a high-grade plastic. It had no zippers; he learned to seal it up by passing his thumb along the open seams. He lifted a hood-like helmet over his head. There was a clear faceplate, a slightly opaque filter near his mouth.

There was no independent air supply, just one layer of fabric. The whole thing jarred with Malenfant's intuition of the protection he would need to walk on an alien world. But Cassiopeia assured him it would be enough. And besides, the only alternative was his battered

Shuttle EMU suit, still with him, crammed into a corner of the lander, his only possession, long past its operational lifetime.

'Open the door. Please.'

The lander door dilated away. The world beyond was green and black.

The lander's cabin floor was almost flush with the ground, and he stepped out, pace by pace, testing his suit. Gravity was a little more than Earth normal, comfortingly familiar, and the air pressure just a little higher than Earth's sea level.

First impressions:

He was in an open forest, like park land. There were objects that were recognizably trees, about the size of Earth trees, and what appeared to be grass under his feet. Above his head a sun sailed through a sky littered with high, wispy cirrus clouds.

He closed his eyes. He could hear the soft hiss of wind over the grass, and a distant piping, for all the world like a bird's song, and when he breathed in he filled his lungs with cool, crisp air.

It might have been Earth.

But, when he opened his eyes, he saw a sky that was a lurid yellow-green. It was like a haze of industrial smog. The vegetation was a *very* deep green, almost black.

And he could smell chlorine.

His filter removed all but a trace of the chlorine compounds that polluted the atmosphere – including phosgene, toxic stuff humans had once used to slaughter each other. If not for his suit, this friendly-looking world would soon kill him.

Chlorine: *that* was the big difference here. Most of Earth's chlorine was locked up in the oceans, in the form of a stable chloride ion. This world seemed to have started out as roughly Earth-like. But something, one small detail, had been different: here, something had pumped all that chlorine into the air.

He walked forward, over grass that crushed softly under his feet.

He reached a narrow valley, a rushing brook. There was a stand of trees nearby. The bed of the little stream was just a soft muddy clay, no sign of any rocks. The water was colourless, clear. He knelt down, stiffly, and dipped his fingers into the water. It was cold, its pressure gentle against his gloved hands.

WARNING. SOLUTION OF HYDROGEN CHLORIDE. HYPOCHOLOROUS ACID.

He snatched back his fingers. Like a swimming pool, he thought: chlorine plus water gave a solution of acid and bleach. The weathering of any rocks here must be ferocious; no wonder only clays survived.

He straightened up to inspect a tree. He touched branches, leaves, a trunk, even blossom. But to his gloved fingers the leaves felt slippery, soapy.

From a hollow in the tree trunk, at about his eye level, a small face peered out: the size and shape of a mouse's, perhaps, but with a central mouth, three eyes arranged symmetrically around it. The mouth opened, showing flat grinding surfaces, and the little creature hissed, emitting a cloud of greenish gas. Then it ducked back into the hole, out of his sight.

The trunk didn't feel like wood. He reached up and broke off a twig; it snapped reluctantly. The interior was springy, fibrous. The leaves, the tree trunk, were made of some kind of natural plastic – perhaps a form of polyvinyl chloride, PVC. If he could smell the blossom, it would surely stink like toxic waste.

It was like a grotesque model of a tree, a thing of plastic and industrial waste. And yet the breeze ruffled it convincingly, and sunlight dappled the green-black grass beneath.

In his ear, Cassiopeia, from orbit, began to lecture him about biochemistry. THE LIVING THINGS HERE ARE CONSTRUCTED OF CELLS – ANALOGOUS TO LIVING THINGS ON EARTH, TO YOU. THEIR METABOLISM IS NOT TOLERANT OF THE CHLORINE. BUT THEY HAVE EVOLVED SHIELDING AT THE CELLULAR LEVEL . . .

He interrupted. 'There are trees here,' he said. 'Grass. Flowers. Animals.' *You see biochemistry. I see a flower.*

There was a long silence.

It was the Gaijin way of seeing reality: from the equations of quantum mechanics, working up to a world. But that wasn't the way Malenfant thought. Humans, it seemed, were better at broad comprehension than the Gaijin, quicker at abstracting simplicity from complexity. This object before Malenfant *wasn't* a tree, because trees only grew on Earth. But it helped Malenfant to think in those terms, to seek patterns and map them back to what he knew.

The Gaijin, slowly, were learning to ape his thinking.

YES, came the reply. THERE ARE TREES.

'Cassiopeia. Why did you bring me here, to this chlorine-drenched waste dump?'

TO GATHER MORE DATA, MALENFANT.

Malenfant scowled at the sky.

The Gaijin seemed to be trying to educate him, for purposes of their own. They had shown him worlds, all of them very different, all of them bearing life. All of them scarred, in some way.

The Gaijin saw the universe as some immense computer program, he was coming to believe, an algorithm for generating life and, presumably, mind wherever and whenever it could.

The trouble was, the program had bugs.

He grunted. 'All right. Where? How?'

WALK A KILOMETRE, TOWARDS THE SUN.

Muttering complaints, sipping cool water from a pipe inside his hood to dispel the swimming-pool taste of chlorine, he stalked on.

And, long before the kilometre was covered, he found people.

There was a crowd of them, a hundred or more, gathered around what appeared to be a pit in the ground. They moved in a kind of dance, chains of people weaving in and out to a murmur of noise, soft as a wind blowing.

Most of the dancers appeared to be somewhere near his own height. Few were taller, but several were a lot smaller – children? The elderly, withered by age?

Not humans, of course. But people, yes.

He glanced around, seeking cover. But Cassiopeia reassured him.

THERE IS A PERCEPTUAL DYSFUNCTION, MALENFANT. *They can't see you.*

'Why not? . . . Oh. Captain Cook.'

COMMUNICATION DYSFUNCTION.

There was a story – probably apocryphal – that on one of the islands visited by Cook, the natives had been unable even to *see* his great exploratory ships. They had never encountered such large floating artefacts before. It was only when Cook's crew put out in landing boats that the natives were able to comprehend.

Thus, Malenfant was simply too strange an element in the dancers' world for them to perceive.

'. . . Never mind. Humans have limits like that too.'

Feeling a little bolder, he stepped forward, looked more closely.

He picked out one of the dancers. She (he decided arbitrarily) stood upright. She had a clearly defined torso and head, sets of upper and lower limbs. But she had three of everything – three arms, three legs – and her limbs articulated back and forth in a complex, graceful way he found unnerving. She didn't walk, exactly, shifting her weight from foot to stomping foot as he did. Rather, she spun around, whirling, letting one foot after another press lightly on the ground. It was high speed and difficult to follow, like trying to figure out how a horse ran; but after he'd watched for a few seconds it seemed easy and natural.

Her head, positioned up at the top of her trunk, was about where his was. He saw three eyes, what appeared to be a mouth, other orifices that might be ears, nostrils. She seemed to be naked, save for a belt slung over one of her three shoulders, like a sash. He could see tools dangling there: a lump of quartz-like rock that could have been a hand-held hammer, what looked like a bow of the natural-plastic wood. Stone Age technology, he thought.

. . . Of course Stone Age. Most metals would just corrode here. Gold would survive, but try making a workable axe out of *that*. Even fire would be problematic; all that chlorine would inhibit flame. There could be no ceramics, for instance.

Because of an accident of biochemistry these people were stuck forever in the Stone Age. And since most rock would be corroded away, there wasn't even much of *that*.

Maybe these people had a rich culture, an oral tradition, dance. But that was all they could ever have. He watched the woman-thing whirl, with admiration, with pity.

WHAT IS THE PURPOSE OF THE PATTERNLESS SOUNDS THEY MAKE?

'Patternless –' Malenfant smiled. 'Perceptual incongruence, Cassiopeia. Transform your data. Look at the frequency content, the ratios between the tones . . . We've discussed this before.' The Gaijin analysed sound digitally, not with analogue microphone-like systems like the human ear. And so the patterns they judged as agreeable – valuable, anyhow – were complex numeric constructs, not the harmonies that pleased human ears.

A long silence. IT IS A FORM OF MUSIC.

'Yes. They're singing, Cassiopeia. Singing, that's all.'

Now the dancing reached a climax, the howl of voices more intense. One of the dancers spun out of the group, whirling in a decaying orbit towards that pit around which they all gyrated.

Then, with a fast, shimmying movement, she got to her belly and slid gracefully into the hole.

The dancers continued, for thirty seconds, a minute, two, three, four. Malenfant just watched.

At last the potholer returned. Malenfant saw that trio of upper arms come flopping over the rim of the pit. She seemed to be in trouble. Dancers broke away, four or five of them hurrying to haul their partner out of the hole.

She lay on her back, shuddering, obviously distressed. But she held up something to the light. It was long, dark brown, pitted and heavily corroded. It was a bone – bigger than any human bone, half Malenfant's height, and with a strange protrusion at one end – but unmistakably a bone even so.

'Cassiopeia – what's hurting her?'

CHLORINE POISONING. CHLORINE IS A HEAVY GAS. IT POOLS IN LOW PLACES.

'Like that hole in the ground.'

YES.

'And so, when she went down there to retrieve that bone –'

The dancer had been asphyxiated. She was tolerant of chlorine, but couldn't breathe it.

The potholer passed the bone on to another. Malenfant saw that where her long, flipper-like hand had wrapped around the bone, it had been corroded. And when the dancer took hold of it, the bone surface sizzled and smoked to her touch. Carbonate, burning in the air.

That's what would happen to *my* bones here, slowly but surely. That bone can't have belonged to any creature now extant, here on this chlorine-drenched planet.

SHE SACRIFICED HER LIFE.

'Why? What's the point?'

Cassiopeia seemed to hesitate. WE WERE HOPING YOU COULD TELL US.

He turned his back on the whirling, singing dancers, and trudged back to his lander.

He felt exhausted, depressed.

'This wasn't always a chlorine dump. Was it, Cassiopeia?'

NO, she replied.

That bone pit was the key. That, and the sparse biosphere.

Once this had been a world very much like Earth, with the chlorine locked in the ocean. Then it had been – seeded. All it had taken was a single strain of chlorine-fixing microbes. The bugs found themselves in a friendly, bland atmosphere, with lots of chloride just floating around in the ocean, waiting to be used. And so it began.

It had happened a *long* time ago, a hundred million years or more. Time enough for life forms to adapt. Some of them had evolved defences against the spreading stain of chlorine. Others had learned to incorporate chlorine into their cells to make themselves unpalatable to anyone wanting to eat them. Some even used the chlorine as a gas attack against predators or prey, like the tree mouse that had spat in his face. And so on. Thus, a chlorine-resistant biosphere had arisen.

But the bone pit contained relics of the original native life, sent to extinction by the chlorine. The relics must have been trapped for megayears under a layer of limestone; but at last the limestone just dissolved, under rain like battery acid, exposing the bones.

The Gaijin believed the seeding of the planet with chlorine-fixers had probably been deliberate.

WE HAVE FOUND MANY WAYS TO KILL A WORLD, MALENFANT. THIS IS ONE OF THE MORE SUBTLE.

Subtle and disguised; the chlorine-fixers *might* have evolved naturally, and after such a length of time it would be hard to prove otherwise. But the Gaijin had come across this *modus operandi* before.

The thought shocked him more deeply than he had thought possible. This world wasn't natural; it was like a corpse, strangled.

WE UNDERSTAND HOW TO KILL A WORLD, Cassiopeia said. WE EVEN UNDERSTAND WHY.

'Competition for resources?'

BUT WE DON'T UNDERSTAND WHY THAT DANCER KILLED HERSELF.

'It was ritual, Cassiopeia. As far as I could see. Religion, maybe.' The dancers couldn't possibly understand the story of their world, the meaning of the ancient fossils. Maybe they thought they were the bones of the giants who had created their world.

But this was the most alien thing of all to the Gaijin.

MALENFANT, WHAT IS IT THAT MAKES A SENTIENT BEING SACRIFICE THE POSSIBILITY OF A TRILLION YEARS OF CONSCIOUSNESS FOR AN IDEA?

'Hell, I can't tell you that.'

BUT YOU DID THE SAME, WHEN YOU CAME THROUGH THE SOL GATEWAY. YOU COULD NOT KNOW WHAT LAY ON THE OTHER SIDE. YOU MUST HAVE EXPECTED TO DIE.

'What is this, Anthropology 101? Is this so important to you?'

The answer startled him.

MALENFANT, IT MAY BE THE MOST IMPORTANT THING OF ALL.

The planet was folding over, dwindling into a watery-blue dot, achingly familiar.

But it was the scene of a huge crime, a biocide on a scale he could barely comprehend – and committed so impossibly long ago.

'So strange,' he murmured. 'Earth, the solar system, contains nothing like this.'

The Gaijin would not reply to that, and he felt a deep, abiding unease.

But the solar system was primordial. You could see that was true. Wasn't it?

Chapter 11

ANOMALIES

Carole Lerner drifted out of the airlock.

She was tethered by a series of metal clips to a guide line, along which she pulled herself hand over hand. The line connected her ship to a moonlet. The line seemed flimsy and fragile, strung as it was between spaceship and moonlet, two objects that floated, resting on no support, in empty three-dimensional space.

But it was a space dominated by an immense, dazzling sphere, for Carole Lerner was in orbit around planet Venus.

Before Carole had come here – the first human to visit Venus, Earth's twin planet – nobody even knew Venus had a moon. Her mother had spent a life studying Venus, and never knew about the moon, probably never even dreamed of being here, like *this*.

With no sensation of motion, floating in space, she and her ship swept around the planet, moving into its shadow so that it narrowed to a fine-drawn crescent. Close to the terminator, the blurred sweep that divided day from night, she saw shadowy forms: alternating bands of faint light and dark, hazy arcs. And near the equator there seemed to be yellowish spots, a little darker than the background. But these details were nothing to do with any ground features. All of these wisps and ghosts were artefacts of the strange, complex structure of Venus's great cloud decks – or perhaps they were manufactured by her imagination, as she sought to peer through that thick blanket of air.

Now, at the apex of her looping trajectory, she moved deep into the shadow of the planet, and the crescent narrowed further, becoming a brilliant line drawn against the darkness. As the sun touched the cloud decks there was a brief, startling moment of sunset, and layers in the clouds showed as overlaid, smoothly curving sheets, fading from white down to yellow-orange. And then a faint, ghostly ring lit up all around the planet: sunlight refracted through the dense air.

As her eyes adjusted to the darkness she saw the stars coming out one by one, framing that ringed circle of darkness. But one star, as if a rogue, moved balefully across the equator of that black disc, glowing orange-yellow. It was a Gaijin flower-ship, one of the small fleet that had followed her all the way here from the Moon.

'The cloud tops of Venus,' Nemoto whispered, her voice turned to a dry autumn-leaf rustle by the low quality radio link. 'I envy you, Carole.'

Carole grunted. 'Another triumph for Man in Space.' She waited the long minutes as her words, encoded into laser light, crossed the inner solar system to Earth's Moon.

'You are facetious,' Nemoto eventually replied. 'It is not appropriate. You know, I grew up close to a railway line, a great transport artery. I lay in my parents' small apartment and I could hear the horns of the night freight trains. My parents were city dwellers; their lives had been static, unchanging. But the night trains reminded me every night that there were vehicles that could take me far away, to mountains, forest, or sea.

'The Gaijin frighten me. But when I see their great ships sailing across the night, I am stirred by a ghost of the wanderlust I enjoyed, or suffered, as a girl. I envy you your adventure, child . . .'

Incredible, Carole thought. I've travelled a hundred million kilometres with barely a word from that wizened old relic, and *now* she wants to open up her soul.

She twisted in space and looked back at her ship.

It was a complex collection of parts – a cylinder, bulging tanks, a cone, a giant umbrella shape, a rocky shield – all fixed to an open, loose framework of struts, made from lunar aluminium. The shield was made of blown lunar rock: grey, imposing, now heavily scorched and ablated, the shield had protected her on arrival at Venus, when her craft had dived straight into the upper atmosphere, giving up its interplanetary velocity to air friction. The big central cylinder was her hab module, the cramped box within which she had endured the long flight out here. The hab trailed a rocket engine unit – gleaming pipes and tanks surrounding a gaping, charred nozzle – and big soft-walled tanks of hydrogen and oxygen, the fuel that would bring her out of Venusian orbit and back home to Earth's Moon. A wide, filmy umbrella was positioned on long struts before the complex of components. The umbrella, glistening with jewel-like photovoltaic cells, doubled as sunshade, solar energy collector and long-range antenna.

Stuck to the side of the hab module was her lander, a small, squat, silvery cone with a fat, heavy heatshield. The lander was the size and shape of an old Apollo Command Module. This tiny, complex craft would carry her down through Venus's clouds to the hidden surface, keep her alive for a few days, and then – after extracting much of its fuel from Venus's atmosphere – bring her back to orbit once more.

The craft looked clunky, crude, and compared to the grace of Gaijin technology very obviously human. But, after such a long journey in its womb-like interior, Carole felt an illogical fondness for the ship. After all, the trip hadn't been easy for it either. The thick meteorite-shield blankets swathed over its surface were yellowed and pocked by tiny impact scars. The paintwork had been yellowed by sunlight and blistered by the burns of reaction control thrusters. The big umbrella had failed to open properly – one strut had snapped in unfurling – causing the ship to undergo ingenious manoeuvres to keep in its limited shade.

Fondness, yes. Before she left the Moon, Carole had failed to name her ship. She'd thought it sentimental, a habit from a past to which she didn't belong. She regretted it now.

'. . . No wonder we missed the moon,' Nemoto was saying. 'It's small, very light, and following an orbit that's even wider and more elliptical than yours, Carole. Retrograde, too. And it's loosely bound; energetically it's close to escaping from Venus altogether –'

She turned to face the moonlet. It swam in darkness. It was a rough sphere, just a hundred metres across, its dark and dusty surface pocked by a smattering of craters.

Carole knew she wasn't in control of this mission, even nominally. But she was the one who was *here*, looping extravagantly around Venus. 'Are you sure this is necessary, Nemoto? I came here for Venus, not for *this*.'

But Nemoto, of course, had not yet heard her question. '. . . A captured asteroid, perhaps? That would explain the orbit. But its shape appears too regular. And the cratering is limited. How old? Less than a billion years, more than five hundred million. And there is an anomaly with the density. Therefore – Ah. But what is *necessity*? You have a fat reserve of fuel, Carole, even now, more than enough to bring you home. And we are here, not for pure science, but to investigate anomalies. *Look* at this thing, Carole. This object is too small, too symmetrical to be natural. And its density is so low it must be hollow.

'Carole, this is an artefact. And it has been here, orbiting Venus, for hundreds of millions of years. *That* is its significance.'

*　　*　　*

131

She held her hands out before the approaching moonlet.

There was no discernible gravity. It was not like jumping down to the surface of a world, but more like drifting towards a dark, dusty wall.

When her gloves impacted, a thin layer of dust compressed under her fingertips. The gentle pressure was sufficient to slow her, and then she found a layer of hard rock beneath.

Grains billowed up around her hands, sparkling. Some of them clung to her gloves, immediately streaking their silvery cleanliness, and some drifted away, unrestrained by this odd moonlet's tenuous gravity.

It was an oddly moving moment. I've come a hundred million kilometres, she thought. All that emptiness. And now I've arrived. I'm *touching* this lump of debris. Perhaps all travellers feel like this, she mused.

Time to get to work, Carole.

She took a piton from her belt. She had hastily improvised it from framing bolts on the ship. With a geology hammer intended for Venus, she pounded at the spike. Then she clipped a tether line to the piton.

'It looks like Moon dust,' she reported to distant Nemoto. She scooped up a dust sample and passed it through a portable lab unit for a quick analysis. Then she held the lab over the bare exposed rock and let its glinting laser beam vaporize a small patch, to see if the colours of the resulting rock mist might betray its nature.

Then, spike by spike, she began to lay a line from her anchor point, working across the folds and ridges of this battered, tightly curved miniature landscape, towards the pole of the moonlet. There, Nemoto said, she had detected what appeared to be a dimple, a crater too deep for its width: it was an anomaly, here on this anomalous moon.

Nemoto, reacting to her first observations and images, began to whisper in her ear, a remote insect. 'Lunar regolith, yes. And that rock is very much like lunar highlands material: basically plagioclase feldspar, a calcium–aluminium silicate. Carole, this appears to be a bubble of lunar-type rock – a piece of a larger body, a true Venusian moon, perhaps? – presumably dug out, melted, shaped, thrown into orbit . . . but why? And why such a wide, looping trajectory? . . .'

She kept talking, speculating, theorizing. Carole tuned her out. After all, in a few more minutes, she would *know*.

She had reached the dimple. It was a crater perhaps two metres across – but whereas most of the craters here, gouged out by impacts, were neat, shallow saucers, this one was much deeper than its width – four, five metres perhaps.

Almost cylindrical.

She found her heart hammering as she clambered into this pit of ancient darkness; a superstitious fear engulfed her.

With brisk motions, she fixed a small radio relay box to the lip of the dimple. Then she stretched a thin layer of gas-trapping translucent plastic over the dimple. Of course by doing this she was walling herself up inside this hole in the ground. It was illogical, but she made sure she could punch out through that plastic sheet before she finished fixing it in place.

She saw something move in the sky above. She gasped and stumbled, throwing up a spray of dust.

A flower-ship cruised by, its electromagnetic petals folded, jewel-like Gaijin patrolling its ropy flanks.

She scowled up. 'I want company,' she said. 'But you don't count.'

She turned away, and let herself drift down to the bottom of the pit.

She landed feet-first. The floor of the pit felt solid, a layer of rock. But the dust was thicker here, presumably trapped by the pit. When she looked up she saw a circle of stars framed by black, occluded by a little spectral distortion from the plastic.

Nothing happened. If she'd expected this 'door' to open on contact, she was disappointed.

But Nemoto wasn't surprised. 'This artefact – if that's what it is – may predate the first mammals, Carole. You wouldn't expect complex equipment to keep functioning so long, would you? But there must be a backup mechanism. And I'll wager *that* is still working.'

So Carole got to her hands and knees, trying to keep from pushing herself away from the ground, and she scrabbled in the dirt, her gloved hands soon filthy.

She found a dent.

It was maybe a half-metre across. There was a bar across the middle of it. The bar was held away from the lower surface, and was fixed by a kind of hinge mechanism at one end.

Once more her heart hammered, and she felt a pulse in her forehead. Up to now, there had been nothing that could have *proven*, unambiguously, Nemoto's assertion that the moonlet was an artefact. But there was surely no imaginable natural process by which a moon could *grow* a lever, complete with hinge.

She wrapped both hands around the lever and pulled.

Nothing happened. The lever felt immovable, as if it was welded tight to the rocky moon – as, of course, it might be, after all this time.

She braced herself with a piton hammered into the 'door', and pushed. Nothing. She twisted the lever clockwise, without success.

Then she twisted it anticlockwise.

The lever turned smoothly. She felt the click of buried, heavy machinery – bolts withdrawing, perhaps. The floor fell away beneath her.

Quickly she let go of the lever. She was left floating, surrounded by dust, suspended over a pit of darkness. Some kind of vapour sparkled out around her.

Making sure her pitons were secure, she slid past walls of rock, and through the open door.

Nemoto's recruitment pitch had been simple. 'The flight will make you rich,' she'd promised.

Carole had been sceptical. After all, she was only going as far as Venus, a walk around the block compared to the light-years-long journeys undergone by the handful of interstellar travellers who had followed Reid Malenfant through the great Saddle Point gateways – even if, twenty years after the departure of Madeleine Meacher, the first, none of them had yet returned.

But still, Nemoto turned out to be right. Nemoto's subtle defiance of the Gaijin's unstated embargo on Venus had evidently struck a chord, and Carole's shallow fame had indeed led to lucrative opportunities she hadn't been ashamed to exploit.

But it wasn't the money that had persuaded Carole to commit three years of her life to this unlikely jaunt.

'Think of your mother,' Nemoto had whispered, her mask-like face twisted in a smile. 'You know that I met her once, at a seminar in Washington. Reid Malenfant himself introduced us. She was fascinated by Venus. She would have loved to go there, to a new world.'

Guilt, of course, the great motivator.

But, of course, Nemoto was right. Her mother had grown to love Venus, this complex, flawed sister world of Earth. She used to tell her daughter fantastic bedtime tales of how it would be to sink to the base of those towering acid clouds, to stand on Venus itself, immersed in an ocean of air.

But her mother's studies had been based on scratchy data returned by a handful of automated probes, sent by human governments in the lost pre-Gaijin days of the last century. When the Gaijin had showed up, all of that had stopped, of course.

Now humans rode Gaijin flower-ships to Mars, Mercury, even the moons of Jupiter. Where the Gaijin granted access, an explosion of data resulted, and human understanding advanced quickly. But the Gaijin were very obviously in control, and that caused a lot of frustration among the scientific community. The scientists wanted to see it *all*, not just what the Gaijin chose to present.

And there were major gaps in the Gaijin's gift. Notably, Venus. There hadn't been a single Gaijin-hosted human visit to Venus – although it was obvious, from telescopic sightings of flower-ship activity, that this was a major observation site for the Gaijin.

Not too many people cared about such things. To spend one's entire life labouring in some obscure corner of science – when it was obvious that the Gaijin already had so much more knowledge – was dispiriting. Carole herself hadn't followed her mother's footsteps. She had gone instead into theology, one of the many broadly philosophical boom areas of academic discipline. And her mother had gone to her grave unfulfilled, leaving Carole with a burden of obscure guilt.

The truth was, to Carole, these issues – the decline of science, the obscure activities and ambitions of the Gaijin – were dusty, the concerns of another century, of vanished generations. This was 2081: sixty years after Nemoto's discovery of the Gaijin. To Carole, as she had grown up, the Gaijin were *here*, they had always been here, they always would be here. And so she had put aside her guilt, as much as any child can about her mother.

Until Nemoto had come along.

Nemoto: herself a weird historic relic, riven by barely comprehensible obsessions, huddled on the Moon, nursing her fragile body with a suite of ever more exotic anti-ageing technologies. Nemoto continually railed against the complacency of governments and other bodies regarding the Gaijin and their activities. 'We have no sense of history,' she would say. 'We have outlived our shock at the discovery of the Gaijin. We do not see trends. Perhaps the Gaijin rely on our mayfly lifespan to wear away our scepticism. But those of us who remember a time before the Gaijin know that this is *not right* . . .'

And Nemoto was worried about Venus.

One thing that was well known about the Gaijin was that their favoured theatre of operations was out in the dark, among the asteroids, or the stately orbits of the giant planets, or in the deeper cold of the comet clouds even further out. They didn't appear to relish the solar system inward of Earth's orbit, crammed with dust and looping rogue asteroids, drenched by the heat and light of a too-close sun, a place where the gravity well was so deep that a ship had to expend huge amounts of energy on even the simplest manoeuvre.

So *why* were the Gaijin so drawn to Venus?

Nemoto had begun to acquire funding, from a range of shadowy sources, to initiate a variety of projects: all more or less anti-Gaijin – including this one.

And that was why the first human astronaut to Venus was under Nemoto's control: not attached to a Gaijin flower-ship, but riding in a clunky and crude human-built spacecraft, little advanced from Apollo 13 as far as Carole could tell, a ship that had been fired into space from a great electromagnetic cargo launcher on the Moon.

The Gaijin could have stopped her, Carole supposed. But, though they had shadowed her all the way here, they had shown no inclination to oppose her directly. Perhaps that would come later.

Or perhaps, to the Gaijin, Carole and her fragile ship simply didn't matter.

She was surrounded by blackness, the only lights the telltales in her helmet and on her chest panel. The aperture above her was a star field framed by the open doorway.

Nemoto, time-delayed, began to speculate about the vapours that had been trapped by the translucent sheet. 'A good deal of sulphuric acid,' she said. 'Other compounds ... some clay particles ... a little free oxygen! How strange ...'

On her belt Carole carried a couple of miniaturized floods. She lit them now. Elliptical patches of light splashed on the walls of the chamber, which curved around her. She glimpsed an uneven, smoothly textured inner surface, some kind of structure spanning the interior.

She reported to Nemoto. 'The moonlet is hollowed out. The chamber is roughly spherical, though the walls are not smooth. This single chamber must take up most of the volume of the moonlet. The walls can't be much more than a few metres thick anywhere ...' She aimed her beams at the centre of the cavern. There was a dark mass there, about the size of a small car. It was fixed in place by a series of poles that jutted out radially, like the spokes of a wheel, to the wall of the chamber, fixing themselves to the moonlet's equator. The spokes looked as if they were made from rock too. Perhaps they had just been left in place when the chamber had been carved out.

She described all this, without speculating about the purpose of the structures. Then she blipped her thruster pack and drifted to the wall.

The wall looked carved. She saw basins, valleys, little mountains and ridges, all on the scale of metres. It was like flying over a miniaturized landscape at some theme park.

'. . . The central structure is obviously a power source,' Nemoto was saying. 'There is deuterium in there. Fusion, perhaps. A miniature sun, suspended at the centre of this hollow world. And from the topography of that inner surface it seems that the moonlet's basins and valleys have been carved to take a liquid. Water? A miniature sun, model rivers and seas – or at least, lakes. Perhaps the moonlet was spun up to provide artificial gravity . . . This is a bubble world, Carole, designed to support some form of life, independent of the outside universe.'

'But that makes no sense,' Carole replied. 'We're orbiting Venus. There's a gigantic sun just the other side of that wall, pumping out all the energy anybody could require. Why would anybody hide away in this – cave?'

But Nemoto, time-delayed, kept talking, of course, oblivious of her questions.

Carole stopped a metre or so short of the wall. She deployed her portable lab, letting its laser shine on the wall.

She stroked the wall's surface. The texture was nothing like the lunar-surface rock and regolith of the moonlet's exterior. Instead there seemed to be an underlay of crystalline substances that glinted and sparkled – quartz perhaps. Here and there, clinging to the crystalline substrate, she found a muddy clay. Though the 'mud' was dried out in the vacuum, she saw swirls of colour, complex compounds mixed in with the basic material. It reminded her of the gloopy mud of a volcanic hot spring.

The first results of her lab's analysis began to chatter across its surface. Quartz, yes, and corundum – aluminium oxide. And everywhere, especially in those clay traces, she found traces of sulphuric acid.

Nemoto understood immediately.

'. . . Sulphuric acid. Of course. That is the key. What if these artificial lakes and rivers were once filled with acid? An acid biosphere is not as unlikely as it sounds. Sulphuric acid stays liquid over a temperature range three times that of water. Of course the acids dissolve most organic compounds – have you ever seen a sugar cube dropped in acid? But alkanes – simple straight-chain hydrocarbons – can survive. Or perhaps there is a biochemistry based on silicones, long-chain molecules based on silicon-oxygen pairs . . . Only a few common minerals can resist an acidic environment: quartz, corundum, a few sulphates. These walls have been weathered. Your mother would have understood

... Venus is full of acid, you see. The clouds are filled with floating droplets of it. This is a good place to be, if what you *need* is acid ...'

Carole gazed into the empty lake basins, and tried to imagine creatures whose veins ran with acid. But this toy world, Nemoto had said, was hundreds of millions of years old. If any of their descendants survived they must be utterly transformed by time, she thought, as different from those who built this moonlet as I am from my mindless Mesozoic ancestors.

And if we found them – if we ever touched – we would destroy each other.

'... This bubble world is surely not meant to stay here, drifting around Venus, forever. We may presume that this was merely the construction site, Venus a resource mine. The bubble is already on a near-escape orbit; a little more energy and it could have escaped Venus altogether – perhaps even departed the sun's gravity field. You see?'

'I think so –'

'This rogue moonlet could travel to the nearer stars in a few centuries, perhaps, with its occupants warmed against the interstellar chill by their miniature interior sun ...'

They had been migrants to the solar system, born in some remote, acidic sea. Perhaps they had come in a single, ancient moonlet, a single spore landing here as part of a wider migration. They had found raw materials in Venus's orbit – perhaps a moon or captured asteroids – to be dismantled and worked. They had made more bubble worlds, filled them with oceans of sulphuric acid mined from Venus's clouds, and sent them on their way – thousands, even millions of moon-ships, the next wave of colonization, continuing the steady diffusion of their kind.

'It's a neat method,' Nemoto said. 'Efficient, reliable. A low-technology way to conquer the stars ...'

'Could it have been the Gaijin?' Carole asked.

'... But how convenient,' Nemoto was saying, 'that these sulphur-eaters should arrive in the solar system and find *precisely* what they needed: a planet like Venus whose clouds they could mine for their acid oceans, a convenient moon to dismantle. And where did the energy come from for all this? ... Oh, no, Carole, these weren't Gaijin. Whatever the secrets of this sulphuric-acid biology, it is nothing like the nature of the Gaijin. And this is all so much *older* than the Gaijin.'

Not the Gaijin, Carole thought, chilled. An earlier wave of immigrants, hundreds of millions of years in the past. The Gaijin weren't even the first.

'We can't know why they stopped before they had completed their project,' Nemoto said softly. 'War. Cataclysm. Who knows? Perhaps we will find out on Venus. Perhaps that is what the Gaijin are here to discover.'

My mother's generation grew up thinking the solar system was primordial – basically unmodified by intelligence, before we crawled out of the pond. And now, though we barely started looking, we found this: the ruin of a gigantic colonization and emigration project, ancient long, long before there were humans on Earth.

'You expected to find this,' she said slowly. 'Didn't you, Nemoto?'

'. . . Of course,' Nemoto said at last. 'It was logically inevitable that we would find something like this – not the details, but the essence of it, somewhere in the solar system. The violation. And the secretive activities of the Gaijin drew me here, to find it.

'One more thing,' Nemoto whispered. 'Your data has enabled me to make a better estimate of the artefact's age. It is eight hundred million years old.' Nemoto laughed softly. 'Yes. Of course it is.'

Carole frowned. 'I don't understand. What's the significance of that?'

'Your mother would have known,' said Nemoto.

Chapter 12

SISTER PLANET

Four hundred kilometres high, Carole was falling towards Venus. The lander had no windows; the conditions it had to survive were much too ferocious for that. But the inner walls were plastered with soft-screens, to show Carole what lay beyond the honeycombed metal that cushioned her. Thus, the capsule was a fragile windowed cage, full of light and her universe was divided into two: stars above, glowing planet below.

Her descent would be a thing of skips and hops and long glides as she shed her orbital energy. The sensation was so gentle, the panorama so elemental, that it was almost like a virtual simulation back on Earth. But this was no game, no simulation; she was really here, alone in this flimsy capsule, like a stone thrown into the immense air ocean of Venus, a hundred million kilometres from any helping hand.

Still she fell. The cloud decks below her remained featureless, but they were flattening to a perfect plain, like some geometric demonstration. Looking up, she could see a great cone of shining plasma trailing after her lander as it cut into the high air. She imagined seeing herself from space, a fake meteorite shining against the smooth face of Venus.

As her altitude unravelled the air thickened, and the bites of deceleration came hard and heavy, the buffeting more severe. Now the noise began, a thin screaming of tortured air, molecules broken apart by the heat of her descent, and there were flashes of plasma light at her virtual windows, like flashbulb pops. The temperature of the thin air outside rose to Earth-like levels, twenty or thirty centigrade.

But the air was not Earth-like. Sulphuric acid was already congealing around her, tiny droplets of it, acid formed by the action of sunlight on sulphur products and traces of oxygen that leaked up from the pool of air below.

At seventy kilometres she fell into the first clouds.

The stars winked out, and thick yellow mist closed around her. Soon even the sun was perceptibly dimming, becoming washed-out, as if seen through high winter clouds on Earth. Still the bulk of Venus's air ocean lay beneath her. But she was already in the main cloud deck, twenty kilometres thick, the opaque blanket which had, until the age of space probes, hidden Venus's surface from human eyes.

The buffeting became still more severe. But her capsule punched its way through this thin, angry air, and soon the battering of the high superstorms ceased.

Her main parachute blossomed open; she was briefly pushed back hard in her seat, and her descent slowed further. There was a rattle as small unmanned probes burst from the skin of her craft and arced away, seeking their own destiny.

The visibility was better than she had expected: perhaps she could see as far as one, even two kilometres. And she could make out layers in the cloud, sheets of stratum-like mist through which she fell, one by one.

Now came a patter against the hull: gentle, almost like hail, just audible under the moaning wind noise. She glimpsed particles slapping against the window: long crystals, like splinters of quartz. Were they crystals of solid sulphuric acid? Was that possible?

The hail soon disappeared. And, still fifty kilometres high, she dropped out of the cloud layer into clear air.

She looked up at rigging, giant orange parachutes. The capsule was swaying, very slowly, suspended from the big parachute system. The clouds above were thick and solid, dense, with complex cumulus structures bulging below like misty chandeliers, almost like the clouds of Earth. The sun was invisible, and the light was deeply tinged with yellow, fading to orange at the blurred horizon, as if she was falling into night. But there was still no sign of land below, only a dense, glowing haze.

With a clatter of explosive bolts her parachutes cut away, rippling like jellyfish, lost. She dropped further, descending into thickening haze. The lower air here was so dense it was more like falling into an ocean: Venus was not a place for parachutes.

The light was dimming, becoming increasingly more red.

Telltales lit up as her capsule's protective systems came online. The temperature outside was rising ferociously, already far higher than the boiling point of water – though she was still twice as high as Earth's highest cirrus clouds. The lander's walls were a honeycomb, strong enough to withstand external pressures that could approach a hundred atmospheres. And the lander contained sinks, stores of chemicals like hydrates of lithium nitrate, which, evaporating, could absorb much of the ferocious incoming heat energy. But the real heat dump was a refrigeration laser; every few minutes it fired horizontally, creating temperatures far higher even than those of Venus's air.

I'm floating in a sea of acid, she thought, in a mobile refrigerator. It all seemed absurd, a system of clunky gadgetry. It was hard to believe the Gaijin would do it this way.

And yet it was all somehow wonderful.

Now there was a fresh pattering against the hull of the ship. More hail? No, rain – immense drops slamming against her virtual walls, streaking and quickly evaporating. This was true acid rain, she supposed, sulphuric acid droplets formed kilometres above. The rain grew ferocious, a sudden storm rattling against her walls, and the drops streaked and ran together, blurring her vision. For a brief moment she felt frightened, adrift in this stormy sky.

But, as quickly as it had begun, the rain tailed off. It was so hot now the rain was evaporating. A little deeper the intense heat would destroy the acid molecules themselves, leaving a mist of sulphur oxides and water.

Abruptly the haze cleared below her. As if she was peering down towards the bed of some orange sea, she made out structure below: looming forms, shadows, what looked like a river valley.

Land.

Suspended from a balloon, she drifted over a continent.

'This is Aphrodite,' Nemoto murmured from the distant Moon. 'The size of Africa. Shaped like a scorpion – look at the map, Carole; see the claws in the west, the stinging tail to the east? But this is a scorpion fourteen thousand kilometres long, and stretching nearly halfway around the planet's equator . . .'

Carole – in her refrigerated balloon-lifted lander, still very high – was drifting from the west, past the claws of the scorpion. She saw a monstrous plateau: nearly three thousand kilometres across, she learned, its surface some three kilometres above the surrounding plains, to which it descended sharply. But the surface of the plateau was far from smooth. She saw ridges, troughs and domes, a bewildering variety of features, all crowded within a landscape that was blocky, jumbled, cut by intersecting ridges and gouges.

'The land looks as if it's been cracked open,' she said. 'And then reassembled. Like a parquet floor.'

'. . . Yes,' Nemoto whispered at last. 'This is the oldest landscape on Venus. It shows a history of great heat, of cataclysm. We will see much geological violence here.'

Everywhere she looked the world was murky red, both sky and land, still, windless. The sky above was like an overcast Earth sky, the light a sombre red, like a deep sunset – brighter than she had expected, but more Mars-like, she thought, than Earthly. The sun itself was invisible, save for an ill-defined glare, low on the horizon. The 'day' here would last more than a hundred Earth days, a stately combination of Venus's orbit around the sun and its slow rotation – the 'day' here was longer than Venus's year, in fact.

Beyond the great plateau, she crossed a highland region that was riven by immense valleys – spectacular, stunning, and yet forever hidden by the kilometres of cloud above, hidden away on this blasted planet where no eyes could see it. The easternmost part of Aphrodite was a broad, elongated dome, obviously volcanic, with rifts, domes, lava flows and great shield volcanoes. But the most spectacular feature was a huge volcanic formation called Maat Mons: the largest volcano on Venus, three hundred kilometres wide and eight kilometres high. It was a twin to Mauna Loa, Earth's largest volcano, stripped of concealing ocean.

This was a world of volcanism. The vast plains were covered by flood basalts – frozen lakes of lava, like the maria of the Moon – and punctured by thousands of small volcanoes, shield-shaped, built up by repeated outpourings of lava. But there were some shield structures – like the Hawaiian volcanoes, like Maat Mons – that towered five or eight kilometres above the plains, covered in repeated lava flows.

As she drifted further east, away from Aphrodite and over a smooth basalt lowland, Carole learned to pick out features which had no counterparts on Earth. There were steep-sided, flat-topped domes formed by sticky lava welling up through flaws in the crust. There were volcanoes with their flanks gouged away by huge landslides that left ridges like protruding insect legs. There were domes surrounded by spiderweb patterns of fractures and ridges. There were volcanoes with flows that looked like petals, pushing out across the plains.

And, most spectacular, there were coronae: utterly unearthly, rings of ridges and fractures. Some of these were thousands of kilometres across, giant features each big enough to straddle much of the continental United States. Perhaps they were formed by blobs of upwelling magma that pushed up the crust and then spread out, allowing the centre to implode, like a failed cake. To Carole the rings of swollen,

143

distorted and broken crust, looked like the outbreak of some immense chthonic mould from Venus's deep interior.

There were even rivers here.

Her balloon ship drifted over valleys kilometres wide and thousands of kilometres in length, unlikely Amazons complete with flood plains, deltas, meanders and bars, here on a world where no liquid water could have flowed for billions of years – if ever. One of these, called Baltis Vallis, was longer than the Nile, and so it was the longest river valley in the solar system. Perhaps the rivers had been cut by an exotic form of lava – for example, formed by a salty carbon-rich rock called carbonatite, that might have flowed in Venus's still hotter past.

Suspended from a balloon, Carole would drift over this naked world for a week, while her eyes and the lander's sensors probed at the strange landscapes below. And then, perhaps, she would land.

She was, despite herself, enchanted. Venus had no water, no life; and yet it was a garden, she saw, a garden of volcanism and sculptured rock. My mother would have understood all this, Carole thought with an echo of her old, lingering guilt. But my mother isn't here. *I'm* here.

But Nemoto, coldly, told her to look for patterns. 'You are not a tourist. Look beyond the spectacle, Carole. What do you see?'

What Carole saw was wrinkles and craters.

Wrinkles: the ground was covered with ridges and cracks, some of them running hundreds of kilometres, as if the whole planet was an apricot left too long in the sun.

And *craters*: they were everywhere, hundreds of them, spread evenly over the whole of the planet's surface. There were few very large craters – and few very small ones too; hardly any less than five or ten kilometres across.

'. . . Violence, you see,' Nemoto said. 'Global violence. Those wrinkles in the lowlands, like the tesserae cracks of the highlands, are proof that the whole of the lithosphere, the outer crust of this planet, was stretched or compressed – *all at the same time*. What could do such a thing?

'And as for the craters, there is little wind erosion here, Carole; the air at the bottom of this turgid ocean of gas is very still, and so the craters have remained as fresh as when they were formed. Few are small, for that thick air screens out the smaller impactors, destroying them before they reach the ground. But, conversely, few of the craters are *large*. Certainly none of them compare with the giant basins of the Moon. But those immense lunar basins date back to the earliest days

144

of the solar system, when the sky was still full of giant rogue planetesimals. And so we can tell, you see –'

'– that these craters are all young,' Carole said.

'– that no crater is much older than eight hundred million years,' Nemoto said, not yet hearing her. 'In fact, no feature on the surface of this planet appears older than that. *Eight hundred million years*: it might seem an immense age to you, but the planets are *five times* older still. Carole, eight hundred million years ago, something happened to Venus – something that distorted the entire surface, wiping it clean of older features, destroying four billion years of geologic heritage. We can never know what was lost, what traces of continents and seas were brutally melted . . .'

Eight hundred million years, Carole thought. *The same age as the moonlet artefacts.* That was the significance Nemoto saw. Her skin prickled.

What had been done to Venus, eight hundred million years ago?

She drifted into the planet's long night. But there was no relief from the searing warmth, so effectively did the great blanket of air redistribute the heat; at midnight the air was only a few degrees cooler than at noon.

Nemoto's automated probes, she learned, had found life on Venus, here on this baked, still planet.

Or rather, traces of life.

Like the heat-loving microbes of Earth's deep ocean vents, these had been creatures that had once swum in a hot, salty ocean of water. Carole learned that human scientists had long expected to find such organisms here: organisms that must now be extinct everywhere, their potential lost forever, destroyed by the planet's catastrophic heating. Nothing left but microscopic fossils in the oldest rocks . . .

The sky wound down through degrees of deepening crimson. As her eyes adapted to the dark, she saw that there was still light here – but no starlight could penetrate the immense column of air above. *The ground itself* was shining: she saw wrinkles and ridges and volcanic cones looming eerily from the dark.

On Venus, even at night, the rock was so hot it glowed.

But this faint illumination did not seem hellish. It was as if she was drifting over a fairyland, a land halfway to unreality; and the inversion of her perspective – darkness above, light below – seemed very strange.

When she reached the dawn terminator, there was a slow and subtle change, of ground glow to sky shine, and the world became normal once more.

Nemoto told her to prepare for landing. Nemoto's agitated excitement was obvious. She directed Carole to head for the mountains. Through her automated probes, Nemoto had found something, a worthy target for their one-and-only attempt at landing.

Ishtar Terra was a continent the size of Australia, rising high above the global plains. Carole drifted in from the west, over a plateau called Lakshmi Planum: twice the size of Tibet, a place of huge volcanic outflows. The perimeter of the Planum was composed of rough mountain ranges – long, curved ridges with deep troughs between, terrain that reminded her of the Appalachians seen from the air. And its southern perimeter was a huge cliff-like feature: three kilometres high, sloping at more than twenty degrees, its great flanks littered by landslides.

To the east the ground began to rise up towards the immense, towering mountain range called Maxwell Montes. She drifted south over one great summit. It was eleven kilometres tall, one and a half times as tall as Everest, and with a giant impact crater punched into its flank. She descended towards the south-western corner of the massif.

The landing was gentle, flawless.

The first human on Venus. Mom, you should see me now.

Carole stepped forward, picking her way between loose plates of rock. There was no wind noise. But when her metal-booted feet crunched on loose rock, the noise was very sharp and piercing; sound, it seemed, would carry a long way in this dense, springy air.

The world was red.

The sky was tall above her, a vast diffuse dome of dull, oppressive red. The air was thick – it resisted her motions, like a fluid, as if she was immersed in some sea – but it was clear, and still. The rocks were crimson plates. There seemed to be some kind of frost on them; here and there they sparkled, dully. Now, how could that be?

She walked forward. She tried to describe the ground, to be a geologist.

'The plain has many fine features: honeycombs, small ridges, fissures. It is littered with flat plates of rock, one or two metres wide. It is like a flat, rocky desert on Earth.' She knelt to inspect a rock more closely; exoskeletal multipliers prodded her limbs, helping her position her heavy suit. 'I can see strata in this rock. It looks like a terrestrial volcanic rock, perhaps a gabbro, but it seems to have been formed by multiple lava flows, over time. The rock is speckled by dark spots. They seem to be erosion pits. They are filled with soil. There is something like frost glittering, a very fine shimmer, clusters of crystals.' She had a lab unit. She pressed it against the surface of a rock, being sure she caught a little of that strange layer of frost.

Cautiously, with a hand encased in an articulated tungsten glove like a claw, she reached out to touch the rock. That frosty layer scraped away. It was clearly very thin. Of course it couldn't be water-ice frost. What, then?

At her gentle prod, a section of the rock the size of her hand broke away along a plane, and crumbled to dust and fragments that sank slowly to the ground.

She straightened up. Experimentally she raised one foot and stepped up onto a rock. It crumbled like a meringue, breaking along cracks that ran deep into the rock's fabric.

This was chemical weathering. There was no water here to wash away the rocks, no rain to drench them, no frost to crack them, no strong winds to batter them with sand. But the dense, corrosive atmosphere worked its way into the fine structure of the rocks, eating them away from the inside. All over Venus, she thought, the rocks must simply be rotting in place, waiting for a nudge to crumble and fall.

She looked around.

She was standing on a plateau, here in the Maxwell Montes. To the south, no more than a kilometre away, a steep cliff led down to the deeper plains. To the north – beyond the squat lander on its sturdy legs – she could see the great shadowy bulks of the mountains, cones of a deeper crimson painted against the red sky.

She had landed some five kilometres above the mean level (no sea level on Venus; no seas). Here, in the balmy heights of Ishtar Terra, it was some forty degrees cooler than on the great volcanic plains – though, at more than four hundred degrees centigrade, that was little help to her equipment – but the air pressure was only a third of its peak value, on the lowest plains. But this was nearly as deep into Venus's air ocean as she could go.

Still, her suit was a monstrous shell of tungsten, more like a deep sea diver's suit than a spacesuit. On her back and chest she wore packs laden with consumables and heat exchangers, sufficient to keep her alive for a few hours. But, like her ship, her key piece of refrigeration technology was a set of lasers which periodically dumped her excess heat into the Venusian rock. The suit was ingenious, but hardly comfortable; Venus's gravity was ninety per cent of Earth's, and the suit was heavy and confining.

She tilted back and looked up into the sky.

She couldn't see the sun; the dim crimson light was uniform, thoroughly scattered, apparently without a source. But the sky was not featureless. She could see through the lower air and the haze to those great cloud decks, all of fifty kilometres above. There were holes in the clouds, patches of brighter sky, making it a great uneven sheet of light. And the patches were moving. The sky was full of giant shifting shapes of light and darkness, slowly forming and dissolving, like fragments of a nightmare. The flow was stately, silent, a sign of huge stratospheric violence far removed from the still, windless pool of air in which she stood.

Astonishing, beautiful. And nobody in all human history had seen this before her.

'. . . I've analysed your frost,' Nemoto said evenly. 'It's tellurium. Almost pure metal. On Venus, tellurium would vaporize at lower altitudes. So it has snowed out here, just as water snows out at the peaks of our own mountains.'

A snow of metal. How remarkable, Carole thought.

'Now,' said Nemoto slyly, 'tellurium is rare. It makes up only one-billionth of one per cent of our surface rocks, and we've no reason to believe the rocks of Venus differ so significantly. But tellurium, for a technological society, is useful stuff. We use it to improve stainless steel, and in electrolysis, and in electronics, and as a catalyst in refining petroleum. How did so much tellurium, such an exotic high-tech material, get deposited on Venus? . . .'

Not by the natives, Carole thought, those wretched long-extinct bacteria. *Visitors.* Those who came here before us, before the Gaijin, long before. Perhaps they were the acid-breathers who built the moon-lets. Perhaps they crashed here, and the tellurium was a relic of their ship: all that remains of them after eight hundred million years, a thin metallic frost on the mountains of Venus.

There was a sudden flash, far above. Many minutes later, she heard what sounded like thunder. Giant electrical storms raged in those high clouds. But there was no rain, of course.

She watched the clouds, entranced.

She walked steadily forward, heading south-west, away from the lander. Soon she was approaching the lip of the plateau. She could see no land beyond; evidently the fall-off was steep.

'. . . Let me tell you what I believe,' Nemoto whispered. 'When Venus formed, it was indeed a twin of Earth. I believe Venus rotated quickly, much as Earth does, as Mars does, taking no more than a few

Earth days to spin on its axis; why should Venus have been different? I believe Venus was formed with a moon, like Earth's. And I believe it had oceans, of liquid water. There is no reason why Venus should not have formed with as much water as Earth. There were oceans, and tides . . .'

With surprising suddenness, she came to the edge.

A cliff face fell away before her, marked here and there by the lobed flow of landslides. This great ridge ran for kilometres to either side, all the way to the horizon and beyond. And the slope continued down – on and on, down and down, as if she was looking over the edge of a continental shelf into some deeper ocean – until it merged with a plateau, far below, and then the planet-circling volcanic plain beyond that.

This was the edge of the Maxwell mountains region. This cliff descended six kilometres in just eight kilometres' distance, an average slope of thirty five degrees. There was nothing like it on Earth, anywhere.

She had to descend to the level of the Lakshmi Planum, six kilometres below, to study Nemoto's puzzle. They hadn't anticipated any surface journey of such length and difficulty; she hadn't brought a surface vehicle, and the lander had neither the fuel nor the capability to fly her deeper into the ocean of air. And so she had to walk.

Nemoto had said she owed it to the human race to accept the risk, to complete her mission. Carole just thought she owed it to her mother, who would surely not have hesitated.

'Of course Venus is closer to the sun; even wet Venus was not an identical twin of Earth. The air was dominated by carbon dioxide. The oceans were hot – perhaps as hot as two hundred degrees – and the atmosphere humid, laden with clouds. But, thanks to the water, plate tectonics operated, and much of the carbon dioxide was kept locked up in the carbonate rocks, which were periodically subducted into the mantle, just as on Earth.

'Venus was a moist greenhouse, where life flourished . . .'

She found talus slopes, rubble left by crumbled rocks. It would require care, but this type of climb wasn't so unfamiliar to Carole. She had hiked in places in the Rocky Mountains that were rather like this, places where chemical weathering seemed to dominate, even on Earth. But the depth would push the envelope of her suit's design. And, of course, there was nobody here to help her up. So she took care not to fall.

After a couple of kilometres she paused for breath. She looked down, across kilometres of steeply sloping rock, to the Planum below.

She thought she could see something new, emerging from the murk: a long dark line, oddly straight, that disappeared here and there among folds in the rock, only to emerge once more further along. As if somebody had reached down with a straight-edge and scoured a deep dark cut into these hot rocks.

There was something beside the line, squat and dark, like a beetle. It seemed to her to be moving along the line. But perhaps that was her imagination.

She continued her careful climb downwards.

'. . . But then the visitors came in their drifting interstellar moonlets,' Nemoto had said. 'And they cared nothing for Venus or its life forms. They just wanted to steal the moon, to propagate their rocky spore. So they stopped Venus spinning.'

At the base of the cliffs she paused for a few minutes, letting her heartbeat subside to something like normal, sipping water.

The black line was a cable. It was maybe two metres thick, featureless and black, and it was held a metre from the ground by crude, sturdy pylons of rock.

'How do you despin a planet?' Nemoto whispered. 'We can think of a number of ways. You could bombard it with asteroids, for instance. But I think Venus was turned into a giant Dyson engine. Carole, I have observed cables like this all over the planet, wrapped east to west. They are fragmentary, broken – after all they are eight hundred million years old – but they still exist in stretches hundreds of kilometres long. Once, I would wager, the surface of Venus was wrapped in a cage of cables that followed the lines of latitude, like geographical markings on a schoolroom globe . . .'

She pressed her lab box against the cable. She even ran her hand along it, cautiously, but could feel nothing through the layers of her suit.

She began to walk alongside the cable. Some of the pylons were missing, others badly eroded. It was remarkable any of this stuff had lasted so long, she thought; it must be strongly resistant to Venus's corrosive air.

'Electric currents would be passed through the cables,' Nemoto whispered. 'The circulating currents would generate an intense magnetic field. This field would be used to couple the planet to its moon – perhaps the moon was dragged within its Roche limit, deliberately broken apart by tides.

'Thus they used the planet's spin energy to break up its moon.

'They rebuilt the fragments into their habitats, their rocky bubbles. The moonlets would be hurled out of the system, each of them robbing Venus of a little more of its spin. I wonder how long it took – thousands, millions of years? ... And, as they worked, they waited for Venus to bake itself to death.

'The climate of Venus was destabilized by the spin-down, you see,' Nemoto said. 'It got hotter. There must have been a paucity of rain, a terrible drought, at last no rain at all ... And finally, the oceans themselves started to evaporate.

'When all the oceans were gone – life must already have been extinguished – the water in the air started to drift to the top of the atmosphere. There, it was broken up by sunlight. The hydrogen escaped to space, and the oxygen and remnant water made sulphuric acid in the clouds.

'And that was what the moonlet builders wanted, you see. *The acid.* They mined the acid out of the ruined air, perhaps with ships like our profac crawlers.

'It's an efficient scheme, if you think it over. All you need is a fat, fast-spinning planet with a moon, and you get a source of moonlet ships, a way to launch them, and even a sulphuric acid mine. Venus, despun, was ruined. But *they* didn't care. They had what they wanted.

'We are lucky they did not select Earth. Perhaps our Moon was too large, too distant; perhaps the sun was too far away ...'

But they didn't finish the job, Carole thought. What great catastrophe, eight hundred million years ago, stopped them? Were some of Venus's great impact craters the wounds left by remnants of that vanished moon falling from the sky, uncontrolled – or even the scars of some disastrous war? ... For Venus, Nemoto said, things got worse still. When all its water was lost, plate tectonics halted. The shifting continents seized up, like an engine run out of oil. The planet's interior heat was trapped, built up – until it was released catastrophically. 'Mass volcanism erupted. There were immense lava floods, giant new volcanoes. Much of the surface fractured, crumpled, melted – and the carbon dioxide locked up in the rocks began to pump into the atmosphere, thickening it further ...'

Something was moving, directly ahead of her.

It was the beetle-like thing that she had observed from the cliff. And it was working its way along the cable, gouging at it with complex tools she couldn't make out, scoring it deeply.

It was a grey-black form, the size of a small car. It was as tall as she was, its surface featureless, returning glinted highlights of Venus's complex sky. And it was based on a dodecahedral core.

151

'Hello,' she said. '*You* haven't been here for eight hundred million years.'

'Gaijin technology,' Nemoto whispered when she saw the image. 'It is here to scavenge. Carole, this ancient cable is a superconductor, working at Venusian temperatures. Remarkable. Even the Gaijin have nothing like this. And what,' she hissed, 'do they intend to do with it? Which of our planets or moons will *they* wrap up, like a Christmas parcel?'

An alarm chimed softly in Carole's helmet. She must soon turn back, if she was to complete her long climb back to the lander in safety.

From here she could see the lower plains, the true floor of Venus, the great basalt ocean that covered the planet, still kilometres below her altitude. She longed to go further, to climb down and explore. But she knew she must not. My mission is over, she realized. Here, at this moment; I have come as far as I can, and must turn back.

She was surprised how disappointed she felt. Earth would seem very confining after this, despite the wealth she expected to claw in from her celebrity. She glanced up at the twisting, pulsing clouds, fifty kilometres up. But no matter how far I travel, she thought, I will always remember this: Venus, where I was first to set foot.

This, and the immense crime I have witnessed here.

'. . . If this happened once, it must have happened again and again,' whispered Nemoto. 'A wave of colonists come to a solar system like ours. They take what they want, ruinously mining out the resources, trashing what remains. And then they move on . . . or are somehow stopped. And then, later, when the planets have begun to heal, others follow, and the process begins again. Over and over.

'I predict we will find this everywhere. We can't assume that *anything* in the solar system is truly primordial. We don't yet know how to look, and the scars will be buried deep in time. But *here*, it is unmistakable, the mark of their wasteful carelessness . . .'

Carole stepped carefully behind the blindly toiling Gaijin beetle machine, and, peering patiently through the ruddy murk, sought scraps of superconductor.

Chapter 13

THE ROADS OF EMPIRE

Different suns, a sheaf of worlds: Malenfant drifted among the stars, between flashes of blue teleport light.

It was a strange thought that because the Saddle Point links were so long – in some cases spanning hundreds of light years, with transit times measured in centuries – there could be whole populations in transit at any moment, stored in Saddle Point transmissions: whole populations existing as frozen patterns of data arrowing between the stars, without thought or feeling, hope or fear.

And he was slowly learning something of the nature of the Saddle Point system itself.

A teleport interstellar transportation system made economic sense – of course, or else it wouldn't have been built. Saddle Point signals were minimum strength. They seemed to be precisely directed, as if lased, and operated just above the background noise level, worked at frequencies designed to avoid photon quantization noise. And the gateways, of course, were placed at points of gravitational focussing, in order to exploit the billion-fold gain available there. He figured, with back-of-the-envelope calculations, that with such savings the cost of information transfer was at least a billion times less than the cost of equivalent physical transfer, by means of ships crawling between the stars.

It was an interstellar transport system designed for creatures like the Gaijin, who relished the cold and dark at the rim of star systems, working at low temperatures and low energies and with virtually no leaked noise. No wonder we had such trouble detecting them, he thought.

But the physics of the system imposed a number of constraints.

Each receiver had to be quantum-entangled with a transmitter. What the Builders must have done was to haul receiver gates to the stars by some conventional means, slower-than-light craft like flower-ships. But it was a system with a limited life. Each gate's stock of entangled states would be depleted every time a teleportation was completed – and so each link could only be used a finite number of times.

Perhaps the Builders still existed, and had sustained the motivations that led them to build the gates in the first place, and so were maintaining the gates. If not, the system must be fragmenting, as the key, much-used links ceased to operate. Perhaps the oldest sections had already failed.

It might be that the hubs, the oldest parts of the system, would be inaccessible to humans and Gaijin, the Builders isolated, forever unknowable.

He wondered if that was important. It depended on how smart the Builders had been, he supposed, how much they understood about what the hell was going on in this cruel universe. He was getting the impression that the Gaijin knew little more than humanity did: that they too were picking their way through this Galaxy of ruins and battle scars, trying to figure out *why* this kept happening.

Confined for most of his time to the habitats the Gaijin provided, Malenfant was a virtual prisoner. After a time – after *years* – he knew he was becoming institutionalized, a little stir crazy, too dependent on the small rituals that got him through the day.

He became devoted, obsessively so, to his suit, his Shuttle EMU, his one possession. He spent hours repairing it and maintaining it and cleaning it. As much as possible he tried to leave his animated photo of Emma in the spacesuit pocket where it had lain for years. He already knew every grain of it, every scrap of motion and sound; he couldn't bear the thought of wearing it out, of it fading to white blankness; it would be like losing his own existence.

After a time it seemed to him he was getting ill. He sensed he was growing weaker. If he pinched his cheek – or even cut himself – it didn't seem to hurt the way it should.

It didn't trouble him, cocooned as he was in the tight confines of his habitats.

He did find out that the Gaijin didn't suffer such problems.

The very basis of their minds was different. *His* consciousness was based on quantum-mechanical processes going on in his brain, which was why his whole brain – and his body, his brain's support system – had to be transported, and was therefore somewhat corrupted by every Saddle Point transition.

Cassiopeia's 'mind' was more like a computer program. It was composed purely of classical information, stuff you could copy and store at will, stuff that didn't have to be destroyed to be transmitted by the Saddle Points. When she went 'through' a gateway, Cassiopeia's program was simply halted. That way she used up fewer of the Saddle Point link's stock of entangled states.

He wasn't enough of a philosopher to say if all this disqualified her from being conscious, from having a soul.

There were other differences.

Periodically he would watch the Gaijin swarming like locusts over the hull of a flower-ship, thousands of them. They would *merge*, in clattering, glistening sheets, as if melting into each other, and then separate, Gaijin coalescing one by one as if dripping out of a solute.

The purpose of these great dissolved parliaments seemed to be a transfer of information, perhaps the making of decisions. If so it was an efficient system. The Gaijin did not need to talk to each other, as humans did, imperfectly striving to interpret for each other the contents of their minds. They certainly did not need to argue, or persuade; the shared data and interpretations of the merged state were either valid and valuable, or they were not.

But how was it possible to say that *this* Gaijin, who came out of the cluster, was the *same* individual as had entered such a merge? Was it meaningful even to pose the question?

To the Gaijin, mind and even identity were fluid, malleable things. To them, identity was something to be copied, broken up, shared, merged; it didn't matter that the *self* was lost, it seemed to him, as long as continuity was maintained, so that each of the Gaijin, as currently manifested, could trace their memories back along a complex path to the remote place that had birthed the first of them.

And, likewise, he supposed, they could anticipate an unbounded future, of sentience, if not identity. A cold mechanical immortality.

He was less and less interested in the blizzard of worlds the Gaijin showed him. Even though, as it turned out, everywhere you looked there was life. Life and war and death. He strove to understand what the Gaijin were telling him – what they wanted him to do.

Chapter 14

DREAMS OF ANCESTRAL FISH

Madeleine Meacher flew into Kourou from Florida.

The plane door slid open, and hot, humid air washed over her. This was East Guiana, a chunk of the north-eastern coast of South America. All Madeleine could see, to the horizon, was greenery: an equatorial rainforest, thick, crowding trees, clouds of insects shimmering above mangrove swamps.

Already she felt oppressed by this crowding layer of life, the dense, moist air. In fact she felt a stab of panic at the thought that this big, heavy biosphere was unmanaged. *Nobody at the controls.* Madeleine guessed she'd spent too long in spacecraft.

Some kind of truck – good grief, it looked like it was running on *gasoline* – had dragged up a flight of steps to the plane. Madeleine was going to have to walk down herself, she realized. It was the year 2131, and, through the Saddle Points, Madeleine had travelled as far as twenty-seven light years from Sol. And here, seventy years out of her time, she was walking down airline steps, as if it was 1931.

Not a good start to my new career, Madeleine thought bleakly.

A man was waiting at the bottom of the steps. He looked about thirty, and he was a head shorter than Madeleine, with crisp black hair and a round face, the skin brown and leathery. He was wearing some kind of toga, white and cool.

She wanted to touch that face, feel its texture.

'Madeleine Meacher?'

'Yes.'

He stuck out his hand. 'Ben Roach. I'm on the Triton project here. Welcome to South America's spaceport.' His accent was complex – multinational – but with an Australian root.

She took his hand. It was broader than hers, the palm pink-pale; his flesh was warm, dry.

They walked towards a beat-up terminal building. There was vegetation here: scrubby, yellowed grass, drooping palms. It was a contrast to the lush blanket she'd glimpsed from the air.

'What happened to the jungle here?'

He grinned. 'Too many fizzers.' He glanced down, then took her hand again. 'Oh. You are hurt.'

There was a deep cut on the index finger; a wound she'd somehow suffered on that creaky old staircase, probably. Madeleine studied the damaged finger, pulling it this way and that as if it were a piece of meat. 'It's my own fault; the plane was so hot I left off my biocomp gloves.' The gloves, like the rest of the body suit Madeleine wore, were made of a semi-sentient mesh of sensors which warned her when she was damaging herself.

'This is the Discontinuity,' said Ben, curious.

'Yeah. Too much teleportation is bad for you.' Eventually, as she played with the finger, she reopened the drying cut.

Ben stared curiously as fresh blood oozed.

Madeleine's employer had set up an office in the spaceport Technical Centre. This housed a run-down mission control centre, a press office, a hospitality area and a dusty, shut-down space museum: tinfoil models of forgotten satellites.

The office itself was cool, light, airy. Too neat. There was rice straw matting on the floor, and scroll paintings on the wall, and flowers. It was all traditional Japanese, though Madeleine could see the 'paintings' were on some kind of softscreen, so configurable.

The office had a view of the full-scale Ariane 5 mock-up that stood outside the entrance to the Technical Centre. Sitting on its mobile launch table, the Ariane looked a little like the old American Shuttles, with a fat liquid-propelled core booster (called the EPC, for *Etage Principal Cryotechnique*), flanked by two shorter strap-on solid boosters. The launch table itself was a lot more elegant than the Shuttle's Apollo-era gantries, though; it was a slim curved tower of concrete and steel, like a piece of modern sculpture, dwarfed by the booster. This mock-up had to be a hundred and fifty years old, Madeleine figured; its paintwork was eroded away, the old ESA markings barely visible. Mould and creepers clawed at the sides of the rocket, a slow, irreversible vegetable onslaught; the booster was drowned in green, as ancient and meaningless as the ruins of a Mayan temple.

Madeleine's employer was sitting on the floor, cross-legged, before a small *butsudan*, a Buddha shelf, under the window. She was a

Japanese, a small, wizened woman, her face imploded, criss-crossed by Vallis Marineris grooves. Her remnant of hair was a handful of grey wisps, clinging to a liver-spotted scalp. She had been born in 1990. That made her more than a hundred and forty years old, close to the record. Nobody knew how she was keeping herself alive.

She was, of course, Nemoto.

Nemoto touched a carved statue. 'A Buddha,' she said, 'of fused regolith from the Mare Ingenii. Once such an artefact would have seemed very exotic.' She got up stiffly and went to a coffee pot. 'You want some? I also have green tea.'

'No. I burn my mouth too easily.'

'That's a loss.'

'Tell me about it.' An inability to drink hot black coffee was the Discontinuity handicap which Madeleine felt most severely.

She studied Nemoto, this legendary figure from the deep past, and sought awe, even curiosity. She felt only numbness, impatience. 'When do you want me to start work?'

Nemoto smiled thinly. 'Straight to business, Meacher? As soon as you can. The first launches start in a month.'

Madeleine had been hired to prepare two hundred rookie astronauts for spaceflight.

'Not astronauts,' Nemoto corrected her. 'Emigrants.'

'Emigrants to Triton.'

'Yes. Two hundred Aborigines, from the heart of the Australian outback, establishing a new nation on a moon of Neptune. Inspiring thought, don't you think?'

Or absurd, Madeleine reflected.

'All you have to do is familiarize them with microgravity. We've established a hydro training facility here, and so forth. Just stop them throwing up or going crazy before we can get them transferred to the transport. I assigned Ben Roach to shepherd you for your first couple of days. He's a smart-ass kid, but he has his uses.'

Madeleine tried to focus on what Nemoto was saying, the details of her outlandish scheme. Triton? Why, for God's sake? Surrounded by strangeness, numbed by the Discontinuity, it was hard to care.

Nemoto eyed Madeleine. 'You feel – disoriented. Here we sit: mirror images, relics of the twenty-first century, both stranded in an unanticipated future. The only difference is in how we got here. You by your relativistic hop, skip and jump across light years and decades – the scenic route.' She grinned. 'And I came the hard way.' Her teeth were black, Madeleine noticed.

She said, 'But we're both damaged by the experience, in our different ways.'

Nemoto shrugged. 'I ended up with all the power.'

'Power over me, anyhow.'

'Meacher, I still need crew for the transport.'

'You're offering me a flight to Triton?'

'If you're interested. Your Discontinuity won't be a serious liability if –'

'Forget it.'

Madeleine stood up. Her left leg buckled and she nearly fell; she had to cling to the desk top. It was as if Madeleine was the old woman. She found she'd been applying too much weight to the leg and the blood supply had been cut off. She hadn't noticed, of course; and that kind of damage was too subtle for the biocomp suit to pick up.

Nemoto watched her, calculating, without sympathy. 'The Triton colony is crucial,' she said. 'Strategic.'

This was the Nemoto Madeleine had heard of. 'You're still working for the future of the species, Nemoto.'

'Yes, if you want to know.'

Madeleine's heart sank. Nemoto would be hard to deal with rationally. People with missions always were.

But only Nemoto would give her a job.

Aside perhaps from Reid Malenfant – and even after all this time nobody knew what had become of *him* – Madeleine had been the first human to leave the solar system. Her experiences in the light of other stars had been astonishing.

Her first return to the solar system had been something of a triumph – although even then she'd been aware of a historical dislocation, as if the world had had a layer of strangeness thrown over it. And she had been shocked by the sudden – to her – deaths of her mother, and of poor Sally Brind, and many others she had known.

At least Frank Paulis's get-rich-slow compound interest scheme had worked out that first time. And she had earned herself a little fame. She was the first star traveller – aside from Malenfant – and that earned her some profile.

But she hadn't been sorry to leave again, to escape into the clean blue light of the Saddle Points, replacing the baffling human world with the cold external mysteries of the stars.

Her later returns had been less enjoyable.

The truth was that as the decades peeled away on Earth, and the novelty wore off, nobody much cared about the star travellers – and few were prepared to protect the interests of these historical curiosities. So, the last time she came back, Madeleine had returned to find that a devaluation of the UN dollar, the new global currency, had wiped out a lot of the value of her savings. And then had come the banks' decision to close the swelling accounts of the star travellers, a step that had been backed by inter-government agencies up to and including the UN.

Meanwhile no insurance company would touch her, or anyone else who had been through the Saddle Point gateways, after the Discontinuity condition had been diagnosed.

Which was why Madeleine needed money.

Nemoto was attached to no organization. Madeleine couldn't have defined her role. But her source of power was clear enough: she had stayed alive.

Thanks to longevity treatments, Nemoto, and a handful of privileged others, had gotten so old that they formed a new breed of power-player, their influence coming from contacts, webs of alliances, ancient debts and favours granted. Nemoto was a gerontocrat, modelling herself on the antique Communist officials who still ran China.

Madeleine wouldn't have been surprised to find it was Nemoto herself, or the other gerontocrats, who lay behind the whole scam. The closure of the star travellers' accounts had given Nemoto a good deal of leverage over Madeleine, and those who had followed in her path. And the strategy had put a block on any ambitions the star travellers might have had to use *their* effective longevity to accrue power back home.

She wondered if the gerontocrats – conservative, selfish, reclusive, obsessive – were responsible for a more general malaise that seemed to her to have afflicted this fast-forwarded world. There had been change – new fashions, gadgetry, terminology – but, it seemed to her, no progress. In science and art she could see no signs of meaningful innovation. The world's nations evolved, but the various supranational structures had not changed for decades: the political institutions that wielded the power had ossified.

And meanwhile, the world still laboured under the old burdens of a fast-changing ecology and resource shortages, and minor wars continued to be an irritant at every fractured joint between peoples.

Nobody was solving these ancient problems. Worse, it seemed to her, nobody was even trying any more. You could no longer, for example, get reliable statistics on population numbers, or disease occurrences, or poverty. It was as if history had stopped when the Gaijin had arrived.

. . . But it didn't *matter*. She wouldn't have changed a thing. The travelling itself was the thing, the point of it all. The rest was ancient history, even to Madeleine herself.

Ben showed her to her apartment. He had to show her how to open the door. In 2131, God help her, you had to work door locks with foot studs.

The East Guiana spaceport, built up by the Europeans in the 1980s, extended maybe twenty kilometres along the coast of the Atlantic, from Sinnamary to Kourou, which was actually an old fishing village. There were control buildings, booster integration buildings, solid booster test stands and launch complexes, all identified by baffling French acronyms: BAF, BIL, BEAP – and connected by roads and rail tracks that looked, from her window, like gashes in the foliage.

Ariane had been nice-looking technology, for its time, a hundred and fifty years earlier. It had been superseded by new generations of spaceplanes, even before the Gaijin had taken over most of Earth's ground-to-orbit traffic with their clean, flawless landers. But when the French released political control of East Guiana, the new government decided to refurbish what was left at Kourou.

So East Guiana, one of the smallest and poorest nations on Earth, suddenly had a space program.

Ariane had kept flying even as history moved on, and nations and corporations and alliances had formed and dissolved, leaving new configurations whose very names were baffling to Madeleine. But Ariane remained, an antique, disreputable, dirty, unreliable launcher, used by agencies without the funds to afford something better.

Like Nemoto.

Maybe, Madeleine thought, it wasn't a surprise that Nemoto, another relic of the first Space Age, had gravitated here.

The residential quarters had been set up in an abandoned solid-propellant factory, a building that dated back to before Madeleine's birth. The cluster of buildings was still called UPG, for *Usine de Propergol de Guyane*. It was a jumble of white cubes spilling over a hill-side, like a Mediterranean village. It was sparsely set up, but comfortable enough. About four hundred people lived here: the Aborigine emigrants, and permanent technical and managerial staff to operate the automated facilities. Once twenty thousand had been housed in Kourou, a fifth of the country's population. The feeling of emptiness, of age and abandonment, was startling.

She slept for a few hours. Then she drifted about her apartment, tinkering.

It was startling how often and how much everyday gadgets changed. The toilet, for instance, was just a hole in the ground, and it took her an age to figure out how to make it flush. The shower was just as bad; it took a call to Ben to establish that to set the heat, you had to put your finger in a little test sink, and let the thing read your body temperature.

And so on. All stuff everybody else here had grown up with. It was like being in a foreign country, wherever she went, even in her home town; she'd long grown tired of people not taking her requests for basic information seriously. And every time she came back from another Einsteinian fast-forward it got worse.

Anyhow, a few minutes after stepping out of the shower, her skin was prickling with sweat again.

She felt no discomfort, of course. The Discontinuity left her with numbness where pain or discomfort should sit. Like a fading-down of reality. She towelled herself dry again, trying not to scrape her skin.

Perhaps it should have been expected. Before the reality of Saddle Point teleportation had been demonstrated, there had been those who had doubted whether human minds could ever, even in principle, be downloaded, stored or transmitted. The way data was stored in a brain was not simple. A human mind appeared to be a process, dynamic, and no static 'snapshot', no matter how sophisticated the technology, could possibly capture its richness. So it was argued.

The fact that the first travellers, including Madeleine, had survived Saddle Point transitions seemed to belie this pessimistic point of view. But perhaps, in the longer term, those doubts had been borne out.

She knew there was talk of treatment for Discontinuity sufferers. Madeleine wasn't holding her breath: nobody was putting serious money into the problem. There were only a handful of star travellers, and nobody cared much about them anyhow. And so Madeleine had to wear a constricting biocomp sensor suit, which warned her when she'd sat still for too long, or when her skin was burned or frozen, and woke her up in the night to turn her over.

Maybe the Gaijin weren't affected the same way. Nobody knew.

She stood, naked, at an open window, trying to get cool. It was evening. She looked across kilometres of hilly country, all of it coated by burgeoning life. There was a breeze, lifting loose leaves high enough to cross the balcony. But the breeze served only to push more water-laden air into her face.

The blanket of foliage coating the hills around the launch areas looked etiolated: the leaves yellowed, stunted, the trees sickly and small by comparison with their neighbours further away. And the leaves at her feet were yellow and black, others holed, as if burned.

She pulled on a loose dress and walked a kilometre to the block containing Ben's apartment.

She glimpsed Aborigines: her trainees, men, women and children, passing back and forth in little groups, engaged in their own errands and concerns. They showed no interest in her. They were loose-limbed people, many of them going barefoot, some of the women overweight; they wore loose togas like Ben's, the cloth worn, dirty, well-used. Their faces were round, a paler brown than she had expected, with blunt noses, prominent brows. Many of them wore breathing filters or sun screen, and their skin was marked by cancer scars.

They were alien to Madeleine, but no more so than most of the people of the year 2131.

Ben welcomed her. He served her a meal: couscous rice with saffron, chunks of soya, a light local wine.

He told her about his wife. She was called Lena; she was only twenty, a decade younger than Ben. She was in orbit, working on the big emigrant transports Nemoto was assembling. Ben hadn't seen her for months.

Madeleine felt easy with Ben. He even took care with the words he used. Language drift seemed remarkably rapid; less than a century out of her time, even if she was familiar with a word, she couldn't always recognize its pronunciation, and had learned it wasn't safe to assume she knew its modern usage. But Ben made sure that she understood.

'It's strange finding Aborigines here,' Madeleine said. 'So far from home.'

'Not so strange. After all East Guiana is another colonial relic. The French wanted to follow the example of the British in Australia, by peopling East Guiana with convicts.' He grinned, his teeth white and young, a contrast in Madeleine's mind to the ruined mouth of Nemoto. He said, 'Anyhow, now we can escape on the fizzers.' He mimed a rocket launch with two hands clasped as in prayer. 'Whoosh.'

'Ben – why Triton? I know Nemoto has her own objectives. But for you . . .'

'Nemoto's offer was the only one we had. We have nowhere else

163

to go. But perhaps we would follow her anyway. Nemoto is marginalized, her ideas ridiculed – most vigorously by friends of the Gaijin. *But she is right*, on the deepest of levels. We used to think we were alone in a primordial universe. Suddenly we find ourselves in a dangerous, crowded universe littered with ruins. There was fear, and deep anger at the discovery of the violation of Venus. It might have been a sister world to Earth – or Earth might have been the victim. With time, the outrage faded – but we remembered; we, a people who have been dispossessed already.'

More leaves blew in from a darkening sky, broken, damaged by rocket exhaust.

Ben told her he came from central Australia, born into a group called the Yolgnu. 'When I was a boy my family lived by a river bank, living in the old way. But the authorities, the white people, came and moved us to a place called Framlingham. Just a row of shacks and tin houses. Then, when I was eight years old, more white men took me away to an orphanage. The men were from the Aboriginal Protection Board. When they thought I was civilized enough, they sent me to foster parents in Melbourne. White people, called Nash. They were rich and kind. You see, it was the policy of the Government to solve their Aboriginal problem once and for all, by making me white.'

All of this stunned her, embarrassed her. She said, 'You must hate them.'

He smiled. 'It had been tried before. They were always frightened, first of the Japanese, then of Indonesians and Chinese, flowing down from the north, with their eyes on Australia's empty spaces, its huge mineral deposits. Now perhaps they fear the Gaijin, come to take their land. And each time they exorcise their fears using us. I do not hate them. I understand them.'

To her surprise, he turned out to hold a doctorate in black hole physics. But he had been drawn back to Framlingham, as had others of his generation. Slowly they had constructed a dream of a new life. Almost all of the people escaping to Triton were from Framlingham, he said. 'It was a wrench to leave the old lands. But we will find new lands, make our own world.'

Ben served her *sambuca*, an Italian liqueur: a new craze, it seemed. *Sambuca* was clear, aniseed flavoured. Ben floated Brazilian coffee beans in her glass, and set it alight. The alcohol burned blue in the fading light, cupped in the open space above the liquid, and the coffee beans hissed and popped. The flames were to release the oils from the beans, Ben said, and infuse the drink with the flavour of the coffee.

He doused the flames and took careful sips from her glass, testing its temperature for her so that Madeleine would not burn her lips. The flavour of the hot liquid was strong, sharp enough to push at the boundary of her Discontinuity.

They sat under the darkling sky, and the stars came out.

Ben pointed out constellations for her, and he traced out other features of the celestial sphere for her, the geography of the sky.

There was the celestial equator, an invisible line that was a projection of Earth's equator on the sky. From here, of course, the equator passed right over their heads. Lights moved along that line, silent, smoothly traversing, like strangely orderly fireflies. They were orbital structures: factories, dwellings, even hotels. Many of them were Chinese, Ben told her; Chinese corporations had built up a close working relationship with the Gaijin. Then he distracted her with another invisible line called the ecliptic. The ecliptic was the equator of the solar system, the line the planets traced out. It was different from the Earth's equator, because Earth's axis was tipped over through twenty-three degrees or so.

. . . Rather, the ecliptic *used* to be invisible. Now, Madeleine found, it was marked out by a fine row of new stars, medium bright, some glowing white but others a deeper yellow to orange. It was like a row of street lamps.

Those lights were cities, Madeleine learned: the new Gaijin communities, hollowed out of the giant rocks that littered the asteroid belt, burning with fusion light. No human had gotten within an astronomical unit of those new lamps in space.

It was beautiful, chilling, remarkable. The people of this time had grown up with all this. But, nevertheless, she thought, the sky is full of cities, and huge incomprehensible ruins. New toilets and telephones she could accept. But even the *solar system* had changed while she had been away, and who would have anticipated that?

She felt too hot, dizzy.

She considered making a pass at Ben. It would be comforting.

He seemed receptive.

'What about Lena?'

He smiled. 'She is not here. I am not there. We are human beings. We have ties of *gurrutu*, of kinship, which will forever bind us.'

She took that as assent. She reached out in the dark, and he responded.

*   *   *

They made love in the equatorial heat, a slick of perspiration lubricating their bodies. Ben's skin was a sculpture of firm planes, and his hands were confident and warm. She felt remote, as if her body was a piece of equipment she had to control and monitor.

Ben sensed this. He was tender, and held her for comfort. He was fascinated by her skin, he said. The skin of a woman tanned by the light of different stars.

She couldn't feel his touch.

She slept badly. In her dreams Madeleine spun through rings of powder-blue metal, confronted visions of geometric forms. Triangles, dodecahedra, icosahedra. When Madeleine cried out, Ben held her.

At one point she saw that Ben, sleeping, was about to knock the coffee pot, and still-hot liquid would pour over his chest. She grabbed the spout, taking a few splashes, and pushed it away. She felt nothing, of course. She wiped her hand dry on a tissue, and waited for sleep.

When they woke they found that the coffee had burned her hand severely.

Ben treated her. 'The absence of pain,' he said, 'is evidently a mixed blessing.'

She'd heard this before, and had grown impatient. 'Pain is an evolutionary relic. Sure, it serves as an early warning system. But we can replace that, right? Get rid of sharp edges. Soak the world with software implants, like my biocomp, to warn and protect us.'

Ben studied her. He said, 'Do you know what the central reticular formation is?'

'Why don't you tell me?'

'It's a small section of the brain. And if you excite this formation – in the brain of a normal human – the perception of pain disappears. This is the locus of the Discontinuity damage. I am talking of *qualia*, the inner sensations, aspects of consciousness. Your pain, objectively, still exists, in terms of the response of your body; what has been removed is the corresponding qualia, your perception of it. Put an end to discomfort, and there is an end to the emotions linked with pain. Fear. Grief. Pleasure.'

'So my inner life is diminished.'

'Yes. Consciousness is not well understood, nor the link between mind and body. Perhaps other qualia, too, are being distorted or destroyed by the Saddle Point transitions.'

But, Madeleine thought, my dreams are of alien artefacts. Perhaps my qualia are not simply being destroyed. Perhaps they are being –

replaced. It was a thought that hadn't struck her before. Resolutely she pushed it away.

'How do you know so much about this?'

'I have ambitions myself to travel to the stars. To see a black hole, before I build my farm on Triton. It is worth my studying what would happen to me . . . Madeleine,' he said slowly, 'there is something I should tell you. Even though Nemoto has forbidden it.'

'What?'

'The Chinese discovered it first, in their dealings with the Gaijin. Some say it is a Gaijin gift, in fact. Nemoto has worked to suppress knowledge of it. But I –'

'Tell me, damn it.'

'There is a cure for the Discontinuity.'

She was electrified. Terrified.

He said, 'You know, the remarkable thing is that the reticular formation is in the oldest part of the brain. We share it with our most ancient ancestors. Madeleine, you have returned from the stars, changed. There are those who think we are forging a new breed of humans, out there beyond the Saddle Points. But, perhaps, we are merely swimming through the dreams of ancestral fish '

He smiled and held her again.

She stormed into Nemoto's office.

Nemoto was busy; an Ariane launch was imminent. She took a look at the bandaging swathing Madeleine's hand. 'You ought to be careful.'

'There's a way to reverse the Discontinuity. Isn't there?'

'. . . Oh.' Nemoto stood and faced the window, the Ariane mock-up framed there. She held her hands behind her back, and her posture was stiff. 'That smart-ass kid. Sit down, Madeleine.'

'*Isn't there?*'

'I said sit down.'

Madeleine complied. She had trouble arranging herself on Nemoto's office furniture.

'Yes, there's a way,' Nemoto said. 'If you're treated correctly before you go through a gateway, the translation can be used to *reverse* the Discontinuity damage.'

'Then why are you hiding this?' Madeleine asked, and then, 'Send me to a Saddle Point.'

Nemoto looked at Madeleine from her mask of a face. 'You're sure you want *this* back? The pain, the anguish of being human –'

'Yes.'

Nemoto turned and sat down; she nested her hands on the table top, the fingers like intertwined twigs. 'You have to understand the situation we face,' she said. 'Most of us are sleeping. But some of us believe we're at war.' She meant the Gaijin, of course, and their great belt cities, their swooping forays through the inner solar system – and the other migrants who were following, still decades or centuries away but nevertheless on the way, noisily building along the spiral arm. 'You must see it – *you*, when you return from your jaunts to the stars. Everybody's busy, too busy with the short term, unable to see the trends. Only us, Madeleine; only us, stranded out of time.'

Something connected for Madeleine. '. . . Oh. That's why you have kept the cure so quiet.'

'Do you see why we must do this, Meacher? We need to explore every option. To have soldiers – warriors – who are free of pain –'

'Free of consciousness itself.'

'Perhaps. If that's necessary.'

Madeleine felt disgusted, sullied. Discontinuity was, after all, nothing less than the restructuring of her consciousness by Saddle Point transitions. How typical of humanity to turn this remarkable experience into a weapon. How monstrous.

She sat back. 'Send me through a Saddle Point.'

'Or?'

'Or I expose what you've been doing. Concealing a cure for the Discontinuity.'

Nemoto considered. 'This is too big an issue to horse-trade with the likes of you. But,' she said, 'I will make you an exchange.'

'An exchange?'

'I'll send you to a Saddle Point. But afterwards you go to Triton with the Aborigines. We have to make sure that colony succeeds.'

Madeleine shook her head. 'It will take decades for me to complete a round-trip through a gateway.'

Nemoto smiled thinly. 'It doesn't matter. It will take the Yolgnu years to reach Neptune, more years to establish any kind of viable colony. And we're playing a long game here. Some day the Gaijin will confront us directly. Some of us don't understand why that hasn't already happened. We need to be prepared, when it does.'

'And Triton is a part of this scheme?'

Nemoto didn't answer.

But of course it was, Madeleine thought. Everything is a part of Nemoto's grand design. Everything, and everyone: my need for money and healing, Ben's people's need for refuge – all just levers for Nemoto to press.

Nemoto said, 'Where?'

'Where what?'

'Where do you want to go, on your health cruise?'

'I don't care. What does it matter?'

'. . . There might be something suitable,' Nemoto said at length. 'There is another alien species, here in the Earth-Moon system. Did you know that? They are called the Chaera. *Their* star system is exotic. It includes a miniature black hole, which . . . well.' She eyed Madeleine. 'Your friend Ben is a black hole specialist. Perhaps he will go with you. How amusing.'

Amusing. Another little relativistic death.

There was a rumble of noise. They turned to the window. Kilometres away, beyond the mangrove swamps, Madeleine could see the booster's slim nose lift above the trees, the first glow of the engines. The light of the solid boosters seemed to spill over the tree line – startlingly bright rocket light glimmering from the flat swamps – as Ariane rolled on its axis.

'There,' Nemoto said. 'You made me miss the launch.'

Chapter 15

COLONISTS

Six months:

Once Nemoto had given her the date of her Saddle Point mission it was all she could think about. The rest of her life – her work in Kourou and elsewhere, her legal struggles to get back some of the money that had been impounded from her accounts, even her developing, low-key relationship with Ben – all of that faded to a background glow compared to the diamond-bright prospect of encountering another Saddle Point gateway, at that specified, slowly approaching date in the future.

She'd met other star travellers, returned from one or two hops into the sky with the Gaijin. All of them were determined to go on. She imagined a cloud of human travellers, journeying deeper and deeper into the strange cosmos, their ties to a blurred, fast-forwarding Earth stretching and loosening.

It wasn't just the Discontinuity. She didn't *belong* here. After all, she couldn't even work the toilets.

She longed to leave.

The Japanese-built lander touched the Moon, its rockets throwing up a cloud of fast-settling dust. There were various artefacts here, sitting on the surface of the Moon, and Nemoto, the spider at the heart of this operation, was waiting for them, anonymous in a black suit.

Ben and Madeleine suited up carefully. Madeleine made sure Ben followed her lead; she was, after all, the experienced astronaut.

She climbed down a short ladder to the surface. She dropped from step to step, in the gentle gravity. She stepped off the last rung onto regolith, which crunched like snow under her weight.

She walked away from the lander.

The colours of the Moon weren't strong: in fact the most colourful thing here was their Nishizaki Heavy Industries aluminium-frame lander, which, from a distance, looked like a small, fragile insect, done out in brilliant black, silver, orange and yellow. The Sea of Tranquillity was close to the Moon's equator, so Earth was directly above her head, and it was difficult to tip back in her pressure suit to see it. But when Ben goes to live on Triton, she thought, the sun will be a bright point source. And Earth will be no more than a pale blue point of light, only made visible by blocking out the sun itself. How strange that will be.

Nemoto was showing Ben the various artefacts she had assembled here. Madeleine saw a set of blocky metal boxes, trailing cables. These were, it turned out, a pair of high-power X-ray lasers. 'A small fission bomb is the power source. When the bomb is detonated, a burst of X-ray photons is emitted. The photons travel down long metal rods. This generates an intense beam. In effect, the power of the bomb has been focused . . .'

These were experimental weapons, it emerged, dating from the late twentieth century. They had been designed as satellite weapons, intended to shoot down intercontinental ballistic missiles.

Madeleine asked, 'And what have the Gaijin paid us for this obscene old gadgetry?'

'That's not your concern.'

The habitat which would keep them alive was another masterpiece of improvisation and low cost, Madeleine thought, like her fondly-remembered *Friendship-7*. It was based on two modules – called FGB, Russian-built, and the Service Module, American-built – scavenged from the old NASA International Space Station. The Service Module had been enhanced with an astrophysics instrument pallet.

Madeleine slipped her gloved hand into Ben's. 'We ought to name our magnificent ship,' she said.

Ben thought it over. '*Dreamtime Ancestor*.'

Nemoto said, 'Come meet the Chaera.'

The last artefact, sitting on the regolith, was a tank, a glass cube. It contained a translucent disc about a metre across, swimming slowly through oxygen-blue fluid.

It was an Eetie: a Chaera, an inhabitant of the black hole system that was the destination of this mission. The Chaera had, after the Gaijin, been the second variant of Eetie to come to the solar system.

Aside from all the dead ones in the past, of course.

Ben stepped forward. He touched the glass walls of the tank with his gloved hand. The Chaera rippled; it looked something like a sting-ray. She wondered if it was trying to talk to Ben.

. . . *The Chaera had eyes*, she saw: four of them spaced evenly around the rim of the stingray shape, dilating lids alternately opening. Human-like eyes, gazing out at her, eyes on a creature from another star. She shivered with recognition.

Through a hairline crack in the Chaera's tank, fluid bubbled and boiled into vacuum.

'You need to understand that the nature of this mission is a little different,' Nemoto said. 'You are going to a populated system. The Chaera have technology, it seems, but they lack spaceflight. The Gaijin made contact with them and initiated a trading relationship. The Chaera requested specific artefacts, which we've been able to supply.' She grunted. 'Interesting. The Gaijin actually seem to be learning to run rudimentary trading relationships, from *us*. Before, perhaps they simply appropriated, or killed.'

Ben said, '*Killed*? Your view of the Gaijin is harsh indeed, Nemoto.'

Madeleine asked, 'What are the Gaijin getting from the Chaera in return for this?'

'We don't know. The Chaera spend their days quietly in the service of their God. And their requirement, it seems, is simple. You will help them talk to God.'

Ben said dryly, 'With an X-ray laser?'

'Just focus on the science,' Nemoto said, sounding weary. 'Learn about black holes, and about the Gaijin. That's what you're being sent for. Don't worry about the rest.'

The Chaera swam like melting glass, glimmering in Earthlight.

Ben Roach seemed to sense her urgency, her longing for time to pass.

He offered to take her to Australia, to show her places where he'd grown up. 'You ought to reconnect a little. No matter how far you travel, you're still made of Earth atoms, rock and water.'

'Aborigine philosophy?' she asked, a little dismissive.

'If you like. The Earth gave you life, gave you food and language and intelligence, and will take you back when you die. There are stories that humans have already died, out there among the stars. *Their* atoms can't return to the Earth. And, conversely, there are Gaijin here.'

'None of the Gaijin have died here.' That was true; the three ambassadors she had encountered on Kefallinia were still there, still functioning decades later. 'Perhaps they can't die.'

'But if they do, then their atoms, not of the Earth, will be absorbed by the Earth's rocks.'

'Perhaps that is a fair trade,' she said. 'We should extend your philosophy. The universe is the greater Earth; the universe births us,

172

takes us back when we die. All of us, humans, Gaijin, everybody.'

'Yes. Besides, there are lessons to learn.'

'Are you trying to educate me, Ben? What is there to see in Australia?'

'Will you come?'

It would eat up time. 'Yes,' she said.

From the air Australia looked flat, rust-red, and littered with rippling, continent-spanning sand dunes and shining salt flats, the relics of dead seas. It was eroded, very dry, very ancient; even the sand dunes, she learned, were thirty thousand years old. Human occupancy seemed limited to the coastal strip, and a few scattered settlements in the interior.

They flew into Alice Springs, in the dry heart of the island continent.

As they approached the airport she saw a modern facility: a huge white globe, other installations. In among the structures she saw the characteristic gleaming cones of Gaijin landers. New silvery fencing had been flung out across the desert for kilometres around the central structures.

The extent of the Gaijin holding, here in central Australia, startled her. The days when the Gaijin had been restricted to a heavily-guarded compound on a Greek island were long past, it seemed.

Ben grimaced. 'This is an old American space tracking facility called Pine Gap. There used to be a lot of local hostility to it. It was said that even the Prime Minister of Australia didn't know what went on in there. And the local Aboriginal communities were outraged when their land was taken away.'

'But now,' she said dryly, 'the Americans have gone. We don't do any space tracking, because we don't have a space program that requires it any more.'

'No,' he murmured. 'And so they gave Pine Gap to the Gaijin.'

'When?'

He shrugged. 'Forty years ago, I think.' Before he was born.

It was the same all over the planet, Madeleine knew. Everywhere they touched the Earth, the Gaijin were moving out: slowly, almost imperceptibly, but it was all one way. And every year there were more weary human refugees, forced to flee their homes.

Few people protested strongly, because few saw the trends. *Nemoto is right*, she thought. *The Gaijin are exploiting our short lives. Nemoto is right to try to survive, to stretch out her life, to see what is being done to us.*

But Ben surprised her. Being here, seeing this, he lost his detachment; he became unhappy, angry. 'The Gaijin care even less about our feelings than the Europeans. But we were here before the Gaijin, long before the Europeans. They are all Gaijin to us. Some of us are fleeing. But maybe one day they will all have gone, all the foreigners, and we will slip off our manufactured clothes and walk into the desert once more. What do you think? . . .'

The plane landed heavily, in a cloud of billowing red dust.

Alice Springs – Ben called it *the Alice* – turned out to be a dull, scrubby town, a grid of baking-hot streets. Its main strip was called Todd Street, a dreary stretch of asphalt that dated back to the days of horses and hitching posts. Now it might have been transplanted from small-town America, a jumble of bars, soda fountains and souvenir stores.

Madeleine studied the store windows desultorily. There were Australian mementoes – stuffed kangaroos and wallabies, animated T-shirts and books and data discs – but there was also, to cash in on the nearness of the Pine Gap reserve, a range of Gaijin souvenirs, models of landers and flower-ships, and animated spider-like Gaijin toys that clacked eerily back and forth across the display front. But there were few tourists now, it seemed; that industry, already dwindling before Madeleine's first Saddle Point jaunt, was now all but vanished.

They stayed in an anonymous hotel a little way away from Todd Street. There was an ugly old eucalyptus outside, pushing its way through the asphalt. The tree had small, tough-looking dark green leaves, and it was shedding its bark in great ash-grey strips that dangled from its trunk. 'A sacred monument,' Ben said gently. 'It's on the Caterpillar Dreaming.' She didn't know what that meant. SmartDrive cars wrenched their way around the tree's stubborn, ancient presence; once, in the days when people drove cars, it must have been a traffic hazard.

A couple of children ambled by – slim, lithe, a deep black, plastered with sunblock. They stared at Ben and Madeleine as they stared at the tree. Ben seemed oddly uncomfortable under their scrutiny.

It's because he's a foreigner too, she thought. He's been away too long, like me. This place isn't his any more, not quite. She found that saddening, but oddly comforting. Always somebody worse off than yourself.

They rested for a night.

At her window the Moon was bright. Fat bugs swarmed around the hotel's lamps, sparking, sizzling. It was so hot it was hard to sleep.

She longed for the simple, controllable enclosure of a spacecraft.

The next morning they prepared to see the country – to go *out bush*, as Ben called it. Ben wore desert boots, a loose singlet, a yellow hard hat and tight green shorts he called 'stubbies'. Meacher wore a loose poncho and a broad reflective hat and liberal layers of sunblock on her face and hands. After all, she wouldn't even be able to tell when this ferocious sun burned her.

They had rented a car, a chunky four-wheel-drive with immense broad tyres, already stained deep red with dust. Ben loaded up some food – tucker, he called it, his accent deepening as he spoke to the locals – and a *lot* of water, far more than she imagined they would need, in big chilled clear-walled tanks called Eskis, after Eskimo. In fact the car wouldn't allow itself to be started unless its internal sensors told it there was plenty of water on board.

The road was a straight black strip of tarmac – probably smart concrete, she thought, self-repairing, designed to last centuries without maintenance. It was empty of traffic, save for themselves.

At first she glimpsed fences, wind-pumps with cattle clustered around them, even a few camels.

They passed an Aboriginal settlement, surrounded by a link fence. It was a place of tin-roof shacks, and a few central buildings that were just brown airless boxes – a clinic, a church perhaps. Children seemed to be running everywhere, limbs flashing. Rubbish blew across the ground, where bits of glass sparkled.

They didn't stop; Ben barely glanced aside. Madeleine was shocked by the squalor.

Soon they moved beyond human habitation, and the ground was crimson and treeless. Nothing moved but the wispy shadows of high clouds. It was too arid here to farm or even graze.

'A harsh place,' she said unnecessarily.

'You bet,' Ben said, his eyes masked by mirrored glasses. 'And getting harsher. It's becoming depopulated, in fact. But it was enough for *us*. We touched the land lightly, I suppose.'

It was true. After tens of millennia of trial and error and carefully accumulated lore, the Aborigines had learned to survive here, in a land starved of nutrient and water. But there was no room for excess: there had been no fixed social structure, no prophets or chiefs, no leisured classes, and their myths were dreams of migration. And, before the coming of the Europeans, the weak, infirm and elderly had been dealt with harshly.

In a land the size of the continental United States, there had been only three hundred thousand of them. But the Aborigines had survived, where it might seem impossible.

As the ground began to rise, Ben stopped the car and got out. Madeleine emerged into hot, skin-sucking dust, flat dense light, stillness.

She found herself walking over a plateau of sand hills and crumbled, weathered orange-red rock, red as Mars, she thought, broken by deep, dry gulches. But there was grass here, tufts of it, yellow and spiky; even trees and bushes, such as low, spiky-leaved mulgas. Some of the bushes had been recently burned, and green shoots prickled the blackened stumps. To her eyes, there was the look of park land about these widely separated trees and scattered grass; but this land had been shaped by aridity and fire, not western aesthetics.

Ben seemed exhilarated to be walking, stretching his legs, thumbs hooked in the straps of a backpack. 'Australia is a place for creatures who walk,' he said. 'That's what we humans are adapted for. Look at your body some time. Every detail of it, from your long legs to your upright spine, is built for long, long walks through unforgiving lands, of desert and scrub. Australia is the kind of land we've been evolved for.'

'So we've been evolved to be refugees,' Madeleine said sourly.

'If you like. Looking at the crowd that seems to be on the way along the spiral arm, maybe that's a good thing. What do you think?'

Walking, he said, was the basis of the Dreamtime, the Aboriginal Genesis.

'In the beginning there was only the clay. And the Ancestors created themselves from the clay – thousands of them, one for each totemic species . . .' Each totemic Ancestor travelled the country, leaving a trail of words and musical notes along the lines of his footprints. And these tracks served as ways of communication between the most far-flung tribes.

Madeleine had heard of this. 'The song lines.'

'We call them something like "The Footprints of the Ancestors". And the system of knowledge and law is called the *Tjukurpa* . . . But, yes. The whole country is like a musical score. There is hardly a rock or a creek that has been left unsung. My "clan" isn't my tribe, but all the people of my Dreaming, whether on this side of the continent or the other; my "land" isn't some fixed patch of ground, but a trade route, a means of communication.

'The main song lines seem to enter Australia from the north or north-west, perhaps from across the Torres Strait, and then weave their way southwards across the continent. Perhaps they represent the routes of the first Australians of all, when they ventured over the narrow Ice Age strait from Asia. That would make the lines remnants of trails that stretch much further back, over a hundred thousand years, across Asia and back to Africa.'

'From Africa,' she said, 'to Triton.'

'Where the land is unsung. Yes.'

They climbed a little further, through clumps of the wiry yellow-white grass, which was called spinifex. She reached out to touch a clump, feeling nothing; Ben snatched her hand back. He turned it over. She saw spines sticking out of her palm.

Patiently he plucked out the spines. 'Everything here has spines. Everything is trying to survive, to hold onto its hoard of water. Just remember that . . . *Look*.'

There was a crackle of noise. A female kangaroo, with a cluster of young, had broken cover from a stand of bushes.

The kangaroos looked oddly like giant mice, clumsy but powerful, with rodent-like faces and thick fur. Their haunches were white against the red of the dirt. When the big female moved, she used a swivelling gait Madeleine had never seen before, using her tail and forelegs as props while levering herself forward on her great lower legs. There was a cub in her pouch – no, Ben said it was called a *joey* – a small head that protruded, curious, and even browsed on the spinifex as the mother moved.

The creatures, seen close up, seemed extraordinarily alien to Madeleine: a piece of different biological engineering, as if she had wandered into some alternate world. The Chaera, she thought, are hardly less exotic.

Something startled the kangaroos. They leapt away with great efficient bounds.

Madeleine grinned. 'My first kangaroo.'

'You don't understand,' Ben said tightly. 'I think that was a *Procoptodon*. A giant kangaroo. They grow as high as three metres . . .'

Madeleine knew nothing about kangaroos. 'And that's unusual?'

'Madeleine, *Procoptodon* has been extinct for ten thousand years. *That's* what makes it unusual.'

They walked on, further from the car, sipping water from flasks.

'It's the Gaijin,' he said. 'Of course it's the Gaijin. They are restoring megafauna that have long been extinct here. There have been sightings of *wanabe*, a snake a metre in diameter and seven long, a flightless bird twice the mass of an emu called *genyornis*. The Gaijin seem to be tinkering with the genetic structure of existing species, exploring these archaic, lost forms.'

They came upon an area of bare rock that was littered with bones. The bones were broken up and scattered, and had apparently been gnawed. Few of the fragments were large enough for her to recognize – was this an eye socket, that a piece of jaw?

'We think they use parsimony analysis,' Ben was saying. 'DNA erodes with time. But you can deconstruct evolution if you have access to the evolutionary products. You track backwards to find the common gene from which all the products descended; the principle is to seek the smallest number of branch points from which the present family could have evolved. When you have the structure you can recreate the ancient gene by splicing synthesized sequences into modern genes. You see?' He stopped, panting lightly. 'And, Madeleine, here's a thought. Australia has been an island, save for intervals of bridging during the Ice Ages, for a hundred million years. The genetic divergence between modern humans is widest between Australian natives and the rest of the population.'

'So if you wanted to think about picking apart the human genome –'

'– here would be a good place to start.'

She thought of the Gaijin she had seen undoing itself, decades back, in Kefallinia. 'Perhaps they are dismantling us. Taking apart the biosphere, to see how it works.'

'Perhaps. You know, humans always believed that when the aliens arrived, they would bring wisdom from the stars. Instead they seem to have arrived with nothing but questions. Now, they have grown dissatisfied with *our* answers, and are seeking their own . . . Of course it might help if they told us what it is they are looking for. But we are starting to guess.'

'We are?'

They walked on, slowly, conserving their energy.

He eyed her. 'For somebody who has travelled so far, you sometimes seem to understand little. Let me tell you another theory. Can you see any cactus, here in our desert?'

No, as it happened. In fact, now she thought about it, there were none of the desert plants she was accustomed to from the States.

Ben told her now that this was because of Australia's long history. Once it had been part of a giant super-Africa continent called Gondwanaland. When Australia had split off and sailed away, it had carried a freight of rainforest plants and animals which had responded to the growing aridity by evolving into the forms she saw here.

He rubbed his fingers in the red dirt. 'The continents are rafts of granite that ride on currents of magma in the mantle. We think the continents merge and break up, moving this way and that, under the influence of changes in those currents.'

'All right.'

'But we don't know *what* causes those magma currents to change. We used to think it must be some dynamic internal to the Earth.'

'But now –'

'Now we aren't so sure.' He smiled thinly. 'Imagine a huge war. A bombardment from space. Imagine a major strike, an asteroid or comet, hitting the ocean. It would punch through the water like a puddle, not even noticing it was there, and then crack the ocean floor.' His lips pursed. 'Think of a scum on water. Now throw in a few rocks. Imagine the islands of dirt shattering, convulsing, whirling around and uniting again. *That* was what it was like. If it happened, it shaped the whole destiny of life on Earth. The impact structures wouldn't be easy to spot, because the ocean floor gets dragged under the continents and melted. After two hundred million years, the ocean floor is wiped clean. Nevertheless there are techniques . . .'

A huge war. Rocks hurled from the sky, battering the Earth. Tens of millions of years ago. The hot dusty land seemed to swivel around her.

It sounded like an insane conspiracy theory. To attribute the evolution of Venus to the activities of aliens was one thing. But this . . . Could it possibly be true that everything she had seen today – the animals, the ancient land – all of it was shaped by intelligence, by careless war?

'Is this why you brought me to Australia? To tell me this?'

He grinned. 'On Earth, as it is in Heaven, Madeleine. We seem to find it easy to discuss the remaking of remote rocky worlds by waves of invaders – even Venus, our twin. *But why should Earth have been spared?*'

'And this is why you follow Nemoto?'

'If the Gaijin understand this – that we live in a universe of such dreadful violence – don't you think they should, at the very least, *tell us?* . . .' Ben found what looked like a piece of thigh bone. 'I'm not an expert,' he said. 'But I think this was a *diprotodon*. A wombat-like creature the size of a rhino.'

'Another Gaijin experiment.'

'Yes.' He seemed angry again, in his controlled, internalized way. 'Who knows how it died? From hunger, perhaps, or thirst, or just simple sunburn. These are archaic forms; this isn't the ecology they evolved in.'

'And so they die.'

'And so they die.'

They walked on, and found more bones of animals that should have been dead for ten thousand years, huge failed experiments, bleached in the unrelenting sun.

The Saddle Point gateway was a simple hoop of some powder-blue material, facing the sun, perhaps thirty metres across. Madeleine thought it was classically beautiful. Elegant, perfect.

As the flower-ship approached, Madeleine's fear grew. Ben told her Dreamtime stories, and she clung to him. 'Tell me . . .'

There was no deceleration. At the last minute the flower-ship folded up its electromagnetic petals, and the silvery ropes coiled back against the ship's flanks, turning it into a spear that lanced through the disc of darkness.

Blue light bathed Madeleine's face. The light increased in intensity, until it blinded them.

With every transition, there is a single instant of pain, unbearable, agonizing.

. . . But this time, for Madeleine, the pain didn't go away.

Ben held her, as the cool light of different suns broke over the flower-ship, as she wept.

Chapter 16

ICOSAHEDRAL GOD

The Saddle Point for the Chaera's home system turned out to be within the accretion disc of the black hole itself. Ben and Madeleine clung to the windows as smoky light washed over the scuffed metal and plastic surfaces of the habitat.

The accretion disc swirled below the flower-ship, like scum on the surface of a huge milk churn. The black hole was massive for its type, Madeleine learned – metres across. Matter from the accretion disc tumbled into the hole continually; X-rays sizzled into space.

The flower-ship passed through the accretion disc. The view was astonishing.

The disc foreshortened. They fell into shadows a million kilometres long.

A crimson band swept upwards past the flower-ship. Madeleine caught a glimpse of detail, a sea of gritty rubble. The disc collapsed to a grainy streak across the stars; pea-sized pellets spanged off *Ancestor*'s hull plates. Then the ship soared below the plane of the disc.

A brilliant star gleamed beneath the ceiling of rubble. This was a stable G2 star, like the sun, some five astronomical units away – about as far as Jupiter was from Sol. The black hole was orbiting that star, a wizened, spitting planet.

Soon, the monitors mounted on the *Ancestor*'s science platform started to collect data on hydrogen alpha emission, ultraviolet line spectra, ultraviolet and X-ray imaging, spectrography of the active regions. Ben took charge now, and training and practice took over as the two of them went into the routine tasks of studying the hole and its disc.

Nemoto had hooked up to the Chaera's tank a powerful bioprocessor, a little cubical unit, which would enable the humans to communicate, to some extent, with the Chaera, and with their Gaijin hosts. When they booted it up, a small screen displayed the biopro's human interface design metaphor. It was a blocky, badly synched, two-dimensional virtual representation of Nemoto's leathery face.

'The vanity of megalomaniacs,' Madeleine murmured. 'It's a pattern.'

Ben didn't understand. The Nemoto virtual grinned.

Ben and Madeleine hovered before a window into the Chaera's tank.

If Madeleine had encountered this creature in some deep sea aquarium – and given she was no biologist – she mightn't have thought it outlandishly strange. After all it had those remarkable eyes.

The eyes were, of course, a stunning example of convergent evolution. On Earth, eyes conveyed such a powerful evolutionary advantage that they had been developed independently perhaps forty times – while wings seemed to have been invented only three or four times, and the wheel not at all. Although details differed – the eyes of fish, insects and people were very different – nevertheless all eyes showed a commonality of design, for they were evolved for the same purpose, and were constrained by physical law.

You might have expected Eeties to show up with eyes.

The Chaera communicated by movement, their rippling surfaces sending low-frequency acoustic signals through the fluid in which they swam. In the tank, lasers scanned the Chaera's surface constantly, picking up the movements and affording translations.

Inter-species translation was actually getting easier, after the first experience with the Gaijin. A kind of meta-language had been evolved, an interface which served as a translation buffer between Eetie 'languages' and every human tongue. The meta-language was founded on concepts – space, time, number – which had to be common to any sentient species embedded in three-dimensional space and subject to physical law, and it had verbal, mathematical and diagrammatic components; to Madeleine's lay understanding it seemed to be a fusion of Latin and Lincos.

Madeleine felt an odd kinship with the spinning, curious creature, a creature that might have come from Earth, much more sympathetic than any Gaijin. And if we have found *you* so quickly, perhaps we will find less strangeness out there than we expect.

Ben asked, 'What is it saying?'

Virtual Nemoto translated. 'The Chaera saw the disc unfolding. "What a spectacle. I am the envy of generations . . ."'

Mini black holes, Madeleine learned, were typically the mass of

Jupiter. Too small to have been formed by processes of stellar collapse, they were created a millionth of a second after the Big Bang, baked in the fireball at the birth of the universe.

Mini black holes, then, seemed to be well understood. The oddity here was to find such a hole in a neat circular orbit around this sun-like star.

'And the real surprise,' said virtual Nemoto, 'was the discovery, by the Gaijin, of life, infesting the accretion disc of a mini black hole. The Chaera. It seems that this black hole is God for the Chaera.'

'They *worship* a black hole?' Madeleine asked.

'Evidently,' said Nemoto impatiently. 'If the translation programs are working. If it's possible to correlate concepts like "God" and "worship" across species barriers.'

Ben murmured wordlessly. Madeleine looked over his shoulder.

In the central glare of the accretion disc, there was something surrounding the black hole, embedding it.

The black hole was set into a net-like structure that started just outside the Schwarzschild radius, and extended kilometres. The structure was a regular solid of twenty triangular faces.

'It's an icosahedron,' Ben said. 'My God, it is so obviously artificial. The largest possible Platonic solid. Triumphantly three-dimensional.'

Madeleine couldn't make out any framework within the icosahedron, or any reinforcement for its edges; it was a structure of sheets of almost transparent film, each triangle hundreds of metres wide. The glow of the flower-ship's hungry ramscoop shone and sparkled from the multiple facets.

'It must be mighty strong to maintain its structure against the hole's gravity, the tides,' Ben said. 'It seems to be directing the flow of matter from the accretion disc into the event horizon . . .'

It was a jewel-box setting for a black hole. A comparative veteran of interstellar exploration, Madeleine felt stunned.

The Chaera thrashed in its tank.

Nemoto said, 'Time to pay the fare. Are we ready to speak to God?'

Madeleine turned to Ben. 'We didn't know about *this*. Maybe we should think about what we're doing here.'

He shrugged. 'Nemoto is right. It is not our mission.' He began the operations they'd rehearsed.

Reluctantly, Madeleine worked a console to unship the first of the old X-ray lasers; the monitors showed it unfolding from its mount like a shabby flower.

The self-directed laser dove into the heart of the system, heading for its closest approach to the hole.

Ben murmured, 'Three, two, one.'

There was a flash of light, pure white, which shone through the Service Module's ports.

Various instruments showed surges, of particles and electromagnetic radiation. The laser's fission-bomb power source had worked. The shielding of *Ancestor* seemed adequate.

The X-ray beam washed over the surface of 'God'. The net structure stirred, like a sleeping snake.

The Chaera quivered.

Ben was watching the false-colour images. 'Madeleine. Look.'

The surface of 'God' was alive with motion; the icosahedral netting was bunching itself around a single, brooding point, like skin crinkling round an eye.

'I can give you a rough translation from the Chaera,' said Nemoto. '"She heard us."'

Madeleine asked, '"She"?'

'God, of course. "If I have succeeded . . . Then I will be the most honoured of my race. Fame – wealth – my choice of mates –"'

Madeleine laughed sourly. 'And, of course, religious fulfilment.'

Ben monitored a surge, of X-ray photons and high-energy particles, coming from the hole – and the core at the centre of the crinkled net exploded. A pillar of radiation punched through the accretion disc like a fist.

The Chaera wobbled around its tank.

'"God is shouting,"' Nemoto said. She peered out of her biopro monitor tank, her wizened virtual face creased with doubt.

The beam blinked out, leaving a trail of churning junk.

The flower-ship entered a long powered orbit which would take it, for a time, away from the black hole, and in towards the primary star and its inner system. Madeleine and Ben watched the black hole and its enigmatic artefact recede to a toy-like glimmer.

The Chaera inhabited the accretion disc's larger fragments.

In the *Ancestor*'s recorded images, Chaera were everywhere, spinning like frisbees over the surface of their worldlets – or whipping through the accretion mush to a neighbouring fragment – or basking like lizards, their undersides turned up to the black hole.

The beam from 'God' had left a track of glowing debris through the accretion disc, like flesh scorched by hot iron. The track ended in a knot of larger fragments.

In the optical imager, jellyfish bodies drifted like soot flakes.

'Let me get this straight,' Madeleine said. 'The Chaera have evolved to feed off the X-radiation from the black hole . . . from "God". Is that right?'

'Evolved or adapted. So it seems,' Nemoto said dryly. ' "God provides us in all things." '

Ben said, 'So the Chaera try to – *shout* – to "God". Some of them pray. Some of them build great artefacts to sparkle at Her. Like worshipping the sun, praying for dawn. Basically they're trying to stimulate X-radiation bursts. All the Gaijin have done is to sell them a more effective communication mechanism.'

'A better prayer wheel,' Madeleine murmured. 'But what are the Gaijin interested in here? The black hole artefact?'

'Possibly,' Nemoto said. 'Or perhaps the Chaera's religion. The Gaijin seem unhealthily obsessed with such illogical belief systems.'

'But,' Madeleine said, 'that X-ray laser delivers orders of magnitude more energy into the artefact than anything the Chaera could manage. It looks as if the energy of the pulse they get in return is magnified in proportion. Perhaps the Chaera don't understand what they're dealing with, here.'

Nemoto translated: ' "God's holy shout shatters worlds." '

The main star was very sun-like. Madeleine, filled with complex doubts about her mission, pressed her hand to the window, trying to feel its warmth, hungering for simple physical pleasure.

There was just one planet here. It was a little larger than the Earth, and it followed a neat circular path through the star's habitable zone, the region within which an Earth-like planet could orbit.

But they could see, even from a distance, that this was no Earth. It was silent on all wavelengths. And it gleamed, almost as bright as a star itself; it must have cloud decks like Venus.

On a sleep break, Ben and Madeleine, clinging to each other, floated before the nearest thing they had to a picture window. Madeleine peered around, seeking constellations she might recognize, even so far from home, and she wondered if she could find Sol.

'Something's wrong,' Ben whispered.

'There always is.'

'I'm serious.' He let his fingers trace out a line across the black sky. 'What do you see?'

With the sun eclipsed by the shadow of the FGB Module, she gazed out at the subtle light. There was that bright planet, and the dim red disc of rubble surrounding the Chaera black hole, from here just visible as more than a point source of light.

Ben said, 'There's a *glow*, around the star itself, covering the orbit of that single planet. Can you see?' It was a diffuse shine, Madeleine saw, cloudy, ragged-edged. Ben said, 'That's an oddity in itself. But –'

Then she got it. 'Oh. No zodiacal light.'

The zodiacal light, in the solar system, was a faint glow along the plane of the ecliptic. Sometimes it was visible from Earth. It was sunlight, scattered by dust that orbited the sun in the plane of the planets. Most of the dust was in or near the asteroid belt, created by asteroid collisions. And in the modern solar system, of course, the zodiacal light was enhanced by the glow of Gaijin colonies.

'So if there's no zodiacal light –'

'There are no asteroids here,' said Ben.

'Nemoto. What happened to the asteroids?'

'You already know, I think,' virtual Nemoto hissed.

Ben nodded. 'They were mined out. Probably long ago. This place is *old*, Madeleine.'

The electromagnetic petals of the flower-ship sparkled hungrily as it chewed through the rich gas pocket at the heart of the system, and the shadows cast by the sun – now nearby, full and fat, brimming with light – turned like clock hands on the ship's complex surface. But that diffuse gas cloud was now dense enough that it dimmed the further stars.

Data slid silently into the FGB Module.

Ben said, 'It's like a fragment of a GMC – a giant molecular cloud. Mostly hydrogen, some dust. It's thick – comparatively. A hundred thousand molecules per cubic centimetre . . . The sun was born out of such a cloud, Madeleine.'

'But the heat of the sun dispersed the remnants of *our* cloud . . . didn't it? So why hasn't the same thing happened here?'

'Or,' virtual Nemoto said sourly, 'maybe the question should be: *how come the gas cloud got put back around this star?*'

They flew around the back of the sun. Despite elaborate shielding, light seemed to fill every crevice of the FGB module. Madeleine was relieved when they started to pull away, and headed for the cool of the outer system, and that single mysterious planet.

It took a day to get there.

They came at the planet with the sun behind them, so it showed a nearly full disc. It glared, brilliant white, just a solid mass of cloud from pole to pole, blinding and featureless. And it was surrounded by a pearly glow of interstellar hydrogen, like an immense, misshapen outer atmosphere.

The flower-ship's petals opened wide, the lasers working vigorously, and decelerated smoothly into orbit.

They could see nothing of the surface. Their instruments revealed a world that was indeed like Venus: an atmosphere of carbon dioxide, kilometres thick, scarcely any water.

There was, of course, no life of any kind.

The Chaera spun in its tank, volunteering nothing.

Ben was troubled. 'There's no reason for a Venus to form this far from the sun. This world should be temperate. An Earth.'

'But,' Nemoto hissed, 'think what this world has that Earth doesn't share.'

'The gas cloud,' Madeleine said.

Ben nodded. 'All that interstellar hydrogen. Madeleine, we're so far from the sun now, and the gas is so thick, that the hydrogen is neutral – not ionized by sunlight.'

'And so –'

'And so the planet down there has no defence against the gas; its magnetic field could only keep it out if it was charged. Hydrogen has been raining down from the sky, into the upper air.'

'Once there, it will mix with any oxygen present,' Nemoto said. 'Hydrogen plus oxygen gives –'

'Water,' Madeleine said.

'*Lots* of it,' Ben told her. 'It must have rained like hell, for a million years. The atmosphere was drained of oxygen, and filled up with water vapour. A greenhouse effect took off –'

'All that from a wisp of gas?'

'That wisp of gas was a planet-killer,' Nemoto whispered.

'But why would anyone kill a planet?'

Nemoto said, 'It is the logic of growth. This has all the characteristics of an *old* system, Meacher. Caught behind a wave of colonization – all its usable resources dug out and exploited . . .'

Madeleine frowned. 'I don't believe it. It would take a hell of a long time to eat up a solar system.'

'How long do you think?'

'I don't know. Millions of years, perhaps.'

Nemoto grunted. 'Listen to me. The growth rate of the human population on Earth, historically, was two per cent a year. Doesn't sound much, does it? But it's compound interest, remember. At that rate your population doubles every thirty-five years, an increase by tenfold every century or so. Of course after the twentieth century *our* growth rates collapsed; we ran out of resources.'

'Ah,' Ben said. 'What if we'd kept on growing?'

'How many people could Earth hold?' Nemoto whispered. 'Ten, twenty billion? Meacher, the whole of the inner solar system out to Mars could supply only enough water for maybe fifty billion people. It might have taken us a century to reach those numbers. Of course there is much more water in the asteroids and the outer system than in Earth's oceans, perhaps enough to support ten thousand *trillion* human beings.'

'A huge number.'

'But not infinite – and only six tenfold jumps away from ten billion.'

'Just six or seven centuries,' Ben said.

'And then what?' Nemoto whispered. 'Suppose we start colonizing, like the Gaijin. Earth is suddenly the centre of a growing sphere of colonization, whose volume must keep increasing at two per cent a year, to keep up with the population growth. And that means that the leading edge, the colonizing wave, has to sweep on faster and faster, eating up worlds and stars and moving on to the next, because of the pressure from behind . . .'

Ben was doing sums in his head. 'That leading edge would have to be moving at lightspeed within a few centuries, no more.'

'Imagine how it would be,' Nemoto said grimly, 'to inhabit a world in the path of such a wave. The exploitation would be rapid, ruthless, merciless, burning up worlds and stars like the front of a forest fire, leaving only ruins and lifelessness. And then, as resources are exhausted throughout the lightspeed cage, the crash comes, inevitably. Remember Venus. Remember Polynesia.'

'Polynesia? . . .'

'The nearest analogue in our own history to interstellar colonization,' Ben said. 'The Polynesians spread out among their Pacific islands for over a thousand years, across three thousand kilometres. But by about AD 1000 their colonization wavefront had reached as far as it could go, and they had inhabited every scrap of land. Isolated, each island surrounded by others already full of people, they had nowhere to go.

'On Easter Island they destroyed the native ecosystem in a few generations, let the soil erode away, cut down the forests. In the end they didn't even have enough wood to build more canoes. Then they went to war over whatever was left. By the time the Europeans arrived the Polynesians had just about wiped themselves out.'

Nemoto said, 'Think about it, Meacher. *The lightspeed cage.* Imagine this system fully populated, a long way behind the local colonization wavefront, and surrounded by systems just as heavily populated – and armed – as they were. And they were running out of resources. There surely were a lot more space dwellers than planet dwellers, but they'd already used up the asteroids and the comets. So the space dwellers turned on the planet. The inhabitants were choked, drowned, baked.'

'I don't believe it,' Madeleine said. 'Any intelligent society would figure out the dangers long before breeding itself to extinction.'

'The Polynesians didn't,' said Ben dryly.

The petals of the flower-ship opened once more, and they receded from the corpse-like planet into the calm of the outer darkness.

It was time to talk to the icosahedral God again. The second X-ray punch laser was launched.

After studying the records of the last encounter, Ben had learned how the configuration of the icosahedral artefact anticipated the direction of the resulting beam. Now Madeleine watched the core squint into focus. The killer beam would again lance through the accretion disc – and, this time, right into one of the largest of the Chaera worldlets.

Millions of Chaera were going to die. Madeleine could *see* them, infesting their accretion disc, swarming and living and loving.

In its tank, their Chaera passenger drifted like a Dali watch.

Madeleine said, 'Nemoto, we can't go ahead with the second firing.'

'But they understand the consequences,' virtual Nemoto said blandly. 'The Chaera have disturbed the artefact a few times in the past, with their mirrors and smoke signals. Every time it's killed some of them. But they need the X-ray nourishment ... Meacher,' she warned, 'don't meddle as you did at the burster. If you meddle, the Gaijin may not allow human passengers on future missions. And we won't learn about systems like *this*. We'll have no information; we won't be able to plan ... Besides, the laser is already deployed. There's nothing you can do about it.'

'It *is* the Chaera's choice, Madeleine,' Ben said gently. 'Their culture. It seems they're prepared to die to attain what they believe is perfection.'

Nemoto quoted the Chaera. 'It knows we're arguing here. "Where there are prophecies, they will cease. Where there are tongues, they will be stilled; where there is knowledge, it will pass away. For we know in part and we prophesy in part, but when perfection comes, the imperfect disappears."'

'Who's the philosopher?' Madeleine asked sourly. 'Some great Chaera mind of the past?'

Ben smiled. 'Actually, it was quoting Saint Paul.'

Nemoto looked startled, as Madeleine felt.

'But there remain mysteries,' Ben said. 'The Chaera look too primitive to have constructed that artefact. After all, it manipulates a black hole's gravity well. Perhaps their ancestors built this thing. Or some previous wave of colonists, who passed through this system.'

'You aren't thinking it through,' virtual Nemoto whispered. 'The Chaera have eyes filled with salty water. They must have evolved on a world with oceans. They can't have evolved *here*.'

'Then,' Madeleine snapped, 'why are they here?'

'Because they had no place else to go,' Nemoto said. 'They fled here – even modified themselves, perhaps. They huddled around an artefact left by an earlier wave of colonization. They knew that nobody would follow them to such a dangerous, unstable slum area as this.'

'They are refugees.'

'Yes. As, perhaps, we will become in the future.'

'Refugees from what?'

'From the resource wars,' Nemoto said. 'From the hydrogen suffocation of their world. Like Polynesia.'

The core artefact trembled.

And Nemoto kept talking, talking. 'This universe of ours is a place of limits, of cruel equations. The Galaxy must be full of lightspeed cages like this, at most a few hundred light years wide, traps for their exponentially growing populations. And then, after the ripped-up worlds have lain fallow, after recovery through the slow processes of geology and biology, it all begins again, a cycle of slash and burn, slash and burn . . . *This is our future*, Meacher. Our future and our past. It is after all a peculiar kind of equilibrium: the contact, the ruinous exploitation, the crash, the multiple extinctions – over and over. And it is happening again, to us. The Gaijin are already eating their way through *our* asteroid belt. Now do you see what I'm fighting against? . . .'

Madeleine remembered the burster, the slaughter of the star lichen fourteen times a second. She remembered Venus and Australia, the evidence of ancient wars even in the solar system – the relics of a previous, long-burned-out colonization bubble.

Must it be like this?

Something in her rebelled. To hell with theories. The Chaera were real, and millions of them were about to die.

And there was – she realized, thinking quickly – something she could do about it.

'Oh, damn it . . . Ben. Help me. Go down to the FGB Module. Get everything out of there you think we have to save.'

For long seconds, Ben thought it over. Then he nodded. 'I'll trust your instincts, Madeleine.'

'Good,' she said. 'Now I have a little figuring to do.' She rushed to the instrument consoles.

Ben gathered their research materials: the biological and medical samples they'd taken from their bodies, data cassettes and diskettes, film cartridges, notebooks, results of the astrophysical experiments they had run in the neighbourhood of the black hole. There was little personal gear in here, as their sleeping compartments were in the Service Module. He pulled everything together in a spare sleeping bag, and hauled it all up into the Service Module.

Madeleine glanced down for the last time through the FGB Module's picture window, at smoky accretion-disc light. The flower-ship skimmed past the flank of 'God'; the netting structure swarmed around the pulsing core.

The Chaera thrashed in its tank.

Ben pulled down the heavy hatch between the modules – it hadn't been closed since the flower-ship had swept them up from the surface of Earth's Moon – and dogged it tight. Madeleine was running a hasty computer program. She called, 'Remember the drill for a pressure hull breach?'

'Of course. But –'

'Three, two, one.'

There was a clatter of pyrotechnic bolts, an abrupt jolt.

'I just severed the FGB,' she said. 'The explosive decompression should fire it in the right direction. I hope. I didn't have time to check my figures, or verify my aim –'

Bits of radiation spat out like javelins as the core began to open.

Nemoto thundered, 'What have you done, Meacher?'

She saw the FGB Module for one last instant, its battered, patched-up form silhouetted against the gigantic cheek of 'God'. In its way it was a magnificent sight, she thought: a stubby twentieth-century human artefact orbiting a black hole, fifty-four light years from Earth.

And then the core opened.

The FGB Module got the X-ray pulse right in the rear end. Droplets of metal splashed across space . . . But the massive Russian construction lasted, long enough to shield the Chaera worldlets.

Just as Madeleine had intended.

The core closed; the surface of the net smoothed over. The slowly-cooling stump of the FGB Module drifted around the curve of the hole. Madeleine saluted it silently.

'The journey back is going to be cramped,' Ben said dryly.

The Saddle Point gateway hung before them, anonymous, eternal, indistinguishable from its copies in the solar system, visible only by the reflected light of the accretion disc.

'You saved a world, Madeleine,' Ben said.

'But nobody asked you to,' virtual Nemoto said, her voice tinny. 'You're a meddler. Sentimental. You always were. The Chaera are still protesting. "Why did you hide God from us?" . . .'

Ben shrugged. 'God is still there. I think all Madeleine has done is provide the Chaera with a little more time to consider how much perfection they really want to achieve.'

'Meacher, you're such a fool,' Nemoto said.

Perhaps she was. But she knew that what she was learning, the dismal, stupid secret of the universe, would not leave her. And she wondered what she would find when she reached home this time.

The blue glow of transition flooded over them, and there was an instant of searing, welcoming pain.

Chapter 17

LESSONS

World after world after world.

He saw worlds something like Earth, but with oceans of ammonia or sulphuric acid or hydrocarbons, airs of neon or nitrogen or carbon monoxide. All of them alive, of course, one way or another.

But such relatively Earth-like planets turned out to be the exception.

He was shown a giant world closely orbiting a star called 70 Virginis. This world was a cloudy ball six times the mass of Jupiter. The Gaijin believed there were creatures living in those clouds, immense, tenuous whales feeding off the organics created in the air by the central star's radiation. But colonists had visited here, long ago. At one pole of the planet there was what appeared to be an immense mining installation, perhaps there to extract organics or some other valuable volatile like helium-3. The installation was desolate, apparently scarred by battle.

Close to a star called Upsilon Andromedae, forty-nine light years from Earth, he found a planet with Jupiter's mass orbiting closer than Mercury to its sun. It had been stripped of its cloud decks by the sun's heat, leaving an immense rocky ball, with canyons deep enough to swallow Earth's Moon. Malenfant saw creatures crawling through those deep shadows, immense beetle-like beings. They were protected from the sun's heat by tough carapaces, and had legs like tree trunks strong enough to lift them against the ferocious gravity. Perhaps they fed off volatiles trapped in the eternal shadows, or seeping from the planet's deep interior. Here the battles seemed to have been fought out over the higher ground; Malenfant saw a plain littered with the wreckage of starships.

Not far from the star Procyon there was a nomadic world, a world without a sun, hurled by some random gravitational accident away from its parent star. It was in utter darkness, of course, a black ball swimming alone through space. But it was a big planet with a hydrogen-rich atmosphere; it warmed itself with the dwindling heat of the radioactive elements in its core, with volcanoes and earthquakes and tectonic shifts. Thus, under a lightless sky, there were oceans of liquid water – and in their depths life swarmed, feeding off minerals from the deeper hot rocks, not unlike the deep-sea animals which clustered around volcanic vents in Earth's seas. Here, though, life was doomed, for the world's core was inexorably cooling, as the heat of its formation was lost. .

But even this lonely planet had been subject to destructive exploitation by colonists; there were signs, Malenfant learned, of giant strip-mine gouges in the ocean floors, huge machines now abandoned, perhaps deliberately wrecked.

Everywhere, he had learned, life had emerged. But every world, every system, had been overrun by waves of colonization, followed by collapse or destructive wars – not once, but many times. Everywhere the sky was full of engineering, of ruins.

And the bad news continued. The universe itself could prove a deadly place. He was taken through a region a hundred light years wide where world after world was dead, land and oceans littered with the diverse remains of separately-evolved life.

There had been a gamma ray burster explosion here, the Gaijin told him: the collision of two neutron stars, causing a three-dimensional shower of high-energy electromagnetic radiation and heavy particles that had wiped clean the worlds for light years around. It had been a random cosmic accident that had cared nothing for culture and ambition, hope and love and dreams. Some life survived – on Earth, the deep-ocean forms, perhaps pond life, some insects would have endured the lethal showers. But nothing advanced made it through, and certainly nothing approaching sentience; after the accident, its effects over in weeks or months, it would require a hundred million years of patient evolution to fix the rent in life's fabric suffered in this place.

But nothing was without cost, he learned; nothing without benefit. The intense energy pulse of nearby gamma ray bursts could shape the evolution of young star systems; primordial dust was melted into dense iron-rich droplets, which settled quickly to the central plain of a dust cloud and so accelerated the formation of planets. Without a close-by gamma ray burst, it was possible that star systems like the solar system could never have formed. Birth, amid death; the way of the universe.

Maybe. But such cold logic was no comfort for Malenfant.

The Gaijin seemed determined to show him as much as possible of this vast star-spanning graveyard, to drive home its significance. After a time it became unbearable, the lesson blinding in its cruelty: that if the universe didn't get you, other sentient beings would.

Sometimes a spark within him rebelled. *Does it have to be like this? Can't we find another way?*

But he was very weak now, very lonely, very old.

He huddled in his shelter, eyes closed, while the years, of the universe and of his life, wore away, drenched in blue Saddle Point light.

There is only so much, all things considered, that a man can take.

III

TRENCHWORKS

AD 2190–2340

The Gaijin had a somewhat mathematical philosophy. Malenfant thought it sounded suspiciously like a religion.

The Gaijin believed that the universe was fundamentally comprehensible by creatures like themselves – like humans, like Malenfant. That is, they believed it possible that an entity could exist that could comprehend the entire universe, arbitrarily well.

And they had a further principle which mandated that if such a being could exist, it must exist.

The catch was that they believed there was a manifold of possible universes, of which this was only one. So She may not exist in this universe.

It – She – was the final goal of the Gaijin's quest.

But until the God of the Manifold shows up, there's only us, Malenfant thought. And there is work to do. We have to fix the bugs in this universe we're all stuck in. Hence, we throw a net around a star.

Hence, my sacrifice.

But, almost from the beginning, we humans fought back. We barely understood a damn thing, and nothing we did alone was going to make a difference, and the whole time we were swept along by historical forces that we could barely understand, let alone control, much as it had always been. We didn't even know who the bad guys were. But, by God, we tried.

At whatever cost to ourselves.

Chapter 18

MOON RAIN

There were only minutes left before the comet hit the Moon.

'You got to beat the future! – or it will beat you. Believe me, I've been there. Look around you, pal. You guys have lasted a hundred and fifty years up here, in your greenhouses and your mole holes. A hell of an achievement. *But the Moon can't support you . . .'*

Xenia Makarova had a window seat, and she gazed out of the fat, round portholes. Below the shuttle's hull she could see the landing pad, a plain of glass microwaved into lunar soil, here on the edge of the green domes of the Copernicus Triangle. And beyond that lay the native soil of the Moon, just subtle shades of grey, softly moulded by a billion years of meteorite rain.

And bathed, for today, in comet light.

Xenia knew that Frank J Paulis thought this day, this year 2190, was the most significant in the history of the inhabited Moon, let alone his own career. And here he was now, a pile of softscreens on his lap, hectoring the bemused-looking Lunar Japanese in the seat alongside him, even as the pilot of this cramped, dusty evacuation shuttle went through her countdown check.

Xenia had listened to Frank talk before. She'd been listening to him, in fact, for fifteen years, or a hundred and fifty, depending on what account you took of Albert Einstein.

'. . . You know what the most common mineral is on the Moon? Feldspar. And you know what you can make out of that? Scouring powder. Big fucking deal. On the Moon, you have to bake the air out of the rock. Sure, you can make other stuff, rocket fuel and glass. But there's no water, or nitrogen, or carbon –'

The Japanese, a businessman type, said, 'There are traces in the regolith.'

'Yeah, traces, put there by the sun, and it's being sold off anyhow, by Nishizaki Heavy Industries, to the Gaijin. Bleeding the Moon even drier . . .'

A child was crying. The shuttle was just a cylinder-shaped cargo scow, hastily adapted to support this temporary evacuation. It was crammed with people, last-minute refugees, men and women and tall, skinny children, subdued and serious, in rows of canvas bucket seats like factory chickens.

And all of them were Lunar Japanese, save for Frank and Xenia, who were American; for, while Frank and Xenia had taken a time-dilated hundred-and-fifty-year jaunt to the stars – and while America had disintegrated – the Lunar Japanese had been quietly colonizing the Moon.

'You need volatiles,' Frank said now. 'That's the key to the future. But now that Earth has fallen apart nobody is resupplying. You're just pumping around the same old shit.' He laughed. 'Literally, in fact. I give you another hundred years, tops. *Look around.* You've already got rationing, strict birth control laws.'

'There is no argument with the fact of –'

'How *much* do you need? I'll tell you. Enough to future-proof the Moon.'

'And you believe the comets can supply the volatiles we need for this.'

'Believe? That's what Project Prometheus is for. The random impact today, which alone will deliver a trillion tonnes of water, is a piece of luck. It's going to make my case for me, pal. And when we start purposefully harvesting the comets, those big fat babies out in the Oort cloud –'

'Ah.' The Lunar Japanese was smiling. 'And the person who has control of those comet volatiles –'

'That person could buy the Moon.' Frank reached for a cigar, a twentieth-century habit long frustrated. 'But that's incidental . . .'

But Xenia knew that Frank was lying about the comets, and their role in the Moon's future. Even before this comet had hit the Moon, Project Prometheus was already dead.

A month ago, Frank had called her into his office.

He had his feet up on his desk. He was reading, on a softscreen, some long, text-heavy academic paper about deep-implanted volatiles on the Earth. She tried to talk to him about work in progress, but he patently wasn't interested. Nor was he progressing Prometheus, his main project.

He had gotten straight to the point. 'The comet is history, babe.'

At first she hadn't understood. 'I thought it was going to supply us all with volatiles. I thought it was going to be the demonstration we needed that Prometheus was a sound investment.'

'Yeah. But it doesn't pan out.' Frank tapped the surface of his desk, and it lit up with numbers, graphics. 'Look at the analysis. We'll get some volatiles, but most of the nucleus's mass will be blasted back to space. Comets are spectacular fireworks, but they are inefficient cargo trucks. However you steer the damn things down, most of the incoming material is lost. I figure now you'd need around a *thousand* impactors to future-proof the Moon fully, to give it a stable atmosphere, thick enough to persist over significant periods before leaking away. And we aren't going to get a thousand impactors, not with the fucking Gaijin everywhere.' He looked thoughtful, briefly. 'One thing, though. Did you know the Moon *is* going to get an atmosphere out of this? It will last a thousand years –'

'*Iroonda.*'

'No, it's true. Thin, but an atmosphere, of comet mist. Happens every time a comet hits. Carbon dioxide and water and stuff. How about that.' He shook his head. 'Anyhow it's no use to us.'

'Frank, how come nobody figured this out before? How come nobody questioned your projections?'

'Well, they did.' He grinned. 'You know I'm never too sympathetic when people tell me something is impossible. I figured there would be time to fix it, to find a way.'

This was, on the face of it, a disaster, Xenia knew. Project Prometheus had got as far as designs for methane rockets, which could have pushed Oort comets out of their long, slow, distant orbits and brought them in to the Moon. The project had consumed all Frank's energies for years, and cost a fortune. He needed investors, and had hoped this chance comet impact, a proof of concept, would bring them in.

And now, it appeared, it had all been for nothing.

'Frank, I'm sorry.'

He seemed puzzled. 'Huh? Why?'

'If comets are the only source of volatiles –'

'Yesterday I thought they were. But look at this.' He tapped his softscreen. He was talking fast, excited, enthusiastic, his mind evidently racing. 'There's a woman here who thinks there are all the volatiles you could want, a hundred times over – *right here on the Moon*. Can you believe that?'

'That's impossible. Everyone knows the Moon is dry as a bone.'

He smiled. 'That's what everyone *thinks*. I want you to find this woman for me. The author of the paper.'

'Frank –'

'And find out about mining.'

'Mining?'

'The deeper the better.' His grin widened. 'How would you like a journey to the centre of the Moon, baby?'

And that was how she first learned about Frank's new project, his new obsession, his latest way to fix the future.

Ten seconds. Five. Three, two, one.

Stillness, for a fraction of a second. Then there was a clatter of explosive bolts, a muffled bang.

Xenia was ascending as if in some crowded elevator, pressed back in her bucket seat by maybe a full G. Beyond her window, stray dust streaked away across the pad glass, heaping up against fuel trucks and pipelines.

But then the shuttle swivelled sharply, twisting her around through a brisk ninety degrees. She heard people gasp, children laugh. The shuttle twisted again, and again, its attitude thrusters banging. This lunar shuttle was small, light, crude. Like the old Apollo landers, it had a single fixed rocket engine that was driving the ascent, and it was fitted with attitude control jets at every corner to turn it and control its trajectory. Just point, twist, squirt, as if she was a cartoon character carried into the air by hanging onto an out-of-control water hose.

Three hundred metres high the shuttle swivelled again, and she found she was pitched forward, looking down at the lunar surface, over which she skimmed. They were rising out of lunar night, and the shadowed land was dark, lit here and there by the lights of human installations, captured stars on dark rock. She felt as if she was falling, as if the ascent engine was going to drive her straight down into the unforgiving rocks. Sunrise. *Wham.*

It was not like Earth's slow-fade dawn; the limb of the sun just pushed above the Moon's rocky horizon, instantly banishing the stars into the darkness of a black sky. Light spilled on the unfolding landscape below, fingers of light interspersed with inky-black shadows hundreds of kilometres long, the deeper craters still pools of darkness. The Moon could never be called beautiful – it was too damaged for that – but it had a compelling wildness.

But everywhere she could see the work of humans: the unmistakable tracks of tractors, smooth lines snaking over the regolith, and occasional orange tents that marked the position of emergency supply dumps, all of it overlaid by the glittering silver wires of mass driver rails.

The shuttle climbed further. The Lunar Japanese around her applauded the smooth launch.

Now Earth rose. It looked as blue and beautiful as when she and Frank had left for the stars. But it had changed, of course. Even from here, she could see Gaijin flower-ships circling the planet, the giant ramscoops of the alien craft visible as tiny discs. She felt a stab of antique resentment at those powerful, silent visitors, who had watched as humanity tore itself apart.

And now, as the shuttle tilted and settled into its two-hour orbit around the Moon, Xenia saw a sight she knew no human had ever seen before today:

Comet rise, over the Moon.

The coma, a diffuse mass of gas and fine particles, was a ball as big as the Earth, so close now it walled off half the sky, a glare of lacy, diffuse light. Massive clumps in the coma, backlit, cast shadows across the smoky gases, straight lines thousands of kilometres long radiating at her. The comet was coming out of the sun, straight toward the Moon at seventy thousand kilometres an hour. She looked for the nucleus, a billion-tonne ball of ice and rock. But it was too small and remote, even now, a few minutes from impact. And the tail was invisible from here, fleeing behind her, running ahead of the comet and stretching far beyond the Moon, reaching halfway to Mars in fact.

Suddenly there was light all around the shuttle. The little ship had plunged *inside* the coma. It was like being inside a diffuse, luminous fog.

'*Vileekee bokh.*'

Frank leaned across her, trying to see. He was seventy years old, physiological; his nose was a misshapen mass of flesh. He was a small, stocky man, with thick legs and big prize-fighter muscles built for Earth's gravity, so that he always looked like some restless, half-evolved ape alongside the tall, slim Lunar Japanese.

'*Eta prikrasna,*' Xenia murmured.

'Beautiful. Yeah. How about that: we're the last off the Moon.'

'Oh, no,' she said. 'There's a handful of old nuts who won't move, no matter what.'

'Even for a comet?'

'Takomi. He's still there, for one,' she said.

'Who?'

'He's notorious.'

'I don't read the funny papers,' Frank snapped.

'Takomi is the hermit out in the ruins of Edo, on Farside. Evidently he lives off the land. He won't even respond to radio calls.'

Frank frowned. 'This is the fucking Moon. How does he live off the land? By sucking oxygen out of the rock? . . .'

The light changed. There was a soft Fourth-of-July gasp from the people crammed into the shuttle.

The comet had struck the Moon.

A dome of blinding white light rose like a new sun from the surface of the Moon: comet material turned to plasma, mixed with shattered rock. Xenia thought she could see a wave passing *through* the Moon's rocky hide, a sluggish ripple in rock turned to powder, gathering and slowing.

Now, spreading out over the Moon's dusty grey surface, she saw a faint wash of light. It seemed to pool in the deeper maria and craters, flowing down the contours of the land like a morning mist on Earth. It was air: gases from the shattered comet, an evanescent atmosphere pooling on the Moon.

And, in a deep, shadowed crater, at the ghostly touch of the air, she saw light flare.

It was only a hint, a momentary splinter at the corner of her eye. She craned to see. Perhaps there was a denser knot of smoke or gas, there on the floor of the crater; perhaps there was a streak, a kind of contrail, reaching out through the temporary comet atmosphere.

It must be some by-product of the impact. But it looked as if somebody had launched a rocket from the surface of the Moon.

Already the contrail had dispersed in the thin, billowing comet air.

People were applauding again, at the beauty of the spectacle, with relief at being alive. Frank wasn't even watching.

It was only after they landed that it was announced that the comet nucleus had landed plumb on top of the Fracastorius Crater dome.

Fracastorius, on the rim of the Sea of Nectar, was one of the largest settlements away from the primary Copernicus–Landsberg–Kepler triangle. The Lunar Japanese grieved. The loss of life was small, but the economic and social damage huge – perhaps unrecoverable, in these straitened times, as the Moon's people tried to adapt to life without their centuries-old umbilical to Earth's rich resources.

Frank Paulis seemed unconcerned. He got back to work, even before the shuttle landed. And he expected Xenia to do the same.

Xenia and Frank had spent a year of their lives on a Gaijin flower-ship, submitted themselves to the unknown hazards of several Saddle Point gateway teleport transitions, and got themselves relativistically stranded in an unanticipated future. On their way home from the Saddle Point radius, Frank and Xenia had grown concerned when nobody in the inner system answered their hails. At last they tapped into some low-bit-rate news feeds.

The news seemed remarkably bad.

Earth had fallen into a state of civil war. There were battles raging around the equatorial region, the Sahara and Brazil and the far east. Frank and Xenia listened, bemused, to reports laced with names they'd never heard of, of campaigns and battles, of generals and presidents and even emperors. Even the nations involved seemed to have changed, split and coalesced. It was hard even to figure out what they were fighting over – save the generic, the diminishing resources of a declining planet.

One thing was for sure. All their money was gone, disappeared into electronic mist. They had landed on the Moon as paupers, figuratively naked.

It turned out to be a crowded Moon, owned by other people. But they had nowhere else to go. And, even on the Moon, nobody was interested in star travellers and their tales.

Frank had felt cheated. Going to the stars had been a big mistake for him. He'd gone looking for opportunity; he'd grown impatient with the slow collapse of Earth's economy and social structure, even before the wars began, long before people started dying in large numbers.

Not that he hadn't prospered here.

The Moon of the late twenty-second century, as it turned out, had a lot in common with early twenty-first century Earth. Deprived of its lifelines from the home world, the Moon was full: a stagnant, closed economy. But Frank had seen all this before, and he knew that economic truth was strange in such circumstances. For instance, Frank had quickly made a lot of money out of reengineering an old technology that made use of lunar sulphur and oxygen as a fuel source. As the scarcity of materials increased, industrial processes that had once been abandoned as unprofitable suddenly became worthwhile.

Within five years Frank J Paulis had become one of the hundred wealthiest individuals on the Moon, taking Xenia right along with him.

But it wasn't enough. Frank found it impossible to break into the long-lived, close-knit business alliances of the Lunar Japanese. And besides, Xenia suspected, he felt cooped up here, on the Moon.

Anyhow, that was why this comet had been so important for Frank. It would shake everything up, he said. Change the equation.

It was either admirable, she thought, or schizophrenic.

After all these years – during which time she had been his companion, lover, employee, amateur therapist – Xenia still didn't understand Frank; she freely admitted it. He was an out-and-out capitalist, no doubt about that. But every gram of his huge ambition was constantly turned on the most gigantic of projects. The future of a world! The destiny of mankind! What Xenia couldn't work out was whether Frank was a visionary who used capitalism to achieve his goals – or just a capitalist after all, sublimating his greed and ambition.

But, swept along by his energy and ambition, she found it hard to focus on such questions.

Bathed in blue-water light, pacing his stage, Frank J Paulis was a solid ball of terrestrial energy and aggression, out of place on the small, delicate Moon. 'You got to beat the future! – or it will beat you. I believed that before I went to the stars, and I believe it now. I'm here to tell you how . . .'

To launch his new project, Frank, feverish with enthusiasm, had hired the Grand Auditorium, the heart of Landsberg. The crater's dome was a blue ceiling above Xenia, a thick double sheet of quasiglass, cable-stayed by engineered spider-web, filled with water. The water shielded Landsberg's inhabitants from radiation, and served to scatter the raw sunlight. During the long lunar day, here in Landsberg, the sky was royal blue and full of fish, goldfish and carp. After five years, Xenia still couldn't get used to it.

Frank was standing before a huge three-dimensional cartoon, a Moon globe sliced open to reveal arid, uninteresting geological layers. Beside him sat Mariko Kashiwazaki, the young academic type whose paper had fired Frank off in this new direction. She looked slim and uncertain in the expensive new suit Frank had bought for her.

Xenia was sitting at the back of the audience, watching rows of cool faces: politicians, business types. They were impassive. Well, they were here, and they were listening, and that was all Frank cared about right now.

'Here on the Moon, we need volatiles,' Frank was saying. 'Not just to survive, but to expand. To grow, economically. Water. Hydrogen, helium. Carbon dioxide. Nitrogen. Maybe nitrates and phosphates to supplement the bio cycles.

'But the Moon is deficient in every essential of life. A molecule of water, out there on the surface, lasts a few hours before it's broken up by the sunlight and lost forever. The Moon's atmosphere is so thin some of the molecules are actually *in orbit*. Frankly, it's no damn use.'

It was true. All this had been well known from the moment the first Apollo astronaut had picked up the first lump of unprepossessing Moon rock, and found it dry as a bone – dryer, in fact.

For a time there had been hope that deep, shadowed craters near the Moon's poles might serve as stores for water ice, brought there by cometary impacts. But, to the intense disappointment of some dreamers, no more than a trace of such ice had been found. As the Fracastorius impact had demonstrated, such impacts deposited little volatile material anyhow. And even if any ice was trapped it wouldn't be there forever; the Moon's axis turned out to be unstable, and the Moon tipped this way and that over a period of hundreds of millions of years – a long time, but short enough that no crater remained in shadow forever.

Dry or not, Moon rock wasn't useless. In fact, it was about forty per cent oxygen by weight. There were other useful elements: silicon which could be used to make glass, fibreglass, polymers; aluminium, magnesium and titanium for machinery, cables, coatings; chromium and magnesium for metal alloys.

But Frank was essentially right. If a mine on Earth had turned up the highest-grade lunar ore, you'd throw it out as slag.

And that was why Frank had initiated Project Prometheus, his scheme for importing volatiles *and* spinning up the Moon by hitting it with a series of comets or asteroids. But it hadn't worked.

'So where do we turn next?' He eyed his audience, as always in command, even before these wary, slightly bemused Lunar Japanese. 'Believe me, we need to find something. The Moon, *your* Moon, is dying. We didn't come to the Moon so our children could live in a box. We came to live as humans, with freedom and dignity.' He threw back his arms and breathed the recycled air. 'Let me tell you my dream. One day, before I die, I want to throw open the damn doors and walk out of the dome. And I want to breathe the air of the Moon. The air we put there.' He began to pace back and forth, like a preacher – or a huckster. '*I want to see a terraformed Moon.* I want to see a Moon where breathable air blankets the planet, where there is so much water the deep maria will become the seas they were named for, where plants and trees grow out in the open, and every crater will glisten with a circular lake ... It's a dream. Maybe I won't live to see it all. But I know it's the only way forward for us. Only a *world* – stable, with deep biological reservoirs of water and carbon and air – is going to be big enough to sustain human life, here on the Moon, over the coming centuries, the millennia. Hell, we're here for the long haul, people, and we got to learn to think that way. Because nobody is going to help us – not Earth, not the Gaijin. None of them care if we live or die. We're stuck in this trench, in the middle of the battleground, and we have to help ourselves.

'But to make the Moon a twin of Earth we'll need volatiles, principally water. The Moon has no volatiles, and so we must import them. Correct?'

Now he leaned forward, intimidating, a crude but effective trick, Xenia thought dryly.

'*Dead wrong*. I'm here today to offer you a new paradigm. I'm here to tell you that the Moon *itself* is rich in volatiles, almost unimaginably so, enough to sustain us and our families, hell, for millennia. And, incidentally, to make us rich as Croesus in the process ...'

It was the climax, the punch-line, Frank's big shock. But there was barely a flicker of interest in the audience, Xenia saw. Three centuries and a planetary relocation hadn't changed the Japanese much, and cultural barriers hadn't dropped; they were still suspicious of the noisy foreigner who stood before them, breaking into the subtle alliances and protocols that ruled their lives.

Frank stood back. 'Tell 'em, Mariko.'

The slim Lunar Japanese scientist got up, evidently nervous, and bowed deeply to the audience.

Earth-Moon and the other planets – said Mariko, supported by smooth softscreen images – had condensed, almost five billion years ago, from a swirling cloud of dust and gases. That primordial cloud had been rich in volatiles: three per cent of it was water, for instance. You could tell that was so from the composition of asteroids, which were left-over fragments of the cloud.

But there was an anomaly. All the water on Earth, in the oceans and atmosphere and the ice sheets, added to less than a *tenth* of that three per cent fraction. Where did the rest of the water go?

Conventional wisdom held that it had been baked out by the intense heat of Earth's formation. But Mariko believed much of it was still there, that water and other volatiles were trapped deep within the Earth: perhaps four hundred kilometres down, deep in the mantle. The water wouldn't be present as a series of immense buried oceans. Rather it would be scattered as droplets, some as small as a single molecule, trapped inside crystal lattices of the minerals with names like wadsleyite and hydrous-D. These special forms could trap water within their structure, essentially exploiting the high pressure to overcome the tendency of the rising temperature to bake the water out.

Some estimates said there should be as much as *five times* as much water buried within the Earth as in all its oceans and atmosphere and ice caps.

And what was true of Earth might be true of the Moon.

According to Mariko, the Moon was mostly made of material like Earth's mantle. This was because the Moon was believed to have been budded off the Earth itself, ripped loose after a giant primordial collision, popularly called the 'big whack'. The Moon was smaller than the Earth, cooler and more rigid, so that the centre of the Moon was analogous to the Earth's mantle layers a few hundred kilometres deep. And it was precisely at such depths, on Earth, that you found such water-bearing minerals . . .

Frank watched his audience like a hawk.

His cartoon Moon globe suddenly lit up. The onion skin geological layers were supplemented by a vivid blue ocean, lapping in unlikely fashion at the centre of the Moon. Xenia smiled. It was typical Frank: inaccurate, but compelling.

'Listen up,' he said. 'What if Mariko is right? What if even *one tenth of one per cent* of the Moon's mass by weight is water? That's the same order as five per cent of Earth's surface water. A hidden ocean indeed.

'And that's not all. Where there is water there will be other volatiles: carbon dioxide, ammonia, methane, even hydrocarbons. All we have to do is go down there and find it.

'And it's *ours*. We don't own the sky; with the Gaijin around, maybe humans never will. But we inhabitants of the Moon do own the rocks beneath our feet.

'Folks, I'm calling this new enterprise Roughneck. If you want to know why, go look up the word. I'm asking you to invest in me. Sure it's a risk. But if it works it's a way past the resource bottleneck we're facing, here on the Moon. *And* it will make you rich beyond your wildest dreams.' He grinned. 'There's a fucking ocean down there, folks, and it's time to go skinny-dipping.'

There was a frozen silence, which Frank milked expertly.

* * *

After the session, Xenia took a walk.

The Moon's surface, beneath the dome, was like a park. Grass covered the ground, much of it growing out of bare lunar regolith. There was even a stand of mature palms, thirty metres tall, and a scattering of cherries. People lived in the dome's support towers, thick central cores with platforms of lunar concrete slung from them. The lower levels were given over to factories, workshops, schools, shops and other public places.

Far above her head, Xenia could see a little flock of schoolchildren in their white and black uniforms, flapping back and forth on Leonardo wings, squabbling like so many chickens. It was beautiful. But it served to remind her there were no birds here, outside pressurized cages. Birds tired too quickly in the thin air; on the Moon, against intuition, birds couldn't fly.

Water flowed in streams and fountains and pools, moistening the air.

She passed Landsberg's famous water-sculpture park. Water tumbled slowly from a tall fountain-head, in great shimmering spheres held together by surface tension. The spheres were caught by flickering mechanical fingers, to be teased out like taffy and turned and spun into rope and transformed, briefly, into transient, beautiful sculptures, no two ever alike. It was entrancing, she admitted, a one-sixth gravity art form that would have been impossible on the Earth, and it had immediately captivated her on her arrival here. As she watched, a gaggle of children – eight or ten years old, Moon legs as long as giraffes' – ran *across* the surface of the pond in the park's basin, Jesus-like, their slapping footsteps sufficient to keep them from sinking as long as they ran fast enough.

Water was everywhere here; it did not *feel* dry, a shelter in a scorched desert. But overhead, huge fans turned continually, extracting every drop of moisture from the air to be cleansed, stored and reused. She was surrounded by subtle noises: the bangs and whirrs of fans and pumps, the bubbling of aerators. And, when the children had gone, she saw tiny shimmering robots whiz through the air, fielding scattered water droplets as if catching butterflies, not letting a drop go to waste.

Landsberg, a giant machine, had to be constantly run, managed, maintained. Landsberg was no long-term solution. The various recycling processes were extraordinarily efficient – they had got to the levels of counting molecules – but there were always losses; the laws of thermodynamics saw to that. And there was no way to make good those losses.

It didn't *feel* like a dying world. In fact it was beginning to feel like home to her, this small, delicate slow-motion world. But the human Moon was, slowly but surely, running down. Already some of the smaller habitations had been abandoned; smaller ecospheres had been too expensive. There was rationing. Fewer children were being born than a generation ago, as humanity huddled in the remaining, shrivelling lunar bubbles.

And there was nowhere else to go.

Xenia had an intuition about the rightness of Frank's vision, whatever his methods. At least he was fighting back: trying to find a way for humans to survive, here in the system that had birthed them. Somebody had to. It seemed clear that the aliens, the all-powerful Gaijin, weren't here to help; they were standing by in their silent ships, witnessing as human history unfolded, and Earth fell apart.

If humans couldn't figure out how to save themselves soon, they might not have another chance.

And if Frank could make a little profit along the way to achieving that goal, she wasn't about to begrudge him.

Well, Frank convinced enough people to get together his seedcorn investment; jubilantly, he went to work.

But getting the money turned out to be the easy part.

There never had been a true mining industry, here on the Moon. All anybody had ever done was strip-mine the regolith, the shattered and desiccated outer layers of the Moon, already pulverized by meteorites and so not requiring crushing and grinding. And nobody had attempted – save for occasional science surveys – to dig any deeper than a few tens of metres.

So Frank and Xenia were forced to start from scratch, inventing afresh not just an industrial process but the human roles that went with it. They were going to need a petrophysicist and a geological engineer to figure out the most likely places they would find their imagined reservoirs of volatiles; they needed reservoir engineers and drilling engineers and production engineers for the brute work of the borehole itself; they needed construction engineers for the surface operations and support. And so on. They had to figure out job descriptions, and recruit and train to fill them as best they could.

All the equipment had to be reinvented. There was no air to convect away heat, so their equipment needed huge radiator fins. Even beneficiation – concentrating ungraded material into higher-quality ore – was difficult, as they couldn't use traditional methods like froth flotation and gravity concentration; they had to experiment with methods based on electrostatic forces. There was of course no water – a paradox, for it turned out that most mining techniques refined over centuries on Earth depended highly on the use of water, for cooling, lubrication, the movement and separation of materials and the solution and precipitation of metals. It was circular, a cruel trap.

They hit more problems as soon as they started to trial heavy equipment in the ultra-hard vacuum that coated the Moon.

Friction was a killer. In an atmosphere every surface accreted a thin layer of water vapour and oxides that reduced drag. But that didn't apply here. They even suffered vacuum welds. Not only that, the ubiquitous dust – the glass-sharp remains of ancient, shattered rocks – stuck to everything it could, scouring and abrading. Stuff wore out *fast,* on the silent surface of the Moon.

But they persisted, and solved the problems, or found old references of how it had been done in the past, when the Lunar Japanese had worked more freely beyond their domed cities. They learned to build in a modular fashion, with parts that could be replaced easily by a guy in a spacesuit. They learned to cover all their working joints with sleeves of a flexible plastic, to keep out the dust. After much experimentation they settled on a lubricant approach, coating their working surfaces with a substance the Lunar Japanese engineers called quasi-glass, hard and dense and very smooth; conventional lubricants just boiled or froze off.

The work soon became all-absorbing, and Xenia found herself immersed.

The Lunar Japanese, after generations, had become used to their domes. It was hard for them even to imagine a Moon without roofs. But once committed to the project, they learned fast, and were endlessly, patiently inventive in resolving problems. And it seemed to Xenia a remarkably short time from inception to the day Frank told her he had chosen his bore site.

'The widest, deepest impact crater in the fucking solar system,' he boasted. 'Nine kilometres below the datum level, all of thirteen kilometres below the rim wall peaks. Hell, just by standing at the base of that thing we'd be half way to the core already. And the best of it is, we can buy it. Nobody has lived there since they cleaned out the last of the cold-trap ice ...'

He was talking about the South Pole of the Moon.

Encased in a spider-web pressure suit, Xenia stepped out of the hopper.

The Moon's Pole was a place of shadows. The horn of crescent

Earth poked above one horizon, gaunt and ice-pale. Standing at the base of the crater called Amundsen, Xenia could actually see the sun, a sliver of light poking through a gap in the enclosing rim mountains, casting long, stark, shadows over the colourless, broken ground. She knew that if she stayed here for a month the Moon's glacial rotation would sweep that solar searchlight around the horizon. But the light was always flat and stark, like an endless dawn or sunset.

And, at the centre of Amundsen, Frank's complex sprawled in a splash of reflected light, ugly, busy, full of people.

Xenia had never walked on the Moon's surface before, not once. Very few people did. Nobody was importing tungsten, and it was too precious to use on suits for sight-seeing. The waste of water and air incurred in donning and doffing pressure suits was unacceptably high. And so on. On the Moon of 2190, people clung to their domed bubbles, riding sealed cars or crawling through tunnels, while the true Moon beyond their windows was as inaccessible as it had been before Apollo.

That thought – the closeness of the limits – chilled Xenia, somehow even more than the collapse of Earth. It reinforced her determination to stick with Frank, whatever her doubts about his objectives and methods.

Here came Frank in his spacesuit, Lunar Japanese spider-web painted with a gaudy Stars and Stripes. 'I wondered where you were,' he said.

'There was a lot of paperwork, last-minute permissions –'

'You might have missed the show.' He was edgy, nervous, restless; his gaze, inside his gold-tinted visor, swept over the desolate landscape. 'Come see the rig.'

Together they loped towards the centre of the complex, past Frank's perimeter of security guards.

New Dallas, Frank's roughneck boomtown, was a crude cluster of buildings put together adobe-style from lunar concrete blocks. It was actually bright here, the sunlight deflected into the crater by heliostats, giant mirrors perched on the rim mountains or on impossibly tall gantries. The 'stats worked like giant floodlights, giving the town, incongruously, the feel of a floodlit sports stadium. The primary power came from sunlight too, solar panels which Frank had had plastered over the peaks of the rim mountains.

She could recognize shops, warehouses, dormitories, mess halls; there was a motor pool, with hoppers and tractors and heavy machinery clustered around fuel tanks. The inhabited buildings had been covered over for radiation-proofing by a few metres of regolith. And

213

there was Frank's geothermal plant, ready for operation, boxy buildings linked by fat, twisting conduits.

The ground for kilometres around was flattened and scored by footprints and vehicle tracks. It was hard to believe *none* of this had been here two months ago, that the only signs of human occupation then had been the shallow, abandoned strip mines in the cold traps.

And at the centre of it all was the derrick itself, rising so far above the surface it caught the low sunlight, high enough, in fact, to stack up three or four joints of magnesium alloy pipe at a time. There was a pile of the pipe nearby, kilometres of it spun out of native lunar ore, the cheapest component of the whole operation. Sheds and shops sprawled around the derrick's base, along with huge aluminium tanks and combustion engines. Mounds of rock, dug out in test bores, surrounded the derrick like a row of pyramids.

They reached the drilling floor. At its heart was the circular table through which the pipe would pass, and which would turn to force the drill into the ground. There were foundries and drums to produce and pay out cables and pipes: power conduits, fibre-optic light pipes, hollow tubes for air and water and sample retrieval.

The derrick above her was tall and silent, like the gantry for a Saturn V. Stars showed through its open, sunlit frame. And suspended there at the end of the first pipe lengths she could see the drill head itself, teeth of tungsten and diamond, gleaming in the lights of the heliostats.

Frank was describing technicalities that didn't interest her. 'You know, you can't turn a drill string more than a few kilometres long. So we have to use a downhole turbine . . .'

'Frank, *eta ochin kraseeva*. It is magnificent. Somehow, back in Landsberg, I never quite believed it was real.'

'Oh, it's real,' Frank said tensely. 'Just so long as it works.' He checked his chronometer, a softscreen patch sewn into the fabric of his suit. 'It's nearly time.'

They moved out into the public area.

Roughneck was the biggest public event on the Moon in a generation. There must have been a hundred people here, men, women and children walking in their brightly coloured surface suits and radiation ponchos, or riding in little short-duration bubble rovers – the richest Lunar Japanese, who could still afford such luxuries. Cameras hovered everywhere. She saw Virtual Observers, adults and children in softscreen suits, their every sensation being fed out to the rest of the Moon.

Frank had even set up a kind of miniature theme park, with toy derricks you could climb up, and a towering roller-coaster based on an old-fashioned pithead rail – towering because you needed height, here on the Moon, to generate anything like a respectable G-force. The main attraction was Frank's Fish Pond, a small crater he'd lined with ceramic and filled up with water. The water froze over and was steadily evaporating, of course, but water held a lot of heat, and the Pond would take a long time to freeze to the bottom. In the meantime Frank had fish swimming back and forth in there, goldfish and hand-some koi carp, living Earth creatures protected from the severe lunar climate by nothing more than a few metres of water, a neat symbol of his ambition.

The openness scared Xenia to death. 'Are you sure it's wise to have so many people?'

'The guards will keep out those Grey assholes.'

The Greys were a pressure group who had started to campaign against Frank: arguing it was wrong to go digging holes to the heart of the Moon, to rip out the *uchujin* there, the cosmic dust. They were noisy but, as far as Xenia could see, ineffective.

'Not that,' she said. 'It's so public. It's like Disneyland.'

He grunted. 'Xenia, all that's left of Disneyland is a crater that glows in the dark. Don't you get it? This PR stunt is *essential*. We'll be lucky if we make hole at a couple of kilometres a day. It will take fifty days just to get through the crust. We're going to sink a hell of a lot of money into this hole in the ground before we see a red cent of profit. We need those investors on our side, for the long term. They have to be here, Xenia. They have to *see* this.'

'But if something goes wrong –'

'Then we're screwed anyhow. What have we lost?'

Everything, she thought, if somebody gets killed, one of these cute Lunar Japanese five-year-olds climbing over the derrick models. But she knew Frank would have thought of that, and discounted it already, and no doubt figured out some fallback plan.

She admired such calculation, and feared it.

Frank tipped back on his heels and peered up at the sky. 'Well, well,' he said. 'Looks like we have an audience.'

A Gaijin flower-ship was sailing high overhead, wings spread and sparkling, like some gaudy moth.

'This is ours,' Frank murmured, glaring up. 'You hear me, assholes? *Ours*. Eat your mechanical hearts out.'

A warning tone was sounding on their headsets' open loops now, and in silence the Lunar Japanese, adults and children alike, were lining up to watch the show. Xenia could see the drill bit descend towards the regolith, the pipe sweeping silently downwards inside the framework, like a muscle moving inside a sheath of flesh.

The bit cut into the Moon.

A gush of dust sprayed up immediately from the hole, ancient regolith layers undisturbed for a billion years, now thrown unceremoniously towards space. At the peak of the parabolic fountain, glassy fragments sparkled in the sunlight. But there was no air to suspend the debris, and it fell back immediately.

Within seconds the dust had coated the derrick, turning its bright paintwork grey, and was raining over the spectators like volcanic ash.

There was motion around her. People were applauding, she saw, in utter silence, joined in this moment. Maybe Frank was right to have them here, after all, right about the mythic potential of this huge challenge.

Frank was watching the drill intently. 'Twenty or thirty metres,' he said.

'What?'

'The thickness of the regolith here. The dust. Then you have the megaregolith, rock crushed and shattered and dug out and mixed by the impacts. Probably twenty, thirty kilometres of that. Easy to cut through. Below that the pressure's so high it heals any cracks. We should get to that anorthosite bedrock by the end of the first day, and then –'

She took his arm. Even through the layers of suit she could feel the tension in his muscles. 'Hey. Take it easy.'

'I'm the expectant father, right?'

'Yeah.'

He took little steps back and forth, stocky, frustrated. 'Well, there's nothing we can do here. Come on. Let's get out of these Buck Rogers outfits and hit the bar.'

'All right.'

Xenia could hear the dust spattering over her helmet. And children were running, holding out their hands in the grey Moon rain, witnesses to this new marvel.

Chapter 19

DREAMS OF ROCK AND STILLNESS

*Her world was simple: the Land below, the Dark above, the Light
that flowed from the Dark. Land, Light, Dark. That, and herself.*

Alone save for the Giver.

For her, all things came from the Giver. All life, in fact.

*Her first memories were of the Giver, at the interface between
parched Land and hot Dark. He fed her, sank rich warm moist substance into the Land, and she ate greedily. She felt her roots dig into
the dry depths of the Land, seeking the nourishment that was hidden
there. And she drew the thin soil into herself, nursed it with hot Light,
made it part of herself.*

*She knew the future. She knew what would become of herself and
her children.*

*They would wait through the long hot-cold bleakness for the brief
Rains. Then they would bud, and pepper this small hard world with
life, in their glorious blossoming. And she would survive the long
stillness to see the Merging itself, the wonder that lay at the end of
time, she and her children.*

*. . .But she was the first, and the Giver birthed her. None of it would
have come to be without the Giver.*

*She wished she could express her love for him. She knew that was
impossible.*

She sensed, though, that he knew anyhow.

Overwhelmed by work as she was, Xenia couldn't get the memory of
the comet impact out of her head. For, in the moment of that gigantic
collision she had glimpsed a contrail: for all the world as if someone,
something, had launched a rocket from the surface of the Moon.

But who, and why?

She had no opportunity to consider the question as the Roughneck
project gathered pace. At last, though, she freed up two or three days

from Frank, pleading exhaustion. She determined to use the time to resolve the puzzle. She went home, for the first time after many nights of sleeping at the Roughneck project office.

She took a long, hot bath, to soak out the gritty lunar dust from the pores of her skin. In her small tub the water sloshed like mercury. Condensation gathered on the ceiling above her, and soon huge droplets hung there suspended, like watery chandeliers. When she stood up the water clung to her skin, like a sheath; she had to scrape it loose with her fingers, depositing it carefully back in the tub. Then she took a small vacuum cleaner and captured all the loose droplets she could find, returning every scrap to the drainage system, where it would be cleansed and fed back into Landsberg's great dome reservoirs.

Her apartment was a glass-walled cell in the great catacomb that was Landsberg. It had, in fact, once served as a *genkan,* a hallway, for a greater establishment in easier, less cramped times, long before she had returned from the stars; it was so small her living room doubled as a bedroom. The floor was covered with rice straw matting, though she kept a *zabuton* cushion for Frank Paulis. Miniature Japanese art filled the room with space and stillness.

She had been happy to accept the style of the inhabitants of this place – unlike Frank, who had turned *his* apartment into a shrine to Americana. It was remarkable, she thought, that the Japanese had turned out to be so well adapted to life on the Moon. It was as if thousands of years on their small, crowded islands had readied them for this greater experience, this increasing enclosure on the Moon.

She made herself some coffee – fake, of course, and not as hot as she would have liked. She tuned the walls to a favourite scene – a maple forest, carpeted with bright green moss – and padded, naked, to her workstation. She sat on a *tatami* mat, which was unreasonably comfortable in the low gravity, and sipped her drink.

There was no indexed record of that surface rocket launch, as she had expected. There was, however, a substantial database on the state of the whole Moon at the time of the impact; every sensor the Lunar Japanese could deploy had been turned on the Moon, the events of that momentous morning.

And, after a few minutes' search, in a spectrometer record from a low-flying satellite, she found what she wanted. There was the contrail, bright and hot, arcing through splashed cometary debris. Spectrometer results told her she was looking at the products of aluminium burning in oxygen.

So it had been real.

She widened her search further.

Yes, she learned, aluminium could serve as a rocket fuel. It had a specific impulse of nearly three hundred seconds, in fact, not as good as the best chemical propellant – that was hydrogen, which burned at four hundred – but serviceable. And aluminium-oxygen could even be manufactured from the lunar soil.

Yes, there were other traces of aluminium-oxygen rockets burning on the Moon that day, recorded by a variety of automated sensors. More contrails, snaking across the lunar surface, from all around the Moon. There were a dozen, all told, perhaps more in parts of the Moon not recorded in sufficient detail.

And each of these rocket burns, she found, had been initiated when the gushing comet gases reached its location.

She pulled up a virtual globe of the Moon, and mapped the launch sites. They were scattered over a variety of sites on the Moon: highlands and maria alike, Nearside and Farside. No apparent pattern.

Then she plotted the contrails forward, allowing them to curl around the rocky limbs of the Moon.

The tracks converged, on a single Farside site. Edo. The place the hermit, Takomi, lived.

It was the first Rain of all.

Suddenly there was air here, on this still world. At first there was the merest trace, a soft comet Rain which settled, tentatively, on her broad leaves, where they lay in shade. But she drank it in greedily, before it could evaporate in the returning Light, incorporating every molecule into her structure, without waste.

With gathering confidence she captured the Rain, and the Light, and continued the slow, patient work of building her seeds, and the fiery stuff that would birth them, drawn from the patient dust.

And then, suddenly, it was time.

In a single orgasmic spasm the seeds burst from her structure. She was flooded with a deep joy, even as she subsided, exhausted.

The Giver was still here with her, enjoying the Rain with her, watching her blossom. She was glad of that.

And then, so soon after, there was a gusting wind, a rush of the air molecules over her damaged surfaces, as the comet drew back its substance and leapt from the Land, whole and intact, its job done. The noise of that great escape into the Dark above came to her as a great shout.

Soon after, the Giver was gone too.

But it did not matter. For, soon, she could hear the first tentative scratching of her children, carried to her like whispers through the still, hard rock, as they dug beneath the Land, seeking nourishment. There was no Giver for them, nobody to help; they were beyond her aid now. But it did not matter, for she knew they were strong, self-sufficient, resourceful.

Some would die, of course. But most would survive, digging in, waiting for the next comet Rain.

She settled back into herself, relishing the geologic pace of her thoughts. Waiting for Rain, for more comets to gather from the dirt and leap into the sky.

Xenia took an automated hopper, alone, to the Sea of Longing, on Farside. The journey was seamless, the landing imperceptible.

She donned her spider-web suit, checked it, and stepped into the hopper's small, extensible airlock. She waited for the hiss of escaping air, and – her heart oddly thumping – she collapsed the airlock around her, and stepped onto the surface of the Moon.

A little spray of dust, ancient pulverized rock, lifted up around her feet. The sky was black – save, she saw, for the faintest wisp of white, glowing in the flat sunlight. They were ice crystals, suspended in the thin residual atmosphere of the comet impact. Cirrus clouds on the Moon: relics of the death of a comet. The mare surface was like a gentle sea, a complex of overlapping, slowly undulating curves.

And here were two cones, tall and slender, side by side, geometrically perfect. They cast long shadows in the flat sunlight. She couldn't tell how far away they were, or how big, so devoid was this landscape of visual cues. They simply stood there, stark and anomalous.

She shivered. She walked forward, loping easily.

She came to a place where the regolith had been *raked*. She stopped, standing on unworked soil.

The raking had made a series of parallel ridges, each maybe six or eight centimetres tall, a few centimetres apart, a precise combing. When she looked to left or right, the raking went off to infinity, the lines sharp, their geometry perfect. And when she looked ahead, the lines receded to the horizon, as far as she could see undisturbed in their precision.

Those two cones stood, side by side, almost like termite mounds. The shallow light fell on them gracefully. She saw that the lines on the ground curved to wash around the cones, like a stream diverting around islands of geometry.

'Thank you for respecting the garden.'

She jumped at the sudden voice. She turned.

A figure was standing there – man or woman? a man, she decided, shorter and slimmer than she was – in a shabby, much-patched suit.

He bowed. '*Sumimasen*. I did not mean to startle you.'

'Takomi?'

'And you are Xenia Makarova.'

'You know that? How?'

A gentle shrug. 'I am alone here, but not isolated. Only you sought and compiled information on the Moon flowers.'

'*What* flowers?'

He walked towards her. 'This is my garden,' he said.

'A zen garden.'

'You understand that? Good. This is a *kare sansui*, a waterless stream garden.'

'Are you a monk?'

'I am a gardener.'

She considered. 'Even before humans came here, the Moon was already like an immense zen garden, a garden of rock and soil.'

'You are wise.'

'Is that why you came here? Why you live alone like this?'

'Perhaps. I prefer the silence and solitude of the Moon to the bustle of the human world. You are Russian.'

'My forebears were.'

'Then you are alone here also. There are some of your people on Mars.'

'So I'm told. They won't respond to my signals.'

'No,' he said. 'They won't speak to anybody. In the face of the Gaijin onslaught, we humans have collapsed into scattered, sullen tribes.'

Onslaught. It seemed a strange word to use, stronger than she had expected. Briefly, she was reminded of somebody else, another reclusive Japanese.

She pointed. 'I understand the ridges represent flow. Are those mountains? Are they rising out of cloud, or sea? Or are they diminishing?'

'Does it matter? The cosmologists tell us that there are many time streams. Perhaps they are both falling and rising. You have travelled far to see me. I will give you food and drink.'

He turned and walked across the Moon. After a moment, she followed.

*   *   *

The abandoned lunar base, called Edo, was a cluster of concrete components – habitation modules, power plants, stores, manufacturing facilities – half-buried in the cratered plain. There were robots every-where, but they were standing silent, obviously inert.

But a single lamp burned again at the centre of the old complex. Takomi lived at the heart of Edo, in what had once been, he said, a park, grown inside a cave dug in the ground. The buildings here were dark, gutted, abandoned. There was even, bizarrely, an ancient McDonald's, stripped out, its red and yellow plastic signs cracked and faded. A single cherry tree grew, its leaves bright green, a splash of colour against the drab grey of the fused regolith.

This had been the primary settlement established by the Japanese government, back in the twenty-first century. But Nishizaki Heavy Industries had set up in Landsberg, using the crater originally as a strip mine. Now, hollowed out, Landsberg was the capital of the Moon, and Edo, cramped and primitive, had been abandoned.

She clambered out of her suit. She had tracked in Moon dust. It clung to the oils of her hand and looked like pencil lead, shiny on her fingers, like graphite. It would be hard to wash out, she knew.

He brought her green tea and rice cake.

Out of his suit Takomi was a small, wizened man; he might have been sixty, but such was the state of life-extending technology it was hard to tell. His face was round, a mass of wrinkles, and his eyes lost in leathery folds; he spoke with a wheeze, as if slightly asthmatic.

'You cherish the tree,' she said.

He smiled. 'I need one friend. I regret you have missed the blossom. I am able to celebrate *ichi-buzaki* here. We Japanese like cherries; they represent the old Samurai view that the blossom symbolizes our lives. Beautiful, but fragile, and all too brief.'

'I don't understand how you can live here.'

'The Moon is a whole world,' he said gently. 'It can support one man.'

Takomi, she learned, used the lunar soil for simple radiation shield-ing. He baked it in crude microwave ovens to make ceramic and glass. He extracted oxygen from the lunar soil by magma electrolysis: melting the soil with focused sunlight, then passing an electric current through it to liberate the oh-two. The magma plant, lashed up from decades-old salvage, was slow and power-intensive, but the electrolysis process was efficient in its use of soil; Takomi said he wasn't short of sunlight, but the less haulage he had to do the better.

He operated what he called a grizzly, an automated vehicle already a century old, so caked with dust it was the same colour as the Moon. The grizzly toiled patiently across the surface of the Moon, powered by sunlight. It scraped up loose surface material and pumped out glass sheeting and solar cells, just a couple of square metres a day. Over time, the grizzly had built a solar farm covering square kilometres, and producing megawatts of electric power.

'It is astonishing, Takomi.'

He cackled. 'If one is modest in one's request, the Moon is generous.'

'But even so, you lack essentials. It's the eternal story of the Moon. Carbon, nitrogen, hydrogen –'

He smiled at her. 'I admit I cheat. The concrete of this abandoned town is replete with water.'

'You *mine concrete*?'

'It is better than paying water tax.'

'But how many humans could the Moon support this way?'

'Ah. Not many. But how many humans does the Moon need? Thus, I am entrenched.'

It struck her as another strange choice of word. There was much about this hermit she did not understand, she realized.

She asked him about the contrails she had seen, their convergence on this place. He evaded her questions, and began to talk about something else.

'I conduct research, you know. Of a sort. There is a science station, not far from here, which was once equipped by Nishizaki Heavy Industries. Now abandoned, of course. It is – was – an infrared study station. It was there that a Japanese researcher called Nemoto first discovered evidence of Gaijin activity in the solar system, and so changed history.'

She wasn't interested in Takomi's hobby work in some old observatory. But there was something in his voice that made her keep listening.

'So you use the equipment,' she prompted.

'I watched the approach of the comet. From here, some aspects of it were apparent which were not visible from Nearside stations. The geometry of the approach orbit, for example. And something else.'

'What?'

'I saw evidence of methane burning,' he said. 'Close to the nucleus.'

'Methane?'

'A jet of combustion products.'

A *rocket*. She saw the implications immediately. Somebody had stuck a methane rocket on the side of the comet nucleus, burned the comet's own chemicals, to divert its course.

Away from the Moon? Or – towards it?

And in either case, who?

'. . . Why are you telling me this?'

But he would not reply, and a cold, hard lump of suspicion began to gather in her gut.

Takomi provided a bed for her, a thin mattress in an abandoned schoolhouse. Children's paintings adorned the walls, preserved under a layer of glass. The pictures showed flowers and rocks and people, all floating in a black sky.

In the middle of the night, Frank called her. He was excited.

'It's going better than we expected. We're just sinking in. Anyhow the pictures are great. Smartest thing I ever did was to insist we dump the magnesium alloy piping, make the walls transparent so you can see the rocks. We have the best geologists on the Moon down that fucking well, Xenia. Seismic surveys, geochemistry, geophysics, the works. The sooner we find some ore lode to generate payback, the better . . .'

The Roughneck bore had passed the crust's lower layers, and was in the mantle. *The mantle of the Moon*: sixty kilometres deep, a place unlike any other reached by humans before.

The Moon was turning out to be *much* easier to deep-mine than the Earth, for it was old and silent and still. There was a temperature rise of maybe ten degrees per kilometre of depth, compared to four times as much as on Earth. The pressure scaled similarly; even now Frank's equipment was subject only to a few thousand atmospheres, less than could be replicated in the laboratory. Strangely, the density of the Moon hardly varied across its whole interior.

But Xenia knew the project had barely begun. If Frank was to find the water and other volatiles he sought, if he was to reach the conditions of temperature and pressure that would allow the water-trapping minerals to form, it could only be at enormous depths – probably beneath the rigid mantle, a thousand kilometres deep, just a few hundred kilometres from the centre of the Moon itself.

She tried to ask him technical questions, about how they were planning to cope with the more extreme pressures and temperatures they would soon encounter. She knew that at first, in the impact-shattered upper regolith, he had been able to deploy comparatively primitive mechanical drilling techniques like percussion and rotary. But faced by the stubborn, hard, fine-grained rocks of the mantle, he had had to try out more advanced techniques – lasers, electric arcs, magnetic induction techniques. Stretching the bounds of possibility.

But he wouldn't discuss such issues.

'Xenia, it doesn't matter. You know me. I can't figure any machine more complicated than a screwdriver. And neither can our investors. I don't *need* to know. I just have to find the right technical guys, give them a challenge they can't resist, and point them downwards.'

'Paying them peanuts the while.'

He grinned. 'That's the beauty of those vocational types. Christ, we could even get those guys to pay to work here. No, the technical stuff is piss-easy. It's the other stuff that's the challenge. We have to make the project appeal to more than just the fat financiers and the big corporations. Xenia, this is the greatest lunar adventure since Neil and Buzz. That party when we first made hole was just the start. I want everybody involved, and everybody paying. Now we're in the mantle we can market the TV rights –'

'Frank, they don't have TV any more.'

'Whatever. I want the kids involved, all those little dark-eyed kids I see flapping around the palm trees the whole time with nothing to do. I want games. Educational stuff. Clubs to join, where you pay a couple of l-yen for a badge and get some kind of share certificate. I want little toy derricks in cereal packets.'

'They don't have cereal packets any more.'

He eyed her. 'Work with me here, Xenia. And I want their parents paying too. Tours down the well, at least the upper levels. Xenia, for the first time the folks on this damn Moon are going to see some hint of an expansive future. A frontier, beneath their feet. They have to *want* it. Including the kids.' He nodded. 'Especially the kids.'

'But the Greys –'

'Screw the Greys. All they have is rocks. We have the kids.'

And so on, on and on, his insect voice buzzing with plans, in the ancient stillness of Farside.

The next day Takomi walked her back to her tractor, by the zen garden.

She had been here twenty-four hours. The sun had dipped closer to the horizon, and the shadows were long, the land starker, more inhospitable. Comet-ice clouds glimmered high above.

'I have something for you,' Takomi said. And he handed her what looked like a sheet of glass. It was oval-shaped, maybe a half-metre long. Its edges were blunt, as if melted, and it was covered with bristles. Some kind of lunar geologic formation, she thought, a relic of some impact event. A cute souvenir; Frank might like it for the office.

She said, 'I have nothing to give you in return.'

'Oh, you have made your *okurimono* already.'

'I have?'

He cackled. 'Your shit and your piss. Safely in my reclamation tanks. On the Moon, shit is more precious than gold . . .'

He bowed, once, then turned to walk away, along the rim of his rock garden.

She was left looking at the oval of Moon glass in her hands. It looked, she thought now, rather like a flower petal.

Back at Landsberg, she gave the petal-like object to the only scientist she knew, Mariko Kashiwazaki. Mariko was exasperated; as Frank's chief scientist she was already under immense pressure, as Roughneck picked up momentum. But she agreed to pass on the puzzling fragment to a colleague, better qualified. Xenia agreed, provided she used only people in the employ of one of Frank's companies.

Meanwhile – discreetly, from home – Xenia repeated Takomi's work on the comet. She searched for evidence of the anomalous signature of methane burning at the nucleus. It had been picked up, but not recognized, by many sensors.

Takomi was right.

Clearly, someone had planted a rocket on the side of the comet nucleus, and deflected it from its path. It was also clear that most of the burn had been on the far side of the sun, where it would be undetected. The burn had been long enough, she estimated, to have deflected the comet, to *cause* its lunar crash. Undeflected, the comet would surely have sailed by the Moon, spectacular but harmless.

She then did some checks of the tangled accounts of Frank's companies. She found places where funds had been diverted, resources secreted. A surprisingly large amount, reasonably well concealed.

She'd been cradling a suspicion since Edo. Now it was confirmed, and she felt only disappointment at the shabbiness of the truth.

She felt that Takomi wouldn't reveal the existence of the rocket on the comet. He simply wasn't engaged enough in the human world to consider it. But, such was the continuing focus of attention on Fracastorius, Takomi wouldn't be the only observer who would notice the trace of that comet-pushing rocket, follow the evidence trail.

The truth would come out.

Without making a decision on how to act on this, she went back to work with Frank.

*   *   *

The pressure on Xenia, on both of them, was immense and unrelenting.

After one gruelling twenty-hour day, she slept with Frank. She thought it would relieve the tension, for both of them. Well, it did, for a brief oceanic moment. But then, as they rolled apart, it all came down on them again.

Frank lay on his back, eyes fixed on the ceiling, jaw muscles working, restless, tense.

Later Mariko Kashiwazaki called Xenia. Xenia took the call in her *tokonoma,* masking it from Frank.

Mariko had preliminary results about the glass object from Edo. 'The object is constructed almost entirely of lunar surface material.'

'Almost?'

'There are also complex organics in there. We don't know where they came from, or what they are for. There is water, too, sealed into cells within the glass. The structure itself acts as a series of lenses, which focus sunlight. Remarkably efficient. There seems to be a series of valves on the underside which draw in particles of regolith. The grains are melted, evaporated, in intense focused sunlight. It's a pyrolysis process similar to –'

'What happens to the vaporized material?'

'There is a series of traps, leading off from each light-focusing cell. The traps are maintained at different temperatures by spicules – the fine needles protruding from the upper surface – which also, we suspect, act to deflect daytime sunlight, and conversely work as insulators during the long lunar night. In the traps, at different temperatures, various metal species condense out. The structure seems to be oriented towards collecting aluminium. There is also an oxygen trap further back.'

Aluminium and oxygen. *Rocket fuel,* trapped inside the glass structure, melted out of the lunar rock by the light of the sun.

Mariko consulted notes in a softscreen. 'Within this structure the organic chemicals serve many uses. A complex chemical factory appears to be at work here. There is a species of photosynthesis, for instance. There is evidence of some kind of root system, which perhaps provides the organics in the first place . . . But there is no source we know of. This is the *Moon.*' She looked confused. 'You must remember I am a geologist. My contact works with biochemists and biologists, and they are extremely excited.'

Biologists? 'You'd better tell me.'

'Xenia, this is essentially a vapour-phase reduction machine of staggering elegance of execution, mediated by organic chemistry. It must be an artefact. And yet it looks –'

'What?'

'As if it *grew,* out of the Moon ground. There are many further puzzles,' Mariko said. 'For instance, the evidence of a neural network.'

'Are you saying this has some kind of a nervous system?'

Mariko shrugged. 'Even if this *is* some simple lunar plant, why would it need a nervous system? Even, perhaps, a rudimentary awareness?' She studied Xenia. 'What is this thing?'

'I can't tell you that.'

'There has been much speculation about the form life would take, here on the Moon. It could be seeded by some meteorite-impact transfer from Earth. But volatile depletion seemed an unbeatable obstacle. Where does it get its organic material? Was it from the root structure, from deep within the Moon? If so, you realize that this is confirmation of my hypotheses about the volatiles in –'

Xenia stopped her. '*Mariko.* This isn't to go further. News of this – discovery. Not yet. Tell your colleagues that too.'

Mariko looked shocked, as Xenia, with weary certainty, had expected. 'You want to *suppress* this?'

That caused Xenia to hesitate. She had never thought of herself as a person who would *suppress* anything. But she knew, as all the star travellers had learned, that the universe was full of life: that life emerged everywhere it could – though usually, sadly, with little hope of prospering. Was it really so strange that such a stable, ancient world as the Moon should be found to harbour its own, quiet, still form of life?

Life was trivial, compared to the needs of the project.

'This isn't science, Mariko. I don't want anything perturbing Roughneck.'

Mariko made to protest again.

'Read your contract,' Xenia snapped. 'You must do what I say.' And she cut the connection.

She returned to bed. Frank seemed to be asleep.

She had a choice to make. Not about the comet deflection issue; others would unravel that, in time. About Frank, and herself.

He fascinated her. He was a man of her own time, with a crude vigour she didn't find among the Japanese-descended colonists of the Moon. He was the only link she had with home. The only human on the Moon who didn't speak Japanese to her.

That, as far as she could tell, was all she felt.

In the meantime, she must consider her own morality.

Lying beside him, she made her decision. She wouldn't betray him. As long as he needed her, she would stand with him.

But she would not save him.

Life was long, slow, unchanging.

Even her thoughts were slow.

In the timeless intervals between the comets, her growth was chthonic, her patience matching that of the rocks themselves. Slowly, slowly, she rebuilt her strength: Light traps to start the long process of drawing out fire for the next seeds, leaves to catch the comet Rain that would come again.

She spoke to her children, their subtle scratching carrying to her through the still, cold rock. It was important that she taught them: how to grow, of the comet Rains to come, of the Giver at the beginning of things, the Merging at the end.

Their conversations lasted a million years.

The Rains were spectacular, but infrequent. But when they came, once or twice in every billion years, her pulse accelerated, her metabolism exploding, as she drank in the thin, temporary air, and dragged the fire she needed from the rock.

And, with each Rain, she birthed again, the seeds exploding from her body and scattering around the Land.

But, after that first time, she was never alone. She could feel, through the rock, the joyous pulsing of her children as they hurled their own seed through the gathering comet air.

Soon there were so many of them that it was as if all of the Land was alive with their birthing, its rocky heart echoing to their joyous shouts.

And still, in the distant future, the Merging awaited them.

As the comets leapt one by one back into the sky, sucking away the air with them, she held that thought to her exhausted body, cradling it.

Eighty days in and Frank was still making hole at his couple-of-kilometres-a-day target pace. But things had started to get a lot harder.

This was *mantle*, after all. They were suffering rock bursts. The rock was like stretched wire, under so much pressure it exploded when it was exposed. It was a new regime. New techniques were needed.

Costs escalated. The pressure on Frank to shut down was intense.

Many of the investors had already become extremely rich from the potential of the ore lodes discovered in the lower crust and upper mantle. There was talk of opening up new, shallow bores elsewhere on the Moon to seek out further lodes. Frank had proved his point. Why go further, when the Roughneck was already a commercial success?

But metal ore wasn't Frank's goal, and he wasn't about to stop now.

. . . That was when the first death occurred, all of a hundred kilometres below the surface of the Moon.

She found him in his office at New Dallas, pacing back and forth, an Earthman caged on the Moon, his muscles lifting him off the glass floor.

'Omelettes and eggs,' he said. 'Omelettes and eggs.'

'That's a cliché, Frank.'

'It was probably the fucking Greys.'

'There's no evidence of sabotage.'

He paced. 'Look, we're in the *mantle of the Moon* –'

'You don't have to justify it to me,' she said, but he wasn't listening.

'The mantle,' he said. 'You know, I hate it. A thousand kilometres of worthless shit.'

'It was the changeover to the subterrene that caused the disaster. Right?'

He ran a hand over his greasy hair. 'If you were a prosecutor, and this was a court, I'd challenge you on "caused". The accident happened when we switched over to the subterrene, yes.'

They had already gone too deep for the simple alloy casing or the cooled lunar glass Frank had used in the upper levels. To get through the mantle they would use a subterrene, a development of obsolete deep-mining technology, a probe that melted its way through the rock and built its own casing behind it, a tube of hard, high-melting-point quasiglass.

Frank started talking, rapidly, about quasiglass. 'It's the stuff the Lunar Japanese use for rocket nozzles. Very high melting point. It's based on diamond, but it's a quasicrystal, so the lab boys tell me, halfway between a crystal and a glass. Harder than ordinary crystal because there are no neat planes for cracks and defects to propagate. And it's a good heat insulator similarly. Besides that we support the hole against collapse and shear stress. Rock bolts, fired through the casing and into the rock beyond. We do everything we can to ensure the integrity of our structure . . .'

This was, she realized, a first draft of the testimony he would have to give to the investigating commissions.

When the first subterrene started up, it built a casing with a flaw, undetected for a hundred metres. There had been an implosion. They lost the subterrene itself, a kilometre of bore, and a single life, of a senior toolpusher.

'We've already restarted,' Frank said. 'A couple of days and we'll have recovered.'

'Frank, this isn't a question of schedule loss,' she said. 'It's the wider impact. Public perception. Come on; you know how important this is. If we don't handle this right we'll be shut down.'

He seemed reluctant to absorb that. He was silent, for maybe half a minute.

Then his mood switched. He started pacing. 'You know, we can leverage this to our advantage.'

'What do you mean?'

'We need to turn this guy we lost – what was his name? – into a hero.' He snapped his fingers. 'Did he have any family? A ten-year-old daughter would be perfect, but we'll work with whatever we have. Get his kids to drop cherry blossom down the hole. You know the deal. The message has to be right. *The kids want the bore to be finished, as a memorial to the brave hero.*'

'Frank, the dead engineer was a she.'

'And we ought to think about the Grey angle. Get one of them to call our hero toolpusher a criminal.'

'Frank –'

He faced her. 'You think this is immoral. Bullshit. It would be immoral to stop; otherwise, believe me, *everyone* on this Moon is going to die in the long run. Why do you think I asked you to set up the kids' clubs?'

'For *this*?'

'Hell, yes. Already I've had some of those chicken-livered investors try to bail out. Now we use the kids, to put so much fucking pressure on it's impossible to turn back. If that toolpusher had a kid in one of our clubs, in fact, that's perfect.' He hesitated, then pointed a stubby finger at her face. 'This is the bottleneck. Every project goes through it. I need to know you're with me, Xenia.'

She held his gaze for a couple of seconds, then sighed. 'You know I am.'

He softened, and dropped his hands. 'Yeah. I know.' But there was something in his voice, she thought, that didn't match his words. An uncertainty that hadn't been there before. 'Omelettes and eggs,' he muttered. 'Whatever.' He clapped his hands. 'So. What's next?'

*   *   *

This time, Xenia didn't fly directly to Edo. Instead she programmed the hopper to make a series of slow orbits of the abandoned base.

It took her an hour to find the glimmer of glass, reflected sunlight sparkling from a broad expanse of it, at the centre of an ancient, eroded crater. She landed a kilometre away, to avoid disturbing the flower structures. She suited up quickly, clambered out of the hopper, and set off on foot.

She made ground quickly, over this battered, ancient landscape, restrained only by the Moon's gentle gravity. Soon the land ahead grew bright, glimmering like a pool. She slowed, approaching cautiously.

The flower was larger than she had expected. It must have covered a quarter, even a third of a hectare, delicate glass leaves resting easily against the regolith from which they had been constructed, spiky needles protruding. There was, too, another type of structure: short, stubby cylinders, pointing at the sky, projecting in all directions.

Miniature cannon muzzles. Launch gantries for seed-carrying aluminium-burning rockets, perhaps.

'. . . I must startle you again.'

She turned. It was Takomi, of course: in his worn, patched suit, his hands folded behind his back. He was looking at the flower.

'Life on the Moon,' she said.

'Its lifecycle is simple, you know. It grows during periods of transient comet atmospheres – like the present – and lies dormant between such events. The flower is exposed to sunlight, through the long Moon day. Each of its leaves is a collector of sunlight. The flower focuses the light on regolith, and breaks down the soil for the components it needs to manufacture its own structure, its seeds, and the simple rocket fuel used to propel them across the surface.

'Then, during the night, the leaves act as cold traps. They absorb the comet frost which falls on them, water and methane and carbon dioxide, incorporating that, too, into the flowers' substance.'

'And the roots?'

'The roots are kilometres long. They tap deep wells of nutrient, water and organic substances. Deep inside the Moon.'

So Frank, of course, was right about the existence of the volatiles, as she had known he would be.

'I suppose you despise Frank Paulis.'

He said mildly, 'Why should I?'

'Because he is trying to dig out the sustenance for these plants. Rip it out of the heart of the Moon. Are you a Grey, Takomi?'

He shrugged. 'We have different ways. Your ancestors have a word. *Mechta.*'

'Dream.' It was the first Russian word she had heard spoken in many months.

'It was the name your engineers wished to give to the first probe they sent to the Moon. *Mechta.* But it was not allowed, by those who decide such things. Well, I am living a dream, here on the Moon, a dream of rock and stillness, here with my Moon flower. That is how you should think of me.'

He smiled, and walked away.

The Land was rich with life now: her children, her descendants, drinking in air and Light. Their songs echoed through the core of the Land, strong and powerful.

But it would not last, for it was time for the Merging.

First there was a sudden explosion of Rains, too many of them to count, the comets leaping out of the ground, one after the other.

Then the Land itself became active. Great sheets of rock heated, becoming liquid, and withdrawing into the interior of the Land.

Many died, of course. But those that remained bred frantically. It was a glorious time, a time of death and life.

Changes accelerated. She clung to the thin crust which contained the world. She could feel huge masses rising and falling far beneath her. The Land grew hot, dissolving into a deep ocean of liquid rock.

And then the Land itself began to break up, great masses of it hurling themselves into the sky.

More died.

But she was not afraid. It was glorious! – as if the Land itself was birthing comets, as if the Land was like herself, hurling its children far away.

The end came swiftly, more swiftly than she had expected, in an explosion of heat and light that burst from the heart of the Land itself. The last, thin crust was broken open, and suddenly there was no more Land, nowhere for her roots to grip.

It was the Merging, the end of all things, and it was glorious.

Chapter 20

THE TUNNEL IN THE MOON

Frank and Xenia, wrapped in their spider-web spacesuits, stood on a narrow aluminium bridge. They were under the South Pole derrick, suspended over the tunnel Frank had dug into the heart of the Moon.

The area around the derrick had long lost its pristine theme-park look. There were piles of spill and waste and ore, dug out of the deepening hole in the ground. LHDs, automated load-haul-dump vehicles, crawled continually around the site. The LHDs, baroque aluminium beetles, sported giant fins to radiate off their excess heat – no conduction or convection here – and most of their working parts were two metres or more off the ground, where sprays of the abrasive lunar dust wouldn't reach. The LHDs, Xenia realized, were machines made for the Moon.

The shaft below Xenia was a cylinder of sparkling lunar glass. The tunnel receded to the centre of the Moon, to infinity. Lights had been buried in the walls every few metres, so the shaft was brilliantly lit, like a passageway in a shopping mall, the multiple reflections glimmering from the glass walls. Refrigeration and other conduits snaked along the tunnel. It was vertical, perfectly symmetrical, and there was no mist or dust, nothing to obscure her view.

Momentarily dizzy, she stepped back, anchored herself again on the surface of the Moon.

Frank rubbed his hands. 'It's wonderful. Like the old days. Engineers overcoming obstacles, building things.' He seemed oddly nervous; he wouldn't meet her eyes.

'And,' she said, 'thanks to all this problem-solving, we got through the mantle.'

'Hell, yes, we got through it. You've been away from the project too long, babe.' He took her hands. Squat in his suit, his face invisible, he was still, unmistakably, Frank J Paulis. 'And now, it's our time.'

Without hesitation – he never hesitated – he stepped to the lip of the delicate metal bridge.

She walked with him, a single step. A stitched safety harness, suspended from pulleys above, impeded her.

He said, 'Will you follow me?'

She took a breath. 'I've always followed you.'

'Then come.'

Hand in hand, they jumped off the bridge.

Slow as a snowflake, tugged by gravity, Xenia fell towards the heart of the Moon. The loose harness dragged gently at her shoulders and crotch, slowing her fall. She was guided by a couple of spider-web cables, tautly threaded down the axis of the shaft; through her suit's fabric she could hear the hiss of the pulleys.

There was nothing beneath her feet save a diminishing tunnel of light. Xenia could hear her heart pound. Frank was laughing.

The depth markers on the wall were already rising up past her, mapping her acceleration. But she was suspended here, in the vacuum, as if she was in orbit; she had no sense of speed, no vertigo from the depths beneath her.

Their speed picked up quickly. In seconds, it seemed, they had already passed through the fine regolith layers, the Moon's pulverized outer skin, and they were sailing down through the megaregolith. Giant chunks of deeply shattered rock crowded against the glassy, transparent tunnel walls like the corpses of buried animals.

The material beyond the walls turned smooth and grey now. This was lunar bedrock, anorthosite, buried beyond even the probings and pulverizing of the great impactors. Unlike Earth, there would be no fossils here, she knew, no remnants of life in these deep levels; only a smooth gradation of minerals, processed by the slow workings of geology. In some places there were side shafts dug away from the main exploratory bore. They led to stopes, lodes of magnesium-rich rocks extruded from the Moon's frozen interior, which were now being mined out by Frank's industry partners. She saw the workings as complex blurs, hurrying upwards as she fell, gone like dream visions.

Despite the gathering warmth of the tunnel, despite her own acceleration, she had a sense of cold, of age and stillness.

They dropped through a surprisingly sharp transition into a new realm, where the rock on the other side of the walls glowed of its own internal light. It was a dull grey-red, like a cooling lava on Earth.

'The mantle of the Moon,' Frank whispered, gripping her hands. 'Basalt. Up here it ain't so bad. But further down the rock is so soft it pulls like taffy when you try to drill it. A thousand kilometres of mush, a pain in the ass.'

They passed a place where the glass walls were marked with an engraving, stylized flowers with huge lunar petals. This was where a technician had been killed in an implosion. The little memorial shot upwards and was lost in the light. Frank didn't comment.

The rock was now glowing a bright cherry-pink, rushing upwards past them. It was like dropping through some immense glass tube full of fluorescing gas. Xenia sensed the heat, despite her suit's insulation and the refrigeration of the tunnel.

Falling, falling.

Thick conduits surrounded them now, crowding the tunnel, flipping from bracket to bracket. The conduits carried water, bearing the Moon's deep heat to hydrothermal plants on the surface. She was becoming dazzled by the pink-white glare of the rocks.

The harness tugged at her sharply, slowing her. Looking down along the forest of conduits, she could see that they were approaching a terminus, a platform of some dull, opaque ceramic that plugged the tunnel.

'End of the line,' Frank said. 'Down below there's only the downhole tools and the casing machine and other junk . . . Do you know where you are? Xenia, we're more than a thousand kilometres deep, two-thirds of the way to the centre of the Moon.'

The pulleys gripped harder and they slowed, drifting to a halt a metre above the platform. With Frank's help she loosened her harness and spilled easily to the platform itself, landing on her feet, as if after a sky-dive.

She glanced at her chronometer patch. The fall had taken twenty minutes.

She got her balance, and looked around. They were alone here.

The platform was crowded with science equipment, anonymous grey boxes linked by cables to softscreens and batteries. Sensors and probes, wrapped in water-cooling jackets, were plugged into ports in the walls. She could see data collected from the lunar material flickering over the softscreens, measurements of porosity and permeability, data from gas meters and pressure gauges and dynamometers and gravimeters. There was evidence of work here, small inflatable shelters, spare backpacks, notepads – even, incongruously, a coffee cup. Human traces, here at the heart of the Moon.

She walked to the walls. Her steps were light; she was almost float-ing. There was rock, pure and unmarked, all around her, beyond the window-like walls, glowing pink.

'The deep interior of the Moon,' Frank said, joining her. He ran his gloved hands over the glass. 'What the rock hounds call primitive material, left over from the solar system's formation. Never melted and differentiated like the mantle, never bombarded like the surface. Untouched since the Moon budded off of Earth itself.'

'I feel light as a feather,' she said. And so she did; she felt as if she was going to float back up the borehole like a soap bubble.

Frank glared up into the tunnel above them, and concentric light rings glimmered in his face plate. 'All that rock up there doesn't pull at us. It might as well be cloud, rocky cloud, hundreds of kilometres of it.'

'I suppose, at the centre itself, you would be weightless.'

'I guess.'

On one low bench stood a glass beaker, covered by clear plastic film. She picked it up; she could barely feel it, dwarfed within her thick, inflexible gloves. It held a liquid that sloshed in the gentle gravity. The liquid was murky brown, not quite transparent.

Frank was grinning. Immediately she understood.

'I wish you could drink it,' he said. 'I wish we could drink a toast. You know what that is? *It's water*. Moon water, water from the lunar rocks.' He took the beaker and turned around, in a slow, ponderous dance. 'It's all around us. Just as Mariko predicted, a fucking ocean of it. Wadsleyite and majorite with three per cent water by weight . . . Incredible. We did it, babe.'

'Frank. You were right. I had no idea.'

'I sat on the results. I wanted you to be the first to see this. To see my –' He couldn't find the word.

'Affirmation,' she said gently. 'This is your affirmation.'

'Yeah. I'm a hero.'

It was true, she knew.

It was going to work out just as Frank had projected. As soon as the implications of the find became apparent – that there really were oceans down here, buried inside the Moon – the imaginations of the Lunar Japanese would be fast to follow Frank's vision. *This*, after all, wasn't a simple matter of plugging holes in the environment support system loops. There was surely enough resource here, just as Frank said, to future-proof the Moon. And, perhaps, this would be a pivot of human history, a moment when humanity's long decline was halted, and mankind found a place to live in a system that was no longer theirs.

Not for the first time Xenia recognized Frank's brutal wisdom in his dealings with people: to bulldoze them as far as he had to, until they couldn't help but agree with him.

Frank would become the most famous man on the Moon.

That wasn't going to help him, though, she thought sadly.

'So,' she said. 'You proved your point. Will you stop now?'

'Stop the borehole?' He sounded shocked. 'Hell, no. We go on, all the way to the core.'

'Frank, the investors are already pulling out.'

'Chicken-livered assholes. I'll go on if I have to pay for it myself.' He put the beaker down. 'Xenia, the water isn't enough; it's just a first step. We have to go on. *We still have to find the other volatiles.* Methane. Organics. We go on. Damn it, Roughneck is my project.'

'No, it isn't. We sold so much stock to get through the mantle that you don't have a majority any more.'

'But we're rich again.' He laughed. 'We'll buy it all back.'

'Nobody's selling. They certainly won't after you publish this finding. You're too successful. I'm sorry, Frank.'

'So the bad guys are closing in, huh. Well, the hell with it. I'll find a way to beat them. I always do.' He grabbed her gloved hands. 'Never mind that now. Listen, I'll tell you why I brought you down here. *I'm winning.* I'm going to get everything I ever wanted. Except one thing.'

She was bewildered. 'What?'

'I want us to get married. I want us to have kids. We came here together, from out of the past, and we should have a life of our own, on this Japanese Moon, in this future.' His voice was heavy, laden with emotion, almost cracking. In the glare of rock light, she couldn't see his face.

She hadn't expected this. She couldn't think of a response.

Now his voice was almost shrill. 'You've gone quiet.'

'The comet,' she said softly.

He was silent for a moment, still gripping her hands.

'The methane rocket,' she said. 'On the comet. It was detected.'

She could tell he was thinking of denying all knowledge. Then he said: 'Who found it?'

'Takomi.'

'The piss-drinking old bastard out at Edo?'

'Yes.'

'That still doesn't prove –'

'I checked the accounts. I found where you diverted the funds, how you built the rocket, how you launched it, how you rendezvoused it with the comet. Everything.' She sighed. 'You never were smart at that kind of stuff, Frank. You should have asked me.'

'Would you have helped?'

'No.'

He released her hands. 'I never meant it to hit there. On Fracastorius.'

'I know that. Nevertheless, that's what happened.'

He picked up the glass of lunar water. 'But you know what, I'd have gone ahead even if I had known. I needed that fucking comet to kick-start *this*. It was the only way. You can't stagnate. That way lies extinction. If I gave the Lunar Japanese a choice, they'd be sucking water out of old concrete for the rest of time.'

'But it would be their choice.'

'And that's more important than not dying?'

She shrugged. 'It's inevitable they'll know soon.'

He turned to her, and she sensed he was grinning again, irrepressible. 'At least I finished my project. At least I got to be a hero . . . Marry me,' he said again.

'No.'

'Why not? Because I'm going to be a con?'

'Not that.'

'Then why?'

'Because I wouldn't last, in your heart. You move on, Frank.'

'You're wrong,' he said. But there was no conviction in his voice. 'So,' he said. 'No wedding bells. No little Lunar Americans, to teach these Japanese how to play football.'

'I guess not.'

He walked away. 'Makes you think, though,' he said, his back to her.

'What?'

He waved a hand at the glowing walls. 'This technology isn't so advanced. Neil and Buzz couldn't have done it, but maybe we could have opened up some kind of deep mine on the Moon by the end of the twentieth century, say. Started to dig out the water, live off the land. If only we'd known it was here, all this wealth, even NASA might have done it. And then you'd have an American Moon, and who knows how history might have turned out?'

'None of us can change things,' she said.

He looked at her, his face masked by rock light. 'However much we might want to.'

'No.'

'How long do you think I have, before they shut me down?'

'I don't know. Weeks. No more.'

'Then I'll have to make those weeks count.'

He showed her how to hook her suit harness to a fresh pulley set, and they began the long, slow ride to the surface of the Moon.

Abandoned on its bench top at the bottom of the shaft, she could see the covered beaker, the Moon water within.

After her descent into the Moon, she returned to Edo, seeking stillness.

The world of the Moon, here on Farside, was simple: the regolith below, the sunlight that flowed from the black sky above. Land, light, dark. That, and herself, alone. When she looked downsun, at her own shadow, the light bounced from the dust back towards her, making a halo around her head.

The Moon flower had, she saw, significantly diminished since her last visit; many of the outlying petals were broken off or shattered.

After a time, Takomi joined her.

He said: 'Evidence of the flowers has been found before.'

'It has?'

'I have, discreetly, studied old records of the lunar surface. Another legacy of richer days past, when much of the Moon was studied in some detail. But those explorers, long dead now, did not know what they had found, of course. The remains were buried under regolith layers. Some of them were billions of years old.' He sighed. 'The evidence is fragmentary. Nevertheless I have been able to establish a pattern.'

'What kind of pattern?'

'It is true that the final seeding event drew the pods, with unerring accuracy, *back* to this site. As you observed. The pods were absorbed into the structure of the primary plant, here, which has since withered. The seeding was evidently triggered by the arrival of the comet, the enveloping of the Moon by its new, temporary atmosphere. But I have studied the patterns of earlier seedings –'

'Triggered by earlier comet impacts.'

'Yes. All of them long before human occupancy began here. Just one or two impacts per billion years. Brief comet rains, spurts of air, before the long winter closed again. And each impact triggered a seeding event.'

'. . . Ah. I understand. These are like desert flowers, which bloom in the brief rain. Poppies, rockroses, grasses, chenopods.'

'Exactly. They complete their lifecycles quickly, propagate as vigorously as possible, while the comet air lasts. And then their seeds lie dormant, for as long as necessary, waiting for the next chance event, perhaps as long as a billion years.'

'I imagine they spread out, trying to cover the Moon. Propagate as fast and as far as possible.'

'No,' he said quietly.

'Then what?'

'At every comet event, the seedings *converge*. Just as they did here. These plants work backwards, Xenia.

'A billion years ago there were a thousand sites like this. In a great seeding, these diminished to a mere hundred: those fortunate few were bombarded with seeds, while the originators withered. And later, another seeding reduced that hundred to twelve or so. And finally, the twelve are reduced to one. This one.'

She tried to think that through; she pictured the little seed pods converging, diminishing in number. 'It doesn't make sense.'

'Not for us, who are ambassadors from Earth,' he said. 'Earth life spreads, colonizes, whenever and wherever it can. But this is lunar life, Xenia. And the Moon is an old, cooling, dying world. Its richest days were brief moments, far in the past. And so life has adjusted to the situation. Do you understand?'

'. . . I think so. But now, this is truly the last of them? The end?'

'Yes. The flower is already dying.'

'But why here? Why now?'

He shrugged. 'Xenia, your colleague Frank Paulis is determined to rebuild the Moon, inside and out. Even if he fails, others will follow where he showed the way. The stillness of the Moon is lost.' He sniffed. 'My own garden might survive, but in a park, like your old Apollo landers, to be gawked at by tourists. It is a – diminishing. And so with the flowers. There is nowhere for them to survive, on the new Moon, in our future.'

'But how do they *know* they can't survive? – oh, that's the wrong question. Of course the flowers don't know anything.'

He paused, regarding her. 'Are you sure?'

'What do you mean?'

'We are smart, and aggressive. We think smartness is derived from aggression. Perhaps that is true. But perhaps it takes a greater imagination to comprehend stillness than to react to the noise and clamour of our shallow human world.'

She frowned, remembering Mariko's evidence about neural

structures in the flowers. 'You're saying these things are *conscious?*'

'I believe so. It would be hard to prove. I have spent much time in contemplation here, however. And I have developed an intuition. A sympathy, perhaps.'

'But that seems *cruel*. What kind of God would plan such a thing? Think about it. You have a conscious creature, trapped on the surface of the Moon, in this desolate, barren environment. And its way of living, stretching back billions of years maybe, has had the sole purpose of diminishing itself, to prepare for this final extinction, this death, this *smyert*. What is the purpose of consciousness, confronted by such desolation?'

'But perhaps it is not so,' he said gently. 'The cosmologists tell us that there are many time streams. The future of the Moon, in the direction *we* face, may be desolate. But not the past. So why not face *that* way?'

She barely followed him. But she remembered the *kare sansui*, the waterless stream traced in the regolith. It was impossible to tell if the stream was flowing from past to future, or future to past; if the hills of heaped regolith were rising or sinking.

He said, 'Perhaps to the flowers – to *this* flower, the last, or perhaps the first – this may be a beginning, not an end.'

'*Vileekee bokh*. You are telling me that these plants are living backwards in time? Propagating – not into the future – but *into the past?*'

'In the present there is but one of them. In the past there are many – billions, perhaps. In our future lies death for them; in our past lies glory. So why not look that way?' He touched her gloved hand. 'The important thing is that you must not grieve for the flowers. They have their dream, their *mechta*, of a better Moon, in the deep past, or deep future. The universe is not always cruel, Xenia Makarova. And you must not hate Frank, for what he has done.'

'I don't hate him.'

'There is a point of view from which he is not *taking* nutrients from the heart of the Moon, but *giving*. He is pumping the core of the Moon full of water and volatiles, and when he is done he will even fill in the hole . . .You see?'

'Takomi.'

He was still.

'That isn't your real name, is it? This isn't your identity.'

He said nothing, face averted from hers.

'I don't think you are even a man. I think your name is Nemoto. And you are hiding here on the Moon, whiling away the centuries.'

Takomi stood silently for long seconds. 'My Moon plants recede into a better past. That, for me, isn't an option. I must make my way into the unwelcome future. But at least, here, I am rarely disturbed. I hope you will respect that.

'Now come,' said Takomi, or Nemoto. 'I have green tea, and rice cake, and we will sit under the cherry tree, and talk further.'

Xenia nodded, dumbly, and let him – her? – take her by the hand. Together they walked across the yielding antiquity of the Moon.

It was another celebration, here at the South Pole of the Moon. It was the day Project Roughneck promised to fulfil its potential, by bringing the first commercially useful loads of water to the surface.

Once again the crowds were out: investors with their guests, families with children, huge softscreens draped over drilling gear, Virtual Observers everywhere so everyone on the Moon could share everything that happened here today. Even the Greys were here, to celebrate the project's end, dancing in elaborate formations.

Earth hovered like a ghost on one horizon, ignored, its sparking wars meaningless.

This time, Xenia didn't find Frank strutting about the lunar surface in his Stars and Stripes spacesuit, giving out orders. Frank said he knew which way the wind blew, a blunt Earthbound metaphor no Moon-born Japanese understood. So he had confined himself to a voluntary house arrest, in the new *ryokan* that had opened up on the summit of one of the tallest rim mountains here.

When she arrived, he waved her in and handed her a drink, a fine sake. The suite was a penthouse, magnificent, decorated in a mix of western-style and traditional Japanese. One wall, facing the borehole, was just a single huge pane of tough, anhydrous lunar glass. She saw a tumbler of murky water, covered over, on a table top. Moon water, his only trophy of Roughneck.

'This is one hell of a cage,' he said. 'If you've got to be in a cage.' He laughed darkly. 'Civilized, these Lunar Japanese. Well, we'll see.' He eyed her. 'What about you? Will you go back to the stars?'

She looked at the oily ripple of the drink in her glass. 'I don't think so. I – like it here. I think I'd enjoy building a world.'

He grunted. 'You'll marry. Have kids. Grandkids.'

'Perhaps.'

He glared at her. 'When you do, remember me, who made it possible, and got his ass busted for his trouble. Remember *this*.'

He walked her to the window.

She gazed out, goddess-like, surveying the activity. The drilling site was an array of blocky machinery, now stained deep grey by dust, all of it bathed in artificial light. The stars hung above the plain, stark and still, and people and their vehicles swarmed over the ancient, broken plain like so many spacesuited ants.

'You know, it's a great day,' she said. 'They're making your dream come true.'

'*My* dream, hell.' He fetched himself another slug of sake, which he drank like beer. 'They stole it from me. And they're going inward. That's what Nishizaki and the rest are considering now. I've seen their plans. Huge underground cities in the crust, big enough for thousands, even hundreds of thousands, all powered by thermal energy from the rocks. In fifty years you could have multiples of the Moon's present population, burrowing away busily.' He glanced at his wristwatch, restless.

'What's wrong with that?'

'It wasn't the fucking *point*.' He glared up at Earth's scarred face. 'If we dig ourselves into the ground, we won't be able to see *that*. We'll forget. Don't you get it? . . .'

But now there was activity around the drilling site. She stepped to the window, cupped her hands to exclude the room lights. People were running, away from the centre of the site.

There was a tremor. The building shuddered under her, languidly. A quake, on the still and silent Moon?

Frank was checking his watch. He punched the air and strode to the window. 'Right on time. Hot damn.'

'Frank, what have you done?'

There was another tremor, more violent. A small Buddha statue was dislodged from its pedestal, and fell gently to the carpeted floor. Xenia tried to keep her feet. It was like riding a rush hour train.

'Simple enough,' Frank said. 'Just shaped charges, embedded in the casing. They punched holes straight through the bore wall into the surrounding rock, to let the water and sticky stuff flow right into the pipe and up –'

'A blow-out. You arranged a blow-out.'

'If I figured this right the interior of the whole fucking Moon is going to come gushing out of that hole. Like puncturing a balloon.' He took her arms. 'Listen to me. We will be safe here. I figured it.'

'And the people down there, in the crater? Your managers and technicians? The *children?*'

'It's a day they'll tell their grandchildren about.' He shrugged, grin-

244

ning, his forehead slick with sweat. 'They're going to lock me up anyhow. At least this way –'

But now there was an eruption from the centre of the rig, a tower of liquid, rapidly freezing, that punched its way up through the rig itself, shattering the flimsy buildings covering the head. When the fountain reached high enough to catch the flat sunlight washing over the mountains, it seemed to burst into fire, crystals of ice shining in complex parabolic sheaves, before falling back to the ground.

Frank punched the air. 'You know what that is? Kerogen. A tarry stuff you find in oil shales. It contains carbon, oxygen, hydrogen, sulphur, potassium, chlorine, other elements . . . I couldn't believe it when the lab boys told me what they found down there. Mariko says kerogen is so useful we might as well have found chicken soup in the rocks.' He cackled. 'Chicken soup, from the primordial cloud. *I won*, Xenia. With this blow-out I stopped them from building Bedrock City. I'm famous.'

'What about the Moon flowers?'

His face was hard. 'Who the fuck cares? I'm a human, Xenia. I'm interested in human destiny, not a bunch of worthless plants we couldn't even *eat*.' He waved a hand at the ice fountain 'Look out there, Xenia. I beat the future. I've no regrets. I'm a great man. I achieve great things.'

The ground around the demolished drill head began to crack, venting gas and ice crystals; and the deep, ancient richness of the Moon rained down on the people.

Frank Paulis whispered, 'And what could be greater than this?'

. . . She was in the Dark, flying, like one of her own seeds. She was surrounded by fragments of the shattered Land, and by her children.

But she could not speak to them, of course; unlike the Land, the Dark was empty of rock, and would not carry her thoughts.

It was a time of stabbing loneliness.

But it did not last long.

Already the cloud was being drawn together, collapsing into a new and greater Land that glowed beneath her, a glowing ocean of rock, a hundred times bigger than the small place she had come from.

And at the last, she saw the greatest comet of all tear itself from the heart of this Land, a ball of fire that lunged into the sky, receding rapidly into the unyielding Dark.

She fell towards that glowing ocean, her heart full of joy at the Merging of the Lands . . .

In the last moment of her life, she recalled the Giver.

She was the first, and the Giver birthed her. None of it would have come to be without the Giver, who fed the Land.

She wished she could express her love for him. She knew that was impossible.

She sensed, though, that he knew anyhow.

Chapter 21

HOMECOMING

After their journey to the stars, Madeleine and Ben returned to a silent solar system.

Over a century had elapsed. They themselves had aged less than a year. It was now, astonishingly, the year 2240, an unimaginable, futuristic date. Madeleine had been braced for more historic drift, more cultural isolation.

Not for silence.

As the long weeks of their flight inward from the Saddle Point radius wore away, and the puddle of crowded light that was the inner system grew brighter ahead, they both grew increasingly apprehensive. At length, they were close enough to resolve images of Earth in the *Ancestor*'s telescopes. They huddled together by their monitors.

What they saw was an Earth that was brilliant white.

Ice swept down from both poles, encroaching towards the equator. The shapes of the northern continents were barely visible under the huge frozen sheets. The colours of life, brown and green and blue, had been crowded into a narrow strip around the equator. Here and there, easily visible on the night side of the planet, Madeleine made out the spark of fires, of explosions. Gaijin ships orbited Earth, tracking from pole to pole, their ramscoops casting golden light that glimmered from the ice and the oceans, mapping and studying, still following their own immense, patient projects.

Madeleine and Ben were both stunned by this. They studied Earth for hours, barely speaking, skipping meals and sleep periods.

Ben, fearful for his wife, his people on Triton, grew silent, morbid, withdrawing from Madeleine. Madeleine found the loneliness hard to bear. When she slept her dreams were intense, populated by drifting alien artefacts.

*   *   *

The Gaijin flower-ship dropped them into orbit around Earth's Moon.

Nemoto came to them, at last. She appeared as a third figure in the cramped, scuffed environment of *Dreamtime Ancestor*'s Service Module, a digital ghost coalescing from a cloud of cubical pixels.

Her gaze lit on Madeleine. 'Meacher. You're back. You were expected. I have an assignment for you.' She smiled.

Madeleine said, 'I don't believe you're still alive. You must be some kind of virtual simulation.'

'I don't care what you think. Anyhow, you'll never know.' Nemoto was small, shrunken, her face a leathery mask, as if with age she was devolving to some earlier proto-human form. She glanced around. 'Where's the FGB Module? . . . *Oh.*' Evidently she had just downloaded a summary of their mission from the virtual counterpart who had travelled with them. She glared. 'You have to meddle, don't you, Meacher?'

Madeleine passed a hand through Nemoto's body; pixels clustered like butterflies. To Madeleine, ten more decades out of her time, the projection was impressive new technology. There was no sign of time-delay; Nemoto – or the projector – must be *here*, on the Moon or in lunar orbit, or else her responses would be delayed by seconds.

Ben asked tightly, 'What about Triton?'

Nemoto's face was empty. 'Triton is silent. It's wise to be silent. But your wife is still alive.'

Madeleine sensed a shift in Ben's posture, a softening.

'But,' Nemoto said now, 'the colony is under threat. A fleet of Gaijin flower-ships and factories is moving out from the asteroids. They're already in orbit around Jupiter, Saturn, even Uranus. They have projects out there, for instance on Jupiter's moon Io, which we don't understand.' Her face worked, her anger visible, even after all this time, her territoriality powerful. 'The Earth has collapsed, of course. And though the fools down there don't know it, the Moon faces long-term resource crises, particularly in metals. And so on. *The Gaijin are winning,* Meacher. Triton is the only foothold we humans have in the outer system. The last trench. We can't let the Gaijin take it.'

And you have a plan, Madeleine realized, with a sinking heart. A plan that involves me. So she was immediately plunged back into Nemoto's manipulation and scheming.

Ben was frowning. He asked Nemoto some pointed questions about her presence, her influence, her resources. What was the political situation now? Who was backing her? What was her funding?

She'd answer none of his questions. She wouldn't even tell them where, physically, she was, before she disappeared, promising – or threatening – to be back.

Madeleine spent long hours at the windows, watching the Moon.

The Moon was controlled by a tight federal-government structure which seemed to blend seamlessly with a series of corporate alliances, which had grown mainly from the Japanese companies that had funded the first waves of lunar colonization. The lunar authorities had let the *Ancestor* settle into a wide two-hour orbit, but they wouldn't let Madeleine and Ben land. It was clear to Madeleine that, to these busy lunar inhabitants, returned star travellers were an irrelevance.

Huge glowing Gaijin flower-ships looped around the Moon from pole to lunar pole.

This new Moon glowed green and blue, the colours of life and humanity. The Lunar Japanese had peppered the great craters – Copernicus, Eudoxus, Gassendi, Fracastorius, Tsiolkovsky, Verne, many others – with domes, enclosing a freight of water and air and life. Landsberg, the first large colony, remained the capital. The domes were huge now, the crests of some of them reaching two kilometres above the ancient regolith, hexagonal-cell spaceframe structures supported by giant, inhabited towers. Covered roads and linear townships connected some of the domes, glowing lines of light over the maria. The Japanese planned to extend their structures until the entire surface of the Moon was glassed over, in a worldhouse. It would be like an immense arboretum, a continuously managed biosphere.

All of this – Madeleine learned, tapping into the web of information which wrapped around the new planet – was fuelled by huge core-tapping bores called Paulis mines. Frank Paulis himself was still alive. Madeleine felt a spark of pride that one of her own antique generation had achieved such greatness. But, fifty years after his huge technical triumph, Paulis was disgraced, incommunicado.

Virtual Nemoto materialized once more.

Madeleine had found out that Nemoto was still alive, as best anybody knew. But she had dropped out of sight for a long period. It was rumoured she had lived as a recluse on Farside, still relatively uninhabited. It had been a breakdown, it seemed, that had lasted for decades. Nemoto would say nothing of any of this, nothing of herself, even of the history Madeleine and Ben had skipped over. Rather, she wanted to talk only of the future, her projects, just as she always had.

'Good news.' She smiled, her face skull-like. 'I have a ship.'

Ben said, 'What ship?'

'The *Gurrutu*. One of my colony ships. It's completed the Earth-Neptune round trip twice already. It's in high Earth orbit.' She looked wistful. 'It's actually safer there than orbiting the Moon. Here, it would be claimed and scavenged for its metals.' She studied them. 'You must go to Triton.'

Ben nodded. 'Of course.'

Nemoto eyed her. 'And you, Meacher.'

Of course Ben must, Madeleine thought. Those are his people, out there in the cold, struggling to survive. It's his wife, still conveniently alive, having traversed those hundred years the long way. But – regardless of Nemoto's ambitions – it's nothing to do with me.

But, as she gazed at Nemoto's frail virtual figure, doggedly surviving, doggedly battling, she felt torn. Maybe you aren't as disengaged from all this as you used to be, Madeleine.

She said, 'Even if we make it to Triton, what are we supposed to do when we get there? What are you planning, Nemoto?'

Nemoto said bleakly, 'We must stop the Gaijin – and whoever follows them. What else is there to do?'

They would have to spend a month in Earth orbit, working on the *Gurrutu*.

The colony craft was decades old, and showing its age. *Gurrutu* had been improvised from the liquid-propellant core booster of an Ariane 12 rocket. It was a simple cylinder, with the fuel tanks inside refurbished and made habitable. The main living area of *Gurrutu* was a big hydrogen tank, with a smaller oxygen tank used for storage. A fireman's pole ran the length of the hydrogen tank, up through a series of mesh floor-partitions to an instrument cluster.

Big, fragile-looking solar-cell wings had been fixed to the exterior. But reconditioned fission reactors provided power in the dimly lit outer reaches of the solar system. These were old technology: heavy Soviet-era antiques, of a design called Topaz. Each Topaz was a clutter of pipes and tubing and control rods set atop a big radiator cone of corrugated aluminium.

There was a docking mount and an instrument module at one end of the core booster, and a cluster of ion rockets at the other. The ion thrusters were suitable for missions of long duration, missions measured in years, to the outer planets and beyond. And they worked; they had ferried the Yolgnu to Triton. But the ion thrusters needed much refurbishment. And they, too, were old technology. The newest Lunar Japanese helium-3 fusion drives were, Madeleine learned, much more effective.

It wouldn't be a comfortable ride out to Neptune. The toilets never seemed to vent properly. There was a chorus of bangs, wheezes and rattles when they tried to sleep. The solar panels had steadily degraded, so that there was never enough power, even this close to the sun. Madeleine soon tired of half-heated meals, and lukewarm coffee, and tepid bathing water.

But forty people had lived in this windowless cavern-slum for the five years it had taken *Gurrutu* to reach Neptune: eating hydroponically grown plants, recycling their waste, trying not to drive each other crazy. The tank had been slung with hammocks and blankets, little nests of humans seeking privacy. Three children had been born here.

Madeleine found scratches on an aluminium bulkhead that recorded a child's growth, the image of a favourite uncle tucked into the back of a storage cupboard.

The ship could have been built in the twenty-first century – even the twentieth. Human research into spaceflight engineering had all but stopped when the Gaijin had arrived. Madeleine thought of the Gaijin flower-ships which had carried her to the Saddle Point radius and beyond: jewelled, perfect, faultless.

But *Gurrutu* was simply the best Nemoto could do. And so it was heroic. With such equipment, Nemoto had reached Neptune – thirty times Earth's distance from the sun, ten times further out than the asteroid belt. Only Malenfant himself, unaided by Gaijin, had gone further – and his mission had been a one-man stunt. Nemoto had sent two hundred colonists.

As she laboured over the lashed-up systems, improvising repairs, Madeleine's respect for Nemoto deepened.

. . . And, while Madeleine worked, the Earth slid liquidly past the windows of the *Gurrutu*.

Those old environmentalist Cassandras had been proven right, Madeleine learned. The climate really had been only metastable; in the end, after forty thousand years of digging and building and burning, humans managed to destabilize the world, tip over the whole damn bowl of cherries, until it settled with stunning rapidity into this new, lethal state.

Madeleine could see patterns in the ice: ripples, lines of debris, varying colours, where the ice had flowed from its fastnesses at the poles and the mountain peaks. There was little cloud over the great ice sheets – merely wisps of cirrus, streaked by winds which tore perpetually around immense low-pressure systems squatting over the frozen poles.

The ice covered most of Canada, and a great tongue of it extended far into the American Midwest, reaching further south than the Great Lakes – or where the Lakes used to be. Chicago, Detroit, Toronto and the other cities were all gone now, drowned. The familiar lobed shapes of the Lakes themselves had been overwhelmed by a new, glimmering ocean that stretched a thousand kilometres inland from the eastern seaboard. And to the west, a ribbon of water stretched up from Puget Sound towards Alaska. The land itself was crushed down under the weight of the ice, and sea water had flowed eagerly into the shallow depressions so formed.

Even to the south of the ice line, the land was grievously damaged. Desert stretched from Oregon through Idaho, Wyoming, Nebraska and Iowa, a belt of immense, rippled sand dunes. It was a place of violent winds, for heavy, cold air poured off the ice over the exposed land, and she saw giant dust storms that persisted for days. At night she saw lights glimmer in that vast expanse, flickering: just camp fires lit by descendants of mid-western Americans who must be reduced to living like Bedouins in that great cold desert.

South of the ice, Earth at first glance looked as temperate and habitable as it had always done. She could see green in the tropical areas, coral reefs, ships plying to and fro through warm, ice-free seas. But nowhere was unaffected. The great rain forests of equatorial Africa and the Amazon Basin had shrunk back into isolated pockets, surrounded by swathes of what looked like grass lands. Conversely, the Sahara seemed to be turning green. Even the shapes of the continents had changed, as glistening sheets of continental shelves were exposed by the falling sea level.

In the southern United States there were still cities: great misty-grey urban sprawls around the coasts and along the river valleys, from Baja California, along the Mexican border, the Gulf of Mexico, to Florida. But New Orleans seemed to be burning continually, great fires blocks wide sending up black smoke plumes that streaked out over hundreds of kilometres. Likewise, there appeared to be a small war raging around Orlando; she made out what looked like tank tracks, frequent explosions that lit up the night.

It was impossible to gather direct news. Presumably all communication was carried out by land lines or with point-to-point modulated lasers; belatedly, it seemed, the inhabitants of Earth had learned the wisdom of not broadcasting their business to the stars. It did appear, though, that some of these wars had been blazing since before the return of the ice.

The most savage conflict appeared to be occurring in north Africa, where the population of Eurasia – hundreds of millions – had tried to drain into the southern European countries and the new North African grasslands. But any orderly relocation had long broken down. Huge black craters scarred the Sahara, some of them glimmering as if with puddles of glass; and, once, she made out the tell-tale shape of a mushroom cloud, rising like a perfect toy from an ochre African horizon.

And – more sinister still – she could see new forms on Earth's long-suffering hide. They were great sprawling structures, spider-like, silvery: not like human cities, more centrally organized, the pieces interconnected, like single buildings spanning tens of kilometres. These were Gaijin colonies. There were several of them in the ice-free middle latitudes, with no sign of human occupancy nearby. There were even a handful on the ice sheets themselves, places no human could survive. Nobody knew what the Gaijin were doing in there.

She felt a cold fury. Couldn't the Gaijin have done something to stop this, to halt the collapse of her world? If not, why the hell were they here?

Ben said he wanted to go to Earth, to Australia, one last time, before he left forever. Madeleine quailed at the idea. *That's not my planet any more.* But she didn't want to oppose Ben's complex impulse.

An automated ground-to-orbit shuttle came climbing up to meet them. Nemoto had found someone who had agreed to host them, if briefly.

They skimmed through morning light towards Australia, approaching from the south. They received no calls for identification; there was no attempt at traffic control, nothing from the ground. It was like approaching an uninhabited planet.

They drifted over Sydney. The city was still populated, its suburbs scarred by conflict, but there was no harbour; Sydney had been left beached in the country's drying interior. The rust-red deserts of the centre appeared still more desiccated than before. But she saw no signs of humanity. Alice Springs, for example, was burned out, a husk; nothing moved there.

They skimmed low over the great geological features south of the Alice, Ayers Rock and the Olgas. These were uncompromising lumps of hard, ancient sandstone protruding from the flat desert, extensively carved by megayears of water flows. To the Aborigines, nomads on this unforgiving tabletop landscape, these formations must have been as striking as the medieval cathedrals that had loomed over Europe. And so the Aborigines had made them places of totemic and religious significance, spinning Dreamtime stories from cracks and folds, until the rocks became a kind of mythic cinema, frozen in geological time. It had been a triumph of the imagination, she supposed, in a land like a sensory deprivation tank.

This had briefly been a centre for tourism. The tourists were long gone now, the western influence vanished in an instant, a dream of fat and affluence. But the Aborigines had remained. From the air she saw slim figures moving slowly over the landscape, round faces turned up to her vehicle, all as it had been for twelve thousand years – just as Ben had once foreseen, she remembered.

Ben peered from his window, silent, withdrawn.

Perhaps a hundred kilometres south of the Alice, they saw a structure of bright blue, a dot in the desert. A tent.

The shuttle dipped, fell like a brick, and skidded to a halt half a kilometre distant from the tent.

Nobody came to meet them. After a few minutes they climbed down to the ground and walked towards the tent.

The land was an immense orange-red table, the sky a sheet of washed-out blue. There was utter silence here: no bird song, no insects. The sun was high, ferocious, the heat tremendous and dry. They walked cautiously, unused to Earth's heavy gravity.

Madeleine felt overwhelmed. Save for a few space walks, it was the first time she had been out of a cramped hab module, out in a landscape, for years.

Ben touched her arm. She stopped. Through the heat haze of the horizon, something moved, stately, silent.

'It looks like a lizard,' she whispered. 'A komodo dragon, maybe. But –'

'But it's immense.'

'Another Gaijin experiment, you think?'

He said, 'I think we ought to keep still.'

The lizard, a Mesozoic nightmare, paused for long seconds, perhaps a minute, a tongue the length of a whip lashing out at something unseen. Then it moved on, turning away from the humans.

They hurried on.

Their host was a woman: an American, small, compact, stern-faced, her thick black hair tied back severely behind her head. She was dressed in a silvery coverall. She was called Carole Lerner.

Lerner looked them up and down contemptuously. 'Nemoto told me to expect you. She didn't tell me you were two babes in the wood.' She eyed them with hard suspicion. 'I have a hoard.'

Ben frowned. 'What?'

Lerner said, 'I'm not about to tell you where. If I die my caches will self-destruct.'

Madeleine understood quickly. Medicine had collapsed, along with everything else, when the ice had come. So no more anti-ageing treatments. Such supplies had become the most precious items on the planet. She held up her hands. 'We're no threat to you, Carole.'

Lerner kept watching them.

At last, sternly, she brought them into the tent, which was blessedly cool, the air moist. She dug out a couple of coveralls, indicated they should put them on. 'These are priceless. Literally. Therm-aware clothing, all but indestructible. Nobody makes them any more. People hand them down like heirlooms, mother to child. Be careful with them.'

'We will,' Madeleine promised.

The tent had no partitions. Ben shrugged, stripped naked, and climbed into his coverall. Madeleine followed suit.

Lerner began to boil water for a drink, and she gave them food, a rehydrated soup, its flavour unidentifiable. She looked about sixty. She was in fact much older than that. She turned out to be *the* Carole Lerner, the woman who had – following another project of Nemoto's – descended into the clouds of Venus, and become the first, and only, human to set foot there.

Ben glanced around, at piles of rock samples, data discs, a few old-fashioned paper books, heavily thumbed, their pages dusty and yellowed.

'My work,' Lerner growled, watching him. 'I'm a geologist. No previous generation has lived through the onset of an Ice Age.'

Ben asked, 'Are there still journals, science institutes, universities?'

'Not on Earth,' Lerner said, scowling. 'I'm caching my samples and notes. Buried deep enough so the animals can't get 'em. And I post my results and interpretation to the Moon, Mars.' She eyed Madeleine, hostile. 'I know what you're thinking. I'm some old nut, an obsessive. Science doesn't matter any more. You star travellers make me sick. You hop and skip through history, and you don't see a damn thing. I'll tell you this. The Gaijin work on long timescales. We're mayflies

255

to them. And that's why science matters now. More than ever. So we can stay in the game.'

Madeleine raised her hands. 'I didn't . . .'

But Lerner had turned her attention to her soup, her anger subsiding. Ben touched Madeleine's arm, and she fell silent.

This is a woman, she thought, who has spent a *long* time alone.

Lerner had a small car, just a bubble of plastic on a light frame, powered by batteries kept topped up by a big solar cell array, and with a gigantic tank of water strapped to its roof. The next day she piled them in and drove them west.

After a couple of hours they reached an area which seemed a little less arid. Madeleine saw green vegetation, trees, tufts of grass, birds wheeling. They came to a shallow creek, dry, which Lerner turned to follow. They passed what appeared to be an abandoned farm, burned out.

They climbed a shallow rise, and Lerner slowed the car, let it run forward almost noiselessly. Finally, as they neared the crest, she cut the engine, and let the car's momentum carry it forward in silence.

As they went over the rise, the land opened up before Madeleine.

There was water, a great calm blue pool of it, stretching halfway to the horizon, utterly unexpected in this dry old place. She could actually smell the water. Her soul felt immediately lifted, some primitive instinct responding.

And it took a full minute of looking, of letting her eyes become accustomed to the landscape, before she could see the animals.

There was a herd of what looked like rhinoceros, lumbering cylinders of flesh, jostling clumsily at the water's edge. But they had no horns. One of them raised a massive head in which small black eyes were embedded like studs. It was quite spectacularly ugly. She saw that it had small, oddly human feet; it trod delicately.

'*Diprotodons*,' Lerner murmured. 'Very common now.'

Madeleine made out kangaroo-like creatures of all sizes, bizarre, overblown animals, some so huge it seemed they could barely lift themselves off the ground – but jump they did, in clumsy lollops. There were creatures like ground sloth, which Lerner said were a variety of giant wombat.

And there were predators. Madeleine saw packs of wolf-like animals, warily circling the grazing, drinking herbivores. Some resembled dogs, some cats.

'It's the same elsewhere,' Lerner said. 'As the ice spreads, the grasslands and forests of the temperate climes are retreating, to be replaced by tundra, steppe, spruce forests.'

'Places these reconstructed creatures can survive,' Ben said.

'Yes. But the Gaijin aren't responsible for everything. In Asia there are reindeer, musk oxen, horses, bison. In North America, the wolves and bears and even the mountain lions are making a recovery.' She smiled again. 'And in the valley of the Thames, I've heard, there are woolly mammoths . . . Now *that* I'd like to see.'

They sat for long hours watching ancient herbivores feed.

They drove on. They drove for hours.

It was only after they had returned to Lerner's camp, with the shuttle parked patiently by, that Madeleine realized she hadn't seen a single human being, not one, nor any sign of recent human habitation, all day.

They stayed three days. Gradually Lerner seemed to learn to tolerate them.

At the end of the last day, Lerner made them a final meal. As the sun sank to the horizon, they sat sipping recycled water in the shade of Lerner's tent.

They swapped sea stories. Lerner told them about Venus. In return, they told her of the Chaera, huddling in the dismal glow of a black hole. And they talked of the changes that had come over humanity.

Lerner said sourly, 'There were a lot of *words:* refugee, relocate, discontinuity, famine, disease, war. Death on a scale we haven't seen since the twentieth century. And people keep right on being born. You know what the average age of humans is now?'

'What?'

'Fifteen years old. Just fifteen. To most people on the planet *this* is normal.' She waved a hand, indicating the depopulated town, the ice-transformed climate, the strange reconstructed animals, the wispy flower-ships that crossed the sky above. 'We're in the middle of a fucking epochal catastrophe here, and people have *forgotten*.' She spat in the dirt, and wiped her mouth with the back of her hand.

Ben leaned forward. 'Carole. Do you think Nemoto is right? That the Gaijin are trying to destroy us?'

Lerner squinted. 'I don't think so. But they don't want to save us either. They are – studying us.'

'What are they trying to find out?'

'Beats me. But then, they probably wouldn't understand what *I'm* trying to find out.'

After a time, Lerner went out to fetch more drink.

In Ben's arms, Madeleine murmured, 'We humans don't seem to age very well, do we?'

'No.'

But then, she thought, humans aren't meant to live so long. Maybe the Gaijin are used to this perspective. *We* aren't. And the feeling of helplessness is crushing. No wonder Lerner is an obsessive, Nemoto a recluse.

Ben was silent.

'You're thinking about Lena,' she said. 'Are you frightened?'

'Why should I be frightened?'

'A hundred years is a long time,' Madeleine said gently.

'But we are *yirritja* and *dhuwa*,' he said. 'We are matched.'

She hesitated. 'And us?'

He just smiled, absently.

Too hot, she peered up at the sky. There was a lot of dust suspended in the air, obscuring many of the stars, and the Moon was almost full, grey splashed with virulent green. Nevertheless, she could see flower-ships swooping easily across the sky. Alien ships, orbiting Earth, unremarked.

And beyond the ships, she saw flickers among the stars. In the direction of the great constellation of Orion, for instance. Sparks, bursts. As if the stars were flaring, exploding. She'd noticed this before, found no explanation. It was strange. Chilling. The sky wasn't supposed to *change*.

Clearly, something was headed this way. Something that spanned the stars, a wavefront of colonizing aliens, perhaps.

'I don't like it here,' she said.

'You mean Australia?'

'No. The planet. The sky. It isn't ours any more.'

'If it ever was.'

Madeleine thought, I'm frightened of the sky. But I can't run away again. I'm involved – just as Nemoto intended.

I have to go to Triton.

To do what? Blindly follow Nemoto's latest insane scheme?

She smiled inwardly. Maybe I'll think of something when we get there.

Lerner brought back a bottle of some kind of hooch; it tasted like fortified wine.

She smiled at them coldly. 'I heard that in Spain and France people have gone back to the caves, where the art still survives, from the *last*

Ice Age. And they are adding new layers of painting, of the animals they see around them. Maybe it was all a dream, do you think? The warm period, the inter-glacial, our civilization. Maybe all that matters is the ice, and the cave.'

As the light failed, and the inhabited Moon brightened, they drank a series of toasts: to Venus, to the Chaera, to Earth, to the ice.

Chapter 22

TRITON DREAMTIME

Even before Neptune showed a disc, Madeleine could see that it was blue, and Triton white. Blue planet, white moon, swimming mistily out of the huge slow-moving dark like exotic deep sea fish.

Neptune swelled into a disc, made almost full by the pinpoint sun behind her. The looming planet was dim, at first just a faintly blue hole against the stars, gradually filling with misty detail as her eyes dark-adapted, becoming a ball of subtle blue and violet, visibly structured. Bands of darker blue girdled the planet, following lines of latitude. There were big storm systems, swirling knots like Jupiter's red spot. And there were thin stripes of white, higher clouds far above the blue, clouds that formed and dissipated within a few hours, surprisingly rapidly. Sometimes, when the angle of the sun was right, she could see those high clouds casting shadows on the deeper layers beneath.

She was a *long* way from home.

It was impossible even to grasp the immensities of scale here. The sun showed as no more than an intense star, bright enough to cast shadows, grey but razor-sharp. The sun's gravity grip was so loosened that Neptune took more than a hundred times as long as Earth to complete a single orbit. And Neptune was surrounded by emptiness more than ten times wider than Earth's orbit around the sun – an emptiness, indeed, that could have contained the whole of Jupiter's orbit.

Out here, in the stillness and cold and dark, the worlds that had spawned were not like Earth. Here the planets had grown immense, misty, stuffed with light elements like hydrogen and helium which had boiled away from the hot, busy inner worlds. So Neptune's rocky core was buried beneath thick layers of opaque gas; the blue was of methane, not water; there were no continents or ice caps here.

But she had not expected that Neptune would be so stunningly Earth-like. She felt tugs of nostalgic longing; for Earth itself, of course, was no longer blue, but a diseased white, the white of encroaching ice.

On the last day of its long flight, the *Gurrutu*, engines blazing, swept around the limb of Neptune. The manoeuvre occurred in complete silence, and as Madeleine watched the huge world swim past her, it was as if she was flying through some cold, dark, gigantic cathedral.

And there was Triton, already bright and growing brighter, a pink-white pearl floating in emptiness.

The final approach to Triton was a challenge for the navigation routines. Triton, uniquely among the solar system's larger moons, orbited Neptune in a retrograde manner, opposite to the spin of Neptune itself. And Triton's orbit was severely pitched up, some twenty degrees out of the plane of the ecliptic. It was thought these eccentricities of Triton were a relic of its peculiar origin: it had once been an independent body, like Pluto, but had been captured by Neptune, perhaps by impact with another moon or by grazing Neptune's atmosphere, a catastrophic event that had resulted in global melting before the moon had learned to endure its entrapment.

Gurrutu entered a looping elliptical orbit. Madeleine watched as a surface of crumpled, pink-streaked water ice rolled beneath the craft. Triton's misty twilight was marked by a single, yellow, man-made beacon: at the site of Kasyapa Township, home to Ben Roach's people. They were not alone in Triton orbit. Many emigrant transport ships, of the same design as *Gurrutu,* still circled here. Others had been driven into the surface, to be broken up for raw materials.

After a day, a small shuttle came up to meet them. Triton's atmosphere, a wisp of nitrogen laced with hydrocarbons, was too thin to support any kind of aircraft; so the shuttle would descend from orbit standing on its rockets, as Apollo astronauts had once landed on the Moon.

As the lander swivelled, the icy ground opened out before her. It was white, laced with pink and, here and there, darker streaks, like wind-blown dust. It was crowded with detail, she saw, with ridges and clefts and pits in the ice, as if the skin of the planet had shrivelled in some impossible heat.

The lander tipped up and fell sharply, entering the last phase of its descent routine. The horizon flattened out quickly, and detail exploded at her. She was descending into a region criss-crossed by shallow ridges, a parquetry of planes and pits in the ice. But there was evidence of human activity: two long straight furrows cut across the random geologic features, a pair of roadways as straight as any Roman road, neatly melted into the ice. And at their terminus, set at the centre of one of the walled ice pits, she saw a small octagonal pad of what looked like concrete, a cluster of silvery tanks and other buildings nearby.

The final landing was gentle. Madeleine and Ben suited up and climbed out of the lander.

The plain around them was still, the fuel tanks and crude surface buildings pale and silent. Under her boots there was a crunch of frost overlaying a harder, whiter rock.

. . . Not rock, she told herself. This was ice, water ice. She scraped at the ice with her boot. It was impenetrable, unyielding, and she failed to mark its surface; it was like a hard, compacted stone. Here, in the intense cold, ice played the part of silicate rocks on Earth. There was an elusive pink stain about the ice, almost too faint to see. Some kind of sunlight-processed organics, perhaps.

She took a step forward, two. She floated and hopped, Moonwalk-style. In fact, she knew, Triton's gravity was little more than half the strength of the Moon's. But she was a big clumsy human with a poor gravity sense; to her body, Triton and Moon were both lumped together in a catch-all category called 'weak gravity'.

She looked up, into a black sky. There was no sense of air above her, no scattering of the sunlight: only a deep starry sky, as if seen from the high desert – but with a dominant bright pinprick at the centre of it. The sun was bright enough to cast shadows, but it was not like authentic sunlight, she thought, more like illumination by a very bright planet, like Venus. The land was a plain of pale white, delicate, a land of midnight stillness, its planes and folds seeming gauzy in the thin light. It seemed a creation of smoke or mist, not of rock-solid ice.

Now she tipped back and peered overhead, where Neptune hung in the sky. The planet appeared as large as fifteen of Earth's full Moons, strung across the sky together. It was half-full, gaunt, almost spectral.

From the corner of her eye she saw movement: flakes of pure white, sparsely descending around her.

'Snow, on Triton?'

'I think it's nitrogen,' Ben said.

Madeleine tried to catch a flake of nitrogen snow on her glove. She wondered how the crystals would differ from the water-ice snow of Earth. But the flakes were too elusive, too sparse, and they were soon gone.

Ben tapped her shoulder and pointed to another corner of the sky, closer to the horizon. There was what looked like a star, perhaps surrounded by a diffuse disc of light.

It was a Gaijin engineering convoy: alien ships, built of asteroid rock and ice, en route to Triton.

The refugee Yolgnu had established their home in the rim wall of a shallow, circular depression called Kasyapa Cavus. This was on the eastern edge of Bubembe Regio, a region of so-called cantaloupe terrain, the complex, parquet-like landscape of the type Madeleine had noticed during the landing. The Cavus had a smooth, bowl-like floor, easy to traverse. There were tractors here, whose big, gauzy balloon tyres seemed to have made no impression on the icy ground. Kasyapa Township was a system of branching caverns. The colonists had burrowed far into the ice-rock, ensuring that a thick layer of ice and spacecraft hull-metal shielded them from the radiation flux of Neptune's magnetosphere, and from the relic cosmic radiation of deep space.

She was given a cabin, a crude cube dug into the ice. She moved her few personal belongings into the cabin – book chips, a few clothes, virtuals of an X-ray burster and a black hole accretion ring. Her things looked dowdy and old, out of place. The wall surface – Triton ice sealed and insulated by a clear plastic – was smooth and hard under Madeleine's hand. After the cool spaces of the Neptune system, she found Kasyapa immediately claustrophobic.

Ben Roach was swallowed up by the family he had left behind, two whole new generations of nephews and nieces and grand-nephews and grand-nieces.

And here, of course, was Lena Roach. She had become a small, precise woman whose silences suggested great depths. She hadn't seen her husband, Ben, for a hundred of her years, for most of her long life. But she had waited for him, built a home in the most unforgiving of environments.

It was immediately clear she still loved Ben, and he loved her, despite the gulfs of time that separated them. Madeleine watched their calm, deep reunion with awe and envy. It was like grandmother greeting grandson, like wife meeting husband, complex, multi-layered.

She explored fitfully, moodily.

It was obvious to her that the colony was failing.

The people were thin, their skins pale. Malnourished, they were spectres in the dim sunlight. People moved slowly, despite the welcoming gentleness of the gravity. Energy was something to be conserved.

263

There was an atmosphere of a prison here. These had once been people of openness, of the endless desert, she reminded herself. Now they were confined here, inside this icy warren. She thought that must be hurting them, perhaps on a level they didn't appreciate themselves.

There were few children.

The people of Kasyapa were welcoming, but she found they were locked into tight family groups. She would always be an outsider here.

Madeleine spent a lot of time alone, cooped up in her ice-walled box. She engaged in peculiar time-delayed conversations with Nemoto; with a minimum of ten hours between comment and reply, it was more like receiving mail. Still, they spoke. And gradually Nemoto revealed the deeper purpose she had concocted for Madeleine.

'These people are starving,' Nemoto whispered. 'And yet they are sitting on a frozen ocean . . .'

Triton was, Nemoto told her, probably the solar system's most remote significant and accessible cache of water, within the Kuiper Belt anyhow. She said that Robert Goddard, the American rocketry pioneer, had proposed – in a paper called 'The Last Migration' – that Triton could be used as an outfitting and launching post for interstellar expeditions. 'That was in 1927,' Nemoto said.

'Goddard was a far-sighted guy,' Madeleine murmured.

'. . . Even if he got it wrong,' Nemoto was saying – had said, five hours earlier. 'Even if, as it turns out, Triton will be used as a staging post for expeditions *from* the stars. And not used by us, but by Eeties. The Gaijin.'

But the ocean under Madeleine's feet, tens of kilometres thick, was useless to the colonists as long as it was frozen hard as rock.

'Imagine if we could melt that ocean,' Nemoto said, her face an expressionless mask.

But how? The sun was too remote. Of course the sunlight could be collected, by mirrors or lenses. But how big would such a mirror have to be? Thousands of kilometres wide, more? Such a project seemed absurd.

'It's not the way humans work,' Madeleine said gloomily. 'Look at the colonists here, burrowing like ants. We're small and weak. We have to take the worlds as they are given to us, not rebuild them.'

'. . . And yet,' came Nemoto's reply many hours later, 'that is exactly what we must do if we are to prevail. We are going to have to act more like Gaijin than humans.'

Nemoto had a plan. It involved diverting a moon called Nereid, slamming it into Triton.

Madeleine was immediately outraged. This was arrogance indeed.
But she let Nemoto's data finish downloading.

It was a remarkable, bold scheme. The rocket engines which had
brought the colonists here would now be used to divert a moon. The
numbers added up. It could be done, Madeleine realized reluctantly.
It would take a year, no more.

It was also, Madeleine thought, quite insane. She pictured Nemoto,
stranded centuries out of her time, isolated, skulking in corners of the
Moon, concocting mad schemes to hurl outer-planet moons back and
forth, an old woman fighting the alien invasion, single-handed.

And yet, and yet . . .

She looked inward. What is it *I* want?

All her family, the people she had grown up with, were lost in the
past, on a frozen world. She was rootless. And yet she had no pull to
join this tight community, had felt no envy of Ben when Lena had
recaptured him, on his arrival here. Her life had become a series of
episodes, as she'd drifted through scenes of a more-or-less incomprehensible history. Was it even possible to sustain a consistent motivation
– to find something to want?

Yes, she realized. It isn't necessary to be picaresque. Look at Nemoto. *She* still knows what she wants, the same as she always did, after
all these years. Maybe the same applied to Reid Malenfant, wherever
he was. And maybe that was why Madeleine was attracted to Nemoto's
projects – not for the worth of the work, but for Nemoto's singular
strength of mind.

She went to discuss it with Ben. His first reaction was like hers.

'What you're proposing is barbaric,' Ben said. 'You talk of smashing
one moon into another. You will destroy both.'

'It's technically feasible. Nemoto's numbers prove that a deflection
of Nereid by the thruster systems from the orbiting transports would –'

'I'm not talking about feasibility. Many things are feasible. That
doesn't make them right. Once Triton is changed, it is changed forever.
Who knows what future, wiser generations might have made of these
resources we expend so carelessly?'

'But the Gaijin are on their way now.'

'We wreck this world, or they do. Is that the choice you offer?'

'Triton is ours to wreck, not theirs!'

He considered. He said at length, 'I will concede your plan has one
positive outcome.'

'What?'

'We are barely surviving here. The Yolgnu. That much is obvious. Perhaps with what you intend –'

She nodded. 'It will work, Ben.'

'There will be a lot of opposition. People have been living here for generations. This is their home. As it is.'

'I know. It's going to be hard for all of us.'

'What will you do now?'

She considered. She hadn't thought it through that far. 'We can send probes to Nereid,' she said. 'Survey the emplacements of the thrust units, perhaps even initiate the work. Ben, those Gaijin are on their way, whatever we do. If we leave this too long we might not be able to do anything anyhow.' She squinted up at the ice roof, imagining the abandoned ships circling overhead. 'We could even begin the deflection, start the thrusters. It will take a year of steady burning to set up the collision. But I'll initiate nothing irrevocable until you get agreement from your people.'

He said sadly, 'You started out your career as a transporter of weapons. And you are still transporting weapons.'

That irritated her. 'Look, Triton is a lifeless planet. There is nothing here but humans, and what we brought.'

He eyed her. 'Are you sure?'

After a couple of months, to Madeleine's surprise, Lena Roach had invited her to 'go walkabout', as she called it, to go see something more of Triton.

Madeleine was a little suspicious. She remained the focus of the colony's intense debate about its future; few people were so open with her that such offers didn't come with strings.

She spoke to Ben.

He laughed. 'Well, you're right. Everybody's got a point of view. Lena has her opinion. But what harm can it do to go out and see some ice?'

Madeleine thought it over for a day.

The Nereid project had begun. Ben had loaned her Kasyapa engineers to detach the engine units from the transport hulks in orbit around Triton, reconfigure them for operation on Nereid, improvise systems to extract fuel from the substance of the moon. She had a small monitoring station set up in her ice cell, which showed her, by telemetry and a visual feed, that sparse array of engines burning, twenty-four hours a day, consuming Nereid's own material as fuel and reaction propellant, slowly, slowly pushing the battered moon out of its looping ellipse. It was good to have a project, to be able to immerse herself in engineering detail.

But she would have a year to wait, even if Kasyapa's great debate concluded in an acceptance of her program. Ben, torn between his lost family and the endless work of the colony, had little time to spend with her. There were few people here, nowhere to escape, little to do. She still spent much of her time alone, in her ice cell, immersed in virtuals, reading up on the dismal history she had skipped over.

Getting out of here would be a good thing. She agreed to go along with Lena.

So they climbed aboard a surface tractor, a big balloon-tyre bubble.

At first they drove in silence, the tractor bouncing gently. Madeleine felt as if she was floating, all but naked, above Triton's ice ground. The sky was a velvet dome crowded with stars, and with that subtle, misty hull of Neptune riding at the zenith above their heads.

Lena was a small, compact woman, her movements patient and precise. She had been just twenty when Ben had departed for the Saddle Point. Her age was over a hundred and twenty years old, but, thanks to rejuvenation treatments, she might have been forty. But she didn't act forty, Madeleine thought; she acted old.

The ground was complex. The tractor's lights showed how the ice was stained pink, as if by traces of blood, and there were streaks of darker material laid over the surface. But here and there the dirty water-ice rock was overlaid by splashes of white, brilliant in the lights; this was nitrogen snow, fresh-fallen.

The land became more uneven. The tractor climbed a shallow ridge, and Madeleine found herself tipped precariously back in her seat. From the summit of the ridge she caught a glimpse of a landscape pocked by huge craters, each some thirty kilometres wide or more. But they weren't like impact craters; many of them were oval in shape.

The tractor plunged into the nearest crater. The ground broke up into pits and flows, like frozen mud, and the tractor bounced and floated in great leaps.

Lena said, 'This is the oldest surface on Triton. It covers perhaps a third of the surface. From orbit, the land looks like the surface of a cantaloupe melon, and that gave it its name. But this is difficult and dangerous terrain.' Her accent was odd, shaped by time, sounding strangulated to Madeleine. 'These "craters" are actually collapsed bubbles in the ice. They formed when the world froze . . . You know that Triton was once liquid?'

'After its capture.'

'Yes.'

'Neptune raised great tides in Triton. There was an ocean hundreds of kilometres deep – crusted over by a thin ice layer at its contact with the vacuum – that stayed liquid and warm, for half a billion years, as the orbit became a circle.'

Madeleine eyed her suspiciously. '*Life*. That's what you're getting at. Native life, here in the tidal melt of Triton.' Just as Ben had hinted. She wasn't surprised, or much interested. Life emerged wherever it could; everybody knew that. Life was a commonplace.

Lena said, 'You know, when we first came here we spread out from Kasyapa, around this little world.'

'You sang Triton.'

'Yes.' Lena smiled. 'We made our roads with orbiting lasers, and we named the cantaloupe hollows and the snow fields and the craters. We were exhilarated, on this empty world. *We* were the Ancestors! But we grew – discouraged. Nothing moves here, save bits of ice and snow and gas. Nothing lives, save us. There aren't even bones in the ground. Soon we found we had to ration food, energy, air. We mapped from orbit, sent out robots.'

'Robots don't sing.'

'No. But there is nothing to sing here . . .'

Madeleine, with a sudden impulse, covered Lena's hand with her own. 'Perhaps one day. And perhaps there was life in the deep past.'

'You don't yet understand,' Lena said, frowning. She tapped a control pad and the motor gunned.

The tractor followed complex ridge pathways, heading steadily away from Kasyapa.

They talked desultorily, about planetary formation, Lena's long life on Triton, Madeleine's strange experiences among the stars. They were exploring each other, Madeleine thought; and perhaps that was the purpose of this jaunt.

Lena knew, of course, about Ben's relationship with Madeleine. At length they talked about that, tentatively.

Lena had known about it long before Ben had left for the stars. She knew such things were inevitable, even necessary, in a separation that crossed generations. She herself had taken lovers, even an informal second husband, with whom she'd raised children. The ties of *galay* and *dhuway* were, she said, too strong to be broken by mere time and space.

Madeleine found she liked Lena. She still wasn't sure if she envied Lena the ties she shared with Ben. To be bound by such powerful

268

bonds, for a lifetime of indefinite duration, seemed claustrophobic to her. Perhaps I've been isolated too long, she thought.

After some hours they reached a polar cap. It turned out to be a region of cantaloupe terrain, where every depression was filled with nitrogen snow. They camped here, near the pole, on the fringe of interstellar space. Overhead, Madeleine saw cirrus clouds of nitrogen ice crystals.

The pole was a dangerous place to walk. She saw evidence of geysers: huge pits blasted clean of snow, and dark streaks across the land, tens of kilometres long, like the remnants of gigantic roads. All of this under Neptune's smoky light, and a rich dazzle of stars.

This was an enchanting world. Madeleine found herself, reluctantly, falling in love with Triton.

Reluctantly, because, she was coming to realize, she would have to destroy this place.

Lena brought her, on foot, to a small unmanned science station, painted bright yellow so it stood out from the pinkish snow.

'We are running a seismic survey,' she said. 'There are stations like this all over Triton. Every time we shake the surface, by so much as a footstep, waves travel through this world's frozen interior, and we can deduce what lies there.'

'. . . And?'

'You understand that Triton is a ball of rock, overlaid by an ocean – a frozen ocean. But ice is not simple.' Lena picked up a loose fragment of ice, and cupped it in her gloved hands. '*This* form is called ice I. It is the familiar form of ice, just as on Earth's surface.' She squeezed tighter. 'But if I were to crush it, eventually the crystal structure would collapse to an alternative, more closely packed, arrangement of molecules.'

'Ice II.'

'Yes. But that is not the end. There is a whole series of stable forms, reached with increasing pressure, the crystal structure more and more distorted from the pure tetrahedral form of ice I. And so, inside Triton, there are a series of layers: ice I at the surface, where we walk, all the way to a shell of ice VIII, which overlays the rocky core . . .'

Madeleine nodded, not very interested.

The snows seemed to be layered. The deeper she dug with her booted toe, the richer the purple-brown colours of the sediment strata she uncovered. This hemisphere was entering its forty-year spring, and the polar cap was evaporating; thin winds of nitrogen would eventually carry all this cap material to the other pole, where it would snow out.

And later, when it was autumn here, the flow was reversed. Triton's atmosphere was not permanent: it was only the polar caps in transit, from one axis to another.

But Lena was still talking. '. . . large scale rebuilding of the planet is the same as –'

Madeleine held up her hands. 'You left me behind. What are you telling me, Lena?'

'That there is evidence of tampering, planetary tampering, from the deepest past, here on Triton.'

Madeleine felt chilled. 'Even here?'

'Just like Venus. Just like Earth. Nothing is primordial. Everything has been shaped.'

That inner layer of ice VIII was no crude seam of compressed mush. It was very pure. And it seemed to have been sculpted.

When they got back to the tractor Lena showed Madeleine diagrams, seismic maps. The core had facets – triangles, hexagons – each kilometres wide. 'It's as if somebody encased the core in a huge jewel,' she said. 'And it must have been done before the general freezing.'

'Somebody came here,' Madeleine said slowly, 'and – somehow, manipulating temperature and pressure in that deep ocean – froze out this cage around the sea bed.'

'Yes.'

'And the life forms there –'

'Immediately destroyed, of course, their nutrient supply blocked, their very cells broken open by the freezing. We can see them, their relics, in the deep samples we have taken.'

Madeleine felt a deep, unreasoning anger well up in her. 'Why would anybody do such a thing?'

Lena shrugged. 'Perhaps it was not malice. *They* may have had a mission – insane, but a mission. Perhaps *they* thought they were helping these primitive Triton bugs. Perhaps *they* wished to spare the bugs the pain of growth, change, evolution, death. This great crystal structure encodes very little information. You need only a few bits to characterize its composition – pure ice VIII – and its regular, repeating structure. It is static, perfect – even incorruptible. Life, on the other hand, requires a deep complexity. It is this complexity which gives us our potential, and our pain. Perhaps, you see, they felt pity.'

Madeleine frowned. 'Lena, did Ben encourage you to show me this? Are you trying to persuade me to back off the Nereid project?'

Lena said, 'Ben and I have different experiences. He travelled to the stars, and saw many things. I worked here. Helping to uncover this strange, ancient tragedy.'

Yes. There was no need to go to the stars, Madeleine saw now. It was *here*, all the time, on Venus and Triton and God-knows-where, and even Earth. The central paradoxical mystery of the universe. Everywhere, life emergent. Everywhere, life crushed. And no explanation *why* it had to be this way. Over and over.

She felt her anger burn brighter. She had made her own decision. This wasn't simply what Nemoto wanted. It had become what *she* wanted. And that burning desire felt good.

Lena smiled, gnomic, wise.

By the time they got back to Kasyapa, the flower-ships had grown in Triton's sky, until at last their delicate filigree structure was visible, just, with the naked eye. The same fucking Gaijin who had watched as Earth had gone to hell.

She sailed up to orbit, boarded *Gurrutu*, and headed for Nereid.

Madeleine first sighted Nereid ten days out. It grew rapidly, day by day, finally hour by hour, until its battered grey hide filled the viewing windows.

Rendezvous with the hurtling rock was difficult. The *Gurrutu* couldn't muster the velocity change required to match Nereid's crashing orbit. So Madeleine had to burn her engines and use tethers, harpooning this great rock whale as it hurtled past, letting her ship be dragged along with it. *Gurrutu* suffered considerable damage, but nothing significant enough to make Madeleine abort.

She entered a loose, slow orbit, inspecting the moon's surface. Nereid was uninteresting: just a misshapen ball of dirty ice, pocked by craters; it was so small it had never melted, never differentiated into layers of rock and ice like Triton, never had any genuine geology. Nereid was a relic of the past, a ruin of the more orderly moon system that had been wrecked when Triton was captured.

But, despite its small size, it massed as much of five per cent of Triton's own bulk. And where Triton's orbit, though retrograde, was neatly circular, Nereid followed a wide, swooping ellipse, taking almost an Earth year to complete a single one of its 'months' around Neptune.

Nereid could be driven head-on into Triton. It would be a useful bullet.

She navigated with automatic star trackers, with radio Doppler fixes on Kasyapa, and by eye, using a sextant. Her purpose was to check the trajectory of the little moon, backing up the automated systems with this on-the-spot eyeballing, which, even now, was one of the most precise navigation systems known.

Nereid was right on the button. But this game of interplanetary pool was played on a gigantic table, and Triton was a small target. Even now, even so close, Nereid could be deflected from its impact.

At times the cold magnitude of the project – sending one world to impact another – awed her. *This is too big for us. This is a project for the arrogant ones: the Gaijin, the others who strangled Venus and Triton.*

But, when she was close enough, she could see the glow of engines on Nereid's far side: engines built by humans, placed by humans. Placed by *her*. She clung to her anger, seeking confidence.

Even now Ben debated the ethics of the situation with his people. Most people here had been born long after the emigration: born in the caverns of Kasyapa, now with children of their own. To them, Madeleine and Ben Roach were intruders from the muddy pool at the heart of the solar system, invaders from another time who proposed to smash their world. *The shortness of human lives, she thought; our curse. Every generation thinks it is immortal, that it has been born into a world that has never changed, and will never change.*

She slept in her sleeping compartment, a box little larger than she was. Inside, however, tucked into her sleeping bag with the folding door drawn to, she felt comfortable and secure. She would track Nereid as long as she could, guiding it to its destination, unless she was ordered to stand down.

She got a number of direct calls from Nemoto which she did not accept. Nemoto was irrelevant now.

At the very last minute Ben came through.

Somewhat to her surprise, the colonists had agreed to let the project go ahead. Ben would arrange for the temporary evacuation of the colonists from Kasyapa, to the hulks of the old transport ships still in orbit, now drifting without their engines.

'Lena is pleased,' he told her.

'Pleased?'

'By your reaction to the crystal shell around the core. The ice VIII. She wanted to make you angry. If the project succeeds then the crystal shell will be destroyed. And the last trace of the native life will surely be destroyed with it.'

Madeleine growled, '*I know*, Ben. I always knew. The Triton bugs lost their war a long time ago, before they even had a chance to voice an opinion. Their memory should motivate us, not stop us. The crystal builders have gone, but the Gaijin are on their way, here, now. Well, the hell with them. This is the trench we've dug, and we aren't going to quit it.'

'If,' he said, 'the Gaijin are the true enemy.'

'They will do for now.'

He smiled sadly. 'You sound like Nemoto.'

'None of us age gracefully. Why didn't you tell me about the native life, Ben?'

His virtual image shrugged. 'Not everybody who's grown up here knows about it. Life is hard enough here without people learning that there is an alien artefact of unknown antiquity buried at the heart of the world.'

She nodded. And yet he hadn't answered her question. Despite all we've been through – even though we're both refugees from another age, and we travelled to the stars together – I'm not close enough for you to share your secrets.

At that moment, she felt the ties between them stretch, break. Now, she thought, I am truly alone; I have lost my only companion from the past. It was surprising how little it hurt.

'Here is another possibility,' Ben said. 'Beyond ethics, beyond this perceived conflict with the Gaijin. You like to meddle, to smash things, Madeleine. You are like Nereid yourself, a rogue retrograde body, come to smash our little community. Perhaps this is why the plan is so appealing to you.'

'Perhaps it is,' she said, irritated. 'You'll have to judge my psychology for yourself.'

And with an angry stab, she shut down the comms link.

Alone in *Gurrutu*, she assembled a complete virtual projection of Triton, a three-dimensional globe a metre across. She looked for the last time at the ice surface of Triton, the subtle shadings of pink and white and brown.

She switched to a viewpoint at Triton's evacuated equator. It was as if she was standing on Triton's surface.

Nereid was supposed to do two things: to spin up Triton, and to melt its ancient oceans. Therefore she had steered the moon to come in at a steep angle, to deliver a sideways slap along Triton's equator. And so, when she turned her virtual head, Nereid was looming low on the horizon: a lumpy, battered moon, visibly three-dimensional, rotating, growing minute by minute.

An icon in the corner of her view recorded a steady countdown. She deleted it. She'd always hated countdowns.

Her imaging systems picked out Gaijin flower-ships in low orbit around the moon, golden sparks arcing this way and that. She smiled. So the Gaijin were curious too. Let them watch. It would be, after all, the greatest impact in the solar system since the end of the primordial bombardment.

Quite a show. And for once it would be humans lighting up the sky.

The end, when it came, seemed brutally fast. Nereid grew from a spot of darkness, to a pebble, to a patch of rock the size of her hand, to, *Jesus*, a roof of rock over the world, and then –

Blinding light. She gasped.

The image snapped back to an overview of the moon. She felt as if she had died and come back to life.

A plume of fragments was rising vertically from Triton's surface, like one last mighty geyser: bits of red hot rock, steam, glittering ice, some larger fragments that soared like cannonballs.

Nereid was gone.

Much of the little moon's substance must already have been lost, rock and ice and rich organic volatiles blasted to vapour in that first second of impact: lost forever, lost to space. Perhaps it would form a new, temporary ring around Neptune; perhaps eventually, centuries from now, some of it would rain back on Triton, or some other moon.

This was an astoundingly inefficient process, she knew, and that had been a key objection of some of the Kasyapa factions. *To burn up a moon, a whole four-billion-year-old moon, for such a poor gain is a crime.* Madeleine couldn't argue with that.

Except to say that this was war.

And now something emerged from the base of the plume. It was a circular shock wave, a wall of shattering ice like the rim of a crater, ploughing its way across the ground. The terrain it left behind was shattered, chaotic, and she could see the glint of liquid water there, steaming furiously in the vacuum and cold. Ice formed quickly, in sheets and floes, struggling to plate over the exposed water. But echoes of that great shock still tore at this transient sea, and immense plates, diamond white, arced far above the water before falling back in a flurry of fragments.

Now, in that smashed region – from cryovolcanoes kilometres wide – volatiles began to boil out of Triton's interior: nitrogen, carbon dioxide, methane, ammonia, water vapour. Nereid's heat was doing its work; what was left of the sister moon must be settling towards Triton's core, burning, melting, flashing to vapour. Soon a mushroom of thickening cloud began to obscure the broken, churning surface. Some of the larger fragments thrown up by that initial plume began to hurtle back from their high orbits, and burned streaks through Triton's temporary atmosphere. And when they hit the churning water-ice beneath, they created new secondary plumes, new founts of destruction.

The shock wall, kilometres high, ploughed on, overwhelming the ancient lands of ice, places where nitrogen frost still lingered. It was not going to stop, she realized now. The shock would scorch its way around the world. It would destroy all Triton's subtlety, churning up the nitrogen snows of the north, the ancient organic deposits of the south, disrupting the slow nitrogen weather, destroying forever the ancient, poorly understood cantaloupe terrain. The shock wall would be a great eraser, she thought, eliminating all of Triton's unsolved puzzles, four billion years of icy geology, in a few hours.

But those billowing ice-volcano clouds were already spreading in a great loose veil around the moon, the vapour reaching altitudes where it could outrun the march of the shattered ice. Mercifully, after an hour, Triton was covered, the death of its surface hidden under a layer of roiling clouds, within which lightning flashed, almost continually.

She heard from Ben that the Yolgnu were celebrating. *This* was Triton Dreamtime, the true Dreamtime, when giants were shaping the world.

After three hours there was a new explosion, a new gout of fire and ice from the far side of the moon. That great shock wave had swept right around the curve of the moon, until it had converged in a fresh clap of shattered ice at the antipode of the impact. Madeleine supposed there would be secondary waves, great circular ripples washing back and forth around Triton like waves in a bathtub, as the new ocean, seething, sought equilibrium.

Nemoto materialized before her.

'You improvised well, Madeleine.'

'Don't patronize me, Nemoto. I was a good little soldier.'

But Nemoto, of course, five hours away, couldn't hear her.

'. . . Triton is useless now to the Gaijin, who need solid ice and rock for their building programs. But it is far from useless to humans. This will still be a cold world; a thick crust of ice will form. But that ocean could, thanks to the residual heat of Nereid and Neptune's generous tides, remain liquid for a long time – for millions of years, perhaps. And Earth life could inhabit the new ocean. Lightly modified anyhow – deep sea creatures, able to live off the heat of Triton's churning core – plankton, fish, even whales. Triton, here on the edge of interstellar space, has become Earth-like. Imagine the future for these Aborigines,' Nemoto said, seductively. 'Triton was the son of Poseidon and Aphrodite. How apt . . .'

This was Nemoto's finest hour, Madeleine thought, this heroic effort to deflect – not just worlds – but the course of history itself. She tried to cling to her own feelings of triumph, but it was thin, lonely comfort.

'One more thing, Meacher.' Virtual Nemoto leaned towards her, intent, wizened. 'One more thing I must tell you . . .'

Later, she called Ben.

He asked, 'When are you coming home?'

'I'm not.'

Ben frowned at her. 'You are being foolish.'

'No. Kasyapa is your home, and Lena's. Not mine.'

'Then where? Earth? The Moon?'

'I am centuries out of my time,' she said. 'Not there, either.'

'You're going back to the Saddle Points. But you are the great Gaijin hater, like Nemoto.'

She shrugged. 'I oppose their projects. But I'll ride with them. Why not? Ben, they run the only ship out of port.'

'What do you hope to learn out there?'

She did not answer.

Ben was smiling. 'Madeleine, I always knew I would lose you to starlight.'

She found it hard to focus on his face, to listen to his words. He was irrelevant now, she saw. She cut the connection.

She thought over the last thing Nemoto had said to her. *Find Malenfant. He is dying . . .*

Chapter 23

CANNONBALL

It had to be the ugliest planet Madeleine had ever seen.

It was a ball the size of Earth, spinning slowly, lit up by an unremarkable yellow star. The land was a contorted, blackened mess of volcano calderas, rift and compression features, and impact craters that looked as if they had been punched into a metal block. Seas, lurid yellow, pooled at the shores of distorted continents. And the air was a thin, smoggy, yellowish wisp, littered with high mustard-coloured cirrus clouds.

On the planet there were no obvious signs of life or intelligence: no cities gleaming on the dark side, no ships sailing those ugly yellow oceans. But there were three Gaijin flower-ships in orbit here, Madeleine's and two others.

Her curiosity wasn't engaged.

All the Gaijin would tell her about the planet was the name they gave it – Zero-Zero-Zero-Zero – the name, and the reason they had brought her here, across a hundred light years via a hop-skip jump flight between Saddle Point gateways in half a dozen systems, a whole extra century deeper into the future: that they needed her assistance.

Malenfant is dying.

Reluctantly – after a year in transit, she had gotten used to her lonely life in her antique *Gurrutu* hab module – she collected her gear and clambered into a Gaijin lander.

Madeleine stepped onto the land of a new world.

Ridges in the hard crumpled ground hurt her feet. The air was murky grey, but more or less transparent; she could see the sun, dimmed to an unremarkable disc as if by high winter cloud. Immediately she didn't like it here. The gravity was high – not crushing, but enough to make her heavy-footed, the bio pack on her back a real burden.

Numbers scrolling across her faceplate told her the gravity was some forty per cent higher than Earth's. And, since this world was about the same size as Earth, that meant that its density had to be around forty per cent higher too: closer to the density of pure iron.

Earth was a ball of nickel-iron overlaid by a thick mantle of less dense silicate rock. The high density of *this* world must mean it had no rocky mantle to speak of. It was nickel-iron, all the way from core to surface, as if a much larger world had been stripped of its mantle and crust, and she was walking around on the remnant iron core.

That wasn't so strange. There were ways that could happen, in the violent early days of a system's formation, when immense rogue planetesimals continue to bombard planets that were struggling to coalesce. Mercury, the solar system's innermost planet, had suffered an immense primordial impact that had left that little world with the thinnest of mantles over its giant core.

At least human scientists had presumed it was primordial. Nobody was sure about such things any more.

She glanced around the sky. She was a hundred light years from home, a hundred light years in towards the centre of the Galaxy, roughly along a line that would have joined Earth to Antares, in Scorpio. But the sky was dark, dismal.

There were no asteroid belts, only a handful of comets left orbiting further out, and two gas giants both stripped of their volatiles, reduced to smooth rocky balls. She was well inside the interstellar colonization wavefront that appeared to be sweeping out along the spiral arm and was nearing Earth, a hundred light years back. And this was a typical post-wavefront system: colonized, ferociously robbed of its resources by one short-sighted, low-tech predatory strategy or another, trashed, abandoned.

Even the stars had been obscured, their light stolen by Dyson masks: dense orbiting habitat clouds, even solid spheres, asteroids and planets dismantled and made into traps for every stray photon. It was a depressing sight: an engineered sky, a sky full of scaffolding and ruins.

Earth's sky was primeval, comparatively. This was a glimpse of the future, for Earth.

She walked further, away from the lander, which was a silvery cone behind her. She was only a few kilometres from the shore of one of those yellow seas; she figured it was on the far side of a low, crumpled ridge.

She reached the base of the ridge and began to climb. In the tough gravity she was given a good workout; she could feel her temperature rising, the suit's exoskeletal multipliers discreetly cutting in to give her a boost.

She topped the ridge, breathing hard. A plain opened up before her: shaded red and black, littered by sand dunes and what looked like a big, heavily eroded impact crater. And off towards the smoky horizon, yes, there was that peculiar yellow ocean, wraiths of greenish mist hanging over it. It was a bizarre, surrealist landscape, as if all Earth's colours had been exchanged for their spectral complements.

And, only a hundred metres from the base of the ridge, she saw two Gaijin landers, silver cones side by side, each surrounded by fine rays of dust thrown out by landing rockets. Beside one of the landers was a Gaijin, utterly still, a spidery statue. Next to the other stood a human, in an exo-suit that didn't look significantly different to Madeleine's.

The human saw her, waved.

Madeleine hesitated for long seconds.

Suddenly the world seemed crowded. She hadn't encountered people since she last embraced Ben, on Triton. She'd certainly never met another traveller like this, among the stars. But it must have taken decades, even centuries, for the Gaijin to organize this strange rendezvous.

She began to clamber down the ridge towards the landers, letting the suit do most of the work.

The waving human turned out to be a Catholic priest, called Dorothy Chaum. Madeleine had met her before, subjective years ago. And inside one of the landers was another human, somebody she knew only by reputation.

It was Reid Malenfant. And he was indeed dying.

Malenfant was wasted. His head was cadaverous, the skull showing through thin, papery flesh, and his bald scalp was covered in liver-spots.

Dorothy and Madeleine got Malenfant suited up, and hauled him to Dorothy's lander. In this gravity it was hard work, despite their suits' multipliers. But Dorothy's lander had a more comprehensive med facility than Madeleine's. Malenfant had nothing at all, save what the Gaijin had been able to provide.

Malenfant had grown old, and had sunk into himself, like a tide going out, an ocean receding. He had managed to keep himself alive a good few years. But his equipment wasn't sufficient any more – and the Gaijin he travelled with sure didn't know enough about human biology to tinker. Not only that, he was suffering from the Discontinuity.

When he had started to die, the Gaijin were confounded.

'So they sent for us,' Dorothy Chaum said, marvelling. 'They sent signals out through the gateway links.'

'How did they keep him alive so long?'

'They didn't. They just preserved him. They bounced his signal around the Saddle Point network, never making him corporeal for more than a few seconds at a time . . .'

Madeleine studied Malenfant. Had he been aware, as he passed through one blue-flash gateway transition after another, of the light years and decades passing in seconds? Malenfant woke up while they were bed-bathing him. Stripped, washed, and immersed in a med tank. He looked Madeleine in the eyes. 'Are you *qualified* to be scrubbing my balls?'

'I'm the best you're going to find, pal.'

But now he was staring at Chaum, the diagrammatic white collar around her neck. 'What is this, the last rites?' He tried to struggle upright, on arms as thin as toothpicks.

Madeleine shoved him back. 'It will be if you don't cooperate.'

He swivelled that gaunt head. 'Where's my suit?'

Dorothy frowned, and pointed to the Gaijin-manufactured envelope they'd bundled up in one corner. 'Over there.'

'No,' he whispered. 'My *suit.*'

It turned out he meant his old NASA-era Shuttle EMU, a disgusting old piece of kit almost as far beyond its design limits as Malenfant himself. He wouldn't relax until Madeleine got suited up, went across to the lander that had brought him here, and retrieved the EMU for him. Then again, it was the only possession he had in the world, or worlds. She could understand how he felt.

He scrabbled in its pockets until he found a faded, much folded photograph, of a smiling woman on a beach.

When they had him in the tank, Madeleine spent a little time working on that gruesome old suit. She could fix the wiring shorts and the cooling-garment tubing leaks, polish out the scratches on the bubble helmet, patch the fabric. But she couldn't make it clean again; the dust of many worlds was ingrained too deep into the fabric. And she couldn't wash out the stink of Malenfant.

All the time, visible through the lander's windows, that Gaijin sat on the surface, as unmoving as a statue, watching, watching, as if waiting for Dorothy or Madeleine to make a mistake.

*   *   *

While Malenfant was sleeping off twenty subjective years of travelling, Dorothy Chaum and Madeleine took a walk, across the battered iron plain, towards the yellow sea.

They were each used to solitude and they were awkward, restless with each other – and with the notion that they'd been summoned here, given an assignment by the Gaijin. It didn't make for good conversation.

Dorothy was a short, squat woman, who looked as if she might have been built for this tough overloaded gravity. She seemed older than Madeleine remembered; her journey here had absorbed more of her subjective lifetime than Madeleine's had.

They passed the solitary Gaijin sentinel.

'Malenfant calls it *Cassiopeia*,' Dorothy murmured. 'He says it's been his constant companion since the solar system.'

'A boy and his Gaijin. Cute.'

Dorothy Chaum's personal star quest seemed to be a sublimated search for God. That was how it seemed to Madeleine, anyhow.

'I studied the Gaijin on Earth,' Dorothy said. Madeleine could see her smile. 'You remember that, on Kefallinia. I got my initial assignment from the Pope . . . I don't even know if there is a Pope any more. The Gaijin have some things in common with us. Sure, they are robot-like creatures, but they are finite, built on about the same scale as we are, and they seem to have at least some individuality. But in spite of their similarity – or maybe because of it – I was immediately overwhelmed by their strangeness. So I was drawn to follow them to the stars, to work with them.'

'And have you discovered yet if a Gaijin has a soul?'

Dorothy didn't seem offended. 'I don't know if that question has any meaning. Conversely, you see, the Gaijin seem fascinated by *our* souls. Perhaps they are envious . . .'

Dorothy stopped dead, and held out one hand. Madeleine saw there was some kind of black snow, or a thin rain of dust, settling on the white of her glove palm. 'This is carbon,' Dorothy said. 'Soot. Just raining out of the air. Remarkable.'

Madeleine supposed it was.

They walked on through the strange exotic air.

Madeleine prompted, 'So you travelled with the Gaijin to try to understand.'

'Yes. As I believe Malenfant did.'

'And did you succeed?'

'I don't think so. What may be more serious,' she said, 'is that I

281

don't think the Gaijin are any closer to finding whatever it is *they* were seeking.'

They reached the shore of the sea. It was a hard beach, loosely littered with rusty sand, and blackened with soot, as if worn away from some offshore seam of coal.

The ocean was very yellow. The liquid was thin and it seemed to bubble, as if carbonated. Further out, mist banks hung, dense and heavy. Seeing this garish sea recede to a sharp yellow horizon was eerie.

They stepped forward, letting the liquid lap over their boots. It left a fine gritty scum, and it felt cool, not cold. Vapour sizzled around Madeleine's feet.

Dorothy dipped a gloved finger into the sea, and data chattered over her visor. 'Iron carbonyl,' she murmured. 'A compound of iron with carbon monoxide.' She pointed at the vapour. 'And *that* is mostly nickel carbonyl. A lower boiling point than the iron stuff...' She sighed. 'Iron compounds, an iron world. On Earth, we used stuff like this in industrial processes, like purifying nickel. Here, you could go swimming in it.'

'I wonder if there is life here.'

'Oh, yes,' Dorothy said. 'Of course there is life here. Don't you know where you are?'

Madeleine didn't reply.

Dorothy said, 'That's where the soot and the carbon dioxide comes from. I think there must be some kind of photosynthesis going on, making carbon monoxide. And then the monoxide reacts with itself to make free carbon and carbon dioxide. That reaction releases energy –'

'Which animals can use.'

'Yes.'

'There is life everywhere we look,' Madeleine said.

'Yes. Life seems to be emergent from the very fabric of the universe which contains us, hard-wired into physical law. And so, I suppose, mind is emergent too. *Emergent monism:* a nice label. Though we can scarcely claim understanding...'

They stepped back on the shore, and walked further across the rusty dirt without enthusiasm.

Then they saw movement.

There was something crawling out of the sea. It was like a crab. It was low and squat, about the size of a coffee table, with a dozen or more spindly legs, and what must be sensors – eyes, ears? – complex little pods on the end of flimsy stalks that waved in the murky air. The whole thing was the colour of rust.

And it had a dodecahedral body.

Madeleine could hear it wheezing.

'Lungs,' Dorothy said. 'It has lungs. But – look at those slits in the carapace there. Gills, you think?'

'It's like a lungfish.'

The crab was clumsy, as if it couldn't see too well, and its limbs slid about over the bone-hard shore. One of those pencil-thin legs caught in a crack, and snapped off. That hissing breath became noisier, and it hesitated, waving a stump in the air.

Then the crab moved on, picking its way over the beach, as if searching for something.

Dorothy bent and, fumbling with her gloved fingers, picked up the snapped-off limb. It looked simple: just a hollow tube, a wand. But there was a honeycomb structure to the interior wall. 'Strength and lightness,' she said. 'And it's made of iron.' She smiled. 'Iron bones. Natural robots. We always thought the Gaijin must have been manufactured, by creatures more or less like us – the first generation of them anyway. It was hard to take seriously the idea of such mechanical beasts evolving naturally. But perhaps that's what happened . . .'

'What are you talking about?'

She eyed Madeleine. 'You really don't know where you are? Didn't the Gaijin tell you?'

Madeleine had an aversion to chatting to Gaijin. She kept her counsel.

Dorothy said, 'This iron world is Zero-Zero-Zero-Zero, Madeleine. The origin of the Gaijin's coordinates, the place their own colonization bubble started. *The place they came from.* No wonder they brought Malenfant here, if they thought he was going to die.'

Madeleine felt no surprise, no wonder, no curiosity. *So what?* 'But if that's so, where are they all?'

Dorothy sighed. 'I guess the Gaijin are no more immune to the resource wars, and the predatory expansion of others, than we are.'

'*Even the Gaijin?*' The notion of the powerful, enigmatic, star-spanning Gaijin as victims was deeply chilling.

Dorothy said, 'If this is a robotic lungfish, maybe life here got pushed back into the oceans by the last wave of visitors. Maybe this brave guy is trying to take back the land, at last.'

The crab thing seemed to have reached its highest point, attained the objective of its strange expedition. It stood there on the rusty beach for long minutes, waving those eye-stalks in the air. Madeleine wondered if it even knew they were here, if it recognized the Gaijin as its own remote descendant.

Then it turned and crawled back into the yellow ocean, step by step, descending into that fizzing, smoky liquid with a handful of bubbles.

'The Gaijin are not like us,' Malenfant whispered. He was sitting propped up by cushions in a chair, wrapped in a blanket. He was bird-thin. They had had to bring him back to his own lander; after so long alone he had gotten too used to it, missed it too much. 'Cassiopeia is constantly in flux,' he said. '"Cassiopeia" is just the name I gave her, after all. Her *own* name for herself is something like a list of catalogue numbers for her component parts – with a breakdown for subcomponents – *and* a paper trail showing their history. A manufacturing record, not really a name. She constantly replaces parts, panels, internal components, switching them back and forth. So her name changes. And so does her identity . . .'

'*Your* cells wear out, Malenfant,' Dorothy said gently. 'Every few years there is a new you.'

'But not as fast as *that*. It's the way they breed, too – if you can call it that. Two or more of them will donate parts, and start assembling them, until you got a whole new Gaijin, who goes off to the store room to get the pieces to finish herself off. A whole new person. Now, where does *she* come from?' He sighed. 'They have continuity of memory, consciousness, but identity is fluid for them: you can divide it forever, or even mix it up. You see it when they debate. There's no persuasion, no argument. They just – *merge* – and make a decision. But the Gaijin are cautious,' he said slowly. 'They are rational, they consider every side of every argument, they sometimes seem paralysed by indecision.'

'Like Balaam's Ass,' Dorothy said, smiling. 'Couldn't decide between two identical bales of hay.'

Madeleine asked, 'What happened?'

'Starved to death.'

Malenfant went on, as if talking to himself, 'They aren't like us. They don't glom onto a new idea so fast as we do –'

Dorothy said, 'Their minds are not receptive to memes. They have no sense of self –'

'But,' Malenfant said, 'the Gaijin are *interested* in us. Don't know why, but they are. And creatures *like* us. Religious types. Folks who

284

mount crusades and kill each other and even sacrifice their lives, for an idea.'

Madeleine remembered the Chaera, orbiting their black hole God, futilely worshipping it. Maybe Nemoto had been right; maybe it hadn't been black hole technology the Gaijin were interested in, but the Chaera themselves. But – why?

Dorothy leaned forward. 'Have the Gaijin ever talked about creatures like us? What becomes of us?'

'I gather we mostly wipe ourselves out. Or think ourselves to extinction. Memes against genes. That's if the colonization wars don't get us first.' He opened his rheumy eyes. 'Earth, the solar system, might be swept aside by the incoming colonists. It's happened before, and will happen again. *But it isn't the whole story*. It can't be.'

Dorothy was nodding. 'Equilibrium. Uniformity. Nemoto's old arguments.'

Madeleine didn't understand.

Malenfant smiled toothlessly at her. '*Why* does it have to be this way? That's the question. Endless waves of exploitation and trashing, everybody getting driven back down to the level of pond life . . . You'd think somebody would learn better. What stops them all?

'If what stopped an expansion was war, you'd have to assume that there are *no* survivors of such a war – not a single race, not a single breeding population. Or, if intelligent species are trashed by eco collapse, you have to assume that *every* species inevitably destroys itself that way.

'You see the problem. We can think of a hundred ways a species might get itself into trouble. But whatever destructive process you come up with, it has to be *one hundred per cent* effective. If a single species escapes the net, wham, it covers the Galaxy at near-lightspeed.

'But we don't see that. What we see is a Galaxy that fills up with squabbling races – and then *blam*. Some mechanism drives them *all* back down to the pond. There has to be something else, some other mechanism. Something that destroys them *all*. A Reboot.'

'A Galaxy-wide sterilization,' Madeleine murmured.

'And,' Chaum said, 'that explains Nemoto's first-contact equilibrium.'

'Yeah,' Malenfant said. '*That's* why they come limping around the Galaxy in dumb-ass ramscoops and teleport gates and the rest, time after time; that's why nobody has figured out, for instance, how to bust lightspeed, or build a wormhole. Nobody lasted long enough. Nobody had the *chance* to get smart.'

Madeleine stood, stretching in the dense gravity of this Cannonball world. She looked out the window at the dismal, engineered sky.

Could it be true? Was there something out there even more ferocious than the world-shattering aliens whose traces humans had encountered over and over, even in their own solar system? – some dragon that woke up every few hundred megayears, and roared so loud it wiped the Galaxy clean of advanced life?

And – how long before the dragon woke up again?

Madeleine said, 'You think the Gaijin know what it is? Are they trying to do something about it?'

'I don't know,' Malenfant said. 'Maybe. Maybe not.'

Madeleine growled, 'If they are just as much victims as we are, why don't they just *tell* us what they are doing?'

Malenfant closed his eyes, as if disappointed by the question. 'We're dealing with the alien here, Madeleine. They don't see the universe the way we do – not at all. They have their own take on things, their own objectives. It's amazing we can communicate at all when you think about it.'

'But,' Madeleine said, 'they don't want to go through a Reboot.'

'No,' he conceded. 'I don't think they want that.'

Dorothy said, 'Perhaps this is the next step, in the emergence of life and mind. Species working together, to save themselves. We need the Gaijin's steely robotic patience, just as they need us, our humanity . . .'

'Our faith?' Madeleine asked gently.

'Perhaps.'

Malenfant laughed, cynically. 'If the Gaijin know, they aren't telling me. They came to *us* for answers, remember.'

Madeleine shook her head. 'That's not good enough, Malenfant. Not from you. You're special to the Gaijin, somehow. You were the first to come out and confront them, the human who's spent longest with them.'

'And they saved your life,' Dorothy reminded him. 'They brought us here, to save you. You were dying.'

'I'm still dying.'

Madeleine said, 'Somehow you're important, Malenfant. You're the key.' Right there, right then, she had a powerful intuition that must be true.

But the key to what?

He held up skeletal hands, mocking. 'You think they're appointing me to save the Galaxy? Bullshit, with all respect.' He rubbed his eyes, lay on his side, and turned to face the lander's silver wall. 'I'm just an old fucker who doesn't know when to quit.'

But maybe, Madeleine thought, that's what the Gaijin cherish. Maybe they've been looking for somebody too stupid to starve to death, like that damn ass.

Dorothy said slowly, 'What *do* you want, Malenfant?'

'Home,' he said abruptly. 'I want to go home.'

Madeleine and Dorothy exchanged a glance.

Malenfant had been a long time away. He could return to the solar system, to Earth, if he wished. But they both knew that for all of them, home no longer existed.

IV

BAD NEWS
FROM THE STARS

AD 3265–3793

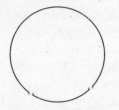

At the centre of the Galaxy there was a cavity, blown clear by the ferocious wind from a monstrous black hole. The cavity was laced by gas and dust, particles ionized and driven to high speeds by the ferocious gravitational and magnetic forces working here, so that streamers of glowing gas criss-crossed the cavity in a fine tracery. Stars had been born here, notably a cluster of blue-hot young stars just a fraction away from the black hole itself.

And here and there rogue stars fell through the cavity – and they dragged streaming trails behind them, glowing brilliantly, like comets a hundred light years long.

Stars like comets.

He exulted. I, Reid Malenfant, got to see *this*, the heart of the Galaxy itself, by God! He wished Cassiopeia were here, his companion during those endless Saddle Point jaunts to one star after another . . .

Again, at the thought of Cassiopeia, his anger flared.

But the Gaijin were never our enemy, not really. They learned patience among the stars. They were just trying to figure it all out, step by step, in their own way.

But it took too long for us.

It was after all a long while before we could even see the rest of them, the great wave of colonizers and miners that followed the Gaijin, heading our way along the Galaxy's spiral arm.

The wave of destruction.

Chapter 24

KINTU'S CHILDREN

Two hundred kilometres above the glowing Earth, a Gaijin flower-ship folded its electromagnetic wings. Drone robots pulled a scuffed hab module out of the ship's stringy structure, and launched it on a slow, precise trajectory towards the Tree.

Malenfant, inside the module, watched the Tree approach.

The bulk of the Tree, orbiting the Earth, was a glowing green ball of branches and leaves, photosynthesizing busily. It trailed a trunk, hollowed-out and sealed with resin, that housed most of the Tree's human population. Long roots trailed in the upper atmosphere: there were crude scoops to draw up raw material for continued growth, and cables of what Malenfant eventually learned was superconductor, generating power by being dragged through Earth's magnetosphere.

The Tree was a living thing twenty kilometres long, rooted in air, looping around Earth in its inclined circular orbit, maintaining its altitude with puffs of waste gas.

It was, Malenfant thought, ridiculous. He turned away, incurious.

He had been away from Earth for twelve hundred years, and had returned to the impossible date of AD 3265.

Malenfant was exhausted. Physically he was, after all, more than a hundred years old. And because of the depletion of the Saddle Point links between Zero-Zero-Zero-Zero and Earth, he had been forced to take a roundabout route on the way back here.

All he really wanted, if he was truthful, was to get away from strangeness: just settle down in his 1960s ranch house at Clear Lake, Houston, and pop a few beers, eat potato chips and watch *Twilight Zone* reruns. But here, looking out at all this orbiting foliage, he knew that wasn't possible, that it never would be. It was just as Dorothy Chaum had tried to counsel him, before they said their goodbyes back on the Cannonball. It was Earth down there, but it wasn't *his* Earth.

Malenfant was going to have to live with strangers, and strangeness, for whatever was left of his long and unlikely life.

At least the ice has gone, though, he thought.

His battered capsule slid to rest, lodging in branches, and Malenfant was decanted.

There was nobody to greet him. He found an empty room, with a window. There were *leaves,* growing around his window. On the *outside.*

Ridiculous. He fell asleep.

When Malenfant woke, he was in some kind of hospital gown.

He felt different. Comfortable, clean. He wasn't hungry or thirsty. He didn't even need a leak.

He lifted up his hand. The skin was comparatively smooth, the liver spots faded. When he flexed his fingers, the joints worked without a twinge.

Somebody had been here, done something to him. I didn't want this, he thought. I didn't ask for it. He cradled his resentment.

He propped himself up before his window, and looked out at Earth.

He could see its curve, a blue and white arc against black space. He made out a slice of pale blue seascape, with an island an irregular patch of grey and brown in the middle of it, and clouds scattered over the top, lightly, like icing sugar. He was so close to the skin of the planet that if he sat back the world filled his window, scrolling steadily past.

Earth was *bright:* brighter than he remembered. Malenfant used to be a Shuttle pilot; he knew Earth from orbit – how it used to be anyhow. Now he was amazed by the clarity of the atmosphere, even over the heart of continents. He didn't know if Earth itself had changed, or his memories of it. After all, his eyes were an old man's now: rheumy, filled with nostalgia.

One thing for sure, though. Earth looked empty.

When he passed over oceans he looked for ship wakes, feathering out like brush strokes. He couldn't see any. In the lower latitudes he could make out towns, a grey, angular patchwork, a tracery of roads. But no smog. No industries, then.

And in the higher latitudes, towards the poles, he could see no sign of human habitation at all. The land looked raw, fresh, scraped clean, the granite flanks of exposed mountains shining like burnished metal, and the plains were littered with boulders, like toys dropped by a child. His geography was always lousy, and now it was a thousand years out of date – but it seemed to him the coastlines had changed shape.

He wondered who, or what, had cleaned up the glaciation. Anyhow, it might have been AD 1000 down there, not 3265.

Two people came drifting into his room. Naked, all but identical, they were women, but so slim they were almost sexless. They had hair that floated around them, like Jane Fonda in *Barbarella*.

They were joined at the hip, like Siamese twins, by a tube of pink flesh.

They hadn't knocked, and he scowled at them. 'Who are you?'

They jabbered at him in a variety of languages, some of which he recognized, some not. Their arms and shoulders were big and well-developed, like tennis players, but their legs were wisps they kept tucked up beneath them. Microgravity adaptations. Their hair was blonde, but their eyes were almond-shaped, with folds of skin near the nose, like Chinese.

Finally they settled on heavily accented English.

'You must forgive stupidity.' 'We accommodate returning travellers –' '– from many time periods, spread across a millennium –' '– dating from Reid Malenfant himself.'

When they talked they swapped their speech between one and the other, like throwing a ball.

He said, 'In fact, I am Reid Malenfant.'

They looked at him, and then their two heads swivelled so that blank almond eyes stared into each other, their hair mingling. For these two, he thought, every day is a bad hair day.

'You must understand the treatment you have been given,' one said.

'I didn't want treatment,' he groused. 'I didn't sign any consent forms.'

'But your ageing was –' '– advanced.' 'We have no cure, of course.' 'But we can address the symptoms –' 'Brittle bones, loss of immunity, nervous degeneration.' 'In your case accelerated by –' 'Exposure to microgravity.' 'We reversed free radical damage with antioxidant vitamins.' 'We snipped out senescent cell clusters from your epidermis and dermis.' 'We reversed the intrusion of alien qualia into your sensorium, a side-effect of repeated Saddle Point transits.' 'We removed various dormant infectious agents which you might return to Earth.' 'We applied telomerase therapy to –'

'Enough. I believe you. I bet I don't look a day over seventy.'

'It was routine,' a Bad Hair Day twin said. They fell silent. Then: 'Are you truly Reid Malenfant?'

'Yes.'

*　　*　　*

The twins gave him food and drink. He didn't recognize any of the liquids they offered him, hot or cold; they were mostly like peculiar teas, of fruit or leaves. He settled on water, which was clean and cold and pure. The food was bland and amorphous, like baby food. The Bad Hair Day twins told him it was all processed algae, spiced with a little vacuum greenery from the Tree itself.

The twins pulled him gracefully through microgravity, along tunnels like wood-lined veins that twisted and turned, lit only by some kind of luminescence in the wood. It was like a fantasy spaceship rendered in carpentry, he thought.

There were a few dozen colonists here, living in bubbles of air inside the bulk of the Tree. They were all microgravity-adapted, as far as he could see, some of them even more evolved than the twins. There was one guy with a huge dome of a head over a shrivelled-up body, sticks of limbs, a penis like a walnut, no pubic hair. To Malenfant he looked like a real science fiction type of creation, like the boss alien in *Invaders from Mars*.

The people, however strange, looked young and healthy to Malenfant. Their skin was smooth, unwrinkled, unmarked save by tattoos; his own raisin-like face, the lines baked into it by years of exposure to Earth's weather and ultraviolet light and heavy gravity, was a curiosity here, a badge of exotica.

They all had almond eyes, folds of yellow skin.

As far as Malenfant could make out this was a kind of reverse colony from the near-Earth asteroids, which had been settled by descendants of Chinese. Out there, it seemed, there were great bubble habitats where everyone had lived in zero gravity for centuries.

Sometimes he thought he could hear a low humming, sniff a little ozone, feel hair-prickling static, as if he was surrounded by immense electrical or magnetic fields that tweaked at his body. Maybe it was so. Electromagnetic fields could be used to stimulate and stress muscles and bones, and even to counter bone wastage; NASA had experimented with such technologies. Maybe the Tree swaddled its human cargo in electricity, fixing their bones and muscles and flesh.

But maybe there was no need for such clunky gadgetry, a thousand years downstream. After all the Tree provided a pretty healthy environment, of clean air, pure water, toxin-free foods: no pollutants or poisons or pathogens here, and even natural hazards – like Earth's naturally-occurring radioactivity in soil and stone – could be designed out. Maybe if you gave people a good enough place to live, this was how they turned out, with health and longevity.

And as for adaptation to microgravity, maybe that came naturally too. After all, he recalled, the dolphins and other aquatic mammals had had no need of centrifuges or electro stimulation to maintain their muscles and bones in the no-gravity environment *they* inhabited. Maybe these space-dwelling humans had more in common with the dolphins than the bony dirt-treaders of his own kind.

The Tree itself had been gen-enged from giant ancestors on the Moon. Humans used the Tree for a variety of purposes: port, observation platform, resort. But the Tree's own purpose was simply to grow and survive, and there seemed no obstacle to its doing so until the sun itself flickered and died.

There was more than one Tree.

In 3265, Earth was encased in a spreading web of vegetation, space-going Trees and airborne spiders, reaching down from space to the surface. And, slowly, systems were evolving the other way. One day there might be some kind of unlikely biological ladder, reaching from Earth to space. It was a strategy to ensure long-term access from space via stable biological means. Nobody could tell Malenfant whose strategy this was, however.

The colonists in this Tree seemed to care for returning travellers like him with a breed of absent-minded charity. Beyond that, the twins' motive in speaking to him seemed to be a vague curiosity. Maybe even just politeness.

The Bad Hair Day twins' variant of English contained a fraction of words, a fifth or a quarter, that were unrecognizable to Malenfant. Linguistic drift, he figured. It had, after all, been a thousand years; he was Chaucer meeting Neil Armstrong.

They asked, 'Where did you travel?'

'I started at Alpha Centauri. After that I couldn't always tell. I kind of bounced around.'

'What did you find?'

He thought about that. 'I don't know. I couldn't understand much.'

It was true. But now – just as Madeleine Meacher and Dorothy Chaum had sought him out, saved his life on that remote Cannonball world without asking his by-your-leave – so the Bad Hair Day twins had thrust unwelcome youth on him. He felt *curious* again. Dissatisfied. Damn it, he'd gotten used to being old. It had been comfortable.

There were no other travellers here.

He soon got bored with the Tree, the incomprehensible artefacts and activities it contained. Lonely, disoriented, he tried to engage the Bad Hair Day twins, his enigmatic nurses. 'You know, I remember how Earth looked when I first went up in *Columbia,* back in '93. 1993, that is. In those days we had to ride these big solid rocket boosters up to orbit, you know, and then, and then . . .'

The twins would listen politely for a while. But then they would lock on each other, mouths pressed into an airtight seal, small hands sliding over bare flesh, their hair drifting in clouds around them, that bridge of skin between them folded and compressed, and Malenfant was just a sad old fart boring them with war stories.

If he was going back to Earth, where was he supposed to land?

He asked the Bad Hair Day twins for encyclopaedias, history books. The twins all but laughed at him. The people of AD 3265, it seemed, had forgotten history. The Bad Hair Day twins seemed to know little beyond their speciality, which was a limited – if very advanced – medicine. It was – disappointing. On the other hand, how much knowledge or interest had he ever had in the year AD 1000?

He got frustrated. He railed at the twins. They just stared back at him.

He would have to find out for himself.

He still had the softscreen-like sensor pack Sally Brind had given him centuries ago, when he set off for the Saddle Point to the Alpha Centauri system. It would work as a multi-spectral sensor. He could configure it to overlay the images of Earth with representations in infrared, ultraviolet, radar imaging, whatever he wanted; he could select for the signatures of rock, soil, vegetation, water, and the products of industrialization like heavy metals, pollutants.

Alone, he found a window and studied the planet.

Earth was indeed depopulated.

There were humans down there, but no communities bigger than a few tens of thousands. There were no industrial products, save for a thin smear of relics from the past, clustered around the old cities and strung out along the disused roads. He couldn't even see signs of large-scale agriculture.

Malenfant studied what was left of the cities of his day, those that had somehow survived the ice. New York, for example.

In AD 3265, New York was green. It was a woodland of birch and oak, pushing out of a layer of elder thicket. He could still make out the shapes of roads, city blocks and parking lots, but they were green rectangles, covered with mosses, lichens and tough, destructive plants like buddleia. On Manhattan, some of the bigger concrete buildings still stood, like white bones poking above the trees, but they were bereft of windows, their walls stained by fires. Others had subsided, reduced to oddly shaped hummocks beneath the greenery. The bridges had collapsed, leaving shallow weirs along the river. He could see foxes, bats, wolves. There were more exotic creatures, maybe descended from zoo stock: deer, feral pigs.

Some of the roads looked in good condition, oddly. Maybe the smart-concrete that was being introduced just before his departure from Earth had kept working. But the big multi-lane freeway that ran up out of Manhattan looked a little crazy to Malenfant, a wild scribble over grassed-over concrete. Maybe it wasn't just repairing itself but actually growing, crawling like a huge worm across the abandoned suburbs, a semi-sentient highway over which no car had travelled for centuries.

Once Malenfant saw what looked like a hunting party, working its way along the coast of the widened Hudson, stalking a thing like an antelope. The people were tall, naked, golden-haired. One of the hunters looked up to the sky, as if directly at Malenfant. It was a woman, her blue eyes empty. She had a neck like a shot-putter. Her face was, he thought, somehow not even human.

When Malenfant left Earth, a thousand years ago, he had left behind no direct descendants. His wife, Emma, had died before they had a chance to have children together. But he'd had relatives: a nephew, two nieces.

Now there was hardly anybody left on Earth. Malenfant wondered if anybody down there still bore a trace of his genes. And if so, what they had become.

For sentimental reasons he looked for the Statue of Liberty. Maybe it was washed up on the beach, like in *Planet of the Apes*. There was no sign of the old lady.

But he did find a different monument: an artefact kilometres across, a monstrous ring, slap in the middle of downtown Manhattan. It looked like a particle accelerator. Maybe it had something to do with the city's battle against the ice. Whatever, it didn't look human. It was out of scale.

There was other evidence of high technology, scattered around the planet; but it didn't seem to have much to do with humans either. For example, when the Tree drifted over the Pyrenees, the mountains on the crease of land between France and Spain, he could see a threading of light, perfect straight lines of ruby light, joining the peaks like a spider-web. His screen told him this was coherent light: lased. There were similar systems in other mountainous regions, scattered around the planet. The laser arrays worked continuously. Maybe they were adjusting the atmosphere somehow: burning out CFCs, for instance.

And he observed flashes from sites around the equator, on Earth's water hemisphere. A few minutes after each flash the air would get a little mistier. He estimated they must be coming every minute or so, on a global scale. He remembered twenty-first century schemes to increase Earth's albedo – to increase the percentage of sunlight reflected back into space – by firing sub-micrometre dust up into the stratosphere: naval guns could have done the job. The point was to reduce global warming. But the dust would settle out: you would have needed to fire a shot every few seconds, maintained for years – decades, even centuries. Back then the idea was ridiculed. But such dust injections would account for the increase in global brightness he thought he'd observed.

This was planetary engineering. All he could see from here were the gross physical schemes. Maybe down on the planet there was more: nanotechnological adjustments, for instance.

Somebody was fixing the Earth. It didn't look to Malenfant like it was anybody human. It would, after all, take centuries, maybe millennia. No human civilization could handle projects of that duration, or ever would be able to. So, give the job to somebody else.

Not every change was constructive.

In southern Africa there was a dramatic new crater. It looked like a scar in the greenery of the planet. He didn't know if it was some kind of meteorite scar, or an open-cast mine, kilometres wide. Machines crawled over the walls and pit of the crater, visibly chewing up shattered rock, extracting piles of minerals, metals. From space, the machines looked like spiders: dodecahedral bodies maybe fifty metres wide, with eight or ten articulated limbs, working steadily at this open wound in the skin of Earth.

Malenfant had seen such machines before. They were Gaijin factory drones, designed to chew up ice and rock. But now they weren't off in the asteroid belt or stuck out on the cold rim of the solar system, billions of kilometres away. The Gaijin were *here*, on the surface of Earth itself. He wondered what they were doing.

He looked further afield, seeking people, civilization.

The most populous place on the planet, it appeared, was some kind of mountain-top community in the middle of Africa. It was, as far as he could remember his geography, in Uganda.

And there was something odd about its signature in his sensor pack. From a source at the centre of the community he plotted heavy particles, debris from what looked like short half-life fission products. And there were some much more energetic particles: almost like cosmic rays.

But they came from a source embedded deep within Earth itself.

The only other similar sources, scattered around the planet, looked like deep radioactive-waste dumps.

The Ugandan community wasn't civilization, but it was the most advanced-looking technological trace on the planet. Population, and an enigma. Maybe that was the place for him to go.

The Bad Hair Day twins showed him a wooden spaceship. It was, good God, his atmospheric entry capsule. It was like a seed pod, a flattened sphere of wood a couple of metres across. It was fitted with a basic canvas couch, and a life support system – just crude organic filters – that would last a couple of hours, long enough for the entry. The pod even had a window, actually grown into the wood, a blister of some clear stuff like amber. He would have to climb in through a dilating diaphragm that would seal up behind him, like being born in reverse.

He spent some time hunting for the pod's heatshield. The Bad Hair Day twins watched, puzzled.

They kept him on orbit for another month or so, giving him gravity preparation: exercise, a calcium booster, electromagnetic therapy. They gave him a coverall of some kind of biocomposite material, soft to the touch but impossible to rip, smart enough to keep him at the right temperature. He packed inside the sphere his sole personal possession: his old Shuttle pressure suit, with its faded Stars and Stripes and the NASA logo, that he'd worn when he flew through that first gateway, a thousand AU from home, a thousand years ago. It was junk, but it was all he had.

He enjoyed a last sleep in weightlessness.

When he awoke the Tree was passing over South America. Malenfant could see the fresh water of the Amazon, noticeably paler than the salt of the ocean, the current so strong the waters had still failed to mingle hundreds of kilometres off shore.

He climbed inside his capsule. The Bad Hair Day twins kissed him, one soft face to either cheek, and sealed him up in warm brown darkness.

He was whiplashed out of the Tree by a flexing branch. A sensation of weight briefly returned to Malenfant, and he was pressed into his seat. When the cast-off was done, the weight disappeared.

But now the pod was no longer in a free orbit, but falling rapidly towards the air.

At the fringe of the atmosphere, the pod shuddered around him. He felt very aware of the lightness and fragility of this wooden nut-shell within which he was going to have to fall ass-first into the atmosphere.

Within five minutes of separation from the Tree, frictional deceleration was building up: a tenth, two-tenths of a G. The deceleration piled up quickly, eyeballs-in, shoving him deeper against his couch.

The pod shuddered violently. Malenfant was cocooned in a dull roaring noise. He gripped his couch and tried not to worry about it.

As the heat shield rammed deeper into the air, a shell of plasma built up around the hull. Beyond the amber windows the blackness of space was masked by a deep brown, which quickly escalated through orange, a fiery yellow, and then a dazzling white. Particles of soot flew off the scorching outer hull of the pod and streaked over the window, masking his view; now all he could see were extreme surges of brightness, as if fireballs were flying past the craft.

From the surface of Earth, the ship would be a brilliant meteor, visible even in daylight. He wondered if there was anybody down there who would understand what they saw.

The oak-like wood of the hull made for a natural heatshield, the Bad Hair Day twins had told him. All that resin would ablate naturally. It was a neater solution than the crude, clanking mechanical gadgets of his own era. Maybe, but he was an old-fashioned guy; he'd have preferred to be surrounded by a few layers of honest-to-God metal and ceramic.

The glow started to fade, and the deceleration eased. Now the windows were completely blacked over by the soot, but a shield jettisoned with a bang, taking the soot away with it, and revealing a circle of clear blue sky.

There was another crack as the first parachute deployed. The chute snatched at the pod and made it swing violently from side to side. He was pressed against one side of his couch and then the other, with the cabin creaking around him; he felt fragile, helpless, trapped in the couch.

Two more drogue chutes snapped open, in quick succession, and then the main chute. He could see through his window a huge canopy of green leafy material, like a vegetable cloud against the blue sky. The chute looked reassuringly intact, despite its vegetable origins, and the swaying reduced.

Malenfant glimpsed the ground. He could even track his progress, with maps in his sensor pack. He'd come down over the island that used to be called Zanzibar, on the east coast of Africa. And now he was drifting inland, to the north-west, towards Lake Victoria. Forest lay like thick green cloth over mountains.

Malenfant felt his couch rise up beneath him. Collapsing sacs pumped compressed carbon dioxide into the base of his seat, preparing to act as a shock absorber on landing. He was pressed up against the curved roof of his pod, with only a small gap between his knees and the roof itself. He felt hemmed in, heavy, hot. Gravity pulled at him, tangibly.

The pod hit the ground.

The parachutes pulled the capsule forward, so Malenfant was tipped up onto his face, and then the pod started to career across rocky ground, rocking backward and forward, spinning and rattling. His head rattled against his couch headrest.

Finally the pod slithered to a halt.

Malenfant found himself suspended on his side, with daylight pouring through the window behind him. The shock absorber was still pressing him against the roof, so he couldn't see outside. He lifted his hands to his face. There was blood in his mouth.

The pod wall dilated, releasing a flood of hot sunlit air into the capsule, so rich in oxygen and vegetable scents it made him gasp.

He began the painful process of climbing out.

His pod had come down on a low pebbly beach. The beach ran in a sinuous light-grey line between the darker grey face of a lake and the living green of a banana grove. From the margin of the lake to the highest hill-top, all he could see was contrasting shades of green, spreading like a carpet.

This was the northern coast of Lake Victoria. It was the closest place to that population centre, with its odd radioactivity signature, that the Bad Hair Day twins would deliver him.

Once he got his balance, he didn't have any trouble walking. He didn't feel dizzy, but oddly disoriented. He could feel his internal organs moving around, seeking a new equilibrium inside him. And he seemed to be immune to sunburn.

But it was odd to be walking around without his pressure suit. Disconcerting. And the sense of openness, of scale, was startling. After all his travels, Malenfant had become an alien, uncomfortable on the surface of his home world.

There was no sign of humanity.

Malenfant made camp in the inert, scorched shell of his pod. He used the bubble helmet of his old NASA pressure suit to collect water from a brook, a little way inland. He ate figs and bananas. He figured if he was stuck here for long he'd try to fish that lake.

The days were short and hot, although there was usually a scattering of cloud over the blue sky. He set up a stick in the sand, and watched its shadow shifting and lengthening with the hours. That way he figured out the time of local noon, and he reset his astronaut's watch. If he was stuck here long enough he might find the equinox, and start filling out a calendar.

The sunsets were spectacular. All that sub-micrometre dust.

The nights were cold, and he would wrap himself up inside the Beta-cloth outer layers of his pressure suit, there on the beach. But he stayed awake long hours, studying a changed sky.

The crescent Moon glowed blue.

The crescent's edge was softly blurred by a band of light, which stretched part way around the dark half of the satellite. There was a thick band of what looked like cloud, piled up over the Moon's equator. On the darkened surface itself there were lights, strung out in lines: towns, or cities, outlining hidden lunar continents. The Moon had a twin light, a giant mirror that orbited it slowly, shedding light on the Moon's shadowed hemisphere, which would otherwise languish in the dark for fourteen days at a time, probably long enough for the precious new air to start snowing out.

And in the centre of the darkened hemisphere which faced him was a dazzling point glow. The point source was Earthlight, reflecting from the oceans of the Moon.

Even a slim crescent Moon, now, drenched the sky with light, drowning out the stars and planets. The wildlife of Earth made use of the new light: he heard the croak of amphibians, the growl of some kind of cat. No doubt this changed Moon was working on the evolution of species, subtly.

The Moon was beautiful, wonderful, its terraforming one heck of an achievement. But to Malenfant it was as unreachable as before Apollo, a thousand years ago. And, even from here, Malenfant could see Gaijin craft orbiting over the lunar poles.

When the Moon set, taking its brilliant light with it, the full strangeness of the sky emerged.

Huge objects drifted against the blackness, green and gold: Trees, spectral patches of life green, and Gaijin flower-ships, their open ramscoop mouths tangles of silvery threads, like dragonflies. There was a chain of lights clustered around the plain of the ecliptic, sparkles in knots and clusters, almost like streetlights seen from orbit. They were Gaijin asteroid-belt cities.

The shapes of the constellations were mostly unchanged, the stars' slow drift imperceptible in the mayfly beat he'd been away. A bright young star had come to life in Cassiopeia, turning that distinctive W shape into a zig-zag. But many more stars had dimmed, to redness or even lurid green – or they were missing altogether, masked by life. This was the mark of the colonization wave, pulsing along the Galaxy's star lanes, an engineered consumption of system after system, heading this way.

And in one part of the sky, loosely centred on the grand old constellation of Orion, stars were flickering, burning, sputtering to darkness. It was evidence of purposeful activity spread across many light years, and it made him shiver. Perhaps it was the war he had come to fear, breaking over the solar system.

In the deepest dark of the nights he made out a huge, beautiful comet, sprawled across the zenith. Even with his naked eye he could see the bright spark of its nucleus, a tail that swept, feathery, curved, across the dome of the sky.

Comets came from the Oort cloud. He wondered if there was any connection between this shining visitor, flying through the heart of the inner solar system, and the sparkling lights he saw around Orion, the remote disturbance there.

One morning he crawled out of his pod, bollix naked.

There was a man standing there, staring at him.

Malenfant yelped, and clamped his hands over his testicles.

The man – no more than a boy, probably – was tall, more than two metres high. His skin was copper brown, covered by a pale golden hair, so thick it was almost like fur, and his eyes were blue. He had muscles like an athlete's. He was wearing some kind of breech cloth made of a coarse white material. He was carrying a sack. There was a belt around his waist, of some kind of leather. It contained a variety of tools, all of them stone, bone or wood: round axes, cleavers, scrapers, a hammerstone.

His neck was thick, like a weightlifter's. He had a long low skull, with some kind of bony crest behind. And he had bony eyebrows, a sloping forehead under that blond hair. He had a big projecting jaw – no chin – strong-looking teeth, a heavy brow ridge shielding his eyes, a flat ape-like nose. He didn't, Malenfant thought, look quite human.

But he was beautiful for all that, his gaze on Malenfant direct and untroubled.

He grinned at Malenfant, and emptied out the sack over the sand. It contained bananas, sweet potatoes and eggs. 'Eat food hungry eat food,' he said. His voice was high and indistinct, the consonants blurred.

Malenfant, stunned, just stood and stared.

His visitor folded up his sack, turned and ran off over the sand, a blur of golden-brown, leaving a trail of Man Friday footsteps on the beach.

Malenfant grunted. 'First contact,' he said to himself. Curiouser and curiouser.

He went to the tree line to do his morning business, then came back to the food. It made a change from fruit and fish.

He settled down to waiting. Man Friday and his unseen compadres surely didn't mean him any harm. Even so, he found it impossible not to stay close to his pod, glaring out at the tree line.

He wondered what he could use for weapons. Discreetly, he got together a heap of the bigger stones he could gather from the beach.

When his next visitors came, it was from the lake. He heard the voices first.

Six canoes, crowded with men and women, came shimmering around the point of the bay. Malenfant squinted to focus his new, improved eyes.

The crew looked to be of all races, from Aryan to Negro. Malenfant spotted a few beautiful, golden-haired creatures like his Man Friday. He saw what looked like the commander, standing up in one of the canoes. He was dressed in a bead-worked head-dress, adorned with long white cock's feathers, and a snowy white and long-haired goat-skin, with a crimson robe hanging from his shoulders. To Malenfant he was a vision out of the Stone Age. But he was hunched over, as if ill.

Empty-handed, Malenfant went down the beach to meet them.

The canoes scraped onto the shore, and the commander jumped out and walked barefoot through shallow water to the dry sand. He stumbled, Malenfant saw, on legs swollen to the thickness of tree-trunks. His face was burned black, and patches of hair sprouted from his scalp like weeds. But his gaze was alert and searching.

He reached out. There was a stench of rotting skin, and it was all Malenfant could manage not to recoil in disgust. To Malenfant, it looked like an advanced case of radiation poisoning. Something, he thought, is going on here.

The commander opened his mouth to speak. His lips parted with a soft pop, and Malenfant saw how his mucous membranes were swollen up. He began talking to Malenfant in a language he couldn't recognize. Swahili or Kiganda, maybe.

Malenfant held up his hands. 'I'm sorry. I don't understand.'

The commander looked startled. 'Good God,' he said, 'a European . . . I never expected to see another European!' His English was heavily accented.

'Not European. American.'

'You're a deep traveller.'

'Deep?'

'Deep in time. Like me. I left Earth the first time in 2191. You?'

'Earlier,' said Malenfant.

'Listen, I'm a kind of ambassador from the Kabaka.'

'Kabaka?'

'The emperor. Among other duties, I meet travellers. Not that they come often.' He noticed Malenfant reacting to his condition. He smiled, his mouth a grisly gash that exposed black teeth. 'Don't worry about this. I fell out with the Kabaka for a while. Most people do. My name is Pierre de Bonneville. I used to be French. I went to Bellatrix with the Gaijin: Gamma Orionis, three hundred and sixty light years away. A remarkable trip.'

'Why?'

De Bonneville laughed. 'I was a writer. A poet, actually. My country believed in sending artists to the stars: eyes and ears to bring home the truth, the inner truth, you see, of what is out there. I rode one of the last Arianes, from Kourou. Vast, noisy affair! But when I got home everyone had left, or died. There was nowhere to publish what I observed, noone to listen to my accounts.'

'I know the feeling. My name's Malenfant.'

De Bonneville peered at him. He didn't seem to recognize the name, and that suited Malenfant.

The golden-haired crewmen poked curiously around the charred husk of Malenfant's reentry pod.

De Bonneville grinned. 'You're admiring my golden-haired crewmen. The Uprights. Kintu's children, I call them.'

'Kintu?'

'. . . But then, we are all children of Kintu now. What do you want here, Malenfant?'

Travellers and emperors, history and politics. Malenfant felt his new blood pump in his veins. He'd been among aliens too long. Now human affairs, with all their rich complexity, were embracing him again.

He grinned. He said, 'Take me to your leader.'

Chapter 25

WANPAMBA'S TOMB

Pierre de Bonneville, with his crew of humans and golden-haired hominids, spent a night on the beach where Malenfant had fallen from
orbit. By firelight, the human crew ate dried fish and sweet potatoes.
The Uprights served the humans, who didn't acknowledge or thank
them in any way.

De Bonneville started drinking a frothy beer he called *pombe*, of
fermented grain. Within an hour he was bleary-eyed, thick-tongued,
husky-voiced.

When they were done with their chores the Uprights settled down
away from the others. They built their own crude fire, and cooked
something that sizzled and popped with fat; to Malenfant it smelled
like pork.

The boy who Malenfant had dubbed 'Friday' turned out to be called
Magassa.

De Bonneville told Malenfant how he had travelled here along
the course of the Nile, from where Cairo used to be. Like Malenfant,
he'd been drawn, on his return from the stars, to the nearest thing
to a metropolis the old planet had to offer. The Nile journey
sounded like quite a trip: in AD 3265, Africa was a savage place once
more.

'Listen to me. The ruler here is called Mtesa. Mtesa is the Kabaka
of Uganda, Usogo, Unyoro and Karagwe – an empire three hundred
kilometres in length and fifty in breadth, the biggest political unit in
all this pagan world. Things have – reverted – here on Earth, Malenfant, while we weren't looking. The people here have gone back to
ways of life they enjoyed, or endured, centuries before your time or
mine, before the Europeans expanded across the planet. You and I are
true anachronisms. Do you understand? *These people aren't like us.*
They have no real sense of history. No sense of change, of the possibility
of a different future or past. The date, by your and my calendars, may

307

be AD 3265. But Earth is now timeless.' He coughed, and hawked up a gob of blood-soaked phlegm.

'What happened to you, de Bonneville?'

The Frenchman grinned, and deflected the question. 'Let me tell you how this country is. We're like the first European explorers, coming here to darkest Africa, in the nineteenth century. And the Kabaka is a tough gentleman. When the traveller first enters this country, his path seems to be strewn with flowers. Gifts follow one another rapidly, pages and courtiers kneel before him, and the least wish is immediately gratified. So long as the stranger is a novelty, and his capacities or worth have not yet been sounded, it is like a holiday here. But there comes a time when he must make return. Do you follow me?'

Malenfant thought about it. De Bonneville's speech was more florid than Malenfant was used to. But then, he'd been born maybe two hundred years later than Malenfant; a lot could change in that time. Mostly, though, he thought de Bonneville had gotten a little too immersed in the local politics – who cared about this Kabaka? – not to mention becoming as bitter as hell.

'No,' he said. 'I don't know what you're talking about.'

De Bonneville seemed frustrated. 'Ultimately you must pay back the Kabaka for his hospitality. If you have weapons with you, you must give; if you have rings, or good clothes, you must give. And if you do not give liberally, there will be found other means to rid you of your superfluities. Your companions will desert, attracted by the rewards of Mtesa. And one day, you will find yourself utterly bereft of your entire stock – and be stranded here, a thousand kilometres from the nearest independent community.'

'And that's what happened to you.'

'When I stopped amusing him, the Kabaka dragged me before his court. And I – displeased him further. And, with a kiss from the Kate-kiro – Mtesa's lieutenant – I was sentenced to a month in the Engine of Kimera.'

'An Engine?'

'It is a yellow-cake mine. I was put in with the lowest of the low, Malenfant. The sentence left me reduced, as you see. When I was released, Mtesa – in the manner of the half-civilized ruler he is – found me work in the court. I am a book-keeper.

'Here's something to amuse you. From my memories of Inca culture I recognized the number recording system here, which is like the *quipu* – that is to say, numerical records made up of knotted strings. The Kabaka has embraced this technology. Every citizen in this kingdom is stored in numbers: the date of her birth, her kinship through birth and marriage, the contents of her granaries and warehouses. I was able to devise an accounting system to assist Mtesa with tax levies, for which he showed inordinate gratitude, and I became something of a favourite at the court again, though in a different capacity.

'But you see the irony, Malenfant. We travellers return from the stars to this dismal post-technological future – a world of illiterates – and yet I find myself a prisoner of an empire which lists the acts of every citizen as pure unadorned numbers. This may look like Eden to you; in fact it is a dread, soulless metropolis!'

The Uprights were laughing together. Malenfant could hear their voices, oddly monotonous, their jabbered speech.

'Their talk is simple,' Malenfant said.

'Yes. Direct and non-abstract. Sweet, isn't it? About the level of a six-year-old human child.'

'What are they, de Bonneville?'

'Can't you tell? They make me shudder. They are physically beautiful, of course. The women are sometimes compliant . . . Here. More *pombe*.'

'No.'

They sat in the cooling night, an old man and an invalid, stranded out of time, as in the distance the Uprights clustered around their fire, tall and elegant.

Malenfant agreed to travel with Pierre de Bonneville to Usavara, the hunting village of the Kabaka, and from there to the capital, Rubaga. Rubaga was the source of those radiation anomalies Malenfant had observed from orbit.

The next day they rowed out of the bay. De Bonneville's canoe was superb, and Magassa, the Upright, drummed an accompaniment to the droning chant of the oarsmen.

Malenfant, sitting astern, felt as if he had wandered into a theme park.

About two kilometres along the shore from Usavara, the hunting village, Malenfant saw what had to be thousands of Waganda – which was, de Bonneville said, this new race's name for themselves. They were standing to order on the shore in two dense lines, at the ends of which stood several finely-dressed men in crimson and black and snowy white. As the canoes neared the beach, arrows flew in the air. Kettle and bass drums sounded a noisy welcome, and flags and banners waved.

When they landed, de Bonneville led Malenfant up the beach. They were met by an old woman, short and bent. She was dressed in a crimson robe which covered a white dress of bleached cotton. De Bonneville kneeled before this figure, and told Malenfant she was the Katekiro: a kind of Prime Minister to the Kabaka.

The Katekiro's face was a wizened mask.

'Holy shit. *Nemoto.*' It was her; Malenfant had no doubt about it.

When she looked closely at Malenfant, her eyes widened, and she turned away. She would not meet his eyes again.

De Bonneville watched them curiously.

The Katekiro motioned with her head and, amid a clamour of beaten drums, Malenfant and de Bonneville walked into the village.

They reached a circle of grass-thatched huts surrounding a large house, which Malenfant was told would be his quarters. They were going to stay here a night, before moving inland. Nemoto left as soon as she could, and Malenfant didn't get to speak to her.

When Malenfant emerged from his hut he found gifts from the Kabaka: bunches of bananas, milk, sweet potatoes, green Indian corn, rice, fresh eggs, and ten pots of *maramba* wine.

Reid Malenfant, cradling his NASA pressure suit under his arm, felt utterly disoriented. And the presence of Nemoto, a human being he'd known a thousand years before, somehow only enhanced his sense of the bizarre.

He laughed, picked up a pot of wine, and went to bed.

The next day they walked inland, towards the capital.

Malenfant found himself trekking across a vast bowl of grass. The road was a level strip two metres wide, cutting through jungle and savannah. It had, it seemed, been built for the Kabaka's hunting excursions. Some distance away there was a lake, small and brackish, and beyond that a range of hills, climbing into mountains. The lower flanks of the mountains were cloaked in forest, their summits were wreathed in clouds. The dome-like huts of the Waganda were buried deep in dense bowers of plantains – flat leaves and green flowers – which filled the air with the cloying stink of over-ripe fruit.

Malenfant heard a remote bellowing.

He saw animals stalking across the plain, two or three kilometres away. They might have been elephants; they were huge and grey, and tusks gleamed white in the grey light of the pre-dawn sky. The tusks turned downwards, unlike the zoo animals Malenfant remembered.

He asked de Bonneville about the animals.

De Bonneville grunted. 'Those are *deinotherium*. The elephant things. Genetic archaeology.'

Malenfant tried to observe all this, to memorize the way back to the coast. But he found it hard to concentrate on what he was seeing.

Nemoto: God damn. She'd surely recognized him. But she'd barely acknowledged his existence, and during this long walk across Africa, he couldn't find a way to get close to her.

After three hours' march, they came into view of a flat-topped hill, which cast a long shadow across the countryside. The hill was crowned by a cluster of tall, conical grass huts, walled by a cane fence. This hill-top village, said de Bonneville, was the capital, Rubaga; the hill itself was known as Wanpamba's Tomb. Rubaga struck Malenfant as a sinister, brooding place, out of sympathy with the lush green countryside it ruled.

In the centre of the hill-top cluster of huts stood a bigger building. Evidently this was the Imperial Palace. To Malenfant it looked like a Kansas barn. Fountains thrust up into the air around the central building, like handfuls of diamonds catching the light. That struck Malenfant as odd. Fountains? Where did the power for fountains come from?

Broad avenues radiated down the hill's flanks. The big avenues blended into lower grade roads, which cut across the countryside. Along these radiating roads, Malenfant saw, much of the traffic – pedestrians and ox-carts – was directed, towards and away from the capital.

Two of the bigger roads, to east and west, seemed more rutted and damaged than the rest, as if they bore heavy traffic. The eastern road didn't ascend the hill itself but rather entered a tunnel cut into the hill-side. It looked like it was designed for delivering supplies of some sort to a mine or quarry inside the bulk of the hill, or maybe for hauling ore out of there. In fact he saw a caravan of several heavy, covered carts, drawn by labouring bullocks, dragging its way along the eastern road. It reminded Malenfant of a twenty-mule team hauling bauxite out of Death Valley.

They proceeded up the hill, along one of the big avenues. The ground was a reddish clay. The avenue was fenced with tall water-cane set together in uniform rows.

People crowded the avenues. The Waganda wore brown robes or white dresses, some with white goatskins over their brown robes, and others with cords folded like a turban around their heads. They didn't show much curiosity about de Bonneville's party. Evidently a traveller was a big deal out in Usavara, out in the sticks, but here in the capital everyone was much too cool to pay attention.

There wasn't so much as a TV aerial or a Coke machine in sight. But de Bonneville surprised Malenfant by telling him that people here could live as old as 150 years.

'We have been to the stars, and have returned. Rubaga might look primitive, but it is deceptive. We are living on the back of a thousand years' progress in science and technology. Plus what we bought from the Gaijin, and others. It is invisible – embedded in the fabric of the world – but it's *here*. For instance, many diseases have been eradicated. And, thanks to genetic engineering, ageing has been slowed down greatly.'

'What about the Uprights?'

'What?'

'What lifespan can they expect?'

De Bonneville looked irritated. 'Thirty or forty years, I suppose. What does it matter? I'm talking about *Homo Sapiens*, Malenfant.'

Despite de Bonneville's claims about progress, Malenfant soon noticed that mixed in with the clean and healthy and long-lived citizens there were a handful who looked a lot worse off. These unclean were dressed reasonably well. But each of them, man, woman or child, was afflicted by diseases and deformities. Malenfant counted symptoms: swollen lips, open sores, heads of men and women like billiard balls to which mere clumps of hair still clung. Many were mottled with blackness about the face and hands. Some of them had skin which appeared to be flaking away in handfuls, and there were others with swollen arms, legs and necks, so that their skin was stretched to a smooth glassiness.

All in all, the same symptoms as Pierre de Bonneville.

De Bonneville grimaced at his fellow sufferers. 'The Breath of Kimera,' he hissed. 'A terrible thing, Malenfant.' But he would say no more than that.

When these unfortunates moved through the crowds the other Waganda melted away from them, as if determined not even to glance at the unclean ones.

They reached the cane fence which surrounded the village at the top of the hill. They passed through a gate and into the central compound.

Malenfant was led to the house which had been allotted to him. It stood in the centre of a plantain garden and was shaped like a marquee, with a portico projecting over the doorway. It had two apartments.

Close by there were three dome-like huts for servants, and railed spaces for – he was told – his bullocks and goats.

Useful, he thought.

The prospect from up here was imperial. A landscape of early summer green, drenched in sunshine, fell away in waves. There was a fresh breeze coming off the huge inland sea. Here and there isolated cone-shaped hills thrust up from the flat landscape, like giant tables above a green carpet. Dark sinuous lines traced the winding courses of deep tree-filled ravines, separated by undulating pastures. In broader depressions Malenfant could see cultivated gardens and grain fields. Up towards the horizon all these details melted into the blues of the distance.

It was picture-postcard pretty, as if Europeans had never come here. But he wondered what this countryside had seen, how much blood and tears had had to soak into the earth, before the scars of colonialism had been healed.

Not that the land wasn't developed, pretty intensely: notably, with a network of irrigation channels and canals, clearly visible from up here. The engineering was impressive, in its way. Malenfant wondered how the Kabaka and his predecessors had managed it. The population wasn't so great, it seemed to him, that it could spare huge numbers of labourers from the fields for all these earthworks.

Maybe they used Uprights, whatever they were.

Anyhow, he thought sourly, so much for the pastoral idyll. It looked as if *Homo Sap* was on the move again, building, breeding, lording it over his fellows and the creatures around him, just like always.

In this unmanaged biosphere, immersed in air that was too dense and too hot and too humid, Malenfant had trouble sleeping; and when he did sleep, he woke to fuzzy senses and a sore head.

There was no way to get coffee, decaffeinated or otherwise.

The next afternoon Malenfant was invited to the Palace.

The Katekiro – Nemoto – came to escort him, evidently under orders. 'Come with me,' she said bluntly. It was the first time she'd spoken directly to Malenfant.

'Nemoto, I know it's you. And you know me, don't you?'

'The Kabaka is waiting.'

'How did you get here? How long have you been here? Are there any other travellers here?'

Nemoto wouldn't reply.

They approached the tall inner fence around the Palace itself. He wasn't the only visitor today, and a procession drew up. The ordinary Waganda weren't permitted beyond this point, but they crowded around the gates anyhow, gossiping and preening.

There was a rumbling roll of a kettle-drum, and the gate was drawn aside; and they proceeded, chiefs, soldiers, peasants, and three interstellar travellers, on into a complex of courtyards.

There was a wide avenue inside the fence, and at the fence's four corners those spectacular fountains thrust up into the air, rising fifteen metres or more. The water emerged from crude clay piping which snaked into the ground beneath the Palace. Maybe there were pumps buried in the hill-side.

Malenfant approached the nearest fountain. He reached out to touch the water – Christ, it was *hot,* so hot it almost scalded his fingers – and Nemoto pulled his arm back. Her hand on his was leathery and warm.

The drums sounded again. They passed through courtyard after courtyard, until finally they stood in front of the Palace itself.

It was only a grass hut. But it was tall and spacious, full of light and air. Malenfant, who had once visited the White House, had been in worse government buildings.

The heart of the Palace was a reception room. This was a narrow hall some twenty metres long, the ceiling of which was supported by two rows of pillars. The aisles were filled with dignitaries and officers. At each pillar stood one of the king's guards, wearing a long red mantle, a white turban ornamented with monkey skin, white trousers and black blouse. All were armed with spears. But there was no throne there, nor Mtesa himself. Instead there was only what Malenfant took to be a well, a rectangular pit in the floor.

Malenfant, Nemoto and the rest had to sit in rows before the open pit.

Drums clattered, and puffs of steam came venting up from the well-mouth, followed by a grinding, mechanical noise. A platform rose up out of the well, smoothly enough. Once again, Malenfant wondered where the energy for these stunts came from. The platform carried a throne – a seat like an office chair – on which sat the lean figure of Mtesa himself. Mtesa's head was clean-shaven and covered with a fez; his features were smooth, polished and without a wrinkle, and he might have been any age between twenty-five and thirty-five. His big, lustrous eyes gave him a strange beauty, and Malenfant wondered if there was Upright blood in there. Mtesa was sweating, his robes a little rumpled, but grinning hugely.

Nemoto, as Katekiro, and Mtesa's vizier and scribes all came forward to kneel at his feet. Some kissed the palms and backs of his hands; others prostrated themselves on the ground. Malenfant found it very strange to watch Nemoto do this.

Through all this, a girl stood at Mtesa's elbow. She was tall, dressed in white, her hair dark, but she had the broad neck and downy golden fur of an Upright. She couldn't have been more than fifteen. She moved like a cat, and – thought Reid Malenfant, dried-up hundred-year-old star voyager – she was sexy as all hell. But she looked troubled, like a child with a guilty conscience.

The main business of the afternoon was a bunch of petitioners and embassies, each of which Mtesa handled with efficiency – and, when he was displeased, brutality. In such cases the 'Lords of the Cord' were called forward: big beefy guards, whose job was to drag away the source of Mtesa's anger by ropes about the neck. It was, Malenfant thought, a striking management technique.

Nemoto, as the Katekiro, was heavily involved in all this: the presentation of cases and evidence, the delivery of the verdict. And each sentencing was preceded by Nemoto placing a dry kiss on the cheek of the terrified victim – a kiss of death, Malenfant thought with a shudder, planted by a thousand-year-old woman.

At last Mtesa turned to Malenfant. Through an interpreter, a dried-up little courtier, the Kabaka asked questions. He showed a child-like curiosity about Malenfant's story: where and when he had been born, the places he had seen in his travels.

After a while, Malenfant started to enjoy the occasion. For the first time in a thousand years, Reid Malenfant had found somebody who actually *wanted* to hear his anecdotes about the early days of the US space program.

Mtesa, it turned out, knew all about the Gaijin, and Saddle Point gateways, and, roughly speaking, the dispersal of humanity over the last thousand years. He wasn't uncomfortable with the idea of Malenfant having been born a millennium ago. But these were abstractions to him, since the Gaijin didn't intervene in affairs on Earth – not overtly anyhow – and Mtesa was more interested in what profit he could make out of this windfall.

Malenfant reminded himself that people were most preoccupied by their own slice of history; Mtesa was a man of his time, which had nothing to do with Malenfant's. Still, Malenfant wondered how many more generations would pass before only the kings and courtiers knew the true story of mankind, while everyone else subsided to flat-Earth ignorance, and started worshipping Gaijin flower-ships as gods in the sky.

Mtesa offered Malenfant various gifts, and an invitation to stay as long as he wished, and dismissed him.

The Katekiro, Nemoto, got away from Malenfant as soon as she could.

That evening, alone in his villa, Malenfant started to feel ill.

He couldn't keep down his food. He felt as if he was running up a temperature. And his hand hurt: there was a burning sensation, deep in the flesh, where the fountain water had splashed him.

In the bubble helmet of his EMU, he studied his reflection. He didn't look so bad. A little glassy about the eyes, perhaps. Maybe it was the food.

He went to bed early, and tried to forget about it.

He pursued the Katekiro, Nemoto. He tried everything he could think of to break through to her.

Eventually, with every evidence of reluctance, Nemoto agreed to spend a little time with Malenfant. She came to his hut, and they sat on the broad, wood-floored veranda, by the light of a small oil lamp and of the blue Moon.

She brought with her a buddha, a squat, ugly carving. It was made, she said, of fused regolith from the Mare Ingenii: Moon rock, worn smooth by time. The wizened little Japanese looked up at the blue-green Moon. 'And now the regolith is buried under metres of dirt, with fat lunar-gravity-evolved earthworms crawling through it. We have survived to see strange times, Malenfant.'

'Yeah.'

They talked, but Nemoto was no cicerone. The only way he could get any information out of her was to let her rehearse her obsession with the Gaijin – not to mention her former employers, Nishizaki Heavy Industries, who she thought had betrayed the human species.

He was astonished to find she'd travelled here, through a thousand years of history, the long way round: not by skipping from era to era as he and the other Saddle Point travellers had done, but simply by not dying. She gave him no indication of what technology she had used to exceed so greatly the usual human lifespan.

A thousand years of consciousness: no doubt this was dwarfed by Cassiopeia and her mechanical sisters, but such a span seemed unbearable on a human scale. He wondered how well Nemoto could retrieve the memories of her own deep past, of her first meeting with him on the Moon, for instance; perhaps she had been forced to resort to technology, to reorder and optimize her immense recollections. And, listening to Nemoto, he wondered how much of her sanity, her personality, had survived this long ordeal of life. She hinted at dark periods, slumps into poverty and powerlessness, even a period – centuries long – when she had lived as a recluse on the far side of the Moon.

However she had been damaged by time, though, she had retained one thing: her crystal-clear enmity of the Gaijin, and the Eeties who were following them.

'When I found the Gaijin I imagined we were destined for a thousand-year war. But now a thousand years have elapsed, and the war continues. Malenfant, when I still had influence, I struggled to restrict the Gaijin. I recruited the people called the Yolgnu. I established Kasyapa Township –'

'On Triton.'

'Yes. It was a beachhead, to keep the Gaijin from expanding their industrial activities in the outer system. I failed in that purpose. Now there are only a handful of human settlements beyond the Earth. There is a colony on Mercury, huddling close to the sun beyond the reach of the Gaijin ... If it survives, perhaps *that* will be our final home. For *the Gaijin are here.*'

A moth was beating against the lamp. She reached up and grabbed the insect in one gnarled hand. She showed the crushed fragments to Malenfant.

Flakes of mica wing. The sparkle of plastic. A smear of what looked like fine engine oil.

'*Gaijin,*' Nemoto said. 'They are here, Malenfant. They are everywhere, meddling, building. And worse are following.' She pointed up to the stars, in a sky made muddy with light by the low Moon. He could pick out Orion, just. 'You must have seen the novae.'

'Is that what they are?'

'Yes. There has been a rash of novae, of minor stellar explosions, like an infection spreading along the spiral arm. It has been proceeding for centuries.'

'My God.'

She smiled grimly. 'I've missed you, Malenfant. You immediately see implications. This is deliberate, of course, a strategy of some intelligence. *Somebody is setting off the stars,* exploding them like fire-crackers. The stars selected are like the sun – more or less. We have seen the disruption of Castor and Pollux in Gemini. Castor is a binary of two A-class stars some forty-five light years away, Pollux a K-class thirty-five light years away. Then came Procyon, an F-class eleven light years away, and, more recently Sirius –'

'Just nine light years away.'

'Yes.'

'Why would anybody blow up stars?'

She shrugged. 'To mine them of raw materials. Perhaps to launch a fleet of solar-sail starships. Who knows?' She said darkly, 'I call them the Crackers. Appropriate, don't you think? The spread seems to have been patchy, diffuse.'

'But they are coming this way.'

'Yes. They are coming this way.'

'Perhaps the Gaijin will defend us.'

She snorted. 'The Gaijin pursue their own interest. *We* are incidental, just another victim species a few decades or centuries behind the general development, about to be burned up in an interstellar war between rapacious colonists.'

Just as Malenfant had seen among the stars. Over and over. And now it was happening here.

... But there was still much mystery, he thought. There was still the question of the Reboot, the greater cataclysm that seemed poised to sweep over the Galaxy, and all its squabbling species.

What were the Gaijin *really* up to, here in the solar system? Nemoto's blunt antagonism seemed simplistic to Malenfant, who had come to know the Gaijin better. They were hardly humanity's friends, but neither were they mortal enemies. They were just *Gaijin,* following their own star.

But Nemoto was still talking, resigned, fatalistic. 'I am an old woman. I was already an old woman a thousand years ago. All I can do now is survive, here, in this absurd little kingdom ...'

Maybe. But, he reflected, if she'd chosen to retire, she could have done that anywhere. She didn't have to come *here,* to this dismal feudal empire, and serve its puffed-up ruler. The grassy metropolis – and the radiation signature, that trace of technology – had drawn her here, just like himself.

He said, testing her, 'I have a functioning pressure suit.'

She scarcely moved, as if trying to mask her reaction to that. She was like a statue, some greater Moon rock buddha herself.

There is, he realized, something she isn't telling me. Something significant.

He was woken before dawn.

De Bonneville's ruined face loomed over him like a black moon, the sweet stink of *pombe* on his breath. 'Malenfant. Come. They're hunting.'

'Who?'

'You'll see.'

A sticky, moist heat hit Malenfant as soon as he left his hut. He walked down the broad hill, after de Bonneville, working through a hierarchy of smaller and more sinuous paths, until there was savannah grass under his feet, long and damp with dew. Wagandans were following them, men and women alike, talking softly, some laughing.

The blue Moon had long set. There were still stars above. Malenfant saw a diffuse light, clearly green, tracking across the southern sky: it was a Tree, a living satellite populated by post-humans, floating above this primeval African landscape.

De Bonneville cast about and pointed. 'There's a track – see, where the grass has been beaten down? It leads towards the lake. Come. We will walk.' And, without waiting for acquiescence, he turned and led the way, limping and wheezing, his pains evidently forgotten in his eagerness for the spectacle.

Malenfant followed, tracking through the long damp grass. They passed a herd of the elephant analogues, the *deinotherium*. They seemed unaware of the humans. From a stand of trees, Malenfant saw the scowl of a cat – perhaps a lion – with long sabre teeth protruding over its lower jaw. De Bonneville said it was a *megantereon*. And he almost tripped over a lizard, hiding in the undergrowth at his feet; it was a half-metre long, with three sharp horns protruding from its crest. It scampered away from him and then sat in the grass, its huge eyes fixed on him.

They passed a skull, perhaps of an antelope, bleached of flesh. It had been cracked open by a stone flake – little more than a shaped pebble – embedded in a pit in the bone. Malenfant bent down and prised out the flake with his fingers. Was it made by the Uprights? It seemed too primitive.

De Bonneville grabbed his arm. 'There,' he whispered.

Perhaps a half-kilometre away, a group of what looked like big apes – muscular, hairy, big-brained – was gathered around a carcass. Malenfant could see curved horns; maybe it was another antelope. In the dawn light the hominids were working together with what looked like handheld stone tools, butchering the carcass. A number of them were keeping watch at the fringe of the group, throwing rocks at circling hyenas.

Malenfant said, 'Are these the hunters you brought me to see?'

De Bonneville snorted with contempt. 'These? No. They are not even hunters. They waited for the hyenas or jackals to kill that *sivatherium,* and now they steal it for themselves . . . Ah. Look, Malenfant.'

To Malenfant's left, crouching figures were moving forward through the grass. In the grey light, Malenfant could make out golden skin, flashes of white cloth. It was Magassa, and more of his people, moving towards the ape-like scavengers.

'*Now,*' de Bonneville hissed. 'Now the sport begins.'

'What are these creatures, de Bonneville?'

He grinned. 'When the ice was rolled back, the Earth was left empty. Various – experiments – were performed to repopulate it. But not as it had been before.'

'With older forms.'

'Of animals and even hominids, us. Yes.'

'So Magassa –'

'– is a once-extinct hominid, recreated here, in the year AD 3265. Magassa is *Homo Erectus.* And there are tigers once more in India, and mammoths in the north of Europe, and roaming the prairies of North America once more are many of the megafauna species destroyed by the Stone Age settlers there . . . Quite something, isn't it, Malenfant? I'm sure you didn't expect to find *this* on your return to Earth: the lost species of the past, restored to roam the empty planet, here at the end of time.'

It sounded, to Malenfant, like characteristic Gaijin tinkering. Just as they had poked around with Earth's climate and biosphere and geophysical cycles, so, it seemed, they were determined to explore the possibilities inherent in DNA, life's treasury of the past. Endless questing, as they sought answers to their unspoken questions. But still, here was a hunting party of *Homo Erectus,* by God, stalking easily across the plains of Africa in this year AD 3265. 'Is anyone studying this?'

De Bonneville looked at him curiously. 'Perhaps you don't understand. *Science is dead,* Malenfant. These are only Uprights. But . . .' He looked more thoughtful. 'I sometimes wonder if Magassa has a soul. Magassa can speak, you know, to some extent. His speech mechanism is closer to nonhuman primates. Still, he can make himself understood. Look into Magassa's eyes, Malenfant, and you will see a true consciousness – far more developed than any animal's – but a consciousness lacking much of the complexity, and darkness and confusion, of our own. Is there still a Pope or a mullah, somewhere on Earth or the Moon, concerned with such issues, perhaps declaring Magassa an abomination even now? But Magassa himself would not frame such questions; without our full inner awareness, he would lack the ability to impute consciousness in other beings, and so could not envisage consciousness in non-human animals and objects. That is to say, he would not be able to imagine God.'

'You envy him,' Malenfant said.

'Yes. Yes, I envy Magassa his calm sanity. Well. They make good labourers. And the women – Wait. Watch this.'

Magassa stood suddenly, whooped, and brandished a torch, which burst into flame. The other Uprights stood with him and hollered. Their high, clear voices carried across the grassy plain to Malenfant, like the cries of gulls.

At the noise, the primitive scavenging hominids jumped up, startled. With bleating cries they ran away from the Uprights and their fire, abandoning the antelope. One of the hominids – a female – was a little more courageous; she reached back and tore a final strip of flesh from the carcass before fleeing with the others, flat breasts flapping.

But now more Uprights burst out of the grass before the fleeing hominids. It was a simple trap, but obviously beyond the more primitive hominids' mental grasp.

At this new obstacle the scavengers hesitated for a second, like startled sheep. Then they bunched together and kept on running. They forced their way right through the cluster of Uprights, who hailed stones and bone spears at them. Some of the weapons struck home, with a crunching violence that startled Malenfant. But as far as he could see all the hominids got through.

All, that is, except one: the female who had hung back, and who was now a few dozen metres behind the rest.

The Uprights closed around her. She fought – she seemed to have a rock in her clenched fist – but she was overwhelmed. The Uprights fell on her, and she went down in a forest of flailing arms.

Her fleeing companions didn't look back.

De Bonneville stood up, his blackened face slick with sweat, breathing hard.

The Upright, Magassa, came stalking out of the pack, with a corpse slung over his shoulder. He had blood on his teeth and on the golden fur of his chest.

The body he carried was about the size of a twelve-year-old child's, Malenfant guessed, coated with fine dark hair. The arms were long, but the hands and feet were like a modern human's. The brain pan was crushed, a bloody mess, but the face was prominent: a brow ridge, a flat ape-like nose, the jaw protruding, big front teeth. That tool was still clutched in the female's hand; it was a lava pebble, crudely shaped.

The head, in life, had been held up. This was a creature that had walked upright.

Magassa dumped the corpse at de Bonneville's feet and howled his triumph.

'And what is *this*, de Bonneville?'

'Another reconstruction: Handy Man, some two million years vanished. Even less conscious, less self-aware, than our Upright friends.'

'*Homo Habilis.*'

'Malenfant, every species of extinct hominid is represented on this big roomy land of ours. I was pleased to see the prey were habilines, this morning – the Australopithecines can run, but are too stupid for good sport –'

'Get me out of here, de Bonneville.'

De Bonneville's ruined eyes narrowed. 'So squeamish. So hypocritical. Listen to me, Malenfant. *This is how we lived.* Sometimes they rape before the kill. Think of it, Malenfant! You and I have travelled to the stars. And yet, all the time, we carried the Old Men with us, asleep in our bones, waiting to be recalled . . .'

The Upright took a rock from his belt and started to hammer at the back of the dead habiline's skull. He dug his fingers into the hole he made, pulled out grey material, blood-soaked, and crammed it into his mouth.

Reid Malenfant knew, at last, that he had truly come home. He turned away from the habiline corpse.

Chapter 26

KIMERA'S BREATH

Soon after the Upright hunt, de Bonneville disappeared. Nemoto warned Malenfant not to ask too many questions.

On his own, Malenfant wandered around the court, the streets outside, even out into the country. But he learned little.

He found it hard to make any human contact. The Waganda were incurious – even of his sleek biocomposite coverall, a gift from the Bad Hair Day space twins, an artefact centuries of technological advancement ahead of anything here.

Most definitely, he did not fit in here. Madeleine Meacher had warned him it would be like this.

Anyhow, he tired quickly, and his hand still ached. Maybe those Bad Hair Day twins hadn't done as good a job on him as they thought.

The days wore on, and his mind kept returning to de Bonneville. When he thought about it, Pierre de Bonneville – for all he was an asshole – was the only person in all this dead-end world who had tried to help him, to give him information. And besides, de Bonneville was a fellow star traveller who was maybe in trouble in this alien time.

So he started campaigning, with the Kabaka and Nemoto in her role as the Katekiro, to be allowed to see de Bonneville.

After a few days of this, Nemoto summoned Malenfant from his villa. Impatient and reluctant, she said she had been ordered to escort Malenfant to de Bonneville. It turned out he was being held in Kimera's Engine, the mysterious construct buried in the hill-side at the heart of this grass-hut capital.

'I do not advise this, Malenfant.'

'Why? Because it's dangerous? I've seen de Bonneville. I know how ill he is –'

'Not just that. What do you hope to achieve?' She looked at him out of eyes like splinters of lava; she seemed sunk in bitterness and despair. 'I survive, as best I can. That's what you must do. Find a place here, a niche you can defend. What else is there? Hasn't your hop-and-skip tour of a thousand years taught you that much?'

'If that's what you believe, why do you want my pressure suit?'

She coughed into a handkerchief; he saw the cloth was speckled by blood. 'Malenfant –'

'Take me to de Bonneville.'

Accompanied by a couple of guards, Nemoto led Malenfant from the Palace compound, and out into Rubaga. They followed streets, little more than tracks of dust, that wound between the grass huts.

After a while the huts became sparser, until they reached a place where there were no well-defined roads, no construction. The centre of the plateau – maybe a kilometre in diameter and fringed by huts – was deserted: just bare rock and lifeless soil, free of grass, bushes, insects or bird-song. Even the breeze from Lake Victoria seemed suppressed here.

It looked, he thought, as if a neutron bomb had gone off.

They marched on into this grim terrain. Nemoto was silent, her resentment apparent in every gesture and step.

Malenfant had been ill during the night, and hadn't got much sleep. He was feeling queasy, shivering. And the landscape didn't help. The ground here was like a little island of death, in the middle of this African ocean of life.

At last they reached the heart of the central plain. They came to a wide, deep well set in the ground. There were steps cut into the rock, spiralling into the ground around the cylindrical inner face of the well. In the low light of the morning Malenfant could see the steps for the first fifty metres or so, beyond that only darkness.

Nemoto began to clamber down the steps. She walked like the stiff old woman she had become, her gaudy court plumage incongruous in the shadows. Malenfant followed more slowly.

He wished he had a gun.

Within a few minutes they'd come down maybe thirty metres – the open mouth of the well was a disc of blue sky, laced with high clouds – and Nemoto rapped on a wooden door set in the wall.

The door opened. Beyond, Malenfant saw a lighted chamber, a rough cube dug out of the rock, lit up by rush torches. At the door stood one of the king's guards. He was a pillar of bone and muscle, overlaid by fat and leathery skin. Nemoto spoke briefly, and the guard, after a hostile inspection of Malenfant, let them through.

The room was surprisingly large. The heat was intense, and the smoke from wall-mounted torches was thick, despite air passages cut into the walls. But the smoke couldn't mask the sweet stenches of vomit, of corrupt and decaying flesh. Malenfant grabbed a handkerchief from his pocket and held it over his face.

Pallets of wood and straw, covered by grimy blankets, were arranged in rows across the floor, and Malenfant had to step between them to make his way. Maybe half of the pallets were occupied. The eyes that met Malenfant's flickered with only the dullest curiosity.

The invalids all seemed wasted by the disease which had afflicted de Bonneville, to a greater or lesser degree. Patches of skin were burned to blackness, and there were some people with barely any skin left at all. Malenfant saw heads free of hair – even eyelashes and eyebrows were missing as if burned off – and there were limbs swollen to circus-freak proportions, and broken and bleeding mouths and nostrils. There were attendants here, but as far as Malenfant could see they were all Uprights: *Homo Erectus,* reconstructed genetic fossils, tall and naked and golden-furred, moving between the sick and dying. There seemed to be no real medical care, but the Uprights were giving out water and food – some kind of thin soup – and they murmured comfort in their thin, consonant-free voices to the ill.

It was like a field hospital. But there had been no war: and besides there were women and children here.

At last Malenfant found de Bonneville. He lay sprawled on a pallet. He stared up, his face swollen and burned beyond expression. 'Malenfant – is it you? – have you any beer?' He reached up with a hand like a claw.

Malenfant tried to keep from backing away from him. 'I'll bring some. De Bonneville, you got worse. Is this a hospital?'

He made a grisly sound which might have been a laugh. 'Malenfant, this is – ah – a dormitory. For the workers, including myself, who service the yellow-cake.'

'Yellow-cake?'

'The substance which fuels the Engine of Kimera . . .' He coughed, grimacing from the pain of his broken mouth, and shifted his position on his pallet.

'What's wrong with you? Is it contagious?'

'No. You need not fear for yourself, Malenfant.'

'I don't,' Malenfant said.

De Bonneville laughed again. 'Of course you don't. Indeed, nor should you. The illness comes from contact with the yellow-cake itself. When new workers arrive here, they are as healthy as you. Like that child over there. But within weeks, or months – it varies by individual, it seems, and not even the strongest constitution is any protection – the symptoms appear.'

'De Bonneville, why did they send you back here?'

'I have a propensity for offending the Kabaka, Malenfant, most efficiently and with the minimum of delay. So here I am again.'

'You're a prisoner?'

'In a way. The guards ensure that the workers are kept here until such time as the Kimera sickness takes hold of their limbs and complexion. Then one is free to wander about the town without hindrance.' He touched his blackened cheeks; a square centimetre of skin came loose in his fingers, and he looked at this latest horror without shock. 'The stigmata of Kimera's punishment are all too obvious,' he said. 'None will approach a yellow-cake worker, and certainly none will feed or succour him. And so there is no alternative, you see, but to return to the Engine, where at least food and shelter is provided, there to serve out one's remaining fragment of life . . .'

'Who is Kimera?'

'Ah, Kimera!' he said, and he threw back his ravaged head. Kimera, it turned out, was a mythical figure: a giant of Uganda's past, so huge that his feet had left impressions in the rocks. 'He was the great-grandson of Kintu, the founder of Uganda, who came here from the north; and it was Wanpamba, the great-great-grandson of Kimera, who first hollowed out the hill of Rubaga and entombed the soul of Kimera here . . .' And so forth: a lot of poetical, mythical stuff, but little in the way of hard fact. 'You know, they had to reconstruct these old myths from the last encyclopaedias, for the people had forgotten them – but don't let the Kabaka hear you say it . . .' De Bonneville's eyes closed, and he sank back, sighing.

Nemoto, nervous, plucked at Malenfant's sleeve. Her mime was obvious. Time was up; they should go; this was an unhealthy place.

Malenfant didn't see what choice he had. All the way out, Malenfant was aware of de Bonneville's gaze, locked on his back.

Outside the grisly dormitory, Malenfant peered into the deeper blackness of the well. 'Nemoto, *what's down there?*'

'Danger. Death. Malenfant, we must leave.'

'It is the Engine of Kimera, whatever the hell that is. You know, don't you? Or you think you know. Rubaga has the only significant radiation-anomaly signature on Earth . . .'

Her face was as expressionless as her Moon rock buddha's. 'If you want to fry your sorry skin, Malenfant, you can do it by yourself.' She turned and walked off, leaving him with the guard.

The guard looked at him quizzically. Malenfant shrugged, and pointed downwards.

He walked to the ledge's rim – a sheer drop into darkness, no protective rail of any kind – and leaned over. There seemed to be a breeze blowing down from above, rustling over the back of his neck, into the pit itself, as if there was a leak in the world down there. Now, he couldn't figure that out at all. Where was the air going? Was there a tunnel, some kind of big extractor?

The only light came from the flames of rush torches, flickering in that downwards breeze, and Malenfant's impressions built up slowly.

He made out a large heap of ore, crushed to powder, contained within a rough open chamber hollowed out of the stone. Maybe that ore was the yellow-cake de Bonneville had talked about. Long spears of what appeared to be charcoal – like scorched tree-trunks – stuck out of the heap from all sides and above. Water was carried in channels in the walls and pipes of clay, and poured into the heart of the heap. He guessed the heap contained a hundred tonnes of yellow-cake; there were at least forty charred trunks protruding from it.

The chamber was full of people.

There were a lot of tall Uprights, many squat habilines, and some Waganda: men, women and children who limped doggedly through the darkness, intense heat and live steam, serving the heap as if it were some ugly god. They hauled at the charcoal trunks, drawing them from the yellow-cake, or thrusting them deeper inside. Or else they hauled simple wheelbarrows of the yellow-cake powder to and from the heap, continually replenishing it. Their illness was obvious, even from here. Peering down from far above, it was like looking over some grotesque ant-hill, alive with motion.

The heap was intensely hot – Malenfant could feel its heat burning his face – and the water emerged from the base of the heap as steam, which roared away through a further series of pipes. There was a lot of leakage, though, and live steam wreathed the heap's ugly contours.

The principle was obvious. The heap was an energy source. The steam produced by the heap must, by means of simple pumps and other hydraulic devices, power the various gadgets he'd witnessed: Mtesa's ascending throne, the fountains. Maybe the water which passed through the system was itself pumped up from some deeper water table by the motive power of the steam.

There had to be a lot of surplus energy, though.

And now he made out a different figure, emerging from some deeper chamber at the base of the pit. It was a woman. She looked like a cross between a habiline and an Upright: big frame, thick neck, head thrust forward. She was wearing a suit, of some translucent plastic, that enclosed her body, hands and head. She was familiar to him, from a hundred TV shows and school-book reconstructions. She was Neandertal: another of humanity's lost cousins.

Holy shit, he thought.

There was a flash of light from the hidden chamber, from some invisible source.

It was blue, a shade he recognized.

Neandertals, and pressure suits, and electric-blue light. Unreasoning fear stabbed him.

He got out of there as fast as he could.

The next day Malenfant visited de Bonneville again. Malenfant brought him a small bottle of *pombe*; de Bonneville fell on this avidly, jealously hiding it from the other inmates of the ward. Malenfant wanted to ask about the Engine, but de Bonneville had his own tale to tell.

'Listen, Malenfant. Let me tell you how I came to this pass. It started long before you arrived . . .'

De Bonneville told him that a gift had arrived for Mtesa, the emperor, from Lukongeh, king of the neighbouring Ukerewe. There had been five ivory tusks, fine iron wire, six white monkey-skins, a canoe large enough for fifty crew – and Mazuri, an Upright girl, a comely virgin of fourteen, a wife suitable for the Kabaka.

'Mtesa's harem numbers five hundred. Mtesa has the pick of many lands; and many of the harem are, as I can testify, of the most extraordinary beauty. But of them all, Mazuri was the comeliest.'

'I think I saw her in the Palace. Mtesa likes her.'

'She has –' de Bonneville waved his damaged hands in a decayed attempt at sensuality '– she has that *animal* quality of the Uprights. That intensity. When she looks you in the eyes, you see direct into her primeval soul. Do you know what I'm talking about, Malenfant?'

'Yes. But I'm a hundred years old,' Malenfant said wistfully.

'Mazuri was young, impetuous, impatient at her betrothal to Mtesa – a much older man, and lacking the vigour of her own kind . . .'

De Bonneville fell silent, in a diseased reverie.

'Tell me about the Engine.'

'The Waganda say the yellow-cake is suffused with the Breath of Kimera,' de Bonneville said, dismissive. 'It is the Breath which supplies the heat. But a given portion of yellow-cake is eventually exhausted of its Breath, and we must extract and replace the cake, continually.'

'What about the tree-trunks?'

'We must insert and extract the trunks, according to the instructions of – ' He quoted a term Malenfant didn't know, evidently a sort of foreman. 'The Breath is invisible and too rapid to have much effect – except on the human body, apparently, which it ravages! The tree-trunks are inserted to slow down the Breath from the heart of the heap – do you see? Then it gets to work on the rest of the yellow-cake. And that is, in turn, encouraged to produce its own Breath in response. It's like a cascade, you see. But the Waganda can control this, by withdrawing their charred trunks; this has the effect of allowing the Breath to speed up, and escape the heap harmlessly . . .'

A cascade, yes, Malenfant thought. A chain reaction.

'And the water? What's that for?'

'The emission of the Breath is associated with great heat – which is the point of the Engine. Water flows through the hill-side, through the Engine. The water is a cooling agent, which carries off this heat before any damage is done to the Engine. And the heat, of course, turns the water to steam, which in turn is harnessed to drive Mtesa's various toy devices and fripperies . . .' Malenfant heard how de Bonneville's voice slowed as he said that, as if some new idea was coming to him.

To Malenfant, it all made sense.

Twentieth century nuclear fission piles had been simple devices. They were just heaps of a radioactive material, such as uranium, into which reaction-controlling moderators, for example carbon rods, were thrust. Technical complexity only came if you cared about human safety: shields, robot devices to control the moderators, a waste extraction process, and so forth. If you *didn't* care about wasting human life, a reactor could be made much more simply.

With a little instruction, a tribe of Neandertals could operate a nuclear reactor. A bunch of children could. *Especially* if you didn't care about safety.

'It's the Breath that makes you ill,' he said.

'Indeed.'

'Why not others? Why not Mtesa himself?'

'The Breath is contained by the hundreds of metres of rock within which the Engine is housed. But, though it is not spoken of, there is much illness among the general population; and there are elaborate taboos about associating too closely with products of the Engine – you shouldn't drink the water which has circulated through the yellow-cake, for instance.'

Malenfant remembered how Nemoto had warned him against inserting his hands in Mtesa's fountains. He felt, now, a renewed itching in his own damaged skin.

Shit, he thought. I must have taken a dose myself.

De Bonneville waved his gnarled hands. 'The Engine is clearly very ancient, Malenfant. The Waganda's legend says it was constructed by an old king, seventeen generations before our own glorious Mtesa. It seems to me the Waganda have learned how to control their crude device, not by proceeding from a body of established knowledge as *we* might have done, but by trial and error over generations – and expensive trial and error at that – expensive in human life, I mean!' But he was tiring, and losing interest. 'Let me tell you of Mazuri . . .'

'You screwed the king's favourite wife. You asshole, de Bonneville.'

'I tried to put her aside, when I left Rubaga to meet you. But when I returned, full of *pombe* and the excitement of the hunt, there she was . . . Ah, Malenfant, those eyes, that skin, that mouth . . .'

He was found out. Mtesa's fury had been incandescent. De Bonneville was expelled from his position in court – dragged, by a rope around his neck, by Mtesa's enthusiastic Lords of the Cord, and subjected to fifty blows with a stick, a punishment severe enough to lame him – and then banished to the lowliest position of Rubaga society: to work in the yellow-cake Engines, buried deep within the hill-side.

De Bonneville grasped Malenfant's arm with his ruined, claw-like hands. 'It was all a trap, Malenfant. One accumulates enemies so easily in such a place as this! And I – I was always impetuous rather than careful . . . I was led into a trap, and I have been destroyed! Seeing you now, a traveller, makes me understand anew how much has been robbed from me by these savages of the future. But –'

'Yes?'

His blue eyes gleamed in his blackened ruin of a face. 'But de Bonneville shall have his revenge, Malenfant. Oh, yes! His determination is sweet and pure . . .'

He confronted Nemoto.

'Nemoto, you know what the Engine is, don't you? It's a nuclear pile. A fucking nuclear pile.'

Nemoto shrugged. 'It's just a heap. Maybe a hundred tonnes of "yellow-cake" – which is a uranium ore – with burnt tree stumps used as graphite moderators. It was a geological accident: yellow-cake seams inside this hollow mountain, and some natural water stream running over the pile, cooling it . . .'

Natural nuclear reactors had formed in various places around the planet, where the geological conditions had been right. What was needed was a concentration of uranium ore, and then some kind of moderator. The function of the moderator was to slow down the neutrons, the heavy particles emitted by decaying uranium atoms. A slowed-down neutron would impact with another atomic nucleus and make *that* decay – and the neutron products of that event would initiate more decays – on and on, in the cascade of collapsing nuclei the physicists called a chain reaction.

Under Rubaga's mountain, the action of water, over billions of years, had washed uranium from the rock and caused it to collect in seams at the bottom of a shallow sea. The uranium had then been overlaid by inert sand, and the rocks compressed and uplifted by tectonic forces, the uranium further concentrated by the slow rusting of surrounding rocks in the air. Thus had been created seams of uranium, great lenticular deposits, two or three metres thick and perhaps ten times as wide, under their feet, right here.

At first there had been no chain reaction. But then water and organic matter, seeping into cracks in the uranium seams, had served as primitive moderators, slowing the neutrons down sufficiently for the reaction process to start.

Nemoto whispered, 'The reaction probably started as a series of scattered fires in concentrations of the uranium ore. Then it spread to less rich areas nearby. It was self-controlling; as the water was boiled by the reaction's heat it would be forced out of the rock – and the reaction would be dampened, until more water seeped back from the surface layers above, and the reaction could begin again.' She smiled thinly. 'And that is what the Neandertal community here discovered. It took them a couple of centuries, but they learned to tinker with the process, inserting burnt wood – graphite – as secondary moderators . . .'

The workers in the pile maintained it with their bare hands. At times the workers had to haul heaps of yellow-cake from one part of the pile to another, or they mixed the yellow-cake, by hand, with other moderator compounds, or they cleared out the coolant-water pipes – the small fingers of children were well adapted for that particular chore. And as well as the regular operation of the pile, they had to cope with accidents, types of which Nemoto listed in the local language: *leakages, spill-outs, crumbles, hot beds, slaps.*

'Why did the Neandertals need to do this?'

'Because of us. *Homo Sapiens*, Malenfant. For a while, after the ice, the Earth was empty. The Gaijin implanted their little pockets of reconstructed pre-humans. But then along *we* came, and it all unravelled as it had before, thirty or forty thousand years ago. You've seen how the locals treat the Uprights, the habilines.'

'Yes.'

'So it was with the Neandertals . . . except *here*. The Neandertals had their uranium, their radioactivity. They laced water supplies. They put tips on their spears . . . It helped keep back the humans, until a smart human leader – a predecessor of Mtesa – came along and struck a deal.'

'So Mtesa supplies human slaves to the Neandertals. To maintain the pile.'

'Essentially. Makes you think, doesn't it, Malenfant? If only the *true* Neandertals, of our own deep past, had discovered such a resource. Perhaps they could have kept us at bay, survived into modern times – I mean, *our* times.'

Malenfant frowned. 'It doesn't sound too stable. A nuclear pile isn't much of a weapon . . . You'd think that Mtesa's soldiers could overwhelm the Neandertals, take what they wanted, drive them out. And the radioactivity – we're all living on top of a raw nuke pile, here. Even those who don't have to go work in that hole in the ground are going to suffer contamination.'

Nemoto grimaced. 'You are not living in Clear Lake now, Malenfant. These people accept things we wouldn't have. The Waganda have built a stable social arrangement around their Engine. They keep their blood-lines reasonably pure by stigmatizing any individual showing signs of mutation or radiation sickness. It's a kind of symbiosis. The Waganda use the Engine's energy. But the Engine maintains itself by poisoning a proportion of the Waganda population. Mostly they use Uprights and habilines anyhow; among the humans, only Mtesa's victims finish up in the Engine.'

Malenfant said, 'Those toys of Mtesa's – the fountains and the Caesar's Palace trick throne – can't absorb more than a few per cent of the pile's energy . . . The rest of it runs that Saddle Point gateway. Doesn't it, Nemoto? And *that* is the true purpose of this place. *This is some huge Gaijin project.*'

'I am no tourist guide, Reid Malenfant. I don't know anything.' She looked away from him. 'Now leave me alone.'

*　　*　　*

Malenfant had trouble sleeping. He felt ill, and at times he felt over-whelmed by fear.

He'd glimpsed a Saddle Point gateway, buried deep in this African hill-side. That was where all the power went. And that downward breeze had been air passing through the gateway, a leak in the fabric of the world.

He felt drawn to the gateway, as if by some gravitational field.

I don't want this, he thought. I just wanted to run home. But I brought myself *here*. I chose to come to this place, kept digging until I found *this*, the centre of it all. A way back into the game. Just like Nemoto.

A way to fulfil whatever purpose the Gaijin seemed to have for him.

I can't do it. Not again. I just want to be left alone. I don't *have* to follow this path, to do anything.

But the logic of his life seemed to say otherwise.

Spare me, he thought; and he wished he believed in a god to receive his prayers.

Malenfant was woken, rudely, by a shuddering of his pallet. His eyes snapped open to darkness, and he sucked in hot African air. For a second he thought he was in orbit: *a blow-out in the Shuttle Orbiter, a micrometeorite that had smashed through Number Two Window* . . .

He was alone in his villa, and the grass roof was intact. He pushed off his cover and tried to stand.

The ground shook again, and there was a deep, subterranean groan-ing, a roar of stressed rock. A quake, then?

Through the glassless windows of the villa, a new light broke. He saw a glow, red-white and formless, which erupted in a gout of fire over the roof-tops of Rubaga. Grass huts ignited as tongues of glowing earth came licking back to ignite the flimsy constructions. He heard screaming, the patter of bare feet running.

That fount of flame came from the heart of the town, Malenfant saw immediately – from the well of Kimera – from the pit of that monstrous Engine.

De Bonneville. It had to be. In some way, he'd carried out his vague threat.

The shuddering subsided, and Malenfant was able to stand. He pulled on his biocomposite coverall and stepped out of the villa.

All of Rubaga's populace appeared to be out in the narrow streets: courtiers, peasants, courtesans and chiefs, all running in terror. The big gates of the capital's surrounding cane fence had been thrown

333

open, and Malenfant could see how the great avenues were already thronged with people, running off into the countryside's green darkness.

Malenfant set off through the capital towards the centre of the plateau. He had to push his way through the panicking hordes of Waganda, who fled past him like wraiths of smoke.

By the time he'd reached the dead heart of the hill-top, even the great grass Palace of Mtesa was alight.

Malenfant hurried into the central plain, away from the scorching huts. He reached the blighted zone with relief; for the first time in many minutes, he could draw a full breath.

The fire of Kimera loomed out of the earth before Malenfant, huge and angry and deadly; and all around the rim of the plain he saw the glow of Rubaga's burning huts. Christ: he was in the middle of a miniature Chernobyl. And it scared the shit out of him to think that there was nobody here, *nobody*, who understood what was going on, nobody at the controls.

He walked on, his feet heavy, his chest and face scorching in the growing heat, his burned hands tingling, and the light of the fire was brilliant before him. He didn't see how he could get any closer. He began to circle the blaze. He stumbled frequently, and his eyes were sore and dry.

I am, he thought, too fucking old for this.

Then he saw what looked like a fallen animal, inert on the ground. Malenfant braved the fire, sheltering his head with his arms, and approached.

It was de Bonneville. He lay face-down in the barren earth of Rubaga. Malenfant could see, from scrabbles in the dirt, that he had walked away from the pit until he could walk no more, then crawled, and at last he had dragged himself by his broken fingertips across the ground.

Malenfant knelt down, and slid his arms beneath the deformed torso. De Bonneville was disconcertingly light, like a child, and Malenfant was able to turn him over, and lay that balloon-like head on his lap.

De Bonneville's blue eyes flickered open. 'Good God. Malenfant. Have you any beer?'

'No. I'm sorry, de Bonneville.'

'You must get away from here. Your life is forfeit, Malenfant, if you confront the Breath of Kimera . . .' His eyes slid closed. 'I did it. I . . .'

'The Engine?'

'It was the water,' he said dreamily. 'Once I made up my mind to act, it was simple, Malenfant . . . I just blocked the pipes, where they admit the water to the well . . .'

'You blocked the coolant?'

'All that heat, with nowhere for it to go . . . You know, it took just minutes. I could hear them crying and screaming, as the burning, popping yellow-cake scorched their bodies and feet, even as they thrust their tree-trunks into the heap. It took just minutes, Malenfant . . .'

De Bonneville, limping on his already damaged legs, had escaped the well minutes before the final ignition and explosion.

'And was it worth it?' Malenfant asked. 'You came back from the stars, to do this?'

'Oh, yes,' de Bonneville said, his eyes fluttering closed. 'For he had destroyed me. *Mtesa*. If I die, his empire dies with me . . . And more than that.' De Bonneville tried to lick his lips, but his mouth was a mass of popping sores. '*It was you*, Malenfant. You, a heroic figure returned from the deep past! From an age when humans, we Westerners, strove to do more than simply survive, in a world abandoned to the Gaijin. You and I come from an age where people *did* things, Malenfant. My God, we shaped whole worlds. You reminded me of that. And so I determined to shape mine . . .'

He subsided, and his body grew more limp.

Dawn light spread from the east, and Malenfant saw a cloud of smoke, a huge black thunderhead, lifting up into the sky.

It was you, de Bonneville had said. My fault, he thought. All my fault. I was probably meant to die, out there, among the stars. It should have been that way. Not *this*.

He cradled de Bonneville in the dawn light, until the shuddering breaths had ceased to rack him.

The morning after the explosion, Malenfant was arrested.

Malenfant was hauled by two silent guards to Mtesa's temporary court, in a spacious hut a couple of kilometres from Wanpamba's Tomb, and he was hurled to the dust before the Kabaka.

His trial was brief, efficient, punctuated with much shouting and stabbing of fingers. He wasn't granted a translator. But from the fragments of local language he'd picked up he learned he had been accused of causing the explosion, this great epochal crime.

Nemoto stood silently beside the Kabaka while the comic-opera charade ran its course. She did this, he realized. She framed me.

To his credit, Mtesa seemed sceptical of all this, irritated by the proceedings. He seemed to have taken a liking to Malenfant, and was shrewd enough to perceive this as an obscure dispute between Malenfant and the Katekiro. *Why are you involving me? Can't you sort it out yourself?*

But the verdict was never really in doubt to anyone.

When it was done, the Lords of the Cord came to Malenfant. Rope was looped around his neck, and he was dragged to his feet.

Nemoto walked forward, hunched over, and stood before him. In English, she said, 'You're to be treated leniently, Malenfant. You won't be working the Engine. You're to be cast –'

'Into the pit.' And then he saw it. 'The gateway. You're forcing me to the Saddle Point gateway. That's what this is all about, isn't it?'

'*You saw the light,* Malenfant. If I thought that pressure suit of yours would fit me, I would take it from you. I would walk into the Engine of Kimera and confront the enigma at its heart, following those mysterious others who come and go . . . But I cannot. It is my fate to remain here, amusing the Kabaka, until the ageing treatments fail, and I die.

'I had to do this, Malenfant. I could see your reluctance to go forward – *even though you brought yourself here,* to the centre of things. I could see you could not bring yourself to take the last step.'

'So you pushed me. Why, for God's sake? Why are you doing this?'

'Not for the sake of God. For history. Look around you, Malenfant. Look at the huge strangeness of this future Earth. Certainly the arrival of Eeties deflected our history – and those exploding stars in the sky tell of more deflections yet to come. But no human has ever been in control of the great forces that shaped a world, of history and climate and geology; only a handful of us have even witnessed such changes.'

'If none of us can deflect history, you're killing me for nothing.'

'Ah.' She smiled. 'But individual humans *have* changed history, Malenfant – not the way *I* tried to, with plots and schemes and projects – but by walking into the fire, by giving themselves. Do you see? And *that* is your destiny.'

'You're a monster, Nemoto. You play with lives. The right hand of this Stone Age despot is the right place for you.'

She raised a bony wrist and brushed blood-flecked spittle from her chin, seeming not to hear him.

He was overwhelmed with fear and anger. 'Nemoto. Spare me.'

She leaned forward and kissed his cheek; her lips were dry as autumn leaves, and he could smell blood on her breath. 'Goodbye, Malenfant.'

The cords around his neck tightened, and he was hauled away.

The rest of it unfolded with a pitiless logic. As a prisoner, condemned, Malenfant had no choice, no real volition; it was easy to submit to the process, to become detached, let his fear float away.

He was indeed treated with leniency. He was allowed to go back to his hut. He retrieved his EMU, his ancient pressure suit in its sack of rope.

He was taken to the rim of the central desolation.

There was a small party waiting: guards, with two other prisoners, both young women, naked save for loin-cloths, with their hands tied behind their backs. The prisoners returned his stare dully. Malenfant saw they'd both been beaten severely enough to lay open the skin over their spines.

I've come a long way, thought Malenfant, for this: a walk into hell, with two of the damned.

Once more he descended the crude spiral staircase.

Soon they were so deep that the circle of open sky at the top of the shaft was shrunk to a blue disc smaller than a dime, far above him. The only light came from irregularly-placed reed torches. The stairs themselves were crudely cut and too far apart to make the descent easy; soon Malenfant was hot, and his legs ached.

The prisoners' faces shone, taut with fear.

They passed two big exits gouged in the rock wall, one to either side of the cylindrical shaft. The air from these exits was marginally less stale than elsewhere. Perhaps they led to the great avenues from east and west which he'd noticed from outside, tunnels which led into the body of the hill-side itself.

A hundred metres down, water spouted from clay founts, elaborately shaped, mounted on the walls. The water, almost every drop of it, was captured by spiral canals which wound around the shaft, in parallel to the stairway. The founts gushed harder as they descended – water pressure, thought Malenfant – and soon the spiral canals were filled with bubbling, frothing liquid, which took away some of the staleness of the still air of the well. But the founts and channels were severely damaged by fire, cracked and crudely repaired; water leaked continually.

Already he was hot and dizzy; a mark of the dose he'd already taken, maybe. He reached towards a canal to get a handful of water.

But a dark, bony hand shot out of the darkness, pushing him away. It was one of the prisoners, her eyes wide in the gloom.

Malenfant watched the narrow, bleeding shoulders of the prisoner as she descended before him. Here she was, going down into hell, no more than a kid, and yet she'd reached out to keep a foreigner from harm.

Deeper and deeper. There was no trace of natural daylight left now.

They reached a point where the two prisoners were released to a dormitory, hollowed out of the rock, presumably to be put to work later. Before they were pushed inside, they peered down into the pit, with loathing and dread. For here, after all, was the Engine which was to be their executioner.

And Malenfant was going on, deeper. The guards prodded at his back, pushing him forward.

At last the descent became more shallow. Malenfant surmised they were approaching the heart of the hollowed-out mountain. They stopped maybe fifteen metres above the base of the well. From here, Malenfant had to go on alone.

By the light of a smoking torch, with a mime, he asked a favour of the guards. They shrugged, incurious, not unwilling to take a break.

Malenfant pulled his battered old NASA pressure suit from its sack.

He lifted up his Lower Torso Assembly, the bottom half of his EMU, trousers with boots built on, and he squirmed into it. Next he wriggled into the upper torso section. He fixed on his Snoopy flight helmet, and over the top of that he lifted his bubble helmet, starred and scratched with use. He twisted it into place against the seal at his neck.

The guards watched dully.

He looked down at himself. By the light of a different star, Madeleine Meacher had spent time repairing this suit for him. The EMU was still a respectable white, with the Stars and Stripes still proudly emblazoned on his sleeve.

. . . But then the little ritual of donning the suit was over, and events enfolded him in their logic once more.

Was this it? After all his travels, his long life, was he now to die, alone, here?

Somehow he couldn't believe it. He gathered his courage.

Leaving the staring guards behind, he walked further down the crude stairwell, deeper towards the fire. The starring of his battered old bubble helmet made the flames dance and sparkle; it was kind of pretty. His own breath was loud in the confines of the helmet, and he felt hot, oxygen-starved already, although that was probably just imagination. His backpack was inert – no hiss of oxygen, no whir of fans – and it was a heavy mass on his back. But maybe the suit would protect him a little longer.

He'd just keep walking, climbing down these steps in the dark, as long as he could. He didn't see what else he could do.

It didn't seem long, though, before the heat and airlessness got to him, and the world turned grey, and he pitched forward. He got his hands up to protect his helmet, and rolled on his back, like a turtle.

He couldn't get up. Maybe he ought to crawl, like de Bonneville, but he couldn't even seem to manage that.

He was, after all, a hundred years old.

He closed his eyes.

It seemed to him he slept a while. He was kind of surprised to wake up again.

He saw a face above him. A dark, heavy face. Was it de Bonneville? No, de Bonneville was dead.

Thick eye ridges. Deep eyes. An ape's brow, inside some kind of translucent helmet.

He was being carried. Down, down. Even deeper into the mountain of Kimera. There were strong arms under him.

Not human arms.

But then there was a new light. A blue glow.

He smiled. A glow he recognized.

Cradled in inhuman arms, lifted through the gateway, Reid Malenfant welcomed the pain of transition.

There was a flash of electric-blue light.

Chapter 27

THE FACE OF KINTU

Long ago, long long ago.

Kintu giant comes down from north.

Nothing.

No earths, no stars, no people. Kintu sad. Kintu lonely. Very lonely. Nothing nothing nothing.

Kintu breathes in. Breathes in what? Breathes in nothing.

Chest swells, big big big. Round. Mouth of Kintu here, Navel of Kintu there. Breathe in, big big big, blow in, all that nothing.

Skin pops, pop pop pop. Worlds. Stars. People. Popping out of skin, pop pop pop. Still breathes in, in in in, big big big.

Here. Now. The Face of Kintu. Here. See how skin pops, pop pop pop, new baby worlds, new life, things to eat. We live where, on Face of Kintu.

The Staff of Kintu. People die, people don't die. Inside the Staff of Kintu. Happy happy happy. Live how long, long time, long long time, forever.

In future, long long time. Kintu throw Staff, long long way. Throw Staff where, to Navel of Kintu. People live on belly of Kintu, long long time, long long way, how happy, happy happy happy.

Everyone else what? Dead.

The transition pain dissipated, like frost evaporating. He felt the hard bulge of the arms which carried him, the iron strength of biceps.

His head was tipped back. He saw the white fleshy underside of a tiny beardless chin. Beyond that, all he could see was black sky. Some kind of wispy high cloud, greenish. A rippling aurora.

His weight had changed. He was light as an infant, as a dried-up twig.

Not Earth, then.

He could be anywhere. Encoded as a stream of bits, he could have been sent a thousand light years from home. And because Saddle Point signals travelled at mere lightspeed, he could be a thousand years away from a return. Even the enigmatic Earth he'd returned to, the Earth of 3265, might be as remote as the Dark Ages from the year of his birth.

Or not.

Now a face loomed over him, as broad and smooth as the Moon, encased in a crude pressure-suit helmet that was not much more than a translucent sack. Obviously hominid. But the face had big heavy eye-ridges, and a huge flat nose that thrust forward, and a low hair-line. Thick black eyebrows, like a Slav, wide dark eyes. Those eye-ridges gave her a perpetually surprised look.

Her. It was a female. Young? The skin looked smooth, but he had no reference.

She smiled down at him. She was, of course, a Neandertal girl.

There was black around the edge of his vision.

He was running out of air. His suit was a non-functioning antique. It was all he had. But now it was going to kill him.

The girl's face creased with obvious concern. She lifted up her hand – now she was holding him with *one arm*, for God's sake – and she started waving her right hand up and down in front of her body. Those thick Russian eyebrows came down, so she looked quizzical.

She was miming, he thought. *Pain?*

'Yes, it hurts.' His radio wasn't working, and she didn't look to have any kind of receiver. She probably couldn't speak English, of course, which would be a problem for him. He was an American, and in his day, Americans hadn't needed to learn other languages. Maybe she could lip-read. 'Help me. I can't breathe.' He kept this up for a few seconds, until her expression dissolved into bafflement.

With big Moonwalk strides she began to carry him forward. Inside his bubble helmet his head rattled around, thumping against the glass.

Now, in swaying glimpses, he could see the landscape.

A plain, broken by fresh-looking craters. The ground was red, but overlaid by streaks of yellow, brown, orange, green, deep black. It looked muddy and crusted, like an old pizza. Much of it was frosted. From beyond the close horizon, he could see a plume of gas that turned blue as it rose, sparkling in the flat light of some distant sun. The plume fell straight back to the ground, like a garden sprinkler.

And there was something in the sky, big and bright. It was a dish of muddy light, down there close to the horizon, a big plateful of cloudy bands, pink and purple and brown. Where the bands met, he could see fine lines of turbulence, swoops and swirls, a crazy water-colour. Maybe it was a moon. But if so it was a hell of a size, thirty or forty times the size of the Moon in Earth's sky.

His lungs were straining at the fouling air. There was a hot stink, of fear and carbon dioxide and condensation. He tried to control himself, but he couldn't help but struggle, feebly.

. . . *Jupiter*. Think, Malenfant. That big 'moon' had to be Jupiter.

And if that was a volcanic plume he'd seen, he was on Io.

He felt a huge, illogical relief, despite the claustrophobic pain. He was still in the solar system, then. Maybe he was going to die here. But at least he wasn't so impossibly far from home. It was an obscure comfort.

But – *Io*, for God's sake. In the year AD 3265, it seemed, there were Neandertals, reconstructed from genetic residue in modern humans, living on Io. Why the hell, he still had to figure.

The blackness closed around his vision, like theatre curtains.

He drifted back to consciousness.

He was in a tent of some kind. It stretched above him, cone-shaped, like a teepee. He couldn't see through the walls. The light came from glow-lamps. Relics of the high-tech past, perhaps.

He was lying there naked. He didn't even have the simple coverall the Bad Hair Day twins had given him in Earth orbit. Feebly he put his hands over his crotch. He'd come a thousand years and travelled tens of light years, but he couldn't shake off that Presbyterian upbringing.

People moved around him. *Neandertals*. In the tent they shucked off their pressure suits, which they just piled up in a corner, and went naked.

He drifted to sleep.

Later, the girl who'd pulled him through the Saddle Point gateway, pulled him through to Io itself, nursed him. Or anyhow she gave him water and some kind of sludgy food, like hot yoghurt, and a thin broth, like very weak chicken soup.

He knew how ill he was.

He'd gotten radiation poisoning at the heart of that radioactive pile. He'd taken punishment in the mucous membranes of his mouth, oesophagus and stomach, where the membrane surfaces were coming off in layers; it was all he could do to eat the yoghurt stuff. He got the squits all the time, twenty-five or thirty times a day; his Neandertal nurse patiently cleaned him up, but he could see there was blood in the liquid mess. His right shin swelled up until it was rigid and painful; the skin was bluish-purple, swollen, shiny and smooth to the touch. He got soft blisters on his backside. He could feel that his body hair was falling out, his eyebrows, his groin, his chest.

He was sensitive to sounds, and if the Neandertals made much noise it set off his diarrhoea. Not that they often did; they made occasional high-pitched grunts, but they seemed to talk mostly with mime, pulling their faces and fluttering their fingers at each other.

He drifted through periods of uneasy sleep. Maybe he was delirious. He supposed he was going to die.

His Neandertal nurse's physique was not huge, but her body gave off an impression of density. Her midsection and chest were large – flat breasts – and the muscles of her forearm looked as thick as Malenfant's thigh muscles. Her aura of strength was palpable; she was much more physical than any human Malenfant had ever met.

But what immediately stood out was her face.

It was outsized, with her eyes too far apart, nose flattened, and features spread too wide, as if the whole face had been pulled wide. Her jaw was thick, but her chin was shallow and sliced back, as if it had been snipped off. Bulging out of her forehead was an immense brow, a bony swelling like a tumour. It pushed down the face beneath it and made the eyes sunken in their huge hard-boned sockets, giving her the effect of a distorted reflection, like an embryo in a jar. A swelling at the back of her head offset the weight of that huge brow, but it tilted her head downward, so that her chin almost rested on her chest, her massive neck snaking forward.

But those eyes were clear and human.

He christened his nurse Valentina, because of her Russian eyebrows: Valentina after Tereshkova, first woman in space, who he met once at an air show in Paris.

Valentina was more human than any ape, and yet she was not human. And it was that closeness-yet-difference which disturbed Malenfant.

He slept, he woke. Days passed, perhaps; he had no way to mark the passage of time.

He got depressed.

He got frightened. He cursed Nemoto for his renewed exile.

He clutched his ruined old spacesuit to his chest, running his aching hands over his mission patch and the Stars and Stripes, faded by harsh Alpha Centauri light. He stared at his fragment of Emma, the only human face here, and wept like a baby.

Valentina tolerated all this.

And, slowly, to his surprise, he started getting better. After a time he was even able to sit up, to feed himself.

Valentina, a dirt-caked bare-assed Neandertal, was curing him of radiation poisoning. He couldn't figure it, grateful as he was for the phenomenon. Maybe there was some kind of nanomachinery at work here, repairing the damage he had suffered at the cellular, even molecular level. He'd already seen evidence of how the Earth was suffused by ancient machinery from beyond the Saddle Points, from the stars.

Or maybe it was just the soup.

Soon Malenfant was able to walk, stiffly.

Most of the Neandertals ignored him. They stepped over and around him, as if they couldn't even see him.

For his part, he watched the Neandertals, amazed.

He counted around thirty people crammed into this teepee. There were adults, frail old people, children all the way down to babies in arms. But, he sensed, it would take a long time to get to know them so well that he could distinguish all the individuals. He was the archetype of the foreigner abroad, to whom everybody looked alike.

The women seemed as strong as the men. Even the children, muscled like Olympic shot-putters, joined in the chores. They used their teeth and powerful jaws, together with their stone tools, to cut meat and scrape hides – meat he presumed must have been hauled through from Earth, through the Saddle Point gateway he'd followed himself. They would bake some of the meat in hearths, if you could call them that: just shallow pits scraped in the ground, lined with fire-heated rocks and covered by soil. But the softer meat was given to the infants – and to Malenfant, incidentally, by Valentina. The adults took their meat mostly uncooked; those big jaws would chomp away at the tough flesh, grinding and tearing, muscles working, making it swallowable.

There was one old guy who showed some curiosity in Malenfant, a geezer who walked with a heavy limp, hunched over so that his belly drooped down over his shrivelled-up penis. Malenfant decided to call him Esau. The Book of Genesis, if he remembered right: *Behold, Esau my brother is a hairy man, and I am a smooth man.*

Malenfant looked into Esau's eyes, and wondered what he was thinking. He wondered *how* he was thinking.

This is my cousin, but far enough removed he represents an alien species, an alien consciousness. The first thing my remote ancestors did, stumbling out of Africa, was to close-encounter the alien, these

Eeties of the deep past: the true first contact. And when the last of the Neandertals lay dying, in some rocky fastness in France or Spain or China, there must have been a *last* contact: the last we'd have for thirty thousand years, until the Gaijin showed up in the asteroid belt.

Hell of a thing, to be alone all that time.

The Neandertals had a portable Saddle Point gateway. When they set it up and used it, Malenfant goggled.

It was a big blue hoop maybe three metres high. They were able to step through it, with the characteristic blue flash, thus disappearing from Io; later they would reappear with sacks of material, much of it rock and meat and metal canisters, maybe containing oxygen. This must be their link to Earth, to the Kimera mine – the way he had been brought here.

He toyed with the idea of going back through, trying to get back to Earth. Escape. But it would only lead him to the Kimera Engine, which would kill him; or if he evaded that, back into the clutches of Mtesa.

Maybe that was a last resort. For now he was stuck here.

What did Malenfant know about Neandertals? Diddley squat. But he did remember they weren't supposed to have speech. Their palates weren't formed correctly, or some such. He'd seen them miming, and they were clearly smart. But speech, so went the theories he remembered, had been the key advantage enjoyed by *Homo Sap*. So here he was, the speaking man in the country of the dumb.

Maybe Reid Malenfant could teach Neandertals to talk. Maybe he could civilize them. He was fired by sudden enthusiasm.

He pointed to Esau. 'You.' At himself. 'Me. You. Say it. You, you, you. Me. Malenfant. My name. Mal-en-fant. You try.'

Esau studied Malenfant for a while, then slapped him, hard. It knocked him back onto the floor.

Malenfant clambered upright. His cheek stung like hell; Esau was *strong*.

Esau rattled through gestures: pointing to him, two fingers to his own forehead, then a fist to Malenfant's forehead. He didn't seem angry: more like he was trying to teach Malenfant something. *Point. Fist to head. Point. Fist.*

'Oh.' Malenfant pointed to himself, then made the fist sign. 'I get it. This is the name you're giving me. A sign word.'

Esau slapped him again. There was no malice, but again he was knocked over.

When Malenfant got up this time, he made the signs, point, fist, without speaking.

So it went. If he spoke more than a couple of syllables, Esau would slap him.

His vocabulary of signs started to grow: ten words, a dozen, two dozen.

He observed mothers with children. They got the slaps too, if they made too much noise. He started to interpret the complex rattle of fingers and gestures as the adults communicated with each other, fluent and urgent. He'd pick up maybe one sign in a hundred.

So much for the speaking man in the country of the dumb. He was like a child to these people.

It was a long time before he found out that the fist-to-head sign, his name, meant *Stupid*.

One day, when he woke up, everyone was clambering into their translucent pressure suits: men, women, children, even infants in little sacklike papooses. A couple of the adults were working at the teepee, pulling at the poles which held it up, taking up the groundsheet.

It was, it seemed, time to move on.

Holding his bubble helmet in front of his genitals, Malenfant cowered against the wall of the collapsing teepee, naked, scared, as the smooth dismantling operation continued around him. Malenfant had no pressure suit: only the NASA antique he'd worn to come here in the first place. What if the Neandertals thought it was still functional? If he stepped out on the surface of Io, the suit would kill him, in fifteen minutes.

Valentina came up to him. She was in her suit already, with the soft helmet closed over. She was holding out another suit; it looked like a flayed skin.

He took it gratefully. She showed him how to step inside it, how to seal up the seams with a fingernail. It was too short and wide for him, but it seemed to stretch.

It *stank*: of urine, faeces, an ancient, milk-like smell. It smelled like Esau, like an old Neandertal geezer.

Somebody had died in this suit.

When he realized that he almost lost his breakfast, and tried to pull the suit off his flesh. But Valentina slapped him, harder than she'd done for a long time. There was no mistaking the commands in her peremptory signs. *Put it on. Now.*

This, he thought, is not the Manned Spaceflight Operations Building, Cape Canaveral. Things are different here. Accept it, if you want to keep breathing.

346

He pulled on the suit and sealed it up. Then he stood there trying not to throw up inside the suit's claustrophobic stink, as the Neandertals dismantled their camp, and the light of Jupiter was revealed.

Morning on Io:

Auroras flapped overhead, huge writhing sheets of light.

The sun was a shrunken disc, low down, brighter than any star in the sky. It cast long, point-source shadows over the burnt-pizza terrain. In the sky Jupiter hung above the horizon, just where it had before, a fat pink stripy-painted football. But now the phase was different; Jupiter was a crescent, the terminator blurred by layers of atmosphere, and the dark side was a chunk out of the starry background, a slab of night sparking with the crackles of electrical storms bigger than Earth, like giant flashbulbs exploding inside pink clouds.

In a red-green auroral glow, the Neandertals moved about, packing up their teepee and other gear, loading it all onto big sled-like vehicles, signing to each other busily. Malenfant picked up his only possession, the remnant of his NASA suit, and bundled it up on the back of a sled.

When they were loaded, the adult Neandertals started strapping themselves into traces at the front of the sled, simple harnesses made of the ubiquitous translucent plastic. Soon everybody was saddled up except the smallest children, who would ride on the top of the loaded sleds.

Nobody told Malenfant what to do. He looked for Valentina, and made sure he got into a slot alongside her. She helped him fit a harness around his body; it tightened with simple buckles.

And then they started hauling.

The Neandertals just leaned into the traces, like so many squat pack horses. And, by the light of Jupiter, they began to drag the sleds across the crusty Io surface. It turned out that Malenfant's sled was a little harder to move than the others, and his team had to strain harder, snapping signs at each other, until the runners came free of the clinging rock, with a jerk.

Valentina's gait, when walking, was – different. She seemed to lean forward as if her centre of gravity was somewhere over her hip joints, instead of further back like Malenfant's. And when she walked her whole weight seemed to pound down, with every stride, on her hips. It was clumsy, almost ape-like, the least human of her features, as far as Malenfant could see.

Valentina wasn't built for walking long distances, like Malenfant was. Maybe the Neandertals had evolved to be sedentary.

Malenfant did his best to pull with the rest. It wasn't clear to him why he was being kept alive, except as some vaguely altruistic impulse of Valentina's. But he sure wanted to be seen to be working for his supper. So he added his feeble *Homo Sap* strength to the Neandertals'.

Thus, hominids from Earth toiled across the face of Io.

The ground was mostly just rock: silicates, big lumps of it under his feet, peppered by bubbles. It was basalt, volcanic rock pumped out of Io's interior. Sulphur lay in great yellow sheets over the rock, crunching under his feet. Io was a rocky world, not an ice ball like most of the other outer-system moons; sized midway between Earth's Moon and Mars, Io was a terrestrial planet, lost out here in Jupiter orbit.

Jupiter changed constantly, a compelling, awesome sight.

Io was, he recalled, tidally locked to its giant parent; it kept the same face to Jupiter the whole time. But the moon skated around Jupiter's waist every forty-two hours, and so the gas giant went through its whole cycle of phases in less than two days. And Jupiter, meanwhile, rotated on its own axis every ten hours or so. He didn't have to watch that huge face for long to see the cloud decks turning, those turbulent bands and chains of little white globules chasing each other around the stripy bands. But there was no Big Red Spot, he was disappointed to find; evidently that centuries-long storm had blown itself out some time in the millennium he'd been away.

Jupiter had a powerful magnetosphere, a radiation belt of electrons and ions locked to the giant planet, within which Io circled. Jupiter's fast rotation made that magnetosphere whip over Io like an invisible storm. That was the cause of the huge auroras which flapped constantly over his head, energetic particles battering at the thin air of this forsaken moon, ripping away a tonne of atmospheric material every second. Malenfant shivered, naked inside his old man's suit, as he thought of that thin, fast sleet of energetic particles slamming down from the sky, pounding at his flesh.

But the Neandertals weren't concerned. They pulled for hours, and the tracks of the three sleds arrowed across the flat landscape, straight towards Jupiter. Malenfant – a hundred years old and still recovering from radiation exposure – could do little but lean into the traces and let the rest carry him along.

He'd built up an impression that the Neandertals worked hard. They used their big gorilla bodies where *Homo Sap* would have used tools. Their bodies were under intense physical stress, the whole time. Malenfant observed that Esau's body, for example, bore a lot of old injuries, scars and badly set bones. It was as if they climbed a mountain or ran a marathon every day of their lives.

But the Neandertals accepted this, an occupational hazard.

The compensation was the very physical nature of their lives. They lived immersed in their world. They were vigorous, intensely *alive*. By comparison Malenfant, as the only available sample of the species *Homo Sap*, felt weak, vague, as if he was blundering about in a mist. He found he envied them.

The Neandertals sang as they hauled – sign-sang, that is. It was a song about the Face of Kintu. Kintu was one of the few words they vocalized, and it was, Malenfant recalled, the name of a Ugandan god, the grandfather of Kimera. The song was about Kintu blowing himself up with breath until stars and worlds popped out over his body, like volcanoes on Io. Kintu was God and the universe for the Neandertals, and the Face of Kintu – it took him a while to realize – was their name for Io itself.

The signing was functional for the Neandertals, for their magic suits had no radios. But it was more than that. It was beautiful when you got to follow it a little, a mix of dance and speech.

He had to be shown how to use his magic suit's sanitary facilities. Basically the trick was just to let go. The suit's surface absorbed the waste, liquid and solid; it simply disappeared into that translucent wall, as if dissolving. Most of it anyhow. On the move, Malenfant had no chance to open his magic suit, this shell he had to share with the stink of a dead old man, and now of his own waste. The Neandertals clearly weren't hung up on personal hygiene. After a couple of days, however, Malenfant was longing for a shower.

After a time, snow fell around the Neandertals, fine little blue crystals that settled over Malenfant's head and shoulders, crisping the basaltic ground.

Valentina nudged him, and pointed. Over the horizon, a geyser was erupting. It was the source of the snow.

The sparkling plume was venting into space, tens of kilometres high. The plume was blue, sulphur dioxide. At the top of the plume the ice glittered brightly: ionized by Jupiter's magnetic winds, the charged molecular fragments shimmered with energy, a miniature aurora. At the base of the plume lava was flowing. Perhaps it was liquid sulphur. As it emerged it flowed stickily, slowly, like molasses, but as it cooled it became runnier, until it pooled down the shallow slopes of the vent, like machine oil.

A volcanic plume, glowing in the dark. It looked like a giant, twisted fluorescent tube: exotic, strange, spectacular. His heart lifted, the way it had when he first beheld Alpha Centauri. He might not understand everything he saw. But, he felt now, it was *worth* coming out here – worth exploring, worth suffering all the incomprehensible shit and endless culture shocks and even getting slapped around by Neandertals – worth it for sights like this.

The march was diverted to skirt the plume's caldera.

Soon the party started to stray into an area where a kind of frost lay over the ground, thick and green-blue, probably sulphur dioxide. The ground started to get significantly colder under Malenfant, and he was shivering.

The party moved away from the frost, seeking warmer ground.

They were walking over hot spots, he realized. But the hot spots must shift. Io, plagued by volcanism, squeezed like a rubber ball in a fist by Jupiter's tidal pumping, was resurfaced by lava flows all the time.

So the Neandertals had to move on, wandering over Io, in search of warmth from the ground.

It was one hell of a lifestyle. But they seemed to be happy.

About twice every Io day the caravan stopped.

The Neandertals didn't always set up camp. They would unload scuffed and scarred pieces of equipment, boxes the size of refrigerators or washing machines. They plugged their magic suits into these, at hip and mouth, for a couple of hours at a time. The mouth socket supplied food, edible mush that tasted of nothing.

Malenfant didn't know how his magic suit kept him supplied with oxygen; he wasn't carrying a tank. The suit must somehow break down the sulphur dioxide air, and scrub out carbon dioxide from his lungs. Maybe the hip socket extracted stored waste, carbon dioxide and urine and faecal matter, for recycling. Anyhow the boxes seemed to recharge the magic suits, making them good for another ten or twelve hours.

The suits just worked, without any fuss. But the Neandertals only had a finite number of magic suits, and seemed to have no way of manufacturing more. If some sad old geezer hadn't died, there would have been no magic suit for Malenfant. What then? Would they have abandoned him? Well, he hadn't been invited here.

He had no idea how old all this equipment was. It was clear to him somebody had set up this Neandertal community on Io. *Somebody.* The Gaijin, of course. Who else?

He had yet to figure out their purpose, however.

Every time the Neandertals stopped they checked over the Staff of Kintu.

This was a metallic rod, about the size of a relay baton. It seemed to be their most precious artefact. It was just a pipe a half-metre long, of a metal that looked like aluminium, and it seemed light. Sitting in Io frost, the adults would pass the Staff from hand to gloved hand, checking its weight, fondling it, signing over it. The songs they sang, about the breath of Kintu, concerned the Staff. Maybe it was some kind of religious totem. But it was too easy to assume that anything you didn't understand must have religious significance. Maybe there was more to it than that.

Malenfant envied them their community. Ignored even by the children, he felt shut out, lonely. He felt eager to learn to talk.

Malenfant observed signs, copied them, and repeated them to Valentina.

At first he had been able to grasp only simple concrete nouns, straightforward adjectives: a hand raised to the mouth for 'food', for instance, or a rubbed stomach for 'hungry'. But, more slowly, he learned to recognize representations of more abstract thoughts. Two forefingers brought together harmoniously seemed to mean 'same' or 'like'; two pointing fingers stabbing each other was 'argument' or 'fight'. There seemed to be a significance in the hand-shapes, their position relative to the body, and accompanying non-manual features like body language, posture and facial expression. And there was a grammar, it seemed, in the order of the signs. Get any one of the elements wrong and the sign made no sense, or the wrong sense.

It seemed to him that several signs could be transmitted at once, using fragments of multiple words. The Neandertals were not constrained to speak linearly, a word at a time, as he was. They could send across whole chunks of information simultaneously, at a much higher bit rate than humans. And, it occurred to him, these new reconstructed Neandertals must have devised their rich, complex language from scratch, in just a few generations. After all, there could be no way of retrieving the lost language of their genetic predecessors, the true Neandertals.

It was a wonderful, rich mode of communication.

He tried to avoid getting slapped. But he was punished if he got the signs too badly wrong.

'You don't know your own strength. I'm an old man, damn it!'

Slap.

When the Neandertals lay down to sleep, out in the open, they did it in their magic suits, out there on the bare surface of Io.

He picked out the constellations – and the pale stripe of another comet, a huge one, its double tail sprawled over the sky. And in the direction of Orion there was something new: bright flares, like distant explosions, scattered over a shield-shaped patch of sky. It was a silent, unending firework show: as if there was a battle going on, out there at the fringe of the solar system, a defensive fight against some besieging invader.

War in the Oort cloud, perhaps. Were the Gaijin battling Nemoto's star-cracking aliens out there, on the rim of the system, defending Sol? If so, why? Surely the Gaijin's motivation had little to do with humanity. If they fought, it was to protect their own interests, their projects.

And, of course, if there really was a comet-scrambling war going on in the Oort cloud, it had one dread implication: that the Crackers were no longer out there, at Procyon or Sirius – but *here*.

Sleep came with difficulty under such a crowded, dangerous sky. In the end he burrowed under his bulky NASA pressure suit, seeking darkness.

After maybe a week, to Malenfant's intense relief, they set up camp once more. It was at a site that had evidently been used before: a rough circle of kicked-up soil, scarred by hearths.

Inside the teepee the Neandertals immediately stripped off. After a week locked into the suits the stink of their bodies almost knocked Malenfant out.

There was a great spontaneous festival of the body. The kids wrestled, the adults coupled. Malenfant saw one girl pursuing an older man – literally pursuing him around the cave, her vulva visibly swollen and bright red, until she'd pinned him down and climbed on top of him. Then they slept together, in great heaps of stinking, hairy flesh. There was no lookout; presumably there were no predators on Io, no enemies.

Malenfant hunkered in a corner, generally ignored, though Valentina and Esau brought him food.

Sometimes – when the light was low, when he caught a woman or child out of the corner of his eye – he thought of them as like himself, like people. But they weren't people. No better or worse than humans. Just different. A different form of consciousness.

It seemed to him that the Neandertals lived closer to the world than he did. That intense physicality was the key. Their consciousness was dispersed at the periphery of their beings, in their bodies and the things and people that occupied their world. When two of them sat together – signing, or working, in peaceable silence – they seemed to move as one, in a slow clumsy choreography, as if their blurred identities had merged into one, in the ultimate intimacy. Malenfant felt he could see the flow of their consciousness like deep streams, untroubled by the turbulence and reflectiveness of his own nature.

Every day was like the first day of their lives, and a vivid delight.

Malenfant wondered how it was possible for such people as these – intelligent, complex, vibrant – to have become extinct.

Extinct: a brutal, uncompromising word. Extinction made death even more of a hard cold wall, because it was the death of the species. It no longer mattered, truthfully, how sophisticated the Neandertals' sign language had been, whether they had been capable of true human-like speech, how rich was their deep-embedded consciousness. Because it was all gone.

The Neandertals had been brought back for this short Indian summer to serve the Gaijin's purposes. But this had not cheated the extinction, because these Neandertals were *not* those who had gone before; they had no memory of their forebears, no continuity. The extinction of the Neandertals, in the deep past of Earth, had buried hope and memory, disconnected the past from the future.

And now, Malenfant feared, the time was drawing close for an extinction event on a still more massive scale, extinction across multiple star systems, so complete that not even bones and tools would be left behind for some future archaeologist to ponder.

Valentina woke him with a kick. She beckoned him, a universal gesture, and handed him his suit.

He got dressed groggily and followed her out of the teepee.

Out on the surface, he relieved himself, and looked around. Io was in eclipse right now, so that the pinpoint sun was hidden by Jupiter. The ground was darkened by the giant planet's shadow, illumined only by starlight, and by an auroral glow from Jupiter, which was otherwise a hole in the sky.

As the warm fluid trickled uncomfortably down his leg, he stumbled after Valentina, who had already set off across the crusty plain.

There were five Neandertals in the party, plus Malenfant. They were all carrying bags of tools. The Neandertals moved at a loping half-jog that Malenfant found almost impossible to match, despite the gravity.

They kept this up for an hour, maybe more. Then they stopped, abruptly. Malenfant leaned forward and propped himself up against his knees, wheezing.

There was something here. A line on the ground, shining silver in the starlight. It arrowed straight for the swollen face of Jupiter.

Malenfant recognized the texture. It was the same material he'd seen trailing from the roots of Trees, in orbit: material that had been found on the surface of Venus.

It was superconductor cable.

The Neandertals, signing busily, pressed a gadget to the cable. Malenfant couldn't see what they were doing. Maybe this was some kind of diagnostic tool. After a couple of minutes, they straightened up and moved on.

As they trotted, the eclipse was finishing. The sun started to poke out from behind Jupiter's limb, a shrunken disc that rose up through layers of cloud; orange-yellow light fled through the churning cloud decks, casting shadows longer than Earth's diameter.

The dawn light caught Io's flux tube. It was like a vast, wispy tornado reaching up over his head. The flux tube was a misty flow of charged particles hurled up from Io's endless volcanoes sweeping in elegant magnetic-field curves into the face of the giant planet. And where the tube hit Jupiter's upper atmosphere, hundreds of kilometres above the planet's cloud decks, there was a continuing explosion: gases made hotter than the surface of the sun, dragged across the face of the giant planet at orbital speed, patches of rippling aurora hundreds of kilometres across.

Io, a planet-sized body shoving its way through Jupiter's magnetosphere, was like a giant electrical generator. There was a potential difference of hundreds of thousands of volts across the moon's diameter, currents of millions of amps flowing through the ionosphere.

Standing here, peering up into the flux tube itself, the physical sense of energy was immense; Malenfant wanted to quail, to protect himself from the sleet of high-energy particles which must be gushing down from the sky. But he stood straight, facing this godlike play of energy. Not in front of the Neandertals, he told himself.

Soon they arrived at a place where the cable was buried by a flow of sulphurous lava, now frozen solid. After a flurry of signs, the Neandertals unpacked simple shovels and picks and began to hack away at the lava, exposing the cable.

Malenfant longed to rest. His legs seized up in agonizing cramps; the muscles felt like boulders. But, he felt, he had to earn his corn. He rubbed his legs and joined the others. He used a pick on the lava, and helped haul away the debris.

He couldn't believe this was the only length of superconductor on Io. He imagined the whole damn moon being swathed by a net of the stuff, wrapping the shifting surface like lines of longitude. Perhaps it had been mined from Venus, scavenged from that ancient, failed project, brought here for some new purpose of the Gaijin.

The Neandertals' job must be to maintain the superconductor network, to dig it out. Otherwise, such was the resurfacing rate on this ferocious little moon, the net would surely be buried in a couple of centuries or so. The work would be haphazard, as the Neandertals could travel only where the volcanic hot spots allowed them. But, given enough time, they could cover the whole moon.

It was a smart arrangement, he thought. It gave the Neandertals a world of their own, safe from the predations of *Homo Sap*. And it gave the builders of this net – presumably the Gaijin – a cheap and reliable source of maintenance labour.

Neandertals were patient, and dogged. On Earth, they had persisted with a technology that suited them, all but unchanged, for sixty thousand years. They might already have been here, on Io, for centuries. With Neandertals, the Gaijin had gotten a labour pool as smart as humans, not likely to breed themselves over their resource limits here, and lacking any of the angst and hassle that came with your typical *Homo Sap* workforce.

Smart deal, for the Gaijin.

All he had to do now was figure out the purpose of the net itself: this immense Gaijin project, evidently intent on tapping the huge natural energy flows of Io. What were they making here?

Without a word to Malenfant the Neandertals jogged off again, along the cable towards Jupiter.

Malenfant, wheezing, followed.

When they got back to the teepee, they found Esau had died.

Valentina was inordinately distressed. She hunkered down in a corner of the tent, her huge body heaving with sobs. Evidently she had had some close relation to Esau; perhaps he was her father, or brother.

Nobody seemed moved to comfort her.

Malenfant squatted down opposite her. He cupped her chinless jaw in his hand, and tried to raise up her huge head.

At first Valentina stayed hunched over. Then – hesitantly, clumsily, without looking at him – she lifted her huge hand, and stroked the back of his head.

She looked up in surprise. Her hard, strong fingers found a bony protrusion. It was called an occipital bun, Malenfant knew, a relic of his distant French ancestry. She grabbed his hand and pulled it to the back of her own scalp. There was a similar knotty bulge there, under her long black hair. Here was one place, anyhow, where they were similar. Maybe his own occipital bun was some relic of Neandertal ancestry, a ghost trace of some inter-species romance buried millennia in the past.

Valentina's human eyes, buried under that ridge of bone, stared out at him with renewed curiosity. Her breasts were flat, her waist solid, her build as bulky as a man's. And her face thrust forward with its great projecting nose, her puffed-up cheekbones, her long chinless jaw. But she wasn't ugly to him. She was even beautiful.

The moment stretched. This close to her, this still, Malenfant was uncomfortably aware of a tightness in his groin.

Damn those Bad Hair Day twins. He hadn't wanted any of this complication.

He tried to imagine Valentina behaving provocatively: those eyes coyly retreating, perhaps, tilting her chin, glancing over her shoulder, parting her mouth, signals common to women of his own species the world over, in his day.

But that wasn't the way Neandertal women behaved. They were *not* coy, he thought.

It may be humans and Neandertals couldn't interbreed anyhow. And for sure, a few hundred millennia of separate evolution had given them a different set of come-on signals. He began to understand how it might have been back in the deep past: how two equally gifted, resourceful, communicative, curious, emotionally rich human species could have been crammed together into one small space – and yet be as mindless of each other as two types of birds in his old back yard. It was chilling, epochally sad.

He thought of Valentina's massive hand grabbing his balls, and what was left of his erection drained away.

The Neandertals held a ceremony.

They pulled back the groundsheet of the teepee, to reveal a brick-red ground. The teepee filled up with a pungent, bleach-like stink: sulphur dioxide.

Briskly the Neandertals dug out a grave. They used their strong bare hands, working together efficiently and co-operatively. A metre or so down they started hauling out dirt that was stained a more vivid orange and blue.

Malenfant inspected it curiously: this was, after all, the soil of Io. The dirt looked just like crumbled-up rock, but it was laced with orange, yellow and green: sulphur compounds, he supposed, suffused through the rock. There were a few grains of native sulphur, crumbling yellow crystals.

The deeper dirt looked as if it was polluted by lichen.

Some of this was colourless, a dull grey, and some of it was green and purple. Malenfant had never been a biologist, but he knew there were types of bacteria on Earth that flourished in environments like this: acidic, sulphur-rich, oxygen free, like the volcanic vents on Earth. Maybe there was actually some photosynthesis going on here. Or maybe it was based on some more exotic kind of chemistry. There could be underground reservoirs where some kind of plants stored energy by binding up sulphur dioxide into a less stable compound, like sulphur trioxide; and maybe there were even simple animals which breathed that in, burning elemental sulphur, for energy . . .

Scientifically, he supposed, it was interesting. But he was never going to know. And he wasn't here for the science, any more than the Neandertals.

And anyhow, Malenfant, life in the universe is commonplace. And so, it seems, is death.

When the grave was dug, they lowered the body of Esau into it. Valentina got down there with him, and curled him up into a kind of foetus shape. The girl surrounded the old man with a handful of arte-facts, maybe stuff that had been important to him: a flute, for instance, carved out of what looked like a femur.

And Valentina tucked the totem rod, the Staff of Kintu, into Esau's dead hand.

After that Valentina stayed in the grave with the corpse a long, long time. There was a lot of signing, back and forth; Malenfant couldn't follow many words, but he could see a rhythmic flow to the signs, as they washed around the grave. They were singing, he suspected.

When at last Valentina clambered out, Malenfant felt his own mor-bid mood start to lift. The Neandertals started to throw Io dirt back into the grave.

Then – just before the grave was closed over, Esau turned his shrunken head, lifted a stick-like arm.

Opened gummy eyes.

The Neandertals kept right on kicking in Io dirt.

... But he was still alive. Malenfant froze, with no idea what to say or do.

Stick to your own business, Malenfant. Be grateful they didn't do it to you.

After that, he found it difficult to sleep. He kept hearing scrabbling, scratching at the ground beneath him.

He was startled awake.

There was a bright electric-blue glow, coming from under the groundsheet, leaking into the teepee's conical space. A glow, coming from the old geezer's grave.

Malenfant had seen that glow before: a thousand astronomical units from Earth, and by the light of other suns, and in the heart of an African mountain, and even here, on Io. It was the glow of Saddle Point gateway technology.

He tried to ask Valentina, the others. But he didn't have the words, and they slapped him away.

A while after that – it might have been a couple of days – the Neandertals lifted the sheet and started to dig out the grave.

To Malenfant's relief, the stink wasn't too bad, and masked by the sulphur dioxide. Maybe the wrong bacteria in the soil, he wondered.

Valentina reached down into the grave and pulled out the metal Staff. She showed no signs of the distress she had exhibited before.

The Neandertals, with little fuss or ceremony, started to refill the grave.

Malenfant got close enough to look inside the grave. *It was empty.* He felt his skin prickle, a kid at Halloween.

He tried to get a look at the Staff. Maybe it was the cause of that electric-blue Saddle Point glow, the disappearance of the corpse. But the girl hid it away.

A party set out along the cables once more, Valentina and Malenfant included. Malenfant kept to himself, ignoring the fantastic scenery, even ignoring the aches of his own rebuilt body.

His head seemed to be starting to work again, if reluctantly. And slowly, step by step, he was figuring out the set-up here.

This arrangement with the Gaijin wasn't all one way. There was a reward for the Neandertals, it seemed, beyond the gift of this remote moon.

He thought about the electric-blue Saddle Point flash that came out

358

of old Esau's grave. Saddle Point teleport gateways worked by destroying a body so as to record its quantum-mechanical structure. Every passage into a gateway was like a miniature death anyhow. Maybe the Staff of Kintu, that little metal artefact, stored some kind of recorded pattern, from the dying old geezer.

Maybe Esau – and perhaps all the Neandertals' ancestors, stretching back centuries – were still, in a sense, *alive*, their Saddle Point signals stored in the Staff. No wonder the Neandertals took such care of the artefact. Maybe that was their reward, to live on in the Staff, until –

Until what?

Until, he thought, they had gathered enough energy, with the huge engines which encased Io. Until Kintu was ready to throw his Staff, all the way to his Navel. Just like in the songs.

He grinned; he had it. That Staff, rattling around in some Neandertal backpack, was no totem. It was a fucking *spaceship*.

And *that* was why they were gathering all this energy, from the natural dynamo that was Io.

Malenfant, excited, grabbed Valentina's arm. 'Listen to me.'

She lifted a hand to slap him.

He backed off and tried to sign. *Wait. Tell me, you tell me. Staff of Kintu, Navel. You go Navel, in Staff. Navel what Navel, what what what.* 'Oh, damn it. What are the Gaijin making here? Antimatter? What is the Navel? Is that where the Gaijin are heading?' She slapped him, knocking him back, but he kept going. *Navel.* 'Kintu has belly, belly, Navel . . . I'm right, aren't I?' *Speak true know true.* 'I –'

She prepared to slap him again.

Beneath his feet the ground felt suddenly hot. It was like standing on a griddle. He backed away, instinctively, until he reached a place where the gritty dirt was cooler.

Valentina hadn't moved. She was looking down, as if baffled. The ground was starting to darken, its shade deepening down from the ubiquitous red. Blue gas erupted around Valentina's feet, like a stage effect.

It was a volcanic plume, opening up right under Valentina.

When the ground started to crumble, he didn't even think about it. He just lunged forwards, fists outstretched. It seemed to take an age to arc through Io's feeble gravity.

He hit her on her shoulders as hard as he could. Despite her greater mass and low centre of gravity, she toppled backwards, and fell away from the vent towards harder ground. She was safe.

Malenfant, on the other hand, was helpless.

He was falling in desperate low-gravity slow-motion, spread-eagled, right down into the centre of the vent, which had opened up into a bubbling pit of dark molten sulphur. He could feel the skin of his chest and face blistering, bubbling like the sulphurous ground. Evidently his magic suit wasn't going to protect him from this one.

He laughed. So it ends here. At least he'd gotten to know the answer. Some of it, anyhow.

There were worse deaths.

The sulphur bubbled up over him, and the pain was overwhelming.

But there was a strong hand at his neck –

After that, only fragments:

Lying flat. No feeling anywhere.

Stars overhead. Vision bouncing. One eye still working? Being carried?

Walls around him, lifting up, a circle of thick-browed faces.

. . . Oh. A grave. *He* was the old geezer now. He tried to laugh, but nothing seemed to be working.

A rain of blackness over him. Dirt. It spattered on his chest, his face. Pain stung where it hit exposed flesh. There were hands working above him, big powerful hands like spades, scooping up dirt to throw over him. Valentina's hands, others.

The dirt landed in his eyes, his mouth. It tasted of bleach.

I'm alive. They're burying me. I'm alive!

He tried to cry out, but his throat was clogged by dirt. He tried to rise, but his limbs had no strength, as if he was swaddled up in bandages.

The dirt rained on his face, a black sulphurous hail. He couldn't even move.

There was something in the corner of his vision. A metallic glint.

A flash of electric-blue light.

Chapter 28

PEOPLE CAME FROM EARTH

A little before Dawn, Xenia Makarova stepped out of her house into silvery light. The air frosted white from her nose, and the deep Moon chill cut through papery flesh to her spindly bones.

The silver-grey light came from Earth and Mirror in the sky: twin spheres, the one milky cloud, the other a hard image of the sun. But the light was still dim enough to allow her to see the changed, colonized stars, as well as the fainter stripes of the comets that hailed through the inner system, one after another, echoes of the titanic war being waged on the solar system's rim.

And beyond the comets the new supernova – the destructive blossoming of the star the astronomers had once labelled Phi Cassiopeiae – was still brilliant, as bright as Venus perhaps, though dimming. When Xenia had been born such a spectacle, a supernova a mere nine thousand light years away, would have been a source of great scientific and public interest. Not today, of course, not in the year AD 3480.

But now the sun itself was shouldering above the horizon, dimming even the supernova. Beads of light like trapped stars marked the summits of Tycho's rim mountains, and a deep bloody crimson was working its way high into the tall sky. Almost every scrap of the air in that sky had been drawn from the heart of the Moon by the great Paulis mines. But now the mines were shut down, the Moon's core exhausted, and she imagined she could see the lid of the sky, the millennial leaking of the Moon's air into space.

She walked down the path that led to the circular sea. There was frost everywhere, of course, but the path's lunar dirt, patiently raked in her youth, was friendly and gripped her sandals. The water at the sea's rim was black and oily, lapping softly. She could see the grey sheen of pack ice further out, though the close horizon hid the bulk of the sea from her. Fingers of sunlight stretched across the ice, and grey-gold smoke shimmered above open water.

There was a constant tumult of groans and cracks as the ice rose and fell on the sea's mighty shoulders. The water never froze at Tycho's rim; conversely, it never thawed at the centre, so that there was a fat torus of ice floating out there around the central mountains. It was as if the rim of this artificial ocean was striving to emulate the unfrozen seas of Earth which bore its makers.

She thought she heard a barking, out on the pack ice. Perhaps it was a seal. And a bell clanked: an early fishing boat leaving port, a fat, comforting sound that carried easily through the still, dense air. She sought the boat's lights, but her eyes, rheumy, stinging with cold, failed her.

She paid attention to her creaking body: the aches in her too-thin, too-long, calcium-depleted bones, the obscure spurts of pain in her urethral system, the strange itches that afflicted her liver-spotted flesh. She was already growing too cold. Mirror returned enough heat to the Moon's long Night to keep the seas from freezing, the air from snowing out. But she would have welcomed a little more comfort.

She turned and began to labour back up her regolith path to her house.

When she got there, Berge, her grandson, was waiting for her. She did not know then, of course, that he would not survive the new Day.

He was eager to talk about Leonardo da Vinci.

Berge had taken off his wings and stacked them up against the concrete wall of her house. She could see how the wings were thick with frost, so dense the paper feathers could surely have had little play. Even long minutes after landing he was still panting, and his smooth fashionably-shaven scalp, so bare it showed the great bubble profile of his lunar-born skull, was dotted with beads of grimy sweat.

She scolded him even as she brought him into the warmth, and prepared hot soup and tea for him in her pressure kettles. 'You're a fool as your father was,' she said. His father, of course, had been Xenia's son. 'I was with him when he fell from the sky, leaving you orphaned. You know how dangerous it is in the pre-Dawn turbulence.'

'Ah, but the power of those great thermals, Xenia,' he said, as he accepted the soup. 'I can fly kilometres high without the slightest effort . . .'

Only Berge called her Xenia.

She would have berated him further, which was the prerogative of old age. But she didn't have the heart. He stood before her, eager, heartbreakingly thin. Berge always had been slender, even compared to other skinny lunar folk; but now he was clearly frail.

And, most ominous of all, a waxy, golden sheen seemed to linger about his skin. She had no desire to comment on that – not here, not now, not until she was sure what it meant, that it wasn't some trickery of her own age-yellowed eyes.

So she kept her counsel.

They made their ritual obeisance – murmurs about dedicating their bones and flesh to the salvation of the world – and finished up their soup.

And then, with his youthful eagerness, Berge launched into the seminar he was evidently itching to deliver on Leonardo da Vinci, long-dead citizen of a long-dead planet. Brusquely displacing the empty soup bowls to the floor, he produced papers from his jacket and spread them out before her. The sheets, yellowed and stained with age, were covered in a crabby, indecipherable handwriting, broken with sketches of gadgets or flowing water or geometric figures.

She picked out a luminously beautiful sketch of the crescent Earth . . .

'No, Xenia,' said Berge patiently. 'Not Earth. Think about it. It must have been the crescent *Moon*.' Of course he was right; she'd lived on the Moon too long. 'You see, Leonardo understood the phenomenon he called the ashen Moon – like our ashen Earth, the old Earth visible in the arms of the new. He was a hundred years ahead of his time with *that* one.'

This document had been called many things in its long history, but most familiarly the Codex Leicester. Berge's copy had been printed off in haste during The Failing, those frantic hours when the Moon's dying libraries had disgorged great snowfalls of paper, a last desperate download of their stored electronic wisdom before the power failed. It was a treatise centring on what Leonardo called the 'body of the Earth', but with diversions to consider such matters as water engineering, the geometry of Earth and Moon, and the origins of fossils.

The issue of the fossils particularly excited Berge. Leonardo had been much agitated by the presence of the fossils of marine creatures, fishes and oysters and corals, high in the mountains of Italy. Lacking any knowledge of tectonic processes, he had struggled to explain how the fossils might have been deposited by a series of great global floods.

It made her remember how, when Berge was small, she once had to explain to him what a 'fossil' was. There were no fossils on the Moon: no bones in the ground, save those humans had put there. But now, of course, Berge was much more interested in the words of long-dead Leonardo than his grandmother's.

'You have to think about the world Leonardo inhabited,' he said. 'The ancient paradigms still persisted: the stationary Earth, a sky laden with spheres, crude Aristotelian proto-physics. But Leonardo's instinct was to proceed from observation to theory – and he observed many things in the world which didn't fit with the prevailing world view –'

'Like mountain-top fossils.'

'Yes. Working alone, he struggled to come up with explanations. And some of his reasoning was, well, eerie.'

'Eerie?'

'Prescient.' Gold-flecked eyes gleamed. The boy flicked back and forth through the Codex, pointing out spidery pictures of Earth and Moon and sun, neat circles connected by spidery light ray traces. 'Remember, the Moon was thought to be a crystal sphere. What intrigued Leonardo was why the Moon wasn't much brighter in Earth's sky. If the Moon *was* a crystal sphere, perfectly reflective, it should have been as bright as the sun.'

'Like Mirror.'

'Yes. So Leonardo argued the Moon must be covered in oceans.' He found a diagram showing a Moon coated with great out-of-scale choppy waves and bathed in spidery sunlight rays. 'Leonardo said waves on the Moon's oceans must deflect much of the reflected sunlight away from Earth. He thought the darker patches visible on the surface must mark great standing waves, or even storms, on the Moon.'

'He was wrong,' she said. 'In Leonardo's time, the Moon was a ball of rock. The dark areas were just lava sheets.'

'Yes, of course. But now,' Berge said eagerly, 'the Moon *is* mostly covered by water. You see? And there *are* great storms, wave crests hundreds of kilometres long, which are visible from Earth – or would be, if anybody was left to see . . .'

They talked for hours.

When he left, she went to the door to wave him goodbye.

The Day was little advanced, the rake of sunlight still sparse on the ice, and Mirror still rode bright in the sky. Here was another strange forward echo of Leonardo's, it struck her, though she preferred not to mention it to her already over-excited grandson: in these remote times, there *were* crystal spheres in orbit around the Earth. The difference was, people had put them there.

As she closed the door she heard the honking of geese, a great flock of them fleeing the excessive brightness of full Daylight.

*   *   *

364

Each Morning, as the sun laboured into the sky, there were storms. Thick fat clouds raced across the sky, and water gushed down, carving new rivulets and craters in the ancient soil, and turning the ice at the rim of the Tycho pack into a thin, fragile layer of grey slush.

The storms persisted as Noon approached on that last Day, and she travelled with Berge to the phytomine celebration to be held on the lower slopes of Maginus.

They made their way past sprawling fields tilled by human and animal muscle, thin crops straining towards the sky, frost shelters laid open to the muggy heat. And as they travelled they joined streams of battered carts, all heading for Maginus. Xenia felt depressed by the people around her: the spindly adults, their hollow-eyed children – even the cattle and horses and mules were skinny and wheezing. The Moon soil was thin, and the people and animals were all, of course, slowly being poisoned besides.

Most people chose to shelter from the rain. But to Xenia it was a pleasure. Raindrops here were fat glimmering spheres the size of her thumb. They floated from the sky, gently flattened by the resistance of the thick air, and they fell on her head and back with soft, almost caressing impacts, and water clung to her flesh in great sheets and globes she must scrape off with her fingers. So long and slow had been their fall from the high clouds that the drops were often warm, and the air thick and humid and muggy. She liked to think of herself standing in the band of storms that circled the whole of the slow-turning Moon.

It reminded her of the day of Frank Paulis's final triumph.

She remembered that first hour it was possible to step outside the domes – the first hour when unprotected people could survive on the Moon, swathed as it was by air drawn up by the great mines that bore Paulis's name – an hour that had come to pass thanks, of course, to Frank's ingenuity, courage, determination and downright unscrupulous dishonesty. Frank, doggedly, had lived to see it, and on that day the authorities let him out of house arrest, just briefly. They wouldn't permit him to be the first to walk out of a dome without a mask – they couldn't bring themselves to be as generous as *that*. But he was among the first. And that was, perhaps, enough. She remembered how he stalked in the fresh air, squat and defiant, sniffing up great lungfuls of the air he had made, and he laughed as the rain trickled into his toothless mouth, fat lunar drops of it.

And, soon after that, he died.

After that Xenia had left, with the Gaijin, for the stars.

When she returned home she found 1300 years of history had worn away, leaving the Earth a cloud-covered ruin, the solar system threatened by interstellar war, the last humans struggling to survive on Mercury and the Moon. Nobody remembered her, or much of the past: it was as if this attenuated, unstable present was all there ever had been, all that would ever be. So she had shed her old identity, settled into the community here.

Thanks to her engineered biology, a gift of the futures she had visited, she had remained young, physically. Young enough to bear children, even. But now, despite the invisible engineering in her flesh, she was slowly dying, of course, as was everybody, as was the Moon.

How strange that the inhabited Moon's life had been as brief as her own: that her birth and death would span this small world's, that *its* rocky bones would soon emerge through its skin of air and ocean, just as hers would push through her decaying flesh.

At last they approached Maginus.

Maginus was an old, eroded crater complex to the south-east of Tycho. Its ancient walls glimmered with crescent lakes and glaciers. Sheltered from the winds of Morning and Evening, Maginus was a centre of life, and long before they reached the foothills, as the fat rain cleared, she saw the tops of giant trees looming over the horizon. She thought she saw creatures leaping between the tree branches. They may have been lemurs, or even bats; or perhaps they were kites wielded by ambitious children.

Berge showed delight as they crossed the many water courses, pointing out engineering features which had been anticipated by Leonardo, dams and bridges and canal diversions and so forth, some of them even constructed since the Failing. But Xenia took little comfort, oppressed as she was by the evidence of the fall of mankind. For example, they journeyed along a road made of lunar glass, flat as ice and utterly impervious to erosion, carved long ago into the regolith by vast spaceborne engines. But they travelled this marvellously engineered highway in a cart that was wooden, and drawn by a spavined, thin-legged mule.

Such contrasts were unendingly startling, to a time-stranded traveller like Xenia. But, she thought with a grisly irony, all the technology around them would have been more than familiar to Berge's hero, Leonardo. There were gadgets of levers and pulleys and gears, their wooden teeth constantly stripped; there were turnbuckles, devices to help erect cathedrals of Moon concrete; there had even been pathetic lunar wars fought with catapults and crossbows, 'artillery' capable of throwing lumps of rock a few kilometres.

But once people had dug mines that reached the heart of the Moon. The people today knew this was so, else they could not exist here. *She* knew it was true, for she remembered it.

As they neared the phytomine, the streams of traffic converged to a great confluence of people and animals. There was a swarm of reunions of friends and family, and a rich human noise carried on the thick air.

When the crowds grew too dense Xenia and Berge abandoned their wagon and walked. Berge, with unconscious generosity, supported her with a hand clasped about her arm, guiding her through this human maelstrom.

Children darted around her feet, so fast she found it impossible to believe *she* could ever have been so young, so rapid, so compact, and she felt a mask of old-woman irritability settle on her. But many of the children were, at age seven or eight or nine, already taller than she was, girls with languid eyes and the delicate posture of giraffes. The one constant of human evolution on the Moon was how the children stretched out, ever more languorous, in the gentle gravity. But in later life they paid a heavy price in brittle, calcium-starved bones.

All Berge wanted to talk about was Leonardo da Vinci.

'Leonardo was trying to figure out the cycles of the Earth. For instance, how water could be restored to the mountaintops. Listen to this.' He fumbled, one-handed, with his dog-eared manuscript. '*We may say that the Earth has a spirit of growth, and that its flesh is the soil; its bones are the successive strata of the rocks which form the mountains; its cartilage is the tufa stone; its blood the veins of its waters . . . And the vital heat of the world is fire which is spread throughout the Earth; and the dwelling place of the spirit of growth is in the fires, which in divers parts of the Earth are breathed out in baths and sulphur mines . . .* You understand what he's saying? He was trying to explain the Earth's cycles by analogy with the systems of the human body.'

'He was wrong.'

'But he was more right than wrong, grandmother! Don't you see? This was centuries before geology was formalized, before matter and energy cycles would be understood. Leonardo had got the right idea, from somewhere. He just didn't have the intellectual infrastructure to express it . . .'

And so on. None of it was of much interest to Xenia. As they walked it seemed to her that *his* weight was the heavier, as if she, the foolish old woman, was constrained to support him, the young buck. It was evident his sickliness was advancing fast – and it seemed that others around them noticed it too, and separated around them, a sea of unwilling sympathy.

At last they reached the plantation itself. They had to join queues, more or less orderly. There was noise, chatter, a sense of excitement. For many people, such visits were the peak of each slow lunar Day.

Separated from the people by a row of wooden stakes and a few metres of bare soil was a sea of growing green. The vegetation was predominantly mustard plants. Chosen for their bulk and fast growth, all of these plants had grown from seed or shoots since the last lunar Dawn. The plants themselves grew thick, their feathery leaves bright. But many of the leaves were sickly, already yellowing.

The fence was supervised by an unsmiling attendant, who wore – to show the people their sacrifice had a genuine goal – artefacts of unimaginable value, ear rings and brooches and bracelets of pure copper and nickel and bronze.

The attendant told them, in a sullen prepared speech, that the Maginus mine was the most famous and exotic of all the phytomines: for here gold itself was mined, still the most compelling of all metals. These mustard plants grew in soil in which gold, dissolved out of the base rock by ammonium thiocyanate, could be found at a concentration of four parts per million. But when the plants were harvested and burned, their ash contained four *hundred* parts per million of gold, drawn out of the soil by the plants during their brief lives.

The phytomines, where metals were slowly concentrated by living things, were perhaps the Moon's most important remaining industry.

As Frank Paulis had understood centuries ago, lunar soil was sparse and ungenerous. And yet, now that Earth was wrecked, now that the spaceships no longer called, the Moon was all the people had.

The people of the Moon had neither the means nor the will to rip up the top hundred metres of their world to find the precious metals they needed. Drained of strength and tools, they must be more subtle.

Hence the phytomines.

The technology was old – older than the human Moon, older than spaceflight itself. The Vikings, marauders of Earth's dark age, would mine their iron from 'bog ore', iron-rich stony nodules deposited near the surface of bogs by bacteria which had flourished there: miniature miners, not even visible to the Vikings who burned their little corpses to make their nails and swords and pans and cauldrons.

And so it went, across this battered, parched little planet, a hierarchy of bacteria and plants and insects and animals and birds, collecting gold and silver and nickel and copper and bronze, their evanescent bodies comprising a slow merging trickle of scattered molecules stored in leaves and flesh and bones, all for the benefit of that future generation who must some day save the Moon.

Berge and Xenia, solemnly, took ritual scraps of mustard-plant leaf on their tongues, swallowed ceremonially. With her age-furred tongue she could barely taste the mustard's sharpness. There were no drawn-back frost covers here because these poor mustard plants would not survive to the sunset: they died within a lunar Day, from poisoning by the cyanide.

Berge met friends, and melted into the crowds.

Xenia returned home alone, brooding.

She found her family of seals had lumbered out of the ocean and onto the shore. These were constant visitors. During the warmth of Noon they would bask for hours, males and females and children draped over each other in casual abandon, so long that the patch of regolith they inhabited became sodden and stinking with their drop-pings. The seals, uniquely among the creatures from Earth, had not adapted in any apparent way to the lunar conditions. In the flimsy gravity they could surely perform somersaults with those flippers of theirs. But they chose not to; instead they basked, as their ancestors had on far-remote Arctic beaches.

Xenia didn't know why this was so. Perhaps the seals were, simply, wiser than struggling, dreaming humans.

The long Afternoon sank into its mellow warmth. The low sunlight diffused, yellow-red, to the very top of the tall sky.

Earth was clearly visible, wrapped in yellow clouds – they were clouds of dust and bits of rock and vaporized ocean, thrown up there by the great impact a hundred years back – clouds which, the scientists used to say, would take centuries to disperse. Now, nobody so much as looked at Earth, as if, now that it could no longer succour its blue satellite, the planet had become unmentionable, its huge wounds somehow impolite. But Xenia could make out a dim cloud of green, swathing the Earth: it was an orbiting forest, Trees that had survived the collision, still drawing their sustenance from the curdled air with superconductor roots.

The comet impact had been relatively minor, on the cosmic scale of such events. But it had been sufficient to silence Earth; nobody on the Moon knew who, or what, had survived on its surface. Xenia wondered if even those Trees could survive the greater and more frequent impacts which many had predicted were the inevitable outcome of the conflict in the Oort cloud, as the Crackers threatened to break through the Gaijin cordon, as warring Eeties hurled giant rogue objects into the system's crowded heart, century after century.

Such musing failed to distract her from thoughts of Berge's illness, which advanced without pity. She was touched when he chose to come stay with her, to 'see it out', as he put it.

Her fondness for Berge was not hard to understand. Her daughter had died in childbirth. This was not uncommon, as pelvises evolved in heavy Earth gravity struggled to release the great fragile skulls of Moon-born children – and Xenia's genes, of course, came direct from Earth, from the deep past.

So she had rejoiced when Berge was born, sired by her son of a lunar native; at least her genes, she consoled herself, which had emanated from primeval oceans now lost in the sky, would travel on to the furthest future. But now, it seemed, she would lose even that consolation.

But she was not important, nor the future, nor her complex past. All that mattered was Berge, here in the present, and on him she lavished all her strength, her love.

Berge spent his dwindling energies in feverish activities. Still his obsession with Leonardo clung about him. He showed her pictures of impossible machines, far beyond the technology of Leonardo's time: shafts and cogwheels for generating enormous heat, a diving apparatus, an 'easy-moving wagon' capable of independent locomotion. The famous helicopter intrigued Berge particularly. He built many spiral-shaped models of bamboo and paper; they soared into the thick air, easily defying the Moon's gravity, catching the reddening light.

She wasn't sure if he knew he was dying.

In her gloomier hours – when she sat with her grandson as he struggled to sleep, or as she lay listening to the ominous, mysterious rumbles of her own failing body, cumulatively poisoned, wracked by the strange distortions of lunar gravity – she wondered how much further humans must descend.

The heavy molecules of the thick atmosphere were too fast-moving to be contained by the Moon's gravity. The air would be thinned in a few thousand years: a long time, but not beyond comprehension. Long before then people would have to reconquer this world they had built, or they would die.

So they gathered metals, molecule by molecule.

And, besides that, they would need knowledge.

The Moon had become a world of patient monks, endlessly transcribing the great texts of the past, pounding the eroding wisdom of the millennia into the brains of the wretched young. It seemed essential to Xenia they did not lose their concentration as a people, their memory. But she feared it was impossible. Technologically they had already descended to the level of Neolithic farmers, and the young were broken by toil even as they learned.

She had lived long enough to realize that they were, fragment by fragment, losing what they once knew.

If she had one simple message to transmit to the future generations, one thing they should remember lest they descend into savagery, it would be this: *People came from Earth.* There: cosmology and the history of the species and the promise of the future, wrapped up in one baffling, enigmatic, heroic sentence. She repeated it to everyone she met. Perhaps those future thinkers would decode its meaning, and would understand what they must do.

Berge's decline quickened as the sun slid down the sky, the clockwork of the universe mirroring his condition with a clumsy, if mindless, irony. In the last hours she sat with him, quietly reading and talking, responding to his near-adolescent philosophizing with her customary brusqueness, which she was careful not to modify in this last hour.

'. . . But have you ever wondered why we are *here* and *now*?' He was whispering, the sickly gold of his face picked out by the dwindling sun. 'What are we, a few million, scattered in our towns and farms around the Moon? What do we compare to the *billions* who swarmed over Earth in the great years? Why do I find myself alive *now* rather than *then*? It is so unlikely . . .' He turned his great lunar head. 'Do you ever feel you have been born out of your time, as if you are stranded in the wrong era, an *unconscious* time traveller?'

She would have confessed she often did, but he whispered on.

'Suppose a modern human – or someone of the great ages of Earth – was stranded in the sixteenth century, Leonardo's time. Suppose he forgot everything of his culture, all its science and learning –'

'Why? How?'

'*I* don't know . . . But if it were true – and if his unconscious mind retained the slightest trace of the learning he had discarded – wouldn't he do exactly what Leonardo did? Study obsessively, try to fit awkward facts into the prevailing, unsatisfactory paradigms, grope for the deeper truths he had lost? Don't you see? Leonardo behaved *exactly* as a stranded time traveller would.'

'Ah.'

She thought she understood; of course, she didn't. And in her unthinking way she launched into a long and pompous discourse on feelings of dislocation: on how every adolescent felt stranded in a body, an adult culture, unprepared . . .

Berge wasn't listening. He turned away, to look again at the bloated sun.

'I think,' she said, 'you should drink more soup.'

But he had no more need of soup.

It seemed too soon when the Day was done, and the cold started to settle on the land once more, with great pancakes of new ice clustering around the rim of the Tycho sea.

Xenia summoned Berge's friends, teachers, those who had loved him.

She clung to the greater goal: that the atoms of gold and nickel and zinc which had coursed in Berge's blood and bones, killing him like the mustard plants of Maginus – killing them all, in fact, at one rate or another – would now gather in even greater concentrations in the bodies of those who would follow. Perhaps the pathetic scrap of gold or nickel which had cost poor Berge his life would at last, mined, close the circuit which would lift the first ceramic-hulled ships beyond the thick, deadening atmosphere of the Moon.

Perhaps. It was cold comfort.

But still they ate the soup, of Berge's dissolved bones and flesh, in solemn silence. They took his life's sole gift, further concentrating the metal traces to the far future, shortening their own lives as he had.

She had never been a skilful host. As soon as they could, the young people dispersed. She talked with Berge's teachers, but they had little to say to each other; she was merely his grandmother, after all. She wasn't sorry to be left alone.

Before she slept again, even before the sun's bloated hull had slid below the toothed horizon, the winds had turned. The warmer air was treacherously fleeing after the sinking sun. Soon the first flurries of snow came pattering on the black, swelling surface of the Tycho sea.

Her seals slid back into the water, to seek out whatever riches or dangers awaited them under Moon core ice.

Chapter 29

BAD NEWS FROM THE STARS

When Madeleine Meacher arrived back in the solar system – just moments after passing through the pain of her last Saddle Point transition – she was stunned to find Nemoto materializing in the middle of her small hab module.

'Nemoto. *You.* What – how –'

Nemoto was small, hunched over, her face a mask of sourness. This was a virtual, of course, and a low-quality one; Nemoto floated in the air, not quite lined up with the floor.

Nemoto glanced about, as if surprised to be here. 'Meacher. So it's you. What date is it?.'

Madeleine had to look it up. AD 3793.

Nemoto laughed hollowly. 'How absurd.'

There was no perceptible time delay. That meant the originating transmitter must be close. But, of course, there had been no way Nemoto could have known which Saddle Point gateway Madeleine would arrive from. 'Nemoto, what *are* you?'

Nemoto grunted impatiently. 'I am a limited sentience projection. My function is to wait for the star travellers to return. I dusted the Saddle Point radius, all around the system. Dusted it with monitors, probes, transmitters. Technology has moved on, Meacher. Look it up. It scarcely matters . . . Listen to what I have to say.'

'Nemoto –'

'*Listen,* damn you. The Gaijin have been fighting the Crackers. Out on the rim of the system.'

'I know that –'

'The war has lasted five centuries, perhaps more. The Oort cloud is deep, Meacher, a deep trench. But now the war is lost.'

The simple, stunning brutality of the statement shocked Madeleine. 'Are you sure?'

Nemoto barked laughter. 'The Gaijin are withdrawing from the solar system. They don't bother to hide this from us. Just as most people don't bother to look up, into the sky, and *see* what is going on . . . Oh, many of the Gaijin remain. Scouts, observers, transit craft like *this* one. But the bulk of the Gaijin fleet – mostly constructed from stolen solar system resources, *our* asteroids – has begun to withdraw to the Saddle Points. The outer system war is over.'

'And the Crackers . . .'

'Are on the way into the inner system. They are already through the heliopause, the perimeter of the solar wind.' The virtual flickered, became blocky, all but transparent. 'The end game approaches.'

'Nemoto, what must I do?'

'Go to Mercury. Find *me*.' She looked down at herself, as if remembering. 'That is, find Nemoto.'

'And what of *you*? Nemoto, what is a *limited-sentience projection*?'

Nemoto raised a hand that was crumbling into bits of light. She seemed puzzled, as if she was finding out for herself as she spoke. 'I am autonomous, heuristic, sentient. I was born sixty seconds ago, to give you this message. But my function is fulfilled. I'm dying.' She looked at Madeleine, as if shocked by the realization, and reached out.

Madeleine extended a hand, but her fingers passed through a cloud of light.

With a thin wail, the Nemoto virtual broke up.

Sailing in from the rim of the solar system, Madeleine used Gaijin technology to study the strange new age into which she had been projected.

There was little Gaijin traffic, just as virtual Nemoto had said.

But she found signatures of unknown ships – solar sail craft, they appeared to be, great fleets of them, a gigantic shell that surrounded the system. They were still out among the remote orbits of the comets for now, but they were converging, like a fist closing on the fat warmth of the inner system.

Cracker fleets, come to disrupt the sun.

Earth seemed dead. The Moon was a fading blue, silent. There were knots of human activity in the asteroids, on Mars – and Triton. And she found signs of refugee fleets, humans fleeing inwards to the core of the system, to Mercury. But no ships arrived at or left remote Triton.

When she understood that, she knew where she must go first.

The Gaijin flower-ship sailed around Triton, its fusion light illuminating smooth plains of ice. It was a world covered by a chill ocean, like

Earth's Arctic, with not a scrap of solid land; but the thin ice crust was easily broken by the slow pulsing tides of this small moon, exposing great black leads of water that bubbled and steamed vigorously, trying to evaporate and fill up all of empty space.

There were six human settlements.

The settlements looked like clusters of bubbles on a pond, she thought. They were sprawling, irregular patches of modular construction – not rigid, clearly designed to float over the tides. Five settlements seemed abandoned – no lights, no power output, no sign of an internal temperature significantly above the background. Even the sixth looked largely shut down, with only a handful of lights at the centre of the bubble-cluster, the outskirts abandoned to the cold.

She radioed down requests for permission and instructions for landing. Only automated beacons responded. The answers came through in a human voice, but in a language she didn't recognize. The translation suite embedded in her equipment couldn't handle it either. She had the Gaijin put her down on what appeared to be a landing site, close to a system of airlocks.

Suited up, she stepped out of the conical Gaijin lander.

Frost covered every surface. But it was gritty, hard as sand. Remember, Madeleine, water ice is rock on Triton

She walked carefully to the edge of the platform, and looked out beyond the bounds of the bubble city. A point source sun cast wan colourless light over smooth ice fields. Neptune was rising over the horizon, a faint, misty-blue ball, making the light on the ice deep, subtle, complex, the shadows softly glowing. Pointlessly beautiful, she thought. She turned away.

She found a door large enough for a suited human. She couldn't understand the elaborate script instructions beside the control panel. But there was one clear device, a big red button: *Press me*. She hit it with her fist.

Radio noise screeched. The door slid back, releasing a puff of air that crystallized immediately. She hurried into a small, brightly-lit airlock. The door slammed shut and the airlock immediately repressurized.

She twisted off her helmet. Air sighed out of her suit, and her ears popped. The air was biting cold. It smelled stale.

She palmed a panel that opened the inner door, and found herself looking into a long, unadorned corridor that twisted out of sight.

Wandering through the corridors, carrying her helmet, she was eventually met by a woman. She was evidently a cop: spindly, fragile-looking after fifteen hundred years of adaptation to low gravity, but she carried a mean-looking device that could only be a hand-gun.

The cop walked Madeleine, luggage pack and all, into the centre of town. The cop's skin was jet black. Madeleine's translator software couldn't interpret her language.

Madeleine caught glimpses of abandoned corridors, and some kind of complex, gigantic machinery at the heart of everything. In one area she passed over a clear floor, water rippling underneath, black and deep. She saw something swimming there, sleek and fast and white, quickly disappearing into the deeper darkness.

The cop delivered her to a cramped suite of offices. Madeleine sat in an anteroom, waiting for attention. Maybe this was the office of the Mayor, she thought, or the town council. There was no sign of the colony's Aboriginal origins, save for a piece of art on the wall: around a metre square, pointillist dots in shades of cobalt red. A Dreamtime representation, maybe.

Madeleine was starting to get the picture. Triton was a small town, at the fringe of interstellar space. They weren't used to visitors, and weren't much interested either.

Eventually a harassed-looking official – another woman, her frizzy hair tied back sharply from her forehead – came into the room. She studied Madeleine with dismay.

Madeleine forced a smile. 'Pleased to meet you. Who are you, the Mayor?'

The woman frowned, and jabbered back impatiently.

But Madeleine smiled and nodded, and tapped her helmet. 'That's it. Keep talking. My name is Madeleine Meacher. I've come from the stars . . .'

Her translator suite was essentially Gaijin. How ironic that seventeen centuries after the Gaijin came wandering unannounced into the asteroid belt, humans should need alien technology to talk to each other.

At last the translator began to whisper.

'At last. Thanks for your patience. I –'

'And I am very busy,' the translator whispered, ghosting the woman's speech. 'We should progress this issue, the issue of your arrival here.'

'My name is Meacher . . .' Madeleine summarized her CV.

The woman turned out to be called Sheela Dell-Cope. She was an administrative assistant in the office of the Headman here – although, as far as Madeleine could make out, the Headman was actually a woman.

'I have a mission,' Madeleine said. 'I bring bad news. Bad news from the stars.'

The woman silenced her with an upraised hand. 'There is the question of your residency, including the appropriate fee . . .'

Madeleine was forced to sit through a long and elaborate list of rules regarding temporary residency. To Dell-Cope, Madeleine Meacher was strange, incomprehensible, a visitor from another time, another place. Now *I* am the Gaijin, Madeleine thought.

She was going to have to apply for an equivalent of a visa. And she would have to pay for each day she stayed, or else work for her air. This was a closed, marginal world, where every breath had to be paid for.

'The work is not pleasant,' Dell-Cope said. 'Servicing the *otec*. Or working with the Flips, for instance.'

That meant nothing to Madeleine, but she got the idea. 'I'll pay.' She had a variety of Gaijin high-tech gadgets that she could use for a fee. Anyhow she wasn't going to be here long, come what may.

As it turned out, the painting on the wall was a representation of an ancient Aboriginal artwork: the Dreaming of a creature of the Australian Outback, the honey-ant. But it was a copy of a copy of a copy, done in seaweed dyes. And, she was prepared to bet, nobody on Triton knew what a honey-ant was anyhow.

She was given a room in a residential area. There seemed to be no hotels here.

The room was just a cube carved out of concrete. It had a bed, some scattered and unfamiliar furniture – spindly low-G chairs – a small galley, and a comms station with an utterly baffling human interface.

Not that the galley was so easy either. She shouted at it and poked it, her favoured way of dealing with new-fangled technology, until she found a way to make it decant a hot liquid, some kind of tea.

There were no windows. The room was just a concrete box, a sarcophagus, a cave. Here in the emptiness on the edge of interstellar space, humans were hiding from the sky.

What are you doing here, Meacher?

What was she *supposed* to do? Simply blurt out her news – that an alien invasion fleet had massed on the rim of the solar system, that it was almost certain to spill into the region of Neptune's orbit soon, that she was here, with her friendly Gaijin, to help these people evacuate to worlds their ancestors had left behind a thousand years earlier? It seemed absurd, melodramatic.

She worked at the comms equipment, striving to make it do what she wanted. It was a strange irony, she thought, that comms equipment, whose purpose was after all to join people together, always turned out to have the most baffling designs, presenting the worst challenges to the out-of-time traveller.

She tried to make an appointment to meet the Headman, but she was stalled. She tried further down the local hierarchy, as best she could figure it out, but got nowhere there either.

Nobody was interested in her.

Frustrated, on a whim, she decided to hunt for descendants of the colonists she had known. With the help of her translator she asked the comms station to find her people with 'Roach' in their surname.

Most of the surnames scrolling before her, phonetically rendered, were unfamiliar. But there were a few families with compound surnames which included the name 'Rush'.

Just around the corner, in fact, in the same floating bubble as this room, there was a man – apparently living alone – with the surname Rush-Bayley.

She spent a frustrating hour persuading the comms unit to leave him a message.

She took long walks through the city's emptiness. Lights turned themselves on, off again when she passed, so she walked in a moving puddle of illumination.

She walked from bubble to floating bubble over bridges of what seemed to be ceramic; when the bubbles shifted against each other, the interfaces creaked, ominously. She encountered few people. Her footsteps echoed, as if she was walking through immense hangars.

Madeleine imagined this place had been designed for ten, twenty times as many people as it held now. And she thought of those other colonies, abandoned on the waters of Triton.

It saddened her that nothing – save a few sentimental tokens like paintings – survived of the Aboriginal culture that Ben's generation had brought here. After all, even fifteen hundred years on Triton were dwarfed by maybe sixty *thousand* years of Australia. But the Dreamtime legends, it seemed, had not survived the translation from the ancient deserts of Australia to these enclosed, high-tech bubbles.

She reached the centre of the kilometres-wide colony. Here, a great structure loomed out of the ice-crusted sea, visible through picture windows. It was mounted on a stalk, and reared up to a great dome-shaped carapace, some hundreds of metres above the ice. It was a little

378

like a water tower. She picked out engineering features: evaporators, demisters, generators, turbines, condenser tubing. Madeleine learned that this tower was based on a taproot that descended far into the ocean, kilometres deep, in fact.

This was the *otec*. The name turned out to be an acronym from old English, for Ocean Thermal Energy Converter. It was a device to extract energy from the heat difference between the deep ocean waters, at just four degrees below freezing, and the surface ice, at more than a hundred below. The *otec* turned out to be the main power source for the colony. It was fifteen hundred years old, as old as the colony itself, and maintained by the colonists with a diligent, monkish devotion. There were other power sources, like fusion plants. But the colonists were short of metal; the nearest body of rock, after all, was the silicate core of Triton, drowned under hundreds of kilometres of water. The colonists were able to fix the *otec*, clunky machinery though it was, with materials they could extract from the water around them.

After a couple of empty days, she found her comms unit glowing green. She poked at it, trying to figure out why.

It turned out there was a message on it, from Rush-Bayley.

Adamm Rush-Bayley was tall, thin, dark. He wore a loose smock-like affair, his skinny legs bare. The smock was painted with vibrant colours, red, blue, green, a contrast to the drab environment.

He turned out to be seventy years old, though he didn't look it.

He looked nothing like Ben, of course, or Lena. Had she been hoping that she could retrieve something of Ben, her own vanished past? How *could* he be like Ben, sixty generations removed?

His family had kept alive Ben's story, however, his name – and the story of the Nereid impact. And so he looked at her with mild curiosity. 'You're the *same* Madeleine Meacher who –'

'Yes.'

'How very strange. Of course we have records.' He smiled. 'There is a public archive, and my family kept its own mementoes. Perhaps you'd like to see them.'

'I was there for the live show, remember.'

'Yes. You must have fascinating stories.' He didn't sound all that fascinated, though, to Madeleine; it seemed clear he'd rather show her the records his family had cherished than hear her testimony from history. The past was a thing to own, to lock away in boxes and archives, not to explore.

It wasn't the first time she had encountered such a reaction.

He made her a meal in his home, which was a multi-chamber cave. The food was shellfish, with what appeared to be processed seaweed or algae as a side dish. They ate off plates made of a kind of paper. The paper wasn't based on cellulose, she learned, but on chitin extracted from the shells of lobsters.

Adamm's clothes were made from seaweed – or more precisely a seaweed extract called algin. Algin could be spun into silk-like threads, and was the basis of virtually all the colonists' clothing and other fabric, and products like films, gels, polishes, paints. There was even algin additive in her food.

They talked tentatively while they ate.

Adamm made a minor living making pearl artefacts. He showed her a pearl the size of her fist that had been sliced open and hollowed out to make a box for a mildly intoxicating snuff-like powder. The pearl was exquisite, the workmanship so-so.

Most of the work he did was for one engineering concern or another; luxury was at a premium here. He could only sell, after all, to his fellow citizens. It seemed to her that nobody was rich here, nobody terribly poor. But this was Adamm's home, and he was used to its conditions.

Most people, she learned, were probably older than they looked to her. Here in the low gravity environment of Triton, and with anti-ageing mechanisms wired centuries earlier into the human genome, life expectancy was around two centuries. And it would have been even higher if not for problems with the colony's life support. 'We have crashes and blooms, diseases, toxicity . . .'

The biosphere was just too small.

Right now Adamm lived alone. He had one child by a previous marriage. He was considering marrying again, trying for more children. But there was a quota.

He listened, without commenting, to her talk of interstellar war. Madeleine had the impression that Adamm was merely being polite to somebody who might have known his ancestors.

She felt herself losing concentration, overwhelmed by cultural inertia.

After the meal, they took a walk.

He guided her to an area like an atrium. It was walled, roofed and floored with transparent sheeting, and for once there was no sense of enclosure. Around her, stretching to a close, tightly curving horizon, was a sheet of ice; above her was Neptune's faint globe, slowly rising as Triton spun through its long artificial day; beneath her feet she could see the Triton ocean, through which pale white forms skimmed.

She said, 'I remember when Neptune hung in the sky, unmoving. Seeing it rise like that is – eerie. But I suppose it makes Triton more Earth-like.'

She glimpsed hostility on his face.

'Travellers like you have returned before,' he said, her translator filtering out any emotion from his voice. 'What does it matter if Triton is *Earth-like* or not? Madeleine, I've never seen Earth. Why would I want to?'

The little clash depressed her. Of course he's right, she thought; 'Earth-like' must sound as alien to Adamm as the accretion-disc home of the Chaera would have to me. Fifteen hundred years; fifty, sixty generations . . . We humans just can't maintain cultural concentration, even over such an insignificant span.

While the Gaijin sail on.

As if on cue, there was a flash in the sky, somewhere beyond the blue shoulder of Neptune.

She grabbed Adamm's hand; he recoiled from her touch. 'There. Did you see that?'

Ne. '. . . No.'

There was nothing to see now, no afterglow, no repeat show. She felt like a kid who had glimpsed a meteor in the desert sky, a flash nobody else had seen. She said defensively, 'It's not just a light in the sky. It might have been the destruction of an ice moon, or a comet nucleus –'

Adamm asked reluctantly, 'This is your war?'

'Adamm, the war isn't mine. But it is *real* . . .'

A sleek white shape broke the water beneath her feet. She stepped back, startled. She saw a smooth, streamlined head, closed eyes, a small mouth – something like a dolphin, she thought. The creature opened its mouth and uttered a cry, high-pitched, complex, like a door creaking.

Then it flipped backwards and disappeared from view, leaving Madeleine stunned, disturbed.

'*War*,' Adamm said sourly. Then he sighed. 'I suppose you mean well. But it seems so – remote.'

'Believe me, it isn't. Adamm, I'm going to need your help. The Headman won't see me. You have to help me convince people.'

He laughed, not unkindly. He pointed down to the black water. 'Start with them.'

'Who?'

'The Flips. Try convincing them. They're people too.'

She peered into the water, stunned.

He walked away. She had no choice but to follow.

The Headman's office loaned her a hard-shelled suit, full of smart stuff and heating elements. She descended into the water, from a bay on the outskirts of the bubble city, through a hole neatly cut in the ice.

She fell slowly, in deepening darkness. She moved around experimentally. She couldn't feel the cold, and the water pressure here on this low-G moon was pretty low, but the water resisted her movements. When the hole in the ice was just a pinpoint of blue light above her, she turned on her helmet lamps. The beams penetrated only a few metres into the murk. She ran a quick visual check of her systems, and glanced upwards to see her tether coiling reassuringly up through the water, her physical link to the world of air and light above.

Deep-sea diving on Triton. She'd never liked swimming, even on a real planet.

She was alone. The colonists didn't take to the water much. Their deep ocean was just a resource, a mine, not a place to explore, still less play.

Something wriggled past her faceplate.

She recoiled. Her chin jammed against her air inlet, and there was a sudden decrease in pressure; her ears popped alarmingly.

She calmed herself down. It had only been a fish. She didn't recognize the species – a native Earth type, or gen-enged for this peculiar environment?

She fell faster.

The murky dust grew thicker. It was probably organic debris, she had been warned: decomposed body parts, drifting down to the deep ocean floor. More critters and plants drifted up past her. There were strands of seaweed, what looked like tiny shrimps, more fish of a variety of shapes and sizes, even what appeared to be a sea horse.

There was a whole biosphere down here, gen-enged from Earth life. There was little photosynthesis: not enough sunlight for that. Most of the energy for life here came from the heat of Triton's interior. So the food chain was anchored in communities of exotic bugs clustered around smoking, mineral-laden vents, cracks in the ocean floor hundreds of kilometres from the light.

. . . She felt it before she could see it, a sudden and unexpected nuzzling at her legs, soft, warm, curious. She twisted around in the water, tether looping.

It was like a dolphin, yes: a small dolphin, sleek body a couple of metres long, streamlined fur pure white, powerful flukes and stubby fins. But it – no, *he*; there was a fully operational penis down there, beneath the sleek belly – *he* had a face that had little in common with a dolphin's: a blunt rounded shape, a wide, stretched mouth, a nose squashed flat and the nostrils extended into two slits. Bubbles streamed from a blowhole at the top of his head. And the eyes were closed; she could make out no brows, no lids.

No eyes, she realized. But what use were eyes, in this deep darkness?

This was a human, of course: or rather, a post-human, gen-enged for this environment, the true, deep heart of Triton, far beneath the cold, attenuated huddles of the surface.

He swum around her smoothly, brushing her legs, feet, arms, chest. She heard a pulsing click, perhaps some form of echo-sounding . . .

He rolled on his back.

Enough analysis, Madeleine.

Without thinking, she reached out with her gloved hand and scratched his corrugated, gun-metal-grey belly. She could feel nothing of the texture of his fur. But the clicks and pops he made deepened, seeming to denote satisfaction.

'Can you hear me? Can you understand? . . .' Are you a Roach too, she thought, some remote, metamorphosed child of Ben and Lena?

For reply he wriggled away and floated there, just out of her reach.

She had to let herself drift a little deeper to touch him again. He let her stroke him a couple more minutes, then wriggled away again. And she had to descend further, reach out again.

And again, and again.

He's testing me, she realized slowly. Playing some game with me. Psychology. Still human enough for that.

And, she saw by the swelling of his impressive penis, it was giving him a kick.

She rose up a little, folded her arms.

When he saw she wasn't playing any more, he rolled on his front and his fins beat at the water, as if in frustration. But then he quickly forgave her, and began rolling around her legs, nuzzling and butting.

More shadows in the water, she saw now: two, three, four Flips. They clustered around her curiously. She wondered if her first companion had called to them, in some manner she couldn't detect. She tried not to flinch as their powerful bodies brushed the equipment that kept her alive; they showed no malevolence, only a kind of affectionate curiosity, and her gear was surely designed to survive encounters like this.

Now one of them – her first friend maybe, impossible to say – began to emit a new kind of sound. It was a kind of whistle, much purer than the echo clicks or the squeaky-door groans she had heard before.

Another joined in, making a whistle that wavered a bit but soon settled on the same pitch as the first. And now she heard a pulsing, overlaid on their simple pure-tone singing. Beats, she thought, the interference of one tone with another.

The other Flips joined in, singing their own notes, producing more beats. As a piece of music it was simple, just a cluster of pure tones in straightforward harmony with each other. But the beats were more complex, an elusive pattern of pulses that shifted, hopping from one frequency to another, sometimes too rapidly for her to follow.

On a whim she activated a feed to her concrete cave room, up in the surface colony, and let the translator suite record the singing. Then she closed her eyes and let herself drift, immersed in song, oblivious even to the gentle touch of the Flips as they swam around her.

. . . The Flips scattered, suddenly, as if in panic, disappearing into the gloom, leaving her alone. She felt shocked, oddly bereft; without the song, the world seemed empty.

But now she heard a new noise: a deep regular thrumming. Something was approaching through the water ahead of her, something massive, a texture that spanned the ocean.

It was a net.

She paced back and forth in Adamm's lounge. 'What kind of people are you? Those Flips are your –'

'Children?' He smiled, languid, sipping a kind of wine whose principal ingredient was seaweed. 'Cousins? Brothers, sisters? Don't be absurd. They are a different species. They became that way by choice. When they first went into the sea, they took tools, ways of extracting metal. They discarded it all, bit by bit. They even discarded their hands, and their eyes, everything that makes us human. They *chose* to go back, you see, back to – mindlessness. It was ideological.'

She wondered how much, if any, of that was true. 'But to hunt them down –'

He studied her curiously. 'Do you imagine we *eat* them? You don't think much of us, do you? The Flips are just a pest. They disrupt the ecology. They interfere with the city's systems, the filter valves for instance . . .'

Perhaps, she thought.

The translator had analysed the Flips' singing.

With no referents, it was impossible to provide a one-to-one translation. But it was obvious the song was full of structure. The suite
identified patterns in the choice of frequencies, the way the beats were
manipulated, in their spacing and timing and intonation and pitch . . .
The suite estimated that an hour of such singing could encode a million
bits. Which was, for comparison, about the information content of
Homer's *Odyssey*.

The Flips couldn't match the richness of whale song of Earth. Not
yet. A few more centuries, she thought, and they'd have it.

So the Song went on after all, here in this watery desert, a place
even more elemental than the Outback.

Adamm was still talking. '. . . And you needn't imagine they are
some kind of cute pet. Some of them have turned predatory, you know.
Ecological niches tend to be filled . . . *They* consume each other. Look,
they're just Flips. They don't matter.'

'And nor did your ancestors, in white Australia.'

His face hardened. 'You created this world, I suppose, with your
stunts, firing moons back and forth. And now you want to destroy it,
evacuate thousands of people.' He smiled. 'History remembers you as
a meddler. Grandiose. Ideas above your capabilities.' But even as he
spoke he seemed distant, as if unable to believe he was challenging
this historical figure – as if he was facing down Columbus, or Julius
Caesar. He gazed out at interstellar darkness, the edge of the system.
'If these aliens are as powerful as you claim, maybe we should just
accept what's going to happen. Like death. You can't fight that.'

She growled, 'No, but you can put it off.' She stood. 'I'm not
interested in your opinion of me, or your analysis. I'm going to see
the Headman, whether she likes it or not. I'll do what I can to arrange
evacuation to the inner system for everybody who wants it. Even the
Flips.'

He eyed her, saying nothing; somehow she sensed this remote grandson of long-dead Ben and Lena wasn't going anywhere, with or without
her.

'Goodbye, Adamm.'

Goodbye, goodbye.

Chapter 30

REFUGE

The Gaijin flower-ship soared on a fast, efficient powered trajectory into the crowded heart of the solar system. The sun grew brighter, swamping the subtleties of the star-laden sky, its glaring light more and more the dominant presence in the universe.

Madeleine felt an unreasonable, illogical sense of claustrophobia. There were no walls here, and there was room for whole planets to swim through the dark; and yet this place felt oppressive, closed in, like the heart of a city. She spent much time with the lander's windows opaqued against the yellow-white glare, drifting beneath a cool, austere virtual Neptune.

The Gaijin refused to carry Madeleine any closer to the sun than the orbit of Earth. She was going to have to proceed on to Mercury in the cramped confines of a lander designed primarily for orbit-to-ground hops.

The few hundred refugees from Triton who had followed her back into the heart of the system would have to endure the same rigours. The transfer into the landers was ill-tempered, chaotic.

It had proved impossible to communicate to the deep-ocean aquatics the need to evacuate. So she had been forced to leave them behind, those dolphin-like post-humans, abandoning them to whatever mysterious fate awaited them, without ever even knowing if they understood what was happening to them.

Just as, perhaps, the retreating Gaijin wondered of her.

As she watched the flower-ship sail away back into the outer darkness, she felt an entirely unexpected pang of loneliness, of abandonment.

She'd always suspected that Malenfant's habit of giving his Gaijin companion a name – of treating Cassiopeia as some analogue of a human individual – was just anthropomorphism, sloppy sentimentality. But the fact was she actually *liked* these aloof, stately, rational

Gaijin a lot more than she liked some humans – notably the racist-type surface colonists she had encountered on Triton. The Gaijin were ancient, much-travelled, had endured experiences unimaginable to most humans; to them, a single, short-lived human and her concerns must seem as evanescent, as meaningless – and yet perhaps as beautiful – as the curl of a thread of smoke, the splash of a single raindrop.

At last, ten days after the Gaijin had left her, planet Mercury sailed into view. She was approaching at an angle from the night side, so to her it was a bony crescent against the black, slowly opening up, its cratering apparent even from a great distance.

She slid into orbit, and was held there while an electronic bureaucracy – run by a governing body called the Coalition – processed her requests to land, machines separated by centuries of technical and social development seeking a way to speak to each other.

Mercury, turning beneath her, was like the Moon's elder brother, just a ball of rock with a pale, thickly cratered surface. But there was no Mercury equivalent of the Moon's great maria; whatever process had formed those great lunar seas of frozen lava hadn't operated here. And there were features unlike anything on the Moon: zones of crumpling, ridges and folds and cracks, like the wrinkled skin of a dried tomato, as if the planet had shrunk after its formation.

The stand-out feature was one immense impact basin, maybe thirty degrees north of the equator. She sailed over a ragged ring of mountains – not a simple rim, but a structure, with the tallest mountains innermost, and lower foothills further out. Inside the ring there was a relatively smooth floor, scarred by ridges, folds and rifts that followed roughly concentric patterns, like the glaze on an old dinner plate. It was a fantastic sight, a basin that took her lander long minutes to skim over on its first approach pass, circles of mountains big enough neatly to encompass the Great Lakes.

And, in the deep shadows right at the huge crater's heart, she saw lights, a hint of order, buildings and tracks. It was a human settlement, here in the deepest scar on the most inhospitable planet in the solar system. She ought to have been uplifted by the spectacle. But that tiny spark in the midst of such ferocious desolation seemed merely absurd.

There was a lot of traffic in the sky.

They were human ships. Most of them were driven by solar sails, filmy and beautiful, wispy shapes that tacked against Mercury's impassive rocky face, the slow evolution of their forms betraying the intelligent control that guided them. The ships rode the hail of photons that came from the huge, nearby sun, a much more effective means of transportation here than at Earth's orbit and beyond.

It was immediately obvious that there were more ships arriving than leaving. But then there was no other place for humans to go, here in the solar system of the year AD 3793; Mercury was a sink of people, not a source.

On the far side of Mercury she saw a type of landscape she'd never seen before: broken up, chaotic, almost shattered. She worked out that it was at the exact antipode of that giant impact structure, the target of converging spherical shock waves that must have travelled around the world; rock-smashing energies had focused here and made the land flex and crumble and boil.

Once Madeleine had hurled moons around the outer solar system. Now she felt awed, humbled, by the evidence of such huge forces. Overwhelmed by a sense of impotence.

She was brought to land near the main human settlement. This was in a wide crater called Chao Meng-Fu, another giant impact structure, this one almost covering the south pole.

The gravity startled her with its strength, around twice that on the Moon. Strange for such a small planet, really little larger than the Moon; Mercury was very dense, another cannonball.

Madeleine suited up. It was straightforward; through the centuries, in contrast to comms units and coffee machines, she'd found that life-critical equipment like pressure suits and airlocks remained easy to operate, its operation obvious.

She stepped out of the tractor. Once again I set foot on a new world, she thought. Do I hold the record?

Within Chao Meng-Fu there were power plants and automated strip-mining robots. The surface structures cowered in rim mountain shadows, avoiding a sun which glared down for one hundred and seventy-six Earth days at a time – an unexpected number; Mercury's 'day' was fixed, by tidal effects, as two-thirds of the little planet's eighty-eight-day year, and so its calendar was a complex clockwork.

She looked up, towards the sun, which was low on the horizon. Filters in her helmet blocked out the disc of the sun itself, but that disc was three times as large as Earth's sun, a bloated monster.

She saw no humans above ground, none at all.

Her arrival at Chao City was processed by crude virtuals. These software robots had been designed to handle the arrival of speakers of incomprehensible languages, from all over the solar system. Their humanity smoothed out, they guided her wordlessly with simple mime and gesture. Chao City was a warren of corridors and tunnels, hastily cut out of the bedrock. It was crowded with a dozen diverse races, a place full of suspicion and territoriality.

She was assigned a poky room, another cave like the one she'd endured on Triton – though this time, at least, carved from familiar silicate rock rather than water ice. How strange it was that humans, on whatever world they settled from one end of the solar system to the other, were driven to burrow into the ground like moles.

The room contained a comms interface unit, inevitably of a very different design from those on Triton, with which, wearily, she battled. At last she found a way to instruct a contemporary analogue of a data miner to find Nemoto – if she was indeed here on Mercury.

The comms unit began to ping softly. After no more than thirty minutes' probing she found out that the sound meant the unit contained a message, waiting for her. *Come see me. Nowadays I live in a crater called Bernini. Not so far away from Chao. You'll enjoy the view.* It named a place and time.

It was from Dorothy Chaum.

She was kept waiting another twenty-four hours. Then she was taken to see somebody called an Immigration Officer. More bureaucracy, she thought with a sinking heart. Just like Triton; a universal human trait.

The Immigration Officer actually tried to speak to her in Latin. *Quo vadis? Quo animo?* – Where are you going? With what intention? She had brought her pressure suit helmet with its embedded translator suite, and the office had similar facilities, and she waited patiently for the equipment to work.

The Officer's name was Carl ap Przibram. He was a native of an asteroid: tall, spindly, with a great eggshell of a skull under thick hair, and long bony fingers, a cliché pianist's. His skin was pale, his features smoothed-out, as if his skin was stretched; perhaps there were folds at his eyes, traces of an Asian ancestry, but any ethnic antecedents from Earth were long mixed and blurred. He seemed profoundly uncomfortable – as well he might, Madeleine thought, as he was effectively operating in multiples of the gravity he was used to.

When they were able to communicate he took her name, requested various identification numbers she didn't have, then asked for a summary of her background. She listed her voyages beyond the stars. Using a workstation built into his desk, he brought up, from some deep database, a record on her, maintained over centuries. Ap Przibram seemed immersed in his job, all the documentation and procedure, utterly uninterested in the reality of the exotic fossil before him. It was a reaction she'd encountered on Triton, and many times before.

He requested that she make a donation of DNA samples. It was logical – a scheme to keep mankind's small, isolated gene pools refreshed – though she'd heard of travellers who had patronized a flourishing black market in traveller genetic samples, notably sperm; the latter-day legend, happily encouraged by some travellers, was that the good stuff from these crude near-barbarians from a thousand years ago was more vigorous, more potent than the etiolated modern vintage.

At last he handed her a piece of plastic embedded with temporary ident codes, preliminary to a full implant; she took it gravely. 'You are welcome here,' he told her.

'Thank you.' She raised the issue of her companions from Triton.

'Their application will be processed as speedily as possible.' He fell silent, his drawn face impassive.

She tapped the desk with a fingernail. She found it hard to read his posture, the language of his face. 'They've flown across the system, across thirty astronomical units, in landers designed for hundred-kilometre orbital hops. Those things are flying toilets. We have children, old people, disabled, ill . . .'

'We are processing their application. Until that is concluded there's nothing I can do.'

His eyes were hollow. The man is exhausted, she thought. He is overwhelmed, as Mercury is; and here I am with more refugees, boat-loads of resentful ice dwellers from Triton. In such circumstances, bureaucracy is a medium of civilized discourse; at least he isn't throwing me out.

She resolved to be patient.

At the appointed time she set off to meet Dorothy. There was a mono-rail link from Chao City to Bernini – slow, bumpy, uncomfortable, real pioneer stuff – and then she had to take a ride in an automated tractor, a thing of giant wire-mesh wheels, over lightly occupied Mercury.

She arrived at what Dorothy had referred to as a solar sail farm.

Outside the tractor she studied the sky.

She could see few stars. Solar-sail ships swam, dimly visible, like sparks from a fire, swarming around Mercury's equator, bringing more refugees. But there was a haze across the sky, a mistiness surrounding that too-large sun disc, and a pale wash further out, like a starless Milky Way. She was seeing the sun's tenuous atmosphere, made visible by the artificial occulting of the central star. And the flat belt of light further out was the zodiacal light, the shining of dust particles and meteorites and asteroids in the plane of the ecliptic. Once Gaijin cities had shone there; now the asteroid belt was deserted once more.

When she cupped her hands around her faceplate she could see the tail of yet another giant comet, smeared milkily over the black dome of the sky. She couldn't see any Cracker ships, of course – not yet – even though, it was said, they had broken through the orbit of Neptune.

As the Oort war had turned sour, Mercury had been annexed by a coalition of nations from the asteroid colonies: the near-Earths, the main belt, even a few from the Trojans in Jupiter's orbit. It was hardly an occupation; nobody but a few hermit types had been living here anyhow. The set-up here was barely democratic – a situation which, to their credit, appeared to disturb the emergency government, the Coalition. But it was functioning.

The colonists had adapted technologies that had once been used in the initial colonization of the Moon: once more, humans were forced to bake their air out of unyielding rock. But there were plans for the longer term – such as a Paulis mine at Caloris Planitia, the giant impact crater she'd observed from orbit. But this was not the Moon. Mercury was all iron core, with a little rocky rind. A different world, different challenges.

Now she picked out a double star, a bright double pinpoint, one partner strikingly blue, the other a pale grey-white . . .

'Earth, of course.' Here was Dorothy standing close by her side, in a suit so coated with black Mercury dust it was all but invisible, despite the brightness of the sun. Her helmet was heavily shielded, just a golden bubble; Madeleine couldn't see her face.

They exchanged meaningless pleasantries, awkward; there were no obvious protocols for a relationship such as theirs.

Then Dorothy loped heavily across the dusty plain. Madeleine, reluctantly, followed.

The regolith crunched under her feet, the noise clearly audible, carried through her suit. In the virgin dust she left footprints, clear and sharp as on the Moon, and the dust she threw up clung to the fabric of her suit. But her footing was heavy here, in this double-Moon gravity. No bunny-hop Moonwalking here.

It was like the Moon, yes – the same undulating surface, heavily eroded, crater on crater, so the surface was like a sea of dusty waves.

But if anything the erosion was more complete here. There were hills – she was close to the rim wall of crater Bernini – but they were stoop-shouldered, coated in regolith. The smaller craters were little more than shadows of themselves, palimpsests, their features worn away.

She hadn't met Dorothy since they had been with Malenfant on the Gaijin's home world, and the three of them had set off to return to the solar system by their different routes. Dorothy seemed different to Madeleine: more closed-in, secretive, perhaps obsessive. Somehow older.

Dorothy paused, and pointed to a hole in the ground. 'Here's where I live. Subsurface shelter. It isn't so bad. Not if you already spent subjective years in spacecraft hab modules.'

At Madeleine's feet was a flattened boulder, its exposed top worn smooth, like a lens. She bent stiffly, scuffed at the soil, and prised the rock out of the dirt. Most of the rock had been hidden in the dirt, like an iceberg. Underneath it was sharp, a jagged boulder.

Dorothy said, 'It probably dropped here a billion years ago, thrown half-way around the planet by some impact. And since then any bits of it that stuck out have just been eroded flat, right here where it landed, layer by layer.'

Madeleine frowned. 'Micrometeorite impacts?'

'Not primarily. At noon it gets hot enough to melt lead. And in the night, which lasts nearly six months, it's cold enough to liquefy oxygen.'

'Thermal stress, then.'

'Yes. Shaped the landscape. Bane of the engineer's life, here on this hot little world. Come on. Let me show you what I do for a living . . .'

They walked briskly through a shallow crater littered with bits of glass.

That, anyhow, was how it seemed to Madeleine at first glance. She was surrounded by delicate glass leaves that rested against the regolith, spiky needles protruding. There was, too, another type of structure: short, stubby cylinders, pointing at the sky, projecting in all directions, like miniature cannon muzzles. It was like a sculpture park.

Dorothy stalked on without pausing. Some of the petal-shaped glass plates were crushed under Dorothy's careless feet; Madeleine walked more carefully. Dorothy said, 'We can just grow sail panels right out of the rock. These things are gen-enged descendants of vacuum flowers from the Moon. I've made myself something of an expert at this technology. Good to have a profession, on a world where you have to pay for the air you breathe, don't you think?' She tilted back her head, her face obscured. 'Next time you see a solar sailing ship, think of this place, how those gauzy ships are born, morphing right out of the rocks at your feet. Beautiful, isn't it?'

They walked on. Madeleine asked about Malenfant.

Dorothy shrugged. 'I got back twenty years before you did. If he came directly back to the system after we parted, as he said he would, he might have arrived here centuries earlier yet. I don't know what's become of him.'

Madeleine studied her. 'You're troubled. The time we had on the Cannonball –'

'Not troubled, exactly. Guilty, perhaps.' She laughed. '*Guilt*: the Catholic Church's first patent.'

'And that's why you work so hard here.'

Dorothy said dryly, 'Analysis now, Madeleine? I also work to live, as must we all ... But still, yes, I failed Malenfant, there on the Cannonball. I used to be a priest. If ever there was a soul in torment, in his own silent, lonely way, it was Reid Malenfant. And I couldn't find a way to help him.'

Madeleine scowled, irritated. 'What happened on the Cannonball was about Malenfant, Dorothy; not you and your guilt. Malenfant was a victim. A tool of the Gaijin, dragged across the Galaxy, part of plans we still know nothing about. Why should he put up with that?'

'Because he knew, or suspected, that it was the right thing to do, if the Gaijin had any hope of changing –' she waved a gloved hand at the damaged sky '– *this*. The rapacious colonization waves, the wars, the trashing of worlds, the extinctions. Even if there was a chance of making a difference, it might have been right for Malenfant to sacrifice himself.'

'But he's just a man, a human. Why should he give himself up? Would you?'

Dorothy sighed. 'I'm not the right person to ask any more. Would *you*?'

'I don't know.' Madeleine was chilled. 'Poor Malenfant.'

'Wherever he is, whatever becomes of him, I hope he isn't alone. Even Christ had the comfort of His family, at the foot of the Cross. You brought refugees here, didn't you?'

Madeleine grunted. 'I'm told that everybody here is a refugee. But here we are as safe as anywhere.'

Dorothy barked laughter. 'You don't get it yet, do you? Obviously you haven't spoken to Nemoto ... *She's* still alive. Did you know that? Centuries old . . . Of all the places to come – *this*, Mercury, as the last refuge of mankind? *Wrong*.'

'Mercury is deep in the inner system. So close to the sun the Gaijin don't want to come here.'

'But the Gaijin are not the enemy,' Dorothy hissed. 'You have to think things through, Madeleine. We think we know how the Crackers work. They manipulate the target star, causing it to nova . . .' A nova: a stellar explosion, releasing as much energy in a few days as a star would have expended in ten thousand years. 'The Crackers feed on the light pulse, you see,' Dorothy said. 'They ride their solar-sail craft out to more stars, scattering like seeds from a burst fungus, sailing past planets scorched and ruined. We used to think novae were natural. A question of a glitch in a star's fusion processes, perhaps caused by an infall of material from a binary companion. Now we wonder if *any* nova we have observed historically has been natural. Perhaps *all* of them, all over the sky, have been the responsibility of the Crackers – or foul species like them.'

And Madeleine started to see it. 'How do you make a star nova?'

'Simple. In principle. You set a chain of powerful particle accelerators in orbit around your target star. They create currents of charged particles, which set up a powerful magnetic field, caging the star – which can then be manipulated.'

'. . . Ah. But you need a resource base to manufacture those thousands, millions of machines. And a place to make your new generation of solar sailing boats.'

'Yes. Madeleine, here in the solar system, what would be the *ideal* location for such a mine?'

A rocky world orbiting conveniently close to the central star itself. A big fat core of iron and nickel just begging to be dug out and broken up and exploited, without even an awkward rocky shell to cut through . . .

'Mercury,' Madeleine whispered. 'What do we do? Do we have to evacuate?'

Dorothy said, comparatively gently, '*Where to*? Meacher, remember where you are. We've already lost the solar system. This is the last bolt hole. All we can do is dig deep, deep down, as deep as possible.'

Something about her emphasis on those words made Madeleine look hard at Dorothy, but her face remained obscured.

'What are you doing here, Dorothy? You're planning something, aren't you? . . .' Her mind raced. 'Some way of striking back at the Crackers – is that what this is about? *Are you working with Nemoto?*'

But Dorothy evaded the question. 'What can *we* do? The Crackers have already driven off the Gaijin, a species much older and wiser and more powerful than *us*. We're just vermin, infesting a piece of prime real estate.'

Madeleine said coldly, 'If you believe we're vermin, you really have lost your faith.'

Dorothy laughed. 'Compared to the Gaijin, even the Crackers, what other word would you use?' She peered up at the sky, her face obscured by scuffed glass. 'Remember, Madeleine. *Tell them to dig deep.* That's vital. As deep as they can . . .'

She went back to Carl ap Przibram to discuss the issue of the Aborigines. Interstellar war or not, *they* still had no other place to go.

'Please be straightforward with me. I appreciate you're trying to help. I don't want to offend you, or imply –'

'– that I'm some kind of immoral bastard,' he said tightly.

The archaic term surprised her. She wondered what thirty-eighth-century oath lay on the other side of the chattering translators.

He said, 'This isn't an easy job. People always find it hard to accept what I have to tell them.'

'I sympathize. But I need you to help me. I'm a long way from home – from my time. It's hard for me to understand what's happening here, to progress the issue.' She pointed to the ceiling. 'There are two hundred people up there. They've come all the way in from Triton, the edge of the solar system. They have absolutely no place to go. They are completely dependent, refugees.'

'*We are all refugees.*'

She grunted. 'That's the standard mantra here, isn't it?'

He frowned at her. 'But it's true. And I don't know if you understand how significant that is. I haven't met a traveller before, Madeleine Meacher. But I've read about your kind.'

'My *kind*?'

'You were born on Earth, weren't you? At a time when there were no colonies beyond the home planet.'

'Not quite true –'

'You are accustomed to think of us, the space dwellers, as exotic beings, somehow beyond the humanity you grew up with. But it isn't like that. *My* home society, on Vesta, was fifteen centuries old. My ancestors spent all that time making the asteroid habitable. Centuries living in tunnels and lava tubes and caves, cowering from radiation, knowing that a single mistake could kill everything they cared about

. . . We are a deeply conservative people, Madeleine Meacher. We are not used to travel. We are not world-builders. We, too, are a long way from home.'

'You got here first,' Madeleine said. 'And now you're driving every-body else off.'

He shook his head. 'It isn't like that. If not for us, *this* – a habitable corner of Mercury – wouldn't be here at all.'

She stood up. 'I know you'll do your job, Carl ap Przibram.'

He nodded. 'I appreciate your courtesy. But you understand that doesn't guarantee I will be able to let your party land here. If we cannot feed them . . .' He steepled his long fingers. 'In the long run,' he said, 'it may make no difference anyhow. Do you see that?'

If the Crackers win, if they come here. *That's* what he means.

He studied her face, as if pleading for help, for understanding.

Everybody does his best, she thought bleakly. How little it all means.

Chapter 31

END GAME

In the final months, events unfolded with shocking rapidity. The great spherical fleet of Cracker vessels sailed inwards, through the huge empty orbits of the outer planets, past abandoned asteroids, at last into the hot deep heart of the system.

One by one, all over the system, beacons were extinguished: on Triton, the asteroids, Mars, human stories concluded without witness, in the cold and dark.

The data miners found Nemoto – or, Madeleine thought, perhaps she consented to be found.

It turned out Nemoto had shunned the underground colonies. She was working on the surface, in an abandoned science base in a big, smooth-floored crater called Bach, some thousand kilometres north of Chao City.

Madeleine used the monorail to get to Bach. The 'rail was still functioning, for now; the encroaching Cracker ships had yet to interfere materially with Mercury in any way. Nevertheless there were no humans operating on the surface of Mercury, nobody amid the blindly toiling robots, diggers and scrapers. And everywhere, tended by the robots or not, Madeleine saw the gleam of solar sail flowers.

In the shade of an eroded-smooth crater wall, Nemoto was toiling at a plain of tilled regolith. Here, one of the glass-leafed arrays had spread out over the heat-shattered soil. Nemoto was hunched over, monk-like, a slow, patient figure, redolent of age, tending her plants of glass and light.

The sun was higher in the sky at this more northerly latitude, a ferocious ball, and Madeleine's suit, gleaming silver, warned her frequently of excessive temperatures.

'Nemoto –'

Nemoto straightened up stiffly. She silenced Madeleine with a gesture, beckoned for her to come deeper into the shade, and pointed upwards.

Madeleine lifted her visor. Gradually, as her eyes adapted, the stars came out. The sky's geography was swamped, in one corner, by the extensive glare of the sun's corona.

But the stars were just a backdrop to a crowd of ships.

They were all around Mercury now, spread out through three-dimensional space, like a great receding cloud of dragonflies, frozen in flight. Loose clusters of them already orbited the planet, looping east and west, north and south, cupping the light. And further out there was a ragged swarm still on the way, reaching back to the hidden sun, around which these misty invaders had sailed.

Their filmy, silvery wings were caught folded or twisted, in the act of shifting better to catch the sun's light. The spread of those gauzy wings was huge, some of them thousands of kilometres across. These were no trivial inner-system skimmers, as humans had built, made to sail in the dense light winds close to the sun; these were giant interstellar schooners, capable of travelling across light years, through spaces where the brightest, largest star was reduced to a point.

Not dragonflies, she thought. Locusts. For not one of those ships was human, Madeleine knew, or even Gaijin. Nothing but Crackers.

'It's remarkable to watch them,' Nemoto breathed. 'I mean, over hours or days. Simply to stand here and watch. You can see them deploying their sails, you know. The sunlight pushes outward from the sun, of course. But they sail in towards the sun by tacking into the light: they lose a little orbital velocity, and then simply fall inwards. But sailing ships that size are slow to manoeuvre. They must have been plotting their courses, here to Mercury, all the way in from the Oort cloud.'

'I wonder what the sails are made of,' Madeleine said.

Nemoto grunted. 'Nothing *we* have ever been capable of. Maybe the Gaijin would know. Only diamond fibre would be strong enough for the rigging. And as for the sails, the best *we* can do is aluminized spider-silk. Much too thick and heavy for ships of that size. Perhaps they grow the sails by some kind of vacuum deposition, molecule by molecule. Or perhaps they are masters of nanotech.'

'They really are coming, aren't they, Nemoto?'

Nemoto turned, face hidden. 'Of course they are. We are both too old for illusion, Meacher. They are wasps around a honey pot, which is Mercury's fat iron core.'

Together, they walked around the spreading array, glass flowers that sparkled with the light of stars and Eetie ships.

Madeleine tried to talk to Nemoto, to draw her out. After all, their acquaintance – never friendship – went back across *sixteen hundred years*, to that steamy office in Kourou, a tank of spinning Chaera on the pre-Paulis Moon. But Nemoto wouldn't talk of her life, her past: she would talk of nothing but the great issues of the day, Mercury and the Crackers and the great Eetie colonization pulse all around them, the huge and impersonal.

Madeleine wondered if that was normal.

But there was nothing *normal* about a woman who had lived through seventeen centuries, for God's sake. Nemoto was probably the oldest human being who had ever lived; to survive, Nemoto must have put herself through endless reengineering, of both body and mind. And, unlike the lonely star travellers, she had lived through all those years on worlds full of people: Earth, the Moon, Mercury. Her biography must run like an unbroken thread through the tangled tapestry of a millennium and a half of human history.

But Madeleine truthfully knew little of this ancient, enigmatic woman. Had she ever married, ever fallen in love? Had she ever had children? And if so, were *they* alive – or had she outlived generation after generation of descendants? Perhaps nobody knew, nobody but Nemoto herself. And Nemoto would talk of none of this, refused to be drawn as she tended her plants of glass.

But in her slow-moving, aged way, she seemed focused, Madeleine thought. Determined, vigorous. Almost happy. As if she had a mission.

Madeleine decided to challenge her.

She walked among the glassy leaves. She bent, awkwardly, and picked up a glimmering leaf; it broke away easily. It was very fine, fragile. When she crushed it carelessly, it crumbled.

Nemoto made a small move towards her, a silent admonition.

Madeleine dropped the leaf carefully. 'I've been reading up,' she said.

'You have?'

'On you. On your, umm, career.' She waved a hand at the leaves. 'I think I know what you're doing here.'

'Tell me.'

'Moon flowers. You brought them here, to Mercury. This isn't just about growing solar sails. There are Moon flowers all over this damn planet. You've been seeding them, haven't you?'

Nemoto hunkered down and studied the plant before her. 'They grow well here. The sunlight, you see. I gen-enged them – if you can call it that; the genetic material of these flowers is stored in a crystalline substrate which is quite different from our biochemistry. Well. I removed some unnecessary features.'

'Unnecessary?'

'The rudimentary nervous system. The traces of consciousness.'

'Nemoto – *why*? Will dying Mercury become a garden?'

'What do you *think*, Meacher?'

'That you're planning to fight back. Against the Crackers. You are remarkable, Nemoto. Even now, even here, you continue the struggle . . . And these flowers have something to do with it.'

Nemoto was as immobile as her flowers, the delicate glass petals reflected in her visor. She said, 'I wonder how they started. The Crackers. How they began this immense, destructive odyssey. Have you ever thought about that? Surely no species *intends* to become a breed of rapacious interstellar locusts. Perhaps they were colonists on some giant starship, a low-tech, multi-generation ark. But when they got to their destination they'd gotten too used to spaceflight. So they built more ships, and just kept going . . . Perhaps the gimmick – blowing up the target sun for an extra push – came later. And once they'd worked out how to do it, reaped the benefits, they couldn't resist using it. Over and over.'

'Not a strategy designed to make them popular.'

'But all that matters, in this Darwinian Galaxy of ours, is short term effectiveness. No matter how many suns you destroy, how many worlds you trash . . . There simply isn't the time to have qualms about such things. And so it goes, as the Galaxy turns, oblivious to the tiny beings warring and dying on its surface . . .'

She walked on, tending her garden, and Madeleine followed.

'You must help us,' said Carl ap Przibram.

Madeleine sat uncomfortably, wondering how to respond. She felt claustrophobic in this bureaucrat's office, crushed by the layers of Mercury rock over her head, the looming nearness of the sun: as if she could somehow sense its huge weight, its warp of space.

He leaned forward. 'For fifteen centuries my people lived like this.' He held up his hands, indicating the close rocky walls. 'In environments that were enclosed. Fragile. Shared.' His face clouded with anger, hostility. 'We didn't have the luxury for – aggression. Warfare.'

Now she understood. 'As *we* did, on "primitive Earth". Is that what you think? But my world was small too. *We* could have unleashed a war which might have made the planet uninhabitable.'

'That's true.' He jabbed a Chopin finger at her. 'But you didn't *think* that way, did you? *You*, Madeleine Meacher, used to ship weapons, from one war zone to another. That was your job, how you made a living.

'You come from a unique time. We remember it even now; we are taught about it. Uniquely wasteful. You were still fat on energy, from Earth's ancient reserves. You managed to get a toehold on other worlds, the Moon. But you squandered your legacy – turned it into poisons, in fact, that trashed your planet's climate.'

She stood up. 'I've heard this before.' It was true; the bitterness at the well-recorded profligacy of her own 'fat age' had scarcely faded in the centuries since, and the travellers, time-stranded refugees from that era, made easy targets for bile and prejudice. But it scarcely mattered *now*. 'Carl ap Przibram, tell me what you want of me.'

'I've been authorized to deal with you. To offer you what we can . . .'

It turned out to be simple, unexpected. Impossible. The Coalition wanted to put her in charge of Mercury's defences: assembling weapons and a fighting force of some kind, training them up, devising tactics. Waging war on the Crackers.

She laughed; ap Przibram looked offended. She said, 'You think I'm some kind of warrior barbarian, come from the past to save you with my primitive instincts.'

He glared. 'You're more of a warrior – and a barbarian – than I will ever be.'

'This is absurd. I know nothing of your resources, your technology, your culture. How could I lead you?' She eyed him, suspicious. 'Or is there another game being played here? Are you looking for a fall guy? Is that it?'

He puzzled over the translation of that. Then his frown deepened. 'You are facetious, or foolish. If we fail to defend ourselves, there will be no "fall guys". In the worst case there will be nobody left *at all*, blameworthy or otherwise. We are asking you because . . .'

Because they are desperate, she thought, these gentle, spindly aster-oid-born people. Desperate, and terrified, in the face of this Darwinian onslaught from the stars.

'I'll help any way I can,' she said. 'But I can't be your general. I'm sorry,' she added.

He closed his eyes and steepled his fingers. 'Your friends, the refu-gees from Triton, are still in orbit.'

'I know that,' she snapped.

He said nothing.

'. . . Oh,' she said, understanding. 'You're trying to bargain with me.' She leaned on the desk. 'I'm calling your bluff. You haven't let them starve up there so far. You won't let them die. You'll bring them down when you can; you aren't serious in your threats.'

His thin face twisted with embarrassment. 'This wasn't my idea, Madeleine Meacher.'

More gently, she said, 'I know that.'

'In the end,' he said, 'none of this may matter. The Crackers have little interest in our history and our disputes and our intrigues with each other.'

'It's true. We're vermin to them.' Anger flared in her at that thought, the word Dorothy had used.

But it's true, she thought.

This, here on Mercury, may be the largest concentration of humans left anywhere. And if the Crackers succeed in their project, it will be the end of mankind. None of our art or history, our lives and hopes and loves, none of it will matter. We'll be just another forgotten, defeated race, just another layer of organic debris in the long, grisly history of a mined-out solar system.

I can't let that happen, she thought. And: I must see Nemoto again.

On the surface of Mercury, Nemoto sighed. 'You know, the Crackers' strategy – making suns nova – isn't really all that smart. When you're more than a few diameters away from your disrupted star it starts dwindling into a point source, and the light wind's intensity falls off rapidly. But if you have a *giant* star – say a red giant – you are sailing with a wall of light behind you, and you get a runaway effect; it takes *much* longer for the wind to dwindle. You see?'

'So –'

'So the best strategy for the Crackers would be to tamper with the sun's evolution. To make it old before its time, to balloon it to a red giant that would reach out to Earth's orbit, and ride out that fat crimson wind. But the Crackers aren't smart enough for that. None of the Eeties out there are *really* smart, you know.'

'Maybe the Crackers are working on an upgrade,' Madeleine suggested dryly.

'Oh, no doubt,' Nemoto said, matter-of-fact. 'The question is, will they have time to figure out how to do it, before *their* race is run?'

'Why haven't you told the refugees what you are up to, Nemoto?'

'Meacher, the people on this ball of iron are conservative. And split: there are many factions here. Some believe the Crackers may be placated. That these Eeties will just leave of their own accord.'

'That's ridiculous. The Crackers *can't* leave. They *must* dismantle the sun to continue their expansion.'

'Nevertheless, such views are held. And such factions would, if they knew of my project, seek to shut me down.'

'So what do we do?'

'The settlers here must go as deep as they can, deep into the interior.'

Just as Dorothy Chaum had said. 'When?'

'When the Cracker ships are here. When all the wasps have swarmed to the honey pot.'

'I'll try. But what of you, Nemoto?'

Nemoto just laughed.

Madeleine leaned forward. 'Tell me what happened to Malenfant.'

Nemoto would not meet her eyes.

She told Madeleine something of what sounded like a long and complicated story, embedded in Earth's tortured latter history, of a Saddle Point gateway in the heart of a mountain in Africa. Her account was cool, logical, without feeling.

'So he went back,' Madeleine said. 'Back through the Saddle Points, back to the Gaijin, after all.'

'You don't understand,' Nemoto said without emotion. 'He had no choice. *I* sent him back. I manipulated the situation to achieve that.'

Madeleine covered Nemoto's cold hand.

'. . . Just as I have manipulated half of mankind, it seems. I exiled Malenfant, against his will.' Nemoto said sharply, 'I believe I have sent him to his death, Meacher. But if it is a crime, it will be justified – if the Gaijin can make use of that death.'

'I guess you have to believe that,' Madeleine murmured.

'Yes. Yes, I have to.'

Her manner was odd – even for Nemoto – too cool, logical; too bright, Madeleine thought.

Madeleine knew that no human could survive more than a thousand years without emptying a clutter of memory from her overloaded head. Nemoto *must* have found a way to edit her memories, to reorder, even delete them – a process which, of course, meant the editing of her personality too.

Perhaps she has attempted to cleanse her memories of Malenfant, her guilt over her betrayal of him. That is how she has been able to achieve such distance from it.

But if so, she was only partially successful. For this action against the Crackers, whatever it is, will kill her, Madeleine realized.

And Nemoto is embracing the prospect.

Madeleine worked hard on Carl ap Przibram, trying to get him to take Nemoto's advice seriously. It wasn't easy, given her lack of any detailed understanding of what Nemoto might be trying to attempt. But at last he yielded, and got her a slot before the Coalition's top council.

It was an uneasy session. It took place in a steamy cave crammed with a hundred delegates from different factions, none of them natives, jammed in here against their will in the bowels of Mercury. There was a range of body types, she observed, mostly variants on the tall, stick-thin low-gravity template; but there were a number of delegates adapted for zero G, even exotic atmospheres, in environment tanks, wheel chairs and other supportive apparatus.

She faced rows of faces glaring with suspicion, fear, self-interest, even contempt. This wasn't going to be easy. But she recognized, here in the main governing council, one of the women from the Triton transports, which had at last been allowed to land. These people were prickly, awkward, superstitious, fearful. But, even in this dire strait, they welcomed refugees, and even gave them a place at the top table.

It made her obscurely proud. *This* is what the Gaijin should have studied, she thought. Not wrinkles in our genome. *This*: even in this last refuge, we refuse to give up, and we still welcome strangers.

She launched into her presentation. She stayed on her feet a good hour as speaker after speaker assailed her. She didn't always have answers, but she weathered the storm, trying to persuade by her steady faith, her unwavering determination.

Not everybody was convinced. That was never going to be possible. But in the end, factions representing a good sixty per cent of the planet's population agreed to concur with Nemoto's advice.

Immensely relieved, Madeleine went back to her room, and slept twelve hours.

The final evacuation was swift.

The remnants of humanity had fled inwards, to Mercury. And now they were converging even more tightly, flowing over the surface of Mercury in monorails or tractors or short-hop sub-orbit shuttles, gathering in the great basin of Caloris Planitia: the shattered ground where, under a high and unforgiving sun, humans had burrowed in search of water.

And, meanwhile, the last of the giant interstellar fleet of Cracker sailing craft were settling into dense, complex orbits around Mercury: wasps around honey, just as Nemoto had said. Data flowed between the Cracker craft, easily visible, even tapped by the cowering humans. These Eeties clearly had no fear of interference, now the Gaijin had withdrawn.

Maybe it would take the Crackers a thousand years to make ready for their great star-bursting project. Maybe it would take a thousand days, a thousand hours. Nobody knew.

Madeleine spent some time with Carl ap Przibram, the nearest thing to a friend she had here.

They had a very stiff dinner, in his apartment. The recycling loops were tight; illogical as it might be, she found it difficult to eat food that must have been through Carl's body several times at least. On the way, she'd decided to invite him to have sex. But it was an offer made more in politeness than lust; and his refusal was entirely polite, too, leaving them both – she suspected – secretly relieved.

Madeleine spent her last day on Mercury inside the Paulis mine in Caloris. This was a tube a half-kilometre wide, the walls clear, the rocks beyond glowing orange-hot. It was the big brother of Frank Paulis's first ancient well on the Moon. This mine had never been completed, and perhaps never would be; but now it served a new purpose as a deep shelter for the remnants of humanity.

Giant temporary floors of spider-silk and aluminium had been spun out over the shaft, cut through by supply ducts and cabling and a giant fireman's-pole of open elevators. Here – safe from radiation and the sun's heat and the shadow's cold – half Mercury's population, a million strong, was being housed in flimsy bubbles of spider-silk and aluminium. The Paulis tunnel wasn't pressurized, of course, and so big flexible walkways ran between the bubbles. The floors were misty and translucent, as were the hab bubbles; and, looking down into the glowing pit of humanity, Madeleine could see people scattered over floor after floor, moving around their habs like microbes in droplets of water, receding into a misty, light-filled infinity.

It was well known she was planning to leave today. In the upper levels many faces were turned up to her – she could see them, just pale dots. She had always been isolated, especially in this latest of her parachute-drops back into human history. Perhaps she was getting too old, too detached from the times. In fact she suspected the displaced Triton colonists rather resented her – as if she, who had guided them here, had somehow been responsible for the disaster that had befallen their home.

Anyhow, it was done. She turned her back on the glimmering interior of the Paulis mine, its cache of humans, and returned to the surface.

She flew up from Mercury, up through a cloud of Cracker ships.

Great sails were all around her. Even partly furled, they were huge, spanning tens of kilometres, like pieces of filmy landscapes torn loose and thrown into the sky. Some of them had been made transparent rather than furled, so that the bright light of the sun shone through skeletal structures of shining threads. And the wings had a complex morphology, each warping and twisting and curling, presumably in response to the density of the light falling on it, and the thin shadows cast by its neighbours.

The Cracker ships sailed close to each other: in great layers, one over the other, sometimes barely half a kilometre apart, a tiny separation compared to the huge expanse of the wings. Sometimes they were so close that a curl in one wing would cause a rippling response in others, great stacks of the wings turning like the pages of an immense book. But Madeleine never once saw those great wings touch; the coordination was stunning.

Madeleine rose up through all this, just bulling her way through in her squat little Gaijin lander. The wonderful wings just curled out of her way.

At ten Mercury diameters, she looked back.

Mercury was a ball of rock, maybe the size of her palm held at arm's length. It looked as if it was wrapped in silvery paper, shifting layers of it, as if it were some huge Christmas present – or perhaps as if immense silvery wasps were crawling all over it. Quite remarkably beautiful, she thought. But, she reflected bitterly, if there was one thing she had learned in her long and dubious career, it was that beauty clung as closely to objects of killing and pain and horror as to the good; and so it was here.

She stretched, weightless. She felt deeply – if shamefully – relieved to be alone once more, in control of her own destiny, without the complication of other people around her.

Nemoto called her from the surface.

'I'm surprised they let you through like that. The Crackers. You're in a Gaijin ship, after all.'

'But the Gaijin are gone. The Crackers clearly don't believe the Gaijin are a threat any more. And they don't even seem to have noticed us humans.' The Crackers are just kicking over the ant hill, she thought, without even looking to see what was there, what *we* were.

'Meacher, how far out are you?'

'Ten diameters.'

'That should be sufficient,' hissed Nemoto.

'Sufficient for what? . . . Never mind. Nemoto, how can you choose death? You've lived so long, seen so much.'

'I've seen enough.'

'And now you want to rest?'

'No. What rest is there in death? I only want to act.'

'To save the species one more time?'

'Perhaps. But the battle is never over, Meacher. The longer we live, the deeper we look, the more layers of deception and manipulation and destruction we will find . . . Consider Mercury, for example, which may be doomed to become a resource mine for the sun-breaking Crackers. Why, if I was a suspicious type, a conspiracy theorist, I might think it was a little *odd* that there should be a giant ball of crust-free nickel-iron placed so *conveniently* right here where the Crackers need it. What do you think? Could some predecessors of the Crackers – even their ancestors – have *arranged* the giant impact that stripped off Mercury's crust and mantle, left behind this rust ball?'

Madeleine was stunned by this deepening of the great violation of the solar system. But, deliberately, she shook her head. 'Even if that's true, what difference does it make?'

Nemoto barked laughter. 'None at all. You're right. One thing at a time. You always were practical, Meacher. And what next for you? Will you stay with the others, huddled in the caves of Mercury?'

Madeleine frowned. 'I'm not a good huddler, Nemoto. And besides, these are not my people.'

'The likes of us have no "people" –'

'Malenfant,' Madeleine said. 'Wherever he is, whatever he faces, he is alone. I'm going to try to find him.'

'Ah,' Nemoto whispered. 'Malenfant, yes. He may be the most important of us all. Goodbye, Meacher.'

'Nemoto? –'

Mercury exploded.

She had to go over it again, rerun the recordings, over and over, before she understood.

It had happened in an instant. It was as if the top couple of metres of Mercury's surface had just lifted off and hailed into the sky.

All over Mercury – from the depths of Caloris Planitia to the crumpled lands at the antipode, from Chao City at the south pole to the abandoned settlements of the north – miniature cannon snouts had poked their way out of the regolith, and fired into the sky. The bullets weren't smart: just bits of rock and dust, dug out of the deeper regolith. But they were moving fast, far faster than Mercury's escape velocity.

The Crackers didn't stand a chance. Mercury rocks tore through filmy wings, overwhelming self-repair facilities. The Cracker ships, like butterflies in a reverse hailstorm, were shredded. Ships collided, or plunged to Mercury's surface, or drifted into space, powerless, beyond the reach of help.

The Moon flowers, of course: they were the key, or rather their dumb, gen-enged descendants, transplanted to Mercury by Nemoto, a wizened, interplanetary Johnny Appleseed. The Moon flowers could make explosive, of aluminium and oxygen, extracted from Moon rock – or Mercury rock – a serviceable chemical-rocket propellant to propel their seed pores. Nemoto had engineered the flowers' descendants to make weapons.

The Crackers had nobody even to fire back at, no way to avoid the rising storm of rock and dust. Even one survivor might have been sufficient to resume the Crackers' mission, for all anybody knew. But there were no survivors. The Crackers had taken a thousand years to reach Mercury, to fly from Procyon and battle through a shell of Gaijin ships. It had taken humans – rock world vermin, contemptuously ignored – a thousand seconds to destroy them.

As she watched that cloud of peppery rock rise from the ground and rip through the gauzy ships – overwhelming them one by one, at last erupting into clear space – Madeleine whooped and howled.

The debris cloud continued to expand, now beginning to tail after Mercury in its slow orbit around the sun. It caught the brilliant light, like rain in sunshine. Maybe Mercury is going to have rings, she thought, rings that will shine like roadways in the sky. Nice memorial. The major features of the surface beneath had survived, of course; no backyard rocket was going to obliterate Caloris Planitia. But every square metre of the surface had been raked over.

She contacted the Coalition.

Every human on Mercury had survived – even those who hadn't taken Nemoto's advice about deep shelter. Already they were emerging, blinking, under a dusty, starry sky.

Every human but Nemoto, of course.

At least we have breathing space: time to rebuild, maybe breed a little, spread out, before the next bunch of Eetie assholes come chomping their way through the solar system. Good for you, Nemoto. You did the best you could. Good job.

As for me – story's over here, Madeleine. Time to face the universe again.

And so Madeleine fled before the hail of rubble from Mercury – still expanding, a dark and looming cloud that glittered with fragments of Cracker craft – fled in search of Gaijin, and Reid Malenfant.

V

THE CHILDREN'S CRUSADE

AD 8800, and Later

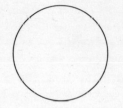

Near the neutron star there were multiple lobes of light. They looked like solar flares to Malenfant: giant, unending storms rising from the neutron star's surface. Further out still, the founts of gas lost their structure, becoming dim, diffuse. They merged into a wider cloud of debris which seemed to be fleeing from the neutron star, a vigorous solar wind. And beyond *that* there were only the Galaxy core stars, watchful, silent, still, peering down as if in disapproval at this noisy, spitting monster.

This was a pulsar. You could detect those radio beams from Earth.

Malenfant had grown up with the story of the first detection of a pulsar. Pre-Gaijin astronomers had detected an unusual radio signal: a regular, ticking pulse, accurate to within a millionth of a second. Staring at such traces, the scientists had at first toyed with the idea it might be the signature of intelligence, calling from the stars.

In fact, when envoys from the stars began to make their presence known, it was not as a gentle tick of radio noise but as a wave of destructive exploitation that scattered mankind and all but overwhelmed the entire solar system – and the same thing had occurred many times before.

We put up a hell of a fight, though, he thought. We even won some victories, in our tiny, scattershot way. But in the end it was going to count for nothing.

It was ironic, he thought grimly. Those old pre-Gaijin star gazers had thought that first pulsar was a signal from Little Green Men.

In fact it was a killer of Little Green Men.

Chapter 32

SAVANNAH

She woke to the movement of air: the rustle of wind in trees, perhaps the hiss of grass, a gentle breeze on her face, the scent of dew, of wood smoke. Eyes closed, she was lying on her back. She could feel something tickling at her neck, the slippery texture of leaves under the palms of her hand. Somewhere crickets were calling.

She opened her eyes. She was looking up at the branches of a tree, silhouetted against a blue-black sky.

And the sky was full of stars. A great river of light flowed from horizon to horizon. It was littered with pink-white glowing clouds, crowded, beautiful.

She remembered.

Io. She had been on Io.

Her Gaijin guides had taken her to a grave: Reid Malenfant's grave, they said, dug by strong Neandertal hands. She had, briefly, despaired; she had been too late in her self-appointed mission; he had died alone after all, a long way from home.

The Gaijin hadn't seemed to understand.

Then had come a blue flash, a moment of pain –

And now, *this.* Where the hell was she? She sat up, suddenly afraid.

She saw a flickering fire, a figure squatting beside it. A man. He was holding something on a stick, she saw, perhaps a fish. He stood straight now, and came walking easily towards her.

She felt herself tense up further.

His head was silhouetted against the crowded stars; he was bald, his skin smooth as leather. It was Reid Malenfant.

She whimpered, cowered back. '*You are dead.*'

He crouched before her, reached out and held her hand. He felt warm, real, calm. 'Take it easy, Madeleine.'

'They put you in a hole in the ground, on Io. Jesus Christ –'

'Don't ask questions,' he said evenly. 'Not yet. Concentrate on the here and now. How do you *feel*? Are you sick, hot, cold? . . .'

She thought about that. 'I'm okay. I guess.' She wiggled her fingers and toes, turned her head this way and that. Everything intact and mobile; nothing aching; not so much as a cricked neck. Her trembling subsided, soothed by a relentless blizzard of detail, of normality. The here and now, yes.

It *was* Reid Malenfant. He was wearing a pale blue coverall, white slip-on shoes. When she glanced down, she found she was wearing the same bland outfit.

He was studying her. 'You were out cold. I thought I'd better leave you be. We don't seem to have any medic equipment here.'

The smell of the fish reached her. 'I'm hungry,' she said, surprised. 'You've been *fishing*?'

'Why not? I mined my old spacesuit. Not for the first time. A thread, a hook made from a zipper. I felt like Tom Sawyer.'

. . . Never mind the fish. This guy is *dead*. 'Malenfant, they buried you. Your burns . . .' But she was starting to remember more. The Neandertals had opened the grave. It was empty.

'Just look at me now.' Emulating her, he clenched his fists, twisted his head. 'I haven't felt so good since the Bad Hair Day twins had a hold of me.'

'Who?'

'Long story. Look, you want some fish or not?' And he loped back to the fire, picked up another twig skewered through a second fish, and held it over his fire of brush wood.

She got to her feet and followed him.

The sky provided a soft light, as bright as a quarter-Moon, perhaps. Even away from that Galactic stripe the stars were crowded. There was a pattern of bright stars near the zenith that looked like a box, or maybe a kite; there was another easy pattern further over, six stars arranged in a rough, squashed ellipse. She recognized no constellations, though.

The grassy plain rolled to the distance, dotted with sparse trees, the vegetation black and silver in the starlight. But where Malenfant's fire cast a stronger light she could see the grass was an authentic green.

Gravity about Earth normal, she noted absently.

She thought she saw movement, a shadow flitting past a stand of trees. She waited for a moment, holding still. There was no sound, not so much as a crackle of undergrowth under a footstep.

She hunkered down beside Malenfant, accepted half a fish and bit into it. It was succulent but tasteless. 'I never much liked fish,' she said.

'Sorry.'

'Where's the stream?'

He nodded, beyond the fire. 'Thataway. I took a walk.'

'During the daylight?'

'No.' He tilted back his head. 'When I woke up it was night, as deep as this.' He glanced up at the sky, picking out a complex of glowing clouds. 'What do you think of the view?'

The larger of the clouds was a rose of pink light. Its heart was speckled by bright splashes of light – stars? – and it was bordered by a band of deeper darkness, velvet blackness, where no stars shone. It was beautiful, strange.

'That is a star birth nebula,' he said. 'It's probably much more extensive. All we can see is a blister, illuminated by a clutch of young stars at the centre – see the way that glow is roughly spherical? – the stars' radiation makes the gases shine, out as far as it can reach, before it gets absorbed. But you can see more stars, younger stars, emerging from the fringes of the blister. That darker area all around the glow, eclipsing the stars behind, is a glimpse of the true nebula, dense clouds of dust and hydrogen, probably containing proto-stars that have yet to shine . . . Madeleine, I did a little amateur astronomy as a kid. I *recognize* that thing; it's visible from Earth. We call it the Lagoon Nebula. And its companion over there is the Trifid. The Lagoon contains stars so young and bright you can see them with the naked eye, from Earth.'

In all her travels around the Saddle Point network, Madeleine had seen nothing like this.

'Ah,' Malenfant said, when she expressed this. 'But we've come far beyond *that*, of course.'

She shivered, suddenly longing for daylight. 'Malenfant, in those trees over there. I thought I saw –'

'There are Neandertals here,' he said quickly. 'You needn't fear them. I think they're from Io. Maybe some of them are from Earth, too. I think they were brought here when they were close to death. I haven't recognized any of them yet. There is one old guy I got to know a little, who died. I called him Esau. He must be here somewhere.'

She tried to follow all that. He didn't seem concerned, confused by the situation. There was, she realized, a lot he needed to tell her.

'We aren't on Io any more, are we?'

'No.' He pointed at the stars with his half-eaten fish. 'That's no sky of Earth. Or even of Io.'

Madeleine felt something inside her crack. '*Malenfant* –'

'Hey.' He was immediately before her, holding her shoulders, tall in the dark. 'Take it easy.'

'I'm sorry. It's just –'

'We're a long way from home. I know.'

'I've got a lot to tell you.' She started to blurt out all that she'd seen since she, Malenfant and Dorothy Chaum had returned to the solar system from the Gaijin's Cannonball homeworld: the interstellar war, the hail of comets into the sun's hearth, the Crackers.

He listened carefully. He showed regret at the damage done to Earth, the end of so many stories. He smiled when she spoke of Nemoto. But after a time, as detail after detail spilled out of her, he held her shoulders again.

'Madeleine.'

She looked up at him; his eyes were wells of shadow in the starlight.

'*None of it matters*. Look around, Madeleine. We're a long way away from all that. There's nothing we can do to affect any of it now . . .'

'How far?'

He said gently, 'Questions later. The first thing *I* did when I woke up was go behind those bushes over there and take a good solid dump.'

Despite herself, that made her laugh out loud.

By the time they'd eaten more fish, and some yam-like fruit Malenfant had found, it was still dark, with no sign of a dawn. So Madeleine pulled together a pallet of leaves and dry grass, and tucked her arms inside her coverall, and quickly fell asleep.

When she woke it was still dark.

Malenfant was hunkered down close to a stand of trees. He seemed to be drawing in the dirt with a stick, peering around at the sky. Beyond him there was a group of figures, shadowy in the starlight. Neandertals?

There really was no sign of dawn, no sign of a moon: not a glimmer of light, other than starlight, on any horizon. And yet something was different, she thought. Were the stars a little brighter? Certainly that Milky Way glow close to the horizon seemed stronger. And, it seemed to her, the stars had shifted a little, in the sky. She looked for the star patterns she had noted last time she was awake – the box overhead, the ellipse. Were they a little distorted, a little more squashed together?

She joined Malenfant. He handed her a piece of fruit, and she sat beside him.

The Neandertals seemed to be a family group, five, six adults, about as many children. They seemed oblivious to Malenfant's scrutiny. They were hairy, squat, naked: cartoon ape men. And two of the children were wrestling, hard, tumbling over and over, as if they were more gorilla than human.

Malenfant asked slowly, avoiding her eyes: 'Why did you come here, Madeleine?'

He seemed stiff; she felt embarrassed, as if she had been foolish, impulsive. 'I volunteered. The Gaijin helped me. I wanted to find you.'

'Why?'

'I got to know you, on the Cannonball, Malenfant. I didn't like the idea of you being alone when –'

'When what?'

She hesitated. 'Do *you* know why you're here?'

'Just remember,' he said coolly, 'I didn't ask you to follow me.' He continued his sketching in the dust, angry.

She shrank back, confused, lost; she felt further from home than ever.

She studied his sketches. They were crude, just scrapings made with the point of his stick. But she recognized the box, the ellipse.

'It's a star map,' she said.

'Yeah. Kind of basic. Just a few score of the brightest stars. But look here, here, here . . .'

Some of the points were double.

'The stars have shifted,' she said.

'Here's where *this* one was yesterday – or before we slept, anyhow. And here's where it is now.' He shrugged. 'The shift is small – hard to be accurate without instruments – but I think it's real.'

'I noted it too,' she said.

'Not just a shift. Other changes. I think there are *more* stars than yesterday. They seem brighter. And they are flowing across the sky –' he swept his arms over his head, towards the bright Milky Way band on the horizon '– thataway.'

'Why that way?'

He looked up at her. 'Because that's where we're headed. Come see.' He stood, took her by the hand and pulled her to her feet, and led her past a stand of trees.

Now she saw the Galactic band exposed to her full view: it was a river of stars, yes, but they were stars that were varied, yellow and blue and orange, and the river was crammed with exotic features, giant dark clouds and brilliant shining nebulae.

'It looks like the Milky Way,' she said. 'But –'

'I know,' he said. 'It's not like this at home . . . I think we're looking at the Sagittarius Spiral Arm.'

She said slowly, 'Which is *not* the arm which contains the sun.'

'Hell, no. *That's* just a shingle, a short arc. *This* mother is the next arm in, towards the centre of the Galaxy.' He swept his arm so his hand spanned the star river. 'Look at those nebulae – see? – the Eagle, the Omega, the Trifid, the Lagoon – a huge region of star-birth, one of the largest in the Galaxy, immense clouds of gas and dust capable of producing millions of stars each. The Sagittarius Arm is one of the Galaxy's two main spiral features, a huge whirl of matter that reaches from the hub of the Galaxy all the way out to the rim, winding around for a full turn. This is what you see if you head inward from the sun, towards the Galaxy centre.'

Under the huge, crowded sky, she felt small, humbled. 'We've come a long way, haven't we, Malenfant?'

'I think we busted out of the edge of the Saddle Point network. We know the network is no more than a couple of thousand light years across, extending just a fraction of the way to the centre of the Galaxy. We must have reached a radius where the Saddle Points aren't working any more. Which is a problem if you want to go further . . . I think this is just the start of the true journey.'

He was speaking steadily, evenly, as if discussing a hiking tour of Yosemite. She felt her self-control waver again. But she didn't want to seem weak in front of Malenfant, this difficult cold man.

'And,' she said, 'where will that *true journey* take us?'

He shrugged. 'Maybe all the way to the centre of the Galaxy.' He studied her, perhaps to see how well she could take this. Then he pointed. 'Look, Madeleine – the Lagoon Nebula, up there, is five thousand light years from Earth.'

And so, therefore, she thought, the year is 8800 AD, or thereabouts. It was a number that meant nothing to her at all. And, even if she turned around now and headed for home, assuming that was possible, it would be another five thousand years before she could get back to Earth.

But the centre of the Galaxy was twenty-five thousand light years from the sun. Even at lightspeed it would take fifty thousand years to get there and back. *Fifty thousand years.* This was no ordinary journey, not even like a history-wrenching Saddle Point hop; the human species itself was only a hundred thousand years old . . .

He was still watching her. 'I've had time to get used to this.'

'I'm fine.'

'Madeleine . . .'

'I mean it,' she snapped. She got up, turned her back and walked away. She found a stream, drank and splashed her face, spent a few minutes alone, eyes closed, breathing deeply.

Perhaps it's just as well we humans can't grasp the immensities we have begun to cross. If we were any smarter, we'd go crazy.

Remember why you came here, Madeleine. For Malenfant. Whether he appreciates it or not, the asshole. Malenfant is strong. But maybe it helps him just to have me here. Somebody he has to look after.

But her grasp of psychology always had been shaky. Anyhow, she was here, whether he needed her or not.

She went back to Malenfant, at his patient vigil.

One of the Neandertal women was working a rock, making tools. She held a core of what looked like obsidian, a glassy volcanic rock. She gave the core one sharp strike, and a flake of it dropped off. A few light strokes along the edge and the flake had become a tear-shaped blade, like an arrow-head. The woman, with a lop-sided grin, gave the knife to one of the males, signing rapidly.

Malenfant murmured, 'She's saying he should be careful of the edge.'

She frowned. 'I don't understand how those guys got here.'

He told her what he'd observed of the Neandertals' burial practices: the mysterious Staff of Kintu.

'So you think the Gaijin were rewarding the dying Neandertal workers for all their labours with this – a soapy Heaven.'

He laughed. 'If they were, they are the first gods in history to deliver on their afterlife promises.'

She paced, feeling the texture of the grass under her feet, the breeze on her face. 'Why is it like *this*? Trees, grass, streams – it feels like Africa. But it isn't Africa, is it?'

'No. But if you ask almost any human, anywhere, what type of landscape they prefer, it's something like *this*. Open grass, a few flat-topped trees. Even Clear Lake, Houston, fits the pattern: grass out front, maybe a tree or two. And you never put your tree in front of your window; you need to be able to look out of your cave, to see the predators coming. After taking us apart for a thousand years, the Gaijin know us well. And our Neandertal cousins. We're a hundred millennia out of Africa, Madeleine, and five thousand light years distant.' He tapped his chest. 'But it's still here, inside us.'

'You're saying they've given us an environment that we're comfortable with. A Neandertal theme park.'

He nodded. 'I think very little of what we see is real.' He pointed at the sky. 'But *that* is real.'

'How so?'

'Because it's changing.'

She slept and woke again.

And the sky, once more, had changed dramatically. She lay on her back alongside Malenfant, gazing up at the evolving sky.

He started talking about how he had travelled here.

'They put me through a whole series of Saddle Point jumps, taking me across the geography of the Galaxy . . . First I headed towards Scorpio. Our sun is in the middle of a bubble in space, hundreds of light years across – did you know that? – a vacuum blown into the Galactic medium by an ancient supernova explosion. But the Saddle Point leaps got longer and longer . . .'

With the sun already invisible, he had been taken out of the local bubble, into a neighbouring void the astronomers called Loop 1.

'I saw Antares through the murk,' he said, 'a glowing red jewel set against a glowing patch of sky, a burst of young stars they call the Rho Opiuchi complex. Hell of a sight. I looked back for the sun. I couldn't find it. But I saw a great sheet of young stars that slices through the Galactic plane, right past Sol. They call that Gould's Belt, and I knew *that* was where home was.

'And when I looked ahead, there was a band of darkness. I was reaching the inner limit of our spiral arm, looking into the rift between the arms, the dense dark clouds there. And then, beyond the rift, I arrived here – in this place, with the Neandertals . . .'

'And the stars.'

'Yes.'

While she had slept, the stars had continued to migrate. Now they had *all* swum their way up towards that Sagittarius Arm horizon, the way Malenfant said they were heading. The opposite horizon looked dark, for all its stars had fled. All the stars in the sky, in fact, had crowded themselves into a disc, centred on a point some way above that brighter horizon – at least she guessed it was a disc; some of it was below her horizon. And the colours had changed; the stars had become green and yellow and blue.

Now, in what situation would you expect to see the stars swimming around the sky like fish?

'This is the aberration of starlight, isn't it, Malenfant? The distortion of the visible universe, which you would see if –'

'If you travel extremely quickly. Yes,' he said softly.

She understood the principle. It was like running in the rain, a rain of starlight. As she ran faster, the rain would hit her harder, in her face, her body. If she ran extremely fast indeed, it would be as if the rain was almost horizontal . . .

'We're on a starship,' she breathed.

'Yeah. We're moving so fast that most of the stars we see up ahead must be red giants, infrared sources, invisible to us in normal times. All the regular stars have been blue-shifted to invisibility. Wherever we're going, we're travelling the old-fashioned way: in a spaceship, pushed up to relativistic speeds. And we're still accelerating.'

She sat up and dug her fingers into the grass. 'But it doesn't *feel* like a starship. Where is the crew? Where are we going? What will happen when we get there?'

'When I found you, I hoped *you* were going to tell *me*.' He got to his feet. 'What do you think we should do now?'

She shrugged. 'Walk. There's nothing to stay for here.'

'Okay. Which way?'

She pointed to the glowing Sagittarius Arm horizon, the place the stars were fleeing, their putative destination.

He smiled. 'And add a couple of kilometres an hour to our eighty per cent of lightspeed? Why not? We're walking animals, we humans.'

Malenfant picked up a sack, which turned out to contain his ancient spacesuit, the wreck she had spent hours fixing up on the Cannonball. Obeying some obscure impulse for tidiness, he scuffed over his dirt-scraped star map. Then they set off.

They passed the Neandertal family, who sat just where they had yesterday.

When Madeleine looked back, the Neandertals were still sitting, unmoving, as the humans receded, and the stars flowed overhead.

The next time she woke, there was only a single source of light in the sky. It was a small disc, brighter than a full Moon, less bright than the sun seen from Earth, tinged distinctly bluish.

Aside from that the cloudless sky was utterly empty.

Malenfant was standing before her, staring at the light. Beyond him she could see Neandertals, a family group of them, standing too, staring into the light, their awkward heads tipped back. Shadows streamed from the light, shadows of people and trees, steady and dark.

She stood beside Malenfant. 'What is it? Stars?'

He shook his head. 'The stars are all blue-shifted to invisibility. All of them.'

'Then what –'

'I think that's the afterglow.' The background heat of the universe, left over from the Big Bang, stretched to a couple of degrees above absolute zero. 'We're going so fast now, just a tad lower than light-speed, that even *that* has been crumpled up by aberration, crushed into a tiny disc. Some spectacle, don't you think? . . .' He held his hand up before him, shading the universe-sun; she saw its shadow on his face. 'You know, I remember the first time I left Earth, en route to the Saddle Point. And I looked back and saw the Earth dwindle to a dot of light smaller than *that*. Everything I'd ever known – five billion years of geology and biology, of sliding continents and oceans and plants and dinosaurs and people – all of it was crammed into a splinter of light, surrounded by nothing. And now the whole damn *universe*, stars and galaxies and squabbling aliens and all, is contained in that little smudge.'

He told her he thought they were riding an antimatter rocket.

'. . . It explains what the Gaijin were doing on Io. Tapping the energy of Jupiter's magnetosphere. Probably turned the whole moon into one big atom-smasher, and picking the antimatter out of the debris.' The antimatter rocket could be a kind called a beam-core engine, he specu-lated. 'It's simple, in principle. You just have your tanks of atoms and anti-atoms – hydrogen, probably, the anti-stuff contained in a magnetic trap – and you feed it into a nozzle and let it blow itself up. The electrons make gamma rays, and the nuclei make pions, all high energy stuff, and some of the pions are charged, so that's what you throw out the back as your exhaust . . . There are other ways to do it. I don't imagine the Gaijin have a very advanced design.'

'It must have taken the Gaijin a long time, an immense project, to assemble the antimatter they needed.'

'Oh, yeah. Hauling those superconductor cables all the way out from Venus, and everything. Big engineering.'

'But,' Madeleine said deliberately, 'there is no way you could haul all of this –' she indicated the plain, the trees '– a ship the size of a small *moon* up to relativistic speeds, all the way to the Galaxy core. Is there?'

He looked into the sky. 'I saw a study which said you would need a hundred tonnes of antimatter to haul a single ragged-assed astronaut to Proxima Centauri. At the time it would have taken *our* biggest atom-smasher two centuries to produce so much as a milligram. I doubt that whatever the Gaijin built on Io was so terribly advanced over that. So – no, Madeleine. You couldn't haul a small moon.'

She studied her hand, pinched the flesh. The pinch hurt. '*What are we*, Malenfant? You think we're some kind of simulations running inside a giant computer?'

'It's possible.' His voice contained a shrug, as if it didn't matter. 'It only takes a finite number of bits to encode a human being. That's because of uncertainty, the graininess of nature . . . If not for that, the Saddle Point gateways wouldn't be possible at all. On the other hand –' He dug into the ground until he came up with a stone the size of his thumb nail. 'If the universe was the size of this rock, then each star would be the size of a quark. There are orders of magnitude of scale, structure, beneath the level of a human. Maybe we're real, but shrunken down somehow. Plenty of room down there.'

She felt a pulse in her head, a pressure. 'But,' she said, 'if we're just emulations in some toy starship, we're dead. I mean, we're no longer us. Are we? How can we be?'

He eyed her. 'The first time you stepped through a gateway you were no longer you. Every transition is a death, a rebirth. Why do you think it hurts so much?'

She felt weak, her legs numb. Carefully, she lowered herself to the grass, dug her hands into the rich cool texture of the ground.

He knelt beside her, took her hand. 'Listen. I don't mean to be so tough on you. What do I know? – I only have guesses too. I've had more time to get used to this stuff, is all.' He went on with difficulty, 'I know you came here to help me. I remember the way you fixed my suit, on the Cannonball. You were – kind.'

She said nothing.

He said, 'I just don't think you can help.' His face was turning hard again. 'Or *will* help.'

That chilled her, his harsh dismissal. 'Help with *what*, Malenfant? Why did the Gaijin go to all this trouble – to train Neandertals to mine antimatter on Io, build a starship, hurl it across light years?'

He looked troubled at that. 'I think – I have this awful feeling, a suspicion – that the purpose of it all was *me*. A huge alien conspiracy, all designed to give *me* a ride across the Galaxy.' He studied her, face emptied by wonder. 'Or is that paranoid, megalomaniac? Do you think I'm crazy, Madeleine?'

Beyond him, perhaps a half kilometre away, she made out a new shadow: angular, gaunt, crisp and precise before the cosmos light.

It was a Gaijin.

'Maybe we'll soon find out,' she said.

They approached the Gaijin. It just stood there impassively, silent.
Madeleine saw how the pencil-thin cones that terminated its legs were
stained green by crushed grass, and that a little quasi-African dust had
settled on the surfaces of its upper carapace.

Malenfant said he recognized it. It was the individual Gaijin he had
come to know as Cassiopeia.

'Oh, really? And how do you know that, Malenfant? The Gaijin
are just spidery robots. Don't they all look alike? . . .'

He didn't try to answer.

Madeleine found the Gaijin's calm mechanical silence infuriating.
She bent down and picked up a handful of dirt. She threw it at the
Gaijin; it pinged off that impassive hide, not making so much as a
scratch. 'You. Space robot. You've been playing with us since you
showed up in our asteroid belt. I don't care how alien you are. No
more fucking *games* . . .'

Malenfant seemed shocked by her swearing. A corner of her found
amusement at that. Malenfant really was a man of his time: here they
were hurtling away from Earth at a tad less than lightspeed, shrunk
to quark-sized copies or else trapped in some alien virtual reality, and
he was shocked to hear a woman swear. But he just stood and let her
rant her heart out. Therapy, for absorbing one shock after another.

She ran out of energy, slumped back to the grass, numbed by
tiredness.

The Gaijin stirred, like a tank turret swivelling. Madeleine thought
she heard something like hydraulics, perhaps a creak of metal scraping
on metal. The Gaijin spoke, its booming voice a good emulation of
the human – a woman's voice, in fact, with a tinge of Malenfant's
own accent.

She said, NO DOUBT YOU'RE WONDERING WHY I ASKED YOU HERE
TODAY.

The silence stretched. Malenfant peered up at the Gaijin doubtfully.

'She made a joke,' Madeleine said slowly. 'This ridiculous alien
robot made a joke.'

Malenfant stared at Madeleine. Then he threw his hands in the air,
slumped back on the grass, and laughed.

Pretty soon, Madeleine caught the bug. The laugh seemed to start
in her belly, and burst out of her throat and mouth, despite her best
efforts to contain it.

So they laughed, and kept on laughing, while the Gaijin waited for them.

And, cradling its precious cargo of mind and hope and fear, the ten-centimetres-long starship hurtled onwards towards the core of the Galaxy, and its destiny.

Chapter 33

THE FERMI PARADOX

They drank from a stream, and ate fruit, and lay on the grass, letting the tension drain out. Madeleine thought she slept for a while, curled up against Malenfant in the grass, like two exhausted kids.

And then – when they were awake, sitting before Cassiopeia – the Gaijin waved a spidery metal limb, and the world dissolved. It melted like a defocusing image: grass and mud and trees and streams running together, everything but the three of them, two humans and a Gaijin, and that eerie universe-sun, so that they seemed to be floating, bathed in a deeper darkness than Madeleine had ever known.

She reached out and grabbed Malenfant's hand. It was warm, solid; she could see him, the folds on his jumpsuit picked out by the cosmic glow. She dug the fingers of her other hand into loamy soil beneath her. It was still there, cool and friable, invisible or not. She clung to its texture, to the pull of the fake world sticking her to the ground.

But Malenfant was staring upwards, past the Gaijin's metal shoulder. '*Look* at that. Holy shit.'

She looked up unwillingly, reluctant to face new wonders.

Above them, a ceiling of curdled light spanned the sky. It was a galaxy.

It was a disc of stars, flatter and thinner than she might have expected, in proportion to its width no thicker than a few sheets of paper. She thought she could see strata in that disc, layers of structure, a central sheet of swarming blue stars and dust lanes sandwiched between dimmer, older stars. The core, bulging out of the plane of the disc like an egg yolk, was a compact mass of yellowish light; but it was not spherical, rather markedly elliptical. The spiral arms were fragmented. They were a delicate blue laced with ruby-red nebulae and the blue-white blaze of individual stars – a granularity of light – and with dark lanes traced between each arm. She saw scattered flashes

426

of light, blisters of gas. Perhaps those were supernova explosions, creating bubbles of hot plasma hundreds of light years across.

But the familiar disc – shining core, spiral arms – was actually embedded in a broader, spherical mass of dim red stars. The crimson fireflies were gathered in great clusters, each of which must contain millions of stars.

The Gaijin hovered before the image, silhouetted, like the spidery projector cluster at the centre of a planetarium.

'So, a galaxy,' said Madeleine. '*Our* Galaxy?'

'I think so,' Malenfant said. 'It matches radio maps I've seen.' He pointed, tracing patterns. 'Look. That must be the Sagittarius Arm. The other big structure is called the Outer Arm.' The two major arms, emerging from the elliptical core, defined the Galaxy, each of them wrapping right around the core before dispersing at the rim into a mist of shining stars and glowing nebulae and brooding black clouds. The other 'arms' were really just scraps, she saw – the Galaxy's spiral structure was a lot messier than she had expected – but still, she thought, the sun is lost in one of those scattered 'fragments'.

The Galaxy image began to rotate, slowly.

'A galactic day,' Malenfant breathed. 'Takes two hundred million years to complete a turn . . .'

Madeleine could see the stars swarming, following individual orbits around the Galaxy core, like a school of sparkling fish. And the spiral arms were evolving too, ridges of light sparking with young stars, churning their way through the disc of the Galaxy. But the arms were just waves of compression, like the bunching of traffic jams, with individual stars swimming through the regions of high density.

And now, Madeleine saw, a new kind of evolution was visible in the disc. Like the pulsing bubbles of supernovae, each was a ripple of change that began at an individual star, before spreading across a small fraction of the disc. Within each wavefront the stars went out, or turned red, or even green; or sometimes the stars would pop and flare, fizzing with light.

'Life,' she said. 'Dyson spheres. Star Crackers –'

'Yes,' Malenfant said grimly. 'Colonization bubbles. Just like the one *we* got caught up in.'

The Gaijin said sombrely, THIS IS WHAT WE HAVE LEARNED.

Life – said Cassiopeia – was emergent everywhere. Planets were the crucible. Life curdled, took hold, evolved, in every nook and cranny it could find in the great nursery that was the Galaxy.

Characteristically life took hundreds of millions of years to accrue the complexity it needed to start manipulating its environment on a major scale. On Earth, life had stuck at the single-celled stage for billions of years, most of its history. Still, on world after world, complexity emerged, mind dawned, civilizations arose.

Most of these cultures were self-limiting.

Some were sedentary. Some – for instance, aquatic creatures, like the Flips – lacked access to metals and fire. Some just destroyed themselves, one way or another, through wars, or accidents, or obscure philosophical crises, or just plain incompetence – which last, Madeleine suspected, might have been mankind's ultimate fate, left to its own devices.

Maybe one in a thousand cultures made it through such bottlenecks.

That fortunate few developed self-sustaining colonies off their home worlds, and – forever immune to the eggs-in-one-basket accidents which could afflict a race bound to a single world – they started spreading. Or else they made machines, robots that could change worlds and rebuild themselves, and sent them off into space, and *they* started spreading.

Either way, from one in a thousand habitable worlds, a wave of colonization started to expand.

There were many different strategies. Sometimes generations of colonists diffused slowly from star to star, like a pollutant spreading into a dense liquid. Sometimes the spread was much faster, like a gas into a vacuum. Sometimes there was a kind of percolation, a lacy, fractal structure of exploitation leaving great unspoiled voids within.

It was a brutal business. Lesser species – even just a little behind in the race to evolve complexity and power – would simply be overrun, their worlds and stars consumed. And if a colonizing bubble from another species was encountered, there were often ferocious wars.

Madeleine said sourly, 'It's hard to believe that every damn species in the Galaxy behaves so badly.'

Malenfant grinned. 'Why? This is how *we* are. And remember, the ones who expand across the stars are self-selecting. They grow, they consume, they aren't too good at restraining themselves, because that's the way they *are*. The ones who *aren't* ruthless predatory expansionists stay at home, or get eaten.'

Anyhow, the details of the expansion didn't seem to matter. In every case, after some generations of colonization, conflicts built up. Resource depletion within the settled bubble led to pressure on the colonies at the fringe. Or else the colonizers, their technological edge sharpened by the world-building frontier, would turn inwards on their

428

rich, sedentary cousins. Either way the cutting-edge colonizers were forced outwards, farther and faster.

Before long, the frontier of colonization was spreading out at near lightspeed, and the increasingly depleted region within, its inhabitants having nowhere to go, was riven by wars and economic crisis.

So it would go on, over millennia, perhaps megayears.

And then came the collapse.

It happened over and over. None of the bubbles ever grew very large – no more than a few hundred light years wide – before simply withering away, like a colony of bacteria frying under a sterilizing lamp. And one by one the stars would come out once more, shining cleanly out, as the red and green of technology and life dispersed.

'The Polynesian syndrome,' Madeleine said gloomily.

'But,' Malenfant growled, 'it shouldn't *always* be like this. Sooner or later *one* of those races has got to win the local wars, beat out its own internal demons, and conquer the Galaxy. But we know that not *one* has made it, across the billions of years of the Galaxy's existence. And *that* is the Fermi Paradox.'

YES, said Cassiopeia. BUT THE GALAXY IS NOT ALWAYS SO HOSPIT-ABLE A PLACE.

Now a new image was overlaid on the swivelling Galaxy: a spark that flared, a bloom of lurid blue light that originated close to the crowded core. It illuminated the nearby stars for perhaps an eighth of the galactic disc around it. And then, as the Galaxy slowly turned, there was another spark – and another, then another, and another still. Most of these events originated near the Galaxy core: something to do with the crowding of the stars, then. A few sparks, more rare, came from further out – the disc, or even the dim halo of orbiting stars that surrounded the Galaxy proper.

Each of these sparks caused devastation among any colonization bubbles nearby: a cessation of expansion, a restoring of starlight.

Death, on an interstellar scale.

Their virtual viewpoint changed, suddenly, swooping down into the plane of the Galaxy. As the spiral arms spread out above her, dissolving into individual stars which scattered over her head and out of sight, Madeleine cried out and clung to Malenfant. Now they swept inwards, towards the Galaxy's core, and she glimpsed structure beyond the billowing stars, sculptures of gas and light and energy.

Her attention came to rest, at last, on a pair of stars – small, fierce, angry. These stars were close, separated by no more than a few tens of their diameters. The two stars looped around each other on wild elliptical paths, taking just seconds to complete a revolution – like courting swallows, Madeleine thought – but the orbits changed rapidly, decaying as she watched, evolving into shallower ellipses, neat circles.

A few wisps of gas circled the two stars. Each star seemed to glow blue, but the gas around them was reddish. Further out she saw a lacy veil of colour, filmy gas that billowed against the crowded background star clouds.

'Neutron stars,' said Malenfant. 'A neutron star binary, in fact. That blue glow is synchrotron radiation, Madeleine. Electrons dragged at enormous speeds by the stars' powerful magnetic fields . . .'

The Gaijin said, PERHAPS FIFTY PER CENT OF ALL THE STARS IN THE GALAXY ARE LOCKED IN BINARY SYSTEMS – SYSTEMS CONTAINING TWO STARS, OR PERHAPS MORE. AND SOME OF THESE STARS ARE GIANTS, DOOMED TO A RAPID EVOLUTION.

Malenfant grunted. 'Supernovae.'

MOST SUCH EXPLOSIONS SEPARATE THE RESULTANT REMNANT STARS. ONE IN A HUNDRED PAIRS REMAIN BOUND, EVEN AFTER A SUPERNOVA EXPLOSION. THE PAIRED NEUTRON STARS CIRCLE EACH OTHER RAPIDLY. THEY SHED ENERGY BY GRAVITATIONAL RADIATION – RIPPLES IN SPACETIME.

The two stars were growing closer now, their energy ebbing away. The spinning became more rapid, the stars moving too fast for her to see. When the stars were no more than their own diameter apart, disruption began. Great gouts of shining material were torn from the surface of each star, and thrown out into an immense glowing disc that obscured her view.

At last the stars touched. They imploded in a flash of light.

A shock wave pulsed through the debris disc, churning and scattering the material, a ferocious fount of energy. But the disc collapsed back on the impact site almost immediately, within seconds, save for a few wisps that dispersed slowly, cooling.

'Has to form a black hole,' Malenfant muttered. 'Two neutron stars . . . too massive to form anything less. This is a gamma ray burster. We've been observing them all over the sky since the 1960s. We sent up spacecraft to monitor illegal nuclear weapons tests beyond the atmosphere. Instead, we saw *these*.'

THERE IS INDEED A BURST OF GAMMA RAYS – VERY HIGH ENERGY PHOTONS. THEN COMES A PULSE OF HIGH-ENERGY PARTICLES, COS-MIC RAYS, HURLED OUT OF THE DISC OF COLLAPSING MATTER,

FOLLOWING THE GAMMA RAYS AT A LITTLE LESS THAN LIGHTSPEED.

THESE EVENTS ARE HIGHLY DESTRUCTIVE.

A NEARBY PLANET WOULD RECEIVE – IN A FEW SECONDS, MOSTLY IN THE FORM OF GAMMA RAYS – SOME ONE-TENTH ITS ANNUAL ENERGY INPUT FROM ITS SUN. BUT THE GAMMA RAY SHOWER IS ONLY THE PRECURSOR TO THE COSMIC RAY CASCADES, WHICH CAN LAST MONTHS. BATTERING INTO AN ATMOSPHERE, THE RAYS CREATE A SHOWER OF MUONS – HIGH-ENERGY SUBATOMIC PARTICLES. THE MUONS HAVE A GREAT DEAL OF PENETRATING POWER. EVEN HUNDREDS OF METRES OF WATER OR ROCK WOULD NOT BE A SUFFICIENT SHIELD AGAINST THEM.

Malenfant said, 'I *saw* what these things can do, Madeleine. It would be like a nearby supernova going off. The ozone layer would be screwed by the gamma rays. Protein structures would break down. Acid rain. Disruption of the biosphere –'

A COLLAPSE IS OFTEN SUFFICIENT TO STERILIZE A REGION PERHAPS A THOUSAND LIGHT YEARS WIDE. IN OUR OWN GALAXY, WE EXPECT ONE SUCH EVENT EVERY FEW TENS OF THOUSANDS OF YEARS – MOST OF THEM IN THE CROWDED GALAXY CORE.

Madeleine watched as the Galaxy image was restored, and bursts erupted from the crowded core, over and over.

Malenfant glared at the dangerous sky. 'Cassiopeia – are you telling me that these collapses are the big secret – the cause of the Reboot, the galactic extinction?'

Madeleine shook her head. 'How is that possible, if each of them is limited to a thousand light years? The Galaxy is a hundred times as wide as that. It would be no fun to have one of these things go off in your back yard. But –'

BUT, said Cassiopeia, SOME OF THESE EVENTS ARE – EXCEPTIONAL.

They were shown a cascade, image after image, burst after burst.

Some of the collapses involved particularly massive objects. Some of them were rare collisions involving three, four, even five objects simultaneously. Some of the bursts were damaging because of their orientation, with most of their founting, ferocious energy being delivered, by a chance of fate and collision dynamics, into the disc of the Galaxy, where the stars were crowded. And so on.

Some of these events were very damaging indeed.

Cassiopeia said, FROM THE WORST OF THE EVENTS THE EXTINCTION PULSE PROCEEDS AT LIGHTSPEED, SPILLING OVER THE GALAXY AND ALL ITS INHABITANTS, ALL THE WAY TO THE RIM AND EVEN THE HALO

CLUSTERS. NO SHIELDING IS POSSIBLE. NO COMPLEX ORGANISM, NO ORGANIZED DATA STORE, CAN SURVIVE. BIOSPHERES OF ALL KINDS ARE DESTROYED . . .

So it finishes, Madeleine thought, the evolution and the colonizing and the wars and the groping towards understanding: all of it halted, obliterated in a flash, an accident of cosmological billiards. It was all a matter of chance, of bad luck. But there were enough neutron star collisions that every few hundred million years there was an event powerful enough, or well-directed enough, to wipe the whole of the Galaxy clean.

It had happened over and over. And it will happen again, she saw. Again and again, a drumbeat of extinction. That is what the Gaijin have learned.

'And for us,' Malenfant growled, 'it's back to the fucking pond, every damn time . . . So much for Fermi's paradox. Nemoto was right. This *is* the equilibrium state for life and mind: a Galaxy full of new, young species struggling out from their home worlds, consumed by fear and hatred, burning their way across the nearby stars, stamping over the rubble of their forgotten predecessors.'

. . . And this is what the Gaijin tried to show me, Madeleine recalled, on my first Saddle Point jaunt of all, to the burster neutron star: the star lichen, fast-evolving life forms wiped out by a stellar fluke every fourteen seconds. It was a fractal image of *this*, the greater truth.

The Galaxy image abruptly receded, the spiral arms and the core and the surrounding halo imploding on itself like a burst balloon. Madeleine gasped at the sudden illusory motion. The world congealed around her: grass and trees and that black sky, all of it illuminated by fierce blue cosmic light. She was flooded with intense physical relief, as if she could breathe again.

But her mind was racing. 'There must be ways to stop this. All we have to do is evade *one* collapse – and gain the time to put aside the wars and the trashing, and get a little smarter, and learn how to run the Galaxy properly. We don't have to put up with this shit.'

Malenfant smiled. 'Nemoto always did call you a meddler.'

BUT YOU ARE RIGHT, said the Gaijin. SOME OF US ARE TRYING . . .

Ahead of them, she saw a group of Neandertals. They were dancing, signing furiously to each other, jumping up and down in the light of the cosmos. Something was changing in the sky, and the Neandertals were responding.

She looked that way. That cosmic light point seemed to be expanding.

432

The unwrapping sky was full of stars. It was the centre of the Galaxy.

Malenfant was confronting the Gaijin. 'Cassiopeia,' he said softly, 'what has all this got to do with me?'

The Gaijin said, MALENFANT, YOU ARE OUR BEST HOPE.

And now the Gaijin turned with a scrape of metal, a soft hiss as her feet sank deeper into the loam.

IT IS RISING.

She turned and began to stalk across the meadow, with that stiff, three-legged grace of hers, away from the stand of trees. Madeleine saw the Neandertals were following, a shadowy group of them, their muscles prominent in the starlight.

Malenfant grabbed her hand.

They walked through a meadow. The grass was damp, cool under her feet, and dew sparkled, a shattered mirror of the stars.

They were all immersed in diffuse shadowless light, in this place where every corner of the sky glowed as bright as the surface of the Moon. The light was silvery, the colours bleached out of everything; the grass was a deep green, the leaves on the trees black. Madeleine wondered vaguely if there was enough nourishment in that Galaxy light to fuel photosynthesis, if life could survive on a rogue, sunless planet here, just eating the dense starlight.

They topped a ridge, and looked down over a broad, shallow valley. There were scattered trees and standing water, ribbons and pools of silver-blue, all of it still and a little eerie in the diffuse starlight.

The Gaijin, Cassiopeia, had stopped, here at the crest. The Neandertals had gathered a little way away, along the ridge, and they were looking out over the valley.

But now one of the Neandertals came shambling towards Malenfant, with that clumsy, inefficient gait of theirs. It was a man, stoop-shouldered, the flesh over his ribs soft and sagging, and sweat slicked over his shoulders. That great brow pulled his face forward, so that his chin almost rested on his chest.

Malenfant said, 'Hello, Esau –'

Esau slapped him, and his fingers rattled, his fist thumping his forehead.

Malenfant grinned, and translated. '*Hello, Stupid.*' Malenfant seemed genuinely pleased to see this old Neandertal geezer again.

But now Cassiopeia stirred, and Madeleine grabbed his arm. 'Malenfant. Look. Oh, shit.'

A new star was rising above the valley, over the newly revealed horizon, brighter than the background wash.

It was a neutron star, a brilliant crimson point. Near the star there were multiple lobes of light. They contained structure, veins and streamers, something like the wings of a butterfly around that ferocious, dwarfed body; they glowed pink and an eerie blue, perhaps through the synchrotron radiation of accelerated electrons.

And there was something alongside the star. It looked like netting – scoop-shaped, like a catcher's mitt, facing the star as if endeavouring to grasp it.

Obviously artificial.

Cassiopeia said, OUR JOURNEY IS NOT YET DONE, MALENFANT. WE MUST PENETRATE THE GALACTIC CENTRE ITSELF. THIS IS WHAT WE WILL SEEK.

Malenfant said, 'This is the site of a gamma ray burster. A future Reboot event. I'm right, aren't I, Cassiopeia?'

THE STAR'S COMPANION IS AS YET SOME DISTANCE AWAY – BILLIONS OF KILOMETRES, IN FACT, TOO REMOTE TO SEE. AND YET THE CONVERGENCE HAS BEGUN. THE COLLISION IS INEVITABLE. UNLESS –

'Unless somebody does something about it,' Madeleine whispered.

That strange artefact continued to ride higher in the sky, like a filmy, complex moon. It was a net, cast across the stars. It must have been thousands of kilometres wide.

Madeleine found it impossible to believe it wasn't a few metres above her head, almost close enough she could just reach out and touch. The human mind was just not programmed to see giant planet-spanning artefacts in the sky. Think of an aurora, she told herself, those curtains of light, rippling far above the air you breathe. And now imagine *that*: it would hang there far beyond any aurora, suspended in space, perhaps beyond the Moon . . .

But there was something wrong: the netting was obviously unfinished, and great holes had been rent into its structure.

Malenfant said, 'It's broken.'

YOU WOULD CALL THIS A SHKADOV SAIL . . .

It would be a thing of matter and energy, of lacy rigging and magnetic fields: a screen to reflect the neutron star's radiation and solar wind. But it was bound to the star by invisible ropes of gravity.

'Ah,' Madeleine said. 'You disturb the symmetry of the solar wind. You see, Malenfant? The wind from the star will push at the sail. But the sail isn't going anywhere, relative to the star, because of gravity. So the wind gets turned back . . .'

'It's a stellar rocket,' Malenfant said. 'Using the solar wind to push aside the star.'

THAT IS THE PURPOSE. WHEN COMPLETE IT WILL BE A DISC A HUNDRED THOUSAND KILOMETRES ACROSS, ALL OF IT LACED WITH INTELLIGENCE, A DYNAMIC THING, CAPABLE OF SHAPING THE STAR'S SOLAR WIND, RESPONDING TO ITS COMPLEX CURRENTS.

Malenfant grinned. 'Hot damn. Somebody *is* fighting back.'

Madeleine asked, 'Who is building this thing? You?'

NOT US ALONE. MANY RACES HAVE COME HERE, COOPERATED ON THE SAIL'S CONSTRUCTION. IT APPEARS TO HAVE BEEN A RELIC FROM A PREVIOUS CYCLE, FROM BEFORE A PREVIOUS REBOOT.

'Like the Saddle Point network.'

Madeleine peered doubtfully at the huge, unlikely structure. 'How can a sail like that move a neutron star – an object more massive than the sun?'

THE THRUST IS VERY SMALL, THE ACCELERATION MINUSCULE. BUT OVER LONG ENOUGH PERIODS, SMALL THRUSTS ARE SUFFICIENT TO MOVE WORLDS. EVEN STARS.

'And will that be enough to stop the coalescence of this binary, to stop the Reboot?'

NOT TO STOP IT. TO POSTPONE IT GREATLY, BY ORDERS OF MAGNITUDE. IF WE CAN DELAY THIS STERILIZATION EVENT –

'We might win time,' Malenfant said.

Madeleine challenged the Gaijin. 'Is this *really* the best option? Haven't you come up with anything smarter?'

Malenfant eyed her. 'Like what?'

'Hell, I don't know. You could use antigravity. Einstein's cosmological constant, the force that makes the universe expand. Or you could interfere with the fundamental constants of physics. For example there is a particle called the Higgs boson, which gives matter its mass. If you took it away, switched it off, you could make your neutron stars lighter, and then just push them aside. In fact, take *all* the mass away and they would fly off at the speed of light. Easy. Give me a lever and I will move the world . . .'

WE HAVE NO SUCH POWERS, said Cassiopeia, and Madeleine thought she detected sadness in that synthesized voice. WE HAVE SEARCHED. THERE IS NO CIVILIZATION SIGNIFICANTLY MORE ADVANCED THAN OUR OWN – EVEN BEYOND THE GALAXY.

IT IS LIKE YOUR FERMI PARADOX. IF THEY EXISTED, WE WOULD SEE THEM. IMAGINE A GALAXY WITH ALL THE STARS FARMED, COVERED BY DYSON SPHERES, THEIR PHYSICS ALTERED PERHAPS TO

EXTEND THEIR LIFETIMES. IMAGINE THE GALAXY ITSELF ENCLOSED BY A DYSON STRUCTURE. AND SO ON. EVEN SUCH CLUMSY ENGINEER-ING, ON SUCH A SCALE, WOULD BE VISIBLE. WE SEE NO SUCH THING, AS FAR OUT AS WE LOOK, AS DEEP INTO SPACE AND TIME.

But it wasn't a surprise, Madeleine thought. How long would it take a galactic civilization to rise – even supposing somebody could survive the wars and assorted despoliation? Because of lightspeed, it would take a hundred thousand years for a message to cross the Galaxy *just once*. How many such exchanges would it take to homogenize the shared culture of a thousand species, born of different stars and biochemistries, creatures of flesh and metal, of rock and gas? A thousand Galaxy crossings, minimum?

But that would take a hundred million years, and by that time the next burster would have blown its top, the next Reboot driven everybody back to pond scum.

So maybe this clumsy net really was the best anybody could do. But still, good intentions weren't enough.

'Tens of millions of years,' she said. 'You'd have to maintain that damn thing for *tens of millions of years*, to make a difference. How can any species remotely like us, or even *you*, maintain a consistency of purpose across megayears? None of us even *existed* in anything like our present forms so long ago.'

. . . BUT, Cassiopeia said slowly, WE MUST TRY.

Malenfant said, 'We?'

YOU MUST JOIN US, MALENFANT.

Madeleine clutched at Malenfant's hand. But he pushed her away. She looked up at him. His face was pinched, his eyes narrow. He was starting to feel scared, she realized, drawn out, as if pulled into space by the thing in the sky, up towards the zenith.

Because, she realized, this is his destiny.

Malenfant stood before the alien robot, silhouetted against Galaxy core light. He looked helplessly weak, Madeleine thought, a raga-muffin, before this representat: of a cool, immeasurably ancient gal-actic power.

Yet it was Cassiopeia who was supplicating before Malenfant, the human.

'You can't do it,' he said, wondering. 'You can't complete this project. There is something – missing in you.'

Cassiopeia said, THERE IS CONTROVERSY.

Madeleine glared up at that filmy structure. There were holes in the netting you could have passed a small planet through, places where thousand-kilometre threads seemed to have been burned or melted or distorted. *Controversy*.

'Wars have been fought here,' Malenfant said bluntly.

THE RACES OF THE GALAXY ARE VERY DIVERGENT. UNITY DIS-SOLVES. THERE IS FREQUENT CONFLICT. SOMETIMES A RACE WILL SEEK TO TAKE THIS TECHNOLOGY AND USE IT FOR ITS OWN PURPOSES; THE OTHERS MUST MOUNT A COALITION TO STOP THE ROGUE. SOME-TIMES A RACE WILL SIMPLY ATTEMPT TO IMPOSE ITS WILL ON OTHERS. THAT USUALLY ENDS IN CONFLICT, AND THE EXPULSION OR EXTERMINATION OF THE AMBITIOUS.

Malenfant laughed. 'Infighting. Sounds like every construction project I ever worked on.'

THERE ARE DIVERGENCES AMONG US.

Madeleine looked up, startled. 'You mean, even among the Gaijin?'

THERE ARE FACTIONS WHO WOULD ARGUE THAT WE SHOULD ABANDON THE PROJECT TO OTHER RACES, CALCULATING —

Malenfant grunted. 'Calculating that the others will finish the job for you — without you incurring the costs of the work. Gambling on the altruism of others, while acting selfishly. Games theory.'

OTHERS SEEK A TIME SYMMETRY . . .

Malenfant seemed baffled by that, but Madeleine thought she understood. 'Like the Moon flowers, Malenfant. If the Gaijin could train themselves to think *backward in time*, then they needn't face this — terminus — in the future.'

Malenfant laughed at the Gaijin, mocking.

Madeleine felt disturbed at this blatant evidence of discord among the Gaijin. Weren't they supposed to merge into some kind of super-mind, make decisions by consensus, with none of the crude arguing and splits of human beings? Dissension like this, so visible, must represent an agony of indecision in the Gaijin community, faced by the immense challenge of the star sail project. Indecision — or schizophrenia.

Malenfant said, still challenging, 'But your factions are wrong. Aren't they? Completing this project isn't a question of a game, theoretical or not. It is a question of sacrifice.'

Sacrifice? Madeleine wondered. Of what — or who?

MALENFANT, YOU ARE SHORT-LIVED — YOUR LIVES SO BRIEF, IN FACT, THAT YOU CAN OBSERVE NONE OF THE UNIVERSE'S SIGNIFI-CANT PROCESSES. YOUR RESPONSE TO OUR PRESENCE IN THE SOLAR SYSTEM WAS SPLINTERED, CHAOTIC, FLUID. YOU DO NOT EVEN UNDERSTAND *YOURSELVES*.

AND YET YOU TRANSCEND YOUR BREVITY. AND YET HUMANS, DOOMED TO BRIEF LIVES, CHOOSE DEATH VOLUNTARILY – FOR THE SAKE OF AN IDEA. AND WITH EVERY DEATH, THAT IDEA GROWS STRONGER.

WE HAVE ENCOUNTERED MANY SPECIES ON OUR TRAVELS. RARELY HAVE WE ENCOUNTERED SUCH A CAPACITY FOR FAITH.

Malenfant stalked back and forth on the hill-side, obviously torn. 'What are you talking about, Cassiopeia? Do you expect me to start a religion? You want me to teach faith to the toiling robots and cyborgs and what-not who are building the neutron star sail – something to unite them, to force them to bury their differences, to persist and complete the project across generations . . . Is that it?'

No, Madeleine thought sadly. No, she is asking for something much more fundamental than that.

She wants you, Malenfant. She wants your soul.

And the Gaijin started talking of mind, and identity, and memes, idea viruses.

To Cassiopeia, Malenfant was scarcely sentient at all. From the Gaijin's point of view, Malenfant's mind was no more than a coalition of warring idea-viruses, uneasy, illogically constructed, temporary. The ideas grouped together in complexes that reinforced each other, mutually aiding replication – just as those other replicators, genes, worked together through human bodies to promote their own reproduction.

Yes, Madeleine thought, beginning to understand. And the most fundamental idea complex was the sense of self.

A self was a collection of memories, beliefs, possession, hopes, fears, dreams: all of them ideas, or receptacles for ideas. If an idea accreted to the self – if it became *Malenfant's* idea, to be defended, if necessary, with his life – then its chance of replication was much stronger. His sense of self, of *him*self, was an illusion. Just a web woven by the manipulating idea viruses.

The Gaijin had no such sense of self. But sometimes, that was what you needed.

Malenfant understood. 'Every damn one of the Gaijin has a memory that stretches back to those ugly yellow seas on the Cannonball. But they are – fluid. They break up into their component parts and scatter around and reassemble; or they merge in great ugly swarms and come out shuffled around. Identity for them is a transient thing, a pattern, like the shadow of a passing cloud. Not for us, though. And that's why the Gaijin don't have *this*.' He stabbed a finger at his chest. 'They don't have a sense of *me*.'

And without self, Madeleine saw, there could be no self-sacrifice.

438

That was why the Gaijin couldn't handle the Reboot prevention project. Only humans, it seemed – slaves of replicating ideas, nurtured and comforted by the illusion of the self – might be strong enough, crazy enough, for that.

Through the dogged sense of his own character, Malenfant must give the fragmented beings toiling here a sense of purpose, of worth beyond their own sentience. A sense of sacrifice, of faith, of self. To help the Gaijin, to save the Galaxy, Malenfant was going to have to become like the Gaijin. He was going to have to lose himself . . . and, in the incomprehensible community that laboured over the strands of the sail, find himself again.

Malenfant, standing before the spidery Gaijin, was trembling. 'And you think this will work?'

No, Madeleine thought. But they are desperate. This is a throw of the dice. What else can they do?

The Gaijin didn't reply.

'. . . I can't do this,' Malenfant whispered at last, folding his hands over and over. 'Don't ask me. Take it away from me.'

Madeleine longed to run to him, to embrace him, offer him simple human comfort, animal warmth. But she knew she must not.

And still the Gaijin would not reply.

Malenfant stalked off over the empty grassland, alone.

Madeleine slept.

When she woke, Malenfant was still gone.

She lay on her back, peering up at a sky crowded with stars and glowing dust clouds. The stars seemed small, uniform, few of them bright and blue and young, as if they were deprived of fuel in this crammed space – as perhaps they were. And the dust clouds were disrupted, torn into ragged sheets and filaments by the immense forces that operated here.

Towards the heart of the Galaxy itself, there was structure, Madeleine saw. Laced over a backdrop of star swarms she made out two loose rings of light, roughly concentric, from her point of view tipped to ellipticity. The rings were complex: she saw gas and dust, stars gathered into small, compact globular clusters, spherical knots of all-but-identical pinpoints. In one place the outer ring had erupted into a vast knot of star formation, tens of thousands of hot young blue stars blaring light from the ragged heart of a pink-white cloud. The rings were like expanding ripples, she saw, or billows of gas from some explosion. But if there had been an explosion it must have been

439

immense indeed; that outermost ring was a coherent object a thousand light years across, big enough to have contained almost all the naked-eye stars visible from Earth.

And when Madeleine lifted her head, she saw that the inner ring was actually the base of an even larger formation that rose up and out of the general plane of the Galaxy. It was a ragged arch, traced out by filaments of shining gas, arching high into the less crowded sky above. It reminded her of images of solar flares, curving gusts of gas shaped by the sun's magnetic field – but this, of course, was immeasurably vaster, an arch spanning hundreds of light years. And rising out of the arch she glimpsed more immensity still, a vast jet of gas that thrust out of the Galaxy's plane, glimmering across thousands of light years before dissipating into the dark.

It was a hierarchy of enormity, towering over her, endless expansions of scale up into the dark.

But of the Galaxy centre itself, she could only see a tight, impenetrable cluster of stars – many thousands of them, swarming impossibly close together, closer to each other than the planets of the solar system. Whatever structure lay deeper still was hidden by those crowded acolyte stars.

The Gaijin still stood on the ridge, silhouetted against the pulsar's glow, hatefully silent.

Malenfant still hadn't returned. Madeleine tried to imagine what was going through his head, as he tried to submit himself to an unknown alien horror that would, it seemed, take apart even his humanity.

Madeleine got to her feet and stalked up to the Gaijin, confronting it. She was aware of Neandertals watching her curiously. They signed to each other, obscurely. *Look at crazy flathead.*

Madeleine shouted, 'Why can't you leave us alone? You came to our planet uninvited, you used up our resources, you screwed up our history –'

The Gaijin swivelled with eerie precision. WE MINED ASTEROIDS YOU PROBABLY WOULD NEVER HAVE REACHED. WITHOUT US YOU WOULD HAVE REMAINED UNAWARE OF THE CRACKERS UNTIL THEY REACHED THE HEART OF YOUR SYSTEM. AS TO YOUR HISTORY, THAT IS YOUR RESPONSIBILITY. WE DID NOT INTERVENE. BUT MOST OF YOU WOULD NOT HAVE WISHED THAT ANYHOW.

'You fucking immortal robots, you're so damn *smug*. But for all your powers, you need Malenfant . . . But why *Malenfant*, for God's sake?'

REID MALENFANT IS SELF-SELECTED. MADELEINE MEACHER, RECALL THAT HE MADE HIS WAY, SINGLE-HANDED, TO THE CENTRE OF OUR PROJECTS *TWICE OVER*, FIRST THROUGH THE ALPHA CENTAURI GATEWAY AND THEN THROUGH IO.

'Reid Malenfant is a stubborn, dogged son-of-a-bitch. But he is still just a human being. Must he die?'

The Gaijin hesitated, for long minutes. Then: HE WILL NOT DIE.

No, she thought. He must endure something much more strange than that. As he seemed to know.

The Gaijin raised one spindly leg, as if inspecting it. MADELEINE MEACHER, IF YOU WISH US TO SPARE HIM, WE WILL COMPLY.

She was taken aback. '. . . What has it to do with me?'

YOU ARE HUMAN. YOU ARE MALENFANT'S FRIEND. *YOU* MADE A SACRIFICE OF YOUR OWN, TO FOLLOW HIM HERE. AND SO YOU HAVE RESPONSIBILITY. IF YOU WISH US TO SPARE MALENFANT, THEN SAY SO. WE WILL COMPLY.

'And then what?'

WE HAVE SADDLE POINT GATEWAYS. WE CAN SEND HIM HOME, TO EARTH. BOTH OF YOU. WE CANNOT AVOID THE TIME DISLOCATION. BUT YOU CAN LIVE ON.

'Even if *he* wants to go on?'

IT IS HARD FOR MALENFANT TO MAKE THE RIGHT CHOICE. FOR ANY HUMAN THIS WOULD BE SO. YOUR DECISION OVERRIDES HIS.

'And if you let him go – then what about the project, the sail?'

WE MUST FIND ANOTHER WAY.

'The Reboot would become inevitable.'

WE MUST FIND ANOTHER WAY.

Madeleine sank to the grass. Shit, she thought. She hadn't expected this.

The notion of saving a Galaxy of sentient creatures from arbitrary annihilation was *too big* – too much for her to imagine, too grandiose. But she had lived through the overwhelming destructiveness of the attempted Eetie colonization of the solar system, found evidence of the other wasteful waves of horror of the deep past. She had *seen* it for herself.

And you once built a world, Madeleine. You've been known to show a little hubris yourself.

If this project succeeds, perhaps humans, and species like them, would never have to suffer such an ordeal again. Isn't one man's life worth such a prize?

But who am *I* to make that call?

. . . There was another option, she thought, that neither of them had expressed, neither she nor the Gaijin.

It doesn't have to be Malenfant. Maybe *I* could take his place. Save him, and progress the project anyhow.

She wrapped her arms around herself. Malenfant is full of doubt and fear. Even now he might not be able to make it, make the sacrifice. But he is out there gathering his strength, his purpose. I could never emulate that.

The Gaijin waited with metallic patience.

'Take him,' she whispered, hating herself as she uttered the words. 'Take Malenfant.' *Take him; spare me.*

And, as soon as she made the choice, she remembered Malenfant's inexplicable coldness when she arrived here.

She had ended up betraying him. Just as, she realized now, he had known she would, right from the beginning.

She buried her face in her hands.

After maybe a full day, Malenfant returned. Madeleine was sitting beside a sluggish stream, desultorily watching the evolution of Galaxy-core gas streamers.

Malenfant came running up.

He threw himself to the grass beside her. He was sweating, his bald pate slick, and he was breathing hard. 'Jogging,' he said. 'Clears the head.' He curled to a sitting position, cat-like. 'This is a hell of a thing, isn't it, Madeleine? Who would have thought it? . . . Nemoto should see me now. My mom should see me now.' The change in him was startling. He seemed vigorous, rested, confident, focused. Even cheerful.

But she could see the battered photograph of his dead wife tucked into his sleeve.

She hugged her knees, full of guilt, unable to meet his eyes. 'Have you decided what to do?'

'There's no real choice, is there?'

Tentatively she reached for his hand; he grabbed it, squeezed hard, his calm strength evident. 'Malenfant, aren't you afraid?'

He shrugged. 'I was afraid the first time I climbed aboard a Shuttle orbiter, sitting up there on top of millions of tonnes of high explosive, in a rickety old ship that had been flying thirty years already. I was afraid the first time I looked into a Saddle Point gateway, not knowing what lay beyond. But I still climbed aboard that Shuttle, still went through the gateway.' He glanced at her. 'What about you? After . . .'

'After you're dead?' she snapped impulsively.

He flinched, and she instantly regretted it.

She told him about the Gaijin's offer of a ride home.

'Take it. Go see Earth, Madeleine.'

'But it won't be my Earth.'

He shrugged. 'What else is there?'

She said shyly, 'I've been thinking. What if we – the sentients of the Galaxy, of this generation – *do* manage to come through the next Reboot? What if this time we *don't* have to go back to the ponds? What if we get a chance to keep on building? If I keep on rattling around the Saddle Point gateways, maybe I'll get to see some of that.'

He nodded. 'Beaming between the stars, while the network gets extended. Onward and onward, without limit. I like it.'

'Yeah.' She glanced up. 'Maybe I'll get to see Andromeda, before I die. Or maybe not.'

'There are worse ambitions.'

'. . . Malenfant. Come with me.'

He shook his head. 'Can't do it, Madeleine. I've thought it over. And I bought Cassiopeia's pitch.' He looked up at the sky. 'You know, as a kid I used to lie at night out on the lawn, soaking up dew and looking at the stars, trying to feel the Earth turning under me. It felt wonderful to be alive – hell, to be ten years old, anyhow. But I knew that the Earth was just a ball of rock, on the fringe of a nondescript galaxy. I just couldn't believe, even then, that there was nobody out *there* looking back at me down *here*. But I used to wonder what would be the point of my life, of human existence, if the universe really was empty. What would there be for us to do but survive, doggedly, as long as possible? Which didn't seem too attractive a prospect to me.

'Well, now I know the universe isn't empty, but crowded with life. And, even with the wars and extinctions and all, isn't that better than the alternative – better than *nothing*? And you know, I think I even figured out the purpose of our lives in such a universe – mine, anyhow. To make it better for those who follow us. What else is there to do?' He glanced at her, eyes cloudy. 'Does that make any sense?'

'Yes. But, Malenfant, the cost –'

'Nemoto said it would be like this. Humans can't change history, except *this* way. One of us, alone, going to the edge . . .'

Suddenly it was too much for her; she covered her face with her hands. 'Fuck history, Malenfant. Fuck the destiny of the universe. We're talking about *you*.'

He put an arm around her shoulders; he was warm, his body still

443

hot from his run. 'It's okay,' he said, trying to soothe her. 'It's okay. You know what? I think the Gaijin are jealous. Jealous, of us wretched little pink worms. Because we got something they don't, something more precious than all the Swiss-Army-knife body parts in the universe, something more precious than a billion years of life.'

But now the Gaijin stood before them, suddenly *there*, tall and stark.

Malenfant said, his voice unsteady, 'So soon, Cassiopeia?'

I AM SORRY, MALENFANT.

Malenfant straightened up, withdrew his arm from Madeleine's shoulders. She felt the reluctance in the gesture. She'd provided him comfort after all, she realized; by caring for her, he had been able to put off confronting the reality of it all. But now, in the silent person of the Gaijin, the reality was here, and he had to face it alone.

But here was old Esau, grinning from one side to the other of his flat face, deep eyes full of starlight. He was signing: the fist to the forehead, then left palm flat upright, supporting the right fist, which was making a thumbs-up gesture. *Hey, Stupid. I'll help you.*

Malenfant signed back. *What help me what what?*

Forefinger and middle finger together, on both hands, held out like a knife; a sharp chop downwards, a stark, unmistakable sign. *To die.*

Chapter 34

THE CHILDREN'S CRUSADE

Cassiopeia embraced him.

He was pulled into her body, articulating arms folding about him. He could smell the burning tang of metal that had been exposed to vacuum, to the light of a hundred different suns. And now finer arms, no more than tendrils, began to probe at his body, his skin, his mouth, his eyes.

Through a mist of metal cilia, he could see Madeleine on the hill-side before him, weeping openly. 'Tell them about me, Madeleine. Don't let them forget.'

'I will. I promise.'

Now warm metal probed at his ears, the membranes of his mouth, even his eyes. Probed and pierced, a dozen stabs of sharp pain. Then came an insidious penetration, and he could taste blood. 'It hurts, Madeleine.' He cried out; he couldn't help it. 'Oh, God!'

But now Esau was before him, signing vigorously. *Stupid Stupid. Watch me me.*

Malenfant tried to focus, as the pain deepened.

Esau sat on the hill-side. By the light of Galaxy-centre stars, he held out a core of obsidian.

Malenfant reached forward. His bare arms trailed long shining tendrils, back to the cold body of the Gaijin, within which he was merging. He could move his fingers, he found. But they glinted, metallic.

Esau was still holding out the glassy rock, thrusting it at him.

Malenfant took the rock. He could feel its rough texture, but remotely, as if through a layer of plastic. He turned it over in his hands.

Esau held up a fresh lump of obsidian, hammers of bone and rock. He signed bluntly to Malenfant. *Same as me, Stupid. Do same as me. Copy.*

Obediently, Malenfant set to work, tapping clumsily at the rock,

445

emulating Esau's movements, practising this most ancient of human crafts twenty-five thousand light years from home.

'The Buddhists have a doctrine of *anatta*,' Madeleine murmured. 'It means, *no self*. Or rather, the self is only temporary, like an idea or a story. "Actions do exist, and also their consequences, but the person that acts does not" ... It won't be so bad, Malenfant. Some people can do this for themselves. Some *choose* it ...'

She was weeping, he saw, the tears leaking out of closed eyes. Weeping for him. But he must not think about her. He tried to bury himself in the tasks. He focused on the work, the movements of his hands and arms. He would think about Madeleine – and put the thought aside. The differences between his own hands and the Neandertal's struck him, frustrating him with his own clumsiness. But he must put aside that thought too.

For brief periods, he got it. It was as if he saw the stone, the tool he was making, with a kind of stunning clarity: *the thing itself*, not the geologic processes which had produced the raw material, not the mysterious interstellar gateways which had brought him and the stone to this place, not even the tool's ultimate purpose. Just the thing, and the act.

But then the spell would be broken, and plans and analyses and self-consciousness would return to clutter up his head, an awareness of Madeleine and Cassiopeia, and Esau, the trees and grass and the heart of the Galaxy, and the *pain*, that penetrated right to his core.

'You have to let it go, Malenfant,' Madeleine whispered. 'Don't think. Live in the now, the present moment. If ideas come up, reflections, memories, hopes, fears, let them go. Butterflies, flitting out the window. Treat everything equally. Don't filter, don't focus. Watch Esau ...'

Esau, yes.

Malenfant was like an observer. But Esau *was* the rock he worked in its deep chthonic richness, in a way Malenfant perhaps could never be. It was a smooth, rolling, fleeting form of awareness, without past or future, memory or anticipation. It was like driving a car while holding a conversation. Like being stoned. Or like being five years old, and every moment a delicious Saturday morning.

Madeleine was still talking, but he could make out no words. She was receding, as if dissolving.

Goodbye, goodbye.

He closed his eyes.

... No, it wasn't like that:

446

Eyes that were closed.

There was a blue flash, a moment of searing pain.

He cried, *'Emma!'*

And then –

Limbs that worked. Tactile, graceful. Tasks that were progressed.

The rope: complex, multi-level, a thing of monomolecular filaments, superconducting threads within. The extension of the rope, the repair of breaks, the tasks of the limbs.

Visual receptors, eyes. A repositioning.

Data nets above, below, all around, a great curving wall. At extremes, a flat-infinite plane, in every direction: the sail.

Above, the spitting neutron star, its envelope of gas.

Here, a body, a spider-like form of many limbs, a dodecahedral box at the centre. Multiple tasks for those limbs. The sail that was repaired, extended; the body that was maintained, adjusted, itself extended; records that were kept; a mesh of communications with others that was maintained, extended.

Other workers.

Some near. Some far. Some as this body, a common design. Millions of them. Some not. Tasks that were progressed.

The structure. Vibrations, the shudder of torn threads. Complex modes, wave forms in space and time.

War, in a remote part of the sail.

A position that was adjusted, an anchoring of the body that was improved and secured.

The work that was progressed in one part of the sail, war in other parts.

The anchoring. The self-maintenance. The work.

The universe, of tasks, of things.

No centre.

. . . And he felt as if he was drowning, struggling up from some thick, viscous fluid, towards the light. He wanted to open his mouth, to scream – but he had no mouth – and no *words*. What would he scream?

I.

I am.

I am Malenfant . . .

No. Not just Malenfant. Malenfant / Esau / Cassiopeia.

The pain!

The shuddering of the net. The anchoring. The work that was progressed . . .

447

No! More than that. *I* feel the shudder. *I* must hold on to the net; *I* must continue the work, in the hope that sanity will prevail, the conflict is resolved, the work is continued, the greater goal achieved.

Thus it must be. Oh, God, the *pain.*

Terror flooded over him. And love. And anger.

He could see the sail.

It was a gauzy sheet draped across the crowded stars of this place. And within the sail, cupped, he could see the neutron star, an angry ball of red laced with eerie synchrotron blue, like a huge toy.

Beautiful. Scary.

And he saw it with eyes beyond the human.

He saw the sleeting rays that flowed beyond the human spectrum: the sail's dazzle of ultraviolet, the sullen infrared glower of the star itself. He saw the sail, its curves, the star, from a dozen angles, as if the whole impossible, unlikely structure was a mote that swam within his own God-like eyeball, visible from all sides *at once*, as if it had been flayed and pinned to a board before him.

And he saw the whole project embedded in time, the sail unfurling, growing, the star's slow, reluctant deflection. He saw its origins – the sail shared design features with the artefact that had been found cupping a black hole in the system of the species called Chaera; perhaps it too was a relic of those vanished builders.

And he even saw it all through the gauzy eyes of mathematics. He could see the brutal equations of gravity and electromagnetism which governed the drag of the star's remote companion, the push of star on sail and sail on star; and he could see, like shining curves extending ahead of and back from this single moment, how those equations would unfold, the evolution of the system through time, out of the past, through the now, and into the future.

Not enough, he saw.

Still the construction of the sail was outpaced by the neutron stars' approach. The project was projected to fail; the stars were mathematically destined to collide before the sail's deflection was done, the great gamma ray burst lethally mocking their efforts. But they must, they would, try harder, the toiling communities here.

. . . And if you see all this, Malenfant, then what are *you*? God knows you're no mathematician.

He looked down at himself.

Tried to.

His gaze swivelled, yes, his vision sparkling with superhuman spectra. But his *head* did not turn.

For he had no head.

A sense of body, briefly. Spread-eagled against the sail's gauzy netting. Clinging by fingers and toes, monkey digits, here at the centre of the Galaxy.

A metaphor, of course, an illusion to comfort his poor human mind. What was he truly? – a partial personality, downloaded into a clumsy robot, clinging to this monstrous structure, bathed by the lethal radiation of a neutron star?

And even now the robot he rode was working, knitting away at the net. This body was working, without having to be told, directed, by *me*, or anybody else.

But that's the way it is, Malenfant. Self is an illusion, remember. You've always been a passenger, riding inside that bony cage of a skull of yours. It's just that now it's a little more – explicit.

Welcome to reality.

But if I'm a robot, why the *pain?*

He looked for Cassiopeia, for any of the Gaijin, reassuring dodecahedral bulks. He saw none, though the unwelcome enhancements of his vision let him zoom and peer through the spaces all around him.

But when he thought of Cassiopeia, anger flooded him. Why?

It had been just minutes since she had embraced him on that grassy simulated plain . . . hadn't it?

How do you *know*, Malenfant? How do you know you haven't been frozen in some deep data store for ten thousand years?

And . . . how do you know this isn't the first time you surfaced like this?

How *could* he know? If his identity assembled, disintegrated again, what trace would it leave on his memory? What *was* his memory? What if he was simply *restarted* each time, wiped clean like a reinitialized computer? How would he *know?*

In renewed terror, lost in space and time – in helpless, desolating loneliness – he tried again to scream. But he could not, of course.

The sail shuddered. Great ripples of disturbance, thousands of kilometres long, wafted through the net. As the waves passed, he saw others shaken loose, equipment hurled free, damaged.

Without his conscious control, he was aware how his body (or bodies? – how do you know you're *even in one place*, Malenfant?) grasped tighter to the fine structure.

He felt a clustering of awareness around him. Other workers here, perhaps. Other parts of himself.

Frightened.

Have faith, he told his companions, his other parts. Or his disciples.

But that was the problem. *They* didn't have faith. Faith was a dangerous idea. The only thing less dangerous, in fact, was the universe itself, this terrible Rebooting accident of celestial mechanics.

All this had happened before. The wars. The destruction. The abandonment of work. The resumption, the patient repairs.

There was a species he thought of as the Fire-eaters. They were related to the Crackers, who had tried to disrupt Earth's sun. But these more ambitious cousins wanted to steal part of the sail and wrap up a hypernova, one of the largest exploding stars in the Galaxy. As best he understood it they would try to capture a fraction of that astonishing energy in order to hurl themselves out of the Galaxy within an ace of lightspeed. And that way, their subjective experience stretched to near-immobility by time dilation, they would outlive this Reboot, and the one after it, and the one after that. He remembered a diversion of resources, a great war, huge damage to the sail, before the Fire-eaters were driven off.

. . . He *remembered*.

Yes. He had surfaced, like this, become Malenfant before, cowering under a sky full of silent, deadly, warring Eeties, in a corner of the sail where the threads buckled and broke.

Surfaced more than once.

Many times.

How long have I been here? And between these intervals of half-remembered awareness, how long have I toiled here, awake but unaware?

Ah, yes, but take a look at where you *are*, Malenfant.

He looked up from the rippling sail, away from the lethal neutron star, and into the complex sky.

He was at the heart of the Galaxy: within the great central cluster of stars, no more than a couple of dozen light years from the very centre. At that centre there was a cavity some twenty light years wide, encased by a great shell of crowded, disrupted stars; the neutron star binary huddled at the inner boundary of this shell.

The emptiness of the 'cavity' was only relative. There was a great double-spiral architecture of stars, like a miniature copy of the Galaxy, trapped here at its heart. The spiralling stars were dragged into their tight orbits around the object at the Galaxy's gravitational core itself:

450

a black hole with a broad, glowing, spitting accretion disc, a hole itself with the mass of some three million suns. It was the violent winds from the vast accretion disc which had created this relative hollowness.

But still the cavity was crammed with gas and dust, its particles ionized and driven to high speeds by the ferocious gravitational and magnetic forces working here, so that streamers of glowing gas criss-crossed the cavity in a fine tracery. Stars had been born here, notably a cluster of blue-hot young stars just a fraction away from the black hole itself. And here and there rogue stars fell through the cavity – and they dragged streaming trails behind them, glowing brilliantly, like comets a hundred light years long.

Stars like comets.

He exulted. I, Reid Malenfant, got to see *this*, the heart of the Galaxy itself, by God! He wished Cassiopeia were here, his companion during those endless Saddle Point jaunts to one star after another . . .

But again, at the thought of Cassiopeia, his anger flared.

And now, his reassembled mind clearer, he remembered *why*.

He had found out after submitting to Cassiopeia's cold, agonizing embrace, after arriving *here*, an unknown time later.

He had learned that even if all went well here – if the wars ceased, if the supplies of raw materials didn't fail, even if the neutron star sail, this marvellous artefact, was completed and worked as advertised – *even then*, it wouldn't do *him* a blind bit of good.

Because it was already too late. For him. And his people.

This binary, yes: this implosion was far enough in the future to affect, with this low-tech solution, robots and nets and solar wind rockets. But *this* wasn't the next scheduled to blow up.

There was *another* coalescing neutron star binary, buried still deeper in the Galaxy's diseased heart, another Reboot. And it was already too late to stop that one, too late to avert the coming catastrophe.

This unlikely sail would work. But it was too long term. The project would avert *the next Reboot but one*.

We were always doomed. All we could do was make it better for the next cycle, advance the project far enough that *they* – the next to evolve from the pond scum of the Galaxy, the next to stumble on the half-finished sail after another few tens of millions of years – *they* would understand a little better than we had, would know what to do, how to finish it.

The first designers of the sail, sometime before the *last* Reboot, had known it. Cassiopeia had known it.

She hadn't thought to tell him, though, before he – died. Maybe she didn't think it was significant. After all a sacrifice was a sacrifice. Maybe he simply hadn't understood; maybe she'd expected him to be able to think it through himself. After all, she could *see* the mathematics.

He remembered how it felt, to find out. It had been the final betrayal. And hence, the anger.

But it didn't matter. In fact, it made his work, the role here, still more important.

Humans, Gaijin, Chaera, all of the current 'generation' of galactic sentients – all of those who contributed to the sail's slow building – they were *all* doomed, no matter what happened here.

But this was all they could do: to make things better for the next time.

And, he told himself, thinking of Madeleine, the alternative to all this pain – a lifeless universe doomed to nothing but meaningless expansion – would be much worse.

Have courage, he told himself / themselves. We have a noble goal. Our death doesn't matter. The future, the children . . . even if they are not *our* children. That is what matters. We will prevail.

He must continue. He must reach out to others, working here. Infect them.

Convert them.

This wasn't a project, after all. It was a crusade.

The net shuddered again. That damn war.

He was dissolving, sinking back. He didn't fight it. It was good.

Malenfant sighed, metaphorically. You don't have to be crazy to work here but it helps.

Blue light that gathered around him. Pain that intensified.

. . . *Cassiopeia*, he flared. Why did you betray me?

No centre.

The universe, of tasks, of things.

The anchoring. The self-maintenance. The work.

Always the work.

EPILOGUE

The Gaijin colony lay quietly beneath its translucent bubble, the bevelled edges of the buildings making the little city look like a scattering of half-melted toys. Beyond the bubble an airless, desolate plain stretched to a clean horizon. Shadows raked the plain.

Looking up, she traced the quasar's fantastic geometry.

The powerhouse at the quasar's heart, barely two hundred light years away, was a pinpoint of unnatural brightness. Twin sprays of electron flux tore from the poles of the powerhouse, straining to zenith and nadir. And swaddling the waist of the quasar was a torus of glowing rubble. This colony world orbited almost within the torus, so that the debris looked like a pair of celestial arms reaching around the powerhouse to touch the fake clouds nestling under the bubble.

The sky was full of dodecahedral frameworks, triangular faces glimmering, drifting like angular soap bubbles.

It was glorious, astonishing.

She had travelled a billion light years from Earth, across the curve of the universe. She wasn't aware of it. She had been in store, or bouncing from gateway to gateway without downloading, since leaving Malenfant.

I am a billion years from home, she thought. Everything I knew is buried under deep layers of past. Humans must have fled Earth, or become extinct. Earth's biosphere itself could not survive so long as this. Perhaps I am the last human.

Perhaps I am, by now, a construct of alien qualia; perhaps I'm not even human any more myself.

Well, I don't have to face that. Not yet.

She looked to the zenith. A scattering of galaxies glimmered through her bubble.

The galaxies glowed green, every one of them.

Life everywhere. Triumphant. Awe, wonder, love surged in her.

It was proof, of course. Just waking up again, emerging from the

Saddle Point network, had been proof. Humans and their allies – or rivals or successors – had beaten the countdown clock, had bust out of the limits of the Galaxy, and gone on, spreading across the universe, building their Saddle Point links.

And if they had got as far as *this*, they must be everywhere. Hell of a thought.

But –

Where to now, Madeleine?

She wondered if Malenfant could have survived, in one form or another, even over such an immense span of space and time. *She* had, after all. She smiled, thinking of Malenfant, the original grey cyborg.

The quasar dipped to the horizon now; optical filters in the bubble around her softened its shape, turning it red. The electron flux was splayed across the sky like brush marks on velvet. The last traces of quasar light touched the sky like cool smoke.

It was so beautiful it hurt.

She turned away, and went in search of Reid Malenfant.

AFTERWORD

A good recent survey of the state of our thinking on extraterrestrial life is Paul Davies' *Are We Alone?* (Penguin Books, 1995). The passages set on the Moon are based in part on conversations with former astronaut Charles M. Duke, who in 1972 walked on the Moon as Lunar Module Pilot of Apollo 16. There really are naturally occurring nuclear reactors; a reference is 'Fossil Nuclear Reactors' by Michel Maurette, *Annual Review of Nuclear Science* v 26, pp319–350 (1976). I published a technical article on the feasibility of the Moon's deep ocean in the *Journal of the British Interplanetary Society* (v 51, pp 75–80, 1998).

Any errors, omissions or misinterpretations are of course my responsibility

Stephen Baxter
Great Missenden
February 2000

I remember with pleasure many personal discussions at Berne with Professor Röthlisberger, Secretary of the International Bureau of Copyright, which gave me a wider and more practical knowledge of continental ideas on the subject. I also thank M. Henri Morel, Director of the International Office, for giving me a welcome, and a free run of the Bureau and Library under his charge.

To my friend and old pupil, W. D. Aston, B.A., LL.B., I am indebted for valued assistance in making references and extracts, and in indexing. Indeed, in the latter parts of the book—particularly on Colonial Law and on that of the United States of America, which were not originally designed as sections of this work—his share has been so substantial that, had they been issued separately, his name also would have appeared on the title-pages.

To render it a work of practical utility as fully as possible, the book has been divided into five distinct parts, each of which is largely complete in itself. This has necessarily led to some duplication, but only such a limited use of subject-matter which belongs to another Part has been made as to render the context intelligible. Special care, by means of carefully arranged and full Contents and Index, has been taken to make the book not merely a text-book on the subject, but ready for purposes of reference.

WILLIAM BRIGGS.

BURLINGTON HOUSE,
    CAMBRIDGE,
        January 3rd, 1906.

PREFACE.

LITTLE apology ought to be needed for the issue of this, the first work in English on the Law of International Copyright, a subject of such importance as to call for exposition in every civilised language. Continental readers possess an excellent account, *Du Droit des Auteurs et des Artistes dans les Rapports Internationaux*, by Dr. Alcide Darras, published the year following that most important of all international agreements on the subject—the Berne Convention of 1886. But the English standpoint differs materially from that of continental nations, as the present chapters on the Berne Convention abundantly show. In a great measure this is due to the constant reference to that scrap-heap of English Copyright legislation, the codifying Literary Copyright Act of 1842. Increasingly liberal interpretations of the Courts bring our domestic legislation a little nearer to the standards of other leading civilised nations, but it still suffers considerably by comparison with them.

The relation of International Law to domestic Law in England differs widely from that which generally obtains on the Continent, and consequently the interpretation of International Law calls for special treatment.

In the preparation of this work I am indebted to Dr. Darras for many suggestions, and also for his kind permission to make use of the many interesting historical instances concerning international piracies of intellectual works.

THE LAW

OF

INTERNATIONAL COPYRIGHT

WITH SPECIAL SECTIONS ON THE COLONIES AND
THE UNITED STATES OF AMERICA

BY

WILLIAM BRIGGS, LL.D., D.C.L.

M.A., B.SC., F.C.S., F.R.A.S.

London

STEVENS & HAYNES

13 BELL YARD, TEMPLE BAR, W.C.

1906

Library of Congress Cataloging-in-Publication Data

Briggs, William, 1861-1932.
    The law of international copyright.

    Reprint. Originally published: London : Stevens
& Haynes, 1906.
    Bibliography: p.
    Includes index.
    1. Copyright, International. 2. Copyright--
Great Britain--Colonies. I. Title.
K1411.6.B75 1986   341.7'582   86-26264
ISBN 0-8377-1941-0 (alk. paper)

THE LAW

OF

INTERNATIONAL COPYRIGHT

*WITH SPECIAL SECTIONS ON THE COLONIES AND
THE UNITED STATES OF AMERICA*

BY

WILLIAM BRIGGS, LL.D., D.C.L.

M.A., B.SC., F.C.S., F.R.A.S.

Fred B. Rothman & Co.
LITTLETON, COLORADO
1986

THE LAW OF

INTERNATIONAL COPYRIGHT.

1P

CONTENTS

Preface   vii

1   A Licence to Lose Money   1
2   'The Greatest Editor in the World'   45
3   Cold Warrior   119
4   Ancient and Modern   167
5   Fortress Wapping   219
6   Fifty-Four Weeks under Siege   253
7   Independent Challenges   300
8   Sturm und Drang   332
9   Simon Jenkins   367
10   Critical Times   416
11   The Heart of Europe   472
12   New Labour, New Journalism   497
13   War in Peacetime   559
14   Dumbing Down?   610

List of Illustrations   651
Notes   653
Bibliography   693
Index   697

PREFACE

This is an official history. It has access to private correspondence and business documents that have not been made generally available to other writers or historians. Some may consider this a mixed blessing and assume that the consequence must necessarily – in the words of the accusation that used to be labelled at *The Times*'s obituaries – 'sniff of an inside job'. It should therefore be stated from the first that at no stage has anyone altered anything I have written or pressured me into adopting a position or opinion that was not my own. It is an official history but not a formally approved or authorized version of events.

Indeed, Rupert Murdoch's relaxed attitude while I probed around in an important part of his business empire contrasted favourably with past precedent in this series. Those commissioned to write the six previous volumes of the official history of *The Times* were closely involved in the paper's life, a conflict of interest that certainly hindered the appearance of objectivity. The first four volumes, covering the period between its foundation in 1785 and the Second World War, were compiled between 1935 and 1952 by a team under the command of Stanley Morison. Morison was the inventor of the world's most popular typeface, Times New Roman. He was also a close friend of the paper's then owner, John Astor, and its editor, Robin Barrington-Ward, who went so far as to describe Morison as 'the Conscience of *The Times*'. Iverach McDonald, who was an assistant editor and managing editor of the paper during the period he described, wrote volume five in 1984. Volume six, covering the years 1966 to 1981, was written in 1993 by John Grigg. He had been the paper's obituaries editor between 1986 and 1987 and was a regular columnist. Grigg, at least, was not directly involved in the events about which he wrote. Instead, he brought the insight and flair of the independent historian of note, attributes for which he will be fondly remembered. For my own part, I cannot claim much personal involvement with the paper during the years covered in this volume. My only first hand experience was garnered during the year 2000, when I was a leader writer. As a historian, my specialist area is British politics in the 1930s.

The Times is not, first and foremost, a national institution. It is a business. Yet I have avoided the temptation to treat it purely as a corporate entity, as if its journalistic and literary output had no more cultural significance than the manufacturing of the paper on which it was printed. Consequently, I have described its journalism within the context of the world events that were its stimulation. The book, therefore, is part business history, part work of reference, part anthology. It is intended to appeal both to those interested in the paper in particular or journalism in general who want to know how *The Times* conducted itself during the period 1981 to 2002.

The book would not have been possible without the knowledge and assistance of *The Times*'s archivist, Eamon Dyas, and his assistant, Nick Mays, at News International's impressively organized Archive Centre and Record Office. Elaine Grant and Karen Colognese were unceasingly helpful in providing assistance from the chairman's office. Journalists too numerous to mention here have accepted my invitations to share what they know over some light refreshment. Their recollections and observations have made this book a pleasure to write. It has also been a relief to discover that the traditions of the Fleet Street lunch are not entirely a thing of the past. It is not the place of an official history to indulge the sort of convoluted tales of uncertain provenance that enliven many a hack's memoir of the Street of Shame's alleged glory days. Nonetheless, despite my preference for primary evidence, I have not omitted gossip where I have been able to cross reference the story and establish its basis in fact. Any errors or misrepresentations remain, of course, entirely my own.

Among the many individuals that have helped me, I should like in particular to thank Richard Spink and Tasha Browning for their indefatigable generosity of spirit. At HarperCollins, Annabel Wright has been a stalwart aid. I have profited enormously from the valuable suggestions made by Andrew Knight and Brian MacArthur whose experience of the newspaper world is exceptional. Rupert Murdoch gave me a considerable amount of his time and I appreciate the unconditional assistance he has given me. I should especially like to thank Les Hinton, executive chairman of News International, who has been a great friend of the project and unfailing in his support and enthusiasm. It is my regret that Sir Edward Pickering, grand old man of Fleet Street and executive vice-chairman of Times Newspapers, did not live to see the completion of the book he commissioned and for which he provided such sagacious advice. I dedicate it to his memory.

Graham Stewart, February 2005

CHAPTER ONE

A LICENCE TO LOSE MONEY

The Problems of Owning *The Times*;
the Thomson Sale and the Murdoch Purchase

I

On 22 October 1980, in its one hundred and ninety-sixth year, *The Times* was put up for sale. It would be closed down if no suitable buyer secured a deal before 15 March – the Ides of March. Staff received notice that their contracts were being terminated.

Superficially *The Times* was a prize, but few who had studied the accounts would have thought so. It resembled the sort of Palladian mansion still occasionally offered for sale through the pages of *Country Life*. Despite the odd seedling protruding from the cornicing, the exterior still looked magnificent and the asking price seemed preposterously low. But those enquiring beyond the inventory of rare and exotic contents (to be auctioned separately) soon discovered why the previous owners no longer felt able to comply with the conditions of this national treasure's preservation order. The lead had come away from the roof, the attic floorboards had collapsed and damp enveloped what had once been a ballroom. The costs of upkeep would be punishing and, with little prospect of a change of usage permit, the likely revenue insufficient. On hearing the news that *The Times* was for sale, the reaction of Rupert Murdoch, the owner of the *Sun* and the *News of the World*, was reported in the press: 'I doubt whether there will be any buyers.'[1]

It was certainly a bad sign that the share price of the Thomson Organisation, *The Times*'s owner, soared by £40 million on the announcement that it was offloading its flagship paper. This was particularly alarming since for sale was not only *The Times* and its three smaller circulation supplements but also the *Sunday Times*, a paper that had been profitable for seventeen out of the past twenty years. But the Sunday market leader had lost 300,000 copies through industrial action the weekend before Thomson's announcement that it was for sale. It had lost 800,000 the weekend before that. No newspaper that lost five million copies in a year as a result of the action of those employed to print it could realize its potential.[2] Together, the papers – *The Times*, the *Times Literary Supplement*, the *Times Educational Supplement*, the *Times Higher Education Supplement* and the *Sunday Times* – that comprised Times Newspapers Limited (TNL) had made after-tax losses of £18.8 million in 1979 and £14.5 million in 1980.[3] In the same interview in which he declared little interest in picking up the bill, Rupert Murdoch was quoted as describing TNL as a 'snake-pit'.

It was hard to see what hard-headed businessman would leap at the opportunity to enter this environment. Certainly, there would be bidders with an interest in either asset stripping or wanting to turn *The Times* into a private toy. Middle Eastern backers expressed interest but, as Sir Richard Marsh, chairman of the Newspaper Publishers' Association (NPA), indelicately put it: 'I think [the idea of] *The Times* being owned by somebody in the Lebanon would be a joke.'[4] Nearer home, there were some circling sharks, among them Robert Maxwell, James Goldsmith and Tiny Rowland, to whom the Thomson board were simply not prepared to sell the paper at any price.[5]

In Westminster there was cross-party alarm. Michael Foot, the Deputy Leader of the Labour Party, who had once been one of Beaverbrook's sharpest pens, declared 'every journalist in the country, I would think, would be deeply shocked at hearing the news' that *The Times* was for sale or closure, adding: 'undoubtedly this has created a crisis of major proportions for the free press in Britain'.[6]

The mood in the non-parliamentary wing of the Labour Movement was also glum. Meeting the members of the Thomson board two days after the announcement of the sale, Joe Wade, general secretary of the National Graphical Association (NGA) print union, whose members made up much of the skilled print labour force at TNL, said that the news 'had wonderfully concentrated people's minds' and that in the last forty-eight hours he had been able to obtain a number of guarantees of continuous production. This was surprising. During 1978–9, his union had preferred to witness TNL's papers being taken off the streets for eleven months rather than make concessions to its management. The shutdown of the papers had cost Thomson £40 million and ended only when management crumbled at the first sight of union guarantees that subsequently proved worthless. But now that his supposed antagonists appeared to be quitting the field, Wade changed his tune: 'the Unions would prefer the *Times* titles to remain with

The Thomson Organisation – better the devil you know'. The thirteenth-hour loyal protestation, if that is what it was, had come too late. The decision to sell was irrevocable. Wade unhelpfully commented to the press: 'the unions frankly had grave doubts whether a realistic proposition would emerge for the transfer of the titles to a new owner'.[7]

In a rare moment of unity, the editor of *The Times* agreed. William Rees-Mogg had been in the chair since 1967, having been appointed shortly after Roy Thomson's purchase of the paper from the Astor family. His father was a Somerset squire, but he was brought up in the Roman Catholic faith of his American mother, a former actress who in her day had performed alongside Sarah Bernhardt. Sent to school at Charterhouse, his precocious abilities won him a Brackenbury scholarship to Balliol College, Oxford, where he was at ease with the college's temporal traditions; he was elected president of the Oxford Union. On going down, he worked first for the *Financial Times* and then at the *Sunday Times* as its deputy editor. He was still only thirty-eight when he became editor of *The Times*. Under his editorship the paper had continued to play to its strengths – in particular the authority of its comment and reflection on world events – while continuing to lag behind the *Daily Telegraph* in the breadth and immediacy of its home news coverage. In particular, Rees-Mogg had maintained the high standard of *Times* leader articles, the most memorable of which were his own work. As a seasoned commentator of the period put it with regard to Rees-Mogg's paper: 'One found oneself every morning in the company of a civilized, slightly barmy, humorous, usually gentle, intelligence, whose most stimulating characteristic was its unpredictability.'[8] This last facet was now to make itself evident as Rees-Mogg decided that it had fallen to him – with the journalists around him – to save *The Times*.

No sooner had the news of the sale broken than Rees-Mogg summoned his editorial staff. As many of the 330 full complement as could crowded around. His deputy, Louis Heren, described the occasion as 'almost like a revolutionary commune'.[9] If a 'person of good character and quality' wanted to buy the papers then that would be acceptable, Rees-Mogg declared. But merely switching ownership from one press baron to another should not be the 'plan to save our future'. Thomson was offering *The Times* and *Sunday Times* for sale together as a package. This, Rees-Mogg argued, was a mistake. If anything was now clear it was that the two papers were 'by their natures so different that neither paper is good for the other'. Not only did they have incompatible audiences, 'the industrial logic which put the *Sunday Times* and *The Times* together was mistaken industrial logic'. In any case, 'if the Thomson family were not able to master this business why should any other individual be any more successful?'. With the example of *Le Monde*, which was run by a journalists' cooperative, the editor proposed bringing the already-formed staff group known as Journalists of *The Times* (JOTT), together with managers, as minority shareholders in a consortium supported by a variety of financial backers. Together they would buy the paper.[10]

It was a bold idea. Some found the editor's newfound conversion to worker participation perplexing, but others were enthusiastic. The paper's Whitehall correspondent, Peter Hennessy, stood up to say, 'I am very pleased about the powerful lead you intend to give us in our struggle and unwillingness to accept any Northcliffe-type buyer.' Northcliffe had bought *The Times* from its original Walter family owners in 1908, popularizing it but interfering in its cherished editorial independence. He had also saved the paper from certain death. Within six years of Northcliffe's acquisition of the paper, its circulation had risen from a mere 40,000 to 314,000 copies a day. It was a sign of what had happened under the two subsequent owners that, despite the massively expanding market during the twentieth century, this 1914 figure was higher than the 298,000 *The Times* was averaging between July and December 1980.

The Times of 23 October 1980 carried as its front-page lead story its own perilous position. Rees-Mogg wrote a signed article on the Op-Ed page (the page for columnists opposite the leaders and letters page) elaborating on his ideas in his speech to the staff. 'Now *The Times* is going to fight for herself,' proclaimed a new agenda: 'the lesson of the Thomson years is that subsidy destroys the commercial operation of newspapers' and that 'I no longer believe in the virtue of a newspaper proprietorship which does not include the people who make the paper as shareholders in the ownership.' 'From now on,' he announced, 'the main thrust of my work will be to try with like-minded colleagues to develop a partnership – commercial not charitable – which can keep *The Times* in being.'[11]

The paper's letter page soon filled with exhortations from readers, often pledging the length of their active service to the paper's circulation by way of qualification, in support of Rees-Mogg's idea of a journalist–capitalist syndicate.[12] Barings became the project's merchant bankers and Sir Michael Swann, Provost of Oriel College, Oxford, and a former chairman of the BBC, chaired the consortium. Lord Weinstock, managing director of GEC and a personal friend of Rees-Mogg, sat on its steering committee. If £10 million of working capital could be raised, fortified by £30 million a year revenue, it was certainly feasible that *The Times* could balance its books if it could cut its expenses by printing outside London's notorious high labour costs. Lord Barnetson, the chairman of the *Observer*, had suggested to Rees-Mogg that printing *The Times* at a provincial 'greenfield' site could be done for £7 million a year. This was a third of the cost of doing it with the current TNL print workers at the paper's London headquarters in Gray's Inn Road.[13]

Of course, it was not that simple. Even if an existing provincial print works, for example the United Newspapers' plant in Northampton, could be engaged, there would be a period of disruption – conservatively estimated at six weeks – before *The Times* could roll out from its new site. Readers' loyalty had already been seriously tested by the eleven-month shutdown the previous year and another lengthy period in which the paper was off the streets was clearly something to be avoided. More importantly, the strategy assumed that the London print unions would sit back while their jobs were transferred to 'brothers' in the provinces. This was not in the spirit of union solidarity. Even if their fellow members in the provinces did decide to handle *The Times*, the print unions could then hold hostage the *Sunday Times* by going on strike at Gray's Inn Road. With this, the whole Thomson strategy of selling the papers together would unwind. Even without these problems, the Rees-Mogg consortium had to convince long-term investors that it could gain access to sufficient and sustainable capital and that a syndicate in which journalists played a part would have the necessary unity of purpose to take hard decisions.[14]

The consortium's best hope was to step in following the Thomson board's failure to attract a serious bid from one of the major media magnates. This Rees-Mogg came to accept, ultimately viewing his plan as a fall-back position,[15] but at the time the Thomson board watched with mounting alarm as the extent of his desire to promote his rescue plan manifested itself. *The Times*'s editor had a journalist's eye for finding ways to maximize publicity (some supposed that this must have had something to do with the early influence of a theatrical mother). Gathering a television crew about him, Rees-Mogg now set off across the Atlantic. There, he hoped, he might find white knights, ready to take a share in his mission to save 'this strange English institution'.

Having arrived in the United States, Rees-Mogg had lunch with Katharine Graham, the proprietor of the *Washington Post*. Despite her liberal politics, she had shown the determination to break a debilitating print workers' strike that threatened to strangle the *Post* in 1975, defeating those besieging her printing plant by flying newsprint into it over their heads. Unlike Times Newspapers' management, she had taken on her industrial tormentors and won. But, joined for lunch by her senior management, even she could not see how *The Times* could get out of its dire situation. Having listened to Rees-Mogg's presentation, the verdict was to the point: 'The *Washington Post* saw *The Times* as a potential disaster area which they didn't want anything to do with,' Rees-Mogg recalled, 'although they were very polite and friendly.'[16]

Rees-Mogg had considered Kay Graham the sort of acceptably independent-minded proprietor *The Times* should be trying to attract. He had not yet spoken of Rupert Murdoch in that light. Indeed, in 1977 he had told the Royal Commission on the Press: 'Mr Murdoch's writ does run in his own building and, much as I respect his energy and vigour, because of his views on the proprietorial function, I would never myself be willing to work for him.'[17] Less than a month before it was announced *The Times* was being put up for sale, Rees-Mogg had encouraged his New York correspondent, Michael Leapman, to write an attack on Murdoch's methods at his *New York Post*. The article, illustrated with a *Post* front-page headline 'PREGNANT MOM IN 911 TERROR' was equally punchy:

> It is nearly four years since Mr Murdoch gave the United States its first true sampling of the journalism of the lowest common denominator. That was when he bought the struggling *New York Post* and filled its senior editorial positions with British and Australian newspapermen, expert in plumbing the depths of bad taste which Americans had scarcely guessed at.[18]

Yet now Rees-Mogg made the trip to the top of the *New York Post* building overlooking the Brooklyn Bridge to discover whether Rupert Murdoch, owner of eighty-four newspapers including the *Sun* and the *News of the World*, was interested in helping to save *The Times*.

The meeting, Rees-Mogg reflected, went well. Murdoch was friendly, courteous and drank not from a mug but from an elegant china tea service. He did not let himself be drawn on exactly what his intentions were but by the time Rees-Mogg returned to Manhattan street level he had gained the impression that Murdoch was sizing up the possibility of a bid for the *Sunday Times*. This was good, for the whole point of Rees-Mogg's consortium plan was that there should be a divorce in the *Times* family. Furthermore, Murdoch appeared to be keen to help the consortium in any practical way, perhaps even printing it at his plant in Worcester. Indeed, 'he was sympathetic to anything that would keep *The Times* alive'.[19]

It was only the third time Murdoch and Rees-Mogg had properly met one another. Previously they had found themselves seated together at a table with the Queen at a celebratory gathering of the Press Club during which Rees-Mogg had noticed the Australian's ability to make the Queen laugh. But their first meeting, in the summer of 1951, had been more prescient. The young Rees-Mogg, already at the age of twenty-three bearing the assumed gravitas of an elder statesman, had been walking up The Turl in Oxford when he was stopped by a 'brash young member of the Labour Club' who wanted to cut him in on a business venture. The Antipodean undergraduate said he was thinking of buying the ailing student newspaper *Cherwell*, and wondered whether Rees-Mogg wanted to invest in his scheme. Venerable title or not, Rees-Mogg replied that *Cherwell* was staid and boring and would never attract sufficient advertising to be an attractive business proposition. The young Murdoch countered that with drive and initiative it could be made attractive by changing the editorial content, bringing it up to date and transforming the finances. 'You'll never make any money out of *Cherwell*' was the young Rees-Mogg's cheerful reply. And with that mistaken prophecy, the two undergraduates went their separate ways.[20]

Twenty-nine years later, two men were determined to put Murdoch's profit-making expertise back in touch with a venerable, occasionally staid, loss maker. The first was one of Fleet Street's most respected figures – Sir Denis Hamilton, editor-in-chief of Times Newspapers Limited. The other was Sir Gordon Brunton, managing director of TNL's parent company, Thomson British Holdings Limited. Both men thought Rees-Mogg's consortium idea was suicidal, but when they had discussed the disposal of Times Newspapers in a secretly convened meeting with Thomson's chairman, Lord Thomson of Fleet, on 18 September 1980, Hamilton had reported the opinion that 'Rupert Murdoch is probably not interested'.[21] One look at the other likely bidders was enough to convince those seated around the table that it was a matter of urgency to get him interested.

Sir Gordon Brunton had got to know Murdoch through the Newspaper Publishers' Association. The two men shared a similar attitude towards dealing with the print unions and, unlike so many of the other Fleet Street proprietors who attended NPA meetings, Brunton believed that if Murdoch gave his word on a particular action he would keep it.[22] Murdoch considered Brunton 'clear-headed and strong-willed'.[23] Besides his godfather role at Times Newspapers, Sir Denis Hamilton was also chairman of Reuters, the board meetings of which Murdoch regularly attended. It was on a flight to Bahrain for one of these meetings that the two found themselves sitting together in the aeroplane. This was a seating coincidence that Hamilton – assuming Murdoch would be taking the same flight – had carefully engineered. The long flight was an unrivalled opportunity to get Murdoch alone and Hamilton did his best to, as he later put it, 'plant as much of a seed as possible – for my fellow directors felt that only a really strong owner who would be prepared to take savage measures, and of whose determination the unions could have no doubt, had any hope'.[24]

In fact, Murdoch had already scented blood. Back in September, he had bumped into Lord Thomson in the Concorde departure lounge at JFK and gained from him, however obliquely, the impression that TNL would not remain within the Thomson empire for much longer. Murdoch, indeed, had greater forewarning that *The Times* would be up for sale than had its editor. But whether the owner of predominately tabloid titles, a man who gave little impression of wanting to join the British Establishment, could be persuaded to take the bait and rescue *The Times* still remained far from clear.

Whichever projection was favoured, *The Times* was not on any rapid course to profitability. Although it had edged into the black during the early 1950s and for one tantalizing moment in 1977, it had been losing money for the vast majority of the twentieth century. A paper with such a track record would have been shut down long ago had it not been for its reputation and the manner in which being the proprietor of *The Times* conveyed a position in public life that had a value of its own. Gavin Astor, who became (alongside his father) proprietor in 1964, described the newspaper as 'a peculiar property in that service to what it believes are the best interests of the nation is placed before the personal and financial gains of its Proprietors'.[25] But a proprietor's belief in his role as a national custodian was not necessarily appreciated by less sentimentally minded shareholders. When Roy Thomson bought *The Times* in 1966 he recognized that it would not be a cash cow and, in order not to trouble shareholders' consciences with it, opted to fund it out of his own exceptionally deep pocket. In 1974 this decision was reversed when the Thomson Organisation's portfolio diversified further into other interests, including North Sea oil, whose profitability dwarfed TNL's losses. The only commercial argument for retaining *The Times* was that as a globally recognized quality brand, it (at least psychologically) added value as the glittering flagship of the Thomson Line. Unfortunately, in becoming a byword for unseaworthiness, it risked very publicly bringing down Thomson's reputation for business savvy and managerial skill. From that moment on, it became a matter of floating it out into the ocean and abandoning ship.

When it came to the announcement of sale, the Thomson board maintained that although they had failed, a new management team might be able to turn the paper around. This was a predictable statement – *The Times* could not easily be sold by asserting it had no viable future whoever owned it. But no serious forecaster believed it could be turned around quickly. Could supposedly 'short-termist' shareholders be expected to understand a new owner's perseverance? In this respect Murdoch offered more hope than some potential bidders because he and his family owned a controlling share of his company, News International Limited. Thus, so long as Murdoch saw a future for the paper, News International could carry *The Times* through a long period of disappointing revenue without its survival in the company being frequently challenged by angry shareholders. And given the profitability of the other stallions in the stable, the *Sun* and the *News of the World*, there was every reason to expect that the banks would continue to regard News International as creditworthy.

On the other hand, appearing to have an excess of available money also threatened *The Times*. Journalists and print workers who regarded their paper as a rich man's toy could be expected to want to joy ride with it. This had been part of the problem with the Thomson ownership of TNL. Roy Thomson was the son of a Toronto barber who described purchasing *The Times* when he was aged seventy-two as 'the summit of a lifetime's work'. An Anglophile, he renounced his Canadian citizenship in order to accept a British peerage (as the future Canadian proprietor of the *Daily Telegraph*, Conrad Black, would later do). He took as his title Lord Thomson of Fleet – the closest a peerage could decorously go towards being named after a busy street. Not only did he describe owning *The Times* as 'the greatest privilege of my life' he announced that in acquiring it, the paper's 'special position in the world will now be safeguarded for all time'.[26] This was a hostage to fortune. Owning STV (Scottish Television) had provided much of the financial base for his British acquisitions and he had once famously described owning a British commercial television station as 'like having your own licence to print money'. He appeared to accept that owning *The Times* was a licence to lose it.

II

Fleet Street, whose pundits were paid daily to indict others for failing to put the world to rights, was noticeably incompetent in managing its own backyard. For those proprietors already ensconced, there was at least the compensation that this created a cartel-like environment. The huge costs of producing national newspapers caused by print unions' ability to retain superfluous jobs and resist cost-saving innovation acted to ward off all but the most determined and rich competitors from cracking into the market. Competition from foreign newspapers was, for obvious reasons, all but nonexistent. The attempts through the Newspaper Publishers' Association to act collectively against union demands were frequently half-hearted. No sooner had the respective managements returned to their papers' head-quarters than new and deadline-threatening disputes would lead them to cobble together individual peace deals that cut across the whole strategy of collective resistance. During the 1970s, it was widely understood that one of the major newspaper groups had resorted to paying sweeteners to specific union officials who might otherwise disrupt the evening print run.

By 1980, Fleet Street's newspapers were the only manufacturing industry left in the heart of London. The print workers came predominantly from the East End, passing on their jobs from father to son (never to daughter) with a degree of reverence for the hereditary principle rarely seen outside *Burke's Peerage* or a Newmarket stud farm. They were members of one of two types of union. The craft unions, of which the National Graphical Association (NGA) was to the fore, operated the museum-worthy Linotype machines that produced the type in hot metal and set the paper. The non-craft unions, in particular NATSOPA (later amalgamated into SOGAT), did what were considered the less skilful parts of the operation and included clerical workers, cleaners and other ancillary staff. Almost any suggested change to the working practice or the evening shift would result in a complicated negotiation procedure in which management was not only at loggerheads with union officials but the officials were equally anxious to maintain or enhance whatever differential existed with their rival union prior to any change. The balance of power was summed up in a revealing and justly famous exchange. Once Roy Thomson, visiting the *Sunday Times*, got into a lift at Gray's Inn Road and introduced himself to a sun-tanned employee standing next to him. 'Hello, I'm Roy Thomson, I own this paper,' the proprietor good-naturedly announced. The *Sunday Times* NATSOPA machine room official replied, 'I'm Reg Brady and I run this paper.'[27] In 1978, the company's management discovered that this was true.

The print unions operating at Times Newspapers, as at other Fleet Street titles, were subdivided into chapels, individual bargaining units intent on maintaining their restrictive advantage. The union shop steward at the head of each chapel was known as the father. He, rather than anyone in middle management, had far more direct involvement in print workers' daily routines. The father was effectively their commanding officer in the field. The military metaphor was a pertinent one for, although the position of father was an ancient one, the Second World War had certainly helped to adapt a new generation to its requirements. Non-commissioned officers who, on returning to civvy street, were not taken into management positions often found the parallel chain of command in the chapel system to their liking.

At Times Newspapers there were fifty-four chapels in existence, almost any one of which was capable of calling a halt to the evening's print run. TNL management's attempt to enforce a system in which a disruption by one chapel would cause the loss of pay to all others consequently left idle had been quashed. And chapels often had equally scant regard for the diktats of their national union officials. When in 1976 the unions' national executives got together with Fleet Street's senior management to thrash out a 'Programme for Action' in which a change in work practices would be accepted so long as there were no compulsory redundancies, the chapels – accepting the latter but not the former – scuppered the deal.[28]

It was not only those paying the bills who despaired of this state of affairs. Many journalists, by no means right wing by political inclination, became resentful. Skilled Linotype operators earned salaries far in excess of some of the most seasoned and respected journalists upstairs. As Tim Austin, who worked at The Times continuously between 1968 and 2003 put it, 'We couldn't stand the print unions. They'd been screwing the paper for years. You didn't know if the paper was going to come out at night. You would work on it for ten hours and then they would pull the plug and you had wasted ten hours of your life.' The composing room was certainly not a forum of enlightened values. When Cathy James once popped her head round to check that a detail had been rendered correctly she was flatly told where a woman could go.[29]

Relations had not always been this bad. The Times had been printed for 170 years before it was silenced by industrial action, the month-long dispute of March to April 1955 ensuring a break in the paper's production (and thereby missing Churchill's resignation as Prime Minister) that even a direct hit on its offices from the Luftwaffe during the Blitz had failed to achieve. But the 1965 strike had affected all Fleet Street's national titles. *Times* print workers had not enjoyed a reputation for militancy until the summer of 1975 when the paper's historic Blackfriars site in Printing House Square was put up for sale and the paper, printers and journalists alike transferred to Gray's Inn Road as the next-door neighbours of Thomson's other major title, the *Sunday Times*. The decision to move had been taken as a cost-cutting measure – although the savings proved to be largely illusory. The consequence of bringing *Times* print workers into the orbit of those producing the *Sunday Times* was far more easily discernable. Even in the context of Fleet Street, *Sunday Times* printers had a reputation for truculence. Partly this was attributed to the fact that they were largely casuals who worked for other newspapers (or had different jobs like taxi driving) during the week and were not burdened by any sense of loyalty to the *Sunday Times*. Industrial muscle was flexed not merely through strike action but by a myriad minor acts designed to demonstrate whose hand was on the stop button. Paper jams occurred with a regularity that management found suspicious. Such jams could take forty minutes to sort out and result in the newspaper missing the trains upon which its provincial circulation depended. But from the print workers point of view, paper jams meant extra overtime pay. Newsagents began referring to the newspaper as the *Sunday Some Times*.[30]

More important than industrial action or sabotage was the effect the print union chapels had on blocking innovation. Muirhead Data Communications had developed a system of transmitting pages by facsimile for the *Guardian* back in 1953 but, because of union hostility, no national newspaper had dared use the technique until the *Financial Times* gritted its teeth and pressed ahead in 1979.[31] By then, *The Times* – in common with all other national newspapers – was still being set on Linotype machines (a technology that dated from 1889). Molten metal was dripped into the Linotype machine, a hefty piece of equipment that resembled a Heath Robinson contraption. As it passed through, the operator seated by it typed the text on an attached keyboard. Out the other end appeared a 'slug' of metal text which, once it had cooled, was fitted into a grid. It would then be copy checked for mistakes. If errors were spotted, a new 'slug' would be typed. Once the copy was finally approved, it would proceed to 'the stone'. There, it would be encased in a metal frame. This was the page layout stage, from which it was ready to be taken to the printing machines. It was an antiquated and occasionally dangerous (the hot metal could spatter the operator) method of producing a newspaper, not least because most of the rest of the world – including the Third World – had long since abandoned Linotype machines for computers. Thomson had purchased the computer equipment but had to store it unused in Gray's Inn Road pending union agreement to operate it. Using computer word processors to create the newspaper text for setting out was a far less skilled task than operating the old linotype machines. In 1980, journalists were still using typewriters. Their typed pages were then taken to the Linotype operator who would retype in hot metal. But with computerized input, journalists could type their own stories directly into the system, negating the need for NGA members to retype anything. This was part of the problem – it would make redundant most of the Linotype operators and, if followed up by other Fleet Street newspapers, would soon threaten the very existence of a skilled craft union like the NGA. Thus the union officials at TNL refused to allow the journalists to type into a computerized system unless their own union members typed the final version of it. In other words, if journalists and advertising staff typed up their text on their own computer screens, NGA members would have to type it up all over again on computer screens for their exclusive use. This was known as 'double-key stroking' and negated any real saving in introducing computer technology.

Management's attempt to break the NGA's monopoly on keying in text in favour of journalists having the powers of direct input was one of the causes of the shutdown of *The Times* for just short of a year between November 1978 and November 1979. Led into battle by TNL's chief executive, Marmaduke Hussey, management attempted to force the print unions to conclude new deals that would pave the way for the computer technology's introduction. When no comprehensive deal emerged, management shut down the papers in the hope of bringing the unions back to the negotiating table. As a strategy it proved a miserable failure. It cost Thomson £1 million a week to keep its printing machines idle and to have a nonexistent revenue from sales or advertising. The fear that *The Times*'s best journalists would be poached by rival newspapers ensured that all the journalists were kept on on full pay to do nothing. This was a clear signal to the print unions that there was no intention to shut down *The Times* permanently. Furthermore, they could also see that, buckling under the costs, the management were increasingly desperate to resume publication. By sitting it out, the printers could drive a harder bargain.

Management did attempt one daring breakout. It was often alleged that it would be cheaper to print the newspaper abroad and airfreight it into

Britain than print it under the restrictive practices of Fleet Street. What was certainly the case was that 36 per cent of advertising revenue in *The Times* came from overseas. So it was decided to print a Europe-only edition that would at least show that the paper was alive and could feasibly be produced elsewhere. A newspaper plant in Frankfurt agreed to undertake the task. This proved most illuminating. In Fleet Street, NGA compositors doing 'piece work' managed to type around 3500 characters an hour. They defended their high salaries by pointing to this level of expertise. But the German compositors in Frankfurt – women (all but barred by the Fleet Street compositors) working in a language that was not their own – managed 12,500 characters an hour (in their own language they could set 18,500).[32] Such statistics told their own story.

But if a point was proved by the exercise, it was the value of brute force. The British print unions persuaded their German brothers to picket the plant. With ugly scenes outside, the German police discussed tactics with Rees-Mogg who was at the Frankfurt site for the launch. They offered to use water cannon on the crowd in order to clear a path for the lorries to transport the first edition out of the plant but they could not guarantee subsequent nights if the situation deteriorated further. Meanwhile, inside the plant, various sabotage attempts were being detected, including petrol-soaked blankets that had been placed near the compressor – potentially capable of causing a massive explosion, which, as Hussey put it 'might have blown the whole plant and everyone in it sky high'.[33] Reluctantly, Rees-Mogg gave the order to abandon production. Once again, management's attempts to circumvent their unions had been humiliatingly defeated.

In November 1979, the TNL management formally climbed down and called off the shutdown. They had failed to secure direct input for journalists or to get the print workers to agree legally binding guarantees of continuous production. The only upside to this humiliation was that management was prevented from installing what would actually have been the wrong typesetting system (a disastrous discovery Hussey made late in the dispute when he visited the offices of *The Economist* and realized his mistake).[34] The shutdown meant that *The Times*, which had long claimed to be Britain's journal of record, had reported nothing for almost a year. Among the events it was unable to comment upon was Margaret Thatcher's coming to power. The total cost to Thomson exceeded £40 million. The unions' concession was that – already obsolete – computer typesetting would be introduced in stages but that NGA operatives would 'double-key stroke' all text.

That *The Times* returned at all after a stoppage of such duration was impressive. That it returned with circulation figures similar to those it had enjoyed before the shutdown was an extraordinary testament to the quality of the product and the extent to which its readers had mourned its absence. Indeed, such was the economics to which Fleet Street was reduced that the eleven-month shutdown left little enduring advantage to *The Times*'s competitors. *The Times*'s absence had increased their market opportunity. The *Daily Telegraph*, in particular, made gains. But gains involved pushing up production levels and this was only achieved at a cost that met the increase in sales revenue. When *The Times* returned, its rivals had to scale production down again but, thanks to union muscle, they were unable to cut back the escalating cost that had been forced upon them in the meantime.[35]

It might have been imagined that the journalists' frustration at the print workers would have bonded them more closely with management in ensuring that *The Times* saw off its tormentors, but the failed shutdown strategy made many of them equally critical of TNL executives.[36] Indeed, the success of the print workers in defending their corner emboldened some of the more militant *Times* journalists to see what would happen if they too pushed at a door that was not only ajar but loudly banging back and forth in the wind.

During the 1970s, salaries for *Times* journalists had lagged behind the spiralling inflationary settlements of the period. But during the shutdown, Thomson had kept faith with its Gray's Inn Road journalists by continuing to pay their full salaries during the eleven months they were not actually doing anything. Furthermore, they were given a 45 per cent pay increase in 1979 to make up for previous shortfalls.[37] Despite this, in August 1980 the journalists went on strike when TNL offered a further 18 per cent pay increase instead of the expected 21 per cent.

Of the 329 members of the paper's editorial staff, about 280 were members of the National Union of Journalists (NUJ). The union meeting at which the decision to strike was made took place when many were away and – although it represented a majority of those who turned up to the meeting – only eighty-three actually voted for industrial action. They were responding to the call of *The Times* NUJ's father of the chapel, Jake Ecclestone, who argued that it was a matter of principle: an independent arbitrator had suggested 21 per cent and in offering only 18 per cent TNL had refused to be bound by independent arbitration. That the NUJ chapel had also refused to be bound by it was glossed over.[38]

While the independent arbitrator had concentrated upon what he thought was the rate for the job, TNL had to deal with a law of the market: what they could reasonably afford. The difference between the two pay offers amounted to £350 a journalist but, if the knock-on effect of subsequent negotiations with the print workers was factored in, then TNL maintained the difference was £1.2 million. There was certainly collusion between print and journalist union officials in calling the strike. Although many journalists crossed the picket line, the NUJ had taken the precaution of getting the NGA to agree to go on strike too if management attempted to get the paper out.

Management had long come to accept that dealing with those who printed the paper was a war of attrition against a tenacious and well-organized opponent. But the attitude now displayed by some who actually wrote the paper was too much to endure in silence. The strike ended after a week but it destroyed the will of the existing management to persevere. When *The Times* returned on 30 August, its famous letters page was dominated by readers of long standing who had loyally waited for their paper's return during the eleven-month shutdown but who now felt utterly betrayed. 'It is impossible to believe in the sense, judgment or integrity of your journalists any longer' was one typically bitter accusation. Subscriptions were cancelled, sometimes in sadness but frequently in anger at the fact that 'you and your staff can have no feeling for your advertisers and readers. Other newspapers do not get into these situations. Your ineptitude beggars belief.'[39] But the most important lecture came not from disgusted of Tunbridge Wells but in the day's leader column, written by Rees-Mogg himself. 'How to Kill a Newspaper' ran the length of the page. It washed the paper's dirty linen in public and some staff disliked the idea that their editor was writing a leader chastising the actions of many of his own colleagues. Jake Ecclestone, 'gifted but difficult', was even named in the sermon that laid out before readers exactly the scale of journalists' pay increases over the previous two years and contrasted it with the extent of the newspaper's losses. Rees-Mogg pulled no punches, claiming that there could be no such thing as dual loyalty, for a journalist 'is either a *Times* man first or an NUJ man first . . . if the strikers do not give their priority in loyalty to *The Times* . . . why should they expect that the readers, or indeed the proprietor, of *The Times* should continue to be loyal to the paper?'[40]

This was very much to the point, for the Thomson board had been meeting to debate that very question. Although it was denied at the time, it was the NUJ strike that tipped the balance in convincing Thomson executives to dispose of *The Times* and, with it, the other TNL titles.[41] Sir Gordon Brunton had called senior colleagues to his beautiful country house near Godalming, Surrey, and it was there that the decision was taken. This was then ratified by the Thomson British Holdings board and, over the telephone, confirmed with Lord Thomson of Fleet. Preferring to live most of his time in Canada, Ken Thomson had taken over the family empire on the death of Roy, his father, in 1976. He felt little of his Anglophile father's obvious pride in owning *The Times*. In the end, the ultimate proprietor did not take much persuading although, naturally, in the press release he stated, 'it grieves me greatly'.[42] It was Harold Evans, editor of the *Sunday Times*, who put it succinctly: 'One can't blame Lord Thomson . . . the poor sucker has been pouring millions into the company and has been signing agreements which have been torn up in his face.'[43] Roy Thomson's dream of securing *The Times*'s future forever had ended after only fourteen years and at a cost of £70 million. The *Spectator*'s media pundit, the historian Paul Johnson, summed up the situation:

> *The Times* . . . is a *femme fatale*: it sent Northcliffe off his rocker, proved too expensive even for the Astors and wrecked Thomson's reputation for business acumen. It could well drag down Murdoch and his entire empire, financially much less solid than Thomson's, if he is fool enough to saddle himself with it.[44]

And yet, on New Year's Eve, the last day in which bids for the paper would be accepted, Times Newspapers received an offer from Rupert Murdoch. It was for a mere £1 million, but it was a declaration of intent.

III

In all, there were around fifty bids, although given the criteria Sir Gordon Brunton and Sir Denis Hamilton had drawn up, less than a handful were seriously considered. The Aga Khan and a plethora of Middle Eastern bidders were ruled out by the decision to ensure that a potential owner had to be either British or from the Commonwealth. At a stretch this would be widened to include suitable (North) Americans. Rejected on personal grounds were Robert Maxwell, Sir James Goldsmith and Tiny Rowland.[45]

In so far as any one man could determine who would buy *The Times*, that man was Sir Gordon Brunton. Lord Thomson fully trusted his chief executive with the task of disposing of his most famous possession. Born in the East End and influenced as a student by Harold Laski, his tutor at the LSE, as well as by his experiences of wartime command in the Royal Artillery and Indian Army in Assam and Burma, Brunton combined formidable business acumen, left-leaning political inclinations and a committed interest in the Turf. He had joined the Thomson Organisation in 1961 and within seven years had risen to become its managing director and chief executive. Given that TNL had ultimately proved to be the one major failing company in Thomson's British operations, it would have been understandable if Brunton had regarded its disposal as a matter of getting the best price in the fastest time with the minimum of fuss. But this was not at all how he saw his task. Rather, he threw his full weight behind finding a buyer who would ensure the survival of the famous newspaper, even if this meant declining a higher but separate bid for the *Sunday Times* on its own. By the 31 December deadline, Rees-Mogg's consortium had proffered a token £1 for *The Times*. Believing that the paper's viability was tied to staying within the TNL family, Brunton was fundamentally at odds with the *Times* consortium's assumption that the daily could have an independent future. Consequently, he was equally dismissive of the attempts of Harold Evans to form a separate consortium to buy the *Sunday Times*. Like Rees-Mogg with *The Times*, Evans had been trying to encourage a range of investors to take a share in the future ownership of the paper he edited. At one stage he had been hopeful that the *Guardian* would be the paper's saviour, although the *Guardian*'s board soon balked at the cost. But even if Evans had succeeded in attracting sufficient support, Brunton was having none of it, making his position clear in a telephone conversation in which Evans recalled the chief executive saying, 'Consortia cannot deal with unions. And I am not selling single titles. I will not see *The Times* shut down.'[46]

In the 1960s, *The Times*'s then owners, the Astor family, concerned by the paper's inability to make a profit, had also concluded that it could not stand on its own. They sought out the possibility of it merging with the *Guardian*. The *Guardian* enjoyed a higher circulation, but there were serious questions over whether the differences in political outlook (and the readership thereby attracted) could be harmonized successfully into one merged paper. When in 1966 the scheme fell through, *The Times* considered merging with the *Financial Times*. This would have created a newspaper of perhaps unsurpassable international authority with a readership profile tailored to suit a quality – and thus very lucrative – advertising market. *The Times* would have formed the main paper with the distinctive pink-papered *FT* inserted inside as its business section. Owned by Pearson, the *FT* was profitable and had established itself as the principal daily record of business and finance. But despite his protestations that owning *The Times* was about preserving the national interest rather than making a profit, Gavin Astor had considered Pearson's price for buying *The Times* inadequate to the point of insulting. Meanwhile, Roy Thomson, owner of the *Sunday Times*, offered over £3 million for *The Times*. Considering the Astor family had bought it for £1.5 million in 1922, this gave some indication of how poor an investment it had proved. But the Thomson bid was far better than that from the *Financial Times*.[47] Thus was given up one of the great opportunities to ensure *The Times*'s market sector pre-eminence so that it could successfully fund its own expansion. Instead, its future would depend upon subsidy from the wealth of its group owner.

In becoming the one hundred and eighty-third newspaper in the Thomson Organisation, *The Times* found itself in the same group as the *Sunday Times*. Despite the coincidence of the same word in the title, there was no shared ancestry between the two papers – both had always had different owners. Roy Thomson had bought the *Sunday Times* from its then owner, Lord Kemsley, in 1959. Only when Thomson purchased *The Times* in 1966 did the two papers find themselves, while still editorially independent from one another, sharing a common proprietor. Although his own experience was in guiding the *Sunday Times* to its extraordinary commercial success, Sir Denis Hamilton prided himself on his role in supporting Brunton's fusion of these two very different newspapers into one company, Times Newspapers Limited. In fact, it was always cohabitation rather than a marriage and the decision to live together at Gray's Inn Road, while not obviously affecting *The Times*'s editorial morality, was widely viewed as corrupting it in other respects. Courteous and high-minded, this was not how Sir Denis saw it and he desperately wanted to avoid seeing what he regarded as one of his life's achievements end in an acrimonious break-up. Thus he shared Sir Gordon Brunton's view that whoever bought the potentially profitable *Sunday Times* would have to be equally committed to shoring up the losses of *The Times*. On no account should their creation, TNL, be broken up. This dovetailed perfectly with Murdoch's plans since he did not think he could buy either paper separately. In the case of the *Sunday Times*, he thought the Monopolies Commission would block his purchase. In view of the daunting scale of its losses, he recalled, 'I would not have had the guts to buy *The Times* on its own.'[48] But if both were sold to him as a joint package, so these barriers were removed: the daily paper's losses could be cancelled out by the Sunday's revenue potential while the Government might permit him to own the Sunday paper if it meant that in doing so he could save the existence of the daily.

Having skimmed down the list, Brunton and Hamilton were left with what they considered were just two serious offers. One was from Rupert Murdoch, the other from Vere Harmsworth, third Viscount Rothermere. Besides its regional papers, Lord Rothermere's Associated Newspapers owned the *Daily Mail* and part-owned the London *Evening Standard*. His great-uncle, Lord Northcliffe, as well as founding the *Daily Mail*, had owned *The Times* between 1908 and 1922, saving it from bankruptcy. But future profit rather than family pietàs appeared to be Rothermere's motivation now. He offered Thomson £25 million for the *Sunday Times* but would knock £5 million off if the price of closing the deal meant that he had to buy *The Times* as well.[49] This was ominous. Rothermere later stated:

> I didn't want *The Times*. I wanted the *Sunday Times*. What we wanted to do was somehow shunt off *The Times* where it would survive as a parish newspaper of the elite. So it would remain that way at a minimum loss situation because none of us could see how it could ever be made commercially viable.[50]

That he should want the *Sunday Times* was hardly surprising. If its troubled industrial relations could be sorted out it would quickly return to great profitability. And buying it certainly seemed less risky than Associated's other plan – launching the *Mail on Sunday*. But the notion that *The Times* could survive as some sort of specialist interest publication with a tiny readership and minimal investment was, from a business perspective, without logic. Ultimately it would not even satisfy its core market: if it was starved of the money necessary to retain experts reporting from home and abroad, why would even an elite turn to it as a reliable source of information? When Brunton asked Rothermere if he could guarantee that he would not close down *The Times* if he bought it, Rothermere admitted he could make no such undertaking.[51]

Rothermere was a victim of his own honesty since, once the deal had gone through, he would have got his hands on the prize of the *Sunday*

Times and could have shut *The Times* down almost immediately, pausing only to transfer its better features and journalists to the Sunday title along the way. That he told the truth may well have been what saved *The Times* from the scrap heap. Brunton's insistence that he would not sell TNL to anyone who did not intend to invest in *The Times*'s future meant that there remained only one other press magnate on the Thomson chief executive's list. But could Rupert Murdoch's motives be trusted?

Murdoch had delayed asking for a prospectus until early December. But once he had decided to move he did so with speed. Two key players were brought in. One was his banker friend Lord Catto, chairman of Morgan Grenfell, who organized a meeting at his flat with Brunton to discuss the deal. Educated at Eton and Cambridge, Catto was the son of the Governor of the Bank of England during its 'nationalization' by the Attlee Government. He had been on the board of Murdoch's News International Ltd since 1969, having played a decisive part in securing Murdoch's first foothold in Fleet Street: ownership of the *News of the World* (by convincing its owners, the Carr family, that their paper would remain safe in their hands if the young Australian became a major shareholder). Catto now had to convince Brunton that *The Times* would be safe in the Murdoch grip. Murdoch's other lieutenant in the operation was his old boarding-school friend, Richard Searby. As boys they had been roommates together at Geelong Grammar School before following one another up to Oxford. A politically well-connected QC in Australia, Searby was sufficiently impressed by Murdoch's seriousness about purchasing *The Times* that, over the course of a telephone call, he offered his services and flew in to London in order to be in the closest position to offer legal advice on the deal.[52]

With Catto and Searby at his side, Murdoch's clear display of interest contrasted favourably with the more languid approach to negotiation displayed by Rothermere who, cocooned in his Parisian tax haven, left most of the negotiating to Associated Newspapers' managing director, Mick Shields. But the crucial difference was that Murdoch stated categorically that he was bidding for all of TNL and fully intended to keep *The Times* as a going concern. He told Harold Evans that Rees-Mogg was mistaken if he had come away from his meeting at the *New York Post* with the impression that Murdoch's interest was in the *Sunday Times* alone.[53] Importantly, Murdoch had Sir Denis Hamilton's support. On 9 January 1981 Hamilton wrote a memo to Brunton giving his views, and those of the national directors of Times Newspapers, that Murdoch was their preferred choice. It was true he had had a 'deteriorating effect' on tabloid standards but this had to be balanced by the fact that he had created a quality broadsheet in *The Australian*. If binding guarantees could be secured regarding editorial independence and quality, then there were no objections to his purchasing Times Newspapers. Hamilton and the directors were much less enthusiastic about Rothermere's bid, suspecting that 'property potential is greater motiv-ation than the development of these papers'. Furthermore, the 'strong and consistent bias towards the Conservative Party' displayed in Rothermere's newspapers was 'incompatible with the independent role of *The Times*'.[54] This contrasted with Murdoch who was 'neither greatly to the left or greatly to the right'.[55] In this last respect, opponents of the political orientation of Murdoch's newspapers in the 1980s might be forgiven for delivering a mirthless laugh.

Initially Harold Evans at the *Sunday Times* had been taken aback by the speed with which Hamilton had come round to seeing Murdoch as a saviour.[56] Yet, while continuing to press the claims of his own *Sunday Times* consortium, Evans wrote to Brunton on 20 January passing on the views of *Sunday Times* staff: 'between Murdoch and Rothermere, it is Murdoch who is preferred by a wide margin'. Subject to the appropriate safeguards, Evans also conceded, 'I myself would choose Murdoch'.[57]

Brunton's task was to keep Murdoch interested without giving him the impression he was the only horse in the race. This was not just because the hint of competition would encourage Murdoch to raise his offer price. Closing down *The Times* would cost its owner £35 million in redundancy payouts. Thomson would have to foot this bill if the paper's ownership was not transferred before the 15 March deadline. If Murdoch believed none of his rivals could secure a deal before that date, he could sit it out and wait for *The Times* to fold, allowing Thomson to pay the costs. After a seemly pause, there was nothing to stop Murdoch then starting a new paper called *The Times* (after all, in Fleet Street's history there had been a number of newspapers of varying longevity called the *Sun*). For this 'new' *Times* he could hire whoever he liked on whatever terms (subject to employment law) fitted in with his own business strategy, including possible adoption of the Rees-Mogg plan of freeing himself from Fleet Street's costs and militancy by printing from a provincial location.

In fact, there was nothing in Murdoch's negotiating stance that suggested this ethically doubtful option formed any part of his strategy. Indeed, the more Hamilton and the Times Newspapers directors contemplated the 'ruthless operator' the more they believed he had 'a personality which probably could relate to *The Times*'.[58] Rees-Mogg was now firmly of the view that Murdoch, rather than his own consortium, was the newspaper's saviour-in-waiting. All that remained was for an appropriate price to be agreed together with his assent to a number of safeguards that would stop him interfering in the paper's editorial content in the way in which he was known to do with the *Sun*.

The negotiations came to a head on 21 January at the elegant Thomson headquarters in Stratford Place, off Oxford Street. The Thomson team refused Murdoch's demand that they should give a written guarantee that the company's assets were worth £17.9 million and that the current losses would be no greater than £14.5 million. There was, Brunton later admitted, 'some blood on the walls'. Murdoch then went downstairs to face the vetting committee that had been drawn up to assess his personal suitability. 'These dignified gentlemen probably thought I was quaking with fear,' he recalled; 'actually I was shaking with anger'.[59] Despite this, he made a favourable impression. The vetting committee consisted of Sir Denis Hamilton together with the two editors, Rees-Mogg and Harold Evans, and the national directors, Lords Roll, Dacre, Greene and Astor (Lord Robens, who was in America, kept in touch by telephone). Murdoch made several assurances: that he would abide by the editorial safeguards drawn up and would not seek to direct editors, even when they pursued views contrary to those expressed in his other titles; that he hoped Harold Evans would continue to edit the *Sunday Times*; that he did not have the resources of Lord Thomson at his disposal. He said that he saw the role of the independent national directors as that of a court of appeal for an editor who felt himself in conflict with his proprietor. Murdoch guaranteed to increase the number of independent directors sitting on the board of Times Newspapers Holdings Ltd. This board alone would have the power to appoint or remove an editor, voting by majority decision. It would also take a majority vote of the directors to approve any subsequent sale of *The Times* or *Sunday Times*.[60]

Harold Evans took great care to ensure the wording of the guarantees. Rees-Mogg took a less legalistic view, believing that, once ensconced, the power of a proprietor was such that little could realistically be done to bind him to guarantees he had chosen, for whatever reason, to disobey. Rees-Mogg maintained, 'I thought therefore a judgment of character had to be made', and in his opinion Murdoch 'would in fact honour the agreements'. Thus the precise wording was not really crucial.[61] The *Spectator*'s press columnist later took a yet more robust view, maintaining that *The Times* would never have seen the light of day if John Walter, the ex-bankrupt who founded it in 1785 with the intention of making money for himself, had been subjected to the proprietorial guarantees forced upon Murdoch.[62] In fact, the Australian was in some respects treated with less condescension than had been Roy Thomson. When he had bought *The Times* in 1966 he had to agree not only to abstain from editorial interference (which was, in any case, never his style) but also that he would not even sit on the newspaper's board (from where, with *de haut en bas* condescension and despite having sold the business, Gavin Astor managed to ensure his appointments continued to exercise a guardian role). Murdoch fully intended to sit on the board of his own company into which he would be pouring money.

The vetting committee voted unanimously in favour of Murdoch. The deal was eventually done after the midnight hour had struck. Subject to securing agreement for job cuts with the unions and that the Government would not refer the purchase to the Monopolies and Mergers Commission, *The Times* and the other TNL titles would become the property of News International. The press releases went out on 22 January. Brunton expressed the hope that the unions would agree with him that Murdoch represented the best hope of keeping TNL together. Murdoch sought to concentrate on the guarantees he had given with regard to independent national directors, to his faith in Harold Evans as 'one of the world's great editors' and to his own intentions:

I am not seeking to acquire these papers in order to change them into something entirely different. I have operated and launched newspapers all over the world. This new undertaking I regard as the most exciting challenge of my life.[63]

The first major newspaper to carry the news was Rothermere's London *Evening Standard*. The banner headline roared out 'MURDOCH BUYS THE THUNDERER'.[64]

Thomson's asking price for Times Newspapers was £55 million. Murdoch's final offer of £12 million was £8 million less than the bid Rothermere had made and £13 million less than Rothermere had proffered for the *Sunday Times* alone. That Brunton nonetheless favoured Murdoch's bid was proof that Thomson was philanthropically more interested in the long-term future of *The Times* than in making money from its sale.

What remained to be seen was whether Murdoch was equally high-minded. True, TNL was making a loss, but such losses could be set against the tax payable on the profits of News International's other press division,

News Group Newspapers (the *Sun* and the *News of the World*). NGN had recorded a £20.3 million pre-tax profit in the second half of 1980. In return for the £12 million Murdoch had paid for TNL, he had gained the freehold of the *Sunday Times* building on Gray's Inn Road (said to be worth at least £8 million) together with other assets such as vehicles and machinery that were roughly computed to be worth nearly £18 million. Of the £12 million paid to Thomson, £8 million was for the Gray's Inn Road property and only £4 million for the shares in Times Newspapers. By keeping the property assets of TNL separate from the publishing subsidiary, News International could shut down the papers with minimal redundancy payouts to the employees and yet liquidate the property assets separately.[65] Brunton believed Murdoch was a man of his word. If he was not, Thomson had sold out to someone who could make a quick profit as an asset stripper.

IV

Murdoch's purchase of Times Newspapers was conditional. If he could not negotiate sufficient job cuts with the unions before 15 March the deal would be off. In this eventuality, the Thomson board would find themselves scrapping around at the last minute for an alternative purchaser in whatever days remained before the official shut-down of the company. In that eventuality it would be a buyer's market and the papers might have to be sold to a proprietor who fell short of Brunton's ideals (although he remained adamant that he would rather see *The Times* put to sleep than handed into the bear hug of Robert Maxwell).[66] There was also a second hurdle. Newspaper takeovers were subject to referral to the Monopolies and Mergers Commission. Purchasing TNL gave News International more than a quarter of the market share in dailies. The Government might block the purchase on these grounds alone. At any rate, there was no prospect of the Monopolies Commission issuing its report before the 15 March deadline for transferral of ownership.

On 19 January, the *Times*'s NUJ chapel had carried overwhelmingly (there was only one vote in opposition and four abstentions) a motion stating that 'any further concentration of ownership of national newspapers in Britain would be against the public interest' and that a potential purchaser should be referred to the Monopolies Commission.[67] Since the newspaper's purchase by either of the major bidders could not do other than concentrated ownership, the union activists appeared to be endangering any future for their paper unless it was from a consortium like that proposed by Rees-Mogg (who was, in any case, now in the pro-Murdoch camp). This stance fortified efforts to block Murdoch's purchase in the House of Commons. The Labour MP Phillip Whitehead was attracting names for an Early Day Motion as opposition, particularly although not exclusively on the left, mounted to the deal.

On the first Saturday after he had made his provisional agreement with Thomson and the TNL directors, Murdoch was shown around the *Sunday Times*'s composing room. Stopping to look at the proof of the paper's leader article on the sale, he spotted a factual omission (the *Daily Star* had not been added to the list of titles owned by Express Newspapers). Instinctively, Murdoch reached for his pen and marked on the proof where the words 'Daily Star' should be inserted. This was his first error. Word soon got around that the proprietor designate had already broken his guarantees and was interfering in the editorial policy of the *Sunday Times*. Had he not had the gall to change a leader article in the full view of the composing room? Evans sent him a note of rebuke. Murdoch quickly apologized, but the incident was a gift to his detractors.

Given the attitude expressed by the NUJ chapel, reassuring the journalists was an immediate priority. With Rees-Mogg standing supportively at his side, Murdoch addressed the editorial staff of *The Times* on 26 January. He had 'great respect' for the paper and reaffirmed his intention not to alter its essential character. There would be more of interest for women with extra sections to make it 'of greater value and appeal at home rather than being taken off to work by commuters' but there would be no sudden attempt to become a mass-market paper. Murdoch repeated that he would stand by his editorial guarantees and that while he would 'complain if the facts are wrong' he had 'no intention of interfering with any opinions in the paper'. He believed that any attempt by him to tear up the guarantees would create 'a terrible public stink' that 'would destroy the paper'. On the paper's financial future he was resolute. It was 'unhealthy' for it to be dependent on a proprietor. Profitability was the best guarantor of independence. But it was the 'biggest challenge in the world' to make *The Times* viable and it would take at least three to four years for it to make a profit. It would not move to his currently idle print works at Wapping. He thought the *Guardian* and *Daily Telegraph* were equal rivals. He apologized for previously calling *The Times* a 'dead duck'. He had meant to say 'sick duck'.[68]

Although the union activists in the paper's NUJ chapel remained sceptical or hostile, opinion was sharply divided and immediately after Murdoch had made his address to them, one hundred journalists on the paper quickly signed a statement supporting his purchase. On the same day, Jake Ecclestone passed on the view of the NUJ meeting to John Biffen, the Secretary of State for Trade and Industry, demanding a referral to the Monopolies Commission.[69]

Looked at at face value, the case for referring the Murdoch bid to the Monopolies Commission was overwhelming. In 1966 Harold Wilson's Government had referred Roy Thomson's purchase of *The Times* even although it would give him control of a mere 6.5 per cent of the national and provincial dailies' circulation. In 1981, *The Times* had only 1.9 per cent of the market share in national daily newspapers but the *Sun* enjoyed a 25.3 per cent share. Together this meant that News International's papers would account for 27.2 per cent. Concentration was yet higher in the Sundays market where the 7.7 per cent share of the *Sunday Times,* when added to that of the *News of the World,* gave News International a 31 per cent share.[70]

On the other hand, such was the relative smallness of their sale, the addition of the *Times* titles made only marginal difference to News International's total market share, especially in the dailies market. In any case, adding the *Sun*'s circulation to *The Times* produced a figure of limited practical meaning since the proportion of readers who regularly bought both a daily tabloid and a broadsheet was tiny. But even if the sales were all added together and treated as one, the company would still not be the market leader. Adding the sales of *The Times* gave News International 4,120,493 daily sales. The Mirror Group had 4,380,000 sales a day. London would still have less of a monopoly newspaper structure than existed in New York, Paris, Bonn or Frankfurt.[71]

Whatever the spin put on the statistics, the 1973 Fair Trade Act stipulated that all major newspaper takeovers should be referred to the Monopolies Commission. But the Secretary of State could overrule this stipulation if the paper concerned was unprofitable and in danger of closing down without a quick transferral of ownership. This section, 58(3) of the Act, was the Thomson–Murdoch 'get out of jail' card and one they were determined to play.

Thomson's submission to the Secretary of State, John Biffen, left little room for ambiguity. On no account would the seller extend the deadline in order to facilitate the Monopolies Commission to undertake its report (which was expected to take a minimum of eight weeks to compile). The proposed agreement with Murdoch rested on consent from the Department of Trade and Industry (DTI) being granted by 12 February otherwise the deal was off. A new potential proprietor would then have to be approached in the time remaining. This would not be easy since 'there is little likelihood that a suitable alternative buyer for TNL as a whole will be identified. There are no signs that any other potential buyer for TNL as a whole has as strong a commitment as NIL [News International Limited] to preserving *The Times* on a long-term basis.' Indeed, if a new serious bidder came forward he would probably be another owner of a media empire, necessitating a fresh Monopolies Commission report to be put in motion and causing yet further delay. The process could last for months with each serious bidder eventually being ruled out in turn until someone sufficiently minor could be found to take on the paper's elephantine problems. Rather than continue losing money while this merry-go-round proceeded at its own leisurely pace, Thomson were not prepared to relent on their decision to close down *The Times* and its sisters, with or without a sale, by 15 March.[72] In other words, the Government could agree to the sale and secure the papers future, or it could demand a referral and risk their destruction.

On 26 January, John Biffen was deluged with visitors. Having only just returned from a trip to India, he was heavily dependent upon the briefing provided by his departmental officials who had spent the last few days working on the legal technicalities of whether the TNL sale necessitated a referral. Sally Oppenheim, his junior minister at the DTI, came over to discuss the matter. Their first visitor was Sir Gordon Brunton. Biffen and Oppenheim insisted that he postpone the sale deadline so that the Monopolies Commission could intervene. Brunton refused point-blank.[73] The next visitor was Rupert Murdoch. He made clear that he would pull out of the deal if it was referred to the Commission. If some thought this a bluff, they were wrong. Murdoch would have pulled out if the deal had been referred.[74] Then came Jake Eccelestone (with Eric Jacobs, his *Sunday Times* counterpart) to put the NUJ case for referral. Finally, Sir Denis Hamilton called, assuring Biffen that Murdoch was the papers' only hope and that he had made guarantees on editorial freedom that no other Fleet Street proprietor had been prepared to make.

This was not the only influence brought to bear. In 1981, Margaret Thatcher and Rupert Murdoch scarcely knew one another and had no communication whatsoever during the period in which *The Times* bid and referral was up for discussion.[75] But, in Woodrow Wyatt, Murdoch and the Prime Minister had a mutual friend. This clearly being the moment to make the most of such a contact, Murdoch got Wyatt to plead his case directly with her.[76] Subsequently, Murdoch assumed that Biffen was 'probably told what to do by Margaret.'[77] In fact the part played by Margaret Thatcher in the decision not to refer the bid was at best a subtle one. Critics of Thatcher and Murdoch have long maintained that there must have been some – even if tacit – understanding in which she used her weight to ensure that he could bypass the Monopolies Commission and buy *The Times* and in return he ensured his newspapers henceforth banged the Thatcherite drum. There is a problem with this theory. Although John Biffen assumed the Prime Minister wanted the bid to go through, he could recall no occasion when she pressed him on the matter. What was more, when 'E' Committee – the Cabinet committee delegated with the task of determining whether to make the referral – convened on 26 January the most outspoken voice in favour of permitting Murdoch's purchase was the decidedly un-Thatcherite Jim Prior. Prior, who was Employment Secretary, wanted the deal to go ahead not least because the unions wanted Murdoch.[78]

Whether adding 1.9 per cent to News International's market share of daily sales constituted a threat to the free working of a competitive market was no longer the issue bothering 'E' Committee. But there certainly remained a presentational problem if the bid was not referred. Lawyers spent the evening working out how the safeguards Murdoch had made to the TNL vetting committee could be legally incorporated into the conditions giving consent for the transfer of ownership to go ahead. The somewhat arbitrary commitment to editorial quality could not be phrased into a legal obligation, but in other respects the guarantees would be made legally binding. Although a fine was more likely, Murdoch would risk a spell in jail if he flouted them.[79]

Biffen was due to give his statement to the Commons on 27 January. By then ninety-two MPs had signed the Early Day Motion demanding a referral to the Monopolies Commission and the Speaker of the House of Commons permitted the Opposition a three-hour emergency debate on the matter.

As Shadow Secretary of State, Labour's John Smith opened the case for referring the sale of what he called '*The Times*, perhaps our most prestigious newspaper'. It was, he believed, 'one of the largest and perhaps the most significant mergers in the history of journalism in the United Kingdom'. He questioned the *Sunday Times*'s supposed unprofitability and cast doubts on the ability of national directors – of whom 'there was a faint air of the Athenaeum' – to keep Murdoch true to his promises. Biffen then made his statement. He conceded the law stipulated that any transferral of a national newspaper must be subject to the scrutiny of the Monopolies Commission but mentioned the let-out clause if, because of the paper's unprofitability, doing so would endanger the paper's life. This was such a case. He had asked Thomson to extend their deadline so that the Monopolies Commission could look into the sale. They had refused. He was not prepared to risk the closure of *The Times* and over four thousand redundancies at TNL by demanding a referral.

Cries of 'disgraceful' resounded around the Commons chamber. Jo Grimond, the former leader of the Liberal Party (and a trustee of the *Guardian*), was outraged: 'Parliament could not have legislation made a nonsense of because people laid down a timetable.' Not content with describing it as 'blackmail' and 'an insult to the nation' the Labour MP (and sometime business associate of Robert Maxwell) Geoffrey Robinson described it as 'a pay-off' for the *Sun* supporting the Conservatives in the general election.[80] But the most penetrating speech in opposition came from the Conservative benches. Jonathan Aitken was Beaverbrook's great-nephew. He was concerned about the method with which the Government had approved the bid but, privately, he also feared that Murdoch was looking for fresh springboards to promote his anti-Establishment and republican views.[81] It was clear Aitken had done his homework when he quoted from an interview Murdoch had given to an American magazine, *More*, in 1977. Murdoch had been quoted as saying it was 'quite correct and proper' that the Monopolies Commission would prevent him from acquiring another 'successful' British daily. 'Successful' was, of course, the key clause, but Aitken had more to add. The guarantees were worthless. Murdoch had 'strewn assurances and safeguards on newspaper and television ownership like confetti' both to the Carr family and in Australia. There were plenty of credible owners for *The Times* – the Rees-Mogg consortium, Lonhro, Associated Newspapers, Atlantic Richfield – which the Thomson board had chosen to ignore because their deal with Murdoch was 'pre-arranged'. Aitken even cast vague doubts upon one of the TNL directors on the vetting committee, who was also chairman of Warburgs (Thomson's merchant bankers), asking 'What is the role of Lord Roll? [laughter on both sides of the House] Is he banker of fees or the bulwark of liberty?' His conclusions were sweeping:

This is a sad day for Fleet Street, which is to see the greatest concentration of newspaper monopoly in its history. It is a sad day for the

Conservative Party, which appeared this afternoon to have abandoned its traditional role of the opponent of large monopolies whenever possible.[82]

Aitken was one of five Conservative MPs (the others were Peter Bottomley, Hugh Fraser, Barry Porter and Delwyn Williams) who defied a three-line whip and voted with the Opposition. It was in vain, and the Commons divided 281 to 239 against referring the sale. Murdoch had won a major battle. Securing the job cuts with the unions remained the only hurdle before Times Newspapers would be in his hands.

But while he had won the vote, not everyone was convinced his case had won the argument. Although he would soon accept Murdoch's shilling, Harold Evans wrote Aitken a letter congratulating him on his speech.[83] There was a widespread belief that it had all been a stitch-up. Aitken had alleged that Thomson had suspiciously ignored several serious bids because it had already decided upon Murdoch. But were the names Aitken reeled off superior bidders? Rees-Mogg himself thought Murdoch a better option than his own consortium. Atlantic Richfield was about to move out of British newspaper ownership. Associated Newspapers could not guarantee *The Times*'s future. The idea that the editorial independence of the paper would be in safer hands with Lonhro's Tiny Rowland was, as the *Observer* would later discover, highly contestable. If Brunton had pre-judged Murdoch's suitability over these alternatives, might it not have been on the basis of an honest assessment of who offered the best future – perhaps the only future – for *The Times*? And if Lord Roll was a 'banker of fees' would he not have urged acceptance of the far higher bid from Rothermere's Associated Newspapers?

The controversy was kept alive when, only a month after Biffen had made his statement in the Commons, the American oil company Atlantic Richfield sold the troubled *Observer* to Outrams, a subsidiary of Tiny Rowland's Lonhro Group. Given that the *Glasgow Herald* was the closest Outrams/Lonhro could claim to owning a national newspaper, Biffen's decision to refer the bid to the Monopolies Commission appeared perverse. Memorably dubbed by Edward Heath the 'unacceptable face of capitalism', Rowland had made himself objectionable to conservatives, socialists and liberals in equal measure and could find fewer defenders than Murdoch. The manner in which the *Observer* had been sold to him created unease, for the first that any of the editor-in-chief, the editor or the board of directors knew of it was after the deal had been done. There was also a more clearly defined question of public interest, in particular whether there was a conflict between the *Observer*'s extensive coverage of African affairs and Rowland's business interests there. The Monopolies Commission could find no evidence to assume that it would and permitted the deal to go ahead subject to the installation of independent directors on a model similar to that adopted at Times Newspapers.[84] The experience was not to prove a happy one. But in February 1981 there remained many who could not see the consistency in the Government's handling of newspaper takeovers.

Whatever the political symmetry between the Thatcher Government and Rupert Murdoch, the decision not to refer the TNL purchase was only legally possible on the grounds of the papers' unprofitability. The Thomson submission to Biffen had claimed, 'neither *The Times* nor the *Sunday Times* are economical as going concerns and as separate newspapers under current circumstances'.[85] That *The Times* was in dire straits was not in doubt. But could that really be said of the *Sunday Times*, whose problems were hoped to be but temporary?

The TNL statistics sent out by Warburgs to prospective buyers had shown that the *Sunday Times* had actually scraped into the black in 1980 and by 1983 would be making projected profits of £13 million. John Smith immediately challenged Biffen on these figures since they appeared at odds with the statement he had given to the Commons. Biffen had to concede that he had based the paper's loss on an estimate of the first nine months of 1980 and not, as MPs had been led to assume, the first eleven.[86] Harold Evans was not alone in resenting the way in which those seeking to avoid a referral had treated his paper. He found that many of his journalists 'objected to being swept into what they saw as a large, alien publishing group on the sole grounds that it was necessary to save *The Times*'.[87] This now became a problem. The NUJ chapel of the *Sunday Times* decided to challenge Biffen's non-referral in court. The action could cost £60,000 – a sum that was far beyond the chapel's reach. Negotiations were opened with Rothermere's Associated Newspapers to see if they would underwrite the expense. The intermediary was Jonathan Aitken. But Associated were hesitant and, with only thirty-six hours to go before the court hearing, the chapel called off the action following Murdoch's promise that two working journalists would be appointed to the TNL Holdings board.[88]

Murdoch could now turn his attention to jumping the final hurdle: agreement with the unions. Historically, he had not been one of the unions' principal bogeymen. In 1969, they had emphatically preferred his bid for the *Sun* to that of Robert Maxwell who promised under his ownership a paper that 'shall give clear and loyal support at all times to the Labour movement' but who wanted to cut the number employed printing the paper.[89] Compared to Rothermere who might close *The Times*, or the Rees-Mogg consortium that wanted to move printing to the provinces, Murdoch seemed the best bet for keeping jobs at Gray's Inn Road. Because of this, Bill Keys (SOGAT), Joe Wade (NGA) and Owen O'Brien (NATSOPA) had written on the day after Thomson had accepted Murdoch's provisional bid to Michael Foot, Labour's Deputy Leader, urging him not to press for a referral to the Monopolies Commission.[90] The appeal fell upon deaf ears, but it was a positive sign of how they regarded Murdoch.

News International and the unions had until 12 February to agree a deal. A 30 per cent cut in the four thousand jobs at TNL was demanded. If enough voluntary redundancies could not be agreed, compulsory ones would make up the shortfall. There would also have to be a wage freeze until October 1982. Murdoch put two of his most doughty negotiators in charge of the talks. One was John Collier. Collier had been a NATSOPA official, working for the *Guardian* back in the days when it still retained *Manchester* in its title. He had joined Murdoch's News Group Newspapers following its purchase of the *Sun*, becoming general manager in 1974. He knew how Fleet Street negotiations worked. In contrast, his accomplice had not even set foot in Britain before. But Murdoch had every confidence in the ex-secretary of the Sydney Ten-pin Bowling Association, Bill O'Neill. He had started as a fifteen-year-old apprentice in the composing room of the Sydney *Daily Mirror*. Like Collier, he had been active in the print union although disgust at the outlook of its pro-Communist officials led him to seek out union responsibilities that were less overtly political. He was still at the Sydney *Mirror* when its owners, Fairfax, sold it to Murdoch. The new proprietor promptly set about reinvigorating the run-down title in a manner similar to his later strategy at the *Sun*. By the mid-seventies, O'Neill had switched to the management side. When, in early 1981, Murdoch asked him what he thought of the intention to buy *The Times*, O'Neill mumbled something about barge poles. Murdoch shot back, 'it's obvious you've been talking to the wrong people', and told him that he should expect to be in London for only as long as it took to finalize the deal with the unions there – which he estimated at two weeks. This was one of Murdoch's less accurate predictions.[91]

In truth, the scope for trimming departments stretched far beyond what was discussed. When a thirty-year old Iowan named Bill Bryson arrived as a subeditor on *The Times*'s company news desk in the dying days of the Thomson ownership he was astonished by the work culture he encountered. His colleagues wandered in to the office at about 2.30 in the afternoon, proceeded to take a tea break until 5.30 p.m. after which they would 'engage in a little light subbing for an hour or so' before calling it a day. On top of this, they got six weeks' holiday, three weeks' paternity leave and a month's sabbatical every four years. Bryson was equally taken aback by the inventive approach to filing expense claims and the casual attitude of the reporters in his section, many of whom stumbled back to the office after a lengthy liquid lunch to make 'whispered phone calls to their brokers'. 'What a wonderful world Fleet Street then was,' Bryson concluded twelve years later when he wrote the episode up with only mild exaggerations for comic effect in his best-selling book on his adopted Britain, *Notes from a Small Island*, adding wistfully, 'nothing that good can ever last'. Suddenly, Murdoch's men – 'mysterious tanned Australians in white short-sleeved shirts' – began roaming around the building armed with clipboards and looking as if 'they were measuring people for coffins'. Soon company news got subsumed into the business news department and Bryson found himself working nights and 'something more closely approximating eight-hour days'.[92]

Despite the extent of the options for where cuts could be made, Collier and O'Neill were faced with a massive task to reach agreement with all fifty-four separate chapels in the twenty-one days between Murdoch's deal being agreed in principle with Thomson and the 12 February deadline. Invariably brinkmanship played its part but on the final day a compromise was reached. The TNL payroll was cut by 563 job losses, a reduction of around 20 per cent. This was achieved by voluntary redundancy at a cost of around £6 million to News International. It was telling that removing a fifth of the workforce did not appreciably lower the quality of the product. Importantly, agreement was reached to print the supplements (the *Times Literary*, *Times Educational* and *Times Higher Education*) outside London. This probably saved the life of the loss-making *TLS*. But the proposed wage freeze would only last for three months, there were no compulsory redundancies and no movement from the unions towards allowing journalists direct input. 'Double-key stroking' would remain. Harold Evans later concluded that the negotiations were 'an opportunity forgone': of the 130 jobs cut from the 800-strong NATSOPA clerical chapel, 110 were actually unfilled vacancies (in itself an extraordinary statistic at a time of soaring unemployment) and the most militant union fathers kept their jobs. But the truth of the matter was that there was little prospect of the newspapers being printed had News International tried to sack the unions' spokesmen. At about this time, Len Murray, the general secretary of the TUC, confided to Murdoch his long-held belief that the Fleet Street proprietors had got the trade unions they deserved. With just a hint of menace, Murdoch replied, 'well, now perhaps the unions have got the proprietor they deserve'. He appeared to mean it. Asked how he would respond to any new bout of industrial action at Gray's Inn Road, Murdoch told the press, 'I will close the place down'.[93] It was an unequivocal response from the man who was being interviewed because he had just officially become *The Times*'s owner.

V

Richard Searby believed Rupert Murdoch's desire to own *The Times* was deep-seated and stretched back to the splendid engraved inkwell that the paper's owner, Lord Northcliffe, had presented to his father.[94] At Geelong Grammar, a boarding school labouring under the tag 'the Eton of Australia', the boys mocked the young Rupert with his father's nickname, 'Lord Southcliffe'. In fact it was his first name, Keith, that Rupert shared with his father.

The friendship between Northcliffe and Keith Murdoch had been forged during the First World War. In 1915 while employed by one of the news agencies, Keith Murdoch had been sent out to cover the Dardanelles campaign where Australian and New Zealand (Anzac) soldiers were suffering heavy casualties. He quickly surmised that the senior command was incompetent and that heroic Anzac troops were being let down by their British counterparts. In fact, he was not on the front line and much of his information came from a dissatisfied reporter from the London *Daily Telegraph*. But if his sources were weak his readership was focused. His report landed on the desk of the Australian Prime Minister and, on reaching London, Keith Murdoch went to *The Times* with his account. Northcliffe, the paper's editorially interfering proprietor, read it and told the driven Australian journalist to pass it to the Prime Minister. Asquith promptly circulated it to his Cabinet.

The commanding officer, General Sir Ian Hamilton, blamed his subsequent removal on Murdoch's coloured account. The Anzacs' withdrawal from the campaign also came to be seen as stemming from what had been written. Keith Murdoch's version would eventually be summarized by his admiring son: 'it may not have been fair, but it changed history'.[95] In the year the son bought *The Times*, he co-financed a film, *Gallipoli*, starring Mel Gibson, in which effete British commanders casually sacrificed the lives of courageous anti-Establishment Australians. Given a choice between truth and legend, the son continued to promote the legend.

From the moment of Keith Murdoch's Dardanelles scoop, he had the attention and support of Lord Northcliffe. The owner of *The Times* became a mentor for the motivated Australian, inspiring him and including him in his influential social circle. And Murdoch learned a good deal from the man who had done so much to create the mass-appeal 'new journalism', launching new titles and rejuvenating old ones like *The Times*. When Murdoch struck out on his own, taking up the editorship of Australia's Melbourne *Herald*, Northcliffe even went over there to sing his praises. The *Herald*'s directors soon had cause to join in: circulation rose dramatically and its editor joined its management board, buying other papers and a new medium of enormous potential – a radio station. Growth would be fuelled by acquisition, creating a business empire in a country in which the print media was entirely localized. It was also a route to making enemies who believed Keith (from 1933, Sir Keith) Murdoch's expansionist strategy not only gave the Herald and Weekly Times Group too much financial clout but also made its managing director a kingmaker in Australian politics as well. The Herald Group's competitors were especially dismayed when with the outbreak of the Second World War he was appointed Australia's director-general of information. The role of state censor was certainly not in keeping with the role he had played in the previous conflict. But when, in 1941, ten-year-old Keith Rupert Murdoch arrived at boarding school, it was to discover to his surprise that it was his father's crusade to bolster the power of the press that was often looked at with mistrust and apprehension.

Though he showed little interest in Geelong's emphasis on team sports, Rupert Murdoch's childhood had been predominately spent outdoors with his three sisters riding and snaring (Rupert persuaded his sisters to skin the unfortunate rodents for a modest fee while he sold on the pelts at a larger mark-up). Home was his parents' ninety-acre estate, Cruden Farm, thirty miles south of Melbourne. The house itself was extended over the years and by the time Rupert was growing up there it resembled the sort of colonnaded colonial residence more generally associated with Virginian old money. But rather than be overexposed to its creature comforts, Rupert spent his evenings between the ages of eight and sixteen in a hut in the grounds. His mother thought it would be good for him.[96]

Cruden was named after the small Aberdeenshire fishing village from which Rupert Murdoch's grandfather, the Revd Patrick Murdoch, had lived and preached. A Minister in the principled and unyielding Calvinism of the Free Church of Scotland, the Revd Murdoch had in 1884 transferred his mission to the fast-expanding metropolis of Melbourne. Widely admired, by 1905 he had risen to the church's highest position in the country – moderator of the General Assembly of Australia. The grandfather on his mother's side provided young Rupert with a contrasting influence: Rupert Greene was an affable half-Irish, free-spirited gambling man. Not surprisingly, commentators came to see Rupert Murdoch as, in some ways, a composite of the two.

In 1950 Murdoch went up to Oxford University. For the most part he enjoyed student life there and later became a generous benefactor of his college, Worcester. But at the time, and despite the efforts of such eminent tutors as Asa Briggs, it was not his Philosophy, Politics and Economics degree course that held his attention. At the Geelong school debating society, he had espoused radical and frequently socialist views. He maintained this stance at Oxford, often attending Union debates where bestrode confidently the young Tory matador, Rees-Mogg of Balliol. Murdoch, however, chose to stand for office in the university Labour Club. The club's president, the young Gerald Kaufman, had other ideas, and had him disqualified for illegally soliciting votes (canvassing being – technically – forbidden). Some thought it was Murdoch who was indulging in gesture politics. He kept a bust of Lenin in his rooms, but they were among the finest in college. He was also one of the few students committed to the triumph of the proletariat to own, in his final year, a car in early 1950s Oxford. He had an eclectic circle of friends in a whimsical philosophical society he joined named after Voltaire. *Cherwell* described him as 'turbulent, travelled and twenty-one, he is known ... as a brilliant betting man with that individual Billingsgate touch. He manages *Cherwell* publicity in his spare time.'[97] Relegated to even sparer time were his studies and in 1953 he went down with a third-class degree.

On coming down, he got his first taste of Fleet Street as a junior sub at the *Daily Express*. The pride of Beaverbrook's titles, the *Express* was at that time close to the summit of its prestige and popularity. Edward Pickering found time to keep a paternal eye on Sir Keith's son as he toiled away on the subs desk. Indeed, Pickering assumed the mentor's role for Rupert Murdoch that Northcliffe had played for his father. And the young journalist appreciated the training, retaining throughout his career the highest regard for the man he would ultimately make executive vice-chairman of Times Newspapers.

In September 1953, Murdoch returned to Australia. But it was not the homecoming of which he had once dreamed. Sir Keith had died the previous year while his son was still up at Oxford. It was a terrible blow. 'My father was always a model for me,' Murdoch later said. 'He died when I was twenty-one, but I had idolized him.'[98] And the son had learned something else from his father's experience: Sir Keith had built up a newspaper empire, but as a manager, not an owner. After death duties had taken a sizeable claim, the money left for his widow Lady (later Dame) Elisabeth, son and three daughters was held in the family holding company, Cruden Investments. The Herald Group persuaded Lady Elisabeth to sell them the Murdoch half-share in the Brisbane *Courier-Mail* on terms that proved highly favourable to the Herald Group. Thus the only proprietorship left for Rupert Murdoch to inherit was a controlling interest in News Limited, owner of a single by no means secure daily, the *Adelaide News* – which was not even the biggest paper in Adelaide – and its sister title, the *Sunday Mail*. The immediate response of the Herald Group was to try and strip him of it. On failing to persuade Lady Elisabeth to sell them the Murdoch stake in News Limited, they announced their intention to drive the *Adelaide News* out of business. Sir Keith had helped make the Herald Group the most important media company in Australia. Its treatment of his family on the morrow of his death caused tremendous acrimony. And it instilled in the son an important lesson about where power lay. He would follow in his father's footsteps, but with one crucial difference – he was determined to own the papers he built up.

The first objective was to see off the Herald Group's assault on the *Adelaide News* and *Sunday Mail*. The attack was repulsed and News Limited became the basis of Rupert Murdoch's acquisitions fund. Within two years of taking the helm he saw its net assets double. After purchasing a Melbourne women's magazine, the loss-making Perth *Sunday Times* became his first newspaper acquisition in 1956, when he was still only twenty-four. He transformed its sales but kept its sensationalist reporting. The purchase of other small local papers followed. Then he bid successfully for one of the two licences for Adelaide's first television channels. His Channel 9 beat the rival Channel 7 to be first on the air and started generating enough revenue to finance far grander dreams of expansion. Sydney's newspaper market was a virtual duopoly of the Fairfax and Packer families but in 1960 Murdoch got a foot in the door when Fairfax sold him the *Mirror*, a downmarket paper which had become something of an embarrassment to the company and which when sold, it was imagined, would be less of a threat if owned by an outsider like Murdoch than by a more direct rival. Instead, the result was a no-holes-barred circulation war in which Sydney's tradition of sensationalist reporting was surpassed.

In 1964 Murdoch launched his first new title. Based in the capital, Canberra, *The Australian* became the country's only truly national newspaper. It was also a serious-minded broadsheet, committed to political analysis and in-depth reporting. In other words, it was a departure from its owner's previous projects. Maxwell Newton, *The Australian*'s editor, recalled that on its first night Murdoch told him, '"Well, I've got where I am by some pretty tough and pretty larrikin methods ... but I've got there. And now," he said, "what I want to do – I want to be able to produce a newspaper that my father would have been proud of."'[99] He stuck with the paper ever after, despite its inability to return a profit.

In 1969, Murdoch made the great leap, breaking into the British market with a newspaper far removed from his product in Canberra. He had originally wanted to take control of the *Daily Mirror*, but purchasing sufficient shares proved impossible. The *News of the World* was a popular Sunday institution, long known as the 'News of the Screws' because of its stories about defrocked vicars and low goings-on in high places (or just low places if it was a slow news day). With six million copies sold each Sunday (down from a peak of over eight million in 1950), the raucous and right-wing publication had the largest circulation of any newspaper in Britain. But by 1968 its Carr family proprietors, giving the outward impression of ennui, found themselves fragmented and receiving the unwelcome attention of Robert Maxwell. In order to prevent Maxwell buying a third of their company's shares, the Carrs opted to sell a 40 per cent stake to Murdoch. This seemed the best policy since, although the thirty-eight-year-old Australian would become managing director, he had promised that he would not seek to increase further his share and that Sir William Carr – or, in time, another member of his family – would continue to be chairman of the company. Within six months of the deal going through, Murdoch duly increased his share, entrenched his control of the paper and forced Sir William, incapacitated by illness, to resign. Murdoch then put himself forward as chairman. He regarded this as a matter of business sense. Others called it sharp practice.

It was the trade unions that provided Murdoch with his greatest coup. Maxwell, having been thwarted in his attempt to acquire the *News of the*

World, hoped to buy the ailing *Sun* from the *Daily Mirror*'s owners, IPC. He would maintain the *Sun*'s left-leaning politics and would not let it challenge the *Mirror* directly for dominance. Delighted, IPC agreed generous terms of sale. But Maxwell also made it clear that in taking on a loss-making paper he would have to cut jobs and costs. The unions objected to this, and Hugh Cudlipp, IPC's chairman, feared it might trigger a wave of union militancy that would disrupt production of the company's highly profitable *Mirror*. Cudlipp had fathered the *Sun* in 1964 as a middle-market broadsheet (it replaced the defunct trade union-backed *Daily Herald* bought by IPC three years earlier) and did not want to contemplate infanticide. So he sold it for the trivial sum of £500,000 (of which only £50,000 was a down payment) to Murdoch, a man who – compared to Maxwell or the alternative of certain death – had the unions' blessing. Over the next three years, the circulation of Murdoch's *Sun* rose from under one million to over three million. The paper's mix of sauce and sensationalism earned its new owner the sobriquet 'Dirty Digger'. But more to the point, he now had his cash cow and could plan for expansion accordingly.

Yet Murdoch's next forays into Fleet Street were unsuccessful. It seemed *The Times* would never come up for sale – Roy Thomson had pledged as much and was not in apparent need of ready cash. But the future of another illustrious title, the *Observer*, edited by Gavin Astor's cousin David, appeared far less certain. In 1976, however, it preferred to sell itself for a mere £1 million to Atlantic Richfield rather than to the downmarket tabloid owner of the *Sun* and the *News of the World*. Like Thomson with Times Newspapers, Atlantic Richfield was a company making large profits from oil exploration that talked the language of moral obligation rather than business opportunity (at least until 1981 when it sold the loss-making paper to Tiny Rowland). In 1977, Murdoch's was one of the raised hands in the crowded bidding for the fallen Beaverbrook empire. The prospect of breathing new life into the once mighty *Daily Express*, where nearly a quarter of a century earlier he had learned the subeditors' craft from Edward Pickering, was naturally appealing. But he lost to a higher bid from Trafalgar House who placed a building contractor, Victor Matthews, behind the chairman's desk of the newly named Express Newspapers.

But by this stage, Murdoch's News Limited had spread to three continents. His first American acquisitions came in Texas when in 1973 he bought the *San Antonio Express* and its *News* sister paper. After a slow start the titles became increasingly profitable. An attempt to launch a rival to the *National Enquirer* proved unsuccessful but he was not to be put off by temporary reverses (he merely transformed his product into *Star*, a women's magazine that by the early eighties returned a $12 million annual profit). The great test of his mettle came in 1976 when Dorothy Schiff sold him the liberal leaning *New York Post*. He paid $10 million for a paper that was haemorrhaging money, but rather than taking time to regroup he immediately pressed ahead, spending a further $10 million to buy *New York* magazine and *Village Voice*.

In the twenty-eight years between his father's death and his acquisition of *The Times*, Murdoch had progressed from owning one newspaper in Adelaide to becoming a major presence across the English-speaking world with annual sales of over A$ 1 billion (£485 million). His News Corporation was valued on the Sydney stock exchange at £100 million. It owned half the shares in its British subsidiary, News International (owner of Times Newspapers and the tabloids of News Group Newspapers). The other half of News International's shares was quoted on the London stock exchange with a value of £35 million. Yet the perceived imperative of keeping personal control had not been squandered in the midst of this expansion. The Murdoch family's holding company, Cruden Investments, still owned 43 per cent of the parent company.[100]

Murdoch was able to pursue a policy of aggressive expansion because of the profitability of his London tabloids and by pointing to a proven track record in turning around under-performing titles. It was enough to secure credit from the banks. But his growing band of critics had come to credit him only with debasing the profession of journalism. Aside from his patronage of *The Australian* (and even here there had been evidence of his interference in editorial policy), he was now held in contempt by those who believed he had built success upon a heap of trash. His titles sensationalized events, trivialized serious issues (when indeed they bothered to report serious issues at all) and frequently allowed their zeal in getting a scoop to overcome questions of taste, fairness and honesty. More than any other, it was Murdoch's name that had become associated with 'tabloid journalism' as a pejorative term.

From November 1970, the *Sun* sported topless women on its page three. Feminists and arbiters of decency loudly condemned this popular move. In fact, it was not exactly a Fleet Street first: as long ago as 1937 the high-minded Hugh Cudlipp, then editor of the *Mirror*'s Sunday sister paper, had reproduced a topless damsel chaperoned by the obtuse picture caption 'a charming springtime study of an apple-tree in full blossom'. Even newspapers owned by such respectable figures as Lord Thomson and edited by

William Rees-Mogg were not immune. Five months after the *Sun* launched its topless page three girls, *The Times* pictured one of them nude in a full-page advertisement for Fisons' slimming biscuits (one reader asked whether the paper's self-regarding 1950s advertising slogan 'Top People Take *The Times*' should be replaced with 'Topless People Take *The Times*'; another wrote, 'I hope this delightful picture has the same effect on *The Times*'s circulation as it does on mine.'). Although it proved a sell-out issue, it did not, however, start a broadsheet trend. In contrast, page three nudity became synonymous with the *Sun*. Those who did not believe mass-circulation newspapers were the place for entertainment or triviality hated Murdoch's winning formula every bit as much as a previous generation had chastised Northcliffe for giving the people what they wanted in place of what was thought good for them. In the case of the *Sun* and the *New York Post*, Murdoch had indeed taken serious-minded newspapers downmarket. But many of his offending newspapers (in particular the *News of the World*, the Perth *Sunday Times* and the Sydney *Daily Mirror*) had been peddling titillation, half-truth and questionable journalistic standards long before his arrival on the scene. But the increasing size not only of headlines – now often involving a comic pun – but also graphic photographs certainly made their wares more pervasive and intrusive.

Murdoch was not interested in the critics of his tabloids. In his eyes they were cultural snobs, seeking to enforce their own tastes on millions of people whose lives were lived in conditions about which the arbiters of taste demonstrated scant concern or understanding. Papers like the *Sun* and the *New York Post* were responding to a need, reflecting what their readers wanted to unwind with in the course of what was otherwise a day of toil. But Murdoch went further in the defence of his titles. They were not just a form of cheap entertainment; they were genuine upholders of a fearless fourth estate. What the cultural establishment branded scandal-mongering was, more often, an attempt to hold to account those in public life for their actions – public and private. While the self-righteous broadsheets lazily reported 'official' news after it had happened, the popular press regularly created the news in the first place, by uncovering what was actually going on behind the veneer of authorized pronouncement. It was, Murdoch asserted:

not the serious press in America but the muck-rakers, led by Lincoln Steffens and his *New York World*, who became the permanent opposition and challenged the American trinity of power: big business, big labour and big government. It was not the serious press which first campaigned for the Negro in America. It was the small, obscure newspapers of the Deep South.[101]

Nor was this a phenomenon of the New World. Having sympathized with the Confederates in the Civil War, zealously advocated the appeasement of Hitler in the 1930s and adopted an understanding attitude towards Stalin in the 1940s, *The Times* had, in its high-minded way, not always walked with angels.

Yet, it was the social and political comment in Murdoch's tabloids that many of his critics found the most pernicious aspect of his influence. The proprietor had long since mislaid his bust of Lenin, but not his dislike of the class system, and in the first three general elections of his ownership, the *Sun* endorsed the Labour Party. But when it came out in support of Margaret Thatcher's Conservatives for the 1979 election, left and liberal commentators perceived they were now up against a formidable foe that was hooking millions of innocent readers to right-wing policies by pandering to their fears and sugaring the poison with smut and light entertainment. It was as if the *Sun* had become the opiate of the people. Two headlines in the paper in the months leading up to the 1979 election became legendary: 'Crisis? What crisis?' misquoted what the Labour Prime Minister, James Callaghan, had said on returning from a summit in Guadeloupe (although it caught accurately the mood he conveyed) while 'Winter of Discontent' soon became the recognized description of the period of industrial strife.[102] In fact the *Richard III* reference had actually been made by Callaghan in a television interview two months earlier, but it was the *Sun*'s usage that gave it wider currency. Despite the evidence – as Callaghan acknowledged – that there was a cultural sea change underway among the electorate in favour of Mrs Thatcher, discontented figures on the left began to believe that their arguments had been defeated not in a reasoned debate but by the cheap headlines of Murdoch's newspapers and their equivalents on the advertising hoardings hired by Saatchi & Saatchi. Given that Murdoch was known to interfere in the line his newspapers took, it was reasonable to assume the right-wing slant was all his doing. In fact, the extent of the *Sun*'s partisan support for Mrs Thatcher was far more a case of its editor, Larry Lamb, dictating the paper's politics to the proprietor. Murdoch's instincts had been far more cautious. But editors were easily dispensable and it was Murdoch who gained the opprobrium, one that got worse the more he came to believe Lamb had made the correct call.

*　　*　　*

This was the background to Harold Evans's determination to have legally watertight safeguards against Murdoch's exercising any editorial interference in *The Times* and *Sunday Times*. And there were plenty of journalists on the payroll determined to assert their independent judgment from the first. The profile of Rupert Murdoch that appeared in *The Times* upon his gaining control of the paper was certainly not effusive. Dan van der Vat described a 'ruthless entrepreneur . . . and pioneer of female nudity' pursuing a strategy of taking his papers 'down-market to raise circulation'. Murdoch was the owner in the United States of 'the downmarket *Star*' who 'transformed in the familiar down-market manner' the *New York Post*. Scraping the barrel to try and find something positive to say, van der Vat's profile concluded that *The Times* and *Sunday Times* 'each have the most demanding readership in Britain, and it is a well-known tenet of Mr Murdoch's philosophy to give the readers what they want'. The leader article, written by Rees-Mogg and entitled 'The Fifth Proprietorship', was less keen to find fault. Sketching the previous four owners of the paper, it noted, 'neither Northcliffe nor Roy Thomson . . . managed to solve its commercial problems. If Mr Murdoch does resolve those problems he will have achieved something which has defied the masters of his craft.' In Rees-Mogg's opinion, the new owner stood 'somewhere between' Northcliffe's 'editorial genius' and Thomson's outlook as 'a business man'. Murdoch was 'a newspaper romantic'.[103]

Less happy with this affair of the heart was the new owner's wife, Anna. Looking forward to bringing up a young family in New York, she did not want to be uprooted and moved to London, a city in which she had previously had bad experiences (in particular the murder of a friend by kidnappers who mistook the woman for their actual ransom target – Anna herself). *The Times*, she conceded, was 'not something that I really want, but if Rupert wants it and it makes him happy I'm sure we'll sort it out'.[104] Nonetheless, for her husband's fiftieth birthday on 11 March 1981, she presented him with a cake iced with a mock front page of *The Times* – into which he excitedly plunged the knife.

CHAPTER TWO

'THE GREATEST EDITOR
IN THE WORLD'

The Rise and Fall of Harold Evans

I

After fourteen years in the chair, William Rees-Mogg had made it clear he would relinquish the editorship once the transferral of *The Times*'s ownership was complete. Thus, the first question facing Rupert Murdoch was whether the new editor should be appointed from inside or outside the paper. It was recognized that existing staff would be happier with 'one of their own' taking the helm rather than an outsider who might sport alienating ideas about improving the product. But it was not the journalists who were footing the losses for a paper that, on current performance, was failing commercially. In making his recommendation to *The Times*'s board of independent national directors, the proprietor had to consider the signal he would be sending out both to the journalists and to the market outside about what sort of paper he wanted by how far he looked beyond the environs of Gray's Inn Road.

There were three credible internal candidates. As early as 12 February, Hugh Stephenson, the long-serving editor of *The Times* business news section, had written to Murdoch asking to be considered for the top job.[1] A left-leaning Wykehamist who had been president of the Oxford Union prior to six years in the Foreign Office, Stephenson had been with *The Times* since 1968. This was an impressive résumé, but not one especially appealing to the new proprietor who was, in any case, not an admirer of the paper's business content. Even quicker off the blocks was Louis Heren, who had made his intentions known to Sir Denis Hamilton the previous day. He was probably the candidate who wanted the editorship most and his success would certainly have been something of a Fleet Street fairy tale. The son of a *Times* print worker who had died when his boy was only four, Louis Heren had been born in 1919 and grown up in the poverty of the

East End before getting a job as a *Times* messenger boy. His lucky break had come when an assistant editor noticed him in a corner, quietly reading Conrad's *Nostromo*. Subsequently, he was taken on as a reporter and, after war service, he developed into one of the paper's leading foreign correspondents, sending back dispatches from Middle Eastern battlefronts where the new state of Israel was struggling for its survival, and from the Korean War and later becoming chief Washington correspondent. If not a tale of rags to riches, it was certainly rags to respectability and, as Rees-Mogg's deputy, he was entitled to expect to be considered seriously. But the fact that he had been, to all intents and purposes, educated by *The Times* posed questions as to whether he was best able to see the paper's problems from an outside perspective. He was also sixty-two years old. When he sent the new owner a list of suggested improvements to the paper, Murdoch replied, without much sensitivity, that he wanted an editor 'who will last at least ten years' and that another rival for the post, Charles Douglas-Home, 'is more popular than you'.[2]

On this last point, Murdoch was well informed. Charles Cospatrick Douglas-Home ('Charlie' to his friends) *was* the popular choice, certainly among the senior staff. He was the man Rees-Mogg wanted as his successor and when the outgoing editor asked six of the assistant editors whom they wanted, five of them had opted for Douglas-Home. The chief leader writer, Owen Hickey, had even taken it upon himself to write to Denis Hamilton assuring him that Douglas-Home was the man to pick.[3] At forty-four, he was the right age and since joining *The Times* from the *Daily Express* in 1965 he had held many of the important positions within the paper: defence correspondent, features editor, home editor and foreign editor. He had been educated at Eton and served in the Royal Scots Greys. He was the nephew of the former Conservative Prime Minister, Alec Douglas-Home, and his cousin, a childminder at the All England Kindergarten, had recently become engaged to the heir to the throne. So he certainly had highly placed 'connections' (a disadvantage in the eyes of those who believed having friends in high places compromised fearless journalism). But 'Charlie' was no society cyphen. He took his profession seriously and had well-formed 'hawkish' views, especially on defence and foreign policy – all likely to endear him to the new, increasingly right-wing proprietor. He was also something of a contradictory figure: a former army officer who no longer drank, a fearless foxhunter who did not eat meat and a gentleman who, like an ambitious new boy in the Whips' Office, had once been caught keeping a secret dossier on the private foibles of his colleagues.[4]

Murdoch interviewed the three 'internal' candidates on 16 February although, since he already had a preferred candidate in mind, he was essentially going through the motions. The man he wanted was not an old hand of *The Times*. Having made such a success steering the *Sun*, Larry Lamb anticipated the call up and was deeply hurt when it did not come. 'I would never have dreamt of it,' Murdoch later made clear, 'he would have been a disaster.'[5] Yet Murdoch's critics, incredulous that he meant what he said about guaranteeing editorial independence, were still waiting to see which other stooge he would appoint. In an article entitled 'Into the arms of Count Dracula', the editor of the *New Statesman*, Bruce Page, informed his readers, 'it is believed in the highest reaches of Times Newspapers that the candidate which [sic] he has in mind is Mr Bruce Rothwell. Rothwell can reasonably be described as a trusted Murdoch aide . . .'[6] But, whatever was now the practice at the *New Statesman*, *The Times* was not ready to be run by a man named Bruce. Murdoch had fixed upon someone very different – a hero in liberal media circles.

Even before the deal to buy Times Newspapers was done, Murdoch had invited Harold Evans round to his flat in Eaton Place and asked him whether he would like to edit *The Times*. It was a probing, perhaps mischievous, question since Evans was at the time still trying to prevent the Murdoch bid for TNL so that his own *Sunday Times* consortium could succeed. But Murdoch could have been forgiven for regarding the avoidance of saying 'no' as a conditional 'yes'.

Harold Evans was the most celebrated editor in Fleet Street. At a time when standards were said to be falling all over the 'Street of Shame', Evans appeared to exemplify all that was best about the public utility of journalism. By 1981, he had been editor of the *Sunday Times* for fourteen years – thereby shadowing exactly the service record of his opposite number, Rees-Mogg, in the adjoining building at Gray's Inn Road. The two editors were the same age but their backgrounds could not have been more different. Two years older than Murdoch, Harold Evans was born in 1928, the son of an engine driver. His grandfather was illiterate. Leaving the local school in Manchester at the age of sixteen, he had got his first job towards the end of the Second World War as a £1-a-week reporter on a newspaper in Ashton-under-Lyme. The interruption of national service with the RAF in 1946 led to opportunity: the chance to study at Durham University (where he met his Liverpudlian first wife, Enid) and later Commonwealth Fund Journalism fellowships at the universities of Chicago and Stanford. By 1961 he had become editor of the *Northern Echo*. Driven by its new editor, the *Echo* started to take its investigative journalism beyond its Darlington readership. Its campaign to prove the innocence of a Londoner wrongly convicted of murder gained it national prominence. One of those who took notice was the editor of the *Sunday Times*, Sir Denis Hamilton, who brought Evans down to London to work alongside him. The following year, 1967, he succeeded Hamilton as editor of the paper. It was a meteoric rise from provincial semi-obscurity. Evans immediately proved himself at Gray's Inn Road. In his new role as editor-in-chief, Sir Denis's patronage and guidance were useful and some of the paper's success was the consequence of his own formula: the paper's colour magazine (a honey pot for advertising) and major book serializations. But Evans built on these strong foundations and, assisted by Bruce Page, Don Berry and others, he entrenched the position of the *Sunday Times* as Britain's principal campaigning and investigative newspaper.

In 1972, Evans drove the campaign with which his name, and that of the *Sunday Times*, will always be associated: the battle to force Distillers Ltd to compensate adequately the victims of its drug, Thalidomide. The immediate reaction – as he well anticipated – was Distillers' withdrawal of £600,000 worth of advertising in the paper. The other equally swift response was an injunction silencing the *Sunday Times*'s attempts to reveal the history of the drug's development and marketing. With great tenacity (and an understanding proprietor in Roy Thomson), Evans continued the fight through the courts and to Strasbourg. Distillers was eventually forced into a £27 million payout to its product's victims. And at last, in 1977, the *Sunday Times* got to print the details of its story (although the print unions decided to call a stoppage that day, ensuring few got to read about it).

Under Evans, the *Sunday Times* was a paper with a liberal conscience. The paper appeared at ease with the more permissive and meritocratic legacy of the 1960s. The cynic within Murdoch may well have thought that he could silence the howls of protest about his being allowed to buy *The Times* by putting such a respected, independent and liberal-minded editor in charge of it. Indeed, to appoint the man who had spent the previous months trying to wreck the News International bid with his own consortium (and who had privately applauded Aitken's attack on it in the Commons) appeared to show a spirit of open-minded forgiveness that few had previously associated with Murdoch's public conduct. Surely the new owner could not be all that right wing or controlling if he put in charge a man who had wanted the *Sunday Times* to be part owned by that tribune of democratic socialism, the *Guardian*? This would certainly be a calming message to convey.

But there was genuine admiration as well. Back in 1972, Murdoch had played his part in the Thalidomide controversy. He had been behind the anonymous posters that suddenly appeared across the country ridiculing Distillers, hoping (unsuccessfuly) that by this means his papers could discuss the company's role at a time when its legal proceedings made doing so contempt of court. Unusually for Fleet Street proprietors, Murdoch understood every aspect of the newspaper business – not just the accounts. Thanks to the efforts of his father and Edward Pickering at the *Express*, Murdoch could sub articles with effortless aplomb. In this respect, he had something in common with Evans – comprehensive mastery of the journalistic craft. For Evans was the author of such tomes as *The Active Newsroom* and *Editing and Design* (in five volumes) which covered almost every aspect of putting together the written (and pictorial) page. The two men also appeared to have a common outlook. They admired American spirit and drive (both later became American citizens) and neither wished to be considered for membership of the traditional British Establishment. Despite his migration to London, Evans still wanted to be considered something of an outsider and this attracted Murdoch. The American academic Martin Wiener had just written his influential book, *English Culture and the Decline of the Industrial Spirit 1850–1980*. Its message appealed to Murdoch who told a luncheon at the Savoy: 'It is the very simple fact that politicians, bureaucrats, the gentlemanly professionals at the top of the civil service, churchmen, professional men, publicists, Oxbridge and the whole establishment just don't like commerce.' Apart from the reference to 'publicists', he had basically reeled off a list of the core *Times* readership. But he was not finished with his castigation: 'They have produced a defensive and conservative outlook in business which has coalesced with a defensive and conservative trades union structure imposing on Britain a check in industrial growth, a pattern of industrial behaviour suspicious of change – energetic only in keeping things as they are.'[7]

With this attitude, it is easy to see why Murdoch hoped for great things from a restless and meritocratic figure like Harold Evans. That he could be given a pulpit in the housemagazine of the Establishment while being sufficiently intelligent to prevent accusations of being a downmarket influence made him, in Murdoch's view, the ideal candidate.

It was up to the independent national directors, sitting on the holdings board of Times Newspapers, to make the final decision. The board consisted of four peers of the realm, Lords Roll, Dacre, Greene and Robens who, before ennoblement, had been Eric Roll, civil servant and banker; Hugh Trevor-Roper, historian; Sid Greene of the National Union of Railwaymen; and Alf Robens of the National Coal Board. Two new directors nominated by Murdoch now joined them: Sir Denis Hamilton and Sir Edward Pickering. Hamilton's appointment was uncontroversial but Dacre objected to Murdoch assuming Pickering would be acceptable without the directors first voting on it. There was an embarrassing delay at the start of the meeting while this was done although it was not entirely to the directors' credit that they appeared to know little about one of Fleet Street's most successful editors and longest serving figures.[8] It had been under Pickering's editorship that the *Daily Express* had achieved its highest ever circulation. Suitably acquainted with his qualifications, the directors hastily assented to Pickering joining them and proceeded on to the main business – the appointment of the new editor. Under the articles of association, the proprietor had the power of putting forward his preference for editor. The directors had the right of veto but not necessarily the option of discussing who they actually wanted. Had they the right of proposition, the editorship would most likely have gone to Charles Douglas-Home. But it was Harold Evans's name that Murdoch put before them.

Not everyone shared his enthusiasm. Marmaduke Hussey, the executive vice-chairman of TNL who had overseen the failed shutdown strategy with the unions in 1979–80, had already assured Murdoch that the intention to make Evans editor of *The Times* and to move his old deputy, Frank Giles, into his vacated chair at the *Sunday Times* was 'the quickest way to wreck two marvellous newspapers I can think of!'. To no avail, Hussey pleaded with him to make Douglas-Home the new editor.[9] Having brought Evans to the *Sunday Times* in the first place and watched over him as group editor-in-chief and TNL chairman, Denis Hamilton was, in principle, well placed to offer his assessment. And it was not entirely favourable. Certainly, Evans had his flashes of inspiration, even genius, but he was temperamental and liable to change his mind. In the course of producing a once weekly product this could be managed, but in editing a daily it could be disastrous. Yet, at the meeting of national directors, Hamilton chose to pull his punches and the opposition to Evans's appointment was instead led by the forthright historian Lord Dacre, who articulated his objections with a pointed vehemence that bordered upon the abusive. But Dacre's blackball was not enough and following his departure to deliver a lecture at Oxford, Murdoch's insistence that *The Times* needed the best and

Evans was the best convinced the rest of the board.[10] So it was that Harold Evans became only the eleventh man to edit *The Times* since Thomas Barnes established the modern concept of the office in 1816, the year after Waterloo.

Evans's appointment caused a buzz throughout Fleet Street. Those with a liking for archaic usage may still have referred to the paper as 'The Thunderer' but as a noun, not a verb. If anything, critics, particularly those who did not read it, thought of it as *The* (behind the) *Times*. Murdoch hoped that the new editor would instil some of the Sunday paper's drive and contemporary feel into the all too respectable daily.

Those happy with the paper as it was greeted this prospect with disquiet. Louis Heren was of the view that 'we were not a daily version of the *Sunday Times*'. But he conceded that the niche was a small one, being 'boxed in by the *Guardian* on our left and the *Daily Telegraph* on our right' while 'the *FT* stood between us and all that lovely advertising in the City of London'.[11] The fact that the paper's readers were sufficiently loyal to return to it after it had been off the streets for almost a year was not, in itself, proof that all was well. In retrospect, Hugh Stephenson took the view that the 1979–80 shutdown 'served to make people realize that the things they really missed about *The Times* were its quirky features – letters, law reports, obits, cross-word. They didn't miss its news, which wasn't particularly good. In most respects the *Daily Telegraph*, the *Guardian* and the *Financial Times* were better newspapers.'[12] This was an assessment broadly shared by the new editor.[13] In 1981, *The Times* was normally four pages longer than the *Guardian* and four pages shorter than the *Telegraph*. But the gap was wider in the statistics that mattered. In daily sales, the *Guardian* had overtaken *The Times* in 1974. Almost since the day of its launch in 1855, the *Telegraph* had given *The Times* a pasting. When Evans took over, *The Times* averaged 282,000 daily sales to the *Telegraph*'s 1.4 million.

Now the drive was on at least to catch up with the *Guardian* again. There would be no repeat of the famous 1957 advertising campaign – 'Top People Take *The Times*' a preposterously exclusive slogan for a campaign supposedly intended to widen circulation. Murdoch believed *The Times* could aim for a half-million readership. Under Hamilton and Evans the *Sunday Times*, with its book serializations and glossy colour magazine, had promoted the new elite of the photogenic. It was as glamorous and of the moment as *The Times* was monochrome and old-fashioned. Evans's *Sunday Times* promoted celebrities and 'big names' while the *Times* old guard were still lamenting the loss of the anonymous *non-de-plume* 'By Our Special

Correspondent'. *Sunday Times* reporters having occasion to cross the Gray's Inn Road connecting bridge that took them into *The Times* claimed to feel they were crossing into East Berlin.

The Times old guard – those horrified by the connotations of the word 'promotion' and ill at ease with the world of the colour supplement – hated the prospect of their paper being turned into a daily *Sunday Times* or a mark two *Telegraph*. They and their spiritual forebears had blocked a 1958 report by the accountants Coopers with its outlandish idea about putting news on the front page (as the *Guardian* had done since 1952), their objections only finally overcome in 1966. Nor did they see what was wrong with a relatively low circulation so long as it was sufficiently upmarket to cover its costs through advertising (as the *FT* did). There was certainly no obvious link between a broadsheet's influence and its sales figures: by the late 1930s, the *Telegraph* had opened up a half-million lead on *The Times*, but it was Geoffrey Dawson who was the politically influential editor, not the *Telegraph*'s Arthur Watson.

Those apprehensive about the forthcoming Evans–Murdoch strategy of going for growth could also point to precedent. Fortified by Thomson's cash injection, Rees-Mogg's editorship had started with radical attempts to modernize the paper by introducing a separate business news section, a roving 'News Team' acting like a rapid reaction force under Michael Cudlipp's direction, bigger headlines and shorter sentences. Circulation had improved dramatically from 280,000 in 1966 to 430,000 in 1969. Meeting in the White Swan pub, twenty-nine members of staff, including the young Charles Douglas-Home and Brian MacArthur, had signed a declaration condemning what they believed was the accompanying cheapening of the paper's authority. But the most telling argument was that the paper was still not making a profit – the boosted revenue from sales being outstripped by the cost of the expansion programme necessary to sustain it. So the expansion policy was abandoned; circulation slipped back towards 300,000 and, by the mid-seventies the paper even – fleetingly – returned a profit.

Now the introduction of a *Sunday Times* man at the helm suggested *The Times* would retrace its steps and repeat the failed 1967–9 growth strategy, but Harold Evans saw his task as editor in less primarily commercial terms. 'At the *Sunday Times* before Hamilton and Thomson,' he later recalled, 'it was a sackable offence to provoke a solicitor's letter,' but after he became editor 'we were in the Law Courts so many times I felt they owed me an honorary wig.' Evans maintained that this became necessary 'because real reporting ran into extensions of corporate and executive power that had gone undetected, hence unchallenged, and the courts, uninhibited by a Bill of Rights, had given property rights priority over personal rights.'[14] This had not been how *The Times* had generally seen its role during the same period. Indeed, when in 1969 the paper caught out Metropolitan policemen in a bribery sting some old *Times* hands were deeply uneasy about their paper going in for the sort of exposé that subverted the good name of the forces of law and order. Others agreed. Three days after the story broke, the paper reported on its front page a meeting of Edward Heath's Shadow Cabinet in which 'it was considered deeply disturbing that to trial by television . . . there might now be added trial by newspaper, with *The Times* leading the way . . . It was agreed that *The Times* appeared to have put the printing of allegations against the police above the national interest.'[15]

With Evans's arrival, it seemed *The Times* would become a disruptive influence again. The new editor proposed what he called 'vertical journalism' as opposed to the 'horizontal school of journalism' with which the paper had become too comfy, whereby 'speeches, reports and ceremonials occur and they are rendered into words in print along a straight assembly-line. Scandal and injustice go unremarked unless someone else discovers them.' Evans believed he was the true inheritor of an older *Times* tradition, 'The Thunderer' of Thomas Barnes, in which 'the effort to get to the bottom of things, which is the aspiration of the vertical school of journalism, cannot be indiscriminate. Judgments have to be made about what is important; they are moral judgments. The vertical school is active. It sets its own agenda; it is not afraid of the word "campaign".'[16]

Evans's style of leadership was markedly different from that of Rees-Mogg. The outgoing editor had always given the impression that it was the paper's commentary on events that was his prime interest. The leader articles written, he was quite content to leave the office shortly after 7 p.m. in order to spend the evening with his family or at official functions and dinners, confident that the team on the 'backbench' could be entrusted with presenting the breaking news stories. Evans could not have been more different. On his first day as editor, he told his staff that he would be on the backbench every night. 'It is called,' he said proudly, 'the editing theory of maximum irritation.'[17] And he was not wrong. As if to make his point, he took off his jacket – a sight unseen during Rees-Mogg's fourteen years in the chair (unfortunately Evans's unattended jacket was promptly stolen).[18]

One who lamented the passing of the baton from Rees-Mogg to Evans was Auberon Waugh. He foresaw what might be in store:

If, in the months that follow, footling diagrams or 'graphics' begin to appear illustrating how the hostages walked off their aeroplane into a reception centre; profiles of leading hairdressers suddenly break on page 12; inquiries into the safety of some patent medicine replace Philip Howard's ruminations on the English language; if a cheap, flip radicalism replaces Mr Rees-Mogg's carefully argued honourable conservatism and nasty, gritty English creeps into the leader columns where once his sonorous phrases basked and played in the sun; if it begins to seem that one more beleaguered outpost has fallen to the barbarians, we should reflect that there never really was an England which spoke in this language of good nature, of friendliness, of fair dealing, of balance. It was all a product of Mr Rees-Mogg's beautiful mind.[19]

II

In 1967, William Rees-Mogg had left the *Sunday Times* to edit *The Times* and brought only three journalists with him from his old paper. But Harold Evans intended a far more dramatic exodus. His first thought was to bring Hugo Young across the bridge to replace the disappointed Louis Heren as deputy editor of *The Times*. Young, a serious-minded Balliol liberal, was the political editor of the *Sunday Times* and Evans thought him a suitable successor when, in seven years or so, he would want to stand down from editing *The Times*. But Frank Giles, the very embodiment of a Foreign Office mandarin whom Murdoch had – to much surprise – appointed as Evans's successor, did not want to lose so capable a lieutenant and dug in his heels, appealing to Murdoch for protection. To Evans's annoyance Murdoch backed his new *Sunday Times* editor. That Evans did not initially want a *Times* man as his deputy was resented and only after Murdoch, Hamilton and Rees-Mogg all advised him strongly did he agree to elevating Charles Douglas-Home into the position. It was a decision Evans would have cause to regret, but having someone the paper's staff respected as deputy editor did much – at first – to calm the feeling that the new editor intended to surround himself with his own clique of non-*Times* men.

The turf war between Evans and Frank Giles continued for several days, the latter resenting what he regarded as his predecessor's aggressive attempt to poach so many of his old paper's best staff. Giles tried to hold on to

Peter Stothard but Evans was adamant that his young protégé should join him. Despite another appeal from Giles to Murdoch, Evans got his way and Stothard became deputy features editor.[20] Features was one of the areas Evans wanted to see given more emphasis and it promised to be a key role in the new paper. Assisted by Nicholas Wapshott, Stothard would work with the new features editor, the thirty-two-year-old Washington correspondent of the *Observer*, Anthony Holden. After persuading Holden – a renaissance man whose interests ranged from poker to writing libretti for opera – to join *The Times*, Evans held out to him the prospect that he would succeed him as editor . . . in good time.

Other senior changes were also made. Fred Emery, who had been reporting from the world's various trouble spots for *The Times* since 1958, became home news editor. In Douglas-Home's place as foreign editor, Evans put the former editor-in-chief of Reuters, Brian Horton. Sir Denis Hamilton's son, Adrian (who had been at the *Observer*), was brought in to run business news in succession to Hugh Stephenson who decided it was time to cut his losses and leave. The following year he became editor of the *New Statesman*. The other disappointed candidate for the editorship, Louis Heren, was given a 'roving brief' as an associate editor. This soon proved – to Heren's distress – to be something of a non-job.

In the event of both Evans and Douglas-Home being out of the office, the acting editor was to be Brian MacArthur. Responsible for news content and its subediting, he was to be the bridge between the day planning and the night editing. MacArthur was already an immensely experienced journalist. Before Evans brought him over from the *Sunday Times*, he had worked at the *Yorkshire Post*, *The Times* (as news editor) and the *Evening Standard*. He had also been the founding editor of the *Times Higher Education Supplement*. These were precocious achievements that Evans admired in a man he thought vaguely resembled 'one of those eighteenth century portraits of a well-fed Cardinal'.[21]

Another key addition to Evans's kitchen cabinet was Bernard Donoughue. The son of a metal polisher in a car factory, Donoughue had gone on to be a policy adviser to Harold Wilson and James Callaghan and was part of the new meritocracy with which Evans felt most at home. Evans wanted Peter Riddell to join the political team under Donoughue's direction. This would have been a powerful infusion of talent, but not even a generous salary could at that stage tempt Riddell away from the *Financial Times*.[22] However, ballast was added when David Watt, director of the Royal Institute of International Affairs and a former political editor and Washington correspondent of the *FT*, was hired to write a weekly column on political and foreign affairs.

It was also necessary to tickle the public. Evans brought in Miles Kington to write what he suggested should be a 'Beachcomber-Way of the World' column.[23] Located on the Court & Social page, the column, entitled 'Moreover . . .', began its Monday to Saturday run in June. Although only 450 words long, it was a tall order for Kington to maintain a daily output of whimsy and a tribute to his skills that he so frequently carried it off week in, week out, for the next five and a half years. It immediately attracted a devoted following, except among its targets. The Welsh trade unionist Clive Jenkins was not amused about a Kington joke that appeared to encourage Welsh Nationalists to burn his house down. Jenkins was furious, demanded an apology on the Court page and assured Evans, 'My lawyers and the police do not think it is "a joke" and as a result we now have surveillance of my home and office.' Evans advised him to stop drawing so much attention to the supposed incitement. But to Anthony Holden Jenkins fumed, 'Who edits Miles Kington? . . . There are some jokes which are so off that they should never be published.'[24] Meanwhile, Mel Calman continued to raise a smile with his distinctive front-page pocket cartoons, as he had four days a week since 1979. But the editor was deluged with complaints when he put caricatures drawn by Charles Griffin at the head of the day's prominent person's birthday column. For some, a cartoon on the Court & Social page was further proof of *The Times*'s apostasy although many of those featured were delighted and asked if they could purchase the original.

The introduction of a resident political cartoonist caused more prolonged debate. Ranan Lurie was an Israeli born US citizen who had trained with the French Foreign Legion and been dropped behind enemy lines in the Six Day War. Having worked for *Life*, *Newsweek*, *Die Welt* and *Bild*, he was the world's most widely syndicated political cartoonist. Like Vicky in Beaverbrook's Express newspapers, Lurie's cartoons often created a dynamic tension by taking a different angle on politics from that being proposed elsewhere in the paper. His draughtsmanship was excellent, his small, rotund figures especially suited to depicting 'hard hats' enjoying a bit of military brinkmanship. But inevitably he was not to everyone's taste, particularly those who believed his art trivialized the news pages on which they were carried. Evans had far more consistent success with the appointment that also gave him the greatest satisfaction. This was the arrival of the relentlessly droll Frank Johnson as parliamentary sketch writer. When it came to material, the House of Commons of the early eighties was to provide Johnson with an embarrassment of riches.

Amid these arrivals came a major departure. Bernard Levin was the most famous columnist on the paper. One of the *enfant terribles* of the sixties satire boom (he was the subject of a famous attempted physical assault while presenting *That Was The Week That Was*, his assailant seeking revenge for a supposedly cruel review of his wife's acting talents), Levin combined a sharp intellect, high-culture sensibilities and a talent for upsetting the full range of vested interests, be they union barons or barristers. Scarcely a week went by without Levin 'going too far this time'. But he had the support of the one person who mattered – the editor. Rees-Mogg had persuaded him to become a *Times* columnist in 1971, ultimately taking the view that 'he alone has the ability to resist the gentle English equity which sometimes drifts like desert sand from one column to the next'.[25] He was not really, therefore, a *Times* man in the established sense of the term and various of the offended vested interests got their revenge by blackballing him from the Garrick Club, where Rees-Mogg was a member.

Evans admired Levin's vituperative prose, if not his ability to punctuate it. Comparing the length of his sentences to 'the corridors of a Venetian palace' Evans failed to persuade him to make more concessions to readers' mental stamina.[26] But the greatest exertion fell upon Levin himself whose column appeared on Tuesdays, Wednesday and Thursdays (he also wrote for the *Sunday Times*). He needed a rest, or at least a lightening of the load. His decision to take a break suited Evans's new features editor, Anthony Holden, who was keen to introduce new blood.[27] Nonetheless, in his final column, Levin helpfully reassured his readers:

My decision is in no way based on any disquiet on my part at the change of editor or proprietor, nor on any lack of confidence in the paper's future, and anyone saying or writing anything to the contrary is, and for all material purposes should be treated as, a liar.

It would not be long before Evans would be pleading with Levin to return. But by then the trickle of famous names from the Rees-Mogg era departing the paper had turned into a flood.

III

On his twenty-first day in the chair, Evans got his first major test on how to handle a major breaking story for *The Times*. During the evening of 30 March 1981 news came through that the American President, Ronald Reagan, had been shot. Evans raced back to Gray's Inn Road and immediately assumed control. His direction proved masterful.

The front page was given over to the story in its entirety (previously even the most momentous news was mixed with other front-page lead stories and continued elsewhere inside the paper). Three sequential picture strips caught like a cine-freeze frame effect, Reagan turning to face his assailant and then going down as he was hit. The headline was itself a cliffhanger: 'President Reagan shot: bullet still in lung'. The subheading quoted Reagan's plucky comment to his wife; 'Honey, I forgot to duck . . . don't worry about me I'll make it.'

Evans's dramatic cover was certainly different from the front page of *The Times* on 23 November 1963 which – with classified adverts still on the front page – merely carried a small three-word 'President Kennedy Assassinated' note at the top right of the paper's masthead. Predictably, some traditionalist readers wrote to complain at what they regarded as Evans's sensationalist, almost tabloid, front page. But had they to hand a *Times* copy of the death of Kennedy they might have been surprised. Although the news of the Kennedy assassination had appeared on page eight (because that was where foreign news was then to be found, regardless of its importance) the actual page layout was surprisingly similar, complete with an action photograph of a security guard leaping on the back of the dying President's car with Mrs Kennedy tending to the slumped figure of her husband. Another photograph showed, closeup, the look of shock on New Yorkers' faces as they learned the news from a tele-type machine in a news agency office window.[28] It was true that Evans ran the headline across the width of the page, whereas in 1963 it had followed the separate column spaces, but this was the only major cosmetic difference. The story's treatment – narrative of the shooting, history of past presidential assassinations, the reaction of world leaders, the next in line – was remarkably similar between 1963 and 1981. Evans merely had the advantage – denied his predecessor – of being able to splash it across a front page.

Unlike Kennedy, Reagan did not die and, by the night's last edition, the headline had been amended to the more hopeful if less dramatic 'Bullet removed from lung'. Nor would the story spawn an industry of conspiracy theories. By 2 April, the paper was in a position to report that the would-be assassin, John Hinckley, was a troubled obsessive, intent on killing the President as a means of proving his (unsolicited) love for the eighteen-year-old-actress Jodie Foster.[29] But if the shooting proved, by a matter of centimetres, not to be a turning point in world politics, it provided the first example of Evans's ability to capture the drama of breaking news and present it in an effective manner. It was commonly agreed across Fleet Street that *The Times* had excelled.

For an editor with an eye for presentation on the page, improving the paper's layout was an immediate priority. Frequently, readers had turned the front page to find a full-page advertisement greeting them on page three. Although this was a prime commercial site, it did not convey the impression that the paper was serious about conveying hard news. When, in 1966, classified ads had finally been taken off the front page, they were moved to the back page. They had remained there ever since. Evans questioned whether such a prominent part of the paper should be given over to small ads for budget travel brochures, secretarial courses and personal announcements. With Murdoch's support, page three was henceforth given over to news while Evans proposed something new for the back page. It was important that the crossword stayed in the bottom left-hand corner where, with paper folded, it could be easily attempted by those lunching on park benches or being jiggled about in congested train compartments. But besides retaining this, the back page was now to be divided in two. The top half would continue main stories carried over from the front page (again, this was easier for tightly packed commuters) alongside the column designed most to sparkle and entertain – Frank Johnson's parliamentary sketch. In the bottom half, Evans introduced what was christened 'The Times Information Service'. This was a daily almanac of eclectic information: weather forecasts, a brief digest of what other newspapers were saying, opening hours for historic houses, even, for some reason, London restaurants offering al fresco dining facilities (there appeared not to be very many of these). 'There is nothing like it in the British press,' Evans boasted, 'it is, indeed, another example of *The Times*, as so often in its history, being the first.'[30]

But there was not a stampede to follow. The quirkiness of the Information Service was both its attraction and, sometimes, the reason for its impracticality. *Private Eye*, the satirical magazine with a mission to persecute Evans whenever opportunity presented itself, tried to sabotage it by encouraging its readers to enter a 'Useless Information Competition'. The *Eye* would pay £10 for each attempt to mislead *The Times* with bogus submissions and add a £5 bonus if the paper actually printed it. On more than one occasion, this childish exercise succeeded, very much to Evans's exasperation.[31]

In overall charge of the redesign was Edwin Taylor, previously Evans's design director at the *Sunday Times* (for which he had won the 1980 Newspaper Design Award). Another recruit from the *Sunday Times*, Oscar Turnill, joined him in the task with Brian MacArthur and Tim Austin, the home news subeditor, assigned to help in the section reorganization. Predictably, there were letters of complaint from readers who regarded any alteration to be, by its very nature, for the worse. Evans found what he called 'this outcry from the more settled members of the community' rather tedious, not least because many of the layout alterations were, if anything, taking the paper back to the 'light face' traditions of Stanley Morison who had established the classic look of the paper in 1932 and invented the world's most popular typeface, Times New Roman.[32] Evans delighted in writing back to the small legion of detractors in order to point out their foolishness with a brittleness that suggested sensitivity to criticism. 'I suspect that if we changed to printing on gold leaf paper there would be murmurs of disapproval in the clubs,' he told one complainer.[33] On occasion, he even took to telephoning his assailants. One of these turned out to be a dentist who was in mid-operation when his receptionist interrupted him with the news there was an urgent call for him on the phone. The patient was then left, mouth stuffed with cotton wool, while his dentist discussed the principles of newspaper layout with the editor of *The Times*.[34]

The next innovation was the introduction of a Friday tabloid section entitled *Preview*. Given the accolades later heaped upon the *Guardian*'s G2 (which *The Times* eventually copied with *T2*) tabloid section, *Preview* was ahead of its time. Covering forthcoming arts and entertainments, it was geared, in particular, to the younger end of the market and was perfectly launched in June 1981 to coincide with a strike at *Time Out* magazine. While falling within Anthony Holden's empire, its driving force was a former *Time Out* journalist, Richard Williams. Evans was delighted with Williams's work and marvelled that Murdoch had given the project financial backing after only a single brief meeting, a speed of decision making that Evans contrasted favourably with the months it took to approve innovations from the Thomson Organisation.[35]

In the month that *Preview* was launched *The Times* axed its least

successful section. *Europa* was a monthly journal, largely comprising economic stories and 'business profiles' that was produced jointly with *Le
Monde*, *La Stampa* and *Die Welt* on the first Tuesday of every month. *The
Times* had got involved in 1973. Britain had joined the EEC and Rees-Mogg
was at that stage a firm enthusiast for the process of European integration
in which political institutions were not enough – *The Times* proclaiming
that 'Europe need a European press'. The fact that *Europa* proved to be a
patchwork of almost hypnotic dullness did not disqualify it from winning
the 1978 Zaccari prize for spreading EEC ideals. But idealism and economics were not compatible partners and it brought Gray's Inn Road nothing but losses. The plug was pulled in June (July was the final issue) 1981
after the previous issue had managed to carry no advertising whatsoever.
The jilted European papers then approached the *Guardian* as a replacement
for *The Times*. When the *Guardian* politely declined the whole project was
wound up.[36]

The demise of *Europa* went largely unnoticed, evidence, if any were
needed, that it should have been wound up years before. More successful
– at least at generating revenue – were the sections produced by the Special
Reports team. These usually appeared (especially throughout the winter
months) twice a week. Around one hundred appeared a year, totalling 650
pages. Most related to holiday or investment opportunities in foreign climes
and had a function in attracting advertising that would not otherwise have
reached *The Times*.[37]

There was one major news occurrence for which the newspaper had
ample time to prepare. The wedding of Charles, Prince of Wales, to Lady
Diana Spencer was to be the event of the year in Britain, a moment of
romance and glamour in which momentarily to forget the country's
deepening recession. It would be the first marriage of a Prince of Wales for
more than a century and only the seventh in almost six hundred years.
Evans was determined that *The Times*'s coverage would outclass the competition. In this he had an ally in the proprietor. Putting aside his republican
inclinations, it was Murdoch who came up with the idea of having a full-
colour front page for the paper's royal wedding edition and to publish a
souvenir magazine.[38]

The result was a sixty-four-page glossy 'royal wedding' magazine. This
was not as profligate as might seem since it attracted twenty-five pages
of advertising suitably tailored to the occasion: the new video recording
machines, the Vauxhall Royale (available in saloon or hatchback), jewellers,
Harrods and a back page emblazoned with the bright livery of Benson &

Hedges. It was the first time *The Times* had produced a colour magazine and, once again, when looking to innovate Evans had turned to his previous paper for the personnel to achieve it. George Darby, associate editor of the *Sunday Times Colour Magazine*, had led the nine-strong production team. Given away free with the paper the day before the wedding, all half a million copies were snatched up. 'If we had printed a million,' Evans declared, 'we'd have sold the lot.'[39] But it was not the first time *The Times* had given away a royal souvenir: in 1897 it had marked Queen Victoria's Diamond Jubilee with a commemorative plate – colour-printed in Germany.

It was on the day of the wedding that the paper achieved its real coup. All newspapers then printed in black and white since none of the Fleet Street machine rooms could handle full-colour reproduction on standard newspaper runs. But *The Times* had an alternative plan to dish its mono-chrome competitors. The photographer, Peter Trievnor, was engaged to catch the bride and groom as they emerged from the great west door of St Paul's Cathedral. With the precision planning of a crack assassin, he lay in wait for them from a seventh floor window in Juxon House, one of the ugly sixties office blocks then rudely jostling the Cathedral. It was calculated that he would only have a few seconds during which the royal couple would be in range. He had previously had two trial runs from the same vantage point on previous days in order to get it right. Even still, the margin for error was considerable especially given the happy couple's unerring ability to wave in a way that obscured one or the other's face. In the event, he managed to get eight shots in the few seconds in which the Prince and Princess passed the chosen spot.

Having taken what he hoped would be *the* photograph at 12.10 p.m., Trievnor raced to the foot of the building where a motorbike was waiting to collect the film. Once processed, it was hurried to Gray's Inn Road where Evans and the design director, Edwin Taylor, selected the image they wanted. The transparency was then biked to where the colour separations were done and from there – by now coming up against heavy post-wedding traffic – to Battersea Heliport. It was mid-afternoon and Reg Evans, the paper's head of editorial services, took it by helicopter to Peterborough where East Midlands Allied Press pre-printed the colour pictures onto reels. These reached Gray's Inn Road at 10.18 p.m. Feverishly the reels were fitted. But they did not work. The registration was terrible and there was static on the newsprint. Anxious moments passed until eventually the quality improved. In time, it was running perfectly and at 1.30 a.m. the first colour front page of *The Times* – indeed, of any national broadsheet – rolled off the press.

The result caused a sensation. The paper was a sell-out. A telegram arrived at Gray's Inn Road – 'Congratulations on a great technical achievement and a beautiful paper this morning. Gavin.'[40] It was from Lord Astor whose newspaper *The Times* had been until 1966. Actually, the revenue from higher sales was cancelled out by the cost of printing in colour, but it might prove merely a loss leader if it gained permanent converts to the paper. The circulation figures for August (which included the royal wedding edition) showed the paper's circulation had leapt to 303,000, up from 268,797 the same time the previous year.[41] What remained to be seen was whether this was a one-off wedding bonanza or a movement that could be sustained.

One change that the wedding brought that did stay was on the paper's masthead. From the first edition in 1785 until 1966 *The Times*'s masthead had borne the royal coat of arms, but this had fallen victim to 'modernization' when the paper was redesigned to carry news on the front page. The presence of the royal arms had accentuated the uneven lengths of '*The*' and '*Times*' and made the masthead appear off-centre at the top of the page. Stanley Morison had wanted to remove it in 1932 but was dissuaded by the strong opposition of John Walter, scion of the paper's founder, who still held shares in the company.[42] But the eventual exclusion of the device was a doubtful improvement since it made the paper's masthead excessively austere and bare. Evans had intended to revive the royal arms for the paper's two hundredth anniversary in 1985 (he had little doubt he would still be in the chair for it) but the huge acclaim from staff and readers to his inclusion of it on the royal wedding edition convinced him that it should stay there forthwith.

In fact, *The Times* had no more right – and never had – to carry the royal arms than any other newspaper. It did not have the necessary royal warrant, a point the College of Arms had, with ineffectual menaces, periodically brought to the editor's attention. Although there was some inconsistency over the years, the paper had tended to use the royal arms of the day, but Evans decided to go back to the original coat of arms of King George III. It is this set of arms – complete with the white horse of Hanover in the bottom right quarter – that has graced each edition of the paper since 1981.

With Gray's Inn Road awash with self-congratulation and the royal couple sailing away on *Britannia* for their honeymoon, Evans chose his moment to slip out of the country for a three-week holiday. He had scarcely rested since his appointment and most impartial observers could only conclude his opening months had been a success, speckled with moments of triumph. In fact, he too was off to get married.

A fifty-two-year-old father of three, Evans had been divorced from his schoolteacher wife, Enid, after twenty-five years of marriage in 1978 and for the past six years had been seen in the company of his fiancée, the up-and-coming twenty-seven-year-old editor of *Tatler*, Tina Brown. The couple married on 19 August at the Long Island home of Evans's friend, the renowned *Washington Post* editor, Ben Bradlee. Bradlee was Evans's best man and, with the bride's parents in Spain, Anthony Holden stepped in to give the bride away. Anna Blundy, daughter of the *Sunday Times*'s fearless foreign correspondent, David Blundy, was maid of honour. However far from Fleet Street, it was still a journalists' wedding. Some months later, Evans dropped a memo to Colin Watson, the obituaries editor, telling him to advise his contributors to 'introduce the subject's marriage(s) if any, at the appropriate chronological moment. A marriage and the support of a wife is often an important point in a person's life and we have come to the conclusion that it is wrong merely to tack on a sentence to say that so and so is survived by various people.'[43]

IV

Mr and Mrs Harold Evans spent part of their honeymoon staying with Henry Kissinger. Evans wanted Kissinger to write a weekly column for *The Times* and, after consultations with Murdoch, promised a financial inducement the scale of which would have been unprecedented in the paper's history.[44] In the meantime, he had been reading the drafts for the second volume of Kissinger's memoirs, *Years of Upheaval 1973–77*, even helping to rewrite certain passages. This was not a role he would have easily taken upon himself with regard to a senior British political figure. In London, Evans was anxious to avoid compromising entanglement between press and politicians, but he enjoyed a more relaxed perspective across the Atlantic and, in later years, he and his wife would happily mix their journalistic careers with the society of, in particular, leading Democrats.

It was a verdict on the past four years rather than a discovery of latent Toryism that had encouraged Evans to vote Conservative in the 1979 general election. Observing him in the morning conferences, Frank Johnson came to the conclusion that Evans, while an enthusiastic campaigner, did not have a considered political position or particular insight into the Westminster village. He had grown up assuming that the welfare state had improved opportunity immeasurably. The arguments propounded by Keith Joseph and the Institute for Economic Affairs, then gripping the radical right of the Conservative Party, had made little impact upon him.

But they had not escaped Frank Johnson, the lone Thatcherite in the editor's trusted circle (Evans used to tease him in the morning conference by summoning his contribution with the cry, 'I call upon the Leader of the Opposition'). Evans and Johnson shared a non-middle class background. Johnson was the son of a pastry chef. Working his way up from local reporting to the *Sun*, he had been a parliamentary sketchwriter for the *Daily Telegraph* before joining James Goldsmith's short-lived *Now!* magazine (fortuitously leaving it for *The Times* only days before that journal's demise). While Evans was a proud Durham University graduate, Johnson was an autodidact with strong interests in opera and history who had been cultivated by the *Telegraph*'s coven of in-house Tory philosophers. 'I believed Britain was in a life or death struggle,' he later reflected, 'and that if Thatcher lost, it was all over for Britain.' He did not sense that Evans, admiring the achievements of the welfare state and sixties progressivism, shared the same sense of urgency. What was more, Evans had placed the paper's political direction in the hands of Bernard Donoughue who, fresh from advising James Callaghan, was opposed to the line Johnson wanted *The Times* to take.[45]

That line was set almost from the first day of Evans's editorship by the paper's analysis of Geoffrey Howe's 1981 Budget. The headline, 'Harsh Budget for workers but more for business', was, according to Paul Johnson in the *Spectator*, 'the headline which we all thought was the copyright of the *Morning Star* and kept in permanent type there'. The subheading, which claimed 'unexpectedly harsh tax increases', did not seem to follow the accurate predictions that the paper had been making on this very subject over the previous days. Meanwhile, the assertion that the Budget was pro-business was contradicted in the business news section where both the City and industry were stated as being distinctly cool about the measures. *The Times*'s handling was, according to Paul Johnson, 'a disaster'. He also detected hyperbole in the headlines of succeeding days such as 'Chancellor under savage attack from all quarters' and a headline on higher education cuts 'Fears of university system collapsing from loss of income'.[46] This was the sensitivity of a Thatcheritie convert, but 'all quarters' and 'collapsing' left little margin for error.

It was certainly difficult to read the front page without concluding a disaster had befallen the country. Fred Emery's report made the most of 'this muddle of severity against consumers with no clear thrust of benefits to business that worries a number of senior Conservatives'.[47] By contrast, the summary of the Treasury's forecasts by the economics editor, David Blake, was in the older, straight-reporting tradition of the principal news page. The leader column was where opinion was supposed to be located. This Evans wrote himself. He rejected both 'the primitive compass of monetary aggregates' and 'crude expansion'. Instead he argued that the country was locked in a vicious circle where rising unemployment was pushing up current expenditure while capital expenditure, a fifth of all public spending as recently as 1974, had fallen to one tenth. The consequence of this for the country's infrastructure was harming business, thereby pushing up social security payments. It was not entirely clear where the editorial thought the balance should be, although Evans's belief that 'prudent control of the money supply' was 'no longer an adequate prescription for policy' implied he was backsliding from Rees-Mogg's commitment to sound money.[48] As Evans assured Michael Foot with a slight sideswipe at one of Rees-Mogg's more distinctive obsessions, 'I cannot promise much but at least there will be no more articles calling for the return of the gold standard.'[49]

The Prime Minister, Margaret Thatcher, believed the Budget's critics had got it wrong. Far from being deflationary, reducing Government borrowing would precipitate a fall in interest rates and a reduction in sterling's overvalued exchange rate.[50] In the short term this proved accurate, with interest rates falling 2 per cent, to 12 per cent, the day after the Budget. By October, though, it was a run on the pound that caused nervousness, and interest rates were hiked back up to a crippling 16 per cent.

At the end of March, 364 economists sent a letter to The Times denouncing monetarism. The signatories included seventy-six present or past professors and five former chief economic advisers to the Government. It was the idea of two Cambridge professors, Frank Hahn and Robert Nield, and academics at thirty-six universities appended their names. Although it became famous as the 'Letter to The Times', the newspaper almost squandered it. David Blake wrote up the story, but its front-page position was anything but prominent and much of it was continued fifteen pages on in the business news section. By the time it attracted a leader article, the following day, it had been downgraded by the altogether more dramatic story of the assassination attempt on President Reagan.

But the letter was important, not only as a counterblast of the learned and eminent against the Government's economic policy but also as a measure of the culture clash between those now in power and the academic community whose stipends were about to be cut. The letter did give grounds for ambiguity. It claimed there was 'no basis in economic theory or supporting evidence for the Government's belief that by deflating demand they will bring inflation permanently under control' or, as a consequence, bring about an economic recovery. In ignoring the alternatives to monetarism, 'Present polices will deepen the depression'.[51]

When the leading article 'An Avalanche of Economists' appeared, it was somewhat more circumspect. It avoided explicitly endorsing the round-robin letter but made clear The Times believed the Treasury's fixation with Sterling M3 concentrated minds upon too narrow a measure of the money supply. Rather, there was now a need for controlled reflation rather than further deflation.[52] The monetarist response appeared in the business pages in an article by Patrick Minford, Professor of Economics at Liverpool University. His article so pleased the Prime Minister that she wrote to congratulate him.[53] Suspecting the 364s' 'apparently political ends', Minford claimed they were more Keynesian than Keynes: Keynes had supported reflation in 1932 when there was sub-zero inflation and less than 1 per cent money supply growth. He had thus advocated price stability. But the public sector borrowing requirement for 1980–81 was an inflationary 4 per cent. Consequently, reducing the PSBR would create the structure for the sort of price stability Keynes had in mind. Recent history suggested incomes policies were not an effective alternative. What was more, Minford even maintained 'there is no evidence that those with sound long-term prospects are going to the wall' since 'the stock market is now increasing the capitalization of even the hardest hit sectors'.[54] Nigel Lawson later wrote of the 364 economists, 'Their timing was exquisite. The economy embarked on a prolonged phase of vigorous growth almost from the moment the letter was published'.[55] This may have surprised the still swelling ranks of the unemployed, but it was true, nonetheless. The standard measure of national output, gross domestic product (GDP), reached its bottom in the first quarter of 1981, at the very moment when the massed ranks of academia staked their reputations to the statement 'present policies will deepen the depression'.

The end of fixed exchange rates in 1972 had freed governments from the necessity of manipulating their balance of payments to stay in check in order to uphold the exchange rate parity. This liberty permitted running up a persistent budget deficit as a means to stimulate demand and fund the welfare benefits of those for whom there remained no demand. But easing discipline in this way quickly drove western governments onto a road to ruin and by the late seventies Whitehall was desperately trying to rein back the PSBR's share of GDP. The squeeze applied by the Thatcher Government's high interest rate policy also had the effect of pushing up the exchange rate because high rates of interest made it attractive for 'forex' traders to buy sterling. At a time when North Sea oil revenues were already giving the pound the credentials of a petrocurrency, the resulting high exchange rate made exports yet more uncompetitive. During 1981, *The Times* became increasingly hostile to the notion that the Government, obsessed by its monetary targets, should have no view on what the appropriate exchange rate should be. In July, a leader column, 'The Price of Floating', attacked the whole post-1972 free-for-all. Railing against 'the ideology of do-nothing monetarism' with its exclusive focus on combating inflation, the editorial maintained that since 'it is doubtful if a sensible exchange rate policy can be maintained unilaterally' it was necessary to restore international cooperation.[56]

Supporting calls for new world central banking institutions to curb the supposed excesses of the foreign exchange markets, Evans wrote a leading article claiming, 'our fortunes and our prospects have been devastated' by 'the experiment with floating rates and the stupendous growth of international mobile funds'. There was 'a currency casino' in operation when 'on the world market the average trading volume in currency is now some 70,000 million dollars *a day*, a volume by which the global trade in goods, services and investment is insignificant'. The leader article mentioned Enoch Powell and Samuel Brittan among the false prophets who had preached floating as a means of ridding the country of its balance of payments problems. In fact, Peter Jay had penned an influential four column *Times* leader article in September 1976 advocating monetarism and a 'cleanly' floating currency only days before he had drafted the speech his father-in-law, James Callaghan, delivered to the Labour Party conference denouncing reflationary politics – a turning point in the country's affairs. But in July 1981, *The Times* renounced its own former position with the excuse that 'the beginning of wisdom is the admission of error' (unfortunately the 'i' was missing from the word 'is' when the sentence was printed).[57]

Margaret Thatcher had told the 1980 Conservative Party conference,

'You turn if you want; the lady's not for turning.' With Evans at the steering wheel, *The Times* now made clear it was performing a very public U-turn. It marked the 1981 party conference debate on economic policy with a damning analysis of monetarism by James Tobin, the Yale professor who had the previous day been named as the winner of the 1981 Nobel Prize for Economics.[58]

'Three million unemployed and still more to come' was the front-page headline for Melvyn Westlake's report that one in eight of the workforce was without a job and that the figure – which excluded a third of a million more on special employment and training schemes – was likely to keep rising at least until 1983. This proved an optimistic forecast. The accompanying leader column concluded that with output below its 1974 level and the national fabric fragmenting:

> It is devastatingly clear that Britain needs massive investment, private and public, to restore its competitive strength . . . The Europeans are valiantly trying to create a pool of lower interest rates to protect their nascent recovery from another surge of American interest rates . . . we need not be flotsam on the high seas.[59]

The paper's position had suffered from the conundrum that if it thought the exchange rate was so overvalued, why was it wanting to see it locked in at such a rate? But a relatively trouble-free realignment of the major currencies within the European Monetary System encouraged the leader column to adopt the line that it was 'a good time for Britain to join'.[60] This allowed the paper to preach currency stability and commitment to the 'European Vision' that Rees-Mogg's paper had encouraged. But it was premature for it to declare, 'the excuse that the pound is now a petro-currency is not valid'.[61] On currency stability, as on 'European Vision', *The Times* would find consistency as difficult to sustain as did the Treasury.

Indeed, it was across the English Channel that the paper needed to look if it wanted to see alternatives to monetarism in practice rather than theory. A golden opportunity was provided by the victory of François Mitterrand over Válery Giscard d'Estaing. Sixteen years had separated Mitterrand from his first challenge (to de Gaulle in 1965) and his taking possession of the Elysée Palace. More importantly, as Charles Hargrove reported from Paris, it was a 'turning point' in French politics. It was the first presidential victory for the left in the twenty-three year life of the Fifth Republic. Indeed, it was the first time the left had been in complete power since Léon

Blum's ill-fated Popular Front in 1936. With the news of Mitterrand's triumph, Ian Murray reported that French customs officers were given urgent instructions to stop attempts to export money from the country: 'The officers have been told to watch particularly for large cars not registered in frontier areas.'[62]

While the Conservatives had abandoned exchange controls shortly after coming to power in Britain, Mitterrand tightened the French State's preventative powers to see capital exported beyond its border. A real socialist experiment was underway. Editorially, *The Times* was caught between fearing the possibility that a far left resurgence in the coming National Assembly elections could lead to a left–Communist coalition and the satisfaction of seeing the fall of Giscard d'Estaing and 'his scandalous relations' with the Central African Empire's Emperor Bokassa.[63] Writing in his column, Ronald Butt suggested Mitterrand's election might 'bring greater flexibility and a greater significance to the European voice' and 'establish for the first time that the European Community is not simply a vehicle for the centre-right' as it had been under its Christian Democrat domination (for even Germany's SPD Chancellor Schmidt 'makes the kind of leader many a British Tory would be glad to own'). The consequence could be a softening in the anti-EEC attitude of Britain's Labour Party.[64]

The British summer of 1981 was one of disorder. From a news reporting perspective, the most graphic examples came on the streets of Ulster and the deprived inner cities of England.

The hunger strikes among Irish Republican prisoners housed in the 'H-Blocks' of the Maze prison near Belfast had started in October 1980 with demands to wear their own clothes, to have the restrictions on their movement within the prison lifted and to be exempted from doing any work. The Government made a concession, permitting 'civilian style' (but not personal) clothing, but was wary of going further for fear that it was all part of an orchestrated IRA campaign to give their terrorists effective run of the prison and to see them accorded 'political prisoner' status. Indeed, a May 1980 report by the European Commission on Human Rights had rejected the bulk of the prisoners' complaints. A letter was smuggled out from an inmate of Wormwood Scrubs to *The Times* endorsing the view that Irish terrorists enjoyed a far laxer regime than British individuals convicted of more minor misdemeanours on the mainland.[65] The hunger strike had been called off in December 1980 when one of the participants lost consciousness. This was followed by a mass 'dirty protest' in which cells were deliberately fouled.

In March the dirty protests ended and the hunger strikes recommenced. By the time the campaign ended, seven months later, ten Republican prisoners had starved themselves to death. But it was the first prisoner to die who captured the public imagination and caused the most serious political upset. Bobby Sands was a twenty-seven-year-old Republican who had served five of his fourteen-year sentence for being caught with a gun in a car. His decision to stand for Parliament, *in absentia*, on an anti-H-Block ticket in the Fermanagh and South Tyrone by-election was given a boost when the Nationalist SDLP opted to stand aside, giving him a direct run against his Unionist opponent. The consequence of uniting the Nationalist and Republican vote was to hand Sands victory by a margin of 1446 votes.

Filing his *Times* report, Christopher Thomas suggested the result had 'dealt a severe blow to the stronghold of moderate Roman Catholic opinion, the Social Democratic and Labour Party, from which it may never fully recover. Recriminations over the party's failure to contest the seat are biting deep.'[66] *The Times*'s leader was in no mood to indulge dangerous games. 'The House of Commons should move at once, that is before the Easter recess, to unseat him,' it announced, continuing, 'that would be an entirely proper thing to do since he is precluded from attending the House for the duration of this parliament.' The clear extent of polarization precluded pushing ahead with early 'attempts to introduce provincial institutions acceptable to the leaders of both communities'. Instead, the Government was faced with no option but to concentrate on 'normalizing' the 'administration of the province within the United Kingdom'.[67]

In May, Sands died. The immediate response was an orgy of rioting in Belfast and protests beyond. But the main legacy was a propaganda coup for Irish Republicanism, attracting the world's media and drumming up financial support from United States citizens. *The Times* did not form up behind the long procession of mourners that followed Sands's IRA-decorated coffin. 'By refusing to submit to Mr Sands's blackmail, the British government bears no responsibility whatever for his death,' the leader column stated. 'He was not in prison for his beliefs, but for proved serious criminal offences. He was not being oppressed or ill-treated. Indeed the opposite was true. The prison rules applying to Northern Ireland allow for a more comfortable existence than do most English prisons.' It ended, 'There is only one killer of Bobby Sands and this is Sands himself.'[68] He did not get an obituary.

The paper's position continued to be stalwartly supportive of the Thatcher Government's inflexible approach, maintaining, 'It has chosen the right ground to stand on – denial of separate political status in name and substance.' As for the 'murderous' IRA leadership, 'Hope is their oxygen. It must be denied them.'[69] Mrs Thatcher would later refer to the need to cut off the IRA's 'oxygen of publicity'. But far from gulping for air, the Republican movement appeared wholly revived. Indeed, the upsurge of tension in Ulster ensured that *The Times* had to send its first itinerant news team there for many years, with Tim Jones and John Witherow joining the permanent reporter, Christopher Thomas. 'Amid mixed scenes of jubilation and despair,' Thomas reported from Enniskillen the victory of the IRA supporting candidate who retained – with an increased majority – the Fermanagh seat on Sands's death. The leader column condemned a situation in which 'the Irish Government and the Roman Catholic Hierarchy of Ireland so conspicuously qualify their condemnation of this extension of terrorist violence by piling the blame on British ministers for allowing it to continue'. In doing so, the hunger strikers were gaining the virtual 'status of martyrdom'.[70]

The IRA ensured that the hunger strike ended in October with a bang. They detonated a nail-bomb on a coach in Chelsea Barracks carrying Irish Guards. The following month the Unionist MP for Belfast South was shot dead while he was holding a surgery for his constituents. An Anglo-Irish summit brassed up the existing ministerial and official collaborations under a new name, 'The Inter-Governmental Council', but by the following spring, when the proposals of the Northern Ireland Secretary, Jim Prior, for 'rolling devolution' of responsibilities held by Whitehall back to Ulster were ready to get underway, they faced opposition from the SDLP and from across the border from the Taoiseach, Charlie Haughey. Sinn Fein made gains in the elections to the Northern Ireland Assembly in October 1982 and the SDLP members refused to take their seats, effectively torpedoing the project. Once again, the Province's future appeared to be wedged in an impasse. It would take time, and a more emollient attitude in Dublin with the election of Dr Garret Fitzgerald, before the next initiative could be sprung upon the Province.

During 1981, political unrest in Ulster was matched by social disorder in Britain's inner cities. In April, petrol bombs were thrown for the first time on the streets of the mainland. The Brixton riots injured 279 policemen and forty-five members of the public. Twenty-eight buildings were set on fire while surrounding shops were systematically looted. News of scuffles in Brixton came late and received minor billing in the following day's paper under the brief headline, 'Police hurt in scuffles with blacks'. But after a weekend of serious rioting and looting, the events dominated Monday 13 April's paper, forcing Michael Leapman's report from Cape Canaveral on the launch of the space shuttle *Columbia* to take second place on the front page. Inside the edition, Martin Huckerby, who had been jostled by the mob, provided a graphic eyewitness report of the chaos in Brixton:

> The only sign of authority was an abandoned fire engine astride the junction, its windows smashed and its wrecked equipment strewn across the road ... Red hot debris dripped from a series of burning buildings along both sides of the road. Amid the roaring of the flames and crashing of collapsing buildings there were screams and shouts. Despite the furnace of heat, figures could be seen running through the smoke, hurling missiles at unseen police.[71]

Elsewhere on the page the various angles were covered: an interview with a white woman who said she had come to fear the brooding violence of her largely black neighbourhood and 'a young, sharply dressed Guyanan black' who approved '"of what's happened. It's the only way people can put across their case".' The police's view was also represented and there was an article on Lambeth Council's attempts to grapple with housing allocation between its white and black areas. The leading article backed the establishment of a broad ranging enquiry – which the Home Secretary, Willie Whitelaw, announced that day would be conducted by Lord Scarman. On 15 April, Op-Ed featured a gripping article by the Indian journalist Sasthi Brata detailing how, blindfolded and threatened, he was taken by a black gang in Brixton to see their amateur bomb-making cottage industry while one of his captors told him: '"There's going to be a lot more, a big lot more, just tell 'em that. We ain't kidding. We goin' burn 'em down, everythin' everywhere."'[72]

Naturally, the immediate aftermath of the riots in Brixton (and those that followed in Southall and the Toxteth area of Liverpool) were dominated by the apportioning of blame. Political activism was pitched against insensitive policing, moral degeneracy against a trinity of overt racism, poor housing and unemployment. The affected areas combined high numbers of immigrants with a level of social deprivation that was all too obvious to see. But to what extent was the Thatcher Government to blame? That *The Times* stated nothing justified the rioters' behaviour was to be expected but it went further, conceding that the wider social issues were relevant and that the Scarman Inquiry should have the widest remit to consider them.

As for the Government, the leader article chose to pick on its inability to articulate and demonstrate a belief that its policies had a positive social dimension worthy of the same priority as the fight against inflation.[73]

But there was also the question of racism. In a leader entitled 'The Soiled Coin', *The Times* believed racist sentiments 'will not be resisted by preaching integration. This is a fallacy of the sixties. It is unrealizable, it is questionable if it is desirable, and it raises more fear and animosity than it dissipates with its overtones of inter-racial sex, marriage and a coffee-coloured Britain.' Social pluralism, it argued, was obtainable without tolerance requiring 'that every Englishman should have a black man for his neighbour or that every Asian should forget his cultural identity'. Rather, while 'the Government cannot be expected to resolve such a complex and volatile problem overnight' it could at least follow the American lead in encouraging the rapid promotion of 'qualified coloureds to positions of obvious authority – in the army, the police and above all the public service – so that the coloured community can identify with those who take decisions as well as those at the receiving end'.[74]

When it was published in November, the 150 page Scarman Report denied the existence of 'institutional racism' in Britain. Militant activists also disliked the report's support for the police who 'stood between our society and a total collapse of law and order on the streets'. But most sides of the community supported the principal recommendations: racist behaviour by police officers to be a sackable offence, better training, greater independent monitoring of the police complaints procedure, new statutory consultative committees with community liaison but no change to the Riot Act. Whitelaw moved immediately to endorse the principles of the report. Much of this was supported by *The Times*, although not Scarman's enthusiasm for 'taking the investigation as well as the adjudication of complaints out of the hands of the police' which was 'a minefield of good intentions'. Instead, ombudsmen and better lay scrutiny of the results of investigation would be preferable. The paper also lamented the failure to reform the Riot Act, taking the view that 'if a riot is in progress the offence is, or ought to be, being in on it. No one should be able to feel that he can join in with impunity provided no further offence can be proved against him.'[75]

But *The Times* also gave space on the Op-Ed page to Darcus Howe, editor of *Race Today*, billing him as 'a militant voice of black dissent'. According to Howe, the fault lay primarily with the way in which the police exercised their powers against the West Indian community. The trigger for the riots, Operation Swamp, had been regarded as a form of licensed harassment by Brixton's youth. Instead, Howe argued for the 'immediate abolition of all powers of stop and search'.[76]

The police countered that without 'stop and search' powers they had little chance of containing the violence and drug-related disorder that was prevalent in the inner cities and the areas dominated by blacks in particular. Yet, over the following fifteen years, the issue of racism slowly receded from the forefront of public debate until reignited towards the end of the century by the influx of asylum seekers and by the police's inadequate handling of the racist murder of a black teenager, Stephen Lawrence. With the resulting Lawrence Inquiry, specific sore points like 'stop and search' not only became live issues again, but Scarman's rejection of 'institutional racism' within the police force would be publicly revoked.

The critical tone adopted towards the Thatcher Government's fixation with setting targets for narrowly defined money supply growth may have given the impression that under Evans *The Times* believed the State was a font of civic largesse. Certainly, the paper took the view that the Government needed to invest more in capital expenditure, citing the view of one with such impeccable monetarist credentials as Milton Friedman that there was no necessary relation between monetary growth and the size of the public sector borrowing requirement. But the paper took a more parsimonious view with regard to current expenditure. The Treasury's demand of a 4 per cent public sector pay increase (at a time when inflation was running in double-digit per cent) was welcomed as an essential contribution to combating inflation. Indeed, the leader column argued that public sector workers had no right to expect the same pay parity with those in 'the risk-taking' private sector. What was more, those working in the nationalized industries should also see their wage increases pruned, 'and that includes the wages of the miners and water workers as well as civil servants. If it means a hard winter, so be it.'[77] In this respect, *The Times* seemed ready to take on the miners before Mrs Thatcher, with memories of their defeat of Edward Heath, was prepared to do.

Not many miners read *The Times*. But on the issue of cuts in higher education, the newspaper was trespassing on the personal finances of a core area of its readership. In March 1980 the Government had announced three-year spending cuts in higher education. By May the following year, it was clear the University Grants Committee had failed to mitigate the full effects and universities braced themselves for falling matriculation rolls and the possibility of whole departments being axed as a consequence of an 8.5 per cent cut being enforced. Their woes were compounded by a fall in the income from foreign students, following the Government's announcement that it would stop subsidizing fees for foreign students who would, in future, be charged the full cost of their course. Diana Geddes, the education correspondent, analysed the 'grim future' facing Britain's universities. As a consequence of the 1963 Robbins Report, the proportion of eighteen-year-olds in higher education had risen from 3 per cent in the early 1950s to 14 per cent by the 1970s. The Government was now putting this process into reverse, having, as Geddes put it, 'abandoned once and for all the Robbins principle that all those suitably qualified by ability and attainment should have the right to higher education'.

The universities were now paying the price for becoming the dependent wards of the State: over 90 per cent of their income came from public funds. But even 'an overdue pruning of dead wood' would be expensive. Redundancy bills alone could reach £200 million. This would wipe out most of the savings from reducing student numbers. Geddes's article suggested that the Government might be better achieving its cuts by instead reducing its contribution to local authority-administered colleges and polytechnics – these 'less respected institutions in the public sector' – many of whose staff did not enjoy the same academic tenure and who would thus be much cheaper to sack.[78] In its leader column, the paper was prepared to accept the wrath of its readership in academia by stating that the cuts were necessary in the economic climate in which the country found itself.[79]

The plights of publicly funded professionals certainly provided a fitting moment for the Social Democratic Party (SDP) to launch itself. Departing the editor's chair in carefree demob spirit, Rees-Mogg had penned one of his last leader articles by endorsing Shirley Williams as the best future hope for 10 Downing Street. The Labour Party's lurch to the left under James Callaghan's successor, Michael Foot, had been demonstrated in January 1981 when a special conference held at Wembley voted to elect future leaders through an electoral college made up principally of trade union block votes and of party activists. The Parliamentary Labour Party would be reduced to the status of minority shareholders. The immediate consequence of this was the breakaway of the moderate 'Gang of Four' (Shirley Williams, David Owen, Roy Jenkins and Bill Rodgers) to form the Council for Social Democracy. In March, the first twelve Labour MPs resigned the whip and the SDP was born.

The 'Gang of Four' were Murdoch's first guests to lunch at Gray's Inn Road. The main boardroom's table was rather long, ensuring a disconcerting distance between each of the quiet revolutionaries. Fearing they might be given short shrift from the proprietor, Evans came away relieved that Murdoch had asked 'polite, probing questions on policy'.[80] Indeed, the SDP's Communications Committee harboured hopes, believing Murdoch was 'usually open to persuasion, if not to be converted, at least to give us a fair crack'.[81] With no established national organization and without the funding of the trade unions or big business, the party's success was dependent upon achieving maximum publicity in order to attract a mass membership quickly. The party's birth was the main front page story in every national daily apart from the *Sun*. *The Times* reported the party's opening press conference under the informative if underwhelming headline 'SDP pleased by initial recruitment response'. Fred Emery and Ian Bradley reported from 'a crowded news conference in London, staged brilliantly for television, and with a claque of applauding supporters'.

The SDP was launched with twelve policy tasks. Several were phrased in the inclusive language common to the public aspirations of all mainstream politicians. But a few distinctive polices stood out. The party differed from Thatcherism through its belief in a long-term incomes policy and a mixed economy in which 'public and private firms should flourish side by side without frequent frontier changes'. In other words, it rejected monetarism as the principal means of curbing inflation and it would not role back the frontiers of the State. It was at odds with the Labour left by wanting to stay within the EEC and NATO and in resisting unilateral nuclear disarmament. It upheld traditional Liberal Party interests in constitutional reform, particularly of the House of Lords and the introduction of proportional representation. Yet overall, its bias was summed up from the first by Bill Rodgers who told the assembled press that the SDP was 'not a new centre party, we are very plainly a left-of-centre party'.[82] As *The Times* put it in its leader, 'with the exception of proportional representation there is no major policy being propounded by the Social Democrats now which was not at least attempted by the Callaghan Government'.[83]

It was natural that there should be curiosity and, indeed, excitement at the launch of a major new force in British politics. The SDP's difficulty was in sustaining it in the months ahead, denied, as it was, the ability of the Government or the official Opposition to set the agenda in Parliament. It needed constant media interest. In this respect, *The Times* was less helpful than might have been expected. Unless there was a by-election campaign underway, the SDP rarely got more than two front-page mentions a week.[84] This was surprising, given the extent to which the SDP gained the reputation of being the journalists' party with high-profile supporters like the

Guardian's Polly Toynbee, Anthony Sampson of the *Observer* and even the *Daily Mirror*'s agony aunt, Marjorie Proops. Tony Benn was convinced the BBC was an 'agency of the SDP'.[85] The chronicler of the *Guardian* would even conclude that the 'chief reason' for the paper's 'success in the early 1980s was that the Social Democratic Party was founded in its pages and the battle for the soul of the Labour party fought out there'.[86] No such claim could be entertained by *The Times*. But the paper's editorial line might have tilted more obviously towards the SDP if Rees-Mogg had continued as editor. He had made clear his belief that Shirley Williams was a figure around which a new national consensus could be constructed. Back in 1972, when the Labour Party appeared close to self-destruction over the Heath Government's EEC entry terms, the Rees-Mogg *Times* had looked favourably on the possible creation of a government of the centre (that is to say, pro-EEC) under the leadership of Roy Jenkins. In the three general elections during which Rees-Mogg was editor (the paper was off the streets in 1979) *The Times* had expressed the hope of seeing an increase in the Liberal Party's seats so that they might prove a moderating force on the two principal parties.

But if *The Times* under Harry Evans did not rush to pledge itself to the SDP's red, white and blue colours, the atmosphere in Gray's Inn Road was nonetheless respectful towards the new party. Its initial by-election performance suggested it was being taken seriously by an electorate fearful of Labour's leftwards lurch and repulsed by the economic and social cost of Thatcher's medicine. At a by-election in Warrington in July, Roy Jenkins achieved a 23 per cent swing to the SDP, almost unseating Labour in its heartland. The Conservative candidate lost his deposit. In October, following the creation of the 'Alliance' with the Liberal Party, a Liberal activist, Bill Pitt, became the first Lib-SDP Alliance candidate to win a seat, taking Croydon North-West from the Conservatives on a 24 per cent swing. Then, in November, Shirley Williams took Crosby from the Conservatives, recording the biggest turnover of votes in any parliamentary by-election. Repeated at a general election on a nationwide scale, it would give the Alliance 533 MPs, Labour 78 and the Conservatives four. The SDP really looked as if it might succeed in its great project, to break the mould of British politics.

By-elections are problematic for newspapers since the lateness of the declaration plays havoc with newspaper production. Nonetheless, Brian MacArthur and his team managed to beat the competition with the speed in which *The Times* led with Bill Pitt's capture of Croydon. Unfortunately, the front page went to press with a pre-arranged victory article, 'Our Credibility Barrier is Broken' by Shirley Williams, to accompany it. By placing a partisan opinion piece by Williams on the front page, the paper appeared to be not only confusing news with comment but almost endorsing her party. This was a genuine slip. Nonetheless, Evans had to field a call the next day from an irate Gerald Long, the uncompromising new managing director of Times Newspapers, demanding an explanation.[87]

Whatever the placement on the front page, nobody could be in any doubt what the back page of *The Times* made of the SDP's progress. That was where Frank Johnson's daily parliamentary sketch appeared. To Johnson the 'Gang of Four' provided a rich quarry for satire. Roy Jenkins was 'a Fabergé of an egghead ... shining, exquisitely crafted, full of delights, a much loved gracious figure who is to the liberal classes what the Queen Mother is to the rest of us'. The SDP, he would later note in 1986, was 'a happy party, fit for all factions', there being:

> the Owenites; the Jenkinsites; the Elizabeth Davidites; those who want a successor to Polaris; those who want a successor to their Volvo; militant Saabs; supporters of Tuscany for August as opposed to the Dordogne; members of those car pools by which middle class families share the burden of driving their children to the local prep school; owners of exercise machines; people who have already gone over to compact discs ... readers of *Guardian* leaders; and (a much larger group) writers of *Guardian* leaders.[88]

But besides the affectionate whimsy, Frank Johnson was also a perceptive judge. He foresaw the strategic weakness in the SDP's condition. As he noted in September 1982, in lacking 'the irrational emotions, the cranky zeal, that drives on the rank and file of the other parties' the SDP's supporters would eventually become demoralized by any faltering in momentum. And that faltering would come. Johnson had been introduced to Maurice Cowling and the school of Tory historians at Cambridge's oldest college, Peterhouse, who rejected Whig and Marxist interpretations of historical progress and inevitability in favour of a 'high politics' view of men and events. Johnson applied this approach in his own analysis. Try as the SDP might to take a rational or scientific approach, he reminded them 'politics is not a "subject" or an academic discipline. It is simply the random play of chance on a few ambitious politicians. No one, no matter how great an authority on "politics", predicted the Falklands war.'[89]

This was not an approach shared by the theorists of the left, where historical inevitability remained the vogue – especially if it could be given a push with the sort of underhand tactics still employed in the Eastern Bloc or Britain's student unions. Twenty-four hours after Labour had won control of the Greater London Council (GLC) on 7 May 1981, its group leader, the moderate Andrew McIntosh, was ousted in an internal coup by the left wing Ken Livingstone. The radical left now had the opportunity to show what they could do with – or to – Britain's capital city. As 'Red Ken' put it to Nicholas Wapshott who interviewed him for *The Times* shortly after the successful putsch, 'if the left GLC fails, it will be a sad day for the left everywhere'. Wapshott did not paint a favourable background for his subject, stating that, 'as the housing chief of Camden, Livingstone's performance was generally considered abysmal' and ended with Livingstone enthusing about his pet salamanders: 'I feed them on slugs and woodlice. They just live under a stone, come out at night and are highly poisonous. People say I identify with my pets.'[90]

The Times was not impartial in its commentary on the left's progress within the Labour Movement. The paper thought it iniquitous and was not slow to say so. When the former Labour Cabinet minister Lord George Brown asked if he could pen articles for the paper, Evans replied affirmatively, suggesting 'we are particularly interested in the Communists making inroads into the Labour Party'.[91] During September, the paper ran extracts from a forthcoming book by David and Maurice Kogan on the activities of left-wing activists in Tony Benn's campaign team, the 'Campaign for Labour Party Democracy' and the 'Rank and File Mobilizing Committee' who were trying to make the party leadership answerable to the activists rather than the Members of Parliament.[92] Labour was now led by the left wing, nuclear unilateralist, Michael Foot. But in September the battle commenced for the Deputy Leadership. Although this was not a position that involved the wielding of great power itself, the belief that Foot, aged sixty-eight, was a caretaker leader turned it into the struggle for the future of the party, one that was made critical by the possibility of it being won by Tony Benn.

Outside the ranks of his supporters, Tony Benn was perhaps the most feared figure in British politics. For those on the right, it would be more accurate to describe him as a hate figure. He certainly frightened *The Times*. Having seen Benn at close quarters during his period working with Callaghan, none was keener to save the Labour Party from him than Bernard Donoughue. With the Deputy Leadership election pending,

Donoughue suggested the moment had come for a hatchet job on Benn in the form of an investigation into his considerable financial interests.[93] This would show the great tribune of wealth redistribution to be a multi-millionaire who had craftily ring-fenced his own money. The piece appeared on 25 September in a profile of the contenders which described Benn as 'a wealthy aristocrat who waged a remarkable campaign to shed his peerage and upbringing'. The profile stated that his 'main assets' were:

> shares in Benn Bros, publishers; large house in Holland Park and farm in Essex; most of the Benn family wealth comes from legacies and trusts connected with his American-born wife, Caroline. The estimated total is several million dollars: city sources confirm the existence of a Stansgate trust in the tax haven of the Bank of Bermuda. No details of amounts or beneficiaries have ever been disclosed.[94]

The following day *The Times* found itself in the embarrassing position of printing an apology attached to Benn's letter of complaint. Evans also wrote a personal letter to him. Benn's letter stated, 'Neither I nor my family have ever owned a farm nor had any assets in any trust in Bermuda or any tax haven in the world . . . I might add that your account of my wife's assets is grossly exaggerated.'[95] So much for 'city sources' – the information had been supplied by two outside informants. The editor dictated a memo to Anthony Holden, Fred Emery and Adrian Hamilton, the business editor, concluding that the lesson to be learned was 'that incidental attacks on someone like this are not worth making. It is only worth attacking or exposing someone, in any event, when we have very high certainty of our evidence.'[96]

The Deputy Leadership result was to be announced at the Labour Party Conference in Brighton. The declaration was expected in the evening so two different leader articles had been pre-prepared depending on the result. The leader assuming a Benn victory concluded that Michael Foot should 'resign immediately'. 'Both from personal self-respect,' it elaborated, 'and for the good of the Labour Party he should resign instead of providing a fig leaf of shabby respectability for the extremists who have now taken over the Labour Party.'[97]

In the event, *The Times* was not able to run that night with either leading article: a strike by the NGA print union prevented the paper from coming out. Thus was missed the chance to report on an evening of great drama. John Silkin had been eliminated in the first ballot. Benn's rival, the former

Chancellor of the Exchequer, Denis Healey, appeared to have victory in the bag when the Silkin-supporting TGWU announced that it would use its 1.25 million block votes in the electoral college to abstain in the second round. Healey duly arrived in triumph at the conference hall only to discover that the TGWU had decided at the last moment to vote for Benn instead. This suddenly made the result a cliffhanger. When the declaration was made, Benn secured 49.574 per cent of the vote. Healey had squeezed home by a hair's breadth.

Unrepentant in defeat, Benn claimed the 'incoming tide' was with him despite the fact that, 'The privately-owned Press without exception have done all they possibly could to discredit the Labour party, its electoral mechanism, Socialism and the arguments we were putting forward in the campaign. To have got Fleet Street down to fifty-point-something in the Labour party is quite an achievement.'[98] At least *The Times* and the rest of the 'privately-owned Press' knew what to expect if ever the great champion of State control ever did surf in on the 'incoming tide'.

Healey's victory prevented a potentially fatal defection of Labour MPs and supporters to the SDP. By a fraction of 1 per cent he probably saved his party. In doing so, he dished the SDP. When *The Times* returned after the strike, its sigh of relief was all but audible. For the contest to be 'a turning point' the moderates within the Labour Party would have to regain their lost ground.[99] Over 80 per cent of party activists in the constituencies had voted for Benn in the Deputy Leadership ballot, but his colleagues in the Parliamentary Labour Party held him in less regard and when Foot made clear he wanted rid of his turbulent priest, Benn failed to be elected by the MPs into the Shadow Cabinet. But he had not finished in his assault on the media. In March 1982, Benn chose a conference of Pan-Hellenic socialists in Athens to announce that British democracy was threatened by its military (in its pursuit of the arms race) and by its media. Britain, he said, did not have a free press because he could not point to a single newspaper that reflected his views. Catching the eye of *The Times* reporter, Mario Modiano, Benn added:

> And *The Times*, dare I say to you, is really disreputable. It does not print truthfully and faithfully what happens and it pretends, because it is printed in small print that it is above argument. But it is a political propaganda instrument like the *Sun*, but it is printed in rather better print and rather shrewder language.[100]

Benn had a particular reason for lumping the *Sun* and *The Times* together. In January 1982, the *Sun* had printed allegations of widespread drunkenness, absenteeism, rota tampering and moonlighting by train drivers. In retaliation, the drivers' ASLEF union called on its members to 'black' not only the *Sun* but – on the grounds it had the same owner – *The Times* as well. Without access to the trains, the paper could not be distributed. The 'blacking' continued even after a promise to revoke it in the High Court had been secured. Ultimately, the dispute kept *The Times* off the streets for five days. Benn told an NUJ branch meeting that unions were right to black newspapers that printed 'lies' about them in a struggle in which 'day after day Fleet Street conducts its campaign against working people'. He accused journalists who did the bidding of their editors and owners instead of reporting facts accurately as being like 'Jews in Dachau who herded other Jews into the gas chambers'.[101] But if Benn had come to the conclusion that new laws were needed to – as he phrased it – ensure wider press diversity, News International drew different lessons from the dispute with ASLEF: the sooner the strike-prone British Rail distribution system could be replaced with a non-unionized road freight service, the better.

V

Harold Evans had descended upon *The Times* like a whirlwind, whisking up copy, tossing forth ideas, upturning traditional – sometimes lazy – ways of doing things; chopping and changing, a centrifugel force pulsating without let-up late into the night. Left in the wake of this force of nature was a fair degree of desolation. To notice this, the editor would have had to look back. And this was not his job. Murdoch had wanted someone who would upturn a few chairs in the cosy atmosphere of the old clubroom and Harry Evans, ably assisted by his young protégé, Tony Holden, succeeded admirably in this rearrangement. It was to be his undoing.

At the time Evans was appointed, Murdoch installed a new managing director at Times Newspapers. While Evans would handle the creative side of the paper, Gerald Long would stabilize its finances. Evans had been able to work his magic at the *Sunday Times* partly thanks to the millions Thomson let him spend in realizing his ideas. But Murdoch was trying to make *The Times*'s books balance and this was not going to be achieved by throwing money around. Thus there might well have been tension between Evans and whoever was assigned to keep his paper on an even financial keel. Nonetheless, in choosing Gerald Long, Murdoch found a character whose individual chemistry was never likely to bond with that of the editor.

Long had been born in 1922, the son of a well-read postman. Sent to the ancient but minor public school of St Peter's, York, he had progressed to Cambridge. During the war, he had been in the Army Intelligence Corps, serving in the Middle East and Europe. After the end of the war he had helped to establish German newspapers in the British-occupied zone of the country. In 1948 he joined Reuters and, after a stint in Paris, became Reuters' chief representative in Germany between 1956 and 1960. When he became chief executive in 1963, Reuters was a loss-making company. But Long had innovative ideas. Taking advantage of developments in information technology, he introduced 'Monitor', a terminal that allowed subscribers to check share prices around the world, thereby creating an electronic dealing floor. 'Monitor' became part of the technology that drove the international financial revolution from the 1960s onwards. And in turning its owner into as much a provider of financial as news services, it transformed Reuters' fortunes. In recognition, Long started to be referred to as the company's 'second founder'. He had been chief executive of Reuters for eighteen years and was looking for a fresh challenge when Murdoch asked him to renovate Times Newspapers. He accepted immediately.

It was not one of Murdoch's more successful transplants. Long had no knowledge of modern newspaper production, editing or advertising. As chairman of Reuters, Sir Denis Hamilton had seen rather more of Long than had Murdoch and did not think the appointment wise. Hamilton accepted that Long had 'a first-class brain' but 'he was not a leader'.[102] Evans was intrigued by this man who was 'something quite special, an intellectual who has seen the world'. Yet he found his irascibility impossible to deal with: 'His normal manner was so aggressive it provoked reaction. It was derived from reading books rather than observing men.'[103] It quickly became clear that he did not get on with the editor. This put the proprietor in a position. Should he side with his editor or his managing director? If neither, would he have to waste time as a court of higher authority, perpetually adjudicating on their disputes?

The precarious financial position of Times Newspapers in 1981 provided the context for the tug of war. The recession was hitting advertising. TNL's cash cow, the *Sunday Times Colour Magazine*, was finding it hard to generate its former yield and selling display advertising was especially tough for a paper like *The Times* whose questionable future had been so frequently in the news. The new advertising director, Mike Ruda, did away with the separate *Times* and *Sunday Times* advertising display sales departments, combining them together on the fifth floor of *The Times* building. Ruda, a fifty-year-old former javelin thrower for South London Harriers, had been in newspaper advertising since 1954. He had been advertising director of the joint *Sun* and *News of the World* ad sales and Murdoch looked to him to introduce some of that drive into Gray's Inn Road. Ruda did not like what he found, later commenting:

> There was very poor morale. There was a notable lack of what I would call professional selling skills and those people – and there were very few of them – who did have any ability, had been suffocated. Drastic action had to be undertaken fairly quickly to get rid of the dead wood.[104]

Ruda set about his task. Among those he brought in to help sell space was Clive Milner, a young advertising rep from the *Observer* who would end up becoming managing director not only of Times Newspapers but also of the entire News International Group. Evans was uneasy about the changes, telling Murdoch he thought integrating *The Times* and *Sunday Times* advertising departments was a questionable idea 'because selling the two papers seems to require entirely different techniques'.[105] Murdoch, however, believed the merger directly benefited *The Times*. It had not enough advertising while the *Sunday Times* attracted more than it had space to print. Integration facilitated diverting some of this surplus to the daily broadsheet.[106] The process of integration continued in other areas and in November 1982 the two papers' circulation offices were brought together. Long was even put in charge of a feasibility study to see what the savings would be if *The Times* building was relinquished and its staff accommodated next door in the suitably refurbished *Sunday Times* building.[107] The very thought of such a cohabitation horrified many *Times* stalwarts for whom a set of floorboards seemed to offer insufficient protection for their paper's editorial independence from the more popular Sunday title. Few in either paper were sorry when the proposal was ditched. It was also a relief to hear Murdoch state that he would not shift the papers to the East End site of Wapping, where he was fitting out a new printing facility for the *Sun* and the *News of the World*.[108]

When it came to industrial relations, *The Times* was done no favours by being within infection range of the *Sunday Times*. At the end of the first week in June 1981, SOGAT called a strike at the *Sunday Times* that cost the paper 400,000 copies. The union had acted in breach of its agreement with News International setting out a specific disputes procedure in which production was supposed to continue while negotiations took place. This was no trivial matter, for it threatened to unwind the agreements by which Murdoch had purchased the papers. Consequently, the TNL board voted unanimously to close both papers unless the union chapels agreed to abide by the disputes procedure. Long accompanied the announcement with the explanation, 'This is not a threat. It is a decision. Anybody who thinks it is a bluff does not know Rupert Murdoch.'[109] This did the trick – for the moment. Talks with SOGAT commenced and a written undertaking to abide by the disputes procedure was procured. It would last all of three months.

When News International bought *The Times*, the paper was produced on Linotype machines, a nineteenth-century, hot-metal technology. In purchasing Times Newspapers, Murdoch had secured agreement with the print unions to switch production from hot metal to 'cold composition' thus doing away with the Linotype machines and molten metal. Henceforth, the Linotype operators would be redeployed to type with computer keyboards, as had long been the norm in the rest of the world. But this did not mean computerized page make-up. Instead the computers were capable only of printing up text galleys that were passed on to a team armed with scalpels, scissors and glue who cut and pasted the lines of text into position on a drawing board. When a full page had been arranged in this way, a negative would be made of it and converted into a photosensitive polymer plate. From this, the newspaper would be run off.

Back in 1974, Marmaduke Hussey had complained that moving to 'cut and paste' cold composition would scarcely be worth the trouble given that it still involved having to employ process engravers who produced the pictorial printing plates. He argued that only a move to full computerized page composition made sense.[110] Eight years later, Murdoch had no more hope than Hussey of getting such a system installed at Gray's Inn Road in the face of union hostility and – it has to be said – the limitations of the technology then on offer. Getting the halfway house of 'cut and paste' accepted was regarded as an achievement in itself even though it had long been the established method throughout the regional presses.

From the first, *The Times*'s switch to cold composition was beset with teething problems. It was not deemed possible to move the paper overnight from hot to cold composition. Instead the process was gradually expanded and it was not until the following year that the entire paper was produced by photocomposition. The initial results were disappointing. It had taken so long to install the 'new' technology that its makers no longer manufactured it. This made finding replacement parts increasingly difficult.[111] Reproduction was so appalling that in October 1981 Evans suggested that the paper should use 'the *Sunday Times* hot metal facilities for the front and back for as long as we possibly can. I say this because converting to cold type on the front page will be the worst advertisement for *The Times* and certainly hinder our sales and our authority.'[112] Rather than employ speed typists, the NGA had insisted Times Newspapers re-employ the old Linotype operators to work the new computer keyboards. Many of them seemed to have inordinate difficulty adjusting to this change. The initial average of fifteen words per minute frankly beggared belief in an industry driven by deadlines. To this was added the introduction of a further stage in the process – the making of a photo polymer pattern plate, compounding delay and minimizing the time available to pick up errors. Readers zealously spotted the resulting mistakes and wrongly attributed them to declining editorial standards. Nor did speed improve much with practice. On one occasion, Evans found himself standing at the paste-up board until half past midnight trying to insert some copy that had been sent two and a half hours earlier. At that time of night, Rees-Mogg, when he was editor, had long since gone home, had dinner and retired safely to bed. Some thought that Evans should have conserved his energies by following his predecessor's example, leaving the trials of the production process to his night staff. But Evans was too involved to delegate when so much was going wrong, complaining to Gerry Long, 'It says something for our deadlines and for our production efficiency in this area that a[n El] Salvador story which was on the front page of the New York *Herald Tribune*, printed in Zurich and flown to Britain, could not be got into the London *Times* last night.'[113]

In the executive dining room, opinion was divided about the extent to which those 'mastering' cold composition were governed by incompetence, laziness or genuine malevolence. Nor were the NGA compositors the only union members treated with suspicion. Denis Hamilton had long been of the view that Reg Brady, the father of the *Sunday Times* NATSOPA chapel, had natural intelligence and would have been a constructive force if the social circumstances of his background had delivered him into managerial rather than union responsibilities. Instead Hamilton had watched while

Brady 'caused more trouble in the machine room than any other man in the history of the newspaper, discovering all manner of disputes and grievances'.[114] Many of Murdoch's most trusted lieutenants, including John Collier and Bill O'Neill, had started off in print union politics before their potential was spotted and harnessed by News Group's management. It was decided to make Brady an offer and, to the fury of his union brothers, he accepted the Murdoch shilling and switched sides.

Brady's fondness for a Soviet fur hat gave him an appropriately Cold War demeanour but, in the event, his defection to the capitalists did not unlock the potential that Hamilton had seen in him. Union officials refused to talk to him, thereby preventing him from playing any constructive role. Indeed, if disarming him prevented Brady from pursuing his previous destructive function, it did not seem to make much difference in the intractable war of attrition at Gray's Inn Road. The closed shop persisted, preventing management from having a free hand in who was employed. Evans was even unable to fill a secretarial vacancy in his own office because NATSOPA sent a succession of clearly unsuitable candidates from which he had to choose. One secretary he did employ, Liz Seeber, was astonished by the ludicrous demarcation rules prescribing her actions. In the first couple of weeks at her job a typewriter broke but, on lifting it from her desk to remove it, 'about three people said "Oh my God, don't do that, you'll bring SOGAT out on strike."' So she had to put it down, ring a SOGAT official and wait until – in their own time – a small deputation arrived armed with a trolley to wheel it away.[115] It was not an environment geared to exercising personal initiative. Furthermore, it provided a cover for laziness and intimidation. In *Notes from a Small Island*, Bill Bryson recounted the misery he used to experience every night as a subeditor on *The Times*'s business news desk when he tried to get hold of the Wall Street report from the SOGAT member whose task it was to receive it in the wire room. When each night the employee failed to take it to his desk, Bryson had to go up to the wire-room door and ask for it. He would invariably be told to go away (although in blunter language) because the employee was eating pizza and could not be bothered to look for it. Sometimes the threat of violence would be implied. Instead, the employee would come down with it when he felt like it – even if this meant it would miss the copy deadline. Obedient to the union's demarcation rules, he would not allow a non-SOGAT member like Bryson to cross the wire room's threshold to look for the incoming report himself. As Bryson later noted, it was just one of the ways the union exerted control on the newspaper industry 'by keeping technological secrets to itself, like how to tear paper off a machine'.[116]

In the Gray's Inn Road machine room the inter-union demarcation rules had far greater implications. There, NGA members had regarded it as a precondition of their superiority that NATSOPA members employed alongside them were not permitted to earn above 80 per cent of their own rate. In September 1981, NATSOPA members were awarded 87.5 per cent of the NGA's £106 per night wage in return for improved productivity and a small reduction in their manning levels. Although the NGA was not offering similar concessions, it nonetheless demanded that its members' wages should rise commensurately in order to restore their 20 per cent advantage. This would have added 28.3 per cent to the NGA payroll and management refused the request. So the NGA went on strike. No *Sunday Times* appeared on 27 September and *The Times* ceased production that evening.

Those turning up for work on the Monday had to cross a twenty-six-man picket line. Eight hours of negotiation at ACAS failed to produce a break-through. In the meantime, all 1400 *Sunday Times* employees were suspended without pay, a decision to extend this to *The Times* being deferred until the following day. Working closely with John Collier, Murdoch threatened the paper with destruction unless the NGA backed down. It was, he said, 'the most serious situation I have ever seen in Fleet Street':

> We are being held up by a small group of men who never work more than half a shift a week for us. It is a straight attempt at hijacking us. If the company gives in on the dispute we will be rolled over by other unions. Unless the NGA back down, I will close *The Times*. We have lost money, millions of pounds. We are still being held up and there is no point in going on. We are simply not putting any more money into the company.[117]

The hopes of putting aside the ghosts of the Thomson years appeared dashed. It was Hussey's shutdown strategy of 1978–9 all over again. But Murdoch had one advantage. In 1978–9, the unions knew Times Newspapers would sooner or later back down rather than see their titles permanently closed down. With Murdoch, it was not possible to be so sure. Unlike Thomson, he could liquidate the company at minimal cost and with the advantage of having separated ownership of the property assets from the newspapers.

This was brinkmanship of the highest order. Earlier in the month the embattled management of the *FT* had threatened to shut their loss-making paper unless a similar differentials dispute was resolved. Now Murdoch was following suit and he personally took charge in the negotiations, accepting Len Murray's invitation to come to the TUC's headquarters, Congress House. It was there, after hours of torturous exploration, that the NGA finally accepted Murray's proposals at 2 a.m. on Wednesday morning. There would be a written (but not legally binding) guarantee of future uninterrupted production and acceptance of an agreed disputes procedure. Murdoch thanked Murray who 'persuaded me not to pull the plug for the last few hours while he worked around the clock to get this together'.[118] After three days off the streets because of a dispute among those printing its Sunday sibling, *The Times* was back in business with the essential battlegrounds of management versus union rights and inter-union demarcation disputes unresolved. 'In recent months, Rupert Murdoch has learnt that he has no special magic in dealing with London print unions,' concluded the *Australian Financial Review*. 'From the point of view of News Corp. shareholders, the danger is that Murdoch will delay closure of *The Times* beyond the point which commercial sanity dictates.'[119]

VI

At best, *The Times* survived the September crisis with a stay of execution. But there was little cause for celebration. Sales continued to be up on the same month the previous year and, while the royal wedding-fuelled circulation surge of July was always likely to be a one-off, new readers were continuing to outstrip the dead and disaffected. In normal circumstances the improvement would be considered to be excellent but Evans's reputation had created an unrealistic level of expectation that detracted from the gains that were made. The editor himself was concerned by a disturbing fall in reader subscriptions.[120] But whatever angle was taken on the sales figures, the more important statistic was that, between July and November 1981, the paper was losing between £250,000 and £374,000 every week. None doubted that Richard Williams had done an excellent job with *Preview*, the new arts listing tabloid section, but it was expensive to run, failing to attract much advertising, and market research showed few signs that it was raising the paper's circulation. When Ken Beattie, the commercial director, circulated a paper at the TNL board meeting calling for *Preview* to be scrapped, Evans did not mince words in a note he sent Beattie: 'I really do think that you have an obligation to consult me as Editor first before the Chairman. You put me in an impossible position if the Chairman is persuaded against the project which is close to my heart and was, I thought, to his. I tell you frankly that I could not continue to edit *The Times* in circumstances like this.'[121]

While Evans was determined to defend – seemingly with his professional life – an innovation like *Preview*, he was less staunch in support of the arts coverage he had inherited in the main section of the paper. He had a succession of disagreements with John Higgins, the arts editor. One battleground was the failure to take television reviewing seriously. Another concerned Higgins's enthusiasm for giving so much space to opera staged outside Britain. Higgins had greatly improved the arts coverage in the *Financial Times* but Evans was less impressed by his efforts in Gray's Inn Road, threatening, 'I will have to see a marked improvement or consider different ways of covering the Arts.'[122] He proceeded to take the *Saturday Review* section out of Higgins's hands but mishandled the appointment of Bevis Hillier who, having been half-promised various competences, was left in a semi-employed limbo. Hillier was so dissatisfied with his treatment that when he was finally given the *Saturday Review* section to edit in January 1982 he resigned a month later with six months' severance pay.

Hillier was not alone in becoming exasperated by the editor's swings between drive and indecision. The political commentator Alan Watkins claimed that Evans would offer him a job whenever they ran into one another, the details 'about which I would hear nothing until we met a few months later, when he would suggest lunch, about which I would likewise hear nothing'.[123] But the journalist Evans most wanted in his paper was the star columnist he had allowed to take a sabbatical – Bernard Levin. 'Not a day goes by,' he told Levin in September 1981, 'without the Editor of *The Times*, in advanced years, being accosted on the streets, in clubs and society dinners, and racecourses and parlours and, in his bedroom before his shaving mirror, about the absence of Mr Bernard Levin from the columns of the newspaper.'[124] Evans's pleading became desperate. He suggested Levin could return as a television critic, a music critic or even a parliamentary sketchwriter (despite the fact that Frank Johnson was winning such acclaim in this role).[125] Evans even suggested that Levin should pay a visit to Gray's Inn Road to 'satisfy yourself that the place is still inhabited by reasonable men'.[126] Levin kept his distance.

Indeed, the trickle of departures among the editorial staff was turning into a torrent. First out of the door was Hugh Brogan, the respected Washington correspondent, who resigned shortly after Evans's arrival in protest at what he anticipated would be Murdoch's certain destruction of the paper's integrity. But Evans soon found himself at loggerheads with the paper's New York correspondent, Michael Leapman, as well. Exasperated by the frequency with which Brian Horton, the foreign editor and French restaurant lover, spiked his copy, Leapman assumed the worst and accused Evans of political censorship.[127] One of Horton's techniques was to unsettle Leapman by sending him dismissive comments about the quality of his grammar. Not that Horton knew better. He covertly obtained the judgments from the literary editor, Philip Howard, who innocently thought Horton was seeking advice on grammatical matters as a form of self-improvement.[128] Leapman, meanwhile, continued to express dissatisfaction and when Evans demanded an assurance of a 'reasonable' attitude from him he resigned,[129] preferring to become 'William Hickey' in the *Express* instead.

As Evans's closest colleague, Anthony Holden, the features editor, became the lieutenant most closely associated with the drive to introduce new blood – by which was also meant the determination to sack old favourites. Marcel Berlins took voluntary redundancy.[130] With this, *The Times* lost a distinguished and authoritative commentator on legal affairs. The leader writer, Roger Berthoud, also packed up and left. Another to seek redundancy was the paper's Whitehall correspondent, Peter Hennessy. This was a grievous blow for Hennessy was, as Patrick Marnham has pointed out, the first journalist to persuade senior civil servants to talk regularly about what was really going on in the corridors of Government.[131] Evans was sorry to see him go but was unable to dissuade him from doing so.[132] In the course of Evans's opening year as editor, more than fifty members of the editorial staff left with redundancy payouts.

Too much was happening all at once. Familiar faces were leaving, less familiar ones arriving. The paper was riddled with mistakes due to the delays caused by switching to cold composition, a change that was not even improving the print quality of the paper. This was not the best moment to reorder the contents, but the editor did so all the same, deciding that, instead of constantly having to shift around the various news, sport and law sections of the paper in order to keep the centre of the paper fixed, the centre pages should float instead. At one stage he even considered the sacrilege of moving leaders and letters to pages two and three. Even without going that far, floating the paper's philosophical core a few pages either way succeeded only in giving the impression that editorial policy was adrift. Readers were not impressed. Nor were the leader writers, increasingly airing their doubts about the editor's variable decisiveness. Owen Hickey, the chief leader writer, tackled Evans directly, assuring him that readers did not want to turn to the centre of their paper and find obituaries on the left and badminton on the right.[133]

The Times was not used to being in a state of perpetual revolution. But this was now the inevitable tension in a paper stretched on the live wire between the two electricity pylons of Rupert Murdoch and Harold Evans. Recognizing his desire to be closely involved, the backbench would try and track Evans down when news broke during the course of the night. Calls would be made across London to establish his whereabouts. Eventually, he would be discovered subbing a sports report elsewhere in the building. The problem was that, called away from his handiwork, he would then forget to return to it, leaving the subeditors unable to ascertain which bits had been sent. They were left with no option but to unpick his work and start again from scratch. No matter how helpful – how the master of the paper – Evans thought he was being, subs did not always welcome his attempts to steer every boat in the paper's flotilla from early morning to late at night. The Times had long published the Oxford and Cambridge exam results, but the editor decided to extend the service to all the universities. Compiling these graduation lists involved an enormous amount of extra work done after the London edition had been put to bed. On one occasion, around midnight, Tim Austin was working on them when Evans arrived back from a dinner in his black tie. Seeing it was Durham, his *alma mater*, Evans volunteered to do the subbing himself. Unfortunately, he got the style wrong and the whole section had to be redone. 'He just did not know when to stop,' concluded Austin; 'he was not the best at delegating.'[134]

The editor's insistence on making his mark in almost every possible part of the paper might have been a tolerable if irritating eccentricity had it only affected his relations with colleagues. The problem was that his interventions were wrecking the paper's deadlines. The Times was becoming increasingly unobtainable in Scotland because the train at King's Cross would not wait while Evans held up production in order to make some needless alteration. This was a question of priorities and the editor appeared to have lost sight of the commercial imperatives at work. The leader writers would deliver their copy on time only for Evans to announce that he would run them through his own typewriter. Aware that another deadline was being missed, Fred Emery would race over to the editor's office to find its occupant kneeling on the floor with a pair of scissors in his hands. He would be cutting up the original copy and trying to insert some extra lines of his own on scraps of paper with glue. Emery did not even believe the editor's additions improved the sense of the original. 'Rhythms and disciplines are crucial to a daily newspaper's morale and professionalism,' Emery believed. When they were destroyed, 'things fall apart'.[135]

There was a journalistic maxim that 'you can edit with a typewriter or a calculator, but not both'.[136] This was exactly the problem at *The Times* in the dying days of 1981. The editor led with the typewriter while his managing director and the proprietor attempted to rule with the calculator. Famous names were departing and, as so often with voluntary redundancy, it was those most marketable to an alternative employer who were going while those who feared leaving the life raft clung on. Yet, Evans persisted in hiring new journalists, often at higher salaries than those they replaced. Each appointment became a battleground, particularly since, in the short term, even the redundancy programme was adding to the paper's costs. One of many disputes concerned finding a replacement for Michael Leapman. Murdoch maintained that *The Times* could not afford its own correspondent in New York in addition to its office in Washington DC. Instead it should seek a saving by using News Group's New York bureau instead. Ignoring both this opinion – which he felt was an attempt to see copy in *The Times* written by employees answerable to Murdoch rather than to himself – and that of Brian Horton, Evans sent out Peter Watson, formally of the Diary column.[137] Evans simply did not see how he could satisfy the proprietor's instruction to improve the paper without being left alone to hire whoever he felt could best achieve it.

At the heart of the matter was Evans's complaint that he was not given a clear budget allocation. A memo from Gerry Long demanding that all company executives seek written authorization for 'any proposed action' was understandably resented.[138] Evans insisted that this was no way to run a newspaper. 'I am a little shaken,' he told Murdoch with restrained anger. 'I do find it difficult to accept the principle of day-to-day approval for detailed items. I can't honestly edit the paper properly without having discretion . . . It makes life difficult and erodes authority if I am not to be the sole channel for your instructions.'[139] It was demeaning for the editor of *The Times* to have to scurry up and down stairs to the proprietor or managing director every time he wanted to spend money. In May 1981, John Grant, the managing editor, had drawn up a £9.1 million budget on inherited staffing levels for the next eleven months.[140] The redundancy programme was supposed to cut that budget substantially and when, on 20 January, Evans was presented with a spending limit – £7,723,000 – along with the warning that he had already crossed it, it was clear there would have to be further job cuts. Evans's defence that 'in terms of real as distinct from money costs, The Times's editorial budget is less than at any time in recent years' fell upon deaf ears.[141] Times Newspapers lost £8 million between June and November 1981, wiping out News International's summer profits. Worse, this came at a time when the finances of News Corp., the parent company, were already being drained through the New York Post's costly circulation war with the rival Daily News. In these circumstances, The Times really did look like a luxury the increasingly transatlantic Murdoch could ill afford.

There was little by way of Christmas cheer. Evans injured himself putting up decorations and took time off to recover. With Charles Douglas-Home away on sabbatical, the paper was edited by Brian MacArthur and Fred Emery. It was at this moment that Evans committed an act that infuriated Murdoch. The proprietor knew that Evans had taken time off to recover from his spell of concussion but, long after he assumed that the editor was back at his desk, he was aghast to discover that he was, in fact, mysteriously in the United States. Evans had intended to keep his transatlantic mission secret but his secretary had forgotten to tell either MacArthur or Emery that this was the case. Hours before Murdoch was due to fly over to London from New York, he telephoned The Times expecting to speak to Evans, only to discover he was unaccountably in America. The proprietor was furious and perhaps not a little suspicious. When Evans hurried back to the office (having been tracked down by MacArthur and warned to return to London immediately), it was to find a bitter letter from Murdoch waiting for him, berating him for the time he had taken to convalesce. Given how manically hard Evans had worked since his appointment, this was unfair, although, in the circumstances in which the paper found itself, the furtive trip to America certainly looked peculiar. Indeed, the letter read more as if the proprietor was issuing a written warning, putting on record that he was distancing himself from his chosen editor. This was ominous. Evans fired back a six-point rebuttal of Murdoch's charges, reasserting his acceptance of the necessity for hard work and pleading, 'I love The Times. We have until now, I thought, had an extremely close liaison.'[142]

From this moment on, suspicion governed Evans's attitude to Murdoch. He began to suspect Murdoch was complaining about him behind his back and that one of those listening was Paul Johnson, whose media column in the *Spectator* was giving Evans critical reviews. Unless he was there in the room to monitor possible interference, Evans was nervous about Murdoch sounding forth on politics to *Times* journalists. On his return from his Christmastide absence, Evans discovered that Murdoch had expressed a preference for economic sanctions against the USSR while chatting to Owen Hickey. Hickey, who was not likely to compromise his intellectual self-certainty to anyone, did not feel Murdoch was leaning on him. But Evans went out of his way to write a leader condemning the policy as a 'romantic notion' and, worse, an 'apocalyptic strategy'.[143] Whether this could be considered an overreaction depended upon how narrowly the proprietor's guarantee not to direct editorial policy could be reasonably defined. To assume he had to take a Trappist vow whenever a conversation touched upon the modern world was clearly ridiculous. The problem was, did all journalists have the strength to put from their mind Murdoch's stated opinions when they filed copy he might read and note?

Evans's predicament was that tensions were now running high not only with Murdoch but with Gerry Long as well. Scarcely anyone had missed *The Times*'s decision to cancel its detailed coverage of the European Parliament but Long also wanted to cut costs by scrapping the paper's Westminster gallery staff and rely on PA reports instead.[144] This would certainly undermine the paper's claims to be offering something more than its competitors and Evans would have none of it. It was not just Evans who had difficulty relating to Long. Frank Giles, the *Sunday Times* editor, also felt 'to describe his nature as complex is about as observant as pointing out that Schubert's Eighth Symphony is unfinished'.[145] Shortly before he assumed the editorship, Evans had a foretaste of Long's eccentricity when he went to the latter's house for dinner. When the discussion turned to how *The Times*'s reputation should be restored, Long became animated, telling Evans, 'The man you need for authority is Penning-Rowsell of the *Financial Times*' and reached from his bookshelves the proof – a copy of Penning-Rowsell's *The Wines of Bordeaux*.[146] This proved to be a portent of his priorities. Although Long proceeded to demonstrate his readiness to sacrifice good journalists in pursuit of cutting costs, he was never prepared to compromise gastronomic standards at *The Times*. On one occasion when Sir Geoffrey Howe, the Chancellor of the Exchequer, came to lunch at Gray's Inn Road, roast lamb was on the menu. When Howe asked for mint sauce, the waitress pulled rank, grandly announcing, 'Mr Long does not allow mint sauce on the fifth floor.'[147]

Evans could not unseat Murdoch, but he could try and undermine Long. The easiest way of doing this was to provide Long with a public platform for self-immolation. Long had suggested the financially imprudent idea of importing a French and a German food critic to eat their way round Britain's most famous restaurants as part of a forthcoming *Times* series of articles on expensive foods.[148] Discovering that the managing director had been in acrimonious correspondence with the leading restaurateur Albert Roux, Evans persuaded Long that publishing the exchange would be a wonderful opening salvo to start the series. Long had dined at Roux's celebrated Le Gavroche restaurant and had asked for the 'farmhouse cheeseboard'. But, horror of horrors, he suspected that one of the cheeses, a St Paulin, was industrially produced, a fact confirmed upon consulting his trusty *Androuet Guide du Fromage*. 'This met at first with an indignant response from your waiter,' Long informed Roux. Perhaps unwisely, the waiter retaliated with the flip put-down, 'if Monsieur knows cheese better than I do, then of course Monsieur is right'. This remark appeared to have straightened the bristles on Long's Lord Kitchener-style moustache. Roux wrote to assure him that the offending cheese was a product 'made by craftsmen on the scale of a cottage industry' thereby generating a fresh debate on Long's second major hobby – semantics. Long replied at great length, also finding fault with the turbot and making clear he was sending the correspondence to Michelin who had recently given Le Gavroche the only three star rating in England. Despite the provocations, Roux attempted to bring the argument to a close, somewhat incredibly assuring Long, 'the fact that you have taken so much trouble to write about food leaves me with endless pleasure', and inviting him and his wife to dine with him. Boorishly, Long declined the offer.

The unintentionally hilarious correspondence appeared in the paper on Saturday 6 February, suitably illustrated with a Calman cartoon of a French waiter intoning, 'I'm a bit – how to say – cheesed off by these complaints.' Running into Anthony Holden in the office, Long asked him what he thought of the exchange. When the features editor replied that it was 'in the great tradition of British eccentrics', Long was uncomprehending, exclaiming, 'Eccentric? What's eccentric about it?'[149] He would soon find out. When Murdoch toured the *Sunday Times* on the Saturday afternoon (supposedly its busiest period), he found its journalists, feet on table, laughing with childlike glee at Long's cheese pantomime. Evans had knowingly published a correspondence that made the managing director appear ridiculous. What was more, he had allowed Long to demonstrate his obsession with expensive dining at exactly the moment he was also calling for six hundred redundancies, mainly among the clerical staff at Times Newspapers. Long may have hoped that his correspondence would lead Michelin to reconsider the three stars awarded to Le Gavroche. But it was Long who was about to find himself downgraded.

Times Newspapers employed 671 clerical workers (excluding managers and juniors). The combined clerical payroll of its daily and Sunday rivals, the *Guardian* and the *Observer*, was 250. It was clear that TNL was grossly overmanned; indeed, it was the principal reason why a company capable of generating nearly £100 million a year in revenue was still so monumentally in the red. Murdoch was blunt with the staff: 'You will say you have heard of *Times* crises before. I say to you here that if the crisis facing us today is not resolved within days rather than weeks our newspaper will have to be closed.'[150] Despite intense hostility to this 'straight forward mugging' from Barry Fitzpatrick, the father of the *Sunday Times* clerical chapel, and rumours that those doing management's bidding by applying for voluntary redundancy would be blacked by their union brothers,[151] negotiations to find the job cuts got underway with the more moderate union officials. It was another torturous exercise and, in the midst of it, Gray's Inn Road was rocked by a second crisis.

A meeting of the TNL board had been convened on 16 December 1981. In Murdoch's absence, Long had taken the chair and, with Evans and Frank Giles present, won universal – if qualified – approval to remove *The Times* and *Sunday Times* titles trademarks from TNL to News International. The stated reason was that September's NGA dispute had demonstrated that without this change *The Times* could not be published if the *Sunday Times* was liquidated. Transfering the titles to News International would give greater flexibility in future industrial disputes.[152] Consent was agreed subject to 'a reasonable price' being paid for them. At a rushed TNL directors meeting held two days before Christmas at the *Sun*'s headquarters in Bouverie Street (with only Long, John Collier, the company's secretary Peter Ekberg and Farrar's lawyer, Geoffrey Richards, present) News International's offer of £1 million for *The Times* and £2 million for the *Sunday Times* was accepted.[153]

The first Evans and Giles heard of the 23 December meeting and its decision to transfer the titles of the papers they edited was on 16 February 1982 when they were sent a copy of the minutes. They were horrified.[154] Why had they not been informed of the meeting? Why was it held at the *Sun*'s headquarters? The impression was clear: Murdoch's henchmen had attempted to 'pull a fast one'. But what was their motive? If TNL was liquidated while still in possession of its principal assets – the titles – it could be bought by another buyer. Evans approached Jim Sherwood of Sea Containers and encouraged him to buy *The Times* from Murdoch.[155] Murdoch promptly rebuffed Sherwood's offer when it was sent to him on 9 February. Transferring the titles to News International would, wrote one chapel father (Peter Wilby), allow Murdoch to liquidate TNL and restart the papers at a later date with a more favourable set of union (or non-union) staffing agreements.[156] This, and the rejection of the Sherwood offer, suggested that if Murdoch did not get the mass redundancy package accepted he really did intend to abolish TNL and relaunch the titles on his own terms, in his own time. It also placed a gun to the head of the unions in the negotiations over cutting six hundred jobs.

Transferring the titles to News International ran counter to Sir Denis Hamilton's strategy of ring-fencing Times Newspapers in the Articles of Association so that, as he put it, 'in no way could it be mixed up with the operational or financial side of News International'.[157] But Evans and Giles could no longer appeal to Hamilton who, seeing the way events were moving, had resigned as chairman of the company's board of directors. The new chairman was none other than Keith Rupert Murdoch. All of a sudden, it seemed Murdoch was doing to Times Newspapers what he had done to the *News of the World* chairman, Sir William Carr – arriving in the guise of a financial white knight, only to seize the keys to the castle. Yet, was it not inevitable that the person paying the bills also wanted outright control of the company? The only prop keeping TNL on its feet was the money being pumped into it by News International. As Richard Searby, chairman of the parent News Corporation, bluntly put it, ownership of the titles was the security it needed if it was to continue backrolling this liability.[158] The City reacted to the news by wiping £4 million from News International's stock market value.

There were two problems with this strategy. First, if Murdoch attempted to close TNL and relaunch *The Times* in a manner that displeased the print unions they could strike at Bouverie Street, bringing down the *Sun* and the *News of the World*, the two sure cash cows that contributed most to keeping his media empire afloat. Secondly, the titles transfer appeared to be illegal under point 2 (iii) of the terms set out by John Biffen unless the board of independent directors' gave their approval, a detail overlooked in the hastily convened and inquorate TNL meeting of 23 December. Biffen had stipulated that a fine or two years imprisonment would apply to Murdoch if he broke the conditions upon which his purchase of TNL had been granted. This included changing the Articles of Association without consent. *The Times* NUJ chapel pressed for the transferral to be disallowed, threatening if necessary to seek a High Court injunction.[159] Rees-Mogg added his voice to the controversy, writing to Biffen and denouncing the attempted titles shift on the BBC's *The World This Weekend*. The independent directors also waded in, Lord Dacre describing it as a 'gross incivility . . . the Proprietor met the national directors on January 12 and said nothing about it' while Lord Greene at least struck a supportive note for the newspaper's reporting of the fracas by claiming 'All I know about it is what is in *The Times*.'[160] Evans had certainly ensured that his paper could not be faulted when it came to washing its owner's dirty linen on both front and back pages. Even if Murdoch's exact motives were unclear, the manner in which Long had acted created a suspicion of shadiness. The Shadow Trade Minister, John Smith, complained that Murdoch was attempting 'a breathtaking subterfuge, which raises very serious questions about his future intentions for both newspapers'.[161] The Conservative former Cabinet minister Geoffrey Rippon asked Mrs Thatcher to consider establishing an enquiry.

Murdoch, Searby and Long had miscalculated. Talks with Department of Trade officials indicated the transfer was probably illegal. Searby got to work on preparing a dignified retreat. The decision to transfer was reversed pending a meeting of the *Times* board of independent directors who duly made clear their opposition to the plan, killing it there and then.[162] Meanwhile, the deadline for achieving the six hundred redundancies had been reached. But when the requests for voluntary redundancy were counted they numbered scarcely more than one hundred and fifty. Murdoch flew back to London.

For ten hours, the unions and management tried to reach agreement, but the gulf remained too wide. Murdoch announced that 210 clerical workers would be sacked on a last in first out basis if the number of voluntary redundancies did not rise commensurately. The unions replied by issuing a joint statement, making clear they did 'not accept the mandatory notices' that were due to be sent out the following morning. The mood at a meeting of NATSOPA clerical workers on 24 February was firmly defiant. In the *Spectator*, the cartoonist Michael Heath drew an egg timer with the words *The Times* on it – the sand had almost run out.[163]

At such a moment it would have been helpful if the editor and the proprietor could have managed the pretence of a united front. Evans tried to woo Murdoch by telling him what he wanted to hear but the latter cold-shouldered him.[164] Back on 10 February, the *Guardian* had reported rumours that Evans's future had been discussed at a meeting of Times Newspapers' board of directors. Had this been true (it was not) it would have narrowed the 'mole' down to those seated around the boardroom table. Murdoch was quick to deny the story, issuing a statement decrying the 'malicious, self-serving and wrong' rumours and praising his editor, whose 'outstanding qualities and journalistic skills are recognized throughout the world'. Not everyone was convinced. *Private Eye*, with its vendetta against 'Dame Harold Evans' (supposedly confusing him with Dame Edith Evans, first lady of the English stage), played up the stories, as did the new William Hickey columnist in the *Daily Express*. Evans was not the sort of Fleet Street editor who took a relaxed view about what rival newspapers wrote about him. He believed in the righteous purpose of the fourth estate and was not prepared to tolerate its failings in regard to himself.

Back in September, Evans had taken such exception to a sloppily researched article about his *Times* editorship in *Harpers & Queen* entitled 'O Tempora! O Mores!' that he forced the magazine's editor to publish a blow-by-blow rebuttal of points of error. These corrections ranged from 'Mr Anthony Holden's mother-in-law is not the Queen's gynaecologist' to 'Mr Holden's wife does not play the harpsichord'. Readers of the glossy fashion magazine were also to be alerted to the fact that 'Mr Peter Watson did not go for a trial for Bristol Rovers' and 'Mr Brian MacArthur has never written a headline "It's a beaut".'[165] Many thought Evans would have been better letting some of this trivia go. But he was even more incandescent when, on 1 March 1982, the BBC's *Panorama* alleged – in a feature on the crisis at *The Times* – that he had moved an illustration of Libyan hit men from an inside page to the front page on Murdoch's instructions. Evans demanded the BBC issue a statement at the beginning of the following week's programme conceding the claim was 'false in detail and inference'.[166] The allegation was indeed untrue, but it had come from someone intent on mischief from inside the newspaper. The BBC ignored Evans's demand. While this was going on, he was also preparing to go to court against *Private Eye* after it accused him of being a 'two-faced hypocrite' who had tried to do a deal with Rothermere's Associated Newspapers for Times Newspapers even after he had approved Murdoch on the vetting committee (but before Murdoch offered him the *Times* editorship). *Private Eye* had a witness, Hugh Stephenson, and its case would have been strengthened had it known that after Evans had approved Murdoch on the vetting committee, he had written to congratulate Jonathan Aitken on his anti-Murdoch speech in the Commons. Nonetheless, Evans was adamant that he had not assisted Associated, and was determined to get legal redress, dismissing Stephenson as 'a disappointed potential Editor of *The Times*'.[167] Richard Ingrams, the *Eye*'s editor, remained determined to find fault with Evans, subsequently grumbling, 'the fellow has a nasty habit of suing for libel, an aspect of the great crusader for press freedom not often noted by his admirers'.[168]

During February, the divisions within Gray's Inn Road ceased being gossip and became hard news. 'There were two teams producing one newspaper,' recalled Tim Austin. One team comprised those loyal to the editor. Primarily there were the two men he had brought in to sharpen features and policy, Anthony Holden and Bernard Donoughue. There were also others like Holden's deputy, Peter Stothard, who had crossed the bridge from the *Sunday Times* with its illustrious editor. They were in no doubt that, left to his own devices, Evans was a genius who was transforming *The Times* for the better. They gave him their total loyalty. It was Evans's great strength that he inspired such emotions in those he appointed and encouraged. It was his weakness that he could not command such loyalty from many of the entrenched *Times* staff he inherited. Those in the latter camp were a more diffuse entity, brought together only by their belief that the paper was descending into chaos and needed to be rescued by someone who understood its (supposed) core values. Much of what they disliked about Evans's editorship were actually decisions driven by Murdoch in his desire to cut costs and modernize the paper. But while they could not get rid of the man whose money was keeping them in employment, they could balance what they saw as his less enlightened traits if there was a new editor who combined a will to stand up to him with a sensibility for stabilizing the atmosphere on the paper. Such a man existed in the deputy editor, Charles Douglas-Home. And it was no secret that he was increasingly disaffected with Harold Evans.

Towards the end of February, just as Fred Emery was poised to go on a skiing holiday, he received a telephone call. 'I'm sorry you're going away,' said the caller, by way of introduction. 'Who's speaking?' demanded Emery, momentarily failing to register the mild Australian accent. The proprietor asked if he could pop in to see him before he went skiing, making clear that it was a matter of some urgency. Intrigued, Emery hurried over, wondering what could possibly be so pressing. Murdoch came straight to the point. 'I'm thinking of changing the editor,' he said, adding that he now believed Douglas-Home should succeed. He wanted to know what Emery thought. Emery asked what his reasons for the change might be and was told, 'Harry is all over the place.' He was particularly concerned about the influence of Bernard Donoughue and the generous terms upon which he had been hired (while maintaining his City interests). Emery admitted that the paper was indeed in chaos. He also supported Douglas-Home's candidature, while adding that there might be a problem with some of the home news reporters who had never forgiven him for keeping a secret dossier on their private lives. Although disabusing Murdoch on the issue of Evans's politics (he was not, as the proprietor suspected, endorsing the SDP), Emery had largely confirmed his suspicions. Emery was thanked and told to proceed with his skiing holiday.[169]

There were several theatres of war, but none more important than that over the leader column. Evans recognized that the chief leader writer, Owen Hickey, was an authoritative commentator. On important issues such as the Middle East and Ireland, Hickey shared Evans's generally pro-Israeli, pro-Ulster Unionist disposition. But Hickey did not contribute much to the leader conferences, preferring to act as if the column was his personal fiefdom where he should be left undisturbed to formulate his own thoughts. Leader writers had long believed themselves to be a higher caste of *Times* journalist and jealously guarded their right to opine. It was Thomas Barnes (editor, 1817–41), who had introduced the unsigned leader article, prompting William Cobbett to rail against its anonymous pronouncements as if 'each paragraph appears to be a little sort of order in council; a solemn decision of a species of literary conclave'.[170] Barnes and his team had 'thundered out' in the cause of reform, giving the paper its 'Thunderer' nickname in the process. But as Evans was aware, the tone had long since become more Delphic. 'If this was the citadel of *The Times*,' he concluded, 'it was stultified by charm.' He parodied the style of one of the leader writers, Geoffrey Smith, along the lines of, 'The crucifixion was not a good thing, but then it was not altogether a bad thing either.'[171]

The reflective and balanced articles were all very well, but Evans wanted to 'get into the engine-room of government policy, leading as well as reacting'.[172] He looked to Bernard Donoughue, whom he had brought in to formulate the paper's political strategy, to provide this. Donoughue succeeded in impressing upon the editor the case for using the paper to attack the Government's economic policies. This raised problems of personality as well as politics. Donoughue and Hickey did not work effectively together.[173] They especially disagreed on Ireland where, despite his Catholicism and his ownership of a farm in the Republic, Hickey remained a conviction Unionist. Nor was Hickey alone in finding Donoughue's manner that of the bully and there was resentment of him as another Evans import who was indulged by his patron more than the longer serving staff. Certainly he looked 'like a tough centre forward in professional football' as Evans put it, gap-toothed and hair sitting 'tightly on his head in orderly rows of crinkly black like the paper one finds in boxes of chocolates'. But he had every claim to authority as the son of a Northamptonshire car factory worker who had gone down with a First from Oxford and, before his thirties were out, was running the Number Ten Street Policy Unit first for Wilson and later for Callaghan. When Thomson had put Times Newspapers up for sale, Donoughue had been Evans's lieutenant trying to cobble together the *Sunday Times* consortium and had briefed MPs to block Biffen's non-referral of Murdoch's bid to the Monopolies Commission.

Donoughue was a man of great talents but, unintentionally, he contributed to Evans's downfall. His role was widely resented by his colleagues who were agreed that he was a disruptive and alien presence at *The Times* (although they were divided over whether they believed his loyalty was first and foremost to the Labour Party – for whom he was assumed to be informally spying – or to his patron, the editor). Evans was a news-driven editor not a political thinker and consequently felt he needed Donoughue to provide ideological direction. But he was asking for trouble in appointing as his political guru a man who fundamentally opposed the line of the chief leader writer, hated the proprietor, appeared addicted to fuelling conspiracy theories and treated established members of staff with rudeness or suspicion. Rightly or wrongly, most traditional *Times* journalists took the view that Evans, like a Plantaganet monarch with foreign favourites, relied too heavily on bad counsel. Their desire to be rid of Evans, was, as much, a will to be shot of Donoughue.

When Donoughue arrived, Hickey had already been a leader writer for twenty-six years and the contrast between the two could scarcely have been more marked. Hickey conveyed a shy, donnish and in dress slightly down-at-heel exterior that conflicted with his early days. At Clifton College – the sports-conscious public school to which his Catholic Irish parents had sent him – he had captained both the rugby and cricket teams. During the war he had served with the Third Battalion of the Irish Guards, losing an eye in Normandy. He maintained that he owed his life to his batman who had carried him from the battlefield. After the war he had gone up to Magdalen College, Oxford, where he continued to play cricket and rugby and went down with a First in Greats. In 1949, William Haley had persuaded him to move from the *Times Educational Supplement* to *The Times* and he had written the paper's leaders opposing the 1963 Robbins Report's call for the rapid expansion of Britain's universities. He had also drafted much of the 1970 'White Swan' letter against Rees-Mogg's efforts to broaden *The Times*'s appeal (which, he believed, meant lowering its standards).[174] But he saved his spiciest writing for the daily round-up he gave each morning to Rees-Mogg on the previous day's paper, with such acerbic observations as 'by-line suggests our reporter was at Hammersmith and Covent Garden simultaneously. A reading suggests she was at neither' and 'Alan Hamilton has been south of the border long enough not to regard artichokes in cans and sardines as delicacies'.[175] He was, in the verdict of the managing editor, John Grant, 'the conscience of the paper'. Increasingly it was a troubled conscience.

Evans wanted to run a *Times* campaign against lead in petrol. Des Wilson, chairman of CLEAR (Campaign for Lead-Free Air), had sent Anthony Holden copies of private correspondence from the Government's Chief Medical Officer to the Government warning of the health dangers – especially to children – of lead in petrol. To Evans there seemed the possibility of a Government cover-up waiting to be exposed, but the reaction of the paper's old guard was summed up by the home news editor, Rodney Cowton, who asked with an air of distaste if he was being ordered to run 'a campaign' on the subject. The increasingly truculent Charles Douglas-Home phrased it even more dismissively, pondering aloud, 'What *is* campaigning journalism?' To his thinking, the concept was suspect, smacking of personal agendas and sensational (unbalanced) reporting. Temporarily out of the office, Evans wanted Holden to make a big issue out of the story, but Douglas-Home pulled rank and used his authority as deputy editor to shunt the story into the obscurity he believed it deserved.[176] It was a direct challenge to Evans's authority. The gloves were off.

Evans now had to face a barrage of jabs and cuts from several directions. Some colleagues, who might have helped absorb the blows, were absent. Emery was hurtling down black runs. The other acting editor over the festive period, Brian MacArthur, had impressed Murdoch and been rewarded with the deputy editorship of the *Sunday Times*. This was *The Times*'s loss. Nor did Evans enjoy the loyalty of many who remained. Louis Heren all but denounced him on BBC television. Equally unhappy about the situation over which Evans was presiding, John Grant, the managing editor, threatened to resign. This spurred Douglas-Home to call on Murdoch to tell him that, if Grant left, he too would go. The prospect of losing both the deputy editor and the managing editor spurred Murdoch to depose Evans more quickly than he had intended. The fact that Granada television's *What The Papers Say* had just awarded him the title of Editor of the Year was a mere inconvenience.

Donoughue had repeatedly challenged Douglas-Home to prove his loyalty to Evans, and the protestations of allegiance were wearing thin.[177] Evans was to paint an unflattering picture of his deputy's behaviour during this period, implying that he was motivated by a self-serving desire to seize the editorship for himself. On the other hand, Evans's critics thought that when it came to being self-serving, Evans still had questions to answer about his own role in accepting the editorship from someone he had made such concerted attempts to prevent owning the paper.[178] But Douglas-Home's motives were less clear-cut than the Evans loyalists assumed. Far from being a sycophant towards the proprietor, he was distinctly wary of him. It was what he regarded as Evans's weakness in the face of Murdoch's ill temper that disheartened him.[179] There was more than a whiff of snobbery from some of the staff who lined up behind the Eton and Royal Scots Greys Douglas-Home over the northerner and his posse of meritocratic henchmen but a principal belief was that 'Charlie' was the man who would stand up to Murdoch, which 'Harry' had supposedly failed to do. It was Evans's misfortune that Murdoch himself now wanted a dose of Douglas-Home as well.

But did Douglas-Home want to work with Murdoch? Far from pulling out all the stops to supplant Evans, he had entered into negotiations to leave *The Times* for the *Daily Telegraph*. Notified of this, Evans had begun to look around for a new deputy and had even approached Colin Welch.[179] Welch, who had resigned as the deputy editor of the *Telegraph* in 1980, was a noted Tory journalist of the intellectual right. If Evans felt Murdoch's pressure to adopt a more right-wing tone in the paper, then he could not have appeased the proprietor more than by contemplating a prominent role for Welch. Having told Evans of his decision to resign, Douglas-Home proposed postponing his actual leaving until the immediate crisis was over (financially it also made sense to wait until the new tax year in April). In the meantime, he received information that would make him pause further – for a well-placed source assured him that Evans was losing his grip on the situation and would soon be leaving Gray's Inn Road himself. The source was Evans's own secretary, Liz Seeber. Given her job description, Seeber was hardly displaying the customary loyalty to her boss, but she had come to the conclusion Evans was presiding over the paper's collapse and that the only way of saving it was to help Douglas-Home stay in the game.

'The atmosphere was so unpleasant, it was a dreadful environment to work in' was how she defended her actions. 'You had people like Bernard Donoughue permanently in and out of Harry's office and you just wanted it to be over; it was no longer running a newspaper, it was Machiavellian goings-on.'[180] Douglas-Home later repaid her efforts by giving a book written by her husband a noticeably glowing review.[181] But even with this flow of information about what Evans was up to, Douglas-Home still wavered. On the anniversary of Evans's appointment, Murdoch telephoned Marmaduke Hussey to tell him, 'I've ballsed it up. Harry is going so I'm putting in Charlie.' Hussey later wrote, 'I knew that already because Charlie had come to see me the night before and was doubtful whether to accept the job. "For heaven's sake," I told him. "I've spent five years trying to secure you the editorship – if you want out now I'll never speak to you again."'[182]

There were certainly some dirty tricks played. Evans loyalists were maintaining that the editor was in a life or death battle to save *The Times's* editorial independence from a proprietor bent on imposing his own (increasingly right-wing) views on the paper. This claim was undermined by the leader writer, Geoffrey Smith, who walked into a BBC studio and read out a memo Evans had sent to Murdoch asking for the latter's view on how the Chancellor's forthcoming Budget should be presented in the paper. The letter was dynamite but it was between the editor and the proprietor, so why was it being read out for broadcast by a *Times* leader writer? It was a typed letter and the answer appeared to rest with the holder of the carbon copy. Whether it had touched the intermediary hands of the deputy editor remained a matter for speculation. But one thing was clear: that members of the staff were cheerfully appearing on radio and television alternately to stab or slap the back of their editor was an intolerable situation. For a week, the chaos at *The Times* dominated the news. *Times* journalists would gather round the television for the lunchtime news, one half of them cheering Geraldine Norman who would be broadcast condemning Evans, the other half cheering Anthony Holden's championing of him. Then they would all return to their desks and get on with the job of producing Evans's newspaper.

Because of their well-placed mole, Evans's critics had access to more than one incriminating piece of evidence. In a first-year progress report of 21 February, Evans had adopted an excessively ingratiating tone towards Murdoch. 'Thank you again for the opportunity and the ideas,' he purred. 'We are all one hundred per cent behind you in the great battle and I'm glad we're having it now.' Evans's upbeat assessment appeared to offer

Murdoch what it could be assumed he wanted. Evans announced that he had approached the right-wing Colin Welch about joining *The Times*, adding a line that seemed designed to appeal to the Australian's socio-political assumptions, 'I did talk to Alexander Chancellor but came to the conclusion he represents part of the effete old tired England.' However, 'there would be mileage I think in your idea of having some international names (like Dahrendorf, Kissinger, Kristol)'. Regrettably, Evans proceeded to speak ill of past or present colleagues: 'You'll perhaps have seen the attack on me in the *Spectator* for getting rid of "stars" but believe me Hennessy, Berthoud and Berlins they mention were all bone idle. So are many of the others who have gone or are going. It is another part of the old-*Times* brigade not wanting to work, Louis Heren stirring it up a bit.'[183] The unfortunate tone of this letter tended to support Douglas-Home's contention that Evans was not always the bulwark for liberty and defender of his staff that his supporters protested him to be.

In fact, if Evans's tone had been intended to please his proprietor, he was to be sorely disappointed. Two days later, 'Dear Chairman' was how he began a huffy note that objected to the 'cursory comment on the detailed report of our first year which I volunteered to you'. To Murdoch's criticism that the editorial line had lacked consistency, Evans shot back, 'You have not, as it happens, made this criticism on several occasions to me but only once (7 January 1982) though I have been made aware of what you have said to other members of the staff when I have not been present.'[184] When it came to the embattled editor, the proprietor's heart had turned to stone.

Tuesday 9 March marked the first anniversary of Harold Evans's appointment as editor. It was hardly a soft news day appropriate for distracting him. It was Budget Day and Evans ensured that *The Times* covered, reported, reproduced and analysed Sir Geoffrey Howe's measures in an impressive level of detail. 'The Chancellor of the Exchequer,' Evans crooned justifiably to Murdoch afterwards, 'has gone out of his way to say that the Budget coverage of *The Times* had restored *The Times* as a newspaper of record for the first time for many years.'[185] Written by Donoughue, the leader took a measured view although the front page headline 'Howe heartens Tories: a little for everyone' was certainly more positive than the previous year's assessment. Rab Butler's death was also front-page news and together with the obituary was accompanied by an article by his one-time acolyte, Enoch Powell. Powell was as insightful as he was admiring of the man thrice denied the opportunity to become Prime Minister. It 'was mere chance', he noted, that Butler's childhood injuries prevented him from serving in either war, 'but to some of us it was a chance that seemed to match an aspect of his character. He was not the kind of man for whom any cause – not even his own – was worth fighting to the death, worth risking everything.'[186]

Having only recently returned from his own father's funeral, Evans was back at Gray's Inn Road and was just preparing to listen to the Budget speech when he was summoned upstairs to see Murdoch. The proprietor announced he wanted his immediate resignation. He had already asked Douglas-Home to succeed him and Douglas-Home had accepted. According to Evans's account of the conversation, Murdoch had the grace to look emotional about the situation. Nonetheless he stated his reasons – 'the place is in chaos' and Evans had lost the support of senior staff. Evans shot back that it was management's decisions that had created the chaos and reeled off a list of the senior staff that remained loyal to him. He had no intention of accepting this summary dismissal. Instead he left, refusing to resign, with Murdoch threatening to summon the independent national directors to enforce his departure.[187]

The independent national directors were supposed to ensure that the proprietor did not put inappropriate pressure on his editor. Instead, Murdoch was threatening to use them as an ultimate force to ensure the editor was removed from the building. Evans had taken the drafting of the editorial safeguards extremely seriously. The following morning he went to seek the advice of one of the independent directors, Lord Robens. The two men met in the Reform Club, Evans confiding his predicament to the ageing Labour peer above the din of a vacuum cleaner engaged in a very thorough once over of their meeting place. Robens considered the matter and suggested that, rather than staying on for six more months of this torture, Evans should go away on holiday. According to Evans's account, Robens advised, 'Don't talk to Murdoch. Leave everything to your lawyer. Relax. We'll stand by you.'[188] The meeting concluded, Evans strode out from the Reform's confident classicism into St James's Park, continually circling the gardens like a yacht with a jammed rudder while he tried to decide whether to fight for his job and the paper's integrity or to go quietly. Eventually he compromised. He would go noisily.

Back at the office, Evans was received by the unwelcoming committee of Murdoch, Searby and Long who pressed him to announce his resignation before the stand-off created yet more appalling publicity for *The Times*. But believing there were higher issues at stake, making an issue was precisely Evans's purpose. The television cameras massed outside Gray's Inn Road and Evans's home. His admirers and detractors organized further public demonstrations of support and disrespect while those inside the building tried to put together the paper, unsure whether to take their orders from Evans or Douglas-Home.

The headline for 12 March ran 'Murdoch: "*Times* is secure".' His threat to close down the paper had been lifted by the agreement with the print and clerical unions to cut 430 full-time jobs (rather than the six hundred requested) and cut around four hundred shifts. Taken together with the savings from switching to cold composition, the TNL wages bill would shrink by £8 million. There would now be one thousand fewer jobs at Gray's Inn Road than had existed when Murdoch had moved in. This was an extraordinary indictment on the previous owner's inability to overcome union-backed overmanning. At the foot of the news story appeared the unadorned statement: 'Mr Harold Evans, the Editor of *The Times*, said he had no comment to make on reports circulating about his future as editor. He was on duty last night as usual.'[189]

In the leader article he wrote, entitled 'The Deeper Issues' (some felt this referred to his own predicament), Evans surveyed the panorama of the British disease: the human waste of mass unemployment, the crumbling inner cities, 'idiot union abuse', the 'bored insularity' of Britain's approach to its international obligations and the failure of any political party to find answers. There was a scarcely repressed anger from the pen of an editor who had just buried his father – an intelligent and encouraging man for whom the limits of opportunity had confined to a job driving trains. But there were also pointed references to Evans's own finest hour (the Thalidomide victims) and an attack on 'the monopoly powers of capital or the trade unions, or too great a concentration of power in any one institution: the national press itself, to be fair, is worryingly over-concentrated'.[190] There was no need to name names.

Saturday's *Times* gave an accurate picture of the situation at Gray's Inn Road – the report was utterly incomprehensible. Murdoch was quoted as stating 'with the unanimous approval of the independent national directors' that Evans had been replaced by Douglas-Home. Lord Robens described this statement as 'a bit mixed up'. Evans was quoted claiming he had not resigned and his staying on was 'not about money, as alleged. It is and has been an argument about principles.' Gerald Long claimed that the independence of the editor had never been in dispute. Holden said it was. Douglas-Home said it wasn't, going on the record to state:

There has been to my knowledge, and I have worked closely with the editor, absolutely no instruction or vestige of an instruction to the editor to publish or not to publish any political article. There has been no undue pressure to influence the editor's policy or decisions.[191]

Times readers could have been forgiven for believing they were looking not at a news report but at a bleeding gash running down the front page of their paper. During the day, the Journalists of The Times (JOTT) group passed a motion that they released to the press calling for Evans to be replaced by Douglas-Home. They found fault with the 'gradual erosion of editorial standards' and Evans's indecision: 'The way the paper is laid out and run has changed so frequently that stability has been destroyed.' Geraldine Norman had been to the fore of getting this motion accepted, much to the disquiet of many of the two hundred subscribing JOTT members whose approval she had not canvassed.[192] A pro-Evans counter-petition was circulated and also attracted support. Nobody wanted another week of this madness.

Meanwhile, Fred Emery had telephoned from the slopes in order to find out what was happening in his absence. Douglas-Home asked him to come back immediately, particularly requesting that he be back in time to edit the Sunday for Monday paper. Emery raced back and found the journalists had become even more polarized during his absence. He also discovered the reason Douglas-Home wanted him back to edit the paper on the Sunday evening. The editor-in-waiting was singing in a choir that evening. In the circumstances, this was a high note of insouciance.

The denouement came the following day, Monday, 15 March, in a series of remarkable twists and turns. Nobody seemed to know whether the editor was staying or going. However, he did periodically emerge to give the impression that he was still in charge. Taking inspiration from a photograph of himself playing tennis, he swung a clenched fist in the air and assured Emery, 'I play to win!' Half an hour later, he had tendered his resignation in the curtest possible letter addressed 'To The Chairman'. It read in its entirety:

Dear Sir,
I hearby tender my resignation as editor of *The Times*.
Yours faithfully,
H. M. Evans

His colleagues found it easier getting accurate news from the far Pacific than from within the building. All they knew was that Evans had overseen a statement in the early editions of the paper reporting that he had not resigned. They were thus surprised when at 9.40 p.m. he curtly announced to the rolling cameras of *News at Ten* that he had indeed quit. His decision to give advance warning to ITN in order to maximize the publicity but not his own journalists dampened the send-off he might otherwise have been accorded.[193] Instead, when he was sure the cameras were in position, he walked out of the building, stopping only to shake hands with the uniformed guard at the reception desk (unsurprisingly, there was no sign of his secretary). Stopped by a television reporter as he got into the back seat of a waiting car, he refused to make further comment beyond observing, with a weary expression, that it was a tale longer than the Borgias.[194]

VII

Harold Evans came home to a party organized by Tina Brown, his wife. His stalwart supporters came to rally round. Anthony Holden had already created a stir that evening at a function for authors of the year (of which he was one). Seeing Murdoch in the corner of the room he stormed over, almost elbowing the Queen to the ground in the process, and proceeded to harangue the newspaper proprietor. The exchange ended with Murdoch assuring him he would never work on any of his papers again and Holden telling him where he could stick them. Such was the excited gravitation towards this verbal brawl that the Queen found herself momentarily deserted and ignored by the room's inhabitants.[195] Holden resigned from *The Times* with immediate effect without taking a penny of compensation. This was a principled stand that impressed Murdoch. Evans, meanwhile, negotiated a pay-off in excess of £250,000. After only one year's employment, this sum was at the time considered so large that it almost (but not quite) dented *Private Eye*'s preening glee at his departure in its 26 March edition, unpleasantly entitled and illustrated 'Dame Harold Evans, Memorial Issue. A Nation Mourns'.[196]

The generous severance terms did not stop Evans writing *Good Times, Bad Times*, an account of his struggles at Gray's Inn Road which was published in 1983. Inevitably, not everyone liked and some did not recognize the picture he painted. His successor as editor, Douglas-Home, refused to read it. He did, however, see enough of the extracts in the press to pronounce, 'that it presented a quite insurmountable question of inaccuracy'.[197] The most damaging charges Evans brought both in his book and in subsequent allegations concerned his relations with the proprietor, especially in matters of editorial independence. Evans believed he had incurred Margaret Thatcher's displeasure and that, in sacking him, Murdoch was enacting a tacit understanding with the Prime Minister as a result of her pressure to ensure his bid for Times Newspapers was not referred to the Monopolies Commission. Perhaps, as Sir John Junor had prophesied to Tina Brown, Murdoch had always intended to sack Evans after a year as soon as he had been the fall guy for unpopular changes Murdoch wanted forced upon the paper.[198] Such was the regard Evans was held in at the *Sunday Times*, Murdoch would have had difficulty removing him from that editorship, but switching him next door suited his purposes perfectly.[199] Many of the changes Evans effected were those Murdoch had himself wanted to see brought about: redundancies, the paper redesigned with new layout, sharper reporting, more sport and less donnish prevarication as a cover for laziness. On this interpretation of events, Murdoch had used Evans and then flung him overboard.

In *Good Times, Bad Times*, Evans stated that early in 1982 Murdoch had visited Mrs Thatcher suggesting that she find for Evans a public post so that he could be levered out of the editorship. According to Evans's account, the Prime Minister had asked Cecil Parkinson, the Conservative Party chairman, to cast around for a job for him and Parkinson had come up with the post of chairman of the Sports Council. Mrs Thatcher, it seemed, was keen to assist Murdoch in finding an easy way to be rid of his turbulent editor.[200] Evans had caused annoyance by running on his front page a story concerning a letter from Denis Thatcher to the Welsh Secretary written on Downing Street paper (though since this was where he lived, it was not clear what other address he could have given) concerning the slow pace of resolving a planning application made by a subsidiary of a company to which he was a consultant. Most commentators considered undue prominence had been given to a rather minor indiscretion (Mr Thatcher had made clear 'obviously nothing can be done to advance the hearing') and even the *Times* leader on the subject placed it third, where it belonged, below Liberal Party defence policy and political developments in Chad.[201] There was also the question of why Evans had printed a letter that had been stolen from the Welsh Office and touted around by a Welsh news agency. But it hardly necessitated a Thatcher–Murdoch conspiracy to do away with him. Under

Evans, *The Times* had opposed the Government's obsession with narrow definitions of monetary policy but, as Tony Benn and Michael Foot could attest, it was far from being an outright opponent of the Conservatives. On most issues and in particular on trade union reform, it was supportive. Indeed, had Rees-Mogg continued as editor, it might have been every bit as sympathetic towards the SDP as the measured approach adopted by Evans. And Evans would later make clear both that, had Argentina invaded the Falkland Islands during his watch, *The Times* would have been stalwart in its support of Britain's armed liberation of the islands and that the paper would probably have endorsed the Conservatives in the 1983 general election.[202] If the Prime Minister wanted the removal of a Fleet Street editor it is hard to see how Evans of *The Times* could be top of her list. Murdoch asserted that the conspiracy theory was ludicrous, maintaining that he 'never ever' discussed getting rid of Evans with Mrs Thatcher. Asked about it in 2004, Cecil Parkinson stated, 'I cannot remember this incident. I certainly have no recollections of searching for a job for Harold Evans.'[203] Murdoch doubted that Thatcher and Parkinson had conjured up the Sports Council chairmanship as a way of facilitating Evans's departure on the grounds that 'they were not Machiavellian enough' and adding, 'I don't think they cared about *The Times*. She didn't.'[204]

Did Murdoch interfere in editorial policy? Donoughue disliked hearing that Murdoch thought his leader articles were too generous towards Tory 'wets' or Social Democrats.[205] Evans chose to disregard the proprietor's expressed hope that *The Times* would take a critical line on the Civil List.[206] Although he certainly gave vent to uncompromising opinions when the conversation turned to political matters, Murdoch always maintained that he had never instructed Evans to take any line in his paper other than one of consistency – a steady course the proprietor claimed was lacking. Douglas-Home was incredulous that Evans could not tell the difference between Murdoch 'sounding off' as opposed to giving orders. In Douglas-Home's experience, Murdoch 'didn't object to anyone standing up to him on policy issues'. Of course it was easier for the more robustly right-wing Douglas-Home to find this to be the case. But he went further, claiming that it was Evans who had endangered his own editorial independence by constantly ringing Murdoch for reassurance.[207] No subsequent *Times* editor ever claimed undue pressure was applied by Murdoch on editorial policy. Murdoch did not prevent Frank Giles from pursuing a far more 'wet' political line at the *Sunday Times*, also a paper whose direction Mrs Thatcher might have been expected to take a keen interest in. Murdoch did not stop Giles from being sceptical about Britain seeking to retake the Falklands by force or from being overtly sympathetic towards the SDP in the 1983 general election. It was not for his politics that he was eventually replaced by Andrew Neil, an outsider whom Murdoch believed would breathe new energy into the Sunday title as he had once hoped Evans would do with the daily.

Understandably, Evans's allegations confirmed the suspicions of all those on the political left who believed Murdoch was a malign influence on news reporting. They had seen it with the *Sun* and its crude caricature of the left. Now they had evidence that it was consuming *The Times*. Staged at the National Theatre, David Hare's 1985 play *Pravda – A Fleet Street Comedy* was widely interpreted as an attack on Murdoch's style of proprietorship. Co-written with Howard Brenton whose *The Romans in Britain* had caused outrage because of its overt depictions of Romans sodomizing Ancient Britons (apparently a metaphor for the British presence in Ulster), *Pravda* depicted the sorry tale of Lambert La Roux, a South African tabloid owner, buying a British Establishment broadsheet only to sack its editor just after he had received an Editor of the Year award. Anna Murdoch went to see the play. After this, her husband's only comment on it was to suggest, with a wink, that Robert Maxwell might find it actionable.

But more seriously, if Evans felt he had been improperly treated by Murdoch he could have appealed to the independent national directors to adjudicate on the matter. Given the lengths to which he had gone to write these safeguards into the contract by which Murdoch bought the paper it was surprising that he did not avail himself of the opportunity to challenge the proprietor in this way. Perhaps he thought the independent directors would not support his case. Even Lord Robens, who had spoken support-ively to him in an alcove of the Reform Club, was not so stalwart behind his back. According to Richard Searby, Robens promptly told Murdoch that he was the proprietor and if he thought Evans should be sacked, he should be sacked.[208] Whatever his reasoning, Evans preferred to make his case in a book instead. The audience was certainly wider.

Deeply involved in the union negotiations and in attempting to overcome the production difficulties during Evans's year in the chair, Bill O'Neill felt that the problem was not one of politics but of personalities. Evans 'con-sidered himself a creator, an editorial genius', O'Neill maintained 'and not someone who would be burdened with incidentals, like the huge losses the title he edited was running. You could not engage Evans in debate. He would agree with everything you put to him.'[209] In his fourteen years as editor of the *Sunday Times*, Evans had benefited from supportive allies in Denis Hamilton and a proprietor, Roy Thomson, who was happy to invest heavily into ensuring Evans's creative talents bore fruit. With his move to *The Times*, he had difficulty adapting to the culture shock of working for a new proprietor who, after initially encouraging further expansion, suddenly demanded urgent economies in order to keep the title afloat. Hamilton's disillusion and departure also robbed him of a calming and understanding influence. Evans complained that 'every single commercial decision of any importance was taken along the corridor in Murdoch's office, while we went through our charades' on the TNL board.[210] But what did he expect? Who was writing the cheques? It was as if Evans had confused editing the newspaper with owning it. As Evans proved at the *Sunday Times* and in his subsequent career in New York (to where he and Tina Brown decamped), he was at his best when he had a generous benefactor prepared to under-write his initiatives. Especially in the dark economic climate of 1981–2, Murdoch was not in the mood to be a benefactor.

Indeed, if Evans was a victim of Murdoch's ruthless business sense, he was most of all a victim of the times. The dire situation of TNL's finances meant Murdoch was frequently in Gray's Inn Road and was particularly watchful over what was going on there. Furthermore, Murdoch and his senior management could hardly absolve themselves totally of their part in the chaos surrounding Evans's final months in the chair. Murdoch had told Evans to bring in new blood and frequently suggested expensive serializa-tions to run in the paper. When the costs of these changes reached the accounts department he then blamed Evans for his imprudence.[211] The failure to agree with the editor a proper budget allocation compounded these problems, although Murdoch refuted Evans's claims that he did not know what the financial situation was, maintaining he 'got budgets all the time'.[212] The swingeing cuts in TNL clerical staff had to be made, but the brinkmanship necessary to bring them about created a level of tension that clearly had negative effects on morale within the building. Murdoch's own manner at this time, frequently swearing and being curt to senior staff, contributed to the unease and feeling of wretchedness.[213] As the years rolled by with the financial and industrial problems of News International receding while he developed media interests elsewhere, so Murdoch spent less time living above the *Times* shop. Therefore, if Evans wanted to be left to his own devices, it was his misfortune to have accepted the paper's editorship at the worst possible moment. Had he been appointed later, at a time when the paper was no longer enduring a daily fight for survival and justification of every expense was no longer necessary, he might have proved to be a long serving and commercially successful *Times* editor. This, after all, was what became of his protégé, Peter Stothard.

Rees-Mogg took the view on his successor's downfall that an editor could fall out with his proprietor or several of his senior staff but not with both at the same time.[214] In the eyes of the old guard, Evans had two principal problems. First, he frequently changed his mind. This had all been part of the creative process when he had edited a Sunday paper, since he had a week to finalize his position, but it made life on a daily basis extremely difficult. The second irritation was that he surrounded himself with his own people who were not, in heart and temperament, '*Times* Men'. For this reason, Donoughue and Holden were disliked in a reaction that overlooked their considerable talents. In the closing months of the drama, Holden would periodically arrive at his office to find childish sentiments scrawled on his door. Invariably they were of an unwelcoming nature.[215] Indeed, the pro-Evans petition circulated in the dying moments of his tenure demonstrated perfectly the essential rift between *The Times* old guard and Evans's flying circus of new recruits. Six of the thirteen senior staff members signed the pro-Evans petition (the other seven were either absent or pointedly refused to endorse him). But of Evans's six senior supporters, five had been recruited by him from outside the paper in the course of the past year. Only one of the seven who did not sign had worked for *The Times* for less than twelve years.[216] *Good Times, Bad Times* concentrated on Murdoch as the assassin. But at the moment of impact there were plenty of other bullets flying from a plethora of vantage points.

Tony Norbury, able to speak from the vantage point of over forty years experience on the production side of the paper, believed that although Evans's demise was inevitable and perhaps necessary, he was nonetheless 'the Editor who saved *The Times*'.[217] In the space of a year, he had brought about great changes and many of them were for the better. The layout was much improved. Circulation was up by 19,000 on the comparable period in 1980. The paper was revitalized. It was no longer in retreat. Probably his greatest legacy was those journalists he brought in who stayed with the paper in the years ahead, among whom Peter Stothard, Frank Johnson, Miles Kington and the medical correspondent, Dr Thomas Stuttaford, were to loom large. Indeed, it would be quite wrong to assume that the old guard were necessarily right in opposing Evans's innovations. Their victory over him in March 1982 was personal and vindictive. It was also temporary. Much of what he attempted to teach the paper about 'vertical journalism' would, in time and in a less frenetic environment, eventually be accepted and adopted.

It was Evans's other concept, the 'editing theory of maximum irritation', that did for him. As one of the senior financial journalists snootily put it, 'What is this silly little man doing running around trying to tell us how to do our jobs?'[218] Evans's mistake was to make too many radical changes too quickly and in a manner that left old *Times* journalists feeling excluded. His attempts to make the paper more like its more popular Sunday neighbour were especially disliked. A critic at the *Spectator* found fault that 'instead of spending the morning in Sir William [Rees-Mogg's] musty but absorbing library we should be outside "in the field" with Mr Evans getting down to what a French investigative reporter once termed "the nitty grotty". It's all lead poisoning from petrol fumes nowadays, and why not? Only that several other papers tell us about that sort of thing all the time.'[219] While the *Sunday Times* was a 'journalists paper with a high-risk dynamic' to break news, *The Times* 'must get its facts and opinions right' and its editor 'must possess great steadiness and consistency . . . He must be patient and move slowly.'[220] Or, as Philip Howard put it, 'The *Sunday Times* and *The Times* are joined by a bridge about ten yards long and somewhere along that bridge Harry fell off.'[221]

One of the few journalists brought in by Evans who did not support him in his time of trial was Frank Johnson. 'I cannot think of a better thing I did in 1981 than ask you to join *The Times*,' Evans wrote to congratulate him when he was named Columnist of the Year at the British Press Awards.[222] But Johnson, who had always admired the old *Times*, was relieved when Douglas-Home took over. With Murdoch's threat to close the paper lifted and Evans, Holden and Donoughue seeking alternative employment, the atmosphere at Gray's Inn Road improved remarkably swiftly. Douglas-Home, the editor most of the senior staff had wanted in the first place (and but for Murdoch would probably have got), was at last in the chair. But what buried the internecine bickering most decisively was a major incident in – of all unlikely places – the South Atlantic. As Britain's armed forces sailed towards the Falkland Islands and an uncertain fate, office politics suddenly looked self-indulgent and thoughts switched back to the job everyone was paid to do – report the news.[223]

CHAPTER THREE

COLD WARRIOR

The Falklands War; the Lebanon;
Shoring up NATO; Backing Maggie

I

The journalists of the Buenos Aires *Siete Dias* had a commendable knowledge not only of their government's intentions but also of how *The Times* of London liked to lay out its front page. Forty-eight hours before the invasion began *Siete Dias*'s readers were presented with an imaginary front page of that morning's edition of *The Times*. It was good enough to pass off as the real thing. The masthead and typeface were accurate. Even the headline 'Argentinian Navy invades the Falkland Islands' was grouped across the two columns' width of the lead report rather than stretched across the whole front page. That was a particularly observant touch. The accompanying photograph of advancing Argentine troops was also in exactly the place the page designers of Gray's Inn Road would have put it – top centre right with a single-column news story hemming it back from the paper's edge. Someone, at least, had done his homework.

The real *Times* of London for that day had an almost identical front-page layout. The only visual difference was that the lead headline announced 'Compromise by Labour on abolition of Lords' – which could have been confidently stated at almost any time in the twenty years either side of 31 March 1982. But the perceptive reader would have noticed something more portentous in the adjacent single column headlined 'British sub on the move'. The story, 'By Our Foreign Staff', claimed that the nuclear-powered hunter-killer submarine, HMS *Superb* 'was believed to be on its way' to the Falkland Islands although the Royal Navy 'refused to confirm or deny these reports'. This was odd. *The Times* was not in the habit of knowing, let alone announcing, the sudden change of course of a British nuclear submarine. In fact, the story had been planted. It was intended to warn the government in Buenos Aires that their invasion intentions had been discovered. But it was too late. The Argentinian troops had already boarded the vessels. The aircraft carrier *Veinticinco de Mayo* had put out to sea.

In the aftermath of a war that caused the deaths of 255 Britons and 746 Argentinians, questions were asked about why London failed to perceive the threat to the Falkland Islands until it was too late. The press had not seen it coming. But they could hardly be blamed when Britain's intelligence community had also failed to pick up on the warning signs. In retrospect, the Government's dual policy of dashing Argentina's hopes of a diplomatic solution while announcing a virtual abandonment of the islands' defence appeared like folly on a grand scale.

Despite talk of there being oil, there had long been little enthusiasm in the Foreign Office for holding onto the barren and remote British dependency, eight thousand miles away and important primarily for the disruption it caused Britain's relations with Argentina, a bulwark against South American Communism where much British capital was invested. The general impression was given that if Buenos Aires wanted the islands that much, they could have them. But the will of the 1800 islanders, stubborn and staunchly loyal subjects of Her Majesty, complicated the matter. In November 1980, Nicholas Ridley, a Foreign Office minister, thought he had the answer when he suggested transferring the islands' sovereignty formally to Argentina while leasing back tenure in the short term so that the existing islanders would not be handed over to an alien power effectively overnight. This idea had been broadly supported in a third leader in *The Times*, written by Peter Strafford, albeit on the condition the Falkland islanders agreed to it.[1] They lost no time in making clear they did not. Their opposition emboldened Margaret Thatcher and the House of Commons, sceptical of the 'Munich tendency' within the Foreign Office, to dismiss the proposal out of hand.

Argentina was a right-wing military dictatorship. During the 1970s 'dirty war', its ruling junta had murdered thousands of its citizens. If the British Government was determined to close the diplomatic door over the islands' sovereignty to such a regime it might have been advisable to send clear messages about London's determination to guard the Falklands militarily. Yet, this is not what happened. The public spending cuts of Margaret Thatcher's first term did not bypass the armed forces. In 1981, John Nott, the Defence Secretary, proposed stringent economies. Guided by Henry Stanhope, the defence correspondent, *The Times* had argued that if there had to be cuts it would be better for the greater blow to fall upon the British Army of the Rhine rather than the Royal Navy since the BAOR's proportionate contribution to the NATO alliance was not as significant as the maritime commitment. Yet, when Nott's spending review was published in June, he proposed closing the Chatham dockyards and cutting the number of surface ships. One of those vessels was HMS *Endurance*, which was to be withdrawn from its lonely patrol of the South Atlantic.

Although it was understandably not described as such, the *Endurance* was Britain's spy ship in the area – as the Argentinians had long assumed. But for those who did not look beyond its exterior, it appeared too lightly defended to put up much resistance to an Argentine assault. Consequently, scrapping the ship appeared to make sense in every respect other than the psychological signal it transmitted to Buenos Aires. It was a fatal economy. Britain appeared to be dropping its guard over the Falkland Islands. The junta saw its chance. Only a small but prophetic letter, from Lord Shackleton, Peter Scott, Vivian Fuchs and five other members of the Royal Geographical Society, printed in *The Times* on 4 February 1982, pointed out the strategic short-sightedness of withdrawing the only white ensign in the South Atlantic and Antarctic seas.[2] The paper did not pick up on the point.

To be fair, there were remarkably few early warning signs. General Leopoldo Galtieri's inaugural speech as Argentina's President in December 1981 contained no reference to reclaiming 'Las Malvinas'. The first indication *Times* readers received that all was not well came on 5 March 1982 when Peter Strafford reported that Buenos Aires was stepping up the pressure over the islands. Strafford speculated that with the Falklands defended by a Royal Marines platoon and local volunteers – a total of less than one hundred men – an invasion was possible 'as a last resort'. But it seemed far more likely that Buenos Aires would apply pressure through the United Nations or by threatening to sever the only regular air service out of the islands which was operated by the Argentine Air Force.

It was not until 23 March that *The Times* again focused its attention firmly on developments when it reported the Foreign Office's confirmation that an illegal detachment of about fifty Argentinians claiming to have a contract to dismantle the whaling station at Leith on South Georgia, a British dependency eight hundred miles south-east of the Falklands, had hoisted their national flag. The Foreign Office was quoted as reacting 'sceptically to the suggestion that the landing on South Georgia last week was instigated by the Argentine Government'.[3]

Whitehall could not be expected to dispatch the Fleet every time a trespasser waved his national flag on some far-off British territory. In the same month in which the 'scrap metal merchants' were posing for photographs on the spectacularly inhospitable and all but uninhabited South Georgia, Thomas Enders, the US Assistant Secretary of State for Latin America, had visited President Galtieri and passed on to the British Foreign Office Minister Richard Luce the impression that there was no cause for concern. Nonetheless, Margaret Thatcher asked for contingency plans to be drawn up and for a reassessment of the Joint Intelligence Committee's existing report on the invasion threat to the Falklands. It was too late. On the evening of 31 March, John Nott passed to the Prime Minister the appalling news: an intelligence report that an Argentine armada was at sea and heading straight for the Falklands. Their estimated date of arrival was 2 April.[4]

The Times had already reported, on the front page for Monday 29 March, 'five Argentine vessels were last night reported to be in the area of South Georgia'. The second leading article that day, 'Gunboat or Burglar Alarm?', warned that the Falklands were probably the real target. It attempted to marry the diplomatic tone taken when the leader column had last addressed the subject in November 1980 that the islanders' future 'can only be on the basis of an arrangement with their South American neighbours' with a belated note of half-warning, 'Britain should help them get the best arrangement possible, and to do that should be prepared to put a military price on any Argentine smash-and-grab raid'.[5] Tuesday's front page reported that 'two other Argentine naval vessels were said to have left port' but that London was still making no official comment. The following day came the leaked report that a nuclear submarine was on its way to the Falklands. On Thursday 1 April, the paper conveyed accurately the atmosphere in the Gray's Inn Road newsroom with a headline that ought to have become famous in its field: 'Impenetrable silence on Falklands crisis'.

Apart from some 'library pictures' of the Falkland Islands' capital, Port Stanley, and rusting hulks in South Georgia's Grytviken harbour, it was not possible to accompany the unfolding saga with 'live' pictures. There was no press cameraman on the islands. However, the *Sunday Times* had dispatched Simon Winchester to follow up on the South Georgia 'scrap metal merchants'. Winchester was in Port Stanley when the Argentine forces landed. On 2 April, *The Times* was able to use his copy, announcing that the invasion was expected any moment and citing the state of emergency alert broadcast to the islanders by their Governor, Rex Hunt. It made for dramatic reading. Ironically, while a paper like *The Times*, famed for its correspondents in far flung places had not got round to getting a reporter *in situ*, the *Sun* – not celebrated for its foreign desk or international postings – did have a man there. Its reporter, David Graves, had set off for South Georgia on his own whim. He too was in Stanley when the shooting started.[6] Unfortunately, neither journalist would be filing from there for much longer. Both Winchester and Graves had to move to the Argentine mainland. There, Winchester, together with Ian Mather and Tony Prime of the *Observer* were arrested on spying charges. Over the next few weeks, the British media was put in the impossible position of trying to report what was happening on a group of islands where they had no reporters.

If the Government had dithered before the invasion, it was resolute – or at any rate its Prime Minister was – in its response. A Task Force would be dispatched to take the islands back if no diplomatic solution had been reached in the time it would take the Royal Navy to reach the Falklands. All the newspapers recognized the necessity of getting their journalists on board the ships, but the Royal Navy was hostile to carrying any superfluous personnel on board – least of all prying journalists. It took considerable pressure from Downing Street to get the Navy to accept the necessity of any press presence.[7] After much bullying, it was agreed that the newspaper journalists would be corralled upon the aircraft carrier HMS *Invincible*, travelling with the first batch of the Task Force. There would be only five places available.

It was left to John Le Page, director of the Newspaper Publishers' Association, to decide which newspapers would make the cut. He opted for the method of Mrs Le Page drawing the winning titles out of a hat. This pot-luck approach produced random results, not least of which was that the *Daily Telegraph* would be the only representative of the 'quality press'. Neither *The Times*, nor the *Guardian*, nor the country's major tabloid, the *Sun*, was selected. This was no way to report a war. Outrage followed with Douglas-Home and his rival disappointed editors demanding representation. Bernard Ingham, the Prime Minister's press secretary, only managed to cool the heat emanating from his telephone receiver by insisting the three papers were included after all.[8]

The Times only heard that a place had been secured for its nominated reporter, John Witherow, at 10.15 p.m on Sunday 4 April. He had to race to catch the train to Portsmouth – for *Invincible* was scheduled to set sail at midnight. Almost the only instructions Witherow received from Gray's Inn Road was to pack a dark suit. There was, after all, the possibility he might be asked to dine with the officers in the wardroom. He at least came better prepared for the rigours of a South Atlantic winter than the *Sun*'s representative who arrived at Portsmouth docks on a motorbike wearing a pair of shorts.[9]

Robert Fisk was *The Times*'s star war reporter, but he was in the Middle East. And as it transpired, he would soon have an invasion on his doorstep to cover. John Witherow was a thirty-year-old reporter on the home news desk, who had come to the paper from Reuters as recently as 1980. The son of a South African businessman, he had been brought to England as a child and sent to Bedford School. Before reading history at York University, he had done two years voluntary service in Namibia where he taught and helped establish a library for the inhabitants and was befriended by Bishop Colin Winter, an outspoken critic of Apartheid. He was hardly the obvious choice but, although there was no certainty that the Task Force would see action, his status as a young and unmarried reporter who was not committed anywhere else at that moment weighed in favour of his being sent on an assignment that could take weeks or months – or even take his life.

Only representatives of the British media were allowed to accompany the Task Force, Margaret Thatcher taking the view 'we certainly didn't want any foreigners reporting what we were doing down there!'.[10] Witherow and his fellow journalists were soon to discover the limitations imposed upon them, their dispatches monitored by MoD minders and by Royal Naval press officers. The minders occasionally prevented details in dispatches leaving the ship only for the same disclosures to be released by the MoD in London. There was to be considerable friction over this and other scores. When either bureaucratic or technical difficulties prevented Witherow getting his dispatches out, the burden of war reporting fell on Henry Stanhope in London. For his information, Stanhope was reliant upon MoD briefings. But in the first weeks of the Task Force's long journey, the focus was on how diplomacy might yet avert shots being fired in anger. Julian Haviland, the political editor, reported the mood in Westminster as did Christopher Thomas from Buenos Aires. Nicholas Ashford filed from Washington and from New York Zoriana Pysariwsky followed developments at the UN.

With the hawkish Charles Douglas-Home in charge, there was never any doubt what line the paper would take. The seizure of the islands was, the leading article declared as soon as the invasion was confirmed, 'as perfect an example of unprovoked aggression and military expansion as the world has had to witness since the end of Adolf Hitler'. Russia would back Argentina and nothing but words could be expected from the UN. If need be, it would be necessary to meet force with force.[11] On Monday 4 April – the day the Task Force left Portsmouth harbour – there was only one leading article, stretching down the page and occupying sixty-eight column inches and more than five and a half feet. It was written by the editor. 'When British territory is invaded, it is not just an invasion of our land, but of our whole spirit. We are all Falklanders now' the paper thundered. The Argentine junta had eliminated its opponents – 'the disappeared ones' as they were euphemistically known. 'The disappearance of individuals is the Junta's recognized method of dealing with opposition. We are now faced with a situation where it intends to make a whole island people – the Falklanders – disappear.' This could not be tolerated. The words of John Donne were intoned. And it was time for the Defence Secretary, John Nott, and the Foreign Secretary, Lord Carrington, to consider their positions.[12]

During the weekend, Margaret Thatcher and her deputy, Willie Whitelaw, had tried to shore up Carrington's resolve to stay. But, as Thatcher put it in her memoirs, 'Having seen Monday's press, in particular the *Times* leader, he decided that he must go.'[13] Nott, however, was persuaded to hang on. For Douglas-Home, the most important task was to bolster the Prime Minister's reserve not to back down. On 2 April, the Foreign Office had presented her with a litany of diplomatic pitfalls if she proceeded with her intention to send, and if necessary, use, the Task Force just as the MoD had listed the military impediments. Her decision to disregard such advice filled many in Whitehall with alarm. It was essential to restrict the strategic decisions to an inner core. An inner 'War Cabinet' was formed to meet once (sometimes twice) a day to conduct operations. On it sat Mrs Thatcher, her deputy Whitelaw, Nott, Carrington's successor at the Foreign Office, Francis Pym and Cecil Parkinson (who, although only Chancellor of the Duchy of Lancaster, could be expected to back his leader's resolve if the Foreign Office tested it).

In New York, Britain's UN Ambassador, Sir Anthony Parsons, had achieved a notable triumph in securing Resolution 502, which demanded an Argentine withdrawal from the islands. The Security Council presidency was in the hands of Zaire and Spain and Panama sympathized with Argentina. Russia, which could have vetoed the resolution outright, had no reason to back a NATO country and was heavily dependent on Argentine grain. Parsons's skill (and a telephone lecture from Mrs Thatcher to King Hussein of Jordan) ensured most of the opposition was neutered into abstention. Only Panama voted against Britain. Yet, while the United States had voted favourably, its true position was equivocal. It could not rebuff its most senior NATO ally, but it did not want to undermine the anti-Communist regime in Buenos Aires. The 1947 Rio Treaty allowed for any American country to assist any other that was attacked from outside the American continent. Washington believed this was a shield against Soviet interference. A British strike could fatally crack the edifice. Indeed, the night the Argentinians had invaded, Jeane Kirkpatrick, Walter Stoessel and Thomas Enders (respectively US Ambassador to the UN; Deputy-Secretary of State; Assistant Secretary of State for Latin America) were among a group of senior US officials who had dined at the Argentine Embassy. Kirkpatrick, in particular, was no friend of Britain. On 13 April she went so far as to suggest 'If the Argentines own the islands, then moving troops into them is not armed aggression.'[14] Could Britain proceed without US endorsement? The lesson of Suez was not encouraging.

The dispatch of the US Secretary of State, Alexander Haig, as a peace broker between Buenos Aires and London bought Washington time to avoid taking sides. President Mitterrand proved a staunch supporter of Britain's claim to take back islands recognized by international law as her own, but not all the European partners were so steadfast. When the EEC embargo on Argentine imports came up for its monthly renewal in mid-May, Italy and Ireland opted out of it. The closer the Task Force got to fighting the more jumpy became the Germans. Beyond the EEC, Britain's greatest allies proved to be Pinochet's Chile, Australia and New Zealand. Auckland's Prime Minister, Robert Muldoon, wrote a personal article in *The Times* making clear 'New Zealand will back Britain all the way'.[15] He offered one of his country's frigates to take the place of a Royal Naval vessel called up for South Atlantic operations.

To Conservatives of Douglas-Home's cobalt hue, reclaiming the Falklands had implications beyond assuring the self-determination of its islanders. It was also about marking an end to the years of continuous national retreat since Suez. It was about proving that Britain was still great and was not, as Margaret Thatcher put it in reply to Foreign Office defeatists, a country ready to accept 'that a common or garden dictator should rule over the Queen's subjects and prevail by fraud and violence'.[16] That Tories saw an opportunity to commence a national revival of self-confidence troubled the left and many liberals. They had no love for a right-wing military junta in Buenos Aires but they worried a triumphant feat of British arms would restore militaristic (right-wing, class-ridden) attitudes. It was little wonder they turned to the UN in the hope of a compromise that would fudge such absolutes as 'ownership' and 'nationalism'. Indeed, Britain at large appeared to be apprehensive. During April and early May, opinion polls suggested there was support for sending the Task Force but considerable doubt about whether reclaiming the islands was worth spilling British blood.[17]

Despite his own stalwart position, Douglas-Home was careful to ensure the widest possible spectrum of views should be aired in the paper. Never shy to criticize, Fred Emery told him 'your leaders have been a sight too romantic, losing sight of the practicalities'.[18] David Watts was in the camp that argued that the islanders had precious little future without Argentine collaboration and that the utility of 1800 Falkland Islanders to the national interest was less than the financial portfolios of the 17,000 British citizens living in Argentina. A full-page pro-Argentine advert was published.[19] The historian and anti-nuclear campaigner E. P. Thompson was given much of the Op-Ed page to explain 'why neither side is worth backing'. He concluded that Mrs Thatcher's 'administration has lost a by-election in Glasgow and it needs to sink the Argentine navy in revenge'.[20] The letters page started to fill. Many disliked Douglas-Home's editorial line. The former Labour Paymaster-General, Lord (George) Wigg got personal:

I have no confidence in improvised military adventures in pursuit of undefined objectives, and my doubts are further emphasized by the attitude of *The Times* which, during my lifetime, has been wrong on every major issue, and I have little doubt that the time will come when your current follies will be added to the long list of failures to serve your country with wisdom in her hour of need.[21]

Sackloads of letters abhorred the idea of a resolution through violence in the South Atlantic. The playwright William Douglas-Home (the editor's uncle) was among those wondering if a referendum could be held to ask the islanders whether they wanted to be evacuated and, if so, to where, 'otherwise a situation might arise in which the Union Jack flew again on Government House with hardly anybody alive to recognize it'. Four to five hundred letters were arriving at Gray's Inn Road every day. Leon Pilpel, the letters page editor, considered that in the past thirty years only two other issues had generated comparable levels of correspondence – the 1956 Suez crisis and the paper's resumption in 1979 after its eleven-month shutdown. In the first three weeks of the crisis the number of letters received suggested that a little over half disagreed with the paper's editorial line and favoured a negotiated settlement rather than using the Task Force. But there were also sackloads of letters from America supporting the Prime Minister's resolve.[22] It was hard to gauge to what extent this reflected most

Times readers' views. Doubtless an anti-war editorial policy would have stimulated a greater torrent of pro-war letters.

Among broadsheets, *The Times* and the *Daily Telegraph* stood alone in unambiguously supporting the Task Force's objectives. Not even all the 'Murdoch Press' (as the left now chose to call it) supported the war. The *Sunday Times*'s editor, Frank Giles, believed '*The Times*'s leaders brayed and neighed like an old war horse'.[23] By contrast, the *Sunday Times* warned its readers that any attempt to retake the islands by force would be 'a short cut to bloody disaster'. Impressed by no force other than that of the market, the *Financial Times* opposed sending the Task Force. Britain, it maintained, should not seek to retain control of an 'anachronism'. Instead it should propose turning the islands over to a UN Trusteeship.[24] The *Guardian* became the main protest sheet against liberating the islands. The paper's star columnist, Peter Jenkins, perfectly encapsulating the *Guardian* mindset by warning, 'We should have no wish to become the Israelis of Western Europe'. The strident tone adopted by the *Sun* – derided for turning from 'bingo to jingo' – particularly confirmed *bien pensant* opinion against liberating the Falklands. Accusations of fifth columnists in the fourth estate raised temperatures further. The *Guardian*'s editor, Peter Preston, denounced the *Sun* as 'sad and despicable' for questioning the patriotism of the *Daily Mirror* and the BBC's Peter Snow.[25] There would be worse to come.

The *New Statesman*, edited by Bruce Page, a noted investigative journalist who had worked with Harold Evans at the *Sunday Times*, baited *The Times* for its 'We Are All Falklanders Now' editorial. 'It is not easy to believe,' the *New Statesman* pronounced, 'that even a government as stupid and amateurish as Mrs Thatcher's can actually be sending some of the Navy's costliest and most elaborate warships to take part in a game of blind-man's bluff at the other end of the world.' The weekly house magazine of the left exploded in a torrent of loathing, which, surprisingly, was directed not against the side led by a right-wing military junta but against 'the thing we still have to call our government – the United Kingdom state . . . so long as it has its dominion over us it will betray us – and makes us pay the price of betrayal in our own best blood'. For its 30 April edition, the *New Statesman* splashed across its cover the most demonic looking photograph of Mrs Thatcher it could tamper with, above the bold capital letter indictment 'THE WARMONGER'.[26]

The peace lobby tried to talk up every diplomatic initiative to avoid the coming confrontation. In contrast, Buenos Aires's offers were met with the

Sun's famous headline suggestion to 'Stick it up your junta!'[27] Al Haig's shuttle diplomacy stumbled on. But as far as Margaret Thatcher and the editorial policy of *The Times* was concerned, it was hard to see what offer would be acceptable that fell short of handing the islands back to their British owner. Not everyone in the War Cabinet saw the matter in such absolutes. The new Foreign Secretary, Francis Pym, supported a compromise he negotiated with Haig in Washington. The Task Force would turn back and the Argentine occupation would end. In its place a 'Special Interim Authority' would be established in Stanley that would include representatives of the Argentine government and a mysterious as yet unknown entity described as the 'local Argentine population'. There would be no explicit commitment to self-determination. Mrs Thatcher stated in her memoirs that she believed the deal would have allowed Buenos Aires 'to swamp the existing population with Argentinians' and that, had it been approved, she would have resigned.[28] But, rather than be seen to be negative, it was decided to wait and see what the junta made of the scheme. On 29 April, they rejected it. The following day, the United States at last came out formally in support of Britain. By then, South Georgia was back in British hands. With Witherow and the other reporters hundreds of miles away on the *Invincible*, there were no journalists with the landing force and the only photograph *The Times* could run with was an old panorama of a peaceful looking Grytviken harbour.

As the prospect of a major confrontation became inevitable, so Douglas-Home spent long periods on the telephone with intelligence officers and assorted defence experts. As Liz Seeber, his secretary, put it, 'He did seem to be remarkably well informed on some things'.[29] D-notices, a system established in 1912, set out the guidelines for the British news media's reporting of national security matters. Whitehall had only just reviewed and extended them two days before the Argentines had invaded. Concerned that Julian Haviland's article citing 'informed sources' that there was already an advance party on the Falklands breached D-notice 6 on 'British Security and Intelligence Services', Douglas-Home discreetly edited the piece before allowing it onto the front page for 27 April. This was an example of self-censorship, without the Secretary of the D-notice committee even being contacted on the subject.[30]

The censors reviewing John Witherow's dispatches from HMS *Invincible* forbade any mention of the Task Force's strengths, destinations, of the capability of the onboard armoury or even the weather. In London, the Vulcan bombing raid on Stanley's airfield was portrayed as a success (despite Argentine film footage that showed the airstrip was still useable). Witherow spoke to one of the personnel in the flight control room who told him the raid had been a disastrous flop. Witherow filed his copy to this effect, only to have the censor change it to read that the mission had been a success. This, however, was an extreme and rare example. Generally, as at Gray's Inn Road, self-censorship helped ensure that little of substance was actually excised from Witherow's copy.[31] Yet, this did not make relations on board *Invincible* easy. Unlike the Army, which had learned through long (and occasionally bitter) experience as a consequence of the Troubles in Ulster, the Navy was not used to dealing with the press at such close quarters. There was also the question over whether naval procedures applied to the journalists on board. It did not go down well that during the first 'Action Stations' Witherow went onto the bridge of *Invincible* protesting that 'as he represented *The Times*, he could go where he liked'.[32] As the Task Force steamed closer to the Total Exclusion Zone around the Falklands, relations between the press corps and their MoD 'minder' broke down completely. Recognizing the problem, the *Invincible*'s captain, Jeremy Black, did his best to help and assigned his secretary, Richard Aylard (later the Prince of Wales's private secretary), to smooth things over with the journalists. Nonetheless, Witherow's copy was vetted four times before it reached Gray's Inn Road. Once the MoD press officer, Aylard and Black had vetted it on the *Invincible*, it was transmitted to Admiral Sir John Fieldhouse's Command HQ at Northwood, Middlesex, where the MoD censors vetted it again. Despite Captain Black's request that, after they had cleared it, Northwood should release the journalists' dispatches at the same time as its own statements, this frequently did not happen.[33]

Transmitting copy from ship to shore was a major problem. Understandably, the journalists' dispatches were the lowest priority of all the information punched out by the *Invincible*'s messenger centre. It took half an hour for the operator to transfer a journalist's dispatch onto tape. Further delays took place trying to transmit it by satellite and the copy frequently got lost in the process, requiring it to be sent again. The whole process frequently took two to three hours – just to send one dispatch. And there were five Fleet Street journalists, all sending in their handiwork. It was hardly surprising that Black objected to 30 per cent of his outgoing traffic being taken up by press copy when he had far more important operational detail to convey. At one stage, there was a backlog of one thousand signals waiting to be cleared. Eventually Black demanded that press copy could only be transmitted at night, when there was usually less operational messaging needing to be sent. This ensured that copy was appearing in *The Times* around two days after it was written. A seven-hundred-word limit was also imposed.[34]

It had been decided that dispatches would be 'pooled' so that all the news media would have access to them. In any case, it proved almost impossible for any of the Fleet Street editors to make contact with their journalists on board ship. Witherow managed to get a brief call through to Fred Emery on 18 May, but this was a rare exception.[35] 'Those of us without experience of war would have done better,' Witherow later reflected, 'if we'd had the office saying "give us 2000 words on how the Harrier pilots spend their time" – we didn't know what they wanted and were just firing into a void all the time.' By the time newspapers were flown on board ship for the journalists to analyse, they were two to three weeks out of date. Witherow concluded that the failure to provide the embedded reporters with better communication channels ended up harming the Task Force's own publicity: 'if they had allowed it, they would have got much better and less spasmodic, coverage'.[36]

Witherow did not find the crew to be particularly pugnacious. 'They knew the ships were hopelessly defended,' he recalled, 'this became apparent when I saw them strapping machine guns to the railings of *Invincible* to shoot down low flying planes.'[37] On 1 May, the Fleet came under air attack. In London, the War Cabinet was concerned about the strike range of the carrier *Veinticinco de Mayo* and the cruiser *General Belgrano*. Although the latter was an aged survivor of Pearl Harbor, it was fitted with anti-ship Exocet missiles and was escorted by two destroyers. The Task Force's commander, Admiral Woodward, feared the carrier and the cruiser were attempting a pincer movement against his ships. On Sunday 2 May the War Cabinet gave to the submarine HMS *Conqueror* the order to torpedo the *Belgrano*. Three hundred and twenty-one members of its crew went down with her.

The *Belgrano*'s sinking was to be the most controversial action of the conflict. But, at first, it was very difficult to establish much information about it. Such was the paucity of information from the MoD, it did not make the newspapers until Tuesday 4 May editions. Even then, *The Times* had to rely on its US correspondent, Nicholas Ashford, for the news that 'authoritative sources in Washington' had confirmed the cruiser had sunk and that as many as seven hundred of its crew might have drowned. Filing from Buenos Aires, Christopher Thomas backed up Washington's claims. All the MoD in London could offer was that they were 'not in a position to confirm or deny Argentine reports'. Witherow, however, did manage to get a dispatch out that concentrated on the Navy's 'compassion' in sparing the *Belgrano*'s escort ships and in searching for survivors. The best the picture desk could procure was a tiny image with the caption 'The General Belgrano in a photograph taken 40 years ago'.[38] A further sixteen days would pass before the dramatic photograph of the ship – listing heavily and surrounded by life rafts – would make it into the paper, halfway down page six.

News that the *Belgrano* had been hit had prompted the infamous 'Got-cha!' headline in the *Sun*. The NUJ had called an eleven day strike and the paper was being brought out by only a handful of editorial staff on whom the excitement and stress were clearly beginning to have a deleterious effect. The paper's combative editor Kelvin MacKenzie pulled the crude headline after the first edition once news of serious loss of life began to permeate the Bouverie Street newsroom, but by the time 'Gotcha!' had been replaced by the more contrite (though less factually accurate) headline 'Did 1200 Argies drown?' the damage had been done.[39] Reacting to the anti-war stance of its rival, the *Daily Mirror*, the *Sun*'s reporting of the conflict was not only stridently patriotic but also frequently couched in language that suggested the war was some sort of game show. In particular, the 'Gotcha!' front page brought the *Sun* considerable opprobrium, but *The Times*, while opting for the lower-case headline 'Cruiser torpedoed by Royal Navy sinks', was equally certain of the need to send her to the bottom of the ocean. Those who pointed out the ship had been torpedoed outside the Total Exclusion Zone were slapped down, the leader column declaiming, 'it is fanciful to imagine that any Argentine warship can put to sea – let alone sail some three hundred miles eastward towards the Falkland Islands – without having hostile intentions towards the British task force'.[40]

The press and political recriminations over the *Belgrano* had only just begun when the news broke that HMS *Sheffield* had been hit – the first British warship to be lost in battle since the Second World War. Witherow's dispatch from *Invincible* led the coverage, describing how the *Sheffield* 'was completely blotted out by the smoke which formed a solid column from the sea to the clouds'. The sea was 'full of warships all manoeuvring at top speed' with the *Invincible*'s personnel spreadeagled on a floor that 'shook with vibrations' as the carrier dodged the incoming assaults.[41] The war situation was now totally transformed. 'The cocktails on the quarterdeck in the tropics seem another existence,' Witherow stated two days later. The quarterdeck 'is now swept by sleet and spray and piled high with cushions from the officers' wardroom, ready for ditching overboard to reduce risk of fire'.[42]

'In military terms, the Falklands war is turning into a worse fiasco than Suez,' announced Peter Kellner, the *New Statesman*'s political editor, adding that *The Times* 'in superficially more measured tones' was as guilty as the rest of 'the jingo press' in getting Britain's servicemen into this mess.[43] As news of the *Sheffield*'s casualties slowly emerged, there was a palpable 'told you so' from those who thought going to war ridiculous. *The Times* published a letter from the acclaimed professor of politics Bernard Crick lambasting 'the narrowly legal doctrine of sovereignty' that had produced the 'atavistic routes of patriotic death when our last shreds of power lie in our reputation for diplomatic and political skill'. Instead of making war, Britain should work 'in consort' with the EEC and its friends to put 'pressure on the USA to control its other allies'.[44]

Conspiracy theorists soon suggested that the *Belgrano* had been sunk in order to derail a peace plan being proposed by Peru. Thatcher later stated that she knew nothing of the Peruvian proposals (which envisaged handing the islands over to a four-power administration) when the order to sink the cruiser was given and, in any case, Buenos Aires proceeded to reject the proposals. *The Times* did not think much of the Peruvian plan, sniffing that it promised to turn the Falklands into 'some latter-day post war Berlin'.[45] But the *Belgrano*'s sinking created an international outcry. President Reagan begged Mrs Thatcher to hold off further action. The Irish Defence Minister declared Britain 'the aggressor'. The Austrian Chancellor opined that he could not support Britain's colonial claims over the islands. At home and abroad, Thatcher's critics demanded she return to the United Nations for a diplomatic solution. But with the South Atlantic winter setting in, and Galtieri scouring the world's arms market for more Exocet missiles, prevarication was not what the Task Force wanted.[46] *The Times* was deeply sceptical of further diplomatic overtures. Nonetheless Pym got to work with Perez de Cuellar, the UN Secretary-General, on a plan to place the islands under the interim (though some concluded indefinite) jurisdiction of the United Nations. Nigel Lawson later wrote that he thought the plan would have commanded a Cabinet majority.[47] Instead, on 19 May, the Argentine junta rejected the proposals. Pym wanted to try again, but his colleagues overruled him. On 21 May, British troops went ashore at San Carlos Bay. The liberation had begun.

The following morning *The Times* led with 'Troops gain Falklands bridgehead' above a photograph of three Royal Marine Commandos running the Union Jack up a flagpole. The image had not quite the vivid urgency of the US Marines planting Old Glory at Iwo Jima, but, compared to the paper's front-page treatment of the campaign until that moment, it was positively dramatic. The day before the landing, Sir Frank Cooper, the permanent under-secretary at the MoD, had deliberately misinformed a press briefing that British strategy would take the form of a series of smash and grab raids at various locations around the islands rather than a single D-Day-style landing.[48] All the papers, including *The Times*, advised their readers accordingly. Thus, news that there was a major invasion thrust in San Carlos Bay came as a complete surprise. The intention behind Cooper's misleading briefing was to throw the Argentinians off the scent. Amphibious landings were precarious at the best of times and if the defending force had guessed the location, the outcome could have been in the balance. Instead, it would take time for the Argentinians to work out that what was going on in San Carlos Bay was something more than one of the smash and grab raids authoritatively traced throughout the British media to a 'senior Whitehall source'.

Although the landing went unopposed, talk of success was premature. The RAF's failure to gain commanding air superiority and the bravery of the Argentine pilots made it far from certain that the campaign would succeed. *The Times* reported an MoD briefing that five – unnamed – warships had been hit together with the Argentine claim that they had sunk a Type 42 destroyer and a Type 22 frigate. Such sketchy detail caused considerable anxiety to all those with loved ones in the Task Force and appeared to be another instance of the press having to deal with a MoD that was self-defeating in its dilatory release of vital information. But on this occasion, it ensured a better initial headline: Fleet Street led with the good news that British troops were ashore, rather than the battering the naval armada was receiving. Only later did it emerge that HMS *Ardent* and, subsequently, HMS *Antelope*, had been lost.

Frustrated in his bid to land with the troops, Witherow had got himself transferred to what less intrepid reporters might consider a precarious posting – on board an ammunition ship moored in the 'bomb alley' of San Carlos Water. In view of the highly inflammable cargo, he was cheerily assured that if the ship was hit, he wouldn't need a lifejacket but a parachute. 'The bombs came within fifty metres. We were feeling a bit nervous,' he recollected; 'whenever the planes came in, everybody let loose, bullets, guns, missiles.' It was a perfect spot to observe the Argentine air force's finest hour. Night-time offered little relief. Fears that Argentine divers might lay mines necessitated the dropping of depth charges: 'You would be lying in your bunk at 4 a.m. right next to the waterline,' Witherow recalled, 'when suddenly BOOM!'[49]

With the bridgehead on East Falkland secured and the British troops beginning to move inland, Witherow became increasingly frustrated. Having journeyed down with the Navy, he had not had an opportunity to make the now imperative links with the Army that those journalists who had travelled later with the troop ship *Canberra* had established. Most prominent in this group was Max Hastings of the London *Evening Standard*. With Hastings and the Army were Michael Nicholson of ITN and the BBC's Brian Hanrahan who were able to file voice reports (pictures would have to wait) from the beachhead. Eventually, Witherow and the other four journalists on the ammunition ship were helicptered onto East Falkland. But within hours, they were told they were too inadequately clothed to proceed with the troops and were going to be sent back to the ship. Deciding anything was better than skulking on a floating powder keg, they attempted to hide behind some bales of wool. They were discovered and escorted from the island. Next they were put on board HMS *Sir Geraint*, a logistical support vessel that promptly sailed back out to sea. For several days Witherow and his companions wondered why their ship appeared to be taking a peculiar course, circling round the aircraft carriers. Eventually they realized the *Sir Geraint* was trying to draw an Exocet missile attack upon itself so as to save the carriers. Having placed the press corps on, respectively, an ammunition ship and a decoy for air assault, it was clear what the Royal Navy thought of their travelling journalists. The land campaign had been going for two weeks before Witherow was next permitted to step ashore with 5 Brigade.

By then the most famous land battle of the war, Goose Green, had been won. Without air support and with little in the way of artillery, 2 Para had attacked and overcome an entrenched enemy nearly three times their size, taken 1400 prisoners and freed 114 islanders shut up in a guarded community hall. It was an impressive feat and earned a posthumous Victoria Cross for Colonel 'H' Jones, the commanding officer who fell with seventeen of his men. But not everyone had played his or her part. With a level of ineptitude far surpassing their usual reticence, the MoD in London had announced the capture of Goose Green eighteen hours before it happened. The BBC's World Service reported the news that the attack was about to take place. In the meantime, the Argentine troops rearranged their defences to guard against an assault from exactly the direction 2 Para were approaching

– supposedly in secrecy.[50] This scandalous lapse was primarily the MoD's fault, but it generated further animosity between the troops and the reporters. In Gray's Inn Road, the fall of Goose Green was not the main story. Instead, Fred Emery decided to lead with the Pope's arrival in Britain because the first steps of a pontiff on British soil were of greater historical significance.[51]

The British Army's objective was now to yomp across East Falkland, eject the Argentines from the defensive positions in the hills to the west and south of Stanley and liberate the capital. Having finally got himself accredited to 5 Brigade, Witherow proceeded to spend some days with the Gurkhas before attaching himself to the Welsh Guards, a regiment he rightly assumed would be in the thick of any fighting. Despite the cold weather, he spent most nights huddled up in barns or sheds or, occasionally, trying to sleep outdoors. The only way he could now get copy to London was to write it down, persuade a helicopter pilot to carry it on his next trip back to HMS *Fearless* (where all journalists' copy was being directed) and then have the ship transmit it to the MoD censors in Northwood from where it would, it was hoped, be passed, unedited, onto Gray's Inn Road. This chain of action only worked if the pilot remembered to pass the copy to someone who knew what to do with it next. Frequently, the copy got mislaid, put aside or discarded at some point along this convoluted process. One of the reports that got lost in transit was a graphic eyewitness account of the horror on board the stricken landing ships *Sir Tristram* and *Sir Galahad* from Mick Seamark of the *Daily Star*. Some felt its loss was convenient.[52]

Witherow was at Bluff Cove when the disaster struck. His dispatch – which did get through – conveyed the essentials that between five hundred and six hundred men from the Royal Marines and the Welsh Guards had been on the ships, awaiting disembarkation when the air attack came. One survivor was quoted as stating, 'People were screaming, trapped in their rooms. People were in agony. There was mangled wreckage in the corridor.'[53] The attack had come on Tuesday 8 June yet such was the MoD's reticence in releasing details that the death toll had still not been confirmed when *The Times* went to press for its Saturday 12 June edition – four days after the ships had been hit. Henry Stanhope was left to report the rumours of forty-six deaths and 130 wounded but that 'the Ministry's refusal to give casualty figures has also prompted wide speculation in Washington where some sources say British casualties in the Tuesday raids are estimated at 300 dead and a large number wounded'.[54] The actual figure was fifty-one fatalities and forty-six injuries.

The MoD's failure to respond quickly with accurate information was not a cause of media incompetence, as was widely assumed at the time, but of military cunning. The Argentinians believed they had inflicted nine hundred casualties and checked the British advance. Determined to foster this misimpression in their opponents' minds, the MoD deliberately briefed the press that losses had indeed been very heavy and the assault on Stanley might have to be postponed. Henry Stanhope dutifully reported this mis-information.[55] The true death toll was withheld until the assault on Stanley had commenced on time and at full strength.[56] As Admiral Sir Terence Lewin later put it, 'The Bluff Cove incident, when we deliberately concealed the casualty figures, was an example of using the press, the media, to further our military operations.'[57]

Witherow moved up with the Welsh Guards as they advanced for the final push. Passing gingerly through a minefield he observed the battle of Mount Tumbledown from 'quite a way back'. Comprehensively defeated in the hills around the capital, the Argentine garrison was now preparing to surrender. Reaching the outskirts of Stanley, Witherow noted that the road ahead appeared to be open. He decided to advance on the city, hoping to be the first journalist – indeed the first person with the Task Force – into the islands' capital. Gallingly, he discovered the omnipresent Max Hastings of the *Evening Standard* had beaten him to it. By the time Witherow's report made it into *The Times* it was as the follow-up to Hastings's cel-ebrated dispatch describing the moment he liberated the Upland Goose Hotel. Taking advantage of the order to 2 Para to halt just outside the city while negotiations were entered into, Hastings had seen his chance and – exchanging his Army-issue camouflaged jacket for an anorak – wandered into the city. Finding an Argentine colonel on the steps of the adminis-tration block, Hastings recorded, 'I introduced myself to him quite untruth-fully as the correspondent of *The Times* newspaper, the only British newspaper that it seemed possible he would have heard of.'[58]

Having innocently printed the MoD's misinformation about delays to the final assault, *The Times* was as taken by surprise by the speed of the Argentine surrender as were MPs who had gathered in the Commons chamber expecting a ministerial progress report only to discover that the Argentines were 'reported to be flying white flags over Port Stanley'. In the preceding hours, the MoD had insisted upon a news blackout from the South Atlantic so that no reporter could get the news of the ceasefire out before the Prime Minister had announced it to Parliament. *The Times* could feel a sense of vindication for the strong editorial line it had taken from the first, the leader column starting, 'In war, only what is simple can succeed' because 'it was clear that it was the sheer simplicity of Britain's immediate response to the original invasion which has sustained the operation over all these weeks and made such an historic victory possible.'[59] Having initially supported the 1956 Suez fiasco, *The Times* had not always made the right call in such matters. Douglas-Home had risked the paper's reputation in taking an unambiguous stance right from the beginning. Notwithstanding the loss of life, it was natural that there was a sense of relief at Gray's Inn Road that the gamble had succeeded in its objective.

In *The Winter War*, the book he co-wrote with Patrick Bishop of the *Observer*, Witherow pointed out that the Falklands campaign was a nine-teenth-century affair in the respect that it was about territory rather than ideology. Moreover, apart from the missiles, 'the basic tools for fighting were artillery, mortars, machine guns and bayonets', weapons that 'would have been familiar to any veteran of World War II'.[60] It thus proved to be markedly different from the British military operations of the following twenty years in which air power and technology would predetermine the outcome on the ground and Britain would be but a junior partner in an American-led coalition. Witherow maintained that Britain's campaign was never a preordained walkover against a bunch of useless conscripts. Argentine equipment had been generally as good as that possessed by the British. Indeed, with supplies being flown into Stanley airport right up to the eve of the surrender (so much for Britain's claim to have disabled the runway) the Argentine troops in the area were better fed and supplied than the British. What was more, they had had plenty of time to prepare defences and 'initially out-numbered their attackers by three to one, a direct inversion of the odds that conventional military wisdom dictates. They had nothing like the logistical problems that beset their attackers.'[61] There had been moments of luck – in particular the failure of so many Argentine missiles to detonate after hitting their target – but it was undeniably a great feat of British arms. Some began to hope that it presaged an end to the long years of managing decline that had inhabited the Whitehall psyche since Suez.

The Franks Report cleared the Thatcher Government of negligence in failing to foresee the invasion but found fault with Whitehall's capacity for 'crisis management'. The extent to which the Government and the MoD in particular had manipulated the news coverage of the campaign rumbled on elsewhere. The Commons Defence select committee provided news-paper editors, Douglas-Home among them, with the opportunity to draw attention to the many deficiencies that MoD restrictions and poor communication links had produced. Many journalists were outraged that senior Whitehall figures like Sir Frank Cooper had consciously misled them into writing that there would be no single D-Day-style landing only hours before such an undertaking got underway. This kind of deceit undermined trust in Government information. Doubtless Sir Frank calculated that the exact veracity of a particular briefing was less important than the survival of several hundred soldiers who would be sent to their deaths if the Argentines were ready to meet the landing party. If this was the calculation then only a public servant with a peculiar set of priorities would have done otherwise. But it was a stunt that could not be repeated too often. If journalists began to disbelieve everything Government officials told them, the whole point of briefings would break down. Operational reasons were also used to justify the slow release of information. The MoD's decision to announce that ships had been hit without naming which and the late release of casualty figures from the Bluff Cove disaster caused distress to anxious relatives and angered all those who believed news involved immediacy of information. Where the balance resided between Whitehall's obligation to provide a free society with truthful Information and its duty not to needlessly endanger servicemen's lives could not be easily resolved.

In the twenty years following the Falklands' campaign, the number of commercial satellites proliferated, permitting war correspondents to communicate swiftly and directly to their offices and readers or viewers. Those reporting from the South Atlantic in 1982 did not enjoy such liberty. They had no alternative but to entrust their copy to the British military who alone had the capability to transmit it back to London and, in the first instance, to the MoD censors. If the armed forces did not like the look of the copy they were under no obligation even to send the dispatch. Whitehall had been able to prevent any foreign press from covering the operation by the simple device of refusing them a berth on any of the ships travelling with the Task Force. But subsequent wars were not fought over inaccessible islands close to the Antarctic. And since they involved joint operations with allies, what reporters with one country's troops could transmit became the effective property of all.

Indeed, the Falklands War would be the last major conflict in which newspaper reports were more immediate than television pictures. The experience of the BBC and ITV crews on the aircraft carrier *Hermes* was even more frustrating than that of the Fleet Street journalists on *Invincible*. Because the British military transmitters were at the edge of their South

Atlantic coverage, satellite transmission rendered pictures of too poor a quality to show. Using commercial satellites ran supposed security risks if Argentina managed to dial in to them and gain potentially useful information. Instead, all film footage had to be flown from the Falklands to Ascension Island before it could be broadcast. This created monumental delays. The first television pictures of the landings at San Carlos were shown on British television two and a half weeks after the event. Some of the footage took twenty-three days to reach transmission. This was three days longer than it took *Times* readers to find out the fate of the Charge of the Light Brigade in 1854.[62]

The quality of *The Times*'s reporting of the Crimean War had been one of the most illustrious episodes in the paper's history. But besides seeing its editorial line vindicated, *The Times*'s coverage of the Falklands' crisis was competent rather than remarkable. It did not, of course, want to compete with the attention-grabbing antics of the tabloids. Nonetheless, its news presentation lacked sharpness. Perhaps it was at its most deficient in its layout. Sometimes the picture selection beggared belief. The front-page headline for 3 June, 'Argentina lost 250 men at Goose Green', was accompanied by a photograph entitled 'Languid lesson: Students basking in Regent's Park, London yesterday'. The photograph that should have been used – of dejected Argentine soldiers being marched out of Goose Green into captivity – appeared on page three where there was no directly related article. Put simply, Douglas-Home had none of the visual awareness of his ousted predecessor. The magic touch of Harold Evans and his design team was noticeably lacking.

Max Hastings of the *Evening Standard* had proved to be the most successful reporter of the conflict, a reality that created enmity from some of the other reporters who felt he had been given preferential treatment on account of his being *au fait* with Army ways. Journalists' squabbling over who got the best coverage appeared petty to soldiers and sailors whose every thought and action had been directed towards a team effort and a common purpose. Three of the journalists, including the representative from the *Guardian*, so hated the experience of covering the war that they quit and had to be brought home before the campaign was over. Witherow had stuck it out. Right at the very last moment, he was almost rewarded with the scoop he had been so long seeking. Having surrendered to General Moore, General Menendez, the Argentine commander-in-chief, was being held in a cabin on HMS *Fearless*. With Patrick Bishop, Witherow managed to sneak into the cabin and began interviewing the defeated general.

Unfortunately, the inquisition had not advanced far when a naval officer walked in, discovered what was afoot and bundled the two reporters out.[63]

The strident jingoism of the *Sun* and the less patriotic 'even-handedness' of the BBC generated the two shouting matches within the media. *The Times* gave little space to the first issue but it refused to join what it termed the 'shrill chorus of complaint' heard from the *Sun* and right-wing Tories who perceived the BBC's attempts to present both sides of the argument as tantamount to treason. The MoD's inability to speed the supply of copy from the South Atlantic inevitably ensured news services turned to other sources – including Argentine ones – to find out what was going on. What else could they do but cite 'Argentine claims' against 'British claims'? However, the *Panorama* presenter Robert Kee had taken the unusual step of writing a letter to *The Times* criticizing the one-sided anti-war tone of one of the offending reports on his own programme.[64] This ensured the end of Kee's *Panorama* career but it was noticeable that *The Times* did not share the *Sun*'s view that there were 'traitors in our midst', especially in the Corporation.

The boost in national newspaper circulation during the conflict was scarcely perceptible. By the end of hostilities, the increase was below 1 per cent. This tended to support the analysts' claim that the tabloid market had long been at saturation point. But if people were not buying more newspapers, it did not mean they were not above switching titles. Looked at over a slightly broader period, comparing the same March to September period of the previous year, *The Times* circulation had risen 13,000 to 303,300. This compared to a 66,000 fall in the *Telegraph* to 1,313,000 while the war-sceptic *Guardian* had risen by over 8 per cent (33,500) to 421,700, increasing the margin of its lead over *The Times*.[65] In sales figures, it was the *Guardian* that, ironically, had the best war.

II

The stalwart position adopted by the new editor came as no surprise to those who knew him. Among those who did not, there was an easy temptation to portray Charlie Douglas-Home as a placeman of the Establishment. He had gone to Eton and Sandhurst but not to university. His middle name was Cospatrick. His uncle, Sir Alec, had succeeded Harold Macmillan as Prime Minister and his defeat in the subsequent 1964 general election was widely interpreted as victory for British meritocracy. His mother moved in

Court circles. His cousin, Lady Diana Spencer, was still in the first year of her marriage to Prince Charles. As the Princess of Wales she carried the hopes not only of a dynasty but also of much of the nation. Even without this connection, Douglas-Home had been a close friend of the Prince of Wales since the 1970s, the two men having been brought together by Laurens van der Post.

Charlie Douglas-Home certainly had the self-confident attributes of one used to privileged surroundings and high-achieving company. In particular, he had a quick and natural wit that put those he met at their ease. But his background also contained its fair share of family problems, dysfunctional relationships and alcoholism. His brother, Robin, was an accomplished pianist (he was regularly engaged entertaining the members of the Clermont Club in Berkeley Square) and a great lover of beautiful women. Married in 1960 to Sandra Paul, the model and future wife of the Tory leader Michael Howard, he subsequently had affairs with Jackie Kennedy, Princess Margaretha of Sweden and, ultimately, Princess Margaret. After he lost the affections of the Queen's sister to Peter Sellers, he committed suicide in 1968, aged thirty-six. Following the funeral, Charlie came across a manuscript for a novel that was thinly disguised as an account of his brother's affair with Princess Margaret. He lit a fire and placed it on it.

Three novels (and a biography of Frank Sinatra) by Robin Douglas-Home had already been published in his brief lifetime. One, entitled *Hot for Certainties*, ruthlessly parodied his parents although he was saved from parental wrath primarily because each recognized the cruel portrait of their spouse but not of themselves. Both Robin and Charlie had developed a love for playing the piano from their mother, a concert pianist and close friend of Ruth, Lady Fermoy, the Queen's lady-in-waiting. Margaret Douglas-Home was also a fantasist whose tall stories gave Charlie an early training in the journalist's requirement not to take statements at face value but rather to interview many people and ask searching questions in order to get a true picture. At Ludgrove, his prep school, he had been one of only two boys considered to have intellectual potential. The other was the boy he befriended and sat next to, the future left-wing writer Paul Foot (despite their subsequent political differences, they remained on good terms). At Eton, where he was a scholar, Douglas-Home's favourite subject had been history and he had been accepted to go up to Oxford. His college, Christ Church, got as far as putting his name on his door, but he never arrived – at the last minute he discovered that his mother had squandered the money that would have sustained him there.

Instead, he took a commission in the Royal Scots Greys and went out to Kenya as the ADC to the Governor, Sir Evelyn Baring. This proved an important early grounding in political decision taking and the tasks of government. He later wrote Baring's biography which he subtitled *The Last Proconsul*. When he returned to Britain, Douglas-Home determined upon becoming a journalist. He began as a crime reporter at the *Scottish Daily Express*. It was a rough but useful training in reporting from the sharp end, with the young recruit catapulted not only into the seamy side of low life in the Gorbals but also into the hard-drinking culture prevalent in the Glasgow offices of Beaverbrook's paper. His great break came first in moving down to London in 1961 as the *Express*'s defence correspondent and then in covering the same portfolio at *The Times* four years later.

By then he had shown himself to be not only fearless in the ganglands of Glasgow but also in pursuit of the country fox. Hunting was a passion he pursued with a physical recklessness that appeared to know few bounds. He parted from his horse regularly, although never for long. His friend since school days, Edward Cazalet, noted that he used to regard it as 'a military exercise on a grand scale: the terrain, the plan, the tactics were invariably analysed to the full. I know of no-one who got more thrill from riding flat out over fences despite the falls he took.' More traditional members of the hunting fraternity were less impressed. They admonished Douglas-Home for wearing his father's pink hunting coat and black cap, which they believed he was not entitled to wear. Never one to put great store by appearance, he merely dyed the coat blue and sewed on his own regimental buttons. The effect was not entirely harmonious. Unfortunately, a senior officer in the regiment witnessed him in this costume and reported him to the colonel, writing along the lines of, 'Whenever in this dreadful coat a button happened by chance to coincide with a button hole, I saw, to my horror, the Regimental Crest.' Douglas-Home was ordered to remove the offending item. He refused. The matter went higher. Still he refused. Finally, a general was brought in to settle matters. At this point Douglas-Home won the argument by observing that if the regimental crest was deemed worthy to grace beer mugs and place mats, it was surely not out of place amid the risks and dangers of the hunting field.[66]

His chosen profession also involved him in dangers potentially greater than the ever-looming prospect of a hunting accident. In 1968, when he was *The Times*'s defence correspondent, he was arrested by Soviet forces after he discovered 25,000 troops waiting, concealed, along the Czechoslovak border.

His report broke in *The Times* on 27 July. Just over three weeks later the tanks he had stumbled upon rolled in to crush the Prague Spring. The experience made a great impression upon him and deepened his intense hostility towards the Communist expropriation of half of Europe. He was also conscious that for many in Britain and the West, the desire to live in peaceful co-existence had deadened their condemnation of left-wing totalitarianism. His wife had been staying in a hotel in Folkestone when the news broke that Soviet forces had arrested her husband. She was promptly asked to leave the hotel. Its manager did not want the custom of the wife of a man who had been arrested.[67]

The treatment of dissidents in Eastern Europe was an issue that deeply concerned both the editor and his wife. Douglas-Home had met and married Jessica Gwynne, an artist poised to embark upon her career as a theatrical set and costume designer, in 1966. Both subsequently became friends of Roger Scruton, the Tory philosopher who edited the *Salisbury Review*. Scruton was in touch with many of Eastern Europe's leading underground *samizdat* thinkers. He was also involved with the Jan Hus Foundation, a support group that had been founded with money from *Times* readers who had been shocked following the paper's reporting of the arrest in Prague of Anthony Kenny, the Master of Balliol, while discussing Aristotle in a dissident's flat. When Douglas-Home became editor of *The Times*, Scruton encouraged him to publish an anonymous article by the Czech dissident Petr Pithart, who later became the Prime Minister of the Czech and Slovak Federation. Accompanied by Scruton, Jessica Douglas-Home made the first of her many trips behind the Iron Curtain in October 1983 to meet with and assist dissidents. Dodging the secret police became part of her routine. Meanwhile, every Tuesday *The Times* published brief biographies of political prisoners from around the world in a series called 'Prisoners of Conscience', written by Caroline Moorehead.

Another writer who shared the Douglas-Homes' loathing for Communism was Bernard Levin. In October 1982, he returned to *The Times* to write his 'The Way We Live Now' column. After a gap of eighteen months, his first article commenced with the words 'And another thing . . .'[68] Levin, a scourge of authority in almost any guise – from the North Thames Gas Board upwards – never shirked from what he saw as his duty to denounce the totalitarian mindset. The son of a Ukrainian Jewish mother and (an absentee) Lithuanian Jewish father, Levin had shaken off the left-wing views of his youth at the LSE and his early days as the *That Was The Week That Was* resident controversialist but not the argumentativeness or iconoclasm.

While he continued to despise many aspects of the traditional British Establishment, in particular almost all the judiciary and most of the politicians, he was unsparing in his criticism of Soviet repression in Eastern Europe. There was no shortage of material for his scorn.

Throughout 1981, Dessa Trevisan in Warsaw and Michael Binyon, the *Times* correspondent in Moscow, had been filing alarming reports about the deteriorating situation in Poland. The economy was in desperate shape and the Solidarity Movement, the Eastern Bloc's first free trade union, was openly challenging the authority of the Communist Party. Moscow had been issuing the Warsaw government with ominous requests to put its house in order and crack down on 'anti-Soviet activities'.[69] There were fears of a repeat of the Prague Spring of 1968 with Soviet tanks this time invading Poland to restore Communist unity. On 13 December 1981, Poland's leader, General Jaruzelski, took the hint and imposed martial law.

For *The Times*, as with all news services, the problem was how to get reports out from a country that had imposed a news blackout. With the Polish borders sealed and all telephone and telex links shut down, it was extremely difficult to get any accurate news out of the country. Peter Hopkirk pieced together some details from 'western diplomatic sources' and a variety of eyewitness reports from businessmen leaving the country as the crackdown commenced. There were troops and armoured vehicles on the city streets but reports varied as to the extent of the strike action in the mines and factories. Roger Boyes, the *Times* correspondent in Warsaw, managed to get out a daily diary of the first four days of martial law and this appeared in the paper on 17 December. Solidarity's leaders had been arrested and Lech Walesa was being held in isolation in a government villa outside Warsaw. 'Chopin martial music and the general [Jaruzelski] on the screen and radio all day,' Boyes noted. Announcers were wearing military uniform. Troops had occupied the Gdansk shipyards and surrounded the Academy of Sciences in Warsaw, some of whose staff were led away. 'Troops are to be seen everywhere with fixed bayonets.'[70]

Prior to the imposition of martial law, *The Times* had taken the view that between offering fresh financial aid 'tied to IMF-type conditions' and witnessing the economic collapse of Poland, the first was preferable. Unlike the second option, it was more likely to detach the country from the Soviet Union. Jaruzelski's actions in December 1981 killed off any hopes in Gray's Inn Road of sending in the investment analysts.[71] Harold Evans (still editor at that time) wrote to Rupert Murdoch, 'You ought to know that *The Times* leader on the West's reaction to Poland last week described the attitude of

Lord Carrington as "flacid and feeble" (among other things) and he has let it be known that he is extremely annoyed.'[72]

Following street scuffles and clashes with the police, 205 arrests were made in Gdansk over the weekend of 30–31 January 1982. More violent demonstrations led to 1372 arrests on 3–4 May and the reimposition of evening curfews in Warsaw for young people. With a Polish Pope in Rome who had become a rallying point against oppression, the Church in Poland was caught in a difficult position – a spiritual power trying to negotiate with a temporal one. As Roger Boyes suggested, 'the perpetual paradox of Church strategy is that the closer it moves to talking to the government, the further it moves from the main body of Catholic believers'.[73] In November, the release of Lech Walesa after 336 days in custody raised hopes that the end of martial law in Poland might be in sight. But still the West held back in refusing aid.

The Polish situation sharpened the debate over whether the West should invest in the Communist east (a debate held in parallel to that over economic sanctions against South Africa). The *cause célèbre* was the construction of the Siberian gas pipeline. British jobs were involved in it. France and Germany wanted it to help with supplying their own energy needs. There were fears that a decision to cease cooperation would provoke Moscow into pressuring Poland to default on her massive debts to British and European banks. During 1982, however, President Reagan, having banned American companies from equipping the gas pipeline, sought to apply US law retrospectively against European companies involved in its construction. Considering the United States was continuing to sell Midwest grain cheaply to the Soviet Union, there was a measure of inconsistency in the President's position. *The Times*, already irritated by Washington's initial irresolution on the Falklands' crisis, was deeply unimpressed, lambasting an idea that 'set a precedent that could undermine the basis of international business trust'.[74] Reagan backed down and the ban was lifted on 21 August 1983, exactly one month after the end of martial law in Poland. In July, Douglas-Home, accompanied by Murdoch, was granted a twenty-minute audience with President Reagan in the White House.

Michael Binyon had been *The Times*'s man in Moscow. Urbane, with the manner of the British diplomats with whom he spent so much of his time, the Cambridge-educated Binyon had arrived in the Soviet capital with his wife and three-year-old child in 1978. Extraordinarily, the paper had had no Moscow correspondent since 1972, a consequence of Soviet obstruction and a serious handicap to the paper's pretensions as a world paper of record. Yet, as Binyon discovered, 'the Russians had a great respect for *The Times*. They thought it was the official voice of Britain in the same way that *Pravda* is for the Soviet Union. They took it very seriously.'[75]

There was virtually no night life in Moscow, only endless ambassadorial receptions. Binyon had the distinction of being touched out of a photograph published in *Izvestia* at a reception for Michael Foot. He was more readily recognized for his work at the British Press Awards in 1981, when he picked up the David Holden prize. According to the judges, his reporting from the Soviet Union had been 'one of the joys of the year. He combines hard reporting, descriptive writing and highly significant detail.' Such observation filled his subsequent book, *Life in Russia*. But in mid-1982 he was moved on to become the paper's Bonn correspondent. His replacement in Moscow was Richard Owen. Owen was thirty-four and had been at *The Times* for only two years, having previously gained a Ph.D. from the LSE and worked for the BBC. He spoke Russian, German, French and some Polish. He was still settling in Moscow when the Tass news agency confirmed Brezhnev's death after eighteen years at the superpower's helm. 'When the end came, and it had been coming for a long time,' reported Owen 'the Soviet leadership seemed temporarily paralysed.' The previous day *The Times* had led with the headline 'Rumours of top leader's death sweep Moscow', based on Owen's observations that 'television schedules were changed without explanation and television news readers appeared dressed in black'. With the official confirmation, *The Times* went through its usual motions: page six cleared for a full-page obituary – 'President Brezhnev: consolidator of Soviet power' – while on the following page Owen assessed the runners and riders. 'One of the main weaknesses of the Soviet system,' he stressed, 'is that it makes no provision for political succession.' Konstantin Chernenko was the favourite followed by Yuri Andropov, while, of the less likely contenders, 'Michael Sergeyevich Gorbachov is perhaps the most interesting Politburo member in the long term . . . He is confident, quiet, efficient, and biding his time.'[76]

In the event, Andropov pipped Chernenko, *The Times* trying to find the crumb of comfort that, having been head of the KGB for fifteen years, he would at least know what was going on in the country.[77] Fifteen months later, Owen was again prophesying a successor when Andropov died in February 1984 (he had not been seen in public since the previous August). The obituary had no option but to focus on his professional CV since – despite being at the forefront of Soviet politics for so many years – details such as whether he had a wife remained unknown (he did, but she made her first public appearance in the wake of his funeral). This time it was the seventy-two-year-old Chernenko who succeeded.

The West's tense relations with the teetering old men of the Kremlin formed the backdrop to the most important non-party political movement of the early 1980s, the Campaign for Nuclear Disarmament. In Britain, the particular rallying call was the arrival of ninety-six US cruise missiles at the Greenham Common air base in Cambridgeshire. A hard core of women 'peace protestors' had been camping out at the air base for fifteen months when, on 12 December 1982, they were joined by a mass demonstration of thirty thousand women who linked hands and circled the perimeter wire of the base. With flowers and poems being inserted in the wire, the tone of the protest harked back to the 'make love not war' hippy movement of the late 1960s, although the women-only nature of the demonstration reduced, to some extent, the opportunities for hedonism available. There were sixty arrests. A CND demonstration outside Parliament led to 141 arrests. Douglas-Home was not much impressed, but the huge scale of national unease over the deployment of US nuclear weapons could not be so easily dismissed as an offshoot of a particular strain of feminism. Uncertainty about the power struggle in Moscow and dislike for the gun-totting tough talk of the ex-Hollywood cowboy (as his detractors so frequently described him) Ronald Reagan produced a broad coalition which feared that the sober reality of MAD (mutually assured destruction) would prove insufficient deterrence against either side attempting a first strike. With Monsignor Bruce Kent as its general secretary, CND drew particular support from many Church groups and individuals. When *The Church and the Bomb*, a report by the Church of England's working party, argued that the retention of Britain's nuclear deterrent was immoral, the editor's brand of muscular Christianity rose to the fore: 'The immorality of possessing nuclear weapons with the improbable intention of using them is only a small fraction of the immorality of actually using them. Set that against the certain rather than probable moral benefits of sustained peace in Europe, and the working party's case falls down.'[78]

The 1982 Labour Party conference voted for the third year in succession in favour of Britain's unilateral nuclear disarmament. The motion, put forward by the SOGAT '82 print union, gained the necessary two-thirds majority to ensure it was binding on party policy (it had, in any case, the support of the party leader). It called for 'developing with the trade union movement a detailed programme for the conversion of the relevant parts of the arms industry to the manufacture of socially-useful products so that no compulsory redundancy should arise from this policy.' Truly, the party was committed to turning swords into ploughshares. Few on the editorial floor at Gray's Inn Road doubted the ability of SOGAT to master the art of turning sophisticated technology into labour-intensive machinery.

III

Like Rupert Murdoch, Harold Evans had been broadly sympathetic towards Israel, putting on record his doubts about some of his leader writers' wish to endorse a Palestinian state at a time when the PLO was not prepared to acknowledge the state of Israel. He had been up against the pro-Palestinian view of, in particular, Edward Mortimer, a leader writer and foreign specialist at The Times since 1973. An Old Etonian, Balliol man and fellow of All Souls, Mortimer's history of Islam, Faith and Power, was published in 1982. Rather pointedly, he stuck up a pro-Palestinian poster in his office.[79] He would later become chief speech writer to the Secretary-General of the UN, Kofi Annan. In June 1982, The Times affirmed its commitment to an independent Palestinian state: 'Lebanon for the Lebanese, must be the slogan; Israel for the Israelis; and a Palestine of some sort, west of Jordan, for the Palestinians.'[80]

In June 1981, Israeli jets struck the Osirak nuclear plant near Baghdad. The Israeli Prime Minister, Menachem Begin, justified it as a pre-emptive strike at a project that was covertly developing Iraq's attempts to gain nuclear weapons, and he had no doubt that such a capability would be used to annihilate Israel. The Israeli attack raised several issues, not all of them subject to definitive answers. Was Iraq really developing such a capability and, if so, would she use it against Israel? Did such a possibility justify a pre-emptive attack of this kind? There was also the diplomatic angle, given the outrage felt by Arab countries and the French government. France had built the reactor and French personnel (one of whom was killed in the attack) were helping to operate it. The Times took the view that the Iraqis probably were acquiring weapons-grade enriched uranium but that the Israeli action would only drive Saddam Hussein into the arms of Syria. The action 'may cause rejoicing in Israel in the short term, but it has not guaranteed Israeli security in the longer term' concluded the leader column.[81] The unpalatable central issue – whether it was in anyone's interest for Saddam Hussein to acquire nuclear weapons – was sidestepped.

Robert Fisk was the paper's Middle Eastern correspondent. Having completed a Ph.D. at Trinity College Dublin on Irish neutrality during the Second World War, he had joined *The Times* in 1971 in his mid-twenties, reporting on the Troubles in Northern Ireland and winning Granada TV's *What The Papers Say* award for Reporter of the Year in 1975. It was while in Ireland that he uncovered a succession of British Army cover-ups, further cementing his dislike of what he saw as the repressive tendencies of authority and officialdom. 'I learned that authority lies, governments lie, ministries of defence lie,' he said of his time in Ulster, adding that his response was to 'keep challenging, to reject and refuse what you're handed'.[82] The police took him in for questioning following their discovery that he had been receiving classified documents from a rogue Army press officer who was later convicted for manslaughter. His subsequent switch away from reporting on Ireland was wrongly attributed to this incident. In fact, he merely wanted a change of scene. But Gray's Inn Road was no place for a man of Fisk's peripatetic courage. He had an ally in Douglas-Home, at that time home news editor, who, despite his own regard for the British Army, always encouraged Fisk to investigate further. In 1976 he was dispatched to the Middle East, finding plenty of trouble to write about in the Lebanon and Iran before covering the Soviet invasion of Afghanistan where he gained considerable access to the Soviet forces. At the IPC awards he had won International Reporter of the Year for two years running in 1980 and 1981. Frequently shot at, 'you reach a point' he laconically observed, 'when one shell looks very much like another'.[83]

Fisk had arrived in the Lebanon just as the Syrians were invading the country. The Lebanon had collapsed into anarchy and the Syrian occupation had the backing of the Arab League and East Beirut's Christian population. It was not long before Damascus's intervention became, in turn, deeply resented and the Christians began to look for a new saviour – Israel. Syria, meanwhile, decided to crush ruthlessly its own fanatical Muslims. In February 1982 there was an insurrection by Sunni fundamentalists in the Syrian city of Hama. With the Syrian government warning foreign journalists they risked being shot by their forces if they tried to travel there, it was impossible to gauge exactly the extent of the uprising and the undoubted ferocity with which it was being suppressed. Fisk, however, decided to get a closer look and took a detour from the road to Damascus. As he approached, he could see the smoke from the ruins of Hama's old city rising but roadblocks prevented him from getting any closer – as they had prevented any other journalist from enquiry. Fisk, however, had a stroke of luck when two displaced Syrian soldiers approached his car and asked if they could hitch a lift with him back to their units. This was his opportunity. With shells whizzing overhead, Fisk's car sped across the battlefront, making it to the Syrians' lines from where Soviet-made T62 tanks were firing across the Orontes river. A mosque was being shelled to pieces; a giant eighteenth-century wooden waterwheel was on fire, water cascading from its shattered structure; huge mortar cannons rocked back and forth, pounding the ancient walled city to obliteration. Bullets pinged and whirled back from the insurgents. The siege, Fisk learned, had been going on for sixteen days. There had been ferocious fighting in the cellars and passageways underneath the city as well as within it at street level. Syrian troops had even been blown up by a new and shocking phenomenon – women suicide bombers who embraced them clutching uncorked grenades. Some troops had defected to the insurgent Muslim Brotherhood.[84]

At Gray's Inn Road there was considerable concern for Fisk's safety, not least when he telegrammed, 'My decision is to stick it out.'[85] The Syrian government was keen to silence him and complained to the British Ambassador in Damascus that Fisk was filing false reports from Hama and other places 'which he had not visited'.[86] Syrian radio denounced him as a liar. *The Times*, however, stood by its reporter's claim to have been the only journalist to have witnessed the scenes of carnage. The following year he returned to Hama to find out what had happened in the aftermath. To his amazement the old city had simply disappeared. Where ancient walls and crowded streets had once stood, now there was only a giant car park. The death toll remained unknown but was estimated at around ten thousand. The Baathist regime had successfully destroyed its militant Islamic opposition.[87] *The Times* was no advocate of instability for its own sake in the area. It believed the Syrian President, Hafez al-Assad, was 'a man of straightforward dealing and statesmanlike behaviour' and warned Israel not to take advantage of Syria's internal problems by invading southern Lebanon.[88]

Instead, with the world's attention on the Falklands War, Israel attacked southern Lebanon following the shooting on 3 June 1982 of the Israeli Ambassador to Britain outside the Dorchester Hotel in London. Israel claimed that since the ceasefire agreed with the PLO in July 1981 she had been subjected to more than 150 terrorist attacks. *The Times* disputed the legitimacy of this *casus belli*, questioning not only the statistics but also pointing out that none of the attacks during this period had come from the northern front.[89] The implosion of Lebanon, once a land of democracy and prosperity, was, of course, a long affair. Civil war in 1975 was followed by occupation by Syria. Hating their Palestinian and Syrian guests, many Lebanese Christians regarded the Israeli invaders as liberators. But in Gray's Inn Road, sympathy with Begin's Israel was wearing thin. Peace with Egypt in 1978 and massive military and financial aid from the United States, far from giving Israel the sense of security necessary for it to make concessions to the dispossessed Palestinians, appeared to have encouraged aggression: the attack on Iraq's nuclear plant in June 1981, the bombing of Beirut the following month and the annexation of Golan in December. In leading articles written by the paper's Middle East expert, Edward Mortimer, both the invasion of the Lebanon and the equivocal attitude to it from Washington were condemned.[90]

The Israeli offensive into the Lebanon temporarily displaced the Falklands' conflict on the front page. Christopher Walker was able to file censored reports on the Israeli advance including a gripping account of the storming of Beaufort castle, the twelfth-century crusader fortress that had been the PLO's main forward position in southern Lebanon for over a decade. Robert Fisk filed daily from Beirut, chronicling the air assault on the city. Transmitting his reports was an arduous business. At five o' clock each morning he would travel south to observe the Israeli advance, often with reporters from the Associated Press bureau, coming under ferocious air attack, before returning to Beirut to file his report from a telex machine in time for it to make the copy deadline at Gray's Inn Road. The situation deteriorated as Beirut became surrounded. The electricity supply was curtailed and food and petrol were not allowed into the city. Fisk kept his generator running by bribing an Israeli tank crew to supply him with fuel at extortionate rates. Filing to London could take hours because, whenever the generator cut out, the telex went down too. At eight o'clock in the evening, the task would be completed and Fisk, exhausted, had anxious moments waiting for Gray's Inn Road to confirm it had indeed received all of his copy. Periodically, a message would be returned thanking him for his report and apologizing for the fact the unions had called another strike and so it would not be appearing after all. When they were printed, his reports were graphic, gripping and made no attempt to be impartial. 'To say that Israel's war against the Palestinians is turning into a dangerous and brutal conflict,' he wrote, 'would be to understate the political realities of its military adventure into Lebanon'[91]

By 14 June, Israeli tanks had linked up with the Christian Phalange in East Beirut. The Palestinians were hemmed in and surrounded. Yet Fisk, still in the city, predicted disaster for the invader: 'a war which was initially supposed to take their troops only 25 miles north of their own border' now appeared poised to degenerate into costly street fighting, 'terrorizing the entire civilian population of West Beirut and killing hundreds of people. Is it a war that will ultimately be worth winning?'[92] From the greater comfort of Gray's Inn Road, Edward Mortimer agreed, adding that 'the inability of the wealthy and supposedly powerful rulers of the Gulf to save Lebanon and the Palestinians from being destroyed with weapons supplied by the United States will add fuel to the brushfire of Islamic revolution blowing in from Iran'.[93]

The disaster came in September. A disengagement force led by US Marines had overseen the evacuation of the PLO guerrillas from West Beirut, a notable triumph for Israel. But it was no harbinger of peace. Scarcely had the US Marines left than chaos returned. On 14 September, Bashir Gemayel, Lebanon's Christian President-elect, was killed in a terror-ist bomb blast on a Beirut Phalangist Party office. Two hours later, Israeli troops moved into West Beirut. The next day they surrounded the Sabra and Chatila camps which were teeming with Palestinian refugees. As early as the 18 September edition of *The Times*, Leslie Plommer was able to report from Beirut that Phalangists had entered the camps, started fires and removed individuals while Israeli troops looked on. Two days later, Fisk filed a report that painted an altogether more serious picture. His dispatch dominated the front page. The shooting, he wrote, had lasted fourteen hours. He estimated the deaths at around a thousand (the actual figure is still disputed, though thought to be between 600 and 1400). Fisk had gained entry to the Chatila camp shortly after the last Phalangists had left: 'in some cases, the blood was still wet on the ground . . . Down every alley way, there were corpses – women, young men, babies and grandparents – lying together in lazy and terrible profusion where they had been knifed or machine gunned to death,' he wrote. The smell of death was everywhere. Having feasted on the dead, flies moved pitilessly to the living. Fisk had to keep his mouth covered to stop them swarming into it. 'What we found inside the camp . . . did not quite beggar description although it would be easier to re-tell in a work of fiction or in the cold prose of a medical report.' It was certainly graphic, men shot at point-blank range, one castrated. 'The women,' Fisk continued:

were middle-aged and their corpses lay draped over a pile of rubble. One lay on her back, her dress torn open and the head of a little girl emerging from behind her. The girl had short, dark curly hair and her eyes were staring at us and there was a frown on her face. She was dead.

Another child lay on the roadway like a discarded flower, her white dress stained with mud and dust. She could have been no more than three years old. The back of her head had been blown away by a bullet fired into her brain. One of the women also held a tiny baby to her body. The bullet that had passed through her breast had killed the baby too.

Further gruesome descriptions followed, the dispatch ending with Fisk moving on from the camp and finding himself with Israeli troops under fire from a ruined building. Taking cover beside a reticent army major, he tried to solicit information on what had happened at Chatila: 'Then his young radio operator, who had been lying behind us in the mud, crawled up next to me. He was a young man. He pointed to his chest. "We Israelis don't do that sort of thing," he said. "It was the Christians".'[94]

Subsequently Journalist of the Year again, Fisk's dispatch from Chatila became famous with the closing statement adopted as its title. It was reproduced in *The Faber Book of Reportage*, an international anthology edited by John Carey in 1987, one of only four historic examples of *Times* journalism to be included.* Fisk also secured an interview with Major Saad Haddad who denied his Israeli-sponsored private army had participated with the Phalangist militia in the massacre. The tone of Fisk's interview was decidedly sceptical. *The Times* leader column was quick to point the finger at Israel's shared culpability: 'Even if they did not actively will the massacre, they are guilty of knowingly creating the conditions in which it was likely to happen.'[95] The following February, the paper devoted extensive coverage, led by Christopher Walker in Jerusalem, to the findings of the Kahan Commission, the Israeli judicial enquiry, into the tragedy. It was highly critical of the Begin administration's general disregard and in particular found fault with Ariel Sharon, the Defence Minister and architect of the Lebanon invasion, who had permitted the Phalangists to enter the camp despite the obvious likelihood that they would slaughter its inhabitants.

---

* Fisk thus joined the illustrious *Times* company of William Howard Russell's report of the Battle of Balaclava and Charge of the Light Brigade, November 1854; Nandor Ebor's dispatch on Garibaldi's liberation of Palermo, June 1860; and James (Jan) Morris on the conquest of Mount Everest, June 1953.

The instant response of *The Times* to the massacre was to argue that, since neither Syrian nor Israeli forces had brought the stability necessary for a civilian government to succeed in the Lebanon, a multinational UN-sanctioned force should be sent. *The Times* wanted full British participation, something Mrs Thatcher was keen to avoid.[96] Reagan, however, responded immediately, ordering eight hundred US Marines back into West Beirut. France and Italy followed as, reluctantly, did Britain. They marched into a trap. On 23 October 1983, two Shia Muslim suicide bombers killed 242 US Marines and 58 French troops stationed in Beirut. In one day, more servicemen had been killed than Britain lost throughout the Falklands War the previous year. In December, French and US jets retaliated, hitting Syrian positions. It was all in vain. In the new year the Lebanese government fell, having lost control of West Beirut. In March, the multinational force packed its bags and left. The Israelis were drawing and redrawing their defence line closer and closer to their own border. The Lebanon was being left to the militias, the Syrians and the undertakers.

IV

While Robert Fisk and other courageous reporters around the world dodged shot and shell to file their copy for *The Times*, the paper continued to be under an industrial life sentence itself. At the NUJ's annual conference at Coventry in March 1982, the union's president, Harry Conroy, warned that the freedom of the press was being undermined by the Thatcher Government, the proprietors and 'the misuse of new technology'. *The Times* had sent its Midlands correspondent, Arthur Osman, to cover the speech but he was barred from entering the conference on the grounds that the NUJ did not allow non-NUJ journalists to cover its affairs. Mr Osman's crime was to be a member of the Institute of Journalists union. First up to condemn *The Times* for having the temerity to employ a member of a different trade union was Jake Ecclestone, long-term scourge of Times Newspapers' management, who had finally left *The Times*'s employment the previous year and taken up the position of deputy general secretary of the NUJ. Those who spoke most volubly about safeguarding the freedom of the press were, it seemed, less keen on the freedom of association.

The Fleet Street paradox was that, although the various print unions hated one another and the various journalist unions hated one another, they remained great believers in trade union solidarity across unrelated industrial sectors. British Rail still had the contract to deliver *The Times*. In June 1982 a rail strike paralysed distribution of the paper. Yet rather than assist the companies that employed their members, the SOGAT print union refused to distribute any newspapers that were switched to road distribution, thereby closing off the only means of circumventing the National Union of Railwaymen's ability to shutdown the press.[97] This was far from being an isolated incident. In August, Fleet Street was silenced by a sympathy strike by the London press branch of the EETPU (electricians' union) in support of a 12 per cent pay claim by NHS nurses. Fleet Street's proprietors, working though the Newspaper Publishers Association, could not see what the going rate for hospital nurses had to do with those employed to produce newspapers and secured a High Court injunction against what was classed as 'secondary action'. Frank Chapple, the EETPU's moderate general secretary, also appealed to his members not to pull the plug on the press. Undaunted, Sean Geraghty, the branch secretary, led his 1300 members out. No national newspaper managed to publish. Geraghty had excluded only the Communist *Morning Star* from the EETPU strike. Despite this thoughtful dispensation, it too failed to appear when SOGAT members halted its production.

Having lost a day's production due to Geraghty's action, Fleet Street braced itself for a longer shutdown when the NGA print union threatened to go on strike if Geraghty went to prison for contempt of court. As the law stood there was no debate about the matter. James Prior's 1980 Employment Act had made secondary action illegal. Geraghty had ignored a High Court injunction to this effect. Yet, the belief by trade unionists that the matter could nonetheless be determined by the effect of industrial action rather than the writ of a court of law was instructive. *The Times* suspected that the NGA's motivation was to test the secondary action legislation by creating a martyr 'like the commotion that attended the jailing of five London dockers who defied the Industrial Relations Court in 1973 and hastened its demise'.[98] In the event, a showdown was avoided. Geraghty was fined £350 and legal costs of £7000.

Yet, this would not prove to be the end of secondary or 'sympathy' action. On 22 September, *The Times*, together with all the other national newspapers, did not appear when the print unions downed tools and joined the TUC's 'Day of Action' in support of health service workers. Douglas-Home was perturbed by the handful of the paper's journalists who joined the boycott work campaign. He was particularly uneasy with the decision of Pat Healy, the social services correspondent, to be adopted as the Labour candidate for Bedford at the next general election, believing that readers would question the impartiality of her reporting. There was, it has to be said, no shortage of precedent for the conscientious journalist becoming a politician and the matter, perhaps wisely, was allowed to rest.

Industrial action silenced *The Times* again between 20 December 1982 and 3 January 1983. The dispute was caused by nine EETPU members who refused to operate new equipment until management renegotiated their terms and cost Times Newspapers more than £2 million. They won the support of their fellow electricians. Murdoch again threatened to close down the paper. Being off the streets was not the best omen for the paper's new year. In the end, management had to abandon its plan to implement a wage freeze on all staff for 1983. Any hope of *The Times* scraping out of the red was lost. When, on 3 January, the paper returned to the streets, a leader article written by Douglas-Home, entitled 'All Our Tomorrows', laid bare the feeling in Gray's Inn Road. It started on a positive, almost lyrical note:

For many people, life without a newspaper would be like music without time – a blur of inchoate sounds, an endless and incompre hensible cacophony. It is newspapers which puncture the march of time, syncopating their narrative of events with commentary, analysis and entertainment. Newspapers comprehend the sound of history in the making, and give it meaning.

But it questioned how long a newspaper could expect to keep its readers' loyalty if it could not keep its side of the bargain:

The British press is only too ready fearlessly to expose bad manage- ment, bad unions, and bad industrial relations wherever they occur, except in its own backyard. The subterfuge and cynicism which poison industrial relations in Fleet Street remain a close secret. That is a strange kind of conspiracy of silence to maintain when the newspaper houses themselves find any other kind of cooperation almost impos- sible to achieve.[99]

The response of the unions was to go back on strike and *The Times* was not published between 27 January and 3 February when SOGAT struck. As part of a pooling of *Times* and *Sunday Times* library resources, manage- ment had appointed a member from SOGAT's supervisory branch, but

SOGAT insisted that management could only employ someone to a library position from the union's clerical branch. Amazingly, this was the demarcation issue upon which SOGAT shut down the paper. Twenty-six days after this dispute was settled, *The Times* was again shut down when members of the Amalgamated Union of Engineering Workers (AUEW) walked out as part of another TUC-endorsed 'Day of Action' – this time in protest at the Government's efforts to ban union membership among national security and intelligence civil servants at GCHQ in Cheltenham.

V

Those who were preoccupied by Douglas-Home's aristocratic credentials or the fact that his uncle had been a 'wet' Tory Prime Minister, did not, at first, realize that he was of a determinedly Thatcherite frame of mind. No one should have been surprised that he took an uncompromising line on the Falklands' crisis, the first issue to dominate the news after he assumed the chair. Defence was his special subject and he was an ex-soldier and military historian. But some were surprised when he continued to take a bullish view of Mrs Thatcher's domestic agenda as well. There were complaints that his leaders were too often uncritical in their support of the Government. The veteran liberal sage Hugo Young believed that, under Douglas-Home, *The Times* developed 'the most right-wing world view in the serious press' in Britain. Young told Douglas-Home that the paper had even come to outdo the *Daily Telegraph* in this respect, 'mainly by virtue of so rarely finding President Reagan to the left of you'.[100] When Douglas-Home asked the Labour MP Clare Short why she had stopped reading *The Times* she told him it had 'deteriorated into a crudely biased, right-wing paper. Someone else used the phrase "up-market *Sun*".'[101] A consequence of this belief was that it was sometimes difficult to coax senior Labour MPs to write for the Op-Ed page, although in Peter Stothard's experience of trying to commission articles from them this was also partly attributable to their disappointment at being offered the going rate of only £150 per article.[102]

The left's dissatisfaction with what they saw as an increasingly partisan and hostile paper was balanced by those on the right who had found the *bien pensant* pieties of the middle ground stale and unchallenging. In an article 'Welcome Back Thunderer' for the *Wall Street Journal*, Seth Lipsky commended the paper's new sense of purpose, supporting the US intervention in Grenada, agreeing that the USSR was 'an evil empire indeed' and condemning the hypocrisy of those who wanted to place sanctions on South Africa.[103] Others agreed that it was time 'The Thunderer' got some fire back in its belly after a long period in which, according to the leader page of the *Spectator*, it had 'tended to support a government only when it was taking an easy way out'.[104]

The appointment of Roger Scruton as a regular columnist in 1983 began a four-year run in which the Tory philosopher and enthusiastic foxhunter succeeded in running to ground his quarry – from trendy dons and churchmen to CND campaigners and modern architects. Scruton was a friend of Charles and Jessica Douglas-Home but it was Peter Stothard, with whom responsibility for columnists fell, who took the brunt of the backlash from the *soi-disant* 'great and the good' at their most outraged. Reflecting on the matter a decade later, Stothard concluded that 'no decision brought me more trouble' than Scruton's weekly philippics since 'barely would a piece have appeared in print before my in-tray was filled with "dump the mad doctor" from all sides of polite society and the political left'.[105] An admirer of Edmund Burke, Scruton was an articulate, intelligent and authentic critic of modernity's failings, which, in the eyes of progressives bent on cultural conformity to their own nostrums, made him something equivalent to a dangerous revolutionary.

Yet, it was with Douglas-Home's leader writing policy that dissent within the ranks of the paper's 'college of cardinals' was most strongly expressed. None were closet fellow travellers: they were as opposed to the Kremlin's world view as was the editor. Nonetheless, two leader writers in particular who specialized in foreign policy, Richard Davy and Edward Mortimer, were increasingly unhappy with Douglas-Home's tendency to see the editorial column as a fire and brimstone preacher's pulpit rather than the open house for mid-term discussion and the expression of honest doubt. 'Until Charlie took over,' Davy lamented, 'the best *Times* leaders started from an independent position and argued their way to a conclusion giving due weight to other views ... He seemed to want leaders to do no more than fulminate about the Soviet threat whereas I wanted to discuss the political and diplomatic problems of dealing with it.' Davy believed that the tired, old men who ran the Kremlin could not last forever and it was necessary to reinvigorate the 1970s spirit of détente. He was horrified when Douglas-Home looked at him blankly and replied, 'What is there to talk about?' To the editor, détente was indistinguishable from appeasement while to his chief foreign leader writer it was a form of diplomacy that 'merely required periodic adjustment to new circumstances and regular checks to keep it in line with military security'. Where necessary, this meant not only attempting to encourage the trapped peoples of Eastern Europe but also to find means of 'improving relations with their ghastly governments at the same time'. There was, of course, no meeting of minds with Douglas-Home on this point and when in 1984 Davy realized that he was no longer going to be given the space to present his more nuanced argument he resigned. Edward Mortimer left shortly thereafter, also disillusioned. With their departures, Mary Dejevsky started writing leaders. She was much closer to the editor's perception of Cold War realities. With hindsight and the opening of previously closed archives, Davy concluded that Douglas-Home was more hawkish than Ronald Reagan – the latter had, after all, established private channels to Moscow even when his public pronouncements remained at their most defiant.[106]

On most political matters, Douglas-Home and Rupert Murdoch were of like mind. Unquestionably, this made the proprietor more benevolent towards his editor than he had been towards Harold Evans. Consequently, the self-confident Douglas-Home felt able to take the sorts of liberties with his boss that it would not have been sensible for Evans to have risked. Douglas-Home was not averse to putting the phone down on Murdoch – particularly if there was an audience to appreciate such lèse-majesté. The belief that their editor had the social confidence not to be intimidated by the proprietor certainly enhanced his popularity among the staff. Many, however, were uneasy about the political repositioning of the paper. Hugh Stephenson, the former editor of *The Times* business section who had gone on to edit the *New Statesman*, felt the political move defied commercial sense, doubting 'whether there is room for two *Daily Telegraphs*'.[107] But Murdoch was an admirer of the *Telegraph*'s sense of mission and identity and believed *The Times* should be equally purposeful. At one stage, Douglas-Home got so tired of hearing Murdoch sing the *Telegraph*'s praises that he shouted back, 'then why didn't you buy the bloody *Telegraph*?'[108]

An unshakeable belief in defence and NATO was at the core of Douglas-Home's views. At a time when Labour was committed to unilateral nuclear disarmament and the Cold War was going though a tense phase, it was natural that he should back the Conservatives. But under his editorship *The Times* became much more sympathetic to monetarist policies at home. The dislike of monetarism red in tooth and claw evident in the leader columns of Harold Evans was cast aside. 'British economic policy should be guided by two rules: the first is that the Government should have a balanced budget and the second is that the growth of the money supply should be roughly similar to that of underlying production capacity' the column now announced. 'Only if the Government adheres to them consistently will it achieve price stability and, in the long run, price stability is the only macro-economic objective which it can deliver.' Yet there were complications associated with pursuing purity in a world of sin. Britain's problem was the same as that experienced by Switzerland in 1978: trying to achieve balanced budgets and price stability when other countries remained profligate turned the currency into such a safe haven for international investors that the exchange rate rose to levels that made manufactured exports prohibitively expensive. Although *The Times* continued to advocate a way round this problem by re-establishing fixed exchange rates it conceded, somewhat lamely, that in the meantime Britain could do little more than 'set an example of good monetary management and encourage other industrial countries to behave the same way'.[109]

Certainly, if everything else depended upon bringing down the cost of money, there was finally some cause for hope. By November 1982, the inflation rate had fallen to 6.3 per cent, the lowest for a decade, but there was still no sign of this having a positive impact upon the unemployment rate. *The Times* leader column could draw comfort from the reality that 'few people would have believed in 1979 that an unemployment total of three million would be accompanied by so little social discontent'[110] but many felt complacent observations of this kind failed to grasp the extent of social disarray. It was not until September 1983 that there was the first recorded fall in unemployment since 1977, the true extent of joblessness masked by a proliferation of training schemes of varying degrees of usefulness.

The recession was reflected in the fortunes of the business pages of *The Times*. Confronted with the necessity of finding economies, the axe fell on *The Times* business news. Anthony Hilton was appointed City editor but the once large supporting staff was decimated. The journalistic range contracted accordingly. Even great culls present opportunities for those who remained and this was the attitude of the new financial editor, Graham Searjeant, who came over from the *Sunday Times* in 1983. Douglas-Home greeted him with words of advice that could have served well many a new boy: 'Never attempt to be definitive, because you will have to write again tomorrow.'[111] Searjeant proved to be one of the most accomplished business commentators of the next two decades, contributing not only in the business pages but also, anonymously, as a leader writer. For the paper as a whole, though, the comprehensive filleting of The *Times* business news – the section the old Thomson ownership had once imagined would rival the *FT* in its coverage – represented a major contraction. It left the *FT* with an almost unassailable advantage in this vital sector of the market for the next decade.

It was thus surprising that The *Times* was endorsing the Thatcherite vision of the enterprise economy while simultaneously cutting back on its own business coverage. The transformation to Thatcherite cheerleader was not swift or unquestioning, however. The bulk of the Government's privatization campaign to roll back the frontiers of the nationalized economy lay ahead in a second term of office. The first attempt, in 1982, left The *Times* noticeably underwhelmed. The privatization of a majority stake in 'Britoil', as the British National Oil Corporation was renamed, was, as its author Nigel Lawson put it, 'the largest privatization the world had ever known'.[112] But with Labour immediately pledging to renationalize the oil assets at the sale price, investors were cautious. This, together with a flotation in November 1982 that badly coincided with gloomy predictions about future oil prices, ensured it was embarrassingly undersubscribed. Neither Adrian Hamilton in the business news section nor The *Times* leader writers were surprised, concluding that 'a decent interval before the next major sale would be judicious'.[113] What was more, the paper still had to be convinced that 'selling assets at a discount' and 'transferring ownership from twenty million taxpayers to a few hundred thousand shareholders, simply to raise a relatively small amount of money' made sense.[114] This was one tune that time and experience would later change.

Whatever the battles over the opinion pieces in the paper, there was still enough of the journal of record spirit within The *Times* to ensure straight, unbiased reporting on the news pages. The political editor was Julian Haviland, whom Harold Evans had appointed after he had spent more than twenty years at ITN. Haviland was reinforced by Tony Bevins, the chief political correspondent, and a team of four journalists working from the House of Commons to report British political news. In any case, despite the claims that it was now a bastion of right-wing prejudices, it was hard to discern too much enthusiasm for the Conservative Party even on the comment pages of The *Times* as the 1983 general election approached. 'Only the conquest of inflation and of the Falklands were measureable successes,' the leader column conceded, 'with the rest having to be taken on trust from a not very eloquent band of ministers.'[115] But the Labour

Party manifesto, immortalized by Gerald Kaufman as 'the longest suicide note in history', put beyond the slightest doubt which party the paper would endorse. Labour's manifesto called not only for the scrapping of Trident, unilateral nuclear disarmament and withdrawal from the EEC, but for the reimposition of exchange controls and the threat to the major clearing banks that if they refused to 'cooperate with us fully ... we shall stand ready to take one or more of them into public ownership'. Nationalization would be extended over electronics and pharmaceutical companies, on all tenanted land and on any private property 'held empty without justification'. Private schools would lose charitable status and were to be 'integrated' into the local authority sector 'where necessary'.[116] There was scarcely a word in the entire manifesto with which The Times columnists and leader writers did not take issue. Claiming to feel sympathy for his predicament, Bernard Levin described Michael Foot as 'lurching between disaster and calamity with all the skill and aplomb of a one-legged tightrope-walker'. He was, Levin maintained, a man 'unable to make his own Shadow Cabinet appointments or indeed to blow his nose in public without his trousers falling down'.[117]

The paper was also critical of the Liberal-SDP Alliance's offering which was 'a worthy compilation of much that has been tried, half-tried or at least seriously considered over the last political generation'.[118] Editorially, the switch from Harold Evans to Douglas-Home probably made little difference to the paper's hostility to Michael Foot's Labour Party, but it ensured a less charitable attitude towards the centre-left alternative. Despite this, subsequent estimates suggested that a third of Times readers voted for the Alliance. With the exception of the Guardian (41 per cent), this was the highest proportion for any national newspaper's readership.[119]

Due to the 1978–9 shutdown, the 1983 general election was the first that The Times had covered since 1974. There was a last minute danger that it would miss out again when Fleet Street was hit by a fresh wave of strikes. A nine-week dispute with its print workers ensured the Financial Times missed the general election. Two hundred thousand copies of the Observer's final edition before election day were lost when the NGA decided to punish the newspaper's editor, Donald Trelford, for not allowing the NGA space in his paper to attack a Conservative Party advertisement. Since the Observer supported Labour, it was hard to see what the NGA's action was intended to achieve. The following night, the NGA members took exception to the main leader in the Daily Express and refused to print it. Early editions of the paper appeared with a blank space where the offending leader should have appeared. In these circumstances, *The Times* could consider itself lucky to escape the unions' *ad hoc* attempt at press censorship.

Nor, happily, did the paper have to contend with any political direction from the proprietor's office. Although Murdoch was in London on polling day, he had not felt the need to be in the country during the election campaign. He did not interfere with *The Times*'s stance (not that he would have felt the need to) and the same was true at the less resolute *Sunday Times* whose editor, Frank Giles, later made clear that 'at no period had Murdoch raised with me the question of our political line. Nor had [Sir Edward] Pickering.'[120]

The Times reported the election result below the headline (which it would have been safe to have prepared in advance) 'Mrs Thatcher back with a landslide'. Julian Haviland's reporting was updated as results came in, though, by 2 a.m., the picture was pretty clear. Tony Benn was ousted in Bristol East, the paper quietly whooping that 'the man who seemed certain to challenge for the Labour Party leadership next autumn has lost his principal power base, a seat in Parliament'. No less significant was the defeat of two of the Gang of Four – Shirley Williams and Bill Rodgers. It was a frustrating night for the Alliance. It received almost as many votes as Labour but the vagaries of the electoral system ensured it made little headway with a quarter of the vote translating into one twenty-eighth of the seats. All but five of the former Labour MPs who had defected to the SDP were defeated. The results were received from Press Association wires and rekeyed. *The Times* managed to publish around 450 results by the time the last election-night edition rolled off the press, which was more than any of its rivals. The Saturday paper was accompanied by a twelve-page supplement produced by Alan Wood, who was covering his seventh general election. It provided short biographies of all 650 MPs, an unprecedented feat. The final tally was Conservatives 397 seats, Labour 209, Alliance 23 (and Others 21). Margaret Thatcher was the first twentieth-century Conservative Prime Minister to win two successive working majorities. It was the worst result for Labour since 1935. Pat Healy, the only *Times* employee standing, found the soil of North Bedfordshire unfertile for Labour.

Michael Foot was the first post-election casualty of his party's disastrous showing at the polls. His oratorical style had amused Frank Johnson who drew attention to the Labour leader's 'peroration trouble' – the habit of inserting an extra subclause into the ending of a speech that forced him to digress, take the tempo down, rewind and recapitulate like the conclusion of a Beethoven symphony. Foot's successor, Neil Kinnock, also proved a gift for Johnson, who played on his supposed 'windbag' tendencies. Editorially, *The Times* was not confident about the new leader, fearing he was still far too left wing. The day after Kinnock won the party leadership, a four-sequence photo shot was spooled across the front page showing him on Brighton beach stumbling into the advancing sea and having to be hauled to safety by his wife Glenys. The caption read: 'Early lesson for new leader: time and tide wait for no man.'[121] Douglas-Home wanted Foot, liberated from the cares of leadership, to write regular book reviews for *The Times*, but, citing various commitments, he politely declined.[122]

Cecil Parkinson had masterminded the Conservatives' 1983 election campaign and was talked of as Thatcher's eventual successor. *The Times* reacted to the revelation that Sarah Keays, Parkinson's former secretary, was expecting his child with a stalwart defence: 'whatever society's aspirations to the contrary, life in this land is full of split homes, illegitimacy, and one-parent families. Why then does the public expect its leaders to preserve the outward forms of a morality which it no longer practises, if it ever did?'[123] But when Parkinson responded to questioning on the matter during the course of an interview on *Panorama*, Sarah Keays decided to offer her side of the story exclusively to *The Times*. Douglas-Home was at Blackpool for the Conservative Party conference, but as soon as the offer was put to him he dispatched a reporting team to visit her in Bath. In the small hours of 14 October, the *Daily Telegraph* journalist Graham Paterson was awoken in his Blackpool hotel room by an irate editorial office in Fleet Street desperate to find out what was going on and furious at having been scooped by its rival.[124] The headline said it all. 'Sarah Keays talks to *The Times* of "loving relationship"' appeared across the top of the paper that morning, over-shadowing the enthusiastic reception Parkinson had received at the Conservative Party conference the previous day. Within hours, Parkinson had resigned. The one hundredth anniversary Conservative Party conference had turned from celebration to deep gloom, with many outraged that *The Times* had sunk to the depths of printing what they took to be the fury of a woman scorned. The familiar cry went up that the 'paper wasn't what it used to be' and 'what is *The Times* coming to?'. The use of a picture of two of Parkinson's daughters looking distressed outside the family home came in for particular attack. The editor was deluged with letters of complaint, one reader who had been subscribing to the paper for sixty years assuring him, 'the tone of *The Times* is beginning to resemble that of the so-called gutter press . . . you have become VULGAR'.[125] Yet Sarah Keays was not paid for her story and, as Douglas-Home told Alastair Hetherington, 'what ground have I got for not publishing it? Answer: only those of protecting the Minister, and that's not my job.'[126] Further offence was caused when the paper quoted Miss Keays's claim that the *Daily Telegraph* had recommended aborting the child. In fact, the *Telegraph* had stated that such an option 'hardly seems a moral advance' and prominent space had to be hurriedly found for the *Telegraph*'s editor, Bill Deedes, to point this out.[127] For its part, *The Times* continued to be sympathetic to Parkinson's predicament. Jock Bruce-Gardyne wrote an Op-Ed appreciation of the fallen minister, 'hounded out by hypocrisy'. Bernard Levin also raised his eyebrows at the moral panic, finding his usual seam of satire in the lofty pronouncements of the *Daily Mirror*, the *Daily Telegraph* and the Bishop of Bath and Wells.

Despite her reputation for supporting 'Victorian values', the Prime Minister was not noted for taking the moral high ground with those she liked and, in time, Parkinson was allowed back into the Cabinet where he proceeded to set in motion the process that would lead to 'Big Bang' – deregulating financial services and opening up the City more widely to global competition. But the 'love child' revelations had ruined his chances of succeeding Margaret Thatcher in Downing Street. The episode's coverage was said – by those with little knowledge of the paper's history – to be symbolic of the way *The Times* under Rupert Murdoch's ownership had departed from its values. It had given supposedly excessive space to a minor scandal, sensationalizing the accusations of a wronged woman. It had also failed to chastise sufficiently the lax moral standards expected of a man in public office who, for some, had committed the additional sin of being a brazen Thatcherite. As the paper approached its bicentenary, questions over its news presentation, priorities and Thatcherite bias threatened to undermine its continuing claim to being a unique national treasure of objectivity and truth. Matters were not helped when the paper announced it had access to the diaries of Adolf Hitler . . .

CHAPTER FOUR

ANCIENT AND MODERN

The Hitler Diaries; the Arts; Sport; Portfolio;
The Times's Bicentenary; Death of an Editor

I

In its one hundred and ninety-eighth year *The Times* made one of its most embarrassing mistakes: it announced it had bought the rights to sixty volumes of Adolf Hitler's private diaries. It would prove to be the most expensive fraud in publishing history. With hindsight, the newspaper's verification procedures appeared astonishingly nonchalant. It helped persuade its parent company, News Corp., to offer $1.2 million for diaries whose contents had been subjected to no more than the most superficial examination. Had the manuscripts been checked, it would have been quickly apparent that they contained little more than bloodless drivel lifted primarily from Max Domarus's published book *Hitler's Speeches and Proclamations*. Some of the entries were positively comic: 'Must not forget tickets for the Olympic Games for Eva'; 'on my feet all day long'; and 'Because of the new pills I have violent flatulence, and – says Eva – bad breath'. *Stern* magazine, from whom News Corp. bought the rights, refused to reveal its sources or to provide a convincing account of the diaries thirty-eight-year provenance. No comprehensive scientific tests had been done on the ink or the paper. These were basic procedures overlooked in the rush to claim a scoop.

Considering that *The Times* had been the victim of a serious hoax in the past, it should have been alive to the consequences of repeating the error. On 18 April 1887 – the first time the paper had run a story under a double-column headline – it had published a letter supposedly written by Charles Stewart Parnell, the Irish Nationalist leader, applauding the murder of the Chief Secretary of Ireland's under-secretary. The letter was subsequently found to be a forgery (its real author, Richard Pigott, fled to a Madrid hotel where he shot himself in the head) and *The Times* was fined

£200,000 – a sum so large that it did almost as much financial damage to the paper as the harm incurred to its international reputation. That misfortune was, perhaps, ancient history by 1983, but the *Sunday Times* had suffered at the hoaxer's hand well within the memory of many of those at Gray's Inn Road. In 1968, when Harold Evans was its editor, the *Sunday Times*'s owners, Thomson, secured for the paper thirty volumes of Mussolini's diaries with a £100,000 advance payment on a promised £250,000. Thomson's historical and forensic experts adjudged the diaries plausible. In reality, they were the work of two old Italian women. Thomson failed to get any of the money back.

The Hitler Diaries that came to light in 1983 were the work of Konrad Kujau, a Stuttgart con man with a number of convictions for petty crime. Had *The Times* been handed the volumes directly by such a shadowy figure at the back door of Gray's Inn Road, basic steps to ensure their veracity would doubtless have been undertaken. Yet, because the newspaper was offered them by *Stern*, a current affairs journal with a serious reputation, it took far too much on trust in believing that Germany's leading magazine was sufficiently professional not to deal in forged goods. The ensuing debacle would descend into an extraordinary and unedifying blame game that pitted *The Times* against the *Sunday Times*, everyone at Gray's Inn Road against the extraordinary misjudgment of the historian Lord Dacre and every rival newspaper into paroxysms of gleeful jeering at the expense of Rupert Murdoch. But the font of woe was *Stern* magazine. It had paid $4.8 million (£3.5 million) for the diaries through a journalist-researcher of twenty-eight years' standing on its payroll, Gerd Heidemann (Kujau's intermediary), and was not afraid to cut corners in order to ensure a return on the investment.

In 1980, Gerd Heidemann had told Anthony Terry, the *Sunday Times*'s European editor, in confidence that he was trying to track down Adolf Hitler's private papers which he believed had been lost in a plane crash on 21 April 1945. Little more was heard for some time although in late 1982 the far-right historian David Irving had contacted the *Sunday Times* with an offer to investigate reports of faked Hitler diaries and assorted memorabilia being traded between a German historian and a man in Stuttgart. Had the paper taken up Irving's offer, a lot of bother and embarrassment might have been saved. But even though this was long before Irving was found guilty by a High Court judge in April 2000 of falsifying history in his portrayal of the Holocaust, he was already regarded as politically too dangerous to employ. Gitta Sereny was sent to investigate instead.

Heidemann showed her round his personal archive in Hamburg but, before she could probe further in Stuttgart, she was ordered back to London as part of a cost-cutting exercise.[1] This proved a false economy.

The next Times Newspapers learned of the matter was when *Stern*'s Peter Wickman and the foreign rights salesman, Wilfried Sorge, came to visit Gray's Inn Road. Douglas-Home was convalescing in Norfolk at the time so *The Times*'s two deputy editors, Colin Webb and Charles Wilson, met the *Stern* team. All were obliged to sign confidentiality contracts. Webb agreed with Brian MacArthur of the *Sunday Times* a division of spoils: *The Times* would break the story and the *Sunday Times* would serialize it. Clearly, though, they would need to be confident that the diaries were genuine and Webb suggested getting Lord Dacre to authenticate them. It was, it seemed, an inspired choice. As an independent director of Times Newspapers since 1974, Dacre could be trusted with what was a commercially sensitive matter while, in his other guise as the historian Hugh Trevor-Roper, he was well placed to pass a professional judgment. This agreed, Webb telephoned Douglas-Home with the news. With as much haste as he could muster, Douglas-Home returned to Gray's Inn Road to take charge of what promised to be one of the paper's greatest scoops.[2]

Educated at Charterhouse and Oxford, Hugh Trevor-Roper had been in British Intelligence during the war and was a member of the team that cracked the code of the Abwehr, the German secret service. At the end of the war he had been put in charge of determining the details of the Führer's demise. This led to his acclaimed 1947 publication, *The Last Days of Hitler*. Another work, *Hitler's Table Talk*, followed and in 1957 he became Regius Professor of Modern History at Oxford. In 1978 he edited *The Goebbels Diaries*. The following year he took up a life peerage as Lord Dacre and in 1980 swapped Oxford for the commodious Master's Lodge of Cambridge's oldest college, Peterhouse. Given this curriculum vitae and his place on the board of Times Newspapers, it would have been perverse for *The Times* to have commissioned anyone else to authenticate the diaries. Yet, his work on the Third Reich was but a part – and not the main part – of his broad-ranging interests. His real area of speciality was seventeenth-century cultural and ecclesiastical history. Crucially, Webb and Douglas-Home were unaware of a key failing – Dacre's post-war researches had been facilitated by Army interpreters. He was not an especially fluent reader of German.

Douglas-Home assured Dacre that his mission to the Zurich bank vault where the diaries were being stored was merely intended to allow him to gauge in general terms the look and feel of the documents and that Times

Newspapers would not require him to pronounce definitively until he had read subsequent typed transcripts of the diaries up to 1941. But, at the last moment, just as Dacre was about to catch his flight, Douglas-Home telephoned again and explained that Murdoch had now been informed and wanted to secure the serialization rights quickly. Therefore, it would be necessary for Dacre to convey his interim impressions by telephone as soon as he had visited Zurich. Reluctantly – fatally – Dacre acquiesced.

Amid great secrecy, Dacre descended into the vault of the Handelsbank in Zurich chaperoned by Wilfried Sorge, Jan Hensmann, the financial director of *Stern*'s parent company, and *Stern*'s editor, Peter Koch. Dacre had been assured that the paper of the diaries had been definitively tested and dated to the correct period. This was untrue. Furthermore, he was assured that *Stern* knew the identity of the Wehrmacht officer who had retrieved the diaries from the wreck of the aircraft in April 1945 and in whose possession they had been kept until offered to the magazine. In fact, *Stern* had merely taken it on trust that their reporter, Gerd Heidemann, knew (but would not disclose) the German officer's identity. The reality was that no such custodian existed and that Heidemann had been dealing directly with Kujau, the forger. Thus Dacre commenced his investigations on the basis of false premises. He was given an afternoon to inspect what was placed before him. Reading the spidery writing proved difficult but he was impressed by the style of the calligraphy and by its deterioration towards 1945. Besides the dairies shown him, there were also supposed to be supplementary archives (in reality, not yet forged) that included documents on a possible son in France, a manuscript for an unpublished book by Hitler about Mad King Ludwig of Bavaria, sketches for an opera entitled *Wieland the Blacksmith* and about three hundred other drawings and water-colours in Hitler's hand. This would have been an extraordinary amount for one man to forge. In quantity, it bore comparison only with the medieval trade in splinters of the true cross. Faced with the prospect of so much material, Dacre found it hard to believe it could have been the work of a lone forger (although he appears not to have thought of a more logical problem – how the real and rather busy Adolf Hitler could have found the time).

Since *Stern* were not planning on going public until 11 May, there was plenty of opportunity for Dacre to withhold a definitive judgment between his first sight of the diaries on the afternoon of 8 April and his chance to visit Heidemann in Hamburg to discuss their provenance and see the rest of the archive in his keeping. Dacre later blamed the turn of events on the pressure he was placed under by Douglas-Home: 'I allowed myself to be bounced by Charles,' he later complained, 'instead of demanding time to check the documents in the normal scholarly way.'³ This was not the recollection of Colin Webb, who believed Douglas-Home did not apply as much pressure as Dacre seemed to imagine. If Dacre really did feel – as he should have felt – that his afternoon's work in the Handelsbank was not enough to give an informed judgment he did himself and everyone else involved great damage by emerging from the vault and immediately getting on the telephone to urge not a qualified opinion but rather to bellow down the receiver in triumph to Douglas-Home, 'Come at once! They're the real McCoy!'⁴

The editor took Dacre at his word. Within moments of being telephoned with the joyous news, Douglas-Home and Rupert Murdoch were organizing their flight over to Zurich in Murdoch's private jet, accompanied by Richard Searby and Sir Edward Pickering. Gerald Long (now deputy chairman of News International) arrived separately from Paris. On arrival in the vault, the material was laid out for the distinguished guests. Wilfried Sorge read extracts out in German with Long providing simultaneous translations into English. It all sounded plausible enough. The tour of inspection duly completed, the News International and Stern delegations got down to business at the Baur au Lac Hotel in Zurich. Murdoch offered $2.5 million for the US rights plus $750,000 for Britain and the Commonwealth. This got a provisional acceptance and the Times party boarded Murdoch's jet bound for London believing the scoop of the decade was in the bag.⁵

Shortly afterwards, Murdoch was not amused when he learned Stern had welched on the handshake. Instead they offered the US rights to Newsweek and asked News International (or, in its ultimate guise, News Corp.) to increase its offer if it wanted to return to the bidding war. With this tactic, Stern underestimated a man who did not like to be double-crossed. When Murdoch arrived at Stern's offices in Hamburg to recommence the negotiations, the German management were horrified to find the Newsweek executives walking in with him. Rather than be strung along against each other, the two companies had decided on a joint package that would split the cost between them. The negotiations recommenced. Despite years of participating in tough diplomacy with unions, commercial rivals and worldly shareholders, Murdoch was aghast at the naked effrontery with which Stern attempted to rip him off. During an adjournment, he discussed the situation with his team which had now been augmented by the arrival of Michael Binyon. Now the Times Bonn correspondent, Binyon had been diverted from the West German capital to Hamburg by the deputy editor's office and told not to tell *The Times*'s foreign desk where he was going (an instruction that led him to assume he was going to a spy's debriefing). Murdoch confided to his advisers that he thought *Stern* were 'a bunch of cowboys.' This assessment was borne out when, in the subsequent negotiating session, *Stern* responded to the repetition of the News Corp.–*Newsweek* offer price, which they had already agreed, by dramatically raising the hurdle again to $4.25 million. At this Murdoch said, 'I'm sorry', got up and walked out of the room. The *Newsweek* team followed him.

Back in their Hamburg hotel, Murdoch, Binyon and the rest of the News Corp. delegation enjoyed a celebratory evening. The Germans' arrogance and negotiating antics had been beyond belief. Murdoch appeared jovial and relaxed, seemingly happy that, as he put it, 'that's the end of all that rubbish'.[6] As soon as they learned that the News Corp. and *Newsweek* teams had packed their bags and left for home, the *Stern* management panicked. Their attempts to solicit rival bids had not met with much success and the further afield they made approaches the greater the prospect that the secret would leak out. Swallowing their pride, they flew out to New York to make Murdoch a new, much lower, offer. Now they were coming to him. It was clear who had the whip hand. Having days earlier offered, with *Newsweek*, to pay $3.75 million, News Corp. now picked up the diaries at the knock-down price of $800,000 for the US and $400,000 (£256,000) for the British and Commonwealth rights.

While Murdoch was gliding his thumb around the *Stern* begging bowl, Lord Dacre was in Hamburg visiting Gerd Heidemann. He wanted to see Heidemann's personal collection of Nazi 'memorabilia'. As he was shown around, Dacre was slowly coming to the conclusion that the custodian of these artefacts was a little peculiar. Besides possessing Hermann Goering's yacht, *Stern*'s long-serving reporter was the proud owner of two pairs of Idi Amin's (extra large) white cotton underpants. He also mentioned that he was in close touch with Martin Bormann who was, apparently, alive and well and living in Switzerland.[7] Clearly Heidemann was at the unhealthy end of eccentricity. Nonetheless, Dacre continued to believe that a serious periodical like *Stern* had gone through the proper processes of authentication. He recorded a piece to camera for the magazine to use when the story was ready to break.

That date was supposed to be 11 May, but *Stern* was panicked into bringing publication day forward nearly three weeks when, on 21 April, its rival, *Der Spiegel*, rang to enquire whether it was true it was in possession of Hitler's diaries. *Stern* could not afford to lose the scoop of breaking the news. This, of course, affected what *The Times* would do. It had been agreed that *The Times*, rather than the *Sunday Times*, would run the story first in Britain. In any case, it had been *The Times* that had taken the initiative from the first and Murdoch noted the extent to which Douglas-Home was 'so excited and thought it was an incredible story'. In contrast, the *Sunday Times*'s editor, Frank Giles, was far less enthusiastic. The two papers remained protective of their respective independence. Murdoch thought this was because Giles 'didn't like it because it came out of *The Times*' and resented the proprietor's insistence that his Sunday paper should serialize it after the daily had made the running.[8] At the *Sunday Times*, Philip Knightley – remembering the Mussolini saga of 1968 – raised his doubts and even contacted Dacre by telephone to seek, and gain, some reassurance.[9] Without enthusiasm, Giles bowed to his proprietor's will.

The positive phraseology on the front page of *The Times* on Saturday 23 April was unfortunate. 'Hitler's secret diaries to be published' ran the front page headline. Readers' attention was drawn to the serialization commencing in the following day's *Sunday Times*. It had fallen to the usually perspicacious Michael Binyon to write the article and, although he mentioned in passing that two leading West German historians (who, unlike Dacre, had not seen the diaries) had cast doubt on their veracity, the tone of the opening sentence – 'Sixty volumes of hitherto unknown diaries kept by Adolf Hitler throughout his 12-year dictatorship have been discovered . . .' – implied there was not much room for doubt. In fact, Binyon's original copy had been much more guarded. His opening sentence had stated that 'hitherto unknown diaries allegedly kept by Adolf Hitler' had been discovered, but Charles Wilson, the pugnacious deputy editor, scored out the qualification. Wilson told Binyon, in blunt language, that News Corp. had not spent $1.2 million on anything 'allegedly' newsworthy.[10]

The comment page that day was almost entirely given over to Lord Dacre to expound upon the 'Secrets that survived the Bunker'. With each assertion the eminent historian dug himself deeper and deeper into a bunker of his own devising: 'I am now satisfied that the documents are authentic,' he informed readers. The sheer volume of material was compelling evidence in itself as was the story behind their salvage from the wreck of the plane sent out on Hitler's birthday in April 1945 to take them to safety. Taken together, this 'seems to me to constitute clear proof of their authenticity'. While others might argue that the sheer scale of the archive was incompatible with Hitler's known aversion to writing, Dacre turned logic on its head: 'If Hitler (as he said in 1942) had long ago found writing by hand a great effort, that may be not so much because he was out of practice as because he already suffered from writer's cramp.'[11]

The Times had its scoop, but the news that the Sunday Times was about to start serialization prompted its rivals into action. The Observer and the Mail on Sunday both paid David Irving to pronounce in their papers that the Sunday Times had bought a forgery. The German Bild Zeitung offered to fly Irving out to interrupt Stern's proposed press conference in Hamburg on Monday. Irving and Douglas-Home locked horns on BBC television over the diaries' authenticity, The Times's editor attempting to pull rank with the words, 'I have smelt them. I'm a minor historian and we know about the smell of old documents. They certainly smelt.'[12] Doubtless they did, although not of what the minor historian imagined. Indeed, while the opprobrium would soon fall in heaps upon Dacre, Douglas-Home was also not above criticism, having allowed his excitement to overcome his better judgment. He had been particularly impressed by an extract in which Hitler had praised the destruction of the synagogues while being sorry about the loss of ancient glass. 'Typical Hitler!' Douglas-Home pronounced.[13] This was rather hasty, but he was about to make a sin of omission, whether or not intentionally, that was to do far more serious damage to the reputation of the Sunday Times – so much so that The Times's role in the fiasco was soon overlooked.

II

Dacre's first doubts struck him on Saturday morning – the same morning in which his lengthy and confidently expressed Times article was gracing breakfast tables the length and breadth of the country. He decided he ought to ring Douglas-Home to tell him. Had he thought about it, the Master of Peterhouse should have recognized it was important to tell Frank Giles at the Sunday Times since its pages of serialization would be going to press later that day. But it was The Times that had commissioned Dacre and its executives were those with whom he had the closest rapport. In any case, it was not unreasonable to assume that if the editor of The Times thought it merited a call he was capable of ringing the editor of the Sunday Times himself. On telephoning The Times, Dacre was put through to Colin Webb, who telephoned Douglas-Home at his home with the news that Dacre was having second thoughts. Eventually Douglas-Home got back to Webb to double-check what had been said. Nobody telephoned the *Sunday Times*. Webb imagined Douglas-Home would do it. Perhaps Douglas-Home imagined Webb had already done it (but did not ask him if this was so).[14] With Sunday's deadline approaching, Dacre thought it odd that nobody at the *Sunday Times* had rung to discuss the situation with him, but he did not take the trouble to pick up the telephone himself. It was certainly a muddle.

It was after 7 p.m. when the sound of a telephone ringing could be heard deep within the Peterhouse Master's Lodge. It was Frank Giles on the line. The first edition of the *Sunday Times* had just gone to press and he was calling from his office where he was having a celebratory drink with his senior colleagues. He was not telephoning to check on Dacre's doubts – he did not realize they existed – but to ask if the eminent professor would like to pen an essay dismissing the sceptics for the following week's paper. Giles's glass-clinking audience froze as they realized the telephone conversation was moving from cheery salutation to staccato interjections and then to longer pauses. The colour drained from Giles's cheeks as he said, 'But these doubts aren't strong enough to make you do a complete 180-degree turn on that? . . . Oh. I see. You are doing a 180-degree turn.' Having been leaning against the wall, Brian MacArthur started sliding slowly down it.[15]

After a quick council of war, MacArthur got through to Murdoch in New York to seek his sanction to stop the presses. But the proprietor, having placed credence on Dacre's original endorsement, was cutting about his eleventh-hour doubts and told MacArthur to publish. He should have added 'and be damned'; 1.4 million copies rolled under the banner headline 'WORLD EXCLUSIVE: How the diaries of the Führer were found in an East German hayloft'.[16]

Frank Giles was distinctly unhappy to discover that neither Douglas-Home nor Colin Webb had passed on Dacre's doubts during the vital hours of Saturday 23 April. When he demanded an explanation, Douglas-Home claimed Dacre had been in such a 'condition of doubt and perturbation' that it had been difficult to gauge exactly what his opinion had been on that day. Giles later concluded:

Like Murdoch, he [Douglas-Home] too seems to have become so immersed in the business of wanting the diaries to be genuine that he was unable to face the possibility that they were not. The rub for me that fateful Saturday was that it was I and the *Sunday Times*, not

Douglas-Home and *The Times*, who had to pay the price for his clouded judgment.[17]

If Dacre's doubts had made an impression upon Douglas-Home, he was carefully concealing it under his patrician demeanour. On the Sunday evening, Robert Fisk went off to a press award dinner at the Savoy accompanied by his Finnish girlfriend, an air hostess with SAS Airlines. A fluent German speaker, she had been reading the diary extracts in the morning paper and was adamant that they were forgeries – Hitler simply did not express himself in the phraseology used, she insisted. The original German was all wrong. As the dinner got underway, Douglas-Home arrived wearing a jacket that he claimed had once belonged to the Kaiser. He pulled up a chair and sat down next to Fisk and his girlfriend. She assured him that he was making a big mistake and that the diaries were forgeries. The editor of *The Times* brushed aside the air hostess's analysis 'no, no I can tell you, they *smell* of history,' he repeated.[18]

Meanwhile, while the public waded through page after page of *Sunday Times* analysis and brief extracts of Hitler's views on Hess, Chamberlain, Himmler and others, Dacre caught a flight to Hamburg accompanied by Paul Eddy, Anthony Terry and Brian MacArthur, who would act as minders and would ensure that if he had anything to denounce in public he should save it for the front page of the following week's *Sunday Times*. Dacre was to dine with the *Stern* executives in the evening as their guest of honour. But he went first to see Gerd Heidemann. When the reporter refused to disclose the identity of the Wehrmacht officer in whose possession the diaries had supposedly rested for the past thirty-eight years, Dacre turned the conversation into an interrogation that ended with Heidemann storming out. Over dinner, Dacre was astonished to discover that Peter Koch claimed not to know the handler's identity either. Could these methodical Germans really have taken so much on trust? It was one thing not to disclose one's sources, quite another not to know who the sources were in the first place. Dacre was taken aback, but did not reveal his hand to his hosts. Afterwards, he came across Sir Nicholas Henderson (Britain's former Ambassador to Bonn and Washington) in the hotel bar. 'Nico' offered an old friend some advice – the diaries were clearly fake and the sooner he denounced them publicly the better. Dacre decided to sleep on it.[19]

The next morning, *Stern*'s press conference commenced in hubristic triumph. There was an introductory film presentation then the sixty volumes of diaries were theatrically brought in procession towards the front of the hall. Flashlights blazed away. Twenty-seven television crews jostled for space alongside swarms of newspaper journalists. It was the very definition of a world 'media circus'. Then the platform party introduced Dacre to the press – and the smooth operation began to fall apart. As the *Stern* management listened with mounting horror, he confessed he had been misled about the diaries having been positively traced all the way back to the plane crash. *Stern* should have scented trouble – of which Brian MacArthur and Michael Binyon had a sniff – by the fact that the press conference's start had been delayed because of Dacre's late appearance (he had initially locked himself in his hotel room and had refused to come out).[20] Douglas-Home had telephoned him that morning and forcefully advised him that 'so long as there was any chance that the diaries might prove genuine' he should not formally denounce their authenticity.[21] In consequence, he veered between restating 'the provisional conclusion that these documents are genuine' and raising the possibility that their authenticity was 'shaky', adding, 'As a historian, I regret that the normal method of historical verification has, perhaps necessarily, been to some extent sacrificed to the requirements of a journalistic scoop.' This fired the starter gun for a descent into anarchy. From the floor, David Irving denounced the diaries. The *Stern* organizers tried to switch off his microphone. Furiously scribbling down the scene for *The Times* from his vantage point in the hall, Binyon observed that, 'As a throng of cameramen and reporters pressed round Mr Irving, a fight broke out when *Stern*'s staff tried to prevent Mr Irving giving a rival press conference in the same room. The hubbub lasted for some time.'[22]

The Times was now moving in tandem with Lord Dacre – which is to say that it was back-pedalling fast. It seemed odd that *Stern* had deployed *The Times*'s expert at their press conference. Where was *their* reputable historian? Who was *their* authenticator? *The Times* started giving equal coverage to both sides of the debate. The letters' page began to fill up. Immanuel Jakobovits, the Chief Rabbi, wrote to express his disgust at the 'mercenary exploitation' which would allow Hitler to justify his crimes, adding, 'In the name of decency, morality and truth, I call upon men of good will everywhere to prevent this proposed affront to the past and depraved threat to the future.' Those less persuaded that they were about to hear Fascism's authentic voice took a more whimsical view. Pointing to the fact the diaries comprised sixty identically bound volumes, one correspondent wondered if Hitler had benefited from a 'large order' discount when making his purchase, while another asked whether there was no identifiable fingerprint on any of the pages. Michael Holroyd wanted to know what efforts *Stern* had made to seek out 'Herr Hitler's copyright holders to obtain their permission to publish and negotiate fees?'.[23]

It would have taken only three days for *Stern* to get the paper and ink of the diaries comprehensively tested. Instead, only half-hearted attempts at verification had been made. The failure to undertake a proper scientific examination was explained away on the grounds that doing so risked news of the diaries' existence leaking out and ruining the scoop. But once the story was in the public domain the requests to undertake proper testing could not be refused. On 6 May, the results came in. There were factual errors and a handwriting expert demonstrated inconsistencies with the real Hitler's style. But what proved conclusive was the discovery that the paper used for the diaries contained a whitener created in 1955 while the ink had been applied within the past two years. Thus the diaries were incontrovertibly fraudulent. As soon as the news reached London, News International issued a press release that stated, 'The *Sunday Times* accepts the report of the German archivists' and would, consequently, be dropping its serialization. There was no mention of *The Times*'s original role and press rivals chose to focus on the *Sunday Times* where Frank Giles had gone off on holiday leaving Hugo Young to pen a much derided note of 'sincere apology' to 'our readers'. Not unnaturally, rival newspapers had great fun at the *Sunday Times*'s expense, many concluding that it was the price paid for being owned by the likes of Rupert Murdoch. The proprietor himself showed extraordinary sang-froid about the whole matter. Charles Wilson was with him when the news was brought to him that the diaries had been confirmed as forgeries. Murdoch digested the news and paused, lost in thought. There was absolute silence. After a moment he made his only comment. 'Well,' he mused, 'you can't win them all.'[24]

The Times reported with measured detachment the news of the forgery on its front page but no leading article ever appeared on the subject. When Robert Harris's compelling book on the subject, *Selling Hitler*, was published in 1986, the *Times Literary Supplement* was the only News International publication to review it (Professor Norman Stone considering it 'a very funny story . . . very well told'). Harris's account was subsequently made into a television series with Alan Bennett playing Lord Dacre and, yet more improbably, Barry Humphries swapping the persona of the Melbourne society housewife Dame Edna Everage for Rupert Murdoch.

In their defence, Times Newspapers and Lord Dacre could point to the extent to which the supposedly reputable *Stern* had deceived them. The tone of certainty expressed in *The Times* on 23 April rested not only on Dacre's overhasty pronouncement but on the claims by *Stern* that 'it had conducted chemical analyses of the paper and ink' that showed them to be appropriate to the period. Without this false assurance, neither Dacre, Douglas-Home nor Murdoch might have been quite so quick to part with their reputations and their money. Nonetheless, at a personal level, it was Dacre who lost most from the episode. He had recanted his authentication days before the scientific tests had determined the diaries' fate. By contrast, David Irving, who had done much to improve his intellectual standing by initially denouncing the hoax had, by then, come round to supporting the diaries authenticity, possibly because they did not implicate the Führer closely in the Holocaust. Irving, however, was a maverick with recognized extremist views. It was Dacre who had a valuable reputation to lose. In the immediate aftermath he claimed to feel 'like an Arabian adulterer, pinioned in the sand and awaiting the next, perhaps fatal, volley of stones'. He tried not to cast the blame elsewhere, later telling Graham Turner, 'I wanted to protect Douglas-Home and, in any case, it would have been undignified. I assumed that the other people involved would admit their errors.' To his disappointment he found that "the only person who behaved quite well in it all was Rupert – he did send me a genuine, if private, letter accepting part of the blame'.[25]

In accepting the request to look at the diaries, Dacre had sought to do *The Times* a favour, an act of charity that rebounded against him. His reputation was battered – to the ill-disguised merriment of much of his academic peer group. After he retired from Peterhouse, waspish under-graduates there gathered once a term to commemorate his Mastership by founding a dining club called 'The Authenticators'. Some dons joined in as guests. Given his various and distinguished career it was a needlessly ungracious final act when *The Times* announced his death on 27 January 2003 under the page two headline 'Hitler diary hoax victim Lord Dacre dies at 89'.[26] It was not how he would have wished to have been re-membered, especially from a newspaper upon whose board he had dili-gently sat between 1974 and 1988. Yet, those at Gray's Inn Road had grounds for feeling he had landed them in a huge mess. However rushed he may have felt in being asked for an opinion, there was no need for him to express such certainty on the basis of only an afternoon looking at manuscripts he could scarcely read. Sadly, because of this he did end up performing the role of useful scapegoat, thereby deflecting criticism from *The Times*'s editorial decision making.

Gerd Heidemann protested he did not realize the diaries were fakes. Nonetheless, he was sentenced to four years and eight months in prison for embezzling a large share of the money *Stern* had paid out through him to what they believed was the diaries' custodian. The custodian was the forger, Konrad Kujau, who appeared to enjoy the attention accorded him in the courthouse and, between sessions, found time to joke with Michael Binyon: suggesting that if he'd known earlier the Bonn correspondent was from *The Times*, he would have knocked off some forged diaries especially for the paper. He was sentenced to four years and six months but released after serving three years. Seeking to build upon his minor celebrity status, he ran (unsuccessfully) to succeed Manfred Rommel, the son of Hitler's field marshal, as Mayor of Stuttgart. He subsequently paid for medical treatment by copying great works of art in a Hitlerian style and opened a gallery of his own derivative work. He died in 2000.

In more than thirty years working at *The Times*, Tim Austin regarded the Hitler diaries as the paper's most embarrassing episode.[27] Still philosophical about the debacle twenty years later, Murdoch felt rather that 'the result was a black eye for me. People concentrated on me rather than Charlie' but that 'It taught us all to be a lot more cautious . . . You learn from these mistakes.'[28] Indeed, to the wider public, with Lord Dacre, Rupert Murdoch and the *Sunday Times* taking most of the flak, *The Times* escaped with little more than flesh wounds, its initial role largely forgotten. But even the *Sunday Times* did not suffer commercially: its circulation was 20,000 higher after the fiasco than it had been before. And as for Murdoch, he got his money back.

III

Book reviews had appeared in *The Times* since its earliest issues (albeit sporadically), but the creation of a separately sold *Times Literary Supplement* in 1914 encouraged the daily paper to cease providing proper competition. It was not until 1955 that *The Times* decided to take the task seriously again with the establishment of a regular books page. From then on, book reviews came to be regarded as every bit as essential a component of the paper as the output of the theatre critics. There was no formal collaboration between *The Times* and the editorially autonomous *TLS*, but the latter's interest in fiction, poetry and other more literary works certainly encouraged *The Times* towards focusing upon non-fiction and, in particular, biography, politics and history. Murdoch's purchase of Times Newspapers in 1981 gave him not only *The Times* and the *TLS* but also a paper whose book reviews had become extremely well regarded – the *Sunday Times*. This was a formidable combination. In the dailies market during the 1970s, only the *FT* was recognized as the serious competitor to *The Times* for the quality of its book reviewing.

During the 1980s, *The Times*'s literary editor was Philip Howard. His father, Peter Howard, had become the youngest man to captain the England rugby team in 1931 (despite the fact he had been born with a joined foot and knee and spent his childhood wearing a leg iron that prevented him playing contact sport) who subsequently became one of Beaverbrook's highest paid journalists. He was also a novelist and co-wrote, with Michael Foot and Frank Owen, *Guilty Men*, the searing indictment on Neville Chamberlain's Government. He subsequently led the Moral Rearmament Movement. When he died in 1965, seventeen heads of state or prime ministers sent condolences. Philip Howard's mother was the former Doris Metaxa, the 1932 Wimbledon women's doubles champion. An Old Etonian and Classics graduate of Trinity College, Oxford, who had served with the Black Watch during his National Service, Philip Howard had been at the paper since 1964 having been offered a job on the condition he proved his *Times* loyalty by accepting a pay cut from what he had received from his previous employer, the *Glasgow Herald*. He subsequently demonstrated himself to be not only a fine home news reporter but also a stylist of great élan whose ruminations on the English language proved to be a hugely enjoyed peculiarity of *The Times*.

The emerging vogue for hiring 'celebrity reviewers' was resisted at *The Times* during the 1980s. Instead, as literary editor, Howard worked with a chief reviewer who was expected to pen the main article each week. In the early 1980s, the paper was able to benefit from the wide range of Michael Ratcliffe (one of Howard's predecessors as literary editor) in this role. Chief reviewer had been a staff position and, as such, was much envied but when Ratcliffe left the paper in 1982, Howard found a worthy replacement in the philosopher and President of Trinity College, Oxford, Anthony Quinton. The author of *Utilitarian Ethics* and *The Politics of Imperfection*, Lord Quinton was also a master of the reviewing art (save for one mistakenly, well-intentioned decision to show his review on a Schopenhauer book to its author prior to publication – resulting in a lawyer's letter attempting to block it). But the demands of a weekly book review eventually proved too great a restriction for someone with Quinton's buzy diary. In 1984, Howard appointed a successor in James Fenton. From his early twenties, Fenton had thrown himself into the literary and journalistic world, maintaining an impressive output in both and later becoming Professor of Poetry at Oxford. His reviews were incisive and often tart. On one occasion he dismissed a book on Renaissance festivals by Roy Strong, the V&A's director and prolific writer on courtly and horticultural themes, as having been breathlessly written 'in a tone of voice that does rather too often remind us of Alan Whicker'.[29] When Fenton escaped to the Philippines and the *Independent*, the distinguished writer and biographer Peter Ackroyd admirably filled his shoes.

During the 1980s, several of Britain's most famous independent publishers were merged and swallowed up into larger conglomerates. Many of the new parent companies were American. To the fore in this respect were Random House and Murdoch's own HarperCollins (a merger of the American Harper & Row with the Scottish Collins). Big was also thought to be beautiful in the high street where new bookshop chains such as Waterstones and Dillons spread across the country. Opinion divided between those who welcomed the money these innovations brought into publishing and bookselling and those who believed such commercialism contaminated the purity of the product. What was undoubtedly true was that quantity increased noticeably, with more books published than ever before. It remained the task of *The Times* books page to sift through for the quality. In this quest, Philip Howard stood determinedly against the subtle bullying of the book industry. He had little time for best-seller lists. He thought they could be easily manipulated by the strategies of publishing houses and, in any case, were usually dominated by the sort of cookery books, lifestyle manuals and showbiz memoirs that rarely made much impact on the paper's literary pages. He successfully resisted Harold Evans's suggestion that a weekly list should appear. Perhaps more importantly, Howard did not share the Thatcherite zeal increasingly animating *The Times*'s more forthright columnists and leader writers as the decade progressed. At one stage, he had to make a spirited stand to stop Douglas-Home shoe-horning Woodrow Wyatt, a long-standing friend of Murdoch and confidant of the Prime Minister, into the post of chief reviewer. A compromise was reached that allowed Wyatt to review regularly but not to the exclusion of the lit. ed.'s preferred choices. Indeed, wherever possible, Howard encouraged a counter-culture of alternative voices on the books page. He also fostered younger writers of promise. Among the literary figures of note who reviewed frequently were Richard Holmes, Victoria Glendinning, Isabel Raphael and later, Sabine Durrant and Sarah Edworthy. Without diminishing the interest in history and biography, every effort was made to ensure new fiction received sufficient coverage, despite the difficulty of spotting which first-time novelists were worthy of attention. But the popular end of the market was not snubbed. Harry Keating, Tim Heald and Marcel Berlins regularly harvested the high-yielding crops of crime and thrillers in a quick and incisive round-up format.

While Howard shouldered the responsibilities of the books pages throughout the 1980s, Irving Wardle did likewise for the theatre reviews, bringing down the curtain on thirty-four years since he started writing for *The Times* (and as chief drama critic since 1963) in December 1989. Rescued from 'a life of skivvying' in a hotel by John Lawrence (arts editor of *The Times*, 1950–69),[30] the Wadham-educated Wardle had spent much of his subsequent career as an enthusiastic supporter of the new generation of playwrights, most famously John Osborne, who challenged what they saw as a staid theatrical Establishment. Wardle looked with favour upon their attempts to say on stage what had formally been mumbled in private. Many of the leading directors of the sixties and seventies were fading away during the eighties and the acting giants of the previous generation – Olivier, Redgrave, Richardson, Gielgud – died or retired. Some promising ventures, like Jonathan Miller's arrival as artistic director at the Old Vic, were stillborn, with Miller departing after a season. However, the emergence of Tom Stoppard, Alan Bennett and Peter Nichols as writers of the first rank was more positive, as was the staging of plays by Racine and Corneille, dramatists whose work had previously been thought unadaptable in English. Other foreign influences came from the Japanese director Yukio Ninagawa and the Canadian Robert Le Page. The latter's *Trilogy of the Dragon* encouraged comparisons with the celebrated directorial debut of Peter Brook.

A major development was the increasing tendency towards theatre of fact, in which plays were inspired or influenced by real lives – such as the death of Steve Biko or T. S. Eliot's first marriage as interpreted in Michael Hastings's *Tom and Viv*. In this respect even Murdoch and *The Times* provided inspiration (of a sort) for David Hare and Howard Brenton whose *Pravda* Wardle bravely gave a broadly favourable review.[31] His critical impressions were not always those of the broader public. Reviewing Trevor Nunn's direction of Andrew Lloyd Webber's *Cats* when it opened, Wardle felt it 'never succeeds in taking fire into an organic work' and deprecated 'an extremely sickly poem called "Memory" (the only textual departure from Eliot) – an attempt to press the poems into the service of Mr Nunn's warm-hearted style of community theatre'.[32] *Cats* closed in London twenty-one years later by which time it was the second highest-grossing musical of all time (after Lloyd Webber's *Phantom of the Opera*). 'Memory' had received more than two million airplays on US radio stations by 1998 alone.[33] Wardle was a fair-minded critic. This was not always the same as being a chronicler of popular tastes.

Between 1983 and 1985 the deputy theatre critic, Anthony Masters, assisted Wardle. By any measure, Masters was a brilliant young man. He had been Senior Scholar at Winchester and a Scholar at King's College, Cambridge, going down with a First in Classics. For *The Times*, he wrote reviews with the wit, enthusiasm and assurance of youth. He appeared to have a brilliant future ahead of him. On the night of 2 January 1985 he filed a review of Peter Coe's adaptation of *Great Expectations* at the Old Vic. The play had gone on for four hours and Masters ended his piece: 'I sympathized with the father I overheard telling his son, "Theatrical performances are usually shorter than this." At least, they usually seem so.'[34] These proved to be Masters's last words for the next day he was found dead at his home. He was thirty-six. Even for the most accomplished craftsmen, writing reviews to a nightly deadline was an immensely demanding task. Masters had found it difficult getting to sleep after he had filed and had started taking medication to help him drift off. The late running of *Great Expectations* had created extra pressure, leaving him only half an hour to write his review. Getting to sleep afterwards would be a great difficulty. The assumption was that he took a greater dose than usual – one from which he never awoke.

David Robinson was *The Times*'s film critic from 1975 to 1990. During the 1970s, the British film industry had all but collapsed. In 1980 a mere thirty-two native feature films were produced. And then, suddenly, a fight back commenced. On its release in 1981, Robinson identified *Chariots of Fire* as 'in most respects the kind of picture for which we have been looking in British cinema in vain for many years' although he found fault with aspects of it, especially the 'rather out-modish' slow-motion shots of Eric Liddell running with his head flung back. This, in fact, proved to be one of the abiding images from British film making in the eighties. It was also the first British film since 1968 to win the Academy Award for Best Picture, giving false hope to those who shared the aspirations of its scriptwriter, Colin Welland, who collected his Oscar with the fateful boast, 'The British are coming!' For a moment it looked possible. *Gandhi* and *The Killing*

Fields followed successfully in the wake. *Withnail & I* would, over time, attain cult status. The creation of Channel 4, with its own film production arm, promised and delivered much. By 1985, British feature film production had risen to eighty releases. But the triumphs were soon shown to be sporadic, with the achievements usually resting more on British acting talent, only sometimes on production or direction and rarely on home funding. One such example came in 1986, when Robinson rightly identified the sumptuous Merchant–Ivory film *A Room With a View* as a 'masterpiece'.[35] At a time when other European governments were lavishing funds on their film industries, the British Government decided to scrap the capital allowance tax relief that allowed for the writing off of production deficits. Almost immediately investment in the British film industry dried up, falling from £300 million in 1985 to £64.5 million in 1989. Meanwhile, Hollywood cleaned up at the box office with a succession of comic or adventure blockbusters (with multiple sequels) industrially churned out for the teenage market. Robinson struggled to conceal his boredom with so many of the decade's major commercial hits – an output that could be summed up by the success of *Friday the 13th (Part 8)*.

On the small screen, Channel 4's launch in November 1982 was the major event in British broadcasting. The first national terrestrial channel since BBC 2 eighteen years earlier, Channel 4's birth was a precarious one. It arrived in the midst of an advertising recession and an industrial dispute that ensured a screen card rather than commercials filled many of the breaks between its programmes. Nonetheless, in an eve-of-launch preview in *The Times*, the new channel's chief executive, Jeremy Isaacs, brimmed with high-minded enthusiasm, assuring Peter Lennon that 'Channel 4 is the last Reithean Channel! Reithean!' On the evidence of the first day's broadcasts – a mixture of quiz shows, soap operas, comedy and a drama about a mentally ill patient – *The Times*'s television critic, Peter Ackroyd, believed it would prove to be 'the SDP of television, mouthing the rhetoric of fashion or of commitment while in fact offering approximately the same material as the other three channels' before settling down 'perhaps as a slightly down-market BBC 2 (if BBC 2 is not itself already the down-market BBC 2)'.[36]

In trumpeting the public service role of Channel 4, Isaacs claimed 'we have six years while the cable people are still digging holes in the ground to impose ourselves'. But a greater challenge would emerge more quickly from satellite television. This was to be another of Murdoch's great gambles. Months of hostile press speculation that Murdoch was orchestrating *The*

Times's criticism of aspects of the BBC and the future of its licence fee in order to promote his Sky satellite company came to a head in a speech by Alasdair Milne, the BBC's director-general. Before an audience of the TV and Radio Industries Club in January 1985, he posed the question: 'Who is the more likely to serve the public interest, the BBC or *The Times*, whose recommendations if acted upon would have the practical effect of enabling its owner Rupert Murdoch to acquire some of the most valuable broadcasting action in the UK?' Douglas-Home was not amused by this apparent slur on his editorial independence and organized a meeting with Milne to repudiate his imputations. He also asked the independent national directors of Times Newspapers to investigate Milne's claims.[37] When the directors asked Milne for a statement he backtracked, admitting, 'I do not of course have the concrete evidence for which you ask because I do not work for *The Times*. The inference I drew from the paper's behaviour over the BBC seemed a reasonable one, and I was not alone in drawing it. But the Editor's explanation was sufficient to lay my fears to rest.' With editor and proprietor both denying collusion, the independent directors had little option but to conclude that there was no evidence to support Milne's innuendo.[38] Hostile entities were less convinced. When the NUJ made its submission to the Peacock Inquiry into the BBC's future funding, it drew attention to the *The Times*'s attacks on the BBC and stated, 'we find it hard to believe, despite Mr Murdoch's denials, that this attitude is unconnected with his own commercial interests in broadcasting'.[39]

The Times's problem throughout the period of its ownership by Rupert Murdoch was that few people outside the paper's editorial office appeared to believe the proprietor honoured his pledges not to interfere in its editorial policy. Murdoch backed Margaret Thatcher, took a tough stance against the Soviet Union and resented the restrictive practices of both left-leaning trade unions and professional vested interests. That this was also *The Times*'s general editorial line appeared suspicious. The paper's outlook was, in reality, the world view of Charles Douglas-Home and those with whom he surrounded himself. Unlike Evans, plucked to edit from outside the paper by Murdoch, Douglas-Home had become editor primarily because he enjoyed the confidence of the overwhelming majority of the newspaper's senior staff. He was very far from being parachuted in by the proprietor. Indeed, no editor in the first twenty years of News International's ownership of *The Times* had grounds for feeling as secure in his post and unconcerned about annoying the proprietor as the socially self-assured Douglas-Home. As we shall see later, it was his successors who would have greater difficulty convincing sceptics that any favourable reference to a programme that appeared on Sky or – when Murdoch's interests spread to Asia – any comment that fell short of ringing condemnation of the Chinese government was not directly, or indirectly, a consequence of the proprietor's views and business interests.

A secondary charge was that if Murdoch did not interfere directly in the editorial line of the newspaper it was because, with the right-wing Douglas-Home in the chair, he did not need to do so. Certainly there was little to cause the proprietor tremendous offence in the leader column where a barrage was kept up not only against the Soviet Union but also against what the Prime Minister infamously referred to as 'the enemy within' – militant trade unions. There was much less Thatcherite zeal among the paper's reporters. The labour editor was Paul Routledge, a straight-talking Yorkshireman and son of a railway worker who had come to *The Times* in 1971 via grammar school, Nottingham University and the *Sheffield Telegraph*. A man of firm socialist convictions, he was acknowledged as one of the journalists with the best sources on the paper. Within Gray's Inn Road, he had won widespread respect not only for the professionalism of his work but also for his steadfastness as father of the NUJ chapel (a large petition was signed forlornly trying to dissuade him from resigning this post following an incident in which he had responded to goading that he was a pacifist by punching his accuser, Jake Eccelestone, in the face). The miners' strike of 1984–5 proved to be an exceptionally busy time for him, for he was not a reporter who believed a story could be investigated from the monastic introspection of his office desk. Instead, he embarked on a gruelling year trailing round the disputes' battlefields and, in making the most of his familiarity with the National Union of Mineworkers leaders, gaining a level of access to the key players that was the envy of rival newspapers. Although the two men were poles apart politically, Douglas-Home had little option but to give Routledge grudging respect. Indeed, Routledge had previously taken him down a coalmine so that he might get a feel for what the miner's life was like (Douglas-Home appeared to relish the occasion, but was noticeably quiet when Routledge proceeded to take him for a drink in a miners' social club). Yet, despite the excellence of Routledge's coverage of the year long dispute, the editor allowed his ideological suspicions to rise to the surface, on one occasion writing Routledge an insulting letter implying that he was not investigating stories relating to the NUM closely enough. The labour editor certainly felt the pressure of working for a paper whose political direction he did not share but he refused to alter the tenor of his reporting. In any case, whatever his differences with the paper's political comment, he did not care for the middle class student revolutionaries posturing in the *Guardian*. Importantly, his copy for *The Times* during the miners' strike was never spiked or fundamentally altered for political purposes.[40]

In fact, while Routledge was sympathetic to the miners' plight and respected hard-left union leaders like the Scottish Communist Mick McGahey, he had little time for Arthur Scargill who he regarded as a self-serving egoist. When an article in the *Daily Express* identified Routledge as one of Scargill's 'tried and tested cronies' who 'flit, almost unnoticed, in and out of the union's Sheffield headquarters, giving their advice and help' and 'flattering and applauding him', both Routledge and *The Times* sued. Not only did the article wrongly state that he was ghost writing the NUM leader's autobiography, it implied he was misusing his position at *The Times* to 'keep the Scargill show on the road'. The *Express* ended up printing an unqualified apology and writing Routledge a cheque (some of the proceeds of which eventually found its way to miners' causes).[41]

If any one publication did most to undermine the belief that *The Times* was an editorially independent newspaper, it was Harold Evans's account of his period in Gray's Inn Road, *Good Times, Bad Times*. Published in late 1983, a year and a half after its author's sacking, it was precisely the ammunition Murdoch's critics sought. There were those who thought it inappropriate that Evans should rush into print against a man who had just given him what all agreed was a very generous pay-off.[42] But given the gravity of the book's most important claim – that Murdoch had wielded the knife because Evans would not bow to his ways, even involving the Prime Minister in a ruse to get Evans an alternative job at the Sports Council – there was no shortage of interested readers. It was launched to a fanfare of publishing hype – embargoes, a press conference and a largely supportive one-hour Channel 4 programme, *Bad Times at The Times*, presented by Melvyn Bragg. It led to demands in the House of Commons for a debate on whether the terms on which Murdoch had bought the paper had been breached. Many were happy to accept it as the authoritative account of the fall of Britain's most celebrated editor and, with him, the integrity of an illustrious newspaper. In contrast, the protestations of those *Times* staff who did not recognize Evans's portrayal were easily dismissed as the self-serving statements of those still on the News International payroll. Aware that its failure to give Evans's book adequate publicity would lend credence to its claims, *The Times* did not stint on reporting the furore it created and *Good Times, Bad Times* was dispassionately reviewed on the books page by Gordon Newton. A distinguished former editor of the *FT*, Newton took the view that 'the life of an editor on a daily paper with its remorseless day by day fight against time is intolerable without the full support of staff and management' and – echoing what Murdoch himself had told staff from the first – the only sure way to a newspaper's independence was in its ability to return a profit. Newton concluded that, 'the story Evans tells is a sorry one from which few if any emerge with credit'.[43] It was certainly bad press for the paper.

It was not just the political slant of the paper that many believed was influenced by the owner. The launch of an upmarket form of bingo in *The Times* in 1984 provided further ammunition for those who felt Murdoch was having a cheapening influence on the newspaper's demeanour. The bingo war in the tabloid press had started in 1981 with the *Daily Star* and had been sufficiently successful to panic the *Sun* and its great rival, the *Daily Mirror*, into following suit. Before long, the *Daily Express* and the *Daily Mail* had entered the fray. Three years later the bingo war was renewed with added ferocity, each of the tabloids promising regular £1 million winners. Not all could prosper in a circulation battle determined by competitive prize money inflation and Murdoch's *Sun* triumphed over the *Mirror*. It seemed a propitious moment for his other most famous title to be the first broadsheet to try something similar.

The principal objective was, of course, to boost circulation, but *The Times* risked undermining its reputation by offering bingo cards wedged between Bernard Levin and business news. For the gimmick to work, it had to be portrayed as something more highbrow. In the previous three years, various half-baked ideas had been floated. Harold Evans had passed onto Murdoch a number of these, including the outline for a competition in which readers would send in their opinions on various subjects together with a £1 fee that went into a kitty payable to the reader 'who, on the same form, has most nearly forecast what British public opinion thinks. The ingenious point of this is that one gets an opinion poll for free and a competition at the same time.' The ingenious point was lost on the proprietor. Apart from anything else, Murdoch 'felt uneasy about *The Times* taking money from readers in a competition'.[44] Evans, however, had another idea to pass on. In July 1981 he wrote to Murdoch to tell him that a solicitor friend who acted for the football pools 'suggests that we run an investment pool in *The Times* business news in which we ask people to predict the performance of various shares over the week'. By October, a putative and decidedly non-bingo-style title for the game had been devised – 'portfolio'. But with the crisis in Gray's Inn Road intensifying, the idea was put aside. It was not until the summer of 1984 that the name was resurrected for what would be a different share price-based competition. By then, Britain's improving economy and rising stock exchange index ensured it suddenly appeared to be cleverly in tune with the national *Zeitgeist*.

Portfolio was launched on 25 June 1984. Readers were issued with a game card with eight numbers on it, the idea being to match the numbers with the share movements of a list of forty companies listed on *The Times*'s prices page. Prizes of £2000 would be given away, with a £20,000 bonus on Saturday to lift sales on the day of the week when circulation was tradition-ally at its lowest. There was no certainty that the concept would appeal to readers, or, more importantly, potential readers. The paper's executives were nervous and it was launched only on a thirteen-week trial basis. Some £1.5 million was invested. Publicity and promotion were paramount. Television advertisements were broadcast featuring a pinstripe-suited and bowler-hatted Mel Smith, one of the comedians on the popular *Not The Nine O'Clock News* sketch show. Two million game cards, designed and shaped to look like a credit card, were distributed. The *Sunday Times* for the day before the game's launch carried extensive advertising together with the first game cards in an envelope, ensuring that the majority of *Sunday Times* readers who did not normally read *The Times* were directly targeted. Cash prizes for the newsagents who supplied the winners encouraged shop-keepers to push Portfolio upon their customers.[45]

The unease among *Times* executives over whether it would capture the public's imagination was matched by disquiet among journalists over the very idea of running such a gimmick. Following a meeting of the NUJ chapel, it was decreed that no journalist was prepared to write any 'news item' promoting it. In the event, the first winner proved suitably news-worthy and ideal for the paper's attempts to stay 'upmarket': Erik Feldman, a seventeen-year-old at Harrow School. The front page showed him being held aloft by fellow pupils waving their boaters and the accompanying (unattributed) article informed readers that *The Times* was the most read newspaper among current Harrovians.[46] This was exactly the sort of puff dressed up as news that many sceptical journalists feared.

Much of the rest of Fleet Street reacted to *The Times*'s descent into City bingo with a mixture of amusement and *faux* head shaking that a once great newspaper had sunk so low. 'It is too painful even to discuss what has become of "The Thunderer"' opined the *Daily Mail*. 'Let's just say it's a good top people's comic.' With a little more mirth, the *Observer* drew attention to *The Times*'s attempts to dress up the game as if it was something respectable and wondered when the paper would be launching a 'Spot the Grouse' competition or a new page three 'Legal Lovelies' (complete with their briefs, of course). In fact, *The Times* had rather more form in the area of promotional gimmickry that those who put it all down to the supposedly populist tastes of the Australian owner realized. Throughout the 1970s, the newspaper had dreamed up competitions inadequately masked by an embarrassing veneer of literary pretence: in 1970 it was 'Rhyme for *The Times*'; in 1972 there was a competition to write a Christmas carol that mentioned six of the advertisers featured in the paper's festive gift guide (the commercialization of Christmas came early that year) and, most contrived of all, a 'teaser' to nominate an appropriate present for three members of the March family in *Little Women* while selecting a quotation from either *Bartlett's Familiar Quotations* or the *Oxford Dictionary of Quotations* that best summed up the choices. Given this pedigree, Portfolio appeared refreshingly honest.

Perhaps surprisingly, the two newspapers that refrained from a full-scale assault on Portfolio were *The Times*'s principal rivals, the *Guardian* and the *Daily Telegraph*. They were perhaps conscious of the danger of giving it publicity and aware of the possibility that, if it worked, they might end up having to try something similar themselves. *The Times* had been closing its circulation gap with the *Guardian* over the course of the past two years. Yet *Guardian* readers did not desert in droves in order to play a bowler-hat version of bingo and sales of the left-leaning paper were dented by only seven thousand in the first six months after Portfolio's launch.[47] Where the game did help *The Times* gain ground was against the market-leading *Daily Telegraph*. This emphasized a trend that was already apparent before the promotion was launched. Indeed, *The Times* had been slowly gaining ground almost continuously since Murdoch had bought the paper and in the summer of 1983 had benefited from a £1.5 million television advertising campaign. In the year to June 1984 (before the launch of Portfolio), *The Times*'s circulation rose 13 per cent against a broadsheet average of 3 per cent. This surge was well timed to take advantage of the improving economic health of the country. Net advertising revenue was up 31 per cent with display advertising volume increasing by more than a third. Times Newspapers was still trading at a post-tax loss but the gap was closing and, for once, it was partly due to improved finances at *The Times*.[48]

The Times's average daily sale in the six months before Portfolio's launch was 381,000. In the first six months after the game commenced, the average soared by 20 per cent to 457,000. In the first half of 1985 it rose further to 480,000 where, despite the decision to continue with the game, it reached a plateau. This was an extraordinary achievement, particularly since it augmented what was already a period of sustained improvement in the paper's circulation. The result was that, three years after Douglas-Home assumed the editorship, the paper had gained nearly 180,000 extra sales, an increase of 60 per cent on the position he inherited in the autumn of 1981. Having been first overtaken by the *Guardian* in 1962, *The Times* was back in second place in Britain's broadsheet sales. Indeed, its circulation was now at the highest in its two hundred year history. Even those who disliked the manner in which the increase had, in part, been attained could not hold back from a measure of rejoicing at this simple fact. Nonetheless, there was room for caution: it remained to be seen whether 'Portfolio' was gaining readers for the paper who, impressed by the accompanying journalistic content, would convert permanently once the game was dropped. What, if there was one, was the paper's post-Portfolio strategy?

In planning ahead, *The Times* found itself asking a familiar question – should it push for more readers and challenge the *Daily Telegraph* for dominance of the broadsheet market, or refrain from stretching itself further and entrench itself around its core readership and its historic role as the journal for predominately London-based 'top people'. The latter option had the advantage that it would involve less change to the essential character of the newspaper and took account of the fact that the more lucrative advertisers preferred to target papers whose readers had the most disposable income. Unfortunately, from the 1960s onwards, this A-B social category had been targeted with increasing effectiveness by the *FT*. But there were problems too with the going for growth option. When Roy Thomson bought *The Times* in 1966 he had decided that the answer lay with expansion. Policies were enacted that ensured circulation duly rose from just over 250,000 in 1965 to 430,000 in 1969. Financially, the consequences were disastrous. Advertisers were not interested in targeting the nation's undergraduates. Thus, while the advertising rates failed to generate the anticipated return, higher promotion and production costs ensured that each 6d copy of *The Times* cost Thomson two shillings to produce. This was an unsustainable policy and the paper had to be allowed to fall back towards a third of a million daily sales. Unfortunately, this switch did not ensure a return to profitability either and Murdoch was not the sort of proprietor who was content to act merely as custodian of a crumbling monument. While acknowledging the problems Thomson had met when he attempted expansion, the paper, it seemed, had little option but to go once again for growth. Portfolio was the motor for this, but it was accompanied by a decision to attract additional custom by keeping the cover price low. In 1980, Thomson's sale prospectus for *The Times* had suggested that the paper would have a cover price of thirty-five pence by April 1983. Yet, News International opted to hold it at twenty pence until February 1985 when a modest three pence was added to the price.

The Douglas-Home *Times* sought to maintain traditional standards, but with sharper news focus, broader coverage and a popular game all for a below-market price. This was clearly a growth rather than retrenchment strategy. The problem was that Gray's Inn Road had hit a production ceiling set by technical difficulties and union restrictive practices that resulted in terrible distribution. Unless these issues could be sorted out, further expansion was impossible.

Ironically, it was a decision to modernize that had made matters worse. Since its first edition in 1785, *The Times*, like all successive papers, had been typeset in hot metal. In 1975, Thomson had taken the decision to move to computer-set photocomposition. Six years elapsed attempting to put that decision into practice. The process finally got underway during Harold Evans's editorship and, by the time Douglas-Home took the chair, almost all the paper was computer-set. On the night of 30 April 1982 and accompanied by the strains of a bagpipe, the last page ever produced by hot metal received its 'banging out'. *The Times* duly became the first national broadsheet to have an entirely electronic composing room. In this it was four years ahead of the *Telegraph* and *Guardian* and six years ahead of the *FT*.[49]

The results were dire. By the summer of 1982, ten thousand copies a day were being lost due to the problems photocomposition created. During May, not a single paper caught the 10.45 p.m. train to the Northeast while Scotland and Wales received an intermittent service and the sight of a copy in Belfast or Dublin before mid-morning became a unifying spectacle of rarity. On some days, the entire distribution for Europe (nine thousand copies a day) had to be cancelled due to the lateness of the papers leaving Gray's Inn Road. It was a shambles. The unions had retained their 'closed-shop' control over those who keyed in the text. Despite a full programme of training, many proved to be not overly dexterous. There was little attempt to accommodate management's requirements. One hundred and fifty-five typesetters were employed in the composing room and in August fifty-four of them were simultaneously on holiday.[50] Even at other times those that were at their keyboards were supposed to proofread what they were keying in, but they were getting so late in finishing that their only chance of meeting the deadline was to skip the checking stage. Hiring additional proofreaders to stand over the typesetters would have turned the 'new technology' into a yet more labour-intensive one. The result was that only a quarter of the paper was being properly proofread, with the law reports, leaders, court and features getting priority and the news pages coming last.[51] Bill O'Neill had to be recalled to sort it out. In the meantime, readers had to put up with an extraordinary number of spelling and other mistakes in the paper, all of which undermined its reputation for accuracy. If *The Times* was to be believed, the Chancellor of the Exchequer was someone called 'Sir Howe', the Prime Minister regularly 'mad a statement to the Commons' and her Education Secretary was a 'Fellow of All Saints'.[52] These embarrassing errors were compounded by ongoing production problems in the print hall that left some editions so far out of register that text and pictures were blurred. It was all a bit unfortunate for a paper being promoted with the advertising slogan, '*The Times* puts it all in focus'.[53]

The production problems had become so acute that Douglas-Home told his management colleagues he was frankly amazed the paper's circulation was going up and that the biggest problem was 'getting the paper out at all'.[54] Moving to computer-set composition certainly brought change to the print hall. The hot-metal process had involved printing from metal chases. It was now replaced by a more complicated system. Computer printouts of text were cut and pasted into place on a page-make-up board in the composing room. The pasted-up pages were photographed onto a sensitized polymer that was used to create a plastic mould. This was baked into a curved shape for casting the metal plates that were clamped onto the print rolls. By 1984, engineers in the print hall were ready to run plastic plates from the rollers. NGA members, however, refused and thus the plastic plates had to be cast back into metal for fixing onto the machines the NGA members operated. If *The Times* wanted to expand the print run, it had not only to sort out the technical problems but also to get its printers to work more productively. In 1983 the unions had finally agreed to print 420,000 copies per night. This total was usually reached well within time and sometimes within two hours of the end of the printers' night shift. But when management asked the unions to keep printing additional copies until their allotted shift was up (rather than merely going home early) the unions demanded more money. The boost Portfolio gave to circulation thus proved expensive, not only in terms of promotion and prize money but also in forcing up the cost of printing an additional half a million copies each night. Ultimately, it encouraged the search for an expanded and less expensive means of printing a bigger and supposedly better paper. This was the road that led inexorably to Fortress Wapping.

IV

Charles Douglas-Home was an editor in a hurry. In the year before he took the chair, he had been afflicted by increasingly severe back pains. At first, it was thought he had slipped a disc but within a year of taking the chair he was diagnosed terminally ill with bone cancer. For as long as it was possible to conceal it, he did not share the news with colleagues. It was not in his make-up to desert his post just because he was in his mid-forties. In 1985, *The Times* would celebrate its bicentenary and he wanted to be there to see it.

The editor was not without support. He had a close and loving family life. He was fortified by a strong Christian faith. Certainly, he was bolstered by capable senior colleagues and, as his health began visibly to degenerate, it was they who carried much of the burden of ensuring business as normal at Gray's Inn Road. The editor and, indeed, *The Times*, were fortunate to have two deputy editors, both appointed in 1982, of considerable ability.

Douglas-Home had learned an important lesson from his service in the Army: that an effective leader needed the close support of those who had experience of commanding in the field (in journalistic terms, those who had made the most of rising through the provincial presses to Fleet Street). The command structure he established around him reflected that belief. When, in the summer of 1982, John Grant announced his intention to retire, the time had come to appoint a new deputy. Fred Emery, the home and foreign executive editor, was obviously qualified in terms of ability but not necessarily of temperament. Despite his regard for Douglas-Home, Emery was not a natural deputy and disliked interference in what he believed to be his own domain. This occasionally manifested itself in the dispatch of somewhat angry and insulting memos to Douglas-Home on the subject.[55] Instead, Douglas-Home decided to look from outside Gray's Inn Road. He chose Colin Webb. By nature calm and even-tempered in a crisis, Webb was someone the editor could trust implicitly. Given the divided and half-mutinous staff Douglas-Home inherited in March 1982, this was important. Two years Douglas-Home's junior, the grammar school-educated Webb had started his journalistic career in his native Portsmouth before working his passage to Fleet Street via a short-service commission as a captain in the Royal Army Pay Corps. Douglas-Home had got to know him in 1969 when Webb ran *The Times*'s home news desk. In 1974 he had left to become editor of the *Cambridge Evening News* and it was from there that Douglas-Home enticed him back with the deputy editorship. Webb was perfect for the role and proved to have sound instincts matched by a steady hand. He saw his primary role as one of 'boundary maintenance', forming a protective ring round the editor.[56] Nonetheless, when Douglas-Home was away from Gray's Inn Road it was Webb who edited the paper.

Colin Webb's temperament was very different from that of Charles Wilson. Glimpsing Charles Wilson at work, the casual observer would not have been surprised to discover he was a major force in Fleet Street but it would certainly have come as a revelation to learn he was to be appointed the third most important journalist at *The Times*. In conversation, he had a deft command of expletives and an imaginative turn of phrase when deploying them. A strong Glaswegian accent gave his abuse an edge of menace that might have been absent if the same invective had been delivered in Liverpudlian, Cockney or Australian tones. Indeed, slight of frame but alert and intense in demeanour, there was much of the bantam-weight boxer about him. During the course of his journalistic career, many a desk, door or even, on one occasion, wall, would feel the full force of his punch as Wilson worked off his anger and frustration. *Private Eye* dubbed him 'Charlie Gorbals'. It was a name that stuck, sometimes with affection.

Chance played its part in Charles Wilson's appointment. Shortly after becoming editor, Douglas-Home had gone up to speak at an annual lunch of Scottish editors. Seated next to him on the top table was Wilson, the start-up editor of a new (and short-lived) Scottish newspaper, the *Sunday Standard*. The following day, Douglas-Home asked him to become executive editor of *The Times*. Given that Douglas-Home's acquaintance with Wilson rested on little more than an agreeable lunch, it was certainly an appointment based primarily upon instinct. As executive editor (soon translated into a second deputy editorship alongside Webb), Wilson was closely involved in selecting what went in the news pages. It involved getting up early in the morning, organizing the news desk, overseeing developments in the afternoon while Douglas-Home was cocooned in his office writing leading articles and spending the evening on the 'backbench', overseeing the pages being put together. It was a long day and a tough job. Douglas-Home was right to trust his instinct about Wilson's suitability for it.

Unlike Douglas-Home, Wilson's school of hard knocks had not been Eton and the Royal Scots Greys. His father, a supporter of the Independent Labour Party, had been a miner since the age of twelve but an injury in the 1930s forced him to leave the pits and to seek employment in a steelworks. After his first wife died, he married his late brother's widow. Charles Martin Wilson – or Charlie as he was better known – was born in 1935, two years before Charles – or Charlie – Cospatrick Douglas-Home. His parents had moved from their Glasgow tenement to a two-bedroom home in a council housing estate. Despite its poverty and industrial heart, Glasgow benefited from several good schools and Charlie did well at the local one, Eastbank Academy. All seemed set for a place at Glasgow University. Instead, everything changed one evening when, after a blazing row with his father, his mother walked out taking Charlie (in his last year at school) and his two brothers with her on the night train to London.

Although there was no journalistic background in the *Daily Express*-reading Wilson family, Charlie had read the papers on his schoolboy paper round, consummating a love affair with the press that never left him. With the prospect of proceeding directly to university removed, he lost no time in getting employment with the press down in London, becoming a copy-boy at the *People*. On reaching his eighteenth birthday, he did two years National Service in the Royal Marines where he won prizes for boxing. As soon as he was out, he got back into the press, switching to regional journalism, starting with the *Melton Mowbray Times* before moving to the *News Chronicle* as its West Country staffer. Bastion of liberal journalism, the *News Chronicle* was in its final year of publication and, when it was forced into a seemingly unlikely merger with the *Daily Mail* (in effect being subsumed by the right-wing paper), Wilson crossed over with it, becoming the *Mail*'s East Anglia staffer. From there, his career took off. He moved to London to become a reporter on the *Mail*'s news desk. By 1961, he was deputy editor during the paper's conversion from broadsheet to tabloid and thereafter switched to another horse in the Rothermere stable, the London *Evening News*. The chance to sit in an editor's chair took him back home to Glasgow when, in 1976, he became editor of the city's *Evening Times*. From the *Evening Times*, Wilson became editor of Outrams's other leading newspaper, the *Glasgow Herald*, and designed and launched the group's venture into weekend journalism, the *Sunday Standard*. Douglas-Home knew he was bringing back down to London a man who understood how newspapers worked.

Despite their different social backgrounds, Douglas-Home and Wilson got on well. The latter saw past the aristocratic pedigree of the editor, admiring instead 'an instinctive news man' who, prior to *The Times*, had honed his skills in the hard-working, hard-drinking environment of the *Daily Express* (initially in its Glasgow office before escaping to Fleet Street) in the early 1960s. Douglas-Home's informality and disinterest in ceremony appealed to Wilson. There was nothing 'effete' about the editor, Wilson concluded years later. He was 'a tough guy' who was not afraid to be ruthless in cutting away dead wood and taking the responsibility of wielding the axe to do it.[57]

The editorial triumvirate of Douglas-Home, Webb and Wilson saw the paper through a period that started with its very future in question and ended with its circulation doubled and its financial prospects more rosy than they had been for a quarter of a century. There was not a single university degree between these three most senior journalists at Britain's most venerable newspaper, but there were plenty of formal academic credentials among the other key lieutenants. The well-read Peter Stothard assumed responsibility for Op-Ed and leaders with George Brock as his deputy. Oxbridge degrees abounded among those who appeared on these pages. Arts coverage continued to be under the intelligent gaze of the opera specialist, John Higgins. Peter Strafford succeeded the long-serving Colin Watson as obituaries editor and Leon Pilpel continued to organize the letters page.

There was a question mark over the future of *The Times* Diary column. Its home had long been across the bottom of the Op-Ed page. In June 1982, the page's editor, Peter Stothard, wanted to make room for more columnists. Henceforth, ads would no longer be permitted there and Stothard felt the Diary could be safely banished too. Yet no one could agree where, if not on the Op-Ed page, the column should appear. It certainly did not look like a worthy squatter on a serious news page and *The Times* in 1982 did not think it had a soft news page.[58] However, the plot to shunt the Diary into obscurity was very effectively spiked by its editor, Robin Young, who alerted readers to the threat of it being moved to a less august berth. The appeal reaped the desired effect – three hundred letters demanding that it stay put.[59] So it remained on the Op-Ed page, albeit recast as a vertical single column on the left edge, rather than languidly occupying the bottom third, 'the basement', of the page horizontally.

Compiling the Diary was always a delicate task. Adopting a reverential line reduced it to a notice board for anyone with a new book, play or exhibition to promote. Yet, in the early to mid-1980s, *The Times* retained a sufficiently high impression of itself to eschew following other newspapers' interest in the doings, preferably salacious, of popular celebrities. This was not just for fear of the laws of libel but on grounds of taste and what was felt appropriate for the supposed paper of record. 'The Diary has got to keep off smut,' pronounced Douglas-Home over a piece by Young that referred to the composer Percy Grainger's inventive sex life.[60] The Diary's compiler (though in fact there was a small team engaged on it) remained anonymous. Only the initials 'PHS' (which stood for Printing House Square – *The Times*'s traditional address) were proffered at its foot. Under this guise, Angela Gordon, a twenty-six-year-old Scot who had started out on the Edinburgh *Evening News* before moving to the *Telegraph*, assumed the editorial mantle in 1984. Nonetheless, some continued to wonder what purpose it served, or, as Lord Dacre put it to Douglas-Home, 'Don't you think that the action of your gossip-writer in soliciting, paying for, and publishing juvenile indiscretions, dirt, trivialities, about the great is rather lowering to your great newspaper?'[61]

One aspect of the Diary that was widely admired was its daily pocket cartoon. Mark Boxer (who traded under the name 'Marc') had been the master of this art there since 1969. Having been the first editor of the *Sunday Times Colour Magazine*, Marc's work drew primarily upon the metropolitan life of which he was himself a rich adornment. His friends included George Melley and Simon Raven and, as an undergraduate in 1953, he had achieved the distinction of being sent down from Cambridge for blasphemy – the first such case since Shelley at Oxford – for a light-hearted but irreverent poem in *Granta*. Inheriting the tradition of Osbert Lancaster, Marc's usual format for a thumbnail cartoon involved a sketch of an upper middle-class couple confidently sharing a blasé opinion. He chronicled what became known as the 'chattering classes'. Sometimes they would be a covert coat- and headscarf- and pearls-wearing couple rasping a reactionary sentiment, although often they were smug Hampstead liberals declaiming the latest fashionable nostrum. Almost invariably, they were apiece with the titbits from the literary and theatrical world that provided the Diary column with so much of its copy. By 1983, Marc had been providing cartoons for the paper for fourteen years and, feeling constrained, moved on, assuming the editorship of *Tatler* and taking his miniature world with him first to the *Guardian* and subsequently the *Telegraph*. He was only fifty-seven when, in 1988, he died of a brain tumour.

Barry Fantoni filled Marc's gap with cartoons for the Diary column. Fantoni's angular, harder-edged figures often conversing either side of the headline on a newsstand, represented a wider social and regional milieu than Marc could carry off convincingly although, perhaps in consequence, there was not a comparable level of penetrating satire. Meanwhile, there was also a change with *The Times*'s principal cartoonist when Ranan Lurie opted to part company on 'fair and pleasant terms'.[62] His skills as a draughtsman had never been in doubt but he had not lived in Britain for long enough to have a feel for its politics, society or humour and critics felt that this was evident in work that often failed to convey the subtle nuances of the national life. His replacement as chief cartoonist proved to be one of the paper's enduring assets, Peter Brookes.

On the front page, the thumb cartoonist between 1979 and his untimely death aged sixty-two in 1994 was Mel Calman. His drawing style could not have been more different from that of Peter Brookes. Calman's figures – composed of a few curved lines and a large nose – lacked individual characteristics and thereby represented 'everyman'. Given how small the box was in which his idea had to be conveyed, the sense of the little man, anxious and perplexed by the weight of the world around him, worked perfectly. Born in Hackney, the son of Russian-Jewish parents, there was a touch of the underdog in Calman's own character. Despite his great gifts for friendship and generosity, he was defensive about having become a cartoonist after failing to get into Cambridge or be accepted for a journalism course. Ironically, his art got more closely to the helpless anxieties of the age than even some of the most perceptive reporters despite the fact that, as one posthumous tribute put it, he 'hated leaving the West End unless it were for New York'. His arrival in *The Times* office every early evening was one of the great rituals through which those who worked there marked the approach of their own deadlines. Calman's appearance on the floor was strangely magisterial, the act of removing his overcoat acquiring the symbolic resonance of the boxer slipping out of his dressing gown. He would go through the motions of consulting the backbench about what was in the news and what would make appropriate subject matter before getting down to work. Moments later, the backbench would watch in awe as he re-emerged, overcoat over arm, to bid his toiling colleagues adieu for the evening. Was it really as effortless as he made out? That, at any rate, was the impression he liked to give, at least until on a royal visit to the building, the Duke of Edinburgh took one look at his handiwork and asked, 'Did you draw these on the bus coming in, then?'[63]

Feature articles, a fast developing area of broadsheet journalism that by *The Times* of the year 2000 merited a whole daily section, received only a single page a day in the paper of the 1980s under the title 'Spectrum'. However (except on Thursdays when book reviews occupied the available space) there was also an additional page devoted to features designed to be of particular interest to women. These were unimaginatively entitled the Monday, Wednesday and Friday pages, while on Tuesdays Suzy Menkes's fashion page appeared. Besides the lead story, there was a diary column, graced by the likes of Joanna Lumley, Penny Perrick and Alan Franks and recipes on Wednesdays and Saturdays by *The Times* cook, Shona Crawford Poole, as well as regular medical briefings.

In some respects, *The Times*'s greatest shortcoming was not – as was regularly claimed – its generally male-orientated outlook (beyond the desig-nated page for women) but its failure to expand a section that particularly appealed to more masculine pastimes. The paper was at its weakest in its sporting coverage. *The Times* had no shortage of quality sports' journalists but the failure to give them the room they needed ensured that in the twenty years before Murdoch bought the paper it competed seriously against its rivals only in its coverage of racing and cricket with rugby union and golf as runners-up.

Norman Fox, who had been reporting football for *The Times* since the propitious year of 1966, became sports editor in 1982. He was subsequently assisted by a deputy, Richard Williams, who succeeded in balancing his tasks on the sports desk with maintaining an interest in the arts features. Indeed, Douglas-Home – whose principal sporting interests were sailing and riding – considered Williams and Peter Stothard the two most promis-ing journalists on the paper.[64] There were, however, other emerging talents. Upon assuming command, Fox began making a number of first-class appointments that would be critical to the paper's back pages in the years ahead. David Hands became the rugby correspondent in 1983, a post for which he was so suited that he was still in it twenty years later. Fox also appointed David Miller as the paper's first all purpose chief sport's writer. This was an important moment for *The Times*, heralding a new era in which sports journalism evolved beyond the core skills of filing match reports and related news events. Henceforth, it would, like philosophy or politics, deserve magisterial interpreters. In December 1982, another Fox appointment, Simon Barnes, began working for the paper and would soon demonstrate that he was a master of this art.

A Bristol University graduate whose father had been the producer of

Blue Peter and head of children's programmes at the BBC, there was something agreeably accidental about Barnes's path into the highest echelons of sports journalism. He had begun as a news reporter on local newspapers and so hated the bullying attitude of his editor that he had determined to apply for the next vacancy that presented itself. This transpired to be on the sports desk. Nonetheless, he was still in his thirties and living in a London bedsit when he finally got his foot inside *The Times*'s door. Norman Fox recognized his talents and suggested he write a weekly column on obscure sports. Thus, Barnes turned his attention to such exhibitions of sporting prowess as bicycle polo and *boules*. It was soon evident that sport, especially at the epic scale, with its polarity of emotions, provided ideal material for his craft as a writer. While politicians and businessmen sought to dissemble and cover themselves up from the critical glare, Barnes liked the way in which sporting figures stood 'emotionally stark naked'.[65] The glory and cruelty were inescapable parts of the spectacle. Barnes's ability to file copy at short notice was widely admired but he had a lyrical and reflective quality that marked him out from the professional space fillers. He edited an anthology entitled *A La Recherche du Cricket Perdu* and was an avid birdwatcher (indeed, a love of Proust and ornithology was something he shared with the paper's nature notes writer, Derwent May). As a spectator of birds as well as of sporting prowess, Barnes wrote books on ornithology that were as acclaimed as his award-winning writing on sport. Crouching in the bushes was not his only means of observing nature. He was drawn to country life and long hours were to be enjoyed surveying the countryside from the saddle of one of his horses.

Indeed, judged by space made available in *The Times*, racing was, by a considerable margin, the most important sport in Britain. The paper was fortunate to have Michael Phillips as its racing correspondent from 1967 and he continued to write on the sport of kings as 'Mandarin' from March 1984 until his retirement in January 1993. Filing copy most days of the week, he was one of *The Times*'s most prolific journalists.

Filing beside Phillips, first as northern correspondent and thereafter as racing correspondent until his (semi) retirement in 1991 was Michael Seely. Seely was the sort of journalist whose life and work became the stuff of Fleet Street legend. He was the son of an eccentric Nottinghamshire squire who had ridden in the Grand National and enjoyed a *ménage à trois* with his wife and a mistress (who was thirty-five years his junior) at Ramsdale Hall in Nottinghamshire. Michael Seely's early career had been marked by a distinct lack of promise. He had gone from Eton into the Grenadier

Guards in 1944 and spent much of the succeeding years woozy through drink. His father disinherited him in 1952 for marrying a 'hostess' he had met in the West End's notorious Bag of Nails nightclub. A second marriage proved more successful and Seely cut back on his alcoholic consumption. Yet, he might have continued as a clerk at the Raleigh bicycle factory had he not got a lucky break to work on the official weekly form book, Race-form. There, his talent was spotted and in his fiftieth year he got his first newspaper posting when he joined *The Times* in 1975. The role of racing correspondent, with its travelling between racecourses and almost daily deadlines, was not naturally suited to a man of Michael Seely's disorgani-zation and general inability to master even the simplest technology – he continued to file in an almost illegible longhand until the 1990s – but, no matter how fine he cut the deadline, the copy was invariably of the highest standard. Having shared with Michael Phillips the Lord Derby Racing Journalist of the Year Award in 1980 he won it outright in 1989.

Around the racecourses, Seely cut an eccentric but much-loved figure. He continued to enjoy a reputation as a *bon viveur* and *roué* while almost constantly mislaying his false teeth. On one occasion he watched helplessly while his dentures were driven over in the Newmarket car park. Upon disinterring the remains, he nonchalantly gave them a light polish and placed them back in his mouth, subsequently alleging that they were now a far better fit. Besides his prose and racing knowledge, his journalistic talent was honed by his charm and friendliness, attributes that ensured he knew what was going on. To mark his retirement in 1991, Simon Jenkins (by then editor of *The Times*) hosted a party for him in the Jockey Rooms at Newmarket to which most of the leading figures in the sport turned up. Charlie Wilson took Jenkins on a tour of the Jockey Rooms' collection of equestrian art, stopping by one painting to helpfully point out which end was the head and which the tail. Seely's successor was Richard Evans. Evans had been on the racing desk for a year, having previously spent three years as media editor and, before that, eight years on the parliamentary and political staff.

Besides golf, which was reported on by John Hennessy, cricket was the other sport in which the paper had a rightly acclaimed reputation. Marcus Williams covered the county game between 1981 and 1995. The Test matches were the preserve of John Woodcock, cricket correspondent from 1954 to 1987 (although he was still writing periodically for the paper into the twenty-first century) who combined the post after 1980 with the editorship of *Wisden*. During this period, one series outshone all others for its mixture of drama and unpredictability: the 1981 Ashes. Ian Botham stepped down after claiming the England captaincy's worst ever record. No sooner had he done so than he transformed himself into a hero of mythic status. England, having not won any of their past twelve Tests, were following on and struggling at 135 for 7 when he stepped out to bat in the Third Test at Headingley. The canny bookmakers Ladbrokes were offering odds of 500–1 on an England victory. Undaunted, Botham batted England back into the game, although when he finally ran out of support at the opposite crease, the 130-run target set Australia was easily obtainable. When they responded, reaching fifty-five for one, the tourists appeared to be sailing to victory. Then Bob Willis struck with the ball, taking eight wickets for forty-three runs, leaving the stunned Australians eighteen runs short of taking a commanding lead in the series. It was only the second time in Test history that a side asked to follow on had proceeded to win the match (it had last happened in 1894). Yet, the epic was not over, for Botham emerged as Man of the Match in the following Test at Edgbaston when he took Australia's last five wickets for one run. It was a moment of sporting glory. Having scarcely recovered from recording the miracle of Headingley, John Woodcock was again given the honour of starting his report of this latest triumph on the front page under a picture of Botham and his successor as captain, Mike Brearley, with arms raised in ecstasy, an image trapped for eternity. 'At times,' Woodcock informed, 'the crowd of 15,000 cheered the home side on as though it was a horse race.' The rarity of such placement in *The Times*'s order of priorities was demonstrated when England retained the Ashes two weeks later at Old Trafford. The front page ran with a picture of Senator Edward Kennedy swinging a softball bat during a festival for the disabled in Boston.[66]

The year 1981 was an exceptionally memorable one for sport in Britain. Besides Botham and Willis's heroics in the Ashes, in athletics Sebastian Coe and Steve Ovett fought it out for the 1500 metres world record and John McEnroe earned his 'superbrat' soubriquet at Wimbledon. In *The Times*, the Wimbledon fortnight was the busy two-week period each year in which Rex Bellamy, the esteemed tennis correspondent between 1967 and 1992, more than proved his worth and left himself with plenty of time to go fellwalking during the remaining fifty weeks of the year. Nonetheless, despite Bellamy's considerable experience, the paper usually thought the championships merited only half a page's coverage a day. It took John McEnroe's famous racket-breaking tantrum during his first-round victory over Tom Gullikson to ensure another rare sporting picture foray onto the front page. The accompanying text alerted readers that McEnroe had 'called the referee a four-letter name'. Inquisitive readers turning to the skimpy report of the match on page ten were doubtless relieved to discover 'it was not a very serious one'. This was the match – although the *Times* report did not have room to record it – in which McEnroe had famously told the umpire, Edward James, 'You guys are the absolute pits of the world.' Unfortunately, James had misheard the taunt and, believing he had been accused of being 'the piss of the world', duly penalized McEnroe for obscenity.[67]

The Times's interest in on-court antics at the All England Club appeared positively indulgent compared with its breathtakingly inadequate coverage of the 1982 Football World Cup in Spain. Not even the fact that England and the holders, Argentina, were both competing while the Falklands War was still being waged between them was sufficient to give it a higher priority. Each day, the championships struggled to receive much more than half a page. England had not been in the World Cup since it had been hosted in Mexico, twelve years earlier. Nonetheless, their fixtures received only one report each – from the necessarily hard-working and self-dependent Stuart Jones, *The Times*'s football correspondent. There was no room for analysis for a team that commenced the competition with a 3–1 victory over France. Readers had to take it on trust that the performance had been 'inspired'.[68] Yet, on the same day, racing coverage received a full page – Royal Ascot being regarded as a bigger sporting event than the World Cup. This was not the behaviour of a newspaper that was serious about broadening its appeal. When, eventually, England was knocked out, *The Times* did condescend to mention the fact, in passing, on the front page, but it was not deemed worthy of a photograph. The paper led that day instead with a picture of Sir Peter Parker standing talking to a fellow British Rail board member in a deserted strikebound foyer of Euston Station. Italy's defeat of West Germany in the World Cup final received an even smaller front-page reference, although it did benefit from an accompanying photograph a little larger than a postage stamp.[69]

In the 1930s, the football game that *The Times* – and its readers – was primarily interested in was played with the oval-shaped ball. Nonetheless, given the constraints of the age, it did provide passable association football coverage, especially for those still following the amateur side of the game, where teams, many prefixed by the world 'old', vied for manly satisfaction in The Isthmian League, The Spartan League and The Arthur Dunn Cup. By the 1980s, though, the paper's coverage of league football had moved on sufficiently to have lost contact with its amateur proponents but had not greatly expanded its professional reportage. Stuart Jones was the only staff employee covering the game although he was assisted in reporting the weekend fixtures by various freelancers and by the subeditors who – with no paper to work on for Sunday – spent their Saturdays reporting from the various football grounds. Generally, Monday's *Times* would devote two-thirds of a page to the weekend's action. Necessarily, clubs outside the First Division (which was then the top division) struggled to make an impact beyond the football results. Readers living in the North were lucky if they even received this courtesy. Unlike its principal rivals, *The Times* did not print in Manchester as well as London. This frequently ensured patchy sports coverage particularly of football results appearing in the northern editions. The chances of anyone in Scotland reading a report on Celtic or Rangers, Hibs or Hearts, was even more remote. It may well have been one of the reasons few people north of the border bought *The Times*.

As the decade wore on, so the paper made gradual attempts to enhance its football coverage. Regrettably, the sport tended to make its greatest impact in the paper for the worst of reasons. 1985 proved to be a terrible year for English football. On 11 May, fifty-six spectators were killed in a fire at Bradford City. A fortnight later, seventy England fans were arrested after going on the rampage in Helsinki and on 29 May, a riot begun by Liverpool fans at the Heysel Stadium in Brussels prior to the European Cup final caused the death of thirty-eight Juventus fans and injured one hundred and fifty more. Two days later, the Football Association prohibited English clubs from competing in Europe, a ban that FIFA extended to cover the rest of the world. The country that had invented the sport was now in quarantine, its competitors rightly keen to be inoculated against the 'British disease' of hooliganism.

V

Edition number 62,025 of *The Times* appeared on 2 January 1985, two hundred years and one day after the paper's first edition. For those who had worked on the paper – to say nothing of loyal readers who had stuck with it over many years through thick and thin – it was a justifiable cause for celebration. With circulation at an all-time record, a much-admired editor in the chair and some of the most famous names in journalism on the payroll, it was hard to conceive that only five years earlier the paper had been widely feared to have only ten weeks left to live.

There was, perhaps, some irony that it had been saved by Rupert Murdoch, a proprietor accused of having an unsentimental approach to the survival of British institutions. Yet, he proved as animated by the bicentenary celebrations for Britain's oldest and most famous national newspaper as everyone else. Indeed, he and his wife, Anna, even hosted a dinner for the descendants of John Walter, the man who invented the paper and whose family had owned it outright until 1908. With the miners' strike continuing to dominate the front page, it was only a small left-hand column that alerted readers to the fact that this was the paper's bicentennial issue. Inside, however, the commemoration began with the enclosure of a free facsimile of the first edition of 1 January 1785: a four-page newspaper given over largely to small ads and self-promotion in which only four of the sixteen columns of text contained actual news. There was certainly nothing particularly portentous about that first edition, a fact that might explain why only one copy had survived the intervening two hundred years to tell the tale. Before entering the care of the British Library, it had been kept by the father of the late eighteenth-century novelist Fanny Burney.

The Times certainly made more of its bicentenary than it had in 1885 when it celebrated one hundred years with nothing more than a single self-effacing paragraph. In 1985, a colour commemorative magazine and wall-chart poster were published together with two books: a large coffee-table tome focusing on the highs (and a few lows) in the paper's history entitled *We Thundered Out* by Philip Howard and *Double Century: 200 Years of Cricket in The Times* edited by Marcus Williams. The latter was formally launched at the bicentennial cricket match at the historic Hambledon ground in Hampshire in June where a Times XI declared on 128 for 3 (helped by an undefeated fifty from guest batsman, Mike Brearley). Their opponents from the publishers Collins (assisted by Bob Willis) had made sixty-six for two when rain stopped play. John Arlott had presided over lunch and in the evening 450 *Times* staff were entertained at a dinner in the Victoria & Albert Museum as Douglas-Home's guests.

The involvement of other bodies in the celebration was the real testament to the paper's enduring place in national life, not least because it showed it was still a marketable asset. The Post Office brought out a celebratory first-day cover of stamps. Wedgwood designed a plate reproducing Benjamin Haydon's painting *Waiting for The Times*. At the Chelsea Flower Show, Anna Murdoch officially named *The Times* rose (a hardy

perennial floribunda with deep crimson-scarlet blooms that had been selected by the paper's gardening correspondent, Ashley Stephenson). It was
subsequently made available in a reader offer. Likewise, Bollinger brought
out a *Times* cuvée. Douglas-Home named a British Rail locomotive (class
86) *The Times* amid great fanfare (the train later crashed, to more muted
reporting). On 31 January, the bicentennial concert was performed at the
Festival Hall, Sir George Solti conducting the Chicago Symphony Orchestra
in a programme of Shostakovich and Bruckner. The British Library's 'Signs
of *The Times* 1785–1985' exhibition ran from March to June. This was a
level of public recognition accorded few other national institutions and no
other newspaper.

There were two television documentaries to mark the bicentenary. Hugo
Young presented the BBC's *The Times at 200*, the Corporation reversing
its earlier disinterest in such a programme when it learned Thames TV
had been given six months' access to film in Gray's Inn Road for a commemorative documentary they were making. The latter, narrated by
Anthony Quayle with the title *The Greatest Newspaper in the World!* (with
a tabloid exclamation rather than a broadsheet question mark), was broadcast on 2 January 1985, three days after Hugo Young's more agnostic
approach to the birthday institution.

The Thames documentary took as its starting point the view of Establishment critics of their supposed house journal: Edward Heath claimed, 'It
doesn't thunder any more, occasionally screams. Today's *Times* has very
little influence'; Dr Anthony Kenny, the Master of Balliol, noted that it was
no longer a journal of record; Lord Mancroft drew attention to the poor
picture reproduction and misprints; the Bishop of Peterborough thought
it was becoming trivial, like the antics of a trendy vicar. Some of the paper's
journalists also felt free to criticize. Michael Binyon expressed regret that
the paper was lacking its former intellectual drive (an observation that
Wilson subsequently assured him was a sackable offence) while the salesroom correspondent, Geraldine Norman, bemoaned the fact that where
once she could write about what she thought was important now she was
expected to reflect what readers were presumed to find interesting. The
view that the paper's golden age was as the house organ of a tiny elite
was firmly slapped down by someone who came from that very class.
Douglas-Home told the cameras 'we don't want to confine the paper to
the mandarin class'. This sentiment was more forcefully expressed by Murdoch, who, in words that closed the programme, condemned 'people who
are elitist at heart', adding 'and if it's going down-market for them then

good, because one of the things that's wrong with this country is its all pervasive elitism'.[70]

Such opinions were not given rein by Murdoch or Douglas-Home when, on the morning of 28 February, they stood at the Gray's Inn Road entrance to greet the Queen and Prince Philip. The visit of the Head of State and her consort was no mere courtesy call. The royal party sat in on the morning editorial conference, Prince Philip proving keen to join the discussion on what the day's top stories were. They then spent a couple of hours being shown round the various departments and returned in the evening to watch the paper being put to bed. In the photocomposition area, Prince Philip enquired how a gap on the sports page was going to be filled. The compositor replied, 'If nothing comes through we'll put in a panel saying: "Read the *Telegraph*. It's best for sport."' Moving on to the publishing hall, the Queen asked one not especially hard-pressed operator what he was doing. He assured her that he was counting the pages in the paper. Philip interjected, 'Haven't you done the crossword yet?'[71]

The visit was marred only by Paul Routledge who repeated a conversation he had with the Queen about the miners. Introduced to the labour editor, the Queen had expressed the view that the miners' strike was all down to one man. Routledge begged to differ, suggesting that it was also about jobs and livelihoods. In the course of a BBC Radio 4 interview about the royal visit, he referred to the incident and stated, 'I think she felt that the dispute was essentially promoted by Mr Scargill.' Repeating the conversation was not only a breach of protocol, it gave the impression the Queen had adopted a political position. Seething with anger, Douglas-Home rushed to limit the damage, disclaiming the interpretation of the Queen's words which, he said, Routledge had only 'half heard'. Few journalists at Gray's Inn Road were less susceptible to bullying than Paul Routledge and it was a sign of how much pressure was placed upon him that he was forced to agree to a statement in which he said, 'The Queen said the strike was very sad. We had a discussion about the focus now being on one man but she never said the strike was promoted by Mr Scargill.' For his pains, Douglas-Home was deluged with 'disgusted' readers demanding that Routledge be sacked (some got carried away and demanded his head). The editor did not wish to lose one of his star reporters and opted instead to issue him with a rebuke while assuring those who wrote in that Routledge was 'fully aware of the shame he has brought on the paper'.[72] Although blown up out of proportion – not least by those who wanted to see some rain fall on *The Times*'s parade day, 'Times editor's apology to the Queen' was the front-page headline on the *Daily Mail* – it was an unfortunate incident in an otherwise good-natured and highly successful visit.

The Queen and Prince Philip were far from being the only guests who came to celebrate the bicentenary. Queen Elizabeth the Queen Mother and Princess Margaret also made royal progressions through Gray's Inn Road during the course of the year. The highlight was the bicentennial gala hosted by Rupert and Anna Murdoch at Hampton Court Palace on 11 July. Any suggestion that *The Times* was no longer special could be dispelled by a guest list that included the Prince and Princess of Wales, the Prime Minister, the leaders of the SDP and Liberal parties (Neil Kinnock had to bow out at the last minute), three former Prime Ministers (Home, Wilson and Callaghan), most of the world's ambassadors to the United Kingdom and six hundred other guests. Indeed, everyone appeared to be there apart from the actual journalists, some of whom took their exclusion as a snub and organized a rival event in a pub called the Hampton Court near Elephant and Castle. The egalitarian spirit of this alternative attraction was somewhat undermined when non-journalist members of staff like the secretaries and clerical employees were declined entry on the grounds they were not proper hacks. This was an example, if one was needed, that in Fleet Street hierarchy was alive and well in some of the most unlikely places. For those who made it to the real Hampton Court, the experience was one to be savoured. Even those used to State occasions were taken aback by the grandeur of the display. Reflecting on the event eighteen years later, Sir Edward Pickering, the executive vice-chairman of Times Newspapers, described it as one of the greatest evenings of his life.[73] The guests perambulated through the main rooms of the palace, navigating a route around string quartets, harp trios and piano duos. The Band of the Scots Guards, with pipes and drums, marched through the courtyards and there was a profusion of period recreations from the London of 1785, including a hurdy-gurdy player, a troupe of acrobats and other entertainments typical of the Vauxhall and Ranleigh pleasure gardens in vogue when John Walter's money-spinning venture first went to press. Dinner was held in the Great Hall. Murdoch proposed a toast to the Queen; Prince Charles proposed a toast to *The Times*. After dinner, the guests made their way down to the riverbank to watch the fireworks. It was, by common consent, a magical evening. Most importantly of all, *The Times* had made it to its bicentenary, an achievement that had looked in great doubt only four years earlier.

VI

For one guest in a wheelchair the gala evening in Hampton Court was particularly poignant. Diagnosed with myeloma, a cancer of the bone marrow, and with his own time running out, Douglas-Home had at least lived long enough to see the newspaper he edited through to its bicentenary. For the past two years, he had been not only acclimatizing himself psychologically to approaching death but also dealing with acute pain. His fortitude inspired his colleagues. By the end of 1982 he had already succumbed to crutches, his degenerative illness compounded when, returning from Scotland in the New Year, he was hit by a swinging car door and knocked over, badly injuring his hip. On arrival back in London, he had to be anaesthetized by an ambulance crew to get him out of his driving seat.

For six weeks in January and February 1983, Douglas-Home edited *The Times* from his bed in the Royal Free Hospital in Hampstead. Propped up by pillows, he continued to write leading articles. Murdoch visited him there twice, expressing his pleasure at the way the paper's fortunes were being turned around and repledging his intention to maintain investment. From all but his closest colleagues, Douglas-Home concealed the truth that he was dying. He thought Murdoch did not know and was certainly keen that it should stay that way. In fact, the proprietor knew from early on, opting to pretend otherwise. It suited both editor and proprietor that it should be this way. Douglas-Home certainly need not have feared being seen as a disposable liability. On the contrary, Murdoch made clear to senior colleagues that he was totally supportive and that everything was to be done to assist him in his last battle. Quietly, Murdoch took steps to ensure that, when the time came, the pension provision was adequate for the family Douglas-Home would be leaving behind.

Even some of the most eagle-eyed reporters were slow to realize that the editor's health and increasingly regular hospitalization were indications that he was suffering from a degenerative illness. Initially, many merely assumed that he had fallen off a horse again. But by late 1984, and without there needing to be any formal announcement, staff gradually became aware that he was involved in a personal battle. As his illness worsened, so he became less mobile. First he hobbled back to Gray's Inn Road on one stick. Then two sticks became necessary. There were moments when the pain was so excruciating that he had to take some conferences while lying flat on his back on his office floor. But he carried on. Then he was confined to a wheelchair. Next, a swelling started to appear across his forehead. This increasing immobility meant that he could not get around all the departments as much as he would have wanted and became increasingly confined to his office, from where he continued to write leaders. His deputies, Colin Webb and Charles Wilson, did much of the floor prowling on his behalf.

For Douglas-Home, part of the process of coming to terms with his physical degeneration was, if anything, to sharpen his appreciation of life. His wife observed in him 'an even greater ability than before to perceive and understand situations which other more restless and preoccupied people often preferred not to see'.[74] Reflecting on the lessons of Christ's birth for what would prove to be his last Christmas Eve leading article, the editor wrote:

> At the darkest moment there is the promise of daylight . . . For the noon day sun the darkness which lies ahead is no external enemy but its own internal guarantee of another noon to come . . . The beauty and the joy of a birth and the joy of life itself should dispel the unusually intense fear of death which seems nowadays to have whole societies in its grip. A wasted life is a living death long before the clock actually strikes the hour. Fear of death is identical with not wanting to live. Both attitudes negate the possibility of life's completeness. They both negate the affirmation of life as an element in the natural order of things.[75]

Douglas-Home's spells in hospital grew more frequent but still he refused to give up. Webb took the morning conference. A telephone was installed for him and this made editing the paper from a hospital bed a little easier. When it was time for the leader writers to gather, Douglas-Home, laid up again in the Royal Free Hospital, 'joined' the discussion with the help of a squawk box attached to his bedside table. The clarity of the speaker box was so good that he claimed to be able to hear Ivan Barnes's eyebrows rasing. He was spending long periods having radium treatment and sometimes his commentary would have to be interrupted while doctors and nurses attended to him. His secretary, Liz Seeber, performed sterling work running his office and easing his burdens. Towards the end, he tended not to see most of the page proofs any more but a messenger was dispatched from Gray's Inn Road with the leader and feature pages for his perusal and approval. Among his private bedside visitors was the Prince of Wales. Although Douglas-Home was actually his wife's relation, Prince Charles had long been a close friend. Laurens van der Post had brought the two men together in a shared interest in spiritual questions. The Prince took as much time out as his duties permitted to visit and wrote encouraging letters both to Charlie and to Jessica Douglas-Home. His sentiments were heartfelt and touching.[76] Those closest to the editor professionally – his secretaries, his deputies Webb and Wilson – also did their best. It was important that he went down editing to the last, and every effort was made to ensure he did so. 'He used *The Times* as his therapy, his inspiration, his reason for living,' concluded Wilson. Although not given to sentimental hyperbole, Wilson never ceased to regard Douglas-Home as a 'great guy, a wonderful man. He was the bravest man I ever met.'[77]

Charles Douglas-Home died in the Royal Free Hospital on 29 October 1985. He was forty-eight. At Gray's Inn Road, *The Times* staff rose as one for a minute's silence for him at 4 p.m. – the moment he would normally have opened the afternoon editorial conference. Tributes poured in from peers and princes. 'His very name spells courage,' said Margaret Thatcher, who also wrote a moving letter to Jessica. Neil Kinnock also sent a kind and touching note. Murdoch offered his own salute: 'Charles walked the corridors of power in continual pain, but with dignity and incredible courage.' From New York, Anna Murdoch even offered to fly over to stay with Jessica and her young family if she thought it would help. A lengthy telegram was received – unsolicited – from President Reagan: 'the United Kingdom, the English speaking world, indeed, all friends of freedom, have suffered a great loss,' announced the President as part of a generous appraisal of his contribution that was followed up with a personal letter to Jessica.[78] In the days and weeks ahead, she was deluged with letters from those who had worked with him and admired the man or, if they were strangers, merely wanted to salute his contribution to public life.

In the *Spectator*, Paul Johnson suggested that among the 'foetid odours' of Fleet Street, 'his personal example' had shown that journalism 'can still be an honourable trade'. The magazine devoted part of its leading article to Douglas-Home, calling forth his 'zest for action and his gift for cheering people up' and painting a wider picture:

The Times he dreamed of and, in a miraculously short time, created, was not the old, shuffling *Times* of the 1930s and 1940s. It was brisk, aggressive, occasionally vulgar (or jolly, to put it another way), sometimes wrong, but never, if he could help it, bland. And people wanted to read it.[79]

More than a thousand mourners attended Douglas-Home's memorial service in St Paul's Cathedral, among them the Prince and Princess of Wales and other members of the royal family, the Prime Minister and senior members of the Cabinet, four earls, eighteen barons and thirty knights. Having helped in the selection of the order of service, Prince Charles read the first lesson. The correspondent for the *UK Press Gazette* described it as 'the most remarkable tribute to a journalist I have ever attended'.[80]

Douglas-Home had inherited a newspaper in crisis and left it reinvigorated and self-confident. In the space of three and a half years he had earned the right to be considered one of its great editors. Commercially and professionally, he had presided over a period in which *The Times* had achieved the most difficult of tricks: rapidly expanding its circulation without greatly demeaning its quality. The growth would not have been possible without the accompanying investment that Murdoch was prepared to put at the editor's disposal, sums which he had balked at giving Harold Evans. Unlike Evans, Douglas-Home had gained and maintained the proprietor's confidence. This had been achieved through strength and independence of mind and certainly not by sycophancy or subservience. As Murdoch later assessed the relationship, 'he was always terribly straight with me and stood up for the paper if I criticized it'. Those criticisms did not touch upon the political slant of the paper (there was little to trouble the proprietor there) but rather in its handling of news. Murdoch wanted *The Times* to 'go for the jugular' of the *Daily Telegraph* in the sharpness and selection of its news coverage. Instead, he had to accept that the editor simply 'didn't buy into that'.[81] There certainly was much the paper could learn from its younger, more popular rival, especially when it came to sporting coverage and news stories with a human angle, but essentially Douglas-Home was right to play to *The Times*'s strengths. It was in this respect that his success could not be attributed to Murdoch's money alone but to the editorial judgments he made alongside Webb and Wilson. As has been noted, the great surge in circulation was well underway before the Portfolio promotion commenced. Only in one area did the need to make budget cuts seriously reduce the quality of the paper and this was in the business pages where the attempt to offer serious competition to the *FT* was abandoned. It would take more than a decade before the damage to this important part of the paper was properly repaired. In other respects, the legacy was a positive one. Aside from his professional judgment, it was in his own conduct that Douglas-Home set the highest standard. 'Even when he was ill, his authority inside the office was unquestioned' was the verdict of Sir Edward Pickering, a man who, with the better part of forty years experience in Fleet Street's senior ranks, had seen his fair share of careers wax and wane. He considered Douglas-Home's swansong 'an act of devotion and courage which I don't think I have ever seen rivalled in any newspaper office'.[82]

Douglas-Home's personal courage inspired those who knew him. His professional judgment nourished *The Times*'s commercial recovery. His editorship, though, had a wider significance in its contribution to the intellectual fortification it provided for the centre-right during a tense period in the Cold War. At the time, this was controversial. Those who took the view that 'serious journalism' was 'journalism which causes serious trouble for people who have real power' had not welcomed Douglas-Home's appointment as editor. The *New Statesman*, edited by Bruce Page, had asserted that Douglas-Home's 'record in serious journalism is wholly negligible' and that 'while Rupert Murdoch's nominee holds the chair at *The Times*, the rich and powerful will never need to toss upon the pillow'.[83] Given that as a reporter in 1968 it had been Douglas-Home who had revealed the concealed presence of 25,000 Soviet troops on the Slovak–Polish border waiting to crush the Prague Spring and been arrested trying to get a closer look, the *New Statesman* clearly set a high bar on what constituted serious journalism. Perhaps this was because exposing and undermining the Conservative and Republican administrations in Westminster and Washington was the great prize for investigative journalists in the 1980s. In his newspaper, Douglas-Home never ceased to provide a platform for Thatcher and Reagan's battery of critics – as any glance at the contributors to the Op-Ed comment page would attest – but his own contribution, expressed through the leading articles he penned himself, was to oppose the widely expressed belief that there was a moral equivalence between liberal-capitalism and Marxist-Leninism and between NATO and the Warsaw Pact. He was an ex-soldier and ex-defence correspondent and this doubtless sharpened his attitude towards the Cold War division. Yet, what gave his contribution weight was his ability as a committed Christian to engage in intelligent argument with those, especially in the churches and peace movements, who demanded rapprochement with Moscow.

For Douglas-Home, this was the greatest issue of the time and he would not have the leading column of *The Times* failing to take a lead on it. In the 1940s, the paper, under the influence of its assistant editor E. H. Carr, had been indulgent towards Communism. It had accepted the Soviet Union's right to determine the politics of Eastern Europe's nations and even announced that Communism and Western democracy had much to learn from each other.[84] Some regarded this as the sort of well-balanced argument they expected from *The Times* leader column. To Douglas-Home it was both misguided and immoral. He thundered against the attitude of a draft statement put before the British Council of Churches in 1985 that maintained 'both Marxism and Western liberalism in their many forms enshrine positive values' and that there was some sort of equivalence between the Soviet Union's incarceration of ten thousand political prisoners and the 'well over 10,000 Americans killed every year by hand guns which Americans have the "right" to carry'.[85]

The crushing of dissenting voices was, to Douglas-Home, the most insidious aspect of Communist totalitarian rule and he could not understand the blasé attitude towards it from so much of the British intelligentsia. During his editorship, *The Times* devoted much space to the fate of Russian and Eastern European prisoners of conscience and Jessica, his widow, continued to be active in promoting the work of democratic dissident groups in Eastern Europe after her husband's death. As far as the outside world was concerned, Douglas-Home's principal contribution was that he gave anti-Communism a stronger voice in one of the world's most influential newspapers. In Britain, and indeed even within Gray's Inn Road, many felt this process undermined *The Times*'s reputation as a paper of judicious and measured observation and that Douglas-Home had reduced it to the status of a partisan periodical from which it never fully recovered. The leader writer Richard Davy later wrote that the extent of Douglas-Home's hostility to compromising with the Soviets 'destroyed the intellectual integrity of the paper'.[86] Certainly, there are dangers in a newspaper adopting a strong position and both Davy and Edward Mortimer had often good grounds for feeling that they were dissenting voices who were being crushed by an editor who had given up on nuanced argument. If Douglas-Home had continued to take a dogmatic line later in the decade, when even Reagan grasped the opportunities for dialogue with Gorbachev, *The Times* would certainly have been culpable of terrible judgment. It can only be speculated how, or whether, Douglas-Home would have adapted to changed circumstances. Instead, he was responding to a Soviet Union that under Brezhnev and Andropov presented a far less amenable face. He did not live to see the collapse of Communism. Unquestionably, some early signs for diplomatic overtures were missed because of his attitude, but, whatever the aspirations of some of its more disaffected journalists, *The Times* was not the house journal of the Foreign Office. The paper had been haunted by its support for appeasing Hitler in the 1930s and Stalin in the 1940s. Douglas-Home laid those ghosts to rest.

VII

From within Gray's Inn Road, the two deputy editors, Colin Webb and Charles Wilson, were the obvious contenders to fill the vacant chair. Colleagues considered Webb to possess a safe pair of hands but recognized that Wilson was the more dynamic candidate. Both had proved themselves more than capable, but Wilson had an advantage. At the end of 1983, Murdoch had bought the *Chicago Sun-Times* for $90 million, to the horror of the paper's staff who feared he wanted to turn it into a sensationalist tabloid. When, in the new year, he found himself needing a replacement editor at short notice he had asked Wilson if he would do him 'a favour' by standing in as the *Sun-Times*'s editor until a suitable American could be found to take over. Wilson replied 'sure' and asked when he would be expected to go to the Windy City. 'My plane is on the tarmac,' replied Murdoch, 'and I'm going back tonight.' Mentioning that his pregnant wife was at home with a broken collarbone, Wilson managed to negotiate a day's leeway. When the new editor arrived for his first day at the *Sun-Times*, Murdoch was on hand to greet him, introduce him to the managing editor and point him in the direction of the executive washroom. This done, Murdoch announced he was off and if Wilson needed anything he should call him in New York. Within minutes of the proprietor's hasty departure, Wilson discovered he had been lowered into 'a bloody cauldron of hate'.[87] *Sun-Times* journalists had been made aware of Harold Evans's claims in *Good Times, Bad Times* and were not encouraged by the verdict of Patrick Brogan, a former pre-Murdoch *Times* journalist of note who had never met him but felt able to pronounce that 'Wilson is very tough, unpleasant, rude to his subordinates. He puts the fear of God in them.'[88] When, at Wilson's first conference, one staff member asked whether the paper would continue to have a Washington bureau, it was clear how little trust existed.

Three months later, when it was time for Wilson to return to London, *Sun-Times* staff circulated a petition asking him to stay. The speed with which he had won over the journalists by his hard work and focus on sharper news presentation impressed Murdoch. And Murdoch soon had a new mission for Wilson in London. Fed up with Fleet Street's industrial relations and technological limitations, he had decided to sack all his print union workers and move his four British newspapers to Wapping in London's East End. It was an immensely risky operation that – if it failed – stood to bankrupt Murdoch. It needed a hard-working, determined and ruthless general who would see it through and carry the troops of *The Times* with him. On 5 November 1985, the independent national directors duly approved Murdoch's recommendation that Charles Wilson should succeed Charles Douglas-Home as the thirteenth editor of *The Times*. 'Ah yes,' Bernard Levin had prophesied when Wilson first arrived, 'the man who knows how to put the razor blade in the snowball.'[89]

CHAPTER FIVE

FORTRESS WAPPING

The Plan to Outwit the Print Unions

I

In the ten years to January 1986, strikes and stoppages plagued Murdoch's News International. During the period, industrial action prevented 296 million copies of the *Sun* and 38 million copies of the *News of the World* from rolling off the presses. One hundred and four million copies of the *Sunday Times* had been lost over the past decade. *The Times* had lost 96.5 million copies.

Financially, losing a day's distribution represented an immediate shortfall of £71,000 to *The Times*, £362,000 to the *Sunday Times*, £470,000 to the *Sun* and £777,000 to the *News of the World*.[1] But this was only a fragment of the total cost. Trade union activists were able to damage News International without actually taking a full day out on strike. Go-slows, refusal to work specific shifts and deliberate tampering with the printing presses ensured that, although the paper was eventually printed, it was released too late to catch the correct trains and ended up being dumped, unsold. The resulting erratic distribution created uncertainty among readers and advertisers alike. It encouraged the latter to turn to alternative and more reliable media in which to reach their audience. While mindful of Kipling's adage 'that if once you have paid him the Dane-geld, you never get rid of the Dane', management frequently found it easier to give in to whatever the demand of the moment concerned rather than face an even more costly loss of production.

The 1970s had proved a disastrous decade in the industrial annals of Fleet Street. The eleven-month suspension of *The Times* was one that merely typified the events of the period. When Murdoch bought the paper in 1981 optimists hoped for a brighter future: the availability of labour-saving technology, a Conservative Government hostile to trade union militancy and the spectre of high unemployment that greeted those who risked their jobs were all indicators that pointed towards management being able to regain the initiative. Yet, the practice proved different from the theory. None of these factors made an appreciable whit of difference to the number of strikes that crippled Fleet Street production.

The one saving grace for executives at Gray's Inn Road was that competitors were equally disabled by union action. In order to cope with the increased demand created by the 1978–79 shutdown of *The Times*, management at the *Daily Telegraph* had added an extra press in their machine room. When *The Times* was revived, sales of the *Telegraph* fell back accordingly, making the extra press redundant. But when in November 1982 management finally summoned the courage to remove the press, the SOGAT chapel begged to differ and responded by shutting down the paper for ten days. The dispute cost the *Telegraph* £1.5 million in lost copies alone.[2] The *Financial Times* suffered an even more devastating blow when its print workers struck in May 1983, closing the paper for ten weeks because the rival NGA and SOGAT shop stewards could not agree the pay differentials between their members (the NGA demanded a reduction in the number of hours worked and a simultaneous pay rise of 24 per cent).[3] These were not isolated incidents. In the twelve months between July 1984 and July 1985, the national dailies lost more than 85 million copies due to industrial action. In the calendar year for 1985, the figure was nearly 100 million.[4]

The *Daily Telegraph* dispute exemplified the extent to which production had been subcontracted to the unions. It was the shop stewards (chapel fathers), rather than management, who determined which casual shift workers were employed and with what frequency. Consequently, production staff were primarily dependent upon the patronage of their chapel fathers for their terms and conditions rather than enjoying any direct relationship with their employers. In this protective environment, the print unions had certainly been able to deliver material benefits for their members. The average wage in 1985 for Fleet Street production workers was around £18,000 a year. This compared with a *Times* journalist's basic salary of £15,050. But at the highest level – such as the Linotype operators (who were still forced upon most national papers), wages in the region of £40,000 per annum could be earned. A few claimed even more. Compositors had developed such a complex pay scale, known as the 'Scale of Prices', that different rates were demanded according not only to the quantity of text typed but even to the point size of the type used. There was even a going rate for creating lines of blank text. And there were additional charges for making corrections, a situation which was an open inducement to make errors in the first place.[5]

That many of those printing *The Times* were earning more than those writing it certainly caused some ill feeling on the part of journalists struggling to meet mortgage payments and the other burdens of middle-class expectation. There was little social intercourse between the two groups. *Times* journalists did not trespass into the areas where their paper was printed and rarely had more than second-hand accounts of what went on under their feet in Gray's Inn Road. Peter Stothard visited the machine room floor only once: 'I was greeted by grown men pretending to be monkeys in a zoo,' he recalled. 'I did not go back. Many managers, I discovered, had rarely entered the alien territory which they were vainly charged to control.'[6] It was hard to see how management could reassert authority without taking measures that would ensure a mass walkout, the shutdown of the presses and another loss of consumer confidence in the newspaper.

The ten-week dispute at the *FT* had been instructive. The paper's management had considered various options to circumvent its union members' stranglehold. The possibility of using the T. Bailey Forman plant in Nottingham (where Christopher Pole-Carew used a non-union workforce) was considered but this still left the unions able to block distribution. In the end, the management concluded it would be best just to concede defeat as the easiest way to curtail a dispute that had already cost them in excess of £6 million.[7] Like Times Newspapers in 1978–9, the *FT* management had tried to take a stand – and lost. Without reliable (non-striking) distributors as well as a permanent alternative print centre manned by non-NGA-, non-SOGAT-trained staff, they could not escape the vice-like grip of the Fleet Street unions. During 1985, Rupert Murdoch set about assembling the assets that would free him from constraint. With them, the aspiration to break free from the torment of working with the print unions began to look dimly, vaguely, but tantalizingly possible. An idea that started with the intention of liberating his tabloids developed to include *The Times*. As for the unions, they had no idea what was about to hit them.

II

In the late 1970s, London's 'Docklands' – the stretch along the River Thames from Tower Bridge out past the promontory of the Isle of Dogs – was at the nadir of its existence. During the nineteenth century the area had been the world's busiest commercial waterway. Nor was this hive of activity dispersed when masts were replaced by funnels or by the flattening of the area by German bombs during the Blitz. Indeed, the Port of London achieved its maximum volume of trade in the early 1960s. But from then on, its decline was dramatic. The development of far larger vessels and container terminals to greet them ensured Tilbury and beyond became a more suitable entrepôt for international cargo and raw materials. More than 150,000 jobs were lost within a decade. London Docks closed in 1969. In an act of finality, its mighty basin was filled in.

During the 1980s, the desolate Docklands were given a new lease of life. Silted-up waterways were cleared and the grime was cleaned from Victorian warehouses that, converted into apartments, gave new 'young upwardly mobile' professionals ('yuppies') the faint notion of living in *palazzi* by the Thames. The Thatcher Government, and in particular the Environment Minister, Michael Heseltine, encouraged development in what was desig-nated as an 'Enterprise Zone'. Construction began on the Docklands Light Railway and towards the end of the decade the first of a series of giant towers went up at Canary Wharf on the Isle of Dogs offering a massive increase in available office space. In time, much of Fleet Street and the City of London would relocate there.

This renaissance of the late 1980s was still but a dim prospect when, in 1977, Bert Hardy, then chief executive at News Group Newspapers, per-suaded Murdoch to acquire an eleven-acre site where the old London Docks had stood at Wapping, east of Tower Bridge. The logic was simple. The cramped and outdated machine room at Bouverie Street (where the *Sun* and the *News of the World* were printed) had reached capacity. Merely rebuilding it would not overcome the limitations of the site, which would yield far more if sold as a land redevelopment opportunity so near to the City. Although the journalists and compositors would stay at Bouverie Street (at least until a final sell-off of their part of the site), the printing of the *Sun* and the *News of the World* would be moved away to the new more spacious brownfield location of Wapping. There the land was cheap by comparison and lorries would not have to negotiate the narrow and congested streets of the old site off Fleet Street. Wapping was Bert Hardy's brainchild and building work began in 1979. Upon acquiring *The Times* two years later, Murdoch truthfully reassured its nervous employees that he had no intention of moving them from Gray's Inn Road to what many of them considered to be the uncharted wasteland of East London. The Wapping plant was being fitted out for tabloid-only production.

Building the great print hall at Wapping necessitated the destruction of five historic warehouses that had been built in 1805. Had the application come any later in the twentieth century, the growing heritage lobby – pointing to the successful conversion of other warehouses – might have succeeded in blocking the destruction. But Labour was still in power when the application was made. The real-estate aspirations of yuppies were not uppermost in the party's mind and the dilapidated warehouses appeared merely to be grim reminders of the sort of exploitative toil that had given dockers a hereditary grievance against their employers. What was more, the Secretary of State for the Environment, Peter Shore, was the local MP. He was keen to see new jobs created in a constituency that, with the closure of the docks, desperately needed to attract fresh sources of employment. So the go-ahead was given and the five monuments to top-hatted Victorian capitalism were hit by the demolition ball. It was a decision many Labour politicians would live to regret – and not for aesthetic reasons.

The print hall that rose on the site could lay a reasonable claim to being one of the most ugly superstructures in London. A charmless box penetrated by a giant concrete ramp, its architects appeared to have an aversion to the art of simple fenestration. Resembling a giant incinerator, it was too utilitarian even to deserve membership of the 'Brutalist' school of design whose concrete monstrosities were at that time finally destroying the public's strained patience with modern architecture. But it was a print hall, nothing more and nothing less, with little thought given to the eventual possibility of relocating journalists there. The building was ready for use in 1984. It had cost £72 million. All that was needed was to get the trade unions to agree to work in it.

Whatever the building's lack of exterior decoration, on the inside it was an industrial marvel. The print hall was state of the art. Vast, like the loading bay of an aircraft carrier, it was also clean and air-conditioned. It was a world away from the Dickensian conditions and Heath Robinson contraptions familiar to Gray's Inn Road or (worse) Bouverie Street. The printing units were bought new as the last in a line of Goss Mark I Headliner letterpress machines, a design that was a decade old but of proven quality and durability.

Health and safety issues that had been a justifiable area of complaint in Bou-verie Street had been addressed and management hoped the new working environment would meet with the approval of the union chapel fathers. As a softening-up episode, an aeroplane was chartered to fly them out to view a similar printing plant in operation in Finland (the original plan was for them to visit print works in Germany, but the German companies politely made it clear that they would not let Fleet Street union officials anywhere near their employees). News International's labour relations negotiator, Bill O'Neill, accompanied the delegation to Finland, noting that many of the union officials seemed far more interested in treating it as a booze-cruise than as a first insight into their working future. For O'Neill, a subsequent trip to France with them proved to be even more of a living hell.[8]

Upon his return to London, O'Neill opened negotiations with the Bouverie Street union chapels in May 1983. The discussions were held at Wapping and the union representatives were given a tour of the plant so that they could see for themselves its capacity and capability. A myth later developed that the unions were kept in ignorance of what had been constructed at Wapping. In fact, News International had not only shown a video of the plant to chapel fathers, more than one hundred of them and their members had been given tours of the building by the end of 1984. The initial management pitch was that, although Wapping would need fewer workers, those who were employed would be better paid. O'Neill made the assurance that 'any reduction in staffing would be achieved by natural attrition or voluntary redundancy' and that there would not be 'any form of compulsory termination' for the remainder who continued on at the Bouverie Street plant.[9] But this was not good enough for the union negotiators. They maintained that, if Wapping and Bouverie Street were to coincide, the former would have to share the same overmanning and restrictive practices as the latter. This completely undermined the financial rationale behind the new plant. While O'Neill calculated that nine men could operate Wapping's three-unit presses, the unions insisted it had to be eighteen (as at Bouverie Street). Lest O'Neill should think the unions a walkover on this matter, he was reminded by them that 'the *Daily Telegraph*'s pressroom lay idle for eight years waiting on our union's agreement'.[10] Apparently this was a source of union pride. Tony Isaacs, the SOGAT 'Imperial Father', did not mince his words, telling O'Neill, 'Your initial overtures are to be likened to the back-street abortionist who not very skilfully performs his operation, removes what he thinks he should, and isn't particularly worried about the survival of the patient.'[11]

How many men it took to stand round a press was far from being the only point of dispute. An engineer assistants' union representative refused even to consider the Wapping proposals, claiming that if he so much as reported them back to his members there would be disruption at Bouverie Street. Others were determined to extract a price. There were even demands for 'relocation money' despite the fact that Wapping was closer to where most of the print workers lived than Bouverie Street. The main problem, though, was that the proposed move reignited the turf war between the NGA and SOGAT over whose members would do what at Wapping. O'Neill's suggestion that demarcation should be the same as had prevailed at Bouverie Street was rejected. The NGA's London deputy secretary wrote to Bruce Matthews, the new managing director of News International, assuring him that, unless the NGA prevailed over SOGAT's competence in supervising machine manager positions, 'there can be no question of the Wapping development coming on stream'.[12] Management's hopes that the first press lines would be running from Wapping by November 1983 soon proved preposterously optimistic.

By February 1984, nine months after the negotiations had begun, O'Neill had come to the conclusion that the unions 'consider[ed] the longer they wait the more anxious the company will become'. The various union chapels raised all manner of excuses to postpone or call off further negotiations unless some other grievance of the moment at Bouverie Street had been settled on favourable terms first. Given the massive cost to News International of the Wapping plant lying idle, the temptation to concede to whatever price the unions named was tempting – as the unions perhaps calculated. The interest charges alone on the plant were running at £10 million a year.[13] And, as the months rolled by, union militancy broadened and strengthened. Although there were no proposals in place to transfer the *Sunday Times*'s production to Wapping, the paper's chapel officials took the pre-emptive measure of announcing they would veto any such move in the future.[14]

O'Neill came to the conclusion that if incentives had no effect, the only way to get movement was for the unions 'to be frightened in some way'.[15] It was not clear how this could be achieved. Rather, when it came to threatening behaviour, the unions packed a formidable punch. O'Neill's meeting with Ted Chard from SOGAT's London Central Branch demonstrated the improbability of reaching agreement with the union whose members ran the publishing room (where the newspapers were bundled and assembled for distribution). Chard listened carefully to what O'Neill had to say about the proposals for jobs at Wapping. When the presentation drew to a conclusion, Chard stood up and asked if he had finished. O'Neill said that he had. 'Right,' said Chard, 'now I will tell you a thing or two. We are leaving here. We will not be back until you have proposals that make some sense.'[16] As he stormed out, his SOGAT delegation rose and followed him out of the door. It was the end of the negotiations, although it should have come as no surprise. Shown round the pristine plant by its technical director, Ken Taylor, a senior SOGAT representative said, 'When will you get it through your thick heads, we will never let you use it, you may as well put a match to it – or we'll do it for you.'[17]

The negotiations to move to Wapping broke down irrevocably on 19 December 1984. In a parallel development, the Scottish union branches also refused to print the *Sun* at the new Kinning Park plant that had been built in Glasgow unless it was turned into a separate Scottish newspaper rather than one whose pages were transmitted from Bouverie Street. Thus News International had built two state-of-the-art print halls, at a cost in excess of £100 million, which they could not use because the unions refused to let their members work in them. Though the chapel fathers thought they had won a great triumph, they would savour it for only thirteen months. It was a Pyrrhic victory that would ensure only their total annihilation. As Rupert Murdoch had prophesied back in 1981, the unions would soon discover they had finally got the proprietor they deserved.

III

The most violent dispute during the 1970s had been outside the Grunwick photo developing plant in north London. There, a small picket of those at issue with the management was regularly reinforced by many thousands of other trade unionists, including the Yorkshire miners, who tried to prevent the non-striking employees from getting in to work there. Postal workers also got involved. By refusing to handle mail to the company, they hoped to strangle it into submission. The scenes – many of them ugly – helped to persuade the incoming Conservative Government to prevent such sympathy action. The 1980 Employment Act made 'secondary action' (by those not directly employed by the company in a dispute) illegal. A further Employment Act in 1982 curtailed unions' legal immunity. Henceforth, they could be held financially liable for breaching the law. Guilt might result in a fine or being subject to injunctions to freeze assets until any contempt of court was purged. The definition of secondary action was tightened further, to include making it illegal to refuse to handle – to black in the parlance – products produced by non-union workforces. Further measures followed with the 1984 Trade Union Act which sought to make unions more transparent and accountable to their members. Legal immunity was removed if unions failed to hold secret ballots prior to calling a strike.

On paper, this was a formidable body of legislation but whether it was operable remained to be seen. SOGAT's National Executive Council wrote to News International's managing director to disabuse him of any thought that the 1982 Act could be deployed, adding that the union wished 'to state emphatically that we are prepared to utilize all the resources of this society in resisting any implementation of the proposed "Act".' Furthermore, they demanded a carte blanche assurance that News International would not initiate legal action. The letter concluded, somewhat threateningly, 'we rely on your good sense in co-operating with us'.[18] In line with TUC policy, SOGAT also announced that its members would not cooperate or participate in any ballots on the 'closed shop' arranged under the provisions of the 1982 Act.[19] Put simply, the union did not intend to recognize the law.

In July 1983, a dispute between the NGA and Eddy Shah's Messenger Newspaper Group based in Warrington became the litmus test of whether the trade union legislation was enforceable. Shah wanted to end the closed shop and recruit non-union labour. In response, the NGA tried to prevent production of his papers and wrote to advertisers requesting them to withdraw their advertisements. NGA members brought production at the *Daily Mirror* to a standstill, forcing its owner, Reed International, to sell its 49 per cent shareholding in the Messenger Group. Although this sort of secondary action was illegal, the NUJ joined the assault, mandating its members not to provide the Messenger Group with any copy.

Fined £50,000 for contempt of court for persisting with secondary picketing, the NGA's response was to refuse to pay up. An all-out siege of Shah's Warrington plant was organized. The fine was increased to £100,000 and the union's assets sequestrated. NGA members in London took revenge by striking on 25 November, shutting down all the national newspapers for the following day. The main attack on Shah's print works came on the night of 29 November from a mob of four thousand 'pickets'. Buildings were set on fire, the police lines broken and the gates repeatedly rammed (employees were on the other side of them trying to prop them up against the blows). Shah was trapped inside, fearing for his life. The situation was only saved by the timely arrival of the riot police. In Fleet Street, Shah's greatest supporter was the young and outspoken new editor of the *Sunday Times*, Andrew Neil. Never one to let deferential niceties get in the way of his principles, Neil took it upon himself to place a post-midnight telephone call to the Home Secretary warning of the dire consequences of letting the mob incinerate Shah. Neil's reward was a shutdown at his own paper when the unions refused to print the 4 December edition unless the leader column's supportive comments towards Shah were toned down. Neil refused to be intimidated by these tactics. When the unions restarted the presses what followed that evening was a suspiciously high number of paper breaks and lost production.[20]

But the tide was turning. Eventually, in January 1984 the NGA agreed to operate within the law having lost more than £2 million of its £10 million assets in fines and fees. Eddy Shah had won. A minor proprietor of regional free sheets had taken on a national print union on principles for which no Fleet Street proprietor had been prepared to risk all. But the implications would stretch far beyond Warrington. Three important lessons had been learned. First, by legally separating his subsidiary organizations into independent companies, Shah had been able to get court injunctions against 'secondary action'. Secondly, the police could be counted upon to help break an illegal siege of a print works. Third, the TUC might donate some financial aid (it gave the NGA £420,000) but it would not organize cross-union resistance.[21]

These lessons were not lost on Bruce Matthews, the straight-talking Australian who Murdoch had brought in as News International's managing director. In January 1985, Matthews made the journey over to Murdoch's house in Old Chatham, upstate New York, and outlined a scheme to switch all four of News International's major newspapers to Wapping and ditch the existing NGA and SOGAT workforce in the process. It was a seemingly fantastical proposition. Matthews had met Tom Rice, the EETPU (electricians' union) national secretary, and was impressed by the way his union had run a Finnish-owned paper mill in Wales after SOGAT had made unreasonable demands. Matthews proposed that EETPU members could operate Wapping. Ultimately, the EETPU would want recognition with sole bargaining rights but initially would be happy just to see its members employed without formal recognition. In one bound, News International would be rid of the NGA and SOGAT forever.

Matthews, a close follower of the Turf, was setting the stakes for an extraordinary gamble. If the NGA and SOGAT realized there were moves afoot to cut them out of working at Wapping they could call strikes at Bouverie Street and Gray's Inn Road that would destroy Murdoch's media empire long before he would have the chance to get production up and running at Wapping. 1985 was a particularly bad time for Murdoch to risk catastrophe. With total debts of $2.6 billion and plans to take on more with the extension into US film and television (what was to become the Fox network), he was reliant on the revenue provided by his British news-papers – revenue that accounted for almost half of News Corp's profits. A major shutdown would finish him. But he was intrigued by Matthews's audacious plan. Murdoch's *modus operandi* was to come to decisions quickly and then stick by his word. He needed no further persuading.

On 10 February, Murdoch summoned the key personnel he would entrust with the operation to his Fifth Avenue apartment in New York and explained to them their mission. The editors of the four papers were not brought in at this stage. However, *The Times*'s deputy editor, Charles Wilson, was invited. Impressed not only by his work at Gray's Inn Road but also by his handling of the fractious journalists in his brief stint editing the *Chicago Sun-Times*, Murdoch had decided Wilson would fulfil a central role. Those who assembled around the table were left in no doubt about the magnitude of what was being proposed. Logistically, the operation was extremely complicated. It was not just a matter of telling a group of electricians which buttons to press. Wapping had been built to print two tabloids, the *Sun* and the *News of the World*. But the idea now was to move the broadsheets, *The Times* and the *Sunday Times*, there as well. This necessitated a change in capacity. What was more, the journalists of all four papers were to be moved to the new site too. This was the second strand of the strategy. The idea was not only to dispense with the services of the NGA and SOGAT but also, in doing so, to achieve what management had failed to win during the 1978–79 shutdown – an end to double-key strok-ing. Henceforth, journalists would be given the technology the unions had denied them – access to computer terminals where they could type their copy straight in without having to get an NGA compositor to do it for them. Wapping would not only be a blow against trade union militancy, it would herald the long-delayed dawn of technological freedom for journalists.

It was one thing to state the objective, but Murdoch proceeded to sketch the means of pulling off the coup. In great secrecy, the computer terminals would be tested and installed at Wapping. A cover story would be created to throw suspicious observers off the scent: it would be pretended that the plant was being set up to launch a new local newspaper, the *London Post*. This fictitious journal would be 'edited' by Charles Wilson who would go through all the motions of starting up the paper as if it was for real. He would even advertise and hire journalists for it. When the plant was finally ready to print its real product – *The Times* and its stable mates – the unsuspecting journalists from the existing papers would be bussed in and Gray's Inn Road and Bouverie Street evacuated. But until that moment, it would be imperative that the journalists were told nothing about what was planned for them. If news of the plot leaked out before it was ready to 'go live', the unions could bring News International down. And in this eventuality, not just News International but the entire national press would remain at the whim of union activism. For those let into the secret that afternoon it was a bold and exciting plan and the prospect of success was intoxicating. Flying back to London on Concorde, Wilson and his co-conspirators made the most of an otherwise almost deserted cabin. In fact, cruising at supersonic speed above the clouds, they had a party.[22]

IV

In 1814, John Walter II, the son of the founder of *The Times*, had wanted to use a modern steam press that could do the printing of the paper far more effectively that the existing machinery. Fearing the Ludditism of his printforce, he had the steam press installed secretly and ran off the first edition without them realizing. Clearly beaten, his workforce agreed to operate the new machinery. One hundred and seventy-one years later, Walter's successor at *The Times* was contemplating the same tactic although, less certain of his print workers ability to perform a tactical retreat, he would not be offering them the option of re-employment. There was also a more recent – American – precedent for what Murdoch was planning. In 1975, Katharine Graham's *Washington Post* had overcome a violent nineteen-week siege by print workers hostile to the introduction of new technology. Graham had ensured new staff were trained to do the strikers' jobs. The striking printers retaliated by setting fire to the press room. Graham broke the siege by hiring helicopters to ferry the printing plates over the pickets' heads. Ultimately the *Post* got through. Whether the British public would greet Murdoch's attempt with the same understanding it had shown towards Kay Graham's initiative remained to be seen. Unlike her, he was not also a benefactor of liberal causes and could more easily be painted as a bottom-line capitalist careless of his responsibilities to organized labour.

One of those who had helped do the groundwork for Kay Graham's victory was an American-domiciled Liverpudlian, John Keating. Keating was now Murdoch's technical director and was instrumental in advising on the installation of the Atex computer typesetting system at Wapping in a $10 million deal. With so much experience of Fleet Street's failures, Murdoch drew on as much international talent as he could find. Christopher Pole-Carew (brought in to advise from the union busting company T. Bailey Forman) and Bill Gillespie were Englishmen, but in this respect they were in a minority. Wapping's operational manager would be John Cowley who, like Bruce Matthews, confirmed Murdoch's penchant for preferring tough Australians to what he frequently assumed were effete Englishmen. Charles 'Gorbals' Wilson was in no danger of being described as either effete or English. The upper-class Englishman Murdoch did admire, Douglas-Home, was certainly not effete. But in common with the other editors involved in the move, he did not play a leading part in the technical discussions primarily because the plan did not involve any alternation to editorial practice. Nonetheless, Douglas-Home was extremely enthusiastic about the plan and Murdoch kept him briefed on developments. As 1985 progressed, Douglas-Home was a man having to carry the burden of keeping two secrets from his close colleagues: his excitement for the Wapping project and the knowledge that he might not live long enough to see it put into operation.

The first sign that inquisitive visitors were no longer welcome at Wapping came in January when barbed wire went up around the site. In the same month, Tony Britton, News Group's labour relations manager, rebuffed Tony Isaacs, the Imperial Father at the *News of the World* machine chapel, when the latter indicated he was ready to restart negotiations for working at Wapping after all. The unions had missed the boat and, having seen an opportunity to escape them for good, Murdoch was not going to send out a rescue craft to pick them up.

Without the involvement of the EETPU in recruiting suitable staff, launching Wapping would have been all but impossible.[23] With 365,000 members, the union was the eighth largest in the TUC. Since 1982, its general secretary had been Eric Hammond, a political moderate who was used to confrontation. His speeches at TUC and Labour Party conferences were usually drowned out by a chorus of jeers and catcalls leading him on one occasion to assure delegates that Hitler would have been proud of them. In the early 1980s, the EETPU's London press branch had been led by the hard-left. But, following a thwarted attempt to merge with SOGAT, the London Branch had lost its power over employment to the area office. Hammond did not forget SOGAT's attempt to poach his members and extinguish the union's Fleet Street presence. He had been shown no inter-union fraternity and would offer none in return. This was the man with whom Murdoch could do business.

Accompanied by Tom Rice, Hammond had his first meeting with Murdoch and Bruce Matthews on 31 January 1985. The secret gathering took place at the house of Murdoch's intermediary, Woodrow Wyatt. It was there that Hammond made the assurance that his electricians could not only set up Wapping but also run it. From this moment onwards, what was never more than a verbal understanding became an article of faith with, in particular, Murdoch's future riding upon it. In April, the collusion began in earnest, with Tom Rice flying out to the United States with Christopher Pole-Carew. Joined by John Keating, they toured several newspaper plants, including *USA Today* and the *Washington Post*, to see the modern technology at work.

Given the need to keep the plot a secret, the hiring of electricians for Wapping could not be done in London. Instead the EETPU did the recruitment in Southampton via an independent employment agency that conducted the interviewing (and vetting). Most of those selected were unemployed EETPU members or their friends and relatives who grasped the opportunity to get a job at what was considered a decent wage. Every day, these men were bussed the eighty miles to work at Wapping and then bussed back again. When, many months later, the plan was eventually revealed, the use of Southampton electricians caused resentment from existing London EETPU members who had been kept in the dark about it. In the view of the SOGAT general secretary, Brenda Dean, this was 'the greatest treachery of all'.[24] But it was inconceivable that Wapping's 'staffing-up' could have been kept secret if job application forms had been distributed across London.

While the covert use of the electricians to get the Wapping plant ready gathered pace, other aspects of the plan were put in motion. Merely getting the plant to function was not, in itself, enough. News International could print any number of newspapers but if they could not get them distributed properly they would just pile up at the plant's front gate. As with its competitors, the company had a contract with British Rail to transport its papers. From the trains the bundles were taken to 250 wholesalers who then distributed them to the country's forty thousand newsagents. But here was a snag: the wholesale workers were all SOGAT members. Thus, if the rail unions and SOGAT refused to handle newspapers coming out of Wapping they could kill the project. With great secrecy, Murdoch's men devised a way round this hurdle: they would pull out of their contractual obligations with British Rail and sign a deal with the Australian road-freight company TNT instead. TNT depots would be used round the country, cutting out the wholesalers, and deliveries would be made directly to the newsagents.

Getting a list of all the newsagents' addresses involved a good deal of surreptitious research and some wholesalers may have experienced the strange sensation of feeling they were being followed as they went about their work. In fact, using lorries was significantly more expensive than using trains. TNT had 1500 vehicles and Wapping's requirement of eight hundred (and up to two thousand new drivers and distributors) was more than they could spare. In return for increasing their fleet accordingly, TNT got News International to underwrite the £7 million additional outlay if the unions did not strike and the train system could be used after all. Even with this agreement, there remained one potential snag: TNT had a closed-shop agreement with the TGWU whose members drove the lorries. If the drivers responded to their union's call not to enter Wapping, News International would be back with the problem of having piles of newspapers and no means of distributing them. But it was a risk that had to be taken. In June 1985, TNT was given a five-year contract. Meanwhile, British Rail knew nothing of the fact they were shortly to be dumped.

By then the computer system had been installed that would revolutionize newspaper editing and production. The decision to buy Atex had been taken in March. Murdoch wanted to use a system that was tried and tested rather than state of the art because only simple processes could be quickly picked up by 'half-trained manpower'.[25] It would be a disaster if the Wapping opportunity was squandered because staff could not figure out how to work the technology within their deadlines. It would have been easier and cheaper to use Atex's UK subsidiary, but the risk of news of the order leaking out was considered too great. Instead, the $10 million order was placed with the US parent company. The mainframes and typesetting equipment were huge and could have attracted attention while being shipped over from Boston, so they were transported in unmarked boxes and routed via Paris just to doubly confuse anyone who was monitoring their progress. Under the direction of Ben Smylie, the American-only staff charged with creating the software and installing the equipment were also flown over, their tracks suitably covered behind them.

Away from the prying eyes of Fleet Street, 'Smylie's People' (as they inevitably became known) got to work assembling the computer mainframes in a dilapidated but suitably anonymous shed by the Thames Barrier at Woolwich – codenamed 'The Bunker'. A small plaque was affixed, announcing that the shed belonged to 'Caprilord Limited', the cover company created to mask Atex's involvement. With a security guard posted to dissuade curious passers-by and the mist rising from the river, the scene had something of an illicit gangland operation about it, not least when the limousine of 'Gorbals' Wilson drew up to appraise the handiwork. Charged with designing the layout of the new offices as well as launching the *London Post*, Wilson was the Murdoch lieutenant who worked closest with the Atex team in getting the editorial floors technologically operational. Murdoch, the Godfather, visited on 20 April. On 1 May the first test run proved successful. At the end of the month the mainframes were transported over to Wapping, in the dead of night, in long, customized lorries. It was a sign of management's jumpiness that a helicopter flying low overhead just as the lorries were passing through the gates caused momentary alarm that the move was being monitored by spies hired by the unions. But the helicopter moved on, allowing the mainframes to be unloaded and installed on the fourth floor, behind doors that needed a special code to open. Weeks of teething problems and reconfigurations lay ahead, but 'Project X' was well underway.

Meanwhile, back at Gray's Inn Road the journalists were still unaware of the major news story that was waiting to burst. In league with the print unions, the NUJ prohibited any of their members from touching the three or four Atex terminals located on the editorial floor, leading one journalist to glance wistfully at the banned technology and murmur, 'I have seen the future and it's got dust on it.'[26] Little did he appreciate what was being installed a few miles to the east. Wilson and Douglas-Home maintained the façade. The situation was the same at the other News International titles. At the *Sunday Times* only the editor, Andrew Neil (who had experience of using Atex at his previous berth at *The Economist*), and James Adams knew what was being planned although Ivan Fallon, the deputy editor, had his suspicions confirmed.[27] But as the scheme proceeded to plan, so it became necessary to pass the 'Wapping Cough' onto a few more key personnel who, under the cover of sick leave, prepared the ground for the move.

In March, the company had publicly stated its intention to launch the new tabloid newspaper for the capital, the *London Post*. This was the biggest of all the ruses. It was not just a cover story for explaining signs of activity at Wapping. On the advice of News International's lawyer, Geoffrey Richards at Farrar & Co., London Post (Printers) Limited was established as Wapping's operating company. Thus, Wapping was given a separate legal identity from News Group in Bouverie Street and Times Newspapers in Gray's Inn Road. Come a strike, this would prove significant since it would allow the trade union legislation against secondary action to be invoked. It was formally announced that Charles Wilson was the *Post*'s editorial director. Oddly, this did not involve his standing down as deputy editor of *The Times*, but this point was passed over, perhaps because Wilson was well known for his multitasking skills. He even went as far as interviewing journalists for positions on the paper. One of those who turned up naively for an interview was Julie Burchill, who was poised to emerge as one of Fleet Street's more outspoken columnists and controversalists. Murdoch never intended the *Post* to see the light of day although if the unions managed, somehow, to prevent *The Times* and the other existing titles from being switched to Wapping, then there was the fallback possibility of launching *The Post* as an interim measure. In these circumstances, it might be the only way of getting Wapping operational. To that extent, the paper was not a complete fiction, but it would only hit the streets if the main plan failed and those responsible for establishing the shadow paper – in particular Charles Wilson – had no intention of letting the main plan fail.[28] Indeed, part of the cunning of the *Post* project was that it incited the unions to play into Murdoch's hands. It was hoped that merely the prospect of the *Post* being printed without their agreement would – at the appropriate moment – provoke the *Sun*, *News of the World*, *Times* and *Sunday Times* printers to come out on strike. In doing so they would provide Murdoch with the grounds to sack them and move his four papers to Wapping where they would be printed by staff happy to work there.

Wilson was the right man for the job. At the *Chicago Sun-Times* he had experienced at first hand how complete editorial control could work. At the *Sun-Times*, suggestions were acted upon at a time when in Fleet Street they would have created only months of consultation, negotiation and eventual cancellation. What was more, unlike Douglas-Home, Wilson understood the technical side of production. He brought a tight group of lieutenants with him to head-up the *Post*: Mike Hoy, Richard Williams, David Banks, John Bryant and (later) Tim Austin. All believed it was the

Post they were working on. Sworn to secrecy, they were installed in a back room at Gray's Inn Road and even accessed the building from a different entrance. In charge of subbing dummies of the paper, Austin was sent across to the *Chicago Sun-Times* for a fortnight's crash course on using the computer technology.[29]

The extent of the conspirators' secrecy seemed extreme: meeting venues were checked for bugs and long-range listening devices; key executives were advised to trim trees and bushes in their gardens in case they camouflaged eavesdroppers and to consider buying a dog. Ex-Royal Navy, Christopher Pole-Carew was in charge of directing the Wapping defences. When, after he had listed the security measures, Murdoch asked if there was anything else, Pole-Carew replied, 'well, that's all we can do, unless we use guns'. This was doubtless intended as a joke, although the nervous glance exchanged by Murdoch and Wilson suggested the need for reassurance. The subsequent proposal that the way to defeat the pickets' interference with small lorries coming into the plant was to file the underside of the lorries' bumpers to razor sharpness was not taken up. Some wondered if Pole-Carew was becoming overzealous.

In fact, the need for vigilance – rather than vigilante-ness – was real. Comings and goings at Wapping were being monitored by Tony Cappi, a SOGAT member, and Terry Ellis of the AUEW. By establishing contacts with those contracted to set up the plant, they were able to gain intelligence reports on what was going on behind the Wapping barbed wire. They discovered that Atex mainframes had been installed. To a sales manager of NAPP Systems, they posed as potential customers interested in purchasing photopolymer printing plates. They were told the company was supplying Wapping. Some of the work could be explained away as ongoing preparation for the *Post*'s launch if or when the unions gave it the go-ahead. But the *Post* was to be a tabloid. In May, Cappi and Ellis learned that the presses were being configured to print broadsheets. Cappi left an urgent message at the office of SOGAT General Secretary Brenda Dean and finally got to speak to her in June. From that moment on, he was a regular supplier of information.[30] In July, Dean had a meeting with the various chapel fathers, but it was not until the following month that, accompanied by SOGAT and NGA officials, she managed to get an appointment to speak with Bruce Matthews and Pole-Carew at Bouverie Street. The extent to which these two men provided obfuscatory answers was evident in the subsequent statement Dean released:

I am pleased to say that they both totally denied that any personnel were being recruited or were currently working in the premises being trained in jobs traditionally done by SOGAT members. The electricians and engineers working in the plant are engaged on the installation of electrical wiring and equipment.[31]

But it was not long before Brenda Dean had cause to doubt the helpful explanations she had received. By September, Cappi's spies had copied the names and numbers of over five hundred people with access to working at Wapping. Dean was in Blackpool for the last day of the TUC conference when she received a telephone call from a spy informing her that dummy runs of the *Post* had been successfully run off the Wapping presses. This was incontrovertible proof that the electricians were doing rather more than a bit of wiring. They were actually printing newspapers. Dean immediately got in touch with Tony Dubbins of the NGA and the various London officials. 'My own view,' she told them, 'is that we should stop the whole of News International tonight.' Dubbins pondered the options. Militants subsequently believed Dean had been slow to ascertain the seriousness of the situation although, according to her own recollection, she said:

Come on! Let's get real about this. Fleet Street stops at the drop of a hat for absolutely bugger all. This is not about money it's about jobs. We need to get home to Murdoch that we're not having it. We want to get to that negotiating table now, before they go any further ... What's wrong with you all? Now's the time to strike! What's wrong with you all?

She was sure that Murdoch was playing for time but, if confronted with the shutdown of all four of his titles, he would have to respond and respond on terms dictated by the unions. Back at home, at tea time on the Saturday, she got a call from SOGAT's general officer, Bill Miles. He said he had had a meeting with Bruce Matthews and the News International management. They had offered negotiations for the unions to work at Wapping and, therefore, the members had decided not to call a lightning strike. 'Of course,' Miles added, 'the chapels have said if you as General Secretary instruct them to come out, they'll stop the job tonight.' There was a short pause. 'Bill,' sighed Dean, 'if they're not prepared to stand up for themselves, I'm not prepared to put the union on the line for them.'

Thus the unions missed their opportunity to bring down Murdoch's media empire at the moment of his greatest vulnerability – while he was heavily in debt because of his expensive acquisitions in the American market and before he was ready to launch Wapping to produce the newspapers that kept him creditworthy. Instead the unions opted to be locked into months of fruitless negotiations during which time Wapping was brought into operational readiness. 'It was like a wife who is told her husband is playing away but refuses to accept it is happening' was how Wilson interpreted the moment of union self-denial.[32] Reflecting on the missed opportunity eighteen years later, Dean could still not comprehend how such a 'major tactical error' could have been made. 'It was a complete reverse of normal animal behaviour from our people,' she concluded. 'Normally they took action first and asked questions after.'[33]

V

The most important twenty months in Fleet Street's history passed between February 1985 and October 1986. In the popular market, News International faced sharper competition from Robert Maxwell's Mirror Group where a redundancy package was ruthlessly forced through. In the mid-market, there was the promise of similar savings at the *Express* while a new newspaper, *Today*, was planned by Eddy Shah using the latest technology and avoiding the traditional print unions. There was a similar situation in the broadsheet market where *The Times* faced new threats not only from its principal rival, the *Daily Telegraph*, which was rescued from bankruptcy, but from the launch of a new newspaper, the *Independent*, proudly trumpeting its sovereignty from traditional press baron ownership. In the space of twenty months, Fleet Street was destroyed as the capital of the newspaper kingdom.

The catalyst for some of these changes was an event Murdoch had originally opposed – the flotation of Reuters. In return for bailing the news agency out in 1941, the various Fleet Street titles, through the Newspaper Publishers' Association, had taken on a 41 per cent share in the company. Diversification into financial services information technology had subsequently made Reuters profitable. Its profits had quadrupled in Gerald Long's last year as its managing director and doubled again in 1982. By purchasing Times Newspapers, Murdoch had doubled his potential shareholding. If it was floated on the stock exchange, it could realize him between £90 and £100 million. As one of the ten directors on the Reuters board, Murdoch thus had an interest in pushing for the company to be floated. But floating Reuters was against the spirit of the terms that had been agreed in 1941 (in a document drawn up by William Haley who was subsequently *The Times*'s editor). What was more, it would give Murdoch no obvious advantage over his Fleet Street rivals since they would all make similar gains. He did not push for Reuters to be floated. But others on the board were intent on liquidating their assets and in 1984 the company was duly quoted on the stock exchange. While Murdoch chose to hold onto his shares, rivals went for the quick profit. The *Guardian* realized £70 million, paying off all its debts as a consequence and laying the groundwork for a new printing plant in London's Docklands. Associated Newspapers, owner of the *Daily Mail* and a range of regional titles, netted the most. By 1990, it had realized £300 million from its Reuters shares and built new print works in Docklands. Across Fleet Street, proprietors now had the ready money to push for expansion.[34]

With these proceeds, plans could be laid for new and less labour-intensive printing plants. Robert Maxwell even raised the prospect of colour printing. A clash with the unions was imminent. In the second half of 1985, the warning shots began to be fired. The new chairman of the Express titles, David Stevens, made no secret of his hopes to move his papers out of Fleet Street and to reduce the payroll. Even more significant from Murdoch's perspective was the determination to cut out waste by Robert Maxwell who, in 1984, had controversially bought Mirror Group Newspapers. A dispute at the *Sporting Life* had led to his Mirror titles being suspended for a fortnight in August 1985. Vowing 'the gravy train has hit the buffers', he retaliated with a major redundancy programme to cut the total of his employees from 7000 to 2100. A two-week closure at the home of his Scottish papers ensued. Maxwell emerged victorious by deploying a mixture of barbed wire, security guards, threats to move from Glasgow and employ non-union workers and the deployment through the courts of the Thatcher Government's trade union legislation.[35] Some thought these methods incompatible with Maxwell's socialist protestations. But while he had used all means available to him to cut the payroll, he did not destroy the principles of chapel power: the absence of legally binding contracts and retention of the closed shop. In common with every other newspaper proprietor, his journalists still did not have direct input of their own material.

Although not one of the beneficiaries of the Reuters largesse, Eddy Shah, survivor of the Messenger dispute, had begun to think beyond the confines of Warrington and was envisaging a far more revolutionary plan. He conceived a new mid-market national newspaper to be called *Today*, edited by Brian MacArthur. Loosely modelled on *USA Today*, it would transmit its papers via satellite to regional printing plants in Heathrow, Birmingham and Manchester. In doing so it would be free from Fleet Street's restrictive practices and could thus be produced at a cost that significantly undercut the existing titles. Extraordinarily, its planners budgeted that it could break even without any advertising on sales of 600,000. What was more, by using the latest technology and printing in colour it would be attractive to readers. Its journalists would have direct input. The union boss who was able to deliver these non-restrictive practices was none other than Eric Hammond of the EETPU. Buoyed up by his successful negotiations with Murdoch, Hammond had approached Shah in April 1985 with a no-strike guarantee that became public three months later.[36] Like Murdoch, *Today*'s founder also planned distribution by road not rail. Eddy Shah threatened not just the traditional print unions but also the traditional press barons. If *Today*'s colour technology worked and the *Sun* failed to be moved to Wapping, Murdoch faced serious competition.

The plans for moving *The Times* to Wapping were in their final stages when, on 27 December 1985, the *Financial Times* broke the news that a paper called the *Independent* was to be launched in the new year. It would be the first new national quality broadsheet to enter the market since the *Daily Telegraph*, 131 years earlier. At first, it was hard to comprehend how serious a threat it would pose. Like opposing groups of First World War sappers mining underneath each other's trenches, the plans for launching the *Independent* and for relocating *The Times* to Wapping had been evolving in total ignorance of the other's existence. The three founding fathers of the *Independent*, Andreas Whittam Smith, Matthew Symonds and Stephen Glover, were all respected journalists at the *Daily Telegraph*. This was significant. *The Times*'s principal rival was in serious trouble. Its owner, Lord Hartwell, had decided to provide it with expensive and modern print works in Manchester and London's Isle of Dogs at a combined cost that soon exceeded £100 million. Union militancy had ensured that the level of overmanning at the *Telegraph* had been such that it made *The Times* look like a comparatively lean operation. This was one of the reasons why the market leader, with daily sales in excess of 1.2 million, somehow managed to be a money loser. The new print works would produce a better paper at a lower cost but in the short term only added to Hartwell's headache: the proposed redundancy scheme alone was estimated at £38 million. Having greatly overstretched his resources – and his Reuters payout – he scraped around for ways to raise money. When the take-up on his share offer was less than expected, the Canadian businessman Conrad Black scented blood. Black bought a 14 per cent stake together with a first-refusal option on any future share offers. Hartwell soon found himself forced into a fresh share issue that Black duly snapped up. By December 1985, Black had secured a majority stake and made Andrew Knight chief executive. For the gentlemanly Hartwell, who since 1954 had been editor-in-chief of a paper his father had bought and vastly improved in 1928, it was undoubtedly sad to see his own position become effectively honorific. Yet, he was to live long enough to see Knight and Black turn the bankrupt company around.[37] With the *Telegraph* saved and poised for rejuvenation and the *Independent* about to be launched, the future for *The Times* looked to be a lean one unless it could reap the advantages involved in Project Wapping.

VI

In 1985, SOGAT's general secretary, Brenda Dean, was forty-three years old and in only her first year in the post. She was the first woman to head a major British trade union. What was more, in taking care of her appearance and with an elegant blonde bouffant (rather, if truth be told, in the manner of Margaret Thatcher), she appeared the antithesis of the traditional union brotherhood. This was both her strength – as far as the public was concerned – and her weakness when it came to dealing with the (resolutely male) Fleet Street chapels. She did not come from a particularly entrenched union background (her father had been a British Railways inspector) and grew up in Salford. This caused some misgivings among those in the London Central branch who considered themselves a class apart and disliked the interference of supposed no-nothing provincials in their affairs.[38] Doubtless, some were also alarmed that she was dating the CBI's director of information. But she was devoted to the union that she had joined not long after leaving school at sixteen to become a shorthand typist. During the 1970s she even turned down the options of a safe Labour seat or membership of the Downing Street think tank in order to manage SOGAT's affairs. Her tenure as secretary of the Greater Manchester branch had coincided with a doubling of the membership. By 1983 she had risen to national president and two years later to the key position of general secretary.

Shortly after taking command of SOGAT, Dean made a ten-day visit to the United States to examine the effect of the introduction of new technology. She concluded in her report that 'opposition is not an option, it is simply a rapid road to de-unionization'. In writing this, she was taking a bold stand for modernization that would involve, in particular, confronting the short-term interests not only of her Fleet Street members but also those of the rival union, the NGA, which was still committed to the absurdity of double-key stroking. There was little love lost. Her first direct experience of Fleet Street negotiating had come shortly after the end of the 1978–9 shutdown at Times Newspapers. She was not impressed. 'It was negotiation with mob instincts,' she concluded. Incredulous at the salaries some of the printers were earning she told the journalist Linda Melvern: 'I don't know what they spend it on. They all live in council houses.'[39] Had she been in a position to enforce such views some years earlier, her union might never have been locked out from Wapping.

Instead the negotiations for the print unions' participation at Wapping recommenced on 30 September with Dean and the other union leaders convening at the Inn on the Park to hear Murdoch's terms. Murdoch's Gulfstream G3 had narrowly avoided Hurricane Gloria on its route before decanting Murdoch, John Keating and Bill O'Neill at Stansted airport. The union bosses could have been forgiven for imagining the trip had affected the chairman's mood. But, assisted in the drafting by Charles Wilson, he had carefully prepared a statement – which *The Times* proceeded to print in full.[40] He made clear that the negotiations would only concern the proposal to print the *London Post*. If successful, the terms could then be extended to embrace printing the *Sun* and the *News of the World* there too. The implication was that *The Times* and *Sunday Times* would continue, as before, to be printed from Gray's Inn Road. The union representatives had to listen while Murdoch made clear he was tired of employing workers who managed twenty hours a week at double the national average wage; tired of some of them getting as much as twelve weeks holiday; tired of a system in which he could only employ whoever the unions offered for a vacancy:

I have strained myself and my colleagues physically, emotionally and financially to build this business and we have been met with nothing but cynicism, broken promises and total opposition . . . The result today is that all national newspaper production departments are over

manned by from fifty to three hundred per cent, with working practices that are a continuing disgrace to us all.[41]

The irony, of course, was that on this occasion it was News International
that would be negotiating in bad faith. Having determined to operate
Wapping without the traditional print unions, Murdoch's men were not
about to undo all the secretive planning by a last-minute U-turn. Instead,
with delays in getting the new *Times* editorial floor ready, the negotiations
would serve a purpose in buying time for Wapping to become operational.
What was more, the talks could be confidently predicted to show the
print unions unwilling to accept the modern working practices the project
demanded.

News International set a three month deadline for the talks to be concluded. In charge of the negotiating team was Bill O'Neill who, after a year
in the United States, made a poor job of hiding his depression at having
to be back in the company of many of those who had made his life a misery
the last time he had attempted to get them to operate Wapping. For their
part, the unions knew enough about 'Project X' to fear the prospect of
a breakdown in the talks. This time they really did want an agreement.
Nonetheless, they reacted in disbelief at O'Neill's insistence that management would determine the appropriate number of men to work a press.
'You are trying to introduce the work practices of an alien continent,' one
of the NGA's team spluttered. O'Neill replied that the far off land was
called 'the real world'.[42]

Between mid-October and the end of the negotiations, O'Neill conducted thirty-two meetings with the unions. He made clear that journalists on
the *Post* would have direct input of their own copy; that there would be
no union 'closed shop' circumscribing who could be employed; that there
would be legally binding contracts; that disputes would be settled by legally
binding arbitration not by strikes (anyone who struck during his contract
period would be sacked without appeal); and that management had the
right to introduce new technology even if it involved cutting staff. In
essence the package heralded the end of the multiple-chapel system that
had plagued attempts to make fast agreements. As to what would have
happened if the unions had agreed to all News International's terms, O'Neill
later conceded, 'while what was presented was not uncommon in U.S.
labour contracts, it was completely foreign and unacceptable at that time
to the unions I was meeting with. They could never have accepted them
and a strike was inevitable'.[43]

Given their previous attitude, it was a sign of how scared the unions were that they were nonetheless prepared to make some major sacrifices. On 22 November, the NGA conceded direct input to journalists in return for a fifty-fifty representation with SOGAT for double-stroking the columns of advertising. For the first time in the history of Fleet Street, journalists' copy would not be needlessly retyped by members of a print union. In other areas there appeared little progress. The unions continued to oppose legally binding contracts. Complaining that he had endured 'seventeen years of hell', Murdoch made clear this was non-negotiable. When Eric Hammond broke ranks to state that the EETPU had no objection to legally binding contracts, the other unions recognized that they were being outmanoeuvred. On 11 December, they reported the EETPU to the TUC, hoping disciplinary action would be taken against its non-collective attitude.[44]

With Brenda Dean in the chair, the print unions – temporarily putting aside their traditional suspicions of each another – debated what to do at a meeting in the TUC's Congress House on 9 December. Various rumours were discussed, including that News International had developed 'connections' with TNT to deliver the newspapers and sidestep the SOGAT distribution system and the apparent presence of one thousand workers recruited by the EETPU who were up to something 'within the Wapping development'. Most alarming of all was the 'information received informally' that a sixty-page dummy equivalent of the *Sunday Times* had been run off the Wapping presses and that 'there was adequate space and machinery to move in all the titles. Indeed there were rumours that *Times* journalists had already been told they would be moving to Wapping.' This last piece of news was wrong – *Times* journalists had heard nothing – but what was most remarkable about the union meeting was the conclusions drawn from the evidence. Through united action, the unions believed they retained the whip hand since 'at the present time, sixty per cent of the worldwide income of News International was raised by *The Sun* and the *News of the World*; the proprietor would not wish to place either in jeopardy'. Consequently the committee drew up a draft proposal for solidarity in opposing Murdoch's humiliating terms.[45]

The deadline for the talks with News International was Christmas Eve. The last meeting before it, attended by the full union top brass, including Dean and Harry Conroy of the NUJ (whose opening gambit was to ask where O'Neill's black shirt was), broke up without any agreement on 19 December. Three days later, O'Neill telephoned Dean to see if she wanted to talk further. She replied that there was no point. The following day, Bill Miles wrote to Bruce Matthews to inform him that the print unions were united in demanding that News International offer all those it currently employed jobs for life with wage increases 'not least [sic] than the annual retail price index'. If there was a transferral to new premises 'you will guarantee that the members of the unions concerned will be offered employment at the alternative premises with full continuity of employment at their prevailing wages and conditions'. If these demands were not met the unions would go on strike.[46]

The demand was fantastic, incredible. Murdoch had hoped the three-month negotiating period would demonstrate the print unions' reluctance to agree legally binding contracts to work at Wapping, but he could scarcely believe his luck when they threatened to bring down the company if all their members were not granted jobs for life. It was hard to conceive what more the unions could have done to publicize their imperviousness to moderation. In doing so they determined to make a stand upon a battlefield whose topography was all against them. Instead of appearing the aggrieved party forced into industrial action by a callous boss's use of blackleg labour from a covert plant, they ensured that Murdoch could be seen as the put-upon businessman calling upon a coalition of the willing against Luddite militants who had silenced his existing plants in the pursuit of wholly unreasonable demands.

In fact, News International's lawyer, Geoffrey Richards of Farrar & Co., had skilfully manoeuvred the unions into this situation. The Wapping plant was legally distinct from News International's other operations. Since a strike at Gray's Inn Road and Bouverie Street on the issue of preventing EETPU members working at Wapping would be illegal under secondary action legislation, the print unions had to make an unacceptable demand ('jobs for life') knowing it would be rejected so that they could legally call a strike that would coincide with Wapping's launch. But they were playing directly into Murdoch's hands. Had they not struck, News International would have had to pay their wages for a further six months while the existing house agreements were still in force. Their decision to strike not only relieved Murdoch of that burden but also of the £40 million redundancy payments to which they would otherwise have been legally entitled.

The print unions opted to strike because they were confident of success. Indeed, their strategy was based upon a fatal assumption that a financially stretched Murdoch could not bring his papers out if the NGA and SOGAT called industrial action. Bill Miles had been looking into the financial structure of News International and concluded that its gearing was far too high for Murdoch to put at risk his Fleet Street cash crop. News Corp. had borrowed $2.6 billion to acquire the American companies that would become its Fox film and television empire. A huge debt burden was being carried. This, it was predicted, was his Achilles heel. Union colleagues complacently assured Brenda Dean that not a single paper would emerge from the Wapping plant without the guiding expertise of SOGAT and NGA members. 'My view,' Dean later admitted, 'was they couldn't sustain a stoppage of two weeks without any papers at all so there would have needed to be a negotiation.' Even if – as she thought more likely – Wapping managed a limited production run, Murdoch would still have to climb down or face financial meltdown.[47] On 13 January 1986, SOGAT's strike ballots were sent out to their members. The siege of Fortress Wapping was about to begin.

VII

The following day *The Times*'s widely respected subeditor, Tim Austin, received a phone call. It was Charles Wilson, on typical form: 'I want to meet you early tomorrow morning. Early for you. I'll meet you eight o'clock at Waterloo. I'll be in my car. Don't miss me. If you do, you're a dead man.' Despite having spent the last few months with Richard Williams and Michael Hoy assisting Wilson on the *London Post* start-up, Austin had no idea what the new *Times* editor was talking about. Nonetheless, he did not want to miss out and arrived two trains earlier than was strictly necessary. Eventually, Wilson's chauffeured limousine drew up. The back seat window glided down. 'Get in,' Wilson commanded, 'I'm taking you to Wapping. That's where we're printing' – Austin finished the editor's sentence – 'the *Post*?' The editor smiled thinly. 'Just wait,' he murmured. The limousine passed over Tower Bridge and turned east along the Wapping Highway and down Virginia Street. Then Austin got his first sight of what he subsequently described as 'this hideous vision of barbed wire, ten-foot-high steel fences and this ghastly building'. 'Just look at that,' Wilson cut in admiringly. 'That place is going to change your life!'[48]

Over the next few days Wilson repeated the journey taking the newspaper's key personnel one at a time to visit the plant on the condition they were sworn to absolute secrecy. Most knew the company had plans for

Wapping – *The Times* had, after all, reported the breakdown in the *Post* negotiations – but only a handful had any idea that a whole new *Times* office had been constructed within an anonymous looking single-storey East End warehouse.[49] The vast majority of the editorial staff remained totally in the dark. The pressure upon Wilson over the past months had been tremendous. He had been dividing his time between *The Times* – which, with Douglas-Home's removal to hospital, he was assuming much of the burden of editing – and the Wapping project where he was giving the impression he was setting up the *Post*, issuing instructions and inter-viewing staff for it as well as designing the layout and overseeing the equipping of *The Times*'s new office. For months without let up, his day started before dawn when he awoke and read the morning's papers. Then he would go to Gray's Inn Road to discuss the day's agenda with the news desk. After the morning conference at 10.30 he would work on administration matters in his office until slipping out to go to Wapping. There he would confer with the Atex staff and continue the direction of laying out *The Times*'s new office. He would return to Gray's Inn Road for the afternoon conference at 4.30 and stay there until the first edition had left the stone after 8 p.m. On his way home, he would call in on the Atex staff for a drink in their Belgravia 'safe house'. That nobody who was not in on the secret knew Wilson was leading this demanding double life was a tribute to his organizational powers and resilience. Nor was it just the journalists who remained in the dark. When the directors of the Times Newspapers (Holdings) board had met on 10 December, they were given scant indication from Murdoch that *The Times* was about to move home. The meeting lasted forty-five minutes. When it next convened, the move had taken place.[50] There was only one major lapse in the security and this came, unaccountably, from Bruce Matthews. The managing director took it upon himself to tell Andrew Knight, the incoming chief executive of *The Times*'s great rival, the *Telegraph*, the details and even the exact timing of the move to Wapping when he met him, for the first time, in late December. He then updated Knight several times during the first fortnight of the new year. 'The information was critically important for us,' Knight subsequently admitted, although, no less amazingly, the news never leaked out from the executive floor of the *Telegraph*'s offices.[51] It was a bizarre and crazy risk for Matthews to have taken which defied any obvious business logic. Fortunately, the leak spread no further.

It was too soon to give the game away to the unions but just the right moment to antagonize them into making a false move that would put them

– in the public's eyes – in the wrong. On the night of 18 January 1986, while the union ballot papers were still being filled in, a twelve-page supplement for the *Sunday Times* was printed at Wapping. In an act of conscious provocation it was an 'Innovation Special' featuring the new plant, its possibilities and confrontational contributions from Murdoch and the editor, Andrew Neil, in a leader column. Murdoch anticipated that printing the supplement would bring an instant shutdown at Gray's Inn Road, where the other sections of the paper were going to press. A police helicopter with search beam hovered above the Wapping plant looking for (non-existent) saboteurs while the company executives, joined by lawyer Geoffrey Richards, stood waiting for the expected enemy to show itself. Suspecting a trap, Brenda Dean issued a statement telling her members to hold fire, before making clear 'we are not prepared to see our members treated like eighteenth century mill-workers or Australian convicts'. Down in the cramped print room at Gray's Inn Road, a heated exchange took place between Bill Gillespie, TNL managing director, and Roy 'Ginger' Wilson of the SOGAT machine room chapel. The result was that the printers brought the main section of the *Sunday Times* out as slowly as possible, achieving only half the print run. It was a final, albeit typical, gesture.[52]

The union high command was not going to be rushed into wildcat action before the confidently predicted results of the official ballots were announced. In any case, they did not want to damage the possibility that through a broad based demonstration of union solidarity they could successfully breach Fortress Wapping. One possibility was that the EETPU members could be persuaded not to work the presses. Another was to convince the journalists to down pencils. The first prospect quickly receded. Although the TUC general secretary, Norman Willis, worked on a plan to get the print unions to make further concessions and for Eric Hammond to come into line, Hammond would not be moved. In his defence, he cited the law. His members had individual contracts to work at Wapping but the EETPU itself had no formal agreement. Thus, in the terms of the trade union legislation on secondary action, the EETPU could not order a strike against a company with which it had no contractual agreement.[53] Bill O'Neill was of the view that even if Hammond had asked his electricians not to work at Wapping, they would have carried on regardless.[54] They wanted the work. They needed the money. As for the journalists, the print unions could expect a show of solidarity from NUJ activists, but could not be confident that journalists whose hard work had so frequently been spiked by militancy in the print room would leap to their aid. At a meeting on 21 January, *The Times* NUJ chapel duly instructed its members that, in the event of a strike by the NGA and SOGAT, journalists were only to do their work 'using existing personnel and technologies' and 'not to enter the Wapping plant.' Since 'existing technologies' involved all articles being double-key stroked by NGA members, the NUJ was effectively serving notice that it would be joining the strike.[55] *Times* staff would have to decide whether they were primarily loyal to their union or to their employer. Given the secretive manner in which their move to Wapping was being planned behind their backs, some felt their employer had yet to demonstrate loyalty to them.

Later the same day, the results of the print unions' ballots were released. Among SOGAT members, the vote was 3534 for striking and 752 against (an 82 per cent yes vote); the margin was similar among NGA members with 843 voting yes and 117 voting no (an 87.8 per cent yes vote).[56] On 23 January, Murdoch agreed to meet Brenda Dean and her colleagues in two hours of talks at the Park Lane Hotel. He offered new five-year contracts for 'some hundreds' of the five thousand print workers currently employed on his four titles so that they could continue printing editions from Bou-veric Street and Gray's Inn Road, but he would no longer entertain print union representation at Wapping. For her part, Dean went as far as she possibly could to make last-minute concessions on management's 'right to manage,' binding arbitration and a prohibition of wildcat strikes. Such concessions were probably too great for her members and too late for Murdoch. The meeting broke up with neither side accepting its opponent's offers. 'It's tragic that they've missed this opportunity,' Murdoch announced to the waiting press; 'we have been begging the unions to come to an agreement at Wapping for six years now. Earlier on we would have given them all sorts of things.'[57] The following day, the print unions' national executives brought their members out on strike. All five and a half thousand of them – printers, typists, telephonists, librarians, clerks, cleaners – were duly sacked.

On the evening of Friday 24 January, Bill O'Neill telephoned Brenda Dean. She confirmed the strike was on and in the course of an amicable conversation made clear she thought it would be over within a fortnight when, unable to print enough newspapers or get them distributed, News International would reopen negotiations. It was easy to understand the unions' optimism. They did not think Wapping had the capacity. They knew it took all ninety press units at Gray's Inn Road to print the *Sunday Times* and that there were only forty-eight available units at Wapping. But what they did not calculate was that the Wapping employees were prepared to work using methods that kept the newsprint flowing without constant stops to reload and that Wapping staff were able to average about fifty thousand copies an hour. This was more than double what NGA and SOGAT members at Gray's Inn Road had felt within their powers to produce.

Yet even if Wapping's electricians managed to bring the papers out, SOGAT was still confident of preventing distribution. Eighteen hundred SOGAT members were employed at the ninety depots of the country's biggest newspaper wholesaler, WH Smith. Dean promised they would black all News International titles. The union also hoped to prevent production at subsidiary plants in Merseyside, Watford and Manchester where the colour magazines for the *Sunday Times* and *News of the World*, together with extra copies of the tabloid's main section, were printed. Furthermore, Dean had met Ron Todd of the TGWU before Christmas to insist that his members did not drive TNT lorries carrying the papers. Approaches were also made to ASLEF and the NUR to prevent rail distribution.[58] On the night of 23 January, the print union and transport union officials met to coordinate disrupting distribution from Wapping. Together they would show Murdoch who was boss. That night, *The Times*'s deputy editor, Colin Webb, was down on 'the stone' and was surprised to witness the print workers' cheerful attitude. 'We're off for a weekends' golf', they assured him; 'see you Tuesday when Rupert gives in.'[59]

VIII

On the morning of 24 January, Rupert Murdoch, Charles Wilson and Peter Stothard stood in *The Times* vestibule at Gray's Inn Road waiting to greet Shimon Peres, the Israeli Prime Minister. A semicircle of angry print workers faced them. One member of the reception committee quipped mirthlessly that the Israeli security guards might have to protect the hosts rather than the guest.[60] Throughout the building, *Times* journalists wondered who, if anybody, was going to print the paper that evening. The editor, whom they looked to for leadership and protection, had told them nothing. There had been no mention of moving to Wapping at the morning news conference chaired by Colin Webb. At 7.30 p.m., a PA wire confirmed that the strike was going ahead as planned. Desperate to find out what was afoot, a demand was made for the editor to address his staff in a room journalists had booked in Holborn. Webb, however, took the view that Wilson should not answer a summons as if to some revolutionary tribunal but, rather, should call the staff to hear him, and to do so on the home territory of Gray's Inn Road.[61] This was psychologically astute. Wilson had been editor for only three months. What was more, he had spent much of the past two years away from *The Times* office, first in Chicago and subsequently hovering around Wapping. Consequently, he had not had a chance to sustain the personal following or natural authority that the late Charles Douglas-Home could have commanded in the situation. Yet, if journalists did not respond to his appeal, not only Wapping but the future of *The Times* would hang in the balance.

It was not until 8.20 p.m. that Charles Wilson finally strode into a room packed with tense journalists. To rise above the scrum he clambered on top of a table. Hush descended. It was noticed that he was visibly shaking. 'The storm has broken tonight,' he declared: 'We have lost tonight's paper. But we do not intend to lose any more editions of *The Times*. It is going to be produced editorially at Wapping – on Sunday night for the Monday paper. I am here to invite you to come along and help us do it.'

He told them to clear their desks of all their possessions – this would be their last day at Gray's Inn Road – and announced the news that the *Sun*'s journalists had just voted overwhelmingly to go to Wapping. *Times* staff refusing to go there would be sacked for breach of contract. Those who went to Wapping would get a £2000 pay rise and free private health insurance for their family. But more to the point, they would be free at last to type their own articles straight into the editorial system. 'At a single key stroke, this gives the journalist his birthright,' he declaimed. 'I implore you to come with us.'[62]

Had the appeal worked? One journalist was heard to whisper 'he's won', but the tone of the questions asked was hostile and there was considerable muttering as the packed meeting dispersed. That the editor had conspired with Murdoch but not involved or even forewarned his own staff was seen as a betrayal. He had put a gun to his journalists' heads, informing them at almost the last possible moment to move everything to some probably hideous site somewhere in the East End of London (of all places) or be sacked. Such dismissive treatment infuriated those who felt they were professionals being hired or fired like casual cleaners. One journalist went up to Wilson and hissed 'I hate you for this'. Greg Neale, *The Times* NUJ chapel father, convened the second chapel meeting of the day at 9.30 p.m.

It took the decision for a mass meeting the following afternoon. The journalists would not be taken for granted.

The last piece of filed copy for the never-to-appear *Times* that evening reported that there would be an-all night vigil at St Bride's, 'the journalists' church' in Fleet Street, for the future of the newspaper industry.[63] Only as the journalists filed out of Gray's Inn Road that night did it really dawn on them they might never return there. Most of the cars had been moved from the surrounding streets and police ringed the building. The magnitude of what was happening only struck one journalist when he spotted the editor's secretary, Liz Seeber, pulling paintings of past proprietors (she could not find a screwdriver) off the panelled editorial walls. Seeber recalled:

> I had my car outside the reception door and Joe [the editor's chauffeur] was down there reclining and having a fag and then he rang me the moment the SOGAT official disappeared around the corner. So I rushed down to the car and shoved the paintings into my car and Joe had the others and we all went off to Wapping at about ten o'clock at night.[64]

But would the journalists – hurt at being taken for granted – follow the oil paintings of Murdoch's predecessors?

CHAPTER SIX

FIFTY-FOUR WEEKS
UNDER SIEGE

The Siege of Wapping and its Consequences

I

'History is rarely so convenient, but the day that production began at Wapping was the day when, to all intents and purposes, old Fleet Street ended.'[1] The assessment by the financial historian David Kynaston has become the accepted judgment on the cold, miserable day of Saturday 25 January 1985.

The events of that day took place in the teeth of opposition not only from the print unions but also from the journalists' representatives. The National Union of Journalists had instructed its members not to go to Wapping. Journalists at the *Sun* and the *News of the World* voted overwhelmingly to disregard the order.[2] But the ballot among *Times* and *Sunday Times* journalists was reckoned to be a close call. *The Times* NUJ chapel met in the 'ballroom' (the term was not descriptive) of the Royal National Hotel in Bloomsbury. Joining Greg Neale, the chapel father, were the NUJ general secretary, Harry Conroy, and his deputy, Jake Ecclestone. The presence of the union's high command demonstrated how seriously they took the matter. But Conroy, a bluff left-wing Glaswegian, was not naturally appealing to the softer spoken sections of the audience while many remembered Ecclestone, a former *Times* chapel father, as the man whose militancy had led to the paper being sold to Rupert Murdoch in the first place. For the moment, though, such splitist tendencies were put to one side and the NUJ platform party told the *Times* journalists to stand shoulder to shoulder with their print union brothers and not to accept potentially open-ended contractual obligations at Wapping. 'You are *Times* journalists,' Greg Neale pointed out, 'and not even Murdoch, even in this political climate, could get support if he'd just sacked the entire *Times* staff.'[3]

In fact, many *Times* staff were energized by the news that Murdoch was poised to free the paper from the print unions' grip, perhaps making it sustainably profitable for the first time in their working lives. Disobeying the NUJ edict, they had already started drifting over to the new *Times* office behind the wire at Wapping to help get the Monday edition ready. Bill Bryson, still subediting the business news pages, was sorry for the many blameless individuals who had suddenly lost their jobs but he could not help basking 'in the glow of a single joyous thought' that he would no longer be involved in the nightly demarcation battle with lazy and violent SOGAT wire-room operators. Other subeditors welcomed the opportunity to be freed from similar battles of will. An NGA compositor had once spat at Peter Brown for indicating where he wanted a minor copy alteration. Brown felt the print unions had squandered the sympathy that would normally have been due them. What was more, given the rumours that Murdoch had a reserve army of Australians waiting to write *The Times* if its staff went on strike, Brown wanted to know what the NUJ's fall-back strategy was if the paper could be brought out without its official staff. To this, there was no convincing answer.[4]

Ranged against the Wapping advocates were colleagues with a variety of grievances. For a few, union solidarity was an important consideration. Harry Conroy threatened to bring NUJ disciplinary action against any member who went to Wapping. But, as speeches from the floor made clear, the principal issue was outrage at the appalling way in which *Times* staff had been treated and taken for granted by their management. Employed to unearth facts and reveal truth, their professional pride had been dented by their inability to detect what their own management had been plotting under their very noses. Indeed, the failure of any journalist in any section of the British media to predict accurately the scale of Murdoch's coup stood as an indictment. Many felt duped. There was also a more selfish angle. Neale's claim that Murdoch could not produce the paper without its journalists had resonance. Some believed that the proprietor's moment of crisis was their moment of opportunity. Given how much Murdoch needed them to support the greatest gamble of his life, why should they meekly assent to do his bidding without pushing for a better offer? If threatened, he might make all manner of worthwhile concessions.

From the outside, not all commentators had sympathy with journalists' wounded pride and sense of self-worth. Paul Johnson, the *Spectator*'s media correspondent, was scathing, lecturing that 'Civilization is not merely created and advanced by individuals; it is promoted and above all upheld by institutions.' Now was not the moment to risk a great paper's future, especially since many of those demanding a show of loyalty from management had not even shown it towards the former mild-mannered Thomson ownership.[5] This was not a sentiment much aired during the hours of debate at the hotel ballroom. Those who had always disliked what they saw as Murdoch's casual attitude to the disposability of his staff believed he had to be taught a lesson. Some argued that his demands were illegal. To find out if this could be true, they summoned the labour lawyer (and future Lord Chancellor) Derry Irvine. Corralled in an upstairs bedroom in the hotel, he gave his opinion that there were no grounds to sue News International for issuing an ultimatum to move to Wapping although there might be an opportunity to claim for unfair dismissal if anyone was sacked. This advice was not as positive as many had hoped. The speechifying continued until midnight by which time the meeting had been in session for ten hours. A motion was passed (by fifty-nine votes to fifty-eight) which, although supporting the principle of going to Wapping (subject to negotiating better terms and conditions), deferred final judgment until a further meeting on Sunday. The opponents would need only one Wapping supporter to switch sides in order to derail *The Times*'s move.[6]

The key event had already taken place that night. The first pickets – up to two hundred – had assembled outside the Wapping plant, but, inside, the Sunday newspapers had been produced. Surrounded by his senior executives, Murdoch had pressed the button that started the presses rolling at 8 p.m. There was clapping and cheering. Few had ever seen the proprietor in such buoyant mood. Then he turned away from his entourage to make a telephone call. The recipient was Bert Hardy, now at Associated Newspapers and the man whose idea building the Wapping plant had been in the first place and whom Murdoch had subsequently sacked. 'We've done it,' Murdoch hollered down the receiver, 'and I'd just like to thank you.' Little more than an hour later, the first editions were leaving the plant. That night three million copies of the *News of the World* (plus 750,000 printed in Glasgow) and 1.2 million of the *Sunday Times* were printed. The former was two million down on Bouverie Street's production run while the latter had a shortfall of around 150,000. But it was good enough. Management collectively sighed with relief.[7] Britain awoke on the Sunday morning to a new dawn in the country's journalism. It happened to be Australia Day.

This was the sobering reality confronting 'refuseniks' as they made there way to the Marlborough Crest Hotel for the conclusion of the NUJ vote. It was a bitter affair. Angela Gordon, the *Times* Diary editor, called for those who had gone to Wapping that morning in order to bring the paper out ahead of the chapel's vote to resign their union membership. Telexes came in from Charles Wilson accepting the demands made in the previous night's motion. Making the obvious deductions, Don McIntyre argued that only by standing firm would a better deal be offered. Greg Neale implored the meeting to vote 'no'. But a show of hands indicated a three to one vote in favour of going to Wapping. By the time the platform party announced the result and Neale his own resignation as chapel father, the first edition of *The Times*, written and produced from Wapping, was already hitting the streets without them.[8] Several long-serving journalists were in tears.

Bringing that first Wapping edition of the paper out with only a skeleton staff defying the NUJ chapel directive not to do so was an especially difficult task. As Charles Wilson put it, it was 'a bit like parachute jumping or the art of seduction. You had better get it right first time because you might never get another chance.'[9] For the past three months the paper's production editor, Tony Norbury, had been working round the clock to get it right. He had spent the last few weeks with a folding camp bed by his side, snatching a few hours sleep each night in between longer and longer shifts. For the final stretch, Murdoch had been helping out as Norbury's general handyman, subbing work, forwarding copy, running errands, issuing instructions, encouragements and occasional oaths. When the moment of truth arrived, as with the *Sunday Times* the evening before, there was a tremendous sense of expectation. Again, the management and production staff encircled Murdoch and started clapping as he pressed the button that started the first edition of *The Times* from Wapping. There was a sound of revving, then of whirling. The presses started to roll. As they did so, the platform party turned to Tony Norbury and gave him a no less deserved round of applause. Sixty-six per cent of the *Times* print run was completed on the first night and much of it left the plant late, ensuring delayed distribution that left large areas of Britain without the paper on the newsstand by the crucial morning rush hour. But it was good enough to ensure subsequent performances and it was 66 per cent more than the print unions had boasted would come out.

Tim Austin was among the coterie of *Times* journalists who had gone to help bring out the first edition from Wapping while his colleagues were still debating whether to join him. When he had finished subbing it, he formed part of a small group who went off to watch the departure of the first edition at about 9 p.m. He recalled the moment of the great breakout:

We stood behind the fence and watched the trucks lining up behind the gate, revving. There were hordes of baying pickets. The noise was fantastic. A huge police presence. The whole of the area was floodlit. Cries of 'Scabs! Scabs! Bastards!' The police were confident their line would hold for the trucks to get out. You could see the driver in the first lorry. He had obviously psyched himself up. The potential for him being damaged severely was pretty clear. They opened the gates and he just put his foot down. I've never seen a lorry accelerate so quickly. By the time he got to the gatehouse he must have been doing thirty miles an hour. If he was going to kill somebody, too bad. He wanted to get out.[10]

II

On Monday morning, the journalists turned up at their new home. The barbed wire and security measures were the first shock. *The Times*'s new office was the second. Allegedly, French Napoleonic prisoners of war had constructed the building as a rum warehouse in 1805. Its former use fleetingly gave heart to those journalists who had not yet discovered that Wapping was to be a 'dry' work environment; others were filled with foreboding at the thought that their office had supposedly been built by forced labour. From the outside it resembled nothing more inspiring than a long, brick, single-storey tram shed, complete with a corrugated-iron roof. A concrete ramp ascending towards a door wide enough to take a stately wheelchair proclaimed the entrance that had been designed for Charles Douglas-Home. Those venturing inside found the interior brightly lit. It needed to be because, with few windows, there was minimal natural light. Older journalists eyed the computer terminals with apprehension. Monitors were switched on; cursors were blinking. It looked complicated. They had never touched such technology before and doubted whether they could master it now. Indeed, some did not like the idea of typing in their own work directly – as if doing so downgraded them from the status of literati to artisan. Standing on the backbench, Charles Wilson harangued the sceptics: 'Don't be so wet. Some of you will learn the new technology in three weeks. Most of you will take three months. And you, Philip Howard, will take three years!' All eyes swivelled towards the distinguished literary editor. Within days of Wilson's exposition on the benefits of the new technology, he noticed that Angela Gordon had brought in her portable typewriter and had set it down neatly on her desk between two discarded computer screens. Leading by example, Wilson stormed over, picked up the offending typewriter, walked over to the entrance to the Gents' lavatory and installed it there as a doorstop. The incident got elaborated with the telling and rival newsrooms were soon agog with the story that *The Times* was being run by a rampaging, half-crazed Glaswegian who, when not throwing typewriters at his staff, was hurling them down lavatories.[11]

The first few days proved uncomfortable. There were not enough computer terminals installed and the largely computer-illiterate journalists found themselves having to share. A fortnight passed before there were enough terminals to go round, by which time the possessive instincts displayed by some towards what was supposedly communal property had become apparent. It was not just the older generation who appeared bamboozled by the technology. 'I had never before learnt even to touch-type (for I had dictated leaders to my secretary, Val Smith, pacing round the desk for what I thought was rhetorical impact),' recalled Peter Stothard, 'and I was not alone. One of our finest "production journalists" found it hard even to operate the teach-yourself cassette tape, let alone the Atex computers.'[12]

The breakdown of trust between management and journalists took even longer to repair. The situation was not as bad at *The Times* as it was at the *Sunday Times*, where members voted to go to Wapping by only sixty-eight votes to sixty, but many felt the editor's office was now enemy territory. The refuseniks obeyed the NUJ stricture not to work at Wapping by continuing to regard Gray's Inn Road as their place of work and refusing to pass the picket line or file copy to the new location. As they well knew, they were courting the sack. Greg Neale's successor as *The Times*'s NUJ chapel father, Clifford Longley, conceded the irony that 'had our agreement been legally binding – an idea alien to our union but favoured by Murdoch – we could have stopped him in his tracks'.[13] Most, reluctantly, accepted their fate and of all News International's seven hundred journalists, only thirty-eight refused to cross the Wapping picket line. But many of the remaining refuseniks were important figures in the life and work of *The Times*. Among them was Pat Healy who had been with the paper for twenty years, Paul Routledge, who had spent almost seventeen years at *The Times*, mostly as labour correspondent (and in the previous six months in Singapore as the paper's South East Asia correspondent), Greg Neale, Donald McIntyre, David Felton and Barry Clement. They were joined by Martin

Huckerby, the assistant foreign editor, with almost fifteen years Gray's Inn Road experience, whom Wilson sacked for writing a hostile article about Wapping in the UK Press Gazette.[14] Ten Times journalists resigned or were dismissed for refusing to go to Wapping from the first,[15] although others were to join the exodus to find friendlier work environments over the following months.

After the difficulties encountered on the first night, the production run of The Times improved remarkably. By Thursday 30 January (day four from Wapping), the paper reached its full production target (518,800 copies) for the first time. The belief that News International would be lost without the print unions was shown up as amazing complacency. Indeed, the basic statistics immediately demonstrated the extent to which the company had been subjected over the years to a print unions' racket. In the old press rooms of Bouverie Street and Gray's Inn Road, it had taken more than two thousand men (there were almost no women) to produce News International's four national newspapers. At Wapping, it was now taking just 670 to do the same task. Despite being of the same vintage as those at the old sites, Wapping's Goss press machines, working at two-thirds capacity, were each churning out forty thousand newspapers an hour with a fraction of the paper breaks that had halted business so frequently and so suspiciously in the past. Reaching production targets despite having fewer machines to work from, management discovered what they had long suspected but had never been allowed close enough to prove – that the print unions at Gray's Inn Road had been running their presses at far below their capacity. Wapping's productivity was impressive. Nine hundred reels of newsprint were consumed daily, each reel containing around five miles of paper and one press consuming a reel every fifteen minutes. Seventy tonnes of ink were used every week. In the publishing room, 132 employees were now doing what had previously taken nearly 1800 print union members to achieve.[16]

It was little wonder that Murdoch was being observed around the site in trainers and jumper 'looking frightfully bouncy and positive about the whole thing'.[17] 'Everybody has been wonderful!' he gushed, in a thank-you message to his staff.[18] The Times letters' page soon filled with correspondence. A few expressed disgust at the 'Thatcherite' agenda of the paper and the actions of its proprietor but most were supportive. There were plaudits from the past, among them from Sir William Rees-Mogg who wrote a letter for publication reflecting on the trouble he had had when editor with the unions. He commended Murdoch's 'courage to break out of this intolerable and corrupting monopoly'. He was not alone. Sir Denis Hamilton later ranked Murdoch's switch to Wapping 'one of the great newspaper achievements of the century'. One *Times* columnist who felt particularly joyful was Bernard Levin, who promptly penned an article – 'Fleet Street – now the truth can be told' – that catalogued what he saw as the horrors of print union power against which 'any attempt to let the outside world know what was happening nightly would have led to an immediate strike'. There was also praise from what were normally assumed to be hostile quarters. Harold Evans was asked to join a television debate on Wapping. The offer was quickly rescinded when he revealed he would commend Murdoch on his brave and necessary action. In the *Spectator*, Auberon Waugh opined that the so-called 'Dirty Digger' should be offered 'a dukedom at very least'.[19] For his part, Murdoch appeared to be enjoying the fray. Asked on BBC 1 whether he would move back to Bouverie Street or Gray's Inn Road, he replied, 'Of course I won't move back. I feel like a man who has been on a life sentence and has just been released. I feel a wonderful sense of freedom.'[20]

His journalists, meanwhile, were not enjoying the same spirit of ecstasy. With each day that passed, the angry crowds of pickets at the gates grew larger. Staff had to telephone a special number each morning to find where the re-enforced buses, complete with grilles and drawn curtains, would pick them up to take them through the gates into the compound. Rendezvousing with buses at ever-changing locations was not suitable for everyone but those who persisted with taking their cars into work were confronted at the gates with pickets slapping sticky labels that, when removed, took the paintwork with them.

It was dispiriting for journalists to run the gauntlet of taunts from those they did not know. But to experience abuse from former friends and colleagues was particularly unpleasant. Former secretaries taunted those they had previously worked for. Indeed, former secretaries taunted remaining secretaries who crossed the picket line. Pat Healy joined the far side of the barricades. Paul Routledge, back from his posting in Singapore, also joined the demonstration in order to give vent to his feelings, although his former colleagues were more unsettled by the presence of Mrs Routledge whose line of invective, although blunter, was more penetrating. Some journalists tried to deflect the verbal taunts. When one picket snarled 'sc-aaaaa-b' at Alan Hamilton, the seasoned reporter asked him to elaborate. 'You're a traitor to the working class,' the picket alleged. 'No, I'm not,' replied Hamilton, 'I'm from Edinburgh.' The picket opted to call him an unprintable part of the female anatomy instead.[21] Like many others, Tim Austin faced a daily taunt of 'I hope your kids die of cancer' as he passed the pickets. The volley of abuse was not confined to the factory gates. Brian Forbes of the picture desk had excrement thrown in his garden and bricks through his window. Doubtless such behaviour was cathartic for those trying to cope with the loss of their jobs but it was also intended to make the lives of Wapping employees such a misery that they would leave the company. The speed with which elements within the anti-Wapping campaign decided to launch intimidation tactics alarmed those who were on the receiving end. The thuggery took a particularly sinister path on 20 February when two men interrupted Christopher Warman, a respected and long-serving *Times* correspondent, as he was enjoying a drink with Don McIntyre and friends near the old Gray's Inn Road offices. Hassled as to whether he worked at Wapping, he conceded that he did. He was then head-butted and a beer glass was smashed into his face, narrowly missing his jugular vein. The assailants ran away leaving him on the floor, covered in blood.[22] It was a frightening moment. He required nine stitches to his neck and face. Yet, as soon as he was out of hospital, he made a point of reporting for work. As the paper's property correspondent, he promptly filed copy on Wapping's new desirable converted warehouse residences. Although Warman conducted himself with extraordinary sang-froid, many of his colleagues were shaken by the incident and wondered when their own time would come.

Murdoch, Bruce Matthews, Bill O'Neill and the four News International editors were given round-the-clock protection by bodyguards from a security firm of ex-Royal Marines. Others found the level of security a mixed blessing. Used to filing his column from home, Miles Kington had always given his copy to his near neighbour, Philip Howard, to take into the office. But Howard's lit. ed. office was temporarily still in Gray's Inn Road. Undaunted, Kington trekked to Wapping to deliver his copy personally only to be turned away at the security gate for not having a pass. For hours, he tried to contact staff he knew behind the wire, but all telephones were recording 'out to lunch' messages (somewhat improbably, since there was nowhere for miles around serving a decent meal). Eventually, Kington whipped up the courage to ask to be put through to the editor. 'Sorry sir,' the security officer at the gate replied, 'I haven't got the number.'[23]

Someone who did need better protection was the EETPU's leader, Eric Hammond. Attending a meeting of the TUC General Council, he was jostled by three hundred abusive protestors outside and, upon reaching the supposed sanctuary of the Congress House foyer, was kicked and punched by several union officials. Verbally, the mugging continued upstairs. Yet, although the General Council voted overwhelmingly to start proceedings for the EETPU's suspension from the TUC, calmer heads argued for caution in expelling the electricians for fear they would start a rival TUC that would attract those working in the new technologies, leaving the TUC with a membership confined to the shrinking heavy industries. Hammond's position was also strengthened by what he subsequently described as a 'trump card' – News International's threat to sue if the TUC instructed his members to stop work at Wapping against a company with which they were not in dispute.[24] Instead the TUC reached a compromise whereby the EETPU members would not be ordered to stop work at Wapping on the condition their union did not assist in further recruitment there or enter into a formal agreement unless it involved the other print unions too. Hammond accepted this, although he was half-minded to encourage the TUC to demand downing tools at Wapping so that he could have sued his fellow union brothers and 'been free of all their directives.'[25]

When the Labour Party's National Executive (the NEC) met on 29 January they called on 'all Labour Party bodies, Labour local authorities, members and supporters to boycott *The Times*' and the other News International titles. Labour's director of communications, Peter Mandelson, then asked *Times* and *Sun* journalists attending the press conference to leave Labour Party premises immediately. Lobby rules prevented a paper from being specifically blacklisted, so Neil Kinnock called off his weekly briefing with the parliamentary lobby journalists and instituted private meetings with each of the non-News International representatives instead. The *Daily Mail* and the *Yorkshire Post* refused to play this game, a stance subsequently taken up by other papers, thereby denying the Labour Party its chance to influence the press.

The Labour Party boycott quickly descended in farce. Nick Raynsford, the party's by-election candidate in Fulham, found it counter-productive and Larry Whitty, Labour's general secretary, had to be dispatched to ask the print union's permission for the purdah to be temporary lifted. Permission was granted, so long as the press conferences did not stray from the strict issue of the by-election. Three Labour MPs threatened to boycott the House of Commons Environment Committee's visit to York unless the presentation on historic buildings by Dr Norman Hammond of the York Archaeological Trust was cancelled. Dr Hammond's crime was to be *The Times*'s archaeological correspondent. Meekly, the Committee agreed.

But Labour's boycott did not catch on behind the Iron Curtain. When George Robertson, a Labour foreign affairs spokesman (and future NATO Secretary-General), attended a Communist-organized conference in his NEC capacity, he awoke each morning in his East Berlin hotel to the choice of the *Morning Star* or *The Times*.

The boycott campaign made little appreciable impact on sales. By the third week, Wilson was trumpeting *Times* daily sales of 485,000 copies, an increase of 13,000 since moving from Gray's Inn Road.[26] Sales of the *Sun* were also marginally up. But by ensuring that no Labour source was prepared to speak to or write for *The Times* it hit at the paper's ability to report comprehensively. Labour MPs like Jack Straw who had written regularly for the paper had to cease doing so. That many of the paper's refuseniks were left-leaning also harmed its breadth. Particularly grievous was the loss of the paper's labour relations staff. On the night *The Times* chapel had debated whether to go to Wapping, Harry Conroy had leaned closer to Don McIntyre and made clear, in broad Glaswegian, that the labour staff would be treated as scabs for the rest of their lives and would never get work elsewhere if they were minded to stay on at *The Times*. Having fully digested this point, the labour correspondent joined the refuseniks.[27] It was easy to see their predicament. The Labour Movement's refusal to cooperate with News International employees (the NUJ even instructed its members at other newspapers not to supply information to any News International journalist) would have made their task extremely difficult even if they had stayed. But their absence, and the difficulty created in trying to cover labour relations in general and Wapping objectively from the new location was shown up at a time when the *Guardian* was able to field Patrick Wintour and the *Financial Times* Raymond Snoddy. Matters were made worse when an article that was partly critical of Murdoch written by the highly regarded centre-left columnist Peter Kellner was spiked. Kellner, the *New Statesman*'s political editor, had been writing a fortnightly column for *The Times* and the decision not to run his piece ensured his resignation, compounding the paper's drain of alternative voices. As some were quick to point out, the episode smacked of crude censorship and reflected poorly on *The Times*'s objectivity.[28]

Yet, such defensiveness was mild compared to the attempt to gag *The Times*. At least thirty-three Labour-controlled local authorities withdrew job advertising from the paper and its siblings. Their decision had a proportionately much more serious effect on the *Times Educational Supplement*, which was the market leader (by a considerable margin) for advertising education vacancies. As such, the boycott must have been counter-productive to those authorities with teaching vacancies to fill. Undaunted, its advocates also intended to sweep staff common rooms and school libraries of the offending literature. The Labour group controlling the Inner London Educational Authority (ILEA) wrote to school and college governors instructing them to table resolutions to cancel *Times, Times Literary Supplement* and *Times Educational Supplement* subscriptions at their institutions of learning.[29]

Whether such activity was in the interests of the teaching profession was open to debate, but the prohibition of *The Times* from public libraries was altogether more serious and illegal. Across the country, Labour-controlled local authorities had interpreted their party's boycott of News International to include preventing public library users consulting *The Times*. The so-called paper of record was removed from public scrutiny in more than thirty local authority areas. Such action was in breach of the 1964 Libraries Act. In some cases, the consequences descended into absurdity. When a barrister, John Riley, went to his public library in Staffordshire, the staff told him they had *The Times* behind the counter but were instructed not to let him look at it. He threatened legal action.

Richard Luce, the Arts Minister, wrote to fifteen councils drawing attention to the illegality of their action. Three responded positively but the rest, including Bradford, Sheffield and a succession of famously left wing London boroughs, refused. Salford did not get round to replying.[30] When Luce failed to take the matter further, News International called upon the advocacy of Anthony Lester QC and David Pannick and took the local authorities to court. The eventual judgment was damning: 'There could hardly be a clearer manifestation of an abuse of power,' Lord Justice Watkins pronounced, than 'to see such irresponsible behaviour' by elected representatives knowingly ignoring the law.[31] This brought the councils into line, with the exception of the London Borough of Brent which continued to refuse to stock *The Times* in its libraries. The council cited a succession of increasingly bizarre defences for why the court's ruling did not apply to it. At one stage, the argument was proposed that the 'racist and sexist' material contained within the paper would conflict with the council's duties under the Race Relations Act. In contrast, the Communist *Morning Star* remained freely available for consultation. It was not until March 1987 that the council finally bowed to the judgment of the High Court, leading Anthony Lester to declare 'at the thirteenth hour the white flag has been hoisted alongside the red flag, over Brent Town Hall'.[32]

Quietly, the Government was delighted by Murdoch's decision to sack his print union workers although Kenneth Clarke, the Employment Minister, broke cover to say he thought the press baron's personal public relations required 'a great deal of continuing attention. He is not an instantly popular figure.' With John Biffen, the Leader of the Commons, seeking to defer a full-scale debate and the Speaker ruling out Tony Benn's attempt to get an emergency debate, left wing Labour MPs were reduced to demanding that the Home Secretary declare Murdoch an 'undesirable alien' who should be banned from Britain 'in the interest of decency and public order'. For his part, Neil Kinnock told a print workers' rally at Wembley that the next Labour Government would curb the monopolistic power of the main newspaper owners and began referring to 'Stalag Wapping' and 'Schloss Murdoch'. He rejected an invitation to discuss the situation with News International management.[33] The rhetoric of the Labour leader during the dispute frequently gave the impression he saw it as a fight to resist foreign influence. Not content to lambast Murdoch's 'intercontinental ballistic management' and conjure up Teutonic images, the future Vice-President of the European Commission maintained that when it came to the concentration of media ownership, the rule should be 'if you're not British – clear out'.[34]

III

One aspect of the Wapping strategy that worked particularly effectively was the switch from rail to road distribution. Using lorries gave *The Times* much greater flexibility in delaying deadlines if late news or a technical glitch needed to be accommodated. Unlike the railways, road freight could wait. It was flexible. It also ensured that there was just one loading period. Forty-foot lorries could drive up the ramp into the loading bay, take the papers on board and be on their way. Previously, the papers had first to be loaded onto vans and unloaded at the station before being reloaded onto trains, offloaded onto vans at the other end and taken to the wholesale depots before being transported to the shops for sale. The decision had been taken to stick with delivering to the existing wholesalers in the provinces but in London TNT handled all aspects of the distribution right down to delivering to the newsagents' front doors. Brenda Dean had hoped that even if the papers were successfully printed at Wapping her instruction to regional SOGAT members to refuse to handle them would cripple distribution. But the attitude of SOGAT workers in the provinces towards their London brothers was made apparent when only wholesale distributors in Liverpool, Coventry and Glasgow obeyed the executive order to black the titles. WH Smith and John Menzies management made clear that employees refusing to handle the papers would be sacked. Such was the apathy of provincial members towards the Wapping strikers that SOGAT members in Watford even continued to produce the *Sunday Times Colour Magazine*. One SOGAT victory proved to be Pyrrhic: refusing to print 1.5 million extra *News of the World* copies done under contract with Express Newspapers in Manchester ensured that the contract was duly cancelled and jobs were lost. Wapping met the extra print run instead. The unions had badly underestimated the new plant's ability to meet demand.

With the attempt to black distribution in Britain failing, SOGAT tried to broaden the theatres of war by persuading unions at foreign mills to go on strike rather than supply Wapping with newsprint. One firm had the contract for 75 per cent of News International's purchase and Wapping would thus have nothing to print its journalism on if foreign unions adhered to the boycott. But workers of the world did not unite on this occasion; they proved unwilling to risk unemployment for the sake of a British labour dispute. SOGAT had to make do with messages of support.[35]

By creating a legally separate entity to handle distribution, News International's lawyer, Geoffrey Richards, had ensured any blacking campaign would be deemed illegal secondary action.[36] Brenda Dean knew that this would be the case and consequently did not bother to hold ballots prior to issuing her order to black the titles. Consequently, the company began recourse to the law. By nightfall on 29 January, High Court injunctions had been placed not only on SOGAT's blacking tactics but also on the TGWU's attempts to order members driving the TNT lorries not to cross the Wapping picket line. Dean remained defiant in the face of the injunction, telling a three-hundred-strong rally in Manchester, her home base, on 31 January: 'If you walk away from your colleagues dismissed in London and their families, you don't deserve to be called trade unionists.' 'Scab newspapers' should be blacked she told the crowd, adding, 'If you don't support your own kind, no one will support you when you need it.'[37] It was not surprising she was desperate to strike a quick and overwhelming blow. As she later confided, the siege of Wapping 'was winnable – or losable – in those first two weeks'.[38] The longer the period in which distribution was not seriously disrupted the more certain would be News International's eventual victory.

On 8 February, three thousand dismissed print workers and activists gathered outside Wapping in a show of strength. Keen to stress the repercussions on the families of those who had lost their jobs, Brenda Dean led a 'Women's March'. Advancing in candlelit formation in the manner of a column of medieval pilgrims, the women adapted the drunken sailor refrain to 'What shall we do with Rupert Murdoch, early in the morning? Burn, burn, burn the bastard . . .'[39] But for all the protesters' anger, the lorries got through. Two days later, the High Court fined SOGAT £25,000 for contempt of court for failing to obey the injunction prohibiting the 'blacking' from the wholesalers. What was more, the union's £17 million assets were sequestrated until it renounced the 'blacking' instruction.

Having stayed silent on the dispute during its first three weeks, *The Times*'s leader column finally chose the sequestration issue to address the news on its doorstep. 'When the obstacles between the paper and its readers include darts, drill bits and blackened golf balls as well as illegal attempts to threaten customers and suppliers it should surprise no one that the force of law is our first defence,' it declared.[40] Such sentiments left opponents cold. Proud trade unionists continued to demand defiance. Ron Todd of the TGWU pointed out 'if the Tolpuddle Martyrs had taken legal advice, they could have saved themselves a trip to Australia' while Brenda Dean stated 'our members are more important than money'.[41] In fact, many members were far from in agreement with her on this point: the campaign on behalf of the 4500 ex-News International employees was preventing the union's 213,000 other members from receiving their pensions, injury claims and other benefits provided from its central funds. This became a source of friction.

It was not just SOGAT that refused to retract in front of injunctions and fines. The NGA, which had also been fined for contempt of court, failed to win the support of members in a ballot to black production of the *Times* supplements (the *TLS*, *TES* and *THES*) printed in Northampton. Regardless of this rebuff, the union's leadership announced it would black the papers anyway since five NGA members involved in putting the supplements' pages to camera had voted (in a supposedly secret ballot) to strike. Fortunately the ability of five men to disrupt the entire supplements division was overcome when their employer (working under contract to News International) moved them to a less strategic department. Nonetheless, Tony Dubbins proudly boasted that his union's initials stood for 'Not Going Away'.[42]

News International hoped that the freezing of union funds would lead to a hasty settlement and the calling off not only of the blacking call but also the picketing of the Wapping plant. Union activists believed the court action demonstrated the need to intensify efforts while there was time. Three thousand pickets (many of them Kent miners) descended on Wapping on the night of 13 February intent on stopping *The Times* and *Sun* from leaving the gates. Five hundred police, including mounted officers, had to be rushed in to keep the exits clear. There were forty-one arrests on that night alone. A month later, tempers were strained further when two pickets were hit and their legs broken by a lorry they were trying to prevent leaving the plant. To misfortune was added bathos: the lorry was carrying copies of the *Sun*'s 'Freddie Starr ate my hamster' edition. Three nights later, the pickets sought to exact their revenge: seven thousand besieged the plant. Iron bars, lead piping, shotgun cartridges and railing spikes were seized by the police from the rioters, who succeeded in tearing down a forty-yard section of the security fence. Fortress Wapping appeared to be on the verge of being overrun and, in scenes worthy of Sergei Eisenstein, it took mounted-police charges to push the surging demonstrators back. The assault managed seriously to delay, but not to prevent, the lorries getting out.

Most evenings passed with incident, but a pattern was emerging in which Saturday nights involved the most serious breakdowns in order with demonstrators attempting to prevent Murdoch's lucrative Sunday titles from leaving the compound. As weeks passed without the prospect of resolution, the siege became a *cause célèbre*, attracting the attention of left-wing activists, students, trade unionists and, increasingly, thugs looking for a bit of violent excitement. Banners were held high proclaiming Class War, the Socialist Workers' Party and the various Trotskyite factions. The Wapping Highway became a major sales venue for the cottage industry of left-wing newspapers. Only the lonely seller of *Labour Weekly* was made to feel unwelcome. By the end of the third month of the siege, there had been 474 arrests. Among this number was the NGA's general secretary, Tony Dubbins, who was charged with obstructing lorries. But of the total number of arrests, it was telling that less than a third were ex-printers.

Moderate voices within the unions were concerned at the hijacking of the printers' cause by those with their own, sometimes violent, agenda. Yet, having determined upon a tactic that centred upon trying to block the entry and exit points of Wapping, the logic was to welcome as many able-bodied protestors as possible. Weight of numbers was the only prospect of the siege working. After all, the unions' other strategies – getting the

wholesalers to black distribution, encouraging readers not to buy the newspapers and persuading the contract printers Bemrose and Odhams not to
produce the colour supplements, had all failed. Indeed, when balloted for
strike action, the SOGAT employees at Bemrose voted twelve to one against
coming out and those at Odhams also rejected their union's call by an
overwhelming margin.[43] Violence was 'certainly not what we are after,'
announced Chris Robbins, SOGAT's London district secretary, although
he added:

> if there are 8,000 people outside Wapping there is little that the police
> can do. We have shown [on 16 March, when the Sunday titles were
> delayed by four hours] that is a sufficient number to stop the papers
> going out. Unlike Orgreave [a reference to one of the bitterest confron-
> tations of the miners' strike] the exits are all in a pretty enclosed
> area.[44]

The intention was clear. But inside the stockade, plans had been devised to
outsmart the siege. News International's strategy would not have been
possible without the active support of the police (a point that particularly
riled those activists who believed the Met was being used politically). Police
sealed a one-mile area around the plant. There were three permanent
roadblocks, augmented where necessary by up to sixteen temporary roadblocks. Because lorries leaving in ones or twos could be picked off, they
lined up en masse behind the walls, ready for a group breakout. Two o'clock
in the morning was the usual time for one of the sets of gates to open and
the lorries to speed their way through the defences, followed by shouts,
threats and projectiles. From there, there was more than one route that
could be taken and, unlike the drivers and the police, the demonstrators
never knew in advance which it would be, ensuring that they had to stretch
their troops thinly across the whole area. But on nights where the unions
were able to deploy mass numbers it often took mounted-police charges to
clear a way through. It was not only the lorry drivers who found themselves
running the gauntlet in this fashion. Those journalists and staff who could
not get out before the demonstrators started gathering at 7 p.m. were often
forced to stay within the compound until 2 a.m. as well. Hours were wasted
sitting in cars with the headlights off and engine running, lined up in
convoy formation awaiting the command to put the foot down and accelerate fast.

There was an obvious downside to this level of security. The more

Wapping's fortifications were piled high, the less agreeable it appeared to journalists and public alike. The *Sunday Express* cartoonist, Giles, depicted it as a concentration camp complete with goose-stepping Nazi guards. The police did not allow any buses or taxis through the one-mile cordon. Residents could pass through only on production of identity cards proving they lived there. They could be forgiven for wishing the plant could be shut down so that they could get a decent night's sleep. Tower Hamlets Council had been inundated with complaints about the night-time noise generated and some hoped this could be used as a pretext for having the police operation scaled back or even the plant forcibly shut. When a journalist from *New Society*, a weekly magazine later subsumed into the *New Statesman*, drove over to Wapping to talk to some of those who had lodged complaints, some pickets came within view. He gave them a sympathetic gesture of solidarity. Unfortunately it was misinterpreted and a brick came smashing through his car window.

IV

The nightly scuffles preoccupied those caught on both sides of the stockade, but it was only one part of a wider battle for public opinion. In this respect, Brenda Dean presented a more appealing face than either Murdoch's barbed wire or the traditional overweight Bolshie shop steward to which Fleet Street had long played host. Soft-spoken and moderate in tone, Dean led the presentation of the unions' case to the media. She was adept at steering the rhetoric away from overpaid (usually NGA) print men trying to maintain Luddite practices and onto the fate of the lower-paid cleaning and clerical workers, often women, who were more obviously blameless victims in the battle of Wapping. Much was made of the suffering inflicted upon their families. By May, SOGAT had spent £250,000 on the boycott campaign. Indeed, the unions spent an estimated total of £400,000 on publicity during the long course of the siege.[45] Newspaper advertisements were placed, three million stickers produced and six million leaflets printed. The 'Don't Buy . . .' logo was embossed on posters, plastic bags and T-shirts. When the time of year came round there was even a not especially festive Christmas card proclaiming 'Christmas Greetings – Please don't buy *The Sun, News of the World, The Times, Sunday Times*' between four pieces of stylized holly. There was also an advert featuring a photograph of a child clutching her teddy bear beside the caption: 'My dad helped Mr Murdoch make millions. Now he wants to put him on the Dole. Don't let him.' This was not all. A pro-strikers' newspaper, the *Wapping Post*, was launched. Edited by Chris Robbins and running to twelve pages, it was promoted by the unions who placed bulk orders with 45,000 copies being distributed throughout the country. It provided a lively mix of articles on 'Mugger Murdoch', police brutality, the health and safety dangers of operating computers, letters and details of forthcoming events with such titles as 'The Truth Behind Barbed Wire' addressed by the likes of the ubiquitous Tony Benn.[46]

How much effect the campaign had in winning over the public was doubtful. To those involved on either side, it was a life or death struggle for the future of the industry. Those not involved were less concerned. Confidential market research commissioned by News International when the siege was four months old suggested that many of those polled did not care whose will prevailed. Of those who did, 39 per cent favoured the management and 33 per cent the unions (although union support had a majority among those who felt strongly on the issue). Less than half could remember – without prompting – the name of someone connected with the dispute with only Murdoch and Dean attaining significant recognition. But the data did show that no perceptible switch in readership away from *The Times* could be discerned and that only 6 per cent thought the unions were winning the dispute.[47]

Within the News International group, only the *Sunday Times* appeared to be losing circulation in the first three months of the move to Wapping, largely due to distribution problems and, perhaps, the desertion of some of its sizeable non-Thatcherite readership.[48] But *The Times* had particular cause for celebration. On 28 March it published on Good Friday for the first time since 1918. None of its competitors appeared – their print unions forbade it. To capitalize, a record print run of 773,948 copies were made of the Good Friday *Times*, a full 120,000 more than the celebrated royal wedding edition in 1981. By May, the paper was averaging 503,000 sales per day, breaking the highest sustained circulation in its history. Taking advantage of the national economic recovery, advertising revenue was up by 25 per cent on the year and classified ads were at their highest level for more than a decade.[49]

The actual paper looked, at first sight, remarkably similar to its Gray's Inn Road predecessor. Close scrutiny revealed it was produced on a marginally smaller paper size but the quality of the printed page was just as good – or rather bad – as before. This was because the presses were no different. Apart from the departure of some quality journalists, there was little difference in content. Peregrine Worsthorne hoped that by reducing production costs, the Wapping revolution would lead to *The Times* abandoning its fight for larger circulation in favour of serving its 300,000 'top readers'.[50] In fact, the paper's management had been so preoccupied with the logistics of the switch in production that strategic considerations of this kind had been deferred. But upmarket or downmarket, others were fearful for what Wapping meant for the competition. 'By saving an estimated £60 million on his annual production costs,' Peter Paterson warned that Murdoch was 'in a position to reduce the cover price of, say, *The Times*, to the destruction of the *Telegraph* and the *Guardian*'.[51] Old Fleet Street was swept with panic when it was rumoured Murdoch was poised to drop not only his papers' cover prices but also their advertising rates.

In truth, to News International's competitors, Wapping was both a threat and a godsend. Wapping printed four mass-market newspapers, including the leading daily and Sunday tabloid, with a 670-strong production staff. By comparison, the *Daily Mail*'s owners, Associated Newspapers, were lumbered with a 3400 production staff and the *Daily Express*'s new owners, United Newspapers, wilted under the weight of a 6800-strong workforce. Clearly, they had to make cuts urgently or risk going under. In the past, such swingeing cuts would have been impossible since the print unions would have gone on indefinite strike, forcing management to back down or compromise. But Wapping provided Murdoch's rivals with just the weapon – or threat of using such a weapon – that they needed. Once it became clear to the unions they were losing the siege of Wapping, they either had to bow to the other proprietors' demands or risk being shut out entirely *à la* Wapping by them too. The *Express*'s owner, Lord Stevens, lost no time in drawing this conclusion. He discovered that Wapping had concentrated union minds wonderfully and 2500 redundancies were soon agreed. Lord Rothermere, proprietor of the *Daily Mail*, had already announced his intention to build a new print works in Docklands but he well understood that Murdoch's coup transformed the scale and urgency with which he had to act. 'Wapping is a watershed – a great historic date in Fleet Street,' Rothermere conceded; 'those who survive are going to be those who have understood this fastest.'[52] Indeed, after years of timid inertia, the speed with which the various proprietors shot out of their respective blocks was remarkable, or, as Charles Wilson put it, 'they were off like rats up a drain'.[53] A week after *The Times*'s move to Wapping, the *Guardian* rushed through an announcement that it would move to Docklands, switch from hot metal to computer typesetting and introduce direct-input by 1987. Within days, Rothermere's Associated Newspapers declared it would do the same by 1988. Then, in July, the *Financial Times* announced it too would go east and that the 'paper of business' would enter the computer age in 1988.

'One after another, the threatened newspaper groups have been able, with no weapon but a pair of binoculars for seeing the smoke pouring from the roaring chimneys of Castle Wapping, to conclude agreements' that their unions would never previously have accepted, noted Bernard Levin in his 'The Way We Live Now' column. Here was a case in which:

> The man who makes a hole in the hedge gets scratched, but those who go through it after him feel no discomfort. It may be that, as Messrs Black, Stevens, Rothermere and the rest go through the hole, they experience a warm glow of gratitude to the man they can see disappearing towards the horizon with brambles sticking out of him all over. If so, I conclude that if they fail to express that gratitude, it can only be because of shyness [54]

If a little *sotto voce*, some of the rival proprietors did salute Murdoch's courage and audacity. One who loudly did not was the *Daily Mirror*'s owner, Robert Maxwell, who criticized his enemy for 'not doing things the British way'. The weight of Maxwell's pronouncement was soon demonstrated when he sacked his Glasgow print workers for refusing to handle a new colour edition, put up barbed wire and guard dogs around the plant and went to court to sequestrate SOGAT's assets. Labour MPs who had hurled abuse at Murdoch for such behaviour were noticeably silent when Maxwell, a Labour benefactor, trod the same path.

Few rival editors were prepared to be charitable towards Murdoch (an honourable exception being Brian MacArthur at Eddy Shah's newly launched *Today*). When News International placed an advertisement stating its case, most newspapers declined to print it. Some, like the *Daily Telegraph*'s editor, Max Hastings, refused supposedly on the grounds that he did not 'want to give space to our principal commercial competition'. Others, like the *Guardian* and the *FT*, were too scared of their own unions' reaction to print it and demanded indemnities against consequent legal action. Only the *Daily Mail*, the Mirror Group and *Today* agreed to carry it.[55] *The Times* was furious at the craven nature of rivals who stood to benefit from Wapping's legacy but were not prepared to print (let alone endorse) an advertisement in its support. 'There are some in the newspaper industry,' the leader column stated accusingly, 'who are still afraid of their unions. This alone ought to speak more than any advertisement in favour of the cause that News International is fighting.'[56]

One head that did not poke far above the parapet was that of Donald Trelford, editor of the *Observer*. Seven of his subeditors also worked during the week for *The Times*. NGA print workers threatened to stop production of the *Observer* unless they were dismissed. Trelford duly did the dirty work. Next, the printers (backed by the paper's NUJ chapel father) threatened to shut down the paper unless an innocuous review of a book about the Victorian travel writer Augustus Hare was pulled. Its crime was that it had been written by *Times* columnist and print union scourge, Bernard Levin. Trelford duly pulled the article and, with it, Levin's contract to review books for the *Observer*.[57] An editor who fearlessly and famously stood up to a bullying owner, Tiny Rowland, on the question of his paper's reporting of African politics was prepared to capitulate tamely before a delegation of union representatives.

Intimidation at the offices of the *Observer* was as nothing compared to that facing those – journalists and printing staff alike – who worked at or collaborated with Wapping. Leaflets were distributed headed 'Roll of Dishonour' listing 'scabs'' names and – ominously – their home addresses. Even those not on the staff payroll were at risk. Fifty demonstrators smashed through a glass door to get at the history professor John Vincent while he was trying to give a lecture to his students at Bristol University. Vincent was subjected to a barracking because he had written articles in *The Times*. It was unlikely that many of the protestors had ever been anywhere near the paper's machine room but worse followed when one hundred demonstrators disrupted Professor Vincent's lecture for the third week running, some hurling mud at him. Another who experienced the wrath of activist agitprop was the former *Times* business editor, Hugh Stephenson, who had gone on to become Professor of Journalism at City University in London. Hardly a Murdoch sycophant, Stephenson found himself the target of his students' wrath and was subjected to a petition condemning him for submitting articles to *The Times* in breach of the NUJ boycott.[58]

Neither Professors Vincent nor Stephenson endured as lengthy a trial as David Selbourne. A noted academic writer of eclectic sweep, Selbourne had for twenty-two years been a lecturer at Ruskin College, the adult higher education college in Oxford that had links with the trade union movement.

When *The Times* published an article by him on Labour's Militant Tendency, he found himself condemned for 'anti-trade union' thinking by the Ruskin Students' Union who ordered him to apologize and not to write such articles again. When he refused to bow to this Maoist instruction, a student picket barred entrance to his lectures. If Selbourne imagined the staff would stand up for his academic freedom of thought he was soon disappointed. The acting principal described Selbourne's *Times* article as 'provocative' and fellow lecturers declared their 'solidarity' with the Students' Union which promptly called for him to be sacked. Although Ruskin was not part of Oxford University it had access to its facilities and the Oxford University Students' Union also weighed in to condemn the turbulent academic. The Association of University Teachers were not much more helpful. Selbourne stated that he was not a Murdoch supporter but that he would write again for *The Times* if commissioned to do so. Ruskin College's Executive Committee censured him and, unable to get any reassurance that it backed his academic freedom, Selbourne resigned his post. So ended a lengthy career there. But his fate did not go unnoticed. In a succession of leader articles, *The Times* drew attention to his case and the Government announced an independent enquiry under Sir Albert Sloman, the former Essex University vice-chancellor, to investigate Ruskin's (taxpayer funded) commitment to academic freedom. It called for the college to revise its disciplinary procedures and make its commitment to academic freedom more explicit.[59]

Meanwhile, the National Union of Journalists continued to side with the dismissed printers. The NUJ's attempts, as *The Times* leader column put it, 'to deprive a newspaper of information, and to obstruct the public reading it', made it as guilty of promoting censorship as those attempting to silence its academic contributors. During April, the NUJ considered what to do about its members working at Wapping.[60] The decision was not as simple as the more militant voices hoped. The desire to punish those who had gone there was balanced by the fear they would tear up their membership cards and provoke a mass exodus. With these considerations in mind, the union's National Executive voted by thirteen votes to twelve against initiating disciplinary proceedings against all the journalists. Instead, the union would only pick on those it suspected of being particularly culpable or cowardly: it would investigate the actions of the four chapel fathers individually. It also barred *The Times* journalist Peter Davenport, reporting its proceedings from its annual conference in Sheffield. The conference itself was certainly worthy of coverage: delegates voted to reverse their National Executive's decision, ensuring proceedings could be initiated against all News International journalists after all. Condolences were also sent to Colonel Gaddafi over the US raid on Tripoli.

V

On 4 April, Murdoch presented the print unions with a free gift. At face value, it was a generous present and – even if mindful of the history lesson of Greeks bearing gifts – the unions could not easily refuse it. But it was an awkward present all the same. The inspiration for it came in a letter published in *The Times* from a Mr D. P. Forbes of Croydon.[61] Murdoch read it and set about investigating its feasibility. He soon realized it contained the kernel of a brilliant idea that could end the dispute on terms that would deliver him victory by an apparent act of magnanimity to his opponents.

In moving to Wapping, Murdoch no longer had any need for Gray's Inn Road and its print facilities. But rather than selling the property and its contents to the highest bidder he could instead give it away to a trade union body on the condition they used it to print a Labour-friendly newspaper employing the very printers Murdoch had sacked. In return for gaining this employment and better representation of left-wing views in the popular press, the unions would call off the siege of Wapping. The proposal, it seemed, could only rebound to Murdoch's credit. If the unions accepted the offer, everyone would be happy. If they rejected the offer, they would be shown up for being intransigent and unwilling to operate the very machinery and manning levels that they were fighting to foist upon News International.

At a meeting with the print unions at the Mayfair Hotel, Bruce Matthews made them the offer. Although they would not be allowed instantly to asset strip it, they were being offered the freehold on a 300,000 square foot building that, on the open market, had a potential value of around £15 million. With it came a two-year contract to print London editions of the *Guardian* worth £1 million per annum. Also included was 'about £40 million' worth of equipment with computerized typesetting technology and sixty Goss Headliner Mark 1 presses (the same as Wapping used). The offer naturally caught the union delegation off guard. Needing time to digest what was suddenly being tendered, they asked for an adjournment. After they returned, Brenda Dean conceded the offer was 'unusual to say the least' and asked for more time to consider it. She warned, however, that it 'did not represent an alternative to jobs and compensation'. The NGA's leader, Tony Dubbins, was far less equivocal. It was not a solution, he protested, because 'the company was offering plant and equipment – not employment'.

Dubbins was certain that the offer was a non-starter designed to sidetrack the unions from their principal aim. They were demanding the right to work at Wapping and, if that proved impossible, to win generous redundancy payments for those who had been sacked. They had never asked to run a paper themselves. But the offer put his union colleagues in a quandary. If they immediately rejected it, they stood to look like wreckers. In any case, they were short of a convincing fallback position. Their attempts to blockade Wapping were failing and, in becoming increasingly violent, were highly risky. Dean's initial fear was that the offer was not as good as it sounded and that Murdoch was trying to 'stage-manage' a deal by appearing on *Channel 4 News* to announce the gift. In the event, with cameras rolling, Murdoch was unrepentant. 'This is an opportunity,' he announced, 'for the TUC to achieve their ambition and at the same time employ the people who previously worked at the plant. It allows the trade union movement the start-up capital free of charge with no interest charges round their neck.' And with the hint of a smile, he added that in permitting a rival newspaper to be born, 'We will risk the competition.' Dubbins remained unimpressed, musing, 'I think people can't help but be somewhat cynical about an offer from Mr Murdoch' who 'has got a cheek in making this offer after sacking 6,000 workers.'[62]

Union trepidation was understandable. Having come to the conclusion that they were supping with the Devil, they were asking for long spoons. But the secret of Murdoch's success should have given them the courage of their rhetoric. He had, after all, built much of his own empire on the profits from the *Sun*, a seemingly unpromising newspaper he had been given virtually for free by Hugh Cudlipp. Might the unions not also make the most of such a golden opportunity? Eager to add to the number of Labour-supporting newspapers, Neil Kinnock thought this new gift should not be casually discarded just because it came from a man the print unions detested. Clive Thornton, the former chairman of the Mirror Group and a director of the proposed left-wing tabloid *News on Sunday*, agreed, arguing that 'if [the unions] have got any imagination they should use it to see the prospects. Murdoch has used his imagination in making the offer. The unions should use theirs too.'[63] But the TUC's general secretary would have none of it. Addressing eight thousand demonstrators in Trafalgar Square before marching them off to besiege Fortress Wapping, Norman Willis snubbed the Gray's Inn Road offer: 'We put print workers before print works. Our priority has to be people not property.'[64]

When negotiations recommenced at the Hyde Park Hotel on 16 April both sides made new bids. News International offered a £15 million ex-gratia payment to its sacked employees. A forty-year-old printer who had been employed for twenty years on £24,000 per annum could expect a £10,000 payout. In return, Brenda Dean put forward TUC proposals in which News International would recognize a 'National Joint Committee' representing all union members (including the NGA and SOGAT) it would employ. This new body (and not the individual unions that comprised it) would have sole negotiating rights on pay and conditions and would recognize management's right to determine staffing levels.[65] Given the cold hostility of the first weeks of the strike, here at least were signs of movement from both sides. But there was now a more fundamental issue at stake: could the union negotiators deliver a deal that their members would accept? From Sydney, Murdoch wrote to Bruce Matthews, asking him to extend the deadline for acceptance of the Gray's Inn Road plant and expressing his concern that 'Brenda has lost control irretrievably.'[66]

There were plenty of signs that the moderates were not in control. On the night of 9 April, about 450 thugs attacked the TNT distribution depot at Byfleet in Surrey, hurling bricks and missiles, throwing nails in the way of the lorry tyres and smashing the windscreens of three lorries trying to deliver copies of The Times to the depot. A TNT manager was grabbed, punched and kicked. The police had to send for reinforcements and an adjacent garden wall collapsed. Two nights later, a further attack by balaclava-wearing individuals was launched upon a John Menzies distri-bution depot at Southend in Essex causing further damage. But it was not until 3 May – the ninety-seventh day of the dispute – that the worst violence erupted when a concerted attack was made to occupy and destroy the Wapping plant itself.

Two marches – one from the west, the other from the east – converged on the Wapping Highway where the police had barricaded the entrance to the site down into Virginia Street. Seven thousand protestors easily outnumbered the 1700 police blocking the entrance. The first charge on the police line at Virginia Street was ferocious. Coming under a hail of bricks, smoke bombs, bottles and sharpened railings, the police were pushed back as the mob surged forward, seized the barricades and pushed on towards the gates to the plant. Fearing the insurgents were on the verge of smashing their way in, the mounted police arrived just in time to push them back to the original line of defence. The police sustained heavy casualties as the volley of projectiles continued to rain down upon them and a detachment in riot gear was sent behind the assailants' line to pull out from the crowd those throwing the missiles. But the 'snatch squad' approaching the mob from Wellclose Square was hopelessly outnumbered. It soon became clear that unless they were rescued quickly their lives would be in danger as the mob closed in upon them. The decision was taken to smash a way through the rioters' lines in order to free the encircled policemen. A second charge by mounted police was ordered. 'We gave no warnings of the charges because there was no time,' the Met's deputy assistant commissioner, Wyn Jones, admitted, adding, 'The officers in the square were in danger.' The charge certainly smashed through some of the demonstrators who were not involved in the violent rampage and truncheons struck a BBC camera crew in the ensuing melee. One hundred and fifty demonstrators were injured in the mounted charges, but the endangered policemen were rescued and the assault on the plant repulsed back to the original defence line along the Wapping Highway. Of eighty-one arrested, twenty-five were print workers. The police that night suffered 175 injuries, some of them spending days in hospital. One WPC was badly burned by a smoke bomb that was thrown at her. Another was hit over the head with a concrete slab. From her hospital bed, she recalled, 'I could hear women shouting "another Yvonne Fletcher. I hope she dies." '[67]

Tony Benn, who had addressed the meeting before the riot began, proceeded to condemn what he described as a 'massive police attack on perfectly innocent people'. In response, The Times leader column was puce with rage, demanding to know:

What would have happened if the police had not been present at Wapping on Saturday? No doubt the crowd would have invaded the plant, destroyed much of the equipment and physically attacked those working there. Many people would have been seriously injured and it is by no means improbable in the circumstances that several people would have been killed.[68]

One consequence was more positive. Brenda Dean, together with NGA representatives, met Scotland Yard's Wyn Jones to discuss ways in which the demonstrations could be run and policed with less violence. Telephone contact was established between union officials and the police officer in charge. But it was little deterrent to the activists who nightly attached themselves to the printers' cause. In the London area alone, twenty-nine separate groups organized money raising and support back-up for the pickets under an umbrella title, the 'Union of Printworkers Support Groups'. The Socialist Workers' Party helped to bring together the various groups who had supported the miners in their year-long struggle. There was also a 'Policing Research and Monitoring Group' in which the Communist Party member and *Marxism Today* contributor Cathie Lloyd was active in logging allegations of police brutality. The National Council for Civil Liberties was also quick to blame the law enforcers for the breakdown of order. The official statistics told a different story. By mid-May, there had been 851 arrests and 332 police officers injured. There had also been 296 incidents involving TNT vans, including ninety-two smashed windows and thirty-five drivers assaulted.[69]

Meanwhile, SOGAT had finally done a volte-face. On 8 May it purged its contempt of court by withdrawing its instruction to wholesalers to black all News International titles. Given the failure of the tactic, it was hardly a major concession, but it did unfreeze the union's £17 million assets. Some felt the union had suffered enough and looked for a more equitable sharing of the hardship. 'The NGA were sitting relatively pretty,' Brenda Dean later asserted. 'We were taking the great burden of the dispute although it was projected as the "print unions" dispute.'[70] The Wapping management saw the strained relations between Dean and Dubbins as an opportunity, believing SOGAT's leadership was far more open to agreeing a negotiated settlement than their NGA counterparts. The decision was taken to treat with them separately. Murdoch's private Gulfstream jet secretly picked up Dean and her deputy, Bill Miles, and flew them, along with Bruce Matthews, to Los Angeles. From there they were taken to the Beverly Hills villa that Murdoch was renting from the James Bond actor, Roger Moore. It was hoped this would provide the right environment to conclude a deal that could then be presented as a *fait accompli* to the NGA leadership. Murdoch offered £50 million to his ex-employees.[71] A deal appeared to be all but agreed. But Dean had to sell it to her members. This she singularly failed to do.

It was easy to understand Dean's timidity. SOGAT's London branches convened their four-thousand members at Westminster Central Hall on 19 May. They agreed a plan to intensify the siege. One branch official was cheered when he suggested setting fire to any ballot papers that excluded reinstatement to work at Wapping. In contrast, when Dean stood up to

Rupert Murdoch announces he is buying *The Times*, flanked by its incoming and outgoing editors, Harold Evans (*left*) and William Rees-Mogg.

Gray's Inn Road, home of *The Times* from 1974 to 1986.

Harold Evans

Sir Edward Pickering, editor for
Beaverbrook and mentor to Murdoch.

The proprietor in his Press Hall.

March 1982, Charles Douglas-Home announces his editorial intentions. Fred Emery *(centre)* reserves judgement.

Lamb to the slaughter. Lord Dacre on his way to Hamburg to tell the world's press that the Hitler diaries are genuine.

Murdoch gives the Queen a crash course in page make-up when she visits the paper for its bicentenary in 1985.

Douglas-Home clears the hedges at a point-to-point.

Facing the final hurdle. Douglas-Home continued editing *The Times* in the last weeks of his life from a hospital bed.

Charles Wilson, editor 1985-1990.

Flanked by Bill O'Neill and Bruce Matthews, Rupert Murdoch briefs the press on the deadlock in talks with the print unions, 19 January 1986.

Peterloo '86: The Siege of Wapping.

The nightly scuffles outside *The Times* during the Wapping dispute resulted in almost 1,500 arrests.

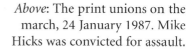

Above: The print unions on the march, 24 January 1987. Mike Hicks was convicted for assault.

'Sc-aaa-b!' The blackleg welcoming committee serenade their former colleagues.

The arson of News International's warehouse in Deptford – the most intense blaze in London since the Blitz.

Times journalists take the honours at the 1988 British Press Awards. *Left to right*: Robert Fisk, Bernard Levin, Howard Foster, John Woodcock, Barbara Amiel and John Goodbody.

Like life on a nuclear submarine, there was little legroom in *The Times*'s elongated and windowless Wapping home. From the upper gantry, Charlie Wilson could berate the ratings.

address her assembled warriors, she was met with a volley of abuse. Her speech was heckled throughout, particularly at those junctures where she counselled moderation and her open-minded attitude towards accepting the Gray's Inn Road offer. It was not the time or place to admit she had been covertly dealing with the enemy while relaxing around Roger Moore's swimming pool.

Dean's failure to tell her members what had been discussed made matters difficult. Murdoch had set a 30 May deadline. On 26 May he flew in for talks with all the principal players (including Norman Willis of the TUC) at the Sheraton Skyline Hotel at Heathrow. As the discussions proceeded, Murdoch added the front part of the *Sunday Times* building to the Gray's Inn Road offer. If new job opportunities became available at Wapping, the sacked print workers would be free to apply for them. But he rejected the unions' idea of a national joint committee on the grounds that its arbitration procedures would not be legally binding. In any case, he questioned whether it would be acceptable to those currently working at Wapping. 'Did they want to belong to the NGA?' he asked, before adding that he doubted it. His £50 million redundancy offer was final: News International 'was not a money fountain'. In seventeen years, its profits had amounted to about £200 million but capital expenditure had been £197 million. Time was short. The unions should accept. This was his final offer.[72] He gave an equally uncompromising response to reporters later that day. He would not sacrifice those currently 'doing a magnificent job' at Wapping since 'our loyalty is to the people who are working for us, not to the people who went on strike'. If the latter rejected his offer then so be it: 'That's it. I am catching the next plane home.'[73]

The union leaders put the package to a vote of their members well aware that Murdoch was not bluffing. Maintaining that the offer 'fell short in every respect' Dubbins recommended his NGA members reject it.[74] In this he was in step with the mood of the union. Indeed, the belligerence at a meeting of eight hundred NGA members was so strongly against even holding a ballot that no one spoke up in favour of accepting the offer. Dean's tactics were somewhat different. She made clear there was little likelihood of a better offer being made if her members voted no, but she did not risk the personal consequences of formally endorsing a yes vote. Even the procedure by which the ballot was held attracted suspicion and attempts at sabotage. No sooner had the voting papers gone out in the post than SOGAT activists launched a High Court injunction attempt to scrap the vote on the grounds that the papers were being sent out to individual members instead of the traditional procedure of being given to the chapel officers for distribution. The legal attempt failed but it would not have made much difference to the outcome. SOGAT members rejected the settlement by 2081 to 1415, the NGA by 648 to 165 and the smallest union involved, the AEU, by 112 to 56. _

Dubbins greeted the news by making clear his union would 'step up this dispute'. Murdoch's reaction was to repeat that there would be no new offer. Gray's Inn Road would now be sold commercially instead, the profits from its sale going into News International's coffers rather than being put at the disposal of the TUC. There would be no new left-leaning newspaper, no jobs for the ex-print workers to take up in producing it. It was, in Bruce Matthews's words, the unions' 'second suicide.'

In fact, there was a perfectly rational explanation for why the vote had gone against reaching an agreement: most of the ex-print workers had already gained employment elsewhere (SOGAT admitted that only a third of its affected members were still eligible for unemployment benefit).[75] Thus they were in no rush to reach a deal. Rather, they would hold out indefinitely, tightening all the while the screw on the Wapping siege until Murdoch, in desperation, came back with a larger payout. To this prospect, Matthews warned, 'if there is an escalation of violence, I think they will isolate themselves from every section of the community.'[76]

VI

On Monday 2 June – even before the results of the ballot had been announced – new and yet more thuggish tactics were being deployed to smash *The Times* and its Wapping stable mates. Instead of concentrating on trying to block the newspapers coming out, the pickets sought to prevent the journalists going in. For two hours between eight and ten o'clock in the morning, about three hundred demonstrators descended upon the plant, taking the twenty policemen by surprise and forcing the main gates to be locked. But the worst scenes were at the rear entrance. Staff turning up for work, including secretaries and other female employees, were punched and harangued. The pickets prevented those arriving by car from reversing by blocking the road behind them with scaffolding and rubble from a nearby building site and subjecting the trapped employees to a terrifying ordeal of intimidation and threatening behaviour.

Late that night, the assault took a yet more sinister path. A News International warehouse at Convoy's Wharf in Deptford where newsprint was being stored was fire-bombed. Two men were seen scrambling over garage roofs and along a wall before making a getaway in a waiting car. Moments later, there was a huge explosion from the warehouse followed by an enormous sheet of flame. The result was the biggest fire in London since the Blitz. The tightly packed newsprint ignited, the steel frame buckled and the roof came crashing in. At one stage the heat was so intense that police feared it would crack the windows and set fire to curtains in a nearby housing estate. Throughout the night, a fireboat pumped 26,000 gallons of water from the Thames every three minutes into the inferno. Two days afterwards, the warehouse's contents were still smouldering. Sifting through the charred remains, police discovered petrol can caps on the floor.

The following morning, Bruce Matthews's secretary received a telephone call from an anonymous caller with some advice for her boss: 'That was a well-organized job last night, wasn't it? Tell him he'll be the next to burn.' Although News International offered a £50,000 reward for information leading to the culprits' arrest and conviction, nobody was ever charged. Whoever were the culprits, what was not in doubt was that they had launched a deliberate attempt to destroy Wapping's store of newsprint. In the event, almost 10,000 tons were destroyed, of which 20 per cent (two weeks' supply) had been intended for Wapping. A lorry and trailers were also incinerated. In all, £7 million of damage was incurred.[77]

A couple of days after the Deptford fire, Eric Hammond answered the telephone to a caller who assured him, 'You and your family are going to burn, you bastard.' He later recognized the voice when he was heckled while giving an interview. It belonged to someone with 'an honoured presence in SOGAT'.[78] At the annual TUC conference in Brighton, Hammond had to be accompanied by bodyguards wherever he went. The *Sunday Times* editor, Andrew Neil, also received death threats, with his home in Onslow Gardens becoming a regular destination for hate mail. When he appeared on the panel of BBC TV's *Question Time*, demonstrators smashed the building's windows and at one point the electricity was cut, plunging the studio into darkness. On another occasion, Neil's attempts to honour an invitation from the Institute of Journalists had to be abandoned when strikers threw smoke bombs into the basement where the meeting was in progress.[79] Marmaduke Hussey had to endure obscene abuse being hurled at him by a picket who accosted him as he was getting into his car. As Hussey levered himself into the driving seat the picket slammed the car door on Hussey's leg. Luckily it was his artificial leg (he had been seriously wounded in the Second World War) and the door 'bounced back with an almighty clang'. The picket was somewhat taken aback.[80]

Throughout the summer, the spate of targeted attacks continued apace. On 19 June, a TNT distribution depot for *The Times* at Snodland in Kent was attacked by masked intruders who shattered windscreens and damaged property. This was not just a hit and run mission by a few desperados: four hundred demonstrators marched on the depot. Six days later, forty men armed with iron bars smashed into a TNT depot in Luton, attacked police officers with bricks and missiles and destroyed vans while two hundred demonstrators picketed outside. A similar assault was launched eleven days later, causing more criminal damage at a TNT depot in Eastleigh, Hampshire.[81] The varied geography of these locations, the premeditated collection of weapons and the size of the supporting demonstration highlighted the organized extent of the campaign being waged against News International and its interests.

Yet, violent methods – whether by or on behalf of the sacked print workers – were a sign of desperation. In rejecting a £50 million financial settlement and having failed to stop or seriously hamper production at Wapping, such measures appeared to be all the activists had left with which to fight. For those enduring the daily abuse and intimidation on their way in and out of work, this was particularly unnerving. But the question now was whether the militant forces within SOGAT would seek to oust Brenda Dean and all other moderating influences within their union. The showdown came in mid-June at the SOGAT annual conference in Scarborough. Dean entered the hall to shouts of 'Judas'. But her speech was uncompromising, making clear that no one branch of 'wreckers' was going to determine the union's destiny as a whole. She rounded on the street-corner chants that alleged she had sold her London members down the river: 'That sort of chant usually comes from those who failed to recognize that there was no longer any river to sell them down.' It was a strong performance and she carried the day. The conference voted to leave the National Executive in charge of handling the dispute rather than devolving it to the militant London chapel. In a decision that would only later take on great significance, the conference also agreed that the union could not take any action that led to its assets being sequestrated a second time. The will of the provincial majority had prevailed – to the disgust of activists from London. The extent of this culture clash was manifest when one London member, in the course of berating Dean, asked her how he was expected to meet his £50,000 mortgage. Dean attempted to explain: 'If I go and tell the rest of the union you need help with that mortgage, you'll get nothing. They're living in houses that don't cost half of that as a total cost.'[82]

The situation was a stalemate. The News International management was not prepared to improve the offer and the union leadership had been given no room for manoeuvre by its members. To *Times* journalists the situation was becoming close to intolerable. Those driving into work sometimes spotted strikers noting down their number plates. Some noticed their photographs being taken. Given what had happened at Deptford, this was an effective form of intimidation. What was more, Wapping in 1986 afforded few of the lunchtime and evening comforts to which journalists were accustomed. Even if there had been pubs or restaurants worth patronizing, it was too risky to do so. Many felt marooned inside the compound, a fate as bad for personal morale as it was for getting out in search of news stories. What made matters worse was the limitations of the office environment. A casualty of the move from Gray's Inn Road was *The Times* library. Six months after the move to Wapping, *Times* journalists were still separated from their paper's books archive and picture library which had been left behind at their former site. In view of staff and space shortage, it was decided to base Wapping's library around the *News of the World*'s holdings with the other papers merely adding what contents they could fit in. This was a short-sighted economy of scale. For the next few years, the paper had to continue to make do with inadequate information resources (although, in truth, whether they were better or worse than the previous *Times* library was debatable). Although improving internet research engines made life easier in the 1990s and there was a sizeable cuttings library, the newspaper still had to rely upon a lamentable range of source material on the communal bookshelves.

Times journalists had other causes of woe. When they moved to Wapping, the basic journalists' salary at the paper was, at £15,050, around £5000 less than the equivalent at the *News of the World* and the *Sun*. There was a good reason for this: the tabloids made money and *The Times* made a loss. But the broadsheet's writers felt they deserved remuneration that represented – to put it mildly – something closer to parity of esteem. On this score, Wapping represented a great opportunity. It threatened to make even *The Times* profitable. The paper's NUJ chapel, led by its new father, the religious affairs correspondent, Clifford Longley, seized the moment to press home the advantage, demanding: 'The time is now right for *The Times* to make good its claim to be the greatest newspaper in the world, which dictates in turn salaries appropriate to that status . . . We feel there-fore that our goodwill has been exploited for many years.' The chapel demanded a pay increase of 25 per cent and proper compensation for those who departed citing they felt themselves 'unable to come to terms with the move to Wapping and/or the introduction of new technology'. The salary demand ignored the fact that the company had increased average pay at the paper by 27.2 per cent between March 1985 and March 1986. As far as Longley was concerned, this was not the point; *Times* staff were still 'at the bottom of the Fleet Street pay league'. The paper's managing editor, Mike Hoy, was incredulous. Inflation was running at around 4 per cent. He assured the NUJ chapel that if they wanted a significantly steeper rise they would have to conclude the sort of agreement that management had demanded from the print unions. This would involve working five days a week (many journalists still managed just four), a no-strike clause, legally binding arbitration and no closed shop.[83]

On 9 June, *Sun* journalists, unhappy with a 3.5 per cent pay offer, narrowly voted to strike. A panicked management swiftly increased the offer to 10 per cent and the threat was averted. *The Times* NUJ chapel followed suit and were duly rewarded with a 'full and final offer' of 10 per cent as well. But the animosity towards not only the managerial but editorial high command was clear when the chapel made a formal complaint to Charles Wilson over the paper's failure to report the original strike vote at the *Sun*. Furthermore, the chapel voted by eighty votes to two to strike if the refuseniks who had declined to cross the Wapping picket line were not reinstated.

This was a serious shot across the bows. Only a third of the paper's NUJ members had attended and voted in the meeting but it only took this number to wreck the paper. Some wondered if the spirit that had animated the active minority of *Times* journalists to go on strike in 1980 – thereby ensuring the paper's sale – had suddenly gripped the chapel once more in this latest period of crisis. Wilson responded by writing a four-page letter to his staff, appealing to them to stay at their desks. Aside from the specifics of the individual refuseniks' cases, *The Times*'s future would be threatened at the very moment it was on the verge of breaking free from the dead hand of those who were making the journalists' lives so unpleasant from the other side of the wire.[84] Longley, however, was making a stand. He spurned the higher pay offer on the grounds that 'we will not discuss money with you while the jobs of six sacked members are at issue. It would be immoral to talk about money.'[85] Yet, in the event, the religious affairs correspondent was deserted by his flock: the chapel voted not to strike over the refuseniks' fate by sixty-three to twenty-eight. In September, Longley became a martyr to his own cause when the NUJ Executive Committee summoned him before a disciplinary hearing on a charge of conduct detrimental to the interests of the union (for not being a refusenik himself). His first reaction was to get a temporary court injunction against the hearing going ahead. When that failed his union found him guilty, but voted narrowly to censure rather than expel him.[86] Perhaps they realized the negative consequences of ridding themselves of a turbulent priest.

While dissent from and between NUJ officials was being seen off, News International had decided, once again, to seek legal redress against the manner in which the siege was being conducted. On 31 July, High Court injunctions were granted that permitted the unions to hold demonstrations only on the condition they passed the Wapping plant and did not seek to block it. Any attempt at the latter would be construed as an official picket that, under the terms of the 1982 Trade Union Act, was limited to six individuals. Mr Justice Stuart-Smith reminded the unions that 'freedom of speech has never extended to intimidation, abuse and threats directed at those going about their lawful business'.[87] Unions who failed to restrict the Wapping picket to six individuals would be liable to fines or resequestration. TNT promptly launched similar injunctions against mass action at their depots. At 2.30 in the morning of 1 August, only a few hours after the High Court had pronounced against mass picketing, a mob of two hundred attacked a TNT distribution depot at Thetford, Norfolk. Besides smashing up vans, the assailants tried to set the depot ablaze by firing flares into the building. In this they were unsuccessful although they did manage to torch bundles of The Times that had just been unloaded.[88]

Having paid a heavy financial penalty the last time they had come up for contempt of court, the unions took this new legal threat seriously and SOGAT's head office ordered its London branch leaders to cooperate with the letter of the law.[89] Indeed, while the NGA and SOGAT leadership were busy trying to get the EETPU expelled from the TUC, they were also receptive to a further attempt to reach a settlement with News International. In late August and early September, they had a series of talks with Bill O'Neill at a hotel near Gatwick. The issue of a national joint committee to represent members of all unions at Wapping was again raised. O'Neill parried that this would be a matter for the existing Wapping employees to decide and 'if pushed now' they would reject the mechanism. O'Neill advised an eighteen-month 'cooling-off period' before the proposal was put to them.[90] In the meantime, the unions should settle. As an inducement, the redundancy offer was increased from £50 million to £58 million. The unions agreed to put it to their members. Once again, the ballot papers went out in the post.

There was confusion over who was still entitled to vote. The majority of the four thousand affected SOGAT members had now got jobs elsewhere. Nonetheless, Dean got her way in insisting that since the settlement concerned them too they had the right to decide it. The vote was announced on 8 October. SOGAT members rejected the improved offer by 2372 votes to 960 while NGA members rejected it by 556 to 116 (and the AUEW members by 107 to 47).[91] News International's attempts to get a package approved collectively had now failed not once but twice. A grand negotiated settlement had proved impossible. Henceforth, the company would try a new tactic, making individual offers over the collective leadership's heads. The dismissed employees would be picked off one by one.

In the fortnight after the vote, management received 180 letters from sacked print workers responding to the prospect of a private settlement.[92] By the time the first anniversary of the strike approached, 1750 had reached agreement. State unemployment benefit was due to end on that date. In order to raise the £2 million need to finance those who continued to be out of work, the SOGAT leadership proposed a six month fifty-eight pence a week levy on all its members nationwide. The membership voted by 51,187 to 44,265 not to contribute.[93] Most, it seemed, had had enough of encouraging the London branch to persist in fighting a war that was clearly lost. On 20 January 1987, a further squeeze was imposed when News International went to court to seek from the unions the costs of Wapping's security measures over the past six months. Events were, it seemed, approaching a denouement. Few appreciated that the worst bout of violence was about to be unleashed.

VII

The massed assault on Wapping that took place on the night of 24 January was timed to commemorate the first anniversary of the strike. But its ferocity was sharpened both by the realization that the resistance of strikers was crumbling and by a tragedy that had taken place the previous fortnight. A nineteen-year-old youth, Michael Delaney, was killed trying to confront a TNT lorry in Stepney. Delaney, who had no connection with the dispute, had gone under the wheels while banging on the side of the truck and shouting 'scab'.[94] Lamentably, *The Times* failed to report the death when it occurred although it did subsequently cover the inquest three months later. A combination of these factors contributed to the dark mood animating those who planned the first-anniversary Wapping attack.

About 12,500 demonstrators marched on the site. The company's security cameras showed a relatively non-violent protest in progress until 7.30 p.m. But the ensuing assault had been carefully planned. The first sign that an orchestrated offensive was being unleashed came when an attempt was made to electronically jam police communications. Then a sting wire was unfurled across the road with the intention of maiming police horses and their riders. There was also an attempt to ignite petrol when five litres were spilled onto the road in front of the police officers. Some rioters overturned a lorry – the same one that had carried the band that had led the march to Wapping – and tried to set it on fire. Missiles were thrown. Uniformed police fell back to be replaced by those in riot gear. An hour later, the police lines had succeeded in pushing the demonstrators back from the top of Virginia Street into the Wapping Highway. Brenda Dean could be heard from the union rostrum lecturing the police to stop harassing the crowd. The security cameras then recorded an unidentified man wearing an armband apparently assuming command of the agitators. He called a group of about twenty-four of them into line. They were all wearing balaclavas and scarves over their faces. This vanguard launched itself at the police, trying to drive them back into Virginia Street. Under a hail of broken bricks and pieces of paving stones, the police line faltered. Mounted police tried to shore up the line and grab some of the activists only to be answered with a hail of thunderflashes, petrol bombs and scaffolding poles. The police sustained many injuries.[95]

Such was the ferocity of the assault that at one point the attackers looked like breaking through into the compound. At the opposite end of *The Times* building, Andrew Neil's office was dangerously close to the main gate. Fearing it was about to be overrun, Neil's bodyguard burst in and tried to persuade him to retreat to the print hall building where he could hide in the last redoubt – locked in behind the steel fire doors at its heart. Neil, who was in mid-meeting, would not be moved. He opted to stay behind with his staff, although he did ask 'them to check that the underground passages connecting our building with the main facility – and our last line of refuge – were open and clear for a dash to safety'.[96]

The audit of war produced sixty-seven arrests (of which thirteen were print workers) and injuries to thirty-nine police officers. Eleven police horses were injured and nine police vehicles damaged. Around thirty demonstrators suffered injuries when mounted police tried to push the surging crowds back. Barbara Cohen, a spokeswoman for a team of observers filing a legal report to the Home Secretary, blamed the police for the problem on the grounds that 'there was barely a visible police presence during the march, which was peaceful and orderly. When the marchers reached Wapping, the sight of rows of riot police equipped for violent conflict raised the tension.' Among the Labour MPs who had addressed the demonstration was Dennis Skinner who told the crowds that Labour's chances of success at the next general election depended upon 'extra-parliamentary activity' to 'win it on the streets'.[97] Certainly, a portion of the streets was ripped up as the pile of discarded weaponry, including chunks of paving stone, assembled by the police the following day demonstrated. A permanent legacy of the night was left in the rows of missing spikes removed from the Wapping Highway's Victorian iron railings. They had been thrown as javelins at the police.

While some in the Labour Movement chose to see the riot as a consequence of police brutality, others were appalled at the discredit it was attaching to the cause. Neil Kinnock described the violence as 'hideous and horrifying' while Norman Willis condemned the 'disgraceful and violent scenes'.[98] Indeed, Willis was now adamant that the strategy of organizing mass demonstrations at Wapping had to stop. The morning after the riot, Dean telephoned Bill O'Neill to request an urgent meeting. O'Neill, who was completing the process of his US naturalization, made clear he could not leave America and wondered if it could wait until he returned. Dean was determined to meet sooner, adding that she wanted the strike brought to an end before her executive met on 5 February. With Bill Miles, she flew to Paris and there caught Concorde to cross the Atlantic.

Dean and Miles met O'Neill in the ground-floor coffee shop of the Hilton at New York's JFK airport. Dean mentioned the decision of the SOGAT annual conference that mandated the union not to act in a way that risked a further sequestration. If News International took SOGAT to court on a further contempt charge, she would be in a position to get her executive to call the strike off without putting the question to the die-hard strikers. Attracted by the force of what had been put to him, O'Neill went to a pay phone to call Geoffrey Richards for his legal advice. While he was trying to get through, a woman picked up an adjacent pay telephone and could be heard speaking into the receiver: 'Could I have "copy"? . . . I want you to know that I've been here for over an hour and it seems as though they have come up with a way to bring this strike to an end . . . They're analysing a formula now and I will stay here and see how it works out.' Dean, Miles and O'Neill froze in panic. How had their meeting been rumbled? The three hurried into the hotel lobby which they found packed with reporters and television cameras. And then they noticed they were being ignored. It transpired that the hotel was also the venue for resolving a Long Island railway dispute. Their relief was palpable. Less than three hours after they had touched down at JFK, Dean and Miles caught another Concorde flight home.[99] In the meantime, the mechanism to end the dispute had been agreed.

Soon afterwards, O'Neill flew back across the Atlantic. On 2 February he and Geoffrey Richards met Dean and Miles for dinner at the home of SOGAT's lawyer. Dean accepted that the strike had been lost long ago and its protraction was only damaging the union's image. A court hearing was set for 6 February. The video footage of the 24 January riot, showing a two-hundred-strong mob trying to smash down the gates to Wapping, supported News International's case that the unions were in breach of their legal undertakings to keep to six pickets. The unions stood to have all their assets sequestrated and to face potentially crippling fines of up to £3 million. Over half of SOGAT's funds had already been spent fighting the dispute and the union's legal advice was to call off the strike or face bankruptcy. SOGAT's existence could be decided by what line its National Executive took. On 5 February, it met. Seven London members argued vociferously against surrender, but they were outnumbered. The final vote was twenty-three to nine in favour of calling off the strike. Dean prepared a press release, explaining, 'a further sequestration would have meant the demise of our union' and adding 'we will never forget this dispute and the ravages of it will be evident for a long time to come'. Then she rang O'Neill. 'I've had a terrible day,' she told him.[100]

With SOGAT's surrender, so collapsed the resistance of its comrades. The NUJ called off its action the following day. All eyes turned to the NGA. Tony Dubbins telephoned O'Neill to plead for a weekend's grace. O'Neill replied that he had but a few hours to submit or face ruin in court. A clerk from Farrar's was waiting at the court with orders to file News International's petition if no news had been received by 3 p.m. The hands of the clock moved slowly around but nothing was heard. Then, a few minutes before three, as O'Neill was preparing to contact the Farrar's clerk, the telephone rang. It was Dubbins offering unconditional surrender. When the news reached the pickets, there was angry talk among some of them about continuing the blockade by unofficial means. This was quickly quelled by the threat of being ejected from the union. At 4 a.m. on Saturday 7 February the official picket packed up and departed. The siege of Wapping was over. It had lasted fifty-four weeks.

VIII

Relief was the overwhelming emotion that swept over *Times* staff as the realization dawned that their daily ordeal was finally over. The paper's leader column summed up the past thirteen months as a period in which 'We were set free from damaging trade union practices inside our gates. We exchanged them for damaging trade union practices outside.'[101] But many, especially at management level, also felt a quiet sense of satisfaction. In 1978, *The Times* had taken on its print unions and, after an eleven-month shutdown, been forced to capitulate to them. It had taken eight years, but here at last was the moment of retribution. Everyone who had crossed the picket line had played his or her part. But in devising and implementing the strategy that made Murdoch's success possible, Charles Wilson, Bruce Matthews, Bill O'Neill and Geoffrey Richards had the most reason to feel proud of their achievement. They were the principal architects of the Wapping revolution. Yet the celebrations were muted. In particular, the dispute had weighed heavily upon Matthews. He had hoped an accommodation might be made to re-employ some of the more moderate print union members but Murdoch was insistent that a complete break had to be made – that, after all, was the point of Wapping and no fresh NGA or SOGAT presence could be recreated there.[102] Tired of the persistent wrangling on both sides of the Wapping barbed wire, in November 1986 a despondent Matthews cleared his desk as managing director before the final victory had been assured. O'Neill took his place. None of the print union members who had been friends with Tony Norbury before the dispute ever spoke to him again. He calculated that Wapping had diminished his social life by 75 per cent. But as the man behind getting *The Times* produced from its new location, he never doubted that he had done the right thing, both for the future of his newspaper and for the unfettering of British print journalism.[103]

Victory had come at a cost. Five hundred and seventy-four police officers had been injured and more than a thousand News International and TNT drivers or their vehicles had been attacked. Some had broken arms. Others had glass in their eyes. One driver had had his windscreen broken twenty-three times. For their part, the protestors had also taken a toll. One young man had been killed. Nearly 1500 people had been arrested, two-thirds of whom were convicted. Police attendance at Wapping had averaged three hundred a day (on crucial nights there had been a thousand protecting the site). The estimated cost of this to the taxpayer exceeded £5 million.[104] News International honoured its £58 million redundancy payout. Depending upon their time with the company, recipients received between £2000 and £30,000 each.

'Little direct good ever comes out of a dispute of this kind – it's a fairly sad story,' was the Employment Secretary Ken Clarke's downbeat verdict on the strike's end, although he did add, 'but I think the lasting effects may be beneficial.'[105] Some of his Cabinet colleagues were more cheerful. Indeed, commentators soon assumed that the greatest victor was not Murdoch and his newspapers but Margaret Thatcher in her battle to smash union power in Britain. She had seen off Arthur Scargill over the mines in a fight that symbolized the fate of the old industries. Wapping demonstrated that the unions would not control the destiny of the new technology-driven industries either.

Certainly, union militancy had been dealt a crushing blow. The NGA and SOGAT began a period of re-evaluation that led to their merger in 1991 as the Graphical, Paper and Media Union (GPMU) with Tony Dubbins as general secretary. Brenda Dean became the new union's deputy leader but retired the following year. Accepting a peerage as Baroness Dean of Thornton-le-Fylde, she became an active member of parliamentary committees, health and higher education boards, the Press Complaints Commission and a variety of other bodies. In 1997, she became chairman of the Housing Corporation. Ironically, one who was disappointed by Wapping's legacy was the union leader who had done so much to make it possible, Eric Hammond. While his members had staffed the plant from the first, he had put off pressing for formal EETPU recognition in accordance with TUC policy. But when, in 1988, the TUC finally expelled the union over its involvement in no-strike deals (and, it was widely presumed, participation in Wapping), Hammond felt free from TUC censure to explore collective bargaining rights there. His attempts were rebuffed, first by O'Neill and subsequently in a painful correspondence with Murdoch.

Hammond could have been forgiven for feeling used. In his memoirs he was moved to write that Murdoch had 'shown no spark of gratitude, even though he couldn't have succeeded without us, and without the support of our people at Wapping'.[106]

Another major union to lose out was the NUJ. In August 1987, a new disputes procedure involving ACAS was agreed at *The Times* that all but banished the grounds for a journalists' strike. For its part, the NUJ had not done much to endear itself. Its National Executive had sought to impose £1000 fines on ninety-five News International employees (forty-eight of them *Times* journalists) for crossing the Wapping picket line during the siege. They were singled out because their names had appeared in news reports (another 320 were acquitted because their names did not).[107] *The Times* NUJ chapel responded by freezing its payments to the union and the fines were eventually dropped but not before irreparable damage had been done. The union was, in any case, in disarray. Among other eccentricities, its accounts had been kept during the 1980s by an official who refused to switch from ledgers to a computer database. Eventually, the accounts were handed over instead to someone whose fake credentials were revealed after the reference he had provided transpired to be the number of a public telephone box.[108] The belief that the union was having difficulty putting its house in order did it much harm. By the 1990s, the once all conquering NUJ had been reduced to but a small bargaining presence in Fleet Street. *The Times* and its Wapping stable-mates opted for total derecognition of the union. The *Daily Telegraph*, *Daily Mail* and *Independent* followed suit.[109] Even the left-leaning *Daily Mirror* refused to recognize the NUJ. This was part of a wider process fuelled by the policies of the Thatcher years and the restructuring of the economy. In 1980, 70 per cent of wages in Britain were set through collective bargaining. By 1998, the figure had fallen to 35 per cent. Only a third of companies established since 1980 recognized unions.[110]

The consequences of Murdoch's victory for British politics or the Labour Movement can be debated. But what can be more easily assessed was the direct effect it had on *The Times* newspaper. By ditching the print unions there was, of course, a huge saving in cutting the surplus workforce. But Wapping also ensured massive improvements to the way the paper's content could be altered at short notice. At the unionized Gray's Inn Road, the paper was limited to making around a dozen significant page changes per night. But at Wapping it was possible to make between thirty and fifty page changes a night and to tinker with a front page that usually changed six times over the course of the evening.[111] It had formerly taken the print union members forty-five minutes to make a single change to a graphic. Wapping's staff could do it in five minutes. Late changes to stories could be done at the press of a button. At Gray's Inn Road, a late change had involved adhering to a lengthy set of union demarcation procedures. First of all, a request would be made to the composing department to come down with a proof. The changes would be marked onto the proof. The proof would then be taken (by hand) back up to the composing department. The comp would then type in the changes and these would be checked again to make sure they had been done correctly (which frequently they were not). A minor change to a story could take thirty to forty-five minutes to enact. Whether the copy or a new headline fitted the allotted space was a matter of trial and error. Wapping's direct-input computers gave journalists an instant 'copy fit' thereby making page planning easy. Correspondents' copy and agency wires could also be brought onto the system at the touch of a button. Previously, they had to wait until a messenger brought them over to the right desk (if he got the right desk) in his own time.[112] Errors and spelling mistakes – once the bane of Fleet Street journalism – could now be quickly corrected. The last edition of *The Times* to come from Gray's Inn Road contained 150 misprints in thirty-two pages. *The Times* of (taking a day at random) 7 May 1987 contained just fourteen in thirty-eight pages. Wapping gave the reader a better product.

Yet the gains were by no means all down to new technology. Although the arrival of computers on the editorial floor greatly speeded up the process of writing and subbing the paper, in other parts of the production process *The Times* was still being produced in an old-fashioned manner. The page make-up techniques and printing presses used at Wapping were essentially those the print unions had operated at Gray's Inn Road. In the Napoleonic vaulted basement of *The Times*'s Wapping home, stylish girls fresh from art college replaced old union lags but they were doing the same task – laying out the pages with scissors and paste. Late changes were often effected by scrambling about on the floor for excised words on tiny trimmed rectangles of paper. Frequently the missing word would be found stuck to someone's shoe. Thus the difference was not in the tools for the job but in the attitude and adaptability of those who wielded them. Wapping's 'paste-up' team cut the time it took from 'last-copy-to-composition' and the last page leaving the stone from sixty-five to ten minutes. What used not to be ready until after 9 p.m. was now completed by 8.10 p.m. And, in the longer term, removing union power at management level did smooth the way for the easier adoption of the technological revolutions of the

1990s – colour, fast redesign, better computer-generated graphics and vastly improved print and picture reproduction.

There was, however, a downside to the move to Wapping and the dispersal of the other newspaper offices that it hastened. By destroying the village of Fleet Street, the geographically tight-knit community that allowed journalists and their contacts to lunch together, dine together and drink together, it reduced not only the convivial quality of life to which many reporters had become accustomed but also their ability to trade contacts and insights from outside the office. The Wapping move did encourage less adventurous journalists to confine the world to what was presented on their computer terminals, rather than going out themselves in search of stories. It is, of course, possible to make too much of this and to overemphasize the extent to which indulging in a long liquid lunch with friends constituted searching for news. On a narrow measure, the destruction of the Fleet Street lunch certainly improved productivity even if a part of the journalistic soul died as a consequence. Health-wise, it was probably a godsend.

Ultimately, what the Wapping revolution delivered could be summed up in one word – flexibility. It gave The Times's production and editorial staff the means to change, alter, innovate and increase the size or quantity of their paper without months of haggling with shop stewards intent on preventing any change without first extracting an inflated price. Murdoch had described the old world from which Wapping permitted him to escape:

> If you wanted to change a column width in The Times it would take you three months to negotiate and £10 a day or a week to everybody in the plant. And in the meantime, having to put up with one hundred typos on page one every second day if people felt they had a bad liver or something.[113]

The barriers to innovation were now swept away. This was not merely a time saving exercise in the nightly rush to press. Strategic changes could at last be enacted. In 1987, The Times came out on Boxing Day for the first time in seventy years (although some readers imagined a Boxing Day newspaper was a disturbing sign of the secular consumerism of the 1980s, The Times had continuously come out on every Boxing Day from 1785 to 1917). Without Wapping, it is hard to envisage the unreformed print unions agreeing to work on such an edition or the rail unions being willing to carry it to its distributors.

Even more importantly, the pagination of the newspaper was expanded.

In the first six months of printing at Wapping, *The Times* was able to raise its number of pages from thirty-four to forty-eight. The only way the presses could handle the bigger paper was to print it in two sections. Thus, while news and comment remained in the main part of the paper, a second section was produced covering business and sport. Complaints flooded in and when, after a year of working at Wapping, Charles Wilson was assured that the capacity had been created to print the whole paper in one section, he took the decision to switch back. The result was a fresh broadside of complaint from readers in support of the two-section paper (many sighting the morning bliss of husband and wife being able to read the different sections over the same breakfast table). This fresh postbag, and the difficulties the presses were having in producing the paper in one section, quickly convinced Wilson to revert to a two-section newspaper. The ability to respond at this speed would have been unthinkable at Gray's Inn Road. Nor was this the end of the matter. As the months progressed, the paper began to expand further. On 3 September 1987, a four-section, sixty-four-page *Times* was launched on Saturday with more pre-print colour than any other national newspaper.[114]

There was also now the possibility that *The Times* could buck its twentieth century history and become a newspaper that actually made a profit. The immediate consequence of moving to Wapping was a threefold increase in News International's profitability. The Wapping plant itself had cost £100 million to build and a further £67 million to equip, but it allowed for the old premises to be sold. Bouverie Street fetched £72 million (the site was subsequently levelled for redevelopment) and *The Times*'s old home, Gray's Inn Road – the building which the unions had turned down for free – was sold to ITN for £70 million.[115] Setting these sales against the expense of construction gave Wapping a net cost of £25 million (which rose significantly a few years later when the plant had to be extended), but, by ditching the print unions, News International had been able to realize job cuts that saved in the region of £65 million each year.[116] Wapping took the company's operating income from £38.4 million in 1985 to £150.2 million in 1987.[117] One estimate suggested it had increased the four newspapers' worth (excluding outstanding debt) from $0.3 billion to $1 billion.[118] The share price trebled. Indeed, in 1987 News International performed better than any other major company on the London stock exchange. Contributing 40 per cent of News Corp.'s global profits, Wapping pump primed Murdoch's expansion into the American television and film network. As we will see later, this encouraged fresh borrowing that almost proved his undoing. Yet, in 2002, Peter Chernin, the News Corp. president, was in a position to reflect that the move to Wapping 'was the most significant labour event in the world during the past forty years', adding that he did not think the company would have survived without it.[119]

Moving to Wapping certainly helped to secure *The Times*'s survival, but it was not just a victory for it, News International and its shareholders. Before Wapping, the print unions had a stranglehold over the management of all Britain's national newspapers. After Wapping, they had a toehold. As Hugo Young, the *Guardian* journalist who was no admirer of Murdoch's politics, nonetheless conceded in 1993, 'What he did for the economics of newspaper publishing, by killing the power of the worst-led trade unions in modern history, has benefited every journalist, advertiser and reader.'[120] At the moment when the siege of Wapping began, *The Times*'s rivals had been attempting to move to new print premises in Docklands but were frustrated by their unions refusal to accept terms that would make the move economic. Wapping enabled them to turn the tables on unions who, overnight, awoke to discover the price for not being shut out entirely was to concede much of their old bargaining power and workforce. The management at the *Daily Mail*'s owners, Associated Newspapers, accepted that Wapping 'was a great help to us. When that happened, if there was any reluctance of our people to come along with us, it disappeared.'[121] Consequently, the company was able to cut its workforce by half without any loss to the production of its papers. Similarly, when the *Daily Telegraph* moved from Fleet Street to Docklands, its management was able to cut the print workforce from 1650 to 678, a wage bill saving of £24 million. The *FT* also made huge economies when it moved its printing works to Docklands in 1988. Its chief executive, Frank Barlow, had argued that the move was essential because of the 'huge cost advantage' that Wapping had given Murdoch.[122] In fighting for his own papers, Murdoch had won a victory for all national newspapers. Of course it might be argued that these results could have been achieved without the Wapping gamble, but the failure of Eddy Shah's innovative and brave venture, *Today* – which eventually had to be rescued from collapse by Murdoch – suggests the process was far from inevitable. The *Independent* would have been launched regardless, but – without Wapping – its founders would have been confronted by many of the industry's old problems. There is no certainty the little infant would have prospered under such rough midwifery. In the opinion of Ivan Fallon, its chief executive eighteen years later, '*The Independent* would not have been possible without the move to Wapping.'[123]

The battle of Wapping won a larger war for all Britain's newspapers. But it is worth contemplating an imaginary scenario where, despite being in a weaker position, other newspaper proprietors did eventually manage, somehow, to overcome the grip of their unions, leaving Murdoch hamstrung in the old world of Fleet Street industrial relations. In this eventuality, it would have been *The Times* that would have found itself plunged into a perilously uncompetitive position, smashed to pieces between a new unencumbered *Independent* and a *Daily Telegraph* rejuvenated by its chief executive, Andrew Knight, both newspapers able to deploy the ways and means to consign 'The Thunderer' to the scrap heap. Wapping also prevented this contingency. It ensured a newspaper that was bigger, quicker, sharper and with fewer mistakes. It offered the prospect of a paper that could even become profitable. It was certainly hard to argue with the most easily measurable consequence – in the decade before the move to Wapping, *The Times* had lost 96.5 million copies through industrial action. In the decade following the move, it lost none.

CHAPTER SEVEN

INDEPENDENT CHALLENGES

Competition from the *Independent*;
the High Tide of Thatcherism; Business; Sport

I

On 7 October 1986, while *The Times* was still under siege at Wapping, a
new direct rival struck at its heart. The *Independent* was the first national
quality daily to be launched since the First World War. Funded by more
than a hundred investors, it had no single proprietor. Its name, backed by
a Saatchi & Saatchi advertising campaign based around the slogan 'It is,
are you?' emphasized its refreshing freedom from the traditional world of
press barons and private agendas. This was something that appealed to
those who had never cared for Rupert Murdoch, the man or his methods.

There were good financial reasons why nobody had started a national
broadsheet for so many years and the venture was, to put it mildly, a risky
one. Max Hastings, the editor of the *Daily Telegraph*, sent the *Independent*
a launch present of a wreath. Charles Wilson was not so cocky. On its first
day, the *Independent* sold 600,000 copies – 130,000 more than *The Times*
had been selling in the preceding days. A desperate fight for circulation
would now commence. Just when it looked as if moving to Wapping and
cutting costs was going to deliver *The Times* from decades of losses, a rival
had arrived that risked taking away its market altogether.

The *Independent* was the brainchild of Andreas Whittam Smith, the
Daily Telegraph's City editor and two *Telegraph* leader writers, Stephen
Glover and Matthew Symonds. Whittam Smith had long been talked about
as a future *Telegraph* editor but, as time passed, a feeling that he was being
passed over and that the Hartwell family were running the paper towards
bankruptcy encouraged him to look to new horizons. With Glover and
Symonds he had begun to plan a new paper in 1985. Given the lax regime
at the *Telegraph* (leader writers were not expected to grace the office until
well into the afternoon) Glover and Symonds were able to devote large

amounts of their day to planning the new paper. It was impossible not to admire the daring of this gang of three. They were accomplished journalists, but had no experience or knowledge about how to finance, produce or distribute their product. Yet, there was no need for them to mislead potential investors about their experience because nobody in the City thought to press them on the matter. They were taken on trust. 'The truth is,' Glover wrote later, 'that the world will nearly always take you at your own apparent estimation of yourself. We were engaged in a glorious bluff.'[1]

The three visionaries were assisted by two enormous strokes of good fortune. The first was that by the time they were ready with their product, they could learn from the mixed performance of Eddy Shah's mid-market *Today* which had been launched seven months earlier in March 1986. They certainly would not be seeking to reproduce the technological hiccups that marred *Today*'s early editions. The *Independent* was not, in any case, troubled by *Today*'s position in the newspaper market since its own primary focus was to gain disaffected readers from the three main broadsheets. The far-greater stroke of good fortune was Murdoch's Wapping revolution that (coincidentally) got underway shortly after Whittam Smith, Glover and Symonds announced their own intentions to launch their paper. By destroying the bargaining power of the print unions and clearing the way for the introduction of new technology, Murdoch slashed the cost of starting up rival newspapers. In consequence, the *Independent* was launched on the back of a mere £18 million with a £3 million overdraft. This was less than a third of the start-up cost of the *Mail on Sunday* in the pre-Wapping environment of 1982.[2] In common with *Today*, the *Independent* contracted its printing out to four (later three) separate companies. Although these still employed union labour, the *Independent* refused to employ any print union members itself, despite the attempts of the NGA to secure a roll in electronic page make-up. As if reducing the cost base and dismantling the union stranglehold was not enough, Murdoch's Wapping battle assisted the *Independent* in a further, more negative, respect. The hardships and ill feelings created by having to work in siege conditions behind barbed wire and the scorn of other journalists ensured that there was a ready supply of disaffected *Times* and *Sunday Times* journalists looking to be tempted into Whittam Smith's feathered perch.

All national newspapers have a continual turnaround of staff but during the Wapping strike the number seeking to depart increased sharply. The first wave bore up the dozen refuseniks who had declined to cross the picket line from the first. They were soon augmented by a continuous trickle of those who subsequently found the courage of their convictions (especially when there were other journalistic jobs offered them) and by those who hated the torment of crossing a battle zone every day to get into work and saw no immediate likelihood of peace breaking out. Wilson was a galvanizing and inspiring figure whose personal courage was recognized by all those who saw him work to bring the newspaper out under the trying conditions of a vicious siege. He was not always so good at recognizing that many members of staff were less keen to spoil for a fight. This was evident from his upbeat assessment that working from behind the wire at Wapping 'had about as much effect as whether or not it was raining' for the life and work of the journalists trapped there.[3] Even for those content to be spat on while making their way through the front gate to work, Wilson's fighting talk was clearly overoptimistic. The Labour Party's refusal even to talk to *Times* journalists and the wariness with which many of those of a left liberal sensibility treated those associated, however indirectly, with Rupert Murdoch did make journalists' lives more difficult. In the first six months of the Wapping siege, 150 journalists left the four News International titles based there. More than thirty of them had worked for *The Times*. When in June 1986 the company placed an advertisement in the *UK Press Gazette* soliciting applications for 'opportunities for general and specialist writers and production staff to add to our success'[4] the appeal read rather more like a desperate plea.

Among the Wapping refuseniks, the loss of Paul Routledge was the highest-profile casualty. Routledge had not wanted to resign, telling the press that he had always had 'a strong feeling for *The Times*. It was the paper I always wanted to work for, and I still do.'[5] But he resolutely obeyed the NUJ's instructions not to work at – or file to – Wapping until the dispute was settled on satisfactory terms. Wilson was reluctant to sack him. Instead Routledge was suspended without pay but with modest expenses to sustain him at his posting in Singapore where Douglas-Home had installed him as South East Asia correspondent. The dispute's prolongation frayed tempers and when Routledge, having left Singapore without permission, chanced to see a Tamil Tiger outrage at Colombo airport and filed an eyewitness report for the *Observer*, Wilson's patience snapped.[6] Sacked, Routledge proceeded to heckle former colleagues on their way into Wapping, an act that cost him several friendships. After toying with working for Maxwell's short-lived *London Daily News*, he defected to the *Observer* where *The Times* Diary editor, Angela Gordon, had also set up shop.

It was the number of his journalists being poached by the *Independent* even before it had been launched that especially worried Wilson. Why were they leaving good jobs on one of the world's most famous newspapers for positions on a paper that did not yet even exist? At Easter, Wilson managed to escape with his family for a brief holiday in Lanzarotte, the first break he had felt able to take in eighteen bruising months. No sooner had he arrived than Mike Hoy, the managing editor, started telephoning him to say defections to the *Independent* were beginning in earnest. By the Friday of his supposedly relaxing family holiday, nine had departed. That day, Wilson was distracted from his sun lounger by a call from the proprietor. 'Hi, Rupert, how are you?' he said, vainly trying to sound upbeat. A growl down the line answered, 'Frustrated. Frustrated because you're there and I'm here.'[7] Murdoch had arrived at Wapping to find his editor absent and the office filled with rumours of defections. It looked bad.

In the end, seventeen *Times* journalists directly defected. Wilson was not concerned by some of the departures, but he was sorry to lose Anthony Bevins, the political correspondent who had been an important factor in *The Times*'s Westminster reporting since 1981. Bevins's leaving was not a surprise (he had clashed with Wilson over the paper's anti-Heseltine handling of the Westland crisis) but it was a disappointment. An LSE-educated Liverpudlian, he was the son of Harold Macmillan's Postmaster-General. (Reginald Bevins had been the only working-class member in that Government and had put up with a lot of condescension for his troubles.) This treatment and two years of voluntary work in Bengal had given Tony Bevins a valuable sense of detachment from the ruling few. His dogged style had been a boon to *The Times* and his disrespect for the hypocrisies of the lobby system and its non-attributable briefings ensured he fitted in well as the first political editor of the *Independent*. There, he was reunited with the former *Times* industrial affairs staff, Don McIntyre, David Felton and Barrie Clement, all of whom had opted to refuse to work at Wapping from the first. Wilson was deeply concerned when told that Miles Kington was also thinking of defecting to the *Independent*. He personally met him at the airport and whisked him away for lunch at the Savoy Grill as a desperate ploy to dissuade him. He failed. After nearly six years of writing his 'Moreover' column five times a week for the paper, it was the first time Kington had actually met Wilson.[8]

There were other high-profile defections. The fashion editor, Suzy Menkes, departed for the *Independent*. Sarah Hogg, the economics editor for the past three years, left to become the new paper's business and finance editor. She told Wilson that she had not felt she was part of his inner circle.

Married to the Tory politician Douglas Hogg, she later became head of the Downing Street Policy Unit to John Major in 1990. In truth, Wilson's inner circle was momentarily contracting. Colin Webb announced his intention to resign the deputy editorship in order to become editor-in-chief of the Press Association. With Webb's departure, Wilson decided to create two deputy editors. One was Peter Stothard who had fulfilled the promise that his mentor, Harold Evans, had first detected in him. His priorities continued to be comment and leading articles. The other was John Bryant. This was an appointment that led to a marked cooling in relations between Wilson and Mike Hoy who, until that moment, had worked amicably with Wilson and might have thought himself a contender for the post. Bryant, however, proved to be an excellent choice. Brought up in the West Country and grammar school-educated, he was, like Wilson, a highly professional 'news man' who, following an apprenticeship at the Edinburgh *Evening News*, had worked at the *Daily Mail*. Both editor and deputy shared a love of sport. While Wilson loved racing, Bryant was an Oxford athletics Blue and a close friend of Roger Bannister, Christopher Chataway and many of the great figures of British track and field. Knowing that Bryant was trying to extract himself from the *Mail* in order to join the *Independent*, Wilson acted fast to bring him to Wapping instead.

While Bryant would prove a worthy replacement for Webb, it was a bad time for Wilson to be falling out with other members of staff. Whatever the bullish persona he attempted to portray on the outside, Wilson was privately deeply worried about the imminent launch of the *Independent*. He knew that Wapping and its accompanying violence had tarnished *The Times*'s image and that Murdoch – painted as an editorially interfering monster by rival newspapers – was the unspoken target of the *Independent*'s title and advertising campaign. It was annoying, given the extent to which Murdoch's Wapping revolution had made the self-regarding ingénue possible, but there was never likely to be much love lost in the circumstances of a circulation war. Bruce Matthews told Wilson he was overreacting.[9] Many industry insiders still thought the new newspaper would quickly implode. The *Financial Times*'s Raymond Snoddy predicted 'Rupert Murdoch will strangle it in its cot before it gets a chance to wave its rattle'.[10]

II

When the *Guardian*'s editor, Peter Preston, held the first edition of the *Independent* in his hands he breathed a sign of relief and observed, 'It looks a bit like *The Times* of five years ago.' It was rather as he had suspected. In April 1986, John Biffen, the Leader of the Commons, had told a lunch held by *Guardian* editorial staff that he had been the guest to lunch at *The Times* the previous week. They had been apprehensive about the *Independent*'s launch although they had no need to be while he found the *Guardian* laid back even though they ought not to be.[11] In the event, Preston's first response was both right and wrong. He was wrong to be relaxed about it. Within eighteen months of the *Independent*'s launch, the *Guardian* had lost 10 per cent of its market. By 1988 the new rival had, from nothing, come to within 100,000 of the *Guardian*'s diminishing 474,000 circulation. Yet, Preston was right to the extent that it had the feel (although with far better print reproduction) of William Rees-Mogg's *Times*. Those who preferred that product were part of its new market and this was a worrying development for Wilson. The attack on *The Times*'s territory came not only in the breadth of the *Independent*'s foreign reporting (with twelve correspondents posted around the globe) but also in the strength of its obituaries and law reports. Many *Times* journalists resented Rees-Mogg's decision to be an *Independent* columnist, seeing it as a slap in the face to his old paper. Others thought it an indictment not on the past editor but on the current paper.

Inevitably, the *Independent* could not keep all the readers that turned to it out of curiosity on its first day. By November, its sales had fallen back to 275,000. *The Times* had lost about ten thousand copies since the arrival of the new competitor and was selling 478,000 a day.[12] In the circumstances, the old paper was holding up surprisingly well against the new, making some of the criticisms of Wilson's editorship appear disingenuous. Wilson, too, began to regain his confidence. He felt the *Independent*'s refusal to report on the monarchy was an own goal – 'well, for *Times* readers that's a nonsense!'[13] The *Independent*'s founders believed the *Telegraph* had weaknesses and that they could take a large share of its readers. It was easy to understand why they worked on this assumption. Not only had their own experience of working at the *Telegraph* made them especially aware of its shortcomings, the statistics markedly pointed to its vulnerability. Between 1980 and 1986, the *Telegraph* had lost almost 300,000 readers while *The*

Times had added 172,000 and the *Guardian* 150,000. Vast though the *Telegraph*'s circulation might be, it was one that was visibly ebbing with each month that passed. Oddly, this was the respect in which Whittam Smith, Glover and Symonds miscalculated. The *Telegraph* proceeded to suffer the fewest losses to the new paper. Indeed, by the time of the *Independent*'s first birthday, the *Telegraph*'s circulation was actually higher than it had been twelve months previously. The *FT* was also undamaged. It was Peter Preston who had the least grounds for passing on birthday congratulations. The crusade for the centre and centre-left readership proved to be the real battleground and it was from the *Guardian* that the *Independent* made the most gains.

This assault on the *Guardian* had at least one bonus for *The Times* – it allowed it to overtake the *Guardian*'s circulation and move into second place in the daily broadsheet market. But the *Independent*'s strengths were there for all to see and few were surprised when it won the *What The Papers Say* 'Newspaper of the Year' award. Aside from the quality of the prose, the design was also crisp. The photographs were by far the best of any newspaper even if there was some truth in Wilson's observation that an addiction to brooding clouds meant they could be described as 'an accumulation of cumulus'. After celebrating its first birthday, its sales began to surge forward again and by late 1988 it was heading towards 400,000. The *Guardian* and *The Times* were now within reach.

The *Independent*'s success was phenomenal. By the spring of 1988 it was making a profit (something *The Times* had proved incapable of sustaining in a century of trying to get it right) and it was even in a position to repay half of the £18 million with which it had been launched. Two years after the *Independent*'s arrival, *The Times*'s sale was still down 32,000 and the *Guardian* had slid 82,000. *The Times*, however, faced another threat that was less worrying to the *Guardian*. Conrad Black's *Daily Telegraph*, led by an aggressive editor, Max Hastings, and Andrew Knight's management team, was taking the painful medicine that the previous Hartwell owner-ship, without the salutary threat of a Wapping manoeuvre, had felt unable to administer. At last it had managed to cut almost 2400 print union employees and reap the benefit of the investment in new presses in Dock-lands. During 1987, the *Telegraph* moved out of danger, declaring a £580,000 pre-tax profit. The following year its profitability soared to £29 million. Meanwhile, in 1988, the *Guardian* showed it too had awoken to the need to adapt to survive with a redesign that featured a new, distinctive, sans-serif typeface. The improvement in its appearance was marked, although there was no immediate reward in circulation gains, despite the decision of its three rivals, including *The Times*, to increase their sale prices from twenty-five to thirty pence.

New print works, fewer print workers, the regaining of management's right to manage and a boom in advertising revenue on the back of the economic recovery drove the national newspapers' surge into profitability in 1987 and 1988. In the year following Murdoch's commencement of the Wapping revolution, the profits of the Mirror Group doubled, the *Express* trebled and even the long-troubled *FT*, 'the pink 'un', announced it was £40 million in the black. The pundits had argued that the Wapping revolution's consequence would be to increase the number of newspapers, but in the immediate aftermath, only *Today* and the *Independent* survived (in the case of *Today* because it was bought and saved by Murdoch), while the *Sunday Today*, the left-wing *News on Sunday* and Maxwell's *London Daily News* all suffered cot deaths. Yet, the market did increase, with a net rise of newspaper sales. The *Independent* in particular managed to generate sales to customers who had previously avoided the broadsheet market. Thanks largely to Whittam Smith's brainchild, the broadsheet market expanded by 11 per cent at the expense of the mid-market titles.

Easily overlooked amid the tumults of congratulation about its journalism, the *Independent* made one serious error from the first: it failed to pursue classified advertising, which was essential to help balance its books. Initially, it only employed six people to attract classified ads.[14] This was madness. The market had jumped 20 per cent in the first six months of 1987. An opportunity to lure business away from the *Guardian* (which, with its attraction to the public sector, led the classified market) was squandered. Advertising revenue also poured into *The Times*. Assisted by the new flexibility offered by Wapping, it was able to add advert-driven supplements with relative ease. It was an area in which *The Times* found itself let off the hook by its new rival. Later, in 1990, at the moment when his paper was poised to overtake *The Times*'s circulation, Whittam Smith would make a far more serious commercial error. By venturing into the Sunday market he would shake the financial foundations of the company, inflict great damage on his original creation and give *The Times* an opportunity to make good its escape. All this, however, looked an improbable outcome in 1988.

III

The scale of the Conservatives' 1983 election landslide and the manner in which Margaret Thatcher conducted her Cabinet were not conducive to an active parliamentary scene. Yet, Westminster reporting remained a central aspect of *The Times*'s political coverage. Much of the work continued to be done by the team scribbling in shorthand the transactions of the lower chamber from the Press Gallery. This was not the only vantage point. The paper's onsite office was a cabin, precariously but perfectly perched on the roof of the Palace of Westminster, between the clock tower of Big Ben and the Commons chamber and accessible only by passing through the Press Bar.

In April 1985, the blast at the Chernobyl nuclear reactor in Ukraine pushed the safety of the nuclear power industry sharply towards the top of the political agenda. In Britain, the Sizewell and Sellafield nuclear repro-cessing plants were already a focus of concern. In December 1985, a member of the all-party Commons Select Committee on the Environment leaked to Richard Evans, a new *Times* lobby reporter, the draft of its chairman's report on the disposal sites for radioactive waste. It stated that the sites were 'primitive in the extreme'. Evans wrote up the story and it was published on 16 December. It informed readers that the Report expressed such 'deep reservations' about the handling of spent nuclear fuel 'that the basis of the processing operation must be called into question'.[15] There was an outcry, but for *The Times* the most serious response came from within the Palace of Westminster. In their private deliberations and proceedings, select committees enjoyed parliamentary privilege. This, Evans had knowingly breached. At Westminster, there was a strong view that he and the paper for which he worked should be punished.

Preparing to face the storm, Evans enjoyed the full backing of his editor and of the Press Council. *The Times* pleaded the well-worn journalistic justification of acting in the public interest. Although it was true that rules had been broken, they were 'now almost invariably unused and in general disrepute' the leading article argued. *The Times* was striking a blow against 'archaic, self-serving secrecy'.[16] As far as both John Biffen, Leader of the Commons, and his Labour shadow, Peter Shore, were concerned, it was *The Times* that was being self-serving. By printing the leak, it had under-mined the confidentiality that was essential to the private deliberations of select committees. The atmosphere in which the committees' members,

coming from the various political parties, could examine evidence imparti-
ally had been damaged. Furthermore, it was not up to a newspaper to decide
which parliamentary rules to obey or what constituted public interest. How
was the public interest served by publishing a draft report when two weeks
later the official report could have been analysed? The once reliable *Times*, it
was argued, had been indulging in nothing more lofty that the commercial
self-interest of a 'scoop'. In May 1986, the parliamentary Committee of
Privileges voted (with only one vote against, that of Tony Benn) to rec-
ommend Evans's expulsion from the Commons for six months and to
prevent *The Times* from replacing him because of its 'serious contempt of
the House'.[17] It would be the first time such a punishment had been carried
out since 1832.

To *The Times*, the reaction appeared disproportionate. The point of
publishing the draft rather than waiting for the published version was to
show how strong the original fears were before they were potentially watered
down – possibly for political reasons – for the final version. Since it was
an MP who had been responsible for the original leak, it could be maintained that the Privileges Committee would have been better searching
more closely for the perpetrator rather than seeking revenge on a young
journalist, a case, if ever there was one, of shooting the messenger. On
20 May, the Commons debated the Privileges Committee's recommendations. Sir Ian Gilmour and Michael Foot provided strong support for *The
Times*'s case, demanding to know why it was acceptable for journalists to try
to discover what went on in Cabinet meetings but not in the deliberations of
select committees. The House agreed, dividing by 154 to 124 not to enforce
the ban on Evans and *The Times*. Significantly, Margaret Thatcher, the
party chairman Norman Tebbit, and four other Cabinet ministers voted
against punishment.[18] This led some conspiracy theorist to ponder whether
the Prime Minister wanted not only to keep in with *The Times* but that
she was also keen to trim the burgeoning authority of select committees'
scrutiny of the Government.[19]

The Prime Minister certainly was in need of all the Fleet Street friends
she could muster. Michael Heseltine, the Defence Secretary, had emerged
as the most flamboyant and charismatic figure in the Cabinet. That he was
no Thatcherite and had developed an alternative philosophy that borrowed
from Japanese corporatism and emphasized the need to regenerate inner
cities made him an ideological as well as a personal challenger for the
leadership. Whenever the Prime Minister appeared vulnerable to the possibility of electoral defeat, Tory faint hearts began to contemplate turning

for salvation to the Defence Secretary instead. The conflict came to a head over his opposition to the efforts of the American company Sikorsky in its bid for a sizeable stake in Westland Helicopters. Heseltine favoured a European consortium and, when Mrs Thatcher demanded he seek Cabinet Office approval before restating earlier pronouncements on Westland's future, he dramatically walked out in the middle of a Cabinet meeting.

The Times was sceptical from the first over Heseltine's role in opposing the Sikorsky bid (which was later accepted by the company's shareholders). Contrasting his attitude with his gung-ho display against CND campaigners at a cruise missile base, The Times noted that, 'the flak-jacketed hero of Molesworth was not as determinedly pro-American as he appeared'.[20] Even before his resignation, the paper's editorial line had cast doubt on his conduct and motives: 'It is hard to escape gracefully from Mrs Thatcher's shadow but it is a journey which all aspiring successors will have to take at some time. The party will prefer not to choose its new organ grinder from its old monkeys and Mr Heseltine knows it.'[21] Three days later he made his dramatic Cabinet walkout. The resulting crisis found the editor and his chief political correspondent at loggerheads. Tony Bevins had developed good contacts with Heseltine and on the news of his resignation assured Wilson, 'She's finished.' Wilson begged to differ. Bevins resented his judgment being dismissed in this fashion and his differences with the paper widened. Surprisingly, Heseltine took heart from The Times's leading article on his resignation, claiming in his memoirs, 'it comes as close as any newspaper of such authority ever would to supporting what a rebel minister had done'.[22] The article, entitled 'A Very Good Resignation', was actually referring to why his walkout might be good for his own leadership chances, rather than endorsing his attempts to interfere in Westland's future ownership.[23] The Times was far from being ready to abandon the Prime Minister, preferring instead to shift the blame onto her press secretary, Bernard Ingham, and the Trade and Industry Secretary, Leon Brittan, who leaked a letter by the Solicitor General referring to 'material inaccuracies' in Heseltine's case against Sikorsky. The leading column called on Brittan to resign in order to save Mrs Thatcher's blushes and when he did so (later that day following a hostile meeting of the backbench 1922 Committee) commented dismissively, 'unlike Mr Heseltine, he has not left a political hole around the cabinet table. And like Mr Heseltine he has no well-prepared hole in the backbenches to which he can rest.'[24] The immediate consequence, though, was that Mrs Thatcher had seen off her most deadly internal enemy – at any rate, for the time being.

By then, Julian Haviland, the paper's political editor, had already departed (he subsequently helped ghost Heseltine's *Where There's A Will*) while the paper's failure to get behind the Tory Jacobite challenger brought forward Tony Bevins's defection to the *Independent*. Philip Webster was promoted to chief political correspondent, Ivan Barnes became parliamentary editor and Robin Oakley became political editor.

Oakley had spent his childhood in Northern Rhodesia (subsequently Zambia) where his father was a civil engineer. At prep school in Surrey and at Wellington College in the 1950s he had dabbled in amateur dramatics and athletics (a back injury blighted his otherwise promising javelin throwing). At Brasenose College, Oxford, in the early sixties he had also followed the horses and, enjoyed a flutter (a passion he would subsequently share with Charles Wilson). It was the desire to gain experience away from London and the Home Counties that led him to turn down a job with the Thomson Group in favour of a graduate traineeship as a subeditor in the *Liverpool Daily Post* where he found himself working alongside Tony Bevins and John Sergeant. He became a parliamentary lobby correspondent for the paper in 1967, moving to the 'Crossbencher' column of the *Sunday Express* three years later which involved mixing and liquid lunching with his political informants. It was also his first experience of working under an invective-peddling Scotsman (John Junor) as editor. Between 1981 and 1986 he found himself working under another strong editor in the shape of David English at the *Daily Mail*. Oakley had built up a reputation as a Westminster insider who was noted for his non-partisan skills as a straight reporter. As such, he began to feel that too long an association with the outspoken *Daily Mail* was damaging his deserved reputation for impartiality. He leapt at the opportunity to succeed Julian Haviland when Wilson offered it to him over breakfast at the Waldorf in September 1986. 'I had dreamed of being Political Editor of *The Times* since my starting days on the *Liverpool Daily Post*', Oakley later recalled, adding that it was 'one of the best jobs in British journalism'.[25]

Unlike Bevins, Oakley valued the workings of the 'lobby'. The term took its name from the members' lobby in the House of Commons where a select group of journalists was permitted to enter and approach or be approached by parliamentary contacts. Talking on 'lobby terms' meant that the conversation was, for the purposes of a newspaper report, non-attributable. For this reason, note taking was discouraged. Lobby correspondents were a small proportion of the total number of parliamentary journalists and, naturally, their privileges generated suspicion. Critics believed The Lobby operated as an exclusive club in which favoured journalists became part of the process by which politicians manipulated the media. One fear was that they were told information in return for pulling punches. In fact, soliciting in the members' lobby was only one means of sharing insider information. Another principal source was the Downing Street press office, led by Bernard Ingham, which provided twice daily non-attributable briefings to political correspondents. The *Independent* and the *Guardian* withdrew from these, believing that they were designed more to mislead than illuminate. *The Times*, however, continued to make the most of the existing channels. Oakley believed that so long as journalists were tenacious in cross-referencing what they were told, the press office was important and that the newspapers that had excluded themselves from Ingham's briefings wasted a lot of time catching up with what had been discussed there. Furthermore, if such briefings did not exist officially, they would inevitably manifest themselves unofficially – and with even less accountability. Indeed, the great benefit of the lobby system was that it allowed MPs of all parties to plant information in newspapers without being identified as the source. Critics regarded this as another invitation to mischief making in which self-interested individuals could bend the ear of a journalist without taking the personal responsibility of making the statement themselves. Inevitably, the device of 'Lobby Terms' was most useful to those MPs who wanted to harm a fellow politician or policy from within their own party. Wilson's successor, Simon Jenkins, was wary about having *The Times* quote disparaging remarks about individuals without quoting the source and, consequently, this practice was cut back.[26] Oakley, however, believed that if attribution were mandatory, politicians would be far more guarded – and less honest – in their conversations with journalists. The result would be a newspaper with diminished responsiveness to the political undercurrents and the creation of a barrier between politicians and journalists in which conversation was restricted to press statements and platitudes.

In October 1986 the Conservatives analysed polling evidence that suggested the public believed the Government was running out of steam. They responded with a variety of new initiates with which to go into the following year's general election. Rearranging the provision of local services was at the core. They put forward proposals to allow schools to opt out of local authority control and council tenants to choose private-sector landlords. Rates, the property-based tax levied by local government, would be replaced by a poll tax of the whole electorate. The privatization programme would also continue, the water and electricity utilities being next for sale. In

December, *The Times* started planning for an assumed general election in either the following May or October. In the event, Mrs Thatcher announced that she would go to the country on 11 June. First there would be the endurance test of a month on the campaign trail.

One who was not surprised by the timing of the election was Robin Oakley. With Labour highlighting Britain's social and economic divisions, he pointed out that 'Mrs Thatcher was determined to rob Labour of the chance of exploiting the conspicuous consumption at the Ascot race meeting in the week of June 18'. This was not as frivolous an observation as might be imagined. The emergence of the young upwardly mobile professional – or yuppie – had become the cultural phenomenon of a period of rising salaries and house prices. It was not just socialists who regarded them with loathing. Bizarrely, *The Times* got involved in a spat with Peregrine Worsthorne, the elegant apostle of High Toryism and editor of the *Sunday Telegraph*, who accused the Conservatives of supporting this 'bourgeois triumphalism'. A *Times* leading article written by Peter Stothard was incredulous, noting, 'It has been remarkable how a few young men have only to make a few hundred thousand pounds in the City and spend it on youthful pleasures for people to start saying that we are witnessing a dangerous exhibition of "bourgeois triumphalism".' Worsthorne responded by writing to *The Times* to condemn it for not urging Mrs Thatcher to disassociate herself from such displays.[27] In its manifestation of heady optimism and growing opportunity – without yet a sense of *noblesse oblige* – Worsthorne had identified the fresh energies that Thatcherism was unleashing. It was certainly a force knocking upon the doors of a closed Establishment and, contrary to its past reputation, *The Times* had become more sympathetic towards prising the portals open. The paper's 1950s advertising slogan, 'Top People Take *The Times*' had come in for much pillorying over the years. But its less well-remembered follow-up, 'Tomorrow's Top People Take *The Times*', now appeared strangely prescient.

With or without the help of the yuppies, the Tories could point to some favourable statistics. Unemployment had fallen continuously for seventeen months (the figure was tantalizingly close to dipping below three million, which it did on the week after the election), there was a public-spending surplus and manufacturing output had struggled back to where it had been in 1979. According to taste, these statistics were either evidence of policies that were working or of how many years they had failed to bear much fruit. Whatever the debate, the Tories went into the month of campaigning with a twelve-point lead in the opinion polls.

With Kinnock at the helm, Labour would not repeat the catastrophe of the 1983 manifesto that was famously dubbed 'the longest suicide note in history'. But Labour went into the 1987 contest as the tax and spend party nonetheless. There were commitments to reverse Nigel Lawson's tax cuts (at a time when the upper rate of income tax had still not been reduced below 60 per cent) and to introduce a wealth tax. The party was also still committed to the dismantling of private education (though it was debatable whether outright abolition would be achieved during the life of the next Parliament). The machinery of State planning would also be re-erected with a pledge to reduce unemployment by one million within two years and to create a National Economic Summit to identify what action Government, employees and unions needed to take to plan for future investment and price control. Unhelpfully, Christopher Walker, reporting from Moscow, pointed out that Denis Healey, the Shadow Foreign Secretary, had emerged from a Soviet briefing to announce that his atheist hosts were 'praying' for a Labour victory.[28]

As the campaign progressed, the Tories proved vulnerable on health issues as did Labour on defence policy and the behaviour of the so-called 'loony left'. With two leaders, David Steel and David Owen (the latter experiencing tense relations with his senior SDP colleagues), the Alliance's greatest problem concerned how to give the misleading impression of unity. Yet, with the exception of one rogue blip, the opinion polls continued to show the Conservatives remained within the electoral comfort zone of above 40 per cent of the popular vote. From a news perspective, the apparent predictability of the result risked diminishing the drama. George Hill subsequently described it as 'a dull campaign, where the main rivalry was between promotional agencies out to win fame and fortune'.[29] As part of the marketing exercise, the pages of The Times were bombarded with full-page adverts promoting the Tories' negative campaign slogan 'Britain's Booming, Don't Let Labour Wreck It'. Labour won the artistic plaudits with an election broadcast dubbed 'Kinnock the Movie', although some thought it too presidential. After Michael Foot's amateurish style of electioneering in 1983, the party had certainly improved its media presentation. The handiwork of Peter Mandelson, two years into his post as director of communications, was beginning to show itself.

Nonetheless, when it came to cajoling the press, there was still much to be learned from the Tories. Having secured interviews with the other party leaders, Oakley was alarmed when Conservative Central Office suddenly decided his interview with Mrs Thatcher could not be squeezed in. This was an extraordinary slap in the face to the newspaper. 'I cashed every outstanding cheque I had at the top of the Tory Party in my efforts to secure the interview', Oakley subsequently wrote. Lord Young eventually managed to get him a twenty-minute slot with the Prime Minister on Monday 8 June. But that very morning Downing Street took umbrage at The Times's front page which featured a photograph of Neil and Glenys Kinnock waving at crowds and a variety of (to Tory eyes) doom and gloom headlines. Young telephoned Oakley and Wilson to say The Times was doing Labour's propaganda for it and the interview was cancelled. As attempts went to bully and manipulate the press, this was pretty unsophisticated. A heated exchange on the telephone ended with the interview being reinstated. Yet, if Mrs Thatcher's heavies hoped The Times would atone for its apostasy they were to be disappointed. When Oakley eventually got to sit down with the Prime Minister, he risked her wrath by following one of her long-winded answers with a demand that, given the short time available, she should keep her answers brief and to the point.[30] The resulting dialogue appeared in The Times on election day.

Besides the reporting of Robin Oakley and Philip Webster, The Times's electoral coverage was enlivened by Craig Brown's sketch writing and lengthier pieces by Barbara Amiel who forwarded her dispatches from Mrs Thatcher's battle bus. As on previous occasions, the focus was not just on policies but also about what was happening in the swing marginal constituencies. Whether Shirley Williams would take Cambridge for the Alliance became a source of intense interest. Few were in any doubt for which party The Times's leading column would declare the paper's allegiance, but its Op-Ed could not be faulted for the spectrum of regular columnists: starting with Ben Pimlott on the left and moving through Jo Grimond, Conor Cruise O'Brien and John Grigg towards T. E Utley and Woodrow Wyatt on the right. As with 1983, The Times was fortunate to make use of the doyen of academic psephologists, David Butler of Nuffield College, Oxford. Professor Butler advised on statistical analysis, providing Op-Ed articles and writing short features as well as assisting with the resulting Times House of Commons guidebook to the new Parliament.

How much effect the reporting of The Times and its rivals had on shaping the electorate's minds was hard to gauge. Television news certainly claimed the limelight. In 1983, only 8 per cent of the public had stated they believed the press provided the most unbiased and complete election coverage. In contrast, 54 per cent thought television provided the most unbiased and 60 per cent the most complete reporting. Although the trend was scarcely new, there was little doubt that newspapers were failing to set the news agenda. Another cerebral pundit hired by *The Times* for the election, Dennis Kavanagh, Professor of Politics at Nottingham University, pointed out that the campaign agenda was largely set on *The Jimmy Young Show* and *Election Call*. By comparison, the 9.30 a.m. press conferences succeeded only in producing what was stale news by the time it was regurgitated on newspaper front pages the following morning.

As far as Labour was concerned, the prioritizing of television and radio over the print media was understandable given the level of savagery meted out by many of the tabloids and mid-market papers. *The Times* was one of the eleven national newspapers that endorsed the Conservatives. Seven opposed Thatcher. The *FT* and the *Independent* opted not to endorse any party. The *FT*'s stance was perhaps the most surprising – especially given that research by MORI suggested that it was the paper with the highest proportion of Tory voters (78 per cent). MORI's polling suggested that 69 per cent of *Daily Telegraph* readers had gone on to vote Conservative, as had 59 per cent of *Times* readers and only just half of *Sun* readers. The Alliance's support among *Times* readers had slipped from 33 per cent in 1983 to 28 per cent. Meanwhile, *Today*, which argued the Alliance's cause, had convinced only a third of its readers of the two Davids' charms – a proportion comparable to the Thatcher-cheerleading *Daily Mail* (and also the agnostic *Independent* whose readers were split almost equally between the three main parties).[31] These figures certainly suggested readers were governed first by their own perceptions and not those of the editorial conference.

On election night, *The Times* was able to speed its reporting with technology that had been denied it in 1983. Back then, NGA members had rekeyed in the results from each constituency from the details provided from the PA. For the 1987 election, the paper was free to use a computerized system that processed the statistics automatically as they came in and was able to provide instant extrapolations on swings and turn them into bar and pie charts. The Saturday *Times* contained a sixteen-page guide to the results in full with short profiles of all the MPs elected. Supporting commentary and analysis were provided by David Butler and Bob Worcester of MORI.

The Conservatives were returned to office with a majority of 101. *The Times*'s headline declared it 'Thatcher's historic victory'.[32] No previous Prime Minister had won three general elections in succession. It was also the first time the Conservatives had gained a majority of working class votes.

This was particularly impressive since economic change was shrinking the working class back to its traditional manual-labouring core. The 2 per cent swing towards Labour in England was remarkably mild given the post-Falklands conditions in which the previous election had been fought. However, the 7.5 per cent swing in Scotland portended trouble ahead north of the border. Oakley concluded sagaciously, 'Ministers will be anxious to know how much that has to do with the introduction of the "community charge" poll tax in Scotland which they have pledged to introduce in England and Wales too.'[33]

The 1987 general election was a disaster for the Alliance and for the SDP in particular. They had entered the year with hope; in February their candidate Rosie Barnes had won a much-publicized by-election that ended a half-century Labour Party tenancy in Greenwich. But the general election was another matter. With defeats for Bill Rodgers at Milton Keynes, Shirley Williams in Cambridge and Roy Jenkins to the left-wing firebrand George Galloway in Glasgow Hillhead, the Gang of Four was now, in parliamentary terms, a gang of one – David Owen. Only four other junior SDP members joined him on the Commons benches. Kinnock's attempts to isolate the hard left had at least succeeded in undermining the point of the 'soft-left' SDP. The Liberals had made no headway and continued to be the party of the rural West Country and the Celtic fringe, although with seventeen MPs they were clearly the senior party in the Alliance. Unlike David Steel, the Liberal leader, David Owen opposed the post-battle prognosis for merger between the two parties. His own members disagreed, and when in August they voted for a merger, Owen resigned and took with him an SDP rump. The divisions within the centre ground were laid bare. From his column in *The Times*, Ben Pimlott described an 'Alliance self-mutilation more pathological than anything witnessed in the Labour Party at the start of the decade'. It was not a pretty spectacle, particularly since it involved those who had so frequently condemned the 'adversarial politics' of the old two party system.[34] After a succession of votes and confusions over what the new name would be (LSD was ruled out for obvious reasons while SLD was soon found to be – in the words of the comedian Rory Bremner – 'not so much a party, more a poor hand at Scrabble') Paddy Ashdown became leader of what was eventually decided would be called the Liberal Democrats. The change of name and leader did not work any spellbinding magic. The opinion polls during 1988 and 1990 suggested the party was struggling to attract 10 per cent support. Owen, meanwhile, stumbled on with his own SDP rump, the once bright hope of democratic socialism reduced to the sidelines of British politics. He finally wound up his SDP group in June 1990 after it won fewer votes than the Monster Raving Loony Party at a by-election in Bootle.

IV

A third term of office and a booming economy gave the Conservatives considerable latitude to enact their programme. Charles Wilson considered his relations with the Prime Minister were 'very good' but they were hardly close and he was a less frequent visitor to Chequers than Douglas-Home had been. In all the period of his editorship, Wilson only spoke to Mrs Thatcher once on the telephone and, although he saw her at some stage most months, this was invariably at a public function in which lengthy private conversation was difficult.[35] Murdoch, his journeys to Britain becoming increasingly infrequent due to the demands of his growing American empire, found he saw Mrs Thatcher little more than once a year.[36] If Britain was being run, as many hostile commentators alleged, by a Thatcher–Murdoch axis then it could only have been coordinated through telepathy.

The interrelation between Downing Street and the press that did exist was primarily conducted between the Prime Minister's press secretary, Bernard Ingham, and Fleet Street's principal reporters. As political editor, Robin Oakley was *The Times* man who saw most of Mrs Thatcher. Not only did he stalk Westminster's corridors, he and the rest of the press pack followed the Prime Minister around the world in the back of her RAF VC-10. It was often a punishing schedule, although it rarely appeared to take much out of Mrs Thatcher who always rose to the occasion for those straining for a glimpse of the Iron Lady. On one occasion in March 1987 on a trip for talks with Gorbachev, she had first gone to light a candle for peace at the Zagorsk monastery near Moscow. Stopping first to visit a Moscow supermarket she bought bread and pilchards. Huge crowds of sturdy Russians pressed around her. Oakley overheard one British diplomat murmuring, 'loaves and little fishes . . . surely not?'.

Back at home, the general election victory in 1987 had revitalized the Government's reforming agenda. Improving choice in public-sector provision was the theme of the modernizers in the Cabinet and health and education were the main targets. The 1988 Education Act transformed

Britain's schools. It created a national curriculum. With the establishment of a funding per capita formula, headmasters and governors gained control of school budgets. Local governments' powers to determine or restrict the size of schools diminished. Preventing local authorities from placing pupils in specified schools widened the scope for parental choice. Schools were permitted to opt out of local authority altogether and become grant-maintained schools funded directly from Whitehall. The widely derided Inner London Education Authority (ILEA) was abolished. New specialist academies, to be called City Technology Colleges, were established. These measures were guided by two principles. The first was that power and funding should be shifted away from local authorities and towards schools and parental choice. The second was that central government should play an enhanced role, not only in ensuring a unified curriculum but also as schools' direct financer. In practice, far fewer schools opted out than the Government had hoped and the elite City Technology Colleges, although successful, proved also to be few in number. The Government's centralizing tendency was widely deplored by those who continued to put their faith in town hall democracy. But the measures had also devolved power to the schools and to parents who now found they had far greater flexibility in choosing their child's education. For this choice to be an informed one, it was necessary to provide them with statistics that demonstrated the varying performances of the institutions in the area. *The Times*'s attempts to provide parents with the information was at first slow and public school-orientated, with the serializing of the *Harper & Queen's Good Schools Guide*. However on 22 June 1987, the education correspondent, John Clare, launched *The Times Good University Guide*, commencing a process that would eventually include schools as well, once more reliable information was made available upon which to base the evidence.

These reforms came amidst what briefly looked like an economic miracle. Britain was experiencing the 'Lawson Boom'. Unemployment had finally fallen below three million and continued to plunge. House prices were soaring. Yet the strict monetarism deployed by Sir Geoffrey Howe, Lawson's predecessor at the Treasury, had been quietly jettisoned now that inflation was under control. The Medium Term Financial Strategy (MTFS) that Howe (and Lawson, who was then Financial Secretary) had originally devised had made M3, the broad measure of the money supply, rather than the exchange rate, the key indicator in the control of inflation. However, M3 targets were easier to set than to adhere to and financial deregulation made it, in any case, a spurious measurement. In the autumn of 1986, the

Treasury effectively abandoned M3 targeting in favour of concentrating on a new exchange rate policy based upon shadowing the Deutschmark. Interest rates went down in the 1988 Budget, encouraging the credit boom further and, ominously, inflationary pressures began to re-emerge. Had the dragon of rising prices not been slain after all? Interest rates had to be hiked up again and Lawson became convinced that the Exchange Rate Mechanism of the European Monetary System was a viable option and hoped to lock sterling into it. The Prime Minister was not so sure and opted for a 'when the time is right' approach to Exchange Rate Mechanism (ERM) membership. The problem was that Lawson did not regard this as a euphemism for never joining.

In the pages of *The Times*, Lawson found a critic in the monetarism economist Tim Congdon. Congdon argued that, far from having failed, targeting M3 'was the key to the government's principal achievement, the reduction in inflation to under five per cent'. Since abandoning this, 'Britain has had the strongest surge in private sector credit in its history and the annual rate of money supply growth has increased from about twelve per cent to over twenty per cent'. This was reminiscent of the 25 per cent supply growth rate of the Heath–Barber boom. Britain was returning to a stop–go cycle. Boom, Congdon claimed, would be followed by bust.[38]

Mortgage payments dominated the explosion in personal credit. Second mortgages were becoming common and unsecured lending was on the rise. Home ownership leapt from 57 to 68 per cent during the 1980s. Council-house building programmes were run down (a description that also fitted the estates that remained while local government fought vainly for funds). The 'right to buy' had proved one of the Thatcher Government's most popular policies with the working class, allowing 1.75 million council tenants to buy their homes between 1980 and 1997. For the first time manual, semi-skilled and clerical workers found themselves able to own their own homes, a prospect unthinkable to previous generations. Renting accommodation, which had been the norm for most working-class households, started to be seen as a mark of failure and many of the council estates that remained deteriorated into 'sink' estates of deprivation and hopelessness. While the majority made the most of their new-found opportunities to prosper through property, the social division evident for those left behind frightened and depressed the critics of Thatcher's 'Home Owning Democracy'.

Part of the problem was that, while the Government took action to dismantle local authorities' grip on housing provision, it was slower to encourage a rejuvenation of the private rental market. Private rent controls had existed since the latter stages of the First World War and were not relaxed until the end of the 1980s. The American libertarian Janet Daley, who began writing for *The Times* in 1988, maintained that it was 'curious that a party devoted to the free market should commit itself so heavily to a system that rewards investment in property (which stultifies the economy), as opposed to investment in industry (which helps it grow)'. The Tories' Mortgage Income Tax Relief had discouraged mobility, she argued, by tying down home owners while Labour's security of tenure for tenants had wrecked the private rental market. The result was a workforce immobilized by the restriction of mortgage or council house.[39]

For most *Times* readers though, the priority was either to get onto the property ladder or stay on top of it. Households' paper value soared. Some looked at the soaring prices and surmised that the boom was unsustainable. But the steeply rising gradient only encouraged those determined to invest yet more heavily before the price went up again. It was a busy few years for *The Times*'s property correspondent, Christopher Warman, who held the post between 1983 and 1991. Warman had joined the paper in 1965 and, having been 'glassed' during the 1986 printers strike, was revered among fellow journalists as the Holy Martyr of Wapping. Yet, while he busied himself with separating genuine property opportunities from the stately piles of estate agents' propaganda that awaited him each morning, the paper, inconceivably, failed to add any extra chairs to the property desk. In doing so, it allowed itself to play third violin behind the *FT* and the *Telegraph*'s property pages. Like travel journalism, the property section was an obvious target for advertising, and this was an avenue the commercial arm of the paper never properly exploited during the 1980s boom. Even the property supplement that began to appear in the Saturday section had a temporary feel about it, being written largely by freelances. Yet, the soaring property prices were central to the Thatcher revolution and its aspirations for a home-owning democracy. While householders believed they held an ever-appreciating asset, their consumer confidence was buffeted. *The Times*'s core readership in London and the Home Counties was exactly where the property boom was most evident. In particular, City bonuses fuelled the speculation yet it was many months after 'Black Wednesday' before talk of a collapse became widespread. In the meantime, Warman was left alone to report on the seemingly ever-expanding opportunities.

Credit cards were also fuelling consumer aspirations. In 1980, banks were lending £934 million of a £2093 million turnover on credit card accounts. By the end of the decade, the figures were £6600 million and £20b million. When the Thatcher Government had come to power in 1979, three million Briton's (7 per cent of the population) owned shares. A decade later the figure stood at nine million (25 per cent). Many had bought into the privatized utilities like British Telecom and British Gas and, while most pocketed a quick profit, by the end of the decade BT was still 20 per cent-owned by private investors. More importantly, it was offering a far better service to its customers. *The Times* met the growing market for personal financial advice more successfully than it did the property boom and on Saturdays a family money section was edited by Jon Ashworth.

Critics viewed the economic and social changes of the 1980s as a mirage built on nothing more substantial than rising house prices and deepening personal debt. Yet these were consequences not causes. The increasing share in employment and wealth of the professions and the service sector at the expense of manual labour was profoundly changing the country. Assessed by the job of the household's head, a third of Britain was middle class in 1980. By 1989 that figure had passed 40 per cent.

In his Budget of March 1988, Lawson cut the standard rate of income tax to 25 per cent. It had not been this low since before the Second World War and was now almost 30 per cent lower than it had been when Mrs Thatcher first took office. Amid squeals from the Opposition benches that it was socially divisive to cut it, the upper rate of income tax was reduced from 60 per cent to 40 per cent. The Prime Minister was convinced this was a moral as well as an economic policy. In May 1988 she outraged her opponents by addressing the General Assembly of the Church of Scotland with a 'Sermon on the Mound' that pointed out that no one would have remembered the Good Samaritan if he had only had good intentions. It was because he had money that he could help.

On the desks of the City's counting houses, *The Times* had ceded supremacy in business and financial coverage to the *Financial Times* in the 1960s. However, the economic boom of the mid-1980s provided it with an opportunity to regain ground. Wilson had long wanted to produce a two-section paper that would be split between a first section of news and comment and a second section of business and sport. Expanding the latter two almost necessitated creating two sections of equal length. The move to Wapping and its less restrictive practices offered the chance to realize his aim. He flew to Hollywood to show Murdoch the proposed redesign. Murdoch approved the decision and the extra expense it involved. Here, it seems, was a mechanism in which the paper could expand its coverage on all fronts. But when the two-section paper was launched the reaction was extraordinarily negative. 'I got more letters than I had ever had before,' recalled Wilson. 'I was very worried.' Flying over to New York, he went to explain to Murdoch that he believed the two-section paper was the right idea but the reader response had been almost universally terrible. Murdoch told him to do whatever he felt right in his bones, promising to back him in that decision. Over the course of the next decade and the various perceptions of three different editors, *The Times* demonstrated remarkable inconsistency in making its mind up whether to arrive daily on the news-stands as a single fat paper or a couple of slim ones and, if the latter, which bits should go in which section. None of the presentational forms ever quite seemed entirely satisfactory.

For Wilson, it certainly appeared to be the right moment to be expanding the business pages. At their head was the debonair figure of Kenneth Fleet who had joined the paper in 1983. He was a well-rounded man, born in 1929 and educated at grammar school and the LSE, who was as impressive at the crease as on the ballroom floor and was particularly interested in the theatre (he was director of the Young Vic from 1976 to 1983 and chairman of the Chichester Festival Theatre from 1985 to 1993). He had pioneered a style of financial journalism that was accessible to the ordinary reader at the *Daily Telegraph* before going on to succeed Nigel Lawson as the City editor of its Sunday sibling. However, he was the sort of editor who reserved his thoughts for his column rather than provide managerial leadership for his department. This was unfortunate since the time for strategic thinking on how to regain the paper's business profile had clearly arrived. During the mid-eighties, the City was engulfed by takeover mania. The biggest attempt came in December 1985 with Hanson Trust's £1.9 billion bid for Imperial Group (which eventually succeeded). 'Big Bang' took place on 27 October 1986. Within a decade, 'gentlemanly capitalism' would be no more. American and German banks became predominant while one by one the old family names succumbed. The City of London began to bear comparison to the Wimbledon Lawn Tennis tournament – Britain provided the desirable venue in which foreigners came to compete and win the trophies. It was nonetheless a process that helped ensure London's eminence as a world financial sector. To chronicle this, *The Times* had the largest team of financial journalists outside the *FT* but ever since the decapitation of *The Times* business news in 1982 it was an accomplished fiddle player straining to gain recognition besides the virtuoso first violinist of the 'pink 'un'. Nothing *The Times* produced could, for example, equal the *FT*'s impressive forty-eight-page 'Big Bang' survey of what it rightly called 'The City Revolution'. This was despite the fact that Wilson wanted his paper to get in on the act and to prioritize financial over industrial coverage. 'Charlie was a typical bull market investor,' reflected Graham Searjeant, a financial editor who had seen it all before.[40]

In the autumn of 1987, Britain was hit by two global forces. On Thursday 15 October, great storms were unleashed upon an unsuspecting southern England. With equal surprise, on the following Monday the stock market experienced the greatest crash of the twentieth century.

After the event, the signs were of course clearer to read than beforehand. On Wall Street, the Dow Jones Index had reached a peak of 2772.42 in August after which it had been sliding. When the New York markets opened on 19 October, the index nose-dived 508.32 points to 1738.41. This represented a decline of 22.6 per cent that compared unfavourably with the 1929 crash of 13.2 per cent. By chance, Christopher Warman had flown out by Concorde to New York to meet the property developer Paul Reichmann on the day of the collapse. Reichmann was financing the Canary Wharf development in London's Docklands and wanted to show Warman what he had achieved in the Battery Park financial district of New York. The view *The Times* property correspondent was given of the Merrill Lynch trading floor that morning did not give him great confidence in Reichmann's financial future.[41] As it did with everyone else, the collapse caught Kenneth Fleet off guard. He was at a dinner at the Savoy as news of events on Wall Street came through. With his usual composure, he telephoned through his copy from the dinner before returning to Wapping, still in his dinner jacket, to finesse his response for the late editions. When the City awoke to do business, it followed in Wall Street's wake, dropping 10.6 per cent and wiping £50 billion off share prices on what became known as 'Black Monday'.

The losses were staggering and even those who could not yet calculate the full economic implications could grasp that a cultural phenomenon, the yuppie, was in the process of being killed off. Charles Bremner filed from New York, where brokers in their familiar red braces and horn-rimmed spectacles stood around in the evening 'trying to come to terms with the unthinkable – the roaring Eighties, the years of easy prosperity, could be over'. A mixture of bewilderment, gallows humour and defiance appeared to be carrying them through towards the uncertainties of the following day's trading.[42] Some estimates put a figure on the paper loss of the stock market crash at a trillion pounds (£1,000,000,000,000). Only

Tokyo escaped the share collapse unharmed. At Wapping, Kenneth Fleet soon became one of the casualties. Wilson felt the business editor had lost his former sharpness, although he stayed on to help in the area where he had come best to perform, as a columnist on the City pages, until 1990. In place of Fleet as business editor, David Brewerton was brought in from the *Independent*. Progress was made with support from John Bell, who provided extensive City news coverage. For some, however, these improvements were not without cost and the atmosphere on the business desk became less agreeable. Seriousness was confused with joylessness. In this respect, the City orientated focus continued to be at the expense of a more rounded survey of a business community that, after a brief renaissance, was about to batten down the hatches for another recession.

V

In editing newspapers, Charles Wilson was a firm believer in the former England manager Alf Ramsay's doctrine that winning teams were those that got it right at the back. In *The Times*'s case, this meant improving the sports pages. Wilson looked to the *Daily Mail* for expertise and found it in that paper's much admired sports editor, Tom Clarke. Hiring Clarke proved one of Wilson's shrewder appointments. Despite the quality of its writers, the paper's sports desk had long been constrained by decades of under-investment. Norman Fox had run a tight ship and necessarily so. When in 1985 his deputy, Richard Williams, was seconded to help set up the move to Wapping, Fox had spent the last months before his retirement with a new deputy, John Goodbody. It was symptomatic of the paper's attitude that Goodbody initially held a position of such responsibility while on a freelance contract and was still filing copy on football and athletics for the *Guardian*. Wilson recognized the need for *The Times* to invest more full-heartedly in Goodbody's talents and, in recognizing his versatility, encouraged him to find sports stories that had the characteristics necessary for front-page treatment. Among other changes made, Richard Evans switched from the parliamentary lobby to the other inside track of the Turf. Evans, indeed, ran a syndicate of *Times* journalists – that included Wilson and Clarke – behind a racehorse named (appropriately for sporting hacks) Sunday for Monday. Sadly, it did not prove to have much by way of winning form, a fact that at least ensured there was no ethical dilemma over tipping it on the racing pages. With Wilson's support, Clarke was able to innovate. Leading figures from the sporting world were commissioned as pundits and commentators with an 'End Column' provided as their forum. Previously, the paper had not taken seriously the idea that players might become columnists. Among those called upon to provide expert analysis was the Aston Villa (and soon to be England) manager, Graham Taylor, for the 1990 World Cup. Only in one area did Wilson want to see less coverage. Those who thought the editor was one of nature's born pugilists were taken aback when he went so far as to suggest *The Times* should cease reporting on boxing, a sport for which he had distaste. After a discussion, Wilson gave way. It would, for instance, have been difficult for the paper to pretend an Olympic sport was not taking place, particularly if one of its famous – or British – exponents was in the ring. An editorial decision of this kind had last been taken in 1982 when Harry Evans had, after a similar period of consultation, decided *The Times* should provide match reports of Graham Gooch's rebel cricket tour of South Africa despite the fact it breached the sporting boycott of the country.

Despite the improvements made by Clarke, two of *The Times*'s own sports writers who made the deepest impression during these years had been recognized and appointed by Fox back in 1983. One was Simon Barnes who conveyed the unshaven and rather casual demeanour of the Barbour jacket-clad countryman but was a consummate professional and able – to any sports editor's joy – not only to fill large spaces with well-honed prose at short notice but to file before deadline. Within a short period, Barnes had moved from covering the dog races and pigeon fancying to expatiating knowledgeably on almost every aspect of modern sport (except boxing – where he shared Wilson's opinion). He also had the greatly prized ability to write about sport in terms that made it of interest to those who avoided recreational activity if they could possibly help it. The other all-purpose sports writer of the period was David Miller. Miller was a prolific journalist, majoring in football, but with a speciality as one who appeared actually to understand the intricacies of Olympics politics. This manifested itself in 1992 with an admiring (and consequently controversial) biography of Juan Antonio Samaranch, the IOC president he esteemed as the Olympic movement's saviour. Like Samaranch, Miller led a peripatetic lifestyle and thought nothing of hurtling around the British Isles and Western Europe at the wheel of a Mercedes in a manner that suggested no sporting fixture could legitimately begin before he had taken his seat in the grandstand.

The end of amateurism in sport's higher reaches meant that winning really did become everything – the players' wages depended upon it. In his first article for *The Times*, Miller examined the consequences of the growth of professionalism. Twenty years previously, he wrote, amateurism had demonstrated not only its inadequacies but also its inequalities: the 'shamateur' status preferred by the All England Club and the 'odious separate door for Players at Lord's'. Even when money was involved in the game, players usually saw little of it. Until 1960, footballers had been subjected to a maximum wage that 'humbled the genius of a Matthews or Mannion with a clerk's wages'. Amateurism's death had put an end to these wrongs, but professionalism had caused a wholesale corruption of sporting values. It had created 'the percentage player and the professional foul', on-court obscenities at Wimbledon, drugs and consumer placement in athletics, match-fixing allegations in Test cricket and 'the most morally corrupt World Cup yet'. To Miller, professional sportsmen had lost sight of ethics that made their endeavour noble: 'Sport at its pinnacle is foremost about glory, and nowhere does the dictionary definition of that word mention winning, only honourable fame. More often than not it is the quality of the loser which determines the fame of the winner'.[43]

By the mid-1980s, professionalism had come to dominate sport. Athletics held out as a pastime for amateurs until 1981 and rugby union until 1995, when the pressures created by the sums to be earned elsewhere – including in rugby league – and the momentum set in train by the belated inauguration of the World Cup in 1987 finally proved too great to resist. The final shoves were given by Kerry Packer and Rupert Murdoch. Packer, who had transformed cricket in the 1970s, was aiming to establish a rival professional World Rugby championship that would lure players away from the amateur game with the prospect of large payments. News Corp.'s £370 million agreement with the Australian, New Zealand and South African authorities for a ten-year television rights' deal meant that the money existed to pay the southern hemisphere's players a competitive salary. 'Yesterday in Paris the nettle was grasped by the International Rugby Football Board,' wrote David Hands, *The Times*'s seasoned rugby correspondent on the decision to endorse professionalism, adding, 'now we await the rash.'[44] Hands foresaw that at the highest levels the sport would change 'from being a player's game' into 'part of the entertainment industry, to be bought and sold by those who dabble in the sporting marketplace'. By becoming 'a weapon in the television ratings war' it would also depend upon 'the cash that only television can inject'.[45] So ended the Five Nations as the British Isles' most important amateur championship.

Yet, long before rugby union went professional, many of its leading players had discovered the opportunities to make money, even legitimately, from the sport without formally drawing an income. The Corinthian spirit in its truest form – where there was neither money nor even much personal fame to be won – was confined to popular fixtures of minority sports like the Boat Race. Between the wars, it was a measure of *The Times*'s perception of its core market that it gave about as much coverage to the annual tussle between the Oxford and Cambridge University crews as it did to any sporting occasion anywhere in the world. Although the paper's priorities had broadened by the last twenty years of the century, the Boat Race's very unusualness as a tough but amateur contest nonetheless continued to keep successive rowing correspondents, Jim Railton and Mike Rosewell, close to the tideway during February and March.

In 1987, the Boat Race became front-page news. Some doubted that even it could retain gentlemanly values when, in the run up to the 133rd race, the Oxford boat was rocked by a mutiny. Five world-class American rowers, mainly imported to the university on short postgraduate courses, rebelled against Oxford's fabled coach, Dan Topolski, and the boat club president, Donald Macdonald. The annual battle of the blues had long had an international flavour among its student oarsmen but some felt that the large number of high-quality foreign imports in recent years had undermined the essentially home-grown and undergraduate nature that gave the contest its charm.

What was at stake was, in the words of *The Times*'s headline, 'The great American disaster and the Great British institution'.[46] Against this, there were countervailing considerations. If the race did not encourage rowers of the highest quality, it could be derided as an anachronism that was amateur in the pejorative sense of the word. One of the mutineers, the cox Jonathan Fish, wrote a column for *The Times* entitled 'Ideas of the Boat Race just a myth' that attempted to set out the Americans' position: 'The mystique of the Boat Race throughout the world is that it represents honesty, fairness and sportsmanship. However, our experiences with the present Oxford University Boat Club hierarchy have shown this not to be true.' Topolski and Macdonald, Fisk suggested, were more interested in defending their own regime and traditions than selecting the fastest possible crew – the technically superior Americans. The build-up to the race, with claim and counter-claim, was exactly suited to *The Times*'s increasing interest in previewing contests. John Goodbody, a Cambridge man, found himself lurking around Oxford boathouses on the trail of Topolski, his former classmate at Westminster School. As it happened, the OUBC coach was not backward in coming forward and used *The Times*'s letters page to state his case and denounce the Boat Race's critics.[47] For everyone – except for the Americans and Cambridge – there was a fairy-tale ending to the saga. Come the great day, the Oxford boat, hastily cobbled together with volunteers from the Isis reserve, rowed to an improbable four-length victory. The events later inspired a film, *True Blue*. Quoting the vindicated Oxford president, David Miller wrote, '"The race is about big hearts, not big reputations." That is the concept which the American experts seemingly could not, and can not, comprehend.'[48]

At the Winter Olympics in Calgary the following February, Britons again demonstrated their preference for the amateur spirit when they applauded the ski jumping effort of Eddie 'the Eagle' Edwards who came a convincing last. In such sports where the British had long given up serious hopes of beating the rest of the world, it was easy to understand why a mere enthusiast like Edwards could be taken to the public's hearts. The national virility test of the Summer Olympics in September 1988 was a different matter entirely.

After the Palestinian terrorism at Munich in 1972, the crippling cost of hosting the Games in Montreal in 1976 and the political boycotts that marred the Moscow Olympics in 1980 and Los Angeles four years later, it was not surprising that the choice of South Korea, struggling to emerge from repressive government and in a state of continual cold war with North Korea, had been controversial. Miller, however, was enthusiastic from the start, writing 'The Koreans have the organization of the Germans, the courtesy and culture of the Orient and the sense of money of the Americans. They can hardly fail.'[49] He was right. It proved to be the first Olympiad in twenty-four years to pass without violence or a major boycott. In this sense the Games were returning to de Coubertin's idealistic notions of international comity. Yet, in another respect, it emphasized the extent to which fair play had given way to winning at all costs. Seoul proved to be the drugs Olympics. There was clearly something peculiar about the final tally in which East Germany won more gold medals than the United States. This proved to have less to do with State investment and the triumph of socialist man than – as was revealed following German reunification – the extent of the GDR's State-sponsored drug programme. During the Olympics, though, it was the 'greatest race of all time', dominated by Canada's Ben Johnson, that attracted the headlines.

Crossing the line in 9.79 seconds, Johnson broke the 100 metres world record in imperious style. He was the fastest man in the world. It was suggested that he had set a record that might not be broken in fifty or a hundred years. While the stadium erupted in joy and salutation, John Goodbody made his way over to Simon Barnes and stated incredulously, 'I don't know about anabolic steroids but that guy is on rocket fuel.' Waiting for Johnson to face the press, Goodbody was seen mimicking to Barnes the action of a man injecting himself.[50] Although such suspicions were commonly expressed within journalistic circles they could not, of course, be printed in the newspaper and Johnson's amazing feat won ovations across the world. Two days later the results of his failed drugs test were revealed. The story broke with impeccably difficult timing. It was almost 7 p.m. in Wapping and Tom Clarke had less than half an hour left before his section deadline. He telephoned Goodbody who was fast asleep in the Seoul Olympic media village (it was four in the morning there), rallying him with the cry 'this is mustard!'. Goodbody immediately swung into action, got confirmation that the wire report on Johnson was true and, within an hour, had filed a report down the telephone that was plastered across the front page. The only interruption to Goodbody's attempt to file had come from Wilson, who, hovering like an excited schoolboy at the copy taker's shoulder, grabbed the receiver and bellowed down the line in broad Glaswegian, 'It's all yer fault, Goodbody, you invented anabolic steroids!'

Goodbody had been at the journalistic forefront of exposing the extent to which there was a lucrative trade in performance-enhancing drugs. His articles were part of a campaign to force legislation making illegal possession of non-prescription steroids, a contribution that was recognized by the British Sports Journalism awards. There had been a long history of horse-doping scandals, steroids in weightlifting and stimulants in cycling, but sports' authorities had been slow to wake up to what was going on in other disciplines, especially athletics. In May 1987, David Jenkins, the 1972 Olympic silver medallist, had gone on trial for running a lucrative anabolic steroid-smuggling operation and at the world athletics championships, the American sprinter Carl Lewis had made allegations against unspecified opponents. Goodbody's articles followed. That the debate was still in its infancy was clear when the paper also published an article by Dr Richard Nicholson that recited evidence that the steroids' medical side effects had been overemphasized – a position that in turn drew a furious rebuke from Ron Pickering in the sport section's 'End Column'.[51] Despite the warnings of Goodbody, Pickering and others, it was Ben Johnson's seventy-two-hour metamorphosis from international hero to global villain that made drugs the central issue in athletics. With Johnson's disqualification, Carl Lewis was moved up into gold position and Britain's Linford Christie into silver. Subsequent drug test revelations would eventually create suspicion about even their achievements. The day after Johnson's race, Florence Griffith-Joyner, the American sprinter celebrated around the world as 'Flo-Jo', won the women's 100 metres and on 28 September, while the shock waves of Johnson's shame were still reverberating, she set a world record in the 200 metres that also looked impregnable to future generations. *The Times* did not feel at liberty to circulate the rumours that these triumphs were also drugs-assisted. The paper was not so reticent when she died from a heart attack in 1998 aged thirty-eight, the obituary quoting an opinion that the glamorous runner was 'a drug addled hermaphrodite'.[52] She had retired, hurriedly, from athletics the year after her 1988 triumphs, aged twenty-nine, on the eve of mandatory random drugs testing – one of the Seoul's major legacies.

The increasingly professional attitude adopted by athletes put winning above other considerations. The drug-fuelled means by which a few of them pursued this goal had the tarnishing effect of putting winners under a cloud of suspicion. It was an extraordinary turnaround. Generations of schoolmasters had upheld the cause of sport because they believed it built character. As Simon Barnes articulated only too clearly, it was also a means of revealing character. Nothing, though, could alter the fundamental human drama of competition. 'The Olympic Games, like all sporting events, are about disappointment,' Barnes wrote when it was time to pack up and leave the Olympic village. 'Every race has more losers than winners, but for winners, there is the strange, unearthly disappointment of victory. To have your dream come true must be the most frightening and disillusioning experience of them all.'[53]

CHAPTER EIGHT

STURM UND DRANG

Poor Morale; Robert Fisk Departs; New Faces;
Thatcher on the Ropes; the Collapse of Communism;
Something for the weekend; Sent to Siberia

I

There was something distinctly odd about the old rum warehouse in which *The Times*'s journalists daily got down to work. Producing a journal that purported to illuminate the ways of the world from a building that had almost no windows was a metaphor worthy of Kafka. After January 1987, the baying hordes outside, shouting abuse and hurling iron railings, had packed off and gone. But the sense of being under siege was not lifted with their departure.

Wapping was home to at least three editors whose reputations for brilliance and brusqueness extended far beyond their offices. In the floors above the giant printing hall, Kelvin MacKenzie appeared to be a law unto himself at the *Sun*, the most iconic, trailblazing and incorrigible of any British newspaper in the 1980s. Strong-willed and abrasive Scotsmen ruled the roost at either end of the long rum warehouse. At its west end was the office of the *Sunday Times*'s editor, Andrew Neil. A *cordon sanitaire* of boilers, pipes and humming power generators separated his domain from that of his compatriot, Charles Wilson, at the east end where *The Times* was based. Life in these quarters was difficult. *Times* journalists felt as if they were toiling on board an unusually elongated hunter-killer submarine patrolled by a gifted but periodically tyrannical captain. At the far end – where the design team, features, sport and business writers were located – there was at least some legroom. However, the closer operations got to Wilson's command post, the more claustrophobic it became. Journalists sat alongside the foreign desk monitoring incoming wire reports and information traffic. A galley of subs separated them from the keyboard-pounding reporters on the home news desk. The advantage of this cheek-by-jowl existence was that there was nowhere to hide – the crew members were always visible and usually within hollering or shoulder-tapping distance. This benefited subs wanting to check changes to stories with their authors. For a hands-on commander like Wilson, it was particularly useful. A mezzanine level had been slotted within the rafters. This doubled as the captain's bridge. From it, Wilson could stand and harangue the ratings stretched out below as far as the eye could see. Those who clambered up to his berth soon discovered that he too was a stranger to comfort. Such was the makeshift nature that the staff lavatories had been erected adjacent to Wilson's wardroom. Potential eavesdroppers were deterred by his periodic habit of giving an almighty kick to the Gents' door as he passed. Those who did squeeze into his personal cabin discovered just how cramped were the conditions from which he charted the paper's course. Its low ceiling was liable to spring a leak whenever there was a heavy downpour. Those most committed to the submarine analogy found this particularly unsettling.

It was not an environment conducive to high morale. Wilson was under tremendous pressure and was well aware that his most able staff members were subject to relentless targeting by the *Independent* to jump ship. Some of the most prized names succumbed. Never had the competition been so intense. What especially alarmed Wilson was when a journalist who was no stranger to hardship and did not even have to work from Wapping decided that he too had had enough. Robert Fisk was *The Times*'s most famous serving reporter. The editor treated his decision to quit as a shattering blow.

Wilson liked Fisk because he admired his courage and professionalism. Politically, the two men had little in common. Fisk had made his reputation at *The Times* during the 1970s when he had been a thorn in the side of the British Army in Ulster. When he shifted his reporting to the Middle East in 1976, the Israeli forces and government came to loathe him no less. To many of Israel's sympathizers in Britain he was a hated figure and accusations of anti-Semitism (which he furiously rejected) were frequently levelled at him and *The Times* for indulging his passions. Yet, he had not regarded Murdoch's purchase of the paper with quite the same foreboding as had some left-leaning journalists. Frequently, he had risked his life to bring out stories from the world's most dangerous region only to discover that the unions had called a strike and the paper had not come out. Four years into News International's ownership, Fisk was still happy to state that Murdoch could have cloven hoofs for all he cared – at least he brought out the newspaper.[1] It was easy to understand why he was sanguine. With

Douglas-Home in the editor's chair, he knew he had a protector who would defend his right to report events in the Middle East as he saw them. 'While Douglas-Home was there, there was no problem, you could write what you liked about the Israelis,' Fisk recalled.[2] He began, however, to sense that Douglas-Home's successor was uneasy about some of the stories he wished to pursue. Wilson looked to balance Fisk's dispatches with columnists who were sympathetic to Israel's case. This should not have been a problem. Fisk, however, took particular exception to what he saw as a personal slur when a columnist was allowed to state that journalists working from West Beirut could not report fairly because they were too scared or embedded with the Muslim militias. A collision course had been set.

The divergence between what *The Times* was saying on its leader page and what its Middle East correspondent was reporting on its front page became increasingly apparent. In April 1986, US warplanes flying from British bases attempted to assassinate Colonel Gaddafi in Tripoli. Instead, they killed around a hundred others including the Libyan leader's adopted daughter. Fisk was there to record the scene of devastation. The leading article, however, defended the raid. Such was the extent of complaints from readers at this line of argument that the paper was forced to write another leader that conceded 'a newspaper which finds itself in marked disagreement with the opinions of its readers must seriously address their concerns if it is to have any hope of influencing them'.[3] Having originally believed that the paper's editorial line was no business of his so long as he was left to report events as he saw fit, Fisk increasingly felt annoyed and perhaps even snubbed by the tone taken on surrounding pages.[4]

Like Douglas-Home before him, Wilson recognized Fisk as a courageous man, prepared to risk his life daily for his profession. Wilson admired toughness. In 1984 he had even gone out to visit him in Beirut. There, he was introduced to Fisk's close friend Terry Anderson, the bureau chief of the Associated Press news agency. Keen to talk to Israeli troops in order to get their point of view, Wilson travelled with Fisk to southern Lebanon. It proved a mistake. One Israeli lieutenant left Wilson in no doubt about his views when he promptly had him arrested. Giving the command 'get these bastards out of here', the officer had the two distinguished *Times* journalists put under armed guard and sent back to Beirut. When they reached the capital it was to discover there had been another suicide bomb attack on the (new) American Embassy.

Filing copy from the Lebanon to London was a particularly frustrating part of Fisk's job. The era of the mobile phone had not arrived and getting through on a landline was a process that could take many hours if achieved at all. Instead, late afternoons and early evenings were spent up in the AP bureau, huddled over a stuttering telex machine whose staccato click-click-clicking replicated the outbursts of rapid machine-gun fire in the streets outside. The AP wire was an old machine using Second World War technology that worked with codes punched out on tape. Whenever the electricity cut out before the complete coding had gone through to London, the whole process would have to be repeated, the tape stuck back together and pushed through the machine with a new code added while Fisk prayed for the requisite twenty minutes of uninterrupted electricity supply. Such orisons were frequently offered up in vain and filing reports that ran to several pages could take hours. There would then be the anxious wait before a telex would come back stating all the pages had been received and understood.

Yet, getting through to London was far from the greatest of Fisk's problems. Various militant factions, most notably the pro-Iranian Islamic Jihad, began kidnapping Westerners. In March 1984, Jeremy Levin, bureau chief of CNN, was kidnapped. Five months later Jonathan Wright, a Reuters correspondent, also fell victim. Both men eventually managed to escape but the seizures continued. In March 1985, Islamic Jihad took Terry Anderson hostage. Others followed, including Terry Waite, the Archbishop of Canterbury's representative, who had tried to negotiate their release. By the spring of the following year, forty-seven foreigners had been abducted over the previous twenty-seven months. Of this number, twenty-six had been subsequently released and five were definitely dead. The fate of the others was in doubt. Faced with this level of danger, all but the most hard-boiled reporters packed up and left. The number of Western journalists based in Beirut fell from more than seventy in 1984 to seventeen in 1986. By then, there was not a single American reporter still around. 'Lebanese and Palestinian gunmen have now almost achieved what the Israelis could never have hoped for,' reported Fisk; 'much of the war in southern Lebanon is now reported only from Jerusalem, where correspondents are in no danger of being kidnapped.'[5] Fisk had no intention of relying on the Israeli government for his information. He saw it as his calling to be a witness on the front line.

Fisk's obstinacy (some mistook it for a death wish) riled those for whom he was also a liability. *The Times* came under pressure from the Foreign Office to have him withdrawn from Beirut and relocated to a place of greater safety. Wilson, however, had a right winger's natural disdain for the

Foreign Office. He demurred and made it clear to Fisk that he trusted his judgment and would stand by whatever he decided to do. From a personal perspective, this was a courageous position to adopt since the editor was likely to face far less criticism for forcing his correspondent to leave than if he allowed him to be captured and killed. When Fisk replied that he was willing to go back and continue reporting, Wilson's reply was characteristic, 'Ok matey. Good luck.'[6]

Back in Beirut, Fisk's life was a misery. Shells continued to rain down on the city, frequently exploding close to him. Long hours were spent in the comfortless refuge of a windowless corridor. The prospect of being kidnapped was as much a probability as a possibility. If the Archbishop of Canterbury's envoy was not sacred, it could be presumed that the life of a *Times* journalist was cheap. To avoid capture, he had to constantly alter his movements, give false names and even make false arrangements. He avoided meeting Western diplomats since this opened him up to allegations of being in cahoots with Western spies. A car circling his building was an extremely worrying occurrence. The prospect of betrayal appeared at every corner. One Lebanese employee at a press bureau asked casually which flight he was catching. Fisk told him. The man disappeared into what had been Terry Anderson's office. Fisk loitered long enough to overhear him whispering down a telephone in Arabic. He was passing on the flight times and movements. Fisk opted not to go to the airport. What was particularly distressing was that his betrayer was the same employee who in 1978 had saved his life.[7]

This was not the environment in which a roaming reporter could operate effectively. Nor was it conducive to embarking upon a relationship either, despite Fisk's hopes of settling down to married life with the *Financial Times* journalist Lara Marlowe. Eventually, Wilson arranged for him to take up a new role as a Paris based features writer for *The Times*. Fisk accepted and enjoyed his new post, but privately he was in a quandary over whether to stay with the paper. He now considered its editorial stance so irksome that he found himself hesitant to mention who his employer was when the subject came up in conversation. *The Times*, he felt, had changed a lot from the liberal-minded journal he had joined in 1971. He disliked its coverage of the Troubles in Northern Ireland, being particularly upset that it had not probed more deeply into security service operations there as he had once done. He was horrified that the paper had urged the BBC and ITV to supply the RUC with film of the brutal murder of two British soldiers in Belfast. This Fisk regarded as a betrayal of journalistic integrity. He was equally opposed to its increasingly hard-line attitude towards the Middle East. He had been appalled by a leading article, 'Death of a Terrorist', that all but supported the Israeli assassination of Abu Jihad. Fisk had long questioned *The Times*'s promiscuous use of the word 'terrorist' when referring to Arab groups but not to Israeli or Lebanese Christian troops in the area.

There was also the question of the proprietor, whose toughness Fisk had previously applauded. 'I do not for a moment think that Mr Murdoch dictates our leaders or our op-ed pages,' he assured Wilson, 'but the organization is so powerful – and has shown itself so ruthless – that many on our editorial staff simply have no inclination to challenge what they think is the received opinion.' The deciding moment came when the USS *Vincennes*, an American warship in the Gulf which mistakenly thought it was under attack, shot down an Iranian passenger jet, killing 290 civilians. *The Times* quickly postulated on why the Iranian airbus was so far off course and even pondered whether a suicide pilot was flying it. Fisk filed a report making use of air-traffic recordings he had heard. This did not tie in with the line the leading article had peddled and Fisk's copy was edited accordingly. Four months later, Fisk resigned 'It is impossible for a reporter to risk his life under fire for a newspaper in which he no longer believes,' he later explained. The *Independent*, he had came to the conclusion, was more like *The Times* he had happily joined in 1971. It was to the *Independent* he would now go.[8]

Wilson was both horrified and hurt at the prospect of his most famous reporter's departure. At a personal level they had always had mutual regard and – with the exception of the *Vincennes* incident – Fisk could certainly not claim that the paper had treated him, or his copy, without due respect. Wilson, however, was not prepared to let him leave without first putting up the sort of fight that between less strong-minded individuals would have been grounds for a terminated friendship. When a personal appeal failed, he threatened Fisk with breach of contract, claiming he would refuse to release him to the *Independent*. In fact, thanks to the Lebanese postal service which had become as dislocated as everything else in that country, the contract had never been received or signed but the editor was not prepared to let this detail stand in the way. Clearly the matter had to be settled and on 18 November 1988 Fisk came to see Wilson at his office. The meeting began in sorrow and ended in anger. According to Fisk's account, Wilson pleaded, 'You have to do your duty to *The Times*', to which the reply came, 'I cannot do duty to a paper which I no longer respect.'

Wilson snapped back, 'I'm not asking you to respect it, I'm asking you to work for it.' Fisk refused, saying simply, '*The Times* lacks honour.' At this, Wilson, agitated and wounded in equal measure, rose to his feet. 'That is personally insulting,' he growled. Fisk explained that, as far as he was concerned, 'some of its leaders are morally bad'. He particularly objected to the excoriating tone of a leading article entitled 'His Infamous Career', written to mark the death of Sean MacBride, the international human rights campaigner who had been the IRA's chief of staff. Whatever the contradictory actions of MacBride's life and work, there was clearly no prospect of a ceasefire in the editor's office at Wapping. Finally, after further traded accusations, the meeting broke up. 'See you soon,' Wilson said. 'No,' replied Fisk, making for the door (which had been locked) and the end of almost eighteen years at the paper. 'It's goodbye, Charles, and good luck.'[9]

II

The disapproving chorus from those who believed *The Times* 'was no longer the paper it used to be' (an *ad hoc* community that appears to have existed since issue two on 2 January 1785) sometimes focused on superficial changes. They grumbled at the increasing size of headlines, the overuse of diagrams and the assumption that popular entertainers are household names even at exclusive addresses. Yet many, especially those who praised the *Independent* for supposedly turning the clock back, felt that Charles Wilson had detached *The Times* from the liberal-Tory moorings to which it had been chained during Rees-Mogg's fourteen years in the chair. For them, Fisk's departure was evidence that the paper no longer tolerated alternative voices. In fact, Wilson was anxious to please. Indeed, he not only wanted to provide a wider forum for middle-of-the-road opinions but also sought to attract back some of the centre-left voices that had stopped writing for the paper at the time of the Labour Party's boycott of the Wapping titles. With the lifting of the edict, attempts were made to re-establish links. During 1987 and 1988 Ben Pimlott wrote regularly for the paper while Jack Straw returned to write the fortnightly column from which he had withdrawn in January 1986. Whether employing Robert Kilroy-Silk as a weekly columnist aided or retarded the process of reaching out to those to the left of centre was perhaps more debatable. Militant activists had ousted him from his Liverpool constituency and *The Times* serialized *Hard Labour*, the account of his travails. His subsequent career as a daytime television host and increasingly populist maverick of the right clouded the image he had first brought to *The Times* in 1987 as a promising and charismatic, if somewhat polemical, voice.

Where the claim that the paper had shifted politically to the right did have most substance was in the opinions emanating from the leader conferences (although the editorial line was not markedly more hawkish than in the days when it had been penned by Douglas-Home). John O'Sullivan – who wrote the Conservatives' 1987 election manifesto – and Frank Johnson – who wrote the 1987 election day leading article commending a Tory vote – were among the leader writers moving the paper to the right at a moment when Max Hastings was attempting to redirect the *Daily Telegraph* away from this ground. In 1987, *The Times* gained a refugee from Hastings's low tolerance for those who preached 'the doctrines of Victorian Conservatism'.[10] This was T. E. Utley. Universally known except in print as 'Peter', Utley had been blind since the age of nine and overcame the inability to read or type to become one of the great comment journalists of the previous twenty years. Dictating trenchantly argued copy to his secretaries, he had advocated Thatcherism back when Margaret Thatcher was a Heath supporter, personally encouraged a younger generation of Tory-minded journalists, and done as much as any man to invigorate the *Telegraph*'s intellectual traditions. His treatment by that paper's new guard certainly demonstrated that there was little romance or gratitude to be dispensed or expected in the modern newspaper world. Wilson, however, welcomed him to Wapping and to the paper for which he had first worked at the outset of his career during the Second World War. *The Times* gained a new advocate for the Ulster Unionist cause on the Op-Ed page to replace Owen Hickey whose leader writing days Wilson had finally drawn to a close. Besides his closely argued essays on the Op-Ed page, Utley also became obituaries editor in succession to John Grigg. Utley appeared set to enjoy a lengthy Indian summer at *The Times*. Sadly, it was not to be; he died the following year, at the age of sixty-seven.

Wilson's switch of Grigg from the obits department to become a columnist was one of the signs that he was aware of the need to reclaim prominent liberal voices for the paper. Grigg was exactly the sort of *Times* man that it was popularly assumed had defected to the *Independent*. He was sympathetic towards the SDP and was, in several admirable respects, the embodiment of a generation described in his friend Noel Annan's book, *Our Age*. His father, Sir Edward Grigg, had been 'Imperial Editor' of *The Times* before the First World War and, after the conflict, had successively advised Lloyd George, become an anti-appeasement Conservative MP and ended up as Lord Altrincham. John Grigg processed through Eton and Oxford (where he won the Gladstone Memorial Prize) and, during the Second World War, the Grenadier Guards. He had unsuccessfully attempted to become a Tory MP in the 1950s and in 1963 renounced the peerage he had inherited from his father in order to pursue his political ambition. It was to remain unfulfilled – possibly because constituency associations were unhappy with an infamous article he had written in 1957 criticizing the Court's stultifying atmosphere. He had dared to describe the Queen's public appearances as those of a 'priggish schoolgirl'. At the time a passer-by in the street punched him in the face. Rudeness, though, was very far from being his stock in trade. A cultivated and engaging man, Grigg brought to *The Times* the historian's erudition to the analysis of political events, focusing particularly on lessons from the period of Lloyd George and the Liberal collapse (perhaps Grigg's greatest achievement was his multi-volume biography of the Liberal war leader who knew his father). The fortunes of the House of Windsor also provided plenty of scope for his historical insight. His column continued until 1995, after which he specialized in reviewing books for the paper. Sir Edward Pickering commissioned him to write volume six of the official *History of The Times* covering the years of Rees-Mogg's editorship, 1966–81, which he completed in 1993. It was widely regarded as the most definitive of the series.

Grigg embodied the understated but authoritative approach of an older generation. Attracting the freshness and vigour of younger voices was no less important. In 1965, the management of all national newspapers had succumbed to an NUJ edict banning the recruitment of any reporter direct from university. Instead, they would first have to work three years on provincial newspapers. This restrictive practice crumbled with the union that had promoted it. Under Peter Stothard's direction, *The Times* was the first national newspaper to establish a trainee journalist scheme for graduates. Thus the paper became the first port of call for ambitious aspiring hacks who wanted to skip the supposed grind of the regional press. Traditionalists demurred at the consequences of this form of gentrification, believing that a stint on a local newspaper provided a far broader education in the basic journalistic skills than could be offered by a swift transition from student digs in Clifton or Cowley to a by-line on a national paper. *The Times*'s scheme however – which included a short spell with a provincial placement – proved a great success in luring intelligent and articulate graduates into journalism who, faced with the alternative of reporting on leaks from the parish pump, might have otherwise been tempted away by the increasingly lucrative alternatives of law, accountancy and the City. 'We were the way in' as Stothard put it.[11] In consequence, he became the minder to a whole new Fleet Street kindergarten of talent.

One who arrived in the guise of a trainee was Toby Young, a precociously witty, socially outgoing and, to all intents and purposes, untameable youth. Another was his Oxford contemporary Boris Johnson who had been President of the Union and a Classics Scholar at Balliol. Both proceeded to make their mark in the paper and, in doing so, encouraged a mailbag from those who felt misrepresented in the articles they penned. Whatever the doubts about the accuracy of their reporting, Young and Johnson could have gone on to become rich adornments of *The Times*. Unfortunately, they fell victim to a reluctance to take the risks involved. Young was sacked for writing freelance articles in the *Mail on Sunday*'s *You* magazine although not before he had hacked into Wilson's confidential files on the database by making the inspired guess that the access codeword would be 'Top Man'. Purporting to be the editor, he proceeded to send vernacularly phrased instructions to various colleagues and departmental heads. Next, he hacked into the database that listed everyone's salary, which he mass copied to every computer screen in the building. In the circumstances, his dismissal was perhaps understandable. Boris Johnson's career at *The Times* was even briefer. He was sacked for making up a quote in an article. He went on to become a star columnist at the *Daily Telegraph*, editor of the *Spectator*, enter Parliament and become the closest thing the fourth estate had to a genuine celebrity.

The Times was better able to hold onto another high-profile journalist, Barbara Amiel. She had been a journalistic sensation in Canada where she had edited the *Toronto Sun* having gone to the country in her adolescence (she had been born in London to a Jewish lawyer and colonel who later committed suicide), fallen out with her family and graduated from Toronto University. By 1980, at the age of thirty-nine, she had already published her autobiography, *Confessions*. Returning to the land of her birth, by the time she arrived at Wapping in 1986 she was on her third marriage and had switched from Marxism to neoconservatism with all the zeal of the convert. Peregrine Worsthorne had turned her down for a job at the *Sunday Telegraph* in part because he mistook her fragrant and carefully coiffured appearance for a lack of seriousness. *The Times* thought otherwise. 'She looks like Gina Lollobrigida and writes like Bernard Levin – and do get it the right way round,' said a friend.[12] *Times* readers of long standing might have thought this was slightly overegging it, at least in regard to the venerable Levin. She certainly had his spark and gifts for invective although could not reasonably be expected (who could?) to match the extraordinary breadth of his cultural range. Others believed her presence tilted the paper's political scales too far to the right.

Of all the appointments Wilson made, none was more surprising or inspired than when, in the autumn of 1988, he hit upon the idea of employing Matthew Parris in succession to Craig Brown as *The Times*'s parliamentary sketchwriter. The appointment was a risk. Aged thirty-nine, Parris had spent seven years on the Conservative backbenches before resigning his seat in favour of a television career which soon came to an abrupt halt when LWT axed *Weekend World*, the Sunday political programme he had presented – it was widely accepted – less adeptly than his predecessor, Brian Walden. Parris's print journalism was limited to three one-off articles for *The Times* over the past six years and a few *Sunday Times* book reviews. There was no doubt that he had the requisite intellect. From a childhood spent partly in Rhodesia, he had gone up to Cambridge, won a fellowship to Yale, been a trainee diplomat at the Foreign Office and worked for Mrs Thatcher at the Conservative Research Department before becoming a Tory MP in 1979 at the age of thirty. After such early precocity, the resignation of his seat and the failure of *Weekend World* suggested talent unfulfilled. When Wilson telephoned him with the offer of *The Times* parliamentary sketch, Parris was even in two minds about accepting. 'I was nearly forty,' he recalled, 'and I had never met with conspicuous success in any job I'd done.' What was more, having been an MP, 'this trudging back, a mere reporter, into a place I had quit as a Member with head held high to be a television star, was a kind of defeat. How could I return except with my tail between my legs? The job seemed a come-down.'[13]

It was, as he later came to accept, his making. Yet so unsure was he initially that he suggested doing it for only twelve months (it ended up being thirteen years). He also agreed to do a weekly Op-Ed column on Mondays. His sketch writing got off to a shaky start. Dispatched to the Liberal Democrats' conference in Blackpool, he filed for the first day. It had to compete with the rather more interesting news of Ben Johnson's drugs shame. The following day Parris did not bother filing at all – unaware that Wapping was expecting daily copy, regardless of whether there was anything worth reporting or not.[14] Within weeks, he had established himself as a crucial feature of the paper. Many of his greatest fans appeared to be his targets for ridicule. Indeed, it was generally his impression that, regardless of their politics, most MPs were so desperate to be noticed and to feel they were important, that they enjoyed a mention in a Parris sketch, almost regardless of how much fun was being had at their expense. In this respect, they were different from peers of the realm. Parris's occasional sketches from House of Lords' debates sometimes provoked personal notes from the close friends of peers (never from the peer personally) writing to let him know how much hurt his jests had caused their target. Working peers toiled long and hard for little public acknowledgement and no proper salary. They did not see why their devotion to public service should be a matter for satire.[15] Disliking causing unnecessary offence, it was little wonder that Parris preferred to look down from the gallery upon the self-promoting politicians of the lower chamber. He was the first columnist to have his handiwork reprinted in the *New Oxford Book of English Prose*.

There were other arrivals. In 1989 a cost-cutting plan that, in everything but the comment section, merged the *Daily* and *Sunday Telegraph* into a seven-day paper caused chaos and resentment within the ranks of Conrad Black's empire. *The Times* benefited from refugees from this miscalculation that included Martin Ivens and Graham Paterson. Wilson might have been presiding over a newspaper that was losing some of its most famous journalists, but he was also responsible for ensuring that it gained new ones who would add lustre to it in the years ahead.

III

Thatcherism's domestic agenda was blown off course by three ill winds: the poll tax, the Chancellor of the Exchequer's faltering grip on the economy and Britain's relations with Europe. The last two became interconnected. After pushing through the legislation to create a single European market, the Prime Minister became much more uneasy about the European Community. She became personally antagonistic towards Jacques Delors, the French socialist who was the European Commission's president. Where Thatcher envisaged the single market as an end in itself, Delors saw it as the prerequisite for an extension of Brussels' competences in other areas, including social legislation. He dared to suggest that, in the future, 80 per cent of legislation would emanate from Brussels. Thatcher had fooled herself into believing the expressions of support for European economic and European monetary union (EMU) that accompanied the Single Act were windy rhetoric. On this she was soon disabused. Europe's idealists were more practical than she realized. The Delors Report set June 1989 as the date for agreement on commencing the process towards EMU. Forewarned that the Prime Minister was about to make her opposition explicit, *The Times* ran for cover, its leading article warning her against making a speech that would give the impression to the country's partners that Britain wanted to be a disruptive player, a notion that would deny 'Mrs Thatcher an unusual opportunity to take a leading role in Europe as it approaches its single market in 1992'.[16] The Prime Minister, however, was not in the mood for such equivocation. Later that day she addressed the College of Europe in Bruges and delivered a speech that would become one of the most important of her career. In it she reaffirmed her belief in nation states and warned that at a time when central control was being seen to fail in Eastern Europe the future lay not with Delors's socialist utopia: 'We have not successfully rolled back the frontiers of the state in Britain only to see them reimposed at a European level.' She wanted the completion of the single market in 1992 to ensure deregulation not centralization and monetary union. These Euro-sceptical shots across the bow were widely resented. Reporting from Bruges, Nicholas Wood quoted a senior European official as calling her remarks 'outrageous and unrelentingly negative'.[17] *The Times* was left to sigh ineffectually, 'she is honest where our partners are idealistic. Their point is that there is a place for ideals.'[18]

The Times was not yet a Euro-sceptic paper although it failed to have the strength of conviction to make clear exactly what sort of a European Community it did envisage. The prospect of creating a single European currency, however, meant that the period for prevarication had passed. The precursor to signing up for the new currency was to stabilize sterling's exchange rate with those of her partners in the Exchange Rate Mechanism. The Prime Minister's problems were compounded not only by Cabinet colleagues who favoured joining the ERM because they wanted to sign up to the single currency but by those – including the Chancellor of the Exchequer – who thought the ERM's anti-inflationary disciplines were the overheating British economy's only hope of salvation. During May 1989, interest rates were pushed up to 14 per cent. The following month inflation hit 8.3 per cent, the highest for seven years. In August, the trade deficit substantially worsened. Despite knowing Nigel Lawson's intentions, Sir Alan Walters, the Prime Minister's personal adviser, described the ERM as 'half-baked' in an article for the *American Economist*. There was an outcry and Mrs Thatcher faced calls to dismiss her adviser. Instead she stuck by him. She lost her Chancellor instead.

Nigel Lawson's resignation was the greatest blow to Mrs Thatcher's Government since Michael Heseltine's dramatic walkout three years earlier. Given Lawson's position, it was altogether more serious and the issue was of rather greater magnitude than who owned Westland helicopters. The following morning the news was splashed across the front page with a large Richard Willson cartoon of Sir Alan Walters falling out of Lawson's collapsing Budget briefcase. Thatcher's decision to stick by Walters had not even saved his skin. His continuation as her adviser would have made life for Lawson's successor all but untenable and he too opted to resign on what Philip Webster and Richard Ford's report described as 'a night of sensation'. 'At 7.45 p.m. in one of the most astonishing scenes enacted in the Commons, Sir Geoffrey Howe, Deputy Prime Minister, told MPs of Lawson's resignation,' the report continued. John Major was promoted to fill Lawson's shoes, despite the fact that he had only been made Foreign Secretary the previous month. Webster described Major as 'one of the most respected Chief Secretaries in recent years'.[19]

Analysing the Lawson resignation, Robin Oakley wrote that although the immediate issue had concerned the differences between Howe and Lawson who supported ERM membership and Thatcher and Walters who did not, it had its roots in

Mrs Thatcher's way of doing things. It is not a case of two people who had stuck together for the sake of the party finally being unable to bear the strain. Lawson was one of the group of four musketeers who used to work with Mrs Thatcher back in opposition days, feeding her the ammunition with which to make an impact at Prime Minister's Question Time. Like Norman Tebbit, another of the four, he was a Thatcherite by conviction, a genuine soul mate.

They had come to find that 'when things go wrong, they feel, she detaches herself from her ministers and talks about them as if they work for somebody else'. Now she had been forced to make Douglas Hurd Foreign Secretary. Given that he did not share her growing hostility to the European project, she would either have to concede political ground to him or retreat further 'into the bunker with that small team of advisers'.[20]

In its leading column, *The Times* put loyalty to the Prime Minister before sensible analysis of what had happened. Minimizing the scale of the crisis, it suggested that Lawson's departure solved the divisive cohabitation on economic policy. Praise for Lawson's achievements was muted: 'His strength of mind was admired, but he has yet to be forgiven for relaxing the fiscal reins last year and allowing the economy to overheat. To that extent his departure will actually strengthen the Government's position.'[21] Three days later, the leading column, entitled 'Panic Over', went so far as to assure Tory backbenchers that 'the drama is over'.[22]

With a challenge to her leadership on the horizon from the backbench 'stalking horse', Sir Anthony Meyer, Mrs Thatcher was interviewed by Robin Oakley and Nicholas Wood in The Times in November 1989. She implied she would fight not only the 1992 election as leader but also the 1997 contest 'by popular acclaim', as she put it (although she would be seventy-two by then). Her eventual successor, she hinted, would probably come from a younger generation (which, if she stayed on beyond 1997, could hardly be doubted). It was, as Oakley and Wood pointed out, 'an astonishing move which can be expected to goad her opponents within the Conservative Party'.[23] In the short term, however, it did not fail. On 5 December, she saw off the 'stalking horse' without having to break into more than a canter. It would take someone altogether more substantial than Sir Anthony Meyer to see her off.

IV

In December 1988, The Times asked its foreign correspondents to speculate on what 1989 held in store. Roger Boyes came closest: 'Romania and East Germany will have leadership crises this year. East Germany is particularly sensitive since there is real pressure for change from below on Herr Erich Honecker, age 75.' As for Romania's even more dictatorial ruler, Nicolae Ceauşescu:

This may be the year of transition as the limits of his power are becoming evident and he has destroyed the machinery of succession . . . The real risk takers are Poland and Hungary, which are trying to run faster and faster to keep up with the rising expectations of their people . . . Hungary is galloping into the new world, with talk of a multi-party system and much else . . . the political implosion of neutral Yugoslavia will become a political factor in the rest of the Balkans; and debt-servicing will be a problem everywhere.[24]

Boyes was certainly well placed to observe a transforming moment in world history. It was Mikhail Gorbachev's attempts to liberalize the Soviet Union that gave the peoples of Eastern Europe hope. Amazingly, *The Times* had been without a correspondent in Moscow for almost a year due to foot-dragging over giving a visa to Mary Dejevsky, who was Wilson's choice to succeed Christopher Walker. Dejevsky's record of writing critically about the Soviet regime told against her. Yet, if the Soviet authorities believed their stalling tactics in issuing a visa would encourage *The Times* to offer up a more amenable journalist instead, they were much mistaken. Wilson refused to play games, insisting that the choice of correspondent would not be a matter for the Soviet government. Undaunted, he even began planning during the summer of 1988 to send a team of *Times* writers over to the USSR to study the changes that were unfolding. Unusually, Mrs Thatcher intervened to secure *The Times* an interview with Gorbachev, her Private Secretary, Charles Powell, speaking to the Soviet Embassy on the matter with 'the Prime Minister's personal instruction'.[25] In April 1989, Wilson was among those Thatcher invited for dinner with Gorbachev.

Getting an inside perspective on the unfolding drama in the Soviet Union was, however, a difficult assignment. Briefly in Moscow in the summer of 1987, Mary Dejevsky had met up with Jewish refuseniks via intermediaries who would arrange to meet her in a specified carriage of a metro station before taking her to their whereabouts. Each had a story of persecution. For eighteen months between May 1988 and November 1989, *The Times* vainly attempted to get Dejevsky a visa. A one-month visa, granted as a goodwill gesture, was issued in December 1988, the words 'only the truth' written above the signature of the Soviet diplomat who issued it. On arrival, even her private telephone was audibly tapped. She had brought with her a Bible that she was going to give to a Moscow worker in a car plant who had written to *The Times* asking for one. 'I handed him his Bible in an opaque, unpatterned carrier bag and we walked down the street, he marvelling that he could meet a Western correspondent without immediate arrest, I that so many precautions still had to be taken. Then we both heard the camera click from a shop window above us.'[26]

When Dejevsky finally got to take up residence in Moscow she still had little idea how long she would be allowed to stay. She was there at the sufferance of the Soviet authorities. Angus Roxburgh, the *Sunday Times* correspondent, had been expelled shortly before her arrival. Dejevsky pondered whether the authorities had deliberately deported Roxburgh so that she would not have a near colleague to compare notes with and in order to break all continuity in News International's reporting operations. Taking up residence in the deserted *Times* flat in the security-enclosed foreigners compound in Moscow, Dejevsky added Gibbons's *Decline and Fall of the Roman Empire* to the bookshelves. She sensed its contents might have contemporary resonance. In the event, she only got halfway through the first volume. The pace of reporting the Soviet empire's implosion left her no time for perusing history books.

During the spring of 1989, the first Soviet multi-candidate elections for the Congress of People's Deputies were held and Gorbachev rid the Soviet Central Committee of many of its old guard. His efforts to produce a new mood of openness in Soviet society were watched with the keenest interest. It had already made possible an extraordinary improvement in relations with the United States. In July 1987, the Kremlin had offered to dismantle medium- and short-range missiles from the USSR's Asian states. The following month, Reagan had responded, suggesting a summit in Washington to ban intermediate nuclear weapons. On 8 December, agreement at Washington was signed, eliminating medium- and short-range nuclear missiles. It was the first mutually agreed disarmament treaty in history. The world appeared to be stepping away from the spectre of nuclear destruction.

Gorbachev, however, was concerned not only with extracting his country from the crippling cost of a nuclear arms race in which it was clear the Soviet Union could no longer compete. In May 1988, he began withdrawing Russian troops from their disastrous campaign in Afghanistan. The last of them was pulled out ignominiously in February the following year. By then Gorbachev had told the UN of his proposals to cut his armed forces by half a million men and to withdraw fifty thousand troops and five thousand tanks from Eastern Europe.

Yet, not everywhere Gorbachev went was he able to foster a new spirit of peace and harmony and those who thought the world was engaged in an overnight embrace of liberalism were about to be rudely jolted. Martial law had been declared in Peking (as *The Times* was still calling Beijing) on 20 May. However, the first serious attempt to enforce it had ended in embarrassment when five thousand inexperienced and nervous soldiers had failed to disperse a crowd of students and other protestors that appeared to be swelling towards 100,000 people. The massed demonstration in Tiananmen Square was particular embarrassing for the party leaders. They had become a focus for the world media, providing an extraordinary spectacle of nascent democracy. Art students had even erected 'The Goddess of Democracy' which consciously resembled the Statue of Liberty in the heart of the square. It was a mortifying spectacle for China's leaders at a time when Gorbachev was visiting for talks. They decided they could tolerate it no longer.

On 5 June, *The Times* splashed its front page with the terrible consequences, 'Peking protesters massacred: Thousands feared dead as tanks crush heroic resistance'. A photograph showed the tank-crushed corpses of students beside the twisted wreckage of their bicycles. The paper's stringer in China, Catherine Sampson, had lain flat on her belly with her notebook from her position on the Peking Hotel's balcony, from where she had watched the atrocity unfold before her eyes. Her report began, 'The people of Peking last night continued their heroic but doomed resistance as some of the tanks and heavy artillery that had crushed the student protest movement less than 24 hours before patrolled the capital.' Unofficial estimates of the death toll had passed one thousand. In the suburbs, university campuses and around the diplomatic quarter there were sporadic bursts of gunfire and resistance. In the darkness, chaos and panic, it was difficult to establish the exact course of events. 'According to one account, tanks and armoured personnel carriers had driven on to the square, indiscriminately crushing the makeshift tents with students still inside. Another report said that when the students had filed out of the square, holding hands, troops had fired at them, felling the first row of 100, and then the second.' The Goddess of Democracy was brought smashing down. Official news reports spoke only of the suppression of a 'counter-revolutionary' riot, without listing casualties.[27] Later, independent estimates suggested around 2600 had perished although nobody was ever really able to speak with authority on the final toll.

Sampson was so traumatized by the horror she had witnessed that, close to collapse, she caught a flight to Hong Kong to be with Mary Dejevsky (in her last weeks there before taking up residence in Moscow) who was filing valuable supplementary reports from the British colony. Dejevsky protected her (not least from an irate foreign desk at Wapping who felt she had deserted her post) and, several days later, Sampson summoned the courage to return to Peking where she reported on the ensuing crackdown. Dejevsky, meanwhile, had been stalwart not only in the defence of her distraught colleague but also on the pages of the newspaper (although Wilson was angry with her not being *in situ* in Peking). As the massacre unfolded, she immediately filed a comment article arguing that the deed would cause the Chinese government the loss of its people's confidence as well as that of foreign investors and the nervous community in Hong Kong which was due to be transferred to Peking's care in eight years time. 'It could also strike the first nail in the coffin of Chinese communism,' she wrote. 'In Peking in the last three weeks I witnessed the spirit of hope and common purpose represented by the student protests. The barricades erected to keep the army out of the city were built and manned by ordinary people, not those of an anti-government persuasion.'[28]

The leading column was unsparing in its criticism. It was written by Rosemary Righter, a forthright intellect who exemplified the most noble traditions of 'The Thunderer'. Righter was an accomplished duellist with the pen against tyranny's swords. Deng Xiaoping, long seen as the leader of reform in China, had opted to hang 'on to power at the expense of his own revolution'. *The Times* argued that Britain should review its 1984 agreement with China over Hong Kong, suspending negotiations on the Basic Law under which the colony was to be governed after the handover. For its part, the Hong Kong government should proceed without delay to introduce democratic institutions while, in Whitehall, the Home Office should review its policy on Hong Kong citizens' entitlement to British residency.[29] When the Government subsequently insisted on restricting entitlement, *The Times* and, in particular its columnist Woodrow Wyatt, were appalled.

Would the Communist old guard clinging onto power in Eastern Europe crush the emerging voices of dissent with equal ruthlessness? On 4 June 1989, just as China's rulers were ordering the suppression of the student protests, Solidarity swept to power in Poland's first free elections since the Second World War and two months later its first post-war non-Communist prime minister took office. There was no bloodshed. Also that August two million people formed a human chain across the three Baltic republics to mark the fiftieth anniversary of their Soviet annexation. It was a potent message of dignified defiance to rule from Moscow. The winds of change were blowing across the continent. In September, Hungary opened its border with East Germany and within four weeks socialists had replaced Communists in power in Budapest.

The flow of migration from East Germany was turning into a flood. Yet, some felt that the events of the Second World War meant that the Soviet Union would never tolerate a united Germany and the toppling of the Communist emblem over East Berlin. As the pressures for political reform and migration mounted in East Germany, two fears loomed large: would its leaders crack down and, if they did not, would Moscow do so on its satellite's behalf? Brezhnev's intimidation of the government in Warsaw in the face of the rise of Solidarity in 1981 was one precedent. But the Brezhnev Doctrine of defending Marxist-Leninism in Eastern Europe, with tanks if necessary, appeared to have disintegrated. Gorbachev was made from more malleable metal. After all, Solidarity had been allowed to form a government in Warsaw. Indeed, far from having their resolve stiffened, the leadership in East Berlin came under pressure from Moscow to pursue a policy of *glasnost* rather than repression. That, at any rate, seemed to make more sense that risking a complete surrender to democratic forces that, if allowed to triumph, could even dismantle the Warsaw Pact, a risk Moscow was not prepared to countenance. The East German regime, however, appeared more resistant to *glasnost* than those who wielded power in the Kremlin. Alarmingly, Egon Krenz, who succeeded Erich Honecker in October 1989, had publicly supported the Chinese government's massacre in Tiananmen Square.

No emblem was more totemic of the Cold War than the Berlin Wall. Two and a half million East Germans had fled to the West while the borders were porous between 1949 and 1961, when the wall was erected to stop them, officially as an 'anti-fascist protection barrier'. Border guards operated a shoot-to-kill policy rescinded only in 1989. Presidents Kennedy and Reagan had both stood before it and condemned it in ringing tones of high oratory. Yet, on 9 November, astonishing news broke. The wall had been breached.

Although the East German politburo announced the wall would remain as a 'reinforced state border', the decision to open crossing points through which all the Democratic Republic's citizens could pass from east to west spelt its doom. Whatever delusions were clung to by Krenz and his circle, *The Times* headline summed up the situation: 'The Iron Curtain torn open: Berliners cross the Wall to freedom.'[30] A photograph showed Berliners actually standing on top of the heavily graffitied structure. Such was the rate of copy and pictures coming through to Wapping on the evening the wall fell that the front page was changed eight times over the course of the night. In nearly thirty-five years at the paper, Tim Austin looked back on it as the most memorable night at *The Times*.[31]

A tide of humanity poured across the border, propelled by curiosity, better shopping, the exercise of a new liberty formally denied or to visit relations they had been separated from for years or generations. Over the first weekend, two million East Germans crossed the border. Holes were widened to accommodate the torrent. Rather than waiting for official sanction, Berliners took chisels to sections. The mayors of the divided city shook hands. Krenz announced free elections. A quarter of East Germans asked for visas. Anne McElvoy led *The Times*'s reporting from East Berlin and she was soon joined by Michael Binyon who arrived in West Berlin in time to witness the influx of 'Oesties' claiming their one hundred Deutsch-mark (£34) 'welcome money' to spend. Many milled about 'unsure of where they were going', Binyon observed. 'They had no idea where the streets went, as East German maps print West Berlin simply as a huge white space.' For some, freedom meant licence. 'One of the most popular attractions were the famous sex shops, which were doing a roaring trade.' A photograph of Leipzigerstrasse showed East Berlin deserted.[32]

Unlike Poland, where there was Solidarity, or in so many other revolutions, the crumbling of Communist power in the German Democratic Republic was the result of mass action but not of an organized opposition. Anne McElvoy was quick to point out the irrelevance of 'New Forum', the hastily cobbled together rainbow alliance. 'An organization which is still debating by lunchtime whether or not to let the Press watch its debate will take at least a year before it knows its own mind on anything else,' she wrote, warning that 'the call for free elections, however, is only meaningful if there are parties worthy to fight them'.[33] It was not exactly clear what East Germans wanted. Were they discontented with the politicians and their policies or did they actually want to replace the whole system of government? Within days the first banners demanding reunification were appearing at rallies in Leipzig, one of the centres for those agitating for reform. How strong the pressure for reunification was could not be easily gauged. Initial opinion polls suggested it was not strong and on 13 November *The Times* reported that 'Herr Krenz, in his conversation with Herr Kohl, appears to have dismissed any talk of reunification'.[34]

Initially, West Germany's Chancellor Kohl gave the public impression that reunification could be years away from realization. In Britain, Margaret Thatcher worried that a hasty endorsement of a united Germany would undermine Gorbachev and thereby hand back the Soviet Union to the rule of the hardliners. There were still 360,000 Soviet troops on East German soil and the other possible option for reuniting Germany – that it would leave NATO and become neutral – was also uncongenial to the Prime Minister's way of thinking. As East Germany went to the polls for its first free elections in March 1990, Thatcher held a private summit to discuss the German question with a team of historians that included Lord Dacre and Norman Stone. Most of the conclusions were positive although the subsequent leaking of a memorandum drawn up listing supposed Germanic character traits made the Prime Minister appear to be trapped in a 1940s mindset. The East German elections, however, produced sensational results: with a turnout of over 90 per cent, the pro-unification Christian Democrat-led 'Alliance for Germany' won 48 per cent and the former Communists were reduced to 16 per cent. From this moment, there was no diverting the emotional tide for one Germany. In June, the Deutschmark became legal tender in the east. On 2 October, Germany was reunified. Anne McElvoy conveyed the scenes in Berlin as its two halves counted down the hours to becoming one again. 'Music rang out on every street corner and fireworks lit up the sky over the Brandenburg gate,' she reported. 'Older Germans burst into tears as midnight approached. "This is the end of a long punishment for my country," said an old man.' The East German Volkskammer convened for its last session. The British, American and French flags were lowered, as the occupying powers ceded their authority to the new free state. The former Chancellor, Helmut Schmidt, penned a column on the Op-Ed page, appealing to his British friends to prevent a new German financial superpower by endorsing a new European central bank and single currency. 'Germany is reborn today, and Europe should rejoice,' proclaimed the leading article written by Daniel Johnson, before proceeding to call for a wider European Community that should incorporate Poland, Hungary and Czechoslovakia.[35] Enlargement of the EC became the Euro-sceptics' solution to what was assumed would be a more powerful Germany just as the Euro-federalists believed the answer came in replacing the Deutschmark with the euro. In the event, both would follow.

The new Germany was, for the first time since the rise of Hitler, surrounded on all sides by democracies. A 'Velvet Revolution' had swept away Communist rule in Czechoslovakia in November 1989. Alexander Dubček, hero of the Prague Spring, had addressed his first rally since the fateful days of 1968. On 10 December, the country's first non-Communist government took office and two days before Christmas the playwright and victim of totalitarianism, Vaclav Havel, was declared the new President. Yet, while Prague celebrated the bloodless means through which it could re-engage with the rest of Europe, events were taking a very different turn in Romania. On 17 December 1989, there were massacres in the Transylvanian city of Timisoara, close to the country's border with Yugoslavia. The Times was faced with a problem. Romania was clearly the lead story but with no reporter inside the country it had to rely on what Dessa Trevisan on the Yugoslav border and Ernest Beck on the Hungarian border were able to glean from a mixture of often second-hand accounts and rumour, together with what was being reported by Tanjug, the Yugoslav news agency. The Romanian state media was making no mention of any atrocities, focusing instead on the state visit to Iran of President Nicolae Ceauşescu, the country's 'Conductor'. Of the available sources of information, Tanjug was the most reliable. Yugoslavia alone had a consulate in Timisoara. From there, unconfirmed reports were streaming in of a second Tiananmen Square massacre. Tanjug was reporting two thousand civilian deaths and the demolition of the city centre. The trouble had started when demonstrators had tried to block the eviction of a popular pastor, Laszlo Tokes, who had criticized Ceauşescu's persecution of the local Hungarian minority.

Romania was a country where even ownership of a typewriter was forbidden without a state licence. *The Times* was cautions about predicting Ceauşescu's demise, a leading article entitled 'Balkan Caligula' pointing out that whereas Gorbachev's support for reform and refusal to enact the Brezhnev Doctrine had undermined the will of the rest of Eastern Europe's regimes to cling to power at all costs, Ceauşescu had isolated his country from Moscow's political influence. Furthermore, 'Romania lacks an obvious institution such as the Catholic Church in Poland around which popular discontent will clearly mobilize.'[36] Pessimism was understandable. Until July 1988, the United States had rewarded Romania with most favoured trading status. The country had paid off most of its debts to the West and the IMF and had embarked upon reducing trade dependence as well. Romania was in the unusual situation of being a creditor with net assets while its citizens lived in penury. Western leverage on Bucharest was thus all but nonexistent. On the Op-Ed pages, Mark Almond, the Oxford don and Romania specialist, warned that the lamb-like collapse of Communism elsewhere in Eastern Europe was likely to make Ceauşescu even more inclined to tough it out. He would draw the parallel instead from the repressive successes of the Tiananmen Square massacre. Indeed, 'the visit to Peking by President Bush's national security adviser, Brent Scowcroft, will probably have persuaded Ceauşescu that the US talks human rights but does business regardless. Gorbachev has now sent an envoy to Peking to pay his respects.' Almond thought it possible that, 'given Gorbachev's growing domestic unpopularity and fundamental failure to reform the Soviet economy, the Ceauşescus may still rule in Romania when *perestroika* is as fond a memory as the Prague Spring'.[37]

The hypothesis was perfectly plausible. However, Almond had overestimated both the intelligence and the tenacity of The Conductor. With news of the massacres at Timisoara spreading, Ceauşescu returned to Bucharest from Tehran and called for a mass pro-government rally that he would address from the balcony of the presidential palace. With the hubris of a regime used to stage-managing emotion, the decision was taken to broadcast the performance live. It was a disastrous miscalculation. With the cameras rolling, the crowd did the unthinkable – Ceauşescu was heckled mid-oration. Visibly losing control, he faltered and stepped back from the balcony. At this very moment, the live broadcast was cut.

As the television coverage came to its abrupt and alarming halt, *The Times*'s reporters were moving across the border. Peter Law arrived in Timisoara where the bodies of more than four thousand victims were being uncovered in a ditch. Michael Hornsby made straight for Bucharest. It seemed the Securitate had shot dead the Defence Minister 'because he had tried to keep soldiers in their barracks'. Fighting was breaking out all over the city between insurgents and army units loyal to a regime whose leader had just been dramatically helicoptered off the roof of The Central Committee building to an unknown fate. The Securitate were using underground passageways to make a bloody stand in The Conductor's absence. Back in Wapping, the dramatic, if conflicting, reports were contributing towards an equally dramatic front page. 'Bloodbath in Bucharest' ran the headline beside a photograph of cheering Romanian troops joining the revolt. It was an image that would not have looked out of place in a 1945 edition of *Picture Post*. A second photograph caught Ceauşescu's helicopter lifting off from the roof of the Central Committee building.[38]

On Christmas Day news spread that both Ceauşescu and his hated wife Elena had been caught, tried for two hours and shot. Michael Hornsby travelled round a Bucharest that was increasingly under the control of the makeshift anti-Ceauşescu alliance, the National Salvation Front. While some signs of normality had returned, there were also lynchings of Securitate members, Hornsby witnessing one of them being shot through the head with his own revolver. 'Others were dragged from cars and beaten to death.'[39]

Whatever the scenes of summary justice in Bucharest, Christmas 1989 was celebrated across Europe with an unusual degree of hope, expectation and, for some, a measure of unease. The process would take another giant stride forward a mere five weeks into the new year when the Soviet Central Committee voted to end the USSR as a one-party state. For all its overuse, it was hard to avoid the metaphor of the toppling dominoes, as first Poland shrugged off Communist rule, then Hungary, East Germany and Czechoslovakia. In the last days of the year it looked as if Romania, too, was poised to follow suit, albeit after blood on the streets. In fact, while it freed itself from the shadow of Ceauşescu, it would shy away from electing a non-Communist government until November 1996. It had been a momentous last six months of 1989 nonetheless. When, back in July, Paris had celebrated the bicentenary of the French Revolution, world leaders had gathered there only six weeks after reform in China had been crushed at Tiananmen Square and half of Europe was still under Communist rule. Reflecting on the 'Year of Revolution', *The Times* observed, 'For Europe, at least, the year of France's revolutionary bicentennial has lived up to the nobler part of its inheritance.'[40]

It was an end to old certainties. The American academic Francis Fukuyama rushed to provide the first of a series of explanations. His suggestion that the world had reached the 'end of history' naturally attracted considerable attention. According to Fukuyama, the future might contain all manner of trouble and strife, but it would not be an ideological battle of wills because the world had arrived at a point where it was merely divided between those countries that had embraced liberalism, those that were in the course of doing so and those for which the day could not long be postponed. Only a few small states with crank rulers still failed to acknowledge that liberal values were not, at least in principle, a good thing. This theory would soon be put to a sterner test by the re-emergence of Islamic fundamentalism, leading other theorists to warn that the world was, in fact, in thrall to a 'clash of civilisations'. This, however, was for the future. Among those in *The Times* who rejected the Fukuyama theory when it was first expounded in 1989 was the Oxford philosopher John Gray who thought not that history had ended but rather that it would rediscover its old rhythms:

> The aftermath of totalitarianism will not be a global tranquilization of the sort imagined by American triumphalist theorists of liberal democracy. Instead, the end of totalitarianism in most of the world is likely to see the resumption of history on decidedly traditional lines: not the history invented in the hallucinatory perspectives of Marxism and American liberalism, but the history of authoritarian regimes, great-power rivalries, secret diplomacy, irredentist claims and ethnic and religious conflicts. It is to this world, harsh but familiar, that we are now returning, and for whose trials we should be preparing.[41]

Daniel Johnson, who joined *The Times* in the new year, wondered whether a diminution of the ideological struggle between capitalism and Communism would topple the primacy of socio-economic historical interpretation in favour of biography and the theory of the 'great man'. 'Over the last decade,' he noted, 'several personalities have emerged in Eastern Europe who seem to possess that titanic quality which the Swiss historian Jacob Burckhardt defined as *historische Grösse*: Gorbachev, Walesa, Havel.'[42] Yet, not even the great men in the last decade of the century appeared able to contain all the tides that swelled around them. Nationalism was replacing Communism in Eastern Europe and was tearing apart the multi-ethnic Soviet Union. Communism in Eastern Europe, it now seemed, had only been sustained for so long by the acknowledged reality that there was a Soviet army of occupation ready to enforce it. It collapsed as soon as its citizens and leaders alike realized that the Brezhnev Doctrine was dead. Bernard Levin wrote, 'the moment Mr Gorbachev made clear that whatever happened in the evil empire he would not lift a finger to help the colonial rulers, he had done the deed – the irreversible deed – that would put paid to communism not only in its colonies but in the mother country itself'.[43] Conor Cruise O'Brien shared this analysis, but believed that these same forces would not triumph in China. There, the situation was different because the army, like the regime, was Chinese. Indeed, much of the armed forces personnel were drawn from the villages where 80 per cent of the population lived. They were far removed from the Western values of the chattering minority in the cities, let alone the students who had been to the fore in Tiananmen Square.[44]

The world had been transformed in a matter of weeks. Reporting revolution on this scale was an enormous test for *The Times*, as for the other papers. Analysis was difficult and speculation about the future almost cavalierly hazardous. Some believed the *Independent* had provided the best coverage of European Communism's collapse. David Walker, a *Times* dissident who defected to the *Guardian*, noted that 'during German unification, for example, it was striking how *Die Welt* cited as a matter of habit not *The Times* but the *Independent*'s views'.[45] Nonetheless, re-examining the paper during this period, *The Times*'s coverage appears impressive. Young and thoughtful reporters like Anne McElvoy provided excellent copy from Berlin. Mark Almond offered weighty analysis on the Op-Ed page. Naturally, the paper's first task of analysis was to assess how the upheavals would shape Eastern Europe and the Soviet Union in the years ahead. It took longer to appreciate that the end of the Cold War would also dramatically change the nature of politics in Western Europe, Britain and the rest of the world. Political parties would have to adapt to new priorities among the voters and there was much (exaggerated) talk of a peace dividend in which huge savings from cutting defence spending could be redirected towards public services. For many in Britain, Margaret Thatcher's unease about German reunification and opposition to deeper integration in the European Community jarred with the spirit of the moment, where European brotherhood animated those with hopes for a continent reborn. French political calculations were perhaps more cynical – the price for a reunited Germany was the abolition of the Deutschmark and the pressing ahead with European economic and monetary union. This ensured that the politics of Western Europe rather than those of the newly liberated Eastern European states would continue to dominate the news and comment pages of *The Times* in the 1990s. Whether a more deeply integrated European Community would facilitate reaching out across the shattered Iron Curtain to a wider Europe beyond remained to be seen.

V

While the editor made preparations for a new decade with his usual unflagging drive and enthusiasm, there was much he could look back upon in the past eighteen months with quiet satisfaction. In particular, the Saturday paper had undergone a remarkable expansion. *The Times* had long been a paper that serious-minded people took with them to work and this was reflected in the circulation figures. Sales had been much better during the weekdays than at the weekends. Enhancing Saturday's sale would need significant investment but advertisers had traditionally been shy of investing in Saturday journalism, preferring the graphic-friendly glossy magazines of the Sunday papers or the daily certainties of the weekday offerings. The paper that did most to change this formula was the *Financial Times*. Although not naturally thought of as the journal with which to relax at the weekend, the *FT* successfully reinvented itself on Saturdays, pioneering the two-section format that emphasized lifestyle-focused journalism. In particular, it had a strong property section. So successful was this weekend edition that the paper began selling more on Saturdays than it did during the week. The *Telegraph* followed suit. Clearly there was a waiting market ripe to be explored and exploited. In Charles Wilson, *The Times* was fortunate to have an editor who understood the challenge.

By the end of 1988, all the national broadsheets had additional weekend sections for the Saturday editions. The *Independent* was the last to do so, but the launch of its second section and a weekend magazine edited by Alexander Chancellor in September 1988 made an immediate impact. Wilson's strategy was different. Rather than introduce a colour magazine he opted to produce a four-section, sixty-four-page edition for Saturdays, one section of which was gravure-printed in colour. There was more of virtually everything too. A family money section took the place of what, during the week, was devoted to company business news. Readers were guided through the proliferation of financial services designed to make every last drop of savings go further. Apart from anything else, this was popular with the advertisers. Where, previously, the 'Saturday' section had merely been tagged onto the main part of the paper, 'Review' became a distinct third section covering the arts, live performances and books. Previewing sporting events rather than just providing match reports for the Monday paper ensured that Saturday's fourth section, covering sport and leisure, was also much more comprehensive than what had been offered in the past. Francesca Greenoak was given more room to tend her gardening column and the general layout was greatly enhanced with watercolour illustrations by Diana Ledbetter. It no longer looked like a grubby old piece of inky newsprint. Indeed, in the last two years of the 1980s, two areas of the paper's Saturday journalism were especially developed: the property section (unfortunately just in time for the market downturn) and the travel pages. In the latter case, the transformation was especially remarkable. What had previously amounted to a couple of articles surrounded by a stamp album of small monochrome ads for weekends in Torquay or Le Touquet sprouted into several pages in which travel writers explored increasingly exotic locations. The quality of the accompanying photography also became more artistic and alluring. This expansion was overseen by the travel editor, Shona Crawford Poole, who had previously been *The Times* cookery writer. Providing the weekend recipes in her place had become Frances Bissell's responsibility while Jane MacQuitty continued to write expertly every Saturday about wine, a task she had been performing without let or hindrance since 1982. Jonathan Meades wrote the restaurant reviews. An atheist of the militant variety, Meades had gone from a minor West Country public school (another bugbear) to RADA 'at the fag end of the Sixties'. But waning aspirations towards the stage were quashed comprehensively by Hugh Cruttwell, RADA's principal, who all too plausibly assured Meades that he had little future until he reached middle age, at which point he would make a good living as a character actor.[46] At thirty-nine, Meades was still approaching this age when he was signed up by *The Times* in 1986, having spent the intervening fifteen years writing for various magazines including *Time Out, Tatler* and *Harpers & Queen*. Although Wilson regretted Meades's 'vituperative excesses' and the amount of column inches he devoted to damning wherever he had been let loose upon,[47] few could doubt that he was an acute critic of the choicest vintage and a writer of exceptional flair and originality. One pub in East Anglia erected a 'Shrine of Hatred' to Meades after a particularly excoriating review.

The Times was broadening its appeal but, given the improving quality of the competition, it had to do this merely to stand still. Wilson's choice as the editor of the Saturday features section, Richard Williams, decided that he preferred the look of the competition and departed for the newly launched (and short-lived) *Sunday Correspondent*. Wilson, who hated losing old comrades, tried to dissuade him and even got Murdoch to offer him a job at Sky, the satellite television company he had launched eight months earlier in February 1989. Williams declined. Indeed, Sky had been one of the contributing factors in Williams's decision to leave *The Times* after thirteen years writing for the paper. In June, after only two months in his post as arts editor, Tim de Lisle had resigned over what he considered the misuse of the arts pages to promote Sky. He had spent an agreeable Bank Holiday Monday afternoon watching a one-day match at Lord's only to discover on his return to Wapping that Mike Hoy had run an advertising puff for a competition across all eight columns of the top of the arts page. Tied in with Sky's forthcoming televising of a popular opera production of *Carmen*, the prize was a satellite dish. De Lisle attempted a damage-limitation operation, cutting down the size of the Sky logo and subsequently demoting down the page the *Carmen* review. This sparked a shouting match with – or rather from – Wilson. De Lisle defended his action by saying he was attempting to save the credibility of the paper. Wilson interpreted this to mean he had used non-objective criteria in laying out the content of his page. De Lisle removed himself to the *Telegraph* and eventually became editor of *Wisden*. It was *The Times*'s loss. Yet the matter was a particularly unfortunate one. News Corp.'s finances were being stretched to the limit by the purchase of what would become the Fox network in the United States as well as by the launch of Sky in Britain. As the economy turned downwards and banks began calling in their loans, it became increasingly possible that News Corp. might go bankrupt. Some journalists were outraged that Wilson appeared to be compromising the integrity of

The Times by providing Sky with what looked like free advertising. *The Times*'s NUJ chapel asked the board of independent directors to examine whether this constituted a breach of the 1981 undertakings Murdoch had made on preserving the paper's editorial independence. Approaches were also made to the Department of Trade and Industry, the Monopolies Commission and the Office of Fair Trading. The independent directors refused to investigate, on the grounds that they only had a remit to do so if the editor asked for it. The editor did not ask for it. One of the directors, the Earl of Drogheda, attempted to calm tempers with the explanation, 'the editor assures us there has been no such interference'. However, de Lisle's self-sacrifice was not in vain. *The Times* was subsequently much more careful about how it covered Sky.[48]

Those who left the chaos of the attempted *Daily* and *Sunday Telegraph* merger in 1989 were horrified by the atmosphere and low morale they encountered on arrival at the rum warehouse. Whenever there was breaking news, Wilson would become a galvanizing force, demonstrating his mastery of command. Journalists who came to him with personal problems were usually treated with sympathy and kindness.[49] But on a day-to-day basis, working successfully with the editor necessitated an imperviousness to jibes and cutting comments. He took to perpetually calling one reporter 'Fingertips' – on the grounds that these were all he was hanging onto his job with. His standard rebuttal to any suggestion or idea he did not like was 'the readers of *The Times* don't want to read about . . . [followed by whatever had been proposed]'. The readers of *The Times* and Charles Wilson appeared to have a lot in common. Problematically, many of the more traditional *Times* hacks believed that this relationship existed only in the editor's imagination. His habit of jabbing a finger at whomever he was addressing lacked insouciance. It was only after much experience that journalists realized his technique of invading their personal space during these dressing downs was only partly a form of intimidation; he was also attempting to discover if they had been drinking at lunchtime. It had certainly been a mistake in the early days of his editorship to inform the fashion editor, Suzy Menkes, that the actress Ali McGraw had an insufficient cleavage for the photographs lined up for the fashion page. This was not in the spirit of the journal of record. Indeed, women journalists particularly disliked his vernacular powers of expression. For a Scot, his use of the English language could be distinctly Anglo-Saxon.

Wilson's many private kindnesses, his vitality and drive, were being overlooked by those who had become tired of his brusque jocularity and his tendency to dismiss or ridicule ideas and propositions without appearing to weigh them properly first. His energy could also be a stimulant for those around him. While many previous editors could have waxed lyrical about what policies had to be enacted in some far-off part of the world they were easily thrown into confusion when confronted by a locked door. Wilson, however, was not the sort of man ineffectually to ask another member of staff if they could go and search somewhere for a key. When on one occasion he turned up for a meeting to find the conference room locked, he merely took a couple of steps back, sized up the narrow gap between the top of the wall and ceiling, leapt up and shinned over a ten-foot-high partition to get in and open the door from the inside. Those who missed this impressive display of their editor's athleticism were at least left to admire its legacy – a series of footprint dents going up the wall. In all his years editing from a rocking chair, William Rees-Mogg never left such an impression.

Wilson had hired some of the finest journalists on the paper, including Graham Paterson, a well-rounded and enthusiastic journalist brimming with ideas, and Mary Ann Sieghart, a young and energetic Op-Ed editor committed to dispelling the belief that the comment pages had fallen into the hands of a Margaret Thatcher support group. He was, however, hampered by the departure of Peter Stothard for Washington DC, in September 1989 when he took up the post of US editor. Stothard retained the somewhat honorary status as deputy editor of the paper, but his removal from Wapping was a handicap for Wilson. Although Murdoch only visited *The Times* five or six times a year, he was aware that there were rumblings of discontent. The two men would, however, speak once a week on the telephone. Wilson enjoyed these chats, which tended to be an opportunity to gossip about the national political scene rather than to map out the future of the paper. 'We had a good relationship' was how he later summed up his dealings with Murdoch, 'and I would have walked on hot coals for him because I admired him then and admire him now.'[50]

For his part, Murdoch considered Wilson 'a hardworking, brilliant, technical journalist like Harry [Evans] but much more decisive'.[51] He certainly owed Wilson a great deal as the lieutenant who had done so much to make the Wapping revolution possible and who had begged, cajoled and inspired *Times* journalists to be a part of it. Yet it was because so many of the older hands at *The Times* and in the industry at large regarded Wilson as one of Murdoch's lieutenants that they wanted a new editor who was seen to be utterly removed from the corporate identity of News International. Even Murdoch came to accept some of the criticisms, later commenting that

Wilson 'didn't have enough respect at the intellectual end of the paper. He was trying to recruit good people but couldn't get them – which was the test.'[52] If *The Times* had still been competing against its old rivals, the *Telegraph* and the *Guardian*, all might have been well. But it was Wilson's misfortune that the *Independent* had arrived and was offering journalists who did not like being shouted at in Glaswegian an alternative and highly respectable berth. During 1989, the financial fate of News International and its parent company, the News Corporation, hung in the balance. Rumours that it was about to collapse were rife. Clifford Longley, Mary Ann Sieghart and (prior to his departure) Richard Williams decided that Murdoch's problems were *The Times*'s opportunity. The three of them began holding private meetings, rather in the manner that Andreas Whittam Smith, Matthew Symonds and Stephen Glover had done in planning the *Independent* when they were still employed by the *Telegraph*. Longley had already talked the situation over with Sir Gordon Borrie, the director-general of the Office of Fair Trading. Together, Longley, Sieghart and Williams drew up proposals to buy *The Times* from News International with the intention of re-establishing it along the lines of the (profitable) business structure that had been adopted by the *Independent*. They approached John Nott, the chairman and chief executive of Lazard Brothers merchant bank, and took soundings from venture capitalists. The response was that the prospectus looked favourable, but it was dependent on Murdoch agreeing to sell. Bravely, Sieghart and Williams decided to go and see him. He listened carefully to their sales pitch, interjecting only with the occasional facial wince. Then he said 'no'. He would not sell. He did, however, ask what they thought was wrong with the paper and was given a fulsome account of its deficiencies compared to the *Independent* and the feeling that it was time for a new editor.[53] The points were noted.

Wilson's nemesis appeared shortly thereafter in the guise of Andrew Knight who Murdoch poached from the Telegraph Group as the new executive chairman of News International in March 1990. When Knight arrived for his first day at Wapping, Wilson telephoned his office at ten in the morning asking to speak to him. He wanted to welcome him and let him know how much he was looking forward to working with him. Knight's secretary said he was 'tied up' and would return Wilson's call when he was free. When he had heard nothing from his new chief executive by lunchtime, Wilson telephoned again and was met with the same reply. He tried again as soon as the afternoon conference was over. Again Knight was too busy to talk to the editor of his group's flagship title. At about 6.30 p.m. Wilson received a call, but it was from Murdoch's secretary. She informed him that he had flown into London and wanted to see him at his flat at 8.30 the following morning. 'I said "fine",' Wilson recalled, 'and I knew that my term was over.' That night he dined for the first time with Neil Kinnock. The bitterness and division of the Wapping dispute had prevented the Leader of the Opposition from being seen breaking bread with the editor of *The Times* for four years. Fittingly, the occasion, long in the planning, had been organized by Brenda Dean's husband. The dinner was à *deux*. The sons of miners got on extremely well, musing on how two men from the same background could have ended up with such different political views. Wilson said nothing about the great issue preying on his mind. It was, he rued, a 'lovely evening'.[54]

The next morning, Murdoch, looking somewhat embarrassed, told Wilson that Andrew Knight wanted a change – he wanted to make Simon Jenkins editor. What was more, Knight wanted Jenkins in Wilson's chair with immediate effect. Wilson was able to extend this to the end of the week, a minor dignity that was the least he was owed. Murdoch wanted to offer more. The fall of the Berlin Wall had opened up seemingly tremendous business opportunities in the former Eastern Europe. There were newspapers with huge circulations that were – it was reasonably assumed – ineptly run and in need of the Murdoch touch. He wanted to make Wilson his East European emissary, or 'International Director'. It appeared to be an intriguing opportunity but if it did not work out by the end of the year he assured Wilson that it would not harm his remaining three-year contract. Murdoch had a reputation for the presumptuous manner in which he sacked long-serving officers, but he also had a record for generosity and consideration in devising the financial terms of the divorce. Wilson stepped over and shook on it. He was back at Wapping in time for the morning conference where he announced he would be stepping aside and that the new editor was Simon Jenkins.

For Wilson, life after *The Times* took some unforeseen twists. It quickly became apparent that News Corp. was in mounting trouble and having difficulty rolling over its debts. One consequence was that fresh investment dried up. Wilson's mission to Eastern Europe increasingly resembled a posting to Siberia. He did not have the budget to make major acquisitions. Murdoch's mooted purchase of *Pravda* was out of the question. Wilson considered buying another Russian paper, *Argumenti i Fakti*, which had a 33.5 million circulation, the largest in the world. 'We could have bought it for peanuts,' he lamented, but the cash was not forthcoming even for that level of investment. When Robert Maxwell telephoned and offered him the editorship of the *Sporting Life*, allowing him to pursue his great love of the Turf, he accepted. Wilson began a new life as an executive in Mirror Group newspapers, becoming managing director in 1992. Some of his old *Times* colleagues raised their eyes to the heavens, murmuring that the appointment only showed what an inappropriate choice he had once been to guide the fortunes of *The Times*. Yet Maxwell was to provide a path back into the broadsheet press. In 1995, the *Independent* that had caused him so much anguish during his *Times* editorship appeared close to collapse, battered by a price war unleashed by Murdoch and ailing from the costs of subsidizing its unprofitable sister, the *Independent on Sunday*. Its new co-owner, the Mirror Group, appointed Wilson to spend six months as the *Independent*'s *de facto* editor with a remit to cut costs before passing onto the thirty-six-year-old Andrew Marr. Inevitably, some who had loved the *Independent* in its glorious early days saw Wilson as a terrible nemesis, brought in to wreak havoc upon his one-time tormentor.

Under Wilson, *The Times* had become less of an institution and more of a newspaper. Its future would have been far more precarious if its editor had pursued any other course. Wilson had Harold Evans's flair for breaking news – clearing the top half of the paper for a dramatic photograph of the space shuttle exploding even before the image was available, for example. Indeed, he was at his best when disasters struck. On these occasions he immediately assumed total mastery of the situation, deploying people to specific tasks with almost military self-assurance. It was typical of him to see things clearly in a crisis. This skill turned out to be an important asset, since his editorship coincided with some terrible disasters: in May 1987 the *Herald of Free Enterprise* sank off Zeebrugge drowning 188 and in December a Philippines ferry sank with 1500 on board, the twentieth-century's worst maritime disaster; the following year the Piper Alpha oil rig exploded killing 166, an Armenian earthquake killed 70,000 and two weeks later Pan Am flight 103, with 258 passengers on board, was blown up by a bomb over Lockerbie, killing a further eleven on the ground. Philip Howard regarded the moment Wilson unsentimentally jettisoned several pages of carefully prepared pre-Christmas quality writing in order to make way for fast and comprehensive coverage of the Lockerbie disaster to be the defining moment when the old *Times* – careful, judicious, slow to judge – died. The observation was not wholly intended as a criticism.[55] 'He was the very best kind of tabloid journalist,' commented Richard Williams, 'and when he was able to bring this to bear on the paper's news coverage it was just what *The Times* needed.'[56]

On the debit side, Wilson had driven away key intellectuals, losing some of the paper's weight in the process. The leader writers were no longer privately referred to as the college of cardinals. Wilson was not someone who conveyed an air of spiritual benediction. But he had brought to the paper new talents, like Matthew Parris and Mary Ann Sieghart, who soon came to be seen as essential. Yet, while some of the old guard may have taken offence, Wilson's dragging *The Times*, kicking and screaming, to places it had little natural inclination to go was not necessarily proof that he was a bad parent to the paper. 'Unless you broadened the audience of *The Times*,' he made clear, 'the paper was going to die.' He taught *The Times* to 'recognize that half of the people who walk round the cities of this country are women'.[57] Married to the magazine editor Sally O'Sullivan, he had a better sense of what women wanted and this was recognized in the way features developed during his editorship. Fashion was given a higher profile and news was not restricted to party political subject matter – which had preoccupied so much of the paper's column inches in the past. Like Harold Evans, he was criticized by those who believed *The Times* was, or ought to be, the home of the crafted essay rather than the ticker-tape machine for breaking news. Sir John Junor in the *Mail on Sunday* and Edward Pearce in the *Guardian* wrote articles defending him from what they saw as the snobbish sentiments of those who believed he had never been cut from *The Times* cloth. He had, they wrote, helped to make the paper more professional and freed it from the cult of deference. These were important achievements.

Much though Wilson had wanted to soldier on, his sacking came at an opportune moment. Although formalities had not been concluded, the Cold War had been won and with it the comment pages of *The Times* needed to adjust to a new era. Similarly, on the domestic front the Thatcher revolution in which Wilson had played his part was collapsing amid the rancour and ruin of the poll tax; the Prime Minister only had eight more bruising months left in Downing Street. At home and abroad, a more emollient style appeared to be required for the future. By contrast, Wilson appeared too closely identified with the decade of struggles – epitomized by the siege of Wapping – that had now drawn to a close. It was time for a change. What was more, he was leaving the paper at an opportune moment in other respects too. News Corp., its parent company, was plunging into a dire financial crisis. During 1990, it looked as if the whole empire might collapse. Cuts would be needed across the board. It was Simon Jenkins who would have to wield the axe.

CHAPTER NINE

SIMON JENKINS

Taking on the *Independent*; Thatcher to Major; War in the Gulf;
News Corp. on the Brink; Redesigning *The Times*;
the Jenkins Experiment Cut Short

I

'The chattering classes will love it' was Murdoch's verdict on his choice of Simon Jenkins as the new editor of *The Times*.[1] This was not meant as a barbed observation. The excesses of the tabloid press – and not least of the *Sun* – had alienated sections of the public and the Government. There was even the prospect of legislation to tighten the fetters on press freedom. To this possibility, Murdoch was vehemently opposed and his appointment of the urbane and Establishment-minded Andrew Knight as News International's executive chairman reflected a desire to emphasize the company's commitment to quality journalism. Knight had been editor of *The Economist* between 1974 and 1986. For the last seven of those years, Jenkins had been the journal's political editor and Knight had formed a high opinion of his skills.

Many senior journalists would have made strenuous efforts to publicize their suitability to edit *The Times*, but Murdoch and Knight were drawn to Simon Jenkins precisely because of his ambivalence towards the paper. This was not because of any unworldliness or lack of drive. Born in 1943, the son of a Welsh Congregationalist minister, the Revd Daniel Jenkins, who was one of the most acclaimed nonconformist theologians of the twentieth century, Simon Jenkins had graduated from St John's College, Oxford, with ambitions to be either a politician or an academic. Journalism, he decided, was the best way of being both. After spells at the *Times Educational Supplement*, the *Evening Standard* and the *Sunday Times*, he became editor of the *Evening Standard* in 1976. Thirty-three was a precocious age to take the helm of a paper that was battling against a hostile takeover from its London rival, the *Evening News*. Jenkins saw off the predator and, in large part, saved the *Standard*'s existence. His reward was to be sacked by the paper's new owners, Trafalgar House. By comparison, *The Economist* proved an agreeably monastic environment but in 1986 he swapped it for the besieged stockade of Wapping, joining the *Sunday Times* as a columnist and as creator and editor of its relaunched books section. In late 1989 he decided to quit in order to become a columnist for the *Independent* instead. It was the decision that was to make him *The Times's* editor. When Murdoch heard the news that Jenkins had been poached by the *Independent* he asked him to call round for a chat. To Murdoch's questioning as to why he wanted to leave the News International stable, Jenkins replied that he thought the *Independent* was a paper that was making great strides forward and the one he most admired. Murdoch asked what was wrong with *The Times*. Jenkins was unsparing in his analysis. The fault, he claimed, was not with Charles Wilson but rather with the strategy Murdoch had set out for him – which was to go after the *Daily Telegraph*'s market. This had been a mistake and, given that circulation was gently sliding, it was not even commercially sensible. The only future for *The Times* was to be like itself, or rather, its former self. This had become more difficult because, while it had been busy focusing on the *Telegraph*, it had left itself open to attack on its flank from Whittam Smith's new paper. Disastrously, the *Independent* was now claiming all the traditional *Times* territory and was increasingly taking its readers too. The *Independent*, therefore, was the paper for which Jenkins wished to be a columnist. Murdoch was not unreceptive to the points being made, even though they represented a critical judgment on his long-standing strategy to target the *Telegraph*'s market. The *Independent* had indeed seized the opportunity to occupy some of *The Times*'s ground. Partly this had been a by-product of the legacy of Wapping – which made starting new newspapers like the *Independent* a much less expensive proposition while simultaneously dumping public opprobrium on Murdoch whose image, in return for making this revolution possible, was now associated with violence, mass sackings and callous Thatcherite zeal. Clearly, he was not going to persuade Jenkins to jilt the firm offer of a column in the *Independent* for one in *The Times*, so he decided on an altogether higher pitch. He suggested Jenkins turn *The Times* into the sort of paper for which he would want to write a column – by becoming its editor. It was a rare journalist who was offered an editorship on such complimentary terms. Nonetheless, Jenkins made clear he would only accept on the condition that Murdoch left him alone to do it his way even if, in the short term, circulation continued to slide. He demanded absolute *carte blanche*. 'Give me two years,' Jenkins requested. Murdoch consented and the deal was done. That evening, Jenkins returned home to talk matters over with his wife, the Texan-born actress Gayle Hunnicutt. He explained the hard task that lay ahead and the conditions upon which he had agreed to work. 'After three years that will be it,' Jenkins assured her, 'because after three years it's either the paper I want to write a column for, in which case I want to write a column for it, or I will have failed.'[2]

II

Few editorial appointments could have been greeted with greater pleasure from journalists, even those writing their tributes in rival newspapers. Almost all agreed that Simon Jenkins was the man to restore *The Times*'s authority. The news crossed the Atlantic. The writer Julian Barnes assured readers of the *New Yorker* that Jenkins's appointment was an appropriate metaphor: 'He first made his name in the early Seventies as a journalist campaigning to save bits of London from the property developers, and helped found an organisation called Save Britain's Heritage. Now he has been handed the biggest heritage-saving job of his career.'[3]

Jenkins was a son of the cloth. His love of ecclesiastical architecture (he was subsequently the author of *England's Thousand Best Churches* which became a bestseller in 1999) was matched by an interest in making *The Times* once again the paper of choice, from the bishop's palace to the provincial vicarage. He considered Whittam Smith to be an editor exuding 'Episcopalian' rectitude. Yet, the problem was not confined even to the Established religion. 'It was significant to me,' he later recalled, 'that the Cardinal Archbishop of Westminster, Basil Hume, had told all his people that henceforth he would write letters to the *Independent* not *The Times* if he wanted to communicate something.' Jenkins set himself a mission to reconvert such backsliders. Recommunicating with the more godless opinion formers was equally pressing. 'I hadn't realised quite how much *The Times* was hated,' he confessed. 'The way the BBC treated the Murdoch press at that time was simply outrageous.' This was not paranoia. The BBC had all but ceased citing *The Times* on round-ups of the morning's papers and *Times* staff were rarely invited onto any programme. This was not a verdict on them or their writing, as Jenkins discovered whenever he complained and received a long and politically tendentious monologue about 'the Murdoch press' in response.[4] The BBC, it seemed, was still implementing the siege of Wapping 'boycott' a full four years after the print unions had abandoned it.

The two main types of reader Jenkins wanted to attract back to *The Times* were those he considered core not only to its circulation but also to its soul. The first was 'the London administrative Establishment'. This group read the paper more for the valuable information it contained than for any particular pleasure. The second group were readers who were generally right of centre in their political views but who were not employed by Government institutions. They nonetheless considered themselves more literary, metropolitan and cosmopolitan than those who subscribed to the *Telegraph*. Attracting them back, without losing readers who liked Wilson's more news-orientated paper, would determine whether circulation held up. This matter could not be disregarded in the headlong race to appeal to a relatively small elite. There were only twenty thousand sales separating the *Independent*, *The Times* and the *Guardian*. The latter was two thousand sales a day ahead of *The Times* while the *Independent* was hard on *The Times*'s heels. Becoming the fourth best-read broadsheet in Britain (with a consequent fall-off in advertising rates) was not an accolade Jenkins wanted to win for his new paper, but unless he could provide dramatic results there was every likelihood that this would be its fate. On his arrival at Wapping, Jenkins summoned his staff onto the news floor and explained to them where he was seeking to position the paper. His speech was short on complacency. Certainly there was a threat on news coverage from the *Telegraph* and on arts and opinion in the *Guardian*. 'But,' he maintained, 'there is only one paper which, five years ago, put its tanks on our lawn and that is the *Independent* . . . the *Independent* is our prime target.' *The Times* would respond by going back upmarket. An impulsive cheer rang out along the length of the building.

The new editor had very clear ideas about what 'going upmarket' involved. It meant less sensationalism. This would involve reducing the size and temper of the headlines as well as writing that was phrased in a more considered and overtly objective style. It would mean fewer but longer articles rather than journalists' copy being hacked into bite-sized morsels. The latter had become all to prevalent over the previous years and was exemplified when David Watts, the paper's Tokyo correspondent, was asked to file two hundred words on the subject of one-hour 'love hotels', a cultural phenomenon related to Japanese society's absence of privacy that demanded the sort of long, reflective 1500-word examination for which space had rarely been forthcoming.[5] Jenkins was particularly concerned by what he considered the deteriorating standard of English in the paper. *The Times* had once been held up to schoolchildren as a model for grammatical correctness. This tradition had ceased due to what the new editor put down to simple sloppiness. He told his staff that he demanded writing that 'will lift the hearts of readers . . . we can more or less correct bad writing; we can edit it down. We cannot correct bad [sub]editing and we have got to pay particular attention to the presentation of writing in the paper. There simply must be no excuse for misprints, misspellings, stylistic errors, solecisms in *The Times*.'[6]

This, indeed, was to be the launch of a crusade that in the months ahead was to do more to cause ructions between editor and staff than possibly any other decision from the chair. Jenkins's announcement that it would be a disciplinary offence for any journalist – sub or otherwise – to let a major error pass into print was to cause much discontent and even fear. Some felt that the editor's definition of a major error included many examples that justified a groan and a quick verbal rebuke rather than a formal written warning. Slang or casual sentence construction was regarded as well within the danger zone. When Jenkins asked Clifford Longley to send a formal warning to whoever wrote 'disintering' in an article he had just spotted four months after the event, Longley wrote back pointing out that the author was none other than Simon Jenkins, adding, somewhat cheekily, 'in the circumstances I see no point in asking you to regard this memo as a rebuke, despite your instruction'.[7] The threat of disciplinary action against anyone responsible for an error was particularly poor for morale on the backbench and on the subs' tables generally. Jenkins did not especially care if this made him unpopular, seeing it as his duty to save the paper's reputation rather than to win the bonhomie of his subs. Yet, what the reader gained in better and more accurately written prose was sometimes lost on occasions when so much time was spent scanning for mistakes that deadlines for the foreign, Scottish and West Country editions were missed.

Updating the in-house 'style guide' was central to ensuring higher standards were met. Jenkins formed a doctrinal conclave of Philip Howard and Bernard Levin to rule on matters of truth and error. However, frequent log jam between the two – who had different ideas about questions of linguistic discipline – ensured that Jenkins ended up making a lot of the judgments himself at a time when he was already extremely busy on the other daily aspects of the paper. The result was a huge improvement on the old greying handbooks of the 1970s that it superseded. Not only did it lay down good basic ground rules for how journalists should write, it included quirky details and elegant forms of writing. Ultimately, though, its idiosyncrasies proved too great and it was comprehensively rewritten by Tim Austin as soon as Jenkins ceased to be editor. It was, at least, a start. While some resented the lengths to which he went, there could be no doubt that the new editor was right to prioritize an area whose failings had caused disproportionate offence to the paper's core highly educated readership and left the impression that *The Times* was indifferent to proper standards and questions of accuracy. True to his word on headline and design sensationalism, Jenkins's eye for linguistic detail was also matched by his visual awareness. In this, he was an editor in the tradition of Harold Evans. He immediately asked David Driver to redesign the paper to make it look more sober and elegant. Its more populist lapses were de-sensationalized. Headlines were reduced in size. Bylines were put in capitals (supposedly giving the named writers greater authority). To anyone of visual sensitivity, the result was a great improvement. The paper once again looked more authoritative then its competition.

Unlike his two predecessors who were internal appointments, Jenkins arrived at *The Times* as its editor. The question thus arose as to how many other outsiders he would bring with him. First of all, he brought in a new managing editor, Peter Roberts. In retrospect, Jenkins believed, 'Without any shadow of doubt, this was the critical appointment I made.' Roberts, who had fulfilled the same role at the *Sunday Times* for the previous twelve years, was by experience and temperament well suited for the job. The position of managing editor was never an easy one since it involved attempting to please the proprietor by finding economies and the editor by providing him with the resources to create the paper he wanted. Roberts was adept at this balancing act, particularly during what would prove in 1990 to be one of the great financial crises to hit the company. 'He took a huge burden off my shoulders,' Jenkins believed, and thereby allowed him the time and space to devote his attentions more fully to editing the paper.[8]

One reliable assistant Jenkins was sorry to lose was the deputy editor he inherited from Wilson: John Bryant went off to edit the troubled *Sunday Correspondent* and, after it folded, the *European*. Jenkins found himself relying heavily on Michael Hamlyn as night editor and brought in David Lipsey who had been a member of James Callaghan's Downing Street staff and subsequently editor of *New Society*. Where Jenkins was particularly active in hiring was in the field of 'specialist' writers. He believed that this was an area that had been badly hit in the aftermath of the move to Wapping and needed reinforcing. Those who remained had been the bedrock of *The Times*'s continued claims to incisiveness – Frances Gibbs who had been legal correspondent since 1982, Richard Ford, a political Correspondent who was moved to home affairs, and Stewart Tendler, who had built up an extensive range of police contacts and informants since becoming crime correspondent in 1978. Jenkins recognized the need to appoint more writers with this level of expertise. To write on science, he hired Nigel Hawkes from the *Observer*. From the BBC came Philip Bassett to write on industrial matters. In October 1990 came the greatest coup of all, when Anatole Kaletsky was hired from the *FT* to write about economics. The most significant fusion of new blood came to the arts pages, however. Marcus Binney was appointed architectural correspondent with a remit to write – initially on Saturdays – about the built heritage, a subject close to Jenkins's heart (Binney was the founder of Save Britain's Heritage) and to many of the paper's readers too. Despite Richard Morrison's relative youth, Jenkins was impressed by his enthusiasm and obvious commitment to improving the coverage. Morrison became arts editor. Within six months, many of the critics were replaced. Benedict Nightingale became chief theatre critic, Richard Cork took over reviewing the visual arts, and later, in 1992, Rodney Milnes was hired as one of the country's foremost authorities on opera. In a crucial area in which the *Independent* had been making gains, these experts began to turn the tide in *The Times*'s favour.

It was not just a question of personnel. Jenkins immediately axed 'Spectrum' the daily features page. He sought, instead, to develop specialist sections of the paper. With Wapping's new presses ready to roll offering added capacity and (sparing) use of colour, advertising-linked supplements for higher education, law, the media, science and technology could be produced. Wilson had increased the amount of material in the paper but – except on Saturdays – had not radically altered the basic structure in which it was presented. With the outsider's eye, Jenkins's approach was to redesign the paper afresh and he was lucky that he arrived just as the technology to realize his vision was being installed.

The other broadsheets had brought out colour magazines on Saturdays. Jenkins believed *The Times*'s failure to follow suit was retarding its growth on the biggest sales day. In June, *Saturday Review* magazine was added with Andrew Harvey as its editor. Although not a 'glossy', it was an attractive colour-printed tabloid that was elegantly designed and featured well-crafted essays. Its upmarket pitch was evident from the first issue's front cover, a work by Piero della Francesca – 'a signature as far as I was concerned,' Jenkins confessed.[9] Within two months, it had helped add twenty thousand new readers at the weekend. A brief foray with a weekend magazine for children, *Prime Time*, made a hopeful start – almost ten thousand young readers responded to its competitions and offers in its first two weeks alone. Unfortunately, it lasted only twelve issues before falling victim to cost cutting in time for Christmas 1990. Yet, the financial squeeze placed on the company in the midst of the economic recession did not retard the drive for other new supplements. In September 1991, the Saturday offering was again improved when *Weekend Times* was launched. With fashion moved into *Saturday Review* and with arts, health and media all getting specialist attention, what remained of general features needed to be reconsidered. Brigid Callaghan came up with a new title *Life and Times* that focused on people in both the wider and narrow sense – from interviews with the famous or noteworthy to lifestyle features, changes in society and choices in the high street. This new section was duly launched in February 1992.

Under Charles Wilson, *The Times* had identified itself closely – some felt too closely – with the Thatcherite cause. Jenkins found disquiet among the leader writers and this was brought to a head within a fortnight of his arrival when one of them, David Walker, penned an article in the *Listener* criticizing the right-wing stance. Walker believed that '*The Times*, with its rhetoric about reforming the very institutions (the law, universities, professions) on which its own idea of authority in culture and society depends, is left incoherent.'[10] It had, effectively, been criticizing the traditional constituencies that Jenkins wanted to wrestle back from the embrace of the *Independent*. This may have been in line with some of the new editor's thinking but Walker won no plaudits for washing the paper's political laundry in public. Jenkins abruptly sacked him for disloyalty. Yet how far he would move towards the Walker worldview and shift the paper's political opinions back towards the centre ground became one of the first tests of his editorship.

Mrs Thatcher's mounting unpopularity certainly made the conditions auspicious for a repositioning, but the new editor's attempts to be seen as master in his own house and not the placeman of Rupert Murdoch also suggested there would be a change in tone. There would, however, be no return to the 'on the one hand . . . and on the other hand' tradition. Jenkins deplored the sort of leaders that 'open with a paragraph of abstract waffle as the writer clears his throat, and ends with a similar paragraph of vague bromide'. Leaders, he felt, should state their intentions from the first and repeat them at the end. He was, however, against the forth estate getting above itself. 'Exhortatory constructions tend to read naively,' he told his fellow leader writers; 'try not to use ought, should and must, especially when referring to authority or government.'[11] The Op-Ed editor, Mary Ann Sieghart, provided him with her assessment of which journalists could provide the best comment copy. Clifford Longley was head of her (surprisingly short) list.[12] Jenkins also thought highly of the religious affairs correspondent and father of the paper's NUJ chapel: Longley became one of his college of cardinals formulating leader writer policy. Joining him was another devout Roman Catholic (although facing more towards the political right), Daniel Johnson. The son of the multi-faceted historian Paul Johnson, he was a specialist in German history and culture (he had a First in History from Magdalen College, Oxford, before crossing the Fens to Peterhouse, later co-editing *German Neo-Liberals and the Social Market Economy*) and had worked at the Centre for Policy Studies before joining the *Daily Telegraph* in 1986, becoming its Bonn and Eastern Europe correspondents. It was a strong team, but none doubted that Jenkins was an editor who would also want to write his own leading articles.

Jenkins declared that he saw *The Times* 'as an independent Conservative paper, which makes up its own mind on policy issues and is open for everyone to put a point of view'.[13] In economic matters Jenkins declared himself an 'enthusiastic Thatcherite'. In social matters he was less supportive while on education policy he considered himself 'quite left wing'. Generally, though, he wanted to edit 'a sceptical Tory paper'.[14] Certainly, there was a pressing piece of legislation ready to receive a sceptical analysis. Laid before Parliament in December 1987, the poll tax bill was due to be implemented in England and Wales on April Fool's Day 1990 – just two weeks after Jenkins had first sat down in the editor's chair. The line he took on the tax would be a marker for how slavishly he would follow the Conservative Government even in its most contentious legislation. It also happened to be fundamental to an issue Jenkins cared passionately about – the reinvigoration of the local government of Britain.

III

The centralization of local government provision had deep roots. Poor relief had passed to central government in the 1920s. Government policy directed the council housing boom of the 1950s and 1960s. The denouement came in the early 1980s when the free-spending ways of left-wing councils underlined their defiance of Thatcherite orthodoxy and forced up local rates to punitive levels, driving professionals and capital out of boroughs that were already deprived. The Government reacted by abolishing local government's setting of supplementary rates in 1982 and introduced rate capping in 1984. The following year, Liverpool City Council had simultaneously demonstrated the irresponsibility of the loony left and the futility of the Government's rate-capping strategy by failing to set a budget. When there was no more money to pay council employees, taxis were hired to deliver thirty thousand redundancy notices, safe in the knowledge that central government would have to foot the bill. Such antics emboldened Neil Kinnock to confront the Militant Tendency within the Labour Party and made the Government equally determined to reduce local government power further, holding town halls directly accountable for the revenue spending that remained within their remit. This was the path that led to the poll tax.

The Government's local government strategy was twofold. Firstly, it was to devolve many of its competences to other bodies. Secondly, it was to make it more responsible towards those who paid for what provisions were left in its gift. At the end of March 1986, the Government dismantled the Greater London Council and England's Metropolitan councils. *The Times* was certainly not sorry to see London's executive functions levered out of the grip of Ken Livingstone, but nor was it enthusiastic that the right policy had been pursued, believing that the GLC's 'deliberative and oversight capacities' should have been retained.[15] Yet, while the GLC's abolition attracted the most attention a far larger revolution was underway. The fate of the inner cities and whether their decline was the fault of central or local government was one of the tests of political opinion in the 1980s. In the 1987 general election Mrs Thatcher had declared it her mission to deal with the problem rather in the way that Gladstone had once put down his tree-cutting hatchet to pronounce that it was his mission to pacify Ireland. Yet, the regeneration – of which London's Docklands was but the most shining example – was achieved not by re-empowering local democracy but by emasculating it further. Regeneration was entrusted to urban development quangoes (quasi-autonomous government organizations) that cut through layers of town hall bureaucracy and better understood how to attract investment. By the 1990s, unelected local quangoes were responsible for spending more money than elected local government. There was an obvious democratic deficit in this state of affairs.

The deficit that the Government chose to address, however, was that affecting the elected branch of local government. While thirty-six million Britons were eligible to vote in local elections, only eighteen million paid local rates and only twelve million paid the property-graded tax in full. The all too apparent consequence had been reckless spending by Labour-controlled councils which, in *The Times*'s opinion, suffered no consequences themselves 'since the majority of their political supporters, paying little or no rates, have no incentive to call them to account'.[16] Rate capping had attempted to prune the worst offenders, but it only encouraged some councils to deliberately set high budgets knowing that any cut could then be blamed on Mrs Thatcher's bean counters. The answer, or so it seemed to her Environment Secretary, Nicholas Ridley, was a poll tax. When the plans were unveiled in December 1987 the poll tax (to be called 'a community charge', although few bothered with the official term) envisaged making almost everyone on the electoral roll pay it. This was far more than the alternative, a local income tax, would have brought into the tax net. For Ridley, this was part of its appeal – it spread responsibility and minimized the poverty trap problem created by high marginal rates for those just within each band. Thus, rather than creating more bands – as even many Tories demanded – the Government preferred a system of rebates for those on low incomes. Even students, pensioners and those of social security would be expected to pay 20 per cent of the poll tax. Whatever effect this would have on reconnecting local government to its community, the more immediate political effect was ably expressed in *The Times* headline 'Ridley unveils poll tax bill to Tory fears'.[17]

Under Charles Wilson *The Times* had sympathized with the poll tax's intention but had worried about its feasibility. Rates had at least had the advantage of being a tax on property that was easy to collect. By comparison, tracking down defaulters that would include students and other peripatetic lodgers would prove a bureaucratic nightmare. The paper had accurately predicted that some might try and dodge payment by removing themselves from the electoral roll, thereby creating a disenfranchised underclass.[18] Yet the true position of *The Times* was one of equivocation.

The new system would be 'at least no more unfair than the old rating system' was hardly a ringing endorsement but nor was it a thundering denunciation.[19] A test run was provided in Scotland, where the poll tax was introduced a year before England. The result was a massive display of discontent and even disobedience. Partly, this was a reflection of the belief among Scots that they were being used as guinea pigs although the truth was rather that they were the tail wagging the dog. It had been Scotland's imminent rates revaluation (which statutorily had to take place every five years there) that had panicked ministers into bringing forward the poll tax proposals. Given the soaring property prices throughout the United Kingdom, it had been assumed in 1987 that a revaluation in England and Wales would have massively increased the amounts property owners had to pay under the old rating system.

In fact, the poll tax was introduced on faulty premises and bad forecasting. It particularly hit Mrs Thatcher's natural constituency – the lower middle class who would pay the same as the wealthy without the rebates offered to those on low income or benefit. It was introduced at a time when the recession was commencing and the middle class belief that the increasing price of property gave them security was just starting to come unstuck. Furthermore, the Government had underestimated how much the effect of higher spending councils would push up the poll tax, ensuring that introduction of charge capping that undermined the local accountability argument that had recommended the new tax in the first place. Higher local taxes were blamed on the Government, not the councils whose alleged profligacy they supposedly reflected. The tax had, in any case, only further weakened the link between the sums town halls raised and spent. Eighty per cent of local government spending was now provided by central government using a uniform distribution formula.

On 31 March, the day before the tax was due to be introduced in England and Wales, a large demonstration organized by the All-Britain Anti-Poll Tax Federation ended in a riot in Trafalgar Square. There were more than three hundred arrests. Nearly four hundred policemen were injured amid fights and fires in the heart of London. The violence was condemned by all responsible groups, but the sense that the poll tax was contributing to a fragmentation of society was widespread. Following on from Brixton, Toxteth, the miners' strike and Wapping, the protest-turned-riot had become one of the abiding images of Thatcher's Britain alongside HMS *Invincible* returning from the South Atlantic, yuppie businessmen in red braces and estate agents' 'For Sale' signs. It provided the occasion for *The*

Times to come firmly off the fence and condemn the poll tax without equivocation:

> So long as the tax remains in place, expediency will require the Treasury, and therefore national taxpayers to bear an ever greater share of local spending, as ministers hurl money at a lengthening line of losers. Since, in the early years of this Government, more local spending was rightly being pushed on to local rates, this reverse move is a real loss to local accountability, and makes a mockery of the prime motive for the charge . . . a brave, but possibly wise, Government might now admit that it had made a mistake and reintroduce rates as from 1991.[20]

Running concomitantly with the poll tax fiasco was the slide in support for the Conservative Party. Nine days before the Trafalgar Square riot, Labour had overturned a 14,700 Tory majority in a by-election in Mid-Staffordshire. The Prime Minister no longer looked impregnable. She was buffeted not only by the poll tax anger and the worsening economic climate but also by discontent among some of her most senior colleagues over her growing Euro-scepticism. The obvious challenger remained in the shape of Michael Heseltine who had languished with ill-concealed impatience on the backbenches since the Westland crisis, the continuing focus for Tory Jacobite hopes and plots. Two days after Jenkins had become editor, *The Times* had run a leading article advising Heseltine to 'put up or shut up'.[21] Yet, at that stage, the considered opinion was that Mrs Thatcher would survive a direct challenge. In April, the acclaimed biographer and Conservative Party historian Lord Blake wrote on the Op-Ed page an examination of the historical record of Thatcher's predecessors and concluded it was highly unlikely that a Conservative leader would be deposed while still in office. 'It will be surprising if any serious potential successor puts his name down as an opponent of Mrs Thatcher in a party election in the autumn,' he prophesied, before adding, 'an attempt to overthrow her would do the party far more harm than any which she can do by remaining . . . When Disraeli overthrew Peel, he doomed his party to 28 years of impotence'.[22]

In the months that followed, however, the Prime Minister appeared increasingly isolated. She had already lost Alan Walters, the last senior figure able to put up intelligent arguments against the Treasury's zeal to lock sterling into the Exchange Rate Mechanism of the European Monetary System. In July, Nicholas Ridley, one of the few Cabinet ministers who had been genuinely enthusiastic about the poll tax, resigned after the *Spectator* published anti-German comments he had made to the magazine's editor, Dominic Lawson, in connection with ceding power to a European central bank. In October, the cause of monetary union was boosted and the diminishing power of the Prime Minister over her Cabinet colleagues laid bare when John Major, the Chancellor, locked sterling into the ERM. Britain, once again, had incarcerated its currency into a house of correction that restricted its ability to float freely. Whenever it looked like sliding below its allotted fixed band (which was set at a 6 per cent margin around one pound equalling 2.95 Deutschmarks) the Treasury was committed to intervening to keep its value up. Major was determined to use a high exchange rate as his tool to fight inflation which, approaching 11 per cent, was back where it had been when Mrs Thatcher had first taken office in 1979. The announcement of ERM membership was accompanied by an entirely political (and consequently ephemeral) interest rate cut to 14 per cent.

The Times did not condemn Major's decision outright, but its tone was decidedly sniffy. Certainly there were arguments for joining the ERM: it would smooth out the currency volatility that affected the half of Britain's manufactured goods exported to the other ERM member states across the English Channel and would act as an anti-inflationary 'discipline'. But the leading column doubted the wisdom of this 'one-club' approach to economic management. 'The German Bundesbank has, in effect, been asked to take the lead role in British monetary policy' the paper noted with the same analysis – but not the xenophobic rhetoric – that had ended Ridley's Cabinet career.[23] It would shortly become apparent that in wrestling with the huge costs of reunification, the German Bundesbank had more pressing concerns than caring about what was good for British interests. In the meantime, Britain could brace itself for worse unemployment. By 15 November, the jobless total had gone back up to 1.7 million and showed no signs of levelling off.

Whether joining the ERM would defeat inflation remained to be seen. The policy had the enthusiastic endorsement of the Bank of England, the CBI, the TUC, the Labour Party, the Liberal Democrats and the *Financial Times*. Some of these supporters appeared to be motivated not just by economic analysis but also by the recognition that joining represented a move towards Britain's engagement with the European Community and no less excitingly a slap in the face to Margaret Thatcher. Major had ridden roughshod over the Prime Minister's proviso that ERM membership could not take place until there was inflation rate convergence in his desperate search for a quick fix solution to Britain's mounting problems. Britain's inflation rate was double the European average. These shortcomings became obvious to critics as the months passed, but *The Times*'s initial assessment that the manner in which Britain was taken into the ERM demonstrated that 'politics has triumphed over economics' and that the timing 'could hardly be less propitious for much of British industry' stood against the grain of received opinion at the time.[24] The *Financial Times*'s analysis that 'both politically and economically, entry is shrewdly timed' did not say much for its judgment in either matter. Its stable mate, *The Economist*, fell into the same category. But it was not alone as opinion writers across the broadsheet spectrum endorsed the move. The relief was expressed with even greater adulation in the mid-market press. The *Daily Mail* was beside itself with joy. Murdoch's *Today* was delighted by the 'historic' move.[25]

On Fleet Street the most prescient writer proved to be Anatole Kaletsky. While the City traders trundled into work on Monday 8 October for the first day of ERM membership, Kaletsky forecast not the 'golden scenario' almost universally being attributed to the move but, rather, a testing time ahead. 'Like every country that chooses to pamper its consumers with an overvalued exchange rate (a policy that Germany and Japan have always tried to eschew) Britain will eventually have to pay a hefty price for deindustrialisation,' he warned. The notion that ERM membership would bring lower interest rates was wishful thinking: 'If international investors begin to catch a whiff of devaluation, either before or soon after a general election, then the supposed support for sterling provided by the ERM rules could turn into a political burden ... Sterling may jump to the top of its target band this morning, as virtually everyone seems to be expecting. But how long it stays there is another matter.'[26]

Acronym-adept pro-Europeans hoped that Britain's entry into the ERM meant the economy was finally being attuned to the prospect of EMU. When the prospect was pushed onto the agenda at a summit of European leaders in Rome at the end of October, Mrs Thatcher made it clear that monetary union would come, in effect, over her dead body. For those tired of her hectoring style, this was not so much a threat as an incitement. It was Sir Geoffrey Howe who decided to wield the knife. His resignation from the Cabinet plunged the Government back into crisis.

Treated dismissively by a Prime Minister who had shunted him from the Foreign Office to the ill-defined post of Deputy Prime Minister, Howe's resignation looked all too predictable in hindsight. Yet this made it no less destructive. He had been the last remaining member of Mrs Thatcher's first Cabinet in 1979. All others had passed by the wayside. Indeed, as *The Times* pointed out, his long-standing commitment to monetarism made him, in some respects, a Thatcherite before Thatcher. However, if he was attempting to instigate a successful challenge to her leadership, the paper believed he would fail. 'The next generation of Tory leaders are certainly in waiting, but they are waiting within the cabinet, not outside it.' The cause of European union was, it reasoned, a poor one to choose. 'Undoubtedly the Europe issue is dividing the party,' the leading column conceded, 'but it is not another tariff reform, nor another appeasement. The debate is over degrees of sovereignty, subsidiarity, even just the mood music of European cooperation.'[27] This was a misjudgment. Like tariff reform and appeasement in the past, it would indeed become the most divisive issue in Tory politics during the 1990s. *The Times*'s failure to perceive the extent of the ideological disagreement led it to discount the danger in which the Prime Minister was about to find herself. This complacency was shattered a fortnight later when Howe delivered his resignation speech in the House of Commons. The front page headline, 'Howe attack leaves MPs gasping', summed up the atmosphere in the chamber and, in a reference to the old claim that an attack by Sir Geoffrey was like being savaged by a dead sheep, Mel Calman provided a pocket cartoon of a fat sheep with the remains of the Iron Lady's legs dangling from its jaws with the simple caption, 'Howe's that?'[28] Within hours, Michael Heseltine announced he would challenge for the leadership.

The next morning, *The Times* carried an interview by Robin Oakely in which the challenger laid out his stall. He was, he boasted, far more of an electoral asset than the existing Prime Minister. Furthermore, he would reform (and presumably abolish) the poll tax and engage positively on Europe (code for sign up to the single currency) so that the City of London did not lose out from EMU. The following day a *Times*/MORI opinion poll appeared to support the first of his claims. It suggested that with Heseltine in Downing Street the Tories would gain a ten-point lead over Labour in the polls. For Tory MPs, anxious at how the poll tax was making their seats dangerously marginal, Heseltine appeared to offer a lifeline.

Ever since Simon Jenkins had assumed the editorship, his paper had been advising Heseltine to get on with his clear desire to stand against the Prime Minister and settle the matter once and for all. On 12 November, the day before Howe's speech, the leading column had teased the potential challenger further by ending, 'If Mr Heseltine fails to throw his cap into the ring, he will thoroughly deserve to have it stuffed down his throat.'[29] Having helped to goad him into a position where Howe's resignation would have made his silence look like cowardice,[30] *The Times* prepared to let him down with an almighty thud. Three days before the first ballot of the 372 Tory MPs, the paper ran an anonymous profile of Heseltine in which he was portrayed as ambitious to a degree unusual even among driven politicians. It suggested that he would have no more of a collective approach to Cabinet government than had Mrs Thatcher. The picture painted was certainly not personally attractive and read, in parts, like a professional hatchet job.[31] Instead, *The Times* rallied to the Prime Minister's tattered standard. The leading article, entitled 'The Case for Thatcher', was written by Simon Jenkins. She was in the fourth year of her third administration and, 'unlike those previously accused of splitting the party, such as Peel or Joseph Chamberlain, she has not radically departed from her last election mandate'. Ousting her, the editorial said, 'would rank even higher in the catalogue of political ingratitude than Churchill's 1945 election defeat, for Churchill was rejected by his opponents, not his erstwhile supporters'. It concluded that so long as Mrs Thatcher made it clear she would henceforth rule through a triumvirate with John Major and Douglas Hurd, 'she can still win the Tories an election. She does not deserve decapitation tonight.'[32]

Did *The Times*'s appeal for loyalty to the leader rally any wavers? Certainly, it did not persuade enough of them. Far less persuasive was the manner of the Prime Minister's election campaign. She spent the last three days of it in Paris for the OSCE summit that effectively ended the Cold War. Although she emerged from the ballot with 204 votes to Heseltine's 152, under the rules the margin was four short of an outright victory. There would have to be a second ballot. From the steps of the British Embassy in Paris, she strode into the glare of the arc lamps to announce she would fight on. But in Westminster, colleagues were already plotting her downfall and Robin Oakley's report described her future as 'in grave doubt'.[33]

The Times's first inclination was to hope that Heseltine would 'honourably stand down'. Since he would not, Mrs Thatcher should face the second ballot. After all, with Douglas Hurd and John Major having intimated that they would not stand against her, she would have a straight fight against Heseltine and had already beaten him once.[34] As the hours passed, so the news from the lobby forced Jenkins and his leader writers to reconsider their advice. The so-called 'men in grey suits' were ganging up on *La Dame de Fer.* News arrived that two-thirds of the Cabinet had allegedly told her it was time to go and panic was spreading that Heseltine might actually win the second ballot. To see this prospect off, *The Times* came up with a new proposal: Mrs Thatcher should stand again but should also release Hurd and Major from their loyalty pledges so that they too could stand. 'The entry of other candidates,' the paper reasoned, 'would almost certainly prevent Mr Heseltine from getting the necessary 187 votes for outright victory.'[35] This was doubtless true, although the result risked demonstrating that the party of government was evenly divided over four different options, none of them commanding a quorum of loyalty on their own. The more obvious option was the one Mrs Thatcher reluctantly felt compelled to adopt. She would fall on her sword so that her revolution might live, at least in some form, under a successor who was not Michael Heseltine.

'Bravura end of Thatcher era' ran the headline on Friday 23 November. Having announced her intention to resign, she had proceeded to give a commanding performance on the floor of the Commons. From his sketchwriter's vantage point above the Speaker's Chair, Matthew Parris watched the scene. Observing Kinnock's stint at the dispatch box made him question whether the right party was holding its leadership election – 'he gulped and blathered, staggering blindly around a verbal grocery shop, knocking tins off shelves'. Mrs Thatcher, by comparison, delivered 'one of her finest parliamentary performances'. Had it not been too late, Parris wondered if 'the mess of pin-striped tumbleweed blowing in the wind behind her might have blown her way after all ... "Why did they sack you?" Labour's Dave Nellist shouted. I looked across at the Tory benches. Not a few of them were wondering the same thing.'[36]

The truth was that the Tory benches were caught between anxiety for what they had done and excitement that the circus had a further performance to run. With Mrs Thatcher's decision to exit, Hurd and Major lost no time in entering the ring. Jenkins went to visit Major, whom he found suffering from toothache. 'Why not wait another term, you're still young?' Jenkins suggested. It was not well received. Major shot back, 'Well, aren't you a bit young to be editor of *The Times*?' Major was right to be confident for he held the best cards. The Brixton born son of a one-time trapeze artist and garden gnome specialist, his credentials fitted perfectly the Thatcherite creed of opportunity and social mobility. He played on this, declaring his wish to create a 'classless society'. At a time when the economy was in difficulties and business and home owners were facing mounting debts they could no longer meet, Major conveyed the demeanour of an approachable bank manager, ever ready to look again at ways to lighten the burden. Given the divisive toxins coursing through the Tory body politik, Major's ability to appear a picture of sweet reasonableness was his great asset. 'I believe in a very broad church Conservatism,' he told Robin Oakley in his pre-second ballot interview in *The Times*. Discerning which hymn sheet Major sang from would preoccupy the paper's finest political minds for years to come. With momentary self-delusion, Thatcher telephoned Jenkins before the second ballot to assure him that Major was 'pure gold, pure gold!'.[37]

In contrast, Hurd resembled the perfect Tory patrician: the son of an MP and sometime agricultural correspondent of *The Times*, educated at Eton and Cambridge (President of the Union), former diplomat, a writer of thrillers in his spare time, a capable and unflappable Home and Foreign Secretary. In the face of Major's classless appeal, Hurd's attempts to play down his background – he went to Eton on a scholarship – were treated with derision. Tories who wanted to bring home the Thatcher revolution felt that Major at least *looked* like the real thing. Mrs Thatcher anointed Major as her successor of choice and, on the morning of the vote, so did *The Times* – the only broadsheet newspaper to do so. Its reasoning was different, airing instead its suspicion that 'by inclination and intellect he sits on the left', but believed his relative youth and demeanour marked him out as the candidate to trump Kinnock's pretensions towards shaping the agenda for the 1990s.[38] Murdoch did not interfere with the editorial position of his broadsheets. In the course of a telephone conversation with Jenkins, he asked, almost in passing, which candidate *The Times* had decided to support. Jenkins was given the impression Murdoch scarcely even knew who Major was at that stage.[39] The 'Murdoch press' went their separate ways. The *Sunday Times* backed Heseltine as did *Today*, edited by David Montgomery. Meanwhile, the *Daily Telegraph* announced its support for Hurd. *The Times*, at any rate, backed the winner. At forty-seven, John Major became the youngest Prime Minister since Lord Rosebery in 1894.

Matthew Parris produced a sketch that painted the month-long internal convulsion as a 'tribal folk mystery'. The tribe had been gripped by panic, 'Michael Heseltine – as much, by now, a totem of dissent as a person – found members of the tribe dancing around him and chanting. He responded.' The tribe's leader, meanwhile had started ranting, then 'one of the elders of the tribe, Sir Geoffrey Howe, began to speak. He spoke almost in tongues: he spoke as he had never spoken.' What followed, Parris suggested, could have been done as a ballet. It had all the elements of a classical drama. Like Chinese opera or Greek tragedy, the rules required that certain human types be represented; certain ambitions be portrayed; certain actions punished. Every convention was obeyed; every actor played out his role. The dramatic unities of time, place and action were fulfilled ... It started with an old leader, who was assassinated as she deserved; then her assassin was assassinated. As he deserved. Then the new leader stepped forward; and here the ballet ended.[40]

IV

On 2 August 1990, Iraq invaded Kuwait. The tiny oil-rich emirate was, per capita, one of the richest countries in the world. Iraq, meanwhile, was burdened with a $70 billion foreign debt, more than half of which was owed to Kuwait and Saudi Arabia. Invading Kuwait had the political objectives of settling a historic argument over a couple of small islands, widening Iraq's narrow front on to the Gulf and demonstrating President Saddam Hussein's pretensions to regional supremacy. It had the economic objectives of wiping away the debts owed to Kuwait and seizing her oilfields. In the days preceding the invasion, *The Times* had reported the breakdown of diplomatic relations and the swelling Iraqi military presence on the Kuwait border. But neither the media nor any intelligence service could work out whether the armed build up was there to coerce the emirate or as a precursor to invading it. The Foreign Secretary, Douglas Hurd, learned that Kuwait was being invaded from the radio news, not British or US intelligence.[41] It was a *fait accompli*. With only the puny Kuwaiti defence forces in the way, the annexation was completed in a matter of hours. Thirty-five British military personnel attached to the emirate were taken prisoner and removed to Baghdad. The Emir's brother was killed. However, the Emir (whose al-Sabah family had been the local rulers since 1759) managed to escape and the Central Bank in Kuwait had time to transfer the national assets to Bahrain. Oil prices soared 15 per cent. The prospect of higher energy costs at a time when Western economies were slowing down was an alarming one.

With more than one million men under arms, Iraq had the seventh largest army in the world, its armaments swelled in particular by arms deals from France, the Soviet Union and China. After eight years of bloody conflict that may have claimed one million lives, its war with Iran had ended in 1988 with no great gain to either side. Saddam had weapons of mass destruction and had used them. In March 1988 he had bombed the Iraqi Kurdish town of Halabja with nerve gases, killing thousands. *The Times*'s Richard Beeston had been one of the first journalists into the ghost town where once fifty thousand had lived only to find it carpeted with dead bodies: 'Like figures unearthed in Pompeii, the victims of Halabja were killed so quickly that their corpses remained in suspended animation', he had written at the time. 'There was the plump baby whose face, frozen in a scream, stuck out from under the protective arm of a man, away from the open door of a house that he never reached.'[42] Thus Saddam was a leader with genocidal tendencies who had every reason to imagine the annexation of Kuwait would pass with only modest protest. Shortly after he had exterminated the Kurds of Halabja, Britain doubled the size of its export guarantee to Iraq and the Americans had provided weapons at a crucial moment when his war with Iran appeared to be going badly.

Saddam, however, had miscalculated. The international community had shrunk from intervening in the fate of Iraqi Kurds or in Iraq's conflict with the Islamic theocracy of Iran, but the attack on Kuwait was an invasion of a sovereign country. This was as stark a contravention of the UN Charter as could be imagined. What was more, the thawing of the Cold War meant that the Security Council was no longer tied into inactivity by the obstruction of the rival superpowers. There was a historic opportunity to show that collective security could act. Given the scale of Iraq's precarious finances and its reliance on exporting oil, it was hoped that economic sanctions – so often ineffective in the past – could at last be shown to work, especially given the possibility of their universal application. On 6 August, the UN voted to impose mandatory sanctions against Iraq that included a worldwide ban on its oil exports and on any arms sales or fresh investment into the country. It was only the second time in the UN's history that economic sanctions on this scale had been imposed. Inauspiciously, the first time had been against Rhodesia in 1967.

Economic sanctions were a means of avoiding taking greater risks. On the day the news of the invasion broke, *The Times* stated that one of Mrs Thatcher's senior aides had indicated Britain would not take military action. Sir Anthony Parsons, who had been Ambassador to Iraq, wrote an Op-Ed article expressing his hopes for economic sanctions since 'it is difficult to imagine military action being taken, whether by the Arab states, one or more of the great powers, or the United Nations. The world of 1990 is far removed from the world of 1945, in which the victorious allies could overawe potential aggressors.' This turned out to be a complete misreading of the situation although the editorial line of *The Times* concurred with Parsons's assessment, suggesting, 'a mostly American counter-invasion to force Iraq to withdraw, as requested by the exiled Emir, is not an option'. Given the size of the Iraqi army and Saddam's threat to turn Kuwait into a 'graveyard' if there was any attempt to liberate it, 'the operation would have to be on a scale not seen since Vietnam'. The very mention of that dreaded word appeared to rule out declaring war. Instead, economic sanctions should be allowed to take hold, since 'Iraq's political and social weaknesses offer a reasonable hope that Saddam Hussein will not last for ever'.[43] With this assessment, *The Times* proved to be wrong on both counts: a war to liberate Kuwait could be fought and won at minimal human cost to the liberators and economic sanctions, as practised then and for many years later, would have no effect in bringing Saddam down.

What frightened the West was that, far from stopping at Kuwait City, the Iraqi forces might press on into Saudi Arabia. If Saddam Hussein achieved this, he would gain control of more than 60 sixty per cent of the world's oil reserves. The extent to which he could hold the developed world hostage hardly needed underlining and for those seeking a resolute response it was fortuitous that President George Bush was meeting Margaret Thatcher (still Prime Minister) in Aspen at the very moment when the Iraqi tanks massed on the Saudi border. On 7 August, the United States began deploying forces to shore up the defence of Saudi Arabia and enforce the embargo through an effective blockade. Yet this was not the same as preparing to liberate Kuwait and as Jimmy Carter's National Security Advisor, Zbigniew Brzezinski, maintained in an article *The Times* had published the previous day, 'there is little stomach for an American lead in the pursuit of genuine military action'.[44] A far more expansive outlook was proposed on the same page, the following day, by the noted Middle Eastern commentator Amir Taheri. He maintained that Saddam Hussein was in a far weaker position than the size of his army suggested. Indeed, an opportunity now existed to foster democracy in the Gulf. 'Kicking Saddam out of Kuwait with his tail between his legs should be just the first step towards creating a new and stable system in the region,' Taheri wrote, for while 'a decade or so ago, there was, perhaps, no credible base for democracy in the Arab states of the Gulf, today, however, all have strong middle classes, many of them western educated and familiar with modern forms of government. Given a chance they could learn the democratic game.'[45] Taheri's arguments fell upon deaf ears in 1990. Yet, thirteen years later, they would make perfect sense to those in the White House and Downing Street as they plotted what they hoped would be a successful endgame to the protracted problem of Saddam Hussein.

The House of Saud's decision to allow US troops on Saudi soil was crucial in changing minds about the possibility and desirability of removing Saddam from Kuwait by force. It was a fateful decision in many ways. Permitting Christian soldiers in the land of Islam's most sacred sites helped to drive Osama bin Laden down the path of hatred that was, in time, to lead to 9/11, the 'War against Terror' and the American decision to occupy Iraq. Such consequences were ill perceived in the summer of 1990. What began as an immediate shoring up of Saudi defences soon expanded into preparations for the military liberation of Kuwait. The appetite of the UN and of other Arab nations (with the notable exception of Jordan) for liberating the emirate state made this transformation possible. Saddam's eccentric diplomacy – on the one hand appealing to Arab solidarity by trying to link a settlement to Palestinian claims while calling for a Holy War to overthrow the Egyptian and Saudi governments and even offering concessions to Iran – did not enhance his regional reputation. There were 1400 British nationals in Iraq. When Saddam had them rounded up so that they could be used as human shields against attack he only hardened British public opinion against him. His decision to be filmed in a display of *faux* affection stroking the hair of one of his captives, a five year old boy named Stuart Lockwood, only gave the impression that he was some sort of twisted pervert.

A month after the invasion, Mrs Thatcher announced Britain would send ground troops to the Gulf. In November, Bush massively increased the US ground forces dispatched to the area. On 29 November, UN Resolution 678 was passed by twelve votes to two (China abstained, only Cuba and Yemen voted against) authorizing a military solution to drive Iraq out of Kuwait unless she withdrew voluntarily by 15 January 1991. With Rosemary Righter influencing the leader-writing stance, *The Times* had swung round in favour of UN-backed armed intervention. This, after all, was a rare opportunity for the UN's principles for international order to be tested. By the time war broke out, twenty-eight Arab, Asian and Western nations had joined the coalition supporting the implementation of the UN's resolutions to free Kuwait. Although *The Times*'s first reflex had been to back economic sanctions, Righter saw that 'giving sanctions time to work' was the mantra used by those determined to avoid war at any cost. As far as she was concerned, the record of such sanctions did not justify the faith the peace campaigners placed upon then, especially given Saddam's indifference to human suffering. 'Not since 1939 has an aggression left so clear a choice to those seeking a just international order' asserted the leading article justifying war: 'The coalition ranged against Iraq represents a step towards the collective enforcement of international law. This experiment must be made to work in the Gulf or countries must arm and ally themselves as best they can against the law of the jungle.'[46]

Britain went to war in the Gulf, unlike in the Falklands, with the united endorsement of the national press. The tabloids vied with each other to take the most jingoistic line (the *Daily Mirror*, which had disliked fighting General Galtieri, was now under the ownership of the pro-Israeli Robert Maxwell). Preferring the economic sanctions route, the *Guardian* was the most reluctant convert to a military solution, yet, whatever their varying levels of enthusiasm, that no national newspaper opposed going to war outright proved to be a moment of remarkable political unanimity in Fleet Street and a far cry from both the Suez and Falklands experiences. For those not given to marching in step with the Tories, endorsing the Government's line was made easier when the less abrasive John Major supplanted Margaret Thatcher only eight weeks before the bombing raids began.

Given Saddam's ruthless record and his threat to launch missiles against Israeli cities, Fleet Street drew up its own dispositions for a long campaign that would stretch resources to the full. With Graham Paterson in command of the newspaper's war coverage, *The Times* finalized its own arrangements eight days before the UN deadline was due to expire. Decisions had to be taken on how many pages could be added and what deadlines could be stretched. The graphics team was put on twenty-four-hour call, ready to illustrate maps with swooping Apache helicopters and guided missiles bursting out of the page. A large body of pre-written analysis was commissioned that examined the military and diplomatic background to the outbreak of hostilities. Rosemary Righter would compose most of the leaders. The defence correspondent, Michael Evans, would spend much of the next couple of months at MoD briefings. Peter Stothard and Martin Fletcher would file from Washington. Among the twelve *Times* reporters filing from the Middle East would be Michael Knipe in Cairo, Christopher Walker in Saudi Arabia and Richard Owen in Jerusalem. Jamie Dettmer would report on the Royal Navy's war from on board HMS *London* and Philip Jacobson, embedded with the 7th Armoured Brigade in

Saudi Arabia, would advance with the Army. The details of the company's life insurance policy were examined.[47] Most important of all, Richard Beeston would tough it out behind enemy lines, as *The Times*'s correspondent in Baghdad.

Much of the official military information was disseminated from the daily briefings held at the coalition headquarters in Riyadh – hundreds of miles from the battlefront. With the experience of the Falklands conflict to draw upon, the MoD drew up a seven-page document providing guidance on what information could be released. It listed thirty-two examples of what journalists should not report without first clearing their copy with the Ministry. The guiding principle, of course, was that no information should be published that could assist the enemy. Detailing size, capability and location of allied units was clearly off limits. The same applied to publishing casualty figures before the Ministry decided it was safe to do so. Reports that included information about ongoing operations and damage to naval vessels or military aircraft were also prohibited without prior clearance if the details had not already been announced officially. Looking at the rules, Christopher Walker expressed the opinion of many reporters who feared 'one of the most sanitised wars this century in terms of immediate reportage'.[48] In return for being 'embedded' with the soldiers and sailors, Jacobson and Dettmer had to remain with their military escort officers at all times. Where need be, copy had 'this report is subject to allied reporting restrictions' tagged to the end of it.

However, in vital respects, the Gulf situation was very different from the Falklands War. Then, the British Government had been able to restrict the coverage of the Task Force's mission to British journalists working for British newspapers and broadcasters. Censoring their work was thus relatively easy within a national framework of agreed rules and understandings and the absence of satellite coverage meant that no instant broadcasts could be sent from the battlefront. No such limitations applied in the Gulf where the world's media descended and where CNN, the world's first twenty-four-hour satellite news broadcaster, was able to transmit words and pictures instantly all over the globe. The 'national interest' was not obviously something that a multinational broadcaster would feel bound to honour. The nature of the British media's contribution was also different. In the Falklands War most of the journalists following the Task Force were employed by newspapers. This was not the case at the outbreak of the Gulf War. In the last days before Operation Desert Storm commenced, ITN had a forty-six-strong team in Saudi Arabia and Baghdad, the BBC had around thirty and there were thirty-five from national newspapers, along with a handful from the regional press and news agencies.[49]

The Times also had its armchair generals in position. The long build-up of coalition forces in Saudi Arabia had given the Iraqis plenty of time to dig in. Yet, Michael Evans predicted that, unlike the Iran–Iraq conflict, Desert Storm would be a war of rapid movement. The five hundred French- and Soviet-made fighter planes of the Iraqi air force would be 'unlikely to survive the first hours of conflict' given the likelihood that they would be the first target of American bombing. Consequently, the Iraqis would have to deal with American air superiority and technological firepower the like of which they had never faced in the long struggle with Iran. American, British and French night-vision equipment would give them a huge advantage in striking during the night. There was, however, the potential for a massive tank battle, with Iraq's 4200 tanks deployed in and around Kuwait against the coalition's three thousand strong force. Evans seemed certain that the coalition would prevail while Air Chief Marshal Sir Michael Armitage went further, writing a column that suggested it could prove to be 'a very short campaign.'[50] These views were far removed from the opinion of peace campaigners and Sir Edward Heath, whose prophecies were apocalyptic.

Shortly before midnight (9.50 p.m. GMT) on 16 January, Operation Desert Storm began, as expected, with intensive aerial bombing. Two days later Iraq launched the first of several Scud missile attacks on Israel cities, including Tel Aviv, in the dead of night. America's deployment of Patriot anti-missile defences – and the inflated claims made for their effectiveness – was intended to quell Israeli demands for revenge. Yet, the fear that the Scuds would inflict great damage – physically and politically – was never far from the minds of those following the conflict. In fact the damage inflicted by the Scuds was minor compared with the ordinance raining down upon the Iraqis. The first couple of weeks of Operation Desert Storm consisted of an unremitting aerial bombardment in which wave upon wave of flight sorties and missiles severed Saddam's communications system. Within two days of the assault commencing, Beeston reported, 'The capital's communications centre is destroyed, hit by four precision missiles. The Presidential Palace lies half in ruins' in a city largely 'deserted and those who have not fled are making plans to do so.'[51] Ineffectual anti-aircraft flak drifted up into the Baghdad night sky and images were beamed back from the nose of US missiles as they homed in with deadly precision upon their target. These were pictures made for television, a moving image world in which the print media could not compete except with the sort of graphics that some readers felt turned the conflict into a comic strip. Those who had expected Baghdad would be carpet bombed like a second Dresden were relieved that technological advances in missile technology had created greater discrimination. But even the smartest bombs could not avoid civilians who found themselves in the way and the ugly phrase 'collateral damage' began to take a gruesome hold over reporting the death of innocent bystanders. Beeston also made clear that some targets were being missed and that anti-Western sentiment from civilians he encountered on the streets was hardening.[52]

An Arab speaker, Beeston was more than equal to the challenge. The son of one of the *Daily Telegraph*'s most highly regarded foreign correspondents, he had avoided university, preferring to go straight into journalism. At the tender age of twenty-one he answering an advertisement to become a reporter in Beirut. There could have been few better training grounds. In this context, his dispatch to Baghdad did not seem to him to involve unnecessary risks. 'It wasn't frightening at all,' he recalled, 'it was exhilarating.'[53] Two days before Operation Desert Storm commenced, Washington had contacted all the media networks and told them to get their journalists out of Baghdad immediately – US forces would be using bunker-busting bombs and their safety could not be guaranteed. Suddenly, Beeston found himself deserted by so many of the reporters who had congregated with him, holed up in Baghdad's Al-Rashid Hotel. Among the British broadsheets, only the representatives of the *Independent* and the *Sunday Times* opted, like Beeston, to stick it out.

Excessive censorship from the Iraqi regime would have devalued the worth of Beeston's commitment to *The Times*. However, Baghdad's officials were in a state of confusion and disorder and proved incompetent censors. He found himself with considerable freedom of movement and the official minder appointed to shadow him and censor his reports let through references to how quickly the Iraqi defence effort appeared to be disintegrating. Only when he attempted to state that there was no water and the hotel was beginning to get a bit smelly did the minder cut in with the gentle admonishment, 'Mr Richard, please take out the "smelly". It is insulting to us.'[54] Beeston felt in surprisingly little danger from the vengeance of the brutal Iraqi state although when he filed more detailed reports about the breaking morale and troop desertions, officialdom finally intervened. He was deported and banned from Iraq for three years. The only way a new *Times* reporter was going to get into the country was with the assistance of the British Army.

The problem was that, aside from a repulsed Iraqi incursion around the

Saudi border town of Khafji, there was still no sign of the promised ground war after almost a month of the conflict's commencement and the ordinance dispatched from 67,000 sorties. Until the frontal assault began, analysts could not prove whether this war of missiles was working or was merely an expensive way to avoid confronting the ultimate necessity of a head-on ground invasion. Neil Kinnock sacked Clare Short, a Labour front-bench spokewomen, for suggested the bombing was about smashing Iraq rather than liberating Kuwait, but the specific event that had provoked her claim also strengthened the sceptics in their belief that all was not going well. On 13 February, two US missiles landed in Baghdad, penetrating ten feet of reinforced concrete and steel bars and exploding inside what had been identified as a military command and control centre directing Iraqi forces but was also a civilian shelter that included a school, a mosque and a supermarket. Graphic scenes were soon broadcast around the world of the charred remains of hundreds of women and children being brought out from the bunker. With Beeston deported, the *Sunday Times*'s Marie Colvin immediately filed her eyewitness report for *The Times*, painting the despair of the relatives as they visited the scene of carnage and discovered the rest of their families had been obliterated.[55]

The opinions of Clare Short and those looking for reasons to condemn the war were one matter. Yet, to the alarm of a number of *Times* journalists cooped up in the rum warehouse, the editor's resolve appeared to be severely shaken during the afternoon conference in which the attack on the shelter was discussed. Jenkins gave the impression he wanted a quick exit strategy to a war that was having calamitous consequences. His change of heart unnerved his colleagues. Martin Ivens and Rosemary Righter were especially determined to prevent *The Times* performing a U-turn halfway through a war it had endorsed. The leading article that emerged from the showdown gave little hint of the private confrontation. It expressed the hope that future targeting would better balance political with military imperatives and that the war had reached a stage when the bombing should concentrate on Iraq's forward positions in the war zone of Kuwait itself.[56] Nonetheless, for many of the senior editorial staff, it was Jenkins's judgment that was seriously questioned. It was, to paraphrase what Margaret Thatcher had previously told George Bush, no time to go wobbly.

With Jenkins's doubts overcome, or at least, outgunned by Ivens and Righter, *The Times* stiffened its resolve for the battle ahead, unmoved by last-minute attempts by Gorbachev to mediate peace before the land war commenced in earnest.[57] The Iraqis began setting the Kuwaiti oil wells alight on 22 February and the sky was soon black with the fumes of five hundred blazing oil installations. Two days later the ground assault into the emirate began. By 27 February, the Iraqis had fled from Kuwait City, a freelance correspondent with the US television network CBS being the first to broadcast the news from the capital that it was back in Kuwaiti hands even before the allied troops had arrived to liberate it officially. *The Times*'s Christopher Walker was not far behind. He discovered a city convulsed by devastation and jubilation. Hotels, public buildings, even the Emir's palace, had been gutted. The cheering crowds were reminiscent of Paris's liberation in 1944 and there was no shortage of Kuwaitis coming forward with their own tales of Iraqi barbarism. Tanks were continuing to sweep into the city 'like a carnival parade', Walker spotting one forgotten Iraqi running along-side the convey, 'frantically signalling that he too wanted to be taken prisoner'. Beyond, 'the roads were littered with Iraqi soldiers' boots and helmets, discarded during their desperate flight north. Iraqi bodies lay scattered under blankets. One soldier lay sprawled face up on the road, legs buckled, anguish still written across his face.'[58]

Much of the allied advance struck not through the emirate at all but up into southern Iraq to secure the western flank. The British 1st Armoured Division was among the mechanized forces hurtling at speed across the desert to reach the Euphrates and trap the half million Iraqi troops falling back in disorder. In particular, the allies wanted to prevent the elite Republican Guard from making it back to Baghdad. The military briefings in Riyadh were suggesting the extent to which it was a rout: there had been 79 American deaths in exchange for smashing 29 Iraqi divisions, 30,000 prisoners had been taken and more than 3000 tanks captured or destroyed. With the bridges blown and allied mastery of the skies secured, there seemed every possibility of not just liberating Kuwait but also of destroying Iraq's ability to be a regional menace altogether. With the allied leader, General Norman Schwarzkopf, warning the Iraqis, 'the gates are closed: there are no ways out', a bitter tank battle ensued west of Basra between almost 500 US tanks and the 300 tanks of the Republican Guard. Again the Iraqis were pulverized. The biggest British armoured assault since El Alamein was also underway. Observing the advance of the 32nd Field Regiment for *The Times*, Philip Jacobson did his best to convey the terrifying nature of the barrage falling upon the Iraqis:

From where I was watching just over a mile away, the flashes were blinding and the earth literally heaved beneath me. As shells passed overhead with a noise like someone tearing heavy canvas, the air pressure changed perceptibly. Then came the double boom of impact and percussion wave, like the slamming of a heavy door. ... We could follow the course of the battle on radio links in our signals vehicle: the voice of Brigadier Patrick Cordingley, commander of the Desert Rats, was on the air continuously, pressing this unit to get a move on towards a new objective, cautioning another not to get carried away before securing an enemy gunpit. A flurry of traffic would indicate that a new attack was under way, yet virtually every voice was calm and composed, even when the first of the British casualties was brought in.[59]

President Bush announced the ceasefire on 28 February, six weeks to the minute since the campaign began and a hundred hours after the ground war's launch. The twin objectives of liberating Kuwait and defeating the Iraqi army had, he said, been met. US airborne troops had come within 150 miles of Baghdad. 'There was no one between us and Baghdad,' Schwarzkopf told reporters. 'If it had been our intention to take Iraq, if it had been our intention to destroy the country, if it had been our intention to overrun the country, we could have done it unopposed.'[60]

The UN resolutions sanctioning Kuwait's liberation did not provide for occupying Iraq. The war had been a remarkable achievement. Britain had suffered twenty-four casualties in action (nine of them from 'friendly fire') while the Iraqi dead and wounded was assumed to exceed 100,000. Before the war began, the Pentagon had warned Bush that there could be ten thousand American casualties. In the event, there was about one coalition soldier death for every one thousand Iraqis killed. The sheer one-sidedness of the 'turkey shoot' on the trapped Iraqi forces militated against prolonging the slaughter. *The Times* supported Bush's 'statesmanlike' decision to call a ceasefire rather than to press on to Baghdad. Writing for Op-Ed, David Owen, the former Foreign Secretary and late leader of the SDP, maintained that if this was not to prove 'to be the single largest mistake of what has otherwise been a brilliantly conducted operation' it was 'our duty to make it impossible for Saddam to continue in power'. Rather than treating with his emissaries for peace terms, his removal and charge with war crimes should be the precondition and sanctions should remain in force.[61]

Instead, it looked, briefly, as if the Iraqis might answer Bush's plea and overthrow Saddam without the need for further intervention. In defeat, Iraq's regional and religious divisions opened up. The Kurds in the north and the Shia Muslims in the south rose against Saddam's Sunni dominated regime, pinning it back to its heartland around Baghdad. Iraqi order appeared to be imploding. Indeed, given the separatist aims of the Kurds, the country risked splitting up altogether. The Shia revolt centred upon Basra but uprisings were being reported across the country. However, after five days of fighting, the Republican Guard gained the upper hand. Despite their presence in the south of the country, the coalition forces stood aside. Initially, *The Times* found it impossible to get any reporters close enough to witness the bloody suppression at first hand but when reports and television pictures of the Kurdish plight eventually did reach London, fears spread that a form of genocide was underway. In freezing conditions, Kurdish families were fleeing to the hills to escape the Iraqi reprisals. If Saddam did not finish them off, the weather might do so. Turkey and Iran sealed their borders.

By the first days of April, reports were appearing that left *Times* readers in no doubt about the extent of the Kurdish plight. The demands for a humanitarian response crescendoed. Some asserted that having been called upon to rise up in the first place only to be denied any military support when they did so, the Kurds' and Marsh Arabs' suffering was largely Britain and America's fault. In an article entitled 'Blood on our hands', Conor Cruise O'Brien wrote in this vein. He was especially incandescent at the UN's refusal – having sanctioned the liberation of Kuwait and the removal of Saddam's weapons of mass destruction – to insist upon creating democracy in Iraq and safeguarding its victims. The coalition, it seemed to him, preferred to keep the despicable Saddam in power than remove him and risk a power vacuum that might result in a disintegrating Iraq. Yet, seeing the dangers of being drawn into a long term commitment to occupy Iraq, Bush was reluctant to protect the Kurds, confiding that he 'did not want one single soldier or airman shoved into a civil war in Iraq that has been going on for ages'.[62] Although *The Times* saw no option but to provide humanitarian assistance, its leading article saw clearly the dangers of interfering in matters of internal sovereignty. With remarkable prescience, it argued:

> The 1990s are certain to be the decade of ethnic distress. The unravelling of communism will lead to thousands of 'economic' refugees crossing frontiers, making calls on the charity and possibly the armies of the world. The liberal dream of global ethnic concord is no more. Nationalism, the '-ism' that defies communism, liberalism and

capitalism alike, remains rampant . . . The nations of the West will be inclined to use their strength, like medieval crusaders, to reorganize the world according to their own high principles, and sometimes their lower ones. The world must be sure it knows what it is about.[63]

John Major, however, was not concerned with the theoretical arguments of the future but the need to address the humanitarian plight of the moment. He secured European support for a plan for creating Kurdish 'safe havens'. This pressured – perhaps shamed – a reluctant Washington into joining in. The deployment in mid-April of 5000 American, 2000 British and 1000 French troops saved an unquantifiable number of lives. In Baghdad, however, Saddam remained. Containing, rather than removing, him became the policy through sanctions and no-fly zones. The UN resolved that his weapons of mass destruction should be destroyed and the process of overseeing the process began. It would not prove to be the end of the affair.

While politicians and commentators talked of a 'new world order' of international cooperation of which the UN resolutions and the liberation of Kuwait were but the bright beginning, the Gulf War had also brought alive the notion of a 'global village' for the news media. From Baghdad's Al Rashid Hotel, Beeston had filed his dispatches to Wapping from a telex machine. Transmitting to satellites from the hotel's roof, CNN had beamed images and reports instantly into homes in ninety-three countries around the world. On 28 January, CNN's Peter Arnett even managed to have a ninety-minute interview with Saddam in which the Iraqi president threatened to use nuclear, chemical and biological warheads against the allies. Satellite television – in which Murdoch was now investing – and the twenty-four-hour rolling news coverage it facilitated had arrived. No other event did more to demonstrate the extent to which power had passed from print to broadcast media. Indeed, while coverage of the war attracted massive viewing figures in Britain, the daily sale of tabloid newspapers actually fell during the period. For its part, *The Times* had performed well. Its late editions were going to press at 3 and sometimes 4 a.m. in order to compete with the television coverage. But it was under no illusions that if it wanted to hold onto its market share in the future it would have to perform two conflicting functions: to be fast in reporting breaking news and to provide more detailed analysis than its broadcasting rivals could muster.

V

The evidence that the future lay with satellite television could not have come at a better time for Rupert Murdoch. While the Gulf War unfolded, his media empire imploded. The roots of News Corp.'s difficulties lay with his purchase in the United States of Metromedia and Fox. He could have funded the purchase by issuing new shares in News Corp., but that would have diluted his control of the company. Having seen the way his father had been treated, Murdoch never lost his belief that family control was the only guarantee of keeping direction of the company. An alternative was simply to borrow the money. In order not to exceed the gearing limit permitted of debt compared to shareholder equity, he had approached Michael Milken, the 'junk bond king', at the bank Drexel Burnham Lambert. Junk bonds offered a high yield because they involved high risk. In March 1986, Milken secured $1.15 billion in junk preferences. This was described as a preference stock – a form of virtual equity – in order not to breach the banks' gearing limit. However, Milken inserted a clause stipulating that if the $1.15 billion could not be repaid within three years (i.e. by March 1989) remuneration for lenders would reflect News Corp.'s latest share price. Thus, as the News Corp. share price went up, so the debt repayment soared. For Murdoch, this proved disastrous. Thanks to the move to Wapping, News International's operating income had gone from £38.4 million in 1985 to £150.2 million in 1987. This had sent News Corp.'s ordinary share price rocketing from around $8.50 in March 1986 to $35 a year later. Thus, the more profitable News Corp. became, the greater in debt it plunged. Unless he wanted to issue more shares and lose control of the company, Murdoch had no obvious way out of this vicious circle. What was more, the classification of the junk preferences as equity prevented him from borrowing from banks to pay them off since he had to stay within his banks' gearing limits. As one commentator put it, 'Wapping had turned Milken's conversion clause into a $3.6 billion nightmare'.[64]

During 1990, the downturn in the Western economies intensified. Banks sought to call in their loans. For News Corp. this was an alarming prospect. The recession hit advertising, seriously depleting revenue. The company's profits were falling, as was its share price. Sky, Murdoch's satellite television venture, was losing in excess of £2 million a week. The situation was not even secure in the tabloid newspaper market. Robert Maxwell's *Daily Mirror* had gained ground on the *Sun*, partly because Maxwell had invested in colour printing. This had forced a reluctant Murdoch to buy colour presses for Wapping as part of a re-equipping and extension to the plant that consumed £500 million. *The Times* was the beneficiary of this investment but in so far as it contributed towards destabilizing the company's finances it was a risky venture. On top of all this, five years of making acquisitions around the world had brought with them debts whose scheduled repayment dates had arrived. The company had in excess of $7 billion in unsecured bank debt and owed $3 billion to its trade creditors. It had to repay $2.6 billion by October 1990. Not only was it in no position to pay this sum back, it needed an extra injection of $600 million merely to keep trading.

A debt rescheduling package was worked out, but by bringing the various transactions together this was a temporary fix that failed to solve a problem: if one of the banks involved was determined to default from the agreement then the whole deal could fall apart. The overused pack of cards analogy was, in this case, all too apt. This was exactly the situation that almost destroyed News Corp. in the first week of December 1990. After much bargaining, the various creditors reached agreement with one small, but awkward, exception. The Pittsburgh National Bank owned 1 per cent of the debt in question and wanted its money back. With great independence of mind, it refused to play its part in the rollover plan even if it meant destroying News Corp. as a consequence. Murdoch's empire, to say nothing of his ownership of *The Times*, was in the hands of a Pittsburgh loan officer who appeared blissfully immune to charm or intimidation down a telephone line. Murdoch assured him that if Pittsburgh National refused to roll over the debt then News Corp. would go out of business. 'That's right,' replied the loan officer. Lest there be any misunderstanding, Murdoch sought qualification: 'You're telling us to liquidate our company?' 'Yes,' came the unabashed reply.[65] It was not clear where else the conversation could go, so, Murdoch attempted to speak to someone more senior. But Pittsburgh National's chairman refused to take his call, referring him back to the loan officer. Only when John Reed, the chairman of Citibank, intervened, calling the Pittsburgh National chairman to assure him that allowing News Corp. to go under risked prompting an international financial crash, did the bank give way to Murdoch's desperate pleas.

This was a temporary respite. In the weeks ahead, News Corp. again appeared close to insolvency with crises breaking on Christmas Eve and New Year's Eve overshadowing the expressions of yuletide felicitations within the Murdoch household. Yet, clinging on proved a sufficient tactic in the short term and by February 1991 the debt override agreement was in place that gave News Corp. three years in which to get its financial house in order. There were other glimmers of hope: the pressure was eased on Sky by its swallowing up of its competitor British Satellite Broadcasting and Murdoch's film company, Twentieth Century-Fox, produced a highly lucrative hit at the box office, *Home Alone* (which Geoff Brown, *The Times*'s critic, not entirely helpfully described as being like fast food because it was 'made to order, with relish but without finesse').[66] For most of the paper's journalists pacing anxiously the length of the Wapping warehouse there was a feeling of helplessness, watching and observing news that, for once, directly affected them. It seemed to be especially hard luck at the very moment when an agreeable arrangement appeared to have been reached – an editor left to do what he liked to take the paper upmarket with a proprietor content to pay the bills. Jenkins was deeply alarmed and concerned and had strenuously to dissuade Clifford Longley from asking Murdoch if he would sell *The Times* to a consortium he was trying to cobble together. Longley saw Murdoch's problems as *The Times*'s opportunity, believing that, freed from News International's care, it could model a new ownership structure based on that which appeared to be suiting the *Independent*. In fact, Murdoch's problems during the winter of 1990–91 were not of so minor a scale that floating off *The Times* would have solved the daunting arithmetic. The only chance of the paper having a new owner was if News Corp. went under. In that scenario it, like all the other parts of the once mighty media group, would be stripped down and sold in the conditions of a fire sale.

Indeed, but for News Corp.'s financial troubles, *The Times* might have found itself with far more managerial autonomy. When Andrew Knight had arrived as executive chairman of News International in March 1990, he had been surprised to discover how complicated the command structure was at the senior levels of the paper compared to what he had experienced running the Telegraph Group for Conrad Black. It was necessary to descend to the fifth tier of management before one came to anyone primarily responsible for *The Times*. Such a layered hierarchy did not necessarily make for clear or responsive decision making. Part of the problem had been created by the specific troubles thrown up by the move to Wapping but the greater issue was that News International consisted of two newspaper groups (NGN for the tabloids and Times Newspapers Limited for the broadsheets) that catered for very different markets and also included Sky, the satellite television venture which was racking up such heavy losses that Knight found himself writing cheques for £2 million (and sometimes

£4 million) a week. Within months of arriving at Wapping, Knight had begun to work on a plan that would effectively split NGN and Times Newspapers into separate companies, a solution that he believed would make the respective managements far more responsive to the titles over which they exercised control. Fate intervened. On holiday with the Murdoch family in Aspen, Colorado, Knight suffered a near fatal skiing accident that forced him to take a lengthy period of recuperation. By the time he recovered, the company was fighting for its life and was hardly seeking the managerial distraction of the kind Knight had envisaged. The moment passed.[67]

The company's attempt to rebuild itself necessarily involved retrenchment. Gus Fischer, News International's managing director, issued the group's editors with an edict demanding a 10 per cent across-the-board cut in budget. This was a crippling blow to Jenkins's upmarket aspirations for *The Times*. He managed to whittle away Fischer's initial recommendation that the paper lose 10 per cent of its staff but the economies when they emerged were still severe. Further investment in promotion was postponed and a redundancy package introduced. The cutback that had the most lasting significance came to the parliament page. Looking for somewhere to cut staff, Jenkins concluded that employing a team to sit in the House of Commons and copy down a transaction of the debates was no longer tenable. *The Times*'s was the only wholly independent newspaper report of parliamentary proceedings, a reporter from the paper always being present in the chamber whenever the Commons was sitting. Each day, an average of thirty-three excerpts from speeches would be printed. The survey evidence suggested it was popular with MPs but Jenkins doubted it was read anywhere much outside the Palace of Westminster's precincts.[68] So ended a famous tradition and, indeed, one of the paper's principal claims to being the 'journal of record'. This tag now largely rested with the continuation of the law reports. It was ironic that the passing of the parliamentary page had happened at the hands of Simon Jenkins rather than Charles Wilson, the supposed downmarket influence who, nonetheless, had not been inclined to take such a risk. Murdoch, too, thought the departure from tradition a mistake, believing it was an important ingredient of what made *The Times* special.[69] On the other hand, he never interfered to tell Jenkins where the mandatory cuts ought to be made instead.

VI

While the Soviet Union and federal Yugoslavia fell apart (see Chapter Thirteen), the architects of the European Community worked to bring a federal union together. For more than thirty years, the Paris–Bonn axis had been the force at the heart of Europe – the place where John Major now stated he wanted Britain to be. Scrapping the impressively powerful Deutschmark in favour of a new single European currency was part of the bargain that Mitterrand extracted from Kohl as the price for acquiescence in unifying Germany.

When John Major became Prime Minister his true views on European integration were unclear (which was one of the reasons why he was seen as the unity candidate). It was not long, however, before he would be called upon to show his hand. The intergovernmental conference called at the Dutch city of Maastricht in December 1991 would determined whether EMU was waffle or a reality. The United Kingdom had the power of veto. Using it risked demonstrating the country's isolation from the rest of Europe, whose members might proceed with their own plans regardless, leaving Britain 'behind'. On the other hand, acquiescing with the federal destiny risked political turmoil at home. This was the dilemma facing a Prime Minister about to go into an election year and still narrowly behind Labour in the opinion polls.

The Times's position was laid out in a leading article that stretched down the entire page. It was uneasy about the headlong rush towards EMU. Indeed, the paper argued that EMU might actually hamper the fruition of European free trade because 'there is no evidence that a diverse continental economy becomes more efficient within a framework of centralized decision-taking and fixed internal pricing than when its component parts can adjust costs, taxes and even exchange rates'. It also condemned the Social Chapter which he claimed was 'centralization gone mad' and 'commercial suicide'. 'In a democracy,' *The Times* began it peroration, 'everybody must know what is being delegated, to whom and why' and a Maastricht treaty could perform an invaluable function in establishing the functions and limitations of the European Community's legal competence. But Britain should 'be outspoken in crying stop' if, instead, its partners tried to overreach themselves. Indeed:

> If no such clarity emerges from Maastricht, the enthusiasm for Euro-
> pean cooperation will vanish in dust by the end of the century. Too

much power stripped from too many electorates and granted to too many international bodies will induce its own reaction: a nationalist upsurge which no amount of central policing will suppress. EMU and political union will collapse in bitterness and fascism. Then Maastricht will seem like a passing madness, a brief shout of concord choked by its own illusions.[70]

The following morning *The Times*'s front-page headline boldly announced 'Major wins all he asked for at Maastricht' alongside the Prime Minister's assessment that it was 'Game, set and match for Britain'. The paper's reporters from Maastricht – George Brock, Michael Binyon and Robin Oakley – adjudged it a triumph for Major who had won on the issues the press had been briefed he would take a stand on: national opt-outs on the Social Chapter and EMU as well as avoidance of a specific federal commitment in the wording. That the agreement fell short of what his continental partners, and in particular France, wanted only seemed to confirm the extent of the diplomatic victory. The leading article, entitled 'A Sort of Triumph' congratulated Major for forcing 'Maastricht to be sensible' and the following day went further, describing his diplomacy as 'an emphatic success' which kept key decision making with the intergovernmental Council of Ministers rather than ceding it to the Commission or any of the other institutions of doubtful accountability.[71] Indeed, Major certainly appeared to have pulled off a short-term triumph, returning 'from Maastricht to a hero's welcome from Tory MPs [who were] in a state of near euphoria' as Philip Webster reported the mood in Westminster. Peter Riddell was similarly impressed by the Prime Minister's political and diplomatic skill.[72] The growing number of Euro-sceptics were relieved that he had not irrevocably committed the country to the Social Chapter and EMU while others, most notably enthusiasts in the business community and the City, safely assumed – as Anatole Kaletsky pointed out – that, come the hour, be it in 1997 or 1999, Britain would sign up for EMU rather than risk being left out in the cold.[73] Whether this would be the right course to take, *The Times* editorial, like the Prime Minister, remained equivocal.[74]

In the meantime, one, or probably two, general elections would intrude. As the spring of 1992 approached, Major opted to go to the polls immediately after a coolly received Budget, with unemployment back up at 2.6 million – nearly one person in ten was now on the dole – and the lowest number of property transactions for a decade. While the recession of the early 1980s had hit hardest areas of Britain that traditionally voted Labour anyway, this time the downturn was affecting the Tory and swing-vote constituencies of London, the South and Southeast. It was not a propitious time for the Conservatives to go to the polls and, having been in power for thirteen years, they could no longer blame past Labour administrations for the country's ills. For some, the feeling that it was time for a change was sufficient to motivate their desire to vote for it. After all, they reasoned, if Labour could not win now, in these favourable conditions, when could it win?

With the salutary experience of three successive election defeats to point to, Neil Kinnock had pushed the Labour Party not only away from the policies that had contributed towards its humiliation in 1983 but even from the pledges with which he had led it to the polls in 1987. Most conspicuously, the commitment to unilateral nuclear disarmament had been dropped though the apparent end of the Cold War downgraded the importance in which defence issues featured among voter concerns. Within a remarkably short period of time, the Labour Party had passed from wanting to withdraw from the European Community to mild Euro-scepticism and now onto positive Europhilia. Labour's nationalization programme had also been dropped. The party's emphasis was, instead, increasing the proportion of the national wealth spent by the public sector.

When, halfway through the election campaign, John Smith, the Shadow Chancellor, unveiled his tax plans, the immediate response was broadly positive. Accompanying analysis from the Institute of Fiscal Studies suggested that it would make 80 per cent of the population better off, which was almost 50 per cent more than were set to prosper under the Tory plans. Some felt Smith had scored a knockout punch against his opposite number, Norman Lamont. Yet, while Lamont reeled, Anatole Kaletsky looked at the figures more closely and started landing some punches of his own. In a series of high-profile articles, he accused Smith of deliberately creating 'a tax structure more punitive to the middle class than any previous Labour government's'. The financial benefit Labour's plans gave to the majority was paltry – often a matter of pence – but the compensating hit on the moderately affluent was enormous. 'Mr Smith,' Kaletsky thundered, 'will ensure a collapse in demand for the goods, houses and services bought by the middle class.' Nor was there even social equity in Labour's proposals: earned income would be taxed at a higher level than unearned income; headteachers and doctors earning £40,000 a year would pay more tax (about £1700 a year more) than a millionaire living on a £100,000 private income. According to Kaletsky, Smith's tax plan would hit hardest those in the south-east who 'could have a crucial impact on the election'.[75] Conservative Central Office seized upon this argument, hoping to woo back this group of disillusioned Tory voters by frightening them with the worse fate John Smith had in store for them. Billboards began to proclaim the new Tory message – 'Labour's Tax Bombshell'.

A Labour victory was certainly not in the interests of News International. The party was committed to an enquiry into the concentration of media ownership in Britain and nobody at Wapping was in any doubt about where the concentration would be pinpointed. Jenkins gathered the leader writers and senior lobby journalists to Le Pont de la Tour restaurant and announced that *The Times* would be endorsing the Conservatives. He paused. Then he asked the assembled to tell him why.

Unlike the two previous general election campaigns, the close nature of the 1992 contest gave added importance to the media coverage. Opinion polls suggested there was a far larger floating vote than had existed in 1987. Mid-campaign, around 80 per cent of readers of *The Times* and its broadsheet rivals were telling pollsters they were interested in the election compared with a little over half of tabloid readers.[76] As the campaign entered its final phase with media pundits declaring that the Tory strategy was lacklustre, Labour appeared to be heading towards a narrow – but clear – win. Matthew Parris, however, wrote to the contrary. Dispatched to the Sheffield Arena to do a sketch for Kinnoch's glitzy rally, he had to file before it had got properly underway. But he had seen enough in the 'media pack' to gain a reasonable idea of the hubris about to follow:

> It is at times of retreat that an army's strengths can best be observed. It is in moments of triumphalism that we first see the seeds of its downfall. It was when Margaret Thatcher employed a train-bearer to carry her gown that we knew her day was gone. And it was in the slick, cynical image-manipulation of Labour's spectacular at Sheffield last night that we first sensed the contempt into which they too must come.

Parris listed the pop endorsements and the needless live broadcast of Kinnock's helicopter touching down, before ending:

> Last night in Sheffield, image throttled intellect and a quiet voice in every reporter present whispered that there was something disgusting about the occasion. Those voices will grow. Peter Mandelson has

created this Labour Party and, on last night's showing, Peter Mandelson will destroy it. 'We will govern,' Neil Kinnock said opening his speech, 'as we have campaigned.'

Oh I do hope not.[77]

Kinnock's excitable performance at Sheffield compared poorly with the old-fashioned manner in which Major fought the campaign, trudging round town centres to stand on a soap box on a street corner. While polls continued to suggest a narrow lead for Labour, they showed that a majority preferred Major to Kinnock. Two days before the polling stations opened, Simon Jenkins wrote a signed article on the Op-Ed page contrasting the leadership styles of the two contenders. They had much in common: 'Neither needed the help of Oxbridge or family or wealth. There was no apprenticeship in the patronage of a great union or the entourage of a Tory grandee. Grammar school and personal ambition looked after them both.' Yet, for all his policy U-turns, 'a search for substance in the verbosity of a Kinnock speech, reveals little more than the foggy egalitarianism that has moved him since he entered the Commons in 1970'. By contrast, Jenkins wrote approvingly that 'Maastricht was John Major's coming of age as a prime minister' and what he lacked in popular appeal he more than made up for by being good at the 'dull business' of government.[78] The full-page Times leading article endorsing the Tories concerned itself with issues rather than personalities, but it did conclude with a final observation that Major 'has emerged during his brief reign as prime minister as a likeable, competent and honest leader of his country'.[79]

On election morning, Oakley's front-page report warned of a 'cliff-hanger'. MORI opinion polls suggested that the Tories were making a late comeback, from a seven-point deficit a week earlier to only 1 per cent behind on the eve of poll. A hung government appeared likely with Ashdown as the power broker. Having endorsed the Tories the previous day and with opinion polls suggesting a strengthening support for the Liberal Democrats, The Times editorial on election morning warned voters against doing anything that made a hung government or its adoption in perpetuity through proportional representation more likely.[80]

In the event, the horse trading of a hung parliament was avoided. After a tense evening in which exit polls had pointed to conflicting results, the early morning editions of The Times for 10 April proclaimed the Conservatives' victory. It was an extraordinary turnaround – although Major restricted himself to the observation that the result had been 'satisfactory'. In fact, the

Tories were the first party to win four general elections in succession since the restricted franchises of the early nineteenth century. Major's twenty-one-seat majority was a slim one but sufficient to govern unaided. Kinnock's achievement was to have made his party almost electable. It was not enough and he immediately announced his intention to step down. The Liberal Democrat breakthrough was once again postponed for another election.

Twelve of the twenty-one daily and Sunday national newspapers endorsed the Conservatives (representing a total sale of over eighteen million) compared to five who backed Labour (8.6 million sales) while four (with 1.5 million copies) refused to endorse any party. Having its polling-day front page announcing 'If Kinnock wins today will the last person to leave Britain please turn out the lights', the *Sun* greeted the results with the proclamation, 'It's the Sun Wot Won It!' Certainly there appeared to be a last-minute swing towards the Tories from readers of Tory-supporting papers which had pulled out all the journalistic stops of persuasion – and abuse – when it looked like Kinnock might win. The extent to which the swing was a consequence of the editorial line was, of course, hard to gauge. MORI identified a 4 per cent swing from *Sun* readers towards the Tories in the final week of campaigning. But there was a 2.5 per cent swing towards the Tories from readers of the Labour-supporting *Daily Mirror*. Having taken an even-handed approach, *Today*'s last-minute endorsement of the Conservatives appeared to make little appreciable difference. The limited influence of the press was best expressed by the *FT* which announced it was time for Labour and saw the proportion of its readers voting Conservative rise by 7 per cent in the final week to 65 per cent.[81] As far as *The Times*'s role in the verdict of 1992 was concerned, Anatole Kaletsky's analysis of Labour's tax plans probably had the greatest effect. The moderately affluent but hard-working families he suggested would be hit hardest by John Smith's proposals resembled a significant section of the newspaper's core readership.

Whether the opinions expressed in the national newspapers swung the election remains a moot point. Yet, the result did nothing to dissuade those at Labour headquarters that – at the risk of style over substance – winning over the media would be central to victory in 1997. For the moment, though, it was Major who appeared to have the bright future before him. Within forty-eight hours of the Tory victory, Peter Riddell was prophesying the coming parliamentary term in which the Conservatives' health and education reforms would reach fruition with most large hospitals becoming trusts, most GPs becoming independent fundholders and a wave of schools seeking grant-maintained status. As for the issue of Europe, 'potential splits within the Tory party over the EC which might have arisen in opposition should be avoidable'. The Conservative Party, Riddell suggested, now appeared 'to be not only the natural party of government but also perhaps the perpetual one, like the Liberal Democrats in Japan'.[82]

VII

On 19 January 1991, in the midst of the Gulf War, *The Times* introduced the greatest change to its front page since replacing advertisements with news there in 1966. A colour photograph appeared. Being *The Times*, the extent of this revolution was modified by demonstrating the amazing new colour facility with a photograph of the night sky. The depiction was, however, Baghdad nocturne. The darkness was broken up with shards of light as the city came under air attack. For *The Times*, it heralded a new dawn.

In the past, colour had largely been restricted to the Saturday supplements and for some advertisements. This had been made possible by using pre-printed gravure colour, but the process was expensive and needed considerable pre-planning. Eddy Shah's *Today* had been the first national daily to use ROP (run of paper) colour printing, although the results had not always been satisfactory. It was in response to Robert Maxwell's decision to print the *Daily Mirror* with colour that the reluctant Murdoch had finally been persuaded to purchase colour presses for Wapping, Knowsley on Merseyside and Kinning Park in Glasgow. Thus *The Times* became the beneficiary of an investment made primarily to boost Murdoch's tabloid sales. For *The Times*, the revolution was more gradual than the dramatic explosions depicted on the first edition suggested. Technological problems and limited colour availability often ensured that the paper was still largely a monochrome product in the months ahead. Annoyingly, when colour was available, it was not always possible to run it on the front page where its use had most visual impact. There were a few readers for whom any obvious improvement was nonetheless a retrograde step, but as colour photography began, however slowly, to manifest itself with increasing frequency in the paper so it gave *The Times* a chance to appeal to a population which, used to colour television, had developed a more bright and visual expectation of news presentation.

Towards the end of the year, the paper underwent another change of appearance. On 25 November 1991, *The Times* changed its typeface. Between 1932 and 1972 it had been set in Times New Roman, a revolutionary font designed by the paper's typographer, Stanley Morison, that established itself as the most popular typeface in the world. In 1972, the paper had adopted the subtly modified Times Europa which was clearer on the Linotype machinery and lighter paper then being used. Changes in typesetting called for the revision of 1991. Times New Roman and its derivatives had been designed for the old hot metal machinery. Times Millennium, the work of Aurobind Patel, was designed with the effect of computer typesetting in mind. The task of overseeing its introduction fell to David Driver, the paper's design editor. By producing less chunky text, it enabled more words to be fitted in while increasing the amount of white space on the page. The result looked smarter and was generally considered stylish although the reader reaction suggested that the vast majority of the public scarcely registered any difference – which was not necessarily a bad sign. It was digitized type for what was becoming a digitized newspaper. On 18 September 1992, the last cut and paste bromide page was made up for *The Times*. Thereafter, the paper was totally set by electronic page make-up.

Where *The Times* was falling behind was in its availability across the European continent. There, the *FT* had led the way, with editions for the European market printed from Frankfurt in 1979, followed by satellite printing in the United States, in New Jersey in 1985 and at a site near Lille in 1988. The results were impressive. By the end of the decade, the *FT* was selling ninety-thousand copies abroad and had effectively seen off the challenge from the *Wall Street Journal*'s Europe edition on the Continent. By 1990, the *Guardian* and the *Independent* were also being printed in Europe and it was essential that *The Times*, with an overseas sale of 22,000 daily, followed suit as soon as the expensive refitting of Wapping could be completed.[83] Jenkins was understandably impatient to see this achieved, not least because the continental editions of *The Times*'s rivals were what nudged them ahead in the circulation figures.[84] Such was his desperation that he even suggested News International should consider buying the imperilled *European*, partly to stop it falling into a rivals' hands and partly to use it as the core for a new-look European first or weekly edition of *The Times*.[85] In the event, it was not until November 1995 that *The Times* transmitted its second edition via satellite to a printing plant near Charleroi in Belgium to reach newsstands across Europe and the Middle East before the morning rush hour.

The editor had good reason to be anxious about sales. In October 1990, *The Times*, having put its price up by five pence, slipped back behind the *Guardian*. In the succeeding months, the *Guardian* started stretching its lead (while the *Telegraph* remained seemingly unassailable with over one million daily sales). More alarmingly, far from being beaten back by Jenkins's upmarket pitch, the *Independent* had cut the daily sales deficit with *The Times* from twenty thousand in January 1990 to four thousand a year later. In April 1992, its daily sales overtook *The Times*. It was a blip and by June *The Times* had regained a 14,000 lead. But the damage was done. Jenkins had promised to repel the *Independent*'s tanks from *The Times*'s lawn. Instead, two years into his tenure (the time in which he had asked to do the job) the *Independent*'s gun barrels were nudging the front door.

Ironically, the moment in which the *Independent* appeared to be on the brink of breaking *The Times* was also the moment when the young pretender to the upmarket readership had critically overstretched itself. Goaded by the prospect of the *Sunday Correspondent* cornering a market in which it believed it had a right to make money for itself, the *Independent* had launched the *Independent on Sunday*. This succeeded in its primary aims of closing down the *Correspondent* and in building a fair-sized circulation for the *IoS* (or *Sindy*) in its own right. But as the advertising recession began to take effect, so problems for the *Sindy* mounted and it began to drain the group's profitability. During 1991, the Sunday paper's loses hovered around £6 million. Resources that could have been deployed by the *Independent* against *The Times* were, instead, redeployed to shore up the Sunday battlefront. Whittam Smith sought a solution by attempting to integrate the Sunday operation with the weekday paper, cutting jobs – among which was that of his one-time friend and fellow *Independent* founding father, Stephen Glover. The *Independent* went from being a profitable business sensation to a desperate organization in search of a moneyed rescuer. It was the perfect moment for *The Times* to counterattack but that would need fresh investment. This was still some months away.

The foundations of hope were News International's improving financial situation. The company was clawing itself back from the brink and Sky, the great money drainer, at last had rosier prospects. During 1992, *The Times* began to expand again. It had more columns of editorial content than its broadsheet rivals.[86] Jenkins had told Murdoch he wanted two years to turn the paper around. It was clear he would need a little more in order to prove his efforts had a commercial return. Murdoch's impatience was assumed when word went round that one of his closest associates, Irwin Stelzer, had joked at a News Corp. conference that *The Times* was the newspaper one hid within one's copy of the *Sun*. In fact, neither Murdoch nor Andrew Knight were determined to be done with Jenkins. Giving him a five-year contract was even mooted. Jenkins, however, was reluctant to commit to more than one year at a time and had, of course, told his wife that he wanted out within the end of his third year.[87] Faced with this, the proprietor and his chief executive began to look for a candidate who wanted to settle into the post for a longer spell. It was their choice of replacement, rather more than their decision to replace Jenkins several months earlier than he had hoped, that caused a breakdown in relations.

Knight believed a possible successor to Jenkins could be Paul Dacre, the editor of the *Evening Standard*. Knight told Murdoch that Dacre had an unparalleled combination of 'drive, intellect and overall grasp'.[88] When they met, Dacre impressed Murdoch with his commanding view of how *The Times*'s fortunes could be improved. Murdoch offered Dacre the editorship. Dacre confirmed he was interested but pointed out that as a matter of courtesy he would not do a deal while his employer, Vere Rothermere, was out of the country.[89] It was then that things started to fall apart. Murdoch telephoned Jenkins to tell him that he thought Dacre could be a worthy successor. The prospect hit Jenkins like a hammer blow. He was aghast at the thought that all the effort he had put into taking the paper upmarket was about to be casually undone. He told Murdoch, in no uncertain terms, that the idea was disastrous and that staff morale would collapse if Dacre was appointed. Murdoch, it seemed, was about to ditch Jenkins's upmarket strategy. Given that Jenkins had originally asked for only two years to do the job he could not really complain at being taken at face value. 'At the time, I was upset not because I was stopping being editor, but because of Dacre,' he later claimed, adding, 'the person I thought should succeed was Peter Stothard'.[90] Tense days passed while Jenkins ruminated on the possibility that all his efforts to save *The Times* from a mid-market fate were about to be thrown away by a proprietor who simply did not understand what was special about his prize possession.

If such a mid-market fate was in store, it was not to come from Paul Dacre. When he told Rothermere that he was considering accepting the job at *The Times*, the Associated Newspapers owner offered him the editorship of the *Daily Mail* instead. Rothermere and Dacre had long worked well together and Dacre decided to stay in the fold by accepting the task of steering the *Mail*.[91] The appearance in the Associated-owned *Evening*

Standard of the news that Dacre had been approached by *The Times* but had rebuffed the offer was acutely embarrassing for Jenkins because it brought into the public domain that his time as editor was up before he had made any such announcement. Dacre went on to preside over a decade of strong growth at the *Daily Mail*, for which success he was loathed by metropolitan liberal opinion. Murdoch, however, appeared unruffled by the rejection and after he had seen the campaigning approach Dacre brought to the *Mail* later reflected that he would not have been right for *The Times*.[92] This was also the opinion of most senior journalists at *The Times*.[93]

With the news of the Dacre offer leaked, it was important to get on with finding a replacement who would accept the job. Various ideas were mooted, including seeking an appointment from outside the industry.[94] Knight telephoned Charles Wilson at his new perch at Mirror Group Newspapers, asking who he thought would make the best editor. Wilson replied that there were two serious candidates, Peter Stothard and John Bryant, and that whichever was not given the office should serve as deputy.[95] On 23 July, it was announced that Peter Stothard would succeed Simon Jenkins when he stepped down as editor in October.

VII

The handling and timing of Jenkins's departure was poor. When he stepped down, the *Independent* was still breathing down *The Times*'s neck and, judged purely by circulation, he had failed in his objectives. Had he stayed on, the *Independent*'s challenge would have crumbled, not least under the weight of its own mounting financial problems. It was finally being confronted with the very problems that had dogged Jenkins, whose editorship had coincided with a spending freeze caused by News Corp.'s near collapse. The budget for promoting *The Times* had been decimated. It was Jenkins's misfortune that he left just as the parent company's fortunes were recovering and a massive investment in the paper would become possible.

The sorrow among staff at his departure was generally less strongly felt than the joy at his initial appointment. Partly, this was because the journalists felt comfortable with Peter Stothard as a replacement. In transforming *The Times* into a newspaper he thought good enough to write for himself, Jenkins had been single-minded and ruthless. This was a way to turn around a newspaper but not to win the affection of its employees. He had not taken the trouble to cultivate friendships. He drew comfort from a wide range of cultural interests and in a personal life that resided outside the windowless warehouse of Wapping. Towards colleagues, Charlie Wilson's line of invective had been far stronger and he had frequently seemed on the point of doing someone a personal injury, but he had also shown a tender streak towards those in trouble or in need of help. For all his occasional roughness, Wilson always had an easy relationship with his backbench: 'like a Field Marshal enjoying the company of his generals', as one of the backbench's most accomplished practitioners, Simon Pearson, put it.[96] Jenkins was far more self-assured in his manner. He had a clear idea about what he wanted and this was not in keeping with a collegiate approach. It did not translate into familiar badinage. The vehemence of his attitude when errors appeared in the paper even earned him the enmity of some who thought his response disproportionate. In this sense, he was a leader more interested in being feared than loved.

Yet, reflecting on his experience of five *Times* editors, the financial editor, Graham Searjeant, took the view that Jenkins was the one who 'saved the paper.'[97] He was right to insist on the highest standards if it was to have any hope of regaining its former reputation for accuracy. Whether *The Times* sunk or swam was ultimately a better judgment of his tenure than whether he was aloof to some of his staff. He had worked incredibly hard. He had stayed in the office well into the evening, taking the 8.30 conference where the first edition was analysed and modified, before leaving for an evening of social engagements only to return to the office at 11.30 to take charge once again. Had he benefited, as his successor did, from a night editor of the skill and self-confidence of David Ruddock, he might have felt able to leave the backbench more to its own devices. He was also hampered by the departure of John Bryant as deputy editor, another journalist who understood the nuts and bolts of putting a paper to bed. Happily, he was able to welcome Bryant back as deputy editor before leaving the chair himself, but Bryant's professional touch was missed for most of Jenkins's editorship.

Jenkins viewed his own two years in the chair with satisfaction: 'We just about stabilised the circulation but the most important thing to me was to reverse the loss of reputation.'[98] He had very effectively spiked the guns of those who asserted that *The Times* lacked its former intellectual vigour. In focusing on hiring specialists, Jenkins helped the paper to regain its reputation as a source of information and good writing, and not just a news-orientated paper written by reporters. This was important. In Anatole

Kaletsky he had hired one of the foremost economic commentators of the age. Another perceptive journalist brought over from the *FT* was Peter Riddell who would similarly play a major and steadying role in the years ahead. In particular, *The Times* regained from the *Independent* the initiative over arts coverage, thanks in no small part to the contributions of Marcus Binney, Richard Cork and Rodney Milnes.

No editor of *The Times* believed he left the paper in a worse position than he found it, but there was much truth in Jenkins's own assessment, that, had he not taken charge in 1990:

> The programme that Whittam Smith undertook in 1986 to wipe out *The Times* would, I think, have been ultimately successful and we stopped it. That is the single biggest contribution I made, by boosting the morale of the paper and hiring particular people who were still all there ten years later. I said to Rupert, 'I've done what I wanted to do, which is what you told me to do – to make it a paper I would want to write a column for.'[99]

He wrote his column for the next twelve and a half years.

CHAPTER TEN

CRITICAL TIMES

The New Editor; the Price War; Sport;
the Arts; Beauty; Science; the Internet

I

Judged by his appointments, Rupert Murdoch did not have a settled idea about what sort of man should be an editor of *The Times*. In choosing Harold Evans he wanted a dynamic leader with a strong news sense who would bring to the paper some of the excitement that he had brought to the *Sunday Times*. Yet, when Murdoch's patience ran out with Evans he turned to Charles Douglas-Home, an editor more in the Rees-Mogg mould, whose primary interest was in considered comment and engagement with ideas. Next, the proprietor turned back in search of a strong news editor, which he found in Charles Wilson. Yet, within five years he had decided that *The Times* needed a less abrasive and more contemplative sage in the shape of Simon Jenkins. Each editor in succession appeared to be either a news editor or an Op-Ed editor writ large. The initial approach to Paul Dacre suggested Murdoch's next instinct was to swing the pendulum back towards a hard news editor with a flair for campaigning journalism. Instead, in selecting Peter Stothard, he performed a volte-face, deciding in favour of another Op-Ed man in succession to Jenkins.

In fact, Peter Stothard appeared to fulfil several requirements. He had the intellectual engagement and breadth of interests that were to be expected of a traditional *Times* editor. Indeed, no previous occupant of the chair had such a grasp or passion for Latin and Greek literature. Yet he had none of the mannered, old-fashioned, donnish demeanour that suggested he would attempt to disengage *The Times* from the modern world. He was forty-one. His father had worked on radar research for Marconi[1] and he had grown up in Essex, going to Brentwood School, which provided a good independent education without being in the senior ranks of the more illustrious public schools. Up at Trinity College, Oxford, to read Classics he had arrived armed with a case containing his father's old blue-green-yellow cricket blazer (not that the son had a well-honed interest in sport) and his grandfather's faded edition of the second six books of Virgil's *Aeneid*. A contemporary there, Stephen Glover (later one of the three founders of the *Independent*) subsequently predicated the myth that Stothard had spent his undergraduate days wandering by the Isis in a kaftan.[2] This was far from the truth for he was neither a college hearty nor a dreamer. Instead, he edited *Cherwell* and counted among his friends there George Brock and the future novelist Sally Emerson and her friend Tina Brown. Indeed, Stothard had developed the characteristics that were looked on with favour at News International. He was astute, intelligent and well educated but belonged to a generation that was meritocratic and open-minded.

One of the legacies to come out of Stothard's period as *The Times*'s comment editor and deputy editor during the 1980s had been his role in scouting out young talent. The training scheme he established brought a new generation of the bright and the ambitious directly from university to *The Times*, a fast-track policy which undoubtedly attracted many to journalism who might otherwise have been lured elsewhere by the increasing financial returns offered by business and the professions. Other newspapers subsequently emulated this policy. The consequence was a marked increase in the number of journalists on major newspapers with excellent degrees from the leading universities – although those who liked their news pages unvarnished and without adjectives came to regret the effect that employing writers with analytical skills and the opinions that came with them had on 'straight' reporting. For Stothard, the short step from Broad Street to Fleet Street had not been so straightforward. After Oxford, he had experimented with various careers. At one stage he was employed by an advertising agency working on the Cadburys chocolate account while his neighbour on the next desk ran the campaign to boost *The Times*'s sales. Out of the corner of his eye, Stothard registered the attempt to sell the struggling paper's charms. Yet it was into broadcast journalism that he next went, spending three years as a BBC trainee working on the *Today* programme. In 1977, he appeared to put the hack's life behind him and, determined upon a career in management, joined Shell. But the journalistic instinct remanifested itself. He began writing a number of scoops in *New Society*. This brought him to the attention of the *Sunday Times*, where he was brought in as a business and political correspondent. There, he became a protégé of Harold Evans. In 1980 Stothard married Sally Emerson and the following year Evans married Tina Brown. Evans took him across the bridge to

The Times. There, Stothard found himself alongside Anthony Holden and Bernard Donoughue as a core member of the editor's praetorian guard. Some were surprised when, unlike Holden and Donoughue, he did not resign when Evans was tipped out of his chair in 1982. Instead, Stothard stayed put and prospered under the incoming Douglas-Home dispensation, becoming features editor and, soon after, chief leader writer. Charles Wilson also thought highly of him, making him deputy editor when Colin Webb left to take up his post at the Press Association. Stothard held onto the title in 1989 when he moved over to Washington DC, to became *The Times*'s US editor.

Stothard gained from the experience of overseeing the paper's American coverage and filing regular and penetrating commentary from Washington even though – or perhaps because – it removed him from the daily skirmishes for power and position at Wapping. *The Times* remained, after all, a paper with an international profile and an American-based owner who expected his executives to have an equally non-parochial attitude. Out in Washington, Stothard had proved that he was not the sort of delicate desk-bound writer who could only thrive within the enclosed and somewhat claustrophobic atmosphere of the windowless rum warehouse off Pennington Street.

Whether from Wapping or Washington, Stothard had spent the 1980s watching the attempt of successive *Times* editors to confront increasing and improving competition, from traditional newspaper rivals, from other media like radio and television and from the new claimant for the paper's core market – the *Independent*. Simon Jenkins had identified the latter as the principal threat. Indeed, he had been appointed as the man to repulse its tanks from the front lawn. In this respect he had failed and by the time he passed the chair on to Stothard, the *Independent*'s position had only strengthened. Circulation between the old and new claimants to informed opinion was running neck and neck.

No sooner had Stothard settled behind the editor's desk than he acted decisively. A wave of sackings was announced. In all, more than twenty journalists were fired. The 'Life and Times' section – which Jenkins regarded as one of his achievements – was axed, having failed to attract much advertising. The prize scalp, however, was that of Clifford Longley. The chief leader writer and religious affairs correspondent had been at *The Times* for a quarter of a century and had been the journalists' NUJ chapel father. *The Economist* credited him with being the last of the *Times* Blackfriars.[3] The manner of the sacking caused ill feeling that went beyond the two protagonists. Relations further deteriorated in early 1994 when *The Times* printed an article by Dr Tim Bradshaw, the Dean of Regent's Park College, Oxford, that named Longley as one of a corps of Roman Catholic journalists who were motivated by malice in their analysis of the Church of England. Backed with legal assistance by his new employers at the *Telegraph* (who had also been criticized in the article), Longley instigated legal action not only against the author and *The Times* but also against Stothard personally. He won damages and his legal costs.[4]

There were other changes. Stothard's arrival as editor coincided with the departure of the political editor, Robin Oakley, who was offered and accepted the same post at the BBC. Peter Riddell replaced him initially, but in a reshuffle in 1993 Philip Webster was made political editor while the post he had held as chief political correspondent since 1986 was passed to Nicholas Wood. Riddell, meanwhile, was free to write his daily political commentary. This was a formula that the other newspapers adopted too (and had its echo in the broadcast soliloquies of the BBC's successive political editors, John Cole, Robin Oakley and, most especially, Andrew Marr). The concern about this development was that it meant mixing up comment and news on the same page with all the resulting possibilities that the former could contaminate the latter. Yet, so long as Riddell's articles were properly displayed as a commentary there was little real danger of it causing any more confusion than Matthew Parris's parliamentary sketches. Riddell certainly had his own view – he was, for example, sympathetic to the pro-European cause – but unlike a celebrity columnist he was not a hired controversialist. His observations could not be faulted for their deliberative qualities or their equanimity of expression.

Stothard, meanwhile, brought on several rising talents. Daniel Johnson became literary editor. Another who appeared destined for great things was Matthew D'Ancona, a Fellow of All Souls and who, like Johnson, had a First in History from Magdalen College, Oxford. Still only twenty-three, his route to *The Times* had been through the graduate traineeship. Initially set to work writing education stories, D'Ancona was identified by the new editor as a journalist with a good political brain who could write on a range of issues. As far as the outside world was concerned, perhaps the greatest sign that all was well came not from the promotion of younger voices but in the return of an older one. In January 1993, William Rees-Mogg returned to *The Times* to write a column for the Op-Ed page on Mondays and Wednesdays. Lord Rees-Mogg of Hinton Blewitt (as he had been since his elevation to the House of Lords in 1988) not only brought all the authority of a senior journalist with forty years experience but also his personal acquaintance with many of the major figures in the political and media Establishment. During the course of the past decade he had been the chairman of several publishing companies, chairman of the Arts Council, vice-chairman of the BBC's board of governors, and chairman of the Broadcasting Standards Commission as well as a director on several company boards, including GEC. Not only was Rees-Mogg's return a boon for the paper, it was a blow to the *Independent*'s desire to be seen as the embodiment of the finest traditions of the pre-Wapping *Times* (Rees-Mogg's earlier stint as a columnist for the *Independent* had hurt many *Times* journalists who treated it as if it was a personal rebuke). The *Independent* was hit further with the departure of Alexander Chancellor who went to New York, from where he filed a weekly Saturday column for *The Times* throughout 1993.

There were also presentational changes to the paper. Some of Jenkins's more conservative design instincts were also jettisoned. Headlines began to increase in size again and colour printing was used wherever there was the capacity to provide it. This reversed Jenkins's more reticent approach that restricted colour photography to images that he thought specifically deserved it. *The Times* was no longer a definitively black and white product. Puffs above the masthead had started appearing on the Saturday editions in 1988 to advertise the highlights within Charlie Wilson's four-section paper. The expansion of special features during the weekdays was an argument in favour of running the puff above (or below – opinion shifted on the question of their placement) the masthead during the week as well. Given the extra sales that could be put on by drawing the attention of passers-by to the paper's contents in this way it was not surprising that when Stothard became editor they were made a fixed daily feature, running below the masthead. The commercial argument could not be countered. Aesthetically, they were an affront. The wider and more garish graphics the puff strip contained, the more the outward appearance of seriousness was debased.

Marketing *The Times* was a difficult process. Those who wanted to read Rees-Mogg on Monday did not necessarily want a huge puff on the front page screaming about goals galore at Stamford Bridge or the pick of the Paris fashion show. Nor could the columns on the Op-Ed page be expected to appeal to the size of audience *The Times* needed to survive. Spending money on television campaigns was a fast route to wasting millions. Targeting a specific audience appeared to make much more sense. An opportunity for this came from an unlikely source. In 1993 the World Chess Federation, FIDE, was plunged into crisis when Russia's Garry Kasparov and Britain's Nigel Short rejected the proposed match fee. Instead they established their own Professional Chess Federation. *The Times* agreed to sponsor the new tournament with a £1.7 million investment that would pit the two men against one another in what would be called *The Times* World Chess Championship. Extensively trailed in the paper, broadcast by Channel 4 and staged at the Savoy Theatre, Stothard envisaged it as a great way of promoting the paper's association with thoughtfulness and strategic thinking. The paper's chess correspondent, Raymond Keene, provided commentary and analysis in *The Times* while Simon Barnes wrote the sketch. There was even a friendly match between Short and Daniel Johnson. The main event, however, turned out less satisfactorily than its promoters had hoped. Short's poor run of form reduced the contest as a sporting spectacle. *The Times* World Chess Championship proved to be a one-off tournament. Stothard was left to conclude, 'Chess politics, I discovered, was probably the most difficult and unpleasant politics of any sort.'[5] The issue of how to get more readers remained. An altogether grander plan was devised.

II

When Rupert Murdoch bought *The Times* in 1981 the intention was to make it profitable within five years. This he achieved. When the paper celebrated its bicentenary in 1985 it had finally moved into the black. Yet, this was to be a temporary phenomenon. The move to Wapping helped ensure News International's strategic profitability although, in the short term, *The Time*'s share of Wapping's start-up costs harmed its own financial figures. Wapping created the conditions in which the paper could modernize and expand – opportunities that required fresh investment rather than cost cutting. The conquering of one costly process – for instance, the reduction of union-protected overmanning in the print hall – was quickly succeeded by the realization of a new expense, like the introduction of colour presses. The revitalized competition, in particular the *Independent* and Conrad Black's *Daily Telegraph*, were also investing in bigger and brighter papers. *The Times* could not stand still and risk the destruction of its market share. The costs continued to spiral accordingly.

A freer market behaved as expected, competition suiting the consumer rather better than the producer.

If *The Times* had a fresh opportunity to balance its books then there was no better period than the latter stages of the Lawson boom when advertising demand was at a premium. The profitability of the *Sunday Times*, with its 1.3 million circulation, ensured that Times Newspapers Limited announced a £20.2 million profit in June 1998. The opportunity existed for *The Times* to be profitable in its own right. Its advertising revenue increased by 38 per cent between 1987 and 1989. Unfortunately, production and editorial (salaries, expenses, etc.) costs soared well above inflation during the period too. The hope that improved advertising sales would bridge this gap proved illusionary. The onset of the recession abruptly ended any thought of pressing on into the black. Advertising revenue was decimated. Businesses stopped advertising for vacancies, luxury products became even more of an unaffordable indulgence and the sun began to set on the holiday market. By 1991–2, advertising was providing only half of the paper's revenue.[6]

The only positive aspect of the economic slowdown was that it was affecting *The Times*'s rivals too. Indeed, during the recession, the paper's advertising department outperformed many of its competitors, showing resourcefulness in reduced circumstances. This was demonstrated by its ability to keep its position in the newspaper advertising market. Its 22 per cent share in 1991 was the same as during the boom time of 1987 and was only 1 per cent behind the leader, the *Telegraph*. Not only did it keep the *Independent* marginalized, *The Times* did significantly better than the *FT* which saw its share slide from nearly a quarter of the market in 1987 to less than a fifth by 1991.

With falling advertising revenue, the paper attempted to recoup its losses by raising the cover price. A paper that had cost its purchaser twenty-three pence on the eve of Wapping in 1986 had gradually crept up to thirty pence during the summer of 1990. From then, as the recession took its toll, the price hikes became more frequent. Between 1990 and 1993 the cost of *The Times* rose from thirty to forty-five pence, a 50 per cent increase. As with advertising rates, the paper's situation was only eased by the reality that its competitors were in no position to outmanoeuvre it. At forty-five pence, *The Times* was the same price as the *Independent* and the *Guardian* and three pence cheaper that the *Daily Telegraph*. On Saturdays, all sold at fifty pence except for *The Telegraph* which cost sixty pence. The *FT*, meanwhile, was retailing during the week at a stately sixty-five pence.

Unsurprisingly, price increases during a period in which recession was forcing households to make economies had a negative effect on sales. Both the broadsheet and the tabloid market contracted. By January 1993, nearly a quarter of a million fewer national broadsheets were being sold every day than in 1989. *The Times* had lost 65,000 daily sales over the period. The question was how to entice the readers back. Simon Jenkins had maintained that it was about producing a quality newspaper. This, indeed, was the conventional wisdom. It was not just *The Times* that was investing in producing extra sections, better print quality and colour. All were seeking to add value to the product. Newspaper strategy had assumed the centrality of building and fostering reader loyalty. This was seen as a matter of investment. Although it was difficult to deny that the price increases had made papers less attractive on the newsstand, opinion in Fleet Street and in the City was still broadly that the national broadsheets were catering for a market that was more quality than price led. The belief that a largely middle class, and in the case of *The Times* often professional, readership would switch brand identity for the sake of saving a few pence a week was widely doubted.

This appeared to be the view among the senior management at News International. Both Murdoch and Andrew Knight were enthusiastic about an idea that Rees-Mogg and Anatole Kaletsky advocated during 1992. They wanted to replace the existing second section (which had eight pages of business news and four of sport) by a completely tabloid pull-out containing forty-eight pages of business and eight of sport. The intention was to trump the *FT* (28 per cent of whose readers were already also reading *The Times*) with a section that would provide yet more detailed analysis of financial sectors. It would also permit *The Times* to increase its cover price towards the *FT*'s level. The idea was eventually dropped because the production cost was simply too expensive.[7] Instead, from 12 October 1992, sport was moved to the back of the main part of the paper and a new second section was created containing business and arts news, controversially countering the previous assumption that business and sport were the subjects men wanted together on their commute to the office. Opinion was sharply divided over whether this new arrangement made sense but it was, at least, not as costly as the innovation floated by Rees-Mogg and Kaletsky.

What was remarkable was how quickly News International challenged the conventional wisdom (including its own) over price versus quality. Within months of taking seriously a plan that would have once again increased the cover price, Murdoch threw himself behind a radical scheme to slash the cover price of *The Times*. Certainly, investment had not been shown to improve the paper's market share. Indeed, despite heavy promotion, its sale had slipped by over 6 per cent in the first six months of 1993 compared to the same period the previous year. Its lead over the *Independent*, at twenty thousand, was uncomfortably small, especially given the financial constraints and lack of promotion with which the latter paper had been forced to operate during the period. The narrow margin looked particularly alarming when it became evident that the *Independent* had plans in motion for rejuvenation focused on improving quality over cost. It was gearing up for an autumn relaunch that would bring expansion, new sections and colour to the news pages. The moment, it seemed, had come in which *The Times* would be comprehensively eclipsed by its newer rival. Such a turn of events would do great psychological damage to *The Times*'s esteem. What was more, as market analysts could relate, once a newspaper started upon a prolonged downward trajectory, it was very difficult to reverse the trend. Identification as only the fourth best-selling broadsheet (behind the *Telegraph*, *Guardian* and *Independent*) would force down advertising rates, reducing revenue and making investment in the product impossible. *The Times* had to act fast before it was sucked into this downward spiral. Most analysts and the executive chairman, Andrew Knight, advised investing in the product. Murdoch decided they were wrong.

Like many important decisions, the one to launch the price war came from what appeared at the time to be a throwaway remark. Murdoch was over in Wapping to see what difference a price cut at the *Sun* was having on sales and bumped into Stothard in a corridor. A brief conversation ensued during which Murdoch proffered the (seemingly) off-the-cuff question, 'Do you think the *Sun*'s experiment would work for *The Times*?' Stothard had independently come to the view that further cover price increases should be resisted but, given the great expense involved in actually making a cut, he had not seriously considered reversing the trend. Nonetheless, almost without pause to weigh the possibilities, he replied that, yes, he thought a price cut could work.[8] It was a bold response. Whether the *Sun*'s economics also applied to the *The Times* had never been properly tested. The tabloid market had been in a long period of declining circulation. Although it remained the market leader, the *Sun* had lost half a million sales in the past five years (1988–93). Yet the paper's price cut in July 1993 to twenty pence proved an immediate stimulant: its sale soared by 368,000 in the following month. This took its share of the tabloid market above 50 per cent, good news for the *Sun* and ultimately for the fortunes of News International upon which *The Times* depended. Yet what appealed to the readers of 'The Sun Says' and page three would not necessarily translate to the paper of Bernard Levin and Court & Social. In any case, some argued that it was not so much more readers, but richer readers, that *The Times* needed.

This was an age-old argument. In a good year, around 70 per cent of *The Times*'s revenue came from advertising. Thus, halving the cover price would have an effect on less than 9 per cent of the paper's revenue. The intention certainly appeared explicable enough – to recoup this loss by gaining new readers and thereby a richer market for advertisers to target. However, experience suggested the equation was not so simple. In 1967 *The Times* had successfully gone in search of new readers but the expense involved in attracting them was greater than the volume of high-quality advertising they brought with them. With costs spiralling out of control, the growth strategy had been abandoned in 1970 and the paper duly contracted, retreating back to serving its core third of a million readers. Unfortunately, that too failed to make the paper profitable. Thus it tried again in 1984, when Portfolio was launched. This time advertising revenue did pick up although because the economy was recovering after a period of deep recession this was to be expected. When, in late 1985, the circulation reached a plateau, many assumed this was the physical limit of the paper's reach.

A new price cut strategy was predicated upon proving the paper did not have a natural plateau that was less than half of what the *Daily Telegraph* sold every day. Yet, if the experiences of 1967–70 were not to be repeated, the 'right sort' of readers had to be attracted. These were the readers who would be especially appealing to advertisers with expensive products to market. If the price cut only attracted students, manual workers and parsimonious pensioners in genteel retirement in Eastbourne, it would never pay its way. The objective was to attract younger professionals with disposable income. Apart from the fact that advertisers preferred them, there was also a longer-term payback if the strategy made lifelong *Times* readers out of those who had forty years of newspaper purchasing ahead of them rather than old-age pensioners who had just a few. The problem was that most analysts believed the only people who would respond favourably to a price cut were the very lower income groups that advertisers spurned.

Thus, cutting the price of *The Times* was a highly risky strategy taken against most of the prevailing wisdom. It would be expensive, especially given the decision that the reduced price would be deducted from the company's share of each sale, and not by reducing the margins of the wholesaler or retailer (for each forty-five pence proffered at the newsagent the retailer would keep twelve pence and, after the wholesaler had taken his cut, News International received back only twenty-sevnty pence). If the paper cut its price to thirty pence, as was now suggested, News International would receive only around twelve pence per copy. Considering it cost nearer thirteen pence to print each copy, this was arithmetic that could not be profitable without encouraging a giant surge in advertising revenue.

Despite all this, Murdoch gave his blessing. Having narrowly escaped bankruptcy in 1990, News Corp. was back in expansionary mode. The satellite television company Sky had bought out its competition to form British Sky Broadcasting (BSkyB) and appeared to be coming out of its financial difficulties. In August 1993, News International announced that profits had soared, year on year, from £48 to £161 million. This was the moment to risk short-term losses assisting *The Times* in order to steal a march on the competition. On 2 August, *The Times* began a trial run of the effect of a price cut by cutting the cover price by fifteen pence to thirty pence to thirty pence in Kent, beyond London's M25 orbital. In the first three weeks, sales went up by almost 14 per cent. This was the confirmation for which Stothard was looking. The decision was taken to repeat the feat throughout the country.

Thus within days of Stothard's corridor chat, a great strategic gamble was being swung into action, backed by a strongly supportive Murdoch and his son-in-law, Alasdair MacLeod, who was *The Times*'s circulation manager and perhaps the single greatest exponent behind the plan. Here was an example of where having the backing of a strong and risk-taking proprietor who was prepared to back his instincts with decisive action in the face of hostile conventional wisdom proved beneficial. It allowed a newspaper to pursue a strategy that would probably not have been open to it if it had been run by a conventional company owned by banks or private investment trusts used to managing though the usual risk-analysis assessments. The daring of the approach was shown by the incredulity of the media analysts. When the news broke that *The Times* was going to cut fifteen pence from its price nationally, the initial industry reaction, as reported by the perceptive Raymond Snoddy in the *FT*, was that Stothard and Murdoch 'must have gone mad'.[9] Alan Rusbridger, the *Guardian*'s deputy editor, made clear his paper would not be following suit. 'Unlike the *Sun* and *The Times*,' Rusbridger sniffed, 'the *Guardian* has no problem in attracting readers prepared to pay what they evidently think is a reasonable cover price.'[10] The *Telegraph* was equally snippy, its managing director stating, 'We think it's sad to see a British institution in such an undignified state, marketing itself not as a paper of record, not for its wide coverage or fine writing, not even for its integrity but "Buy Me, I'm Cheap".'[11] Some of this was the natural badinage of competitors, but for the most part the tone of dismissive condescension was genuine.

A less sanguine attitude animated the *Independent*. When the news broke that *The Times* was dropping its price, the *Independent* took the controversial step of issuing a front-page condemnation. It accused Murdoch of a 'cynical' predatory pricing policy that was deliberately seeking to 'drive this newspaper, *The Independent*, and *The Independent on Sunday* out of business'. 'Without any new editorial ideas', the statement continued, 'and without any belief in *The Times* as a newspaper, Murdoch has decided to crush his nearest rival with the power of money.' The *Independent*, it made clear, would not be prepared to enter this price-cutting war: 'Unlike the *Times*, *The Independent* has to earn its living in the world. Because it has to, it has a genuinely independent liberal voice, something which *The Times* lost the moment Mr Murdoch became its owner.'[12] Three days after *The Times*'s price cut went nationwide, Newspaper Publishing, the *Independent*'s owners, delivered a submission to the Office of Fair Trading (OFT) alleging Murdoch was improperly trying to destroy their business by using the profits from other divisions of his empire to give his (loss-making) *Times* an unfair advantage against its competitors. The assumption was that, once he had achieved his goal of removing the *Independent* as a competitor, he would then increase the cover price and maximize his profits. This operated against competition law and the ultimate losers would be the newspaper-reading public.

These were strong allegations and difficult to prove. The law defined predatory pricing as the attempt by a company that had a 'dominant' position in its market to set its price with the intention of destroying its competition. Yet, not only was *The Times*'s share of the broadsheet market very much a minority one, even if Murdoch's other mass-selling tabloids were included in a survey of the total market, the company still had a minority share. Only in satellite broadcasting did Murdoch's Sky enjoy a dominant position and he maintained that the money to fund *The Times*'s price cut did not come from that sector of his empire. This was not the only problem facing those trying to use the law to block the price cut. Investigations by the Office of Fair Trading could not be concluded quickly and indeed it was necessary that there should not be a recourse that allowed any company immediately to halt a competitor offering an alternative product more cheaply. The problem for Murdoch's accusers was that by the time a predatory pricing policy was shown to have succeeded in its aims, it could be too late to do much about it. Since the introduction of the 1980 Competition Act, the OFT had only undertaken seven formal investigations and five times come to the conclusion that no offence existed. There had never previously been a complaint regarding newspaper pricing.

Murdoch found the *Independent*'s accusations highly hypocritical. 'I think it's a bit rich of Andreas Whittam Smith,' he shot back, 'particularly when he was only able to launch his paper because of what we did at Wapping. He also closed the *Sunday Correspondent* and tried to do the same to *The Observer*.'[13] Whittam Smith's moral high ground had indeed been undermined by his own actions. He had deliberately launched the *Independent on Sunday* in order to destroy the new *Sunday Correspondent*, duly forcing it to fold. In trying (and failing) to buy the *Observer*, he had fuelled speculation that the only reason he wanted to own directly competing Sunday newspapers was in order to strangle the two-hundred-year-old *Observer* so that his own sickly infant could survive. 'I wasn't going to be lectured by them,' fumed Stothard, accusing Whittam Smith of talking 'the most sanctimonious nonsense. The only clear, unequivocal case of a paper doing something to close another paper down was the launch of the *Independent of Sunday* in order to close *The Correspondent*.' By contrast, Murdoch had a reputation for investment rather than closure. He had saved *Today* from the scrapheap and was only eventually persuaded to terminate its life when, having spent millions, it proved impossible to turn around. Indeed, as far as Stothard's analysis was concerned, the complaints against *The Times* had come a bit late: 'the time that we were really predatory pricing was when *The Times* was racking up massive losses'. Neither Northcliffe, nor the Astors, nor the Thomsons had sold the paper at its true cover price, being prepared instead to subsidize its losses from money they had made elsewhere. 'Did anybody complain when the owners of *The Times* were pumping millions of pounds into saving *The Times* from a fate at the hands of the market?' asked Stothard rhetorically. On this reading of the evidence, 'we had been predatory pricing for a hundred years' without complaint. Stothard suspected that what the critics now 'objected to was the success of the paper and its attraction to their readers. I found these arguments hypocritical.'[14]

The thirty-pence *Times* was launched on 6 September 1993. By the end of the week, sales had gone up by more than a quarter. It was in that same week that Murdoch announced the expansion of BSkyB with an eighteen-channel package that doubled the number of satellite channels available in Britain. He had also acquired the Star TV satellite in Asia which was technically accessible to two-thirds of the continent's population. To those who had long looked at Murdoch's rise with feelings of dread, he appeared to be launching assaults on all fronts in a battle for global media domination. One of those particularly horrified that Murdoch appeared to be taking over the world, one satellite dish at a time, was Ann Clwyd, Labour's heritage spokeswoman, who declared *The Times*'s decision to cut its price 'an affront to democracy' and urged an investigation by the Monopolies Commission to prevent 'this degree of influence in Britain's press and broadcasting'. It was not just Labour politicians who were alarmed. Peter Bottomley, the deputy chairman of the Conservative Back-bench Media Committee, also expressed concern.[15]

Where were Murdoch's guns actually pointing? The *Daily Mail* and the *Daily Express* had just increased their cover price when *The Times* launched its offensive and it was from the mid-market, rather than the broadsheet competition, that the most immediate gains appeared to be made. Murdoch's initial approach to Paul Dacre the previous year with the offer of *The Times* editorship certainly suggested that he had his sites on attracting middle-market readers to the more venerable title. Yet it was not just a question of coaxing readers away from other papers. Attracting those who had ceased buying any newspaper was a major contributing factor to *The Times*'s dramatic rise. The emphasis on investing in the quality of the product had, it seemed, blinded newspaper executives to the price sensitivity of the market. Broadsheet readers were just as keen on saving pennies as tabloid browsers. This explained why *The Times* was able to stretch its lead over the *Independent* by 110,000 and by almost 40,000 over the *Guardian* even though the latter's circulation statistics remained buoyant. During October, there were 100,000 more copies of national broadsheet newspapers being bought every day than there had been in August. Far from seeking to wipe out all signs of competition, *The Times*, it seemed, was helping to grow a market that had appeared in gradual decline. This was a repeat of what the *Independent* had successfully done upon its launch in 1986.

In the first months, neither the *Daily Telegraph*, the *Guardian* nor the *FT* suffered greatly from the launch of the cut-price *Times*. The only significant losers were the *Independent*, which was down 20 per cent, and the mid-market *Daily Express*, down 9 per cent. The *Telegraph*'s sales remained surprisingly stable, averaging just over one million.[16] The *Independent*'s attempted fightback in October 1993 with a new-look two sections with colour printing failed to reverse its slide. The price war had come at a moment when the *Independent* was in crisis, its finances drained by the launch of the *Independent on Sunday*. Andreas Whittam Smith, who at one stage had been sufficiently confident to muse that the *Independent* might buy *The Times*, was forced to go cap in hand to Mirror Group Newspapers. Although he remained editor and chairman of the new board, the paper was independent in name only since its fortunes were now at the mercy of the owners of the *Daily Mirror* (whose sales were taking a pounding from the cut-price *Sun*) and backed up by significant shareholdings from *El Pais* and *La Repubblica*. It was not the sort of proprietorial commune the *Independent*'s founders had envisaged. Nonetheless, the new arrangement was a lifeline, bringing the investment the paper need. What it had lost, besides its innocence, was its sense of momentum, a force which only months earlier had looked like elevating it above *The Times*. In February 1994 the *Independent*'s sales fell below those of the supposedly niche-market *FT*. By then it was trailing *The Times* by 175,000. The tables had been most effectively turned.

The *Daily Telegraph* had reacted to the price cut of its principal rival with a degree of sang froid bordering on complacency. With a forecast £60 million profit for 1993 its position at the head of the broadsheet market doubtless appeared unassailable. Its managing director had even argued its rising cover price was an asset on the grounds that it was 'a premium price for a premium brand'. In fact, the *Telegraph*'s half-century domination of the broadsheet market rested on exactly the sort of tactic Murdoch was now pursuing. In 1930, the *Telegraph* had halved its price from twopence to a penny. Its sales soared past the million mark leaving behind *The Times* to cater for its small, if influential, metropolitan catchment area. It had taken a long time for *The Times* to catch on. The *Telegraph*'s problem – whatever the talk of 'premium brands' – was that in the space of the past eight years it had gone from being the cheapest national broadsheet to the most expensive of the four (the *FT*, retailing at sixty-five pence, cost more, but it catered for a targeted market). The *Telegraph*'s initial ability to withstand the price assault bolstered the arguments of those in its ranks who believed there was no need to panic. Of Murdoch's efforts, Neil Collins took the view, 'there must be something better you can do with £40 million than hand it to your customers'. But by June 1994, after nine months of withstanding the assault, it was clear to those assembled at the *Telegraph*'s offices in Canary Wharf that their paper's sales were starting to slide and that delaying matters could be catastrophic. Retailing at eighteen pence more than its direct rival, the *Telegraph* risked pricing itself out of the market. They persuaded Conrad Black to cut the price.[17]

On the evening of the *Telegraph*'s price cutting announcement, Stothard was at a party thrown by the publisher Lord Weidenfeld when Black, looking gruff, came up to him. 'What you and Rupert Murdoch don't understand,' he warned, 'is just how rich I am.' To Stothard these sounded like the words of a man who was not quite as rich as he would like to be.[18] Black's patience and his pockets did transpire to be limited. The *Telegraph*'s cut in price attracted back lost readers but provoked a far more negative response from the City where its share price dived from 540 pence to 349 pence, wiping £264 million from its market capitalization. The crash also put the spotlight on Conrad Black who had raised £73 million by selling shares at 587 pence only the previous month while sticking to the line that the *Telegraph* would not enter the price war. Feeling misled, financiers were furious at his volte-face and he suffered the indignity of having Cazenove, his corporate stockbroker, state they were terminating their relationship with the Telegraph Group. Max Hastings would later write in defence of Black's claim that he had not consciously deceived investors[19] and the Stock Exchange also cleared him of impropriety. Nevertheless, the affair damaged Black's reputation in the City. Critics were quick to dredge the episode back up when, in 2004, his business affairs came unstuck.

In June 1994, Black may have hoped that sanctioning a price cut would bring *The Times*'s offensive to a halt. He was wrong. Stothard and Murdoch immediately agreed to meet fire with fire. Thus *The Times* responded by cutting again, taking the cover price down to twenty pence and immediately wrong-footing the *Telegraph*. Between them, Hollinger and News International were writing off around £80 million in lost revenue from circulation. Many in the City believed it was madness. *The Times* now cost the same as the *Sun*. 'I am watching with the bemusement that I sometimes reserve for a bad pantomine,' commented Peter Preston, the *Guardian*'s Editor.[20] The *Independent*, having taken the most high-minded line of all, dipped its toe in the water with a one-off twenty-pence edition on Monday 23 June. It boosted sales on the day, but few were so impressed that they came back for more at full price the following morning. Black, meanwhile, made informal approaches to Murdoch to call the price war off.[21] The moves were rebuffed. Regardless of how rich Black claimed to be, the evidence was that Murdoch was richer. While the £45 million cost of the price war reduced News International's operating profits to £96.2 million in the year to June 1994, this was more than balanced by the surging profitability of BSkyB and News Corp.'s television and film divisions in the United States.[22] Over the summer of 1994, *The Times* felt sufficiently confident to increase its advertising rates by 15 per cent, a decision that reflected the extent to which gaining sales was also making it a more desirable vehicle for advertisers. Year on year, *The Times*'s circulation was up 40 per cent in the first six months of 1994.

The attempts of competitors to prevent the price war continuing was dealt successive blows in 1993 and 1994 when the OFT reported that there was no evidence of predatory pricing. Nonetheless, while *The Times*'s sale continued to soar, there were casualties at Wapping. Andrew Knight continued as News International's chairman, but the executive powers of the post had passed to August ('Gus') Fischer. The Swiss-born Fischer was far more of a technocrat than the urbane, editorially minded Knight, whose social and political contacts nonetheless continued to make him a formidable defender of the company's interests against further regulation. John Dux, an energetic Australian and former editor of the *South China Morning Post*, continued as managing director until March 1995 when a crisis over the short supply (and correspondingly high price) of newsprint reached such severity that it forced the newspapers to temporarily cut pagination. Voices were raised that the shortages should have been foreseen and better planned around. The crisis precipitated Dux's replacement by his compatriot David Flynn. Gus Fischer also fell by the wayside. Bill O'Neill momentarily stepped back in as Murdoch's eternally safe pair of hands before Les Hinton was appointed executive chairman later in the year. He proved a remarkably stabilizing influence on the Wapping atmosphere.

Ignoring the impressions of those such as Stephen Glover who wrote that, 'Even in this free-market age there is something undignified about *The Times*, of all papers, desperately marketing itself as though it were a soap powder',[23] Stothard was buoyed up by the evidence that once the paper got into readers' hands they were impressed by the product. 'We were in a risk-taking mode,' he later confided. When it was suggested to him that for one day only *The Times* could be offered free in a deal sponsored by Microsoft, he agreed to it. There appeared not to be a conflict of interest since Microsoft would have no editorial say in the content. Instead, the computer software company would merely underwrite the sales' cost in return for the advertising gains of being seen as the paper's sponsor. The free paper duly appeared on 24 August 1995 with a supplement attached advertising Microsoft's new Windows 95 software. A giant print run of 1.5 million was produced to anticipate the inevitable demand the offer of the free paper would create. Circulation was up 8 per cent in the days following the free issue and was still 3 per cent up by the end of the month. 'I think we probably did get something out of it because we could show the paper to a lot more people,' Stothard reflected, before adding, 'would I have done it again? No.'[24] In terms of boosting sales without the cost of promotion, it was a cheap and easy success. Yet it was a mistake insofar as it risked *The Times*'s reputation. It had become, even if only for one day, a 'give-away' product. This tarnished the brand name for quality. Furthermore, despite the avowal that Microsoft had been rewarded with no say in what was printed in the paper, it allowed detractors to suggest that editorial integrity might nonetheless be strained by reliance on the benevolence of a single company. Although this did not happen in practice, it was certainly a most unfortunate possibility in theory. The deal certainly appeared to make commercial sense for Microsoft. *Media Week* magazine reflected that it was 'widely regarded as the most magnificent media coup in recent memory'. Others were sniffy. 'Worth every penny – *Times* for free,' jibed a headline in the *Guardian*.[25]

In November 1995, with circulation approaching 700,000 – double what it had been when the price war had begun just twenty-five months earlier – the decision was taken to raise *The Times*'s price to thirty-five pence. The *Telegraph* promptly upped its cover price to forty pence. Yet this was not a sign that Murdoch was preparing to call off the assault. In June 1996, *The Times* slashed its Monday cover price to ten pence. The intention here was to attract a new market for the paper's revamped sports coverage, which had been invested heavily in and was, at last, ready to take on the *Telegraph* at its strongest point. As a means of attracting new readers, the ten-pence offer was a resounding success. Sales on Mondays soared to 1.2 million, while the paper was selling in excess of 700,000 on the other weekdays. Yet the numbers buying on the Monday and then becoming new, regular readers for the rest of the week were not of a scale to suggest that the price war could bring benefits indefinitely. Not prepared to wait, *The Times*'s competitors launched a fresh appeal to the Office of Fair Trading. There were two principal allegations. They argued that by continuing the price war into a fourth year, the tactic could no longer be defended as being merely a typical promotion exercise and that the ten-pence Monday edition must surely constitute selling the paper at a loss. The critics' case was strengthened by rumours that the *Independent* was about to fold. Having

started the loss-making *Independent on Sunday*, the paper's financial difficulties were not, of course, purely the fault of Rupert Murdoch, but the
prospect of the paper's death was held up as evidence that *The Times*'s
price cut was destroying competition. In the House of Lords, a cross-party
group led by Lord McNally, a Liberal Democrat peer, attempted to ride to
the rescue. The Government was proposing new legislation that intended
to harmonize British law with the principals of European law. The peers
voted by 121 to 93 to amend the Competition Bill in a way that, they
hoped, would make price wars like that being waged by *The Times* illegal.
Among those voting with the Liberal Democrats were twenty-three Labour
peers in defiance of their party whip.

The argument made by McNally dovetailed with that put forward by
the *Independent*, that 'the media is a special case in competition law'.[26] The
Government took the contrary view with Margaret Beckett, the President
of the Board of Trade, maintaining that the McNally proposal was 'unwork-
able in law and practice'. The amendment had attempted to prohibit any
price cut that intended to 'injure or eliminate' competition. A law that
prevented a company pursuing a business strategy that injured its rivals
was not a recipe for innovation in the newspaper market or good value for
the customer. The amendment was duly removed from the bill during its
committee stage in June 1998. The following May, John Bridgeman, the
OFT's director-general issued what was the fourth report into *The Times*'s
pricing policy. The ten-pence paper on Monday was criticized (although
the price had subsequently been increased to twenty pence in January 1998)
but once again the complaints that the paper had been engaged in predatory
pricing with the explicit intent of eliminating a competitor were rejected.[27]

By then, it had become clear that *The Times* was not going to overtake
the *Telegraph*, encouraging some to believe that the latter, in remaining the
best-selling daily broadsheet, was winning the war. It was a sign of *The
Times*'s success that an offensive commenced amid derisive comments that
it would make little headway ended up being questioned because it had
not left its opponent for dead. In this sense, it had altered the perspectives
on what was possible. By 1997, *The Times* had doubled its circulation while
the *Telegraph* had only kept its head above the one million mark by means
that went beyond lowering the cover price. It invested in a vast subscription
scheme to try and lock in 300,000 readers at a cut-price rate. This was
hugely costly to the *Telegraph*, whose profits had fallen from around £60
million in 1993 to £1 million by 1996.[28] On the newsstands, it was *The
Times* that was making the advances as was clear by the fact that it was

selling almost as many copies a day at the full cover price as was the *Telegraph*. This was an extraordinary turnaround.

No treaty or proclamation marked the price war's end. The cover price simply went up in five-pence hikes. Given the turn-of-the-century collapse in revenue because of the advertising recession, the need to claw back some revenue from cover-price sales became inevitable. Nonetheless, it was not until the autumn of 2002 that *The Times* was retailing at the forty-five-pence rate at which it had been priced on the eve of the great gamble nine years earlier. By 2002, circulation had fallen back but remained above 600,000. It had been selling only 354,000 copies when it last sold for forty-five pence. During the intervening period a vast new readership, dwarfing anything the paper had ever attracted in the past, had been enticed by a low price to try it out. The triumph of Stothard's *Times* was not that people bought it because it was cheap but that so many opted to stay with it when the price went back up.

III

Dangerously, *The Times* had begun its great push for new readers before it had sorted out the problems on the backbench that had beset Simon Jenkins's editorship. Nonetheless, changes began to be made that effectively addressed the problem. Tim Austin was appointed chief revise editor. As such, he very successfully eradicated the misspellings, inconsistent punctuation and general lapses from perfection that had riled Jenkins, while making his corrections without the same amount of drama. Most importantly of all, Andrew Knight suggested to Stothard that he might be able to lure David Ruddock over from the *Telegraph* as night editor. Taking up his new position in 1994, Ruddock was a no-nonsense professional whose style of enlightened despotism on the *Telegraph*'s backbench had been a central component to that paper's success. Recognizing a man searching for a new challenge, Knight hoped Ruddock would perform the same task at *The Times*.

Ruddock got to work with relish, gaining the ear of Peter Roberts, the managing editor, to ring the changes. The four-day week enjoyed by subeditors working late nights was abolished, reducing the amount of work done by 'casuals'. The computer system was modified to allow the editor to read copy prior to its being made available on the page. It was a privilege his opposite number at the *Telegraph* had long enjoyed. 'It's the first time I've been able to read what's going on' a delighted Stothard told his new night editor. Smoking was abolished in *The Times* building. This made a significant change to the work environment. The rum warehouse was a long, open-plan shed with few windows (none of which opened anyway) but, worst of all, it had poor air conditioning. For the past eight years its inmates had been cooped up inside within a blue haze of smoke. The decision soon came to be seen as an improvement.

There were further staff changes, among them Tom Pride, who was brought in as a copy taster, and Simon Pearson – whose talent Ruddock early identified as making him a worthy successor when the time came – moved from the foreign subs desk to the position of home chief Sub. Away from the paper, Ruddock was an outspoken and hospitable man with a particular interest in the Peninsular War. From his command point on the backbench, he led by example, working tirelessly from 1 p.m. to 1 a.m., encouraging and exhorting the troops around him for another attack. On one memorable occasion he told the home news editor, James MacManus – a patrician figure not easily cast for a life in domestic service – that he was the waiter and that he, Ruddock, required a menu each night from which he might choose what to put into the paper. This was not how MacManus had seen the relationship. There was no shortage of *plats du jour* but Ruddock generally had a clear idea of what was to his taste and what was not. He inherited a paper that ran six different editions every night. Each edition saw a refining of the copy that had appeared in its predecessor, with reactions to breaking news (and a chance to snoop on what was in the first editions of the rival newspapers) as well as tailoring content to the area the edition was being sent to (more Scottish news in the edition that went north of the border, more West Country news for the edition that was despatched there, and so on).

Stothard took a great interest in the features, the leaders and the main decisions about what was going to be in the following day's newspaper. He usually left the office after the first edition was completed at 8 p.m. He was content to leave John Bryant and David Ruddock to take decisions about breaking news developments as they came in during the night. News that had important political implications for its treatment was a different matter. Nonetheless, at some stage on most nights Stothard would be telephoned for his deliberation on a specific matter than had arisen. Generally, he knew that Bryant and Ruddock were more than capable of handling matters as they arose. It was an understanding that allowed Stothard to adopt a far less interventionist approach to the wording of the news pages than, for instance, Simon Jenkins, had felt at ease to permit. Stothard was also spared the burden of having to shoulder managerial problems by Peter Roberts who Jenkins had appointed managing editor. Roberts continued to oversee the budgetary, contractual and personnel issues even though he was dying of cancer. Despite increasing pain, he carried on until September 1996, dying the following year aged sixty-two. In his place, James MacManus picked up the baton. The price war and the paper's expansion were exciting times in which to be in command of resources and MacManus threw himself into the task with customary flair. When he subsequently moved over to direct the Times supplements' operations, Stothard's friend and colleague George Brock took charge. It proved another successful re-lationship.

Thanks to the improving economic situation, these were good years in which to be managing editor. The prospectus provided by Dick Linford, News International's chief financial officer, proffered opportunities for growth. At its commencement in 1993, the price war had seriously dented *The Times*'s finances. Circulation soared but not the revenue to accompany it because the cover price had been discounted so heavily. Consequently, circulation revenue had halved by 1995. This was a tactical retreat that made possible the strategic advance when new readers continued to stick with the paper after its cover price edged back up. By 1997, with the cover price hiked to 35 pence, circulation revenue was 20 per cent higher than its level at the end of 1993. Even more importantly, advertising revenue increased by 139 per cent over this period as a direct result of the 106 per cent increase in circulation. This was dramatic. Advertising, which had generated half of *The Times*'s revenue in 1993, was, by 1997, contributing two-thirds of the paper's income. What had been lost in cover price discounts had more than been made up in ad sales. By 1997, *The Times*'s losses were less serious than before the price war began. Although still not profitable, the paper's finances continued to improve thereafter and by 2000, advertising had risen again and was accounting for 70 per cent of revenue. The *Sunday Times*, meanwhile, was recording healthy returns that ensured that Times Newspapers Limited posted a £22 million profit that year. This was to be the high point, for the arrival of the new millennium was followed by a major slump in advertising that hurt media empires throughout the western world and Wapping found itself, once again, with its hatches battened down. For the most part, though, *The Times* spent the last years of the twentieth century with far more financial room to manoeuvre than it had enjoyed for any prolonged period in the previous hundred years.

IV

The price cut changed the content of *The Times* less than might have been imagined. Rather, Stothard had set most of the changes in motion before the great bid to increase its market share had got underway. It was these changes that made it a more attractive read for those cajoled into trying it by its sudden cheapness.

Features and columnists were among the principal means through which readers developed what they imagined was almost a personal rapport with their paper's journalists. This bond was at its strongest on Saturdays. Two columnists in particular succeeded in generating a loyal following. One was John Diamond. His column ran for nine years in *The Times Magazine*. His work, which had generally been light-hearted in tone, took on a new profundity in March 1997 when he was diagnosed with throat cancer. For such a naturally gregarious man, it was a particularly cruel assault. As the cancer gradually took hold, robbing him of his voice, his column became his means of expression. Relaying his treatment and facing up to the prospect of death, Diamond retained a sense of self-deprecation that gained him the admiration of readers and colleagues alike. The column was not merely his personal therapy; it served to give hope and understanding to thousands of people facing personal hurdles of their own. By the time of his death in 2001, aged forty-seven, readers were writing to him in extraordinary numbers. Another journalist who developed a particular rapport with readers was John Morgan. Between 1997 and 2000, the dapper boulevardier offered advice on modern manners on the back page of the weekend section of the paper. His achievement was his ability to be amusing and approachable while offering sound recommendations that were never stuffy and rarely antiquated in tone. This was central to the column's success since many of those writing fell into one of two categories. Those from more traditional backgrounds felt insecure about what was correct behaviour in the baffling environment of contemporary Britain where the breaking down of barriers had brought confusion about appropriate conduct. Others, products of post-sixties modernity, wanted guidance on how to behave in a more dignified – but non-snobbish – way. Themes ranged from how to open automatic doors for women, whether breast-feeding was acceptable in public and whether those who ate and drank less than their companions in a restaurant should complain if the bill was split equally. Morgan wrote with self-assurance but never arrogance while guiding readers through the social minefield of how to avoid causing unnecessary offence to other people. Growing up in Perth, he had acquired metropolitan sophistication rather than having been born into it. He died in July 2000, aged forty-one, after falling from a window in his small (but elegantly appointed) third-floor bachelor set in Albany, off Piccadilly. A generous host and lavish spender, he had become increasingly worried about his financial situation. Friends, however, believed he would have chosen a more dignified means of exit. A coroner's court inquest returned an open verdict. *The Times* was inundated with letters from readers conveying their sympathy and sadness at his loss.

In other areas the paper continued to build on its foundations. Tom Clarke had transformed the paper's sports coverage but Stothard, who was able to disengage his own disinterest from sporting endeavour from his recognition that it should be given an even higher profile, decided he wanted a change of personnel. In Clarke's place, David Chappell, supported by Keith Blackmore as his deputy, was entrusted with the sports section. Defeating the *Telegraph* at the game it played best would not be easy, for, as Stothard conceded, 'Male sports enthusiasts are one of the most conservative groups in terms of trying to get them to switch and get hooked on a new paper.'[29] The brief period in which *The Times* sold for ten pence on a Monday was specifically designed to maximize the audience for *The Times*'s improved sports coverage. Slowly, *The Times*'s score incremented, although at a Boycott rather than a Botham run rate.

Certainly, the England cricket team could have done with either player in their prime. For a while it looked as if the country's saviour would come from abroad. In May 1988, Worcestershire's twenty-one-year-old Zimbabwean-born batsman, Graeme Hick, made light of a slow outfield to score 405 not out, the highest first-class score made in England in the twentieth century. Hick would be available to play for England from 1991 and great things were expected. In the event, great things were nearly achieved. He emerged to become one of England's finest county batsmen, ranking among the ten highest run makers in the game, but he never quite achieved greatness for his adopted country at Test level. Marcus Williams filed from around the county grounds and, later, as sports editor, proved to be in both longevity and experience the backbone of the paper's sports desk. When he had arrived at the paper in 1980, the *Telegraph* reported from all the first-class county matches while *The Times* contented itself with reports from four or five during the season. Under Williams, the paper made good this shortcoming and followed its rival's lead in covering all the matches.

Having reported Test matches for *The Times* since 1954, John Woodcock had (alongside Richie Benaud) a reasonable claim to having watched more Test match cricket than any other man in history. In 1987 he finally relinquished his place as chief correspondent, although since he was still writing more occasional cricket commentary for the paper into the twenty-first century it was perhaps a matter of his merely dropping down the batting order. There was much that still enthralled him about the game although he was no fan of some of the innovations – the 'pyjama games' and overindulgence of one-day matches and anything that could be ascribed to the influence of Kerry Packer. When allegations were made that Ian Botham had taken drugs, Woodcock turned with a sigh to John Goodbody and asked, 'Dear boy, where will it end?' Goodbody looked back at the friendly and sagacious face and retorted with resigned worldliness, 'I think, on the front page.'[30]

The arrival of Michael Atherton as England's captain appeared to offer hope. Circumstances, however, were against him. He came to the helm midway through the losing Ashes series of 1993. The following April, the Trinidadian Brian Lara, aged twenty-four, beat Garfield Sobers's thirty-six-year record Test score of 365 (not out) by scoring 375 against England in Antigua, watched by Alan Lee, by then *The Times*'s cricket correspondent. When Atherton resigned after losing a close series to the West Indies in 1998, the statistics looked poor, but he proved to be England's longest-serving captain and was the catalyst for the positive changes gradually ushered in after 1999 by Nasser Hussain and the coach, Duncan Fletcher. In good time for this late English renaissance, Christopher Martin-Jenkins joined *The Times* as its chief cricket correspondent in 1999 after eight distinguished years reporting from the boundary for the *Telegraph*. One of the most respected voices in the game – his calm, analytical summaries continued to be heard on the radio's *Test Match Special* – his move to *The Times* reinforced the extent to which it had closed the gap with the *Telegraph* in the battle for providing the best sports coverage.

At Wapping, the sports desk consisted largely of subs hammering and moulding the constant flow of dispatches from the field reporters into their allotted space. John Goodbody, one of the prolific sports writers who did

Simon Jenkins

Andrew Knight

Bernard Levin at home.

Downtown Kabul. Matthew Parris at ease with the locals.

Peter Stothard, editor 1992-2002.

John Bryant, distance runner and deputy editor.

Rosemary Righter, an accomplished duellist with the pen against tyranny's swords.

Simon Barnes with a friend.

Lynne Truss. Sport for all.

Caitlin Moran.
Testimonies of youth.

Peter Brookes,
master cartoonist.

Gentlemen of *The Times* pay Tony Blair a house call during the 1997 election campaign. Clockwise from Blair are Peter Stothard, Anatole Kaletsky, Alastair Campbell (Blair's press secretary) and Peter Riddell.

Above: Michael Gove

Left: Anatole Kaletsky

Clockwise from top left: Mary Ann Sieghart, Sandra Parsons and Patience Wheatcroft.

Arts editor Richard Morrison always cast a cultured eye.

Halabja, northern Iraq, 1988. Richard Beeston uncovers the victims of Saddam's chemical weapons attack on his Kurdish subjects.

Above: Sam Kiley. Genocidal Hutus in Rwanda assumed he was a friendly French paratrooper on a secret mission.

Left: A light in the darkness. Anthony Loyd files from the Afghan battlefront in 2001.

Afghanistan: Janine di Giovanni comes under fire on the road to Tora Bora.

The last word. Peter Stothard bids farewell after ten years as editor, applauded by his deputy editor, Ben Preston, Ben Macintyre (seated) and George Brock, managing editor.

report for daily duty at Wapping, spent most of his working day on the news rather than the sports desk. Not all sports reporters resembled in appearance the fit athletic specimens it was their calling to write about, but Goodbody was one whose sporting days were not confined to the dim and selectively remembered past. His form was certainly impressive. He had broken British junior weightlifting records and was a member of Britain's national judo squad in 1970 before going up four years later as a mature student to Trinity College, Cambridge. There, he became the university's leading shot putter. A month after he won his Blue he was displaying the multi-tasking skills that would serve him well in his subsequent career. He spent the morning of his part one English Tripos exam answering questions on Henry James and D. H. Lawrence before speeding over to the Crystal Palace trackside for an afternoon at the Olympic athletics trials deconstructing Brendan Foster and Geoff Capes for the benefit of *Sunday Mirror* readers. Having joined *The Times* shortly before the move to Wapping, he continued to cut a toned figure, happily thriving on five hours sleep a night. In August 1991, at the age of forty-eight, his first attempt to swim the English Channel ended three miles from the French coast when he had to be pulled from the water, semi-conscious and suffering from hypothermia. He concluded that the wrong grease and training forty to fifty hours a week in cold water had made him lose too much useful body fat. Undaunted, he tried again and fourteen days later became the oldest Briton for twelve years to achieve the crossing. Simon Jenkins, then editing the paper, was so impressed that he persuaded Goodbody to write a report of his account for the front page.[31]

An audit of which sporting figure's picture appeared most frequently in *The Times* during the late 1990s revealed that one player was far ahead of his field. This was Tim Henman. Most major sports produced a range of stars and superstars but if any one of them failed to be man of the match there was always another team member to be immortalized scoring the goal or flashing the cricket bat. For many Britons, however, Tim Henman was the face of tennis, or at any rate that of the annual Wimbledon championships that in Britain commanded greater interest than the three other Open tournaments put together. Rex Bellamy having retired from the reporters' vantage point on Centre Court, it fell to tennis correspondents Julian Muscat and Alix Ramsay to have the pleasure, or mental ordeal, of reporting on Tim Henman's various attempts to win Wimbledon. The prospect first became a serious possibility when he reached the semi-final in 1998, blocked from becoming the first Briton to make the final since

1938 only by Pete Sampras, the greatest tennis player of the decade and, perhaps, of all time. Henman's struggles as the nearly man of SW19 – he reached the semi-finals four times in five years between 1998 and 2002 – carrying the fevered hopes of millions of otherwise unhysterical middle-class Britons on his shoulders, was the psychological human drama that always brought out the best in Simon Barnes's journalism.

During the 1990s, the progress of both Murdoch's BSkyB satellite television and football went hand in hand. Winning coverage rights to Premiership games helped transform Sky's fortunes. The previous decade had been a low point for the sport, albeit as much for the hooliganism and general unpleasantness that took place off the pitch as for the quality of play on it. The yobbery of Liverpool supporters had caused the death of Juventus fans at the Heysel Stadium, provoking a sense of national shame and ensuring the banning of English clubs from European championships. In 1988 the Government seriously considered forcing all football supporters to be registered and presented with identity cards so that troublemakers could be more easily prevented from attending matches. Tragedy had stalked the grandstand at Bradford City, which became an inferno, and the terraces of Hillsborough where ninety-six Liverpool fans were crushed to death. Established in the Hillsborough tragedy's aftermath, the Taylor Report's recommendations were enacted, forcing league grounds to become all-seater venues and to carry out improvements that made match attendance less of a threatening experience. At the time, many clubs, dependent on gate receipts, questioned how they could afford the expense of the change and the reduced number of paying supporters they would subsequently be able to squeeze through the turnstile. The Government even felt compelled to announce it would divert funds from the betting tax to support the upgraded facilities. In fact, far from hurting the clubs' finances, the improvements came just in time to take advantage of the sport's economic renaissance. In 1992, the Premier League was created. Murdoch's decision to buy the broadcasting rights for Sky transformed the sport. Suddenly, the leading teams were able to benefit from a huge cash injection, the sums from Sky being supplemented by the greatly enhanced opportunities for sponsorship as other companies raced to gain from the exposure. The growth could be seen clearly enough through the increasing sums clubs were prepared to pay for players. In July 1988, Tottenham Hotspur had provoked gasps by purchasing Paul Gascoigne for a record fee of £2 million. A decade later, Alan Shearer cost Newcastle United £15 million with Shearer receiving a £500,000 signing-on fee and a guaranteed annual salary of £1.5

million for five years. The Premiership's principal clubs spent £68 million on new signings in 1995 and the figure had passed £100 million two years later. Some maintained that this revolution came at the expense of the less successful clubs. Others argued that far from extinguishing the non-Premiership teams, the Sky deal helped grow the market. With greater variation in kick-off times and the spread of matches to Sundays, supporters found their viewing choices – on the screen as well as at the ground – widened.

The process was mutually beneficial. The broadcasting deal rescued Sky's previously perilous bank balance. Murdoch's commercial interest in the people's game appeared to approach new heights when in 1999 he made a bid for Manchester United. The deal was blocked by the Government but, by then, the proprietor's business interest in the sport had already manifested profound repercussions for *The Times*. Although there was never any tie-in between the newspaper and Sky, Murdoch's experience of watching the expanding market for football coverage had made him conscious that it was a growth area from which even the most elevated sections of his media empire could benefit. During the spring of 1996, Murdoch paid a visit to *The Times* and asked which big events were coming up. Various forthcoming attractions were mentioned but those that prompted the proprietor's interest fell into one category which he summed up in the phrase – later adopted in the paper and elsewhere – 'the great summer of sport'. Without pausing to digest what had been said, Murdoch made clear that funds would be made available for a massive expansion of *The Times*'s sports section.[32] At its heart was Euro '96 – the European football championships – to be hosted by England in June. With Murdoch's encouragement, the paper would now be able to provide a far higher level of in-depth coverage than it had accorded any previous soccer tournament. Through Sky, he had learned how well football sold and was sure that *The Times* could not afford to miss this extraordinary growth market. This proved a defining moment in the development of the paper. The football coverage shot up from four to nine pages. The expansion was well timed: Euro '96 proved a turning point in the fortunes of football in Britain. There was little sign during the tournament of the unappealing sideshows of hooliganism and bad sportsmanship that had previously tarnished the sport's image. Instead, it proved a tremendous spectacle of the British summer. *The Times* rose to the moment with Rob Hughes, its football correspondent, ably supported by a team that featured the man-marking skills of Oliver Holt, Alyson Rudd and David Maddock. By the time England were defeated in a penalty shoot-out in a thrilling semi-final by the eventual champions, Germany, the country had – in the parlance of the moment – 'gone footie mad'.

The legacy was a noticeable upsurge in interest in the game even from among those who might previously have imagined logging a 4-4-2 formation was something to do with train spotting. Bankers and accountants crammed into pubs to watch the match, rubbing shoulders with the sport's less fair-weather devotees. Even ascending a couple of floors in the office lift the next morning would be treated as a sufficient moment to impart some second-hand observation about the match and, for this, the broadsheets provided their fair share of primary information. The high level of interest in *The Times*'s coverage certainly suggested soccer was becoming gentrified and was even a suitable subject for front-page photography. In this respect David Beckham, a player in danger of being recognized as a celebrity in his own right, became the pin-up of tabloids and broadsheets alike. With money, glamour and excitement all coming together, it was noticeable that football was finally beginning to interest large numbers of women too. This was a change *The Times* was quick to discern. In the past, the concept of the female sports' journalist was poorly grasped. There were rare exceptions, especially in sports with a strong female following like show jumping: after fifteen years as equestrian correspondent, Pamela Macgregor-Morris passed over to Jenny MacArthur in 1983. During the mid-nineties, though – and accentuated by the popular reaction to Euro '96 – the paper turned to journalists like Alison Kervin and Alyson Rudd not only to report on matches but also to become columnists and pundits. Rudd and Lynne Truss, whose 'Kicking and Screaming' column began during the European championship, lifted the lid off the lad culture of soccer. Kervin became an interviewer as well as a reporter, sports coverage having become almost as much about previewing events and analysing the chief protagonists as about filing match reports. *The Times* invested not just in women writing about men's sport but also about their own. Sarah Potter, a specialist on women's cricket, reported extensively on women in all walks of sport.

In any contest between the football World Cup and the Olympic Games, Simon Barnes was of the opinion that the latter remained the greatest show on earth. For all its passion and drama, he found 'the monoculture of football dispiriting'. Its commercialism only inflated its sense of self-importance and covering the World Cup often involved observing a succession of similar narratives. In contrast, he believed that 'the Olympics represent the search for greatness in such a variety of forms', adding, 'and with twice the number of sexes'.[33] Throughout these years – far removed from the overt idolatry, huge salaries and satellite television coverage that was transforming football – the rower Steve Redgrave was winning Olympic gold. At the Atlanta Games in 1996 his performance with Matthew Pinsent in a coxless pair proved to be the only gold medal Britain gained in any discipline in what was, in all other respects, a dismal display of the nation's sporting prowess that left Great Britain on a par with Burundi and Ecuador. Some blamed the poor performance on Britain's seemingly insatiable obsession with football to the exclusion of other sports. Others blamed the lack of funding available for those other sports – although the two points were not mutually exclusive. The sale of school playing fields also came in for particular scrutiny. Yet Barnes refused to join the national browbeating. He pointing out how, but for a millimetre here and a bit of bad luck there, Britain might easily have performed creditably at Atlanta and he doubted that money alone was the key. After all, because of Wimbledon's profitability, 'Tennis gets more than three times as much money as the rest of all the governing bodies of sport put together receive from the Sports Council, and there are more than 100 of them. Henman apart, tennis has for years been a disaster area.'[34] Nonetheless, when Team GB went on to gain eleven gold medals four years later at the Sydney Olympics, many cited the increased funds made available through the National Lottery as a reason. It was there, at Sydney that Redgrave, having transferred with Pinsent to a coxless four, rowed into sporting legend by winning his fifth gold in successive Olympics, a record in an endurance sport. The timing of the race ensured that Barnes had to sprint for the line too, since he only had twenty minutes to file eight hundred words to catch Wapping's printing deadline. It proved a rare occasion in which the expectation was so high he pre-prepared some of his lines, including the opening sentences parodying the hero's previous request to be shot if ever he returned to the river: 'Anyone who sees Steve Redgrave in a boat again has my full permission to knight him. He won his fifth gold medal in five Olympic Games this morning in the greatest five-and-a-bit minutes of sport any of us will ever see.'[35] This remained Barnes's conviction in the sober light of day. Reflecting on his thirty years in sports journalism in 2004, he still considered Redgrave's feat the finest moment of them all.[36]

V

It was not just in the sporting arena that the National Lottery made its mark. Despite the moral objections to the state promotion of gambling and the potential repercussions for hooking some of the most socially disadvantaged and desperate, it proved a popular success. Twenty-five million tickets were sold at its launch in November 1994. Indeed, *The Times* even pondered whether it might prove the most popular development of the Major years.[37] For every pound the punter spent, a little over five pence went to each of five causes – sport, the arts, national heritage, charities and a fund to celebrate the millennium. Such was its popularity – at one stage more than thirty million people indulged in a weekly flutter – that by the summer of 1997, over £3.5 billion had been raised for these five causes.[38] Less surprisingly, the distribution of the largesse provoked a succession of resentments especially among those who claimed to speak for the generally less affluent gamblers who wanted their money to go to children's homes and animal sanctuaries rather than the deep and badly holed pockets of the Royal Opera House. Thanks to a number of grants to high-profile arts and heritage projects, it looked like one of the most effective mechanisms ever developed to take from the poor in order to give to the more cultured elements within the middle class. The truth, however, was that most of the money went not to grand assertions of high culture but towards helping relatively small projects, not least in deprived parts of the country.

The Times and the 'arts lobby' had long since ceased to be natural partners because of the latter's unending pleas for Government subsidies. The persistent proffering of the begging bowl did not greatly prick the conscience of a newspaper given to free market strictures. It was naturally attractive to the paper that the funds pouring in from the National Lottery could offer a means through which the arts might be given a boost without persistently beggaring the taxpayer. There remained, however, a problem. The Lottery's cultural largesse was targeted at capital projects – like the construction or upgrading of theatres or art galleries – but not at underwriting ongoing running costs. All was well where the new cultural facilities generated an increased market to support its output. Tate Modern proved perhaps the most prominent success in this regard and a museum of pop music in Sheffield the greatest failure. The number of potential white elephants alarmed *The Times* and it pointed out that 'there is no point in building splendid new venues if they place an intolerable strain on a subsidy system that can barely cope with present demands'.[39] The danger was that artistic dreams were running ahead of the market to sustain them. Despite the investment in improving auditoria and related facilities, the patronage of classical concerts was not obviously larger in 2002 than it had been in 1982. Many theatre companies experienced similar fortunes.

It was the financial difficulties of the Royal Opera House that placed *The Times* in a particular dilemma. On the one hand it represented the sort of high culture the paper's more refined writers wanted to see promoted. On the other hand, the paper could not easily sustain its criticism of the arts lobby's benefit dependency while making an exception for what was a fringe interest of – for the most part – the more exulted social classes. Furthermore, 'the House' appeared to have lost its way artistically and was trailing behind the English National Opera based at the Coliseum. The will of the arts editor, Richard Morrison, prevailed in the paper, with his argument that if Rome and Milan could only afford one opera house each there was little hope that London could successfully sustain two. Thus, the Coliseum (also in need of investment), should be sold and the ENO could share Covent Garden with the Royal Opera.[40] This line continued to fuel the ongoing correspondence in *The Times* letters' page. In the end, the Royal Opera House benefited from a large – and controversial £78 million cheque from the National Lottery as part of a £214 million restoration project. By the end of the decade, it had regained the artistic initiative and had, in the overused pun, put 'the House' back in order.

Being a critic for *The Times* had long been among the most prized positions on the paper. Yet, as in so many other areas, the scope for complacency had been squeezed in 1986 by the advent of the *Independent*. In terms of space provided for arts coverage, the ingénue trumped the past master. While the erudite John Higgins had presided over the arts coverage, *The Times* continued to hold its own in quality, but after he was moved to the obituaries department in 1988, the paper faced intense competition from its new rival which was making vigorous attempts to poach key reviewers. Richard Williams's focus was sharpest at culture's more popular end and for a while Mary Ann Sieghart had the impossible task of trying to run both Op-Ed and the arts coverage. It took a heated discussion between Charlie Wilson and Higgins's protégé, Richard Morrison, for the editor – whose recreations were more the Turf than the Tate – to appreciate that greater investment in covering the arts had become an urgent priority. An orchestral trombonist and organist and Cambridge music graduate, Morrison got his way and, having joined the paper as a classical music reviewer in 1984, he was rewarded on the arrival of Simon Jenkins with the post of arts editor. The rank conferred upon him generalissimo powers over everything from the visual arts to theatre, dance and music. Not given to wanton idleness, he combined this marshalling task with continuing to file reviews himself.

Whether for a concert or the theatre, attending the first night of a performance that might go on past ten o'clock created tremendous pressure on the critic to file before the copy deadline – which was usually around 10.30 p.m. If there was time, the theatre critic Benedict Nightingale would dash into his car and hurtle from the West End to Wapping where he would file his piece and oversee it being subbed onto the page. Sometimes there was not even time for this and he would sit in his parked car typing up his judgment, a communication problem made easier by the advent of the laptop computer and e-mail. Yet, even if the review could be filed by 10.30 p.m., the early editions going up to Scotland, the North or abroad had long since left the presses. Their readers would receive the critics' verdict a day after the more privileged browsers of London and the South-east who got the first-night review the morning after it had happened. Those who lived on the distribution boundaries between the different editions were often the worst served by this unfortunate but inevitable arrangement. They might miss the expected review on the Monday by receiving an earlier edition and then miss it on its second showing if they were sold a later edition on the Tuesday. Morrison regularly found himself soothing miffed readers who had unwittingly been caught by this hazard and wanted to know why the paper had not covered an important occasion at the Barbican or the first night of a new and much-heralded production at the National.

Indeed, readers in the provinces often felt that the paper's artistic coverage was too focused upon events in London. *The Times* was sensitive to this complaint although it was constrained in its reaction by the greater consideration that most important works were premiered in London, a city that was by a considerable margin the country's cultural megalopolis. Rather than using regional reviewers, the paper believed it was necessary to judge provincial productions by more easily verifiable metropolitan standards. The result was a large bill for rail fares and overnight accommodation but this was probably better than being reliant on unverifiable opinions and the possibility of regional pride clouding judgments. Certainly there was much to applaud. This was the period in which Simon Rattle, the conductor of the City of Birmingham Symphony Orchestra, became one of the most discussed figures in the British arts scene. It was during the summer – when the Proms, the Edinburgh Festival and Bayreuth coincided – that the critics found themselves at their most peripatetic. The really intensive challenge was provided by the Proms since every concert had to be reviewed. Increasingly, this amounted to covering two separate concerts at the Royal Albert Hall each night. The reviewer just had time to nip out for a sandwich and file a review for the first concert before having to return to the auditorium for the second concert – which almost invariably went on past the copy deadline, ensuring publication in the following edition.

The knowledge and dedication of the classical music reviewers was peerless. Barry Millington and Noel Goodwin filed throughout the period covered in this book as did Hilary Finch who began reviewing in 1980 and was, in particular, a discerning writer on chamber music. Debra Craine began her career as the paper's dance critic in 1989. John Allison began filing in 1994 and Geoff Brown switched from watching the silver screen to the orchestral stage in 1999. Fortunately, reviewing was an area of journalistic activity that involved making highly personal and subjective comments without obedience to the same libel laws that operated over other parts of the paper. While the regular critics betrayed their own tastes, they proved to be above the sort of suspicions that occasionally animated the literary world, especially in the non-fiction market, of giving favourable reviews to the works of friends. Certainly there were a number of caustic remarks that caused injury over the period, but generally artists of whatever discipline held back from responding directly to a poor review. There were a few exceptions. A Higgins review of Jonathan Miller's production of *Tosca* did provoke the good doctor's immortal riposte that it was 'impertinent in the eighteenth-century sense of the term'. Meanwhile, the meaning of at least one review got lost in translation. Having spent the evening attending an indifferent operatic performance, Stephen Pettitt filed his column down the telephone line referring to what the Innererklang Music Theatre Company had billed as 'Mouth Music'. Unfortunately, the copy taker miss-heard and typed 'Mouse Music'. The misunderstanding was then compounded when the review appeared the next morning under the headline 'I can smell a rat'.[41]

Ideologically, the great battle concerned whether the critic's primary duty was to explore and interpret the cultural cutting edge or to review performances that were of interest to a wider range of *Times* readers. Certainly, Paul Griffiths felt most at ease when analysing works that were 'difficult'. A brilliant and insightful critic who started reviewing classical concerts for the paper in 1973, Griffiths maintained an extraordinary turnover until 1996 when he departed for the *New York Times*. He was an extoller of the cutting edge, interpreting for a knowing readership the works of Stockhausen and Boulez in the manner of Aaron expounding the thoughts of Moses. The fading allure of these heroes from the concert hall repertoire did not dim his admiration for them and he also championed Harrison Birtwistle. Attending the premiere in the Coliseum of Birtwistle's *The Mask of Orpheus*, Griffiths could not contain his excitement: 'I remarked here a couple of years ago that Birtwistle's earlier *Punch and Judy* was the one perfectly satisfactory reinvention of opera since Stravinsky. Now there is another,' he crooned, before concluding, 'the world afterwards is different'.[42]

Hailing Birtwistle certainly suggested *The Times* was not diverted by the popularizing tendencies manifested in the phenomenon of mass-selling compilations of the Three Tenors, the injection of sex appeal through the marketing techniques of the pop world or the advent of a commercially viable radio station, Classic FM. While moving away from the belief that the challenging work was almost by definition the most demanding of attention, *The Times* did not feel called upon to cover whatever was popular. If there was dumbing down in the paper it did not happen in the arts pages. For those interested in culture as a challenging experience the problem, in so far as there was one, was not of *The Times*'s making. During the nineties, British composers of the calibre of Judith Weir, John Tavener and James MacMillan continued to write exciting – even inspirational – works. Yet, in matters of international renown, the country could not quite summon a composer of the stature of Benjamin Britten. Indeed, by the last years of the twentieth century, the most ambitious modern composers were to be found in the United States rather than Europe. It was American minimalists like Philip Glass, John Adams and Steve Reich who demonstrated that there was no necessary contradiction between the avant-garde and the popular.

When it came to opera, Simon Jenkins had been determined that *The Times* could only afford the best. The best was Rodney Milnes, the esteemed editor of *Opera* magazine who had translated the libretti for the ENO's productions of Dvořák's *Rusalka* and Janáček's *Osud* as well as *Tannhauser* for Opera North, and was probably London's only working journalist to be a Knight of the Order of the White Rose of Finland (unfortunately he was only allowed to wear the decoration when in the Finnish President's presence). There was, however, a hitch. Milnes was unsure whether the newspaper that opposed increased state funding of the arts was where he would feel at ease. 'Do you really want a 1950s leftie?' he queried. Jenkins and Morrison insisted that indeed they did and Milnes duly came on board. It was a great moment for the paper's critical credentials. It certainly proved well worth the ensuing periodic disagreements over arts funding policy, with Milnes later admitting, 'My eight years working with Richard Morrison were among the happiest in my life.'[43] True, there was the wearisome saga of the Royal Opera House's difficulties prior to its triumphant reopening in 1999 but on a sweeter note, there was also much to celebrate at the ENO and in the emerging talents of David McVicar, Deborah Warner and Richard Jones.

Milnes was certainly not a critic whose enthusiasm for the arts' cause clouded his critical judgment. He was generally underwhelmed by the emergence of country house opera during the 1990s, believing that Garsington and the Grange were as much about social class as about artistic quality and, as such, were turning the clock back to a dimmer period in the country's cultural history. He had a far higher opinion of what Glyndebourne offered, especially after 1994 when its Michael Hopkins-designed auditorium provided it with facilities that finally surpassed the better sort of boarding-school pantomime. There were extensive trips, too, across the United States, Russia and Europe in order to bring his judicious observations of the world's great performances within the reach of every reader of The Times. His audience, indeed, stretched far beyond the confines of the paper. The Italian press's timidity towards criticizing La Scala meant that – on the sham pretext of displaying British journalism's impertinent streak – they contrived instead to reprint Milnes's forthright demolition when Milan's great opera house failed to meet the mark. At La Scala for a production of Gluck's Armide, he wrote, in a review more memorable than the performance, that it had been an evening of 'witless operatic baroquery' contrived at such expense that it tested even his patience with limitless subsidy. The qualities of the opera itself were totally lost in the ostentatious display of wealth. He took one look at the array of costumes on La Scala's stage and assured his readers 'there cannot be an ostrich left in all of Africa with a feather on its hind quarters'.[44]

There was a glorious episode in The Times in 2000 when Milnes – the last single he had bought was one by Gerry and the Pacemakers – accepted the inspired suggestion that he write a critical analysis of Madonna. A weekend was spent exploring her music. Bemused, he concluded that she was an accomplished performer, had better pitch (if far more limited in range) than some opera singers but was labouring with an awful repertoire, most of which she wrote herself.[45] Milnes never let his erudition cloud his powers of expression. Alas, in July 2002, after ten years as *The Times* opera critic, an attack of deep-vein thrombosis forced him to take his own bow, elegantly signing off his last review from a joyful Glyndebourne performance of *Carmen*.

By then, the reviewers' craft had been made a lot more difficult by the diversification of serious music. 'World music' – which rarely penetrated the ears of an earlier generation of *Times* critics – opened up new avenues, quickly becoming standard fare on the South Bank and in the arts pages of the *Guardian*. *The Times* came to give it due, if not comprehensive, attention. The broadening range of musical options called for ever-stricter discernment on what was covered. The space available, though, continued to expand. *The Times* that News International bought in 1981 devoted on average only a single page a day to the arts, in which theatre, gallery, film and music reviews jostled for attention around a main feature. By the end of the eighties this had expanded significantly and during the nineties coverage increased again. The notion that ownership by Rupert Murdoch had somehow lowered the tone was demonstrably nonsense. By 2002, *The Times* devoted far more coverage to reviewing serious classical music than any of its competitors. With the rhythms of world music energizing its soul, the *Guardian*, indeed, had fallen back to averaging only about two classical reviews a week. To state that *The Times* remained the foremost daily record of classical music in Britain would smack of the sort of bombastic immodesty that was alien to its reviewers' nature. Suffice it to say that it had no superior.

All of this, of course, was for the benefit of a select and discerning audience. By the mid-1990s, classical music made up only a little over 7 per cent of album sales in Britain, about half the combined sale of easy listening, country, folk, jazz, blues and reggae. Seventy-eight per cent of sales were accounted for by pop, rock and dance. One estimate put the British music industry's worth at £2.5 billion a year, which was more than was being contributed to the economy by the country's shipbuilding yards, electronic components and water supply.[46] *The Times* had long recognized the importance of covering jazz music. Not even the departure of Richard Williams in 1989 could dim the paper's ongoing interest and, happily, Clive Davis continued to provide readers with weekly direction on which recordings to purchase and concerts to attend. Where a great effort was made to broaden the paper's coverage was in the realm of pop and rock.

Despite his own preference for Glyndebourne over Glastonbury, John Higgins recognized that the tastes of a younger generation needed attention and in 1985, with Nicholas Shakespeare as his scout, he appointed David Sinclair to review rock music. Sinclair, a session musician who had played drums with London Zoo and the CBS-signed band TV Smith's Explorers, was at that time writing for *Kerrang!* (before it became fashionable) and had worked at the BBC on *The Rock and Roll Years*. In one respect it was a courageous appointment in that Sinclair regarded most of the contemporary music scene as a 'wasteland'. The perfumed pop of the New Romantics and Duran Duran held little appeal for a Rolling Stones admirer whose affinity with *The Times* dated from Rees-Mogg's famous 1967 leading article 'Who Breaks a Butterfly on a Wheel?' which defended the band against a possible jail sentence for drugs possession. However, having a prevailing culture to kick against was an energizing motivation for any critic and Sinclair's wry and perceptive journalism comfortably outlived many of the pop world's more transitory acts. It was a bonus too for the paper to have a reviewer who could take turns between writing in the house style and beating the Stones's Ronnie Wood at snooker. Despite this, his first interview with Mick Jagger was not a success. The conversation had produced some amusing copy – Jagger was on cocksure form and full of anecdotes about some irreverent banter he had recently had with Murdoch – but unfortunately, just as the piece was going to press, Higgins noticed that the iconic rocker had also just given an interview with the *Independent*. Rival newspapers interviewing the same man was an unconscionable solecism. Sinclair's *tête-à-tête* was pulled.

Nonetheless, the rivalry with the *Independent* was to prove helpful for *The Times* in broadening its survey of contemporary culture. When Sinclair arrived, the paper's rock journalism consisted, at most, of two short live concert reviews a week. Yet, faced with the *Independent*'s challenge the following year, this quickly increased to include album releases, interviews and broader features. Lining up behind Labour's boycott of the Wapping titles, a few rock artists who, like Paul Weller, were active in the 'Red Wedge' movement, refused to have anything to do with *The Times*. Generally, though, Sinclair was able to make the most of the increasing amount of space being made available in the paper. He did not encounter the subversive demands that band and record company publicists tried to enforce upon the eager young freelancers of the youth press. Even in the irreverent priorities of rock, *The Times* was accorded a surprising degree of respect.

Spawning acts like the Smiths and New Order, Manchester mounted a claim to being the capital of Britain's music scene during the 1980s. Tony Wilson offered himself as the city's impresario, setting up Factory Records. His Hacienda nightclub became the headquarters of the Rave culture and its hedonistic excesses. Briefly a new generation of bands like the Happy Mondays and the Stone Roses promised to take popular music in new directions before fizzling out in self-destruction and diminishing inspiration. Certainly, the hypnotic beats of Acid House and Rave were facilitated by the easy availability of drugs, in particular Ecstasy, that gave partygoers the ability to dance for several hours without tiring, although the side effects became a contentious issue and a source of minor moral panic. The loudness of the music and its pill-popping followers fuelled the phenomenon of illegal raves in which an underground network of promoters could, at short notice, seek to evade the attentions of the police and the rights of private property by organizing all-night events in fields. That thousands of young people could find their way to these illicit sites, despite there being little official publicity before the forces of law and order got wind of them, was certainly an indication of the movement's scale and organizational élan.

While rave culture took hold in Britain, from America came Rap and Hip-Hop – the music of the Afro-American inner city. For Sinclair, though, the most exciting movement emerging from the United States was the proliferation of guitar bands from Seattle in the early 1990s. Appealing to the so-called slacker generation, the foremost exponents of this nihilistic 'grunge rock' was the band Nirvana until its acclaimed and tortured lead singer, Kurt Cobain, put himself out of his misery in 1994. 'Let no one underestimate Cobain's importance,' wrote Sinclair in his lament, adding that there was 'an eternity now left to consider the songs on Nirvana's four albums'. It was the disaffected attitude of a younger generation that those too old to jump around to 'Smells Like Teen Spirit' regarded with something approaching distaste. Bernard Levin – whose musical ear was not well adjusted to grunge – was incredulous at Sinclair's obsequies, concluding of them that, 'The heathen in his blindness bows down to wood and stone.'[47]

Cobain's death closed one musical chapter yet within weeks a new one had opened. It was British and possessed what grunge had lacked – a decent dose of irony. 'Britpop' burst upon the scene with the releases of Blur's third album *Parklife* and Oasis's debut *Definitely Maybe*. The media was encouraged to pitch this as a rivalry between the rough Mancunians of Oasis versus the southern art school graduates in Blur. Enjoying the occasion and the music, Sinclair nonetheless felt that Blur were not quite equal to the adulation. In reviewing *Parklife* he noted that it reminded him of London bands of the sixties like the Kinks and the Small Faces, although sourer and combining 'occasionally grating cockneyisms with a ton of disaffected attitude'.[48] As for *Definitely Maybe*, it might have little depth but, nonetheless, 'as an uncomplicated celebration of youthful brio this is an album that takes some beating'.[49] The hype surrounding the manufactured battle between Blur and Oasis certainly appeared at odds with their claims to stand apart from the conformities of the music industry. It worked all the same. Oasis's second album, *What's The Story (Morning Glory)*, became the biggest selling album in British history. 'Britpop has succeeded where punk failed,' suggested Sinclair, 'essentially by stealing the clothes of the old guard. Rather like new Labour portraying itself as the party of low taxation and sound economic management, the new bands have, generally speaking, got where they are by abandoning any notion of being a "radical alternative".'[50] Indeed, it was not long before Tony Blair and his circle began to laud such bands, as if there was a link between Britpop and its other artistic bedfellows – what American magazines like *Newsweek* and *Vanity Fair* had latched onto as 'Cool Britannia' – and the modernizing agenda of New Labour. The irony was that the British music scene had been at its peak during the years of the Major Government and wilted almost as soon as Tony Blair had formally embraced it at a Downing Street party he hosted for its luminaries, including Oasis's Noel Gallagher and Creation Records' Alan McGee in July 1997. Shortly thereafter, the death of Diana, Princess of Wales, overshadowed the launch of Oasis's third album. The interment of Britpop was announced. Indeed, the immediate effect of the Princess's death was to ensure that an updated version of Elton John's 'Candle In The Wind', a song originally written about Marilyn Monroe in 1973, became history's biggest selling recording.

By then, Britpop was, in any case, eclipsed by a new phenomenon spilling beyond the arts pages and onto the news section – the Spice Girls. They were a chirpy all-female band propelled by a male manager called Simon Fuller and a cry for 'girl power' which, although lacking a coherent philosophy, nonetheless resonated with the sort of impressionable teenagers (and pre-teens) who were still buying singles. By March 1997 they had become the first band to reach number one in the charts with their first four releases. 'Wanabee', their debut single, reached number one in more than thirty countries including the United States. Spending time with them in Dublin, Sinclair found interviewing them 'one of the most enjoyable afternoons' of his professional career. It had been his experience that, on closer inspection, many rock superstars appeared socially awkward and unforthcoming. An interview he had conducted with the singer Prince in New York had been like getting blood out of a stone while George Harrison had appeared to be a shy, introverted man with frightened eyes and – given John Lennon's fate – an understandably intense interest in his security. The Spice Girls, however, were different. They were friendly, flirtatious and seemingly normal and went out of their way to make the gentleman from *The Times* laugh.[51] Briefly laying claim to a form of global domination, Geri Halliwell's assertion (in, of all places, the *Spectator*) that the group were children of the Thatcher revolution even made the more serious newspapers toy with the notion that they had some cultural significance. 'In the wacky world of pop,' Sinclair mused, 'expressing support for the Tories remains the ultimate taboo. If the Spice Girls can carry that off, they can get away with anything.'[52]

The extraordinary – if brief – appeal of the Spice Girls masked the descent of mainstream pop in the last years of the decade towards no less manufactured but far less impressive 'boy bands' and female artists of dehumanized plasticity. That their looks and dance routines had more substance than their music was emblematic of the general level of inanity. Their appeal appeared to be strongest towards the pre-teen age group. Music for a more streetwise generation came instead from those like the Prodigy, the Chemical Brothers and Fat Boy Slim who used 'sampling' technology to mix pre-recorded sounds and music extracts into a new blend. The intention was not to record songs to be learned, sung and remembered but to produce spontaneous rhythm sounds for dancers packed into clubs like London's Ministry of Sound. Sinclair viewed this disinterest in posterity as a return to 'the original virtues of pop: disposable, ephemeral, effortlessly of the moment'. Popular music's heroic age – of Dylan, protest and social change – had related to a particular moment in history that had passed for good. As a consequence, 'Pop is now in the process of reverting to its pre-rock'n'roll function as entertainment with no revolutionary or ideological symbolic strings attached. Thus, while pop in 2000 will continue to be everywhere in evidence it will be nowhere in substance.'[53]

Indeed by the arrival of the twenty-first century, the pop industry's finances were being undercut by technology that allowed millions of would-be customers to download (usually illegally) music onto their computers or walk around with a pocket Ipod programmed with several thousand tunes. The sheer omnipresence of the music helped to undermine its distinctive qualities. With younger listeners getting out of the habit of buying recordings in shops there was much for the music industry to worry about. Yet the fall in compact disc sales was matched by a trend back towards live performances and an experience distinct from the ease of access that technology provided. With this increase in demand, rock concert ticket prices were able to rise to a level that made the cheaper seats at the Royal Opera House a competitive alternative. The same could be said for season tickets to the Premier League football clubs. Between highbrow art and lowbrow entertainment, market forces had become the great leveller.

The Times chose to engage with this process. Writing from her parent's council house in Wolverhampton, Caitlin Moran became, at seventeen, the paper's youngest regular journalist when she was given a brief to pick over the lighter end of popular culture. Aged thirteen, she had won the Dillons' Young Reader/Writer of the Year Award and three years later she not only became the *Observer* Young Reporter of the Year but also had her first novel, *The Chronicles of Narmo* (an anagram of Moran), published. Anxious to attract a fresh voice that could appeal to adolescents and young people, both Simon Jenkins (contrary to his usual instincts) and Richard Morrison encouraged her to write in her own way even though this meant almost physically restraining several subeditors from imposing the house style upon her idiosyncratic expression. One truth was evident: the paper had come a long way since a subeditor corrected – and destroyed the credibility of – an insightful Richard Williams's review of punk rock by unhelpfully changing the album title in the article to *Anarchy In The United Kingdom*. In truth, Moran's accessible manner would not have found favour in *The Times* of an earlier generation – not that the old journal might have been the worse for the occasional dash of such individuality. Ignoring the increased space made available for reviewing classical music, traditional readers doubtless found the space given to the musings of the precocious teenager from Wolverhampton as evidence that the paper was indeed adopting a dumbing down attitude. Popular culture in the paper might be tolerated when it was judiciously dissected from the traditional lofty artistic standpoint of the reviewer. Moran's charm was that she discussed the modern world of pop, celebrity and weekend television with indulgent familiarity rather than intellectual analysis. The question of whether it could be justified as art appeared irrelevant. Moran was celebrating what for many millions of people was the essence of modern life.

The diverse choices opened up by the unbridled consumerism also confronted the visual art world. The spread of a technologically advanced media age in which even the least receptive inhabitants were bombarded by images – in newspapers, on television, on cinema screens, on advertising hoardings – was perhaps the greatest challenge facing art since the birth of photography. Paint on canvas would remain a principal medium of expression but a new generation of artists was turning to a wider range of visual resources that included video, film installation and computer-based image manipulation.

Well placed to comment on these developments was Richard Cork who Simon Jenkins personally appointed *The Times*'s chief art critic in 1991. Cork had previously been the *Listener*'s critic and was the 1989–90 Slade Professor of Fine Art at Cambridge, his alma mater, where he had lectured on the avant-garde art of the Great War. He had already gained a considerable reputation as an author, with books that ranged from the two-volume *Vorticism and Abstract Art in the First Machine Age* to the *Social Role of Art* and a study of David Bomberg. Other works, including books on Jacob Epstein and his collected journalism, would follow.

While newspapers like *The Times* always endeavoured to cover major exhibitions around the world, the day-to-day emphasis was, appropriately, on what most readers would have a reasonable chance to view in Britain. Happily for Cork and his audience, the nineties proved to be a decade in which some of the most important art was being made in London. In some respects this was surprising. After the boom of the mid-eighties, art prices had dived and the beginning of the new decade appeared to be a time of great uncertainty for emerging talent. Adversity, however, failed to dampen creativity and a new generation elbowed its way to the fore. There was no guiding principle unifying what was dubbed 'BritArt'. Some of its exponents had been at Goldsmiths College together, although the majority had not. What they tended to have in common was a lack of youthful idealism and a fascination with decay and death (in this respect, the work of Francis Bacon was a major influence). As one of the selectors for the 1995 British Art Show, Cork played his part in bringing them to public attention. The exhibition proved immensely popular. The great breakthrough proceeded two years later. After successive summers in which the Royal Academy's exhibitions had failed to engage with a wider public, its decision to open *Sensation* in the autumn of 1997 put the old institution back at the centre of British art. *Sensation* displayed works by young British artists (yBas) collected by their greatest patron, Charles Saatchi. The most controversial work was that by Marcus Harvey whose giant painting of Myra Hindley composed from hundreds of children's handprints, radiated menace.

Damien Hirst, the supposed *enfant terrible* of the generation, was also represented. His 1991 work, a tiger shark suspended in a tank of formaldehyde,
became perhaps the yBas' most widely recognized work. Cork believed it
shared a 'kinship with the work of George Stubbs'. Hirst's other works,
including sliced pigs and cows' heads swarmed over by flies, expressed his
interest in mortality. Also on display was a tent inscribed with the names
of everyone its creator, the self-reverential Tracey Emin, had ever slept with.
Visitors were invited to crawl inside. Meanwhile, Sarah Lucas's *Sod You Gits*
expressed contempt for tabloid images of female sexuality.

Sensation lived up to its name. Hostile critics found fault with the yBas'
often crude or self-indulgent subject matter and their fixation with 'shock
art'. Traditionalists condemned the prevalence of conceptual installations
in which the artist had played little part in personally crafting the work.
Richard Cork had no time for such quibbles, delighting instead that 'the
rebels have stormed the bastions of conservatism' and hoping that if this
led to some Royal Academicians carrying out their threat to resign then so
much the better since the institution 'has spent much of the 20th century
condemning the most vital impulses in modern art . . . The show's arrival
is a welcome sign that the Academy has belatedly decided to atone for its
disgraceful, antiquated intolerance in the past.' Cork even ranked Rachel
Whiteread's *Ghost* (a mould created of a typical London living room) as
'among the classic British sculptures of the present century'.[54]

A media storm and the reaction of some of the public certainly suggested
that art still had the power to shock. It was not just the tabloids and
self-declared philistines that came to mock. Even Simon Jenkins thought
the yBas' work was rubbish:

> Van Gogh famously wrote of his garbage dump: 'My God, it was
> beautiful.' But he portrayed garbage through the medium of his art.
> This exhibition (or most of it) takes garbage and, like the Dadaists,
> puts it in a museum. Art is merely a custodial function, an act of
> redefinition. The artist is a wordsmith.
>
> . . . The stuff is mostly the usual mutilations, deformities, sex
> organs and banalities of the Adrian Mole school of sculpture. The
> catalogue clothes them in the pretension now obligatory for event
> art. They are 'grizzly Gothic macabre' or 'post-colonial neo-Victorian'
> or 'a democracy of material and meaning'. If medicine or law
> described its work in the gibberish used by artists, half Britain would
> be dead or in jail.

Indeed, as far as Jenkins was concerned, *Sensation* appeared to be less about the content of what was on display than about the person who had given it meaning by purchasing it. The public were merely being asked 'to admire Mr Saatchi's taste, not because anyone can tell a good dead sheep from a bad one, but because Mr Saatchi says Mr Hirst is a good dead-sheep artist. He has sanctified objects and their finders or creators by the act of his patronage.'[55]

Similar objections were made, often by those with less artistic sensitivity than Simon Jenkins, to the works short-listed for the Turner Prize. During the nineties, public interest in this competition soared, thanks in part to Channel 4's decision to turn it into a television event but also to the new market BritArt's exponents had helped create. Artists like Damien Hirst and Tracey Emin became personalities in their own right – which in the latter's case was appropriate given how much of her work was autobiographical. Her appearance, drunk on television drowning out with a string of obscenities Cork's efforts to discuss modern art's subtleties, only added to her renown. There was nonetheless a danger that the media interest was transforming the yBas from artists into celebrities whose personal antics were given as much attention as their creativity. For good or ill, art had certainly made itself relevant in this sense of catching the new millennial *Zeitgeist* of 'celebrity culture'. Indeed, an audience existed not only to lap up exhaustive coverage of the lives and loves of modern artists and popular entertainers (or, at any rate, the image their publicists proffered) but even descended into the hero worship of the genuinely talentless publicity seekers who appeared on 'reality television' shows like Channel 4's extraordinarily successful *Big Brother*. 'This is television for its own sake, pure television,' warned *The Times*'s critic, Paul Hoggart, even before the first series of *Big Brother* had begun. 'It features people who are on television because they want to be on television, and who want to be on television because they want to be on television even more.'[56] Undaunted, more Britons voted in the *Big Brother* contestant eviction nights than in the European parliamentary elections. Whether this was a verdict on Brussels or Britain was open to debate.

There were others who deplored the mixture of celebrity trappings and shock art that the Turner Prize appeared to promote in place of more meaningful expressionism. In *The Times*, the sculptor Sir Anthony Caro criticized the 'anything goes' attitude that tolerated what he regarded as the transient and self-indulgent quality of much of the younger generation's work. The arts lobby was appalled at such effrontery, as if criticizing the new aesthetic orthodoxy was a form of heresy, and Caro's office received several telephone calls from the Tate Gallery trying to get his remarks withdrawn.[57] Caro had made his observations to Dalya Alberge, who had arrived at *The Times* from the *Independent* in 1994. As the new arts correspondent, it was her brief to cover stories of interest for the news pages. This proved a useful point of contact for those wishing to publicize the looming fate of endangered art works and several were saved as a direct consequence of their being brought to the attention of concerned *Times* readers. Yet the controversies of the contemporary art scene were never far away. On the day in which the 2000 Turner Prize winner was to be announced, Alberge accused one of the nominees of plagiarism. Glenn Brown's giant canvas, *The Loves of Shepherds*, was an almost identical copy of Anthony Robert's jacket illustration for a science fiction paperback novel of 1974.[58]

The Times did not just report on art, it helped make it. In 1998, the paper joined forces with Artangel to pay for a new work of art – the first occasion in which a national newspaper had commissioned an artwork from inception. Cork was on the panel that included Rachel Whiteread and Brian Eno to sift through seven hundred proposals. Trust was eventually placed in Michael Landy, a yBa whose work dealt with issues of modern consumerism. The resulting installation, entitled *Breakdown*, was three years in the planning and certainly caused a stir. During a fortnight in February 2001, Landy filled an empty former C&A department store in Oxford Street with all his personal possessions, more than seven thousand in all, ranging from his car, his art collection (which included works by Hirst and Emin), love letters and even his remaining postage stamps and the money in his bank account. 'Everything Must Go' posters on the windows gave a hint of what was about to happen to them. As 45,000 visitors filed through, Landy and a team of blue overall clad assistants placed each object on a moving assembly line, proceeding to smash them to pieces and put them through a shredder. A sizeable crowd formed outside watching the artist divest himself of all his worldly possessions. The end product finished up in a landfill site. At any rate, Landy had suffered for his art.

What was evident was the extent to which Britain entered the twenty-first century with London's place in the firmament of contemporary visual art well established. It had become what New York had been in the 1970s and Paris in the more distant past. In Europe, the Venice Biennale was perhaps the major rival, although the variety of galleries and shows in London was without peer. Most of all, the success of Tate Modern was phenomenal. Cork was spoilt for choice. Beside the yBas, a slightly older generation of sculptors like Antony Gormley and Anish Kapoor had risen to prominence. Yet, notwithstanding Gormley's impressive *Angel of the North* near Gateshead and the construction of new modern galleries like nearby BALTIC (for which Cork voted in favour in his other guise as the chairman of the Arts Council's visual arts committee) and the Lowry in Salford, British art remained predominantly associated with events in London. If anything, Cork was of the view that the process by which London sucked talent from elsewhere was accelerating.

When in 1998 Daniel Johnson departed for the *Telegraph*, Peter Stothard made the unorthodox appointment of himself as the new literary editor and for the next year managed to find the time to match books with reviewers while also editing the rest of the paper. Working for him was Erica Wagner who had arrived as Johnson's secretary. Stothard was impressed by her knowledge and abilities and eventually appointed her to take the reins – although not before mischievously announcing at a staff party that he had finally agreed to step down from the job he had come to love, that of editor ... literary editor. His knowledge and appreciation remained nonetheless. He expressed his admiration for Ted Hughes in moving comment articles he penned under his own name at the time of the Poet Laureate's death and memorial services.[59] Only months earlier he had broken one of London's best-kept literary secrets when he revealed in *The Times* that Hughes had written an eighty-eight poem verse narrative, *Birthday Letters*, that chronicled his troubled relationship with Sylvia Plath. The paper also won the serialization rights of what Andrew Motion regarded as Hughes's greatest work, 'as magnetic as Browning's poems for Elizabeth Barrett, as poignant as Hardy's Poems 1912–13'.[60]

Despite the expertise and deep interest of Erica Wagner and Peter Stothard, it was dramatic rather than literary *tour de forces* that continued to receive daily attention in the paper. It was never going to be easy finding a replacement for Irving Wardle, who stepped down after twenty-seven years as *The Times*'s chief theatre critic in 1990, but Benedict Nightingale proved a worthy successor. Having spent the last few years in the United States, Nightingale was especially able to provide a fresh perspective on the state of British theatre. His mother, Evelyn, had been the first wife of Evelyn Waugh (he had sought revenge following their divorce by unfairly portraying her as Brenda Last in a *Handful of Dust*). After Charterhouse and the universities of Cambridge and Pennsylvania, Nightingale had embarked upon a career as a drama critic at the *Guardian*, *New Statesman* and *New York Times* followed by three years as Professor of English, Theatre and Drama at the University of Michigan.

Returning to London, Nightingale despaired at the inability of playwrights to examine social and political attitudes unless through 'reflex indignation and doctrinaire disapproval'. He feared that theatre had become insufficiently dangerous, that it was no longer, as Tom Stoppard said after seeing John Osborne's *Look Back in Anger* in 1956, 'the place to be'.[61] Nonetheless, while finding faults, Nightingale was enthusiastic about David Hare's state-of-the nation trilogy scrutinizing the Church in *Racing Demon*, the legal system in *Murmuring Judges* and politics in *The Absence of War* which featured a People's Party leader bearing distinct similarities to Neil Kinnock. He especially commended Stoppard's *Arcadia*. Hare, Stoppard, Michael Frayn and Harold Pinter were playwrights with distinctive voices. This was lacking in the new generation emerging in the mid-1990s who were disengaged from the old ideologies and assumptions. If they had anything in common, it was what Nightingale dubbed their contribution to the 'Theatre of Urban Ennui'. There was much to praise in the work of Jez Butterworth, Judy Upton and Patrick Marber. Doubt and less formulaic thinking appeared to be one solution to what Nightingale had previously condemned about the doctrinaire works that had predominated when he arrived back in London from the United States. But there was a concern that, as he put it, 'the generation between the youthful Marbers and McDonaghs and Pinter, Stoppard and even Hare lacks distinction. Where is the dramatist large-minded enough to deal with the spiralling dilemmas produced by scientific progress, cultural globalisation, political nationalism and personal rootlessness?' Indeed many of the best dramatists, like Conor MacPherson, Martin McDonagh and Billy Roche, hailed from across the Irish Sea.

Financially, some of the West End's greatest successes during the decade came from musicals and revivals. Some saw the success of these forms of entertainment as evidence of how sickly British theatre had become – reduced to being fed on a drip by replaying dead playwrights' back catalogues and by musicals that similarly relied on a compilation of hits from long defunct pop groups like Queen and Abba. Given the financial risks of staging in the West End, it was perhaps understandable that impresarios often preferred the tried and tested to risking all with an innovative work by an obscure hopeful. However, some revivals, like Stephen Daldry's adaptation of *An Inspector Calls*, found a new resonance that was rightly rewarded and, as Nightingale observed, 'in a reductionist era, when the psychological and behavourial sciences are annexing the human spirit, isn't there something exhilarating in the size, imagination, verbal energy and moral fullbloodedness of, especially, the Greek, Jacobean and Spanish classics?'.[62] In 1999 twenty-four million people visited the theatre in Britain, rather more than attended league football matches. The Almeida and the Donmar Warehouse rose to prominence, the latter finding an inspiring director in Sam Mendes. And while the RSC lurched into crisis under Adrian Noble, Richard Eyre and Trevor Nunn, successive directors of the National Theatre, helped it go from strength to strength. Nightingale remained convinced that British theatre's successes were made possible by state subsidy and, without it, there would be a collapse. This, he thought, was the main reason why the West End was more lively than its American equivalents. It was, as he also recognized, not the only reason. The British film industry was far less dominant than Hollywood. While the top American actors were sucked into movie making, British theatre audiences could still benefit from performances from great actors at the peak of their powers.

At the cinema, Hollywood production values certainly ensured that the nineties was the decade of large budgets and technologically advanced special effects. Both came together in James Cameron's *Titanic*, which cost $200 million to make and confounded expectations that it would suffer the stricken liner's fate. The world's most expensive film became the world's most profitable one. Men allegedly enjoyed it as a disaster movie while women supposedly were attracted to the love story at its heart. 'Yet for all the sluggish script and the enormous weight of the special effects, this movie behemoth still has the power to shake us rigid and touch the soul,' wrote *The Times*'s film critic, Geoff Brown.[63] Yet all too frequently, spending on film making had come to exceed subtler considerations. By the end of the century, Hollywood's average marketing budget per film had reached $25 million. Fittingly, a tiny budget horror movie, *The Blair Witch Project*, proceeded to gross among the most substantial receipts. Indeed, violent and often psychopathic behaviour played a starring role in many of the more noteworthy films of the decade with Quentin Tarantino's *Reservoir Dogs* and *Pulp Fiction* – whose 'very gusto keeps total nihilism at bay' according to Brown – proving the most impressive.[64]

As the century drew to a close, Britain appeared to be providing many of the great actors but failing to make any serious challenge on Hollywood's grip on production. Inadequate funding and lack of distribution rights remained gripes although when National Lottery money was invested it mostly subsidized commercial (and worse, artistic) flops. There were, of course, periodic triumphs when a film scored highly in both departments. Anthony Minghella's *The English Patient* and John Madden's *Shakespeare in Love*, co-scripted by Tom Stoppard, received their due at the Oscars. The great commercial success was the 1994 romantic comedy *Four Weddings and a Funeral* which helped turn its star, Hugh Grant, into the poster boy for England's bumbling, self-effacingly witty English white upper-middle class. Brown admired the blend of 'tart modern manners with old-fashioned romance' and its bottling of the 'key Merchant–Ivory ingredients: elegance, posh clothes, snob appeal' alongside the repressed emotions displayed in Grant's character. Others were less delighted. As with the Merchant–Ivory productions of E. M. Foster's novels during the 1980s, that this was the image of Britain still being portrayed across the world to large and enraptured audiences only damned it further among those who wanted to see the country given a cooler, non-elitist, multi-ethnic, cutting-edge international profile. They were to be further antagonized when *Four Weddings*'s writer, Richard Curtis, followed up his success five years later with a similar format in *Notting Hill*. Less prone to post-imperial angst, the public, like the critic in *The Times*, Nigel Cliff, enjoyed the return, relieved that Hugh Grant was still on form, 'playing Hugh Grant as only he can'.[65]

Yet Britain's cinematic contribution to the nineties was not all floppy hair or period-piece corsetry. Working-class grit featured in the comedies *Brassed Off* and *The Full Monty* which dealt with the post-Thatcher, post-industrial landscape of the North of England with its threatened sense of community and punctured male pride, while *East is East* demonstrated there was a mainstream audience for a wry look at multicultural Britain. A film with the unpromising title of *Trainspotting* was the work that attained the greatest cult status. Directed by Danny Boyle from the novel by Irvine Welsh, it concerned the trials of four drug-abusing losers from the non-postcard side of Edinburgh with particularly plausible performances from Ewan McGregor who played Renton, the character attempting to go straight, and Robert Carlyle as the psychotic Begbie. Its amorality and 'sense of life ripped from the gutters' was not to Geoff Brown's taste, although he accurately conceded that younger audiences would enjoy its adrenalin rush.[66] By turns comic, endearing, revolting and surreal, *Trainspotting* blended fine acting, a quotable script, a hip soundtrack, a modicum of violence and all the tricks that also gave Tarantino such a transatlantic following – but with a Scots accent.

There were voices untamed by Received Pronunciation, too, in the fashion world. John Galliano was building his reputation, as was Alexander McQueen, an East End 'bad boy' with a Penchant for buttock baring. Their extravagant and colourful designs caused a sensation and helped to push fashion journalism into the news pages of the paper. That British designers were conquering the fashion world but that London was still not its capital was evident when both men went off to Paris to work for Dior and Givenchy. British designers, like British actors and directors, appeared to have internationally recognized talents but lacked a home industry of sufficient scale and investment to sustain them. Instead, their creativity was applauded in foreign currencies.

This was nonetheless an exciting period in the fashion world and *The Times* was particularly fortunate in 1998 to attract the fashion features director of *Vogue*, Lisa Armstrong, to assume command over its coverage. 'It is entirely to the point,' Nigella Lawson had written three years earlier, 'that the Princess of Wales once appeared, in model pose, on the front of *Vogue*: where once covergirls wanted to be princesses, now princesses want to be covergirls.'[67] By the time of Lisa Armstrong's arrival at *The Times* the age of the supermodel was giving way to a fresh inter-relationship between fashion, film stars and the cult of celebrity. Designers could get as much exposure from seeing their creations worn by an actress attending the Oscars or a premiere – especially in terms of front- or news-page coverage – than from the catwalk recognition of a leading fashion show. Likewise, sporting the work of an acclaimed designer could vastly improve the public profile of an actress, as Liz Hurley discovered when she wore what became popularly referred to as 'that dress' by Gianni Versace. If any event demonstrated the democratization of fashion it was the media reaction to Versace's murder in July 1997. It was on the front page of *The Times* and was the subject of no fewer than thirteen articles in the paper that and the following day. The violent nature of his death played some part in the extent of the exposure, but the response from the tabloids – for whom the life and work of expensive fashion designers had not traditionally been considered close to readers' hearts – was more extraordinary. The *Sun* devoted nine pages of coverage on the first day alone. High fashion had moved beyond the preserve of the chic, the wealthy and the cultivated.

The reasons for this democratizing process were, in part, economic. Clothes had become cheaper. What was more, within days of a top fashion designer's new collection appearing on the catwalk and in photo spreads across the newspapers, low-cost derivatives were available in the high streets for those with more modest budgets. It was even possible to purchase skirts or handbags that were closely influenced by leading designs in supermarkets. Buying into a 'label' became particularly important for those whose interest was primarily in making a social statement. Fashion houses like Gucci invested large sums in promoting their brand names. For some, there was a danger that brand advertisement was supplanting attention to design. The process through which the smaller fashion companies continued to be swallowed up by the larger ones helped foster these commercial empires. A phenomenon developed in which high-quality brands were devalued precisely because they were adopted as the badges of the masses. A more general trend was that the clothes to bare flesh ratio swung increasingly towards the latter with fewer and skimpier fabrics predominating as the decade wore on. By the century's end, *The Times*'s coverage had never been better or its reputation higher, with Lisa Armstrong and her team at the forefront of the effort to make it a paper of broader interest to women. The glossy monthly fashion magazines continued to have the pictorial advantage, but because they were tied to production schedules that necessitated feature planning weeks or even months in advance, they lacked the daily newspapers' versatility. *The Times*'s Saturday magazine was able to respond with glossy space for photo shoots as well, but it remained in the newspaper section, especially after the launch of the *T2* tabloid in 2000, that the higher quality in writing was put to best effect. There was no shortage of material. As Armstrong pointed out, 'ultimately, fashion is about expression'.[68]

Attractiveness was not the only form this articulation took. Given the breadth of its embrace and the money involved, the fashion world continued to have a dark side that gobbled up and spat out those it manipulated. In the early nineties, the preference for unhealthily thin waif-like models was blamed for an upsurge in anorexia and eating disorders among young girls. Particularly noxious was the so-called 'heroin chic' look that used etiolated models who appeared listless and dazed on drugs – often because they were. This destructive look was featured not only in British magazines like *i-D* and *The Face* but was even read as a possible subtext for Corinne Day's pictures of Kate Moss that appeared in *Vogue*. It soon went transatlantic and entered the advertising mainstream with companies like Calvin Klein using models who, to put it mildly, conveyed neither health nor happiness. If, in this respect, *The Times* was not at the forefront of a fashion movement then that was a point in its favour. Fearing that elements within the fashion world were effectively promoting drugs in order to sell their product and exploiting young girls, the trend was much criticized in works like Michael Gross's *Model: The Ugly Business of Beautiful Women* and in a 1997 speech (after the fad had largely passed) by President Clinton. It was certainly not a look that *The Times* actively promoted although, as Lisa Armstrong subsequently attested, 'after the sublime vacuousness of 1980s fashion photography, with its cartoon notions of glamour' the approach of the early nineties was more an attempt at social commentary and as revolutionary as punk had been in the 1970s at 'peeling back traditional layers of fashion artifice'.[69]

Health scares and symptoms of illness were the preserve of the former Norfolk Tory MP, Dr Tom Stuttaford. *The Times*'s medical correspondent since 1982 and expert columnist since 1991, he was one of the most prolific, knowledgeable and popular writers on the paper. His briefings provided valuable diagnosis, delivered with authority and accessibility. They were also particularly strong in advice on preventative medicine. The issues of dieting and healthy eating were also regularly examined by Nigel Hawkes, the science editor. Hawkes was a natural sceptic and as such saw it as a scientific duty to probe rather than give unquestioning credence to each new theory, fad or headline-grabbing scare. He questioned the nutritionists' craze for portraying fats, salt and sugar as dangerous health risks. Indeed, as he subsequently observed, obesity increased during a decade in which fatty foods were trimmed from the national diet. The French, meanwhile, ate more fat and more cholesterol than either the British or the Americans but suffered only half as many heart disease-related deaths.[70] He was similarly alarmed at what he believed were scare stories demonizing gene-modified crops as dangerous 'franken foods'. Always he wanted to examine more closely the scientific evidence for such claims. In Britain, at least, he was battling against a tide. Environmentalism proved to be one of the most potent ideologies of the post-Communist era. Depressing stories of pollution and species depletion dominated the ever-increasing workload of successive environment editors, Michael McCarthy and Nick Nuttall.

No environmental issue attracted so much alarm as the belief that the planet was being wrecked by man-induced global warming. No sooner had the fear of nuclear annihilation been diminished by the Cold War's thaw than this new threat to life on earth rose to become almost an accepted wisdom. One who begged to differ was Hawkes. An Oxford metallurgy graduate who had worked for *Nature* and subsequently the *Observer* before joining *The Times*, he had in the 1970s reported the contentions of leading scientists that the earth was destined for a second Ice Age. He suspected the new global warming claims were alarmist and based on unreliable computer predictions drawn from too little real information. He wanted to know, if the equation was so simple, why temperatures had decreased when carbon emissions had multiplied in the previous decades of the century. 'Global warning has turned into an inverted pyramid of implications resting on a handful of facts,' he wrote when chiding Margaret Thatcher for her claim that the world had to act decisively to curb carbon emissions. 'Fortunately, the human appetite for sacrifices is limited and its attention-span is short,' Hawkes prophesied. 'A couple of cold winters will take the froth off the debate, and allow us the time we need to discover whether or not the earth is really warming up.'[71] The cold weather, however, did not come to Hawkes's rescue, and as the accumulation of information improved during the decade, he tempered his scepticism on the subject. Nonetheless, it disturbed him that it was always the worst-case scenarios that attracted the headlines while research that suggested temperature change might be less severe, or even had some countervailing benefits, was largely ignored by the media. At heart, he believed environmentalism was an ideology that cherry picked the facts to support its case and disregarded those that challenged it. It was, he thought, not a very scientific approach.

On 1 January 1996, *The Times* was launched on the Internet. In April a new supplement, *Interface*, edited by Keith Blackmore, was started and ran weekly for the next five years. It kept readers abreast of developments in cyberspace and explored the expanding horizons of information technology during a period in which there was much excited talk about how such developments were creating a 'new paradigm' in world economics. Stothard recognized the website's importance, but did not allow himself to be diverted by some of the hyperbolic claims being made about how the print edition would recede into history. He not only believed that the paper edition had a future but that it should remain the centre of his attention. In Stothard's opinion, the online edition reproduced the paper's content rather than provided an alternative or enhanced service.

Stothard's measured approach contrasted with the competition. The *Daily Telegraph* and the *Guardian* had both launched websites the year before *The Times*. In particular, the *Guardian*'s editor, Alan Rusbridger, channelled considerable resources into *Guardian Unlimited*, which offered readers far more material than was available in the print edition. This was an expensive investment but one that it was hoped would eventually produce a return once increasing proportions of the world turned first to their computers, pocket screens and even mobile telephones for information rather than to newsprint. When the dot.com bubble burst in 2000, Stothard's attitude looked more sagacious than those who had got caught up in a modern equivalent of tulipmania and other past speculative catastrophes. Wild expectations that the Internet would ensure exponential growth as a virtual poster site for advertisers withered almost overnight. Unfortunately, News Corp. had begun to invest heavily and was among those financially damaged when the collapse occurred. Development programmes for *The Times*'s online edition had to be curtailed. The future, it seemed, was not on the world wide web after all.

It was at this moment, when expansion gave way to retrenchment, that a new online business development officer arrived at Wapping. The Dutch-born Annelies Van Den Belt had experience of the necessity for a cool head in a crisis, having previously run operations for the *St Petersburg Times* and the *Moscow Times* in the midst of Russia's economic turmoil. Collapsing online advertising revenue disabused any who retained the notion that *Times Online* would generate vast returns. Yet, while finding ways of cutting costs, Van Den Belt rolled out a strategy for generating fresh sources of subscriber revenue. An online version of the paper, instantly available around the globe, was particularly valuable to British expats and others with an interest in Britain who lived in parts of the world where the paper edition was obtainable a day late, if at all. This market would later, in 2004, be offered a full subscription-only digital edition, or e-paper, that reproduced the paper edition exactly on the screen, allowing the viewer all the casual browse and page-turning navigation that the headline-driven online edition lacked. This was a service that was withheld from the British market. For that home market, the strategy was one of introducing rolling charges rather than full upfront subscription. Charging for accessing home or breaking news was not sensible when online users could surf rival news sites for information of broadly comparable quality freely. In this respect, there was competition not only from the other online broadsheets but also from the BBC's news website, which, being licence-fee funded, had vast resources at its disposal and was likely to remain free as part of the Corporation's public service remit. Instead, *The Times*'s task was to identify which parts of the paper represented a unique product for which online users would be prepared to pay a charge. Thus, basic access would be free but there would be a charge for specialist content. The first area identified in this way was the crossword. *Times Online*'s 'crossword club' succeeded in attracting enough subscribers to more than cover its costs. Other areas followed. A large proportion of internet use concerned business research and *Times Online* was able to generate money by charging for access to its archive and to law reports. Improved palm-size technology offered other downloading opportunities. Sport and business alerts could be sent to mobile phones for a charge. By 2002, subscription revenue was accounting for 20 per cent of the site's overall revenue. All the classified advertisements for jobs, holidays and promotions that appeared in the print edition became available in the online format. Display advertising provided additional revenue. While the reckless enthusiasm of the late 1990s had subsided, there was every reason to assume that the sums generated in this way would accumulate substantially in the years ahead.

Halfway through the twenty-first century's first decade, it was too early to make a judgment on whether *The Times's* cautious approach was the right one. *Times Online* employed less than a third of the staff engaged in producing *Guardian Unlimited*. While the British broadsheets continued to make most of their content free to home users, the *Financial Times* had decided to make most of its content available only to subscribers. In the short term at least, this proved expensive. *FT.com* consumed a large share of its owner Pearson's £184 million investment in internet services in 2000 alone.[72] Such figures dwarfed what *Times Online* consumed. The *Guardian* and *FT* were laying down enormous investments in the hope of establishing a secure grip on a potentially lucrative future market. One early consequence was that the *Guardian*, with a strong American following, was the most popular British broadsheet on the web. Whether this market share could be sustained once subscription fees were eventually hiked up remained to be seen. *The Times* had opted for a middle way and in doing so moved into second position in the number of hits its website recorded, behind the *Guardian*. There were advantages in having a reduced outlay of expense. By 2004, *Times Online* had even broken into profit. The death of the paper edition certainly did not appear remotely imminent, but the electronic edition had nonetheless established its place as a fundamental component of *The Times's* future.

CHAPTER ELEVEN

THE HEART OF EUROPE

Losing Faith in the Tories; Euro-Scepticism; Blair

I

Peter Stothard was four days into his editorship when sterling was forced out of the Exchange Rate Mechanism. Having been in the United States for almost all of Major's administration up until that point, he had returned at the very moment the Government's credibility collapsed. The result, Stothard later maintained, was that 'I never saw a good day of the Major government.'[1]

Sterling exited the ERM on Black Wednesday, 16 September 1992. It was a humiliation for Norman Lamont, the Chancellor of the Exchequer, yet it was understandable that John Major believed sterling's exit from the ERM was not a resigning matter. Joining the system had, after all, been Major's principal act while Lamont's predecessor at the Treasury. Despite advice to the contrary, he had even insisted on the high sterling to Deutschmark parity. If it was a resigning matter, then there would be fingers pointing at the Prime Minister.

As a discipline that drove out inflation, ERM membership had already succeeded in its task, yet the Government had remained committed to it nonetheless partly because it had no alternative economic strategy and also because a free-floating currency was incompatible with the Maastricht criteria for joining the euro. By March 1992, 1200 businesses a week were folding. There were 40 million square feet of unwanted commercial property in London alone. As Britain prepared for autumn, unemployment reached 2.8 million. The Conservatives' reputation for economic competence was in tatters. Regardless, the Government persevered with a policy that necessitated raising interest rates to defend sterling's overvalued parity at a time when British business, deep in recession, needed a reduction in the cost of borrowing and a cheaper currency with which to trade. Repeatedly, the leading columns of The Times advised Major to renegotiate the terms while there was still a chance.[2] The Prime Minister, however, was nothing if not a man of his word. In the last days, despite all the signs that sterling's rate within the ERM was unsustainable, the Government wasted £3.3 billion and the Bank of England parted with £25 billion of its reserves in a forlorn attempt to stop the currency falling through the floor of its fixed trading bands.

'With one bound we are free,' whooped Anatole Kaletsky, whose financial analysis had been promoted to the front page during the crisis. While others, engulfed by the sense of national defeat, prophesied further bad economic news, he argued that letting sterling float and cutting interest rates would ensure an economic recovery. He did not disguise his disdain for the incompetence of 'the political and business establishment, the prime minister, the captains of industry, the City bankers and above all, the Treasury knights' whose abrogation of financial sovereignty to the Bundesbank had ensured 'a million people have lost their jobs. Hundreds of thousands have been made homeless and bankrupt.' Kaletsky, indeed, was one of a select few who had warned of the dangers from the moment Major had – to the acclaim of informed opinion – first taken Britain into the ERM nearly two years earlier.

Major had an opportunity, if he wished to take it, to set a new course that put a positive spin on a floating currency and low interest rates and turned its back on immediate aspirations to join a single European currency. His failure to do so crushed any lingering Euro-sceptics' hope that he was secretly on their side but had merely been playing a long game for tactical reasons. In consequence, he had to contend with the virulent enmity of daily denouncements from Euro-sceptics, either, if they were his own back-benchers, to the television cameras on College Green, or, if they were writers, in the pages of papers like *The Times*.

The official HMSO version of the Maastricht Treaty was not published until May 1992, more than six months after it was signed. Constitutional lawyers pored over its implications. At the time of its signing, *The Times*, like all other British media organizations, had no means of knowing its exact content and had to rely on the interpretation Major and his press office put on it. Once fuller details became available, *The Times*'s ardour cooled substantially. Simon Jenkins, who had applauded Major's efforts in December 1991 from the editor's chair, was among those who felt duped. In his new role as a *Times* columnist, he denounced Maastricht as 'the worst treaty since Versailles'.[3] Be that as it may, it was now clear to both Jenkins and Peter Stothard that the Prime Minister so believed his own propaganda about winning 'game, set and match' at Maastricht that no argument or event would disabuse him of the notion. Even before Black Wednesday, the Danes, on 2 June, had stunned all Europe by daring to reject the Treaty in a national referendum. Their veto invalidated it. Twenty-four hours after the verdict of Copenhagen, nearly one hundred Tory MPs had signed an early-day motion calling for a 'fresh start' and a change in Europe's direction. They were dumfounded when their Prime Minister reacted to the news by suggesting that it was the Danes – rather than the EU – who needed to think again.

Over a very short period of time, Euro-scepticism had gone from being perceived as a modern variant on flat earth-ism to a respectable analysis of the disengagement between politicians and public. Four days after sterling fell through the ERM trapdoor, the French referendum called by President Mitterrand to demonstrate the strength of his country's pro-Europeanism recorded a 'yes' majority to Maastricht of just over 1 per cent. If support for the European project had waned so much in the country that had led it for the past thirty-five years, it was hardly surprising that the Danes had – by an equally narrow margin – voted against it. Nor were they the only ones. Despite the adherence of the German political elite and the constitutional bar on referenda, opinion polls suggested most Germans were opposed to scraping the Deutschmark. In Britain, there could have been no more personalized example of how the intellectual mood had changed among Tory-minded journalists than in the case of William Rees-Mogg. During his editorship of *The Times* between 1967 and 1981, he had been a strong advocate of Europeanism and regarded his paper's support for British membership of the EEC (as it then was) as among the greatest legacies of his years in the chair. Although he remained a supporter of that decision, his enthusiasm for integration had waned considerably. Not content to assault Maastricht repeatedly from his perch on the Op-Ed page, he mounted a High Court challenge to its becoming law.

Major was adamant that there would be no referendum in Britain. Spades were handed out for what promised to be a lengthy bout of parliamentary trench warfare. The Tory Party conference in October descended into a shouting match and a Commons revolt in November reduced the Government's majority to three. When, in the new year, the bill to approve the Maastricht Treaty entered its committee stage, five hundred amendments and one hundred new clauses were proposed by Euro-sceptics content to wear the Government down in this war of attrition. The old contemptibles who had opposed Heath's original entry made up the core of the Tory rebellion in the Commons but they had been joined by a younger generation of dogged sceptics that included Bill Cash and Michael Spicer. It was these two MPs who led what became effectively a party within a party, complete with London HQs, separate financing and a back room full of eager young men down from Oxbridge whose youthful idealism to liberate Britain from Brussels echoed a previous generation's zeal to free Spain from Fascism. Although Stothard had always resisted getting too close to any one politician or interest, he had enjoyed gatherings of the Conservative Philosophy Group and other Thatcherite think tanks during the 1980s and found himself similarly drawn to the cabals and coteries that formed around the Euro-sceptic banner. Brushing aside those who thought Bill Cash was too driven on the subject, Stothard enjoyed Cash's company, noting, 'at least he had some strong arguments'.[4]

Rees-Mogg's legal challenge failed on 30 July 1993 and three days later Maastricht was formally ratified. The Danes, too, had been persuaded to reconsider their objection while Austria, Finland and Sweden were poised to join an EU increased from twelve to fifteen member states. Yet, at Westminster and Wapping, the Euro-sceptics appeared unwilling to concede defeat and their hounding of the Prime Minister continued. On 28 November 1994 (the night Norway rejected joining the EU in a referendum), Major only won a Commons division on increasing Britain's contribution to the EU budget by threatening to resign if the vote was lost. Given the unpopularity of his party this was leadership through suicide pact. Even still, eight Tory MPs rebelled. When the whip was withdrawn from them another MP opted to join them. The Government no longer had a Commons majority. In December, the vote on imposing VAT on domestic fuel was lost. In the words of Norman Lamont (who Major had finally got round to replacing with the pro-European Ken Clarke), the Government appeared to be in office but not in power.

II

Unlike Margaret Thatcher, John Major was an assiduous reader of the press. Given his thin-skinned reaction to criticism, this was perhaps a mistake. Across Fleet Street he could count on very few allies. Stewart Steven at the *Evening Standard* and Bruce Anderson, the *Spectator*'s political editor, argued his corner but elsewhere the collapse in support for the Tory

Government from once-friendly newspapers was astonishing. Among the senior journalists at *The Times*, Stothard, Daniel Johnson and Martin Ivens all took great exception, in particular, to Major's failure to steer a more Euro-sceptic course. Anatole Kaletsky shared their contempt and Mary Ann Sieghart represented for him the worst of both worlds – a Euro-sceptic and New Labour supporter. *The Times*, though, was not governed by a party line. In their columns, Woodrow Wyatt and Matthew Parris bravely gave the Prime Minister the benefit of the doubt while Peter Riddell, the political editor, was a committed supporter of his attempts to keep Britain positively engaged in the process of European integration. Riddell, indeed, took a completely different line from that emanating from the editorial conferences and argued that Maastricht would 'in time, be seen as the start of a new, more diverse EC'.[5] Thus, Major retained the support of some of the most widely read columnists in the paper. He had one other advocate. The deputy editor, John Bryant, shared his love of sport and believed *The Times* was not giving him a fair chance. Indeed, he suspected that many of those who despised him so vehemently were motivated by a deep-seated social and educational condescension towards the Prime Minister whose degree came from the university of life. 'They had pretty much decided that they didn't like him because he was too downmarket' was Bryant's assessment of his colleagues' attitude.[6]

Neither Major nor his private office made much attempt to court *The Times*. Stothard thought Major's reticence was perhaps to his credit. Major did occasionally provide Stothard with warm gin and tonic around the Cabinet table, but he received far less attention from the Prime Minister than he had from his predecessor, even though he had then held far more junior rank at the paper. Even Sarah Hogg, head of the Downing Street Policy Unit, did not attempt to call in old favours despite having worked with Stothard at *The Times* prior to the move to Wapping. She did, however, express surprise that Major and Stothard did not get on given that, as far as she could see, they came from similar backgrounds – an observation that caused the Oxford Classicist's eyebrow to rise.[7]

It was Simon Jenkins who launched the articles in *The Times* that caused particular upset in Downing Street. He was the first journalist to refer (in an otherwise supportive article) to an alleged Prime Ministerial breakdown. 'Certainly he wobbled inside Admiralty House on Black Wednesday, by some accounts wobbled alarmingly,' Jenkins wrote. This fired the starting gun for others to repeat rumours that were circulating throughout Westminster. On 21 October 1992, Graham Paterson and Andrew Pierce wrote a lengthy article entitled 'Can Major Take the Strain?' Using unnamed 'friends' of the Prime Minister as its sources, it stated that Major was not eating properly and was lonely in the evenings because his wife preferred to live in Huntingdon. A professor of organizational psychology was quoted stating that such unstable eating patterns 'indicate a man in the second phase of a stress disorder'. There was certainly more supposition in the article than was consistent with being the journal of record. The worst slur, however, concerned the events of Black Wednesday. 'There is a deep reluctance from Mr Major's close colleagues and civil servants to divulge anything about the prime minister's bearing during that day,' Paterson and Pierce winked. 'But for five weeks one question has been asked again and again in Westminster and Fleet Street: did he crack up?' One man who had spent time with Major during that day was Norman Fowler, the party chairman (and a former *Times* journalist). He immediately took the unusual step of denouncing the article as 'nasty and malicious'. A well-briefed *Daily Mail* was particularly vociferous in attacking *The Times*'s efforts, providing its readers with a point-by-point refutation of the claims made by Paterson and Pierce.[8] Stothard remained convinced that his source was 'impeccable'.[9] In his autobiography, Major described the rumours as a 'malicious invention'.[10]

The attacks intensified. At the *Daily Telegraph*, Max Hastings had spiked a commissioned article by Paul Johnson that argued in fine polemical style that Major was not fit to be Prime Minister.[11] Stothard published it in *The Times* instead. Rees-Mogg soon came to share Johnson's contempt for Major, writing:

> He seems to be the most over-promoted of the seven [post-war Tory Prime Ministers]. He is not a natural leader; he cannot speak; he has a weak Cabinet which he has chosen; he lacks self confidence; he has no sense of strategy or direction. Even on Europe he does not stand for any great issue . . . His ideal level of political competence would be deputy chief whip, or something of that standing.[12]

The dislike for Major, for his European policy and for his failure to come to grips with the sleaze allegations that were engulfing so many of his colleagues tended to diminish his Tory critics' appreciation for those parts of his agenda that took Thatcherism forward. Yet plans to privatize British Rail, deregulate London buses, reduce the Post Office's monopoly and produce Audit Commission league tables on councils' performance were drawn up nonetheless. John Major had launched his Citizen's Charter back in July 1991. It aimed to apply the language of rights and expectations to consumers' use of public sector services. The intention was to increase choice, quality, value for money and accountability. Patients and parents would be permitted to see league tables of how their local health and education authorities were performing. NHS patients who had waited over two years for an operation would be entitled to treatment within the next three months or have the health authority pay for them to be treated privately. For the first time, there would be a legal requirement for schools to be independently inspected regularly. Public utilities would be forced to give compensation for poor service. Passengers would receive refunds if their trains were cancelled or subject to unreasonable delays and the emergency services would be subject to new 999 response target times.

There was, however, a downside. The granting of contractual rights to users of public services and the separation of powers between providers and scrutinizers necessitated the creation of a new army of inspectors and regulators to monitor and enforce standards. Some of these, like the 'Cones Hotline' (a service that allowed drivers to report delayed road works) quickly became the butt of jokes and condescension. More importantly, a new level of bureaucracy was created that proved expensive and a time-consuming distraction to the public sector employees it was trying to hold to account but was sometimes frustrating their professional judgment. This regulatory burden continued to impose itself when some of the utilities, like the railways, were privatized. For those that remained within the public sector, it was all part of a wider Tory strategy to create internal markets in areas of the economy that could not be privatized and, in doing so, to make them more responsive to consumer rather than producer interests. The policy had started in the 1980s, when local authorities were forced to offer out some of their services to 'competitive tender'. During the summer of 1991, the programme was rolled out in what became a central feature of the Government's domestic legislation. School and hospital league tables became popular measures by which the public could gain information on the provision of services in their area. Slowly, the number of patients waiting very long periods for NHS treatment was reduced. Before the new standards and inspections were enforced, some schools did not even trouble themselves to provide parents with annual reports on their child's progress. Chris Woodhead, appointed the Chief Inspector of Schools, became a familiar scourge of the so-called 'trendy teacher'. When his Office of Standards in Education (Ofsted) compiled evidence that illuminated low standards in many schools, the Association of Teachers and Lecturers union responded by calling for Ofsted to be abolished. *The Times*, though, saluted Woodhead's efforts and the drive to make the performance of schools as well as hospitals more transparent.[13] In November 1992, *The Times* was able to publish an official table of national school GSCE and A-level performances for the first time.

Accompanying the new world of Charter Marks and regulatory bodies, the Tories turned their attention once again to higher education. Having expressed his determination to make Britain a classless society, Major declared that 'at the heart of our reforms is the determination to break down the artificial barrier which has for too long divided an academic education from a vocational one'.[14] Polytechnics would be allowed to call themselves universities. Indeed, the Government, with Ken Clarke as its Education Secretary bringing the changes onto the statute book, wanted to see a third of young people receiving higher education degrees by the end of the decade. Although *The Times* later became a great critic of expanding entrance to higher education beyond what it regarded as the limitations of its applicants and the grade inflation that accompanied it, the paper did not rush to criticize the move. Taking a free-market approach to the issue, it hoped that the transformation from polytechnics into universities would enhance competition for students and resources – a process that need not mean a dilution in standards.[15] Certainly, the polytechnics leapt at the opportunity to upgrade their status. Within a very short space of time, a higher education system with almost one hundred universities was created. For *The Times*, one consequence was the decision taken following the 1992 graduation ceremonies to end the practice of printing degree results. In one sense, this abandonment marked yet another retreat from the paper's pretensions to be the journal of record (albeit that until 1986 it had only bothered to print non-Oxbridge degrees if they were first-class honours). However, the increasing number of degree-awarding institutions meant either causing offence by only persisting with publishing the results from the traditional universities or giving the paper during the summer months the appearance of a metropolitan telephone directory.

The greater consequence of the expanding number of universities concerned how potential students could differentiate between what they offered. In a phrase that doubtless made degree holders from the likes of Imperial, UCL, Bristol and Edinburgh wince, *The Times* declared that 'until now, Britain has been different: outside Oxford and Cambridge, a university degree has carried much the same weight, whatever its source'.[16] This was a gross exaggeration and a glib insult, but the expansion of degree-awarding bodies certainly made the claim that all universities were equal far less tenable. To differentiate, in 1992 *The Times Good Universities Guide* led the way with the first ranking of them according to various criteria that ranged from the qualifications of the staff, the amount of library spending per head and the quality of student accommodation. It was a major undertaking, beset with problems of comparing potentially non-compatible statistics and deciding what weighting should be attributed to which measurements. The task was entrusted to Tom Cannon, a former director of the Manchester Business School. His efforts were made yet more difficult by the deliberate obstruction of some of the institutions concerned. Indeed, many vice-chancellors (and not just those of the worst-performing universities) vehemently denounced the attempt to create a ranking system even though something similar had existed in the United States for more than a decade. The chairman of the Committee of Vice-Chancellors and Principals and his equivalent on the Committee of Directors of Polytechnics responded with an open letter that stated, 'We believe the tables are wrong in principle, flawed in execution and constructed upon data which are not uniform, are ill-defined, and in places demonstrably false.'[17] They had a point: raw statistics were a most imprecise science and no guarantee of the 'value added' strengths of what was on offer. Nonetheless, they were more useful to the consumer who, able for the first time to compare so much information in one place, no longer had to rely on the only real alternative guide – hearsay and snobbery, real or inverted. The first *Times* ranking placed Cambridge ahead of Oxford by only a fraction of a point and the two ancient institutions continued this closely contested pre-eminence, followed by the science-only Imperial College London, throughout the ensuing decade. At the other end of the scale, the universities propping up the ranking, all former polytechnics, continued to protest that the points system took insufficient account of the problems they laboured with and, indeed, by branding them failures, only added to the divisiveness of higher education. In response to this, *The Times* stood firm: having opted to join the league of universities, 'they must expect to be judged against the best'.[18]

III

Everything that the ERM's supporters claimed would happen if sterling was allowed to float failed to happen. Instead, 1993 began with interest rates falling to 6 per cent (their lowest level since 1977) and inflation to 1.7 per cent (the lowest for a quarter of a century). The 'feel good' factor took longer to return. With the housing market remaining stagnant, heavily mortgaged families that had bought during the 1980s boom were locked into negative equity. It was a gloomy portfolio for The Times's new property correspondent, Rachel Kelly. Dissatisfaction with the Government's health policies continued. In August 1993, the number on NHS waiting lists passed one million. The Scott Report into arms sales to Iraq and the Nolan Report into standards in public life did little to lift the reputation of senior Tories. Sleaze allegations chipped further at their integrity. The Defence Minister, Michael Mates, had to resign over his links with the fugitive businessman Asil Nadir, while several MPs, most prominently Neil Hamilton, were linked to payments from Mohammed Fayed, Harrods' owner. The sex scandals caused the greatest titillation, in particular David Mellor's dalliances with a resting actress and the death while engaged in a sex act of a rising star, Stephen Milligan. Collectively, they reduced to ruins Major's 'Back to Basics' campaign which The Times described as his 'last despairing stab at a big idea'.[19]

The public's response, towards which no popular newspaper could be indifferent, had become remarkably hostile to the Conservative Party. In the local elections of May 1993, the party was left in control of only one county council. Supposedly safe seats were transformed in by-elections to huge majorities for the Liberal Democrats, further frustrating Major's ability to retain a Commons majority. A MORI opinion poll in September 1993 suggested that only a third of Times readers supported the Tories. Forty-three per cent of them backed Labour and 20 per cent the Liberal Democrats. The share was not much different in the FT and the Conservatives did not even quite scrape a majority among Telegraph readers. Most alarmingly for Major, his party was down to 22 per cent of Sun readers.[20] The constituency that Margaret Thatcher had put together had been lost.

It was an atmosphere conducive to satire. The television show Spitting Image depicted Major from early on as a grey figure pushing his peas around the plate. It was the Guardian's Simon Hoggart and its cartoonist,

Steve Bell, who established the memorable image of Major with his shirt tucked into a visible pair of Y-fronts. *The Times*'s cartoonist, Peter Brookes, preferred to depict the Prime Minister as a slightly goofy looking man dominated by a large pair of spectacles. The non-transparent nature of the glasses suggested there was not much of a personality behind them. One who resisted the temptation to kick a man when he was down was the parliamentary sketchwriter, Matthew Parris. Like many ex-Tory MPs, Parris had no love for the Tory Party, although he remained a Conservative by instinct. His sketches were never partisan in the party sense and he got on well with many Labour MPs. Nonetheless, originally a member of the 'blue chip' generation of Tory MPs himself, he found it difficult to caricature them with the same ease with which he had got to work with the larger than life figures of the Thatcher years. 'There I was,' he later wrote, 'my gang in power, chronicling their noontide, their late afternoon, their internal mutinies and finally their sunset and night.' Indeed, Parris was sufficiently close to the Prime Minister to draft a section of his 1994 conference speech, a conflict of journalistic interests that a past editor of *The Times*, Geoffrey Dawson, had once more controversially performed on behalf of Stanley Baldwin.[21] This was, perhaps, one of the benefits of his decision to remain on a freelance contract. Like John Bryant, Parris regarded Major's treatment by the press as 'downright nasty . . . And I think his dignity and politeness in the face of adversity and mockery were heroic.'[22] If partisanship made him pull the occasional punch in his sketch, then this was perhaps a necessary relief from the unending attack to which the Major Government was prey from almost every other corner of the newspaper. During 1994, opinion polls suggested it was the most unpopular government since polling began.

IV

The Times's disillusionment with John Major had not been accompanied by any great enthusiasm for John Smith. The leader of the Labour Party and the editor of *The Times* had little in common. Smith once asked Stothard to join him for a drink in the House of Commons. It was not a success: Stothard was underwhelmed by the Leader of the Opposition 'pouring half a glass of red wine down his shirt' at six in the evening.[23] On 12 May 1994, Smith died of a heart attack. It was Tony Blair's ascendancy that made a difference to the relationship between Labour and *The Times*. Peter and Sally Stothard had got to know Tony and Cherie Blair in the 1980s when the Blairs bought their Islington house. Happily, the relationship survived this transaction.

Matthew Parris had reacted very differently on his first acquaintance with Blair. Introductions had been arranged in the late 1980s by the Blairs' new friend, Mary Ann Sieghart, who invited them and Parris for dinner. Parris was less than impressed, finding the MP for Sedgefield strangely hollow, unlike his wife who was the far more substantial personality.[24] This assumption had not changed much by the time Tony Blair emerged to run for the leadership. Watching him make his bid during a speech in Bloomsbury, Parris observed:

Seating in the hall was divided into the three sections eligible to choose the Labour leader: one third BBC, one third print journalists and one third Labour Party . . . Blair delighted most journalists. His skills would serve in those amusement arcade 'Grand Prix' screen games. His own screen, the Autocue screen, and his gaze rigid with concentration, Mr Blair drove at gathering velocity round a track littered with the death traps of policy commitments, swerving to avoid every one, fuelled by a tank full of abstract nouns.[25]

It was nonetheless a strategy that impressed Stothard. In 1995, Labour delegates were persuaded to remove Clause Four, their party's historic commitment to state ownership of the means of production. Blair assured them, 'Today a new Labour Party is being born. Our task now is nothing less than the rebirth of our nation.' A new start was certainly made with News International. That year, Blair travelled to Australia to speak to the News Corp. seminar on Hayman Island. Considering the Labour Party's boycott campaign during the Wapping dispute, the occasion was seen as a defining moment in which the symbolism of past disagreements was buried. Blair, indeed, had travelled an awfully long way to prove the point.

Believing in John Major's depth and Tony Blair's shallowness, Parris's view continued to be far more distrustful than the open minded attitude of his editor. His sketch for Blair's second party conference speech as leader in 1995, noted:

Blair offered the New Testament. Within moments he was quoting Christ. Near the end he declared (twice): 'Be strong and of good courage.' The tone was positively messianic. Mr Blair has yet to declare: 'As God said and rightly . . .' but he will.[26]

In May, Parris was called to take tea with Major, who floated the idea of his 'put up or shut up' resignation strategy. Parris advised against such an unorthodox move. Unsure whether Major had shared with him the idea in confidence, he chose not to break it in the paper.[27] However, Major duly resigned the party leadership and dared any rival to challenge him. Michael Portillo thought about doing so, but drew back. It was John Redwood, the Welsh Secretary, who left the Cabinet to do so.

Five years earlier, Parris had christened Redwood and Portillo 'vulcans' although it was with Redwood that the title stuck, greatly to his personal distress. It was a theme Parris revisited when he turned up for Redwood's opening press conference only to find himself debarred from entering by organizers who claimed the hall was full. Watching it on television, he reported the scene in his sketch:

Television viewers yesterday watched the first Tory leadership campaign in history to be launched from the bosom of Teresa Gorman. Viewers were startled by the strange green-clad torso behind John Redwood as he spoke at his press conference yesterday. No head was visible in the frame.

I can reveal that it belonged to Mrs Gorman. We would recognise that bust anywhere. Once, as Redwood parried, a hand could be seen tugging at her lapels, drawing them together like green curtains across the cleavage. We trust the hand belonged to Mrs Gorman.

As for the candidate, Parris successfully ridiculed him:

How did he view Wales? 'It-is-a-beautiful-country,' said the Vulcan, because that is what Earthlings say about Wales. Instructed by his minders to display humour, Redwood told us he was a 'jobseeker.' He followed this with the smile he has now learnt to do very nicely: a triumph of muscular control . . . What, we wondered, would be his final word?

'No extra charge!' he declared. Mr Redwood must have seen this in a supermarket, recorded it as a useful idiomatic phrase, and inputted it onto the wrong disk-drive in his logic system.[28]

When his colleagues voted on 4 July 1995, Major defeated his challenger by a sufficient although, in the circumstances, hardly crushing manner. Redwood received eighty-nine votes and there were twenty abstentions.

Meanwhile, Conrad Black replaced Max Hastings with the more firmly anti-Major Charles Moore as editor of the *Daily Telegraph*. This was followed by a raid on *The Times* for some of its best staff. Anne McElvoy was inveigled away to the *Spectator* and Matthew D'Ancona was poached by the *Sunday Telegraph*. D'Ancona's departure did not alter *The Times*'s hostility to the Government, but it did raise the possibility that it would mix a right wing attack on its European policies with a Blairite attack on domestic issues. Mary Ann Sieghart was proving to be an articulate and forceful advocate of Blair's 'third way'. As the only senior *Times* leader writer who knew Tony Blair well, she was able to speak authoritatively on his agenda without risk of contradiction. The chief leader writer, Rosemary Righter, disagreed with her, but because her own speciality was foreign policy she was keen to find a strong intellectual who could shoreup the paper's defences against falling for Blair's charms. The answer came in the guise of D'Ancona's friend and Oxford contemporary, Michael Gove. An Aberdonian, Gove had attended Robert Gordon's College, a regular feature in the surprisingly intense world of Scottish schools debating contests. Proceeding up to Lady Margaret Hall, he had been elected president of the Oxford Union. To Gove, journalism was the natural means of keeping his formidable debating skills in fine fettle. Like Stothard, another minor independent schoolboy and Oxford graduate, he had worked at the BBC (on the *Today* and *On The Record* programmes) and was looking to escape into print journalism. Believing that he had identified the next leader of the Conservative Party, he had also begun writing a biography called *Michael Portillo: The Future of the Right*. When *The Times* considered serialization, Gove met and made a favourable impression on Martin Ivens. In January 1996, he was duly appointed a leader writer, at the age of twenty-eight. A few months later, the leader team was strengthened further with the arrival of Tim Hames, an Oxford don of light blue hue who would also come to play a prime role in the paper's political positioning. Daniel Johnson was moved from the literary editorship over to become comment editor. These changes stalled, at least for the moment, the prospect of *The Times* falling for the charms of Tony Blair.

In fact, the dynamics of Stothard's inner circle were complicated. Michael Gove and Mary Ann Sieghart were both Euro-sceptics and, for the most part, social liberals. Yet the former was a trenchant Tory, committed to maintaining the Act of Union with Scotland and Ulster and man of evangelical convictions, while the latter was an equally strong advocate of New Labour who had a personal rapport with the Blairs. Daniel Johnson provided a more traditional voice of social and religious Conservatism. Like Bernard Levin before him, Anatole Kaletsky had a sparkling mind and prevented leader conferences from proceeding along conventional lines by the elasticity of his thinking. On foreign policy, Rosemary Righter combined an uncompromising neo-conservative world view with a strong belief in the principles of the United Nations (thus ensuring she was often highly critical of the UN in practice). Michael Binyon, on the other hand, was relied upon to represent the unflappable perspective of the Foreign Office and was, alone among the group, noticeably less hostile to the causes of Brussels and the Palestinians. During previous editorships, Stothard had watched 'a lot of aggression take place in and around the leader department' yet among his own college of cardinals he recognized that 'the general spirit was exceptionally good. They were very fine representatives of their causes, all good humoured, good hearted people' despite the daily ding-dongs that took place between them.[29]

The political commentator least amenable to the attractions offered by either of the main parties was, perhaps, the cartoonist, Peter Brookes. Having studied at London's Central School of Art and Design, Brookes was an expert draughtsman whose rare achievement was an ability to parody his subject matter while still drawing them with great accuracy and attention to detail. He began at *The Times* in 1981 as an illustrator to the main columnists on the Op-Ed page. After a while, he concluded it would be more satisfying to conjure up his own commentaries rather than, for example, reproduce Bernard Levin's views in visual form. From 1993, he became the paper's political cartoonist. His method was to arrive at the office in good time for the morning conference when the main news stories were discussed. He would then spend the rest of the morning and early afternoon toying with ideas in pencil. Once he had decided on his cartoon, usually by about 4.30 p.m., he had a couple of hours to translate it onto paper in pen and ink before the page was ready to go to press. For the Saturday edition, he added his box of watercolours in order to produce 'Nature Notes'. This was a weekly bestiary that depicted public figures as animals, annotated with informative behavioural notes. Eventually, colour came to the Op-Ed page as well, specifically so that the daily Brookes cartoon could be unveiled in the best of lights. Neither Tory, nor Euro-sceptic, nor taken in by the blandishments of New Labour, his political prejudices were often far removed from those emanating from the editor's office and this helped create an important ideological counterpoise in the heart of the paper. His real achievement, though, was the piquant wit he brought to contemporary events. While the quality of his artistry was without equal, it was always the idea he was conveying that was the central component of his success.

As colleagues reassembled at Times House in the New Year – an election year – Stothard was musing about the implications of change. Did this mean he would take *The Times* where it had never gone before by endorsing the Labour Party? He gathered the leader writers and senior political staff for a private meeting in the Reform Club where the options were laid before them. It was Stothard's technique in leader conferences to set up opposing views and watch the two antipathetic sides battle it out to a conclusion. The same format was deployed at the Reform Club. Michael Gove made the case for endorsing the Tories and Mary Ann Sieghart did likewise for Labour. Gove maintained that what was at the core of Blair's programme was constitutional reform and this, unlike issues of funding and provision, was so revolutionary that it could not be undone five years later if *The Times* did not like the consequences. As a Scottish Unionist, Gove was deeply uneasy about Labour's plans for devolution within the British Isles but he was especially concerned about the likelihood of being taken into the euro and a far deeper form of integration than even Major was prepared to stomach. Blair's plans were irreversible and bad. Furthermore, Gove questioned whether the modernizers were really in control? He doubted that a Cabinet containing Frank Dobson and Margaret Beckett in key portfolios was likely to think the unthinkable in reforming the welfare state. Sieghart took a different line. She too was averse to taking Britain into a European single currency, but Blair would hold a referendum on that issue so it was not a defining issue for how people should vote at the general election. *The Times*, she argued, had set Blair a number of hurdles that he – and more importantly his party – would have to cross on issues like the unions and education before they could be endorsed. These hurdles had been very impressively cleared. Given how far Labour had come and the distance the Tories had slipped, she maintained that the question of whether the paper endorsed Labour was 'if not now, then when?'. The meeting broke up with no final decision taken. Unusually for an ambitious and sharp-witted young Tory, Gove was a man of generous spirit and unfailing old-fashioned courtesy. He thought that Sieghart had possibly 'won on points.'[30]

The decision lay with the editor and with him alone. He recognized that the Conservatives had run out of steam. Yet, given the limited practical programme set out by Tony Blair – albeit accompanied by much evangelical rhetoric – the Tories certainly seemed to have as much to offer a new parliamentary term as New Labour in terms of proposals for domestic reform. Instead, it was the issue of Europe that remained at the forefront of Stothard's mind. He might have been more inclined to overlook Blair's enthusiasm for Brussels if he had known that once Gordon Brown became Chancellor he would kick the euro issue into touch for the next two parliaments. This, however, was far from clear in the first months of 1997. A Labour victory, it seemed, was the surest way of bringing about a referendum to join the euro within the lifetime of the next parliament. It would be a campaign in which the Government, the most well-known and popular Tory politicians and the Liberal Democrats would all be campaigning for a 'yes' vote. The prospect filled him with as much woe as it did Michael Gove. On the other hand, the other principal issue vexing the editor was not one of policy but of personality. With Michael Howard and Peter Lilley he was on good terms, but he had a shortage of respect that bordered on contempt for John Major. Bumping into the Prime Minister in Australia House shortly before Christmas in 1996, Stothard had told him that *The Times* was about to bring him some good news with an opinion poll that suggested he had gained some ground against Labour. 'For me personally or for the party?' was Major's instant reply.[31] Such comments made Stothard despair. He was also staggered when Lady Thatcher assured him that 'Tony Blair is a man who won't let Britain down'.[32] In any case, having very effectively given the impression he thought the Prime Minister lacked the intellectual rigour to hold the office, he could hardly clear his throat and endorse him for a further five years of political purgatory.

On 17 March, Major announced there would be a general election on 1 May. He had put off the date until the last moment, hoping that the improving economic climate would demonstrate the Tories were not economically incompetent after all. Stothard had still given no indication as to which way his mind was made up between Labour and Conservative, yet there was an alternative that gave him a way out of his dilemma. The businessman and millionaire Sir James Goldsmith had founded the Referendum Party. Its specific aim was expressed in its title, but it was unapologetically a party campaigning against Britain being swept up into the integrationist impulses of the European Union. Around Goldsmith, a group of youthful, right-wing enthusiasts had constellated, as had a few more glamorous figures, drawn in part by the leader's charisma and wealth. For its part, most of the mainstream media regarded Goldsmith with a mixture of fear and loathing. Stothard did not share this aversion and Goldsmith paid a couple of visits to Times House in the run up to polling day. The editor even got Gove to write a profile of Goldsmith, specifically requesting that it should not be the hatchet job that others had done when entrusted with the task. Gove opted to suggest that 'it would be more dignified for Sir James to claim an intellectual victory now than to endure an electoral massacre this spring'. Gove particularly resented Goldsmith's intention to field candidates even against MPs with strong Euro-sceptic track records.[33] Nobody who knew Stothard imagined that he would do anything as eccentric as committing The Times to the maverick pronouncements of the Anglo-French multimillionaire but it was a sign that he was open to unorthodox thinking as election day drew near. It was Hywell Williams, John Redwood's adviser, who suggested that since the editor clearly thought Britain's relations with the EU was the most important issue facing the country, The Times should fight it as a 'coupon election' – endorsing those candidates of whatever party had a history of opposing further integration in general and the euro in particular. Meanwhile, Stothard asked the archives to send up all the paper's twentieth-century general election endorsements. He read them and passed them onto Tim Hames, asking for his historical insight, adding implausibly by way of explanation, 'the twentieth century is not really my period'.[34]

Accompanied by the acclaimed watercolourist Matthew Cook to record the scene, Stothard, Riddell and Kaletsky arrived at 10 Downing Street for their pre-polling day interview with the Prime Minister. In the full-page write-up for the paper by Stothard, Europe appeared to have been the only issue that intruded upon the discussion, save for an almost throwaway sentence, 'he sees the achievement of low inflation as essentially his own, the top item in the ledger of his achievements'.[35] Despite repeated interrogation from Kaletsky, Major nonetheless refused to say what his gut feeling was towards joining the euro, explaining 'what I will do is what I happen to think is in the best interests of the country. It may not actually be what my innate instincts might be. I don't know what judgment I am going to reach.' Major was in a difficult position. If he ruled out joining the euro in the lifetime of the next parliamentary term he would retain – or perhaps regain – the loyalty of two-thirds of his party. Yet, if he pursued this course, he risked losing the support of those Cabinet ministers he actually liked and, in particular, the two most senior members of his government, Michael Heseltine and Kenneth Clarke. It was an unenviable choice, but adopting a wait and see policy gave the impression that the Prime Minister did not have the strength of character to tell his own party whether he actually had an opinion on one of the biggest issues in the economic and political life of the nation – scrapping the national currency and surrendering ultimate budgetary control via the stability pact to the European Union. His equivocation only sharpened the contempt in which his critics at *The Times* – and elsewhere – held him. It was certainly not a display of leadership and, given the discord it was fuelling, some frankly had come to wonder if it was even an effective course of party management.

This last point was thrown into focus when Tory MPs started disavowing their leader's wait and see (it had been rechristened 'negotiate and decide') policy. Major responded to demands for clarity with the desperate appeal, 'don't bind my hands'. Stothard made up his mind, deciding, in the words of a subsequent leading article drafted by Michael Gove, that, 'The party machines do not wish to be bound, but the voters should not have to choose blind.'[36] With only six days to go before polling day, Stothard told Gove what was afoot, entrusting him with leading a small team to draw up within forty-eight hours a comprehensive list of who the Euro-sceptic candidates were. This was a tall order that involved much delving into reference sources and checking on pressure group affiliations. Among the inducements for pro-Europeans to use vaguely Euro-sceptical language in their campaign literature was the prospect of money from the businessman Paul Sykes to help Euro-sceptic candidates' campaign expenses. Gove's team were not prepared to endorse anyone who deployed weasel words like being unable to 'foresee' adopting the euro. Discovering Labour candidates' views on the matter was even more difficult because few cared to deviate from the line of obfuscation being encouraged from their party's headquarters at Millbank. Nonetheless, on Monday 28 April – four days before election day – *The Times* published its list of the candidates it endorsed. The two-page spread was framed by a Richard Willson cartoon depicting a Bayeaux tapestry-style montage with the heads of the leading politicians superimposed on the figures. So that the Euro-enthusiasts could be depicted as being under attack and Major subjected to an arrow in his eye, it was the Euro-sceptics who, oddly, were the Norman cavalry.

The Times decided to list not only those candidates it considered Euro-sceptic but also those with firmly Europhile records, 'whom sceptical voters should not support'. Where a Europhile Tory was being challenged by a candidate from the pro-euro Liberal Democrats, *The Times* advocated voting for the latter on the grounds that 'the Commons will be just as Europhile whether the Tory or Liberal Democrat candidate wins, but if the Tory loses the Tory party as a whole will become more sceptical'.[37] There were also some exceptions. *The Times* refused to endorse Sinn Fein's Gerry Adams or the Tory Neil Hamilton, who was at the centre of the much-publicized fight over allegations that he took cash for questions. The Europhile Tam Dalyell was endorsed on the grounds that he was opposed to devolution for Scotland. Inevitably there was a flurry of telephone calls from anxious Tory candidates keen to protest their Euro-sceptic credentials in order to be added to the list. 'If I lose, you'll have a hand in it,' warned the candidate for Hampstead and Highgate while another, soon to be former, MP, hollered down the telephone, 'This is a scandal: you could cost me the election.'[38] Some injustices were done, although in other cases it appeared that it was only the prospect of being hanged that concentrated a candidate's mind.

Endorsing candidates according to their view on the great issue of the day rather than the party they represented was a complete break from past custom. It did, however, solve Stothard's problem over feeling unable to endorse the Conservatives but reticent to declare for the untested and euro-friendly Blair. Some thought *The Times* had made a serious misjudgment. They questioned whether Europe was an issue that trumped all others. The opinion polls certainly suggested it was bread and butter issues that would determine the result. *The Times* had embarked upon a policy where it found itself endorsing far left Labour candidates like Jeremy Corbyn and Tony Benn with whom it had nothing else in common but an aversion to Brussels. Indeed many of the left-wingers the paper endorsed opposed joining the single currency on the sort of anti-capitalist economic arguments that were anathema to the paper's general outlook. Furthermore, the leading column was also highlighting the cause of specific candidates – usually in marginal seats – who it felt deserved to be elected on account of their contribution to public life. These included politicians like the Liberal Democrat Simon Hughes who supported the euro. Critics were not shy in pointing out these glaring inconsistencies. It came to overshadow the considerable work the paper had made to highlight the other aspects of the general election campaign. *The Times* was the only newspaper to publish the major parties' manifestos in full. Indeed, Stothard later suggested, 'Endorsement is not the main point.' What Labour had been far more interested in was having their policies given 'a fair crack of the whip' in the news pages and across the paper generally. This *The Times* provided.[39]

Nonetheless, the decision of *The Times* to endorse a platform rather than a party took the paper's journalists by surprise. It was the editor's decision alone and was not debated at any leader conference. Mary Ann Sieghart was particularly bewildered, having believed Labour was about to be endorsed. She promptly did some moonlighting for the *News of the World*, helping to write its leader column endorsing Blair.[40] On Tuesday 29 April, *The Times*'s decision ran across the top of the front page and was elaborated upon in a full-page leading article written by the editor. It contained a note of historical self-justification that sought to minimize accusations that the paper was breaking with tradition. In the early years of the twentieth century, the paper had put aside its Liberal instincts in order to defend the causes of the Empire and opposition to Irish Home Rule. It had not taken a hard line in the 1945 election and had been neutral in 1955. Thereafter its Tory endorsements had been accompanied by a plea to shore up the Liberal Party. 'Our strong support of Lady Thatcher in the 1980s was, in this regard, counter to our traditions, not central to them,' it assured readers. While the paper had admired strong leaders, 'John Major, by contrast, has been a true man of his parliamentary machine. His skills are those of the whip. His proudest boasts have been for his powers of negotiation.' In contrast, there was much to commend Blair who had acted quickly to re-educate his party, 'but we do not put our name to what is still a tower of dreams'.[41]

Murdoch was as much taken by surprise as everybody else. Indeed, the division of opinion within his newspaper empire hardly gave credence to the common orthodoxy that News International's owner pulled the political strings. The *Sunday Times* reluctantly endorsed the Conservatives while the *Sun*, rather more confidently, proclaimed the case for Labour. The line adopted by *The Times* appeared eccentric or unashamedly individualist, according to taste. Yet, even though Murdoch privately thought the Euro-sceptic endorsement was a mistake,[42] he did not attempt to dissuade Stothard nor did he use the broadly unfavourable backlash following the paper's pronouncement to undermine him. Indeed, it would have been hard to find a more politically 'hands-off' proprietor in all Fleet Street. Conrad Black's *Daily Telegraph* was the only daily broadsheet to declare for the Tories. *The Times*'s columnists went their separate ways. Accusing Major of 'pathetically ineffectual leadership', Kaletsky described his government as 'the least electable in 50 years'.[43] Rees-Mogg cast around for reasons to vote Conservative, arguing that having been promised a free vote on the euro, a Tory majority would ensure a euro-sceptic parliament.[44] Woodrow Wyatt argued that the polls could be wrong, that many old socialists would abstain rather than vote for Blair and that 'against all the pollsters, and chumps like the pornographic bestseller and disloyal Edwina Currie . . . I believe that John Major, who has fought brilliantly, is on course for a majority of around 30–40'.[45] Eschewing the rancour that so many felt for the collapsing regime, Simon Jenkins wrote a notably fair-minded piece on election eve, noting 'there is no greater compliment to the Thatcher–Major era than the thinness of today's Labour manifesto'.[46]

On election morning, *The Times*'s MORI poll suggested Labour would get 48 per cent and the Tories 28 per cent with the Liberal Democrats on 16, suggesting a Labour majority of between 180 and 200. In the event, the respective percentages were 44, 31 and 17 and the majority was 177. 'Landslide victory for Labour' ran *The Times*'s headline once most of the results were in, below an architrave of Tory portraits – Portillo, Lang, Forsyth, Rumbold, Hamilton, Mellor, Waldegrave, Rifkind, Lamont – each looking dejected, each with the caption 'OUT' splashed across the top. Five Cabinet ministers and eighteen other ministers lost their seats. The Conservative Party, which had gone into the election committed to preserving the United Kingdom against Blair's plans for devolution, was left with no MPs outside England.

What was particularly embarrassing for *The Times* was that the landslide predominantly swept away Tory Euro-sceptics, leaving Euro-friendly chieftains like Kenneth Clarke and Michael Heseltine untouched. There was little evidence that voters had actively endorsed Europhile candidates, merely that they had treated it as a traditional general election fought on party lines and domestic issues, and not as a surrogate referendum on deeper European integration. In this mood, the vast majority of *Times* readers simply ignored their paper's appeal. If the Euro-sceptic voters' guide had any effect then, perhaps, it assisted some in identifying a like-minded candidate from one of the main parties in their constituency, thereby redirecting some protest votes away from Goldsmith's Referendum Party or the UK Independence Party (both of which performed below expectations in the ballot). How many – if any – MPs owed success to this assault on the fringe vote may be contested. At any rate, it had no bearing on the overall result. This was a humiliating rebuff to *The Times*'s editorial stance – not that this consequence was dwelt upon in the leading column whose attention seamlessly switched to the prospects for the new administration. It was a demonstration of how impotent the press could be once the public had already made its mind up on a subject. 'If I could rewrite the traditions of the paper, I would not endorse' at general elections was Stothard's subsequent reflection.[47]

V

The end of eighteen years of Tory rule and the prospects for a new style of government under a young, fresh faced Prime Minister who talked the language of hope and rebirth would now become the focus for *The Times*. Yet not to be overlooked was the relative success of the third party. With forty-six MPs, the Liberal Democrats had produced their best result since Lloyd George's Liberal Party went to the polls promising a Keynesian-style New Deal in 1929. The other, more pressing matter concerned how the Conservatives – whose share of the vote had not been so low since they were led by the Duke of Wellington in 1832 – would regroup. Major immediately announced his intention to stand down, sensibly opting to spend his first day of freedom watching cricket at The Oval. It was the cue for a bloody leadership fight to commence. Matthew Parris was perturbed that 'the party I used to respect' had been gripped by 'some sort of fever' that was turning it away from being led by 'grown ups' who challenged Labour for the middle ground, preferring to become a sort of 'Tory Likud' that instead aimed at predominance on the fringe. The notion that they might find salvation under John Redwood's leadership was, Parris wrote, 'laughable' although it was clear he saw nothing amusing about the prospect.[48] The leading column, however, leapt to pour cold water on Clarke or Heseltine's claims to the succession, positing that they were 'deeply associated with the election debacle'.[49] Having argued that the issue of Europe was the determining factor in the general election, the paper could hardly demand a Europhile victory in the ensuing leadership contest. Portillo, who Michael Gove had tipped as the next leader, had been removed from the contest by his own electors in Enfield Southgate. On 3 May, Heseltine's aspirations were felled by a heart scare that dispatched him to hospital. Within days, John Redwood had entered the leadership race with an article in *The Times* entitled 'I can't defend the past; I can unite the party' in which he maintained that having resigned from the Major Cabinet he was the only candidate who would not have to spend the next few years apologizing for it.[50] In fact, it was Redwood's decision to resign from the Cabinet in 1995 that created an opportunity for a young man of promise, William Hague, to fill Redwood's shoes at the Welsh Office and, in doing so, enter the 1997 election as a candidate with Cabinet experience. Even on the morning after the general election disaster, Andrew Pierce had written up Hague as the leader the Tories might turn to in order to 'skip a generation'.

This initially improbable prospect suddenly took hold. Having originally made a verbal agreement to back Michael Howard by standing as his deputy (and, in effect, heir apparent) Hague soon began to believe he could win under his own steam. Howard's hopes were dealt a further blow by the outspoken maverick Ann Widdecombe, who attacked him over his sacking of the prison chief, Derek Lewis, and announced to a stunned Commons chamber that there was 'something of the night' about the former Home Secretary.

The scale of the election landslide naturally encouraged some to think the Tories needed a complete reinvention. Coming from a younger generation, Hague's profile appeared perfect for this role. Yet, in urging the party to elect Ken Clarke as their leader, Simon Jenkins pointed out that there was no need to assume that the Tories would be out of office for a generation. On the contrary, although exaggerated in seats secured by the vagaries of the electoral system, Blair had actually won only 1 per cent more of the popular vote than had Major in 1992. The gap was thus by no means unbridgeable within the space of one parliamentary term of office. Jenkins was baffled by the defeatism of Tory MPs who were 'behaving as if they lost the argument as well as the election. They did not. They won the argument, which is why they lost the election ... New Labour is one of the Tory party's great achievements.'[51] After Howard and Lilley trailed in the first ballot of MPs, Redwood and Clarke agreed to work together to dish Hague. The decision astounded Westminster and its lobby correspondents. References to the Molotov–Ribbentrop pact abounded. 'We can say a sad farewell to John Redwood as a valid figure in Conservative policies,' wrote Rees-Mogg. 'He was the Robespierre of the Right, the dark-blue Incorrupt-ible ... In the twinkling of an eye he has destroyed himself.'[52] 'Absurd is how the axis between Mr Clarke and Mr Redwood will look to the country and absurd is what it is,' huffed the leading article.[53] Lady Thatcher felt likewise, and endorsed William Hague. The following day, he romped to victory by 92 votes to 70. Aged thirty-six, he was the youngest Tory leader since William Pitt the Younger (of whom he later became a biographer) two hundred years before.

Few, including The Times which backed him, knew where Hague intended to take the party. All that was known for sure was that he was young, fresh, virtually untainted by the infighting of the Major years and, unlike Clarke, was no enthusiast for joining the euro. In the circumstances, this appeared to be a promising start. If he lacked stature then he had time, it seemed, to acquire it and develop some new policies along the way. Yet, escaping the shadows of the past five years of infighting and 'Tory sleaze' remained a daunting prospect. The day after Hague was elected leader, Jonathan Aitken's libel case against the *Guardian* collapsed. Having been prepared to let his daughter Victoria provide him with a false alibi under oath, the former Chief Secretary to the Treasury faced charges of perjury and perverting the course of justice for which he would serve seven months in jail and be declared bankrupt. There were heavy clouds hanging over the bright Tory dawn. *The Times* was ready to look out towards a different horizon.

CHAPTER TWELVE

NEW LABOUR, NEW JOURNALISM

Living with New Labour; Devolution in Print and in Politics;
the People's Princess; Bernard Levin Takes His Bow; Pennington Street;
Media Law, the PCC and Libel; China Calling; the Ashcroft Affair;
the Editor Takes Time Out; *T2*; the Shine Comes off the Spin;
Labour Endorsed

I

'Tony Blair will have to be a great Prime Minister if he is not to be a great failure' wrote Rees-Mogg the day after the general election.[1] The first weeks certainly promised that the new leader would live up to the high expectations created by a landslide that gave him untrammelled political authority. Six days after the election victory, Gordon Brown, Blair's new next-door neighbour as Chancellor of the Exchequer, announced the first surprise: handing interest-rate policy over to an independent Bank of England. Socialists wondered why such an immediate and momentous change had not been included in the election manifesto and, indeed, why one of the first actions of a Labour Government after eighteen years in opposition was to denationalize an instrument of economic management. *The Times* was delighted. An independent central bank was a precondition of joining the euro but the move also weakened one of the single currency supporters' stronger arguments – that British governments had long debauched sterling for short-term political ends. Whatever his feelings about the single currency, Brown had shown himself to be a decisive Chancellor in pursuit of a liberalizing policy that even the Tories had lacked the courage of their convictions to enact.

Brown had the latitude of benign conditions in which to operate. During the summer of 1997, inflation stood at only 3.3 per cent while unemployment, at 1.55 million (5.5 per cent of the workforce), was far below the average on the European continent. This rosy economic prospect had been assisted by the legacy of the Tory reforms that removed rigidities in the labour market, reducing costs to employers of hiring – and firing – staff. Yet the easy employment prospects for the vast majority were matched by pockets of persistent unemployment for a few, who, having been jobless for long periods, had difficulty getting back onto the ladder of opportunity. The Blair Government's 'New Deal' programme was designed to offer a training scheme from which they could get back into work, paid for by a – politically opportunistic – windfall tax on the profits earned by the privatized utilities whose very success had become as much a source of public anger as had their previous losses and ineptitude as wards of the State.

For *The Times*'s political strategists the most momentous decision came on 27 October when, after mounting speculation, Brown informed the Commons chamber that Britain would not join the euro in the current parliament but would hope to do so in the following one. For Stothard, this was a huge relief. The prospect of Blair using the momentum of his election landslide to roll the country into precipitously scrapping sterling had subsided entirely. What happened in a subsequent parliament remained a distant prospect. In the event, Brown (or the failure of the opinion polls to show mounting popular enthusiasm) ensured that Britain would stay out of the euro during Labour's second term too. When eleven members of the European Union welcomed in 1999 with the new currency, Britain would not be among them. The great moment in European unity was marked by fireworks in the sky rather than by a crisis at the shopping tills or money markets. The widespread disorder that some Euro-sceptics' prophesied failed to materialize and the new currency's adoption had an impressively tranquil passage in the period of transition. Yet, the pro-euro campaigners' assertions that a Britain outside the euro zone would suffer from foreign investors deserting its shores and the City of London losing its primacy similarly proved to be scares without foundation. Equally adrift was their claim that a single currency would have an anti-inflationary effect by making price differentials transparent across the Continent. In fact, the new currency provided an opportunity to round prices upwards. Indeed, in the first years of operation the economies of the euro zone – and in particular of a Germany buckling under the costs of reunification and an expensive labour market – were outperformed by a Britain left to the protection of its own currency. Continuing economic growth buttressed Labour's claims to competence and popularity with the electorate. It frustrated the Prime Minister's attempts to convince the Chancellor or the general public of the urgency of joining the euro bloc.

II

The announcement in October 1997 that Britain would not – for the moment at any rate – boldly go into the euro zone came a month after the new Government had recast the political structure of the United Kingdom. On 12 September, 74.3 per cent of Scots voted in a referendum for their own Parliament with 63.5 per cent assenting that it should have tax-raising powers. In Wales seven days later the vote for a more modest assembly without the power to tax was won by the unconvincing margin of 0.6 per cent (a mere 6721 votes). Meanwhile, a post-general election ceasefire by the IRA was deemed sufficient to bring Sinn Fein into talks over Ulster's future, raising expectations that a political settlement could yet be achieved on the basis of a power-sharing assembly at Stormont. Following in quick succession, these developments, taken together with plans to abolish the hereditary element within the House of Lords, appeared to be signs of a new radicalism in British politics, in which Blair dedicated his service to the reform and modernization of the constitutional settlement.

The irony was that Blair appeared to be less excited by the reform agenda than many of his colleagues. In particular, the establishment of a Scottish Parliament created a rival power structure to the centralization of authority he appeared to believe was necessary to create the 'New Britain' of which he so frequently, and ambiguously, spoke. He had inherited the Scottish devolution agenda from his predecessor, John Smith, and during the election campaign had committed a rare and inexplicable gaff by insisting it would be little more than a parish council. When Stothard, accompanied by Peter Riddell and Anatole Kaletsky, had interviewed Blair in the last hours before polling day, the Labour leader denied that his constitutional proposals would be his greatest legacy, claiming 'the improvements in education will be much more important than that'.[2] There were those at Wapping who begged to differ. Given the scale of Blair's majority and the period of introspection it forced upon the official Opposition, George Brock assumed that 'the only interesting politics over the next few years will be in Scotland'.[3] The question underlying the managing editor's prophecy was how a London paper like *The Times* could make itself attractive to a Scottish readership whose lives would increasingly be determined by a legislature meeting in Edinburgh.

The situation had been bad enough even before the first workmen arrived on the Holyrood site to build Scotland's own Parliament building.

Scots had long preferred their own broadsheet newspapers – in particular the *Glasgow Herald* and the *Scotsman* – to the clipped accents from distant Fleet Street. Sales of *The Times* north of the border were pitiful. As with the sale in Ireland, they numbered only a few thousand during the 1980s although circulation began to pick up after 1993 with the commencement of the price war. Part of this long tradition of failure could be laid at the door of the paper being perceived not merely as an English product but one too closely associated with the closed world of Whitehall, the Establishment and the affairs of the Church of England's General Synod. A decade of ownership by Murdoch or even five years with Charlie Wilson at the helm had failed substantially to shift this perception. In truth, it was not just a matter of anti-Home Counties resentment. Middle-class Scots in Edinburgh's New Town or Morningside had their own professional hierarchy as might be expected in the capital of a nation that had always retained its own legal and ecclesiastical sovereignty. Political devolution now threatened to make *The Times* even more redundant north of Berwick-upon-Tweed. After all, Scots could hardly be expected to want a product that focused on issues of domestic policy that were no longer applicable to them while being denied more than occasional references to the laws that did affect them from Holyrood.

A fleeting examination of the balance books suggested the Scottish market could be written off, yet this made no sense for a newspaper that considered itself a British product committed to the maintenance of the Act of Union. Furthermore, Scotland clearly had a readership profile that indicated there were converts to be won if only a London paper could speak to them in a broader brogue. Merely adding a few extra Scottish news items would not address this: they would never be enough for non-current readers to notice and turn to the paper. What was needed was a distinct Scottish edition. This involved considerable investment but, as the process of Scottish devolution got underway, Stothard and Brock drew up plans for just such an innovation. It would not be a completely new paper for certain features, like the comment, leaders, letters and obituaries pages, would remain standard on both sides of the border, but a new Scottish editor would be appointed to oversee the replacement of those news items that would have little resonance with Scottish readers with stories that were relevant to them. The sports pages could also be altered to provide fuller coverage of Scottish teams and individuals. Once it was launched, Scottish readers of this edition would get the best of both worlds – a full portrait of Scottish news combined with all the aspects that made *The Times* the sort of journal of world news against which the *Herald* or the *Scotsman* could never field the resources to compete.

It was a far more complicated process than at first it appeared. Subediting a Scottish edition did not simply involve cutting out news about Eton and pasting in a tale about Fettes. The fact that health and education politics had passed to the Holyrood Parliament's competence did not preclude the possibility that patients in the Edinburgh Infirmary might still want to know about health policies that governed the wards of Guy's Hospital. Likewise, it was important that the Scotland edition did not become a sink estate for Scottish news to be tidied away from English eyes. The Home Counties were generously populated by parents with offspring up at Scottish universities. What was clearly needed was a Scottish editor with an eye for getting the balance right and such a man was found in John Mair. Born in the small clifftop fishing village of Portknockie, east of Inverness, Mair, an Aberdeen University graduate and a discerning lover of poetry, had joined *The Times* as a production sub in 1981 and spent the succeeding seventeen years taking increasing responsibility on the backbench, where he became deputy night editor. Assisted by a single sub, he would, as the new Scottish editor, continue to be based at Wapping. This was necessary for ease of access to Stothard and the rest of the editorial high command including those, like Michael Gove, who had a good grasp of Celtic affairs. The actual reporting, however, would be done from the paper's Edinburgh office, from where Jason Allardyce and Gillian Harris operated, supplemented by Shirley English in Glasgow.

Effective coverage of the Holyrood Parliament would be the most important division between the Scottish and English editions. For north of the border, Angus Macleod was appointed political editor. Aside from its committee work, the new Parliament had full sessions in the chamber on Wednesdays and Thursdays and Magnus Linklater – who had been a *Times* columnist since 1994 – became the sketchwriter for these occasions. As the son of Eric Linklater, the Orcadian-born biographer, soldier and comic novelist, he had a natural sense of place within the Scottish cultural Establishment although, as an Old Etonian, graduate of the universities of Freiburg, the Sorbonne and Cambridge and a member of the MCC, his attachment to the principle of Scottish devolution came with none of the anti-Sassenach baggage that sometimes accompanied the more strident exponents of Scottish exceptionalism. In any case, he had spent most of his journalistic career in London where he had worked with Harold Evans at the *Sunday Times* before moving over to become successively managing editor of the *Observer* and editor of the *London Daily News*. It was only with the collapse of Maxwell's attempt to take on the *Evening Standard* that he moved up to Edinburgh as editor of the *Scotsman* between 1988 and 1994. Writing from his Georgian residence in the heart of Edinburgh's New Town, Linklater was one of nature's true-born Whigs. He was a man of liberal and humane sentiments who combined his journalism with a love of opera, fishing and antiquarian bookshops. He wished the Holyrood venture well without feeling obliged to ignore its shortcomings – except in the matter of the new Parliament's construction costs, which he defended, confident in the belief that it would prove to be an architectural wonder capable of comparison with the Sydney Opera House. While his Holyrood sketches only appeared in the Scottish edition, his weekly column – usually on matters emanating from Scotland's political adventure – appeared in the English editions as well. Like Brock, Stothard took the view that the Holyrood experiment was too interesting a development to be confined to a Scots only audience.

The editions going north began to be re-edited with additional Scottish content in late 1998. Going to press at 6 a.m., the edition for 7 May 1999 carried the full results of the new Parliament's first elections as the front-page lead. A formally distinctive and branded Scottish edition hit the newsstands on 22 July. The first task was to make the best of a logistical problem. Increasing sales of the *Sun* (which already had a Scottish edition) had swamped any spare capacity at News International's Kinning Park printing plant in Glasgow. Consequently, the new *Times* paper had to be printed from the company's Knowsley plant in Merseyside. This created some difficulty for the first print run which went up to the north of Scotland without some of the late-starting Scottish sporting fixtures, although the second edition – which covered the vast majority of the readership in the 'central belt' – left late enough to provide a comprehensive service. Certainly, the product looked as professional as its English counterpart and, on average, contained only around six to twelve article alternations a day. Yet, judiciously selected, these were enough to satiate the target market – those Scots who wanted more home news within a newspaper that was still primarily British in tone and international in scope. Improvements continued to be made. In 2001, some of the more obscure London arts reviews were replaced with reports from Robert Dawson-Scott on what was showing in Scotland's galleries and theatres. Helped by a special price cut, the effect on circulation north of the border was dramatic. *The Times* saw its Scottish sale soar and by 2000 its circulation had passed the thirty thousand mark. The *Telegraph* also launched a Scottish edition along similar lines and recorded comparable gains. Nonetheless, by 2002 *The Times* had opened up a six-thousand-lead over its rival and had become comfortably Scotland's leading Fleet Street broadsheet. Perhaps surprisingly, the *Independent* and the *Guardian* (which might have expected a ready market in a part of the country whose employment patterns and politics favoured a strong public sector) opted only to increase the Scottish content in the editions they sent north rather than to follow *The Times* and *Telegraph*'s path of a full-blown Scottish edition. Their continuing failure to make headway in Scotland suggested they had missed their chance. In contrast, for a paper whose politics remained unionist, *The Times* had demonstrated great versatility in adapting to the new landscape created by Scottish devolution. It was a costly endeavour but it reaped an important dividend.

III

Within weeks of taking office, Tony Blair had shown his faith in the future (whatever it might hold) by giving the go-ahead to the £750 million Millennium Dome, a project that it was hoped would embody everything positive and progressive about what style journalists had taken to calling 'Cool Britannia'. In July 1997, a party hosted in Downing Street for some of the brightest and most recognizable figures in the arts was widely interpreted as a Prime Ministerial attempt to associate himself with the new mood of optimism that sought to be unencumbered with the weight of tradition and history. It was not just post-election triumphalism that gave the Labour Government a sense that 1997 was a year of renewal. On 30 June the story of the British Empire effectively came to a close in Hong Kong when, in a ceremony no less moving for being rain-drenched, the Prime Minister and the Prince of Wales attended the handover of the last significant colony to the People's Republic of China. In *The Times*, a poignant leader article saluted Britain's record there but questioned whether it was living up to its responsibilities for its remaining possessions, the 'few small islands, once staging posts on the shipping routes to the colonies, that are either too small or too remote to make their way alone in the world':

With the loss of Hong Kong, Britain, which once administered the biggest Empire the world has ever seen, now has responsibility for fewer than 180,000 people in the remaining dependent territories. France still has three times as many citizens in its overseas departments, and has long given them full integration with metropolitan France. For these remaining few, Britain retains political and moral responsibility. Sadly the record here is poor. Drug-taking and money-laundering in the Caribbean, arguments over sovereignty in the Falklands and Gibraltar and the most appalling neglect of St Helena, Britain's Atlantic Alcatraz, betray official irritation at being saddled with these pinpricks from a bygone age. There will be no more transfers of sovereignty. It is time now that the old ideals of Empire were properly applied to the small territories where Britain still holds sway.[4]

Eight weeks later, on 31 August, came news that genuinely staggered the world. Diana, Princess of Wales, and one of her lovers, Dodi Fayed, were killed along with their driver in the Pont de l'Alma tunnel, Paris. Seven freelance photographers had been in pursuit and were arrested on manslaughter charges by French police (and later acquitted). Stothard was spending the weekend with Michael Portillo on the estate adjoining Balmoral when the news broke. He raced back to London with a leader written on a British Airways breakfast menu. In the meantime, Brian MacArthur who was editing the Sunday for Monday paper, had already begun masterminding the operation and, by common consent, pulled off a remarkable achievement. Over the next few days newspapers became, as Simon Jenkins observed, more like magazines as they sought not only to piece together the events that caused her death but also to assess her life and the extraordinary reaction to her premature demise. On the Sunday, the BBC provided all-day coverage. There were more than enough eulogies to fill it. No one else in the history of broadcasting had received this level of distinction.

Although some found it excessive, the saturation media coverage appeared to encourage an outpouring of public grief that was far removed from the decorous respect that had marked the passing of King George VI or Sir Winston Churchill. About sixty million flowers – more than one for every person in the kingdom – were laid at makeshift shrines at the west end of The Mall and, more especially, around the late Princess's former home at Kensington Palace. This spectacle of contagious grief also contained a vengeful element intent on blaming both the press for hounding her to her doom and the royal family, first for stripping Diana of her royal title when, on her divorce, she ceased to be royal, and for failing to display publicly the sense of contrition and show of mental distress that was convulsing the millions of people who had never met her. Some republican sentiments were expressed and a potentially serious display of disloyalty towards the Queen and the Prince of Wales was possibly avoided only by a belated loosening of protocol – the royal standard was lowered to half-mast above Buckingham Palace and the Queen was persuaded to make a television broadcast the day before the funeral in which she spoke of Diana's great gifts.

Noting the prevalence of young people among the grieving crowds, Simon Jenkins mused that:

The young seek role models not among the contented but among those before whom the world has dangled every pleasure and yet snatched it away . . . People seem to take comfort in watching the famous find life as hard as they do themselves . . . The word used time and again by those queueing at St James's yesterday was that she represented 'comfort'.[5]

In his funeral oration, Earl Spencer expressed the views of the vengeful, attacking not only the press which had hunted her, but, in an extraordinary display of lèse-majesté, the royal family. He had ensured that no tabloid editor was invited to the funeral. Given his late sister's reliance on the 'red tops' to print information she leaked to them this insistence bemused those in the media who had first-hand experience of her *modus operandi*. In contrast, the broadsheet editors, with whom she had dealt far less frequently, were admitted to Westminster Abbey, even though in *The Times*'s case this meant receiving a stiff cream envelope from the Lord Chamberlain addressed to someone called Peter Pennington Esq – as if the editor had, like a peer of the realm, assumed the name of his territorial domain.

Certainly, those seeking to chronicle each twist of the Prince and Princess of Wales's matrimonial break-up would not find *The Times* to have been Fleet Street's primary source. For Peter Stothard, the most insightful episode in his relations with Diana had occurred the first time he had been granted a private lunch with her in a Park Lane restaurant on 18 May 1994. He was astonished by her forthrightness and ability to impart so much information in so short a period. Within the first five minutes she had already slipped into the conversation a damaging observation about her husband. 'She was as charming that day as everyone always says that she is. But she did not move outside the lines that she had most clearly defined,'

Stothard recalled in an article about that first lunch, published three days after her death:

> Inside those lines were the very aspects of her life which most people keep outside in discussion with newspaper editors – her husband, his mistress, her in-laws, her own fragile sense of herself. Within minutes I felt I was talking to someone I knew. By the time that she had toyed her way through her foie gras and lamb, I knew things about her that I did not know about my closest friends.

Stothard had not until that moment taken an interest in what he considered mere royal gossip and had assumed that much of what had been printed in the popular press was 'misleading, false, fourth-hand, or worse'. It suddenly became clear to him how much of it was directly attributable to its royal source. To Stothard's unease, the Princess began to tell him a story about how she had helped a tramp who had fallen into the Regent's Park Canal and that she was going to visit him in hospital in the afternoon. What was Stothard supposed to make of – or with – this story? 'I had missed enough "royal exclusives" in my life to be far from sure that I had not just somehow missed this one too,' he later related. 'That prospect obviously worried her as well. I did not seem interested enough. Some bits of her story did not fit together as well as a true story should. Yet it seemed churlish to cross-examine a Princess.' With paparazzi gathering outside the restaurant, the editor and the Princess slipped away in the *Times* limousine so that she could be conveyed to the hospital without attracting any media attention. Later that day, Stothard received a letter from Diana thanking him for the 'rescue' adding, 'Today of all days it meant a great deal to me not to be photographed.' Yet, intriguingly, the following morning the newspapers carried full accounts of how she had saved the tramp in the canal. *The Times* also carried the story even although Stothard had not mentioned it to anyone.[6]

Predictably, the reaction of readers when Stothard related the occasion of his lunch with the late Princess was divided. Those who found the outbreak of national hysteria unsettling were delighted to have their suspicions confirmed that she had been a manipulative figure, ready to brief the press one moment then affect hurt at the intrusive publicity the next. Other readers felt that the editor of *The Times* ought not to be telling tales before her body was even formally laid to rest. In any case, she was hardly the only member of what she had memorably called a 'crowded' marriage to have briefed the press. Many of the hostile observations about her in the press during her life had derived from sources within the Prince of Wales's circle of friends. *The Times* was not the first port of call for either side of the warring couple to leak a story. The *Sun* and the *Daily Mail* were regarded far more fertile ground. For *The Times*, the issue had been whether to repeat what was appearing elsewhere and risk accusations of publishing royal tittle-tattle or ignore it and miss stories concerning two of the world's most famous people, one of whom was destined to be Britain's Head of State. Stothard related that, 'The problem was that my perception that the stories were mostly true was at odds with the perception of most *Times* readers that they were mostly false and were being presented either as just selling newspapers, idle gossip or in pursuit of some republican agenda.' This last point was a particularly invidious charge given Murdoch's personal republican leanings. Any *Times* report or comment that showed the House of Windsor in a less than perfect light could be accused of being prompted by the proprietor's supposed views on the subject. In fact, Murdoch did not even raise the subject of *The Times*'s approach to monarchy with his editor. 'I never ever had a discussion with him about that at all,' Stothard stated after his retirement from the editorship.[7] While reserving its right to find fault with individuals, *The Times* remained true to the coat of arms on its masthead and loyal to the concept of monarchy.

For its part, the monarchy appeared to be relaxed about the occasionally irreverent treatment it received from *The Times*. 'That's Mr Hamilton. Don't talk to him; he'll only write terribly rude things about you,' the Queen once instructed a Nigerian in full tribal costume who she spotted about to engage in conversation Alan Hamilton, *The Times*'s royal tours veteran, in the garden of the British High Commissioner's residence in Abuja. The admonishment delivered, the Queen turned to Hamilton and gave him a knowing, sympathetic look before bursting into a smile. 'I took this as a compliment,' the sardonically droll Scotsman reflected; 'at least she reads the stuff.'[8]

IV

With each successive *Times* editor, Bernard Levin, perhaps the nation's most famous columnist, had developed an affectionate rapport. He would not depart for a holiday without leaving several articles already written to cover his absence. From distant parts, he would send the editor amusing mementos. From one trip to California in 1993 he sent Stothard a headline cutting from the *Santa Barbara News-Press* proclaiming, 'Suit says newspaper editor "went berserk"' to which he appended his own pithy leg-pull. Levin was genuinely loved by those who knew him and revered by those who did not. He had become as much a fixture of *The Times* as the crossword at the back. Yet, as the decade wore on, he presented Stothard with a problem. His memory was beginning to fail. There were occasions when he would attempt to file again on the same subject he had written about at length only days before. There remained flashes of the old brilliance but as he started a long and cruel battle with senile dementia so the quality of his column became uneven. Neither Stothard nor Bryant wanted to confront the issue, although letters from concerned readers were beginning to arrive in the editor's office suggesting that releasing Levin from his twice-weekly obligations would be an act of mercy. Both the editor and deputy editor admired and revered a man whose many acts of quiet thoughtfulness were witnessed by all who felt themselves privileged to be counted among his friends. Yet, for most of the inmates of Wapping, Levin appeared self-contained to the point of being withdrawn. He would spend long hours in his small glass cell of an office, peering out with sad eyes, his lugubrious expression fleetingly met by those hurrying past on their way to talk to someone else. Although he was initially reluctant to speak about it, he knew his mental powers were starting to fail him and at times appeared distressed to the point where colleagues feared he would end it all with tablets and champagne. Instead, he chose to struggle on until Stothard grasped the nettle and persuaded him that he must scale down his output. Levin filed his last regular column on 10 January 1997, a lament for the declining quality of new plays and the impact this would have on the West End, without which there would be 'a great hole in the fabric of our land'.[9] It was suggested he should write more at his leisure for the weekend section and this he did for the rest of the year, criticizing the Chinese government, the persecutors of smokers and, finally, in 1998, his reflections on the Court of Appeal's posthumous quashing of Derek Bentley's conviction for murder – a *cause célèbre* he had long championed. It would prove to be his last piece. After it, the efforts of memory proved too great and the country was denied any further observations from a man who had bestrode his profession. His battle with dementia lost, he died in 2004.

There were changes of location as well as personnel. In March 1998, *The*

Times moved its address for only the fourth time in its history. On this occasion, the move could not have been shorter, since it merely involved crossing from the south side of Pennington Street to the north side. The Napoleonic rum warehouse was too small to contain all the paper's departments and decamping across the road to the newly built six-storey office block was a matter of necessity. Despite its undistinguished architecture, some had come to appreciate the old building's bunker-like qualities and the fact that its long, open-plan interior allowed a virtually unobstructed view of everyone in the office at the same time. While journalists toiled on tomorrow's copy, all the past editions were stored, leather-bound, under their feet in the catacombs of the brick vaults below. Its unusualness had become its principal charm and, for some, the hassle of moving a matter of metres away to a new building that lacked a decent sense of history hardly seemed worth the effort. How much of an improvement the new building was quickly became a matter for debate. Despite moving from a largely windowless shed to new glass and brick office block designed by the fashionable architect Rick Mather and rejoicing in the preposterous name of 'La Lumière', many journalists were unimpressed by their new residence and soon rechristened it 'La Gloomy Air'. The building was quickly given an official rebranding as 'Times House'. Before long, however, the welcoming air turned stale as the extent of the drainage problem in the lavatories and a rat infestation became apparent. Some, of course, joked that from a professional standpoint this was appropriate.

Aesthetically, the new residence was less than exciting, representing the styleless architectural interlude that followed the exuberant if tacky postmodernism of the 1980s. The newsroom was successfully accommodated in one large, open-plan ground floor. The leader writers enjoyed greater seclusion on the floor above where the various associate editors were given small glass compartments in which to pretend they enjoyed privacy. Stothard fared better and was able to move into an office that was finally large enough to hold small conferences and accommodate his extensive personal library of historical and biographical tomes. He, at least, was given wooden bookshelves. Elsewhere in the building they were made of metal, fitted with fold-down shutters and painted blue to resemble outsized deposit boxes. There was no reason to believe their designer had any acquaintance with the shape and dimensions of a book. This was not the least of the disappointments. A dank central courtyard became the equivalent of the school bike shed for the paper's resident smokers. On higher levels, steel gantries and a metal staircase that resonated with the constant clinkety-clank sound of its users' feet conveyed the sights and sounds of being on a Panamanian registered oil tanker. Deeper within the building, even the carpeted zones appeared to have been designed for steerage class. Some of the connecting corridors were so narrow that it was impossible for two people to pass each other without doing a forty-five-degree twist of the pelvis. This militated against hanging the treasures of the past on the walls and it was not until 2004 that oil paintings of the Walter, Northcliffe and Astor owners were hung in the entrance foyer as a first and much needed concession to decoration. An enclosed glass footbridge was constructed over Pennington Street and the old warehouse in order to link *The Times* 's new residence with the facilities – including the reference library, restaurant and gym – that it shared with the other newspapers in the group above the print hall. The design of the enclosed bridge ensured that it funnelled scorching heat in summer and arctic chill in the other three seasons. Oddly, the new home's peculiarities invested it with a welcome, if unintended, degree of eccentricity.

Meanwhile, the old rum warehouse *The Times* left behind became the repository for various News International departments, including the Archive and Record Centre. *The Times*'s archives had first been opened to historical researchers on a limited basis during Rees-Mogg's editorship. The driving force behind improving the conditions in which they were kept and making them more readily available to the public came from the venerable Sir Edward Pickering who, at the age of eighty-six, remained one of Murdoch's most trusted and respected executives. With 'Pick's' backing, the company invested in new temperature-controlled storerooms for the paper's documents in an archive that filled over a kilometre of shelving space. At last, a proper budget was assigned to conserving the paper's heritage and even to procure further relevant material at auction. With Eamon Dyas as chief archivist, *The Times* became in June 1998 the first national newspaper to offer outside researchers free and comprehensive access to its historic collection. 'Pick' had made many contributions to the paper's welfare since his appointment as Times Newspapers' executive vice-chairman in 1982. In particular, he had been a sagacious source of advice to successive editors and enjoyed the trust and indeed admiration of Murdoch who considered him his 'first great mentor'. There were, after all, no other 1950s Fleet Street editors still in senior management positions as the twentieth century drew to a close. Indeed, Sir Edward came to the view that he was too old to retire, stayed at his post and died in harness at the age of ninety-one in 2003, an acknowledged giant of Fleet Street. Of his many services to *The Times*, his support for the ongoing project of writing the paper's official history and the creation of a properly endowed Archive Centre were among the tangible monuments. The access provided to scholars greatly enhanced *The Times*'s claims to be the historian's paper of record.

V

Despite the quality of gentlemen going into it, the journalistic world into which Sir Edward Pickering had first ventured before the Second World War was still widely regarded as a trade. By the time of his death, it had clear pretensions to becoming a profession. For those at the broadsheets, salaries had finally reached a level of professional standing and the proportion of those with university degrees had greatly increased. Many even had degrees in journalism. Yet, among the public, the reputation of journalism had enjoyed no such assent. Inexplicably, the papers that were most popular with the public were those that were also held up to have descended deepest into the gutter. During the 1900s, the Press Council's ability to police Fleet Street was increasingly questioned by the Street of Shame's periodic, and high-profile, excesses. Founded in 1953, the Council's chief sanction was that, where it found fault, it could force newspapers to publish its adjudications. Without an agreed code of conduct, its judgments perhaps inevitably lacked consistency and neither journalists, editors nor aggrieved parties appeared to place confidence in it.

Cleaning up the press was not an easy task. Much of the criticism, in particular of the popular press, was directed at its right-wing bias and lowbrow tastes. Yet, drawing up statutory powers to curb such editorial judgments was to stray into dangerous and authoritarian waters in which the law would intrude into value judgments better left – for all their shortcomings – to the forces of competition. Indefensible harassment and deliberate misrepresentation was a different matter. Those who felt they had been libelled had recourse to the courts (at any rate, if they had the time and money). Fleet Street's broadsheet and tabloid editors were united in favouring self-regulation over statutory intervention, but the Press Council's failure to produce speedy, consistent and authoritative judgments ensured that it was no longer the vehicle to guarantee the former. In the House of Commons, various private members' bills proposed a statutory right of reply and the protection of privacy. Nothing better assisted the cause of those demanding a right of privacy than the actions of journalists from the *Sunday Sport* who, in 1990, barged into a hospital to photograph and attempt to interview the comic actor Gordon Kaye as he lay seriously injured on a life-support machine. Believing that, as the law stood, it was within its rights to publish the pictures taken, the *Sport* demonstrated its careless arrogance by responding to a reprimand for its actions with the headline 'Bollocks to the Press Council'. By then, the Government had already decided to act and had appointed Sir David Calcutt QC, the Master of Magdalene College, Cambridge, to chair an enquiry into the press and privacy. The six other members of his committee included Simon Jenkins, who had recently been appointed *The Times*'s editor.

Fleet Street's editors had traditionally been opposed to drawing up a code of ethics but the possibility of having one forced upon them brought an abrupt change of tune. In line with other newspapers, in 1989 *The Times* appointed its former managing editor and deputy editor, John Grant, as its readers' representative, charged with investigating readers' complaints and alleged errors or misrepresentations. Calcutt issued his report in May 1990. It called for the Press Council to be replaced by the Press Complaints Commission (PCC). It would implement a code of practice (the code itself was drawn up and agreed by a committee of editors). For newspapers, the most important part of the report was that it did not sanction a privacy law. But Calcutt made clear the press was on probation. If self-regulation did not work, statutory regulation should follow.

Promoting greater responsibility from the tabloids was the main goal of the PCC, but it was not long before *The Times* fell foul. A *Times* Diary article in May 1991 had alleged that Bernie Grant, the Labour MP, had encouraged a US congressman to boycott the Queen's address to Congress because of racism in Britain.[10] The source for the story in Washington DC, was a good one and when Bernie Grant failed to return *The Times*'s telephone call, the allegation was printed without securing his side of the story. When it was published, the MP categorically denied it. When the PCC subsequently condemned *The Times* for its tardy checking of facts, the newspaper quickly responded by making amends in line with the code of practice.[11] Some of the tabloids, however, appeared to regard a rap on the knuckles as an incitement to behave more outspokenly. The *Sunday People* reacted to complaints about its publication of a photograph of the Duke of York's infant daughter, Princess Eugenie, naked (she was bathing within a private walled garden at the time) by republishing it with a telephone hotline for readers to say whether or not they found it offensive under the caption 'Come on Andy where's your sense of fun?'. The crude excesses of a few risked a statutory backlash that could do far more to gag the serious journalism upon which a free society rested.

There was certainly no shortage of salacious copy to promote, much of it provided by the royal family. The efforts of the PCC's chairman, Lord McGregor, to bring the press to book had been swiftly handicapped by the Princess of Wales. McGregor's attempts to protect her dignity were undermined when it was revealed that the source for many of the stories, particularly those he condemned in Andrew Morton's *Diana: Her True Story*, serialized in the *Sunday Times*, was none other than Diana herself. The tabloids' blood sport at the expense of the royal family continued unabated. When David Mellor, the Heritage Secretary, was provoked into warning that the press 'was drinking in the last chance saloon', the *Sunday People* destroyed Mellor's career by revealing his affair with a resting actress, complete with various inaccurate but highly embarrassing details provided by the publicist Max Clifford.

Meanwhile, Calcutt had been asked to review the workings of the PCC. In 1993 his second report concluded that the self-regulation he had helped put in place had failed and that with 'no realistic possibility' of getting its house in order the PCC should be replaced by a statutory tribunal presided over by a judge armed with powers to block publication, fine miscreants and force published retractions. In particular, there would be legal restraints on such staples of investigative reporting as the use of electronic bugging and long-lens photography. Calcutt's proposals represented what, in effect, resembled a privacy law. In common with the rest of Fleet Street, *The Times* was appalled, accusing the 'blinkered' Calcutt of producing a report that ranged 'between the supercilious and the hostile. In that respect it is certainly a document of its time.'[12] The paper had already made clear its belief that statutory regulation, and in particular a privacy law, 'would be a delight to all those with something infamous to hide and a grave blow to the freedom of the press'.[13] *The Times*'s upholding of this freedom was strengthened by its commitment to freedom of expression on its own pages. Among *Times* columnists, Calcutt found a champion in Woodrow Wyatt. Wyatt, who managed to combine a reverence for the royal family with a close friendship with Rupert Murdoch, used his column to condemn the *Sunday Times* for peddling Andrew Morton's book. What was more, he advocated the sort of French privacy legislation that would have made its publication illegal.[14] Wyatt maintained that *The Times* leader column's reaction to Calcutt smacked of hysteria: 'the US press vigorously attacks the president, his administration and his opponents without restraint. It is not in the least cowed by US privacy laws on Calcutt lines,' he argued.[15]

An alternative argument questioned whether a privacy law was workable. Rees-Mogg observed that Calcutt's proposals against using telephoto lens would not prevent foreign paparazzi having photographs published (indeed, many of the worst intrusions upon the royal family had been taken while abroad) and if there was to be a prohibition on bugging then it should include that undertaken by the State.[16] The Government, too, was reluctant to go as far as Calcutt deemed necessary but *The Times*, conscious that press criticism of the Government and its members' private antics had lost it friends at Westminster, feared some form of retribution. The paper even opposed the less stringent findings of the National Heritage Select Committee, arguing its proposals for a press ombudsman, regional complaints offices and the replacement of the PCC with a more powerful Press Commission stood a chance of being implemented 'because some ministers want to placate parliamentarians and some parliamentarians want to protect their friends'.[17]

In the event, the Government settled for a more modest restructuring of the PCC that put disinterested parties in the majority. Attention was focused upon the PCC's code of practice which was designed to promote responsible journalism. Drawn too tightly, it could threaten legitimate investigative freedom. Thus it attempted to find a balance by permitting newspapers to breach eight of its sixteen rules if they could establish it was in the 'public interest' to do so. Exposing criminality or wrongdoing, safeguarding public health and safety and correcting misleading statements were three areas that were commonly accepted to be within 'the public interest'. The code stated that the public interest extended beyond these areas but decided it would be overly proscriptive to set the parameters and better to take it on a case by case basis. This left considerable room for editorial manoeuvring. To what extent were the private lives of public figures covered by the 'public interest'? Newspapers could certainly claim so when it came to the royal family or politicians. When the *Daily Mirror* published photographs of the Duchess of York – separated from but still married to the Duke – in an intimate setting with her financial adviser, *The Times* argued that 'the best defence the duchess and the rest of the royal family can throw up against intrusion is to show greater discretion in their private behaviour'. While it accepted that publishing the photograph might demonstrate a 'lack of taste', it was wrong 'to expect a legal fiat to lay down the bounds of good taste in a matter such as this'.[18] The paper had a similar attitude to politicians. The tabloids had a field day exposing the sex lives of Conservative MPs, justifying doing so not on grounds of prurience (although this was a large part of it) but because, as members of a party allegedly committed to family values, there was a public interest in exposing them as hypocrites. *The Times* did not take the lead in exposing the private lives of public figures, although it was happy to report them once other newspapers had already published the details. It did not have a scoop in this area until 2003 (outside the scope of this volume) when, having secured the rights to Edwina Currie's diaries, it broke the news that the former Health Minister had had an affair with John Major. Neither party (and least of all Ms Currie) lodged a complaint about the exposure.

In the spring of 1998, however, *The Times* found itself at the centre of a storm when it serialized Gitta Sereny's book *Cries Unheard* about the child killer, Mary Bell. In *Albert Speer: His Battle with Truth*, Sereny had written an acclaimed study of Hitler's architect and wartime planner who had escaped the death penalty at Nuremberg. In it, she carefully unpeeled the seemingly ambiguous relationship he had had towards the crimes of the Nazi regime he had served so well *Cries Unheard* attempted to understand how, at the age of eleven, Mary Bell had strangled two young boys. The book dwelt on the deprivation and abuse that Bell had experienced as a child.

With memories fresh about the murder of the toddler Jamie Bulger by two young boys, an atrocity that had gripped and horrified the public, Sereny's theme had resonance. As a book, its intent was far removed from the titillation of some true-crime literature. Nonetheless, its publication and *The Times*'s serialization caused uproar. Sereny had written the book with Bell's participation – help for which the ex-convict was paid. Bell, it was argued, had therefore profited from her crimes. Tony Blair waded into the furore by describing the payment to Bell as 'repugnant'. Furthermore, given the stigma that her crime had placed upon her, Bell had been granted a life injunction on her release from jail that prevented her from being identified. Benefiting from this, she had been able to start a new life under an assumed identity and had brought up a daughter who was unaware of her mother's grim past. *Cries Unheard* and its serialization in *The Times* provided the tabloid press with an excuse to hunt Bell down. Her cover was blown and, in the face of considerable media harassment and unwanted publicity, she was forced to tell her daughter the truth.

The affair raised many questions. The greatest fury was directed at the antics of the tabloid press whose rapacious desire to expose Bell appeared to come from low and sensationalist motives. Some, however, believed that by cooperating with the book Bell had brought the attention upon herself. Others felt that Sereny herself was guilty of prurience and could not stand aloof from the consequences of her own book just because it was written in an anguished and high-minded style. *The Times* was disparaged for publishing its contents and paying Sereny serialization rights that increased her profit and, potentially, the sum Bell demanded for cooperation. Among rival newspaper editors, none was more scandalized by *The Times*'s decision than Charles Moore who told his readers, 'I felt that this was a situation that a quality newspaper such as the *Daily Telegraph* must avoid.' He assured them that if the *Telegraph* had behaved as *The Times* had done, he would have opened himself up to suspicions of being motivated 'by the desire for profit, sales, sensation, controversy' and risked his paper being found in breach of the PCC's code of practice.[19] This was prophetic. Complaints were duly brought against *The Times* under Clause 16 (ii) of the code which prohibited newspapers paying convicted or confessed criminals for their stories unless there is an identifiable public interest defence. Here then, was the 'public interest' catch-all put to the test.

When, in July 1998, it issued its report, the PCC cleared *The Times* of wrongdoing on the grounds that the payment was in the public interest since it sought to explore the penal system's treatment of child criminals. When the House of Lords debated the issue, Lord Wakeham, the PCC chairman, went further, claiming 'the public interest oozes from every pore of the book and in turn from the extracts from it which was serialised in the newspaper'. Although he conceded that the public interest should not be confused with what the public might be interested in, Wakeham considered what Sereny 'had to say was important and deserved a wide audience'.[20]

Legally, the issue of criminals benefiting from their crimes was a difficult one. The PCC also cleared the *Express* and the *Mirror* for paying two nurses, Deborah Parry and Lucille McLauchlan, convicted of murder in Saudi Arabia, for their stories as well as the *Telegraph* for serializing a memoir by Sean O'Callaghan, a convicted IRA terrorist who had subsequently rejected violence and become a police informer. The existing law permitted the Home Secretary to confiscate money made from criminals writing memoirs. The Government recognized that it was an area of law in need of review but there were difficulties in tightening it up, not least since the European Convention of Human Rights (entrenched in English Law by the 1998 Human Rights Act) guaranteed freedom of expression for everyone, including criminals.

It was in branding a Russian businessman an alleged mafia boss that *The Times* found itself testing the libel laws in the wake of the Human Rights Act. During 1999, the paper published a series of more than forty articles analysing organized crime and the theft of Russian assets since the collapse of the USSR, but it was two articles written in the autumn on 1999 by David Lister, with assistance from James Bone from the paper's New York bureau, that unwittingly made an important contribution to British law.

Lister and Bone's article named Grigori Loutchansky as an 'alleged . . . Russian mafia boss' under investigation in the Bank of New York money-laundering scandal. A second report suggested he had provided a chauffeur and staff in Israel for Lev Chernoi, another Russian businessman who was under investigation for money laundering.[21] According to his own testimony, Loutchansky first heard from a report on Russian television that *The Times* of London had linked him to organized crime. He decided to sue for libel and try to clear his name.

David Lister was a twenty-five-year-old Cambridge history graduate who had worked for the *Evening Standard* before joining *The Times*. In August 1999 he had been tipped off by a former detective with the National Criminal Intelligence Service and the National Crime Squad that a British investigation was pending into Loutchansky's alleged role in the Bank of New York money-laundering scandal. A supplementary source was Jeffrey Robinson, the author of a book on international organized crime, who told him that the Russian businessman was also being investigated by the FBI. According to Lister's notes, Robinson had even suggested that Loutchansky and Semion Mogilevich had sold Scud missiles to the Iraqi regime. Naturally, Lister decided to follow up these intriguing leads and asked a high-ranking FBI intelligence officer who was on secondment at Interpol's headquarters in Lyons if Loutchanksy was being investigated over the Bank of New York scandal. According to Lister, she had laughed nervously and replied, 'I believe it would be fruitful to write about it.' A trawl of published reports turned up allegations that Loutchansky's firm, Nordex, had been established with KGB money and that it had possible links with the Russian mafia.[22]

Some facts were easily verifiable. A businessman in his mid-fifties with joint Israeli and Russian citizenship, Loutchansky's career had resembled the twists and turns of a fairground roller coaster. At twenty-nine he had become pro-rector at the Latvian State University of Riga. Charged with embezzling various items including university furniture, he had been convicted in 1983 for embezzlement, forgery and abuse of power. He was given a seven-year sentence, part of which was spent in Siberia. After his release he had become general manager of Nordex, a Vienna-based company that claimed to trade in fertilizer. Despite this innocuous sounding line of business, in December 1994 Michael Howard, the Home Secretary, had refused him entry to Britain on the grounds that his presence 'would not be conducive to the public good'. Jack Straw, Howard's Labour successor at the Home Office, renewed the ban. This was not the only black mark. In 1996, *Time* magazine described Loutchansky as 'a man considered by many to be the most pernicious unindicted criminal in the world'.[23]

Given what had already been said about him in the United States, Loutchansky's decision to sue *The Times* for libel was a surprise to some. He claimed it was not about money but about clearing his name. Despite upholding the general ban on his entry into the country, Jack Straw allowed him to come to London on a temporary visa to testify against the newspaper. What followed was a trial of the utmost importance. A standard libel trial would have involved *The Times* trying to prove justification – in other words that its allegations were true. The problem for *The Times*, however, was that it did not have the evidence to prove the allegations were true. Like many of those who made allegations involving international money laundering, *The Times* had to concede that such evidence as might exist was held by authorities – like MI6, the Home Office, British and foreign police investigation departments – which were not in a position to disclose what (if anything) they knew. Thus, *The Times* opted for a 'qualified privilege' defence instead. In doing so, the paper was testing a new precedent in libel law. Historically, press 'privilege' from the rigours of British libel law had primarily protected parliamentary and court reporting but its scope had been greatly widened in a landmark ruling made in 1999. This was the so-called 'Reynolds Defence' when the House of Lords had ruled in a dispute between the *Sunday Times* and the former Irish Taoiseach, Albert Reynolds, that a newspaper could print information it could not verify as true if it met ten criteria set out by Lord Nicholls of Birkenhead for responsible journalism where there was a legitimate public interest. In Lord Nicholls's judgment, qualified privilege was a permissible defence even if there were factual inaccuracies published, if the reporting was in good faith using reliable and impartial sources and reasonable attempts to establish their veracity had been taken.

The trial of 'Loutchansky v Times Newspapers' began on 19 March 2001 in the High Court. The presiding judge was Charles Gray who, in a noted career as a libel barrister, had defended high-profile clients against media accusations, winning record damages for Lord Aldington from Nikolai Tolstoy but unsuccessfully defending Jonathan Aitken against the *Guardian*. *The Times*'s counsel was Richard Spearman QC while Desmond Browne QC appeared for the plaintiff. It was the first jury trial on a 'qualified privilege' case since the Reynolds verdict. However, the jury's role was restricted to determining whether they believed Lister's claims that he had shown proper diligence in compiling his report. It was up to the judge to rule whether the qualified privilege defence was valid.

Since the publication of the original articles, *The Times* had been busy collecting information to support the allegations. However, in a decision upheld by the Court of Appeal, Mr Justice Gray declared inadmissible any evidence gathered after the original claims were made. Consequently, the court was denied knowledge of affidavits from the Israeli Interior Ministry opposing the renewal of Loutchansky's passport and regarding the reasons for the Home Secretary's ban on his coming to Britain, as well as a communication between the US Department of State and the embassy in Tel Aviv that led to his being denied a US visa, and reports compiled by the police forces of Israel, Austria and Interpol. With Peter Stothard watching from the back of the courtroom, Loutchansky took the stand and implied that his 1983 conviction was a trumped-up charge by the KGB who were concerned at his pro-democracy sentiments and, indeed, that it was his 'feeling' that '*The Times* newspaper had somebody behind them in all this action. It's something to do with the people who stand behind them.'[24] His QC clashed repeatedly with Lister, attempting to undermine his journalistic professionalism. Certainly, *The Times*'s defence would have been stronger if it had provided Loutchansky with a proper forum to reply to the allegations when they were first made. Unfortunately this had not been done. Despite using an internet search engine, Lister had failed to locate Loutchansky's London or American lawyers nor had an attempt to locate him in Moscow borne fruit. The plaintiff's counsel also sought to belittle the credibility of Lister's anonymous sources. An attempt by Lister to assert why they might consider their lives endangered was halted by the judge. By comparison, James Bone, who had a first-class law degree from Cambridge, appeared almost to enjoy being cross-examined by Desmond Browne.

When the moment came to return a verdict, the jury found generally in favour of Lister's honesty as a reporter. Of the fifteen questions they were asked, they found on ten counts in his favour, on two counts against and recorded three failures to reach a verdict. Importantly, on the substantive questions of the Interpol officer's words, and those of the other main informants, Lister's testimony was upheld. The verdict from the judge proved a different matter. On 27 April, Mr Justice Gray accepted that the claims were 'very serious' but that there was 'no great urgency' to report what, he asserted in news terms, were 'low grade' stories and that *The Times* did not have a duty to publish. He believed newspapers enjoyed qualified privilege from the laws of libel only when they would be open to legitimate criticism if they failed to publish the contentious information. *The Times* was also forced to remove from its internet archive the offending articles, the judge taking the view that a website effectively involved constant republication of the libel every time it received a hit. This judgment had huge implications for archive management in the electronic age, creating – in contrast to the printed newspaper – an unlimited timescale of liability.

The Times immediately made a submission to the Court of Appeal to reverse the decision. In the summation of the *Guardian*'s editor, Alan Rusbridger, the judge appeared to have concluded, 'that the subject matter was in the public interest, but that *The Times* had no duty to report it'.[25] In December, the Appeal judges ruled that Mr Justice Gray had applied 'the wrong test' on the question of the paper's duty to publish and sent the case back to him for reconsideration. However, Gray proceeded to restate his original judgment that *The Times* did not enjoy qualified privilege and threw out its attempt to enter a new plea of justification; he would not permit a new libel trial in which the paper hoped to prove its allegations were true by reference to an Italian police report – Operation Spiderweb. This infuriated the paper, which had in the meantime acquired a 232-page report compiled by the public prosecutor in Bologna into alleged international money laundering that referred to various companies apparently linked to Loutchansky.[26]

London had been dubbed 'the libel capital of the world' in the 1990s, but newspaper lawyers like *The Times*'s Alastair Brett looked forward to the new century as one in which the scales of justice would tilt in investigative journalism's favour. The European Convention's defence of freedom of expression, written into British law by the 1998 Human Rights Act and the Reynolds judgment the following year, were interpreted as moves in this direction. Mr Justice Gray's judgment in the case of 'Loutchansky v Times Newspapers' suggested otherwise. Furthermore, the judgment that an online archive represented constant re-publication had repercussions for the British media that its American counterparts were spared: in the United States the limitation date was set by the day an article was first transferred to an electronic database or website.[27]

Yet the lack of a considerable body of case law meant that there was likely to be much movement in the years ahead. In the case against Loutchansky, *The Times* had marred its claim to qualified privilege by failing to withhold publication until the accused had been given the opportunity to give a full rebuttal. In this respect, the paper published in haste and repented at leisure. Although it did not reach the courts, an example of a *Times* journalist successfully guarding his integrity had taken place on 30 January 1999 when the paper's football correspondent, Matt Dickinson, interviewed the England football coach, Glenn Hoddle. During the course of their talk, Hoddle – who believed in reincarnation – had expressed the opinion that people with disabilities were being punished for sins in a previous life.[28] The response was a public uproar and, facing the sack, Hoddle claimed Dickinson had misrepresented his comments and that he would be issuing a writ. Tony Blair even managed to get involved, announcing that Hoddle should resign but only if he had been honestly reported. Fortunately, Dickinson's shorthand skills ensured he had a very full note of what had been said and a BBC tape was produced in which Hoddle could be heard expressing similar views for an interview on Radio Five Live the previous year. Hoddle dropped his threat of legal action and was duly sacked while Dickinson's scoop was applauded and *The Times* was vindicated in the treatment of his article. In this there was a lesson that needed to be impressed upon Fleet Street and beyond. Because the Hoddle interview had been conducted using good journalistic practices Dickinson had been able to defend himself and the paper from the threat of legal action. In the Loutchansky case, however, the judge had convinced himself that *The Times* reporting had fallen short of such standards. Whatever the subsequent development of qualified privilege, the guidelines established by judges and law lords promised to shape the conduct of responsible journalism in the years ahead. The consequences of failing to follow best practice were to be graphically demonstrated when, in 2003, Andrew Gilligan, a reporter for the BBC Radio 4's *Today* programme, aired his impression of what he had been told by the Iraqi weapons inspector David Kelly without being able to furnish a comprehensive record of the conversation. The consequences were unfortunate for all concerned.

VI

The difficulties experienced by journalists trying to establish the reliability of information in Britain were not as great as those faced by foreign correspondents reporting from the world's remaining one-party states. Totalitarian governments were content to impart an official line on events (or even deny their existence) to foreign journalists, but this was no guarantee of accuracy. States that retained an iron grip on the supply of information were successful in censoring or banning reputable news agencies, papers and broadcasters from uncovering a truer picture of events. But such tactics failed to crush a subculture of rumour and gossip whose purveyors constantly sought out foreign journalists. The problem was that publishing unverifiable rumours was no more responsible than merely parroting the version of events narrated by State officials. Establishing if the rumours had any basis in fact in countries where reporters were not at liberty to probe at will or where potential witnesses were too frightened to talk on the record tested the resourcefulness of the most seasoned foreign correspondents.

No greater challenge could be provided than the enclosed world of Communist North Korea. In 1992, posing as a university lecturer, David Watts managed to get into the country on a special tour that featured an odd selection of fellow travellers, including a trade unionist from Bradford who periodically lectured his hosts about the need to make their society more Communist. Viewing the demilitarized zone from the North Korean side was a revelation. A twenty-four-foot high anti-tank wall (not visible from the southern side) ran the width of the country. Attempts by the north to tunnel under it had been thwarted. At another post, fifteen-foot-high loudspeakers blaring out Souza marches and the sound of automatic weapons fire serenaded the North Koreans. Watts was astonished by what he took to be the lack of military preparedness on North Korea's part. A modern expressway had been constructed from the border to Pyongyang and during the entire journey only four vehicles were spotted on it. There was little sign in the countryside that the world's most socialist state had provided much public transport: just children wandering barefoot on their way to school with the possibility of a lift from an army lorry. On arrival in Pyongyang, Watts discovered a capital city with great tower blocks, many of which, on closer inspection, appeared to be empty. A 105-storey, pyramid-shaped hotel had been constructed on the suggestion of Kim Il

Sung's heir, Kim Jong Il, but it had never been finished because the shape was useless for installing lifts. Gaining reliable sources of information proved impossible. Watts could only record as the observant tourist he purported to be. He did catch the eightieth-birthday celebrations for the 'Great Leader'. Most of the foreign dignitaries were from African states bearing gifts. 'A BBC man proffered a corporation T-shirt,' Watts noticed. 'Unsure of its ideological appropriateness, it was accepted only to be returned because it was not properly wrapped.'[29]

North Korea's profile in the news varied according to the level of tension in the demilitarized zone and the evidence that it was acquiring nuclear weapons. China, where a fifth of the world lived, was emerging from its Maoist introversion as a major power through the market reforms of Zhao Ziyang and Deng Xiaoping, and necessitated a continual reporting presence. Had Stothard but known it when he assumed the chair, it was The Times's reporting of the politics of this part of the world that was to prove one of the most controversial aspect of his editorship. Indeed, it was to tarnish the paper's reputation across wide sections of the British public and beyond.

In 1993, The Times appointed two new correspondents in China: James Pringle replaced Cathy Sampson in Beijing and Jonathan Mirsky established himself in Hong Kong. Pringle had been the paper's stringer In Cambodia and Thailand. He had previously reported China's affairs during Mao's Cultural Revolution for Reuters and Newsweek. It was not unusual in one-party states for the securing of journalists' visas to be a protracted war of attrition and months passed before the Chinese authorities would grant him one, despite approaches to the Chinese Ambassador and press attaché in London who passed the matter onto the Ministry of Foreign Affairs in Beijing which, in turn, complained at the 'slanderous and uninformed' tone of some Times editorials.[30]

Mild was the manner of Beijing's unease over Jimmy Pringle compared to the suspicion with which it regarded Jonathan Mirsky. Mirsky was an American academic specializing in Oriental Studies who had studied at Columbia and Cambridge and taught at Dartmouth and Pennsylvania universities before the Vietnam War provoked his decision to quit American shores. Through his friendship with Conor Cruise O'Brien, he had gone to China as a reporter for the Observer. It was while filing for that paper that he witnessed the horror of the Tiananmen Square massacre. He was in the Square close to the portrait of Mao when the soldiers opened fire on the crowd. He witnessed soldiers beating the protestors. An officer shot those forced to the ground. Suddenly he realized the soldiers were fixing upon him. He tried to make clear that he was a journalist and gestured that he was leaving. A soldier swore at him and, turning to his comrades, screamed at them to kill him. Mirsky was grabbed by two of the soldiers while a couple more started beating him. Desperately he tried to hold onto a balustrade, aware that once they had kicked him to the ground he would get a bullet through the skull. At the very moment in which he was making his last efforts to stay upright an Italian vice-consul and his friend, a young Australian reporter, were scurrying across the Square to make good their escape. As they did so they caught sight of the desperate Mirsky, arms flailing. Without pausing to weigh up the danger, the two men turned back to rescue him. The Australian, no more than an acquaintance of Mirsky's, managed to get a hold of him as he was being pushed down. 'Come on, Jonathan, let's go now,' he said with remarkable coolness and jostled him free. A hail of bullets followed in their path as they hurried away. The Australian, whose name was Robert Thomson, had saved Mirsky's life. In 2002, he became editor of *The Times*.[31]

Like many who had witnessed the distressing scenes in Tiananmen Square, Mirsky found it difficult to maintain an objective view of the Chinese government he vehemently distrusted. Keen to stay on as a reporter, it was not an easy posting for one determined to explore beyond the explanations provided by the press briefings. He regularly had to navigate round the obstruction and admonishments of his official minder. Rather more ominously, he had to endure unknown people emerging from the shadows on street corners to accuse him of spreading lies and warning him of the consequences before turning away, back into the anonymity of the crowd. Who were these people? How did they know who he was or what his movements were? In particular, his trips to Tibet provoked this form of harassment. His telephone was tapped and his mail opened. In 1991, after he had covered John Major's first visit to China, the authorities made it clear they had had enough of Mirsky's journalism. They threw him out of the country.

Stothard's decision to employ such an authentic thorn in the flesh of the Beijing government was a courageous one. It certainly showed no regard for the commercial interests of the proprietor, Rupert Murdoch, who was beginning to invest in what he hoped would be a pan-China satellite television empire – for which he needed Beijing's approbation. Unabashed, Stothard made Mirsky East Asia editor and, when the latter queried whether there might be a potential clash with Murdoch's business interest in appeasing the Chinese authorities, Stothard assured him that he was a free agent who could write whatever he liked. That Beijing had refused Mirsky a visa to travel in the country was not an insurmountable problem. With Pringle filing from Beijing, Mirsky could base himself in Hong Kong, which still had four years left as a British colony. With the date of the handover approaching, Hong Kong would be as much a story as what was going on in the Chinese capital. Stothard was an enthusiastic supporter of the new (and last) Governor of the colony, Chris Patten, and his attempts to force through democratic reforms before Hong Kong was handed back to China. That Mirsky shared these sentiments was a further recommendation. Others were also pleased by the appointment. Douglas Hurd, the Foreign Secretary, went so far as to assure Mirsky of his delight that *The Times* was dispatching someone who he knew could be relied upon.[32]

It was not long before Richard Owen, *The Times*'s foreign editor, found himself summoned before the Chinese press attaché in London in order to be told of their embassy's acute irritation at Mirsky's reporting. An article by him that caused particular offence concerned allegations of cannibalism in Guangxi province during the Cultural Revolution and the state-created famine of 1959–61 that killed between sixteen and forty million people. Nor was Mirsky the only miscreant. There were also complaints about an article by Bernard Levin that thundered against the Foreign Office's selling out of Hong Kong, or, as he put it, 'the brave, beautiful, blazing bulwark against tyranny into bondage'. 'The people of China are ruled by brutes and tyrants,' Levin had continued, warming to his theme, before adding that Beijing's occupation of Tibet 'was a crime hardly less dreadful than those of the Nazis; it encompassed the utter destruction of a culture (and, more to the point, of the human beings, too) that had endured for countless centuries'.[33] The embassy's complaints were politely noted and, it seemed, ignored.

Whether Britain was about to betray its Hong Kong subjects to a repressive regime was hotly debated on the pages of the paper. The 1984 Sino-British Declaration established that China would leave Hong Kong's constitutional laws intact for at least fifty years after the handover in 1997. Deng Xiaoping summed up this settlement as 'one country, two systems'. Yet the pretence of mutual trust had been subsequently rocked by two events. The 1989 Tiananmen Square massacres raised the spectre that Beijing would crush dissent in Hong Kong, imprison political opponents and imperil its economy by undermining the freedoms upon which its success was built. At the time of the massacre, one million Hong Kong citizens marched through the streets of the colony to protest. Many of them had fled from Chinese Communism in the first place and were fearful for their future once the colony was reabsorbed. In turn, China had cause to accuse Britain when Chris Patten set in motion plans to give the colony a fully elected legislature (it had been partly elected since 1991) and a Bill of Rights. Such reforms, coming so late in Britain's ownership of the colony, naturally infuriated Beijing which proceeded to denounce Patten as a 'strutting prostitute', a 'criminal of a thousand antiquities' and a 'tango dancer'. Nonetheless, the reforms had the strong endorsement of The Times, not only from its man on the spot, who knew Patten very well and got stories directly from him, but also at Wapping where the editor and the chief leader writer, Rosemary Righter, were keen to hold Beijing to account.

On 18 September 1995, Hong Kong's first wholly elected Legislative Council ushered in a pro-democracy majority that put the colony on a likely collision course with her future overlords. The Beijing-backed and funded party won only seven of the sixty seats on the Legislative Council and Li Peng, the Chinese Prime Minister, insisted that his country would not abide by the result. Predictably, The Times's leading article stated that the vote had vindicated Patten's reforms.[34] From Beijing the talk was of reneging on the commitments in the 1984 declaration as well as replacing the elected Legislative Council with an appointed body. Describing China's threats as 'arrogant', The Times backed John Major's warning that Britain would involve her allies, the UN and the International Court of Justice, if China made any attempt to revoke the institutions and safeguards guaranteed by the 1984 Agreement.[35] Incurring the strong rebuke of the Chinese Ambassador, The Times also expressed intense hostility to China's threats towards Taiwan, which in 1996 held its first democratic presidential elections (which Beijing interpreted as a step towards declaring the independence that Taiwan already effectively had in practice). Appealing to Clinton not to waver in the United States' defence of Taiwanese integrity, the leading column made clear that 'China is the provoker. The greatest risk lies in turning a blind eye.'[36]

In 1973, The Times had sponsored a politically ground-breaking exhibition of Chinese treasures at the Royal Academy. In September 1996 it did so again, by sponsoring The Mysteries of China at the British Museum. Featured were exhibits unearthed in recent archaeological discoveries from the Neolithic era of 4500 BC to the end of the Han dynasty in the third century AD. As part of the cultural exchange surrounding the Mysteries sponsorship, four board members of the People's Daily were flown over at company expense. They were entertained at a Times reception at which

John Major made a fleeting visit. After dinner, they were given a parting gift of that evening's *Times*. It was, perhaps, an unfortunate present. On its inside pages were two stories about China, one by Bronwen Maddox headed 'Clinton gambles on Far Eastern trade taming the tyranny of Peking' and a second, by Mirsky, entitled 'President warns China against bullying'.[37]

Although he had officially retired in 1990 and had been in uncertain health thereafter, the death in February 1997 of China's 'Paramount Leader', Deng Xiaoping, was recognized as having far more than merely symbolic significance. A survivor of the Long March generation who had finally become unchallenged leader in 1978, Deng had straddled the contradictions of encouraging the private sector while retaining the iron commitment to one-party rule that guided the Tiananmen crackdown. *The Times* tried to do justice to both sides of his legacy. While there were doubts about which successors would establish themselves, the obituary hailed Deng as the saviour of the Communist Party and progenitor 'over the most ambitious and successful market and free enterprise reforms ever undertaken by a socialist country' which ensured 'that millions of Chinese reaped tangible benefits'. Mirsky provided a lengthy assessment too, suggesting that Deng was not interested in ideas, and 'probably went to his grave thinking that technology was the secret of Western power, a blindspot in the leader of a country which professed to be ideologically driven'. He was, Mirsky concluded, 'like a Mafia capo di tutti capi, boss of bosses, who thought of China as Cosa Nostra, the Party's creation, and was ready to crush under a tank any young man or women with a mimeograph who thought they could transform China – as Dr Mimeograph once dreamt of doing – and did'.[38]

Three months later, Stothard flew out to Beijing accompanied by Les Hinton, News International's executive chairman, and James Pringle. There was a possibility that Stothard might be granted an interview with President Jiang Zemin. With Hong Kong's handover just over a month away, this would have been a notable scoop for *The Times*. China's leaders were not in the habit of offering impromptu interviews to foreign journalists and a request was made to see in advance what the questions would involve. Stothard submitted some proposals (the content of which had been suggested by Mirsky), adding that he wished the discussion to spread beyond them. In the event, President Jiang opted not to see *The Times* but Stothard was granted an audience with the deputy prime minister, Zhu Rongji, instead. He was duly invited into the Zhongnanhai, the enclosed complex of offices and gardens where the country's leaders worked. Zhu could not have been more welcoming, even stating that he had been a reader of *The Times* since childhood and that its editor should feel free to ask whatever he liked, being, as he was, among friends. Possibly he did not appreciate that his guest accepted this courtesy literally. When the deputy prime minister provided reassurance that Hong Kong would enjoy press freedom under China's rule, Stothard asked why, in that case, dissidents like Wei Jingsheng and Wang Dan were imprisoned. Astonished, Zhu stood up and told him that was not the sort of question friends ask one another, reminding the editor that it was supposed to be a friendly chat not an inquisition. Within minutes the audience was over.[39] Stothard had not got his interview and when he returned to Wapping few of his colleagues were even aware that he had been in China at all.

On 30 June 1997, Hong Kong was duly handed over in a ceremony attended by Blair and the Prince of Wales. Save for a few isolated possessions, the event marked the end of the British Empire and *The Times* gave it the comprehensive treatment it deserved. Mirsky was the only journalist among the small group of well-wishers allowed onto the quayside to bid Patten farewell as he boarded the Royal Yacht *Britannia* with the Prince of Wales to sail off towards the Philippines. Barely an hour later, a Boeing 747 touched down at Kai Tak airport bearing President Jiang, the first chairman of the Chinese Communist Party to touch Hong Kong soil.

As *The Times*'s leader column noted, China's future ascendancy would be dictated by how she responded to her new responsibility over the former colony.[40] Beijing did not want the liberal-minded elements in the Hong Kong success story to contaminate the Communist one-party state on the mainland. Hong Kong's elected Legislative Council was immediately replaced with an appointed one in a ceremony controversially attended by Patten's British critics, among them Sir Edward Heath and Lord (formally Sir Geoffrey) Howe. The reformers' hope was that Beijing also recognized that it could not afford to kill its golden goose; on the eve of the handover Hong Kong was handling 60 per cent of external investment in China. A political crackdown could have serious economic consequences for the precedence was clear: the Hong Kong stock market had slumped 30 per cent on the news of the Tiananmen Square massacre. Hong Kong's recession began the day after the RY *Britannia* passed beyond its harbour. Ironically, the downturn was caused not by China's assumption of authority but by the Thai baht which collapsed on 2 July, bringing in its wake an Asia-wide financial crisis. A year after reunification with China, the Hong Kong stock market had halved in value. By then, Mirsky was back in London.

Approaching retirement age and with the handover achieved, he had stepped down as South East Asia editor in November 1997. To his surprise, George Brock, *The Times*'s managing editor, asked him not to retire altogether and instead extended his contract so that he might continue to write on Chinese affairs for the paper.

Whatever awaited Hong Kong's longer term future or how serious the immediate economic recession, the former colony did not experience the sudden Tiananmen-style bloodbath that some had feared. There seemed some possibility that the principle of one country, two systems might be acknowledged. Inevitably in this state of affairs, news stories about the province became less frequent – despite Mirsky's attempts to get them in the paper – while attention switched to those parts of the world in greater crisis. Yet, for *The Times* and its Far East coverage, this was a brief lull before the storm for, early the next year, it found itself embroiled in a bitter dispute about its Chinese coverage and the behind-the-scenes dealing of its owner, Rupert Murdoch, which would do immense damage to the paper's reputation.

In a pointed leader in June 1996, *The Times* had warned that China's potential as a magnet for Western investment was making foreign leaders – in particular Helmut Kohl – wary of criticizing its record on human rights.[41] This was a brave observation given the commercial pressures on Rupert Murdoch to behave similarly. In 1993, he had bought Star television, a Hong Kong-based satellite broadcaster. The potential was enormous and with his investment in Sky starting to pay off in Britain, he announced that satellite television would prove 'an unambiguous threat to totalitarian regimes'. Beijing promptly banned all private ownership of satellite dishes. This concentrated Murdoch's mind. Shortly after the deal for Star TV went through, he sold Hong Kong's leading English language newspaper, the *South China Morning Post*, to a Chinese-Malaysian tycoon. The paper, reputedly the most profitable in the world, was an influential voice in the region – Murdoch, indeed, had described it as '*The Times* of Southeast Asia'.[42] The sale was not without financial logic. News Corp. had bought it in 1987 for HK\$ 2.4 billion and sold it six years later for HK\$ 6 billion. The paper's sale recouped two-thirds of the cost of buying Star, whose prospects would bloom if Beijing removed the obstacles to its expansion. It was widely assumed that jettisoning the *South China Morning Post* with its independent editorial line was one way in which Murdoch might bring about a more accommodating attitude from Beijing. This, at any rate, appeared to be his motivation when in 1994 he dropped BBC World Service

TV from the Star TV satellite that was received into thirty-eight Asian countries. The decision to drop the BBC, which scandalized almost every section of the British media, went unrecorded in *The Times*.

This was not the only shortcoming in the paper's reporting. Harper-Collins, the publishing house owned by News Corp., had commissioned Chris Patten to write *East and West*, an account of his governorship. It was due to be published in September 1998, but in July the previous year Murdoch had told HarperCollins executives that he thought it would be better if they paid Patten back his advance and suggested he took his book to another publisher. Murdoch was no fan of Patten's politics and was anxious that the book's publication would be interpreted as a declaration of hostility by the Chinese government. It was not a courageous position to adopt. The manner in which executives at HarperCollins implemented it made it look exceptionally inept. In February 1998 they dropped *East and West* with the phoney claim that it was too boring to be published. This flatly contradicted the opinion of the book's editor, Stuart Proffitt, who resigned and subsequently won compensation for constructive dismissal. All too predictably, the person least harmed by the fallout was Patten himself. HarperCollins had to pay him substantial damages and his book was published by Macmillan instead. For Murdoch, the financial penalty was paltry compared to the scale of the public relations disaster. Patten's successful claim for damages dominated the news in the broadsheets. Beyond Wapping, Fleet Street was cock-a-hoop. 'Murdoch is forced to apologise' ran the *Telegraph*'s front-page headline with ill concealed glee. The *Telegraph*'s leading article overreached itself, accusing Murdoch of being 'the biggest gangster of them all'. Nobody would have expected *The Times* to lead the denunciation, but its attempt to ignore the issue was a serious editorial misjudgment. Tardily, it reported the news on 28 February in an article that focused on News Corp.'s side of events. In consequence, it had opened itself up to allegations of self-censorship. These were not slow to materialize. The paper had never bid for the serial rights to *East and West*. This was a perfectly understandable decision that some now chose to construe as being done in deference to Murdoch. Stothard immediately rebutted the suggestion as 'outrageous and absolutely not true'[43] but rival newspapers, under pressure from *The Times*'s cut in price, knew they had found a weapon with which to fight back. The issue threatened to seriously tarnish the paper's principal asset – its credibility.

Stothard responded to criticisms over *The Times*'s inadequate coverage by admitting that he had misjudged the Patten book's importance and in particular the level of attention competitors would give it. But he refuted any suggestion that he was acting on the proprietor's orders – the subject, he said, had not even been touched upon in the telephone conversation he had had with Murdoch earlier in the week. Furthermore, he attempted to explain that because those tipping off the press had gone first with their stories to rival newspapers, *The Times*'s coverage had been less complete and had constantly struggled to catch up. He admitted, though, that of the many 'difficult calls' he had to make as editor, he had not called this one correctly.[44] Indeed, he had not. On 6 March, *The Times*'s media editor, Raymond Snoddy, wrote an article that confronted the problem. 'No national newspaper in the UK covers its own affairs really well,' he admitted. *Guardian* readers received little information about the manner of their paper's purchase and financing of the *Observer* while the *Independent* was coy about its own attempts to squeeze out of business the Sunday competition. 'Why, even *The Times* has been known, occasionally, to appear to avert its gaze when some activity of Mr Murdoch is being criticised by ill informed souls,' wrote Snoddy with just a hint of whimsy before going on to suggest that the *FT* (his former employer) had the best record of independent judgment from the interests of its owners.[45] This certainly was objective journalism.

Nonetheless, with a price war in full cry, the *Daily Telegraph* had no intention of letting the matter pass. Under intense pressure from *The Times*'s fast-increasing sales, it began to run derogatory references to its rival and its owner as a matter of course. This quickly descended into crassness. A surprisingly lengthy report in the *Telegraph*'s news pages about Murdoch's purchase of an American baseball team even suggested he might 'vulgarise' the Los Angeles Dodgers in the same way that he had *The Times*. A war of letters broke out between Stothard and the *Telegraph*'s editor, Charles Moore, after the latter took umbrage about an article by Brian MacArthur that pointed out the extent of the *Telegraph*'s gratuitous digs at its commercial rival.[46] The *Telegraph*, however, had another trump card to play – a disgruntled *Times* employee.

On 20 January 1998, Jonathan Mirsky had attended a round circle meeting of the Freedom Forum in London, an intimate gathering assembled for the benefit of a visiting group of young Chinese journalists. Told it was off the record, several of the British journalists there felt sufficiently relaxed to start bemoaning aspects of their own newspapers' East Asian coverage. Emboldened, Mirsky duly joined in, giving vent to his frustrations that so much of his filed copy had never made it into *The Times*. Unfortunately for Mirsky, the supposedly off-the-record meeting was duly reported on the Freedom Forum's website. What was worse, the website report left off the other journalists' gripes about their employers except for what Mirsky had said about *The Times* – which was published in detail. He was accurately quoted as attributing his spiked copy to 'the general junkification of the paper' but also to his belief that it was done to protect the proprietor's Far Eastern business empire. '*The Times* has finally decided, because of Murdoch's interests, not to cover China in a serious way,' Mirsky suggested. When a member of the audience questioned whether he was endangering his job with such criticisms, Mirsky waved the concern aside with the reply, 'I'm too old and too famous for them to do something really terrible to me.'[47] This was rather naive.

For a while nothing happened. The website of the Freedom Forum was not a major Fleet Street news source. All this changed on the morning of 4 March 1998, when Mirsky got out of bed and went to his front door to pick up the newspapers. Across the front page of the *Daily Telegraph* ran the headline '*Times* man hits at censor Murdoch'. Hot on the heels of HarperCollins's dropping of the Patten book, Mirsky's quotes provided a great story for the press. The *Telegraph* devoted its lead editorial column to condemning *The Times* over what it decided was its failure to report the Patten fiasco fully and the allegations levelled by Mirsky. That the paper had been outspoken in its support for the Patten reforms was not mentioned. The *Telegraph*'s leading article ended with words that went beyond the usual badinage traded by rival papers: 'Such suppression is not "a pretty minor story", and anyone who thinks it is is well suited to work for Mr Murdoch, but not for a proper newspaper.'[48]

Mirsky had landed himself and his newspaper in a mess. He could not deny he had made his comments, or even that they had been misinterpreted. What he had said was accurately reported. He thus had to substantiate his claims. This he proceeded to do. *The Times*, he noted, had not interviewed the Chinese dissident Wei Jingsheng when he visited London despite the fact that other broadsheets had done so. He also highlighted Stothard's kowtowing to Beijing's demand to know what questions he proposed asking President Jiang Zemin before an interview was granted, an action that had, in Mirsky's inelegant expression, 'lowered ourselves into our own toilet'.

Whatever the aversion to stoking an unseemly public squabble, Stothard had no option but to issue an immediate statement contradicting Mirsky's allegations. 'I have never taken an editorial decision to suit Mr Murdoch's interests' the editor declared, 'nor have I ever been asked to.' Spectators of the feud had to decide whether they trusted the editor's word on this, given that he was hardly likely to announce he was the proprietor's lackey, or the opinion of his China specialist who, having been several thousand miles away at the time, was not necessarily well placed to comment on office politics back home. Where Stothard was successful was in demonstrating where Mirsky lacked precision in his statement of the facts. His claim that *The Times* was downplaying stories about China and Hong Kong could hardly be made to fit the statistics. During 1997, the paper had run 218 articles on China (a figure that was comparable with the number published in the *Telegraph*). Of the 218 articles, Mirsky had written 124 and James Pringle, in Beijing, 94. Furthermore, *The Times* had run six leading articles on China or Hong Kong since May and not, as Mirsky asserted, none. There had also been no shortage of columnists on the Op-Ed page, most noticeably Bernard Levin, who had been unstintingly critical of the Beijing regime. Mirsky cited two occasions when he believed Stothard had personally spiked his articles shortly before he was due to meet Chinese officials in London.[49] Yet, in the context of the great volume of copy filed, this hardly suggested a concerted attempt from on high to silence the South East Asia editor.

Where Mirsky was correct was in his observation that the paper's coverage of Hong Kong's politics had fallen off since the handover of the colony. To this there was an obvious explanation – it was no longer such a major news story. Mirsky, however, believed there was considerable evidence of Chinese bad faith in the months after the handover and questioned the journalistic values that decided otherwise. He was frustrated that Stothard, and Graham Paterson, failed to see the worth in the articles he was proposing. Nonetheless, he had forty-eight articles published following the handover and, as has been noted, *The Times* chose to respond to Mirsky's retirement in November 1997 not with a sigh of relief but with a fresh contract for him to continue writing on an occasional basis on Chinese affairs. Meanwhile, James Pringle was continuing to file from Beijing.

Re-examining *The Times*'s editorial stance on China for this volume, it is difficult to find evidence to support Mirsky's serious allegations although it is understandable that competitors, in particular the *Telegraph*, chose to give the claims top billing. Certainly, Mirsky had filed a considerable amount of copy that had never made its way into the paper. This was not unusual for foreign correspondents, most of whose dispatches are never found the space to be published. As Stothard, who had filed his fair share of unused copy during his stint in Washington DC, put it, most foreign correspondents 'have moments when they feel isolated from office life and see imagined reasons why their rivals' copy should be preferred to their own'.[50] Mirsky was not only tremendously knowledgeable about his subject, but he was a noted journalist who had been named International Reporter of the Year for his coverage of the Tiananmen emergency. He could be forgiven for believing his unpublished copy had been spiked in deference to Rupert Murdoch rather than to the limitations of space. When even the literary editor, Erica Wagner, started turning down his offers to review books on subjects that he was eminently suited to write about, he had reason to suspect he had been effectively blacklisted. Stothard's verdict was harsher. Most of Mirsky's unpublished copy had not been used because the foreign desk and its subeditors thought it unusable. Whether this was a judgment on Mirsky or the editorial desks at Wapping was a matter of opinion.

It was an undignified end to Mirsky's career at *The Times*. Despite the damage caused, George Brock did not want him to resign, not least because it would look as if he had been sacked. Nonetheless, go he did on 11 March, the day the paper's board of independent directors met and concluded there was no substance in his allegations. Mirsky was rightly furious that they had come to this judgment without troubling to ask for his side of events. Brock had told him that he could not simultaneously stay on the paper while using its letters' page to launch a frontal attack on its editorial integrity and so, when he was finally at liberty, the letters' page published his rebuttal of Brian MacArthur's claim that 'he could not write in a journalistic manner'.[51] He turned down a sizeable sum from the *Sunday Telegraph* to rubbish his former employers, opting instead for a better-mannered explanation in the *Spectator*. Nonetheless, for the vast majority who did not read the paper and assumed its writer on Chinese affairs was a whistle-blower, the episode did immense damage to *The Times*'s reputation as an independent organ and once again raised the spectre of supposed editorial interference from the proprietor. In fact, the paper's level of Chinese coverage owed rather more to the personal interests of its editor than the business concerns of its proprietor. *The Times* rediscovered a more consistent and critical tone towards China and the space to give it justice after 2002, when Stothard was succeeded as editor by Mirsky's Tiananmen Square Samaritan, Robert Thomson, despite there being no change in the proprietor or the extent of his Far East business interests.[52]

VII

It was not long before New Labour found its funding arrangements sub-jected to the same scrutiny that had sliced through the Tories' layer cake of sleaze. In November 1997 the Government's intention to exempt Formula One from the forthcoming ban on tobacco advertising was questioned when it emerged that Formula One's owner, Bernie Ecclestone, had given £1 million to the Labour Party. Two days before Christmas 1998, Peter Mandelson, the Trade and Industry Secretary, was forced to resign over the revelation that he had received an undeclared £373,000 home loan from Geoffrey Robinson, the Paymaster-General, whose complicated business affairs with the late Robert Maxwell were the subject of a DTI investigation. Robinson also had to resign. In 1999, Stothard was particularly outraged that the BBC governors should consider appointing Greg Dyke as the new director general of the BBC. Dyke had helped fund Blair's party leadership election campaign and, to Stothard, this fatally compromised his suitability. In this, *The Times* stood shoulder to shoulder with William Hague who made submissions against the appointment. The campaign was in vain and in June, Dyke was appointed.

The financial and personal relationships between what the press were increasingly dubbing 'Tony's Cronies' contrasted with the efforts the new Tory leadership claimed to be making to clean up the Conservatives' act. During the Major Government, the *Sunday Times* had been to the fore in criticizing the clandestine way in which the Conservative Party solicited funds from shadowy individuals, particularly foreigners. When he became Tory leader in June 1997, William Hague had made clear the party would no longer accept foreign donations. Issuing its report the following year, the Neill Committee into standards in public life grappled with the issue of what constituted an overseas donor (and decided it was someone who was ineligible to be a British-registered voter) and recommended tight rules on trusts, requiring that they be 'genuinely UK-based' to qualify as a 'permissible source'.

Legislation was proposed that would put the Neill Committee's findings on a statutory basis but doubts remained whether the Conservatives really were, as Hague suggested, complying with the spirit of the proposals. In May 1999, Tom Baldwin arrived at *The Times* as its new deputy political editor, having made a name for himself over the previous two years at the *Sunday Telegraph* were he had helped to expose Ecclestone's funding links with Labour. He had not even settled into his new berth before he was called upon to investigate a story that would pitch *The Times* and the Tories into a five-month war of words, recrimination and the prospect of a gruelling court case that threatened to bring down either Peter Stothard or William Hague.

'Massive donations make Tories "the plaything of one man"' ran *The Times* headline on 5 June 1999. In the article, Tom Baldwin reported that 'two authoritative sources' within the Conservative Party had told the paper that the party Treasurer, Michael Ashcroft, had been bankrolling the party to the tune of up to £360,000 a month. Baldwin speculated (inaccurately) that this represented an investment of about £4 million a year. It was not difficult to see why such a man would have been welcomed with open arms by Conservative Central Office. Having ploughed resources into an unwinnable 1997 general election campaign, the Tories had posted an £11 million deficit in 1998. Political disarray had lowered morale and donations had collapsed, creating a yawning chasm. The party certainly needed the largesse of generous friends like Michael Ashcroft to help fill it. However, Baldwin's article suggested that this level of reliance upon one man was not only unhealthy but also stood to get worse. An unnamed official was cited as complaining that the party Treasurer's 'abrasive style and controversial reputation within the City' was a reason for the reticence of other donors to come forward. 'For every penny we don't receive,' the official was quoted as saying, 'he becomes even more powerful. We cannot let the party become the plaything of just one man.'[53] The implication was clear: the once mighty Conservative Party had been sold at a rock bottom price to a person with a controversial business history who was known in the City as the 'piranha'.

The *Sunday Times* had ranked Ashcroft Britain's fourteenth richest man. Nonetheless, he spent much of the time out of the country. He was not only a resident of Florida and Belize but was the latter's High Representative to the United Nations. Who was he and what was his motivation in bailing out the bankrupt Tories in Britain? So began a line of *Times* investigation that by its end had assumed the dimensions of a campaign or, to its critics, a witch hunt. At its heart were two questions. The first was whether Michael Ashcroft was using his role as Treasurer and principal donor to wield undue influence in the counsels of the Conservative Party. *The Times* never uncovered any evidence that this was the case. Indeed, those who worked at Conservative Central Office were certain that he did not.[54] At most, his political ambition appeared limited to the personal aspiration of a peerage.

This was hardly a scandal. There was a long tradition that major political donors ended up being ennobled sooner or later although Ashcroft's prospects did not look good – the political honours scrutiny committee had already rejected him once. The second contention was the one upon which the paper chose to focus. Ashcroft was reckoned to be a billionaire and was viewed in the City by some with circumspection. As a Belize-based tax exile he lived in a country with notorious lax rules in financial matters. Attempts to tighten Belize's rules had been thwarted by the country's ruling People's United Party which he helped fund. He enjoyed extraordinary concessions there. To Stothard, it seemed 'a little odd to us that William Hague should appoint to the Tory party Treasurership a man who not only spent most of his time abroad and paid his taxes abroad but was a fully accredited official of a left-wing government'. It was, he later reiterated, 'an absolute issue of public interest to pursue this'.[55]

Pursue it *The Times* conscientiously proceeded to do. Ashcroft's route to extraordinary personal wealth had been a rocky one. Self-made and eschewing university or the social connections of the City Establishment (in itself, perhaps a reason why he was treated with some lofty suspicion), he had accumulated his first million by the age of thirty-one. Inevitably, such a man could not fail to make enemies along the way. He had been criticized by a Department of Trade and Industry report into the Blue Arrow affair and had aroused suspicions by basing his operations like ADT and Carlisle Holdings in offshore tax havens. *The Times*'s reporter, Damian Whitworth, was dispatched to Belize to snoop around. He was staggered by the extent of the Tory Treasurer's business influence in the country and noted the general impression of the locals that he was 'the big man in town'.[56] The paper also sent Dominic Kennedy to Panama in the hope of uncovering further evidence of Ashcroft's financial interests. Important leads started to come in from other sources. *The Times* was passed copies of official Foreign Office documents. These were published over the front page on 13 July. One, dating from October 1996, had been written by Charles Drace-Francis, who was then head of the West Indian and Atlantic Department at the Foreign and Commonwealth Office. It stated that Ashcroft, 'now has about $1 billion in cash and would obviously like to have his own bank to put it in – but cannot use the Belize Bank'. A second was a telegram the following April from the British High Commissioner in Belize referring to the difficulty of knowing whether to believe the 'rumours about some of Ashcroft's business dealings'.[57]

The Times now felt it was in a position to become more aggressive in tone. 'Is it without significance that such a man would resist regulations intended to tackle crime because his own financial interests, albeit legitimate, might suffer?' the leading article posed in relation to how Belize's lax regulations made it conducive to drug- and money-laundering operations.[58] David Mackilligin, the former High Commissioner to Belize, wrote a letter to *The Times* calling on William Hague to launch his Ethics and Integrity Committee enquiry into the activities of a man who 'cannot escape responsibility for establishing a system that makes Belize a much more tempting target for drug-runners'.[59] Hague was certainly in an unenviable position. The stream of criticism against his party Treasurer appeared to link the Tories in the public mind with the sort of sleaze that the new Conservative leader had stated was in the past. Yet, the party's precarious finances would be further imperilled were he to ditch Ashcroft. Indeed, without the backing of Ashcroft's millions, there were fears that the party's line of credit would expire altogether. Hague opted to resist rather than succumb to the demands for an enquiry, choosing instead to echo Ashcroft's claim that he was the victim of a 'smear'. The Tory chairman, Michael Ancram, also went on the offensive claiming a 'political campaign' was being waged against the party and challenged the paper to divulge how many of its supposedly incriminating documents came from political appointees within the Government.[60] Ancram's anger was understandable. The other newspapers had started to follow *The Times*'s lead and, although the *Daily Telegraph* stood somewhat aloof, were generally supporting the call to probe further.

Worse was to follow. Independently of *The Times*'s probe, Toby Follett, a freelance journalist, had been working on an investigation for Channel 4. He contacted the paper suggesting they pooled their resources. He had a source in the US Drug Enforcement Administration. The first results appeared across the front page of the paper of Saturday 17 July, with the revelation that Ashcroft's name was among those that appeared in four separate reports by the US Drug Enforcement Administration into possible drug smuggling and money laundering in Belize. Readers who persevered with the article, written by Tom Baldwin and Andrew Pierce, would have noted that Ashcroft had never even been interviewed and no charges had been brought against him. But the headline and its implications raised the temperature between the warring factions. For those for whom the slightest whiff of smoke necessarily pointed to a blazing inferno, this certainly sounded suspicious. *The Times* did, however, hold the presses and print Ashcroft's furious rebuttal, 'I make this categorical statement: I have never been involved in drug trafficking or money-laundering. My business affairs are entirely proper and no amount of smear, rumour or innuendo will alter that fact.' He continued that he was adding *The Times* to his list of enemies and that having set up 'Crimestoppers' in 1987, an organization that had been responsible for 29,000 arrests, 'I clearly do not condone wrong-doing'.[61]

The Times, however, was beginning to mine a deep seam with the DEA's reports on Belize. It showed a Labour MP, Peter Bradley, its DEA copies and on 21 July he used parliamentary privilege to cite their contents on the floor of the House of Commons. *The Times* published his speech verbatim. The imputation some wanted to make from the content was clear when another Labour MP with a more outspoken record, Dennis Skinner, caused uproar in the Commons chamber by declaiming without any con-crete evidence, 'The Tory Opposition are receiving a million pounds a year from one of the biggest drug-runners in the West.'[62] That very day, Ashcroft issued a writ for libel against *The Times*, Stothard, Baldwin and Follett, accusing them of 'perhaps the most one-sided, partial and coloured account of anyone's affairs ever produced by a newspaper in a free country'. The most famous libel lawyer in the country, George Carman QC, accepted Ashcroft's brief, Geoffrey Robertson QC stood poised and ready to defend News International's corner. The legal and media worlds prepared them-selves for what was immediately billed as 'the clash of the titans' and the most expensive libel trial in history. A figure of £100 million total costs was plucked from nowhere and was soon repeated as if it was the predeter-mined fee. Yet there was hardly a need for exaggeration. Whatever the final rate, either *The Times* or the Conservative Party's Treasurer faced a massive bill and a ruined reputation.

Did *The Times* have its own agenda, as Ashcroft and Ancram alleged? Day after day, the paper was giving massive coverage to its investigation. Those who had been on the paper in 1982 might have recalled the moment when Rodney Cowton challenged the then editor Harold Evans that he appeared to be running a 'campaign'. The issue then had been lead in petrol. Seventeen years on, the attack launched by Stothard, Evans's protégé, was far more personal. The prominent role in the reporting taken by Tom Baldwin was commented upon adversely by those with partisan suspicions. Whatever his well-established talents as a news bloodhound, he was known to be unsympathetic to the Conservatives. Ben Preston, the son of the former *Guardian* editor, Peter Preston, had taken over as news editor and was also assumed to be no Tory die-hard. An official in the Foreign Office was supposed to have leaked documents to the paper. Where there political forces at work behind the scenes? And why was the paper sharing some of its documentation with the Labour Member of Parliament for The Wrekin? Whatever Baldwin's links with the Downing Street press office, the evidence that *The Times* was doing the Labour Government's bidding was, however, hard to sustain. It had just endorsed voting Tory in the European parliamentary elections and had vehemently opposed Greg Dyke, a man who helped fund Blair's leadership campaign, being appointed as the BBC's director-general.[63] Those who assumed the campaign against Ashcroft was a politically-motivated assault on the integrity of the Conservative Party might have been surprised to learn that the initial motivation appeared to come not from Wapping's New Labour admirers but from those with Tory leanings. The domestic politics leader writer, Tim Hames, and George Bridges, a young recruit to the leader team who had been a speechwriter for John Major, were among those who had mentioned the concerns they had heard about Ashcroft's role as the party's banker of first and last resort. They were reporting worries expressed to them by senior Conservative contacts, not from anyone on the left. Nor were they alone. Stothard remained on good terms with leading Conservative politicians on the modernizing wing of the party. Whether from a high-minded opposition to the party becoming 'the plaything' of a wealthy businessman or from a political desire to undermine Hague, they voiced to the editor their concerns about the Tory Treasurer. Stothard fully recognized that the campaign would damage the Tory leadership and that this might help Labour in the short term, but he believed that in opposing an overconcentration of power in one man, the paper was doing the Tories a favour in the longer term. This assumed that kicking the party when it was down was the best way to restore it to its feet.[64] Yet, aside from the journalistic urge to get to the truth, it was not hard to understand why Stothard pursued the matter. Ashcroft was not the only one over whom a cloud of suspicion hung. Ignoring the rumours, Hague was also standing by Lord Archer of Weston-super-Mare as the party's prospective candidate for the London mayoral election. 'The role of kept woman is never dignified but the Tory party is playing particularly fast and loose in its choice of sugar daddy,' added Michael Gove in his column, proceeding also to admonish the influence of Archer as another 'opportunist who gave the Tory party a whiff of the casbah'. It saddened Gove that, 'The party once ruined by Mandy Rice-Davies is now behaving like her.'[65]

Not everyone at *The Times* was happy with the manner in which the campaign was developing. Having been present when the match was lit, Tim Hames increasingly occupied himself on issues that allowed him to stand well back from the coming explosion. The deputy editor, John Bryant, had early on decided that the paper was becoming fixated with its anti-Ashcroft campaign and was losing a sense of proportion in its attempts to get him. In particular, he was uneasy about relying on Toby Follett for information. Stothard, however, would not be reined in. Any hope that the paper might call off its attack had already collapsed. Acting in a private capacity, the PR guru Lord (Tim) Bell had arranged for Stothard to meet Ashcroft over breakfast at the Savoy. The meeting had been civil, with the Tory Treasurer explaining how he was seeking to introduce financial prudence into the free-spending environment of Conservative Central Office. Yet, essentially a man with a shy manner, he did not handle his case with much subtlety. He was reluctant to give *The Times* an on-the-record interview. When the paper asked the Conservative Party questions about financing, its requests were forwarded to Ashcroft's lawyers. Not only did this appear suspiciously defensive, it tended to re-enforce the allegation that the Party was indeed his personal fiefdom.

Probing by *The Times* caused the Conservative Party further embarrassment in November when the paper revealed that the party bank account was receiving around £1 million a year in direct transfers from funds in Ashcroft's Belize Bank Trust Company. The Neill Committee had ruled that this means of payment fell into the category of a foreign donation and a draft bill was being drawn up to make it illegal. It was certainly at odds with the statement the party had made to the Neill Committee the previous year when it claimed it had not received any foreign donations since the general election. *The Times*'s revelation forced Conservative Central Office to admit it was using different guidelines to those set out by Neill. Whether the Neill Committee had grasped that the Tories were using their own different criteria when they made their original boast that they were complying with a no-foreign-donations policy was another matter.[66] What especially alarmed Michael Ancram was the question of how *The Times* had gained access to information on private Conservative Party bank account details. Claiming that it 'appeared to be the latest of a series of dirty tricks being perpetrated by those who will stop at nothing in order to keep this government in power' he asked the Metropolitan Police to investigate who had hacked into the bank accounts.[67] Stothard denied the paper had been involved in any such impropriety. This was, technically, true. To help its defence against the libel suit, it had hired private detectives to investigate Ashcroft and had not chosen to get involved in the methods by which they obtained results.

Ashcroft appeared to believe that *The Times* – lacking hard information to accuse him of being a money launderer or drugs trafficker – was instead printing titbits from Drugs Enforcement Administration files in a manner intended to create a climate of guilt by association. Rejecting Ashcroft's interpretation, *The Times*'s defence was that it was reporting facts and matters about which the public had a right to know. It was merely and quite properly drawing attention to questions that needed to be answered by a person in his position. Yet stating that he had been named in four separate DEA reports had little meaning if the references did not include specific allegations. What *The Times* did publish certainly looked like scraps: a drugs dealer, Thomas Ricke, had channelled some of his ill-gotten gains through the Belize Bank that Ashcroft controlled; Ashcroft had been seen boarding a plane that the DEA believed had been used in drugs operations (although he had innocently hired the plane from a leasing company). The question remained whether these apparent coincidences merited the extensive billing the paper was giving them. Ashcroft asked *The Times* to print the DEA files unedited and in full. *The Times* failed to do so.[68]

Whatever the eventual verdict, a court case was going to be cripplingly expensive. The risk of defeat for *The Times* was a terrifying prospect while Ashcroft could only win after a lengthy period in which every aspect of his business empire – no matter how innocent – would come under detailed scrutiny. It was not as if winning hundreds of thousands of pounds in damages – which he described as 'petty cash' – was vital to him. He was, after all, a billionaire. What was important for both his business and personal interests was for his name to be cleared of the serious imputations contained by *The Times*'s leaking of DEA files. The allegations were, it seems, putting business pressure on him from banks reluctant to roll over loans until his name had been cleared. There were other pressures on him, including his desire for a peerage, which demanded a compromise solution rather than risk more in the public glare of the High Court. Hague's loyalty towards him was steadfast – or, as *The Times* saw it, unquestioning. As Ashcroft later confirmed, Hague 'made clear a newspaper was not going to hound me out. He never put pressure on me.'[69] Yet it was certainly not in the Conservative Party's interest for courtroom claims and counterclaims to keep the story in the news, stretching (with George Carman's temporary indisposition) towards the next general election. The party already had enough bad courtroom publicity to contend with from Jonathan Aitken,

Neil Hamilton and Lord Archer of Weston-super-Mare. Allegations of sleaze had contributed to one general election humiliation and Hague did not wish a second election campaign to be similarly derailed. Murdoch too had no more desire than anyone else to fight a long war of attrition that risked the reputation of his flagship newspaper when a propitious and satisfactory truce could save all the combatants a great deal of hardship. One possibility was to get the respective legal teams to thrash out a compromise. A cheaper and perhaps less protracted alternative was to find an honest broker who would bring Murdoch and Ashcroft together as two men of the world having a tycoon-to-tycoon discussion about how the unfortunate matter might be settled amicably. Jeff Randall, a former *Sunday Times* executive who was editor of the *Sunday Business*, offered himself in this role and it was he who brought Murdoch and Ashcroft together. Preliminary positions established, Murdoch referred a formula to Stothard for his comments and approval and their respective fax machines rumbled into life. Stothard was hosting a reception for *Times* colleagues at the Reform Club when a waiter arrived with a card marked 'urgent message'. It announced that a Mr Michael Ashcroft, in New York, wished to speak to him on the telephone.

Peace was declared in time for Christmas. On the paper's front page of 9 December 1999 ran a 347-word statement under the headline '*The Times* and Michael Ashcroft: Correction.' Three brief paragraphs – including the statement that 'the issues raised by *The Times* have resulted in a substantive and useful debate on foreign donations to political parties' – built up to the denouement: '*The Times* is pleased to confirm that it has no evidence that Mr Ashcroft or any of his companies have ever been suspected of money laundering or drug-related crimes.' The paper applauded the announcement that the Tory Treasurer would be reorganizing his affairs in order to return to live in Britain. Ashcroft recognized 'the public concern about foreign funding of British politics' while 'the openness and account-ability of political funding by all parties will remain a central issue for investigation and comment by *The Times*'. The notice ended, 'With this statement, *The Times* intends to draw a line under the "The Ashcroft Affair". Litigation between the parties has been settled to mutual satisfaction, with each side bearing its own costs.'[70]

'To draw a line' was an interesting phrase. As was quickly spotted, there was no word of apology or retraction. Ashcroft was dropping his litigation for damages and an order for his legal costs. The declaration that the paper had no evidence of criminality was, after all, no more than a statement of fact. It was the perceived hint of innuendo that had provoked Ashcroft into issuing a writ. Those looking for a victor were better advised to conclude that neither of the protagonists had lost. With consummate diplomacy, Jeff Randall declared it 'an honourable score draw'.[71] Surprisingly, this was not quite the end of the matter as far as *The Times* was concerned. Follow-up investigations started before the settlement in December were only finally put on hold after the Tory Treasurer threatened to sue for breach of contract. In the short term, Ashcroft's reputation recovered: when news broke that he had settled with *The Times*, shares in his public company Carlisle Holdings leapt, making him £36 million richer than he had been the day before. In the longer term, he made other gains. In March 2000, he was finally cleared for a peerage after agreeing to move to Britain and renounce his post as Belizean ambassador to the UN. In October he took his seat in the House of Lords as Lord Ashcroft of Belize. Three years later he gained access under the Data Protection Act to fifty-six files held by the Foreign and Commonwealth Office and the Department for International Development which included derogatory and unfounded comments. The departments issued a formal apology and agreed to pay considerable costs.[72] Others fared less well. Following an enquiry, Drace-Francis departed from the Foreign Office and subsequently got a job in an Edinburgh kilt shop. Jonathan Randel, a US drugs agency analyst working in Atlanta, was charged with selling classified documents to Toby Follett (who then passed them to *The Times*; the paper admitted paying Randel's expenses) and in 2003 was sentenced in an Atlanta court to a year in jail.[73]

How the reputation of *The Times* emerged from the imbroglio was hotly debated. In the sense that it had never directly alleged anything that it had to retract, its investigation could not be faulted. It had shone a light on an important and – until that moment – underanalysed figure in British politics, asking valid questions about the manner in which he related his Conservative Party role with his financial arrangements and commitments to another government. The investigation had commenced with genuinely proper motives. The speed with which it uncovered information of an interesting and at times headline-grabbing nature (especially in regard to the DEA references) had, however, encouraged what, from a more objective standpoint, appeared to be a less than appropriate tone. Indeed, the coverage developed a hectoring tendency that gave the impression the hunt was being pursued with a sense of gleeful expectation. Articles by Tory-minded journalists and by the editor himself explaining that the motives were high-minded and not politically partisan were lost amid this raucous tenor. *The Times* had published eighty-one articles relating to the Ashcroft affair in the forty-seven days between the paper making its first foray and its report that Ashcroft was suing for libel. By the time a legal settlement had been reached in December, the tally had almost reached 170. More than thirty of these articles had been splashed across the front page. This was a lot of coverage for a man who had not been charged with any crime and, but for the paper's campaign, was not a publicly well-known figure.

Critics felt that the sheer ferocity with which Ashcroft was pursued smacked of the worst excesses of 'attack journalism'. They believed the patient sniffing of the bloodhound had given way to the snarling aggression of the Rottweiler. There were a small number of examples in the paper's history where it had adopted this approach with the intention of exposing wrongdoing, but, generally speaking, the Ashcroft affair was a noticeable departure from the paper's tradition. Once the paper was under threat of a potentially crippling legal writ, the determination to look under every stone overwhelmed other considerations. Information had been shared between Tom Baldwin and Government and parliamentary sources in a manner that made The Times look as if it was in cahoots with a Labour conspiracy against the Tory Treasurer. A major problem was that The Times had less experience than some other newspapers in running this kind of personal investigation and found itself relying on private investigators and other third parties. They employed methods of gathering information that risked tarnishing – by association – the name of a reputable newspaper. It certainly was not consistent with the measured reporting of established fact associated with being the journal of record. Those who believed this tag had long prevented the paper from fulfilling its proper role to search out truth through disclosure and investigation were delighted. To them, the old reticence had merely made it the lapdog of the powerful. Stothard was named the 1999 Editor of the Year and The Times the Newspaper of the Year at the What the Papers Say awards. It was a high note upon which to end the century. Applauding its 'world-class credentials', the judges commended it for getting 'a taste for setting the news agenda'. The Ashcroft saga was part of this, the citation stating admiringly: 'having got the story, The Times just wouldn't shut up. Even when Ashcroft issued a writ for libel, the paper and its editor carried on.' The result had been to give the Conservative Party 'a bloody nose'.[74] Trying to affect an air of congratulation was the award's presenter, William Hague.

VIII

Stothard had certainly shown the courage of his reporters' convictions in pursuing the Ashcroft story in the face of the threat of legal action that, had Ashcroft won, could have cost News International (or, rather, its insurers) tens of millions of pounds in damages and costs. Such a result would have ensured not only the abrupt termination of Stothard's editorship but, more importantly, it would have inflicted a wound to his paper's integrity (and its parent company's interest in continuing to bail it out) from which it would have difficulty recovering. That he remained the undaunted journalist in pursuit of the story despite these pressures was a testament to his extraordinary audacity and tenacity. Had *The Times* lost in the High Court, this courage would have been decried as criminal recklessness with the fate of a great and famous newspaper.

Instead, *The Times* faced the new century with confidence, producing an outstanding edition for the millennium complete with a section in which the paper's senior writers cast their eyes over the circuitous march of civilization, the point reached, and, more speculatively, the path ahead. It was the Whig interpretation of history writ large. It was also an exceptionally impressive product.

Stothard returned to his office in January 2000 with every reason to feel confident. Those outside the inner circle wondered how much longer he would last in the chair. Murdoch's previous *Times* editors had lasted one year, three years, five years and two years respectively. Stothard was now in his eighth year. The impression that the deal to end the Ashcroft affair had been done by the trio of Murdoch, Jeff Randall and the Tory Treasurer without final reference to the *Times*'s editor led rival newspapers to assume there had been a proprietorial withdrawal of confidence. Nothing could have been further from the truth, as Murdoch assured him. It was on the assumption that he had a lengthy future ahead, rather than through any intimations of mortality, that he reshuffled his inner cabinet. The great casualty was the deputy editor, John Bryant. A man of wide-ranging interests and great professional competence, Bryant's heart had not been in the Ashcroft affair and this may have rankled with Stothard. It was an abrupt end to ten years of stalwart service. Stothard, however, felt that it was time for a change. Like Rees-Mogg before him, he was not the sort of editor who believed it necessary to hover around the backbench until midnight. Instead, he had been content to concentrate on the argumentative rather than strictly factual parts of the paper and to leave the office shortly after, or even before, the first edition had gone to press. Thus, much of the task of organizing and bringing out the news pages of the paper had been in the hands of David Ruddock and John Bryant who worked late into the night. The recent departure of Ruddock had prompted Stothard to express the desire to 'take back control' of the paper and his decision to sack Bryant can best be understood as part of this process. The young, calm and collected home news editor, Ben Preston, ascended into Bryant's vacated position. In Preston's place, Michael Gove, now thirty, became home news editor and Graham Paterson stepped into Gove's shoes to run Op-Ed. Invariably there was gossip that Stothard was attempting to set up the succession with either Gove or Preston emerging to take the crown according to how they performed with their new responsibilities. Both were still extraordinarily young to be in such positions of seniority. That Preston, aged only thirty-six, was to be deputy editor after only seven years with the paper (initially as an education reporter) was a clear sign of favour. Others read the reshuffle differently and believed Stothard was giving Gove – a strategist at home in the officers' mess environment of the leader writers and columnists – the opportunity to earn his campaign medals commanding the infantry battalions of the news room.

These ruminations gathered momentum when, in March 2000, Stothard suddenly announced he was 'taking time off to work on special projects'. It was suggested that he was going to look into internet operations. There was immediate speculation that this was one of Murdoch's euphemisms for giving him the sack. Those who had been around in 1990 remembered when Charlie Wilson had been put in charge of East European acquisitions. An almost audible whoop of delight could be heard from Conservative Central Office whose denizens assumed they had claimed his scalp and that the final score in the Ashcroft affair was that Ashcroft remained as Treasurer and Stothard was sacked as editor. BBC Radio 4's *Today* programme reported this claim as if it was established fact. Rival newspapers assessed the runners and riders for his job. The speed with which speculation was reported as fact ably demonstrated the unprofessional shortcomings of too much modern opinion-driven journalism.[75] It did, however, force to the surface the truth. Having hoped to keep the matter to the privacy of his immediate family since being diagnosed in February, a reluctant Stothard was forced to stand on a chair in the newsroom and tell his stunned colleagues the truth. He had to undergo chemotherapy for a neuroendocrine tumour of the pancreas. He would be back.[76]

To his dejected staff Stothard offered a cheerful prognosis of his recovery prospects but the truth was that he was stepping into lightly chartered medical territory. The form of cancer was a rare one and opinion was divided on the treatment. Some specialists even counselled against chemotherapy in favour of a policy of wait and see. Stothard opted to risk a more proactive line of assault on the tumour. There was no certainty that he would recover. He was, at forty-nine, one year older than Charles Douglas-Home had been when a tumour claimed him. It was in such a situation that the editor of *The Times* could take comfort in the attitude of the proprietor. As Douglas-Home's family could attest, Murdoch's fidelity was at its most steadfast when assisting highly regarded colleague in such circumstances. Stothard also received the unwavering support of Les Hinton, News International's executive chairman. The longer he was away from Wapping, the more important this was since it dampened down unhelpful and destabilizing speculation.

There was no favourable moment to be confronted by a potentially fatal tumour but the timing was particularly unfortunate given that Stothard had just embarked upon new ventures that needed paternal guidance. One was the launch on 13 March 2000 of *Times2* (subsequently shortened to *T2*) a tabloid-sized features section modelled on the highly successful *G2* section of the *Guardian*. Attempts to learn lessons from the *Daily Mail's* appeal to women readers by improving the quality of features had met with mixed results. Christina Appleyard and Sandra Parsons had been hired from the *Mail* to improve *The Times's* offering. Having learned her craft in the *Mail's* abrasive environment, Appleyard's style caused friction with her new colleagues and she departed amid some acrimony. Sandra Parsons, however, proved a popular and accomplished recruit whose infectious enthusiasm and natural talents were soon evident in the marked improvement in the features pages. Stothard believed that she needed a less cramped canvas to display her work. He envisaged a section that would become a new focal point for women readers (as the sports section was for men) while also providing the space for lengthier and more substantial essays and reportage – the sort of journalism that had a structured beginning, middle and an end – for which the news pages had never provided a sympathetic neighbourhood. This was a major and expensive innovation (it assumed yet greater significance when, four years later, the whole paper went tabloid) that involved new deadlines and printing arrangements. Unfortunately, it commanded little support from management. Not only did its launch coincide with a downturn in the advertising market, but the advertising department chose to concentrate its sales efforts elsewhere. In its first months and with Stothard *hors de combat*, *Times2* struggled to assert its identity, unsure whether it was the depository of weighty storytelling or a conveyor belt for lifestyle features. Such indecision hampered attempts to hook a core readership. Preston did his best to support it, but the enormous range of responsibilities suddenly foisted upon him meant he could not devote as much energy to it as it needed. In this respect, Stothard's absence in its crucial first months undoubtedly contributed to its unsettled infancy by denying Sandra Parsons the well-placed advocate she needed at a time when the new section faced indifference from many news-focused journalists and a management busy battening down the hatches as the advertising recession began to hit. This was the economic force that also meant that the old business and sport second section had to be integrated back into a single main broadsheet section. This was not a satisfactory solution, as the mounting number of letters from businessmen made all too clear.

These were new and serious structural problems that would have taxed even an editor of Stothard's experience. Instead they fell to the acting editor, Ben Preston. Preston had only been deputy editor for a fortnight when Stothard had started disappearing for long and unexplained periods. No less alarmingly, Preston had barely enjoyed his new elevation for six weeks before he found himself running the paper outright. The role of acting editor would have been difficult even for a man with decades of executive-level familiarity. It involved all the responsibilities of the editor's job while denying the opportunity to make major long-term strategic decisions. Murdoch certainly saw no reason to distract the new man at the helm. Indeed, Preston was several months into his period in charge before the occasion of the annual News International budget discussions provided him with an opportunity to discuss developments with the proprietor face to face. At any rate, his primary task was thus not to take the paper down new and exciting avenues or to recreate it according to his own perceptions so much as to keep it on an even keel until such time as Stothard might return. In the circumstances, he performed his task with remarkable assurance. The two men were different in so far as Preston's chief focus was the news pages while Stothard's great loves were books, leaders and comment. Yet, had they not been told, few readers in the twelve months between March 2000 and 2001 would have had any reason to suspect their paper's fortunes was being directed not by its official editor but by a young deputy who had been thrown in at the deep end. Among his most important contributions,

Preston impressed his journalists by a calm, unflappable demeanour that was an important asset during a period of uncertainty.

While Stothard had drawn a line under the Ashcroft affair, Preston presided over a period in which the Conservative Party battled in vain to regain the confidence of *The Times*, let alone the wider public. Hague continued to be dogged by questions over his judgment. With Lord Archer of Weston-super-Mare's disgrace following false alibi claims, there was no shortage of commentators who asserted Hague had brought the disaster upon himself. The general view was that he should never have allowed a man over whom there had long hung such a cloud of suspicion to stand as the party's London mayoral candidate. Liberal opinion was also unimpressed when, in April 2000, he responded to the jailing of Tony Martin – who had shot dead an unarmed intruder in his farmhouse – by calling for the law to be strengthened to support those defending their property. Four months later, Hague's boast in *GQ* magazine that he regularly drank fourteen pints a day as a teenager was treated with the same derision as had been meted out to an earlier trip to the funfair for which the Tory leader had donned a baseball hat with his name on it.

In July 1998, *The Times* had set out its attitude to the party in a long leading article written by Michael Gove entitled 'Mods and Rockers'. It made clear that, 'If the Tories are to win office, then liberals must first win the battle of ideas within their party. In this conflict, *The Times* is a committed supporter of those who lead the liberal charge.' A telling sign of which side MPs were on could be discerned by whether they supported an equal age of consent for homosexuals and heterosexuals, the article argued. On this, as in other areas, including the reform of the House of Lords, the party would be better engaged working to make change acceptable rather than being sidelined in pointless opposition:

> Wise Conservatives deal with the world as it is, not as it should be or once was. They respect the changing landscape and are sensitive to its contours. Having spent the Eighties telling other British institutions that they must adapt to compete the Tories must now make the same transition.[77]

The paper recognized that, however tentatively, Hague was nudging his party in a more modern direction. However, the great hope for revival was the subject of Gove's biography, Michael Portillo. Since losing his supposedly safe seat in the most celebrated moment of the 1997 general election, the flamboyant Anglo-Spaniard had undergone a period of reflection and conversion, emerging as a liberal-minded figure well suited to the image-driven priorities of the media glare. When, in September 1999, Alan Clark died, creating a vacancy in the Tory's safest and most sophisticated seat, Kensington and Chelsea, all eyes turned to Portillo. Three days later, *The Times* made an extraordinary scoop when in an interview, Ginny Dougray coaxed from him an admission that he had 'homosexual experiences' as an undergraduate at Peterhouse.[78] The next day he put himself forward for the Kensington and Chelsea constituency. This was certainly a test of the party's liberal sympathies and his subsequent election suggested the Tories might indeed be proceeding along the route that Stothard, Gove and Tim Hames hoped would ensure their recovery.

By then, the expectations invested in Portillo were all the greater because of waning confidence in Hague. The belief that the Tory leader was gradually shifting the party towards fresh and open-minded thinking had been dashed on the back of an apparent success. In June 1999 the Tories had gained the most number of seats in the European elections. It was not a portent of great things: only a third of Britons had troubled themselves to vote and those who did were assumed to be marking their dislike either as a mid-term protest vote against Blair or Brussels, or both. Nonetheless, Hague interpreted his party's relative success in the poll as a sign that, by appealing to the core vote, the Tories could at least regain some of the ground they had ceded during the Major years. He reshuffled the Shadow Cabinet towards the right, sacking Peter Lilley and bringing in Ann Widdecombe as Health spokeswoman. Widdecombe had a following among some party members although her abrasive style was hardly atuned to winning over moderate opinion. When, in October 2000, she called for on-the-spot fines for casual drug users, even her fellow Shadow Cabinet colleagues torpedoed her policy by stepping forward to confess to youthful experiments with cannabis. A strategy of enthusing party members at the expense of the uncommitted multitudes was, in any case, a sign of limited ambition. In April, *The Times* revealed that Conservative Party membership had fallen to 325,000, a figure that was the lowest since the First World War.[79]

By the time Stothard was welcomed back into the editor's chair, in March 2001, fully restored in health and vigour, the last embers of warmth for the Conservative Party appeared to have gone out from within him during his period of convalescence. Serious illness had softened his admiration for the practical and goal-getting Tory mentality. He appeared increasingly sympathetic to those who talked a more collectively minded language.

While the attack on the Government continued on the Op-Ed pages from the paper's conservative columnists, Gove, Parris and Rees-Mogg, rival newspapers regarded the treatment Downing Street received on the news pages as perhaps the most generous in Fleet Street. Alastair Campbell appeared to be more comfortable trusting Philip Webster and Tom Baldwin with exclusive information than most of their broadsheet competition. Inevitably, this caused some inter-newspaper jealousy and it was not long before Webster and Baldwin were being accused of painting Government policies in a favourable light in return for scoops. Such was the supposed favouritism that when Webster was given the scoop that the Queen would be appointing Andrew Motion as the next Poet Laureate – a leak that did not amuse Buckingham Palace – rivals wrongly assumed that he had been fed the information directly from Downing Street.[80]

There was a long tradition of Prime Ministerial press officers showing partiality towards journalists with whom a rapport had been developed while cold-shouldering those who had been marked out as hostile commentators. The Blair administration, however, was the most adept – or shameless – exponent. The belief that Webster and, in particular, Baldwin, allowed themselves to get too close to Campbell in return for disclosures was a damaging accusation refuted primarily by the Downing Street press secretary's complaints about the treatment the Government received in *The Times*'s reporting. This had started long before either Blair or Campbell had gained the keys to Downing Street. On the backbench, David Ruddock had frequently had to endure Campbell telephoning, often several nights a week, to complain about what he had just read in the first edition. Ruddock would explain that he would investigate the complaint and report back. Almost invariably, the story would prove accurate but this would not prevent a tirade of hectoring invective down the telephone line from Campbell. In the meantime, Ruddock would find PA wires being published announcing that *The Times* had withdrawn their allegations when the paper had done no such thing. 'He was such a bore and a bully,' Ruddock recalled of Campbell's nocturnal menaces, 'that I ended up refusing to speak to him.'[81] The frequency and the vitriolic manner of expression were much worse than *The Times* experienced from any previous party press office. It far exceeded the efforts even of Bernard Ingham, the unabashed press voice of Margaret Thatcher, and bore no relation whatsoever to the muted tone occasionally emitted from Major's team.

The impression that the Government was more spin than substance was fuelled when, in July 2000, *The Times* printed leaked documents between the Prime Minister and his pollster, Philip Gould. In the first extract, a memo of 29 April, Blair requested that he be 'personally associated' with 'eye-catching' initiatives to refute claims that the Government was soft on law and order and family issues. Naturally, this was given front-page treatment, the article by Andrew Pierce and Philip Webster stating that 'it conveys the impression of a worried, interventionist Prime Minister, completely consumed by the importance of improving the Government's message, and of his own image'. The day after its publication, another leaked memo was received in which Gould was quoted highlighting the extent to which 'the New Labour brand has been badly contaminated. It is the object of constant criticism, and even worse, ridicule.' This document was also sent to the *the Sun*. A third leak of Prime Ministerial correspondence was published on 27 July with a memo from Blair arguing that, having taken the political decision to join the euro, it was time to make the economic argument more forcefully if a referendum was to be won on the issue.[82] These were embarrassing disclosures that provided ammunition for Blair's opponents, within and without the Labour Party.

The contradiction at the heart of the Government's legal and constitutional reforms was that power was being transferred with one hand but clawed back by another hand. Authority was being devolved, creating new checks on Downing Street. But the latter used its control of patronage to attempt to ensure loyalty from those it was entrusting with these new powers. The hereditary peers (save for a rump temporarily reprieved) were removed from the House of Lords, but there was noticeably less haste in reforming the upper chamber to strengthen its powers. In the meantime, the number of Labour life peerages was swelled by a huge expansion in appointments of those the Government considered its supporters. Having introduced devolution to Wales, Blair responded to the disgrace of Ron Davies, the First Minister, by enforcing the appointment of one of his own loyalists, Alun Michael, despite the Welsh Labour Party's obvious preference for the more independently minded Rhodri Morgan. In a similar vein, Frank Dobson was cajoled into becoming Labour's candidate in the elections for London's new mayor, despite the support for the maverick Ken Livingstone among the party's activists. Accusations of media manipulation – or 'spin' – and 'control freakery' abounded and the Government found itself defending these aspects of its record almost as much as the policies of its legislative programme. On *The Times*'s comment pages, an inflammatory article entitled 'Third Way, or Reich?' by the academic Max Beloff attempted to draw parallels between the methods in which Hitler and Blair removed the obstacles to their absolute power through blandishments towards Establishment dupes in order to remove the constitutional checks and balances. 'Once in power, Hitler showed little interest in the details of policy – not for him files or Cabinet meetings, let alone parliamentary-style debate,' Beloff declaimed. 'A small body of acolytes acted as a buffer between Hitler and the world just as the Downing Street staff now protects Mr Blair'.[83] This was an extreme interpretation and the Prime Minister was soon to discover that his power was not so absolute. In February 2000, Alun Michael stepped down as Welsh First Minister, having lost the confidence of his party who duly turned to Rhodri Morgan. In May, Frank Dobson, Labour's shoe-in for London major, was humiliated by coming third in the election, behind the Tories' Steve Norris and the winner, Ken Livingstone, who had stood as an independent and had been expelled from the Labour Party for his temerity. The low turnouts in the Scottish, Welsh and, especially, London elections suggested devolution had yet to interest a largely apathetic electorate.

Voter disenchantment with politics at all its levels was much in evidence as the country moved into an election year. The exact timing and nature of the election campaign was complicated by a serious outbreak of foot and mouth disease in February 2001. Troops were deployed the following month to assist with the containment of the disease amid scenes of massive cattle burning and fresh apprehensions about the state of British farming. Blair's plans had to be postponed for a month, until, on 8 May, he announced the general election would be held on 7 June.

The chaotic scenes in the countryside apart, few governments could have hoped for more benign conditions with which to go to the polls. Unemployment, the scourge of the Thatcher age, had fallen below one million to its lowest level for twenty-six years. Low interest rates brought the cost of mortgage borrowing to its lowest level for forty years. The property boom, upon which so many households' long-term financial plans rested, continued unchecked. Whatever the disputes over spin, the possibility of joining the euro or the Government's legislative programme, these were the material improvements that were extending choice and opportunity to ever more people in their daily lives and aspirations. With the nation's finances, Gordon Brown exuded a reassuring air (not borne out by the Exchequer's increasing borrowing figures) of Presbyterian prudence. The opinion polls pointed to another Labour landslide.

From a news perspective, these were not the ingredients for an exciting election campaign. Indeed, there was a common perception that the contest did not begin to engage the public until John Prescott, the Deputy Prime Minister, responded to provocation by punching an aggressive demonstrator. For Matthew Parris, *The Times*'s principal campaign sketchwriter, it was the Prime Minister who had got off to a deplorable start with the manner in which he launched his bid for re-election. 'With a Cross behind him, sacred stained glass above him, the upturned faces of 500 schoolgirls in pink and blue gingham before him, and to the strains of a choir singing "I who make the skies of light/I will make the darkness bright/Here I am", Mr Blair launched his campaign at the St Saviour's & St Olave's church school in Southwark', began Parris's sketch. Entitled 'And lo came a demi-idol seeking votes', the sketch was accorded the rare honour of a front-page placing:

> . . . Wild rumours swept the audience that Phoenix the calf was coming on with Blair. Then, to girlish screams normally reserved for adolescent pop idols, Tony Blair strode calfless on to the chapel stage, positioned himself between the Cross and the cameras and beneath the motto 'Heirs of the past, makers of the future', flung off his jacket to further screams, and sat down in shirtsleeves, legs apart, arms spread like a sumo-wrestler. A girls' choir sang 'We are the children of the future', which was not the case . . .
>
> > 'A time to love, a time to share,
> > A time to show how much we care',
>
> sang the girls. Alastair Campbell clapped caringly.
>
> Of Mr Blair's speech, the less said the better. We are not used to seeing a Prime Minister, with a Cross behind him, to an audience of children in their own school chapel, attacking the Opposition. 'What did you think of that?' my *Daily Mail* colleague said to a small black girl after the speech. 'Pack o' lies,' said the perceptive child.
>
> . . . Beside me, and before the closing hymn – yes, hymn – Alastair Campbell sneezed. I tried to say 'Bless you.' The words stuck in my throat.[84]

To Parris's thinking, the first Blair administration, with the attempt at leader idolatry and the media manipulation that the Prime Minister tolerated from his closest servants, had debased the political currency. The result was an electorate disengaged and cynical towards those in public office. There was no sign that the Conservative opposition were any more capable of commanding respect. Hague's perceived lurch to the right during the week of campaigning and his insistence that voting Tory was the only way to save the pound failed to move the terms of the debate in his direction.

Although *The Times* had attempted to portray the euro as the great issue at the previous election, there was little prospect of it endorsing Hague's Conservative Party in 2001. Stothard had, by his own estimation, now been disappointed by a ninth consecutive year of Tory leadership. The liberal conscience of the paper was in the keeping of the chief domestic politics leader writer, Tim Hames, whose light blue empathies had also been bleached by the experience of recent years. He drafted for Stothard *The Times*'s leading article announcing the paper's endorsement. It stretched the length of the leader page and was published two days before election day. It was entitled, simply, 'In Our Time'. Unlike in 1997, there would be no equivocation as to which party to endorse. There was little danger of the country being bounced into joining the euro, it argued, so there was no longer any need to make this the criterion (as Hague sought to do) for casting a vote. Rather, 'the task for those who toil in politics today is largely that of consolidating the core aspects of Thatcherism and extending them to fresh areas of policy'. Labour had yet to flesh out convincing policies on health, but in only four years it had ensured that 'the central tenets of the economic settlement of the 1980s – a fierce resistance to inflation, a recognition that taxation at a certain level inflicts more harm than good and a distrust of trade union power' were better entrenched than they had been four years ago. Making the Bank of England independent had 'laid down roots of iron'. For all the incomplete thinking, Blair was 'likely to blend Thatcherite means with social democratic ends in a manner that will benefit public services'. *The Times* had never ventured to say so before and thus had no precedent to fall back on as it prepared for the inevitable peroration. Thus, it ended by observing that Enoch Powell, William Gladstone, Joseph Chamberlain and Winston Churchill 'all transferred in or out of the Conservative Party in their time. In our time, in this election, it is Labour which deserves the votes of reformers.'[85]

Four and a half years after Mary Ann Sieghart had stood in the Reform Club and asked her colleagues the question 'if not now, then when?' the paper had finally found the strength to say – with some internal dissenters – that the time had indeed come. Even then, the logic was somewhat different: that Blair would complete the Thatcher revolution more convincingly than a fractured and unconvincing Conservative Party. For this analysis, Stothard received a few letters of congratulation and, inevitably, a far heavier postbag from the disgusted and disappointed. Some came in the form of well-argued criticisms of his logic, many stated that they had no wish to subscribe any more to a newspaper that had deserted the Tories, sometimes adding, disingenuously, that the paper had lost its independent voice. One reader, whose letter was published, made clear that he had never voted Conservative in his fifty-three-year life but such was his objection to 'The Thunderer' telling him who to vote for that he would vote Tory as a mark of protest. He thought there were many other readers who would do likewise.[86]

Two days later, it transpired there were not. The election day *Times* carried a MORI poll that pointed to another massive Labour victory, with 45 per cent of the vote, as opposed to 30 per cent for the Tories and 18 per cent for the Liberal Democrats. Health and education were cited as the two most important issues; Europe came tenth equal. 'Blair heads for second landslide' ran the non-risky headline.[87] *The Times* was busy throughout the night as the results came in and the final edition carried an impressive listing of the declarations (the complete results appeared in a twenty-two-page election supplement on Saturday). The vote, when it was finally tallied, showed 42 per cent for Labour, 33 per cent for the Tories and 19 per cent for the Liberal Democrats which, in parliamentary seats, translated into 413, 166 and 52 respectively. Blair had a majority of 167. Four years in which to rebuild after the collapse of 1997 had resulted in the Tories recording a net gain of one seat. Hague immediately accepted his share of responsibility and stepped down. The Peter Brookes cartoon that morning told a different story, one that was more in keeping with the leading column's line of thinking. The ghostly apparition of a bouffant-haired lady with a handbag was stepping into Number Ten. The caption read simply 'Back Again'.[88]

Blair returned to work with a mandate marred only by a turnout that, at below 60 per cent, was the lowest since 1918. Re-engaging the public to the purposes of politics would be one of his greatest tasks. After nine years in which *The Times* had been largely at odds with the government of the day, it had reverted to type and become, once again, the paper most clearly identified with the ruling Establishment. Nonetheless, the roots of the attachment were shallow. The paper appeared to be endorsing Blair personally and the small coterie upon whom he relied. Empathy for the rest of his party was less clearly apparent. There could be no clearer sign of how presidential British politics had become. For their part, the Conservatives remained fractious and ineffective. With Hague stepping down, Portillo, the modernizers' hope, did not even make the final ballot. Instead, Ken Clarke made a last stand to move his party back towards the pro-European tenets to which Sir Edward Heath had once committed it. On 13 September 2001, he was comprehensively defeated by Iain Duncan Smith, an MP with no Cabinet experience who nonetheless had the benefit, in the party member's opinion, of opposing the euro. His victory was not the main news event that day. Like all politics around the world in the months and years that followed, it was overshadowed by terrible events that had taken place in Washington DC and New York two days previously, on 11 September 2001.

CHAPTER THIRTEEN

WAR IN PEACETIME

The Peace Process in the Middle East and Ireland;
Intervention or Isolation?: Bosnia, Somalia, Rwanda, Kosovo, Chechnya;
the New World Order Versus the Rise of Fundamentalism; 9/11;
the War on Terror; Stothard Steps Down

I

'Hallelujah! We study war no more because war is no more,' the President of Harvard University declared, when the appointment of a professor of security studies was vetoed.[1] It was a precipitous hope, as the world looked forward to embarking upon the last decade of the twentieth century, that the Cold War's end made such scholarship redundant. In July 1990, NATO's London Declaration announced the conflict was over and four months later, the Conference on Security and Cooperation in Europe* convened in Paris and agreed a non-aggression treaty between its thirty-four national signatories together with a commitment to cut conventional forces in Europe by nearly a third – the most detailed arms control agreement ever negotiated.

What was true was that the thaw between the East and the West prompted much talk of new, and generally more hopeful, paradigms in international affairs. Francis Fukuyama argued that the age of ideological conflict was receding and a new post-historical world emerging where liberal democracies would speak peace unto liberal democracies and problems and crises would be subject to technical and managerial tinkering rather than the assertion of clashing dogmas. Extrapolating recent events certainly pointed in this direction. The shift towards democratic forms of government was not confined to Eastern Europe's seismic convulsion in

---

* Later renamed the Organization for Security and Cooperation in Europe (OSCE).

1989 and 1990. Around the globe, more than thirty countries had swapped authoritarianism for democracy in the twenty years up to the fall of the Berlin Wall. The crumbling of the ideological divide aroused expectations that the Security Council of the United Nations could be freed from the prospect of one or more of its permanent members instinctively vetoing affirmative action. More than forty years after it had emerged from the rubble of the Second World War as the forum for a new international comity, the UN, at last, had an opportunity to become the agent of world peacemaking. The sanction it gave in 1990 to the liberation of Kuwait would have been unthinkable during the previous decade. What was more, the success of the operation with so little loss of life to the US-led coalition forces – in marked contrast to what the doomsayers had prophesied – encouraged those who believed that peacemaking could be an attainable and relatively cheap forward policy if the world's great nations were persuaded to cooperate rather than actively hinder it. President George Bush spoke optimistically of a 'new world order' while his Secretary of State, James Baker, announced 'our new mission to be the promotion and consolidation of democracy'.[2]

South Africa offered hope. After more than four decades of especially repressive white minority rule, apartheid was dismantled with as little state-sanctioned bloodshed as had accompanied the withering of European Communism. Commentators who anticipated an immediate and vicious backlash from the incoming African National Congress were confounded by the dignified tone of Nelson Mandela. Inaugurated President on 10 May 1994, Mandela promised that his beautiful country would never again become 'the skunk of the world'. Despite spending twenty-seven years in detention, he recognized that the republic's many problems would not be solved by the expulsion or degradation of its white and business-orientated community. As The Times's Southern Africa correspondent, Michael Hamlyn, noted, Mandela felt unable even to acknowledge his wife, Winnie, sitting next to him on the rostrum at the inauguration ceremony to which he had, nonetheless, sent a VIP ticket to James Gregory, his white former jailer on Robben Island.[3] The scars of South Africa could not be healed by the sentiments of redemption alone but, whatever its shortcomings, the Truth and Reconciliation Commission made a better job of burying enmities without developing historical amnesia than many other countries were able to achieve in the years following the toppling of old regimes.

Nowhere was the search for peace more urgent that in the Middle East. The Intifada had begun in late 1987 in the Gaza Strip and spread throughout the Occupied Territories. Between 1987 and 1994, 192 Israelis had been killed by Palestinians, 822 had died in inter-Arab attacks and 1306 Palestinians had been killed by Israelis.[4] One of the effects of exiling Yasser Arafat in Tunis was that the PLO leadership was sidelined by the new generation of Islamic fundamentalists in Hamas and Islamic Jihad who were determined to pursue their holy war against the Jews with even more senseless ferocity than the PLO. The chances of securing any meetings of minds between Israelis and those determined to wipe their nation from the face of the earth were all but unimaginable. Arafat's relationship with other Arab powers had also been damaged by his decision to back Saddam Hussein's occupation of Kuwait. Yet, at the moment when the PLO leadership appeared at its weakest, the United States began to press Israel to view these old adversaries as a potential force for moderation. This was how the latter now appeared, at any rate in comparison to the fanatics of Hamas (in 1989 Arafat had announced that the 1964 PLO Charter's denial of Israel's right to exist was 'null and void'). A sign of this new approach was evident when Palestinian negotiators with links to the PLO were allowed to participate in the 1991 Madrid peace talks. The breakthrough came in September 1993 when, after rounds of secret negotiations in Oslo, the Israeli Prime Minister, Yitzhak Rabin, and Arafat agreed the White House accord, shaking hands under the gaze of President Clinton. It was, in the literal sense of the term, a peace process. Limited Palestinian autonomy would be created in the Gaza Strip and around Jericho in the West Bank under an elected Palestinian council. A timetable was established to finalize the status of East Jerusalem and even to settle the relationship between Israel and what, it seemed, would emerge as a Palestinian state. 'The handshake was neither warm nor lingering,' The Times's leading article admitted, yet, 'Peace, the oldest message from the Middle East, the eternal hope behind so many wars that have wracked the region, came a step closer.'[5] The following year the PLO was handed authority for Jericho and Palestinian police assumed security over the area.

The 1994 Nobel Peace Prize was shared between Arafat, Yitzhak Rabin and the Israeli Foreign Minister, Shimon Peres. Israel and Jordan formally ended their forty-six-year state of war. Yet, while many Israelis believed that it took a strong man with a fearsome reputation like Rabin – the former general who had led Israel's lightning 1967 conquest of the occupied territories – to guarantee a plausible order for peace to take root, a few believed he was selling out on all they held dear. Despite the efforts of a Jewish fundamentalist to derail the peace process by massacring Muslims at prayer in Hebron, in September 1995 Rabin and Arafat made further progress, agreeing on West Bank self-determination from which Israeli troops would be withdrawn. By the end of the year, Nablus and Bethlehem were to be among the towns under Palestinian control. By then, Rabin was no more, gunned down in November at a Tel Aviv peace rally by a Jewish extremist. Shimon Peres succeeded as Prime Minister and, in February the following year, Yasser Arafat became President of the Palestinian Authority. Despite this, Rabin's assassination had created a new climate of uncertainty and vulnerability. Islamic suicide bombings undermined both the Israeli government's ability to safeguard its citizens and the belief that the Palestinian Authority was anything other than a front behind which terrorists could operate at will. Israelis responded in 1996 by voting in a new Likud administration under Benjamin Netanyahu that was committed to maintaining the policy of Jewish settlements on the West Bank. For its part, the Palestinian Authority proved to be a byword for corruption.

Netanyahu's government lost power in 1999. A further attempt to find agreement was made between his successor, the Labour Party's Ehud Barak, and Arafat at Camp David in 2000. Israel appeared prepared to make concessions that would cede the vast majority of the West Bank to Palestinian control but not to lose access to the holy sites in East Jerusalem and to trade some Israeli land for keeping some West Bank settlements. This proved to be a sticking point for Arafat who not only demanded his share of the ancient city but, allegedly, also raised the right of the Palestinian refugees (and their descendants) of 1948 to return to their former homes and properties in Israel. The talks collapsed. *The Times*, at any rate, believed it knew where to apportion blame. 'Mr Arafat has passed up a Palestinian state that would include 90 per cent of his goals, plus the certainty of economic support,' bemoaned the leading article, written by Rosemary Righter:

Instead, he has gone home insisting that he will unilaterally declare a Palestinian state, on September 13, that will cover only a morcellized 40 per cent. Basking in the praise of Arabs who have never seen a defeat they did not call victory, Mr Arafat may not yet see what he has lost – both in American goodwill, and on the ground. But his negotiators do see it. They left Camp David insisting that the talks will go on and that they saw in the outcome 'seeds that will grow very fast'. They know that, nurtured by revived Palestinian militancy, the seeds of war could sprout fast too. Mr Barak's position is difficult;

Mr Arafat's is perilous. Before September 13, this Houdini of the Middle East must measure the depth of the abyss.[6]

It was not quite the end. Talks in Taba, in January 2001, proved to be Arafat's last chance to negotiate a settlement. In the event, he failed, once again, to grasp the opportunity. The Israeli people responded by voting out Barak. In his place they turned to a Likud administration under the hard-line Ariel Sharon, whose failure to prevent the Sabra and Chatila massacres of 1982 continued to hinder his claims to statesmanship. Arafat was once again seen as part of the problem rather than key to a solution. He found himself hemmed in and under effective Israeli house arrest in Ramallah on the West Bank. President Clinton's successor, George W. Bush, endorsed a new 'road map' for peace that envisaged a Palestinian state in the West Bank with a democratic leader (though not Arafat) if the bloody attacks on Israel stopped. Plans were one matter, delivery quite another. Arafat's health deteriorated and it became clear that it would take a new Palestinian leader to establish any basis of trust with his Israeli interlocutors. Hope remained. But it was yet to triumph over experience.

Closer to home, a different peace process also struggled to bring harmony where there had been discord. The 1985 Anglo-Irish Agreement failed to assuage the arguments of the gunmen. Atrocities continued to stain the late 1980s in Ulster. In 1988, the IRA marked Remembrance Day in Enniskillen by detonating a bomb there, killing eleven and injuring sixty-one as they gathered around the memorial to the fallen of two world wars. In March the following year, two British corporals who found themselves confronted by mourners at an IRA funeral were beaten to death on the street. Having narrowly failed to blow up Margaret Thatcher in the Brighton Grand Hotel in 1984, the IRA's first attempt to murder John Major had come within two months of his becoming Prime Minister. On 7 February 1991, an IRA van sped up Whitehall and fired two mortar bombs at 10 Downing Street while Major was with his War Cabinet (it was the middle of the Gulf War). One bomb landed in the 10 Downing Street garden, smashing windows. Two others landed close by without exploding. Subsequent outrages were even less discriminate: a bomb in central Manchester in December 1992 wounded sixty-four while fifty were injured and two children killed by a bomb placed in Warrington's town centre in March 1993. The following month, the IRA struck the City of London, inflicting £1 billion worth of damage and forcing the introduction of a 'ring of steel' to protect one of the world's greatest financial centres.

It was against this background that the search for a negotiated solution recommenced. In November 1993, it was revealed that the British Government had held secret talks with the IRA. A further effort at rapprochement with Dublin was also attempted. In May 1993, the Queen met Mary Robinson in London. It was the first meeting between the British and Irish heads of state since 1937. In December, Major and the Irish Taoiseach, Albert Reynolds, agreed the 'Downing Street' peace accord. Sinn Fein were offered the chance to join the peace process if their terrorist accomplices ended the armed struggle. This appeal was met, if not quite in the desired form of words, in August 1994 when the IRA declared a 'complete cessation of military operations' – after a quarter-century of Troubles that had claimed three thousand victims. Loyalist terror groups followed suit in October. In January 1995, British troops ended daytime patrolling of Belfast's streets. On the last day of January, the Prime Minister's office fielded a telephone call from Stuart Higgins, the editor of the *Sun*. He asked, speculatively, if Major was planning to meet the Sinn Fein leader, Gerry Adams. When asked why he should imagine this, Higgins replied that he was guessing that there must be some big story brewing because the Wapping print hall appeared to be preparing an unusually large print run of *The Times*'s Irish edition. The *Sun*'s editor did not know what *The Times* was up to, but thought Downing Street might be able to tell him. Clearly, something was afoot and when Downing Street discovered *The Times* had gained access to a draft of the framework document drawn up by the British and Irish governments for Ulster's constitutional future, feverish attempts were made to prevent publication. During the evening, Christopher Meyer, Major's press secretary, made several telephone calls to Stothard begging him not to publish the details before the final terms were officially released, arguing that doing so imperilled the peace process. Unmoved, *The Times* went ahead with its scoop, although the Government's statement was added to the later editions. The front page report was written by Matthew D'Ancona, a Roman Catholic with Unionist sympathies, who stated that the draft terms brought 'the prospect of a united Ireland closer than it has been at any time since partition in 1920.' Given that the draft included proposals for strong north-south executive bodies it was a fair comment. With Unionists duly alarmed and John Hume, the SDLP leader calling for everyone to 'shut up', Major went so far as to deliver a television address to reassure the people of the province. The Prime Minister had every cause to be alarmed and not just for the peace of Ulster. His dwindling parliamentary majority at Westminster had forced him to be reliant on the goodwill of

Ulster Unionist MPs. In his autobiography, Major accused the scholarly D'Ancona of being 'an ambitious young journalist' and his disclosure evidence of 'malign behaviour.' It certainly gave Unionist politicians the opportunity to make clear to Major that the sort of terms revealed in *The Times* would be unacceptable as a basis for a settlement.[7]

The final draft of the framework document was published on 22 February. It proposed an Ulster legislative assembly and a revocation of the Republic's constitutional claim on the province. The cross-border aspects that had caused such fury in the leaked draft remained, although in a more carefully circumscribed form. While accepting that much remained vague and uncertain, *The Times* gave qualified support to the process.

However vague remained the details, *The Times* supported the concept. The IRA was less trusting. Despite the acceptance of the Ulster Unionist leader, David Trimble, that the decommissioning of IRA weapons was not a precondition of the talks, Republicans remained suspicious that a new assembly would be another means of turning back the clock to a province under permanent Stormont Unionist majority rule. In February 1996, they returned to violence, killing two in a blast in London's Docklands and injuring two hundred in Manchester. Coded warnings paralysed railway stations and motorways during the 1997 general election campaign and it was not until Tony Blair had been elected that a new ceasefire was declared. Sinn Fein was duly rewarded with a seat at the peace talks. In 1998, the party joined a new power-sharing assembly at Stormont. In return for supposedly removing the armalite from their ballot-box strategy, convicted terrorists (both Republican and loyalist) were conditionally released from prison. The following year, Chris Patten issued a report that wound up the RUC, replacing it with a new police service whose structure was supposed to reassure nationalist apprehensions.

There were those who wanted some clarity on what Ulster's new state of constructive ambiguity actually involved. Despite the Patten Report, Sinn Fein continued its policy of non-compliance with the new police service and the scale of the IRA's decommissioning, although secret, was clearly symbolic rather than substantive. A splinter group, the 'Real IRA' killed twenty-eight and injured 220 by detonating a bomb in Omagh, Co. Tyrone. Unease continued in the Unionist community. David Trimble had been elected First Minister of the Northern Ireland Assembly but had to find a means of reaching out to unionism's disaffected voices. Attempts to curtail the Orange Order marching season had already become a flashpoint, particularly, at Drumcree. Furthermore, devolving authority to a power-sharing executive in which the main parties were all guaranteed key portfolios appeared to encourage voters to register their apprehensions by endorsing the more extreme parties. Thus, the nationalist SDLP haemorrhaged votes to Sinn Fein while Trimble's pro-agreement but deeply divided Ulster Unionists lost ground to the fundamentalists in the Revd Ian Paisley's DUP. A process intended to make the politicians behave in a more consensual way actually encouraged the electorate to vote increasingly for the hardliners. The IRA's continual dalliance with illegal activity led to Stormont's temporary suspension.

The experience of post-apartheid South Africa was uppermost in the minds of those trying to drive the peace process forward and there was no shortage of precedents for terrorists being brought into mainstream politics. The fall in the number of fatal shootings (although punishment beatings and kneecapping continued unabated) raised expectations that more normal living conditions in Ulster would breed more normal politics. The first leading article after the 1998 Agreement saluted the deal, but the piece's author, Michael Gove, was deeply uneasy about the terms and became more alarmed once the details emerged. He almost succeeded in persuading Stothard to oppose the Agreement.[8] When nationalist objections had curtailed the marching season two years before, Orange Order Unionists were pitted against the security forces in ugly scenes at Drumcree. Stothard had sent Gove over there to cover the event at a time when most of the media were reporting it in a light highly unsympathetic to the Unionist cause. Gove empathized with Unionist fears, 'the sense that Ulster is a province under siege has been a persistent feature of life in Northern Ireland', he wrote. He quoted sympathetically the opinion of the Drumcree marchers which summed up their attitude succinctly: '"Only a couple of years ago Sinn Fein were murdering innocent people; now they're treated like film starts and lords of the manor. It proves violence works. Of course we're angry."'[9] In the succeeding years, while the peace process switched repeatedly between gears and indeed was repeatedly flung into reverse, Gove continued to provide commentary that balanced sympathy for David Trimble's predicament with doubts about the price paid for appeasing Sinn Fein-IRA. Gove was perplexed by the double standards of commentators who called for life prison sentences for child molesters but supported the British Government's release of 'some of the UK's most morally culpable mass murderers after sentences which would be considered lenient for robbers'. 'The price of the "peace" negotiated on Good Friday in 1998 has been the freeing of hundreds of Barabbases to satisfy the mobs which call themselves paramilitary organisations,' Gove maintained. 'How can the rule of law maintain respect if it is applied arbitrarily?' Furthermore, he believed there was 'a clear moral difference' between the democratic emancipation of Nelson Mandela's ANC and the embrace offered to both Republican and Unionist gunmen whose role had been to disrupt the workings of a democracy. 'The fate of terrorists, we are told, is to end up dancing with duchesses at Lancaster House,' he began his peroration. Yet, in this instance, 'ministers are not executing another skilful diplomatic pas de deux' but 'dancing on the graves of children'.[10]

II

There was no shortage of symbolism when the thirty-four countries of the Conference on Security and Cooperation in Europe met to bury the Cold War hatchet in Paris in November 1990. History was punctuated by peace treaties signed in Paris and the most famous – or notorious – had been agreed at Versailles. 'Can permanent peace in Europe at last be celebrated today?' asked the leading article in *The Times* commemorating the latest endeavour to settle the Continent:

> Unfortunately not. In burying the Yalta status quo, the popular revolu-
> tions in central and Eastern Europe and the Soviet Union itself have
> unleashed local, national and regional tensions, fed by ethnic rivalries,
> disputed borders and the fragility of renascent democratic processes.
> These instabilities, though preferable to Yalta's sleep of the living dead,
> make the celebration of continental peace premature.[11]

At the time Rosemary Righter composed these lines, the three Baltic States had unilaterally declared their independence, but the Soviet Union was still in existence. It would survive, at least officially, for another year of troubles during which Gorbachev was briefly toppled in a coup by hardliners only to be reinstated by the man who delivered him and humiliated him within the space of hours, Boris Yeltsin. A Russian, as opposed to Soviet, identity would now elbow itself to the fore. On 2 December 1991, Ukraine voted for independence, destroying Gorbachev's hopes of a new, looser confederation surviving. Two days before Christmas, and within days of the superpower's seventieth year, the headline on *The Times*'s front page proclaimed simply, 'The Soviet Union is no more'. It fell to the paper's Moscow correspondent, Mary Dejevsky, to pronounce its end: 'The world's second superpower and communist prototype ceased to exist at the weekend by common consent of its unhappy constituents', her front-page lead began. A temporary fig leaf was created in its stead, a Commonwealth of Independent States, but its 'only one central structure agreed so far is the strategic nuclear command – a fitting legacy for a regime built on military power'.[12] On Christmas Day, Gorbachev stood down, handing over his control of nuclear weapons to Russia. In a leading article entitled simply, in the manner of an obituary, 'Mikhail Gorbachev', *The Times* paid tribute to him, recalling the words of the Chinese philosopher Lao-Tzu: 'When the best leader's work is done, the people say, "we did it ourselves!"'[13]

In the autumn of the following year, Dejevsky reflected, 'somewhere between the winter of 1989 and the summer of 1991, the mass fear which held the Soviet Union in thrall dissolved'. The menace of the KGB lost its hypnotic effect to dictate thoughts and actions. 'For the onlooker it was like watching one of those accelerated films of a plant's life, but on a grander scale: the fall of an empire in four months and four days, as the ascendant Russia stripped the authority, then the power and finally the dignity, from the unsustainable Union and its leader, Mikhail Gorbachev.'[14] By then, another multi-ethnic socialist federation was being rent asunder, in the Balkans.

Between 1991 and 1995, Europe experienced its bloodiest conflict since the end of the Second World War. Yugoslavia was a federation of six republics, three religions and two alphabets that, with Josip Tito's death in 1980, had no leader who inspired the requisite awe and confidence to keep it together. A (frequently amended) constitution, a Communist doctrine and opposition to becoming a Soviet satellite proved, by the end of the decade, unequal to the appeals of nationalism and disillusion with economic underperformance. This was all too evident when, in 1990, multi-party elections came to the constituent republics. Croatia turned to the nationalist, Franjo Tudjman. In Bosnia-Herzegovina, the winner was Alija Izetbegovic's Muslim Party of Democratic Action (SDA). Both Tudjman and Izetbegovic had previously been imprisoned by the Yugoslav authorities, Tudjman for questioning the scale of pro-Nazi war crimes committed by the Croats and Izetbegovic for his Islamic proselytizing. Serbia, too, voted to move away from pieties of multi-ethnic sentiment. Its new President, Slobodan Milosevic, frightened the other members of the Yugoslav federation with his increasingly nationalistic and bellicose rhetoric, although in this he was, if anything, surpassed by the leading opposition party in Belgrade.

Confronted by these assertions of national and religious identity, the federal authorities withered. In July 1990, the Slovene assembly declared independence, a verdict endorsed by 94.6 per cent in a subsequent referendum on the proviso that a looser arrangement could not be agreed instead. The one federal institution that did have the will to assert itself, the army (the JNA), prepared to intimidate this Slovene Spring into submission. In Belgrade, however, Milosevic was content to let Slovenia secede. Apart from any other consideration, Slovenia's departure would enhance Serbian predominance in the remaining federation. Meanwhile, the Serb minority were encouraged to create their own enclave in Croatia so that if that republic also seceded the borders of greater Serbia would be stretched further. The ethnic Serbs boycotted a Croat referendum that returned a massive majority in favour of independence. Croatia followed Slovenia's declaration of independence. Pulled out of Slovenia, the JNA clashed with the lightly armed but tenacious Croatian National Guard and bombarded Dubrovnik and Vukovar. An armistice was agreed on 2 January 1992. By then, Germany had unilaterally recognized Slovenia and Croatia. The promptitude of Helmut Kohl's government was surprising. Although Germany had recently advocated moves towards a common European foreign and security policy during the Maastricht negotiations, it was quick to act independently when pressured by Croatia's Catholic co-religionists in Germany. Kohl's European partners, with varying degrees of reluctance, followed suit. The same process took place in Bosnia, its ethnic Serb minority boycotting the republic's referendum – which went overwhelmingly in favour of independence – in March 1992. The EU duly recognized Bosnia. In May, Slovenia, Croatia and Bosnia-Herzegovina were all admitted to the UN.

The Balkans were the tectonic plates where Catholic, Muslim, Orthodox, European, Slav, Ottoman and Asian rivalries rubbed against one another. During the 1990s they were also the battleground for conflicting notions of *realpolitik* and international justice. The multi-ethnic Bosnia was a microcosm of the varying struggles of identity, power and interdependence reflected in the so-called 'international community'. In response, the latter had to grapple with whether to impose a solution of its own devising or whether to let nature – in its Darwinist form of war – take its course. The former could only be achieved by the threat, or use, of significant force.

An alternative was to try to find ways of ameliorating the worst of the fighting that was taking place until such time as saner voices could prevail over the combatants. As early as September 1991, the UN had imposed an arms embargo on all Yugoslav republics. Sanctions against Serbia were imposed in May 1992 and made more severe the following April. Closely prescribed in its activities (which were entirely defensive), a UN Protection Force (UNPROFOR) had been deployed in Croatia in early 1992 and Bosnia during the summer of 1992. The Bosnian Muslim argument for keeping the country as a single entity had an attraction to an outside community keen to set a precedent. Permitting Bosnia's disintegration threatened the redrawing along ethnic lines of many of the other Balkan states too – Serbian Kosovo and bits of Macedonia might fight to join Albania; part of Serbia could go to Hungary. UNPROFOR had no mandate to use its own arms to ensure Bosnia was kept together but this was the principle behind the UN and EU co-sponsored Vance–Owen peace plan of January 1993. It proposed dividing Bosnia into ten semi-autonomous provinces within a new Bosnian state with weak powers. In its leading column, *The Times* endorsed the plan and suggested that if any of the warring parties rejected it, the UN should authorize its enforcement by 'all available means'.[15] In the event, the Vance–Owen proposals were acceptable to the Croats (who stood to make gains from it) and the Muslims but were resoundingly rejected by a referendum by the Bosnian Serbs.

Rebuffed, Lord Owen conceded sadly that his plan had no future. Bosnia appeared to have not much of one either. The Bosnian Serbs had been besieging Sarajevo since April 1992 and had forged together their enclaves into Republika Srpska, displacing where necessary Muslims and Croats to do so. Meanwhile, the Muslims and the Croats formed their own separate Bosnian states. These three entities fought against one another, although they sometimes allied as a matter of convenience with one to better attack the other. Money and expediency as well as hate and grand strategy dictated military tactics. Serb and Croat successes appeared to doom any prospect of a single republic remaining when the dust settled. Suffering most from the UN-imposed arms blockade, the Muslims' position became the most precarious. Unwilling to engage their pursuers directly, the UN preferred to enhance UNPROFOR's role, creating 'safe havens' in Sarajevo, Gorazde, Srebrenica, Tuzla, Zepa and Bihac. It also empowered Nato with ensuring a 'no-fly zone' to military aircraft and using its own air power to defend, if necessary, the safe havens. There were strong voices raised against allowing 'mission creep'. Led by the United States and the EU, the international community was reluctant to enter a bloody war in pursuit of an uncertain settlement that involved fighting one or more enemies who had a far better native grasp of the defensive possibilities of the terrain. Russia retained sympathy for the Serbs and watched even such ineffectual NATO military preparations as did take place with great suspicion. The memory of the gunshot in Sarajevo in 1914 that ricocheted into the First World War was the most powerful break on the various great powers plunging headlong into a fresh Balkan conflict.

On 16 April 1993, Srebrenica fall to Bosnian Serb forces. As the first reports of the city's fall appeared in *The Times*, Simon Jenkins delivered in his column a resounding rejection of the view articulated three days earlier by Margaret Thatcher that Britain and the UN were in danger of becoming 'accomplices to a massacre' unless they broke their arms embargo in order to provide the Muslims with the means to defend themselves. Jenkins thought this idea was profoundly mistaken. Arming the Muslims would merely provoke the Russians into shipping more arms to the Bosnian Serbs. Nor should the West intervene directly. On their own, NATO air strikes would not work and nor was sending in ground troops a good idea. Citing the failure of the 1982–4 peacekeeping mission to the Lebanon, Jenkins believed ground troops would only ensure NATO ended up becoming associated with anti-Serb atrocities prior to an inevitable and humiliating withdrawal. 'Wars end when one side is beaten,' he assured his readers. 'The Muslims are not going to win this ghastly war. It is irresponsible for the outside world to help to prolong it, however grotesque the Serbs' behaviour.'[16] Politicians also had to consider what implications military intervention might have in boosting the Russian nationalist resurgence against Yeltsin, a point made in a letter *The Times* published from Professor Geoffrey Lee Williams that, 'Crudely put, does Boris Yeltsin matter more to the West than the fate of a phantom state? Greater Serbia is now a fact. To put the vanquished Muslims before the wider interests of the West would be foolish in the extreme.'[17]

Filing for *The Times* from within the besieged city of Sarajevo, Richard Beeston tried to report events with a similar level of detachment while privately horrified at what the 'international community' was failing to prevent. 'All of us grew up in the Cold War era believing that there were rules governing how international politics was run and intervening in internal conflicts really was not on the table,' he later recalled. Having reported from Beirut and Baghdad, Beeston was not squeamish, yet even he conceded that, 'Bosnia was the first time I saw horrific events being perpetrated on our doorstep.' For him, this did make matters worse and led him to question the old assumptions. 'I used to get the flight in from Rome and within twenty minutes you would be in medieval Europe with women being raped and having their heads cut off and we were sitting by and Douglas Hurd was talking about "a level playing field." It was just shocking and it made a huge impact to see these atrocities taking place. I hope it did not show in my writing.'

Journalists took it in turns to cover the Bosnian war from the front line. Beeston's initial impressions were shaped by the experience of his first trip into Sarajevo. Geography rendered it acutely vulnerable. The city was in the bottom of a valley with high mountains around it from where the Bosnian Serb forces entrenched their artillery. Beeston decided to break into the besieged city by travelling with the aid convoys bringing in flour to keep its bakeries going. The closer the trucks got, the more the shots rained down upon them. Tyres were blown, forcing the convoy to stop. Risking all to the cross-wires of a sniper, drivers leapt out to change the tyres before making it safely into Sarajevo. On his arrival, Beeston discovered a city that resembled 'a scene from Hieronymus Bosch of old men cutting bits of wood from the trees in the park to warm their houses, snow everywhere, girls prostituting themselves to Ukrainian peacekeepers to get petrol or a couple of cans of tomatoes'. 'When you see a culture that is so close to yours and people of similar values, it's extraordinary to witness this sort of savagery,' Beeston later confessed. 'It makes you think anything is possible. You really stare into the dark pit.' He proceeded on to the Holiday Inn where many of the world's reporters had set up operations. The top floors had been destroyed by shellfire but the bottom lounge area still functioned as a hacks' doss house. 'They were a fairly colourful collection of journalists,' he admitted.[18]

While the Holiday Inn crowd traded war stories and scuttled back and forth along 'sniper's ally', two other *Times* journalists, Tom Rhodes and Bill Frost, were filing reports from their perambulations in and around Vitez, where an UNPROFOR detachment of British troops was based. In the spring of 1993 they met Anthony Loyd, an itinerant freelancer who was trying to purge his personal demons by throwing himself into the thick of the action. They encouraged him to file some copy for *The Times*. So began the career of one of the most intrepid war correspondents in the paper's history.

Although it was not obvious from the long hair that gave him the look of a hippy, Anthony Loyd came from a multinational military family. Dropping out of Eton at the age of fifteen (he had hated the place and had been caught with drugs) and with little in the way of academic qualifications, he had spent five years as an officer in the Royal Green Jackets. He had seen service – although not as much of it as he believed he would have liked – in the Gulf War. Indeed, it had proved an anticlimactic end to his Army career and he had difficulty adapting to civilian life. He was treated for severe depression. The war in Yugoslavia, he later admitted, offered 'either a metamorphosis or an exit. I wanted to reach a human extreme in order to cleanse myself of fear, and saw war as the ultimate frontier of human existence.'[19] Taking a photojournalism course 'as his passport to war', he arrived there and immediately got as close to the action as he could. He kept a lucky charm in one of his pockets – a First World War bullet that had been pulled out of his great grandfather, the one-eyed, one-handed Adrian Carton De Wiart VC. Loyd had been taught Serbo-Croat before he arrived. He also considered that his Army training was an advantage he had over those journalists who were unfamiliar with the risks of the front line since it gave him 'a much better understanding of war and how to deal with men pointing guns at you'.[20]

Loyd's only journalistic training was as a photographer. His dispatches were eyewitness depictions of what he saw and experienced rather than dispassionate analyses of grand political strategy. The latter task could be crafted as competently from the information technology environment of Wapping as from the vantage point of a shallow trench ducking incoming ordnance. The potential drawback with Loyd's desire to risk all with the combatants was that of the journalist getting too close to the story, losing a sense of objectivity in consequence. Like many outsiders, he felt the nationalistic tensions had been whipped up by culpable Serb and Croat politicians disinterring the historic language of 'Četnik,' 'Ustaša' and 'Turk' for their own ends. The Muslims alone appeared to be committed to a less overtly sectarian compromise. It was they who were subjected to the worst violence.[21] There were moments, indeed, when Loyd too showed signs of wanting to become a combatant once more. Yet, unlike the more dispassionate reporting of those removed from the fray, there was no better means of bringing the war's realities home to *Times* readers and, indeed, a wider polity beyond. In one particularly memorable dispatch, he described how the Croats had captured three Bosnian Muslim soldiers, strapped anti-tank mines to their chests, roped up their hands and sent them back across no-man's land towards their own lines. Ominously, a wire attached to their torsos unravelled a little more with each gingerly taken step back towards their comrades. Realizing what was about to happen, the Muslim officer defending the trench ordered his men to open fire on them. His men refused to shoot their comrades. Moments later, the human bombs detonated. A month passed before their remains could be retrieved – by members of the Coldstream Guards. The Croat deputy commander from the brigade responsible rationalized the crime to Loyd: 'It's a dirty war. Insanity becomes normality here.'[22]

Loyd was intoxicated and horrified by the mindless depravity he encountered and admitted to taking heroin as a means of escape. He was not the only one to find the tasks of depicting the conflict a bruising personal challenge. *The Times* and the Imperial War Museum cooperated to sponsor the Scottish-based painter, Peter Howson, as the official British war artist. Howson, who specialized in strong figurative images of the Glaswegian working and under classes in all their physical power and abject hopelessness, travelled to Bosnia in June 1993. He found the atmosphere so tense that, even with sketchpad in hand, he sometimes feared to stare at anyone and was so unnerved by what he did glimpse that he became ill and returned home early. However, he summoned up the courage to return for a second trip in December. The result was a series of powerful depictions and searing images. One large canvas, *Croatian and Muslim*, featured the brutal rape of a woman whose head had been thrust down a lavatory bowl. It was considered too graphic for reproduction in *The Times* or even to be retained by the Imperial War Museum.

On 5 February 1994, a mortar bomb killed sixty-eight and wounded two hundred in Sarajevo's market place. Although it remained unclear who had fired it, the Bosnian Serbs were blamed at the time. Responding to the atrocity, NATO finally decided to break the siege by air power and ordered the Bosnian Serbs to pull back their artillery or face strikes. When they refused, it was Boris Yeltsin who persuaded them to withdraw in return for the deployment of Russian peacekeeping forces in the area. Yeltsin had saved NATO from military action that could have escalated beyond the level of commitment the politicians envisaged and, into the bargain, he managed to elbow Russia's way into the conflict zone. The Contact Group was formed, consisting of the United States, Britain, France, Germany and Russia. In particular, the United States put diplomatic pressure on Tudjman and Izetbegovic to agree to a joint Muslim–Croat province. In doing so, this at least gave them a common foe against whom to unite. The Americans also acquiesced in allowing the Muslims to receive arms shipments, in breach of the UN embargo. In July, the Contact Group published proposals to end the Bosnian war by ceding 51 per cent of its land to the Muslim–

Croat federation and 49 per cent to a Bosnian Serb state. Yet, despite Slobodan Milosevic's efforts, the Bosnian Serbs' assembly voted against surrendering any territory they had already conquered. Thanks to the ferocity of their 'ethnic cleansing' they had gained control of 70 per cent of Bosnia and did not see why they should hand any of it back.

This was to prove a costly mistake by the Bosnian Serb leader, Radovan Karadzic. Milosevic cut off all trade other than food and medicine from Serbia to the Republika Srpska and Yeltsin's desire to wash his hands of such troublesome associates was only tempered by the pro-Serb popular outpourings of his fellow Russians. NATO, meanwhile, resorted to air strikes. While Sarajevo enjoyed a four-month ceasefire at the beginning of 1995, elsewhere the situation deteriorated. In May, Bosnian Serbs captured 350 UN peacekeepers protecting the 'safe haven' of Gorazde. Twenty of them became 'human shields', chained to potential NATO targets. The UN's strategy had been ridiculed in the most open and provocative manner. While, on 31 May, President Clinton announced he was prepared to commit some ground troops in Bosnia, it was clear that his reluctance to get wholly engaged meant the numbers involved would be small and their presence temporary. The fear of 'mission creep' continued to play on Clinton's mind, as it did on that of the British Government. Within days, Clinton was rowing back from his apparent commitment. *The Times* was unimpressed by the lack of a coherent strategy in Washington.[23]

Fleet Street was virtually united in believing something must be done and that something meant supporting armed force to push the Bosnian Serbs back. Continuing to offer an alternative voice in *The Times*, Simon Jenkins despaired of what he believed was this collective delusion. The UN was, he argued, 'reduced to sending troops to relieve troops, as Kitchener was sent to rescue Gordon in Khartoum'. Giving the Bosnian Serbs 'a bloody nose' – the minimum position upon which most British editorializing appeared to agree – would only inflame matters whereas 'the sooner we get out, the sooner this wretched war will come to its eventual end'.[24] That the situation was deteriorating was not in doubt. On 11 July, Bosnian Serb forces captured the UN-designated 'save haven' of Srebrenica. The four hundred Dutch peacekeepers protecting the enclave ran away when the Bosnian Serbs threatened to execute thirty-two of their captured comrades. Twenty thousand Muslim refugees fled the Bosnian Serb advance. Those who did not made a bad error. The Bosnian Serbs separated Srebrenica's Muslims, conveying the women and children to Tuzla. The eight thousand men were murdered.

The atrocity, the single worst war crime in post-war European history, demonstrated the abject failure of the UN mission. Even before the news of the mass murders had been received, *The Times* voiced its support for French calls to retake Srebrenica by force.[25] Reliance on constant referral to the UN had disabled attempts to respond quickly to situations on the ground. Henceforth the UN effectively ceded its military operational authority to NATO. On 23 July 1995, 1200 British troops were dispatched to keep the road open to Sarajevo and the UN's arms embargo had long since ceased to hold back the supplies reaching the Muslims. On 5 August, the Krajina Serbs came under fierce assault from a Croat offensive (assisted by American advice). Twenty-five thousand Serbs were thrown out of their homes. As the Russians were not slow to point out, the West's silence or even connivance with the Croats' ethnic cleansing of the Krajina Serbs was at variance with the active measures finally taken to safeguard the Bosnian Muslims from their Serb neighbours. Bosnian Muslims also attacked in a concerted movement with the Croat offensive and, at last, the Serbs found themselves on the receiving end, and in retreat. NATO spent the first two weeks of September launching air strikes against the Bosnian Serb positions around Sarajevo. Cruise missiles disabled their communications network in western Bosnia. The Serb heavy artillery was finally withdrawn from around Sarajevo. After 1300 days, the siege was lifted.

The Bosnian Muslim soldiers were advancing into formerly Serb-held territory and in the autumn Anthony Loyd joined one of their elite brigades as it set about securing a narrow twelve-mile salient to turn the Serb flank. It proved a stretch too far. The brigade had been fighting for three weeks without relief and was exhausted. It was at this moment that the Serbs counterattacked. When he had joined the Green Jackets, Loyd had found many of his comrades were partly motivated by a desire to find out what killing was like. Now he tried to convey to *Times* readers sitting comfortably in their homes what it was like almost getting killed. 'Fear overtakes us like a sudden fever. My heart is about to pump itself out of my chest cavity and my brain is emptying of rational thought. My only urge is to run,' he wrote. The unit was collapsing around him and under attack on three sides. 'The air is shrieking with flying metal and whizzing shot.' Desperately he tried to scramble for cover:

There are 600 yards of open ground to the nearest treeline, and it is being raked with anti-aircraft fire. Speed is our only hope and in our fear we throw down whatever equipment we can. Even a flak jacket is ditched in the grass: 25lb of body armour is little use against the shells exploding round us.

I know the rules of this battlefield: I know what happened to the Croats who surrendered in Vukovar and to the Muslims who gave up in Srebrenica. They are dead, and I do not believe for a moment that a press card will save me from a shallow grave. My fear turns to dread at the thought of the captors' mutilating knives. I envy the soldiers running beside me for their pistols. One of my three comrades has prepared a grenade in case one of us should be too badly wounded to go on.

The Serbs were at the edge of the hamlet, rounds were cracking out from through the trees. Loyd could not conceive how he was going to evade death:

I think of my mother and sister, of a group of close friends, of people whom I have loved and who have loved me. Some stillness comes to me. It has been a good life and I accept that I am ready to die. But I don't stop running.

In the trees I am surprised to find myself alive. We gather our breath, sprawling occasionally on the ground as shells whine overhead. Although in cover at last, we are still about ten miles from the Bosnian lines that are holding firm, and the Serbs are closing in. Our thoughts begin to gel. We are together again; four journalists and 14 Bosnian soldiers. What happened to the others, I do not know. Across the plain, artillery is ripping into the ground around the route taken by most of the fleeing group.

Loyd spent the next four hours moving 'through an empty landscape of deserted hamlets, dead livestock and fallen crucifixes, growing more confident in the silence around us' before eventually reaching the safety of the Bosnian lines in the darkness.[26]

For the Bosnian Serbs this was a minor victory in a campaign suddenly filled with reverses. With sanctions being lifted from Serbia, Milosevic had decided to pressure the Bosnian Serbs into ending the struggle. What was more, from their perspective the strategic position was deteriorating. The Croat and Muslim offensives drove the Bosnian Serb control of the country back from 70 to 50 per cent. Suddenly, the Contact Group's 1994 offer of 49 per cent no longer appeared so demeaning. What was more, from

Belgrade Milosevic acted to undermine the Bosnian Serbs' room for manoeuvre by subsuming their position within a negotiating team that he led. He met Croatia's Franjo Tudjman and the Bosnian Muslim leader, Alija Izetbegovic, for peace talks at Dayton, Ohio, in the first three weeks of November. After days of unrelenting bargaining, an agreement to end the Bosnian war was reached. Bosnia-Herzegovina would become a nominally united entity with central authorities but divided between two autonomous regions, a Bosnian Serb republic and a Muslim–Croat federation that included Sarajevo and Gorazde. A sixty-thousand-strong NATO Implementation Force (IFOR) would keep the peace. 'The fact that the toughest disputes at Ohio were over territory would seem to spell one word: partition,' noted The Times's leading article when the deal was done. While war weariness might help the situation, 'If Nato merely patrols buffer zones, it will do no more than put this conflict on ice ... Bosnia will be stable only when the internal frontiers erected in Ohio cease to matter to Bosnians of all persuasions. However precariously founded this agreement may be it must, after such atrocious suffering, inspire hope. It cannot yet inspire confidence.'[27]

It was unclear how many people had been killed in the wars that dismembered Yugoslavia between 1991 and 1995 although the figure of a quarter of a million was the most frequently cited estimate. More than three million people had been uprooted, many with their homes destroyed. Having pontificated about 'the hour of Europe', the EU had failed in its first real attempt at a unified foreign policy. In truth, it could not even police its own back yard. The UN had proved incapable of directing operations and had, in the end, effectively ceded power to NATO. The latter had, itself, been rent asunder by its members' different notions of how much military risk to take. Two hunderd and fourteen soldiers had been killed and a further 1500 wounded trying to represent the UN's divided will in Bosnia. The lessons The Times drew were that, 'As we have long argued, this was a war that could be halted only when mediation was backed by effective firepower ... Had the West been much more decisive, much earlier, this would not be such an unsatisfactory peace.'[28]

III

In the new year, twenty thousand United States soldiers arrived to join their NATO partners to help keep the Bosnian peace. *The Times* was convinced that the Dayton accord would not hold unless Washington showed itself to be firmly committed with troops on the ground. The American reticence was, however, understandable. President George Bush's commitment to a new world order had met with a terrible reversal in one of its first tests – the war-torn state of Somalia. Backed by a UN Security Council Resolution, in December 1992 Bush had dispatched US forces there, the first wave of what would be a total deployment of more than 37,000 UN-backed troops sent in order to try and save Somalia from itself. There, rival warlords presided over bloody anarchy. Into this instability other organizations, including al-Qaeda, would come to insinuate them-selves, but the original American invasion was a peacekeeping mission whose primary motivation was humanitarian. With famine gripping much of the country, one and a half million Somalis faced death through star-vation. Only the deployment of troops appeared to be any guarantee that the foreign aid would reach those in need and not be looted by the warring militias.

Watching the US deployment was *The Times*'s Africa correspondent, Sam Kiley. He had been born in Kenya, the son of a journalist who had been exiled from South Africa because of his reporting. After a brief stint on the Johannesburg *Star*, Kiley went up to Oxford, becoming president of the OUDS – the dramatic society. Along with his student contemporary Boris Johnson, he was one of the first graduates Peter Stothard selected for *The Times*' trainee scheme. Ever eager for a challenge, by August 1991 he was the paper's man in Nairobi. It was a post to which he was temperamen-tally suited: 'Africa Correspondent for *The Times* of London is the best job bar none in English language journalism', he concluded after he had spent eight years in the position. The paper had maintained a South Africa bureau but had not covered the rest of sub-Saharan Africa adequately for decades. Despite this, Kiley found that he enjoyed the best of all worlds, with 'the prestige of *The Times* and a continent to cover with foreign editors who let you pursue your story'. Single-handedly, he transformed the paper's cover-age without ever becoming jaded or losing his sense of intrepidness. Indeed, he could hardly believe his good fortune, noting of his daily toil, 'You get paid to have adventures and go to amazing places and meet bizarre people.'[29]

He had none of the starry-eyed idealism of the gap-year backpacker, admitting he preferred his own culture 'to the primitive world of tribalism' and the odiousness of most African leaders. What he loved was the heroism of individuals and the continent's 'Monty Pythonesque sense of the absurd. A well-timed joke can secure your life, or an interview with a president.'[30] For an enterprising journalist, these were ideal conditions in which to establish a reputation.

Staying alive was the first prerequisite. Somalia was so dangerous that even Kiley, an imposing figure, travelled with a bodyguard at all times. As he passed round the stalls of a Mogadishu arms bazaar, he was tossed primed grenades to catch while a drug-crazed child fired a shot at him from behind. 'There is nothing like the cold terror one feels when coming close to being killed in a part of the world for which the rest of the planet has little sympathy,' he confided.[31] Yet it was thanks to the information coming from him, and the small cadre of other reporters like him, that the world got to hear anything at all about what was happening to their fellow human beings in a country whose glorious beaches had once be promenaded by wealthy Italians. What worried him about the dispatch of US troops was that they soon showed themselves nervous about taking casualties and, in doing so, advertised to the Somali warlords their weakness. A possible opportunity to use overwhelming force and to disarm the groups was missed in favour of a minimalist strategy of using troops to guard the relief convoys and each other. Even the self-defence was ineffective. When the UN Secretary-General, Boutros Boutros Ghali, arrived in Mogadishu to see the aid distribution for himself, he quickly had to turn on his heels and flee the country, surrounded by a stone-throwing crowd.

There were at least thirteen major warlords of which General Muhammad Farrah Aidid was considered the most important. By the middle of 1993 it was clear that Operation Restore Hope was going badly. The Americans were supplemented by smaller forces from twenty-two other nations acting under a UN mandate. In June, 23 Pakistani UN peacekeepers were killed. US gunships responded by launching attacks on what they identified as Aidid targets, yet the occupiers (as many chose to see the UN presence) could not even gain mastery of Mogadishu and by July, the UN mission had succeeded in killing more than two hundred civilians in its botched attempt to smash Aidid's compounds. Kiley stayed close to the action. He had established contact with Ali Hassan Osman, one of Aidid's key aides, and observed the fire fights, one bullet coming within an inch of smashing through his bald dome. The American bungling was spectacular –

on one occasion they absailed into a UN development programme building which they mistook for one of Aidid's hideouts, arresting UN employees within. Worse was to follow. On 3 October, an attempt to drop around 120 elite US forces into a bustling sector of Mogadishu to abduct senior Aidid associates went badly wrong. Two Blackhawk helicopters were shot down, eighteen Americans were killed and a further seventy-eight wounded. By December, the Americans were ferrying Aidid to peace talks in Addis Ababa rather than into custody. In March 1994, President Clinton pulled American troops out of Somalia. Several hundred of Aidid's ill-disciplined thugs had beaten 37,000 troops dispatched by the 'international community', backed by helicopter gunships and AC130 bombers. A year later, the rest of the UN mission, which had been cowering in its heavily fortified compounds, was called home. They left behind a country in as bad, or possibly worse, a condition as they had found it. In return, they had lost more than one hundred peacekeeping troops (thirty of them US troops) and spent billions of dollars in the process. Washington's preparedness to take the fore in UN operations where there was no clear national self-interest was diminished. The Bush doctrine for the 'new world order' had not even lasted three years.

Worse atrocities took place in central Africa. In April 1994, a ceasefire between Rwanda's two main tribes collapsed when the small country's president was killed when his plane was shot down. It triggered an outbreak of genocide by the majority Hutu on the Tutsi who, although a minority, had not been forgiven for exercising disproportionate influence during Belgian colonization. The revenge exceeded imagination. By June, around 800,000 Tutsis (and moderate Hutus) had been murdered. The killing was led by Hutu militias, known as the Interahamwe. In turn, Hutu villagers rose up and murdered their Tutsi neighbours on pain of being themselves killed if they refused to partake in the act of collective madness. What was especially astounding was that, unlike the Nazis and their industrialized methods of annihilation, the Interahamwe relied on machetes and bashing skulls against tree stumps. The only break in their productivity came when tired or aching arms had to be rested.

The genocide lasted one hundred days and was brought to an end not by the intervention of the international community but by an invasion of Tutsi forces from Rwanda's neighbouring countries. This, in turn, precipitated the flight of two million Hutus out of the country, fearing vengeance. From his base in Burundi, Kiley had begun driving in and out of Rwanda (it was too dangerous to spend more than several days at a time there) in May. Driving up to the front line, he had to abandon his car in the middle of a minefield and walk his way out – in the darkness. On other occasions, he made his way into the areas where the Hutus were running amok. To his horror, he discovered that the French – who led Operation Turquoise, the humanitarian relief expedition – were flying supplies to the Interahamwe. Furthermore, he believed that the relative ease with which he was able to move around Hutu-controlled areas was because he physically resembled a French commando and was thus assumed to be helping Hutu operations. 'Vous êtes sur une mission?' the Interahamwe asked at checkpoints. 'Oui,' he replied confidently and marched on. He witnessed at first hand massacres in a concentration camp.[32]

Kiley believed culpability was widely shared among all those who did too little. The Clinton administration had fought shy of even employing the word 'genocide'. Kiley believed that 'well-trained and armed Western soldiers could have stopped the slaughter in a matter of days'. His greatest fury, though, was directed at the Hutus' chief patron, France. French policy makers were obsessed with the notion of the threat to Francophone Africa if the partly English-speaking Tutsi forces took power. Some French units were genuinely engaged in relief – indeed, Kiley had helped direct one officer to a scene of slaughter where there were still Tutsis hiding among the dead and in urgent need of help – but he surmised that other French officers had arrived believing they were there to shore up the Hutu government from Tutsi rebels.[33] Not only were the Hutus supplied with French arms (in breach of the UN embargo) but, even more brazenly, French forces rescued one of the genocide's prime organizers, Colonel Theoneste Bagosora, and ferried him over to Cameroon where they thought (wrongly) he would be safe from extradition. Partly for his reporting on Rwanda, Kiley won the 1996 *What The Papers Say* award for best foreign correspondent.

Regardless of the debate over whether prompt action could have prevented the hundred days of madness in Rwanda, it was not in dispute that the international community had been weighed in the balance and found wanting. The failure to intervene to stop the murder of 800,000 Rwandans appeared to be of a piece with the failure to prevent the slaughter of perhaps 200,000 or more Bosnians. Tony Blair assured the 2001 Labour Party conference that if another Rwanda happened, 'we would have a moral duty to act there'.[34] Problematically, there was no shortage of other claimants for direct intervention. African countries whose natural resources ought to have made them rich instead discovered that the fount of wealth watered little but corruption and warfare. Kiley witnessed the anarchy of Zaire in the last years of President Mobutu's rule. Mobutu and his cronies had run a kleptocracy, plundering the wealth of a country rich in copper, cobalt, zinc and diamonds. The President's own wealth was estimated at £6 billion. Kiley toured Kikwit, a city of 300,000 that had been without running water for two years. The tarmaced streets were breaking up under the force of nature beneath and the bush was reclaiming suburban gardens. The city, like Zaire itself, was returning to the jungle.[35] This did not prevent covetous looks from its neighbours. Most of them invaded. One of the first was Rwanda. It used the excuse of crushing Interahamwe rebels who had crossed into Zaire as its reason for occupying a diamond-rich sector of the country. Clearly, the scramble for Africa had not ended with the lowering of European flags over the continent. In 1997 Mobutu was toppled by Laurent Kabila and Zaire was renamed Democratic Republic of Congo. It was no improvement. Kabila was assassinated in 2001. The country continued to be exploited and fought over, not least by its neighbours. In the four years after 1998, aid agencies estimated that the death toll – direct and indirect – from war in Kabila's country was heading towards three million.

Part of the international community's problem was that the African states proved unable to police their own region effectively or without self-interest. Even well-intentioned interventions were mishandled. Covering South Africa's inept 1998 attempt at restoring order by invading Lesotho, Kiley was stopped at a checkpoint, mistaken for one of the invaders and shot. The bullet entered his right shoulder; his face was peppered with fragments of windscreen. Despite his injury and loss of blood, he managed to swing the car into reverse and retreat – under a hail of gunfire – before making it to a South African medic at the border. He lived to tell the tale: 'I have always wondered what it would be like to be shot. It hurts. It is like being hit with a sledgehammer.'[36] Patched up, he soon found far worse atrocities in Sierra Leone, a once prosperous British colony whose democratic government in Freetown was under pressure from Foday Sankoh's coalition of guerrillas and gangsters who raped and maimed those who stood between them and the country's diamond mines. Kiley wrote a commentary in *The Times*, appealing for Britain and the UN to lead a rescue mission. If humanitarian reasons were not considered sufficient, he asked whether the prospect of a new regime in Freetown being 'able to shop their arms, drugs, and knocked-down nuclear warheads under Sierra Leonean flags of convenience' was a good enough reason to intervene.[37] The following year, Tony Blair committed British troops to shoring up Freetown's embattled democrats against their homicidal opponents. The operation was unquestionably one of the Blair government's major foreign policy successes. It came on the back of another effort to intervene in the affairs of an increasingly lawless province. Once again, war had come to the Balkans. Over Kosovo, Blair was not prepared to offer the same half-measures that had failed the peoples of Bosnia.

Serbia regarded Kosovo as not only an integral party of its territory but also a province whose spiritual and historical significance was core to Serb identity. This the international community recognized. The Dayton accord reaffirmed that Kosovo was part of Serbia. However, a fast-expanding birth rate among its ethnic Albanian Muslim population had taken their proportion to 90 per cent of the province by 1992 where it had been two-thirds thirty years earlier. During the 1970s and 1980s, relations between the ethnic Albanian and Serb inhabitants of Kosovo deteriorated. In 1989, Slobodan Milosevic seized his opportunity to profit from the discontent by leading a rally of more than one million Serbs at the site of the battle of Kosovo Polje on its 600th anniversary (the historic defeat had ensured the Orthodox Serbs were subjected to five centuries of Muslim Ottoman rule). Tito had granted Kosovo a substantial measure of autonomy within Serbia. Milosevic, however, put the process into reverse, clawing back power to Belgrade in the new Serbian constitution of 1989. Like Tito before him, Milosevic ruled out the ethnic Albanians' aspiration for secession.

The heavy-handed and repressive treatment of Kosovo's Albanians marginalized their more moderate politicians. By 1998, a new force had come to prominence – the Kosovo Liberation Army (KLA). The KLA was armed in part from money raised by its émigré community's involvement with organized crime. Its tactics were not only to confront Serb authority but also to attract international attention and support by deliberately inciting Serb special forces into committing reprisal atrocities. It was an astute assessment, given the ease with which the supposed forces of law and order duly demonstrated their prevalence for acts of extreme thuggery against entire villages and families. These acts generated far more international condemnation than the KLA's smaller, more cynical, acts of provocation. By May 1998, 40 per cent of Kosovo was in the KLA's hands and Serb attempts to combat the insurgency created a stream of refugees. Here, it seemed, was a fresh Serb act of ethnic cleansing. Only the threat of NATO air strikes forced Milosevic to permit monitors from the OSCE. In the new year, with revelations of a fresh Serb outrage in the village of Racak in which forty-five fleeing ethnic Albanians were shot and hacked to death, Milosevic and the Albanian Kosovar leadership were persuaded to negotiate at Rambouillet. There, even although the KLA were still refusing to disarm, the Contact Group ordered Milosevic to agree to a referendum in Kosovo within three years (which would all but certainly result in a vote to secede) and to permit NATO troops throughout Serbia. These were humiliating terms. Milosevic was not prepared to accept them. With his refusal, NATO prepared, for the first time in its history, to attack a sovereign country whose boundaries were recognized in international law. The action did not have direct UN sanction.

On 24 March 1999, Operation Allied Force began with air sorties and missile attacks on Serbia's air defence and communications structure. Despite the firepower at its disposal, NATO was disadvantaged by having to agree policy between all nineteen member governments. Although military strategists had raised doubts about whether a war could be won by aerial bombing alone, the governments could not agree on invading with their armies. Clinton had publicly pledged that American troops would not be deployed. This may have given Milosevic hope that he could ride out the storm. He also looked to Russian assertiveness to frighten off any decision that did involve a ground invasion. In one respect, the NATO assault played into the Serb nationalists' hands. Far from preventing their violent harassment of the Albanian Kosovars, the Serbs found that being under attack provided them with a perfect cover to intensify their ethnic cleansing of the province. Within days of Operation Allied Force commencing, Kosovo's stream of refugees turned into a mass exodus with more than 300,000 being displaced or fleeing from their homes. The numbers swelled beyond 700,000 in the succeeding weeks. Sam Kiley was stationed on Albania's border with Kosovo where he reported 'a damburst of people'[38] flooding over while Stephen Farrell described similar scenes from his position on the Macedonian border.

In Wapping, the leader writers had laid out *The Times*'s own grand strategy the previous June. 'Only a clear readiness to make a substantial ground deployment before any peace agreement will demonstrate that Nato means what it says' the editorial warned. 'The only possible resolution for Kosovo is autonomy within Serbia; any intervention would be to preserve Serbia, not destroy it.'[39] The chances of Kosovo remaining thereafter a part of Serbia would, it believed, be better served if Milosevic gave way to a new regime better able to present a more liberal, multi-ethnic future. As the air war gathered momentum, the paper also stated its preference that once victory had been secured, turning Kosovo into an interim international protectorate was a lesser evil than the alternative – partition in which the province would become Albanian save for a few Serb enclaves.[40] As for the conduct of the military operation, *The Times* believed not only in the air war but that the weight of ordnance dropped needed to be stepped up if troops were not to be committed for a ground invasion. It especially despaired of Clinton's public refusal to contemplate a ground attack. This only convinced the Serbs that they could avoid defeat by sitting out the aerial bombardment, it argued. Throughout the campaign – and especially after the air war showed few signs of achieving victory on its own – *The Times* repeatedly argued that NATO needed to proceed in a manner that ensured Belgrade took seriously the prospect of a ground invasion. In leading articles written by Rosemary Righter and Tim Hames, the paper also left its readers in no doubt that a ground war was preferable to what might prove the only alternative – a humiliating admission of defeat.[41]

For *Times* journalists on the ground the situation was acutely dangerous. Anthony Loyd was filing from Pristina, Kosovo's capital, in the last days before the war commenced. The previous week a London-based source had warned him that an ultra-nationalist Serb group in Kosovo had put a price on his head. 'The threat was vague and unformed, so I stayed on,' Loyd concluded. Nonchalance was to be one of the war's first victims. He realized he was in trouble when his potential armed guard turned out to be a plainclothes policeman who had once beaten him up. Loyd slipped away the next morning intending to get behind the KLA's lines but he was stopped at one of their checkpoints and forced back. On his return journey to Pristina he received a call on his mobile phone warning him that the Serb police were searching for him. In Kosovo in 1999, the police were a licensed death squad, murdering and maiming at will. Heeding the warning this time, Loyd headed off back towards KLA-held territory. He was stopped at a Serb checkpoint. 'Screaming and with guns levelled' they encouraged him to retrace his steps. After a further tip-off – 'the police are after you' – in Pristina, he drove south towards the Macedonian border. There he found streams of refugees being pushed back by Macedonian guards taunting them that 'Albania is for the Albanians'. Loyd crossed the border, relieved, but conscious that 'the difference between me and two million Kosovo Albanians was that I could escape'.[42]

The refugees' plight dominated the news coverage. Some commentators suggested the numbers involved were being greatly exaggerated. It was thus important that, in Janine di Giovanni, *The Times* had a courageous reporter moving among the tidal wave of dismal humanity. 'They are coming across the freezing border on bicycles, or walking, pushing babies in prams,' she filed from Rozaje on the Kosovo-Montenegro border. 'They're in their slippers. They wear plastic bags on their heads to shield them from the snow. They carry whatever they can.' Many had fled from Pec, Kosovo's second city. One woman was quoted stating, 'they took all the sick people who were Albanians out of the hospital. My neighbour, a Serb, who I've known for years, came and became my enemy. They killed doctors, teachers, anything alive.' Another man said simply, 'It is history that has done this.' In her report, di Giovanni added a note of urgency of her own: 'These people appear to be left to fend for themselves. As I write this from the mountain-top checkpoint, it is freezing cold and those left outside will not survive the night.'[43]

Janine di Giovanni was an American of Italian descent who had moved to London in 1985. She had reported the Bosnian war for the *Sunday Times*, meeting her future French husband in the siege-bound journalists' barracks of the Sarajevo Holiday Inn. She was acclimatized to acute danger. She was also one of the first journalists to get back into Kosovo after the Serb onslaught in the last days of March 1999. Surrounded with two French colleagues on a mountainside by Serb troops, she was marched at gunpoint down the hill and then stopped by other Serb troops who became almost demented with anger when they examined the passports and found an incriminating photograph of di Giovanni's colleagues working with UN peacekeeping troops. One soldier spoke a little Italian. Di Giovanni attempted to reason with him, mentioning that her parents were Italian. 'You we arrest,' he replied, 'the French we kill.' She was at a loss to understand what followed. After driving towards Pec for about twenty minutes, the Serbs stopped the car, returned the journalists' possessions and kissed di Giovanni on the cheek. '"Italiana," they said, "never come back here."'[44]

By April, NATO had taken the war into a yet more serious dimension by hitting Belgrade with cruise missiles. A heavily populated European capital city was now under direct attack. Twelve days later NATO mistakenly hit a train carrying civilians and, two days later, killed up to seventy-five Kosovan Albanian refugees it mistook for a Serb convoy. The longer the air war went on, the more *The Times* became uneasy about the political resolve supporting it. Far from finding a formula that brought Russia more closely into decision making, the leading article of 7 May argued, 'The Alliance is nearing the point where Serb forces have been so damaged that Nato troops could be committed at acceptable risk.' In this assumption, the paper was trusting NATO's estimates of damage done, when it would have been better believing the Serbs' assessment. Nonetheless, the leading article continued, 'It has never been clearer that the best prospect for peace worthy of the name is to give war a chance.'[45] Later that day, a NATO missile smashed into the Chinese Embassy in Belgrade.

It was important that *The Times* did not just print reports filed from those caught up on the KLA side of the lines. The paper also stationed Tom Walker in the Serbian capital where he reported the effects of NATO bombing on a terrified and angry population. He was joined by Eve-Ann Prentice. At the end of May, Prentice was travelling with a small group of journalists in south-west Kosovo when NATO jets hurtled towards her on a mission to bomb a nearby road tunnel. 'I heard a phenomenal noise and thought it was the last thing I would hear on Earth,' she recalled. 'I was thrown to the ground, and was amazed when the thick-grey black smoke cleared to discover that I was still alive.' One of the cars had been taken out, as had its driver/interpreter. As the next wave of jets thundered in, Prentice scrambled into a water culvert. More bombs exploded all around. She had cut legs and was badly shaken. Eventually she and her remaining companions were rescued by Serb troops and ended up being comforted and given generous hospitality at one of their army bases. She subsequently discovered that the commanding officer had wanted to release her overnight into the sniper infested mountains but Milosevic had personally radioed the camp ordering that the journalists should be well treated. His motives were not necessarily governed by altruism alone.[46]

Blair was moving towards seeking a ground invasion but Clinton remained reluctant to perform a U-turn. Meanwhile, the KLA continued in their efforts to secure the province. Janine di Giovanni had not been especially impressed with the martial quality of some of those she had seen at a training camp at Papaj on the Albanian border. She considered them a 'motley bunch, wearing uniforms donated by Germany and T-shirts provided by the Love Parade, a gay annual celebration in Berlin'.[47] By early May, Anthony Loyd was back in Kosare, in southern Kosovo, with the KLA and discovered that their quality as a fighting unit had much improved.[48] By mid-May, di Giovanni had advanced with a KLA unit into south-west Kosovo, frequently flinging herself face down in ditches as first NATO jets (by mistake) dropped cluster bombs on them and then the Serbs pinned them down with a relentless bombardment, killing and wounding fighters with whom she found herself sharing every hardship and cigarette.

In fact, the war was moving towards its endgame not so much because of the tactics deployed as by the fears of what might follow. On 19 May, Clinton's hostility to a ground invasion publicly softened. Attempts by the

Russians to mediate were supplemented by a delegation led by the Finnish President, Martti Ahtisaari. The belief that Clinton was finally moving towards a ground invasion concentrated both Russian and Serbian minds. NATO's bombing campaign was suspended on 10 June when Milosevic began pulling his forces out of Kosovo. While NATO prepared to dispatch fifty thousand troops to police the peace, Russia asserted its right to involvement by speeding troops stationed in Bosnia over to Pristina airport. With extraordinary recklessness, the NATO commander, General Wesley Clark, ordered the deployment of British paratroopers and Gurkhas to Pristina to confront and repel the Russians. With Tony Blair's backing, General Sir Mike Jackson, the British commander, refused amid heated talk of risking a third world war.

As the peacekeeping force, K-For, began to establish itself in Kosovo, the extent of the violence the province had endured became more apparent. Michael Evans, *The Times*'s defence editor, inspected a torture chamber under a Serb Interior Ministry police station in Pristina. 'The smell of death and suffering is everywhere. The claustrophobia is overwhelming,' he wrote. Implements of medieval barbarity lay around. Pornography was strewn about everywhere as were boxes of industrial-strength condoms. There was a metal-framed bed with a restraining leather strap and a mattress riddled with bullet holes. In the main chamber he found on a ledge a baby's single blue shoe. 'Is it possible they tortured babies, too, in this hole?' he wrote in despair.[49] There were other discoveries of a different kind. Far from having been pulverized by the NATO bombing, the Serb forces retreated in good order. The claim that 122 tanks had been destroyed was demonstrably false. Three damaged T55s were found while the Serbs admitted another ten had been hit. Around four hundred Serb soldiers (but more than a thousand civilian Serbs) were killed, not much of a return on 11,000 strikes and 29,000 sorties against Serbia. As Eve-Ann Prentice had witnessed and reported at the time, the basic utilities had remained operational in Pristina even after two months of the bombing campaign.[50] Milosevic's will appeared to have crumbled not because of the military success of the aerial bombing but because he feared there would be a ground invasion and that Russia could no longer be counted upon to prevent it. The figure of 100,000 missing (presumed murdered) ethnic Albanian men that had been bandied about during the campaign was also shown to have been without foundation. *The Times*, at least, had never endorsed such a high figure. With the conflict's end, the estimate was downgraded to ten thousand and possibly less.

Three thousand six hundred Russian troops participated in K-FOR. Despite the peacekeeping force's best endeavours, the future looked bleak for Kosovo. It offered hope for the displaced Albanians to return to the towns and villages from which they had been driven but the prospects for reconciliation and economic revival remained poor. The former KLA continued to act in its dual role of part police force, part local mafia. The level of organized crime was uncontainable. The future for the non-Albanians was dire. Within a year of the end of the NATO air war, 100,000 Kosovo Serbs had fled the region. Tom Walker filed reports that shielded *Times* readers from none of the horrors perpetrated against them. Nothing was sacred. Monasteries were desecrated, as were nuns. K-FOR found itself having to defend those who remained against the vengeance of Albanians intent on pursuing an 'ethnic cleansing' agenda of their own.

The military occupation of Kosovo, as of Bosnia, was clearly no temporary arrangement. Bosnia-Herzegovina was governed by a myriad different authorities. Given the network of corruption within the country, it was not an obvious magnet for foreign investment. In Ulster, as in Bosnia-Herzegovina, the 'peace process' involved diminishing, rather than strengthening, direct accountability in the hope that this reduced the appeal to sectarian partisanship. Political systems of extraordinary complexity were envisaged in order to ensure power sharing. Yet a lack of accountability was not in itself conducive to good government. In Bosnia's case, effective power rested not with any representative body but with the High Representative, the international community's viceroy in the region. Kosovo, too, looked certain to remain similarly governed in the years ahead. Being run by foreigners was not in itself the key to a long term solution, but it did curtail the level of violence.

With his Serb assertiveness, Milosevic had successfully contributed to the ruination of the constituent parts of what had once been Yugoslavia. In so doing, he had also despoiled his beloved Serbia. For most of the previous eight years, Serbia had been subject to economic sanctions. The economy was in a state of collapse. His actions in Kosovo had led to it being occupied by a multinational force and, with the flight of much of its Serb minority, a question mark remaining over its future as even a nominal part of Serbia. *The Times* had argued that the best hope of maintaining Kosovo within Serbia lay with Milosevic's removal from power in Belgrade. This proved to be one of the aftertremors of the Kosovo war. On 24 September 2000, Milosevic committed his final act of defiance by refusing to concede defeat to Vojislav Kostunica, the opposition candidate who appeared to have won the presidential election. The consequence was not supine acceptance from a cowed people but mass protests and the beginnings of a general strike. On 5 and 6 October, more than half a million protestors assembled in Belgrade. The Parliament building was set on fire. Milosevic was finally forced out after thirteen years of miscalculation. On 9 October, international sanctions against Yugoslavia were lifted. The following year Milosevic was flown to The Hague to stand trial charged with war crimes before the newly convened International Criminal Tribunal for the former Yugoslavia. The new world order was being rebuilt, this time as a legal entity.

IV

During the 1980s, policy makers in Washington DC, had watched the Soviet Union's military difficulties in Afghanistan with ill-concealed glee. They saw the Soviet withdrawal as a Cold War victory for the forces of Communist containment. The Islamic world saw it differently and took heart, drawing the lesson that Islamic warriors could defeat the technologically superior forces of foreign imperialism (albeit when armed and bankrolled by the United States and Saudi Arabia). Afghanistan had other legacies. Resisting the Soviet invader not only proved a useful military training ground for the native tribesmen but also for the thousands of co-religionists who joined the jihad against the infidel.

The collapse of Soviet Communism only sharpened the fault line between the Orthodox and Muslim peoples of the Caucasus. In 1992, Moscow intervened to shore up the forces of its embattled satellite government in Tajikistan, retaking the capital, Dushanbe, and driving the state's Islamic insurgents back to the Afghan border where their cause was kept alive with arms and money from friendly Arab states. In Northern Ossetia and Chechnya, ethnic sensitivities continued to be tense between the Russian settlers and the native Muslims. The latter had been deported by Stalin and had returned, after the dictator's death, to find their land and status much diminished. In 1992, Muslims from Ingushetia fought Orthodox Ossetians for control over disputed property. Russian 'peacekeeping' forces assisted the Ossetian destruction of Ingush villages in Northern Ossetia.

In Chechnya, the regime of Dzhokhar Dudayev was a byword for corruption. Market day in the capital, Grozny, more closely resembled an arms bazaar. In 1994 Dudayev responded to the increasingly militant Islamism of the Caucasus by proposing to make Chechnya an Islamic state operating Sharia law. Moscow looked on with alarm, concerned that Chechnya was becoming – like the West Bank was to Israel – a safe haven for terrorist operatives. In 1994, a mismanaged coup led by Russian troops posing as mercenaries ended in disaster. A formal invasion followed. Grozny was shelled. Armoured columns were lost in its streets as locals took it in turns to destroy the ill-conceived Russian advance with the private arsenal at their disposal. Anatole Leiven had been in Grozny reporting the attack for *The Times* and was joined by Richard Beeston. In January 1995, Beeston was relieved in turn by Anthony Loyd. 'The Russian gunners are operating with total disregard for humanitarian principles and killing their own people en masse as a result, in salvoes on a scale I have never seen before,' Loyd reported from his vantage point on the ground floor of a stone building. 'For the wounded lying in the ruins there is no place of safety, no morphine, and very few bandages. The dead are just left to rot.'[51] Appalled by the Russian army's indiscriminate actions, he was also staggered by its 'blinding incompetence.' Conscripts and tanks were dispatched into urban areas where they were easily blown up by rocket-propelled grenades.

The Chechens' problem, as Loyd pointed out, was that 'successful guerrilla campaigns rely on superpower backing: the Chechens have none'.[52] America might have been happy to pay for the Soviet Union to be embarrassed in Afghanistan, but helping Chechens destabilize Boris Yeltsin was a different proposition entirely. While London and Washington felt they had the motive and the firepower to protect the Muslims of Kosovo against Milosevic, safeguarding the Muslims of Chechnya by preventing the Kremlin from suppressing revolt in its backyard was neither possible nor desirable. The new wars for human rights, however trumpeted in lofty rhetoric, did not have universal application. *Realpolitik* remained the ultimate break on action. The Chechens took assistance from Islam's itinerant guerrillas instead, a fact that further muted Western interest in their cause. Loyd interviewed the Chechen commander, General Aslan Maskhadov, in his bunker as well as his fighters, one of whom took pride in the fact that his capital had held out for thirty-seven days before being overrun by the Russians while Berlin in 1945 had lasted only a fortnight.[53] Despite hoisting the Russian flag over the ruins of the presidential palace, the occupiers soon discovered the cost of attempting to hold the city.

Comparing it to his experiences in Bosnia, Kosovo or (in 2001) Afghanistan, Loyd found being on the front line in Chechyna 'by far the most terrifying experience of my life'. He was familiar with death, barbarism and mutilation, but in Grozny 'the intensity of violence was much greater'. Covering the other conflicts, his main concern had been 'the normal things like being shot by a sniper or stepping on a mine', but crouching in central Grozny while the Russians blasted the city into concrete shards involved witnessing hundreds of humans being killed and wounded in minutes. What was more, he found himself in this situation for hours at a time.[54] In April 1996, Dudayev was killed by a missile that tapped onto his mobile phone signal. In July 1996, the Chechens took back Grozny. Yeltsin tried to get out of the mess, and Chechyna was granted autonomy. It proved in no position to exercise the freedom wisely. Real power had long since switched to its warlords and assorted criminals. Money from Muslim sources in the Middle East, where the struggle was seen as another jihad, helped ensure that terrorism continued to flourish. Yeltsin's successor, Vladimir Putin, met fire with fire. In 1999, Russia reinvaded. Ten years after the first attempt to seize Grozny, half of Chechnya's one million population was assumed dead or exiled. The Russian army was suffering higher losses than it had endured in Afghanistan. While much of the British public paid fleeting attention to the disorders in the Caucasus, *The Times* continued its mission to gather what information it could from a part of the world that had become inaccessible to all but the most intrepid and cunning reporters. The leader-writing team was bolstered by the arrival of Vanora Bennett, a journalist with extensive Russian experience and the author of *Crying Wolf*, a study of Chechnya's woes. Loyd returned to the country in October 1999 in time to catch the worst of Putin's onslaught. Russian bombing had intensified the previous month. There had been more than three thousand kidnappings there since August 1996 and the Chechens, reinforced by Islamic fundamentalists, had produced gruesome videos showing the victims being tortured to death. It was estimated that of the fifty foreigners who entered Chechnya in 1998, thirty-eight were taken hostage. These were not good odds. Loyd decided to hire some gunmen to protect him. Even that was a gamble and he conceded that in 'moments of intense paranoia' he wondered if they had worked out what his ransom was worth. At one point, he was the only Western journalist in the country. Without him, there was little prospect of accurate facts emerging from its borders, which Russian troops had sealed. He was arrested trying to get back into the country in the company of an American photographer friend and a wealthy Bangladeshi who had a fax purportedly from Vladimir Putin granting him permission to enter Chechnya. Loyd only just had time to eat the page of his notebook containing the name of the contact he was due to meet before he was dragged off to detention under suspicion of being a spy. One officer conducted an overnight interrogation while wearing a balaclava and playing an Elvis Presley cassette of *Love Me Tender*. Another began the session by putting Loyd's British passport into a drawer and whispering with almost caricature villainy, 'Without it you have no identity. You do not exist. And that is what we can do to you if we wish – make you disappear.' It was, Loyd conceded, not a promising start.[55] Finally, after three days of unrelenting cross-examination, he was released.

Loyd's brush with the Russian intelligence community did not put an end to *The Times*'s effort to uncover the truth about what was going on. Janine di Giovanni was one of only two journalists (the other was a German photographer) still in Grozny when it fell to the Russians again in February 2000 after a 102-day siege. Her situation was precarious. 'Unlike Bosnia, Kosovo or East Timor,' she admitted, 'there are no aid workers inside Chechnya, no medical relief teams, no United Nations.' She was placing her survival entirely in the hands of Chechen rebels who had a habit of taking outsiders hostage prior, often, to killing them. Grozny's fall did not end the struggle. The rebels who survived the city's bombardment escaped by walking across a minefield. With the Russians left to occupy the pile of rubble that had once been a capital city of 400,000 people, di Giovanni moved to the village of Alkhan Kala where she was given hospitality. This place, in turn, became surrounded by Russian troops, closing in for the kill. Local women dressed her up as a headscarf-wearing peasant and, in this disguise, she made her getaway with two of them and a baby in a car that was driven down an icy road at full speed. As she looked back, she 'saw the column of Russian tanks with their guns mounted, moving steadfastly into the village, the soldiers cockily hanging off the sides'.[56] She survived to collect the *What The Papers Say* award for Foreign Correspondent of the Year.

V

Despite the bloodshed in the Balkans, the Caucasus and in Africa, the twentieth century ended with considerable evidence that Western values had indeed triumphed after all. Except in agriculture, where it suited the producers (if not the consumers) of the United States and the EU to be dyed-in-the-wool protectionists, trade barriers were continuing to come down. Instant global communications helped to ensure the triumph of the market. Membership of its quasi-governing body, the World Trade Organisation (as GATT was rebranded), was the badge of all nations with aspirations towards economic respectability. Even the formerly Maoist republic of China prepared for accession. Nor was the world merely being made safe for capitalists. Political liberalism also received official endorsement. The UN's courts trying those implicated in the horrors of Rwanda and the former Yugoslavia were the first fruits of a new international jurisprudence. Most nations of the world, including Britain, began signing up to create an International Criminal Court, investing it with the powers to try those suspected of crimes against humanity, war crimes or genocide from any country that failed to prosecute them itself. The former President of Chile, Augusto Pinochet, found himself arrested while in Britain for a hospital operation on the basis of a warrant from a Spanish judge who believed he was implicated in political murders that had taken place during his period of power in South America.

Not everyone in the West was excited by these developments. The left protested against the economic liberalism of globalization. Gatherings of the World Trade Organisation were accompanied by riots on the streets as left leaning and anarchist protesters from all nations congregated to condemn globalization. At the same time, the right was apprehensive about a committee of liberal lawyers sitting in judgment over the world's politicians and soldiers. There were anomalies, not least in Ulster where liberals tended to support the political imperative of sharing power with murderous gangsters rather than the legal imperative of holding them accountable for their crimes. Whether the world would be made safer by legal incursions on the exercise of *realpolitik* remained to be seen. Despite the qualms, the process went ahead unchecked. Yet this new order was not remotely taking over the whole planet. In the Muslim world – covering one-fifth of humanity – the *pax liberalis* was not so keenly felt. Its military, monarchical and dictatorial regimes were not swept away by the march of democracy that pinned red-blooded Communism back to North Korea, Cuba and a handful of other enclaves. Secularly administered Turkey was one of the few Muslim countries that remained fully democratic throughout the 1990s.

Indeed, the Muslim world confounded the West less because it was moving in the slow lane towards liberal values than because large tracts of it appeared to be moving in the opposite direction. There, the headway was being made by Islamic fundamentalism.

As the Islamist threat began to assert itself, there were attempts in the West to explain this anger as a product of resentment at economic inequality. In short, selfish capitalist hubris had brought forth a nemesis from the disempowered. On closer inspection, there were considerable problems with this overly simple analysis. In some of the countries where fundamentalism flourished most ardently, oil was reversing the master and servant relationship with the energy-dependent West. Perversely, the fuel for Islamic fundamentalism came from modernization. Many of those who came to prominence as terrorist leaders were first-generation university graduates from lower-middle-class, but not poor, families. Some, like Osama bin Laden, came from backgrounds of ostentatious wealth accumulated through Saudi Arabia's building boom. Like so many other revolutionary movements, the Islamist revival was in large part, a youth movement. As well as providing educational opportunities, the process of modernization boosted the birth rate. A swelling and youthful population in Arab countries migrated to cities. In these sprawling, anonymous urban environments, faith became a pronounced and militant badge of identity. It was in the cities that so many of the charitable, educational and medical organizations upon which inhabitants came to rely were provided by religious, and often hard-line Islamist movements. Indeed, religious charity successfully filled the void left by corrupt state governments that failed to provide reliable or comprehensive services themselves. Thus, civil society was a product of faith, rather than the font of state or secular provision.

Islamic fundamentalism was concerned not only with confronting the infidels living in Israel and its supporting states in the West; it developed out of a sense of outrage at the inefficiency, corruption and self-serving worldliness of its own region's temporal rulers. The Arab nation states created out of the vanquished and vanished Ottoman Empire at the end of the First World War failed to engage the emotional loyalties of their subjects in the same way as those in the Christian world had done. Instead, loyalties remained strongest either at the local levels of family, village and tribe or at the pan-national level of Islamist and Arab awakening. Furthermore, whatever the claims of the various Islamic nation states to lead the Muslim world, none of them attained pre-eminence. None proved able to assert commanding leadership over the others. The consequence not only prevented a strong mediating regional power being able to settle neighbourly disputes (thereby insuring the West intervened) but also underlined the power of Islam as a force greater than any temporal power among the faithful.

As the Islamist revival began to assert itself towards the end of the 1970s, the response from many of the Arab governments was one of appeasement. Radical clerics spreading their message in the mosques of the sprawling cities to impressionable youths generally received less persecution than liberal reformers committed to democracy. Some organizations, like the Muslim Brotherhood, were actively funded and encouraged by regimes such as Saudi Arabia. The accommodation of Islamism by nervous regimes was not confined to Arab states. In the 1970s, Bangladesh dropped its secular constitutional commitments. Pakistan adopted the sharia as its supreme law. Elsewhere, Suharto's Indonesia increasingly Islamicized its laws and Malaysia developed a twin secular and Islamic legal system.

The Islamic revolution in Iran in 1979 suggested that fundamentalism was winning, spurred by Ayatolah Khomeini's instruction that, 'To kill and be killed is the supreme duty of every Muslim.' The suicide bombs directed at the US presence in Beirut – and Reagan's response to scuttle out – suggested that the fearlessness of faith was more than a match for Western technological superiority. The Iranian commentator Amir Taheri provided thoughtful perspectives on the Op-Ed page of *The Times*. In 1989, he reflected that the decade had witnessed the challenge of Islamic fundamentalism but not its victory. Iran failed to overcome Iraq and Baghdad remained under the control of Saddam Hussein's Ba'athist regime. Neither Egypt nor the Lebanon became a theocracy. Pakistan elected a woman, Benazir Bhutto, and elections in Malaysia, Jordan and Tunisia restricted, rather than hastened the path of the extremists. 'Today, the Islamic fundamentalist movement is almost everywhere in retreat,' Taheri believed. But he was not complacent. He warned that it would 'return with a vengeance' if the Muslim states turned away from the process of democratization.[57]

The Arab nations' inability to sort out their own affairs was laid bare when in 1991 the American-led coalition delivered a drubbing to the Iraqi forces. Even though many Islamic governments had sided with the UN-endorsed coalition to free Kuwait, the attitude of their populations was very different. This was not just what Western commentators described with intriguing imprecision as the mood on the 'Arab street'. Even many Arab intellectuals regarded Western military action in their part of the world as a far greater outrage than Saddam Hussein's original boundary transgression. The presence of infidel troops in Saudi Arabia, the land of Islam's holiest sites, was especially singled out as an abomination. Resentment at the West intensified. Subsequent aerial bombing missions over Iraq, intended to enforce the no-fly zones and the UN resolutions, enjoyed little support from Arab governments, even those that had sanctioned the original mission into Kuwait.

Meanwhile, Algeria appeared to be on the brink. The Islamist FIS's challenge for power was only halted by the cancellation of the 1992 elections. Western protests at this retreat from democratic principles were understandably muted. However, Afghanistan joined Iran and Sudan as the third country to be swept up by the fundamentalists when, between 1994 and 1996, the Taleban, a theocratic movement of merciless severity whose warriors had been trained in Pakistan, gained control over the majority of the country. They beat back the mujahidin tribes that, having seen off the Soviet invasion, made the mistake of reverting to infighting among themselves. The spectre of Osama bin Laden began to cast a shadow, at first fleetingly, over the pages of *The Times* in 1997 when Christopher Thomas, filing from Kandahar, drew attention to bin Laden's presence in the city with his three wives in tow. 'Mr Bin Laden is living near the derelict airport,' Thomas wrote, 'hidden from view because, even for Taleban, which claims to have ended his terrorist activities, he is an embarrassment.'[58] Embarrassment or not, it was soon evident that Mr bin Laden had not gone into retirement. On the contrary, his al-Qaeda terrorist network broadened its focus from undermining insufficiently fundamentalist Arab regimes to hitting the United States and its interests. Al-Qaeda was blamed for a lorry bomb that had killed nineteen Americans at a barracks in Saudi Arabia and wounding nearly four hundred others in June 1996. This was but a foretaste of what was to come. In February 1998, bin Laden announced he was launching a 'pitiless' war against 'Jews and Crusaders'. He proved as good as his word when, in August, al-Qaeda lorry bombers blew up the American embassies in Nairobi and Dar es Salaam, killing 224 – overwhelmingly in Nairobi – of which twelve were American and injuring five thousand, most of whom were locals. Failing to kill bin Laden with air strikes, by November, the US was offering $5 million for his capture. He remained at large. In October 2000, al-Qaeda struck again with a suicide attack on the USS *Cole* while it was docked in Aden, killing seventeen and injuring thirty-nine American sailors.

On 11 September 2001, the principal leader writers were enjoying lunch with the independent directors of the Times Newspapers Holdings Board when news was brought to Les Hinton, the company's executive chairman, that there had been an attack on the heart of America. Hinton broke the news to his guests. Apologizing, the leader writers cast aside their napkins and made their way as promptly as decorum allowed out of the dining room. When they returned to their office it was to discover that a succession of hijacked planes had slammed into the Pentagon in Washington DC, and both towers of the World Trade Center in New York.

Another journalist who would not easily forget where he was when the news broke was *The Times*'s new US editor, Nicholas Wapshott. Inconveniently, he was in the middle of the Atlantic Ocean. He had opted for the majestic leisureliness of taking up his duties by arriving in America with his family on the *QE2*. For *The Times*, this was potentially a disaster. The outgoing US editor, Ben MacIntyre, had already departed and now his replacement was quite literally all at sea. Managing to telephone Wapping from on board, Wapshott announced that he would file from the ship, only to discover that the office had decided he could not be of much practical use. Matters for the new US editor then got worse. Rather than docking in the lea of Manhattan, the *QE2* was diverted to Canada, drifting him yet further away from the action. Nor was Wapshott the only *Times* journalist caught off guard by al-Qaeda's lightning strike. Having spent the previous three years reporting Westminster politics, Roland Watson was in his first fortnight as the paper's new Washington correspondent and, like George W. Bush, was down in the Deep South when news of the attack broke. Unlike the President, Watson did not have Air Force One to whisk him away and, with all flights grounded because of the emergency, he had to drive as fast as he could to New York in time to cover the aftermath. En route, he checked into a motel room near Savannah, Georgia where he set up a temporary office to file copy to Wapping. The motel receptionist became suspicious of the stressed looking guest who was feverishly trying to place calls, was receiving faxes about missile defence and refused to let an employee into his room to change the towel. Listening at the door she thought she overheard him saying something like 'Falcon thirty-one secure'. She called the FBI.[59]

It was James Bone who saved *The Times* from the humiliation of having no staff reporter *in situ* to cover one of the most dramatic news stories in living memory. By chance, he had been several streets away – just emerging from a newsagent – when the first plane cruised into the north tower of the World Trade Center and was an eyewitness as the flames licked down it. Twenty minutes later, he stared in disbelief as the southern tower was hit. He watched as helpless souls jumped from the inferno to their certain deaths, and this proved the starting point for his report that led *The Times* the following day. He conveyed the unfolding horror, quoted witnesses and reported everything that could be seen at the time without the temptation to coat it with grandiloquent prose. It was not a story that needed varnishing. While those around him turned to get away, Bone knew he had to get as close as possible. He explained how, 'immediately after the two attacks, thousands of people streamed north up Broadway to get away. As I struggled against them I recognised something in the smell of the debris and smoke.' He watched as the towers crumbled to the ground, rumbling and engulfing the scattering crowds in a pall of smoke.[60] The pictures told the rest of the story. Bone maintained a tone of straight, factual reporting that could only be described as immensely professional. Having been almost caught out, *The Times* ended up having one of the best eyewitness reports of any newspaper.

Inevitably, graphic photographs dominated the paper. *The Times*, like most of its competitors, opted to dominate the front page with the image of the explosion at the moment of impact between plane and tower. On inside pages, Michael Binyon and Richard Beeston, the diplomatic editor, provided a profile of the immediate chief suspect, Osama bin Laden. News of the catastrophe and its implications appeared on pages one to six, augmented by a twenty-four-page special supplement with further comment and analysis provided in *T2*. There, Sandra Parsons and her team wrestled impressively with an even shorter deadline, helped by the extraordinary literary velocity of Giles Whittell who had just returned from his posting in Moscow. In the space of an afternoon, the entire newspaper was rewritten. Never in its history had *The Times* been forced to change and expand so much of its content in so little time.

Indeed, if a newspaper's mettle is tested by its response in a moment of acute flux and crisis, *The Times* passed with honours. The tone remained calm, serious and devoid of hysteria or hyperbole. The leading article stretched the length of the page and avoided repetition, dim cliché or hot-headedness. It and its successor the following day called for the US to retaliate in a manner that would retain the world's sympathy. It did not rule out an invasion of Afghanistan if attempts failed to persuade the Taleban to hand bin Laden over, but it suspected that 'unless an attack killed bin Laden and the great majority of his followers, it could do more harm than good'. However distasteful Islamic fundamentalism might be, 'religious revivalism does not in itself imperil others. The distinction must be drawn between fundamentalism and the Islamist extremists whose weapons include terror.'[61]

'Good will prevail over evil' ran the front-page headline for 13 September as horror gave way to resilience. Articles by Ehud Barak, Michael Portillo and the former presidential hopeful Gary Hart framed the Op-Ed page. As evocative as any sentiment was the Peter Brookes cartoon. It bore no comment, just a drawing of the world. It was upside down. Over the following days, *The Times* continued to provide strong and comprehensive coverage, with text on the news pages interspersed with short 'brief lives' of those mostly unknown but to their friends, family and God. Their hopes and aspirations were listed. One story after another spoke understatedly of the decency and quiet heroism of ordinary people.

On 14 September, President Bush declared a war on terror. Bin Laden was the prime suspect and the first target. So began the period of diplomatic and military build-up that was to create a new special relationship between Bush and Blair. Philip Webster travelled more than forty thousand miles with the Prime Minister on his trans-global mission in the month following the attacks. Attention switched to the best means of prosecuting this new kind of war. In 1998, President Clinton had responded to the Nairobi and Dar es Salaam embassy attacks by launching cruise missiles against supposed al-Qaeda bases in Sudan. These had clearly proved not much of a deterrent. Yet, given the Soviet army's experience in Afghanistan, invading the mountainous and unforgiving country to flush bin Laden out of his base was a potentially costly and perhaps disastrous option. Against this drawback had to be weighed the risk to the world's only superpower being seen as too impotent even to prevent a third-world theocracy from entertaining the most wanted criminal on the planet. For *The Times*'s leader writers this was a crucial point and consequently there was unanimity among them that the war on terror would have to be prosecuted even if it meant a ground invasion of Afghanistan. The counterblast was provided by Simon Jenkins. The prospect of waging a war on terror disheartened him. It is a 'small wonder', he wrote, 'that Mr Bush and Mr Blair react by declaring a Hundred Years' War on an abstract noun'.[62] Writing within hours of the 9/11 attacks for the following day's paper, he expressed his outrage as strongly as every other journalist at the mass murder by the terrorists but questioned the wisdom of retaliation. Throughout his period as one of *The Times*'s foremost columnists, he had preached the doctrine of avoiding military engagement in conflicts for which there was no clear viable solution. He was not going to change his mind now. 'To react to an atrocity by abandoning the customary self-control of democracy is to help the terrorist to do his work,' he maintained. For all its barbarity, al-Qaeda's attack on America 'does not tilt the balance of world power one inch. It is not an act of war . . . Maturity lies in learning to live, and sometimes die, with the madmen.'[63]

The Times, however, like the Pentagon and the MoD, was soon preparing for war. At the very least, this involved removing the Taleban from power and, if possible, trapping bin Laden and his supporters there before they could flee. The campaign would not only be expensive for its prosecutors but also for newspapers which were struggling to cope with the budget-shrinking effects of the deepening recession in the advertising market. As Stothard recognized, *The Times* had no option but to provide comprehensive coverage regardless of the cost. Citing the tenacity of those fighting for their faith, the difficulty of the terrain and the grim experience of successive invaders, including the Russians, there was no shortage of experts prophesying disaster. Yet none of the critics satisfied *The Times*'s leader writers that there was an alternative means of ridding Afghanistan of the Taleban and their notorious guest.

It quickly became clear that the war's critical experts had misunderstood American tactics. Unlike the Russians, the Americans were not proposing a massed invasion with the intention of conquering the country themselves. Rather, their objective was 'regime change' in Kabul with the fighting on the ground carried out by the tribes of the Northern Alliance. Small detachments of British and American special forces would assist the Northern Alliance's efforts and provide laser-targeting for what would be America's major contribution – precision aerial bombing of Taleban and al-Qaeda positions. The critics' point had been that the Soviets had got bogged down fighting a wily and formidable foe, the mujahidin, yet the Anglo-American plan was to enlist and bribe these very fighters to win for them. There were two potential pitfalls with this strategy. The tribes and rival warlords of the Northern Alliance had a history of mutual acrimony. Their internal hatreds were one of the reasons they had lost so much of the country to the Taleban in the first place. They had been fighting the Taleban for six years and during that time had suffered continuous reverses. The second problem was that, while they might be able to regain the initiative in their northern Tajik heartlands, it was assumed they would meet stern resistance from the Pashtun peoples of the south. The Pashtuns were far more supportive of the Taleban. The third problem was articulated by Simon Jenkins:

I hope the word ethical never again crosses the lips of a British government minister. Not in modern history can Britain have forged a public alliance with such unsavoury characters as Abdul Rashid Dostum, Abdul Malik, Ismail Khan, Mohammad Ustad Atta and other northerners, mostly financed by heroin. These men have given a new dimension to the word terror.[64]

On 7 October, American bombing commenced. Anthony Loyd reported from the Northern Alliance's lines near Bagram airport, south of Kabul. He could not help thinking, 'Their morale has improved immensely since their sudden promotion to incidental ally of a superpower.'[65] Janine di Giovanni was based at the Northern Alliance's headquarters. Afghanistan appeared to be a landscape marked out by the landmarks of unending conflict. 'At the foot of the hill, among the scattering of 100m tank shells and alongside the shadow of a giant T55 tank, are Greek ruins dating from the time of Alexander the Great, the leader of a Western military power that made its mark in Afghanistan 2,300 years ago,' she wrote with more than a hint of foreboding. 'Yesterday soldiers from the Northern Alliance took positions behind giant stone urns that once belonged to Queen Hairum to fight yet another battle in Afghanistan.'[66]

The defence editor, Michael Evans, provided expert military analysis. *Times* reporters who were on the receiving end had much to contend with. By early November, Loyd's level of discomfort worsened under the onslaught of acute dysentery. Janine di Giovanni described how, after seventeen days in Afghanistan, the only bath available to her was a dust bath. 'The tension here is not just getting the story,' she admitted. 'It is the fight for survival – finding a place to sleep, grabbing the first bowl of goat-tasting rice, finding a generator that works to charge your satellite phone.' The dust swirled 'into typhoon-like proportions, blinding you, getting in your equipment, making you constantly filthy and irritable.' The result was a dose of bronchitis, a hacking cough and swollen glands. In this, at least, she was not alone. Surveying a foul-smelling shack where fellow reporters were taking refuge, she compared it to 'a giant Victorian tuberculosis clinic'.[67]

Whatever the travails of the press corps, the war was going extraordinarily well for the Northern Alliance. By 9 November, it had captured the strategically important town of Mazar-i Sharif. The belief that the Taleban had solidly entrenched support in the country was shattered. They too were reliant on the intervention of foreigners to fight their battles. This became apparent to *The Times* journalist Ian Cobain who was reporting from the Alliance's positions near Saregh. He watched while 'two ageing T54 tanks trundled slowly up the side of the escarpment to join in the bombardment and fired round after round into the Taleban positions'. One of the tank commanders shouted with undisguised joy, '"These aren't Afghans I'm killing, they're all Chechens and Pakistanis." In Russian, he added: "I'm having a wonderful afternoon."'[68] On 13 November, the Northern Alliance reached the outskirts of Kabul and discovered the Taleban had abandoned their capital.

The success of the Northern Alliance confounded even the war's greatest supporters. Indeed, the very speed of their advance worried those who believed a stronger Anglo-American military presence was urgently needed on the ground in order to ensure fair play. Although there were already special service units operating, the first British troops to arrive officially in Afghanistan were not flown in until 16 November. On his own preferred battleground of the Op-Ed page, Simon Jenkins countered that Kabul had been liberated many times and its sense of joy had never lasted long. 'Afghanistan's history says that this adventure will end in tears. In Kabul we must fight more than terrorism. We must fight history.'[69] Another principal columnist saw events very differently. 'Sometimes war works,' concluded Anatole Kaletsky as the news of the Taleban's flight was digested. He could not resist a dig at all the experts who had insisted the campaign would be a disaster from the first payload being dropped. Ridding Afghanistan of a regime that created more refugees than Rwanda and the Congo combined was a positive good. What was more, the sight of the Taleban running away had destroyed the belief that Islamic fundamentalists were somehow invincible: 'The sudden collapse of the Taleban has proved more clearly than ever that even Muslim fundamentalists are fundamentally human. They try to be on the winning side. They shun defeat. They respect power. They respond to military force and financial incentives. The defeat of the Taleban has shown to the entire Muslim world that the mullah's vision of an ultra-orthodox Islamic Utopia is a catastrophic delusion.'[70]

There was something else gained by the decision to confront the Taleban: intelligence on al-Qaeda. Wondering through the newly liberated Kabul, Anthony Loyd asked to be directed to where the Arabs had lived. He was pointed towards four houses that had, it transpired, been at the centre of al-Qaeda's operations. What the looters had left were the most valuable items – documents. The al-Qaeda operatives had left in a hurry. There was evidence that some documents had spilled onto the floor as they attempted to cart them away. An attempt to set fire to the remainder had fizzled out. There was a profusion of letters, military manuals and aircraft magazines. There were Canadian passport applications, notes on how to blow up bridges and how the air-conditioning systems of apartment blocks worked.

There were details on how to manufacture the toxic biological agent, ricin. There were also notes on how to detonate a dirty bomb using TNT to compress plutonium into a critical mass in order to ensure a nuclear chain reaction and, ultimately, a thermonuclear reaction. 'This was only what was left behind by frightened men escaping the advance of the Mujahidin,' Loyd mused. 'The sensitive material is still with them.'[71]

The war, meanwhile, moved south. A fierce fight took place at Kunduz where the surrounded Taleban made a forlorn stand. They took a pounding. Those that were left surrendered in late November. Kandahar fell, and the last pretence of Taleban rule with it, on 7 December. This war objective secured, the American forces could concentrate on eliminating al-Qaeda's bases in the mountains around Tora Bora. Bin Laden and his closest associates were believed to be holed up there, somewhere in the underground complex of passageways and caves. Janine di Giovanni moved over to Tora Bora to observer operations, while the American air force began dropping 15,000-pound 'daisy cutter' bombs in an attempt to blast out the defenders. By 17 December, however, when the last caves were completely overrun, there was still no sign of bin Laden. Troops continued to comb the area until January, but the assumption was made that he had slipped into northern Pakistan. He would live to fight another day.

What remained unclear was whether the Taleban had been removed permanently from Afghanistan or whether it was merely lying low, waiting for its chance to return when the Americans became bored of the hassles of peacekeeping and departed. On his arrival in Kabul, Loyd had entered a barber shop and asked for a clean shave. 'This may hurt a little, I'm afraid,' replied the barber, flicking open a cut-throat razor. 'Until today it's been five years since I've done a clean shave.' The Taleban's prohibition of male beardlessness had been brutally enforced. Loyd discovered, though, that not many customers were rushing to exercise entirely their new freedom. Most wanted a trim rather than a clean shave. One barber explained why: 'People here are not sure that the Taleban will not return.'[72]

Chaos in the future on the scale of that which had blighted the past was always going to offer the Taleban its best opportunity to make a comeback. The first signs, though, could not have been encouraging to them. In Kabul, Hamid Karzai became interim leader of a shattered nation. By 2004, he became the democratically elected President of Afghanistan. Bush and Blair had brought about regime change in Kabul. In the first months of 2002, the process had yet to come to Baghdad.

VI

The war on terror coincided with a collapse in the advertising market. Over the short space of a few months, the revenue pouring into *The Times* dried up. Like its rivals, the paper could not survive unsupported for a long period on the proceeds of its cover price alone. What was more, if this was to be rapidly hiked up to make good some of the sudden advertising shortfall, all the gains of the 1990s price war would be swiftly reversed. The downturn was particularly ill timed given the fresh expenses involved in covering the war on terror. Rightly, this was given priority, ensuring that other projects had to be curtailed. The most severe budget freeze was imposed since the drastic economies forced upon Simon Jenkins in 1990. Worryingly, the disintegration of the advertising market was not just a British phenomenon. It hit the United States, too, ensuring that the paper could not look to plug the gap from a fresh display of News Corp.'s financial indulgence. Given how quickly the brakes were slammed on, *The Times* managed to maintain a surprisingly unchanged face to its public.

Indeed, it was during this period that the structural problems created in 2000 by the change of formats were put right. To considerable relief, *The Times* was returned to a two section broadsheet format (one for news and comment, the other for business and sport) with *T2* continuing to provide arts and features in an additional and distinctive daily tabloid booklet. Stothard's illness had removed from the scene one of *T2*'s principal architects just at the moment it had been launched. It had taken considerable work by its editor, Sandra Parsons, to mould the tabloid section into an established and popular formula. Yet, by 2002, the task had been largely achieved. Meanwhile, the reintroduction of the business and sport broadsheet section had other implications. The configurations of the printing presses demanded that the two broadsheet sections had to be of equal pagination. Yet, with comment, obituaries and Court & Social all in the first section, this would have meant there was more business and sports reporting than pages of news. It was Ben Preston who devised the solution of shunting Op-Ed and the leader page to the end of the news section and moving obits and Court & Social to the new business and sport second section. There was a minor outcry among some traditional readers who believed that commemorating the passing of the great and the good and reporting the fate of Accrington Stanley made for uneasy bedfellows. But, on the whole, the decision was beneficial and offered traditional readers more, rather than less, of the 'paper of record' formula. In calling the new expanded section 'The Register,' a conscious nod was made to *The Times*'s original 1785 title, the *Daily Universal Register*, and the distinctive masthead heraldry that had accompanied the old name was also resurrected. Three pages for obituaries could now be provided, restoring to *The Times* a clear lead in column inches over its rivals in this area. A 'Lives Remembered' column was also expanded to allow those who had known the deceased to add their own reminiscences.

With 'The Register' launched, sport and business reunited and *T2* beginning to assert itself, Stothard could claim to have presided over both innovation and restoration. The financial clouds created by the advertising recession were the immediate worry but it was unclear, in early 2002, how long the inclemency would prevail. In all other respects, the paper had every reason to be confident. The job done, it was a favourable moment for Stothard to step aside. His tenth anniversary in the chair – by far the longest of any *Times* editor under Murdoch's ownership – was approaching and he intimated to the proprietor that he would not want to remain much beyond that date. Murdoch accepted Stothard's decision. He had met the managing editor of the US edition of the *FT*, Australian Robert Thomson (who had saved Jonathan Mirsky's life in Beijing in 1993) who was credited with transforming the paper's increasing global appeal in its fight to challenge the supremacy of the *Wall Street Journal*. Believing that *The Times* had only a short opportunity to attract someone of Thomson's calibre before a rival did so, Murdoch decided to act. When Thomson accepted, Stothard was informed that the succession was assured and that he could safely step down. It was the end of an era and an appropriate moment for this volume of the paper's history to close. Great changes lay ahead, including the decision of the paper to scrap its broadsheet size in favour of a tabloid format it preferred to describe as 'compact'. There would be other changes: more foreign correspondents were appointed (more, indeed, than at any time in *The Times*'s history) and the paper continued to expand its coverage in other areas as well. It is too early to write with detachment on these and other dramas that will, eventually, shape the opening chapters of a future volume of the history of *The Times*. On 21 February 2002, Peter Stothard announced he was stepping down to the full complement of his editorial staff assembled around him in the newsroom. He retired amid the sort of scenes of emotion and goodwill from his colleagues that few editors had come to expect, let alone experience. There was genuine pleasure when it was announced that, as the new editor of the *Times Literary Supplement*, he was not moving so far away after all. Colleagues had found much in him to admire personally. His dignified struggle with cancer and the manner of his recovery had naturally attracted respect. He had been a guiding presence at the paper for twenty years and an editor for almost ten of them. Yet, he had been more than just an emblem of continuity during years of change and strain. He had worked hard to expand *The Times*'s range and been rewarded with a doubling of its circulation. He had been fortunate in some respects as well. Charlie Wilson had been dogged by a rival, the *Independent*, that was closing fast on *The Times*'s heels. This threat quickly receded during Stothard's editorship, in part because of the hirings made by his predecessor, Simon Jenkins, and by business decisions made by the *Independent*'s management. This was not the only good fortune. Unlike Harold Evans or Simon Jenkins, Stothard's period in the chair had coincided with the parent company's preparedness to invest heavily in the paper rather than cut its budget back. The price war had been a major factor in the paper's upward ascent. Only when the cover price was raised significantly higher would it be clear how many readers had been truly hooked to its contents. However, in attracting a younger but affluent readership, the demographic trends were moving steadily in *The Times*'s favour and many media forecasters believed that Murdoch's long cherished hope that it would supplant the *Telegraph* as the market leader still looked attainable in the longer term. Time would tell.

The paper had expanded its coverage in almost all directions. Sport had made large gains, as had features. Perhaps Stothard's two most important appointments were William Rees-Mogg and Patience Wheatcroft. The return of Rees-Mogg as a columnist sent out a strong signal that, despite the changes being made, the paper had not lost touch with its traditions and fundamental decency. Wheatcroft began a quiet revolution on the business pages, bringing the *FT* under intensive challenge in the home market for the first time in two decades. Nonetheless, the successes of *The Times* during the Stothard years were down to many people of whom only a small number were familiar to the readership. Rosemary Righter had maintained the intellectual rigour of the anonymous leading articles without succumbing to the self-doubting prevarication that had occasionally made balanced debate appear a higher priority than reasoned argument. David Ruddock had been an able master of the backbench, producing night after night a *news*paper that was sharp and unpredictable. Two successive deputy editors, John Bryant and Ben Preston, and managing editors, Peter Roberts and George Brock, had also been the hidden hands tailoring the garment to measure. From his chief revise editor's desk, Tim Austin had quietly turned many a journalistic sow's ear into a silk purse.

The paper had certainly not shirked from controversy and had not always escaped from the fray unbloodied. It campaigned against Greg Dyke becoming the BBC's director-general. Dyke was appointed nevertheless. A lengthier campaign had been launched that questioned Michael Ashcroft's suitability as Treasurer of the Conservative Party. Ashcroft too had survived. The long affair with the 'natural party of government' had been ended although the flirtation with the new claimant to that title appeared of uncertain duration and highly conditional. The great ideological battle over joining the euro was deferred, although, if the opinion polls were accurate, The Times's opposition resonated with much of the population at large. Responding to the vacuum and new alarms created by the Cold War's end, the paper endorsed military intervention in foreign wars.

Naturally there were those who maintained, as they and their great-grandfathers always had, that the paper was a pale shadow if its former self. Those who believed the cost charged for doubling the circulation was the vulgarization of the paper's content claimed that this was the true legacy of Peter Stothard's editorship. It is a contention that will be analysed in the concluding chapter. Among those who knew him personally, it was hard to equate the charge with the man. One of his favourite poems was New Year Letter, written by W. H. Auden in 1940 from the United States as he contemplated the coming fall of Europe. Mourning the lack of leadership, the poem professed the need for a 'voice within the labyrinth of choice'. Providing the voice had been Stothard's achievement in expanding The Times.

CHAPTER FOURTEEN

DUMBING DOWN?

An Overview of the Paper's Performance, 1981–2002

I

For whose benefit has all this effort been directed? Throughout the first twenty-one years in which *The Times* was owned by Rupert Murdoch, it was dogged by two particularly unrelenting criticisms. The first claim was that the paper dumbed down. In other words, it stepped back from its historic position as the journal of record by reducing the quantity and quality of its serious news analysis in favour of more populist, less political, material. The second criticism was related to this first line of attack. It is that, by dumbing down, *The Times* has ceased to be distinct from its competition. Instead of catering for a small but well-informed audience – a 'ruling few' – it is just another newspaper, appealing to the same market as the rest of the quality press. In this interpretation, gaining more readers has been at the expense of providing more elevated journalism.

In assessing the validity of these complaints it is perhaps best to start with the question of the paper's audience. Part of the problem has always been in defining what a typical *Times* reader looked and behaved like. With whatever level of fairness, the other newspapers attracted recognizable stereotypes among their readers – the public sector employee, wearing his corduroy jacket and CND badge, who read the *Guardian*; the Tory-voting Labrador owner and WI volunteer who stood loyally by the *Daily Telegraph*. In contrast, *The Times* never stirred quite the same partisan passions. It appeared to see its own role as that of a moderating counsel to all those in positions of authority. A problem with this was that *The Times*'s supposed stereotype, a civil servant wandering purposefully down Whitehall in a bowler hat and striped trousers, was a sight that had not been seen in public since the early 1960s. At any rate, his descendants – if they had not switched to the *FT* – could hardly be sufficiently numerous to swell *The Times*'s circulation from 280,000 when Murdoch bought the paper in 1981 to nearly 700,000 in 2002. Indeed, Murdoch was hardly the newspaper owner to make courting the British Establishment his life's ambition. He regarded with distaste the notion that the paper existed merely to entertain and inform the 'ruling few'. Matthew Parris, who as a *Times* columnist throughout the 1990s received between twenty and a hundred letters a week from readers, was certainly of the view that there was nothing predictable about them. Some were wealthy but:

> most strike me as neither rich nor poor, and a notable group are of above average education and below average income: young people and old (especially elderly ladies), who in material terms have quite a struggle and for whom an intelligent newspaper represents a vantage point from which to survey the world of ideas, research and the arts. Perhaps my correspondents are untypical, but I am struck by how unmaterialistic most who write to me are: life to them is about more than money.[1]

Throughout the twentieth century, such readers had been attracted to *The Times*, albeit in smaller numbers in total than were reading it by the end of the century. In his study of the paper during the late 1960s and 1970s John Grigg defined them as the 'cultivated and idiosyncratic, but obscure, people'.[2] If the paper was attracting them in increasing quantities – as the raw evidence suggested – then, far from being a point of criticism, it was a positive sign. They may not have been the most commercially attractive stratum of society, but they were some of the most discerning people in the country.

In any case, such readers did not replace the 'ruling few' that were the historic core of *The Times*'s market. They supplemented them. During the years of the Major Government, a higher proportion of MPs still read *The Times* than any other paper.[3] When the smug advertising slogan 'Top People Take *The Times*' was first plastered across billboards in 1957, the 'top people' in question were those classified as social grade 'A'. 'A' grade readers came from households where the chief income earner's occupation could be categorized as higher managerial, administrative or professional. Bishops, board directors and senior managers of large companies with more than two hundred employees, established doctors and barristers and the highest officer ranks (colonel to field marshal) within the armed forces were all, for example, in this category. When Murdoch bought *The Times*, only 3 per cent of the population could be so described, yet more than a fifth of *The Times*'s readers were among them. Although nothing could dislodge the *Telegraph*'s sheer weight of numbers, *The Times* had the highest proportion of any broadsheet newspaper. By 2002, the percentage of Britons who were in the 'A' social grade still only comprised 3 per cent of the population. Yet *The Times* – while broadening its appeal to other social groups – remained the broadsheet newspaper with the highest proportion of 'A' grade readers. While the largest growth in new readers had come from the other social categories, the total number of 'A' grade readers had increased over the period from 186,000 to 273,000. The consequence of twenty-one years of Rupert Murdoch's ownership was that more 'top people' were taking *The Times* than had ever done so before, even compared to when it had been owned by such gentleman proprietors as the Astor family. Indeed, their increasing numbers (up almost 47 per cent) between 1982 and 2002 was far more significant than the growing numbers of 'A' grade households in the country at large (whose numbers had risen 21 per cent).

Social class 'A'

('A' class readers as a percentage of paper's readership; total number of 'A' class readers)

	1982		1992		2002	
	%		%		%	
The Times	21	186,000	17	174,000	15	273,000
Financial Times	19	137,000	19	120,000	13	74,000
Daily Telegraph	14	462,000	12	292,000	13	323,000
Independent		n/a	12	132,000	12	69,000
Guardian	8	116,000	8	104,000	8	105,000
Adult population	3	1,352,000	3	1,344,000	3	1,645,000

Source: National Readership Survey (readers per average issue; Monday to Saturday, January to December 1982, 1992, 2002)

What was especially noteworthy was that the number of these so-called 'top' readers contracted during the 1980s. The paper had twelve thousand fewer of them in 1992 than in 1982. The dramatic increase came thereafter. Thus the era of the 'price war' not only – as might be expected – attracted poorer or less loftily employed readers to *The Times*, but also increased in absolute terms the number of 'top people' readers attracted to it as well. Whether or not Peter Stothard dumbed down the paper's content during the period of his editorship, the allegation that he dumbed down the readership cannot be sustained. To retain a higher social profile than the *Financial Times*, while simultaneously appealing to a far broader swathe of the public, was no small achievement.

The reality was thus different from the appearance. It was in this latter respect that the dumbing down allegation had superficial appeal. At a cosmetic level, *The Times* of 2002 certainly looked less high minded than it had done twenty or thirty years before. Where once the printed word had been crammed into every available inch of the page (as if wartime paper rationing was still in place), the newspaper belatedly evolved and adapted to the challenge of television by becoming more visually appealing and less cluttered in its appearance. Technological advance allowed for larger pictures (with better definition) and for colour printing. Some readers considered the latter a vulgarity when it first appeared in 1991 but, by any objective criteria, it was a significant step forward. Visually, the paper certainly had moved towards a format closer to that favoured by glossy magazines and tabloids. Headlines got bigger. Banner headlines were appropriate for stories of national importance or for a breaking crisis, but the overuse of large text smacked of sensationalism and devalued the journalistic coinage. Furthermore, large font sizes for headlines forced the subeditors to describe the article's message in fewer words. Inevitably, this encouraged inexactitude and exaggeration. Perfectly well-balanced articles became controversial because of the prejudicial and inaccurate headline with which they were lumbered. Another dumbing-down trait was the use of puns in headlines. Although often entertaining, overuse undermined the gravity of the page – especially when more serious news items were cohabiting there.

It was not difficult to understand why many thought the paper was lowering its standards when the front page became the least decorously laid out part of the whole paper. Given how impenetrable the front page of Douglas-Home's *Times* had been, this shift was not entirely for the worse. For those of an aesthetic disposition, though, one newcomer really did lower the neighbourhood's tone. The placing of a puff strapline above (or periodically below) *The Times* masthead was intended to draw the attention of non-committed passers-by to interesting features buried in the pages within. That *The Times*'s rivals all adopted the same approach suggested they too saw the commercial necessity of selling their product's internal wares more openly. At *The Times*, the process began in earnest in 1988 as a means of demonstrating the increasing variety of sections contained within the Saturday paper. With Peter Stothard's arrival in the editor's chair, the practice became a daily occurrence. What was more, the width of the puff band expanded and eventually its superimposed images began to burst beyond the strap boundaries. Suddenly, the elegant lettering of *The Times* masthead, with its Hanoverian coat of arms, was daily jostled by the raised arm of an ecstatic footballer or the bald head of a cartoon character. Like a famous department store taking lessons in shop-window display from an out-of-town supermarket, this did nothing for the dignity of the paper.

These were questions of style and, perhaps, taste. But what had become of the substance? Had *The Times* really reduced the quantity or quality of its content as its critics alleged? The popular perception, reinforced by media pundits like Stephen Glover, was that the greatest period of dumbing down occurred during Peter Stothard's editorship when the paper's circulation doubled. Not everyone believed gaining more readers was good for *The Times*'s mental health. This was the same 'more will mean worse' argument that had animated Kingsley Amis's denunciation of expanding the number of universities and students in 1960 (a process that had subsequently grown the 'quality' newspaper market). At *The Times*, there was certainly more. The paper's circulation had gone up not only by lowering the price hurdle for purchasers but also by expanding the coverage it provided. There were over four million column centimetres of journalism (excluding advertisements and inserts) in *The Times* during 1992. In 2002, the figure had jumped to nearly 6.7 million column centimetres. Thus, *The Times* of 2002 had over 2.5 million more column centimetres of journalistic material in the year Peter Stothard departed the editorship than when he took up the position.[4] This was a substantial increase. Home news had increased from 625,929 column centimetres in 1992 to 923,551 in 2002. European and world news had increased during the same period from 348,042 to 397,049. This was a less spectacular jump but nonetheless ran counter to the popular assertion that *The Times* had reduced its international coverage over the years. The business pages – hardly a 'dumb' section of the paper – had risen by more than 60 per cent. Sport had recorded an even more spectacular growth.

Column centimetres of journalism in *The Times*
*(Including editorial and supplements; excluding all inserts,
classified advertisements and promotions)*

	1992	2002	% change
Total	4,153,279	6,659,982	+ 60.3
Home news	625,929	923,551	+ 47.5
World news	348,042	397,049	+ 14.0
Parliament	113,441	55,198	− 51.3
Business/finance	550,482	895,525	+ 62.6
Sport	714,705	1,234,524	+ 72.7

Source: Author's calculations based on data from Nielsen Media Research.[5]

The raw numbers, of course, did not tell the whole story. The issue was not just one of quantity but of quality. The space devoted to home news doubled over the decade but some of this increase was accounted for not by more intensive political or investigative journalism but by an increasing predilection for 'human interest' stories. These might range from salacious disclosures in the High Court involving some private tragedy or a celebrity divorce to the sort of 'fancy that?' style of story that could be summed up in the headline 'Long day for Santas but that's ho ho ho business'.[6] The number of stories involving animals showed a marked rise. This development was put down by some to Stothard's interest in wildlife. The tone of these animal and human interest articles was often whimsical and they shed a light on some aspect of British eccentricity that might otherwise have gone unrecorded. Occasionally, the focus looked more prurient. Personal tragedies tended to make for better stories if accompanied by a picture of the dead/missing/pregnant teenager. The photograph was larger if the victim was pretty or middle class. When critics derided the journalistic quality of *The Times*, it was often this sort of reporting they had in mind. Against such observations, two points need to be made. First, such articles were usually supplementing, rather than replacing, the more traditional news items. Second, the idea that *The Times*'s role was to report the machinations of the powerful and influential but to ignore stories about ordinary people living and working beyond the metropolitan elite, suggested a rather narrow interest in the world in all its variety and diversity. The paper was there to appeal to and reflect a large community, not behave as if its constituency was a nineteenth-century rotten borough.

It was possible to exaggerate the extent to which 'human interest' stories were taking a hold of the paper, although the impression was helped by the increasing likelihood of their being placed in the front few pages of the main section rather than further back. A reader trying to locate Peter Riddell's political commentary had first to flick through several pages in which the small type of the news articles made less visual impact than the outsize photographs of the actress Kate Winslet smiling from a red carpet or the entertainer Michael Barrymore looking troubled. This did give the impression that the paper had a populist sense of priorities. It was certainly a change from *The Times* of former decades. The front news pages of the 1970s and early 1980s contained tightly packed political stories. Yet, on closer inspection, a significant proportion of the political news in *The Times* of that period was the work of the labour desk. Edition after edition was packed with news of strikes, industrial problems and successive governments' attempts to intervene in them. These stories became a casualty not of an editorial decision but of their increasing infrequency once the Thatcher reforms began to have their effect on changing the climate of Britain's industrial relations and depoliticizing the disputes that remained. Consequently, the work of successive industrial correspondents, Edward Townsend and Ross Tieman, and industrial editors, Derek Harris, Philip Bassett and Christine Buckley, increasingly appeared not in the news pages but in the business section.

Much of the shift of industrial/political stories from news to business happened during the 1980s. A different rebalancing of power was responsible for the reduction of other political news stories in the 1990s. In the home news section of the paper, the coverage of British politics and Parliament halved between 1992 and 2002. In drawing comparisons, it should be remembered that 1992, unlike 2002, was a general election year. However, by 1992 Simon Jenkins's decision to terminate the parliamentary page had already been made. Saving money was not the only reason behind his decision to do away with the paper's attempt to provide readers with a potted version of *Hansard*. Reporting the legislature's debates made sense in the past but its relevance had ebbed as far as contemporary politics was concerned. Britain was increasingly governed not from the chambers of the Houses of Parliament but – as Jenkins well comprehended – from Downing Street, Whitehall, a multitude of quangoes and through EU directives and regulations emanating from Brussels. From a journalistic perspective, this created problems: these other governmental organizations were not as transparent as the Palace of Westminster and publishing on-the-record information was more difficult. This did have a deleterious effect on the comprehensiveness of political reporting.

By 2002, *The Times* had five journalists lurking around Westminster's precincts where twenty years earlier it employed twelve just to report the Commons debates for the Parliament page. Nonetheless, when parliamentary politics most mattered, such as on key Commons divisions or in political crises, *The Times*'s coverage was as comprehensive as it had ever been. Nobody reading it during Peter Stothard's tenure could have complained there was insufficient coverage of the European debate. The reporting and analysis of Budget statements became increasingly detailed. Peter Riddell had as good a feel for the business of government as any of the paper's past political editors. Indeed, on closer inspection the supposed past 'golden age' tarnished easily. In terms of general election coverage, *The Times* had improved remarkably over the last half-century. In the run-up to the 1951 general election, *The Times* offered only one page a day (it was then only a twelve-page paper) of reports on the coming election. A week before polling day in February 1974, it had expanded sufficiently to provide election reports on the front page and on one and a half pages inside, supplemented with Op-Ed and leader page comment (out of a total paper of twenty-eight-pages). By comparison, during the 1997 general election campaign, the fifty-six-page *Times* was regularly committing eight pages of coverage every day in addition to a level of in-depth scrutiny, outside specialists' analysis and interviews that was simply unimaginable a quarter of, let alone half, a century before.

Nor was the reporting of general elections a rare aberration against the trend. The average *Times* edition of 1951 only devoted half a page to home news and two-thirds of a page to foreign news. The business section ran to three columns. Far from being the repository of fine writing, most of the content was short 'news in brief'-style articles for which the source was usually information provided by wire services and official announcements. Analysis was largely restricted to the anonymous proclamations of the leading articles. By 1974, *The Times* was moving much closer to the paper of 2002 in its approach to news gathering and content. Yet, even allowing for a format that crammed more words onto the page (and was consequently harder to read), its offering was much more narrowly focused than what was made available by the paper edited by Peter Stothard.

Much of *The Times*'s historic reputation had been built on the strength of its foreign reporting. It was, after all, the paper of William Howard Russell, Henri de Blowitz and Louis Heren. During the 1980s and 1990s the main allegation against the overseas reporting was less that it had dumbing down by introducing too many human interest stories so much as that it had simply lost its authority. Such a charge was, necessarily, a matter of opinion and, with hindsight, it was not clear what was so impressive about a paper's past judgment that backed appeasing Hitler in the 1930s and Stalin in the 1940s. Naturally, there were those who believed appeasing Israel and taking a tough line on the Arab states were mistaken opinions adopted by the modern paper although the foreign desk received far more – often abusive – calls from readers who were convinced the paper was too critical of successive Israeli governments. All the paper could do was assess the situation to the best of its ability and, having taken every effort to establish the facts, stand by what it reported.

In the areas where the paper's foreign coverage could be quantified, there was no question that it had improved since its acquisition by News International. The paper's foreign news coverage took up more space in the first years of the twenty-first century than at any period in its history. It also had more foreign correspondents reporting from around the globe than at any previous time. Even after taking account of inflation and other increments, the resources the company ploughed into foreign news reporting dwarfed what had been invested in previous decades. Such was the financial squeeze pursued by the Thomson management that when one of the paper's most experienced foreign correspondents, David Watts, joined *The Times* in 1974, he discovered that the foreign desk staff were forbidden from making international telephone calls, even when in direct pursuit of a story. Instead, they had to wait for a possible informant to call them. A paper riding on its reputation for foreign coverage was temporarily reduced to a policy that could only be described as 'call us, we won't call you'. Unsurprisingly, in Watts's opinion, the quality of the paper's foreign journalism had improved immeasurably over the succeeding thirty years.[7]

When *The Times* had been understaffed and underresourced during the Astor and Thomson proprietorships, great reliance had been placed on the reports arriving from the news agency wire services. The result was that, on almost any given day, the paper carried brief news reports from a wide variety of different countries. Details even of a relatively minor change in the Sudanese cabinet might appear. This gave the impression of a paper devoted to publishing the detailed business of government from countries large and small. Peregrine Worsthorne once lovingly recalled that as a trainee foreign sub at *The Times* in the late 1940s he had been given a dressing down for failing to spot a minor mistake in the published list of the Sudanese government's new members – the junior minister of posts' name had been inaccurately rendered from the Arabic. To Worsthorne, this episode demonstrated how much a paper that once prided itself on its accuracy had subsequently lowered its standards. Yet the incident also highlights the extent to which *The Times*'s foreign reporting often comprised little more than copying verbatim (with or without mistakes) an official press release. In what respect was this insightful journalism? *The Times* of the 1990s certainly contained fewer references to the intricacies of the Khartoum regime's musical chairs and, in this sense, the paper could be accused of being less of an international journal of record. But those who really needed to know the identity of the current junior minister responsible for Sudan's postal service could far more easily contact its embassy or find it out through an internet search rather than hope it might be listed somewhere in *The Times* that day. The notion that the paper's primary role in the 1990s should still have been – as Worsthorne comprehended it half a century earlier – to provide the 'essential information needed by the then governing and administrative classes to carry out their official duties' was one that technology had comprehensively superseded.

In fact, the unvarnished statements that comprised so much of *The Times*'s international coverage in the 1940s and 1950s had not been entirely abolished fifty years later. The old agency wire-based tradition continued in the 'news in brief' columns running down the margins of the page and this left most of the expanse of paper for much longer and more perceptive articles than had been the vogue in the past. Such changes called upon the expertise of far more reporters filing from the countries they were actually writing about (and using knowledgeable local stringers where necessary). David Watts's understanding of the complexity of the Asia-Pacific countries, Roger Boyes's reports from central and Eastern Europe, Richard Owen in Rome and Charles Bremner in Paris all combined to provide a deep knowledge of their adopted countries with a fluid and engaging writing style. This was something *The Times* of previous generations often lacked. Indeed, as Worsthorne pointed out, 'the most important qualification for being a journalist when I began fifty years ago was not an ability to write'. Such was *The Times*'s aversion to analysis rather than the straight repetition of published information that 'intellectuals, therefore, were frowned upon as well as writers'.[8] In retrospect, foreign reporting in *The Times* has become a far more sophisticated profession. Aside from covering political developments, correspondents have also been given the space to paint in their articles a 'slice of life' from the countries and cultures that are their speciality. Such insights were rarely accorded to *Times* readers back in the 'golden age'. Where the focus remains narrowly political, innovations like Bronwen Maddox's daily 'Foreign Editor's Briefing', instituted in 2001, greatly enhanced the paper's breadth of international analysis. Anyone interested in comparing *The Times* then and now need only look at its coverage of the signing on 25 March 1957 of the Treaty of Rome, which, in creating the EEC, was one of the most important political developments of the twentieth century. The event was accorded one news item, on column six of the foreign news page (page eight), under the headline 'Further steps in uniting Europe'. There was no picture (the photograph used that day was of voters going to the polls in Belize) and, in order of priorities, it was accorded the fifth most important priority status on that day's page. About half of its 350-word commentary was taken up listing the names of the signatories and describing the décor of the hall in which the agreement was reached. No unaware reader would have understood why the German Chancellor was prophesying it to be 'a historic date in European affairs'.[9] Nor would the reader have been any the wiser seeking elucidation in other pages of the paper. The leading article that day decided the passage of the Shops Bill in the House of Lords was more worthy of its attention. Indeed, apart from one brief article on 11 March and a reprinting – without comment or analysis of any kind – of the basic provisions in the agreement on 20 March, *The Times* failed utterly in the months either side of the Treaty's signing to bother with the story of the EEC's creation even although it was clearly regarded on the Continent as a development of the utmost significance. Judged by such slipshod standards, it is the foreign coverage of the pre-Murdoch *Times* that appears surprisingly dumbed down.

A year after News International's purchase, the fortunes of the paper's business section had fallen markedly. For the next fifteen years, successive business editors were unable to regain the level of coverage that *The Times* business news had provided in the 1970s. This was a period of sudden but long-lasting decline. Indeed, the notion that the paper was a serious rival to the *Financial Times* could not be sustained. *The Times* had neither the range nor the depth. By the late 1990s, however, it was clawing ground back fast. This was partly a response to investment but also a mood of optimism and professionalism that prevailed following Stothard's appointment of Patience Wheatcroft as business editor. The improvement was rewarded in the readership statistics. One serious survey in March 2002 suggested that *The Times* was leading the way with business readers classified in the A-B social grades with 274,000 business readers as compared to 239,000 for the *FT* and 235,000 for the *Daily Telegraph*.[10]

In the areas of home, foreign, business and sports news, direct comparisons can be attempted between what *The Times* was providing at different stages of its development. Much of the dumbing down debate, however, involves subject matter that was given far less priority prior to 1981. This was a response to interconnected social, economic and cultural changes. The consumer choices available in the free-market sector of 1990s Britain far exceeded the more limited (and even State-rationed) choice of the post-war high street. This was not just a matter of supermarkets offering ten different varieties of stuffed olive where once there had been none. The number of books published had soared. Deregulation policies and advances in cable, satellite and digital technology broadened the television, radio, computer and internet options in homes across the country. Knowledge and appreciation of wine was no longer confined to the privileged or to aficionados. The quality of restaurants and interest in cooking grew exponentially. Cheaper air travel and the growth of the tourist industry brought travel to exotic or luxurious locations within the budget of young people where once it had been the preserve of the rich or reckless. A profusion of unit trusts and investment options was on offer to those with even relatively modest savings. *The Times* would have been involved not only in commercial suicide but also in a dereliction of duty if it had not broadened its coverage in all these areas. But for those who regarded any journalism not engaged in the reporting of serious news as a dumbing down exercise, there was much to condemn in the resulting proliferation of pages and supplements that guided *Times* readers through the bewildering array of consumer choices. Doubtless some who wanted to keep the pleasures of Positano to themselves shivered at the thought of a newspaper article directing hordes of new *Times* readers to the delights of the Amalfi coast. On this logic, the more information the paper provided, the less exclusive it became.

The Times in the post-war period had not disdainfully turned its back on consumerism. It happily printed small estate agent advertisements for houses in Surrey, garage salesrooms, stockbroking firms or holiday offers of bed and board in Torquay. This was not considered to be pandering to tawdry tastes. Yet, when the paper expanded the column inches it gave to seriously discussing the property market, assessing the performance of a new range of cars or pension plans, or reporting from an exotic holiday location, so arose the accusations of going downmarket and indulging in the worst excesses of 'lifestyle' journalism. This was particularly galling considering how knowledgeable and refined in taste were so many of the journalists involved. The restaurant critic, Jonathan Meades, went in search of high standards of cuisine, not fast food. The wine critic, Jane MacQuitty, did not overindulge on supermarket plonk. Anne Ashworth did not cater, primarily, for those with a poor credit rating.

Saturdays became the day in which most of these 'lifestyle' articles appeared. As the 1990s commenced, the increasing availability of colour printing meant that magazine supplements could be produced that rivalled what had once been the virtual monopoly of the Sunday Times whose colour magazine had famously revolutionized weekend journalism back in 1962. Bigger and glossier, The Times on Saturday mimicked many of the attributes that had made the Sunday Times the country's market leader. Some readers, indeed, appeared to be under the misconception that the Sunday Times was The Times on Sunday although The Times never quite found the formula to attract the scale of readership amassed by the other News International-owned broadsheet. Nonetheless, by the early 1990s, The Times was among the broadsheets whose combined Saturday market had surged 18 per cent higher than their weekday sales. In February 1997, the Saturday broadsheet market finally overtook the Sunday market. The Times played its part in this process. By 1995, it was selling almost a fifth more copies than during weekdays. It had long been a tough assignment for one man to edit a six-day newspaper, especially when, by the mid-nineties, the Saturday paper had expanded to eight sections. Consequently, the Saturday paper had its own editor and in the latter half of the decade Nicholas Wapshott directed the operation. Wapshott had joined The Times in 1976 and, after a spell as the Observer's political editor, had taken charge of the new-look Saturday Times Magazine in 1992. Under his command, the Saturday paper continued to broaden its range. Not all the accusations of dumbing down were mistaken. In the main news section, there was, on average, less hard political news. This was partly a response to what was considered to be the different demands of the weekend readership. It was also a reflection of the minimal parliamentary and political business conducted on Fridays. The colourful and breezy style of Play, an arts and entertainment magazine started in September 2000, did not suit lengthy or serious review articles. At the same time, cost-cutting measures in the wake of the collapse of the advertising market diminished what could be offered elsewhere in the paper and many readers found themselves denied the sort of serious literary and artistic review section that rival newspapers were offering on Saturdays. It was a deficiency put right when, in 2004, *Play*'s stop button was pressed and the more upmarket *Weekend Review* launched.

The Times on Saturdays was much more successful at attracting women readers than during the week. When Robert Thomson succeeded Peter Stothard, the paper's male-to-female readership ratio was still around 60:40 but on Saturdays it was heading towards sexual equality. In particular, the glossy full-colour *Times Magazine* proved the right medium for fashion and beauty photography and journalism. During the week, the paper had long attempted – not always successfully – to entice more female readers by producing feature pages perceived to be of interest to them. Like *The Times*, the *Daily Mail* had made enormous circulation gains in the second half of the 1990s and this achievement was, in part, attributed to the strenuous efforts it had made to appeal to female readers. There were lessons to be learned from this and, with Sandra Parsons in charge, *The Times*'s new features *T2* tabloid section was started in 2000 amid hopes of similar success. It got off to an uncertain start but by the time the whole paper had followed it down a tabloid path, it was competing favourably with the opposition. In an age when instant news was available from so many other media providers, Parsons's pages were a principal reason for customers continuing to pay the cover price for *The Times*. They helped give the paper its distinctive flavour. Features were no longer an after-thought. They had become an essential ingredient.

To those of a certain age and sex, the dumbing down and the feminiza-tion of *The Times* were one and the same. Female-orientated features were often of the 'human interest' variety and might involve ruminations on such intangible and abstract subject matter as emotions and relationships rather than hard facts and world politics. Whether putting a picture of a pretty actress on the front page appealed more to male or female readers was a moot point. At any rate, as Peter Stothard once reminded Jonathan Mirsky when he complained about the pro-glamour picture priority, the boost in sales generated by having a famous catwalk model smiling out from the front page was what helped to pay the expense of keeping the eminent China scholar as the paper's correspondent in Hong Kong.[11] A newspaper that daily repeated the same images of pensive politicians enter-ing and leaving front doors might also be accused of failing to provide a balanced view of the state of mankind. *The Times* could certainly be accused of getting the balance wrong and the increasing use of page three for 'soft news' stories ahead of more solemn events was a case in point. Likewise, some argued (not altogether convincingly) that there was a place for reports from Paris Fashion Week, but it was not in the main news section of the paper. These were not new developments, however. Before Rupert Murdoch bought *The Times*, page three had not been the place for hard news but for full-page advertisements and fashion spreads appeared cheek by jowl with overseas news. Indeed, some of the old paper's layout priorities were far less explicable than the blurring of hard and soft news in the 1990s. Sport used to appear in the middle of the paper. Thus, the earnest reader had to flick past several pages devoted to ballgames before reaching the leading articles and weightier analysis. It was not until 1981, when Harold Evans sensibly reordered the contents, that the action from Anfield and Aintree was moved to the back pages.

The extent to which *The Times* was 'feminized' during the 1990s could be hotly contested. Covering everything from militant feminism (which was poorly catered for) to pedicure and manicure advice, the term was as imprecise as an observation that the paper in the 1930s was heavily masculine. Back in that period, the business pages were almost inescapably written by men for men. By 2002, society's stratification was less clearly delineated. There was no longer anything especially male orientated about a company report. Instead, a more worthwhile judgment on how *The Times* had become less male orientated can be made not so much by categorizing the content as by those who produced and commissioned it. In 1981, women represented a small minority of *The Times*'s complement of senior journalists. Some of them had built high reputations, like Geraldine Norman, who was fearless in exposing corruption and poor practice in the salesroom world. They were at the helm, though, of only three principal departments – fashion, features and Court & Social. By 2002, the position was transformed. The business pages were edited by Patience Wheatcroft, *T2* was edited by Sandra Parsons, Bronwen Maddox was foreign editor, Anne Ashworth edited the money section, Rosemary Righter was bowing out after many years as chief leader writer, Erica Wagner was literary editor, Cath Urquhart was travel editor, Lisa Armstrong presided over fashion and Brigid Callaghan edited the internet edition, *Times Online*. Alice Miles and Mary Ann Sieghart influenced the paper's politics and, alongside Libby Purves, were regular columnists. For the most part, this blow for equality made little difference to the finished product: there was nothing definitively feminine about a Wheatcroft business page or the thunder rumbling from a Righter leading article.

Indeed, if articles could be easily divided according to their gender appeal, the 1990s was also the decade in which sports coverage – which had a far higher male readership – increased by more than 70 per cent. Even this statistic needed qualification. During the decade, the paper turned increasingly to women sports journalists, several of whom became major columnists. Nonetheless, most of the sporting subject matter retained an overwhelmingly male following. Richard Williams believed 'the single most noticeable factor' in the history of broadsheet newspapers over the past twenty years was the growth of their sports coverage.[12] Football saw the biggest growth with *The Times* following in the wake of its proprietor's identification of soccer coverage as a lucrative growth market. Besides the daily reports, a popular development commenced in 2000 with the publication of monthly football handbooks to accompany the league season. These were soon supplemented with similar productions for rugby union's Six Nations championship, the Ashes and Formula One. There was hardly a sport whose coverage was not substantially improved by the end of the century when compared to ten, let alone twenty, years earlier. In 1984, *The Times*'s coverage of the Los Angeles Olympics rarely exceeded one page a day. By the time of the 2000 Olympics in Sydney, there was, on top of all the usual number of sports pages, a daily twelve-page supplement of Olympic reports. For the many *Times* readers who had no interest in sport, this expansion looked excessive. This was not, in itself, a reason for cutting back. After all, a large proportion of readers had no interest in what was contained within the business section, although this was hardly an argument for restricting its development. The notion that the expanding coverage accorded to sport was a sign of the paper dumbing down was difficult to sustain, given that the growth of the second section was not at the expense of the main news and comment section. Only when sport intruded into the main section for no better reason than that its practitioners had become well-known celebrities could the charge be made that the overall effect was not an improvement in the depth and reach of the newspaper.

II

A history of *The Times* in the last years of the twentieth century naturally seeks to discern the principal changes and developments. However, the paper's continuing appeal has not been determined purely by its zeal for experimentation. The great trend of the Murdoch years has not so much been *The Times*'s dumbing down or wising up, but rather the enduring strength of old staples. In this respect, the letters and obituary pages lead the field. Even those who believed *The Times* had lost its former authority continued to hold its letters page in esteem. Its autonomous spirit, not least as a forum for dissent against the paper's editorial line, was what Roy Jenkins assured Peter Stothard 'has led some of us to remain faithful to *The Times* even when less enthusiastic about other aspects of the paper'.[13]

The irony was that the most famous page in *The Times* was the one not actually written by its journalists. It was the task of Leon Pilpel in the 1980s and Ivan Barnes in the 1990s to sift through 250 to 300 letters a day (and between 60,000 to 70,000 a year) in order to find the sixteen or so that would make it into the newspaper. Periodically, the letters' editor would be deluged. Barnes had to struggle with a thousand letters a day arriving on his desk during the Gulf War. Improvements in communications technology also increased the volume of literary traffic. The first letter sent by email was published in 1997 and by 2002 the volume of emails necessitated a new secondary 'debate' section where they could be published in 'The Register'. Three assistants and three secretaries provided the letters' editor with help and every missive, no matter how barmy, received an acknowledgement. Pilpel would arrive early and read through the entire first post before his assistants arrived, putting to one side those he thought had potential. He had a straightforward criterion for acceptance: 'It should reflect the intelligent after-dinner conversation that you would expect to find among educated folk,' adding 'with the occasional off-beat subject thrown in.' Over the decades, while the art of letter writing declined in Britain, the proportion of those suitable for publication in *The Times* remained constant. Pilpel considered that of an average daily postbag, about 8 per cent were usually publishable.[14]

Pilpel was a former Guards officer and graduate of Trinity College Dublin who had joined *The Times* in 1953 as a subeditor on the home news desk before taking over responsibility for the letters page in 1980. As Brian MacArthur put it, he may have been a largely anonymous journalist to the reading public but he had the power to 'gainsay the mighty or uplift the unknown, start or end national controversies, or solve some of the diverting mysteries and riddles of British life such as why so few ingredients of British salads are grown in Britain'. His subediting skills were important since many letters benefited from being cut down to size. Unlike the *Daily Telegraph* and the *Independent*, *The Times* did not solicit letters, a practice Pilpel regarded as 'bogus'.[15] Exclusivity was also a prerequisite. No letter would be published that was being simultaneously offered to another newspaper. Occasionally, Pilpel would spot a letter he had rejected for publication appearing a few days later in the *Telegraph*. Letters containing personal abuse or vicious invective were also not considered for publication nor were those making specific charges against the royal family since royalty, by convention, could not reply. There were, of course, ways of getting round restrictions. In July 1986 the *Sunday Times* published allegations that a rift had developed between the Queen and Margaret Thatcher. At contention was supposedly the Queen's fear that her Prime Minister's opposition to sanctions against South Africa risked breaking up the Commonwealth. The Queen was also said to be at odds with the more strident aspects of Thatcherism's domestic agenda. Predictably, an almighty row ensued. The principal source for the allegations was Michael Shea, the Queen's press secretary. His defensive assertion that his observations had been misconstrued led two of Times Newspapers' directors – Lords Drogheda and Dacre – to join the calls for Andrew Neil, the editor of the *Sunday Times*, to be sacked. Buckingham Palace took the unusual step of rebutting the *Sunday Times*'s claims in the letters page of *The Times*. William Heseltine, the Queen's private secretary (it was assumed with her approval), wrote at length, making clear that it was 'preposterous to suggest that any member of the Queen's Household, even supposing that he or she knew what her Majesty's opinions on Government policy might be (and the Press Secretary certainly does not), would reveal them to the Press.' The next day, Neil replied at even greater length, denying that the article had gone beyond what Shea had originally intimated. The damage had been done, Neil asserted, because individuals at the Palace 'were playing with fire and did not have the wit to blow it out before it burned them'.[16] Shea stepped down from his post the following year. Neil lasted another seven.

Despite its designation, the famous 1981 letter from 364 economists denouncing Mrs Thatcher's monetarist polices was, in fact, never published on the letters page. Its contents appeared in articles on the news and business pages instead. This was an exception. Topicality dictated that some letters had to be used immediately in the next day's edition. Others were held back while a larger correspondence accumulated so that the best could then be grouped together to create a debate. There was never any danger of a shortage although a section heading, 'Enigma of the Liberal Vote', remained for many years on standby to cover all eventualities. Recurring themes over the years represented the preoccupations of many *Times* readers – cuts in university and research funding, student debt, the state of Britain's railways and her relations with her European partners. There was also the phenomenon of the recurring letter writer. One of these was Vice-Admiral Louis le Bailly whose contributions on an impressive breadth of interests frequently found their way onto the page. Another was Henry Button – a particular mine of information on Oxbridge ephemera. The publication of an academic league table would almost invariably bring forth another Button missive establishing different criteria such as Cambridge's propensity to have more of its chancellors executed than Oxford's (the margin, apparently, was seven to one) or that William Henry Waddington, who rowed for Cambridge in the 1848 Boat Race, was Prime Minister of France from February to December in 1879.[17] Errors in the newspaper provided opportunities for the sharp-eyed, the knowledgeable and the pedant. Articles that claimed something was the 'first' or someone the 'oldest' all but incited letters that pointed out earlier and older examples. For those interested in the arcana of knowledge, *The Times* letters' page provided essential reading matter. There was, for example, a lengthy correspondence on the development and demise of the water-powered organ.[18] A 1981 Diary column about the forthcoming final reunion of veterans of the Boer War led to a particularly sprightly letter from a Mr A. D. Bowers, born in 1882, who announced he was the only veteran who fought 'practically naked, butt end and bayonet' in the last major engagement of the war, the Battle of Tweefontein. 'I have been to most of the reunions since 1901,' he added helpfully.[19] Replying to a leading article decrying the decline of classical language teaching in schools, Frances Morrell, the leader of the Inner London Education Authority, submitted a three-paragraph letter in Latin. It duly appeared as sent. With a little help from the resident classicist, Philip Howard, *The Times* was able to provide an explanation for non-comprehending readers on the home news pages. At any rate, 'Carolo Wilsoni salutem' provided a welcome change to that usually proffered to the editor.[20]

There was an established tradition of the short, whimsical letter. These often generated surprisingly large postbags in turn. Readers continued to write to announce they had heard the first cuckoo of spring even though *The Times* had stopped publishing anything on this subject in 1953. When Miles Kington mused on the fictional characters suggested by village names, the paper was inundated with suggestions. One correspondent wrote in to say that there was a signpost in the Lincolnshire Wolds that stated, 'To Mavis Enderby & Old Bolingbroke', to which someone had added '– a son'.[21] Yet, the extent of the place names correspondence was modest compared to that which followed a personal appeal from the Rector of Barton-le-Cley. He had recently acquired a new horse and asked readers to propose for it a suitable name that would act as an alibi for when the bishop wished to see him. Two hundred and fifty suggestions came in. One letter suggested the excuse, 'I'm afraid the Rector is unable to see you – he's just fallen from Grace.' In the end, he played safe, and settled for being away on 'Sabbatical'.[22]

The letters page could be both thoughtful and whimsical but the question of whether it retained its former importance invariably cropped up. In 1968, J. W. Wober published an analysis of it in *New Society*. His thesis, rather grandiloquently phrased, was that the page 'shared something with the real or mythical forum and agora of ancient cities in which both rulers and ruled spoke their minds' and that while in Parliament, politicians spoke directly to themselves and their colleagues, in the letters pages of *The Times*, politicians, experts and electors all spoke together. By analysing letters written during a single month for each year between 1953 and 1967, Wober demonstrated that slightly more than a third had been written by members of the elite (which he classified as senior figures in Church, State, the professions etc.,). It was not unreasonable to assume that since the period of Wober's study the importance of having a letter published in *The Times* had diminished. During these years other information and comment disseminating media had proliferated, from radio phone-ins to television discussion programmes and internet chatrooms. In 2004, Wober undertook a new statistical analysis that brought his examination of the paper up to date. He discovered that almost 37 per cent of published letter writers were still representatives of elite groups – a proportion that was almost exactly the same as before. Top people still wrote to *The Times*. Indeed, there had been a significant increase in letters from senior figures in education, the armed forces and the police. Despite the grumbles of those who disliked *The Times*'s editorial line, it was still less politically partisan than its competitors – the right-wing *Telegraph*, left-wing *Guardian* or increasingly left-leaning *Independent*. This helped to bolster its claims to be a national debating chamber. As a regular place of interaction between the powerful and the public, Wober suggested that its only real rival was BBC 1's *Question Time*. The number of letter-writing MPs had fallen off but it had increasingly become a forum for the new quangocracy to raise issues with the wider public. In this respect, *The Times* had adapted well to the changing anatomy of British governance.[23]

The letters page was not the only healthy veteran. If there is an area in which British journalism has found dominion then it is in death. The quality and quantity of the daily obituary notices published by the four main broadsheet newspapers far outshines the scant efforts of the European press where only the most eminent are accorded special consideration. Even the great newspapers of the United States provide an obituary service whose quality is uneven compared to the daily monuments to past life erected from newspaper offices in London.

From its beginnings, *The Times* printed death notices and, periodically, tributes to the deceased. Nonetheless, it was not until the middle of the nineteenth century that the term 'obituary' took hold and an editor to work systematically on them was not appointed until after the First World War. For the next sixty years *The Times* obituary reigned supreme as the foremost newspaper assessment of the departed. From the perspective of the early twenty-first century, this appears to have been yet another 'golden age' to have been in a somewhat lower carat than legend relates. World leaders were accorded excellent assessments – the obituaries of Hitler and Churchill still read well despite the passage of time – but the standard format for all lesser mortals was merely a two column section squeezed to the right of the Court & Social announcements. This level of coverage was better than any other newspaper provided at the time. Nonetheless, it was scanty compared to what was deemed appropriate by the 1990s.

The space limitations were only part of the problem. Nowhere did the tag of 'paper of record' hang more soberly than over the obituaries department where the perceived necessity of listing the details of a public servant's career could get in the way of a lively anecdote or telling story. The extent to which *Times* obits moved away from prosaic recitations of the offices held by public servants and embraced non-Establishment figures marked the paper's belated acknowledgment that it was more than the notice board of the policy-making class and that society had become a far broader entity. When Bob Marley, 'the embodiment of reggae', died in 1981 his brief obituary notice came fourth in the pecking order, behind Sir Anthony Milward, Judge William Openshaw and Arturo Jemolo, the commentator on Italian Church and State relations.[24] Indeed, the attempt to give more weight to those who had contributed to popular culture proved controversial. In 1984, Gavin Stamp accused *The Times* of being 'pathetically trendy' for giving Dennis Wilson, a founding member of the Beach Boys, an obituary that stretched to seven column inches.[25] This was a third of the length of what the former chief education officer for Birmingham had been accorded that day. Stamp's concerns were premature. The process of reaching out to the more popular arts proved to be a slow-moving one. As late as 1988, a familiar figure like the comic actor Kenneth Williams could have his entire *Carry On* film career summed up in two sentences, the second of which was 'Smut, like beauty, was in the eye of the beholder.'[26]

It was not just a question of taking a dismissive view of popular entertainers. If any part of the old *Times* considered itself a department of the state apparatus it was the Court & Social page and this was reflected by those deemed worthy of an obituary notice. The emphasis was on public servants rather than those who had made their mark in the private sector. Obituaries of prominent businessmen were particularly weak. During the 1980s, attempts were made to widen the remit. Lord (Keith) Joseph and Sir Charles Pickthorn were engaged to suggest businessmen who should be included.[27] Yet, despite this effort, the results were still inadequate. Assessing the career of someone like Julius Strauss in only 363 words inevitably meant the analysis of his real contribution had to be summed up in two sentences: 'In 1963 he helped to found the Eurobond market, which since then has grown from zero to $5000 billion. The word "Eurobond" was probably invented by him, though there are two other claimants: the late Sir Siegmund Warburg and the late Sir George Bolton.'[28] There was no room to explain the significance to the modern world economy of this development.

Only in extreme circumstances had the old *Times* spoken ill of the dead. The avoidance of the 'hatchet job' was a commendable approach that reflected well on the paper's detachment from petty score settling with those who could no longer sue. But when it came to commemorating the 'great and the good' the lack of any attempt in the early 1980s at even mild objectivity was telling. This was particularly evident whenever a leading Conservative politician of progressive inclinations passed into history. The admiring obituary in 1982 of 'one of the most accomplished and influential statesmen of the century', Rab Butler, excellently conveyed his great strengths and the reasons for his importance while, for example, skating over his wartime defeatism and hostility towards Churchill in 1940 with the cryptic sentence, 'His removal from the Foreign Office was surprisingly delayed until the summer of 1941.'[29] The clue was planted in the word 'surprisingly' but it was so discreet as to cause no upset to any of Butler's friends and admirers and to deliberately leave most readers none the wiser. Similarly, the obituary for Sir Edward Boyle, who was also 'one of the most distinguished Conservatives of his generation', was written in such glowing terms that the casual reader would have been unaware there was any controversy over his commitment to axing grammar schools and replacing them with comprehensives. Over the succeeding twenty years the analysis became far more honest. By 2000, the death of Lady Plowden – who Boyle had appointed to chair the report that recommended child-centred teaching in primary schools, the very embodiment of progressive 'trendy teaching' – received a more balanced assessment which, without denigrating her as a person, at least mentioned that her legacy was controversial.[30]

This changing approach might be viewed as part of a social process in which the deference culture was diminished. It was also a response to improved competition. Throughout the first half of the 1980s, *The Times* had suffered from a lack of serious opposition from its rivals. By the mid-1980s, the paper was still providing more obituary space each day than the *Telegraph* did in a week while the *Guardian* averaged half a column on two days a week. All this changed in 1986 when the *Daily Telegraph* appointed Hugh Montgomery-Massingberd as its obituaries editor and the new *Independent* devoted double the space to obituaries than *The Times* had felt was required. Within a matter of months, the *Telegraph* and *Independent* were comprehensively outclassing *The Times* in an area in which it had previously reigned supreme. By 1990, the *Independent* was averaging five and a half columns to three and a half in *The Times*.

The Times, however, fought back. John Higgins was switched from the arts pages to run obituaries where he was assisted by three full-time members of staff commissioning and subbing the page. They made regular use of around fifty specialists who provided copy on the senior figures in their area of acquaintance or expertise. More than five thousand obituaries were kept on file and periodically updated so that they were ready for use when the time came. Few spent longer in the queue than the Queen Mother's obituary, rewritten in 1987 by the then obituaries editor, John Grigg, and updated eight years later, which was one of a small minority that it was deemed sufficiently important to be kept 'live' in the computer. It was accessible only through the catchline 'Mumsie'.[31]

In 1993, the improvements continued when Anthony Howard took over the helm. The son of a canon, Howard had been educated at Westminster and Christ Church, Oxford. He had succeeded Jeremy Isaacs as chairman of the Oxford University Labour Club and, putting partisan feelings aside, had joined Michael Heseltine's slate to run the Union. He had determined upon a career at the Bar but National Service – including being dispatched to the Canal Zone during the Suez Crisis – intervened and he returned, instead, set upon a career in journalism. Over the next thirty years he prospered at the *Guardian* and the *Observer* and as editor of the *New Statesman* and the *Listener*. He was also a noted political historian, editing Dick Crossman's diaries (and subsequently writing his biography) as well as a life of Rab Butler. In charge of *Times* obits, Howard took a methodical approach. The amount of space set aside for an archbishop, a bishop, a dean or an archdeacon was virtually set in stone. Junior clergy had to have demonstrated some special reason to justify inclusion at a time when the *Telegraph* was developing a distinct market as the celebrator of the eccentric vicar. It transpired that it was the death of a bishop that prompted Howard into making an uncharacteristic slip that landed the paper in trouble. When he learned of the death of the Revd Brian Masters, Bishop of Edmonton, he was determined to write the obit himself. To many, the north London bishop's death pealed no particular bell of recognition. Howard, however, was determined to damn a churchman who opposed the ordination of women and wrote an astonishingly vituperative assessment. Calling the bishop 'one of the last relics' and 'like a clone to Graham Leonard' (the Anglo-Catholic Bishop of London), the tone of the piece was unforgiving and contained such comments as, 'The best that could be said for his sermons was that they tended to be short.'[32] The general feeling was that it was an ill-judged piece. Indeed, it generated more letters of complaint than any other obituary during the period. Uniquely, the Bishop of London denounced it from the pulpit of St Paul's Cathedral.

Frontal assaults of this kind were an aberration. Speaking ill of the dead, particularly in an article that would be published when the corpse was scarcely cold, was generally recognized as a task that had to be undertaken with delicacy. However, the issue of the love that dare not speak its name was especially contentious. In 1976, *The Times* had caused outrage by mentioning in Tom Driberg's obituary that he was homosexual, although it was hard to see how any worthwhile assessment of his life could have been made without mentioning the fact. In contrast, the 1983 obituary of Anthony Blunt, while balanced in its attention to his professional achievements and his treachery, made no reference to his private life or sexual preferences. Hugo Vickers wrote in the *Spectator* that the Blunt obituary reminded him of the highest praise he had ever heard for a *Times* obituary: 'Hmm, sniffs of an inside job.'[33] Three years later the paper's obituary of the ballet dancer Robert Helpmann caused fresh outrage by describing him as 'a homosexual of the proselytizing kind, he could turn young men on the borderline his way'.[34] The then obituaries editor, the normally liberal-minded John Grigg, found himself the target of outrage from the ballet world at the 'monstrous' and 'shabby' slur. Sir Frederick Ashton declared it was 'absolutely not' the Helpmann he knew while Dame Ninette de Valois thought the reference 'extremely distasteful'. The council of Equity, the actors' union, tabled its 'revulsion at the scurrilous attack'.

Sins of omission, real or assumed, also caused controversy. Simon Jenkins and John Higgins were involved in an acrimonious correspondence with Michael Thornton who was indignant that his obituary of the gardening journalist Peter Coats was published omitting his suggestion that Coats was the gay lover of Field Marshal Wavell. Coats had been Wavell's ADC at the Viceregal Lodge in Delhi during the Second World War and, before publishing a claim that would certainly cause consternation and demands of a retraction, Jenkins wanted better proof than Thornton's evidence that Coats had told him of the relationship. Thornton, a source for (in John Higgins's words) 'where show business rubs shoulders with what used to be London Society', made clear he would never write obituaries for the paper again. Even in the version published, the obituary led to a letter being printed from Wavell's daughter disavowing the passage that stated 'the relationship between them was close, Wavell depending on Coats's judgment in many matters. This influence over her husband was not much liked by the viceroy's wife.'[35]

During the 1980s, there was rarely room to give more than a passport-sized photograph of the obituary's subject matter. As the space expanded, so there was a conscious effort to find more expressive images. The decision to accompany the obituary of the former Labour Cabinet minister Lord (Fred) Mulley with the famous photograph of him dropping off to sleep next to the Queen during an air show to mark her Silver Jubilee was certainly defensible in terms of drawing the reader's attention by commemorating the act for which the deceased politician was most famous. However, it caused outrage among his parliamentary colleagues on both sides of the House. Peter Stothard was inundated with letters expressing disgust that the paper had chosen to draw attention to a momentary lapse at the expense of a career devoted to public life. Charles Anson, the Buckingham Palace press secretary, even wrote to make the editor aware that the Queen had thought it unfair and unkind. This was, to all intents and purposes, a royal rebuke. Shamefaced, *The Times* published an apology for its error of judgment that, Anson assured Stothard, had been placed before Her Majesty for gracious inspection.[36]

The rule that criminals were not deserving of obituaries was imperfectly observed. Bobby Sands, the IRA hunger striker, had not been given an obituary despite the fact that when he died in 1981 he was an elected MP and a source of international interest. Yet, other criminals, especially those who had held public office somewhere else in the world, were sometimes accorded recognition. Stothard was keen for the 'no criminals' rule to be applied strictly. Infamous figures like the moors murderer Myra Hindley or Fred West received no recognition when they died. The same applied in 2000 to Reggie Kray even though an obituary had been prepared for him on the justification that his place in 1960s East End gangland culture made him an infamous figure in Britain's history. The rule had been stretched to its ultimate extent earlier that year with the fatal shooting of Arkan, the Serb war criminal who had played his grisly part in the disintegration of Yugoslavia. His assassination was deemed to merit a leading article but, because of the protocol, not an obituary. Only when Stothard retired as editor was the rule relaxed so that those whose infamy had political or social implications beyond the mere depravity of their actions would receive attention.

At least in the decade up to 2002, *The Times* avoided the ultimate solecism of publishing the obituary of someone who was still living. The obituaries staff read the death notices (known as the 'hotch') every day to check nobody important had died and one of the aspects that Tony Howard found most difficult was having to check that the subject matter really had shuffled off the mortal coil. This involved phoning the deceased's nearest relatives in order to enquire, in a sympathetic tone, whether the rumours were true. Working beside Howard was Ian Brunskill who had originally joined the paper's arts pages. Together, they clawed back *The Times*'s position as the primary dictionary of the departed. The number of notices waiting on file gradually rose to around six thousand although, as the space in the paper increased, so the number of staff assisting the obituaries editor rose from four to six, supplemented by about 150 key contributors. Howard had a regular naval source who provided biographies of Royal Navy sailors and an Army source who did likewise for old soldiers. Other institutions, especially the Church and the major universities, also had their discreet observers.

Following on from Op-Ed, the leaders and letters pages, obituaries enjoyed a prime place that Howard was tenacious in defending despite periodic attempts to move it to the second section. Eventually, it was Ben Preston who persuaded Brunskill, Howard's successor, to move obituaries to the second section in return for much more space. This materialized in the form of 'The Register'. Far from being a demotion – as some at first feared – it represented a major expansion and *The Times* re-emerged as the paper with the greatest volume of obituary journalism. Brunskill relaxed Howard's strict demarcation policy that equated rank to column inches. The greater space availability had other positive consequences. The number of foreigners commemorated was increased, despite the occasional complaints of readers who thought the section existed purely as a monument to British worthies. Even before 'The Register' was launched, the effect expanding the space availability had on the quality of analysis could be glimpsed by looking at how the paper analysed the lives of two refugees from Hitler's Europe who made a particularly notable contribution to Britain's cultural life – Sir Nikolaus Pevsner, who died in 1983, and Sir Ernst Gombrich, who died in 2001. Both obituaries were rightly admiring in tone but the extra space that the Gombrich obituary was able to utilize ensured that, in contrast to Pevsner, there was room to analyse the art historian's views as well as record his achievements.[37]

Despite being invented in 2002, 'The Register' resembled a conservation area within a larger urban conurbation that had weathered surrounding change while preserving its own character intact. Supplemented with the announcements of the Court & Social page, it was certainly the living embodiment of the 'journal of record'. In truth, this was less a matter of conservation as of improvement. The standards of the obituary columns had been raised considerably. The days had passed when some of them consisted of little more than – in Brunskill's description – 'adding verbs to a "Who's Who" entry'.[38] Indeed, the paper entered the twenty-first century with obituary notices that had as good a claim as any to being the finest being published, day in day out, anywhere in the world. They had certainly come a long way since the 1930s when the paper's obituaries editor, Frederick Lownes, occupied his time looking out of the window of the Garrick Club in search of the passing visages of famous people looking ill.

The pace of change remained sedate elsewhere in the Court & Social section of the paper. Indeed, the Court page's staff had, somehow, managed to avoid the direct input into computer terminals directive to which all other journalists had succumbed when the paper made its moonlit flit to

Wapping in 1986. Instead, they enjoyed the distinction of being the only journalists who received a daily visit from a subeditor who would read back to them what they had written. It was dignified, but was not efficient. Eventually, in the late 1990s, the nettle was grasped and direct input enforced. It made almost no difference to the layout of a page that, along with the law reports, changed less than any other section of the paper. Indeed, Court & Social and the law reports remained the strongest emblems of maintaining the 'journal of record' tradition. Below the royal coat of arms, the Court Circular announced the daily movements of the royal family with an unceasing adherence to protocol and the correct usage of the upper or lower case. 'University News' reported fellowship and professorial appointments in a manner unchanged since 1921. Parliamentary group luncheons, livery guild dinners and lectures at the likes of the Royal Geographical Society were all accorded notices. Even attendees at memorial services of the great and the good continued to be recognized in serried ranks of small type. For traditionally and punctiliously minded readers, these remained welcome reminders of the continuities of British social, metropolitan and intellectual life and a bulwark against the brasher displays accorded the new elite of celebrities and other supposed false idols. Despite strong competition in this department from the *Daily Telegraph*, placing a notice of a birth, forthcoming marriage or death in *The Times* remained *sine qua non* for those wishing to share personal news with a larger, sometimes imagined but often real, community of those who also turned to the same page for solace or curiosity. A sense of kinship was fostered and authority bestowed upon those whose names graced its page. The appearance was, of course, that of old-fashioned values decorously expressed, although the Personal Column was essentially also one of the most commercially minded parts of the paper.

Usually accompanying the Court & Social section were other familiar features that stood testimony to *The Times*'s seriousness of purpose. *The Times* brought together an impressive range of expert writers. Michael J. Hendrie, *The Times*'s astronomy correspondent, offered regular updates – complete with an accompanying diagram – of the movement of the planets and where to see the brighter stars of the night sky. Meanwhile, Professor Norman Hammond, the archaeological correspondent since 1967, had become one of the paper's longest serving regular contributors. His columns demonstrated his breadth and versatility although he was a particular authority on Mayan civilization. His digs in the Mayan lowlands had, indeed, contributed towards an international recognition that included lengthy periods at the universities of Cambridge and Rutgers as well as visiting professorships at the University of California at Berkeley, at Jilin in China, Bonn University and at the Sorbonne. A succession of other specialists also provided regular copy. One of the most influential figures in the heritage lobby, Marcus Binney, wrote with great erudition and passion on architecture and the preservation of civilization's bricks and mortar. Between August and December every year since 1981, Angus Nicol swung into action as the piping correspondent. *The Times*, indeed, must surely remain the only newspaper south of Berwick-upon-Tweed to profit from a regular bagpipe columnist. The ornithologist and Proust expert, Derwent May, closely observed birds and their habitats. Signing off with the initials DJM, May's Nature Notes had appeared every Monday since 1982 and became daily when 'The Register' was launched in 2002. His style was governed by his observations of the changing seasons: 'Lesser spotted woodpeckers are beginning to make their spring call in the treetops: it is a thin piping note, like a faint car alarm going off' was a typical mode of introduction, rather in the manner of a Cold War spy affecting small talk, before eventually signing off with an equally conspiratorial rejoinder, 'On London plane-trees, there are strings of prickly-looking seed-balls, many of which will go on dangling there until the leaves come out in April.'[39] These columns enjoyed a devoted following.

The Times's range of expert correspondents extended to the more cerebral games and pastimes. From 1986, the chess correspondent was Raymond Keene. Keene was a grandmaster with a long list of accomplishments that included becoming British Chess Champion in 1971 and was eight times a member of the English Olympic team between 1977 and 1980. The organizer of several world championships, he was the natural choice to oversee the 1993 Kasparov vs Short contest that was sponsored by *The Times*. He became the paper's daily columnist in 1995 and also found time to write more than 110 books on chess, which was a world record. Such was his mental ability that, in 1990, Lancashire police asked him to solve a chess-based puzzle that a computer designer had devised while being detained on suspicion of murdering an ex-girlfriend. Handed a puzzle that involved four chess pieces, a board drawn in the outline of a map and a series of moves, the police believed the suspect was providing them with the coordinates for the shallow grave of the disappeared woman. Keene examined it and concluded that her remains might be buried in Ireland, north-west of Limerick. No body was ever located, however, and the suspect was released.[40] Meanwhile, as bridge correspondents, both Robert Sheehan and his successor, Andrew Robson, dealt a daily hand to a large and conscientious following among the readership. Robson, a former World Junior Champion, was one of the youngest players to win the European championship in 1991 and was the first English player to win a US major, which he did two years running. The author of *Common Mistakes: And How to Avoid Them* also started the Andrew Robson Bridge Club, which became the largest in the land.

Nonetheless, the undisputed monarch among *The Times*'s daily offering of games and brainteasers was the crossword. The first had appeared in 1930 and a second, concise crossword, was added in 1983. The paper had also instituted an annual championship in 1970. When Dr Helen Ougham, a scientist at the Institute of Grassland and Environmental Research at Aberystwyth, won it in October 1995 (the first woman to do so) she solved the four puzzles in an average of eleven minutes. As crossword editor between 1983 and 1995, John Grant presided over a team of twelve regular compilers that included a former Scrabble champion, an ex-IBM executive, a French horn player, a retired Army officer, a postman and Brian Greer, a lecturer at Queen's University, Belfast, specializing in the psychology of mathematics education. Having been on the team for twenty years, it was Greer who succeeded Grant as editor in 1995 when the paper celebrated its 20,000th crossword. There was only one serious error – in March 1986, puzzle number 17,005 was published with the wrong grid. 'More than a hundred readers nevertheless solved it on grids of their own devising,' Grant recalled, 'and even suggested it was more fun that way.'[41] More than seventy years after its inception, *The Times* crossword not only remained a national institution, it retained its reputation as perhaps the most recognized test of daily mental agility. This, in itself, was no small achievement.

III

Anthony Howard believed that the journalist's working life had changed remarkably – and not necessarily for the better – since he was first enlisted into its ranks in 1958. Instead of getting out and about in search of stories, reporters had become 'largely dependent on the information revolution. You scan the Internet, you look at what all the news agencies have to say – all there supplied and ready-processed on your desk.' He pitied Wapping's 'galley-slaves' with 'sandwiches to eat at their desks, crouched over their terminals from 10.30 till 6.30, never seeing anyone, working the phone quite hard, but never actually going out into the real world'. Lobby correspondents, operating from the bars and corridors of Westminster and Whitehall, were a rare exception.[42] There was some accuracy in Howard's depiction of desk-bound journalism. In fairness, the revolution in information technology meant there was usually far more readily accessible material to be had by staying close to one's computer screen than by standing around expectantly in pubs. In this respect, perhaps *The Times* had not moved on so far from its established mid-twentieth-century role as the great information interchange in which experienced subeditors polished other agencies' wire reports and disseminated officially released information. Yet even that was only partly true. Then, as in the early twenty-first century, the great disclosures still came through personal contacts and a questing spirit that was not easily put off by obfuscation. Front-line journalists like Anthony Loyd, Richard Beeston and Janine di Giovanni could hardly be accused of a reticence to go deep into hostile territory in search of stories at no small risk to their own welfare. They were in the tradition of the celebrated and fearless reporters who had brought such fame to *The Times* in bygone days. Technological advances greatly assisted foreign correspondents' means of communication. During the 1980s, they still had to get back to an office where they could file their copy through the fraught and time consuming medium of the telex machine. Even in the early 1990s, getting hold of London could take hours. Mary Dejevsky recalled her attempts to cover the Ukrainian independence referendum in December 1991. She tried to file from Lvov, only to be told there was a thirty-six hour wait for an available foreign telephone line. 'There was nothing you could do except go to the post office and yell at people or hope that London called you,' she recalled.[43] Her only option was to fly to Kiev and try from there. Fog, however, ensured that the planes were cancelled, so she had to hire a black-market car and drive for eight hours through the snow and rain in order to get the story out. Such experiences were typical until the advent of mobile phones and electronic filing shrunk the world.

There was always something romantic about the notion of the foreign correspondent sending dispatches from exotic locations but those reporting from domestic shores were no less capable of winkling out information from some of its most concealed crevices. Indeed, in the last twenty years of the twentieth century, the amount of information leaked to journalists from those in official positions seemed far greater than in any previous age. Not all these disclosures were totally unsolicited. Often they were the result of a long period in which trust had been developed through mutual acquaintance. Such was the success of the fourth estate's ability to live by disclosure that some wondered whether it was irreparably damaging the culture of trust that made public governance possible.

Sometimes the criticism has not been that increasingly sedentary journalists have missed stories but rather that they have not taken sufficient care to establish the facts before rushing with indecent haste to claim a scoop. The Hitler diaries fiasco was a case in point. Earlier in the century, *The Times* could not always have been accused of rushing to judge. It had sufficient time to report in relative depth on the news pages the dropping of the first atom bomb on Hiroshima in 1945, yet it opted not to bother changing the leader column on that day to discuss what was potentially the most momentous event in world history – one that might virtually bring it to an end. From a modern perspective, this reluctance to comment appears reticent to the point of sheer laziness and, had it been the *modus operandi* in response to 9/11, readers would have questioned why they were purchasing a paper that could not rise to a challenge that was eagerly being met by the twenty-four-hour rolling news services of television, radio and the internet. In short, such a detached attitude would no longer be considered acceptable. Yet, *The Times*'s Blackfriars of 1945 would have argued that taking time to ponder such a major development was less unprofessional than rushing in with a gut reaction when a period of careful consideration was the only response equal to the moment. This was a mode of thought made famous by Zhou Enlai when he answered a question about the meaning of the French Revolution with the answer, 'It is too early to tell.' Zhou, however, was not in the business of selling newspapers.

Such a detached attitude, even if desirable, is no longer possible. The market will look for alternative news sources that will provide near-instant responses. Reticence is not of itself an attribute. It has to be accepted that analytical journalism can never be more than the daily practice of risk assessment. If historians cannot agree about the cause and effect of events that took place deep in the past despite the advantages of hindsight and a steady accretion of information in the meantime, it is not reasonable to assume that those writing the first draft of history for the morning's newspapers will have a monopoly on truth or wisdom. Looking back with the advantages of fifty years' experience in Fleet Street, William Rees-Mogg made the assessment that, 'Any journalist who gets his judgments right more than half the time is doing quite well. Our job is to make the best judgment that can be made on the first day, when the cork has come out of the bottle but the wine has not yet been poured.'[44] It is debateable whether the greater reticence in reacting to events made by the mid-twentieth-century *Times* ensured it any better diagnostic results. The ability of *The Times* of 2001 to respond to the unimaginable calamity of 9/11 by producing within a matter of hours a paper whose reporting and analysis remained calm, measured and authoritative in its tone was a tribute to how its journalists had maintained standards of the highest professionalism despite the increased pressures placed upon them by expectant readers. Indeed, by the twenty-first century, the question of whether 'fast news' was a good thing was, in any case, entirely academic. Flashing up-to-the-minute news on the paper's website was an implicit requirement, not an optional extra. Internet users had the ability to surf rival sites at the click of an electronic mouse in search of the most up-to-date news and comment. News providers who hesitated lost.

A failure to provide a virtual paper on the web was not a viable option when the rivals all chose to do so. In terms of attracting the major advertisers, newspapers had been losing market share to television throughout the period covered in this book.[45] It remained to be seen whether launching websites would prove to be the alternative visual medium that allowed them to claw some of that share back. The *Guardian* made a huge investment in its online version during the 1990s and succeeded in attracting a large audience from the United States in particular. Online services proved to be the most effective means yet invented of disseminating newspapers around the world. Among the British broadsheets, *Times Online* moved into second place ahead of *FT.com*. Meanwhile, despite having the highest sales of any broadsheet newspaper, the *Telegraph*'s website slid into fourth position. Charging to read the online paper ran the risk of diverting readers to rival free sites and the launch of the BBC's online news service made it difficult for newspapers to introduce registration fees. Naturally, there were fears that if readers could access the material for free, the paper would lose revenue. However, the research suggested that around a half of *Times Online* users were not regular readers of the print edition. Thus, while the paper was inevitably losing sales to those – often in office environments where the internet costs were borne by the business – who were browsing without charge on their computer screens, it was also gaining a new audience from those who would not have bothered to look at it at all if the only means of doing so involved interacting with a newsagent. This new market created opportunities for advertisers seeking space on the virtual paper as well as for hooking new readers to its printed format.

Internet 'fast news' did not undermine the traditional role of *The Times*; rather, it re-enforced the necessity of in-depth journalism to offer a more rounded product. Breaking news on the internet or the 'soundbite' journalism favoured by the visually dependent medium of television could not compete with the weightier analysis the newspaper provided at its best. Even this was a question of finding a balance. Simon Kelner, who, as editor of the *Independent*, pioneered the tabloid-sized quality daily (or 'compact') and put partisan opinion on its front page, suggested that in the future newspapers would respond to the internet and television twenty-four-hour rolling news challenge by evolving into 'viewspapers' instead.[46] Newspaper would become, in effect, daily opinion-led magazines. Was this the future of *The Times*? If so, it would mark the end of its more than two-hundred-year mission to inform. It is hard to imagine its reputation could be other than irrevocably tarnished. In fact, the Kelner prophecy seemed an excessively pessimistic one. When a longer perspective is eventually provided, 9/11 might be seen as a defining moment for quality newspapers. People immediately switched on the television to view the vivid and appalling images and to keep abreast of the breaking news. Yet the next morning and in the days and weeks thereafter, sales of broadsheet newspapers, including *The Times*, soared. Even when the news was at its most graphic, the print media was still seen to provide what the more visual electronic media could not.

IV

Before Murdoch acquired the title, buying *The Times* was a morning ritual for some who believed it was a badge that could be displayed as evidence of having joined an exclusive club rather than because they thought it was necessarily the best all-round newspaper. After the siege of Wapping, the *Independent* was portrayed as the new *Times* – embodying the old paper's qualities but without the associations of being owned by a Reagan-admiring Australian-American tabloid magnate. 'It is, are you?' became the motto on the new badge for those who liked to be thought of as independent-minded people with a newspaper under their arm that proclaimed that very quality. In one sense, by 2002 the *Independent* had indeed begun to resemble the pre-Murdoch *Times*. It had a circulation of only a quarter of a million, could not afford to invest as much in journalism as its rivals and – despite its title – was dependent for survival on being bankrolled by a foreign domiciled proprietor. As has been noted, the proportion of 'A' grade readers that were attracted suggested that the *Independent* never quite managed to topple *The Times* at the upper end of the market. But unquestionably many newspaper purchasers liked the idea of a paper that declared independence from its masthead, even in the days when it was actually in the grip of the Mirror Group. In contrast, a paper owned by Rupert Murdoch was assumed not to be independent. There was a natural self-interest in *The Times*'s commercial rivals portraying it as the mouthpiece of its owner. By questioning the objectivity of the paper's judgment, these attacks hit at the heart of its appeal. Every editorial decision, from backing the Conservatives to backing New Labour was, sooner or later, attributed to Murdoch's hidden hand. Differences of opinion not only between his British newspapers but also with his own supposed opinions were disregarded or overlooked.

Those at the helm of other News Corp.-owned assets might have had different experiences, but a detailed survey of the first twenty-one years of Murdoch's ownership of *The Times* can only conclude that the interesting feature is how little, rather than how much, he has influenced its editorial politics. The one editor who complained about coming under pressure to justify the paper's opinions was Harold Evans although there was no occasion when a change of line actually ensued. The suggestion that the decision to replace Evans as editor was largely due to political differences is hotly disputed. The issue of *The Times*'s Chinese coverage and whether there was a conflict of interest with News Corp.'s Far East business aspirations has been examined in Chapter Twelve. There are also a few other scattered complaints: a belief among some that there is a pro-Israeli bias that emanates, however indirectly, from the proprietor's opinions, or the ordeal of the education correspondent, John Clare, who once had to endure a lengthy monologue in which Murdoch vehemently expounded his own (conflicting) views on the subject.[47] Compared to the evidence that the proprietor has not interfered in the paper's politics, these charges hardly sweep all before them. The 'Murdoch press' was not, for instance, delivered on a plate to Tony Blair. According to Murdoch's recollection of events, he did not even know what party *The Times* was going to support in the 1997 general election and was surprised to read it had opted to back a specific cause instead. This is also the recollection of the editor at the time. Peter

Stothard, indeed, claimed that he had never received a political instruction: 'In all the time I've been writing, I can't remember ever having heard the words "that's a great leader" or "that's a terrible leader"' from Murdoch. Far from being the recipient of unsolicited comments on the line the paper took, Stothard admitted, 'I don't think I've ever seen an email from Rupert.' Telephone conversations, when they occurred, usually took the form of Murdoch ringing for an informal chat about how everything was going on the paper and what was making the news in Britain. Indeed, by the 1990s, the proprietor's trips to Wapping were not frequent. New York was his base and the film, television and satellite divisions of his business increasingly occupied his time. It was as likely that Sky's fortunes would take him to London as any pressing matter with his broadsheets. *The Times* was one of more than 175 titles he owned in three continents. Even if he was minded to interfere, the sheer scale of his other international commitments restricted his opportunities to do so. Partly because of his expanding interests, the editors of *The Times* in the 1990s saw or heard much less of their proprietor than did their predecessors in the 1980s.[48]

This was not just Stothard's experience. Simon Jenkins recalled that Murdoch was 'scrupulous' about not breaking his guarantees on editorial independence. 'I didn't have one discussion with Rupert on editorial policy,' Jenkins maintained. Yet this is not to say the proprietor exercised benign neglect. He remained a nuts and bolts newspaperman, easily annoyed by a bad picture headline or squashed 'basement' article layout. He never forgot the lessons taught him as a young trainee on the *Daily Express*'s backbench by Edward Pickering. While Murdoch left his *Times* editors to get on with their political postures, Jenkins discovered, 'He was obsessive about where the pictures were going and where the money was going and this and that was going.' On occasions when he did come over to *The Times*, he had the unnerving habit of leafing through the morning's paper while mumbling dismissive observations about how poorly it was laid out or the priority given to different articles. 'In many ways,' conceded Jenkins, 'that's more demoralizing than having someone telling you whether you've got to be pro or anti abortion.'[49]

Successful partnerships between editor and proprietor depended upon a mutual understanding of what was to be rendered unto Caesar. The proprietor had to keep out of the politics of the paper and (despite his inclinations to be a chief sub) the daily decisions that were matters of editorial judgment. In turn, the editor had to recognize that major strategic decisions with budget implications had to be agreed with the proprietor.

There was nothing exceptional in this division of powers. It was in areas of grand strategy that Murdoch made his personal mark on the paper, deciding whether it could afford to undercut its rivals in cover price, invest in more business pages to take on the *FT* or change the number of sections in which it was printed. It was at this level that he intervened. Given his enthusiastic endorsement of investing in more sports pages, it might be contested that Murdoch's influence was as much manifested in expanding the paper's coverage of the Euro '96 football championship as its opposition to the euro currency.

Murdoch was not interested in owning *The Times* as a ticket into the British Establishment and nor was it deployed effectively as his prime weapon in exerting political power. As far as he perceived it, Margaret Thatcher cared much more about where the massed battalions of the *Sun* were going to attack.[50] During the government of her successor, *The Times* did little to endear itself to those in power, yet nor did it align itself with the official Opposition either. It could not even quite bring itself to endorse the party that was obviously going to win the 1997 general election by a landslide majority. If the paper's wires were pulled to a particular and cynical strategy, it was hard to comprehend what the agenda was. Rather, Murdoch's motivating interest in *The Times* seemed to relate more clearly to its central place in the history and development of his first and greatest hobby – newspapers. It was the paper from whose offices his father had once worked, the paper whose life had been saved in 1908 by Sir Keith Murdoch's friend and patron, Lord Northcliffe. In Britain, at least, the populist Northcliffe is the press baron with whom Keith Rupert Murdoch has been most frequently compared.

Murdoch made his name as an owner of tabloids who then bought his way into broadsheets. Nicholas Coleridge has suggested, 'had he acquired his papers in a different order – if *The Times*, the *South China Morning Post* and *The Australian* had come first – and he'd only then moved on to buy the tabloids, the world's perception of him would be substantially different ... But that is an idle scenario, since in the Murdoch empire it has always been the profits of the tabloids that have funded the loftier acquisitions.'[51] Of course, his purchase of *The Times* was not conceived in a fit of sentimentality alone. It came as part of a package that included the highly profitable *Sunday Times*. Furthermore, *The Times* was, and remained, the company's flagship newspaper and, as such, added value – however indirectly – to the international prestige of News Corporation. Reflecting in June 2002 on the growth of News Corp. from an Australian newspaper group to a global media organization, its president, Peter Chernin, stated his belief that acquiring *The Times* in 1981 'was the real transforming purchase of the company'.[52] Yet it was never just another deal. Murdoch enjoyed a challenge. Earlier that same month, he had been asked in an interview what he thought would be his lasting contribution as a patron of the popular arts. Without pausing for thought, he answered, 'Saving *The Times*.'[53]

V

Was *The Times* still an influential newspaper in the manner in which it could make that boast earlier in the twentieth century? It was the experience of Les Hinton, executive chairman of News International from 1995, that politicians tended to approach him more frequently about what the *Sun* was writing about them, while bankers and lawyers were far more likely to want to discuss something published in *The Times*.[54] The *Sun* unquestionably had the weight of numbers on its side and that was no small matter in a democracy. The great strength of *The Times* was not just in its news reporting (other papers were also good at that) but also in the quality of its 'specialist' writers. Frances Gibbs as legal correspondent, Michael Evans as defence correspondent and Ruth Gledhill as religion correspondent not only reported news, they wrote from the perspective of deep knowledge of their subject and personal acquaintance with those who were at its forefront. The possession of such expertise was central to the paper's ability to convey authority.

In contrast, the importance of the leading article has declined markedly since the 1950s when a *Times* editorial really was judged according to its contribution to the thinking of those who ran the country. That it should count for less before the bar of world opinion half a century later is hardly surprising. Having declined as a world power, the British view counted for less and thus, consequently, so did the pronouncements of its most famous newspaper. And within Britain, the growing plurality of published and broadcast opinion naturally diminished the claim of any one voice to speak with overweening authority. This increasing plurality of opinion also undermined the status of the leading article within *The Times* itself. In the 1950s, the paper published news reports and leading articles, but not much independent comment. The growth of the columnist – of which Bernard

Levin, Matthew Parris and Simon Jenkins shone brightly in the paper's constellation – significantly broadened the forum for debate. Surmounting this, the often daily political editor's briefing by Peter Riddell, foreign editor's briefing by Bronwen Maddox and business editor's briefing by Patience Wheatcroft created additional poles for authoritative comment. Taken collectively, they reduced the leading column to the ruminations that come out of a process of consensus decision making. This was not of itself a detraction. It made the leaders special and distinct from the personal perspectives of the star columnists.

The academic attainments and intellectual breadth of the principal leader writers of the past twenty years – Owen Hickey, Peter Stothard, Rosemary Righter and Tim Hames – hardly suggested the fine art had passed into the hands of crude hacks. Were these cultivated minds wasting their erudition on leading articles that only they and those they hoped to impress actually read? On a day-to-day basis, a *Times* leader rarely made the 'political weather' among those for whom it was primarily aimed – the top policy and opinion formers in the country. Yet where *The Times* stood on major issues at key moments still ensured it was an important barometer of informed opinion. Perhaps this was because the paper's politics were less predictably partisan than those of the *Telegraph*, the *Guardian* or (increasingly) the *Independent* while, if voting for Neil Kinnock was any judge, the editorial line in the *FT* appeared to have little impact in swaying informed opinion. During the 1990s no other broadsheet's leading articles could be seen to have consistently carried more weight than those of *The Times*.

One assumption remains. It is that in the late 1960s and 1970s *The Times* was a liberal Conservative newspaper propped up by an indulgent proprietor, Lord Thomson, and that thereafter it was a more strident newspaper forced into an excessively commercial approach by the rapacious bottom-line capitalism of its owner, Rupert Murdoch. In fact, much changed so that much could stay the same. After twenty-one years of ownership, Murdoch had become almost as indulgent as the traditional proprietors he was supposed to have replaced. He had pumped millions of pounds, with surprisingly mild complaint, into a newspaper that still failed to make great profits for his company. Even the paper's political outlook had changed less than might be imagined. In backing first Margaret Thatcher and, after about 2000, Tony Blair, it was performing its traditional twentieth-century function as a moderating rather than an instinctively hostile counsel to the government of the day. The period of the Major Government, which it attacked from a principled but non-party perspective, was the break from habit in this respect. Like Rees-Mogg personally, it had become disillusioned with the cause of European federalism (although not the notion of a European family of nations) and remained sympathetic to an Israeli state that continued to find itself surrounded by Middle Eastern enemies. In general tone, *The Times* of 2002 resembled closely the paper Rees-Mogg and the Thomson family handed over to News International in 1981: a liberal Conservative newspaper still, generally free market in outlook and intolerant of those who pandered to gut prejudices whether from left or right. Indeed, its endorsement of Labour in the 2001 general election called into question whether it was even light blue. Like the new Establishment and the pages of the *FT*, it contained shades of soft fuchsia. In this, the paper was a product of its times.

What, therefore, would a historian in fifty or a hundred years time deduce from the changing pattern of *The Times*'s interests and obsessions between 1981 and 2002? A declining interest in the proceedings of parliamentary government would be obvious, although not of executive authority. A broadening in artistic and cultural perspectives would be a growth area, not least the seriousness with which middlebrow or popular forms of entertainment and expression were increasingly accorded attention. There would be much more evidence that women played a larger part in writing and reading the paper. Continuity would be found in the editorialising of the leader page, the columnists and the preoccupations of letter writers. The business pages would also contain much that was familiar, although better written and with more imaginative graphics. The phenomenal growth of interest in sport – and in particular the doings on and off the football pitch – would be of particular note. The historian would be struck not only by a less cluttered layout, with wider margins of space and bigger headlines but also by how much more visual it had become in its presentation. High-resolution photographs that might stretch across a third of a page had replaced grainy images ranging in size from the postage stamp to a small postcard. The newspaper had responded to the visual power of its deadliest rival, television. These changes would be even more apparent if a historian compared *The Times* of 2002 with that of the inter-war or early post-war years. There would be difficulty in locating writers in the old paper capable of blending satire and penetrating insight with the literary brio of Matthew Parris. Nor would a mid-century equivalent of Simon Barnes be easily identified in the sports section. The inter-war business pages would certainly not be read for pleasure. The cryptic crossword would be just as vexing.

Explaining his reasons for starting his newspaper, John Walter, the founder of *The Times*, informed his readers in the first edition on 1 January 1785 that it 'ought to be the register of the times, and faithful recorder of every species of intelligence; it ought not to be engrossed by any particular object; but, like a well covered table, it should contain something suited to every palate'.[55] Times moved on, but the founder's vision was honoured.

LIST OF ILLUSTRATIONS

FIRST PLATE SECTION

Rupert Murdoch announces he is buying *The Times*, 22 January 1981, with
   Harold Evans (*left*) and William Rees-Mogg © Times Newspapers Limited
Gray's Inn Road, home of *The Times* from 1974 to 1986 © Times Newspapers
   Limited

Harold Evans © Times Newspapers Limited
Sir Edward Pickering © Times Newspapers Limited
Rupert Murdoch as *Times* proprietor in his Press Hall © *The Sunday Times*

Editor Charles Douglas-Home addresses his staff, March 1982 © Times
   Newspapers Limited
Lord Dacre heads to Hamburg to tell the world the Hitler diaries are genuine
   in April 1983 © Press Association
Rupert Murdoch and the Queen mark *The Times's* bicentenary in 1985
   © Times Newspapers Limited

Charles Douglas-Home at a point-to-point © Jim Meads
Charles Douglas-Home in his hospital bed © Times Newspapers Limited

Charles Wilson, editor 1985–1990 © Times Newspapers Limited
Rupert Murdoch briefs the press on the deadlock in talks with the print
   unions, 19 January 1986 © Graeme Cookson

The Siege of Wapping, 1986
A scuffle outside *The Times* during the Wapping dispute, 17 February 1986
   © News Group Newspapers

Print unions march down Fleet Street in January 1987 © Press Association
Striking News International workers shout at former colleagues during the
   Wapping dispute © Press Association Photos
The arson of News International's warehouse in Deptford, 2 June 1986

Times journalists take the honours at the 1988 British Press Awards © Times
   Newspapers Limited
The Times's Wapping office © Peter Trievnor

SECOND PLATE SECTION

Simon Jenkins © Times Newspapers Limited
Andrew Knight © Times Newspapers Limited

Bernard Levin © Times Newspapers Limited
Matthew Parris in Kabul © Times Newspapers Limited

Peter Stothard © Times Newspapers Limited
John Bryant © *Daily Mail*
Rosemary Righter © Martin Beddall
Simon Barnes © Times Newspapers Limited

Lynne Truss © Martin Beddall
Caitlin Moran © Times Newspapers Limited
Peter Brookes © Peter Brookes

The *Times* team interviews Tony Blair during the 1997 election campaign ©
    Times Newspapers Limited
Anatole Kaletsky © Times Newspapers Limited
Michael Gove © Times Newspapers Limited

Mary Ann Sieghart © Times Newspapers Limited
Sandra Parsons © Times Newspapers Limited
Patience Wheatcroft © Times Newspapers Limited
Richard Morrison © Times Newspapers Limited

Richard Beeston in Iraq © Majid Karimian
Anthony Loyd in Afghanistan © Seamus Murphy
Sam Kiley © Times Newspapers Limited

Janine di Giovanni under fire in Aghanistan © Miami Herald/Andrew Bosch
Peter Stothard says farewell, March 2002 © Times Newspapers Limited

While every effort has been made to trace the owners of copyright material reproduced herein, the publishers would like to apologise for any omissions and will be pleased to incorporate missing acknowledgements in any future editions.

NOTES

CHAPTER ONE: A LICENCE TO LOSE MONEY (PP. 1–44)

1. *Financial Times*, 23 October 1980; *UK Press Gazette*, 27 October 1980.
2. *Listener*, 30 October 1980.
3. Price Waterhouse's audit for the TNL Directors' Report (Hamilton 9762/6).
4. *UK Press Gazette*, 27 October 1980.
5. Sir Gordon Brunton to the author, interview, 8 April 2003.
6. *The Times*, 23 October 1980.
7. Times Archive, Box 9383.1.
8. Patrick Marnham in *Spectator*, 20 February 1982.
9. Louis Heren on *Panorama*, BBC TV, 17 November 1980.
10. William Rees-Mogg, undated memo [22 October 1980], Box. 9335.
11. William Rees-Mogg, 'Now The Times is going to fight for herself', *The Times*, 23 October 1980.
12. In particular, see *The Times*, letters page, 28 October 1980.
13. Harold Evans, *Good Times, Bad Times*, pp. 97, 108.
14. John Grigg, *The History of The Times*, vol. VI: *The Thomson Years*, p. 554; Evans, *Good Times, Bad Times*, p. 108; *Listener*, 30 October 1980.
15. William Rees-Mogg to the author, interview, 3 December 2001.
16. William Rees-Mogg to the author, interview, 3 December 2001.
17. Quoted in Piers Brendon, *The Life and Death of the Press Barons*, p. 247.
18. Michael Leapman in *The Times*, 27 September 1980; Michael Leapman, *Barefaced Cheek*, p. 190.
19. William Rees-Mogg to the author, interview, 3 December 2001; Leapman, *Barefaced Cheek*, pp. 184–6; Evans, *Good Times, Bad Times*, pp. 96–7.
20. William Rees-Mogg to the author, interview, 3 December 2001; William Rees-Mogg in *Independent*, 29 October 1990.
21. Minutes of ad hoc committee on TNL, Thomson British Holdings Ltd, 18 September 1980. Hamilton Papers 9758/4.
22. Sir Gordon Brunton to the author, interview, 8 April 2003.
23. Rupert Murdoch to the author, interview, 4 August 2003.
24. Denis Hamilton, *Editor-in-Chief*.
25. Quoted in Simon Jenkins, *The Market for Glory*, p. 53.
26. *Newsweek*, 3 November 1980.
27. Sir Gordon Brunton to the author, interview, 8 April 2003.

28. Linda Melvern, *The End of the Street*, p. 175.
29. Tim Austin to the author, interview, 4 March 2003.
30. Marmaduke Hussey, *Chance Governs All*, pp. 129, 132.
31. *Financial Times*, 18 February 1986.
32. Bill O'Neill, *Copy Out* manuscript.
33. William Rees-Mogg to the author, interview, 3 December 2001; Hussey, *Chance Governs All*, p. 164.
34. Andrew Knight to the author, 2 December 2004.
35. Simon Jenkins, *The Market for Glory*, p. 149.
36. And the feeling appeared equally hostile among staff at the *Sunday Times*: Harold Evans to Sir Gordon Brunton, memo, 9 February 1980.
37. *The Times*, 30 August 1980.
38. Ibid.
39. Letters from Alan Reid and T. C. M. Powell, *The Times*, 30 August 1980.
40. William Rees-Mogg, unsigned leader, 'How to Kill a Newspaper', *The Times*, 30 August 1980.
41. Sir Gordon Brunton to the author, interview, 8 April 2003.
42. Lord Thomson of Fleet, press release, 22 October 1980. File 9335.
43. Harold Evans at a luncheon talk to Morgan Grampian journalists, quoted in *UK Press Gazette*, 27 October 1980.
44. Paul Johnson, *Spectator*, 31 January 1981.
45. Grigg, *The Thomson Years*, pp. 554, 556; Sir Gordon Brunton to the author, interview, 8 April 2003; Denis Hamilton, *Editor-in-Chief*, p. 179; Evans, *Good Times, Bad Times*, p. 125.
46. Evans, *Good Times, Bad Times*, pp. 89–91, 111, 125.
47. Iverach McDonald, *The History of The Times*, vol. V: *Struggles in War and Peace 1939–1966*, pp. 409–28; Jenkins, *Market for Glory*, p. 53.
48. Rupert Murdoch to the author, interview, 4 August 2003.
49. Sir Gordon Brunton to the author, interview, 8 April 2003.
50. Quoted in S. J. Taylor, *An Unlikely Hero*, p. 180.
51. Sir Gordon Brunton to the author, interview, 8 April 2003.
52. Richard Searby to the author, interview, 11 June 2002.
53. Evans, *Good Times, Bad Times*, p. 122.
54. Sir Denis Hamilton to Sir Gordon Brunton, 9 January 1980, Brunton Papers.
55. Sir Denis Hamilton to the Directors of TNHL, 16 January 1981. Hamilton Papers.
56. Evans, *Good Times, Bad Times*, pp. 106–7.
57. Harold Evans to Sir Gordon Brunton, 20 January 1981, (underlining as in original), Brunton Papers.
58. Denis Hamilton to Directors of TNHL, 16 January 1981. Hamilton Papers.

59. Quoted in the *Sunday Times*, 15 February 1981.

60. Minutes of the TNL Editorial Vetting Committee, 21 January 1981, file A759-9335.

61. William Rees-Mogg to the author, interview, 3 December 2001.

62. Paul Johnson, *Spectator*, 20 April 1985.

63. Statements by Sir Gordon Brunton and Rupert Murdoch, press releases, 22 January 1981, Hamilton Papers A759-9335.

64. *Evening Standard*, 22 January 1981.

65. *Sunday Times*, 15 February 1981; *Daily Telegraph*, 29 September 1981.

66. Sir Gordon Brunton to the author, interview, 8 April 2003.

67. *The Times*, 20 January 1981.

68. Record of Murdoch's remarks to staff, 26 January 1981, Hamilton Papers A759-9335; *The Times*, 27 January 1981.

69. *The Times*, 27 January 1981.

70. Market share breakdown in memo of 26 January 1981 in Hamilton Papers.

71. Paul Johnson, *Spectator*, 31 January 1981.

72. James Evans (Director, The Thomson Organisation) to John Biffen, 26 January 1981; Thomson submission to the Department of Trade and Industry.

73. Sir Gordon Brunton to the author, interview, 8 April 2003.

74. Rupert Murdoch to the author, interview, 5 August 2003.

75. Ibid.

76. Woodrow Wyatt, *Journals of Woodrow Wyatt*, Vol. I, p. 372, diary entry, 14 June 1987.

77. Rupert Murdoch to John Grigg, Grigg, *The Thomson Years*, p. 573.

78. Lord Biffen to the author, interview, 1 August 2003.

79. Hamilton Papers 9758/4; *The Times*, 28 January 1981; *Sunday Times*, 15 February 1981.

80. *Hansard*, 27 January 1981; *The Times*, 28 January 1981.

81. Jonathan Aitken to the author, interview, 27 May 2003.

82. *Hansard*, 27 January 1981.

83. Jonathan Aitken to the author, interview, 27 May 2003.

84. *The Times*, 26 February 1981; Alan Watkins, *A Short Walk Down Fleet Street*, pp. 178–9; Jenkins, *Market for Glory*, pp. 169–70.

85. Thomson submission to the Department of Trade and Industry.

86. John Biffen to John Smith, 3 February 1981, letter reprinted in *The Times*, 4 February 1981.

87. Evans, *Good Times, Bad Times*, p. 143.

88. Ibid., pp. 151–3; *Sunday Times*, 18 February 1981.

89. Jenkins, *Market for Glory*, p. 58.

90. *The Times*, 13 February 1981.

91. O'Neill, *Copy Out*.

92. Bill Bryson, *Notes from a Small Island*, pp 46–7.

93. O'Neill, *Copy Out*, p. 15; *Sunday Times*, 15 February 1981; Evans, *Good Times, Bad Times*, p. 182; Grigg, *The Thomson Years*, p. 576; *The Times*, 13 February 1981.

94. Richard Searby to the author, interview, 11 June 2002.

95. Quoted in William Shawcross, *Murdoch*, p. 38.

96. Shawcross, *Murdoch*, pp. 47–9; Rupert Murdoch to the author, interview, 4 August 2003.

97. Quoted in Shawcross, *Murdoch*, p. 61.

98. Murdoch quoted in *Chief Executive* magazine; quoted in *TNL News*, November 1982.

99. Maxwell Newton in 'Six Australians: Profiles of Power', Australian Broadcasting Corporation, 1 January 1966, quoted in Neil Chenoweth, *Virtual Murdoch*, p. 32.

100. *Sunday Times*, 15 February 1981; *Daily Telegraph*, 30 September 1981.

101. Rupert Murdoch, speech at Melbourne University, 15 November 1972.

102. *Sun*, headlines, 11 January and 30 April 1979.

103. Leading article, 'The Fifth Proprietorship', *The Times*, 13 February 1981.

104. Quoted in Leapman, *Barefaced Cheek*, p. 174.

CHAPTER TWO: 'THE GREATEST EDITOR IN THE WORLD' (PP. 45–118)

1. Hugh Stephenson to Denis Hamilton, 13 February 1981, Hamilton Papers 9383/12.

2. Quoted in Michael Leapman, *Barefaced Cheek*, p. 203.

3. Owen Hickey to Denis Hamilton, 11 February 1981, Hamilton Papers 9383/12.

4. John Grigg, *The History of The Times*, vol. VI: *The Thomson Years*, p. 376; Leapman, *Barefaced Cheek*, p. 201.

5. Rupert Murdoch to the author, interview, 4 August 2003.

6. Bruce Page, 'Into the arms of Count Dracula', *New Statesman*, 30 January 1981.

7. Rupert Murdoch to the annual lunch of the Advertising Association, quoted in *TNL News*, April 1981.

8. Richard Searby to the author, interview, 11 June 2002; Leapman, *Barefaced Cheek*, pp. 204–5.

9. Marmaduke Hussey, *Chance Governs All*, p. 179.

10. Sir Edward Pickering to the author and Richard Searby to the author, 11 June 2002; Rupert Murdoch to the author, 4 August 2003; Denis Hamilton, *Editor-in-Chief*, p. 181; Leapman, *Barefaced Cheek*, p. 205.

11. Louis Heren, February 1981, *Quarterly of the Commonwealth Press Union*.

12. Hugh Stephenson, 'Not the age of The Times', *New Statesman*, 11 January 1985.
13. Harold Evans, *Good Times, Bad Times*, pp. 188–9.
14. Evans in *British Journalism Review*, vol. 13, no. 4, 2002.
15. Michael Leapman, *Treacherous Estate*, 1992, p. 51.
16. Evans, *Good Times, Bad Times*, p. 340.
17. *TNL News*, April 1981.
18. *Spectator*, 20 June 1981.
19. Ibid., 28 February 1981.
20. Harold Evans to Frank Giles, 27 and 29 April 1981, Evans files.
21. Evans, *Good Times, Bad Times*, p. 253.
22. Evans Day File, 29 April 1981.
23. Evans Day File, 6 April 1981.
24. Clive Jenkins to Harold Evans, 3 July 1981 and Evans to Jenkins 12 July 1981; Jenkins to Anthony Holden, 3 July 1981, Evans Day File, 3 July 1981.
25. *The Times*, 23 October 1980.
26. Evans, *Good Times, Bad Times*, p. 263.
27. Anthony Holden to the author, interview, 9 April 2003.
28. *The Times*, 23 November 1963.
29. Ibid., 2 April 1981.
30. Evans to Rupert Davenport-Hines (and others), 14 June 1981, Evans Day File.
31. *Private Eye*, 28 August 1981; Evans to Anthony Whitaker, 23 October 1981, Evans Day File, A327/3692.
32. Evans Day File, 22 May 1981.
33. Evans to N. P. L. Price, 27 May 1981, Evans Day File.
34. Anthony Holden to the author, interview, 9 April 2003.
35. Ibid.
36. Gerald Long to Herbert Kremp (joint editor-in-chief *Die Welt*), 15 June 1981, Evans file 1, A153-658; *TNL News*.
37. John Grieg to Harold Evans, 9 March 1981 Evans box 1.
38. Evans, *Good Times, Bad Times*, pp. 271, 274.
39. Evans, press release, 30 July 1981.
40. Lord Astor to Gerald Long, 30 July 1981, A153-655.
41. *TNL News*, August 1981.
42. Jack Lonsdale, letter in *TNL News*, October 1981.
43. Evans to Colin Watson, 10 January 1982, Evans Day File A759/9329.
44. Evans to Henry Kissinger, 21 May 1981, Evan Day File.
45. Frank Johnson to the author, interview, 15 January 2003.
46. Paul Johnson, *Spectator*, 11 March and 21 March 1981.
47. Fred Emery, *The Times*, 11 March 1981.

48. *The Times*, leading article (by Harold Evans), 11 March 1981; Evans *Good Times, Bad Times*, p. 214.
49. Evans to Michael Foot, 26 March 1981, Evans Day File A327/3626.
50. Margaret Thatcher, *The Downing Street Years*, pp. 137–8.
51. *The Times*, 30 March 1981.
52. *The Times*, leading article, 'An Avalanche of Economists', 31 March 1981.
53. Thatcher, *The Downing Street Years*, p. 138.
54. Patrick Minford, *The Times*, 7 April 1981.
55. Nigel Lawson, *The View from No. 11*, 1992, p. 98.
56. 'The Price of Floating', leading article, *The Times*, 8 July 1981.
57. 'The Ottawa Opportunity', leading article, *The Times*, 17 July 1981; see Grigg, *The Thomson Years*, p. 390; Edmund Dell, *The Chancellors*, p. 427.
58. James Tobin, *The Times*, 14 October 1981.
59. 'Britain's Economic Legacy', leading article, *The Times*, 27 January 1982.
60. 'The Flexible Side of EMS', leading article, *The Times*, 6 October 1981.
61. 'Wanted: European Vision', leading article, *The Times*, 2 December 1981.
62. Charles Hargrove and Ian Murray, *The Times*, 11 March 1981.
63. 'The Choice for France', leading article, *The Times*, 12 May 1981.
64. Ronald Butt, *The Times*, 14 May 1981.
65. Letter to the editor, *The Times*, 30 May 1981.
66. Christopher Thomas, *The Times*, 11 April 1981.
67. Leading article, *The Times*, 11 April 1981.
68. Ibid., 5 May 1981.
69. 'If Ireland Is To Be United', leading article, *The Times*, 2 July 1981.
70. 'Fermanagh Does It Again', leading article, *The Times*, 22 August 1981.
71. Martin Huckerby, *The Times*, 13 April 1981.
72. *The Times*, 13 April 1981; Sasthi Brata, *The Times*, 15 April 1981.
73. Leading articles, *The Times*, 14 April, 7 July and 13 July 1981.
74. 'The Soiled Coin', leading article, *The Times*, 10 July 1981.
75. 'The Scarman Report', leading article, *The Times*, 26 November 1981.
76. Darcus Howe, *The Times*, 26 November 1981.
77. 'Moonshine and Money' and 'A Hard Winter', leading articles, *The Times*, 17 September and 20 October 1981.
78. Diana Geddes, *The Times*, 30 March 1981.
79. 'Universities Under the Knife' and 'The Cost of University Cuts', leading articles, *The Times*, 3 July and 10 October 1981.
80. Evans, *Good Times, Bad Times*, pp. 218–19.
81. Ivor Crewe and Anthony King, *SDP: The Birth, Life and Death of the Social Democratic Party*, p. 261.
82. *The Times*, 27 March 1981.
83. 'The Gang Becomes a Party', leading article, *The Times*, 27 March 1981.
84. Crewe and King, *SDP*, p. 257.

85. Ibid., p. 254.
86. Geoffrey Taylor, *Changing Faces: History of The Guardian, 1956–1988*, p. 213.
87. *The Times*, 23 October 1981; Evans, *Good Times, Bad Times*, p. 289.
88. Frank Johnson, 'A Happy Party, Fit for all Factions', *The Times*, 16 September 1986.
89. Frank Johnson, *The Times*, 15 September 1982.
90. Nicholas Wapshott's interview with Ken Livingstone, *The Times*, 14 May 1981.
91. Evans to Lord George Brown, 2 July 1981, Evans Day File.
92. *The Times*, 23 and 23 September 1981.
93. Bernard Donoughue, 10 September 1981, Evans Day File 1/17.
94. *The Times*, 25 September 1981.
95. Tony Benn, letter to the editor, *The Times*, 26 September 1981.
96. Evans to features, home and business editors, 29 October 1981, Evans Day File 1/17.
97. Evans Day File, A327/3626.
98. Tony Benn, quoted in the *Daily Telegraph*, 28 September 1981.
99. 'Unfinished Business', leading article, *The Times*, 1 October 1981.
100. Tony Benn, quoted in *The Times*, 13 March 1982.
101. Ibid., 27 January 1982.
102. Hamilton, *Editor-in-Chief*, p. 182.
103. Evans, *Good Times, Bad Times*, p. 324.
104. Michael Ruda, interview, 'The Greatest Paper in the World', Thames Television, broadcast 2 January 1985.
105. Evans to Murdoch, 3 December 1981, Evans Day File.
106. Rupert Murdoch to the author, interview, 4 August 2003.
107. *TNL News*, April 1981; Murdoch's report to the TNL board, 9 June 1981.
108. *TNL News*, April 1981.
109. Ibid., July 1981.
110. Marmaduke Hussey, memorandum, 9 December 1974, Grigg Papers.
111. *TNL News*, September 1984.
112. Evans to Bill O'Neill, 20 October 1981, Evans Day File.
113. Evans to Gerald Long, cc. Bill Gillespie, John Collier, 29 January 1982, Evans Day File.
114. Hamilton, *Editor-in-Chief*, pp. 171–2.
115. Liz Seeber to the author, interview, 18 July 2002.
116. Bill Bryson, *Notes from a Small Island*, pp. 47–8.
117. Murdoch, quoted in the *Financial Times*, 30 September, and the *Daily Telegraph*, 29 September 1981.
118. Murdoch, quoted in *The Times*, 2 October 1981; *TNL News*, October 1981.

119. *Australian Financial Review*, reproduced in *TNL News*, November 1981.

120. Evans to Ken Beattie (TNL commercial director), 4 November 1981, Evans Day File A327/3626.

121. Evans to Ken Beattie, 21 October and 29 October 1981, Evans Day File.

122. Evans to John Higgins, 17 November 1981, Evans Day File A327/3626.

123. Alan Watkins, *Spectator*, 23 July 1983.

124. Evans to Bernard Levin, 2 September 1981, Evans Day File.

125. Ibid., 6 August 1981, Evans Day File.

126. Ibid., 12 November 1981, Evans Day File.

127. Evans to Michael Leapman, 11 June 1981, telex 125912.

128. Philip Howard to the author, interview, 5 December 2002.

129. Evans to Michael Leapman, 29 June 1981, Evans Day File.

130. Anthony Holden to the author, interview, 9 April 2003.

131. Patrick Marnham, *Spectator*, 20 February 1982.

132. Evans to Peter Hennessy, 10 January 1092, Evans Day File A759/9329.

133. Evans, *Good Times, Bad Times*, p. 293.

134. Tim Austin to the author, interview, 4 March 2003.

135. Fred Emery to the author, interview, 24 January 2005.

136. Made famous by *Vanity Fair* editor Graydon Carter, quoted in Toby Young, *How to Lose Friends and Alienate People*, p. 143n.

137. Evans, *Good Times, Bad Times*, pp. 329–31.

138. Gerald Long to department heads, 19 June 1981 (reissued 5 January 1982), ref. A751/9253/42.

139. Evans to Murdoch, 16 September 1981, Evans Day File, A327/3626.

140. Minutes, editorial management meeting, 4 May 1982, ref. 3629/3/4.

141. Evans to Murdoch, undated draft, January 1982, Evans Day File.

142. Ibid., 11 January 1982, Evans Day File.

143. Evans, *Good Times, Bad Times*, pp. 319–23.

144. Evans to Charles Douglas-Home, no date, February 1982, Evans Day File.

145. Frank Giles, *Sundry Times*, p. 221.

146. Evans, *Good Times, Bad Times*, p. 172.

147. Anthony Holden to the author, interview, 9 April 2003.

148. Evans to Anthony Holden, 23 November 1981, Evans Day File A327/3626.

149. Leapman, *Barefaced Cheek*, p. 228.

150. Murdoch, personal message to all *The Times* and *Sunday Times* staff, 8 February 1982.

151. *TNL News*, March 1982; Evans to Gerald Long, 18 February 1982, Evans Day File.

152. Minutes of TNL directors' meeting, 16 December 1981, ref. 6968/1; Evans to Long, 16 February 1982, Evans Day File.

153. Minutes of TNL directors' meeting, 23 December 1981, ref. 6968/1.

154. Evans to Long, Frank Giles to Long, 16 February 1982, ref. 6968/1.
155. Evans, *Good Times, Bad Times*, p. 359.
156. Peter Wilby (Father of the *Sunday Times* NUJ chapel) to Sir Edward Pickering, 20 February 1982.
157. Denis Hamilton, *Editor-in-Chief*, p. 183.
158. Richard Searby to Sir Edward Pickering, 17 February 1982.
159. *TNL News*, March 1982.
160. *The Times*, 15 February 1982.
161. Ibid., February 1982.
162. Richard Searby to Sir Edward Pickering, 19 February 1982; Minutes of TNHL board meeting, 22 February 1982.
163. *Spectator*, 27 February 1982.
164. Evans to Murdoch, 21 and 23 February 1982. Evans Day File.
165. Evans to Willie Landels, 24 September 1981, Evans Day File A327/3626.
166. Evans to Elwyn Parry Jones (producer, *Panorama*), 2 March 1982, Evans Day File A759/9329.
167. Evans to Tony Richmond-Watson, 26 February 1982, Evans Day File 1759/9329; also Evans to Long, 9 March 1981, and Evans to Murdoch, draft memo, undated [February] 1982.
168. Richard Ingrams, *Spectator*, 5 November 1983.
169. Rupert Murdoch to the author, interview, 4 August 2003.
170. Quoted in Evans, *Good Times, Bad Times*, p. 222.
171. Evans, *Good Times, Bad Times*, p. 228.
172. Ibid., p. 229.
173. Bernard Donoughue, *The Heat of the Kitchen*, p. 286.
174. Obituary of Owen Hickey, *The Times*, 5 December 2000. In the spirit of his anonymous work, Hickey had requested not to be given an obituary. The request was ignored.
175. Owen Hickey to Rees-Mogg, 13 November and 23 December 1980.
176. Peter Stothard to the author, interview, 8 November 2004; Anthony Holden to the author, interview, 9 April 2003.
177. Donoughue, *The Heat of the Kitchen*, pp. 288–9.
178. *Spectator*, 5 November 1983.
179. Frank Johnson to the author, interview, 15 January 2003.
180. Liz Seeber to the author, interview, 18 July 2003.
181. Philip Howard to the author, interview, 5 December 2002.
182. Hussey, *Chance Governs All*, p. 179.
183. Evans to Murdoch, 21 February 1982, Evans Day File.
184. Ibid., 23 February 1982, Evans Day File.
185. Ibid., 11 March 1982, Evans Day File.
186. Enoch Powell, *The Times*, 10 March 1982.
187. Evans, *Good Times, Bad Times*, p. 369.

188. Ibid., p. 377.
189. *The Times*, 12 March 1982.
190. 'The Deeper Issues', leading article, *The Times*, 12 March 1982.
191. *The Times*, 13 March 1982.
192. Leapman, *Barefaced Cheek*, p. 235; Evans, *Good Times, Bad Times*, pp. 393–4.
193. Tim Austin to the author, interview, 4 March 2003; Fred Emery to the author, interview, 24 January 2005.
194. 'The Greatest Paper in the World', Thames Television, broadcast 2 January 1985.
195. Anthony Holden to the author, interview, 9 April 2003.
196. *Private Eye*, 26 March 1982.
197. Douglas-Home to Michael Leapman, 11 November 1983, Douglas-Home Papers.
198. Evans, *Good Times, Bad Times*, pp. 177–8.
199. Evans to the author, interview, 25 June 2003.
200. Ibid.; Evans, *Good Times, Bad Times*, pp. 1–2.
201. *The Times*, 17 and 18 September 1981.
202. Harold Evans to the author, interview, 25 June 2003.
203. Lord Parkinson to the author, 2 July 2004.
204. Rupert Murdoch to the author, interview, 5 August 2003.
205. Donoughue, *The Heat of the Kitchen*, p. 288.
206. Evans to the author, interview, 25 June 2003.
207. Notes of discussion between Alastair Hetherington and Douglas-Home, 31 October 1983, Douglas-Home Papers.
208. Richard Searby to the author, interview, 11 June 2002; similarly rendered in Rupert Murdoch's interview with the author, 4 August 2003.
209. Bill O'Neill, *Copy Out* manuscript.
210. Evans, *Good Times, Bad Times*, p. 312.
211. Evans to the author, interview, 25 June 2003.
212. Rupert Murdoch to the author, interview, 4 August 2003.
213. Anthony Holden to the author, interview, 9 April 2003.
214. Rees-Mogg, 'The Greatest Paper in the World', Thames Television, broadcast 2 January 1985.
215. Anthony Holden to the author, interview, 9 April 2003.
216. *Sunday Times*, 14 March 1982.
217. Tony Norbury to the author, interview, 27 April 2004.
218. Quoted in Donoughue, *The Heat of the Kitchen*, p. 287.
219. Patrick Marnham, *Spectator*, 20 February, 1982.
220. Paul Johnson, *Spectator*, 20 March 1982.
221. Philip Howard, 'The Greatest Paper in the World', Thames Television, broadcast 2 January 1985.

222. Evans to Frank Johnson, 12 March 1982, Evans Day File.
223. Frank Johnson to the author, interview, 15 January 2003.

CHAPTER THREE: COLD WARRIOR (PP. 119–166)

1. John Grigg, *The History of The Times*, vol. VI: *The Thomson Years*, p. 549.
2. From Lord Shackleton and others, letters to the editor, *The Times*, 4 February 1982.
3. *The Times*, 23 March 1982.
4. Peter Hennessy, *The Prime Minister*, p. 413.
5. 'Gunboat or Burglar Alarm?', leading article, *The Times*, 29 March 1982.
6. Peter Chippindale and Chris Horrie, *Stick It Up Your Punter*, pp. 128–31.
7. Bernard Ingham, *Kill The Messenger*, p. 285.
8. Charles Douglas-Home, evidence to the House of Commons Defence Select Committee, 18 July 1982; Geoffrey Taylor, *Changing Faces: History of the Guardian, 1956–1988*, p. 225.
9. *Guardian*, 11 July 1988; Miles Hudson and John Stanier, *War and the Media*: A Random Searchlight, p. 169.
10. Hudson and Stanier, *War and the Media*, p. 170.
11. 'Naked Aggression', leading article, *The Times*, 3 April 1982.
12. 'We Are All Falklanders Now', leading article, *The Times*, 5 April 1982.
13. Margaret Thatcher, *The Downing Street Years*, p. 186.
14. *The Times*, 14 April 1982.
15. Ibid., 20 May 1982.
16. Thatcher, *The Downing Street Years*, p. 181.
17. Max Hastings and Simon Jenkins, *The Battle for the Falklands*, p. 161.
18. Fred Emery to Charles Douglas-Home, 29 April 1982, ref. A751/9256/9/2.
19. The advertisement was sponsored by a group describing themselves as Argentine citizens residing in New York State, *The Times*, 24 April 1982.
20. E. P Thompson, 'Why Neither Side Is Worth Backing', *The Times*, 29 April 1982.
21. Lord Wigg, letters to the editor, *The Times*, 6 April 1982.
22. Leon Pilpel in *TNL News*, May 1982.
23. Frank Giles, *Sundry Times*, p. 224.
24. David Kynaston, *The Financial Times: A Centenary History*, pp. 463–6.
25. Taylor, *Changing Faces*, pp. 228–33, 234–5.
26. *New Statesman*, 'Mad Margaret and the Voyage of Dishonour', 9 April 1982; *New Statesman*, 30 April 1982.
27. Chippindale and Horrie, *Stick It Up Your Punter*, p. 136.
28. Thatcher, *The Downing Street Years*, pp. 205–8, 211.
29. Liz Seeber to the author, interview, 18 July 2002.
30. *The Economist*, 22 May 1982.

31. John Witherow to the author, interview, 9 August 2002.

32. Quoted in David E. Morrison and Howard Tumber, *Journalists at War: The Dynamics of News Reporting During the Falklands Conflict*, p. 144; Hudson and Stanier, *War and the Media*, p. 170.

33. John Witherow to the author, interview, 9 August 2002; *The Economist*, 22 May 1982; Charles Douglas-Home, evidence to the House of Commons Defence Select Committee, 18 July 1982.

34. Robert Harris, *Gotcha! The Media, The Government and the Falklands Crisis*, pp. 35–6.

35. Emery to Douglas-Home, 18 May 1982, ref. A751/9256/9/2.

36. John Witherow to the author, interview, 9 August 2002.

37. Ibid.

38. *The Times*, 4 May 1982.

39. Chippindale and Horrie, *Stick It Up Your Punter*, p. 137.

40. 'For a Better Peace', leading article, *The Times*, 5 May 1982.

41. *The Times*, 5 May 1982.

42. Ibid., 7 May 1982.

43. Peter Kellner, *New Statesman*, 7 May 1982.

44. Professor Bernard Crick, letters to the editor, *The Times*, 6 May 1982.

45. 'You Cannot Joke With War', leading article, *The Times*, 12 May 1982.

46. Thatcher, *The Downing Street Years*, pp. 216, 221; *The Times*, 5 May 1982.

47. Nigel Lawson, *The View From No. 11*, pp. 126–7.

48. Harris, *Gotcha!*, p. 111.

49. John Witherow to the author, interview, 9 August 2002.

50. Hudson and Stanier, *War and the Media*, p. 175.

51. Fred Emery to Charles Douglas-Home, ref. A751/9256/9/2.

52. Hudson and Stanier, *War and the Media*, p. 173.

53. *The Times*, 11 June 1982.

54. Ibid., 12 June 1982.

55. Ibid., 10 June 1982.

56. Hastings and Jenkins, *The Battle for the Falklands*, pp. 320–21.

57. Quoted in Harris, *Gotcha!*, p. 118.

58. Hastings and Jenkins, *The Battle for the Falklands*, p. 349.

59. 'The Truce', leading article, *The Times*, 15 June 1982.

60. John Witherow and Patrick Bishop, *The Winter War*, p. 17.

61. Ibid., pp. 18, 26.

62. Harris, *Gotcha!*, p. 56.

63. Hudson and Stanier, *War and the Media*, p. 178.

64. Robert Kee, letters to the editor, *The Times*, 14 May 1982.

65. Taylor, *Changing Faces*, p. 237.

66. Address by Edward Cazalet at Charles Douglas-Home's Memorial Service, 25 November 1985.

67. Jessica Douglas-Home, *Once Upon Another Time*, p. 11.
68. *The Times*, 22 October 1982.
69. Ibid., 19 September 1981.
70. Ibid., 17 December 1981.
71. 'Can We Help Poland?', leading article, *The Times*, 23 September 1981; 'What the West Should Do', leading article, *The Times*, 17 December 1981.
72. Harold Evans to Rupert Murdoch, 17 January 1982, Evans Day File A759/9329.
73. *The Times*, 13 August 1982.
74. 'Trade Across the Curtain', leading article, *The Times*, 16 November 1982.
75. Michael Binyon, quoted in *TNL News*, September 1982.
76. *The Times*, 12 November 1982.
77. 'Enter Mr Andropov', leading article, *The Times*, 13 November 1982.
78. 'The Morality of Deterrence', leading article, *The Times*, 19 October 1982.
79. Harold Evans to Owen Hickey, Richard Owen, Brian Horton, 5 November 1981, Evans Day File; Harold Evans, *Good Times, Bad Times*, p. 237.
80. 'Lebanon for the Lebanese', leading article, *The Times*, 14 June 1982.
81. 'Israel's Pre-Emptive Strike', leading article, *The Times*, 9 June 1981.
82. Robert Fisk to the author, interview, 21 September 2004.
83. *TNL News*, March 1983.
84. Robert Fisk to the author, interview, 21 September 2004; Robert Fisk, *Pity the Nation*, pp. 183–7.
85. Telegram from Robert Fisk, 25 February 1982, HME 1/19.
86. Brian Horton to Harold Evans, 5 March 1982, HME 1/19.
87. Fisk, *Pity the Nation*, pp. 183–7.
88. 'The Best Assad We Have', leading article, *The Times*, 15 February 1982.
89. 'Israel Erupts', leading article, *The Times*, 8 June 1982; 'An Unbalanced Policy', leading article, *The Times*, 10 June 1982.
90. 'An Unbalanced Policy', leading article, *The Times*, 10 June 1982.
91. *The Times*, 8 June 1982.
92. Ibid., 15 June 1982.
93. Edward Mortimer, 'Why the West should fear the shame of the Arabs', *The Times*, 8 June 1982.
94. *The Times*, 20 September 1982.
95. 'After the Massacre', leading article, *The Times*, 20 September 1982.
96. Ibid.
97. Brenda Dean to all Fathers of chapel working under NPA Agreement, 25 June 1982, 6985/21.
98. 'An Unlawful Interruption', leading article, *The Times*, 12 August 1982.
99. 'All Our Tomorrows', leading article, *The Times*, 3 January 1983.

100. Hugo Young to Douglas-Home, 16 February 1985, Douglas-Home Papers.
101. Douglas-Home/Clare Short correspondence, 26 March and 2 April 1985, Douglas-Home Papers.
102. Peter Stothard to Douglas-Home, 13 April 1983, Douglas-Home Papers.
103. Seth Lipsky, 'Welcome Back Thunderer', *Wall Street Journal*, 14 November 1985.
104. Leading article, *Spectator*, 2 November 1985.
105. *The Times*, 4 March 1993.
106. Richard Davy to the author, 2 January 2005.
107. 'Not the Age of *The Times*', *New Statesman*, 11 January 1985.
108. Rupert Murdoch to the author, interview, August 2003. Other accounts render the expletive variously.
109. 'The International Framework', leading article, *The Times*, 11 February 1983.
110. 'Beyond the Budget', leading article, *The Times*, 8 February 1983.
111. Graham Searjeant to the author, interview, 11 January 2005.
112. Lawson, *The View From No. 11*, p. 208.
113. 'The Pains of Privatisation', leading article, *The Times*, 22 November 1982.
114. 'Selling at a Discount', leading article, *The Times*, 28 October 1982.
115. 'The Love that Labour Lost', leading article, *The Times*, 6 June 1983.
116. *The New Hope for Britain*, Labour Party 1983 general election manifesto.
117. *The Times*, 1 December 1982.
118. 'All Their Tomorrows', leading article, *The Times*, 8 June 1983.
119. Ivor Crewe and Anthony King, *SDP: The Birth, Life and Death of the Social Democratic Party*, p. 498.
120. Giles, *Sundry Times*, p. 230.
121. *The Times*, 3 October 1983.
122. Michael Foot to Douglas-Home, 15 September 1983, Douglas-Home Papers.
123. Leading article, *The Times*, 7 October 1983.
124. Graham Paterson to the author, interview, 18 September 2002.
125. Enid M. Macbeth to the Douglas-Home, 15 October 1983, ref. 3627/2/12. Mrs Macbeth was, however, won over by Douglas-Home's reply and wrote to tell him she would be continuing with the newspaper-reading habit of her lifetime after all (letter, 25 October 1983).
126. Douglas-Home to Alastair Hetherington, undated, Douglas-Home Papers.
127. *The Times*, letters to the editor, 15 October 1983; W. F. Deedes, *Dear Bill*, p. 283.

CHAPTER FOUR: ANCIENT AND MODERN (PP. 167–218)

1. *Sunday Times*, 1 May 1983; Robert Harris, *Selling Hitler*, pp. 234–6.
2. Colin Webb to the author, interview, 20 February 2003.
3. Lord Dacre to Graham Turner, interview, *Daily Telegraph*, 28 January 2003. He made similar claims to Frank Giles: Frank Giles, *Sundry Times*, pp. 245–6.
4. These were the exact words Douglas-Home told Webb that Dacre had used when Webb – away on holiday – spoke to the editor by telephone the following day. Colin Webb to the author, interview, 20 February 2003.
5. Harris, *Selling Hitler*, pp. 261–5.
6. Michael Binyon to the author, interview, 25 November 2002.
7. Harris, *Selling Hitler*, pp. 284–7.
8. Rupert Murdoch to the author, interview, 5 August 2003.
9. Harris, *Selling Hitler*, pp. 288–91, 302–3.
10. Michael Binyon to the author, interview, 25 November 2002.
11. *The Times*, 23 April 1983.
12. Harris, *Selling Hitler*, pp. 306–7.
13. Michael Binyon to the author, interview, 25 November 2002.
14. Colin Webb to the author, interview, 20 February 2003.
15. Harris, *Selling Hitler*, p. 314.
16. *Sunday Times*, 24 April 1983.
17. Frank Giles, *Sundry Times*, pp. 243–4.
18. Robert Fisk to the author, interview, 21 September 2004.
19. *Sunday Times*, 1 May 1983; Harris, *Selling Hitler*, pp. 316–18.
20. Michael Binyon to the author, interview, 23 April 2004.
21. Lord Dacre to Charles Douglas-Home, 22 August 1984, Douglas-Home Papers.
22. Harris, *Selling Hitler*, pp. 321–3; *The Times*, 26 April 1983.
23. Letters to the editor, *The Times*, 26–28 April 1983.
24. Charles Wilson to the author, interview, 19 February 2004; Robert Fisk, also in the room at the time, recalled Murdoch saying 'nothing ventured, nothing gained'. Robert Fisk to the author, interview, 21 September 2004; Webb found Murdoch equally relaxed at this time: Colin Webb to the author, interview, 20 February 2004.
25. Lord Dacre to Graham Turner, interview, *Daily Telegraph*, 28 January 2003.
26. *The Times*, 27 January 2003.
27. Tim Austin to the author, interview, 4 March 2003.
28. Rupert Murdoch to the author, interview, 5 August 2003.
29. *The Times*, 29 November 1984.
30. Irving Wardle to the author, 10 June 2004.

31. *The Times*, 3 May 1985.

32. Ibid., 12 May 1981.

33. *Independent on Sunday*, 12 May 2002.

34. *The Times*, 3 January 1985.

35. Ibid., 11 April 1986.

36. Ibid., 1 and 3 November 1982.

37. Douglas-Home to Lord Dacre, 25 April 1985, Douglas-Home Papers.

38. *The Times*, 19 June 1985.

39. *Guardian*, 13 September 1985.

40. Charles Douglas-Home to Paul Routledge, 26 October 1984, Routledge Papers; Paul Routledge to the author, interview, 22 June 2004.

41. *Daily Express*, 3 April 1984; Alastair Brett (Times Senior Legal Assistant) to Sir Larry Lamb, 3 April 1984, Routledge Papers.

42. For example, Paul Johnson and (the far from pro-Murdoch) Charles Moore in *Spectator*, 5 and 12 November 1983.

43. *The Times*, 3 November 1983.

44. Harold Evans to Rupert Murdoch, 29 July 1981, Evans Day File A327/3625.

45. *TNL News*, July 1984.

46. *The Times*, 26 June 1984.

47. Geoffrey Taylor, *Changing Faces: History of The Guardian, 1956–1988*, p. 312.

48. *TNL News*, December 1984.

49. Ibid., April and June 1982; *Observer*, 13 July 1986.

50. Minutes of Times Editorial Management Meeting, 2 June 1982, ref. 3629/3/4.

51. Charles Douglas-Home to Murray Hedgcock, 14 September 1982; Minutes of Times Editorial Management Meeting, 29 June 1982, ref. 3629/3/4.

52. *The Times*, 27 January 1982, 19 January 1983; see also Hugo Young, *Listener*, 3 January 1985.

53. Charles Douglas-Home to Sir Edward Pickering, 3 March 1983, ref. A751/9256/13.

54. Minutes of Times Editorial Management meeting, 29 June 1982, ref. 3629/3/4.

55. For example, Emery to Douglas-Home, 6 April and 24 May 1982, and undated memoranda, ref. A751/9256/9/2.

56. Colin Webb to the author, interview, 20 February 2003.

57. Charles Wilson to the author, interview, 19 February 2004.

58. Minutes of Times Editorial Management meeting, 2 June 1982, ref. 3629/3/4.

59. *The Times*, 4 June 1982; memo, ref. 3629/3/18.

60. Douglas-Home to Fred Emery, 21 June 1982, ref. A751/9256.
61. Hugh Trevor-Roper (Lord Dacre) to Douglas-Home, 9 August 1985.
62. Ranan Lurie to Douglas-Home, 17 April 1982, ref. 3629/3/10.
63. *The Times*, 12 February 1994.
64. Liz Seeber to the author, interview, 18 July 2002.
65. Simon Barnes to the author, interview, 25 January 2005.
66. *The Times*, 3 and 18 August 1981.
67. Ibid., 23 June 1981; see Richard Evans, *John McEnroe: Taming the Talent*.
68. Ibid., 17 June 1982.
69. Ibid., 6 and 12 July 1982.
70. *The Greatest Paper in the World!*, Thames Television, broadcast 2 January 1985.
71. *TNL News*, March 1985.
72. Douglas-Home to various correspondents, March 1985, ref. 1749/9248/2; Paul Routledge to the author, interview, 22 June 2004.
73. Sir Edward Pickering to the author, interview, 15 January 2002.
74. Jessica Douglas-Home, *No End of a Lesson*, p. 13.
75. 'The Nativity', leading article (by Douglas-Home), *The Times*, 24 December 1984.
76. The correspondence, consulted for this volume, is in the care of Jessica Douglas-Home.
77. Charles Wilson to the author, interview, 19 February 2004.
78. *TNL News*, November 1985; letters in the possession of Jessica Douglas-Home.
79. *Spectator*, 2 November 1985.
80. *TNL News*, December 1985.
81. Rupert Murdoch to the author, interview, 5 August 2003.
82. *TNL News*, November 1985.
83. 'The Way the Wind Blow', leading article, *New Statesman*, 19 March 1982.
84. See Iverach McDonald, *The History of The Times*, vol. V: *Struggles in War and Peace, 1939–1966*, pp. 104–8, 133–41.
85. 'Far from their Flock', leading article (by Douglas-Home), *The Times*, 27 March 1985.
86. *Independent*, 9 March 1998.
87. Charles Wilson to the author, interview, 19 February 2004.
88. Quoted in William Shawcross, *Murdoch*, pp. 214–15.
89. Liz Seeber to the author, interview, 18 July 2002.

CHAPTER FIVE: FORTRESS WAPPING (PP. 219–252)

1. News International statistics, presented by Michael Burton QC in the High Court, 10 February 1986.
2. Duff Hart-Davis, *The House the Berrys Built: Inside the Telegraph, 1928–1986*, p. 278.
3. David Kynaston, *The Financial Times: A Centenary History*, pp. 475–81.
4. Suellen Littleton, *The Wapping Dispute: An Examination of the Conflict and its Impact on the National Newspaper Industry*, p. 18.
5. Littleton, *The Wapping Dispute*, pp. 13–14, 17.
6. Peter Stothard, *The Times*, 26 January 1996.
7. Kynaston, *The Financial Time*, p. 481.
8. Bill O'Neill, *Copy Out* manuscript.
9. Ref. 10030/1.
10. Ibid.
11. Tony Isaacs (Imperial Father, *News of the World* machine chapel) to Bill O'Neill, June 1983, quoted in Sarah Benton and Mark Hollingsworth, 'A Plot Conceived and Planned Six Years Ago', *New Statesman*, 6 February 1986.
12. Bill O'Neill to N. F. Robbins (deputy secretary, NGA London region), 28 November 1983; N. F. Robbins to Bruce Matthews, 9 November 1983, ref. 10030/1.
13. Littleton, *The Wapping Dispute*, p. 59.
14. Ibid.
15. Bill O' Neill, memorandum, 13 February 1984, ref. 10030/1.
16. Quoted in O'Neill, *Copy Out*.
17. *Sunday Times*, 6 April 1986. See O'Neill, *Copy Out*.
18. G. H. Willoughby (SOGAT London Central branch secretary), 14 June 1982, 6984/21.
19. E. R. Chard (SOGAT London Central branch secretary) to Bill Gillespie, September 1984, ref. 6985/21.
20. Andrew Neil, *Full Disclosure*, pp. 76–8.
21. Littleton, *The Wapping Dispute*, pp. 33–4.
22. Charles Wilson to the author, interview, 19 February 2004.
23. Bill O'Neill to the author, 1 October 2002.
24. Baroness Dean to the author, interview, 1 April 2003.
25. Quoted in Charles Wintour, *The Rise and Fall of Fleet Street*, p. 219.
26. Quoted by Charles Wilson, speech to the Guild of Newspaper Editors, 8 May 1987.
27. Neil, *Full Disclosure*, p. 102.
28. Richard Searby to the author, conversation, 11 June 2002; Jenkins, *Market for Glory: Fleet Street Ownership in the Twentieth Century*, p. 194; Neil, *Full Disclosure*, pp. 97–8, 101.

29. Tim Austin to the author, interview, 4 March 2003.
30. Linda Melvern, *The End of the Street*, pp. 221–32; Littleton, *The Wapping Dispute* p. 66.
31. Brenda Dean, statement, 30 August 1985.
32. Charles Wilson to the author, interview, 19 February 2004.
33. Baroness Dean to the author, interview, 1 April 2003.
34. Donald Reed, *The Power of News: The History of Reuters*, pp. 412–14, 427, 432–5; John Lawrenson and Lionel Barber, *The Price of Truth*, p. 27; Denis Hamilton, *Editor-in-Chief*, pp. 185, 187; David Kynaston, *The Financial Times*, p. 500; Rupert Murdoch to the author, interview, 4 August 2003; Geoffrey Taylor, *Changing Faces: A History of the Guardian, 1956–1988*, p. 298; S. J. Taylor, *An Unlikely Hero*, p. 209–10.
35. Roy Greenslade, *Press Gang*, pp. 401–2; Jenkins, *Market for Glory*, pp. 176–7.
36. Eric Hammond, *Maverick*, p. 77; Jenkins, *Market for Glory*, pp. 187–90; Littleton, *The Wapping Dispute*, pp 35–6.
37. Hart-Davis, *The House the Berrys Built*, pp. 292–327; Greenslade, *Press Gang*, pp. 409–14.
38. Baroness Dean to the author, interview, 1 April 2003.
39. Brenda Dean, quoted in Melvern, *The End of the Street*, p. 176.
40. *The Times*, 1 October 1985.
41. Rupert Murdoch, statement, *The Times*, 1 October 1985.
42. O'Neill, *Copy Out*.
43. Bill O'Neill to the author, 1 October 2002.
44. Hammond, *Maverick*, pp. 84–5; *The Times*, 11 December 1985.
45. Minutes of the TUC Printing Industries Committee, 9 December 1985.
46. H. W. Miles to Bruce Matthews, 23 December 1985, file 6985/21.
47. Baroness Dean to the author, interview, 1 April 2003.
48. Tim Austin to the author, interview, 4 March 2003.
49. Colin Webb to the author, interview, 20 February 2002.
50. Minutes of the TNHL board, 10 December 1985, ref. A909/11192/2. The minutes make just one Delphic reference that 'the Chairman referred briefly to proposed greenfield operations at the new printing plant of News International plc at Wapping'.
51. Sadly, Matthews took his reasoning to the grave; Andrew Knight to the author, interview, 2 December 2004.
52. Wyatt diary; Geoffrey Richards to Bill Gillespie, 13 January 1986, ref. 10030/2; *London Sogat Post*, February 1986; *The Times*, 13 January 1986; *Sunday Times* 19 January 1986; Neil, *Full Disclosure*, p. 109.
53. *The Times*, 11, 15 and 16 January 1986; Littleton, *The Wapping Dispute*, p. 80.

54. Bill O'Neill to the author, 1 October 2002.
55. *The Times*, 22 January 1986.
56. Ibid., 22 January 1986.
57. Ibid., 24 January 1986.
58. *London Sogat Post*, February 1986.
59. Colin Webb to the author, interview, 20 February 2003.
60. *The Times*, 26 January 1996.
61. Colin Webb to the author, interview, 20 February 2003.
62. Charles Wilson to *Times* staff, notes taken by Martin Huckerby, quoted in Melvern, *The End of the Street*, pp. 81–2.
63. Melvern, *The End of the Street*, p. 85.
64. Liz Seeber to the author, interview, 18 July 2002.

CHAPTER SIX: FIFTY-FOUR WEEKS UNDER SIEGE (PP. 253–299)

1. David Kynaston, *The Financial Times: A Centenary History*, p. 500.
2. *Sun* staff voted 101 to 8 in favour; *News of the World* staff voted 43 to 2.
3. Quoted in Linda Melvern, *The End of the Street*, p. 89.
4. Peter Brown to the author, interview, 27 April 2004.
5. *Spectator*.
6. *Financial Times*, 27 January 1986; *New Statesman*, 6 February 1986; Melvern, *The End of the Street*, pp. 86–9.
7. *Financial Times*, 27 February 1986; *The Times*, 27 January 1986; *Campaign*, 11 September 1987; Melvern, *The End of the Street*, pp. 155–6.
8. Melvern, *The End of the Street*, pp. 90–94.
9. Charles Wilson to the Guild of Newspaper Editors, 8 May 1987.
10. Tim Austin to the author, interview, 4 March 2003.
11. Philip Howard to the author, interview, 5 December 2002; Charles Wilson to the author, interview, 19 February 2004; *New Statesman*, 6 February 1986.
12. *The Times*, 26 January 1996.
13. Ibid., 5 February, 1986.
14. Suellen Littleton, *The Wapping Dispute: An Examination of the Conflict and its Impact on the National Newspaper Industry*, p. 80; ref. B067/12503/9; *Journalist* NUJ newspaper, February 1986, vol. 69, no. 2; Charles Wilson to *Times* staff, 13 June 1986, B067/12503/7.
15. There were eight refuseniks – Barrie Clement, Dave Felton, Paul Griffiths, Pat Healy, Don McIntyre, Greg Neale, Paul Routledge and Pam Spooner. In addition, Derek Pain resigned and Martin Huckerby was dismissed.
16. 'Citizen Murdoch,' *Panorama*, BBC TV, 19 January 1987; News International in-house Wapping production video, 30 April 1987. ·

17. Liz Seeber to the author, interview, 18 July 2002.
18. Rupert Murdoch to all staff, 3 February 1986, ref. 10030/2.
19. William Rees-Mogg, letter to the editor, *The Times*, 30 January 1986; Rees-Mogg was no less supportive in private: William Rees-Mogg to Charles Wilson, 24 April 1986, A749/9242/J; *Spectator*; Denis Hamilton, *Editor-in-Chief*, p. 184; Bernard Levin, *The Times*, 3 February 1986; Harold Evans to the author, interview, 25 June 2003.
20. *The Times*, 3 February 1986; *Financial Times*, 3 February 1986; *Guardian*, 3 February 1986.
21. Alan Hamilton to the author, interview, 29 April 2004.
22. Chris Warman to the author, interview, 29 April 2004.
23. Tim Austin to the author, interview, 4 March 2003; O'Neill, *Copy Out* manuscript; *Spectator*.
24. *The Times*, 29 January 1986; Eric Hammond, *Maverick*, p. 90–91.
25. Hammond, *Maverick*, pp. 93–4.
26. *Sunday Times*, 16 February 1986.
27. Paul Routledge to the author, 22 June 2004.
28. Peter Kellner to the author, 4 March 2003; *Guardian*, 12 and 17 February 1986; critics included Murdoch's fault-finders from the right: Charles Moore in the *Spectator*.
29. *The Times*, 4 March 1986; minutes of the TNHL board, 9 December 1986, ref. A909/11192/2.
30. *The Times*, 20 June 1986.
31. *Times Law Report*, 6 November 1986.
32. *The Times*, 18 and 20 March 1987.
33. Ken Clarke to the Parliamentary Press Gallery, 12 February 1986, quoted in *The Times*, 15 February 1986; *The Times*, 14, 18 and 21 February, 14, 15 and 27 March 1986.
34. Neil Kinnock to the SOGAT conference at Scarborough, *Today*, 12 June 1986.
35. Brenda Dean to SOGAT members, May 1986, B067/12503/2; however, the International Graphical Federation (to which forty-three print unions were affiliated worldwide) did call on its member not to handle any News International print work that might be attempted abroad. This proved a needless precaution: *Financial Times*, 18 February 1986.
36. Under Section 17 of the 1980 Employment Act; *Guardian*, 11 February 1986.
37. *Guardian* and the *Financial Times*, 11 February 1986.
38. Baroness Dean to the author, interview, 1 April 2003.
39. *The Times*, 10 February 1986, 'Citizen Murdoch', *Panorama*, BBC TV, 19 January 1987.
40. 'Using the Law', leading article, *The Times*, 19 February 1986.

41. *The Times*, 11 February, 20 February 1986.
42. *The Times*, 22 February 1986; Littleton, *The Wapping Dispute*, p. 92; *The Sunday Times*, 2 March 1986.
43. *Financial Times*, 21 April 1986; *Guardian*, 22 April 1986.
44. *Guardian*, 21 March 1986.
45. Brenda Dean to members, May 1986, ref. B067/12503/2; Littleton, *The Wapping Dispute*, p. 116.
46. See for example, *Wapping Post*, 7 June 1986.
47. Market research by ARC/Everett, results circulated on 24 April 1986 on the basis of telephoning 750 nationally representative individuals.
48. ABC Figures suggested the *Sunday Times*'s circulation had fallen by 200,000 between January and April 1986; Neil, *Full Disclosure*, p. 149.
49. Charles Wilson to *Times* staff, 13 June 1986, B067/12503/7.
50. *Spectator*, 1 March 1986.
51. *Spectator*.
52. *Sunday Times*, 9 March 1986.
53. Charles Wilson to the author, interview, 19 February 2004.
54. *The Times*, 18 March 1986.
55. *Sunday Times*, 6 April 1986.
56. 'A Very Dangerous Error', leading article, *The Times*, 8 April 1986.
57. *Sunday Times*, 23 February 1986; *The Times*, 2 May 1986.
58. *The Times*, 27 February, 12 March 1986 and 13 February 1987.
59. David Selbourne's offending article, 'No Muzzling Militant', was published in *The Times* on 26 March 1986; *Guardian*, 14 October 1986; *The Times* 23 October 1986; leading articles, 'The Selbourne Affair', 16 October 1986, 'A Non-Academic Inquiry', 17 March 1987, 'Verdict on Ruskin', 7 October 1987, *The Times*.
60. 'The Reputation of Journalism', leading article, *The Times*, 22 April 1986.
61. D. P. Forbes, letters to the editor, *The Times*, 27 February 1986.
62. Minutes of meeting between News International and union representatives, Mayfair Hotel, 4 April 1986, ref. B067/12503; *The Times*, 5 April 1986.
63. *Sunday Today*, 6 April 1986.
64. *The Times*, 7 April 1986.
65. Minutes of meeting between News International and union representatives, Hyde Park Hotel, 16 April 1986, ref. B067/12503; *Financial Times*, 17 April 1986.
66. Rupert Murdoch to Bruce Matthews, 29 April 1986, ref. B067/12503/3.
67. *The Times*, 5 and 7 May 1986.
68. 'When the Police Face Riots', leading article, *The Times*, 5 May 1986.
69. *The Times*, 14 and 22 May 1986.

70. Baroness Dean to the author, interview, 1 April 2003.
71. Neil, *Full Disclosure*, pp. 152–3.
72. Minutes of meeting held between News International and union executives at the Sheraton Skyline Hotel, Heathrow, 26 May 1986, ref. B067/12503/5.
73. *The Times*, 27 May 1986.
74. Ibid., 5 June 1986.
75. Simon Jenkins, *The Market for Glory: Fleet Street Ownership in the Twentieth Century*, p. 203.
76. *The Times*, 7 June 1986; *Sunday Times*, 8 June 1986.
77. *The Times*, 4 and 5 June 1986; *Guardian*, 4 June 1986.
78. Hammond, *Maverick*, pp. 95, 97–8.
79. Neil, *Full Disclosure*, pp. 134–9.
80. Marmaduke Hussey to John Collier, 18 July 1986, ref. B067/12503/2; Marmaduke Hussey, *Chance Governs All*, p. 193.
81. *The Times*, 21 June, 26 June, 7 July 1986.
82. *Today* and *The Times*, 10 June 1986; Baroness Dean to the author, interview, 1 April 2003.
83. *The Times* NUJ chapel, 1986 – Claim for Renewal of House Agreement; minutes of meeting with Mike Hoy, *Times* chapel meeting, 17 March and 14 April 1986.
84. Charles Wilson to *Times* staff, 13 June 1986, ref. B067/12503/7.
85. Minutes of meeting with Mike Hoy (managing editor) and *The Times* NUJ chapel, 12 June 1986, ref. B067/12503/7.
86. *The Times*, 9 September 1986; *Guardian*, 13 September 1986.
87. *The Times*, 1 August 1986.
88. Ibid., 2 August 1986.
89. Danny Sergeant (SOGAT general president) to London branch leaders, 18 August 1986, ref. A909/1193/2.
90. Minutes of meetings between News International and union representatives at the Copthorne Hotel, Gatwick, 22 and 29 August, 7 September 1986, ref. B067/12503/2.
91. Littleton, *The Wapping Dispute*, p. 114.
92. Minutes of TNL Executive meeting, 22 October 1986, ref. B067/12503.
93. *Guardian*, 14 January 1987.
94. Ibid., 26 April 1986.
95. Details from security camera footage, ref. 10030/5; *The Times*, 26 January 1987.
96. Neil, *Full Disclosure*, p. 140.
97. *The Times*, 26 January 1987.
98. *Guardian*, 27 January 1987.
99. O'Neill, *Copy Out* manuscript.

100. Littleton, p. 120; *The Times*, 6 February 1987; SOGAT Press Release, 5 February 1987, ref. 10030/5; O'Neill, *Copy Out*.
101. 'Hard Lessons of Wapping'; leading article, *The Times*, 6 February 1987.
102. Rupert Murdoch to the author, interview, 5 August 2003; Charles Wilson to the author, interview, 12 February 2004.
103. Tony Norbury to the author, interview, 27 April 2004.
104. Littleton, *The Wapping Dispute*, p. 135.
105. Kenneth Clarke on *Channel 4 News*, quoted in *The Times*, 7 February 1987.
106. Hammond, *Maverick*, p. 79.
107. *The Times*, 12 January 1987; *Guardian*, 21 January 1987; *Financial Times*, 16 February 1987.
108. *The Times*, 10 October 1990.
109. This decision was reversed at the *Daily Telegraph* in 2003 and at the *Independent* in 2001.
110. *Guardian*, 5 June 2000.
111. Charles Wilson to the Guild of Newspaper Editors, 8 May 1987.
112. David Flynn to Charles Wilson, 3 April 1986, ref. 9841/5.
113. Rupert Murdoch in *British Journalism Review*, vol. 10, no. 4, 1999.
114. Times Newspapers Holdings Board, Report, 7 June 1988, ref. A909/11192/2.
115. Littleton, *The Wapping Dispute*, p. 134.
116. Estimate in *UK Press Gazette*, cited in Jenkins, *Market for Glory*, p. 203.
117. Neil Chenoweth, *Virtual Murdoch: Reality Wars on the Information Highway*, p. 63.
118. Estimate by John Reidy, vice-president of Drexell Burnham Lambert Bank, interview with Robert Harris, broadcast on *Panorama*, BBC TV, 19 January 1987.
119. Peter Chernin, speech of 21 June 2002, quoted in O'Neill, *Copy Out*.
120. Hugo Young in *Guardian*, 2 September 1993.
121. Bill Pressey, production general manager, Associated Newspapers, quoted in S. J. Taylor, *An Unlikely Hero*, p. 246.
122. *The Times*, 10 July 1986.
123. Ivan Fallon to the 'UK Newspapers: Declining Medium or Growth Opportunity' conference organized by ABN Amro, London, 30 April 2004.

CHAPTER SEVEN: INDEPENDENT CHALLENGES (PP. 300–331)

1. Stephen Glover, *Paper Dreams*, p. 33.
2. David Kynaston, *The Financial Times: A Centenary History*, p. 501.
3. Charles Wilson to the author, interview, 19 February 2004.

4. *UK Press Gazette*, 23 June 1986.
5. Ibid., 19 May 1986.
6. Charles Wilson to Paul Routledge, 6 June 1986, Routledge Papers.
7. Charles Wilson to the author, interview, 24 February 2004.
8. Philip Howard to the author, interview, 5 December 2002.
9. Charles Wilson to the author, interview, 24 February 2004.
10. *Financial Times*, 25 September 1986.
11. Geoffrey Taylor, *Changing Faces: History of The Guardian, 1956–1988*, pp. 328–9.
12. Report to the Board of Times Newspapers Holdings Limited, 9 December 1986, ref. A909/11192/2.
13. Charles Wilson to the author, interview, 24 February 2004.
14. *Campaign*, 30 October 1987.
15. *The Times*, 16 December 1985.
16. 'Our Privilege', leading article, *The Times*, 22 May 1986.
17. 'First Report from the Committee of Privileges, Session 1985–86', House of Commons, 1 May 1986.
18. The Cabinet ministers were Kenneth Baker, Kenneth Clarke, Nicholas Ridley and Paul Channon. Two Cabinet minister voted in favour of the ban. Forty-one 'Government payroll' MPs voted for *The Times* and only fifteen for the ban.
19. 'Atticus', *Sunday Times*, 25 May 1986.
20. 'The Prime Minister's Task', leading article, *The Times*, 27 January 1986.
21. 'Mr Heseltine's Joystick', leading article, *The Times*, 7 January 1986.
22. Michael Heseltine, *Life in the Jungle*, p. 311.
23. 'A Very Good Resignation', leading article, *The Times*, 10 January 1986.
24. 'Excesses of Loyalty' and 'The Prime Minister's Task', leading articles, *The Times*, 24 and 27 January 1986.
25. Robin Oakley, *Inside Track*, pp. 118–21.
26. Robin Oakley to Simon Jenkins, no date but c. 1990, ref. 13262/6.
27. 'A Campaign Lesson', leading article, *The Times*, 10 June 1987; Peregrine Worsthorne, letters to the editor, *The Times*, 12 June 1987.
28. *The Times*, 12 May 1987.
29. Ibid., 31 December 1987.
30. Robin Oakley, *Inside Track*, pp. 139–41.
31. Brian MacArthur, *Sunday Times*, 23 August 1987; Ivor Crewe and Anthony King, *SDP*, p. 498.
32. *The Times*, 12 June 1987.
33. Ibid.
34. Ibid., 29 December 1987.
35. Charles Wilson to the author, interview, 19 February 2004.
36. Rupert Murdoch to the author, interview, 5 August 2003.

37. Robin Oakley, *Inside Track*, pp. 237–8.
38. *The Times*, 20 October 1987.
39. Ibid., 22 March 1991.
40. Graham Searjeant to the author, interview, 11 January 2005.
41. Christopher Warman to the author, interview, 13 October 2004.
42. *The Times*, 20 October 1987.
43. Ibid., 3 January 1983.
44. Ibid., 28 August 1995.
45. Ibid., 5 December 1995.
46. Ibid., 10 February 1987.
47. Dan Topolski, letters to the editor, *The Times*, 20 February 2004.
48. *The Times*, 30 March 1987.
49. Ibid., 3 October 1988.
50. *The Times*, 20 September 2003; John Goodbody to the author, interview, 22 November 2004.
51. *The Times*, 27 and 28 May and 18 and 24 September 1987.
52. Ibid., 22 September 1998.
53. Ibid., 3 October 1988.

CHAPTER EIGHT: *STURM UND DRANG* (PP. 332–366)

1. Robert Fisk on *The Times* at two hundred, BBC TV.
2. Robert Fisk to the author, interview, 21 September 2004.
3. 'The Case for the Raid', leading article, *The Times*, 18 April 1986.
4. Robert Fisk to Charles Wilson, 11 November 1988, ref. 011846.
5. *The Times*, 17 March 1986.
6. Robert Fisk, *Pity the Nation*, p. 618.
7. Robert Fisk to the author, interview, 21 September 2004.
8. Robert Fisk to Charles Wilson, 11 November 1988, ref. 011846; 'Beyond the Aegis', leading article, *The Times*, 5 July 1988; Robert Fisk to the author, interview, 21 September 2004; Fisk, *Pity the Nation*, p. 635.
9. Robert Fisk, Record of meeting with Charles Wilson, 18 November 1988, Fisk Papers; 'His Infamous Career', leading article, *The Times*, 18 January 1988.
10. Max Hastings, *Editor*, p. 64.
11. Peter Stothard to the author, interview, 15 November 2004.
12. Richard Siklos, *Shades of Black: Conrad Black and the World's Fastest Growing Press Empire*, p. 279.
13. Matthew Parris, *Chance Witness*, p. 369–70.
14. Ibid., pp. 371–2.
15. Matthew Parris to the author, interview, 25 January 2005.
16. 'A Vision of Europe', leading article, *The Times*, 20 September 1988.

17. *The Times*, 21 September 1988.
18. 'European Thatcherism', leading article, *The Times*, 21 September 1988.
19. *The Times*, 27 October 1989.
20. Ibid.
21. 'Breaking Point', leading article, *The Times*, 27 October 1989.
22. 'Panic Over', leading article, *The Times*, 1 November 1989.
23. *The Times*, 24 November 1989; Oakley, *Inside Track*, pp. 131–3.
24. *The Times*, 31 December 1988.
25. Charles Powell and Charles Wilson correspondence, 5 October 1988 and 2 March 1989; Charles Wilson to Margaret Thatcher, 27 February 1989, ref. 13262/1.
26. *The Times*, 14 September 1992.
27. Ibid., 5 June 1989.
28. Ibid.
29. 'Message from the Square', leading article, *The Times*, 5 June 1989.
30. *The Times*, 10 November 1989.
31. *TNL News*, March 2003.
32. *The Times*, 13 November 1989.
33. Ibid., 14 November 1989.
34. Ibid., 13 and 14 November 1989.
35. *The Times*, 3 October 1990; *The Times*, 2 October 1990; 'The German Challenge', *The Times*, 3 October 1990.
36. 'Balkan Caligula', leading article, *The Times*, 19 December 1989.
37. *The Times*, 20 December 1989.
38. Ibid., 23 December 1989.
39. Ibid., 26 December 1989.
40. 'Year of Revolution', leading article, *The Times*, 30 December 1989.
41. *The Times*, 28 December 1989.
42. Daniel Johnson, *The Times*, 7 April 1990.
43. *The Times*, 29 December 1989.
44. Ibid., 22 and 29 December 1989.
45. *Guardian*, 26 November 1990.
46. *Independent*, 30 January 2002.
47. Charles Wilson to Richard Williams, 3 April 1987, ref. 9838/5/2.
48. Tim de Lisle to the author, interview, 8 February 2005; *Independent*, 16 August 1989; *Guardian*, 16 August 1989 and 2 March 1998.
49. Graham Paterson to the author, interview, 18 September 2002.
50. Charles Wilson to the author, interview, 24 February 2004.
51. Rupert Murdoch to the author, interview, 4 August 2003.
52. Ibid., 5 August 2003.
53. Clifford Longley to the author, interview, 3 September 2004; Mary Ann Sieghart to the author, interview, 20 January 2004.

54. Charles Wilson to the author, interview, 19 and 24 February 2004.
55. Philip Howard to the author, interview, 5 December 2002.
56. Richard Williams to the author, interview, 12 May 2004.
57. Charles Wilson to the author, interview, 24 February 2004.

CHAPTER NINE: SIMON JENKINS (PP. 367–415)

1. Recollection of John Bryant. John Bryant to the author, interview, 15 October 2004.
2. Simon Jenkins to the author, interview, 20 December 2004; Rupert Murdoch to the author, interview, 2003; Andrew Knight to the author, interview, 2 December 2004; Andrew Knight to Rupert Murdoch, 25 September 1992, ref. 015729.
3. Julian Barnes, *Letters from London 1990–1995*, p. 40.
4. Simon Jenkins to the author, interview, 20 December 2004.
5. David Watts to the author, interview, 17 August 2004.
6. Brian MacArthur, Paper Round, *Sunday Times*, 25 March 1990.
7. Clifford Longley to Simon Jenkins, 16 April 1991, ref. 14269/16.
8. Simon Jenkins to the author, interview, 20 December 2004.
9. Ibid.
10. *Guardian*, 26 November 1990.
11. Simon Jenkins to leader writers, memorandum, 5 May 1990, ref. 13261/6.
12. Mary Ann Sieghart to Simon Jenkins, 18 March 1990, ref. 13261/6.
13. *Independent*, 20 June 1990.
14. Barnes, *Letters from London*, p. 41; Simon Jenkins to the author, interview, 20 December 2004.
15. 'Only One of London's Problems', leading article, *The Times*, 28 March 1988.
16. 'Community Charge', leading article, *The Times*, 17 December 1986.
17. *The Times*, 5 December 1987.
18. 'Community Charge', leading article, *The Times*, 17 December 1986.
19. See, for example, 'A Misleading Debate' and 'Many Names, Not Many Friends', leading articles, *The Times*, 7 October and 5 December 1987; 'Making it Work', leading article, *The Times*, 20 January 1990.
20. 'Community Charging', leading article, *The Times*, 29 March 1990.
21. 'Untrivial Pursuit', leading article, *The Times*, 19 March 1990.
22. Robert Blake, *The Times*, 7 April 1990.
23. 'Taking the Plunge' and 'Averting Stagflation', leading articles, *The Times*, 6 and 19 October 1990.
24. 'Taking the Plunge', leading article, *The Times*, 6 October 1990.
25. *The Economist*, 13 October 1990; *Daily Mail*, 6 October 1990; *Today*, 6 October 1990.

26. *The Times*, 8 October 1990.
27. 'Sir Geoffrey Resigns', leading article, *The Times*, 2 November 1990.
28. *The Times*, 14 November 1990.
29. 'Heseltine Must Stand', leading article, *The Times*, 12 November 1990.
30. Michael Heseltine, *Life in the Jungle*, pp. 360–61, 373.
31. *The Times*, 17 November 1990.
32. 'The Case for Thatcher', *The Times*, 20 November 1990.
33. *The Times*, 21 November 1990.
34. 'Her Life in Their Hands', leading article, *The Times*, 21 November 1990.
35. 'A Wider Field', leading article, *The Times*, 22 November 1990.
36. *The Times*, 23 November 1990.
37. Simon Jenkins to the author, interview, 20 December 2004.
38. 'Best of Three', leading article, *The Times*, 27 November 1990.
39. Simon Jenkins to the author, interview, 20 December 2004.
40. *The Times*, 28 November 1990.
41. John Campbell, *Margaret Thatcher*, vol. 2, p. 662.
42. *The Times*, 22 March 1988.
43. Ibid., 3 August 1990; 'Iraq's Naked Villainy', leading article, *The Times*, 3 August 1990.
44. Ibid., 6 August 1990.
45. Ibid., 7 August 1990.
46. 'No Choice But War', leading article, *The Times*, 16 January 1991.
47. David Lipsey memo, 8 January 1991, ref. 14269/13/2.
48. John Major to David Livsey, associate editor, 11 January 1991, ref. 013522; Brian MacArthur, Paper Round, *Sunday Times*, 13 January 1991; *The Times*, 16 January 1991.
49. Brian MacArthur, Paper Round, *Sunday Times*, 13 January 1991.
50. *The Times*, 16 January 1991.
51. Ibid., 18 January 1991.
52. Ibid., 2 February 1991.
53. Richard Beeston to the author, interview, 10 January 2005.
54. Ibid.
55. *The Times*, 14 February 1991.
56. 'Direct Hit in Amiriya', leading article, *The Times*, 14 February 1991.
57. 'Saddam's Smokescreen', leading article, *The Times*, 22 February 1991.
58. *The Times*, 28 February 1991.
59. Ibid., 28 February 1991.
60. Ibid.
61. Ibid., 1 March 1991.
62. Quoted in Anthony Seldon, *Major: A Political Life*, p. 163.
63. 'Helping the Kurds', leading article, *The Times*, 6 April 1991.
64. Neil Chenoweth, *Virtual Murdoch*, p. 64.

65. Quoted in Chenoweth, *Virtual Murdoch*, p. 69.
66. *The Times*, 6 December 1990.
67. Andrew Knight to the author, interview, 2 December 2004.
68. John Warden, *The Times Parliamentary Report: A Survey of MPs*, July 1986, ref. 9837/11.
69. Rupert Murdoch to the author, interview, 5 August 2003.
70. 'To Maastricht', leading article, *The Times*, 9 December 1991.
71. 'A Sort of Triumph' and 'Job Well Done', *The Times*, 11 and 12 December 1991.
72. *The Times*, 12 and 13 December 1991.
73. Ibid., 11 December 1991.
74. 'Where Britain's interests lies by then is impossible now to say, which was precisely Mr Major's point': 'Job Well Done', leading article, *The Times*, 12 December 1991.
75. Anatole Kaletsky's articles in *The Times*, 17, 18 and 24 March 1992.
76. Brian MacArthur, *The Times*, 31 March 1992.
77. Matthew Parris, *Chance Witness*, pp. 378–81; *The Times*, 2 April 1992.
78. *The Times*, 7 April 1992.
79. 'Major's First Term', leading article, *The Times*, 8 April 1992.
80. 'Moments of Inertia', leading article, *The Times*, 9 April 1992.
81. Brian MacArthur, Paper Round, *Sunday Times*, 12 April 1992.
82. *The Times*, 11 April 1992.
83. Brian MacArthur, Paper Round, *Sunday Times*, 2 July 1989.
84. Simon Jenkins to Andrew Knight, 27 June 1991, ref. 18643.
85. Simon Jenkins to Andrew Knight and John Dux, 6 December 1991, ref. 18643.
86. *The Times* had a 27.4 per cent share of the week's editorial columns; *Independent*, 26.4 per cent; *Telegraph* 24.7 per cent; *Guardian*, 21.4 per cent; source: Media Monitoring Service.
87. Andrew Knight to the author, interview, 2 December 2004.
88. Andrew Knight to Rupert Murdoch, 15 July 1992, ref. 023746.
89. Andrew Knight to the author, interview, 2 December 2004.
90. Simon Jenkins to the author, interview, 20 December 2004.
91. Paul Dacre to the author, conversation, 8 February 2005.
92. Rupert Murdoch to the author, interview, 4 August 2004.
93. Various opinions expressed to the author, 2000–2004.
94. Andrew Knight to Rupert Murdoch, 15 July 1992, ref. 023746.
95. Charles Wilson to the author, interview, 24 February 2004.
96. Simon Pearson to the author, interview, 13 July 2004.
97. Graham Searjeant to the author, interview, 11 January 2004.
98. Simon Jenkins to the author, interview, 20 December 2004.
99. Ibid.

CHAPTER TEN: CRITICAL TIMES (PP. 416–471)

1. Peter Stothard wrote a touching portrayal of his father in 'There will be no obit', *The Times*, 31 December 1997.
2. This became a regular claim made in Stephen Glover's Media Studies column for the *Spectator* even though he wrote to Stothard to admit it was not true; Stephen Glover to Peter Stothard, 27 May 1993, Stothard Papers.
3. *The Economist*, 7 August 1993.
4. *The Times*, 29 January 1994; *Independent*, 7 February 1994.
5. Peter Stothard to the author, interview, 15 November 2004.
6. *The Times* Summary of Annual Performance, Andrew Knight Papers, ref. 015729.
7. Anatole Kaletsky to Andrew Knight, 20 August 1992, ref. 023746; Andrew Knight to John Dux and Peter Stothard, 3 March 1994, ref. 021472.
8. Peter Stothard to the author, interview, 15 November 2004.
9. *Financial Times*, 2 September 1993.
10. *Guardian*, 2 August 1993.
11. *Daily Telegraph*, 2 September 1993.
12. *Independent*, 2 September 1993.
13. *Financial Times*, 2 September 1993.
14. Peter Stothard to the author, interview, 15 November 2004.
15. *Independent*, 2 September 1993; *Daily Telegraph*, 2 September 1993.
16. Source: ABC, *Financial Times*, 26 August 1994.
17. Max Hastings, *Editor*, pp. 355–61.
18. Peter Stothard to the author, interview, 15 November 2004.
19. *Independent*, 25 June 1994; Hastings, *Editor*, pp. 360–62.
20. *Independent*, 24 June 1994.
21. Hastings, *Editor*, p. 363.
22. *Daily Telegraph*, 26 August 1994.
23. *Evening Standard*, 10 May 1995.
24. Peter Stothard to the author, interview, 15 November 2004.
25. *Media Week*, 5 January 1996; *Guardian*, 22 August 1992.
26. *Independent*, 15 November 1997.
27. *The Times*, 22 May 1999; *Independent*, 22 May 1999.
28. *The Times*, 16 July 1997.
29. Peter Stothard to the author, interview, 15 November 2004.
30. John Goodbody to the author, interview, 22 November 2004.
31. *The Times*, 4 September 1991.
32. Marcus Williams and John Goodbody to the author, interviews, 18 November 2004; Keith Blackmore to the author, interview, 25 November 2004.
33. Simon Barnes to the author, interview, 24 January 2005.

34. *The Times*, 3 August 1996.
35. Ibid., 23 September 2000.
36. Ibid., 6 November 2004.
37. 'A Jackpot to Be Won', leading article, *The Times*, 23 October 1993.
38. John Major, *John Major: The Autobiography*, p. 409.
39. 'A Risk for the Lottery', leading article, *The Times*, 4 November 1994.
40. 'Grandees' Opera', leading article, *The Times*, 1 July 1998.
41. *The Times*, 25 May 1988.
42. Ibid., 23 May 1986.
43. Rodney Milnes to the author, interview, 30 November 2004; Richard Morrison to the author, interview, 16 November 2004.
44. *The Times*, 12 December 1996.
45. Ibid., 28 November 2000.
46. According to a British Phonographic Industry analysis and an estimate in the *Sunday Business*: *The Times*, 19 February 1997.
47. *The Times*, 11 April and 14 May 1994.
48. Ibid., 30 April and 14 May 1994.
49. Ibid., 26 August 1994.
50. Ibid., 27 December 1996.
51. David Sinclair to the author, interview, 25 November 2004.
52. *The Times*, 27 December 1996.
53. Ibid., 1 January 2000.
54. Ibid., 16 September 1997.
55. Ibid., 13 September 1997.
56. Ibid., 15 July 2000.
57. Ibid., 10 June 1999; Dalya Alberge to the author, interview.
58. *The Times*, 28 November 2000.
59. Ibid., 30 October 1998 and 14 May 1999.
60. Ibid., 17 January 1998.
61. Ibid., 30 December 1991.
62. Ibid., 1 January 2000.
63. Ibid., 22 January 1998.
64. Ibid., 20 October 1994.
65. Ibid., 12 May 1994 and 20 May 1999.
66. Ibid., 22 February 1996.
67. *The Times*, 21 September 1995.
68. Lisa Armstrong to the author, interview, 11 January 2005.
69. *The Times*, 11 September 2000.
70. Nigel Hawkes to the author, interview, 2 February 2005; *The Times*, 28 February 1991.
71. *The Times*, 8 November 1990.
72. Ibid., 19 December 2000.

CHAPTER ELEVEN: THE HEART OF EUROPE (PP. 472–496)

1. Peter Stothard to the author, interview, 15 November 2004.
2. See, for example, 'Disbanding Sterling', leading article, The Times, 30 December 1991; 'Good Money After Bad', leading article, The Times, 11 September 1992.
3. The Times, 7 October 1992.
4. Peter Stothard to the author, interview, 15 November 2004.
5. The Times, 4 June 1992.
6. John Bryant to the author, interview, 15 October 2004.
7. Note by Peter Stothard, 10 December 1997, Stothard Papers.
8. The Times, 21 October 1992; Daily Mail, 22 October 1992.
9. Peter Stothard to the author, interview, 15 November 2004.
10. John Major, John Major: The Autobiography, p. 339; the same conclusion is reached in Anthony Seldon, Major: A Political Life, p. 317.
11. The Times, 28 October 1992; Guardian, 28 June 1993.
12. The Times, 10 May 1993.
13. See, for example, 'Must Try Harder', 'Childish Rites', 'The Test for Teachers', leading articles, The Times, 6 February, 5 and 9 April 1996.
14. The Times, 21 May 1991.
15. 'The Polys Are Coming', leading article, The Times, 21 May 1991.
16. 'The Ranking of Universities', leading article, The Times, 14 October 1992.
17. The Times, 13 October 1992.
18. 'The Ranking of Universities', leading article, The Times, 14 October 1992.
19. The Times, 30 December 1994.
20. Source: MORI, July–September 1994.
21. Matthew Parris, Chance Witness, pp. 404, 410–11; Graham Stewart, Burying Caesar: Churchill, Chamberlain and the Battle for the Tory Party, pp. 69, 160.
22. Matthew Parris, Chance Witness, pp. 408–9; Matthew Parris to the author, interview, 25 January 2005.
23. Peter Stothard to the author, interview, 15 November 2004.
24. Matthew Parris to the author, interview, 25 January 2005.
25. The Times, 23 May 1994.
26. Ibid., 4 October 1995.
27. Matthew Parris, Chance Witness, pp. 411–14.
28. The Times, 27 June 1995.
29. Peter Stothard to the author, interview, 15 November 2004.
30. Michael Gove to the author, interview, 7 October 2004; Mary Ann Sieghart to the author, interview, 20 January 2005.

31. Note made by Peter Stothard, 6 January 1997, Stothard Papers.
32. Ibid., 23 January 1997, Stothard Papers; Peter Stothard to the author, interview, 8 November 2004.
33. *The Times*, 10 February 1997.
34. Tim Hames to the author, interview, 12 October 2004.
35. *The Times*, 21 April 1997.
36. 'Sceptical Voters', leading article, *The Times*, 28 April 1997.
37. *The Times*, 28 April 1997.
38. Ibid., 1 May 1997.
39. Peter Stothard to the author, interview, 15 November 2004.
40. Mary Ann Sieghart to the author, interview, 20 January 2005.
41. 'Principle Not Party', leading article, *The Times*, 29 April 1997.
42. Rupert Murdoch to the author, interview, 5 August 2003.
43. *The Times*, 22 April 1997.
44. Ibid., 24 April 1997.
45. Ibid., 29 April 1997.
46. Ibid., 30 April 1997.
47. Peter Stothard to the author, interview, 15 November 2004.
48. *The Times*, 28 April 1997.
49. 'Tories in Trauma', leading article, *The Times*, 3 May 1997.
50. *The Times*, 6 May 1997.
51. Ibid., 11 June 1997.
52. Ibid., 19 June 1997.
53. 'Push-Me-Pull-You', leading article, *The Times*, 19 June 1997.

CHAPTER TWELVE: NEW LABOUR, NEW JOURNALISM (PP. 497–558)

1. *The Times*, 2 May 1997.
2. Ibid., 25 April 1997.
3. John Mair to the author, interview, 29 November 2004.
4. 'End of Empire', leading article, *The Times*, 1 July 1997.
5. *The Times*, 3 September 1997.
6. Ibid., 2 September 1997; Peter Stothard to the author, interview, 8 November 2004.
7. Peter Stothard to the author, interview, 8 November 2004.
8. Alan Hamilton to the author, 7 December 2004.
9. *The Times*, 10 January 1997.
10. Ibid., 17 May 1991.
11. Ibid., 9 August 1991; 'Discipline of the Press', leading article, *The Times*, 10 August 1991.
12. 'Perils for the Press', leading article, *The Times*, 15 January 1993.
13. 'Discipline of the Press', leading article, *The Times*, 10 August 1991.

14. *The Times*, 16 June 1992.
15. Ibid., 12 January 1993.
16. Ibid., 11 January 1993.
17. 'A Fine Mess', leading article, *The Times*, 25 March 1993.
18. 'Royalty Uncovered', leading article, *The Times*, 21 August 1992.
19. *Daily Telegraph*, 28 April 1998.
20. Lord Wakeham to the House of Lords, *Hansard*, 27 January 1999.
21. *The Times*, 8 September and 14 October 1999.
22. Ibid., 28 April 2001.
23. *Time Magazine*, 8 July 1996.
24. *The Times*, 28 April 2001.
25. Ibid., 4 May 2001.
26. Ibid., 27 November and 13 December 2002.
27. *The Times*, Law Supplement, 21 May 2002.
28. Ibid., 30 January 1999.
29. *The Times*, 21 April 1992.
30. Richard Owen (foreign editor) and David Watts to Peter Stothard,
    10 January 1994, ref. 026672.
31. Jonathan Mirsky to the author, interview, 8 September 2004.
32. Ibid.
33. Richard Owen to Peter Stothard, 30 March 1995, ref. 026672; *The Times*,
    29 and 10 March 1995.
34. 'Voice of Hong Kong', *The Times*, 19 September 1995.
35. 'China's Obligations' and 'Beyond 1997', leading articles, *The Times*,
    10 January and 5 March 1996.
36. 'Stand by Taiwan' and 'The Taiwan Truth', leading article, *The Times*,
    6 February and 19 March 1996; Jiang Enzhu (Chinese Ambassador to
    Britain), letters to the editor, *The Times*, 28 March 1996.
37. *The Times*, 21 November 1996.
38. Ibid., 20 February 1997.
39. Ref. 026672; *The Times*, 5 March 1998.
40. 'Hopes for Hong Kong', leading article, *The Times*, 30 June 1997.
41. 'The China Trap', leading article, *The Times*, 26 June 1996.
42. Rupert Murdoch to Michael Sandberg (chairman, Hong Kong and
    Shanghai Bank), quoted in William Shawcross, *Murdoch*, p. 287.
43. *Daily Telegraph*, 7 March 1998.
44. *Guardian*, 5 March 1998.
45. *The Times*, 6 March 1998.
46. Ibid., 27 March 1998; Charles Moore to Peter Stothard, 30 March,
    31 March and 6 April 1998; John Bryant to Charles Moore, 3 April 1998,
    and Peter Stothard to Charles Moore, 6 April 1998, ref. 029076.
47. *Free!*, The Freedom Forum Online, 22 January 1998.

48. *Daily Telegraph*, 4 March 1998.

49. *Spectator*, 21 March 1998.

50. *The Times*, 5 March 1998.

51. Note of meeting between Jonathan Mirsky and George Brock, 10 March 1998, ref. 026672; letters to the editor, *The Times*, 2 April 1998.

52. Jonathan Mirsky to the author, interview, 8 September 2004.

53. *The Times*, 5 June 1999.

54. Daniel Finkelstein to the author, conversation, 16 July 2004.

55. *The Times*, 4 October 1999; Peter Stothard to the author, interview, 29 November 2004.

56. *The Times*, 12 June 1999.

57. Ibid., 13 July 1999.

58. 'Bunkered down', leading article, *The Times*, 15 July 1999.

59. David Mackilligan, letter to the editor, *The Times*, 16 July 1999.

60. *The Times*, 16 July 1999.

61. Ibid., 17 July 1999.

62. Ibid., 22 July 1999.

63. 'A Single Issue', leading article, *The Times*, 9 June 1999.

64. Michael Gove to the author, interview, 7 October 2004; Tim Hames to the author, interview, 12 October 2004; Peter Stothard to the author, interview, 29 November 2004; John Bryant to the author, interview, 25 January 2005.

65. *The Times*, 13 July 1999.

66. Ibid., 24 November 1999.

67. Ibid.

68. Lord Ashcroft to the author, interview, 18 January 2005.

69. Ibid.

70. *The Times*, 9 December 1999.

71. *Guardian*, 10 December 1999.

72. *The Times*, 6 June 2003.

73. Ibid., 10 August 2002; *Guardian*, 28 January 2002; *Atlanta Journal-Constitution*, 15 December 2003.

74. *The Times*, 26 February 2000.

75. As Roy Greenslade was quick to point out: *Guardian*, 3 April 2000.

76. Peter Stothard to *Times* staff, notes for speech, 29 March 2000, Stothard Papers.

77. 'Mods and Rockers', leading article, *The Times*, 6 July 1998.

78. *The Times*, 8 September 1999.

79. Ibid., 20 April 2000.

80. Ibid., 19 May 1999; Peter Oborne and Simon Walters, *Alastair Campbell*, p. 243.

81. David Ruddock to the author, interview, 14 October 2004.

82. *The Times*, 17, 19, 20 and 27 July 2000.
83. Ibid., 9 February 1999.
84. Ibid., 9 May 2001.
85. 'In Our Time', leading article, *The Times*, 5 June 2001.
86. Chris Metz, letters to the editor, *The Times*, 7 June 2001.
87. *The Times*, 7 June 2001.
88. Ibid., 8 June 2001.

CHAPTER THIRTEEN: WAR IN PEACETIME (559–609)

1. Quoted in Robert W. Merry, 'The Great Friedman-Huntington debate', *The International Economy*, 22 December 2002.
2. Samuel P. Huntington, *The Clash of Civilizations and the Remaking of World Order*, 1998, pp. 29–35, 192–3.
3. *The Times*, 10 and 11 May 1994.
4. Ibid., 9 December 1997.
5. 'A Chance for Hope', leading article, *The Times*, 14 September 1993.
6. 'The Earth Moved', leading article, *The Times*, 27 July 2000.
7. *The Times*, 1 February 1995; Seldon, *Major*, pp. 526–30; Major, *Autobiography*, pp. 466–71.
8. Michael Gove to the author, interview, 7 October 2004.
9. *The Times*, 11 July 1996.
10. Ibid., 25 July 2000.
11. 'The Peace of Paris', leading article, *The Times*, 19 November 1990.
12. *The Times*, 23 December 1991.
13. 'Mikhail Gorbachev', leading article, *The Times*, 26 December 1991.
14. *The Times*, 14 September 1992.
15. 'Forces for Peace', leading article, *The Times*, 26 January 1993.
16. *The Times*, 17 April 1993.
17. Geoffrey Lee Williams, letters to the editor, *The Times*, 17 April 1993.
18. Richard Beeston to the author, interview, 10 January 2005.
19. Anthony Loyd, *My War Gone By, I Miss It So*, p. 115.
20. Anthony Loyd to the author, interview, 2 February 2005.
21. Anthony Loyd, *My War Gone By, I Miss It So*, pp. 112, 115.
22. *The Times*, 24 November 1993.
23. 'Fireflies In June', leading article, *The Times*, 5 June 1995.
24. *The Times*, 31 May 1995.
25. 'Run Out of Town', leading article, *The Times*, 12 July 1995.
26. *The Times*, 4 October 1995.
27. 'Hope Hotel', leading article, *The Times*, 22 November 1995.
28. 'Bosnia, Ohio', leading article, *The Times*, 24 November 1995.
29. Sam Kiley to the author, interview, 3 February 2005.

30. *The Times*, 26 September 1998.

31. Ibid., 14 July 1992.

32. Sam Kiley to the author, interview, 3 February 2005.

33. *The Times*, 22 August 1994 and 9 April 1998.

34. Ibid., 3 October 2001.

35. Ibid., 31 July 1993.

36. Ibid., 24 September 1998.

37. Ibid., 15 July 1999.

38. Ibid., 2 April 1999.

39. 'Winging It', leading article, *The Times*, 16 June 1998.

40. 'To Will The End', leading article, *The Times*, 8 April 1999.

41. See, in particular, 'Phase Three' and 'Facts on the Ground', leading articles, *The Times*, 5 April and 17 April 1999; the case for war was laid out in 'War Over Kosovo', leading article, *The Times*, 25 March 1999.

42. *The Times*, 25 March 1999.

43. Ibid., 1 April 1999.

44. Ibid.

45. 'Give War a Chance', leading article, *The Times*, 7 May 1999.

46. *The Times*, 1 June 1999 and 2 July 2001.

47. Ibid., 8 May 1999.

48. Ibid., 3 May 1999.

49. Ibid., 18 June 1999.

50. Ibid., 22 May 1999.

51. Ibid., 25 January 1995.

52. Ibid., 4 February 1995.

53. Ibid., 8 February 1995.

54. Anthony Loyd to the author, interview, 2 February 2005.

55. *The Times*, 2 November 1999.

56. Ibid., 2 February 2000.

57. Ibid., 22 December 1989.

58. Ibid., 10 May 1997.

59. Ibid., 2 October 2001.

60. Ibid., 12 September 2001.

61. 'Still the Enemy', leading article, *The Times*, 13 September 2001.

62. *The Times*, 14 November 2001.

63. Ibid., 12 September 2001.

64. Ibid., 14 November 2001.

65. Ibid., 9 October 2001.

66. Ibid., 8 October 2001.

67. Ibid., 19 October 2001.

68. Ibid., 12 November 2001.

69. Ibid., 14 November 2001.

70. Ibid., 15 November 2001.
71. Ibid.
72. Ibid.

CHAPTER FOURTEEN: DUMBING DOWN? (PP. 610–650)

1. Matthew Parris, *Chance Witness*, p. 477.
2. John Grigg, *The History of The Times*, vol. VI: *The Thomson Years*, p. 579.
3. Source: MORI, 1992.
4. Author's calculation from the raw data provided by *The Times* Strategic Planning Department.
5. The author would like to thank Kat Hounsell and Susannah Donnelly for help in compiling this data.
6. *The Times*, 14 December 1995.
7. David Watts to the author, interview, 6 January 2005.
8. Peregrine Worsthorne, 'Dumbing Up', in Stephen Glover (ed.), *The Penguin Book of Journalism*, pp. 116–18.
9. *The Times*, 26 March 1957.
10. Source: Premier TGI for the British Market Research Bureau survey focusing on business readers in the A–B social grades.
11. Jonathan Mirsky to the author, interview, 8 September 2004.
12. Richard Williams to the author, interview, 12 May 2004.
13. Lord Jenkins of Hillhead to Peter Stothard, 25 September 1995, ref. 019975.
14. *The Times*, 4 April 1990.
15. Leon Pilpel to Simon Jenkins, 22 March 1990. ref. 13262/2.
16. William Heseltine letter, 28 July 1986, and Andrew Neil letter, 29 July 1986, *The Times*; Andrew Neil, *Full Disclosure*, pp. 195–207.
17. Henry G. Button, letters to the editor, 17 August and 8 April 1993.
18. Letters to the editor, *The Times*, 4, 16, 17, 22 and 23 September 1987.
19. A. D. Bowers, letters to the editor, *The Times*, 20 May 1981.
20. *The Times*, 21 March 1987.
21. Miles Kington, 'Moreover . . .', *The Times*, 11 January 1985; Pat Adams, letters to the editor, *The Times*, 18 January 1985.
22. Revd I. H. G. Graham-Orlebar, 26 April 1980 and 13 May 1980; Linnea Cliff Hodges (1 May 1990), letters to the editor, *The Times*.
23. J. M. Wober, 'Top people write to The Times', *British Journalism Review*, vol. 15, no. 2, 2004.
24. *The Times*, 13 May 1981.
25. *Spectator*, 3 March 1984.
26. *The Times*, 16 April 1988.
27. Peter Utley to Charles Wilson, 27 October 1987, Wilson Papers.

28. *The Times*, 24 October 1986.
29. Ibid., 10 March 1982.
30. Ibid., 1 October 1981; *The Times*, 2 October 2000.
31. John Higgins to Simon Jenkins, 16 May 1990, ref. 13262/3.
32. *The Times*, 24 September 1998.
33. Ibid., 28 March 1983; *Spectator*, 17 March 1984.
34. *The Times*, 29 November 1986.
35. Besides Coats's boasts to Thornton, there were also various hints in the diaries of Cecil Beaton and Sir Henry 'Chips' Channon – the latter whom the published obituary did identify as one of Coats's partners. Michael Thornton to Simon Jenkins, 15 August 1990, and John Higgins to Simon Jenkins, 29 August 1990, ref. 13262/3. *The Times*, 10 August 1990; Lady Joan Robertson's letter in *The Times*, 16 August 1990.
36. *The Times*, 16 and 21 March 1995; Peter Stothard correspondence files, ref. 019975.
37. *The Times* 19 August 1983 and 6 November 2001.
38. Ian Brunskill to the author, interview, 16 November 2004.
39. For example, *The Times*, 30 January 1995.
40. *The Times*, 21 July 1990, 27 and 28 November 1991.
41. Ibid., 30 October 1995.
42. *The Journalist's Handbook*, p. 36.
43. Mary Dejevsky to the author, 30 November 2004.
44. *The Times*, 1 January 2000.
45. Brian MacArthur, *Sunday Times*, 17 April 1988; Brian MacArthur, *The Times*, 2 July 2004.
46. Speech at the Stationers' Livery Hall, 8 November 2004, reported in *Guardian* (online) 9 November 2004.
47. *Daily Telegraph*, 5 March 1998.
48. Peter Stothard to the author, interview, 15 November 2004.
49. Simon Jenkins to the author, interview, 20 December 2004.
50. Rupert Murdoch to the author, interview, 4 August 2003.
51. Nicholas Coleridge, *Paper Tigers*, p. 504.
52. Peter Chernin's presentation to Bill O'Neill, 21 June 2002, quoted in O'Neill, *Copy Out* manuscript.
53. Rupert Murdoch to James Harding, *Financial Times*, 11 June 2002.
54. Les Hinton to the author, 23 November 2004.
55. John Walter's appeal 'To the Public', *Daily Universal Register*, 1 January 1785.

BIBLIOGRAPHY

Newspapers and periodicals

Australian Financial Review
British Journalism Review
Campaign
Daily Express
Daily Mail
Daily Telegraph
Daily Universal Register
The Economist
Evening Standard
Financial Times
Guardian
Hansard
Independent
Independent on Sunday
International Economy
Journalist
Listener
London Sogat Post

Media Week
New Statesman
Observer
Private Eye
Quarterly of the Commonwealth
Press Union
Spectator
Sun
Sunday Telegraph
Sunday Times
Sunday Today
The Times
TNL News
Today
UK Press Gazette
Wall Street Journal
Wapping Post

Books

Barnes, Julian, *Letters from London, 1990–1995*, London: Vintage, 1995

Brendon, Piers, *The Life and Death of the Press Barons*, London: Secker & Warburg, 1982

Bryson, Bill, *Notes from a Small Island*, New York: Doubleday, 1999

Campbell, John, *Margaret Thatcher*, vol. 2: *The Iron Lady*, London: Jonathan Cape, 2003

Chenoweth, Neil, *Virtual Murdoch: Reality Wars on the Information Highway*, London: Secker & Warburg, 2001

Chippindale, Peter, and Horrie, Chris, *Stick It Up Your Punter: The Uncut Story of the Sun Newspaper*, London: Mandarin, 1999

Coleridge, Nicholas, *Paper Tigers: The Latest, Greatest, Newspaper Tycoons and How They Won the World*, London: Heinemann, 1993

Conroy, Harry, *Off the Record: A Life in Journalism*, London: Argyll Publishing, 1997

Crewe, Ivor, and King, Anthony, *SDP: The Birth, Life and Death of the Social Democratic Party*, Oxford: Oxford University Press, 1995

Curtis, Sarah (ed.), *The Journals of Woodrow Wyatt*, vol. 1, London: Macmillan, 1998

Dell, Edmund, *The Chancellors: A History of the Chancellors of the Exchequer, 1945–90*, London: HarperCollins, 1996

Di Giovanni, Janine, *Madness Visible: A Memoir of War*, London: Bloomsbury, 2004

Donoughue, Bernard, *The Heat of the Kitchen*, London: Politico's Publishing, 2003

Douglas-Home, Jessica, *Once Upon Another Time: Ventures Behind the Iron Curtain*, Wilby: Michael Russell, 2000

Evans, Harold, *Good Times, Bad Times*, London: Weidenfeld & Nicolson, 1983

Evans, Richard, *John McEnroe: Taming the Talent*, London: Bloomsbury, 1990

Fisk, Robert, *Pity the Nation: Lebanon at War*, Oxford: Oxford University Press, 2001

Frost, Gerald (ed.)., *No End of a Lesson: Leading Articles from The Times Under Charles Douglas-Home*, Worcester: Alliance Publishing, 1986

Giles, Frank, *Sundry Times*, London: John Murray, 1986

Glover, Stephen, *Paper Dreams*, London: Jonathan Cape, 1993

— (ed.), *The Penguin Book of Journalism*, London: Penguin, 2000

Greenslade, Roy, *Press Gang: How Newspapers Make Profits from Propaganda*, London: Macmillan, 2003

Grigg, John, *History of The Times*, vol. VI: *The Thomson Years*, London: Times Books, 1993

Hamilton, Denis, *Editor-in-Chief: Fleet Street Memoirs*, London: Hamish Hamilton, 1989

Hammond, Eric, *Maverick: The Life of a Union Rebel*, London: Weidenfeld & Nicolson, 1992

Harris, Robert, *Gotcha! The Media, the Government and the Falklands Crisis*, London: Faber & Faber, 1983

—, *Selling Hitler*: The Story of the Hitler Diaries, London; Faber & Faber, 1986

Hart-Davis, Duff, *The House the Berrys Built: Inside the Telegraph 1928–1986*, London: Hodder & Stoughton, 1990

Hastings, Max, *Editor: An Inside Story of Newspapers*, London: Macmillan, 2002

— and Jenkins, Simon, *The Battle for the Falklands*, London: Pan, 1997

Hennessy, Peter, *The Prime Minister: The Office and its Holders*, London: Penguin, 2000

Heseltine, Michael, *Life in the Jungle: My Autobiography*, London: Hodder & Stoughton, 2000

Hudson, Miles, and Stainer, John, *War and the Media: A Random Searchlight*, Stroud: Sutton, 1997

Huntington, Samuel P., *The Clash of Civilizations and the Remaking of World Order*, New York: Simon & Schuster, 1997

Hussey, Marmaduke, *Chance Governs All*, London: Macmillan, 2001

Ingham, Bernard, *Kill the Messenger*, London: HarperCollins, 1991

Jenkins, Simon, *The Market for Glory: Fleet Street Ownership in the Twentieth Century*, London: Faber & Faber, 1986

Kynaston, David, *The Financial Times: A Centenary History*, London: Viking, 1988

Lawrenson, John, and Barber, Lionel, *The Price of Truth: The Story of the Reuters Millions*, London: Mainstream Publishing, 1985

Lawson, Nigel, *The View from No. 11: Memoirs of a Tory Radical*, London: Bantam Press, 1992

Leapman, Michael, *Barefaced Cheek: The Apotheosis of Rupert Murdoch*, London: Hodder & Stoughton, 1983

—, *Treacherous Estate: The Press After Fleet Street*, London: Hodder & Stoughton, 1992

Littleton, Suellen, *The Wapping Dispute: An Examination of the Conflict and its Impact on the National Newspaper Industry*, Avebury: Avebury Business School Library, 1992

Loyd, Anthony, *My War Gone By, I Miss It So*, New York: Doubleday, 1999

Major, John, *John Major: The Autobiography*, London: HarperCollins, 1999

McDonald, Iverach, *The History of The Times*, vol. V: *Struggles in War and Peace 1939–1966*, London: Times Books, 1984

Melvern, Linda, *The End of the Street*, London: Methuen, 1986

Morrison, David E., and Tumber, Howard, *Journalists at War: The Dynamics of News Reporting During the Falklands Conflict*, London: Sage Publications, 1988

Neil, Andrew, *Full Disclosure*, London: Macmillan, 1996

Oakley, Robin, *Inside Track*, London, Bantam Press, 2001

Oborne, Peter, and Walters, Simon, *Alastair Campbell*, London: Aurum Press, 2004

Page, Bruce, *The Murdoch Archipelago*, London: Simon & Schuster, 2003

Parkinson, Cecil, *Right at the Centre: An Autobiography*, London: Weidenfeld & Nicolson, 1992

Parris, Matthew, *Chance Witness: An Outsider's Life in Politics*, London: Viking, 2002

Porter, Henry, *Lies, Damned Lies and Some Exclusives*, London: Chatto & Windus, 1984

Reed, Donald, *The Power of News: The History of Reuters, 1849–1989*, 2nd edn, Oxford: Oxford University Press, 1992

Seldon, Anthony, *Major: A Political Life*, London; Weidenfeld & Nicolson, 1997

Shawcross, William, *Murdoch*, New York: Simon & Schuster, 1993

Siklos, Richard, *Shades of Black: Conrad Black and the World's Fastest Growing Press Empire*, London: Heinemann, 1995

Silber, Laura, and Little, Allan, *The Death of Yugoslavia*, London: Penguin, 1996

Simms, Brendan, *Unfinest Hour: Britain and the Destruction of Bosnia*, London: Penguin, 2002

Stewart, Graham, *Burying Caesar, Churchill, Chamberlain and the Battle for the Tory Party*, London: Weidenfeld & Nicolson, 1998

Taylor, Geoffrey, *Changing Faces: History of The Guardian, 1956–1988*, London: Fourth Estate, 1993

Taylor, S. J., *An Unlikely Hero: Vere Rothermere and How the Daily Mail Was Saved*, London: Weidenfeld & Nicolson, 2002

Thatcher, Margaret, *The Downing Street Years*, London: HarperCollins, 1993

Watkins, Alan, *A Short Walk Down Fleet Street*, London: Duckworth, 2000

Wintour, Charles, *The Rise and Fall of Fleet Street*, London: Hutchinson, 1989

Witherow, John, and Patrick Bishop, *Winter War: Falklands Conflict*, London: Quartet, 1982

Young, Toby, *How to Lose Friends and Alienate People*, London: Little, Brown, and Company, 2001

INDEX

A

The Absence of War (David Hare) 463

Abu Jihad 337

ACAS (Advisory Conciliation and Arbitration Service) 89–90

Ackroyd, Peter 182, 185

Active Newsroom 49 *see also* Evans, Harold

Adams, Gerry 491, 564 *see also* Sinn Fein

Adams, James 234

Adams, John 450

AEU (Amalgamated Engineering Union) 282

Afghanistan 348, 591, 598, 600 603

Africa 581 *see also* Apartheid; Congo; Rwanda; Sierra Leone; Somalia; South Africa, Sudan

Aga Khan 17

Aidid, General Muhammad Farrah 580–581

Aitken, Jonathan 30–32, 48, 101, 496, 519, 542

al-Assad, Hafez 151

al-Qaeda 579, 598, 601, 604–605

Alberge, Dalya 461

Algeria 598

Allardyce, Jason 501

Allison, John 449

Almond, Mark 354, 357

Amiel, Barbara 315, 341

Amis, Kingsley 614

ANC (African Congress Party) 560

Ancram, Michael 538, 539, 541

Anderson, Bruce 475

Anderson, Terry 334–336

Andropov, Yuri 147, 216

Anglo-Irish Agreement 563

Annan, Kofi 149

Annan, Noel 339

Anson, Charles 634

Antelope, HMS 134

Apartheid 124 *see also* South Africa

Appleyard, Christina 548

Arab League 150

Arafat, Yasser 561–563

Arcadia (Tom Stoppard) 463

Archer of Weston-super-Mare, Lord (Jeffery) 540, 543, 550

Ardent, HMS 134

Argentina 119–121, 125–126, 129, 133 *see also* Falklands War; Galtieri, General Leopoldo

Arlott, John 207

Armide (C.W. Gluck) 451

Armstrong, Lisa 466–468, 624

Arnett, Peter 398

Ashcroft, Michael 536–546, 609

Ashdown, Paddy 317, 407

Ashford, Nicholas 124, 131

Ashworth, Anne 622, 624

Ashworth, Jon 322

ASLEF (Associated Society of Locomotive Steam Engineers and Firemen) 83, 250

Associated Newspapers 20, 30, 31, 32, 101, 239, 272–273, 298

Associated Press 152, 334–335

Astor family 17, 18–19

Astor, David 40

Astor, Gavin (later Lord) 8, 19, 24, 63

Astor, Lord (John Jacob) 23

Atex computers 231, 233–234, 236, 247, 258

Atherton, Michael 440

Atlantic Richfield 30, 31, 40

AUEW (Amalgamated Union of Engineering Workers) 158, 236, 288

Austin, Tim 11, 60, 93, 102, 180, 235–236, 246, 256, 261, 372, 435, 609

The Australian 22, 39, 41, 646

Australian Financial Review 90

Aylard, Richard 130

B

Bad Times at The Times 188

Baker, James 560

Baldwin, Tom 535–536, 538–540, 545, 552

Baltic States 567

Bank of New York 517

Banks, David 235

Barak, Ehud 562, 600

Baring, Sir Evelyn 143

Barings Bank 4

Barlow, Frank 298

Barnes, Ivan 212, 311, 626

Barnes, Julian 369

Barnes, Rosie 317

Barnes, Simon 201–202, 326, 330–331, 421, 442, 444–445

Barnes, Thomas 51, 53, 103

Barnetson, Lord (William) 5

Bassett, Philip 373

BBC (British Broadcasting Corporation) 186, 529–530

Beattie, Ken 90

Beck, Ernest 353

Beckham, David 444

Beckett, Margaret 434, 487

Beeston, Richard 387, 390, 392–393, 398, 571–572, 592, 600, 640

Begin, Menachem 149, 152, 154

Belgrano see General Belgrano

Belize 537–539, 541, 544

Bell, John 325

Bell, Lord (Tim) 541

Bell, Mary 515–516

Bell, Steve 482

Bellamy, Rex 204, 441

Beloff, Max 553–554

Benaud, Richie 440

Benn, Tony 78, 80–83, 114, 164, 265, 271, 279, 309

Bennett, Alan 178, 183

Bennett, Vanora 593

Berlins, Marcel 92, 108, 183

Berry, Don 48

Berthoud, Roger 92, 108

Bevins, Anthony 162, 303, 310–311

Bhutto, Benazir 597

Bicentenary of *The Times* 206–210

Biffen, John 27–29, 31, 32, 99–100, 104, 265, 305, 308

'Big Bang' 323–324

Bild Zeitung 174

Biko, Steve 183

bin Laden, Osama 389, 596, 598, 600–602, 605

Binney, Marcus 373, 415, 638

Binyon, Michael 145, 146, 171–173, 177, 180, 208, 352, 404, 486, 600

Birtwistle, Harrison 450

Bishop, Patrick 138, 140

Bissell, Frances 359

Black, Conrad (Lord Black of Crossharbour) 9, 241, 306, 343, 431, 485

Black, Captain Jeremy 130

Black Monday 324–325

Black Wednesday 474, 476–477

Blackmore, Keith 439, 469

Blair, Tony
  ascendancy 482–483
  and Bush 601
  constitutional reform 487, 499, 553–554
  devolution 499
  general election
    (1997) 491–493
    (2001) 555–557
  Kosovo 588
  Mary Bell furore 515
  Millennium Dome 503
  New Labour 455, 488
  As Prime Minister 493, 497

Sierra Leone success 583–584
Tony's cronies 535
The Blair Witch Project (dirs Daniel Myrick and Eduardo Sánchez) 464
Blake, David 66
Blake, Lord (Robert) 379
Bluff Cove 136–137, 139
Blum, Léon 70
Blundy, Anna 64
Blur 454–455
Bokassa, Emperor Jean-Bedal 70
Bone, James 517, 519, 599–600
Borrie, Sir Gordon 363
Bosnian War 568–573, 574–578, 579, 584 590 *see also* Dayton Accord; Kosovo; NATO; Serbia
Botham, Ian 204, 440
Bottomley, Peter 31, 429
Boutros Ghali, Boutros 580
Bouverie Street 222–226, 229–230, 249, 255, 297 *see also The Sun*; *The News of the World*
Boxer, Mark (Marc) 199
Boyes, Roger 145–146, 346, 619
Doyle, Danny 465
Bradlee, Ben 64
Bradley, Ian 77
Bradley, Peter 539
Bradshaw, Dr Tim 419
Brady, Reg 11, 87–88
Bragg, Melvyn 188
Brassed Off (dir. Mark Herman) 465
Brata, Sasthi 73
Brearley, Mike 204, 207
Bremner, Charles 324, 619
Brenton, Howard 115, 183
Brett, Alastair 520
Brewerton, David 325
Brezhnev, Leonaid 147, 216, 350–351, 357
Bridgeman, John 434
Bridges, George 540
Briggs, Asa 37
British Press Awards 147
British Rail 83, 156, 232–233
British Satellite Broadcasting 401

Britoil 162
Brittan, Leon 310
Brittan, Samuel 68
Britten, Benjamin 450
Britton, Tony 231
Brock, George 198, 404, 417, 437, 499, 529, 534, 608
Brogan, Hugh 92
Brook, Peter 183
Brookes, Peter 200, 482, 486–487, 557, 601
Brown, Craig 315
Brown, Geoff 401, 449, 464–465
Brown, Lord George 80
Brown, Glenn 461
Brown, Gordon 488, 497, 554
Brown, Peter 254
Brown, Tina 64, 112, 113, 116, 417, 418
Bruce-Gardyne, Jock 166
Brunskill, Ian 635
Brunton, Sir Gordon 7, 17–18, 20–25, 28, 31
Bryant, John 235, 304, 372, 413, 415, 436, 476, 482, 508, 541, 546–547, 608
Bryson, Bill 33, 88, 253
Brzezinski, Zbigniew 388
Buckley, Christine 616
Burchill, Julie 235
Bush, George 388, 389, 395, 560, 579, 581
Bush, George W. 563, 599, 601
Butler, David 315, 316
Butler, Rab 108, 631, 633
Butt, Ronald 70
Butterworth, Jez 463

C

Calcutt QC, Sir David 512–513
Callaghan, Brigid 624
Callaghan, James 43, 68, 76, 80
Calman, Mel 56, 200, 382
Cameron, James 464
Campbell, Alastair 552

Canary Wharf 324
Cannon, Tom 480
Capes, Geoff 441
Cappi, Tony 236–237
Carey, John 154
Carlyle, Robert 465
Carman QC, George 539
Caro, Sir Anthony 460–461
Carr, E.H. 215
Carr family 30, 39
Carr, Sir William 99
Carrington, Lord (Peter) 125, 146
Cash, Bill 475
Cats (Andrew Lloyd Webber) 183–184
Catto, Lord (Thomas) 21
Cazalet, Edward 143
CBI (Confederation of British
    Industry) 380
CBS Broadcasting 395
Ceausescu, Nicolae 346, 354–356
Chancellor, Alexander 108, 359, 420
Channel 4 185
Chappell, David 439
Chapple, Frank 156
Chard, Ted 225–226
Chariots of Fire (dir. Hugh Hudson) 184
Charles, Prince of Wales, marriage
    61–63
Chechnya 591–594
Chemical Brothers 456
Chernenko, Konstantin 147–148
Chernin, Peter 298
Cherwell 7, 37
Chicago Sun-Times 217, 235–236
China 187, 348–350, 356–357,
    523–534 *see also* Hong Kong
Christie, Linford 331
The Church and the Bomb 148
Churchill, Sir Winston 11
Clare, John 318, 644
Clark, General Wesley 589
Clarke, Kenneth 265, 293, 475, 489,
    493, 494–495, 558
Clarke, Tom 325–326, 330, 439
CLEAR (Campaign for Lead-Free Air)
    105

Clement, Barry 258, 303
Cliff, Nigel 465
Clifford, Max 513
Clinton, Bill 468, 527, 561, 575, 581,
    583, 585–586, 588–589, 601
Clwyd, Ann 429
CND (Campaign for Nuclear
    Disarmament) 148, 159, 310
CNN (Cable News Network) 391,
    398
Coats, Peter 6334
Cobain, Ian 603
Cobain, Kurt 454
Cobbett, William 103
Coe, Peter 184
Coe, Sebastian 204
Cohen, Barbara 290
Cold War 160, 215, 357, 387, 405, 559,
    567, 609
Cole, John 419
Coleridge, Nicholas 646
Collier, John 33–34, 88, 89, 98
Collins, Neil 430
Columbia space shuttle 73
Communism 144–146, 156, 215–216,
    354–357, 522, 526, 527, 560, 591
Competition Bill 434
Conference on Security and
    Cooperation in Europe 559, 567 *see
    also* OSCE
Congdon, Professor Tim 320
Congo, Democratic Republic of 583
Conroy, Harry 155, 244, 253–254,
    263
Conservative Party 126, 162, 163–165,
    219, 312–317, 318, 375, 550
Ashcroft affair 535–544
general elections 162–164, 312–316,
    318, 346, 406–409, 488–493
higher education 479
hostility towards 481
internal markets 478
leadership challenges 483–484, 494,
    557–558
local government strategy 376–377
membership 551

Poll Tax 377–382
The Times's attitude toward 550
Conservative Philosophy Group 475
Cook, Matthew 489
Cooper, Sir Frank 134, 139
Cork, Richard 373, 415, 458–462
Cowley, John 231
Cowling, Maurice 79
Cowton, Rodney 105, 539
Craine, Debra 449
Crawford Poole, Shona 201, 359
Credit cards 321–322
Crick, Bernard 133
Cries Unheard (Gitta Sereny) 515–516
Croatia 569–570, 573, 577
Cruden Investments 38, 41
Cudlipp, Hugh 40, 41, 277
Cudlipp, Michael 52
Currie, Edwina 515
Curtis, Richard 465
Czechoslovakia 355 *see also* Eastern
    Europe

D

Dacre, Lord (Hugh Trevor-Roper) 23,
    50, 100, 168–180, 352, 627
Dacre, Paul 412–413, 416, 429
Daldry, Stephen 463
Daily Express 38, 40, 101, 143, 163,
    188, 189, 307, 429, 516
Daily Mail 20, 189, 190–191, 209, 262,
    272, 295, 381, 413, 429, 477, 507,
    623
Daily Mirror 39–40, 132, 166, 189,
    227, 390, 399, 408, 514, 516
Daily Mirror (Sydney) 33
Daily News 95
Daily Star 26, 136, 189
Daily Telegraph 3, 15, 26, 44, 51, 106,
    128, 141, 158, 160, 165–166,
    191–192, 214, 220, 224, 240–241,
    295, 298, 305–306, 358, 421, 425,
    426, 429–431, 434, 469, 516,
    530–533, 632, 642
Daley, Janet 321

Dalyell, Tom 491
D'Ancona, Matthew 419, 485, 564–565
Darby, George 62
Dardanelles campaign 35–36
Davenport, Peter 275
David Holden Prize 147
Davies, Ron 553
Davis, Clive 452
Davy, Richard 159–160, 216
Dawson, Geoffrey 52, 482
Dawson-Scott, Robert 502
Day, Corinne 467
Dayton Accord 578, 579, 584 *see also*
    Bosnian War; Kosovo; NATO
de Blowitz, Henri 618
de Cuellar, Perez 133
de Lisle, Tim 360–361
Dean, Brenda 232, 236–238, 241–242,
    244–246, 248–249, 265–267, 270,
    276, 278–281, 284, 288, 290–291,
    293, 364
Deedes, Lord (Bill) 166
Dejevsky, Mary 160, 347–349, 568,
    640
Delaney, Michael 288–289
Delors, Jacques 343–344
Deng Xiaoping 350, 523, 525, 527
Dettmer, Jamie 390–391
di Giovanni, Janine 586, 588, 594, 603,
    605, 640
Diamond, John 438
Diana, Princess of Wales 61–63, 142,
    504, 513
Dickinson, Matt 521
Distillers Ltd 48–49
Dobson, Frank 487, 553–554
Docklands 222, 272–273, 298, 306
Domarus, Max 167
Donne, John 125
Donoughue, Bernard 55, 65, 80–81,
    102–104, 106–108, 114, 117, 118,
    418
*Double Century: 200 Years of Cricket in
    The Times* (ed. Marcus Williams)
    207
Double-key stroking 13–14, 34

Douglas-Home, Charles
background 46, 141–144
on CND (Campaign for Nuclear
Disarmament) 148
editor-in-waiting 46, 50, 52, 54, 95,
102–103, 105–107
and Evans's leadership 105–106,
108
Good Times, Bad Times 112–113
marriage 144
as *Times* editor 416, 418
appointment 107, 109–111
assessment of editorship 213,
214–215, 216–217, 416
and the BBC 186–187
bicentenary celebrations 208–9
cancer and death 195, 211–217
Falklands War 123, 124–127, 129,
138, 158
finding supportive staff 195–198,
418
Hitler Diaries 169–171, 173–177,
179
increase in sales 192–3
labour disputes 156–161
leader writing policy 159–60
Murdoch's influence 114, 160
and newspaper layout 140
and Ronald Reagan 146, 158
Thatcherite 158
Wapping 231
see also full listing for *The Times*
Douglas-Home, Jessica 144, 213, 216
Douglas-Home, Robin 142
Douglas-Home, William 127
Dougray, Ginny 551
Drace-Francis, Charles 537, 544
Drexel Burnham Lambert Bank 399
Driver, David 372, 410
Drogheda, Lord 627
Drugs 329–331, 454, 538–539, 542,
551
Dubbins, Tony 237, 267–268,
276–277, 280–282, 292, 293
Dubcek, Alexander 353
Duncan Smith, Iain 558

Durrant, Sabine 183
Dux, John 432
Dyke, Greg 535, 609

E

East is East (dir. Damien O'Donnell)
465
East Germany 346, 350–353, 355 *see
also* Eastern Europe
East Midlands Allied Press 62
East and West (Chris Patten) 530–531
Eastern Europe 215–216, 340, 346,
350–357, 403, 559 *see also* Baltic
States; Czechoslovakia; East
Germany; Hungary; Poland;
Romania
Ebor, Nandor 154n
Ecclestone, Bernie 535
Ecclestone, Jacob 15–16, 27, 28, 155,
187, 253
Eddy, Paul 176
Editing and Design (Harold Evans) 49
Education Act (1988) 318–319
Edwards, Eddie 'the Eagle' 329
Edworthy, Sarah 183
EETPU (Electrical, Electronic,
Telecommunications and Plumbing
Union) 156–157, 228, 231–232,
237, 240, 244, 248, 261, 287, 293
Egypt 152, 597
Ekberg, Peter 98
Eliot, T.S. 183–184
Elizabeth II, Queen 112, 209–210, 627,
634
Ellis, Terry 236
Elton, John 455
Emerson, Sally 417, 418
Emery, Fred 55, 66, 77, 81, 94, 95,
102–103, 105, 111, 127, 131, 136,
195
Emin, Tracy 459, 460
Employment Act (1980) 156, 226
Enders, Thomas 122, 126
The English Patient (dir. Anthony
Minghella) 465

English, Shirley 501

English Culture and the Decline of the Industrial Spirit (Martin Wiener) 49

English National Opera 447

Eno, Brian 461

ERM (Exchange Rate Mechanism) 320, 344, 379–381, 472, 481

Euro-sceptics 344, 404, 473–475, 476, 485, 490, 493, 495

European Community 343, 358, 380, 403, 620 *see also* European Union

European Convention of Human Rights 517, 520

European Monetary System 69 *see also* ERM

European monetary union (EMU) 344, 358, 380–381, 403–404

European Union 475, 489–490, 498, 570 *see also* European Community

Evans, Harold
  background 47–51
  Active Newsroom 49
  Editing and Design 49
  Good Times, Bad Times 112–113, 117, 188–9, 217
  and Israel 149
  marriage 64
  and the Mussolini hoax 168
  negotiations for *The Times* purchase 31, 32, 34
  in New York 116
  and Poland 145–146
  and *Sunday Times* 17, 18, 21–24
  Murdoch's influence 95–99, 101, 113–115, 118, 644
  thalidomide campaign 48–49
  supports Murdoch's Wapping action 260
  as *Times* editor
  appointment 52
  assessment of editorship 102, 104, 106–108, 111, 113–118
  budget allocation 94–95
  cold composition 87–88
  Denis Thatcher's planning application 113

dirty tricks 107

downfall 116–118

and Gerald Long 83–4, 96–98

growth strategy 52–53

incurring Thatcher's displeasure 113–114

in the Law Courts 52–53

lead in petrol campaign 105, 539

leader column battles 103–105

leadership 44, 53–4, 58–9, 92–94, 102, 106–108, 140

'maximum irritation' theory 53, 118

Parliamentary Privileges 308–309

Portfolio 189–190

personal attacks and allegations 101–102

political position 64–69, 77, 79

redesigning the layout 59–61

royal wedding 62–63

staff changes 54–57, 109–115, 416, 418

transfer of TNL titles 98–100

'vertical journalism' theory 53, 117–118

see also the full listing for *The Times*

Evans, Michael 390, 392, 589, 603, 647

Evans, Reg 62

Evans, Richard 203, 308–309, 325

Evening Standard 20, 24, 135, 475

Express Newspapers 26 *see also* *Daily Express*; United Newspapers

Eyre, Richard 464

F

Faber Book of Reportage (John Carey) 154

Fair Trade Act (1973) 27

Faith and Power (Edward Mortimer) 149

Falklands War 79, 114, 118, 119–141, 152, 155, 205, 391

Fallon, Ivan 234, 298

Fantoni, Barry 200

Farrell, Stephen 585

Fat Boy Slim 456

Fayed, Dodi 504
Fayed, Mohammed 481
Feldman, Erik 190
Felton, David 258, 303
Fenton, James 182
Fieldhouse, Admiral Sir John 130
Financial Times 12, 18–19, 90, 91, 96,
    128, 162, 163, 181, 192, 214,
    220–221, 240, 273, 298, 306–307,
    316, 322, 358, 380–381, 408, 410,
    422, 426, 429
 FT.com 471, 642
Finch, Hilary 449
Fischer, August 402, 432
Fish, Jonathan 328
Fisk, Robert 124, 150–155, 176,
    333–338
Fitzgerald, Dr Garret 72
Fitzpatrick, Barry 98
Fleet, Kenneth 323–325
Fletcher, Martin 390
Flynn, David 432
Fletcher, Duncan 440
Follett, Toby 538–539, 541, 544
Foot, Michael 2, 33, 66, 76, 80–81,
    114, 147, 163–165, 181, 314
Foot, Paul 142
Forbes, Brian 261
Ford, Richard 345, 373
Foster, Brendan 441
Foster, Jodie 59
Four Weddings and a Funeral (dir.
    Richard Curtis) 465
Fowler, Lord (Norman) 477
Fox, Norman 201–202, 325–326
Fox film and television 229, 297, 360,
    399, 430
Franks, Alan 201
Franks Report 138
Fraser, Hugh 31
Frayn, Michael 463
Freedom Forum 531–532
Friedman, Milton 75
Frost, Bill 572
Fuchs, Vivian 121
Fukuyama, Francis 356, 559

The Full Monty (dir. Peter Cattaneo)
    465
Fuller, Simon 455

G

Gaddafi, Colonel Muammar 334
Gallagher, Noel 455
Galliano, John 466
Gallipoli (dir. Peter Weir) 35–36
Galloway, George 317
Galtieri, General Leopoldo 121–122,
    133 see also Argentina; Falklands
    War
Gang of Four see SDP
Garrick Club 57
Gascoigne, Paul 442
GCHQ Cheltenham 158
Geddes, Diana 76
Gemayel, Bashir 153
General Belgrano 131–133
General elections
  (1979) 14
  (1983) 162–164, 405
  (1987) 312–318, 405
  (1992) 346, 404–409
  (1997) 487–493
  (2001) 554–556
Genocide see Iraq; Kosovo; Rwanda;
    Serbia; Srebrenica massacre
Geraghty, Sean 156
Germany 350, 569 see also East
    Germany; Kohl, Helmut
Gibbs, Frances 373, 647
Giles, Frank 50, 54, 96, 98–99, 114,
    128, 164, 173–175, 178
Giles (Sunday Express cartoonist) 270
Gillespie, Bill 231, 248
Gilligan, Andrew 521
Gilmour, Sir Ian 309
Giscard d'Estaing, Válery 69–70
Glasgow Herald 31
Gledhill, Ruth 647
Glendinning, Victoria 183
Glover, Stephen 240, 300–301, 411,
    417, 432, 614

Glyndebourne 452
Goldsmith, Sir James 2, 17, 65,
    488–489, 493
Gooch, Graham 326
Good Times, Bad Times (Harold Evans)
    112–113, 117; 188–189, 217
Goodbody, John 325, 328, 330,
    440–441
Goodwin, Noel 449
Goose Green 135–136
Gorbachev, Mikhail 147, 216, 318,
    347–348, 351–352, 354, 357, 394,
    567–568 *see also* Cold War; Gulf
    War; Reagan, Ronald; Russia; Soviet
    Union; Thatcher, Margaret
Gordon, Angela 199, 255, 258, 302
Gormley, Antony 462
Gould, Philip 553
Gove, Michael 485–487, 489–490, 501,
    540, 547, 550–552, 565, 566–567
GPMU (Graphical, Paper and Media
    Union) 293
Graham, Katharine (Kay) 5–6,
    230–231
Grainger, Percy 199
Grant, Hugh 465
Grant, John 94, 105, 195, 512, 639
Graves, David 123
Gray, John 356
Gray's Inn Road
  closure threat 35
  demarcation rules 89, 294–295
  Murdoch offers freehold to print
    unions 276–278, 281–282
  new site talks 5, 223
  poor morale 85, 102
  print capacity 249
  property assets 25
  sold to ITN 297
  TNL papers 19, 33, 52
  see also Good Times, Bad Times; Print
    unions, industrial action/strikes
The Greatest Newspaper in the World!
    208
Greene, Lord (Sidney) 23, 50, 100
Greenoak, Francesca 359

Griffin, Charles 56
Griffith-Joyner, Florence 331
Griffiths, Paul 449–450
Grigg, John 315, 339–340, 611,
    632–633
Grimond, Lord (Jo) 30, 315
Gross, Michael 468
Grunwick dispute 226
Guardian 12, 18, 26, 51, 60, 61, 78, 79,
    98, 101, 128, 140–141, 163,
    191–192, 239, 273, 276, 305–306,
    312, 370, 390, 410, 426, 429, 433,
    531, 642
Guardian Unlimited 469, 471
Gulf War 388–398 *see also* Iraq
Gullikson, Tom 204

H

Haddad, Major Saad 154
Hague, William 494–495, 535, 537,
    538, 540, 542–543, 545, 550–551,
    556, 557
Hahn, Frank 66
Haig, Alexander 126, 129
Haley, Sir William 104, 239
Halliwell, Geri 456
Hama, Syria 150–151
Hamas 561
Hames, Tim 485, 540–541, 551, 556,
    586, 648
Hamilton, Adrian 55, 81, 116, 162
Hamilton, Alan 260, 507
Hamilton, Neil 481, 491, 543
Hamilton, Sir Denis 7–8, 17, 19–20,
    21–23, 28, 84, 87, 99, 116
  choosing a *Times* editor 45 46, 48, 50
  Wapping move 260
Hamlyn, Michael 372, 560
Hammond, Eric 231–232, 240, 244,
    248, 261–262, 283, 293
Hammond, Professor Norman 262,
    637
Hands, David 201, 327
Hanrahan, Brian 135
Happy Mondays 454

Hard Labour (Robert Kilroy-Silk) 339

Hardy, Bert 222–223, 255

Hare, David 115, 183, 463

Hargrove, Charles 69

Harrison, George 456

Harmsworth, Vere *see* Rothermere, 3rd Viscount

HarperCollins 182, 530

Harpers & Queen 101

Harris, Derek 616

Harris, Gillian 501

Harris, Robert 178

Harrow School 190

Hart, Gary 601

Hartwell, Lord (Michael Berry) 240–241, 300, 306

Harvey, Andrew 373

Harvey, Marcus 458

Hastings, Sir Max 135, 137, 140, 273, 300, 306, 339, 431, 477, 485

Hastings, Michael 183

Haughey, Charles 72

Havel, Vaclav 353, 357

Haviland, Julian 124, 162, 164, 311

Hawkes, Nigel 373, 468

Heald, Tim 183

Healey, Denis 82, 314

Healy, Pat 157, 164, 258, 260

Heath, Edward 31, 75, 78, 208, 528

Heath, Michael 100

Heidemann, Gerd 168–170, 172, 176, 180

Henderson, Sir Nicholas 176

Hendrie, Michael J. 637

Henman, Tim 441

Hennessy, John 203

Hennessy, Peter 4, 92, 108

Hensmann, Jan 170

Herald and Weekly Times Group 36, 38

Heren, Louis 3, 45–46, 51, 55, 105, 108, 618

Heseltine, Michael 222, 309–310, 379, 382–385, 489, 493–494

Heseltine, William 627

Hetherington, Alastair 166

Hick, Graeme 439

Hickey, Owen 46, 93, 96, 103–104, 339, 648

Hickey, William (Michael Leapman) 92, 101

Higgins, John 91, 198, 447, 449, 453, 632, 634

Higgins, Stuart 564

Hill, George 314

Hillier, Bevis 91

Hilton, Anthony 161

Hinckley, John 59

Hinton, Les 432, 527, 548, 598–599, 647

Hirst, Damien 459, 460

Hitler, Adolf 553–554

Hitler Diaries 167–180, 641

Hitler's Speeches and Proclamations (Max Domarus) 167

Hoddle, Glen 521

Hogg, Sarah 303–304, 476

Hoggart, Paul 460

Hoggart, Simon 481

Holden, Anthony 55, 56, 60, 64, 81, 92, 102, 105, 107, 112, 117, 118, 418

Holmes, Richard 183

Holroyd, Michael 178

Holt, Oliver 443

Homosexuality 633–634

Honecker, Erich 346, 351

Hong Kong 503–504, 523, 525–529, 532–533

Hopkins, Michael 451

Hopkirk, Peter 145

Hornsby, Michael 355

Horton, Brian 55, 92, 94

Howard, Anthony 632–633, 635–636, 639–640

Howard, Michael 142, 488, 495, 518

Howard, Philip 92, 118, 181–183, 257, 261, 365, 371, 628

Howe, Darcus 74

Howe, Sir Geoffrey 65, 96, 319, 345, 381–382, 385–386, 528

Howson, Peter 574
Hoy, Mike 235, 246, 285, 303, 304, 360
Huckerby, Martin 73, 258–259
Hughes, Rob 443
Hughes, Simon 491
Hughes, Ted 462
Human Rights Act (1998) 517, 520
Hume, Cardinal Archbishop Basil 369
Hume, John 564
Humphries, Barry 178
Hungary 355 see also Eastern Europe
Hunnicutt, Gayle 369
Hunt, Rex 122
Hurd, Douglas 383, 384–385, 386, 525, 572
Hussain, Nasser 440
Hussein, Saddam 149, 386–390, 396–398, 561, 597 see also Gulf War; Iraq; Kuwait
Hussein, King of Jordan 125
Hussey, Lord (Marmaduke) 13–14, 50, 86, 89, 107, 283

I

Imperial War Museum 574
Independent 238, 240, 298, 300–304, 305–307, 312, 316, 333, 337, 357, 359, 363, 365, 370, 410, 411, 420–424, 427, 429, 430, 433–434, 453, 607, 632, 643
Industrial action 1, 3, 5, 10–14, 48, 60, 81, 83, 85, 89, 152, 155–158, 163, 187, 219–220, 223–225 see also Murdoch; NGA; NUJ; SOGAT; The Times; Wapping
Ingham, Bernard 123, 310, 312, 318, 552
Ingrams, Richard 102
An Inspector Calls (Stephen Daldry) 463–4
Institute for Economic Affairs 65
Institute of Fiscal Studies 405
Institute of Journalists 155, 283
International Criminal Court 591, 595

Internet 468–471, 642–643
IPC (International Press Corporation) 40
IRA (Irish Republican Army) 70–72, 338, 499, 563–566 see also Adams, Gerry
Iran 387, 597–598
Iraq 149, 386–397, 481, 597 see also Gulf War
Ireland see Northern Ireland
Irvine, Derry (later Lord Chancellor) 255
Irving, David 168, 174, 177, 179
Isaacs, Jeremey 185
Isaacs, Tony 224, 231
Islam 150–151, 155
  Intifada 560
  fundamentalism 595–598, 604 see also al-Qaeda; bin Laden, Osama
Islamic Jihad 335, 561
Israel 149, 150–155, 334, 560–563 see also Middle East
Ivens, Martin 343, 394, 476, 485
Izethegovic, Alija 568, 578
Izvestia 147

J

Jackson, General Sir Mike 589
Jacobs, Eric 28
Jacobson, Philip 390–391, 395
Jagger, Sir Mick 453
Jakobovits, Chief Rabbi Immanuel 177
James, Cathy 11
James, Edward 205
Jaruzelski, General Wojciech 145
Jay, Peter 68
Jenkins, Clive 56
Jenkins, David 330
Jenkins, Peter 128
Jenkins, Roy (Lord Jenkins of Hillhead) 76, 78, 79, 317
Jenkins, Simon
  editor-in-waiting 364, 366
  as Times columnist 471, 473, 476, 493, 571, 575, 601–604, 648

Jenkins, Simon – *cont.*
  as *Times* editor
    analysis of *The Times* 368–371, 374, 417, 418
    assessment of editorship 413–415, 416
    background 367–368
    leader writers 374–375
    Murdoch's influence 645
    obituaries 634
    'paper of choice' 369–372
    paper's finances 363, 401–402
    party for Michael Seely 203
    sceptical Tory paper 374–375
    standard of English 371–372, 435
    three-year contract 411–415, 607
    see also the full listing for *The Times*
Jiang Zemin 527–528, 532
JIC (Joint Intelligence Committee) 122
John Paul II, Pope 136, 146
Johnson, Ben 329–330
Johnson, Boris 341
Johnson, Daniel 353, 357, 375, 419, 421, 462, 476, 485–486
Johnson, Frank 56, 59, 65, 79, 91, 117, 118, 164–165, 339
Johnson, Paul 17, 65, 96, 213, 254, 477
Jones, Colonel 'H' 135
Jones, Richard 451
Jones, Stuart 205–206
Jones, Tim 72
Jones, Wyn 279
Joseph, Lord (Keith) 65
Journalists of *The Times* (JOTT) 4, 111
Junor, Sir John 113, 366

K

Kabila, Laurent 583
Kahan Commission 154
Kaletsky, Anatole 373, 381, 404–405, 408, 415, 423, 473, 486, 489, 492, 499, 604

Kapoor, Anish 462
Karadzic, Radovan 575
Karzai, Hamid 605
Kasparov, Garry 421
Kaufman, Gerald 37, 163
Kavanagh, Professor Dennis 316
Keating, Harry 183
Keating, John 231, 242
Keays, Sarah 165
Kee, Robert 141
Keene, Raymond 421, 638
Kellner, Peter 133, 263
Kelly, David 521
Kelly, Rachel 481
Kelner, Simon 643
Kemsley, Lord (James Gomer Berry) 19
Kennedy, Dominic 537
Kennedy, John F. 58
Kennedy, Edward 204
Kenny, Dr Anthony 144, 208
Kent, Monsignor Bruce 148
Kervin, Alison 444
Keys, Bill 33
Khomeini, Ayatolah 597
Kiley, Sam 579–583, 585
Kilroy-Silk, Robert 338–339
Kingston, Miles 56, 117, 261, 303, 629
Kinnock, Glenys 165, 315
Kinnock, Neil 165, 213, 262, 265, 277, 290, 314, 315, 317, 364, 376, 394, 405–408
Kirkpatrick, Jeane 126
Kissinger, Henry 64
Knight, Andrew 241, 247, 299, 306, 363–364, 367, 401–402, 412, 424, 432, 435
Knightley, Philip 173
Knipe, Michael 390
Koch, Peter 170, 176
Kogan, David and Maurice 80
Kohl, Helmut 352, 403, 529
Kosovo 584–590 *see also* Bosnian War; Dayton Accord; Kosovo; NATO; Serbia
Kostunica, Vojislav 590

Krenz, Egon 351–352
Kujau, Konrad 168, 170, 180
Kuwait 386–389, 394–395, 560–561,
    597 see also Gulf War; Hussein,
    Saddam; Iraq

L
Labour Party 2, 76, 78, 80–82, 148,
    160, 162–164, 262–263, 290, 302,
    338, 376, 379, 380, 382 see also
    Blair, Tony; Foot, Michael; Kinnock,
    Neil
  Clause Four removal 483
  funding arrangements 535
  general elections
    (1983) 162–164, 405
    (1987) 312–8, 405–407
    (1992) 404–409
    (1997) 487–493
    (2001) 554–556
  Government and spin 552–553
  euro decision deferred 498
  New Deal 498
  and The Times 552
  Times endorsement 556
Lamb, Larry 43, 47
Lamont, Lord (Norman) 405, 472, 475
Landy, Michael 461
Lara, Brian 440
Laski, Harold 18
The Last Proconsul (Charles Douglas-
    Home) 143
Law, Peter 355
Lawrence, John 183
Lawrence, Stephen (Lawrence Inquiry)
    75
Lawson, Dominic 380
Lawson, Nigel (Lord Lawson of Blaby)
    67, 133, 162, 314, 319, 322,
    344–346, 421
Lawson, Nigella 466
Le Page, John 123
Le Page, Robert 183
Leapman, Michael 6, 73, 92, 94
Lebanon 149, 150–155, 334–336, 597

Ledbetter, Diana 359
Lee, Alan 440
Lee Williams, Professor Geoffrey 571
Leiven, Anatole 592
Lennon, John 456
Lennon, Peter 185
Lester, Anthony 264
Levin, Bernard 57, 91, 144–145, 163,
    166, 218, 260, 273, 274, 341–342,
    357, 371, 454, 486, 507–508, 525,
    533, 647
Levin, Jeremy 335
Lewin, Admiral Sir Terence 137
Lewis, Carl 330–331
Lewis, Derek 495
Liberal Democrats 317, 481, 488, 494
Liberal Party 78, 163, 317, 380 see also
    Liberal Democrats
Life in Russia (Michael Binyon) 147
Lilley, Peter 488, 495, 551
Linford, Dick 437
Linklater, Magnus 501
Lipsey, David 372
Lipsky, Seth 158–159
Lister, David 517, 519–520
Livingstone, Ken 55, 80, 376, 553–554
Lloyd, Cathie 280
Lloyd Webber, Andrew 183
London Daily News 307
London Post 230, 234–236, 242–243,
    246
Long, Gerald 79, 83–84, 86, 94, 96–98,
    100, 109, 110, 171
Longley, Clifford 258, 285–287, 363,
    371, 375, 401, 418–419
Lonhro mining company 30, 31
Look Back in Anger (John Osborne)
    463
Loutchansky, Grigori 517–521
Lownes, Frederick 636
Loyd, Anthony 572–574, 576–577,
    586, 592–594, 603–605, 640
Lucas, Sarah 459
Luce, Richard 122, 264
Lumley, Joanna 201
Lurie, Ranan 56, 200

M

Maastricht 403, 472–475, 569
MacArthur, Brian 52, 55, 60, 78, 95, 105, 169, 175–177, 240, 273, 504, 534, 626
MacArthur, Jenny 444
MacBride, Sean 338
McCarthy, Michael 468
McDonagh, Martin 463
Macdonald, Donald 328
McElvoy, Anne 352–353, 357, 485
McEnroe, John 204–205
McGahey, Mick 188
McGee, Alan 455
McGregor, Ewan 465
McGregor, Lord (John) 513
Macgregor-Morris, Pamela 444
McIntosh, Andrew 80
Macintyre, Ben 599
McIntyre, Don 256, 258, 261, 263, 303
MacKenzie, Kelvin 132, 332
Mackilligin, David 538
MacLeod, Alasdair 426
MacLeod, Angus 501
MacManus, James 436–437
MacMillan, James 450
McNally, Lord (Tom) 434
Macpherson, Conor 463
McQueen, Alexander 466
MacQuitty, Jane 359, 622
McVicar, David 451
MAD (mutually assured destruction) 148
Madden, John 465
Maddock, David 443
Maddox, Bronwen 527, 620, 624, 648
Madonna 451
Mail on Sunday 20, 174, 301
Mair, John 501
Major, John 345, 380–381, 383, 384–385, 390, 398, 403–404 see also Conservative Party
  Back to Basics campaign 481
  and China 524, 526, 527
  Citizen's Charter 478

  Edwina Currie affair 515
  Downing Street peace accord 564–565
  ERM (Exchange Rate Mechanism) 472–473
  Euro-sceptics 475–476
  general elections
    (1992) 404–408
    (1997) 488–493
  IRA mortar bomb 563
  leadership challenge 484–485
  Maastricht treaty 474–475
  and Thatcherism 477–478
  unpopularity 475–477, 481–482
Mancroft, Lord (Benjamin) 208
Mandarin see Phillips, Michael
Mandela, Nelson 560, 567
Mandelson, Peter 262, 314, 406–407, 535
Marc see Boxer, Mark
Marber, Patrick 463
Marlowe, Lara 336
Marnham, Patrick 92
Marr, Andrew 365, 419
Marsh, Sir Richard 2
Martin-Jenkins, Christopher 440
Marxism Today 280
The Mask of Orpheus (Harrison Birtwistle) 450
Masters, Anthony 184
Mates, Michael 481
Mather, Ian 123
Matthews, Bruce 225, 228, 231–232, 236–237, 245, 247, 261, 278, 282–283, 292, 304
Matthews, Lord (Victor) 40
Maxwell, Robert 2, 17, 25, 33, 39–40, 115, 238, 239, 273, 365, 390, 535
May, Derwent 202, 638
Meades, Jonathan 359–360, 622
Media Week 433
Mellor, David 481, 513
Melvern, Linda 242
Menendez, General Mario 140
Mendes, Sam 464
Menkes, Suzy 201, 303, 361

Merchant-Ivory productions 465
Messenger Newspaper Group 227, 240
Metromedia 399
Meyer, Sir Christopher 564
Meyer, Sir Anthony 346
Michael, Alun 553–554
Middle East 333–337, 560 *see also*
    Egypt; Israel; Lebanon; Palestine;
    Saudi Arabia; Suez; Syria
Miles, Alice 624
Miles, Bill 237, 245, 290–291
Milken, Michael 399
Miller, David 201, 326–327, 329
Miller, Jonathan 183, 449
Millington, Barry 449
Milne, Alasdair 186
Milner, Clive 85
Milnes, Rodney 373, 415, 450–452
Milosevic, Slobodan 568–569, 575,
    577–578, 584–585, 588–589
Miners' strike 187–188, 209
Minford, Professor Patrick 67
Minghella, Anthony 465
Mirror Group 27, 238–239, 307, 365,
    430 *see also Daily Mirror*
Mirsky, Jonathan 523–525, 527–529,
    531–534, 607, 623
Mitterrand, François 69–70, 126, 403,
    474
Mobutu, (Joseph) Mobutu Sese Seko
    583
Modiano, Mario 82
Le Monde 4, 61
Monopolies and Mergers Commission
    19, 24, 25, 27–30, 31–33, 104, 361,
    429
Montgomery, David 385
Montgomery-Massingberd, Hugh 632
Moore, Charles 485, 516, 531
Moore, General J.J. 140
Moorehead, Caroline 144
Moran, Caitlin 457
More 30
Morgan, John 438–439
Morgan, Rhodri 554
Morison, Stanley 60, 63, 410

Morning Star 156, 263, 264
Morrell, Frances 628
Morris, James (Jan) 154n
Morrison, Richard 373, 447–451
Moss, Kate 467
Mortimer, Edward 149, 152, 153,
    159–160, 216
Morton, Andrew 462, 513
Motion, Andrew 462, 552
Muirhead Data Communications 12
Muldoon, Robert 126
Murdoch, Anna 115
Murdoch, Sir Keith 35–36, 38, 646 *see
    also* Northcliffe, Lord (Alfred)
Murdoch, (Keith) Rupert
  background 36–42
  media empire/purchases/shares
    Adelaide TV channels 38
    The Australian 22, 39, 41, 646
    Chicago Sun-Times 217, 235–236
    co-finances *Gallipoli* 35–36
    Cruden Investments 38, 41
    Fox film and television 229, 297,
      360, 399, 430
    Los Angeles Dodgers 531
    News of the World 39
    pan-China satellite TV empire 524,
      529, 534, 644
    Perth *Sunday Times* 38
    Reuters shareholding 238–9
    scale of international commitments
      645
    Sky television 186, 360–361, 399,
      401, 411, 426, 427, 442–444
    South China Morning Post 529, 646
    Sydney *Daily Mirror* 33
    Today 307, 381, 428
    TNL purchase 1–2, 6–9, 17,
      19–29, 32, 40, 100 *see also News
      of the World; Sun; Sunday Times;
      The Times; Times Educational
      Supplement; Times Higher Education
      Supplement; Times Literary
      Supplement*
    transfer of TNL titles 99–100
    TV sports deal 327

Murdoch, (Keith) Rupert – *cont.*
  see also News Corporation; News
    International Ltd.; News Limited
  and Israel 149
  mastery of journalistic craft 26, 37,
    39–40, 49
  and the monarchy 7, 507
  political orientation 21–23, 43, 164,
    492, 644
  and Reagan 146
  profile 44
  and the SDP 76–77
  and Thatcher 28–29, 43, 113–114,
    186
  and *The Times*
    Ashcroft affair 543, 546
    bicentenary 207–210
    choosing editors 45–47, 217–218,
      368–369, 416, 607 *see also The
      Times*, editors: Douglas-Home,
      Charles; Evans, Harold; Rees-Mogg,
      William; Stothard, Peter; Wilson,
      Charles
    Douglas-Home's cancer 211,
      213–214, 548
    'dumbing down' 38, 40–42, 189, 531,
      613–625
    East and West (Chris Patten) 530–531
    editorial influence 21, 26, 38–39,
      41–44, 59, 83, 85, 96, 114–116,
      186–187, 298, 337, 532, 534
    and Evans showdown 101, 102–103,
      105–112, 114, 116
    Hitler Diaries 168, 170–173, 175,
      178–180
    nuts and bolts newspaperman 645
    price cutting 422–430
    purchase of *The Times* 1–2, 6–9, 17,
      19–29, 32, 40, 100
    reasons for saving *The Times*
      646–647
    Sherwood's offer 99
    Stothard's cancer 548
    and trade unions 35, 89, 90,
      187–188, 276–278, 281–282
    see also full listing for *The Times*

  and Wapping
    computer technology 231, 233–234,
      236, 247, 258
    distribution 233, 244, 250, 265–266,
      278
    first edition 256–257
    increase in profitability 297–298
    Innovation Special 248
    London Post 230, 234–236, 242–243,
      246
    moving day 250–252
    planning the move 228–230
    conspirators 231–238, 246–248
    praise for Murdoch 259–260, 273
    price of victory 292–299
    public opinion 270–276
      siege/pickets/intimidation
      255–260, 267–270, 274, 278–280,
      282–287, 289–292, 301–302
    subsequent fallout 301–304, 307
    union negotiations 231–238,
      242–246, 248–256, 276–288
Murmuring Judges (David Hare) 463
Murray, Ian 70
Murray, Len 35, 90
Muscat, Julian 441
Muslim brotherhood 597 *see also*
  Islam, fundamentalism
Muslim-Croat federation 574–575 *see
  also* Bosnian War

N

Nadir, Asil 481
NAPP Systems 236
National Council for Civil Liberties
  280
National Lottery 446–447, 465
NATO (North Atlantic Treaty
  Organization) 160, 352
  Bosnian war 571, 575–576
  Implementation Force (IFOR) 578
  K-For 589–590
  Kosovo 584–589
  non-aggression treaty 559
  Sarajevo bombing 574

NATSOPA (National Society of Operative Printers, Graphical and Media Personnel) 10, 33, 34, 88–89, 100
Neale, Greg 251, 253–254, 256, 258
Neil, Andrew 115, 228, 234, 248, 283, 289, 332, 627
Neill Committee 535, 541
Nellist, Dave 384
Netanyahu, Benjamin 562
New Order 453
New Society 629
New Statesman 47, 128, 133, 215, 270
New York Post 6, 21, 41–42, 44, 95
New Yorker 369
News Corporation
  advertising market 606
  East and West (Chris Patten) 530
  financial difficulties 95, 360–361, 364, 366, 399–401, 413, 426
  Hitler Diaries 167, 171–173, 178
  profits 229, 246, 297–298, 426, 432
  saving The Times 646–647
  share value 41
  and TNL 99
  TV sports deal 327
  see also News International Limited
News Group Newspapers (NGN) 25, 41, 231
News International Limited
  ASLEF dispute 83
  boycotts 263–265, 273–274
  cover prices 193, 411, 423, 426–432
  departure of journalists 302–303, 368
  ex-gratia payments 278, 280 281
  job cuts 33, 34–35, 297
  market share of sales 27–29, 238
  operating income 399
  price versus quality 423–424
  profits 95, 116, 219, 297–298, 362, 411, 426, 432
  purchase of TNL 25, 48, 86
  share value 41, 99, 297
  transfer of TNL titles 98–99

Wapping 227–230, 232–235, 237, 243–246, 255, 261, 263, 267–269, 271, 285, 287–288, 290–291
  see also Hitler Diaries; News Corporation
News Limited 38, 40
News on Sunday 277, 307
News of the World 9, 21, 25, 27, 39, 42, 85, 99, 219, 222, 229, 231, 235, 242, 244, 253, 255, 492 see also Bouverie Street
Newspaper Publishers Association (NPA) 2, 7, 10, 156, 238
Newspaper Publishing Limited 427 see also Independent
Newsweek 171–172
Newton, Gordon 189
Newton, Maxwell 39
NGA (National Graphical Association) 2, 10, 12–14, 25, 33, 87, 89–90, 98, 156, 163, 220, 253–254, 274 see also print unions
  mergers 293
  Murdoch offers Gray's Inn Road freehold 276 277
  Wapping 225, 227–229, 236–237, 242–245, 248–250, 267, 270, 278, 280–282, 287, 291
NHS (National Health Service) 156
Nicholls of Birkenhead, Lord (Donald) 518
Nichols, Peter 183
Nicholson, Dr Richard 330
Nicholson, Michael 135
Nicol, Angus 638
Nield, Robert 66
Nightingale, Benedict 373, 448, 462–464
Ninagawa, Yukio 183
Nirvana 454
Noble, Adrian 464
Nolan Report 481
Norbury, Tony 117, 256, 292
Norman, Geraldine 107, 111, 208, 624
Norris, Steve 554
North Korea 329, 522–523

Northcliffe, Lord (Alfred) 4, 20, 35–36, 42, 646
Northern Echo 47–48
Northern Ireland 150, 336, 563–566
Northern Ossetia 591
Notes from a Small Island (Bill Bryson) 88
Nott, John 120, 122, 125, 363
Notting Hill (dir. Richard Curtis) 465
Nuclear
 deterrents 148
 disarmament 160, 163, 348
 waste 308
 weapons 149, 348
NUJ (National Union of Journalists) 15, 25–26, 32, 83, 155, 186, 190, 227, 234, 248–251, 253–254, 255–256, 257–265, 275, 285–287, 291, 294, 302, 340
NUM (National Union of Mineworkers) 187
Nunn, Trevor 183–184, 464
NUR (National Union of Railwaymen) 156, 250
Nuttall, Nick 468

O

Oakley, Robin 311–315, 317, 318, 345–346, 382–383, 385, 404, 407, 419
Oasis 454–455
O'Brien, Conor Cruise 315, 357, 397
O'Brien, Owen 33
Observer 5, 31–32, 40, 98, 163, 174, 191, 274, 302, 428, 523, 531
OFT (Office of Fair Trading) 427–428, 432–434
Oil prices 386, 388
Olympic Games 329–331, 444–445, 625
O'Neill, Bill 33–34, 88, 115, 194, 224–226, 242–244, 248–249, 261, 287, 290–291-3, 432
Operation Desert Storm 391–393 *see*

 also Gulf War; Iraq; Hussein, Saddam; Kuwait
Oppenheim, Sally 28
Orange Order 565–566
Osborne, John 183, 463
OSCE (Organization for Security and Cooperation in Europe) 584
Osman, Arthur 155
O'Sullivan, John 339
O'Sullivan, Sally 366
Outrams 31
Ovett, Steve 204
Owen, David 76, 314, 317–318, 396, 570
Owen, Frank 181
Owen, Richard 147, 390, 525, 619

P

Packer, Kerry 327, 440
Page, Bruce 47, 48, 128, 215
Pakistan 597
Palestine 149, 152–153, 335, 561–563 *see also* PLO
Pannick, David 264
Panorama 101, 165
Parker, Sir Peter 205
Parkinson, Cecil 113–114, 125, 165–166
Parris, Matthew 342–343, 366, 384, 385–386, 406–407, 419, 476, 482, 483–484, 494, 552, 555–556, 611, 648
Parsons, Sandra 548–549, 600, 606, 623–624
Parsons, Sir Anthony 125, 387–388
Patel, Aurobind 410
Paterson, Graham 165, 343, 362, 390, 476–477, 533, 547
Paterson, Peter 272
Patten, Chris 525–526, 528, 530–532, 565
Paul, Sandra 142
Peacock Inquiry 186
Pearce, Edward 366
Pearson group 19

Pearson, Simon 436
Penning-Rowsell, Edmund 96
Peres, Shimon 250, 561–562
Perrick, Penny 201
Peru 133
Peterborough, Bishop of 208
Pettit, Stephen 449
Phillips, Michael 202–203
Pickering, Sir Edward 37–38, 40, 49, 50,
    164, 171, 210, 215, 510–511, 645
Pickering, Ron 330
Pierce, Andrew 476–477, 494, 538
Pigott, Richard 167
Pilpel, Leon 127, 198, 626–627
Pimlott, Ben 315, 338
Pinochet, Augusto 595
Pinsent, Sir Matthew 445
Pinter, Harold 463
Pithart, Peter 144
Pitt, Bill 78
Pittsburgh National Bank 400
Plath, Sylvia 462
PLO (Palestine Liberation
    Organization) 151, 152–153, 561
Plommer, Leslie 153
Poland 145–146, 350, 355
Pole-Carew, Christopher 221, 231–232,
    236
Porter, Barry 31
Portillo, Michael 484, 485, 504,
    550–551, 557–558, 600
Potter, Sarah 444
Powell, Enoch 68, 108, 556
Pravda – A Fleet Street Comedy (David
    Hare) 115, 183
Prentice, Eve-Ann 588–589
Prescott, John 555
Press Association 164, 250, 552
Press censorship 163–164
Press Council/Complaints Commission
    511–514, 516
Preston, Ben 539, 547, 549–550, 606,
    608
Preston, Peter 128, 305–306, 431
Pride, Tom 436
Prime, Tony 123

Prince 456
Pringle, James 523, 527, 533
Print unions 10–13, 25
  closed shops 86–89, 155–156,
      193–194, 219–220, 239–240, 243
  computer technology 13, 86–88, 229,
      231, 233–234
  double-key stroking 13–14, 34, 229,
      242, 244
  industrial action/strikes 1, 3, 5,
      10–14, 48, 60, 81, 83, 85, 89, 152,
      155–158, 163, 186–187, 219–220,
      223–225, 230, 239, 243–245,
      248–250
  legally binding contracts 244–245
  Murdoch offers Gray's Inn Road
      freehold 276–278, 281–282
  redundancies 272
  and TNL sale 31–34
  Wembley rally 265
  see also Gray's Inn Road; Murdoch;
      NGA; NUJ; SOGAT; Wapping
Prior, James 29, 72, 156
Private Eye 59–60, 101–102, 112, 196
The Prodigy 456
Proops, Marjorie 78
Property boom 320–321
Pulp Fiction (dir. Quentin Tarantino)
    464
Punch and Judy (Harrison Birtwistle)
    450
Purves, Libby 624
Putin, Vladimir 593
Pym, Francis 125, 129, 133
Pysariwsky, Zoriana 124

Q
Quinton, Lord (Anthony) 181–182

R
Rabin, Yitzhak 561–562
Race Today 74
Racing Demons (David Hare) 463
Railton, Jim 328

Ramsay, Alix 441
Randall, Jeff 543–544, 546
Random House 182
Raphael, Isabel 183
Ratcliffe, Michael 181
Rattle, Sir Simon 448
Raynsford, Nick 262
Reagan, Ronald 58, 67, 133, 146, 148, 155, 160, 213, 215–216, 348, 597
Recession 380, 399, 404–405, 422–423, 472–473
Redgrave, Sir Steven 445
Redwood, John 484, 489, 494
Reed, John 400
Rees-Mogg, William
 and Blair 497
 Evans's downfall 117
 'How to Kill a Newspaper' 16
 on judging news 641–642
 Maastricht treaty 474–475
 and Major 477, 492
 and Murdoch 7, 37, 44, 259
 and the sale of The Times 3–7, 18, 21–23, 31
 as Times columnist 419–420, 423, 514, 552, 608
 as Times editor 52, 53–54, 57, 61, 66, 76, 78, 105, 114, 474
 Times Europe edition 14
 transfer of TNL titles 100
Referendum Party 488
Reich, Steve 450
Reichmann, Paul 324
Reservoir Dogs (dir. Quentin Tarantino) 464
Reuters 7, 84, 238–239, 335
Reynolds Defence (Albert Reynolds) 518–521, 564
Rhodes, Tom 572
Rice, Tom 228, 232
Richards, Geoffrey 98, 235, 245, 248, 266, 290, 292
Riddell, Peter 55, 408–409, 415, 419, 476, 489, 499, 617, 648
Ridley, Nicholas 120, 377, 379–380
Righter, Rosemary 350, 389, 390, 394, 485–486, 526, 562, 567, 586, 608, 624, 648
Riley, John 264
Rippon, Geoffrey 100
Robbins, Chris 269, 271
Robbins Report 76, 105
Robens, Lord (Alfred) 23, 50, 109, 110, 115
Roberts, Anthony 461
Roberts, Peter 372, 435, 437, 608
Robertson, George 263
Robertson QC, Geoffrey 539
Robinson, David 184–185
Robinson, Geoffrey 30, 535
Robinson, Jeffrey 517
Robinson, Mary 564
Robson, Andrew 639
Roche, Billy 463
Rodgers, Bill 76, 164, 317
Roll, Lord (Eric) 23, 30, 31, 50
Romania 353–356
The Romans in Britain (Howard Brenton) 115
A Room with a View (dir. James Ivory) 185
Rosewell, Mike 328
Rothermere, Lord (Harold) 20–21, 22, 24, 272, 412
Routledge, Paul 187–188, 209, 258, 260, 302
Roux, Albert 97
Rowland, Tiny 2, 17, 31–32, 40, 274
Roxburgh, Angus 347
Royal Commission on the Press 6
Royal Geographical Society 121
Royal Opera House 447, 451
Ruda, Mike 85
Rudd, Alyson 443–444
Ruddock, David 414, 435–436, 547, 552, 608
Rusbridger, Alan 426, 469, 520
Ruskin College 274–275
Russell, William Howard 154n 618
Russia 568, 591–593 see also Soviet Union
Rwanda 581–584

S

Saatchi, Lord Charles 458, 460
Saatchi & Saatchi 43
Samaranch, Juan Antonio 326
Sampras, Pete 442
Sampson, Anthony 78
Sampson, Catherine 349, 523
Sands, Bobby 71, 635
Satellite television 185–186, 360–361,
    399, 427, 429, 432, 442–444 see also
    Sky television; Star TV
Saudi Arabia 388–389, 596
Scargill, Arthur 188, 209, 293
Scarman, Lord (Scarman Report)
    73–75
Schiff, Dorothy 41
Schmidt, Helmut 70, 353
Schwarzkopf, General Norman 395,
    396
Scotland
  devolution 499
  Holyrood Parliament 501–502
  Times edition 500–502
Scott, Peter 121
Scott Report 481
Scottish Daily Express 143
Scowcroft, Brent 354
Scruton, Roger 144, 159
SDP (Social Democratic Party) 76–79,
    82, 102, 114, 163–164, 317–318
Seamark, Mick 136
Searby, Richard 21, 35, 99–100, 109,
    115, 171
Searjeant, Graham 161–162, 324,
    415
Seeber, Liz 88, 106–107, 129, 212,
    252
Seely, Michael 202
Selbourne, David 274–275
Selling Hitler (Robert Harris) 178
Serbia 568–571, 576–577, 590 see also
    Bosnian War; Dayton Accord;
    Kosovo; NATO
Sereny, Gitta 168–169, 515–516
Sergeant, John 311

Shackleton, Lord (Edward) 121
Shah, Eddy 227–228, 238–240, 273,
    298, 301
Shakespeare in Love (dir. John
    Madden) 465
Shakespeare, Nicholas 453
Sharon, Ariel 154, 563
Shea, Michael 627
Shearer, Alan 442
Sheehan, Robert 638
Sheffield, HMS 132–133
Sherwood, James 99
Shields, Mick 21
Shore, Peter 223, 308
Short, Clare 158, 394
Short, Nigel 421
Siberian gas pipeline 146
Sieghart, Mary Ann 362–363, 366,
    375, 447, 483, 485, 487, 492, 556,
    624
Sierra Leone 583
Siete Dias 119
Silkin, John 81–82
Sinclair, David 153 156311, 103,
    473
Single currency see also ERM; EMU
Sinn Fein 499, 564–566 see also IRA
Sino-British Declaration 525
Sir Galahad 136
Sir Tristram 136
Skinner, Dennis 290, 539
Sky television (British Sky
    Broadcasting) 186, 360–361, 399,
    401, 411, 426, 427, 442–444
Sloman, Sir Albert 275
Slovenia 569
Smith, Geoffrey 103, 107
Smith, John 29, 32, 100, 405, 408, 482,
    499
Smith, Mel 190
The Smiths 453
Smylie, Ben 234
Snoddy, Raymond 263, 304, 426,
    531
Snow, Peter 128
Sobers, Garfield 440

SOGAT (Society of Graphical and Allied Trades) 10, 33, 86, 88, 148–149, 156–158, 220, 224–228, 232–233, 236, 241–242, 244–245, 248–250, 253, 265–269, 270–271, 278–284, 287–288, 290–291, 293 *see also* print unions
Solidarity Movement 145, 350–351
Somalia 579–581
Sorge, Wilfried 169–171
South Africa 124, 159, 560, 566, 583, 627
South China Morning Post 529, 646
South Georgia 121–123, 129
South Korea 329
Soviet Union (USSR) 146–147, 159, 186–187, 215–216, 347–348, 350, 355, 357, 403, 567–568 *see also* Russia
The Spectator 17, 65, 96, 100, 108, 118, 213, 254, 260, 475, 633
Spice Girls 455–456
Spicer, Sir Michael 475
Der Spiegel 172
Spitting Image 481
Srebrenica massacre 575–576 *see also* Bosnian War; NATO; UN
La Stampa 61
Stanhope, Henry 120, 124, 136–137
Star TV 429, 529–530
Steel, David 314
Stelzer, Irwin 412
Stephenson, Hugh 45, 51, 55, 101, 160, 274
Stern magazine 167–174, 176–180
Steven, Stewart 475
Stevens, Lord (David) 239, 272
Stoessel, Walter 126
Stone, Professor Norman 178, 352
Stone Roses 454
Stoppard, Tom 183
Stothard, Peter
  'bourgeois triumphalism' 313
  Op-Ed commissions 158–159, 198
  print room visit 221
  'promising' journalist 55, 102, 117, 201, 304, 417
  US editor 362, 390
  Wapping strike 250
  principal leader writer 648
  as *Times* editor
    appointment 412–413
    assessment of editorship 607–609
    background 416–417
    Ashcroft affair 536–546
    cancer treatment 547–548, 551
    and China 523–534
    Conservative Philosophy Group 475
    'dumbing down' 613–614
    editorial structure 436
    election year (1997) 487–492
    endorses Labour 556–557
    and John Major 476, 488–490
    leaders 648
    literary editor 462
    Murdoch's influence 114, 531–534, 645
    newspaper pricing 428, 431–432
    obituaries 634
    online edition 469–470
    and Princess Diana 505–506
    sackings 418–419
    staff re-shuffle 546–547
    stands down 607–609
    and Tony Blair 483
    trainee scheme 340–341
    war on terror 602
    Times Literary Supplement editor 608
  see also the full listing for *The Times*
Strafford, Peter 120–121, 198
Straw, Jack 263, 338, 518
Strong, Roy 182
Stuart-Smith, Mr Justice (Sir Murray) 287
Stuttaford, Dr Thomas 117, 468
STV (Scottish Television) 9
Sudan 598
Suez 138
Sun 22, 25, 30, 33, 41–43, 77, 647 *see also* Bouverie Street
  and ASLEF 83, 250
  bingo 189
  circulation 27, 40, 263, 399

Evans's thalidomide campaign 48–49
Falklands War 123–124, 128, 129,
   131, 141
finances 9
general election (1992) 408
journalists' salaries 285–286
Kinning Park Plant 226
price cut 424–425
and Princess Diana 507
print unions 99
tabloid excesses 367
Versace's murder 466
Wapping 85, 219, 222, 225–226, 229,
   235, 242, 244, 253, 268
Sun-Times see Chicago Sun-Times
Sunday Express 270
Sunday Sport 512
Sunday Times
  book reviews 181
  circulation 27, 51, 86, 180, 271, 422
  election campaign (1983) 164
  finances 84–85, 422
  Hitler Diaries 168, 173–176, 178,
    180
  industrial relations 1, 12, 20, 86, 89,
    98, 219
  Innovation Special 248
  'the journalists' paper' 118
  and Murdoch 26
  Mussolini diaries 168
  the Queen and Thatcherism 627
  sale 1–3, 6, 18–22, 25, 29, 32
  Wapping 234–235, 242, 247–249,
    253, 255
Sunday Today 307
Sunni fundamentalism 150
Swann, Sir Michael 4
Sykes, Paul 490
Symonds, Matthew 240, 300–301
Syria 150–152, 155

T
Taheri, Amir 388–389, 597
Taleban 598, 602–605
Tanjug (news agency) 354

Tarantino, Quentin 464
Tavener, John 450
Taylor, Edwin 60, 62
Taylor, Graham 326
Taylor, Ken 226
Tebbit, Norman 309
Terry, Anthony 168, 176
TGWU (Transport and General
   Workers Union) 233, 250, 266
Thalidomide controversy 48–49
Thatcher, Denis 113
Thatcher, Margaret 14, 28–29, 43, 68,
   75, 113–114, 213
  Bosnian war and the arms embargo
    571
  carbon emissions 469
  East Germany 352–353
  Evans and the Sport Council 113–114
  Exchange Rate Mechanism 320,
    344–346
  Falklands War 120, 122, 124–126,
    129, 133, 137, 138
  general elections 14, 162–164,
    312–316, 318, 346
  German reunification 358
  leadership challenge 366, 374,
    379–384
  Lebanon war 155
  and the miners 75
  monetarist policies 627
  and the Monopolies Commission
    28–32
  and moral high ground 166
  and Murdoch 28–29, 43, 113–114,
    186
  Privileges Committee 309
  South African sanctions 627
  tribute to Douglas-Home 213
  Westland Helicopters 310
Thatcherite policies 65–68, 71, 73, 75,
   78, 160–162, 186–187, 215, 265,
   293–294, 312–313, 318–320,
   343–346, 376–388
'*The Times* at 200' 208
Thomas, Christopher 71–72, 124, 131,
   598

Thompson, E.P. 127
Thomson British Holdings 7, 17 *see also* Thomson Organisation
Thomson, Kenneth (2nd Baron Thomson of Fleet) 17–18, 83
Thomson Organisation
finances 2, 4–5, 8, 14
sale of *Times/Sunday Times* 1–5, 9, 16–19, 25, 28–30, 32
Thomson, Robert 524, 534
Times editor 607, 623
Thomson, Roy (1st Baron Thomson of Fleet) 3, 7–11, 17, 24, 27, 40, 41, 89, 116, 192–193
Thornton, Clive 277
Thornton, Michael 634
Tieman, Ross 616
Time magazine 518
Time Out 60
The Times (please see main index for additional page references)
Business concerns and management
advertising 42, 84–85, 90, 192, 194, 263–264, 272, 307, 421, 424–425, 430, 437, 470–471, 549, 605
Archive and Record Centre 510, 520–521
bicentenary 206–210
boycotts 263–265, 267, 338, 370
circulation 4, 15, 27, 41, 51–52, 63, 90, 117, 141, 189, 191–192, 194, 198, 206, 263, 271–272, 305–306, 358, 411, 423–425, 433–435, 437, 614
consequences of Wapping revolution 301–304, 307
cover price 272, 411, 422–435, 437
innovation and expansion 294–299
'La Lumiere', new office 509–510
marketing 420–421
mergers 18–19
Microsoft deal 432–433
no-smoking policy 436
Portfolio competition 189–194, 425
readership 49, 610–613

redundancies 98–100, 110, 113, 116, 161, 402
Sale and purchase by Murdoch 1–7, 6–9, 17–23, 25, 26, 28–31, 32, 40, 100, 188, 308–9, 363, 401–402 *see also* Times Newspapers Limited
tabloid press bingo war 189
Coverage
Business news
'Big Bang' 323–324
Black Wednesday 477
monetarism 65–70, 75, 114, 160–161, 319–320, 627
Sky TV 360–361
Education
higher 75–76, 479–480
Ofsted 478–479
Europe
European monetary union (EMU) 344, 358, 380–381, 403–404
Euro 403, 472
Euro-sceptics 344, 404, 473–475, 476, 490–491, 493
Europa 61
European Community 344–345, 403
European Parliament 96
Exchange Rate Mechanism (ERM) 320, 344, 379–381, 472–474
Maastricht treaty 403–404, 473–474, 476
Single currency 344, 403, 473
Foreign affairs
Afghanistan 602–604
Berlin Wall 351–352
bin Laden, Osama 598
Bosnian War 570–572, 574–579, 585–589
Chechnya 592–593
China 348–349, 354, 523–534, 644
Deng Xiaping obituary 527
Cold War 160, 215, 357, 387, 559, 567, 609 *see also* Soviet Union
Gorbachev tribute 568
Crimean War 140
Croatia 574–575

Eastern Europe 346–347, 350–357
East and West (Chris Patten)
  530–531
Falklands War 119–137, 140–141,
  152, 205
Hitler Diaries 167–180, 641
Hong Kong 350, 503–504, 525–526,
  528
Human Rights Act and libel laws
  (Loutchansky case) 517–521
Iraq 149, 387–388, 389–398
  Kurds 387, 397
Islamic fundamentalism 597
Israel 149, 150–154, 334, 337, 561
Kuwait 386–389
Lebanon 149, 150–155, 334–337
Mirsky and Freedom Forum
  controversy 531–534
Palestine 149, 153, 335, 561, 562
Poland (Solidarity) 145
Prisoners of Conscience 144
Romania 353–355
Rwanda 581–584
Sierra Leone 583
Somalia 580
South Africa 159
Soviet Union 147, 159, 347–348
Tiananmen Square 348–349
Versace's murder 466
Vincennes incident 337
Home news
BBC 186, 535, 540, 609
Brixton riots 72–75
Calcutt enquiry 513–514
Charles Stewart Parnell forgery
  167–168
Cries Unheard, Mary Bell
  serialization 515–516
devolution 499–500, 553
Princess Diana's death 504–507
environment 468
global warming 469
labour disputes, militant trade
  unions 75, 186–187
Loutchansky v Times Newspapers
  517–521

National Lottery 446–447
Northern Ireland 70–72, 150, 336,
  338, 339, 564–567
nuclear weapons 148
pop culture 455–457
Press Complaints Commission
  513–514, 516
racism 74
radioactive waste 308
reality TV 460
Thatcher, Denis, planning
  application 113
Politics
Conservative Party
Archer, Lord (Jeffrey) and London
  mayoral election 540
economic policy 320–322
Hague, William, and modernisation
  550–1
Heseltine, Michael, resignation
  310
donations, the Ashcroft affair
  536–545, 609
Howe, Geoffrey
  Budget Day 108
  resignation 382
leadership challenges 382–384,
  483–4, 494–495
Major, John, 476–477, 481–482,
  489–490
Parkinson, Cecil, and Keays, Sarah
  165–166
Poll Tax 375, 376–382
Portillo, Michael, 551
privatization 162
public spending cuts 120–121
Thatcherism 158, 162, 344
trade union reform 114, 157
unemployment 161
general elections
  (1979) 14
  (1983) 162–165
  (1987) 313–316
  (1992) 406–408,
  (1997) 489–493
  (2001) 555–557

The Times – cont.
Politics – cont.
Labour Party
Blair, Tony, 483
Brown, Gordon 497
devolution 499–500, 553
Government leaks 552–553
tax plans 405
'Third Way, or Reich' 553
House of Commons, Parliamentary
Privileges 309
Referendum Party 488–489
Scoops
Andrew Motion, Poet Laureate 552
Ulster framework 564–565
Sports
Increased coverage 625
Glen Hoddle interview 520–521
Football and economic renaissance
327, 442–444, 646
Terrorism
Fukuyama theory 356–357
War on terror 601–602
World Trade Center bombing
599–601, 642, 643
Editors (in order of appointment) *see*
Evans, Harold; Douglas-Home,
Charles; Wilson, Charles; Jenkins,
Simon; Stothard, Peter; Thompson,
Robert
Gray's Inn Road
closure threat 35
demarcation rules 89, 294–295
Murdoch offers freehold to print
unions 276–278, 281–282
new site talks 5, 223
poor morale 85, 102
print capacity 249
property assets 25
sold to ITN 297
TNL papers 19, 33, 52
Journalists/journalism
computer technology 258, 294–296,
435
defections/departures 54–57, 91–92,
94–95, 333, 343, 360, 485

'dumbing down' 38, 40–42, 189–91,
208, 531, 613–625
editorial structure 401, 645–646
Evans's departure 110
'feminization' 623–624
good journalistic practices 520–521
information technology 640–643
library 285
life-style articles 622–623
move to Wapping 249, 253–256,
257–265
Murdoch's editorial influence 21, 26,
38–39, 41–44, 59, 83, 85, 96,
114–116, 186–187, 189, 198, 337,
531–532, 534, 613–625, 644
salaries 15–16, 94, 220, 285–286
self-censorship 129–130, 530
trainee scheme 340–341, 417, 579
'The Thunderer' 103
Layout
changes 58–63, 92–93, 113, 117, 372
and the Falklands War 140
first colour page 61–63
headlines 338, 370, 372, 420, 613
masthead 63, 119, 420, 613–614
nude advertisement 42
visual appearance 613–14
Legal actions
Routledge and the miners' strike 188
Loutchansky case 517–521
Longley case 419
Press awards
Lord Derby Racing Journalist of the
Year 203
What the Papers Say 105, 582, 594
Printing
Atex computers 231, 233–234, 236,
247, 258
cold composition 86–87, 92, 110
colour 409, 420, 613, 622
computer-setting 193–194, 294–296
corrections and misprints 284–285
electronic page make-up 410
in linotype 10–13, 86–87, 220
production problems 193–195,
219–220

steam press 230
typeface change 410
Profitability 84–85, 95, 98–99, 116, 191, 422, 437
cover price 272, 411, 422–435, 437
Sections & editions
Archaeology 637
Architecture 373, 638
Arts 91, 198, 423, 446–452, 458–462
Astronomy 637
Book reviews 180–183, 189, 419, 462
Bridge 638–639
Business pages 161–162, 214, 323–325, 423, 620–622
Cartoons 56, 59, 97, 199–200
Chess 421, 638
Cinema 184–185, 464
Columnists 438
Cookery 201, 359
Court & Social 56, 637–639
Crossword 59, 639
Diary column 198–200, 512
Education 75–76, 263–264, 263, 318 319, 479 80
Europe edition 14
Family money 322
Fashion 201, 303, 361, 466–468
Features 55, 201, 373, 438, 548, 607
Female interest 201, 623–624
Foreign editions 410
Gardening 207–208, 359
Health 467–468
Information Service 59
Innovation Special 248
Interface 469
Jenkins's changes 373–374
Law 373, 637
Letters 626–630
Life and Times 374
Lives Remembered 607
Magazine 438, 623
Millennium edition 546
Modern manners 438–439
Moreover 56
Music 447–457
Nature notes 638

Obituaries 315, 339, 606–607, 630–636
Parliamentary proceedings 308–312, 402
Play 622
Preview 60, 90–91
Property 320–321, 359, 481
Royal reporting 61–63, 112, 142, 209–210, 504, 513, 627, 634
The Register 607, 626, 636–638
Religious affairs 258, 285, 375, 41–419
Restaurants 359–360
Rock music 453–457
on Saturday 359
Saturday Review 91, 373–374
School league tables 479
Science 468–469
Scottish edition 500–503
Special Reports 61
Sports coverage 201–206, 325–331, 359, 423, 433, 439–445, 607, 625
T2 tabloid 467, 548–549, 606, 623
Television 185 186
Theatre 183–184, 462–464
'The Way We Live Now' 144
Times Online 470–471, 624, 642
Travel 321, 359
Two and four section paper 297, 322–323, 359, 420, 606
Universities 34, 75–76, 93, 319, 479–480, 637
Weekend Review 623
Weekend Times 374, 438, 622
Wine 359
Sponsorship
Artangel 461
Mysteries of China exhibition 526–527
World Chess Championship 421
Wapping
boycott campaign against *The Times* 262–264
as catalyst for change 238–241
conspirators 231–238, 246–248
eleven-acre site 222–230

The Times – cont.
Wapping – *cont.*
first edition 256–257
'Fortress Wapping' 195, 219–252
increase in profitability 95, 297–298, 400
'Innovation Special' 248
move rejected by Murdoch 85
moving day 250–252
praise for Murdoch 259–260, 273
price of victory 292–299
public opinion 270–276
road distribution 233, 244, 250, 265–266, 278
siege/pickets/intimidation 255, 256–260, 267–270, 274, 278–280, 282–287, 289–292, 301–302
union negotiations 231–238, 242–246, 248–256, 276–288
Times Educational Supplement, sale of 2, 34, 263
The Times Good Universities Guide 319, 479–480
Times Higher Education Supplement 34
Times House of Commons 315
Times Literary Supplement 2, 34, 178, 180, 608
Times New Roman 60
Times Newspapers Limited (TNL) 19–24
and the BBC 186
computerization 13
finances 84–85, 95, 98–99, 116, 191, 422, 437
Hitler Diaries 169–170
House of Commons, TNL Sale, 26, 29–31, 188, 308–309
Holdings board 32, 49–50, 247
independent directors 31
industrial relations 5, 10–14, 15–16, 86, 90, 157, 221 *see also* print unions; Wapping
Loutchansky v TNL 518–521
Monopolies Commission 27–32
redundancies 98, 116
sale 1–7, 17–23, 25, 28–32

tax losses 2
transfer of titles 98–99
Titanic (dir. James Cameron) 464
TNT 233, 244, 250, 265, 278, 284, 287, 289, 293
Tobin, James 69
Today 238, 240, 273, 298, 301, 307, 381, 428
Todd, Ron 250, 267
Tokes, Laszlo 354
Tom and Viv (Michael Hastings) 183
Topolski, Daniel 328
Townsend, Edward 616
Toynbee, Polly 78
Trade Union Act (1984) 227, 239, 248, 287
Trafalgar House 40
Trainspotting (dir. Danny Boyle) 465
Trelford, Donald 163, 274
Trevisan, Dessa 145, 353
Trevor-Roper, Hugh *see* Lord Dacre
Trievnor, Peter 62
Trilogy of the Dragon (Robert Le Page) 183
Trimble, David 565–566
Truss, Lynne 444
TUC (Trades Union Congress) 90, 156, 158, 227–228, 231, 244, 261–262, 278, 287, 293, 380
Tudjman, Franjo 568, 578
Turner, Graham 179
Turnill, Oscar 60
Twentieth Century Fox 401

U

UK Press Gazette 214, 259, 302
Ukraine 567
United Nations 387, 389, 396, 397, 486
failure of mission 575–576
international jurisprudence 595
Protection Force (UNPROFOR) 570, 572
resolutions 597
Security Council 560
Somalia 580

Unemployment 404, 472–473, 554
United Newspapers 5, 272
University Grants Committee 75
Upton, Judy 463
Urquhart, Cath 624
United States
  aid to Israel 152
  and al-Qaeda 602
  and Baltic States 570
  and Bosnian war 574, 579
  Drug Enforcement Agency 538, 542
  and Gulf War 388, 389, 392, 396,
    560
  intervention in Grenada 159
  and Middle East 152–153, 561
  and Somalia 579–581
  and Taleban 602–605
  see also Bush, George; Bush, George W.;
    Clinton, Bill; Reagan, Ronald
USA Today 232, 240
Utley, T.E. (Peter) 315, 339

V
Van Den Belt, Annelies 470
van der Vat, Dan 44
Versace, Gianni 466
Vickers, Hugo 633
Vincent, Professor John 274

W
Wade, Joe 2–3, 33
Wagner, Erica 462, 534, 624
Waite, Terry 335
Wakeham, Lord (John) 516
Walden, Brian 342
Walesa, Lech 145–146, 357
Walker, Christopher 152, 154, 314,
    347, 390–391, 395
Walker, David 357, 374
Walker, Tom 588, 590
Wall Street Journal 158, 410
Walter family (Times owners) 4
Walter, John 23, 63, 207, 210
Walter, John II 230

Walters, Sir Alan 344–345, 379
Wapping
  Archive and Record Centre 510
  Atex computers 231, 233–234, 236,
    247, 258
  boycott campaign 262–264
  as catalyst for change 238–241
  colour presses 400
  conspirators 231–238, 246–248
  eleven-acre site 222–230
  first edition 256–257
  Goss press machines 259
  increase in profitability 95, 297–298
  move rejected by Murdoch 85
  moving day 250–252
  praise for Murdoch 259–260, 273
  price of victory 292–299
  production runs 253–255, 259–260,
    271–272, 296–297
  public opinion 270–276
  re-equipping 400
  road distribution 233, 244, 250,
    265–266, 278
  siege/pickets/intimidation 255,
    256–260, 267–270, 274, 278–280,
    282–287, 289–292, 301–302
  subsequent fallout 301–304, 307
  The Times's new residence 509–510
  union negotiations 231–238,
    242–246, 248–256, 276–288
Wapping Post 271
Wapshott, Nicholas 55, 80, 599, 622
Wardle, Irvine 183–184, 462
Warman, Christopher 261, 321, 324
Warner, Deborah 451
Washington Post 5–6, 230, 232
Watkins, Alan 91
Watkins, Lord Justice 264
Watson, Arthur 52
Watson, Colin 64, 198
Watson, Peter 94
Watson, Roland 599
Watt, David 55
Watts, David 127, 370, 522–523, 618,
    619
Waugh, Auberon 53–54, 260

We Thundered Out (Philip Howard)
207
Webb, Colin 169, 171, 174–175,
195–196, 198, 212–214, 217, 250,
304, 418
Webster, Philip 311, 315, 345, 404,
419, 552, 601
Weekly Times Group 36
Wei Jingsheng 528, 532
Weidenfeld, Lord (George) 431
Weinstock, Lord (Arnold) 4
Weir, Judith 450
Welch, Colin 106, 108
Welland, Colin 184
Weller, Paul 453
Welsh, Irvine 465
Die Welt 61, 357
Westlake, Melvyn 69
Westland Helicopters 310
What the Papers Say 106
Wheatcroft, Patience 608, 620, 624
White Swan letter 105
Whitehead, Phillip 26
Whitelaw, Lord (William) 73, 74,
125
Whiteread, Rachel 459, 461
Whittam Smith, Andreas 240,
300–301, 411, 415, 428, 430
Whittell, Giles 600
Whitty, Larry 262
Whitworth, Damian 537
Widdecombe, Ann 495, 551
Wiener, Martin 49
Wigg, Lord (George) 127
Wilby, Peter 98
Williams, Delwyn 30
Williams, Hywell 489
Williams, Marcus 203, 439–440
Williams, Richard 60, 90, 201, 235,
246, 325, 360, 363, 365, 447, 452,
457, 625
Williams, Shirley 76, 79, 164, 315,
317
Willis, Bob 204, 207
Willis, Norman 248, 278, 281, 290
Willson, Richard 345, 490

Wilson, Charles
acting editor of the *Independent* 365
background 196–198
deputy editor 212–14
Hitler Diaries 169, 173, 178
East European emissary 364–365
and Thatcher 310, 318
personality 332–334, 337–338,
361–363, 414
Seeley's retirement party 203
Sun-Times editor 217–218
as *Times* editor
assessment of editorship 365–6
appointed editor 218
'Big Bang' 324–5
'dumbing down' 208
expanding the paper's size 322–323,
358
increase in sales 263
journalists' pay offer 286
Independent launch 300–303, 608
and 'nemesis' (Andrew Knight)
362–363, 365
new offices 257–265
promoting Sky TV 361–362
skilful editor 365–366
and Thatcher 318
Wapping 229–230, 231, 234–235,
238, 242, 246–247, 250–251, 256,
272, 292
Wilson, Des 105
Wilson, Harold 27
Wilson, Roy 'Ginger' 248
Wilson, Tony 454
Winchester, Simon 122–123
Winter, Bishop Colin 124
The Winter War (John Witherow and
Patrick Bishop) 138
Wintour, Patrick 263
Witherow, John 72, 123–124, 129–132,
134–138, 140
Wober, J.W. 629–630
Wood, Alan 164
Wood, Nicholas 344, 346, 418
Wood, Ronnie 453
Woodcock, John 203–204, 440

Woodhead, Chris 478–479
Woodward, Admiral Sandy 131
Worcester, Bob 316
World Trade Center bombing 599, 642, 643
World Trade Organization 594–595
Worsthorne, Sir Peregrine 272, 313, 618–619
Wright, Jonathan 335
Wyatt, Woodrow 28–29, 182, 232, 315, 350, 476, 492, 513

Yeltsin, Boris 567, 571, 574–575, 592–593
Yorkshire Post 262
Young, Hugo 54, 158, 178, 208, 298
Young, Lord (David) 315
Young, Robin 198
Young , Toby 341
Yugoslavia 568, 591 *see also* Bosnia; Croatia; Dayton Accord; Eastern Europe; Serbia; Slovenia
Yuppies 313

Y

yBas (young British artists) 458–461
Years of Upheaval 1973–77 (Henry Kissinger) 64

Z

Zaire (Congo) 582–583
Zhao Ziyang 523
Zhu Rongji 527–528